The World Treasury of Science Fiction

OF Science Fiction

EDITED BY

David G. Hartwell

With a Foreword by
Clifton Fadiman, General Editor

Little, Brown and Company

Boston ■ Toronto ■ London

First edition

Acknowledgments of permission to reprint previously copyrighted material appear on
pages 1079-1083.

Library of Congress Catalog Card Number: 88-82960

Book Design and Composition by The Sarabande Press

Published simultaneously in Canada
by Little, Brown & Company (Canada) Limited

Printed in the United States of America

CONTENTS

Foreword

This volume forms one of a continuing series of World
Treasuries published in cooperation with the Book-of-
the-Month Club. Each of these Treasuries gathers, from
as many literatures as possible, previously published, high-
order writing of our time, fiction or nonfiction. Each covers a
specific field or genre of general interest to the intelligent
reader. Each has been constructed and edited by a recognized
authority in the field.

The underlying purpose of the series is to meet the expectations of the thoughtful modern reader, one conscious of the
striking change that has taken place in our view of the world.
That change has run counter to parochialism. It recognizes
the contribution made by thinkers and prose artists of the
Orient as well as the Occident, of those who use languages
other than English. Hence *World* Treasuries.

The series is planned to cover a great variety of fields, from
the life sciences to religious thought, from science fiction to
love stories to mystery and detection, and will be issued over
the next several years.

Clifton Fadiman
General Editor

Introduction

This book is the largest and most ambitious collection of science fiction from all over the world ever compiled. It represents the state of the art today. The selections date from the modern period, 1939 to the present. The majority are from the past thirty years, for science fiction did not become an international literary form until the 1950s and did not become truly widespread even in the West until the 1970s. Thus this anthology could not have been assembled until now.

Science fiction is largely a twentieth-century phenomenon. The term was coined in 1929 to signify the birth, phoenixlike, of a new genre from the ashes of an older one, "scientific romance." Hugo Gernsback, the pulp editor and writer who fathered the new genre, pointed to the works of Edgar Allan Poe, Jules Verne, and H. G. Wells for exemplars of science fiction. In the editorial of the first issue of *Amazing Stories* (April 1926), he defined it as "charming romance intermingled with scientific fact and prophetic vision." For a fuller description of what science fiction is and where it has come from, the reader might consult this writer's book, *Age of Wonders* (1984).

Gernsback initially referred to his new genre by many names, one of which, scientifiction, was used commonly until the 1960s. For our purposes, though, there is one other aspect of the naming to be considered. In a historic speech before the 1941 World Science Fiction Convention (actually a gathering of a couple of hundred American fans in Denver), Robert A. Heinlein proposed that the initials SF, the common abbreviation for science fiction, be fused with the broader name "speculative fiction," and SF it has remained, especially because speculative fiction was the rallying cry of the young Turks of the 1960s. This aspect of the name SF reflects an ambiguity toward science that is easily discerned in the literature.

Amazing Stories, Thrilling Wonder Stories, Astounding Stories of Super Science—American pulp magazines with these titles dominated the new genre from the start. The British were the first to experience the invasion of American SF, in the form of pulp magazines used as ballast in freighters and then sold for pennies in British Woolworth before World War II. A few British writers responded by creating their own fantastic stories for this new market; the first British SF pulp magazine, *Tales of Tomorrow,* was founded in the late 1930s but perished in the early days of World War II. However, such writers as C. S. Lewis had noticed the new genre. They combined some of its characteristics with other influences, notably the quite healthy Wellsian tradition (Wells himself was still alive and quite an important man). Thus was created a steady though small stream of distinctive British SF, like Lewis's *Perelandra* trilogy, especially the first volume, *Out of the Silent Planet* (1938).

It was clear, however, that the real action lay in the United States, in the magazines filled with intellectual ferment and all kinds of excitements (except sex—that was reserved for the garish artwork and the advertisements in the back). In this collection I have included examples of energetic stories by John W. Campbell, Jr., and John Berryman from this pulp period, charged with wonder. This SF was a kind of born-again message from converts to the idea of an awesome, technophilic future.

The magazines went out much like the idealistic messages sent into space, in the faint hope that some other intelligence out there in the plurality of worlds in the universe would receive them and respond. But just as early U.S. radio broadcasts, and later television, were beamed in every direction, however weakly, American SF was sent out indiscriminately. It preached a gospel of technological and social optimism.

These early stories did find an audience, usually young, male, and uninitiated into any literary culture. For the most part the readers were interested in science and technology, especially in the rapidly expanding technology of the present and near future, the technology of the atom and of space travel, both wildly visionary in their time and yet related to real science in the real world. No matter how crudely executed—and much was indeed very crude—the vision was communicated to engineers and scientists and to the children who would grow up to be engineers and scientists, eager to transform and improve a world torn by war and poverty. Other than technical material, they had no literature that reflected their concerns and their visions of what they might accomplish, given the tools. American SF said to its audience, "Look, here's a strange predicament, pretty unlikely but interesting—and if we just use our knowledge and our tools to build a neat gadget, the problem is solved."

There was a time lag before the messages were received and translated into other tongues because World War II disrupted communications from the late 1930s through the late 1940s. Most of the prewar U.S. magazines died during this period. But by the end of the war, American SF was ready to boom again, this time under the leadership of a firmly entrenched editor, John W. Campbell, Jr., and his flagship magazine, *Astounding Stories*. Campbell had spent the war years as the new leader of SF, developing young writers and creating what came to be known as the Golden Age of the 1940s. But SF was growing so fast and so strong that by 1950 two influential new magazines, *Galaxy* and *The Magazine of Fantasy & Science Fiction*, had been founded and were seriously challenging the Campbell aesthetic, the former from a sociological, the latter from a literary, point of view. This was certainly a good thing for the international appeal of SF, since the human chauvinism of Campbellian SF (in Campbell's magazine, humans were always smarter, better than aliens) was often nearly indistinguishable from American chauvinism and was therefore certain to disturb a significant number of foreign readers.

Throughout the 1950s and 1960s, SF flourished intermittently in the United States, spreading to television and the movies, to hardcover and then to paperback books, all disseminated worldwide. But it was always difficult to tell whether the message was being received in the non-English-speaking world and whether it was garbled in transmission. Few translations of foreign SF appeared in English, even fewer were published in the United States.

Perhaps the most significant result of the decline of Campbell's *Astounding* was the rise in satirical SF and the concomitant rise in influence of a small group of New York fans turned writers, most of whom had been members of a club called the Futurians in the late 1930s and 1940s. The group included Isaac Asimov, Donald A. Wollheim, Damon Knight, James Blish, Frederik Pohl, Cyril M. Kornbluth, Virginia Kidd, Judith Merril, and Robert A. W. Lowndes. Among them, they have accounted for a large percentage of the effective communications between American SF and the non-English-language world. Starting as members of an idealistic teenage fan club, they have carried through their careers definite leftist leanings and a deep utopian optimism. Thus each one of the primary members has become a strong independent force for worldwide communication through SF, often as publishers, editors, writers, and public figures visiting many countries. Their efforts are strongly represented in this book, often behind the scenes, as translators or as editors who commissioned and published original translations.

Internationalism has been appealing to the Anglo-American SF community since the 1940s; for more than four decades the colorful fan, agent, and Esperantist Forrest J Ackerman, for example, has traveled widely to spread the greetings of American SF. In the 1970s there was a large enough international science fiction community among the peoples of the developed nations for Harry Harrison to call a conference in Ireland in order to found World SF, the world SF professional organization, which now awards prizes for translations in many languages and promotes the cross-fertilization of SF literatures, inviting international responses to English-language SF.

There is not yet a really identifiable third world SF. The underdeveloped countries have not responded to the technologically optimistic appeal of SF, perhaps because that visionary future filled with mechanical wonders seems so far beyond their present resources.

Until the 1970s and 1980s, the international response was most often a repetition of the messages sent from the United States in the 1930s and 1940s, at best accurate, at worst filled with literary static or extraneous matter. To the discredit of the West, we did not hear from Eastern Europe because until recently our antennas were not pointed in that direction. Yet it was from there that some of the most important messages were being returned, in the works of Stanislaw Lem and of Arkady and Boris Strugatsky. Here were serious attempts at true SF of the highest quality, but new and different in approach and often in sensibility. In England and the United States more translations from the Russian have been published than from any other language, but until quite recently very little attention was paid to any of them, because the first wave of translations was poorly done, and the stories usually met political criteria first and literary standards second. While most SF from communist countries has been didactic in the particular direction of socialist utopianism, to the detriment of storytelling, the best of it equals the best Western science fiction.

The stories in this collection demonstrate the range of responses to the dissemination of U.S. science fiction since the primitive days of the 1920s and 1930s. In the works of many British writers emerging in the late 1950s, like Brian Aldiss and J. G. Ballard, it is easy to observe a clear reaction against the technological optimism, naive materialism, and empire-building consciousness of the U.S. literature. By the early 1960s there was a distinct rift opening between United States and British SF. This rift was institutionalized in the mid-1960s under the banner of the "New Wave." A young editor, Michael Moorcock, took the helm at *New Worlds*, a leading British SF magazine, and proclaimed a break with the American tradition, holding up Ballard as the exemplar of the new literature. The idea of a new literature and revolutionary reform spread to the United States in the late 1960s, and many modernist and postmodern literary techniques were incorporated for the first time into SF. Since the New Wave, SF has, in general, been written to a higher literary standard.

The reaction in the 1960s against the standards of American SF is just as clear in other literatures, as evidenced by the work of, say, Josef Nesvadba or Italo Calvino. It is probably not too far off the mark to say that only the Soviets took the attitudes of American SF entirely seriously and attempted to build upon them as foundations, and that in Europe only the French had a strong tradition of literal SF adventure, going back to Jules Verne, that allowed SF to take hold and writers to produce stories reflecting the attitudes toward scientific method and technological wonder so characteristic of American science fiction. The rest of the world seems to have taken the Campbellian SF of the Golden Age of the 1940s and the flowering of Heinlein, Clarke, and Asimov as some kind of joke or as a repository of imagery to be used for purposes other than SF.

To be fair, the same attitude of bemused rejection—surely no one could be expected to take this stuff seriously—has characterized the general reaction in the United States of mainstream literary culture at all levels to science fiction. So much early science fiction was unsophisticated politically, shallow sociologically, lacking in rounded characterization or psychological depth, stylistically uninteresting, and most of all, so unreal on the one hand (space travel and atomic power were considered fantastic and laughable when most of the classics of Heinlein, Asimov, Clarke, and Bradbury were published), and so concerned with the gritty realities of science and technology on the other, that a majority of educated readers had no interest in learning how to read the genre, a practice easily picked up by children and teenagers—by taking every detail literally at first, until given other directions by the text. This is just the reverse of the way we approach the prose literature of this century; we teach ourselves to read with a sensitivity to metaphor and subtext, assuming that that is the route by which the essential communication between reader and text will take place. The rationalist traditions of SF demand, however, that the reader first experience the text as a literal report of something that, by a thin thread of possibility, could be true, given a specified set of circumstances, at some other time, in some other place. SF gives the reader the experience of the fantastic, of magic and wonder, then explains or implies how that wonder could be generated through real science and technology. SF is inherently optimistic because, a priori, it assumes a future, whether dismal or colorful.

I do not, of course, deny the metaphorical level of SF texts. I simply state the obvious, which somehow seems to have been lost in several decades of critical discussion: In a work of science fiction the reader must grant the premise that whatever is stated as the case in the story is literal and true. For instance, in Gérard Klein's "Valley of Echoes," the reader must believe that we are two hundred years in the future, exploring the planet Mars, not merely in some surreal landscape that embodies a metaphor for the human condition. The vehicle, in other words, has just as much weight as the tenor in SF. This is equally true in contemporary science, when we are asked to believe that something is both a wave and a particle. Still, given the hasty writing of the magazine days, when writers lived on the penny-a-word prose they generated, and given the comically hyperbolic covers of the magazines and the paperbacks, it is easy to understand why so many serious people have found it hard to take SF seriously—although, as Theodore Sturgeon was wont to remark, rarely has a literature been judged so exclusively by its worst examples.

The international response to SF is best measured, it seems to me, by analogy to other aspects of American popular culture—jazz, rock 'n' roll, movies, and comics. France is the country where Jerry Lewis is a genius and A. E. Van Vogt is literature. French SF is a hybrid of high literary art and pulp and comic-book sensibilities, too often in conflict in the same story. The selections in this book are exceptions to this and to that extent not characteristic. The British have always considered SF part of contemporary literature—although often, inferior literature, like most of the stuff the Americans write. Ballard and Aldiss are important British writers, and Kingsley Amis, in *New Maps of Hell*, wrote the first significant mainstream book of criticism on science fiction in the late 1950s. But one feels a kind of gloom emanating from British SF, characteristic, as Brian Aldiss has remarked, of a civilization that has, for the time being, given up on Empire and technological advance. There are vigorous SF publishing industries in Germany, Italy, Spain, and Scandinavia, but too little native writing of high quality. The same holds for the countries of South America. Japan has taken a great interest in SF in recent years, but the traditions of narrative that we take for granted in fiction do not obtain in Japanese SF and very little has been translated into English. Chinese SF is in the process of forming in the 1980s, but no works have been translated yet. Only the Soviets have gained faith in science and technology over recent decades, and it is from the Soviet Union that the preponderance of foreign SF emanates.

Many commentators, including Darko Suvin and Franz Rottensteiner, have noted that the primary force behind Soviet SF is utopian social aspiration. Indeed, this seems to provide an impetus precisely parallel to the imperial dreams of U.S. SF of a future made better through the application of scientific knowledge and technology, a future filled with wonders. Most of the rest of the world sees SF as a repository of images that can be used in any fantastic context. This attitude—so foreign to the core idea of U.S. science fiction—will undoubtedly have an increasing influence upon SF writers who aspire to literary eminence, even in the United States, whose science fiction literature the acerbic Polish critic and writer Stanislaw Lem has declared a hopeless case, redeemed only in the works of Philip K. Dick.

SF has been written off with repeated vehemence, perhaps because it challenges so many preconceptions about what is good in literature by being outside the normal criteria and yet popular and influential. Such a writer as Kurt Vonnegut, Jr., was recognized as important as he was disavowing any connection with genre SF, just as earlier Ray Bradbury allowed himself to be winnowed out of the field he had grown up in by friendly critics who said, in effect, "This is so good it can't possibly be SF." It is high time readers discard such preconceptions, which have prevented the recognition of many works of varied strengths and, sometimes, depth and profundity.

This is a rich book, filled with ideas and images, wonders and excitement. It offers many hours of thought-provoking reading, which will, I hope, lead you to investigate the world of SF in more depth and with more satisfaction. It contains a large variety of stories, providing a mixture of American and international SF. I confess to frustration that this volume could not contain three times as much material, for the world of SF has much more to offer.

David G. Hartwell
Pleasantville, New York

The World
Treasury
of Science
Fiction

Harrison Bergeron

Kurt Vonnegut's first novel, Player Piano *(1952), was offered by the Science Fiction Book Club and sold as SF in paperback as* Utopia 14. *In the 1950s Vonnegut published his short stories in both slick fiction and SF magazines, attended the Milford SF-writing workshop, wrote* The Sirens of Titan *(1959), a Hugo Award nominee, about travel in space and time, then* Mother Night *(1961), a mainstream novel on the same theme as Robert A. Heinlein's* Double Star *(1956). But he publicly disavowed the appellation of SF writer, just as Ray Bradbury had earlier in the 1950s allowed that label to be lifted from his works, for the cultural and literary prejudices of the 1950s and early 1960s denied serious attention and monetary rewards to science fiction writers, regardless of merit. The situation has changed enough for Vonnegut to say, recently, "When I began to write stories about things I had seen and wondered about in real life, people said I was writing, hey presto, science fiction. Yes, and people who write faithfully about American urban life today will find themselves writing, hey presto, science fiction. This is nothing to be ashamed about—and never was."*

"Harrison Bergeron" was first published in The Magazine of Fantasy & Science Fiction *in 1961. It has all the outrageous wit and moral force of Vonnegut at his best.*

* * *

The year was 2081, and everybody was finally equal. They weren't only equal before God and the law. They were equal every which way. Nobody was smarter than anybody else. Nobody was better looking than anybody else. Nobody was stronger or quicker than anybody else. All this equality was due to the 211th, 212th, and 213th Amendments to the Constitution, and to the unceasing vigilance of agents of the United States Handicapper General.

Some things about living still weren't quite right, though. April, for instance, still drove people crazy by not being springtime. And it was in that clammy month that the H-G men took George and Hazel Bergeron's fourteen-year-old son, Harrison, away.

It was tragic, all right, but George and Hazel couldn't think about it very hard. Hazel had a perfectly average intelligence, which meant she couldn't think about anything except in short bursts. And George, while his intelligence was way above normal, had a little mental handicap radio in his ear. He was required by law to wear it at all times. It was tuned to a government transmitter. Every twenty seconds or so, the transmitter would send out some sharp noise to keep people like George from taking unfair advantage of their brains.

George and Hazel were watching television. There were tears on Hazel's cheeks, but she'd forgotten for the moment what they were about.

On the television screen were ballerinas.

A buzzer sounded in George's head. His thoughts fled in panic, like bandits from a burglar alarm.

"That was a real pretty dance, that dance they just did," said Hazel.

"Huh?" said George.

"That dance—it was nice," said Hazel.

"Yup," said George. He tried to think a little about the ballerinas. They weren't really very good—no better than anybody else would have been, anyway. They were burdened with sash-weights and bags of birdshot, and their faces were masked, so that no one, seeing a free and graceful gesture or a pretty face, would feel like something the cat drug in. George was toying with the vague notion that maybe dancers shouldn't be handicapped. But he didn't get very far with it before another noise in his ear radio scattered his thoughts.

George winced. So did two out of the eight ballerinas.

Hazel saw him wince. Having no mental handicap herself, she had to ask George what the latest sound had been.

"Sounded like somebody hitting a milk bottle with a ball peen hammer," said George.

"I'd think it would be real interesting, hearing all the different sounds," said Hazel, a little envious. "All the things they think up."

"Um," said George.

"Only, if I was Handicapper General, you know what I would do?" said Hazel. Hazel, as a matter of fact, bore a strong resemblance to the Handicapper General, a woman named Diana Moon Glampers. "If I was Diana Moon Glampers," said Hazel, "I'd have chimes on Sunday—just chimes. Kind of in honor of religion."

"I could think, if it was just chimes," said George.

"Well—maybe make 'em real loud," said Hazel. "I think I'd make a good Handicapper General."

"Good as anybody else," said George.

"Who knows better'n I do what normal is?" said Hazel.

"Right," said George. He began to think glimmeringly about his abnormal son who was now in jail, about Harrison, but a twenty-one-gun salute in his head stopped that.

"Boy!" said Hazel, "that was a doozy, wasn't it?"

It was such a doozy that George was white and trembling, and tears stood on the rims of his red eyes. Two of the eight ballerinas had collapsed to the studio floor, were holding their temples.

"All of a sudden you look so tired," said Hazel. "Why don't you stretch out on the sofa, so's you can rest your handicap bag on the pillows, honeybunch." She was referring to the forty-seven pounds of birdshot in a canvas bag, which was padlocked around George's neck. "Go on and rest the bag for a little while," she said. "I don't care if you're not equal to me for a while."

George weighed the bag with his hands. "I don't mind it," he said. "I don't notice it any more. It's just a part of me."

"You been so tired lately—kind of wore out," said Hazel. "If there was just some way we could make a little hole in the bottom of the bag, and just take out a few of them lead balls. Just a few."

"Two years in prison and two thousand dollars fine for every ball I took out," said George. "I don't call that a bargain."

"If you could just take a few out when you came from work," said Hazel. "I mean—you don't compete with anybody around here. You just set around."

"If I tried to get away with it," said George, "then other people'd get away with it—and pretty soon we'd be right back to the dark ages again, with everybody competing against everybody else. You wouldn't like that, would you?"

"I'd hate it," said Hazel.

"There you are," said George. "The minute people start cheating on laws, what do you think happens to society?"

If Hazel hadn't been able to come up with an answer to this question, George couldn't have supplied one. A siren was going off in his head.

"Reckon it'd fall all apart," said Hazel.

"What would?" said George blankly.

"Society," said Hazel uncertainly. "Wasn't that what you just said?"

"Who knows?" said George.

The television program was suddenly interrupted for a news bulletin. It wasn't clear at first as to what the bulletin was about, since the announcer, like all announcers, had a serious speech impediment. For about half a minute, and in a state of high excitement, the announcer tried to say, "Ladies and gentlemen—"

He finally gave up, handed the bulletin to a ballerina to read.

"That's all right—" Hazel said of the announcer, "he tried. That's the big thing. He tried to do the best he could with what God gave him. He should get a nice raise for trying so hard."

"Ladies and gentlemen—" said the ballerina, reading the bulletin. She must have been extraordinarily beautiful, because the mask she wore was hideous. And it was easy to see that she was the strongest and most graceful of all the dancers, for her handicap bags were as big as those worn by two-hundred-pound men.

And she had to apologize at once for her voice, which was a very unfair voice for a woman to use. Her voice was a warm, luminous, timeless melody. "Excuse me—" she said, and she began again, making her voice absolutely uncompetitive.

"Harrison Bergeron, age fourteen," she said in a grackle squawk, "has just escaped from jail, where he was held on suspicion of plotting to overthrow the government. He is a genius and an athlete, is under-handicapped, and should be regarded as extremely dangerous."

A police photograph of Harrison Bergeron was flashed on the screen— upside down, then sideways, upside down again, then right side up. The picture showed the full length of Harrison against a background calibrated in feet and inches. He was exactly seven feet tall.

The rest of Harrison's appearance was Halloween and hardware. Nobody had ever borne heavier handicaps. He had outgrown hindrances faster than the H-G men could think them up. Instead of a little ear radio for a mental handicap, he wore a tremendous pair of earphones, and spectacles with thick wavy lenses. The spectacles were intended to make him not only half blind, but to give him whanging headaches besides.

Scrap metal was hung all over him. Ordinarily, there was a certain symmetry, a military neatness to the handicaps issued to strong people, but Harrison looked like a walking junkyard. In the race of life, Harrison carried three hundred pounds.

And to offset his good looks, the H-G men required that he wear at all times a red rubber ball for a nose, keep his eyebrows shaved off, and cover his even white teeth with black caps at snaggle-tooth random.

"If you see this boy," said the ballerina, "do not—I repeat, do not—try to reason with him."

There was the shriek of a door being torn from its hinges.

Screams and barking cries of consternation came from the television set. The photograph of Harrison Bergeron on the screen jumped again and again, as though dancing to the tune of an earthquake.

George Bergeron correctly identified the earthquake, and well he might have—for many was the time his own home had danced to the same crashing tune. "My God—" said George, "that must be Harrison!"

The realization was blasted from his mind instantly by the sound of an automobile collision in his head.

When George could open his eyes again, the photograph of Harrison was gone. A living, breathing Harrison filled the screen.

Clanking, clownish, and huge, Harrison stood in the center of the studio. The knob of the uprooted studio door was still in his hand. Ballerinas, technicians, musicians, and announcers cowered on their knees before him, expecting to die.

"I am the Emperor!" cried Harrison. "Do you hear? I am the Emperor! Everybody must do what I say at once!" He stamped his foot and the studio shook.

"Even as I stand here—" he bellowed, "crippled, hobbled, sickened—I am a greater ruler than any man who ever lived! Now watch me become what I *can* become!"

Harrison tore the straps of his handicap harness like wet tissue paper, tore straps guaranteed to support five thousand pounds.

Harrison's scrap-iron handicaps crashed to the floor.

Harrison thrust his thumbs under the bar of the padlock that secured his head harness. The bar snapped like celery. Harrison smashed his headphones and spectacles against the wall.

He flung away his rubber-ball nose, revealed a man that would have awed Thor, the god of thunder.

"I shall now select my Empress!" he said, looking down on the cowering people. "Let the first woman who dares rise to her feet claim her mate and her throne!"

A moment passed, and then a ballerina arose, swaying like a willow.

Harrison plucked the mental handicap from her ear, snapped off her physical handicaps with marvelous delicacy. Last of all, he removed her mask.

She was blindingly beautiful.

"Now—" said Harrison, taking her hand, "shall we show the people the meaning of the word dance? Music!" he commanded.

The musicians scrambled back into their chairs, and Harrison stripped them of their handicaps, too. "Play your best," he told them, "and I'll make you barons and dukes and earls."

The music began. It was normal at first—cheap, silly, false. But Harrison snatched two musicians from their chairs, waved them like batons as he sang the music as he wanted it played. He slammed them back into their chairs.

The music began again and was much improved.

Harrison and his Empress merely listened to the music for a while— listened gravely, as though synchronizing their heartbeats with it.

They shifted their weights to their toes.

Harrison placed his big hands on the girl's tiny waist, letting her sense the weightlessness that would soon be hers.

And then, in an explosion of joy and grace, into the air they sprang!

Not only were the laws of the land abandoned, but the law of gravity and the laws of motion as well.

They reeled, whirled, swiveled, flounced, capered, gamboled, and spun.

They leaped like deer on the moon.

The studio ceiling was thirty feet high, but each leap brought the dancers nearer to it.

It became their obvious intention to kiss the ceiling.

They kissed it.

And then, neutralizing gravity with love and pure will, they remained suspended in air inches below the ceiling, and they kissed each other for a long, long time.

It was then that Diana Moon Glampers, the Handicapper General, came into the studio with a double-barreled ten-gauge shotgun. She fired twice, and the Emperor and the Empress were dead before they hit the floor.

Diana Moon Glampers loaded the gun again. She aimed it at the musicians and told them they had ten seconds to get their handicaps back on.

It was then that the Bergerons' television tube burned out.

Hazel turned to comment about the blackout to George. But George had gone out into the kitchen for a can of beer.

George came back in with the beer, paused while a handicap signal shook him up. And then he sat down again. "You been crying?" he said to Hazel.

"Yup," she said.

"What about?" he said.

"I forget," she said. "Something real sad on television."

"What was it?" he said.

"It's all kind of mixed up in my mind," said Hazel.

"Forget sad things," said George.

"I always do," said Hazel.

"That's my girl," said George. He winced. There was the sound of a riveting gun in his head.

"Gee—I could tell that was a doozy," said Hazel.

"You can say that again," said George.

"Gee—" said Hazel, "I could tell that one was a doozy."

Forgetfulness

A revolutionary writer and editor, John W. Campbell, Jr., was the first man to set out to have a career in science fiction. He imposed his ideas on the field first through writing, both under his own name and his pen name, Don A. Stuart, then through his editorship of Astounding Science Fiction *from 1937 until his death in 1971. "Forgetfulness" is one of the last Stuart stories, published in the June 1937 issue of* Astounding *only months before Campbell became its editor and created what is generally referred to as the Golden Age of SF in the late 1930s and 1940s.*

Campbell developed a whole stable of new young writers willing and eager to meet his rigorous standards—Isaac Asimov, Robert A. Heinlein, L. Sprague de Camp, A. E. Van Vogt, Theodore Sturgeon, and Alfred Bester, among them. He also attracted the established writers, such as Clifford D. Simak, Edward E. Smith, and Jack Williamson, to fashion the dominant model of contemporary science fiction, a compound of scientific method, technological optimism, and clear journalistic prose, a problem-solving literature imbued with depth of feeling and humanity.

"Forgetfulness" is the earliest story in this book, one of the founding works of the modern field. According to Lester Del Rey, another Campbell writer who has gone on to become a major influence, it is "one of the high points of all science fiction." Less sophisticated in some ways than many other selections, it remains a great original.

*   *   *

Ron Thule, the astronomer, stood in the lock gate and looked down across the sweep of gently rolling land. Slowly, he breathed in the strange, tangy odors of this planet. There was something of a vast triumph in his eyes, and something of sorrow. They had been here now scarcely five hours, and the sun was still low in the east, rising slowly. Out beyond, above the western horizon, a pale ghost of the strange twin world of this planet, less than a third of a million miles distant, seemed a faint, luminous cloud in the deep, serene blue of the sky.

It was triumph, for six long years of travel, at a speed close to that of light, lay behind them; three and a half light-years distant was Pareeth, and the crowding people who had built and launched the mighty two-thousand-five-hundred-foot interstellar cruiser that had brought this little band of one hundred. Launched in hope and striving, seeking a new sun with new planets, new worlds to colonize. More than that, even, for this new-found planet was a stepping-stone to other infinities beyond. Ten years of unbroken travel was the maximum any ship they could build would endure. They had found a planet; in fact, nine planets. Now, the range they might explore for new worlds was extended by four light-years.

And there was sorrow there, too, for there was a race here now. Ron Thule turned his eyes toward the little clustering village nestled in the swale of the hills, a village of simple, rounded domes of some opalescent, glassy material. A score of them straggled irregularly among the mighty, deep-green trees that shaded them from the morning sun, twenty-foot domes of pearl and rose and blue. The deep green of the trees and the soft green of the mosslike grass that covered all the low, rounded hills made it very beautiful; the sparkling colors of the little gardens about the domes gave it further enchantment. It was a lovely spot, a spot where space-wearied, interstellar wanderers might rest in delight.

Such it was. There was a race on this planet the men of Pareeth had found after six long years of space, six years of purring, humming atomic engines and echoing gray, steel fabric that carried and protected them. Harsh utility of giant girders and rubbery flooring, the snoring drone of forty quadrillion horsepower of atomic engines. It was replaced now by the soft coolness of the grassy land; the curving steel of the girders gave way to the brown of arching trees; the stern ceiling of steel plates gave way to the vast, blue arch of a planet's atmosphere. Sounds died away in infinitudes where there was no steel to echo them back; the unending drone of the mighty engines had become breezes stirring, rustling leaves—an invitation to rest.

The race that lived here had long since found it such, it seemed. Ron Thule looked across the little village of domes to the largest of them, perhaps thirty feet across. Commander Shor Nun was there with his archæologist and anthropologist, and half a score of the men of this planet. Rhth, they called it.

The conference was breaking up now. Shor Nun appeared, tall and powerful, his muscular figure in trim Interstellar Expedition uniform of utilitarian, silvery gray. Behind him came the other two in uniform— young, powerful men of Pareeth, selected for this expedition because of physical and mental perfection, as was every man of them.

Then came Seun, the man of Rhth. He was taller, slimmer, an almost willowy figure. His lean body was clothed in an elastic, close-fitting suit of golden stuff, while over his shoulders a glowing, magnificently shimmering cape of rich blue was thrown. Five more of these men came out, each in a golden suit, but the draped capes glowed in deep reds, and rich greens, blues and violets. They walked leisurely beside the men of Pareeth. An unconscious force made those trimly uniformed men walk in step between the great, arching trees.

They came near, and Shor Nun called out, "Is the expedition ready?"

From the forward lock, Toth Mour replied, "Aye, commander. Twenty-two men. What do these people say?"

Shor Nun shook his head slightly. "That we may look as we wish. The city is deserted. I cannot understand them. What arrangements have you made?"

"The men you mentioned are coming. Each head of department, save Ron Thule. There will be no work for the astronomer."

"I will come, Shor Nun," called out the astronomer, softly. "I can sketch; I would be interested."

"Well enough, as you like. Toth Mour, call the men into formation; we will start at once. The day varies in length, but is some thirteen hours long at this season, I am told."

Ron Thule leaped down to the soft turf and walked over toward the group. Seun looked at him slowly and smiled. The man of Rhth looked taller from this distance, nearly six and a third feet in height. His face was tanned to a golden color that came near to matching the gold of his clothing. His eyes were blue and very deep. They seemed uncertain—a little puzzled, curious about these men, curious about the vast, gray bulk that had settled like a grim shadow over the low hill. Half a mile in length, four hundred feet in diameter, it loomed nearly as large as the age-old, eroded hills it had berthed on. He ran a slim-fingered hand through the glinting golden hair that curled in unruly locks above a broad, smooth brow.

"There is something for an astronomer in all this world, I think." He smiled at Ron Thule. "Are not climate and soils and atmospheres the province of astronomy, too?"

"The chemists know it better," Ron Thule replied, and wondered slightly at his replying. He knew that the man of Rhth had not spoken, simply that the thought had come to be in his mind. "Each will have his special work, save for me. I will look at the city. They will look at the buildings and girders and the carvings or mechanisms, as is their choice. I will look at the city."

Uneasily, he moved away from the group, started alone across the field. Uneasiness settled on him when he was near this Seun, this descendant of a race that had been great ten millions of years before his own first sprang from the swamps. Cheated heir to a glory five million years lost.

The low, green roll of the hill fell behind him as he climbed the grassy flank. Very slowly before his eyes, the city lifted into view. Where the swelling curve of the hill faded softly into the infinite blue of the sky, first one little point, then a score, then hundreds appeared, as he walked up the crest—the city.

Then he stood on the crest. The city towered before him, five miles away across the gently rolling green swale. Titan city of a Titan race! The towers glowed with a sun-fired opalescence in the golden light of the sun. How long, great gods of this strange world, how long had they stood thus? Three thousand feet they rose from the level of age-sifted soil at their bases, three thousand feet of mighty mass, stupendous buildings of the giants long dead.

The strange little man from a strange little world circling a dim, forgotten star looked up at them, and they did not know, or care. He walked toward them, watched them climb into the blue of the sky. He crossed the broad green of the land, and they grew in their uncaring majesty.

Sheer, colossal mass, immeasurable weights and loading they were—and they seemed to float there on the grace of a line and a curve, half in the deep blue of the sky, half touching the warm, bright green of the land. They floated still on the strength of a dream dreamed by a man dead these millions of years. A brain had dreamed in terms of lines and curves and sweeping planes, and the brain had built in terms of opal crystal and vast masses. The mortal mind was buried under unknown ages, but an immortal idea had swept life into the dead masses it molded—they lived and floated still on the memory of a mighty glory. The glory of the race—

The race that lived in twenty-foot, rounded domes.

The astronomer turned. Hidden now by the rise of the verdant land was one of the villages that race built today. Low, rounded things, built, perhaps, of this same, strange, gleaming crystal, a secret half-remembered from a day that must have been—

The city flamed before him. Across ten—or was it twenty—thousand millenniums, the thought of the builders reached to this man of another race. A builder who thought and dreamed of a mighty future, marching on, on forever in the aisles of time. He must have looked from some high, wind-swept balcony of the city to a star-sprinkled sky—and seen the argosies of space: mighty treasure ships that swept back to this remembered home, coming in from the legion worlds of space, from far stars and unknown, clustered suns; Titan ships, burdened with strange cargoes of unguessed things.

And the city peopled itself before him; the skies stirred in a moment's flash. It was the day of Rhth's glory then! Mile-long ships hovered in the blue, settling, slow, slow, home from worlds they'd circled. Familiar sights, familiar sounds, greeting their men again. Flashing darts of silver that twisted through mazes of the upper air, the soft, vast music of the mighty city. The builder lived, and looked out across his dream—

But, perhaps, from his height in the looming towers he could see across the swelling ground to the low, rounded domes of his people, his far descendants seeking the friendly shelter of the shading trees—

Ron Thule stood among the buildings of the city. He trod a pavement of soft, green moss, and looked behind to the swell of the land. The wind had laid this pavement. The moving air was the only force that maintained the city's walks. A thousand thousand years it has swept its gatherings across the plain, and deposited them as an offering at the base of these calm towers. The land had built up slowly, age on age, till it was five hundred feet higher than the land the builder had seen.

But his dream was too well built for time to melt away. Slowly time was burying it, even as long since time had buried him. The towers took no notice. They dreamed up to the blue of the skies and waited. They were patient; they had waited now a million, or was it ten million years? Some day, some year, the builders must return, dropping in their remembered argosies from the far, dim reaches of space, as they had once these ages gone. The towers waited; they were faithful to their trust. They had their memories, memories of a mighty age, when giants walked and worlds beyond the stars paid tribute to the city. Their builders would come again. Till then, naught bothered them in their silence.

But where the soft rains of a hundred thousand generations had drained from them, their infinite endurance softened to its gentle touch. Etched channels and rounded gutters, the mighty carvings dimming, rounding, their powerful features betrayed the slow effects. Perhaps—it had been so long—so long—even the city was forgetting what once it was. They had waited, these towers, for—

And the builders walked in the shade of the trees, and built rounded domes. And a new race of builders was come, a race the city did not notice in its age-long quiet. Ron Thule looked up to them and wondered if it were meant to be that his people should carry on the dream begun so long ago.

Softened by the silence, voices from the expedition reached him. "—diamond won't scratch it, Shor Nun—more elastic than beryl steel. Tough—" That was Dee Lun, the metallurgist. He would learn that secret somehow. They would all learn. And Shor Nun, commander, executive, atomic engineer, would learn the secrets that their power plants must hold. The dream—the city's life—would go on!

Ron Thule wandered on. No duty his, today; no responsibility to study carefully the form and turn of sweeping line, the hidden art that floated ten millions of tons of mass on the grace of a line. That for the archæologist and the engineer. Nor his to study the cunning form of brace and girder, the making of the pearly walls. That for the metallurgist and the chemist.

Seun was beside him, looking slowly about the great avenues that swept away into slim canyons in the distance.

"Your people visited ours, once," said Ron Thule softly. "There are legends, the golden gods that came to Pareeth, bringing gifts of fire and the bow and the hammer. The myths have endured through two millions of our years—four and a half millions of yours. With fire and bow and hammer my people climbed to civilization. With atomic power they blasted themselves back to the swamps. Four times they climbed, discovered the secret of the atom, and blasted themselves back to the swamps. Yet all the changes could not efface the thankfulness to the golden gods, who came when Pareeth was young."

Seun nodded slowly. His unspoken thoughts formed clear and sharp in the astronomer's mind. "Yes, I know. It was the city builders. Once, your sun and ours circled in a system as a double star. A wandering star crashed through that system, breaking it, and in the breaking making planets. Your sun circled away, the new-formed planets cooling; our Sun remained, these worlds cooling till the day life appeared. We are twin races, born of the same stellar birth. The city builders knew that, and sought your worlds. They were a hundred thousand light-years distant, in that time, across all the width of the galaxy, as the two suns circled in separate orbits about the mass of the galaxy.

"The city builders went to see your race but once. They had meant to return, but before the return was made they had interfered in the history of another race, helping them. For their reward the city builders were attacked by their own weapons, by their own pupils. Never again have we disturbed another race."

"Across the galaxy, though. The Great Year—how could they—so many stars—"

"The problem of multiple bodies? The city builders solved it; they traced the orbits of all the suns of all space; they knew then what sun must once have circled with ours. The mathematics of it—I have forgotten—I cannot develop it. I am afraid I cannot answer your thoughts. My people have forgotten so many things the city builders knew.

"But your people seek entrance to the buildings. I know the city, all its ways and entrances. The drifting soil has covered every doorway, save those that once were used for the great airships. They are still unblocked. I know of one at this level, I think. Perhaps—"

Ron Thule walked slowly back toward the group. Seun was speaking with Shor Nun, and now they angled off across the city. Their voices hushed; their footfalls were lost in the silence that brooded endlessly over the towers. Down timeless avenues they marched, a tiny band in the valley of the Titans. The towers marched on and on, on either side, up over low hills, beyond the horizon. Then, before them, in the side of one of the milky walls a great opening showed. Some five feet above the level of the drifted soil, it led into the vast, black maw of the building. The little party grouped at the base, then, laboriously, one of the engineers boosted and climbed his way to the threshold and dropped a rope to a companion.

Seun stood a bit apart, till Shor Nun lifted himself up to the higher level and stood on the milky floor. Then the man of Rhth seemed to glow slightly; a golden haze surrounded him and he floated effortlessly up from the ground and into the doorway.

The engineers, Shor Nun, all stood frozen, watching him. Seun stopped, turned, half-smiling. "How? It is the *lathan*, the suit I wear."

"It defies gravity?" asked Shor Nun, his dark eyes narrowing in keenest interest.

"Defies gravity? No, it does not defy, for gravity is a natural law. The city builders knew that. They made these suits shortly before they left the city. The *lathan* simply bends gravity to will. The mechanism is in the filaments of the back, servant to a wish. Its operation—I know only vague principles. I—I have forgotten so much. I will try to explain—"

Ron Thule felt the thoughts parading through his mind: Nodes and vibrations, atoms and less than atoms, a strange, invisible fabric of woven strains that were not there. His mind rebelled. Vague, inchoate stirrings of ideas that had no clarity; the thoughts were formless and indistinct, uncertain of themselves. They broke off.

"We have forgotten so much of the things the city builders knew, their arts and techniques," Seun explained. "They built things and labored that things might surround and protect them, so they thought. They labored generations that this city might be. They strove and thought and worked, and built fleets that sailed beyond the farthest star the clearest night reveals. They brought here their gains, their hard-won treasures—that they might build and make to protect these things.

"They were impermanent things, at best. How little is left of their five-million-year striving. We have no things today, nor any protecting of things. And we have forgotten the arts they developed to protect and understand these things. And with them, I am sorry, I have forgotten the thoughts that make the *lathan* understandable."

Shor Nun nodded slowly, turned to his party. Ron Thule looked back from this slight elevation, down the long avenue. And his eyes wandered aside to this descendant of the mighty dreamers, who dreamed no more.

"Seek passages to lower levels," said Shor Nun's voice. "Their records, their main interest must have centered near the ancient ground level. The engineers—we will seek the lowest, subsurface levels, where the powers and the forces of the city must have been generated. Come."

The opalescent light that filtered through the walls of the building faded to a rose dusk as they burrowed deeper into the vast pile. Corridors branched and turned; rooms and offices dust littered and barren opened from them. Down the great two-hundred-foot corridor by which they had entered, ships had once floated, and at the heart of the building was a cavernous place where these ships had once rested—and rested still! Great, dim shapes, half-seen in the misted light that filtered through wall on translucent wall.

The room blazed suddenly with the white light of half a dozen atomic torches, and the opalescent walls of the room reflected the flare across the flat, dusty sweep of the great floor. Two-score smooth shapes of flowing lines clustered on the floor, a forgotten company of travelers that had stopped here, once; when the city roared in triumphant life. A powdery, gray dust covered their crystal hulls.

Slowly, Shor Nun walked toward the nearest of them, a slim, thirty-foot-long private ship, waiting through eternity for a forgotten hand. The open lock at the side lighted suddenly at the touch of his foot, and soft lights appeared throughout the ship. Somewhere a soft, low humming began, and faded into silence in a moment. "Drus Nol—come with me. Seun, do you know the mechanism of these ships?"

The man of Rhth hesitated, then shook his head slowly. "I cannot explain it." He sighed. "They will not function now; they drew their power from the central plant of the city, and that has ceased operation. The last of the city builders shut it down as they left."

The men of Pareeth entered the ship hesitantly, and even while they walked toward the central control cabin at the nose, the white lighting dimmed through yellow, and faded out. Only their own torches remained. The stored power that had lain hidden in some cells aboard this craft was gone in a last, fitful glow. Somewhere soft, muffled thuds of relays acted, switching vainly to seek charged, emergency cells. The lights flared and died, flared and vanished. The questing relays relaxed with a tired click.

Dust-shrouded mechanism, etched in the light of flaring torches, greeted their eyes, hunched bulks, and gleaming tubes of glassy stuff that, by its sparkling, fiery life must be other than any glass they knew, more nearly kin to the brilliant refraction of the diamond.

"The power plant," said Shor Nun softly, "I think we had best look at that first. These are probably delayed; there might still be some stored power in the central plant they could pick up and give us a fatal shock. The insulation here—"

But the city builders had built well. There was no sign of frayed and age-rotted insulation. Only slight gray dust lay in torn blankets, tender fabric their movements had disturbed.

Seun walked slowly toward the far end of the room, rounding the silent, lightless bulks of the ancient ships. The dust of forgotten ages stirred softly in his wake, settled behind him. The men of Pareeth gathered in his steps, followed him toward the far wall.

A doorway opened there, and they entered a small room. The archæologist's breath whistled: the four walls were decorated with friezes of the history of the race that had built, conquered and sailed a universe—and lived in domes under sheltering trees.

Seun saw his interest, touched a panel at his side. Soundlessly, a door slid from the wall, clicked softly, and completed the frieze on that wall. The archæologist was sketching swiftly, speaking to the chemist and the photographer as he worked. The torches flared higher for a moment, and the men moved about in the twenty-foot room, making way for the remembering eye of the little camera.

As Seun touched another stud, the door slid back into the wall. The room of the ships was gone. Hastily, the men of Pareeth turned to Seun.

"Will that elevator work safely to raise us again? You said the power was cut off—"

"There is stored power. Nearly all has leaked away, but it was designed to be sufficient to run all this city and all its ships, wherever they might be, for seven days. There is power enough. And there are foot passages if you fear the power will not be sufficient. This is the lowest level; this is the level of the machines, the heart of the city—nearly one thousand feet below the level at which we entered."

"Are the machines, the power plant, in this building?"

"There is only one building, here beneath the ground. It is the city, but it has many heads. The power plant is off here, I think. It has been a long time since I came this way. I was young then, and the city builders fascinated me. Their story is interesting and—"

"Interesting—" The thought seemed to echo in Ron Thule's mind. The story of the conquest of the universe, the story of achievement such as his race could only dream of yet. They had dreamed—and done! And that, to their descendants, that was—*interesting*. Interesting to this dark, strange labyrinth of branching corridors, and strange, hooded bulks. Production machinery, he knew, somehow, production machinery that forgotten workmen had hooded as they stepped away temporarily—for a year or two, perhaps till the waning population should increase again and make new demands on it. Then great storerooms, bundled things that might be needed, spare parts, and stored records and deeds. Libraries of dull metal under gray dust. The unneeded efforts of a thousand generations, rotting in this quiet dark that he, Ron Thule, and his companions had disturbed with the moment's rush of atomic flame.

Then the tortuous corridor branched, joined others, became suddenly a great avenue descending into the power room, the heart of the city and all that it had meant. They waited still, the mighty engines the last of the builders had shut down as he left, waited to start again the work they had dropped for the moment, taking a well-earned rest. But they must have grown tired in that rest, that waiting for the resurgence of their masters. They glowed dimly under the thin blankets of grayed dust, reflecting the clear brilliance of the prying light.

. . .

Shor Nun halted at the gate, his engineer beside him. Slowly, Seun of Rhth paced into the great chamber. "By the golden gods of Pareeth, Drus Nol, do you see that insulation—those buss-bars!"

"Five million volts, if it's no better than we build," the engineer said, "and I suppose they must be busses, though, by the stars of space, they look like columns! They're twenty-five feet through. But, man, man, the generator—for it must be a generator—it's no longer than the busses it energizes."

"When the generator operated," Seun's thoughts came, "the field it created ran through the bars, so that they, too, became nearly perfect conductors. The generator supplied the city, and its ships, wherever in all space they might be." And the further thought came into their minds, "It was the finest thing the city builders had."

Shor Nun stepped over the threshold. His eyes followed the immense busses, across in a great loop to a dimly sparkling switch panel, then across, and down to a thing in the center of the hall, a thing—

Shor Nun cried out, laughed and sobbed all at one moment. His hands clawed at his eyes; he fell to his knees, groaning. "Don't look—by the gods, don't look—" he gasped.

Drus Nol leaped forward, bent at his side. Shor Nun's feet moved in slow arcs through the dust of the floor, and his hands covered his face.

Seun of Rhth stepped over to him with a strange deliberation that yet was speed. "Shor Nun," came his thought, and the man of Pareeth straightened under it, "stand up."

Slowly, like an automaton, the commander of the expedition rose, twitching, his hands falling to his sides. His eyes were blank, white things in their sockets, and horrible to look at.

"Shor Nun, look at me, turn your eyes on me," said Seun. He stood half a head taller than the man of Pareeth, very slim and straight, and his eyes seemed to glow in the light that surrounded him.

As though pulled by a greater force, Shor Nun's eyes turned slowly, and first their brown edges, then the pupils showed again. The frozen madness in his face relaxed; he slumped softly into a more natural position—and Seun looked away.

Unsteadily, Shor Nun sat down on a great angling beam. "Don't look for the end of those busses, Drus Nol—it is not good. They knew all the universe, and the ends of it, long before they built this city. The things these men have forgotten embrace all the knowledge our race has, and a thousand thousand times more, and yet they have the ancient characteristics that made certain things possible to the city builders. I do not know what that thing may be, but my eyes had to follow it, and it went into another dimension. Seun, what is that thing?"

"The generator supplied the power for the city, and for the ships of the city, wherever they might be in space. In all the universe they could draw on the power of that generator, through that *sorgan* unit. That was the master unit; from it flowed the power of the generator, instantaneously, to any ship in all space, so long as its corresponding unit was tuned. It created a field rotating"—and the minds of his hearers refused the term—"which involves, as well, time.

"In the first revolution it made, the first day it was built, it circled to the ultimate end of time and the universe, and back to the day it was built. And in all that sweep, every *sorgan* unit tuned to it must follow. The power that drove it died when the city was deserted, but it is still making the first revolution, which it made and completed in the first hundredth of a second it existed.

"Because it circled to the end of time, it passed this moment in its swing, and every other moment that ever is to be. Were you to wipe it out with your mightiest atomic blast, it would not be disturbed, for it is in the next instant, as it was when it was built. And so it is at the end of time, unchanged. Nothing in space or time can alter that, for it has already been at the end of time. That is why it rotates still, and will rotate when this world dissolves, and the stars die out and scatter as dust in space. Only when the ultimate equality is established, when no more change is, or can be will it be at rest—for then other things will be equal to it, all space equated to it, because space, too, will be unchanged through time.

"Since, in its first swing, it turned to that time, and back to the day it was built, it radiated its power to the end of space and back. Anywhere, it might be drawn on, and was drawn on by the ships that sailed to other stars."

Ron Thule glanced very quickly toward and away from the *sorgan* unit. It rotated motionlessly, twinkling and winking in swift immobility. It was some ten feet in diameter, a round spheroid of rigidly fixed coils that slipped away and away in flashing speed. His eyes twisted and his thoughts seemed to freeze as he looked at it. Then he seemed to see beyond and through it, as though it were an infinite window, to ten thousand other immobile, swiftly spinning coils revolving in perfect harmony, and beyond them to strange stars and worlds beyond the suns—a thousand cities such as this on a thousand planets: the empire of the city builders!

And the dream faded—faded as that dream in stone and crystal and metal, everlasting reality, had faded in the softness of human tissue.

. . .

The ship hung motionless over the towers for a long moment. Sunlight, reddened as the stars sank behind the far hills, flushed their opalescent beauty with a soft tint, softened even the harsh, utilitarian gray of the great, interstellar cruiser above them into an idle, rosy dream. A dream, perhaps such as the towers had dreamed ten thousand times ten thousand times these long æons they had waited?

Ron Thule looked down at them, and a feeling of satisfaction and fulfillment came to him. Pareeth would send her children. A colony here, on this ancient world would bring a new, stronger blood to wash up in a great tide, to carry the ideals this race had forgotten to new heights, new achievements. Over the low hills, visible from this elevation, lay the simple, rounded domes of the people of Rhth—Seun and his little clan of half a hundred—the dwindling representatives of a once-great race.

It would mean death to these people—these last descendants. A new world, busy with a great work of reconquering this system, then all space! They would have no time to protect and care for these forgetful ones; these people of Rhth inevitably would dwindle swiftly in a strange, busy world. They who had forgotten progress five millions of years before; they who had been untrue to the dream of the city builders.

It was for Pareeth, and the sons of Pareeth to carry on the abandoned path again—

CONCLUSION OF THE REPORT
TO THE COMMITTEE OF
PAREETH
SUBMITTED BY SHOR NUN,
COMMANDER OF THE FIRST
INTERSTELLAR EXPEDITION

—thus it seemed wise to me that we leave at the end of a single week, despite the objections of those members of the expedition personnel who had had no opportunity to see this world. It was better not to disturb the decadent inhabitants of Rhth in any further degree, and better that we return to Pareeth with these reports as soon as might be, since building operations would soon commence on the twelve new ships.

I suggest that these new ships be built of the new material *rhthite*, superior to our best previous materials. As has been shown by the incredible endurance of the buildings of the city, this material is exceedingly stable, and we have found it may be synthesized from the cheapest materials, saving many millions in the construction work to be undertaken.

It has been suggested by a certain member of the expedition, Thon Raul the anthropologist, that we may underestimate the degree of civilization actually retained by the people of Rhth, specifically that it is possible that a type of civilization exists so radically divergent from our own, that it is to us unrecognizable as civilization. His suggestion of a purely mental civilization of a high order seems untenable in the face of the fact that Seun, a man well-respected by his fellows, was unable to project his thoughts clearly at any time, nor was there any evidence that any large proportion of his thoughts were to himself of a high order of clarity. His answers were typified by "I have forgotten the development—" or "It is difficult for me to explain—" or "The exact mechanism is not understood by all of us—a few historians—"

It is, of course, impossible to disprove the assertion that such a civilization is possible, but there arises in my mind the question of advantage gained, it being a maxim of any evolutionary or advancing process that the change so made is, in some manner, beneficial to the modified organism of society. Evidently, from the statements made by Seun of Rhth, they have forgotten the knowledge once held by the mighty race that built the cities, and have receded to a state of repose without labor or progress of any kind.

Thon Raul has mentioned the effect produced on me by close observation of the *sorgan* mechanism, and further stated that Seun was able to watch this same mechanism without trouble, and able to benefit me after my unfortunate experience. I would point out that mental potentialities decline extremely slowly; it is possible that the present, decadent people have the mental potentialities, still inherent in them, that permitted the immense civilization of the city builders.

It lies there, dormant. They are lost for lack of the driving will that makes it effective. The *Pareeth*, the greatest ship our race has ever built, is powered, fueled, potentially mighty now—and inert for lack of a man's driving will, since no one is at her helm.

So it is with them. Still, the mental capacity of the race overshadows us. But the divine fire of ambition has died. They rely wholly on materials and tools given them by a long-dead people, using even these in an automatic and uncomprehending way, as they do their curious flying suits.

Finally, it is our conclusion that the twelve ships under consideration should be completed with all possible speed, and the program as at present outlined carried out in full; i.e., seven thousand six hundred and thirty-eight men and women between the ages of eighteen and twenty-eight will be selected on a basis of health, previous family history, personal character and ability as determined by psychological tests. These will be transported, together with a basic list of necessities, to the new planet, leaving in the early months of the coming year.

Six years will be required for this trip. At the end of the first year on the new planet, when some degree of organization has been attained, one ship, refueled, will return to Pareeth. At the end of the second year two ships will return from Rhth with all data accumulated in that period. Thereafter, two will sail each year.

On Pareeth, new ships will be manufactured at whatever rate seems practicable, that more colonists may be sent as swiftly as they desire. It is suggested, however, that, in view of the immense scientific advancements already seen in the cities of Rhth, no new ships be made until a ship returns with the reports of the first year's studies, in order that any resultant scientific advances may be incorporated.

The present crew of the *Pareeth* have proven themselves in every way competent, courageous and coöperative. As trained and experienced interstellar operators, it is further suggested that the one hundred men be divided among the thirteen ships to sail, the *Pareeth* retaining at least fifty of her present crew and acting as guide to the remainder of the fleet. Ron Thule, it is specifically requested, shall be astronomical commander of the fleet aboard the flagship. His astronomical work in positioning and calculating the new system has been of the highest order, and his presence is vitally needed.

> Signed by me, SHOR NUN,
> this thirty-second day after
> landing.

UNANIMOUS REPORT OF THE
COMMITTEE OF PAREETH ON
THE FIRST EXPEDITION TO THE
PLANET RHTH

The Committee of Pareeth, after due consideration of the reports of Folder R127-s6-11, entitled "Interstellar Exploration Reports, Expedition I" do send to commander of said expedition, Shor Nun, greetings.

The committee finds the reports highly satisfying, both in view of the successful nature of the expedition, and in that they represent an almost unanimous opinion.

In consequence, it is ordered that the ships designated by the department of engineering plan as numbers 18834–18846 be constructed with all such speed as is possible.

It is ordered that the seven thousand six hundred and thirty-eight young people be chosen in the manner prescribed in the attached docket of details.

It is ordered that in the event of the successful termination of the new colonizing expedition, such arrangements shall be made that the present, decadent inhabitants of the planet Rhth shall be allowed free and plentiful land; that they shall be in no way molested or attacked. It is the policy of this committee of Pareeth that this race shall be wards of the newly founded Rhth State, to be protected and in all ways aided in their life.

We feel, further, a deep obligation to this race in that the archæologist and anthropological reports clearly indicate that it was the race known to them as the city builders who first brought fire, the bow and the hammer to our race in mythological times. Once their race gave ours a foothold on the climb to civilization. It is our firm policy that these last, decadent members of that great race shall be given all protection, assistance and encouragement possible to tread again the climbing path.

It is ordered that the first colony city on Rhth shall be established at the spot represented on the accompanying maps as N'yor, as called in the language of the Rhth people, near the point of landing of the first expedition. The nearby settlement of the Rhth people is not to be molested in any way, unless military action is forced upon the colonists.

It is ordered that if this condition shall arise, if the Rhth people object to the proposed settlement at the spot designated as N'yor, arbitration be attempted. Should this measure prove unsuccessful, military penalties shall be exacted, but only to the extent found necessary for effective action. The colonists shall aid in the moving of the settlement of the Rhth people, if the Rhth people do not desire to be near the city of the colonists.

In any case, it is ordered that the colonists shall, in every way within their aid, advance and inspire the remaining people of Rhth.

It is further ordered that Shor Nun, commander, shall be plenipotentiary representative of the committee of Pareeth, with all powers of a discretionary nature, his command to be military and of unquestioned authority until such time as the colony shall have been established for a period of two years. There shall then have been established a representative government of such nature and powers as the colonists themselves find suitable.

It is then suggested that this government, the State of Rhth, shall exchange such representatives with the committee of Pareeth as are suitable in the dealings of two sovereign powers.

Until the establishment of the State of Rhth, it is further ordered that—

The grassland rolled away very softly among the brown boles of scattered trees. It seemed unchanged. The city seemed unchanged, floating as it had a thousand thousand years halfway between the blue of the sky and the green of the planet. Only it was not alone in its opalescent beauty now, twelve great ships floated serene, motionless, above its towers, matching them in glowing color. And on the low roll of the hill, a thirteenth ship, gray and grim and scarred with eighteen years of nearly continuous space travel, rested. The locks moved; men stepped forth into the light of the low, afternoon sun.

To their right, the mighty monument of the city builders; to their left, the low, rounded domes of the great race's descendants. Ron Thule stepped down from the lock to join the eight department commanders who stood looking across toward the village among the trees.

Shor Nun turned slowly to the men with him, shook his head, smiling. "I did not think to ask. I have no idea what their life span may be. Perhaps the man we knew as Seun has died. When I first landed here, I was a young man. I am middle-aged now. That time may mean old age and extinction to these people."

"There is one man coming toward us now, Shor Nun," said Ron Thule softly. "He is floating on his — what was that name? — it is a long time since I heard it."

The man came nearer leisurely; time seemed to mean little to these people. The soft, blue glow of his suit grew, and he moved a bit more rapidly, as though conscious of their importance. "I—I think that is Seun," said the archæologist. "I have seen those pictures so many times—"

Seun stood before them again, smiling the slow, easy smile they had known twelve years before. Still he stood slim and straight, his face lined only with the easy gravings of humor and kindliness. He was as unchanged as the grassland, as the eternal city. The glow faded as he settled before them, noiselessly. "You have come back to Rhth, Shor Nun?"

"Yes, Seun. We promised you that when we left. And with some of our people as well. We hope to establish a colony here, near the ancient city; hope some day to learn again the secrets of the city builders, to roam space as they once did. Perhaps we will be able to occupy some of the long-deserted buildings of the city and bring life to it again."

"A permanent colony?" asked Seun thoughtfully.

"Yes, Seun."

"There are many other cities here, on this planet, nearly as large, equipped with all the things that made this city. To my race the quiet of the unstirred air is very dear; could you not as easily establish your colony in Shao—or Loun—any of the other places?"

Shor Nun shook his head slowly. "I am sorry, Seun. We had hoped to live near you, that we might both discover again those forgotten secrets. We must stay here, for this was the last city your people deserted; here in it are all the things they ever built, the last achievements of the city builders. We will aid you in moving your colony if you wish, to some other meadowland near the sea. All the world is the same to your people; only this city was built in this way; it was the last to be deserted."

Seun exhaled softly, looked at the ten men of Pareeth. His mind seemed groping, feeling for something. His deep blue eyes misted in thought, then cleared slowly as Ron Thule watched. Slowly, they moved from man to man of the group, pausing a moment at the anthropologist, catching Shor Nun's gaze for an instant, centering slowly on Ron Thule.

Ron Thule looked into the deep eyes for a moment, for a long eternity — deep, clear eyes, like mountain lakes. Subtly, the Rhthman's face seemed to change as he watched the eyes. The languor there changed, became a sense of timelessness, of limitlessness. The pleasant, carefree air became, some-how—different. It was the same, but as the astronomer looked into those eyes, a new interpretation came to him. A sudden, vast fear welled up in him, so that his heart contracted, and a sudden tremor came to his hands. "You have forgotten—" he mumbled unsteadily. "Yes—but you—"

Seun smiled, the firm mouth relaxing in approval. "Yes, Ron Thule. That is enough. I sought your mind. Someone must understand. Remember that only twice in the history of our race have we attempted to alter the course of another's history, for by that you will understand what I must do."

Seun's eyes turned away. Shor Nun was looking at him, and Ron Thule realized, without quite understanding his knowledge, that no time had elapsed for these others. Now he stood motionless, paralyzed with a new understanding.

"We must stay here," Seun's mind voice spoke softly. "I, too, had hoped we might live on this world together, but we are too different. We are too far apart to be so near."

"You do not wish to move?" asked Shor Nun sorrowfully.

Seun looked up. The twelve great interstellar cruisers hovered closer now, forming, almost, a roof over this conference ground. "That would be for the council to say, I know. But I think they would agree with me, Shor Nun."

Vague pictures and ideas moved through their minds, thoughts emanating from Seun's mind. Slowly, his eyes dropped from the twelve opalescent cruisers to the outstretched palm of his hand. His eyes grew bright, and the lines of his face deepened in concentration. The air seemed to stir and move; a tenseness of inaction came over the ten men of Pareeth and they moved restlessly.

Quite abruptly, a dazzling light appeared over Seun's hand, sparkling, myriad colors—and died with a tiny, crystalline clatter. Something lay in his upturned palm: a round, small thing of aquamarine crystal, shot through with veins and arteries of softly pulsing, silver light. It moved and altered as they watched, fading in color, changing the form and outline of light.

Again the tinkling, crystalline clatter came, and some rearrangement had taken place. There lay in his hand a tiny globe of ultimate night, an essence of darkness that no light could illumine, cased in a crystal surface. Stars shone in it, from the heart, from the borders, stars that moved and turned in majestic splendor in infinite smallness. Then faded.

Seun raised his eyes. The darkness faded from the crystal in his hand, and pulsing, little veins of light appeared in it. He raised it in his fingers, and nine of Pareeth's men fell back. Ron Thule looked on with frozen, wooden face.

A wave of blue haze washed out, caught and lifted the men and carried them effortlessly, intangibly back to the lock, through the lock. From the quiet of the grasslands they were suddenly in the steel of the ship that clanged and howled with alarms. Great engines bellowed suddenly to life.

Ron Thule stood at the great, clear port light of the lock. Outside, Seun, in his softly glowing suit, floated a few feet from the ground. Abruptly, the great atomic engines of the *Pareeth* shrilled a chorus of ravening hate, and from the three great projectors the annihilating beams tore out, shrieking destruction through the air—and vanished. Seun stood at the junction of death, and his crystal glowed softly. Twelve floating ships screamed to the tortured shriek of overloaded atomics, and the planet below cursed back with quarter-mile-long tongues of lightning.

Somewhere, everywhere, the universe thrummed to a vast, crystalline note, and hummed softly. In that instant, the green meadowland of Rhth vanished; the eternal city dissolved into blackness. Only blackness, starless, lightless shone outside the lock port light. The soft, clear note of the crystal hummed and beat and surged. The atomic engine's cry died full throated. An utter, paralyzed quiet descended on the ship, so that the cry of a child somewhere echoed and reverberated noisily down the steel corridors.

The crystal in Seun's hand beat and hummed its note. The blackness beyond the port became gray. One by one, six opalescent ships shifted into view in the blackness beyond, moving with a slow deliberation, as though forced by some infinite power into a certain, predetermined configuration. Like atoms in a crystal lattice they shifted, seemed to click into place and hold steady—neatly, geometrically arranged.

.   .   .

Then noise came back to the ship; sounds that crept in, afraid of themselves, grew courageous and clamored; pounding feet of men, and women's screams.

"We're out of space," gasped Shor Nun. "That crystal—that thing in his hand—"

"In a space of our own," said Ron Thule. "Wait till the note of the crystal dies down. It is weakening, weakening slowly, to us, but it will be gone, and then—"

Shor Nun turned to him, his dark eyes shadowed, his face pale and drawn. "What do you know—how—"

Ron Thule stood silent. He did not know. Somewhere, a crystal echoed for a moment in rearrangement and tinkling sound; the universe echoed to it softly, as the last, faint tone died away.

"Shor Nun—Shor Nun—" a slow, wailing cry was building up in the ship. Scampering feet on metal floors became a march.

Shor Nun sobbed once. "That crystal—they had not lost the weapons of the city builders. Space of our own? No—it is like the *sorgan*: It rotates us to the end of time! This is the space we knew—when all time has died, and the stars are gone and the worlds are dust. This is the end of the nothingness. The city builders destroyed their enemies thus—by dumping them at the end of time and space. I know. They must have. And Seun had the ancient weapon. When the humming note of the crystal dies—the lingering force of translation—

"Then we shall die, too. Die in the death of death. Oh, gods—Sulon—Sulon, my dear—our son—" Shor Nun, commander, seemed to slump from his frozen rigidity. He turned abruptly away from the port light toward the inner lock door. It opened before him suddenly, and a technician stumbled down, white faced and trembling.

"Commander—Shor Nun—the engines are stopped. The atoms will not explode; no power can be generated. The power cells are supplying emergency power, but the full strength of the drive does not move or shake the ship! What—what is this?"

Shor Nun stood silent. The ship thrummed and beat with the softening, dying note of the universe-distant crystal that held all the beginnings and the endings of time and space in a man's hand. The note was fading; very soft and sweet, it was. Through the ship the hysterical cry of voices had changed; it was softening with the thrum, softening, listening to the dying thread of infinitely sweet sound.

Shor Nun shrugged his shoulders, turned away. "It does not matter. The force is fading. Across ten million years the city builders have reached to protect their descendants."

The note was very low—very faint; a quivering hush bound the ship. Beyond the port light, the six sister ships began to move again, very stealthily away, retreating toward the positions they had held when this force first seized them. Then—

Shor Nun's choked cry was drowned in the cries of the others in the lock. Blinding white light stabbed through the port like a solid, incandescent bar. Their eyes were hot and burning.

Ron Thule, his astronomer's eyes accustomed to rapid, extreme changes of light, recovered first. His word was indistinct, a cross between a sob and a chuckle.

Shor Nun stood beside him, winking tortured eyes. The ship was waking, howling into a mad, frightened life; the children screamed in sympathetic comprehension of their elders' terror.

White, blazing sunlight on green grass and brown dirt. The weathered gray of concrete, and the angular harshness of great building cradles. A skyline of white-tipped, blue mountains, broken by nearer, less-majestic structures of steel and stone and glass, glinting in the rays of a strong, warm sun with a commonness, a familiarity that hurt. A vast nostalgia welled up in them at the sight—

And died before another wave of terror. "Darun Tara," said Shor Nun. "Darun Tara, on Pareeth. I am mad—this is mad. A crazy vision in a crazy instant as the translating force collapses. Darun Tara as it was when we left it six long years ago. Changed—that half-finished shed is still only three quarters finished. I can see Thio Rog, the port master there, coming toward us. I am mad. I am five light years away—"

"It *is* Darun Tara, Shor Nun," Ron Thule whispered. "And the city builders could never have done this. I understand now. I—"

He stopped. The whole, great ship vibrated suddenly to thwang like the plucked, bass string of a Titan's harp. Creaks and squeals, and little grunting readjustments, the fabric of the cruiser protested.

"My telescope—" cried Ron Thule. He was running toward the inner lock door, into the dark mouth of the corridor.

Again the ship thrummed to a vibrant stroke. The creaking of the girders and strakes protested bitterly; stressed rivets grunted angrily.

Men pounded on the lock door from without. Thio Rog, Ton Gareth, Hol Brawn—familiar faces staring anxiously in. Shor Nun moved dully toward the gate controls—

Shor Nun knocked gently at the closed, metal door of the ship's observatory. Ron Thule's voice answered, muffled, vague, from beyond.

The commander opened the door; his breath sucked in sibilantly. "Space!" he gasped.

"Come and see, come and see," the astronomer called softly.

Shor Nun instinctively felt his way forward on tiptoe. The great observatory room was space; it was utter blackness, and the corridor lights were swallowed in it the instant the man crossed the threshold. Blackness, starred by tiny, brilliant points, scattered very sparsely, in every direction.

"Seun took the telescope, but he left me this, instead. I understand now; he said that only twice had they attempted to alter a race's history.

"This is space, and *that* is Troth, our own star. Watch—"

The star expanded; the whole of this imageless space exploded outward and vanished through the unseen walls of the observatory. Troth floated alone, centered in the invisible room. Seven tiny dots of light hung near it, glowing in its reflected light.

"And that is our system. Now this is the star of Rhth—"

Space contracted, shifted and exploded, leaving one shining, yellowish star, attended by five brightly visible worlds.

"The other planets are too small or too dimly illumined to see. When I came there was a new system displayed. This one."

Another planetary system appeared.

"That is the system of Prother."

"Prother!" Shor Nun stared. "Five and a half light-years away—and planets?"

"Planets. Uninhabited, for I can bring each planet as near as I will. But, Shor Nun"—sorrow crept into the astronomer's voice—"though I can see every detail of each planet of that system, though I can see each outline of the planets of Rhth's system—only those three stars can I see, close by."

"No other planetary systems!"

"No other planetary system that Seun will reveal to us. I understand. One we won, on the right of our own minds, our own knowledge; we reached his worlds. We had won a secret from nature by our own powers; it was part of the history of our race. They do not want to molest, or in any way influence the history of a race—so they permitted us to return, if only we did not disturb them. They could not refuse us that, for it would be a breach in their feelings of justice.

"But they felt it needful to dispossess us, Shor Nun, and this Seun did. But had he done no more, our history was altered, changed vitally. So—this he gave us; he has shown us another, equally near, planetary system that we may use. We have not lost vitally. That is his justice."

"His justice. Yes, I came to you, Ron Thule, because you seemed to know somewhat of the things that happened." Shor Nun's voice was low in the dark of the observatory. He looked at the floating planets of Prother. "What is—Seun? How has this happened? Do you know? You know that we were greeted by our friends—and they turned away from us.

"Six years have passed for us. They wanted to know what misfortune made us return at the end of a single year, for only one year has passed here on Pareeth. My son was born, there in space, and he has passed his fourth birthday. My daughter is two. Yet these things have not happened, for we were gone a single year. Seun has done it, but it cannot be; Seun, the decadent son of the city builders; Seun, who has forgotten the secrets of the ships that sailed beyond the stars and the building of the Titan Towers; Seun, whose people live in a tiny village sheltered from the rains and the sun by a few green trees.

"What are these people of Rhth?"

Ron Thule's voice was a whisper from the darkness. "I come from a far world, by what strange freak we will not say. I am a savage, a rising race that has not learned the secret of fire, nor bow, nor hammer. Tell me, Shor Nun, what is the nature of the two dry sticks I must rub, that fire may be born? Must they be hard, tough oak, or should one be a soft, resinous bit of pine? Tell me how I may make fire."

"Why—with matches or a heat ray—No, Ron Thule. Vague thoughts, meaningless ideas and unclear. I—I have forgotten the ten thousand generations of development. I cannot retreat to a level you, savage of an untrained world, would understand. I—I have forgotten."

"Then tell me, how I must hold the flint, and where must I press with a bit of deer horn that the chips shall fly small and even, so that the knife will be sharp and kill my prey for me? And how shall I rub and wash and treat the wood of the bow, or the skin of the slain animal that I may have a coat that will not be stiff, but soft and pliable?"

"Those, too, I have forgotten. Those are unnecessary things. I cannot help you, savage. I would greet you, and show you the relics of our deserted past in museums. I might conduct you through ancient caves, where mighty rock walls defended my ancestors against the wild things they could not control.

"Yes, Ron Thule. I have forgotten the development."

"Once"—Ron Thule's voice was tense—"the city builders made atomic generators to release the energy bound in that violent twist of space called an atom. He made the *sorgan* to distribute its power to his clumsy shells of metal and crystal—the caves that protected him from the wild things of space.

"Seun has forgotten the atom; he thinks in terms of space. The powers of space are at his direct command. He created the crystal that brought us here from the energy of space, because it made easy a task his mind alone could have done. It was no more needful than is an adding machine. His people have no ships; they are anywhere in space they will without such things. Seun is not a decadent son of the city builders. His people never forgot the dream that built the city. But it was a dream of childhood, and his people were children then. Like a child with his broomstick horse, the mind alone was not enough for thought; the city builders, just as ourselves, needed something of a solid metal and crystal, to make their dreams tangible."

"My son was born in space, and is four. Yet we were gone but a single year from Pareeth." Shor Nun sighed.

"Our fleet took six years to cross the gulf of five light-years. In thirty seconds, infinitely faster than light, Seun returned us, that there might be the minimum change in our racial history. Time is a function of the velocity of light, and five light-years of distance is precisely equal to five years of time multiplied by the square root of minus one. When we traversed five light-years of space in no appreciable time, we dropped back, also, through five years of time.

"You and I have spent eighteen years of effort in this exploration, Shor Nun—eighteen years of our manhood. By this hurling us back Seun has forever denied us the planets we earned by those long years of effort. But now he does not deny us wholly.

"They gave us this, and by it another sun, with other planets. This Seun gave not to me, as an astronomer; it is his gift to the race. Now it is beyond us ever to make another. And this which projects this space around us will cease to be, I think, on the day we land on those other planets of that other sun, where Seun will be to watch us—as he may be here now, to see that we understand his meanings.

"I know only this—that sun I can see, and the planets circling it. The sun of Rhth I can see, and those planets, and our own. But—though these others came so near at the impulse of my thoughts, no other sun in all space can I see so near.

"That, I think, is the wish of Seun and his race."

The astronomer stiffened suddenly.

Shor Nun stood straight and tense.

"Yes," whispered Seun, very softly, in their minds.

Ron Thule sighed.

JOHN BERRYMAN

Special Flight

In the early days of the Campbell era there was a constant search for new talent. One of the writers who responded to the challenge of Astounding *was John Berryman. I include this story to represent something of the breadth of SF at the inception of the modern period. It also gives a good idea of the sources of such later media avatars as* Star Trek, *with its heroic captain and international crew who relate to one another through tough and witty dialogue. Here is space adventure with a sincere concern for science and a real attempt at technological detail to increase verisimilitude. Some of the details are just plain wrong (there is never a lack of gravity in the ship) and some today seem quaint (the use of slide rules), but this is typical early hard SF.*

*　　*　　*

Schwab gravely unfastened the buckles on his corset, one by one, and finally peeled the garment off. "You know," he observed, holding it up and looking at it as though he had never seen it before, "I don't think I'd mind this job half so much if I didn't have to wear that thing. I swear it's doing something to my subconscious." Sympathetic laughter from the rest of the *Monitor*'s crew ran around the crew room. Space flying had its price, and part of it was wearing "strait-jackets," and heavy corsets.

Captain Feathers, a little slower about his undressing than the navigator, was still tugging idly at a zipper that refused to slide. "Agh," he breathed heavily, "it sure is good to have a trip like that one. Not a murmur out of the rockets, no detours, just a nice smooth ride in an elevator." He leaned back and stretched his shoulders.

"What's the matter, Cap, getting old?" the navigator cracked.

"Not old, Schwab," he replied with a smile; "just weary."

"You'll be another Lex Cloates before you know it!" Schwab shot back at him from the shower door. "You'll be making each trip at maximum allowable acceleration just to get it over with!"

Feathers chuckled a little at the vagaries of some of the men who flew spaceships to the Moon. It wasn't an easy life. The battering of the rockets, the racking of occasional high accelerations, all tended to age a man unless he kept in the peak of physical condition. He wondered to himself whether the dream of flying passengers to the planets would ever materialize. The short haul back and forth to the Moon, ferrying the precious ores from the rich mines, was hard enough on a man. Shaking away his moody thoughts, he stood up, calling across to Buchanan, the computer, as he did: "Hey, Buck, what've you and your squaw got on for tomorrow night? How about some bridge?"

The computer paused at the shower door. "Why, I'd like to, Pete," he replied, "but I'm scheduled out at six the morning after that, I think. I can't make it very late." A chorus of denials broke out. "Everything's cancelled for three days, dope," Schwab yelled from inside the shower. "The Perseids get here 6 a.m. tomorrow. Hines told me the last ship left over two hours ago. Everybody pulled out for the Moon."

Buchanan began to laugh. "That's a scream. First vacation I've had in six months and I forgot all about it. All right, then, Pete, tomorrow night's O.K." The showers began to hiss as the quicker ones jumped in and started the water. Feathers had just begun to struggle with his corset when the phone rang. He picked it up. "Yeah? Crew room." His face lit with concern. "What's that again? Slower, Harry." The headphone squeaked again. "Good Lord! That's terrible. Is it coming over the ticker?" He waited an instant for an answer, and then snapped: "I'll be right up." He slapped the phone back on the pedestal again, and leaped to the shower room, where the other nine of the *Monitor*'s crew were luxuriating under the needlelike jets.

"Hey!" Feathers bawled. "Hey! Shut off that water!" A few complied, and in a moment all was quiet, the men looking around shower curtains at the corset-clad captain. "Listen, men," he said, speaking rapidly. "There's been a serious accident on the Moon. Something went haywire at No. 2 Mine. Hines just phoned. I'm beating it up to his office to take a look at what comes in on the teletype from headquarters, and you men better hang around on the ready. I don't think there's another ship in the port; everybody else is up at Mines City." He ran back to his locker as a ripple of exclamations ran over the men. Most of them leaped for towels, while Feathers, who hadn't got wet, slipped into his captain's dungarees and dashed out of the room, tugging at the sticky zipper that exposed his bare chest.

The dispatcher's glass-fronted office was on the ground floor of the Administration Building, and lit, at that late hour of the night, by only one green-shaded lamp on Hines' desk. The dispatcher was hunched up in his swivel chair, leaning forward, nervously reading the tape that was streaming from the teletype. His head snapped up as Feathers opened the door. "Hi, Pete," he got out in a quavering tone, "this is awful!" Feathers went to the desk.

"What's the story, Harry?" he asked. The dispatcher passed him the tape with shaking hands. His voice seemed strained, unnatural, as he replied: "All hell must have broken loose at No. 2. Bliss got a phone call through to Mines City a few minutes ago and said that maybe forty men were caught in some sort of an explosion in the smeltery. Hey! Here comes some more now!" He snatched the tape away from Feathers and leaned over to read the purple printing on the yellow ribbon.

22,347E—06.30 AUG 10 GMT—BLISS REPORTS FROM NUMBER TWO THAT SMELTER POT APPARENTLY EXPLODED. FORTY SMELTER HANDS TRAPPED. ADVISED THAT TRACTOR WAS DUE AT NUMBER TWO AT THAT TIME FOR REGULAR PICKUP. AM MAKING INQUIRY. PLEASE ADVISE.

HENDERSON.

Hines looked up. "God, that molten metal all over the place. Wonder how any got out?" Feathers' face grew stony, granitelike in the green light of the lamp shade. He lit a cigarette. The teletype began to clack again. Hines read aloud:

"22,348E—06.34 AUG 10 GMT—BLISS REPORTS TRACTOR WAS IN SMELTERY DOME AT TIME AND WAS BURIED UNDER THE MELT. OPERATOR KILLED. ADVISES FORTY-ONE DEAD NONE INJURED. INDICATES NO IMMEDIATE EMERGENCY.

HENDERSON."

Hines' agitated face was turned to Feathers, eerie in the light as he stood up. "None injured. Those poor guys never had a prayer. What do you think happened, Pete?"

"Hell, I don't know. What do they mine there?"

"No. 2? That's tantalum, I think. Oh, that must have been frightful! That pot was filled with molten magnesium. They dissolve the tantalum out of its ores with that. When that stuff hit the air, it must have yanked every molecule of oxygen out."

Feathers walked off into the shadows of the office, out to the window that formed the front, looking out to where the floodlighted *Monitor* stood erect in her loading cradle. Her silvery sides gleamed, and from the gaping hole that was her after hatch, he could see the cranes unloading the pigs of metal, impure alloys about to be sent to the big refineries at Martin's Creek, the Arizona desert town that had built itself around the Earth's only spaceport. Just as the teletype began to clack again, Schwab came in, followed by Prentiss, the computer's mate. All four leaned over the machine, reading the tape as it passed out in short jerks as the operator rattled off a phrase at a time.

22,349E—06.36 AUG 10 GMT—BLISS REPORTS EXPLO-
SION HURLED PART OF MELT ON TO ROOF OF TANK
SHED. BOTH DOMES AT NUMBER TWO CUT OFF FROM
OXYGEN. ASKS AID WITHIN TWELVE HOURS. DETAILS
FOLLOWING.

HENDERSON.

(FOLO.)

Here followed a detailed account of the predicament of the remaining hundred and ten men at the No. 2 workings. In smelting the tantalum ores, through the use of molten magnesium as a solvent for the refractory metal, pressure created through boiling the magnesium had apparently burst the pot. The huge caterpillar-tread tractor used to collect the ingots of metal from the several mines that surrounded Mines City, the Moon's spaceport, had just loaded up after its call at No. 2 and was about to leave when caught in the torrent of incandescent metal. Those who were not in the mine shaft itself, or in the barracks dome, were all killed. The remaining hundred and ten, however, had been cut off from their supplies of oxygen by the explosion, which had covered the tank shed and its contents of compressed-oxygen cylinders with a great blob of the liquid metal.

The rest of the *Monitor's* crew had straggled in in the meantime, and after they had apprised themselves of the situation, the men scattered themselves around in the shadowy corners of the room, sitting on desks and filing cabinets, waiting for more news. Hines, behind his desk, showed a shiny, sweaty face in the desk lamp's cloistered glow. Cigarettes cut little red holes in the darkness of the corners, and soft murmurs of speculation stole around the office. Outside the glass front the *Monitor* was still the centre of buzzing activity, as the last of her metal cargo was being swung down.

The clattering of the phone burst in on the tense silence like a bomb. Hines snatched it up. "Yes?" he quavered. He listened for a moment. "Right away, you mean?" The crew sat like statues, listening. More monosyllables from the dispatcher. With a final, "Yes, sir, right away," he hung up and swung around to the expectant group.

"That was Turner. Those guys have to have another tractor right away. He says to load that one that was scheduled to go up next week, and cart it up tonight!" Silence greeted his breathless announcement. Faces loomed whitely in the shadow as they looked from man to man.

"What ship?" Schwab finally drawled.

"Well, it'll have to be the *Monitor*. Everything else is up there. They were pulling out every couple of hours all day to beat the Perseids. Last ship left almost three hours ago."

Schwab looked slowly to his left and right, and before Feathers, who was about to say something, could speak, the navigator slowly said: "That'll be nice. The ship hasn't been serviced, injector pistons haven't been lapped, and there's a meteoroid storm in the offing. Yeah, nice trip, eh, boys?"

Feathers cut in: "You'd better get me Turner on the phone, Hines. I'd better talk to him."

The dispatcher dialled the number and handed the instrument to the captain. "Hello," he spoke into it, "Mr. Turner? Captain Feathers speaking. . . . Yes, sir. We're the only ship in port. Just got back about an hour ago, maybe a little longer. . . . Yes, sir, we've been reading it as it came off the ticker. . . . That's what I wanted to speak to you about, sir. We're nowhere near ready to leave; we need to . . . Oh, certainly, I understand that. I know it's their only chance, but what do you mean by right away? The ship needs some service. Those injectors—" He paused, dragging deeply on his cigarette as Turner interrupted him, his voice squeaking in the headset.

Turner finally finished. "Well, there's something in what you say, but I'd like to see a little done to them. But what's this about radio silence? . . . Don't the papers or newscasters know anything about it?" The crew sat up; that was something new. "Oh, I see. O.K., we'll do that. But there's one more thing: what about this Perseid storm?" Feathers' eyes wandered unseeing over the tense faces of his crew as they leaned forward nervously, half obscured in the dim light. "Yes, sir. I understand that, but it seems to me that it would be suicide to fly through the Perseid storm. . . . All right, I'll call them, then, and have them ring you. Thanks a lot." He hung up, but said nothing for a moment.

"Well?" Hines demanded querulously. "What did he say?" Feathers snubbed his butt in an ash tray. "Turner says that tractor is absolutely the only hope those men have. They have to cart oxygen some way from Mines City to No. 2, and with the tractor up there buried in tantalum and magnesium, they can't use that. It's a good forty miles, too." He looked around the group. "Another thing, not a word of this to anybody; don't even phone your wives. They haven't let this out yet. We can't even use our radio on the way up."

"Say, what's he handing us?" Schwab broke in. "What did he say about those meteoroids?" A chorus of assents to his question broke out. Feathers shook his head. "He said to call the Observatory and find out from them the latest possible hour of leaving. I think that guy expects us to go, no matter what they say at the Observatory. He made some crack about our having the only new detector-calculator in the whole fleet, and that that should get us through any meteoroid storm. What do you think about that, Buck?" he asked the computer.

"Hah!" Buchanan shot back, with scorn. "That machine may be pretty good at finding rocks in the sky and shoving us away from them, it may even be the best in existence, like the manual says; but it can only do five body problems, and they come in bigger batches than that at the height of the storm. Don't you think so?" he asked his mate.

Prentiss assented. "That's right, Captain. After all, that is the first one they ever installed in a spaceship, and we've only had it this one trip. We aren't too familiar with it yet."

"Yeah," Buchanan began again. "Besides that, we didn't have a peep out of the detectors the whole trip, both ways. We've never even seen the darned thing work. It may be good, and fast, and then again it may be another queery. I don't know." He mumbled into incoherence, shaking his head as though affairs had got beyond his understanding.

"You see what I mean," Prentiss continued. "Even we don't know how well the thing works."

Buchanan interrupted him: "Oh, I imagine it works like they say, but it would have to be better than it is to get us through the Perseid storm."

Listening intently to all that was being said, Feathers had at the same time dialled a number. His connection completed, he began speaking into the mouthpiece. "Hello. I'm calling for Turner. Is it possible for a ship to leave tonight and yet beat out the Perseid storm, and if so, what's the latest safe hour of departure? . . . Well, can't you tell me that? Can't you . . . Yes, yes," he interrupted testily, "I know all that, but this is imperative. . . . Well, get the old dope out of bed. I'm holding the wire. . . . All right, call me back, then. This is an emergency, stupid!"

"Those damn astronomers!" he swore. "They're all alike. The universe is Lord knows how many billion years old, so they figure they have at least that long again to do anything!"

"What'd they say?" the navigator queried.

"Oh, some old sap answered the phone and said the chief astronomer would have to be consulted, and would I call in the morning! They'll let me know in a few minutes." He appropriated the swivel chair that Hines had left while he paced back and forth, and leaned far back. "Say," he observed, as his announcement raised no comment, "whether we can go or not, it wouldn't hurt any to have them load that tractor. That'll save a little time."

Hines waved his hand. "I forgot to tell you," he said to Feathers, "Turner already gave the order. It should be being piled in now." He bent down to peer through the window, and up. Three of the largest cranes were cooperating in loading the forty-foot vehicle into the *Monitor*'s after hold. A long hose was draped out of the smaller central hatch. Feathers inquired as to the latter.

"Oh, I guess they figure that if you're going, you might as well take a load. It'll take some time to tie that tractor down in there." Schwab, who had been unusually quiet for some time, exploded at this. "Hey, what the hell? Turner acts like we're going, no matter what. Well, you boys can count me out. This whole thing sounds like a contest to see who can think up the easiest way to get killed. You boys can be heroes. I'm keeping one foot on the ground tonight."

Campbell and McCleod, Scotch engineer and engineer's mate, joined the discussion at Schwab's outburst. "Aye," yelled the engineer, "those injectors will be overmeterin' inside of an hour, and we'll all get our guts jerked out. I'm in nae mood for the ride!" The pent-up feelings of the crew broke as a babel of voices rose to condemn or approve his sentiment.

Feathers remained silent—not an extraordinary performance for him— not moving till the phone rang again. Quiet fell with a thud. "Hello," Feathers said softly. "Yes, Feathers speaking. . . . Oh, I see. Well, that's not so bad. . . . At 2 p.m. Greenwich mean time, August 10th. What is that by our time? . . . Uh-huh. Well, that leaves us about seven hours yet, doesn't it? . . . Will you please get in touch with Turner? . . . Thanks. Oh, one more thing: what about the Moonlets? Will there be any detours? . . . No, there's no flight forecast for tomorrow, no operations were scheduled. . . . Yes, will you phone as soon as you get that, please, for a take-off." He paused, covering the mouthpiece as he called to Hines: "When will we get off, at this rate, Harry?"

"By midnight, I guess."

"Hello. For a take-off at 12 midnight, mountain time, August 9th. . . . Yes, that's it." He placed the phone back on the pedestal, turning to face the crew. "It isn't so bad, men," he announced. "The Observatory says that Turner cancelled operations almost a day early in order to avoid any possible meetings with the strays that usually precede the main body of the storm, and that we will easily avoid the front of the meteoroids if we get off by 6 a.m. tomorrow. I still think we should scram as soon as possible."

Schwab was on his feet in an instant. "Say, listen here," he demanded ungrammatically, "we still haven't figured anything about those injectors. You know they ought to be lapped thirty-six hours after every flight. Those babies are worn from this last jaunt. We'll never get there without them being serviced. For Pete's sake, can't those boys on the Moon figure out anything?"

Feathers rubbed the stubble on his jaw and looked around the crew. "The worst of our worries is out of the way," he observed slowly. "We may have a little trouble with those injectors. I don't deny it, but for the love of Mike, Schwab, there's a hundred and ten men depending on us for their lives! This is no time to worry about a rough ride! We're going!"

Schwab walked up next to the desk, where the light from Hines' green-shaded lamp made him clearly visible to all. "I hate to remind you," his slow, acid tones ground out, "of what happened the last time some wise guy sent a ship out without lapping the injector pistons. Wallace and his gang are still out there, floating around, nobody knows where. I'm afraid I don't appreciate Turner's invitation to become part of the matter making up Feathers' Comet!" He stopped, staring defiantly at Feathers. The captain remained silent. "Damn it all!" Schwab cried. "Do all you guys want to be heroes? That's cheap stuff, and you know it. Listen here, Hines," he rasped, buttonholing the dispatcher, "you're the dispatcher here. Nothing can leave unless you O.K. it. What do you say? Are you going to let these saps make the score ten more at No. 2?"

Hines' pallid face peered over at Feathers, and then he croaked: "I'll check you out. It's O.K. by me."

Feathers didn't give Schwab another chance to remonstrate. "All right, men, get back into your strait-jackets. Inspection in the control room in ten minutes."

Campbell stepped forward. "Cap," he began, and as Feathers nodded, said: "Those injectors won't be so bad, Schwab. We didn't cut a one out on the way in. We'll make it. I'll nurse them like a mother, I will!"

The navigator snarled incoherently.

Feathers spoke again: "Schwab, you wait here a minute. The Observatory is sending through the dope on the detours for Moonlets in a few minutes. You'll want that." The other eight started back to the crew room to strap their corsets and protectors back on, and Feathers and Schwab waited in front of the dispatcher's desk. "Hey," Feathers called after the retreating men, "I don't care how hungry you are, don't eat anything. We may have a rough trip, and I don't want any of you guys getting sick on me."

The navigator started to remonstrate once again with his chief as the three sat waiting for the call from the Observatory, but the captain cut him short. "Now listen, Schwab, I've had about enough of this. What's the matter with you? You'd think that after two years of this you'd be used to it. You've been on rough rides before. You didn't die. Now cut the chatter and get that sour look off your puss, or does it belong there?"

The reprimand seemed to make Schwab bitterer. "O.K., chief. Just as you say. The Rover Boys to the rescue. But wait till a few of those Perseids show up early. *We shouldn't be flying*, and you know it!" Then he shut up, his dour countenance growing, if that were possible, more tart. The word came at last, giving Schwab one little bit of satisfaction. None of the Moonlets would intercept the *Monitor's* course from a midnight take-off. Schwab found something to gripe about, however. "What the hell," he complained. "No Moonlets to navigate around, what do you need me for? I'd better stay home." Feathers' scorching glance conveyed that he would stand for no more. The two stepped out of the door and walked in silence across the concrete apron towards the loading dock, conscious of the clinging August heat of the desert.

Schwab glanced over to where the long launching ramp could be seen, bathed in the blue-white glare of enormous lights as it stretched its two-mile length up the slope. Then he bowed his head again, fixing his fierce gaze on the concrete apron as he swore softly to himself, not even glancing up at the towering hull of the *Monitor* as they approached it. Feathers' eyes shot up to the shiny spaceship, rising a hundred and fifty feet over his head, where its chromium-plated bulk reflected in bright, tiny points the myriads of lights that are strung around a spaceport, and mirrored in a dazzling streak the floor lights that blazed down upon the launching ramp. Now that the after hatch had been closed, the smooth, round hull was apparently unbroken by a port or hatch for almost its entire length. The nose, however, appeared transparent, for it was here that the control room periscopes stared out into the void. Below the quartz plates of the nose, protected by the heavy meteoroid wall, lay the control room, and beneath that, nine more decks for cargo and machinery. The stern driving rockets were hidden by the loading cradle, giving the *Monitor* the appearance of a long, thin egg held upright in an egg cup.

As they reached the loading cradle, the glowering Schwab followed the still-silent Feathers up the ladder to the *Monitor's* "back door," her lowest hatch, really an airlock, opening on I deck. They entered the lift and shot up the length of the spaceship to the control room on A deck.

II

The lift door slid open and the two men stepped into the control room. Buchanan, the computer, and Prentiss, his mate, were bending over the newly installed calculator, while the rest of the crew was disposed around the room in various postures and positions. Pease, first mate, stepped from behind the chart table and handed Feathers the manifest. "Cap," he greeted him, "all's secure. They stuck in some canned goods and five hundred gallons of milk to keep cool beside the tractor." Feathers nodded silently as he signed the paper, and walked over to the calculator.

"Well, Buck," he began, "is that thing all right?"

"Sure," the computer replied. "She's a beauty. We can get five body approximations on this as easy as we got three on the old one."

Eyeing the complex "shuffler" from its shiny new International Business Machines label to the intricate complexity of the photo-electric sorters, Feathers cracked: "Something tells me it had better do all the Fuller brush man said it would. I'm expecting a little trouble this trip."

Schwab's explosive "Hah!" jerked Feathers' head around. "Oh, yes?" he asked. "Where's Campbell? He was here a minute ago."

"He's down checking the rockets, chief," Clement, navigator's mate, replied.

Schwab yanked himself out of his seat behind the navigator's desk and stamped towards the lift. "All I've got to say," he ground at the floor, "is that that thing better be fast, and it better be good. I just can't wait till a few Perseids pull in a little ahead of their time. They aren't so hot on arrivals and departures." He snapped a glance back at the frowning Feathers. "You know what they need, don't you, Cap? A smart dispatcher like Hines to tell them when to pull in here!" He swung the lift door open viciously as it rose from I deck, and leaned out of the cage to call, finally: "Who's taking her out, Cap, firsts or seconds?"

Feathers sucked in a deep breath. "I guess I'll take her out, Schwab." He looked over to the others. "You seconds better go below for a little rest. We'll change watches every hour unless the going gets too rough." Schwab allowed the door to slam shut and the lift whined as it dropped him to the bunk room on B deck. Smiling and shaking his head, the captain dialled the engine room on the phone. "Hello, Campbell?" he finally said. "Well, what about those injectors?" His pained grin revealed that the engineer's opinion of said injectors, in spite of his optimistic sentiments in the dispatcher's office, was at extremely low ebb. When Campbell's profanity had run itself into incoherency, Feathers tried again: "Is there anything you can do with them?" Again the headset crackled as Campbell indicated his general dissatisfaction with the situation. "All right, listen, I'll be down in a couple of minutes. I want to check over the service records." He hung up after a few more words. "Agh," he grunted to the ventilator screen, "I'd hate to have another ride like that one two months back."

The computer and his mate nodded their agreement. Two months previously the injectors of the *Monitor*, apparently poorly lapped in by the shop crew, had begun to overmeter, injecting excess charges of fuel into the rocket chambers. In order to prevent enormous accelerations from being achieved, four chambers eventually had to be cut out, and the majority of the flight made in a jarring madhouse.

Getting out from behind the control board, Feathers asked: "How long before we get off, Buck?" Prentiss replied for his superior: "Less than an hour, now, Captain." The captain walked to the lift door. As he pressed the button and waited for the cage to rise from B deck, he said: "Run through the instrument checks for me, will you, Pease? I'm taking a look around below." The lift dropped him quickly through eight decks. Campbell was not in sight as he stepped out, so, with a word to McCleod, Feathers went down the spiral stairway that led to J deck. He was still checking over the service record sheet when the squeak of Campbell's rubber-soled shoes on the steel-webbed stairs made him look up.

"Hi, skipper," the Scotchman grinned, "and what do ye find?"

Feathers smiled wanly. "Nothing, Willy," he replied. "Pretty even distribution of failures."

The engineer knelt down on the deck, and began to examine the throttle setting on the injector atop No. 1 tube, carefully entering on a slip of paper the setting. He made his way around the circle of eight heads that protruded slightly through the deck, ducking under the huge girders that all but filled the tiny space. With worries over the chance of running into a meteoroid storm fairly well dispersed, Feathers, not to mention certain members of his crew, was still concerned over the fuel injectors.

Mounted atop each rocket chamber, so that they could be serviced in flight, the injectors were really tiny metering devices, Lilliputian pumps designed to force an infinitesimal, but rigidly constant, quantity of water—the fuel of the atomic rockets—into the presence of the catalyst plate with every blast of the rockets. Formed of the hardest alloys, and machined within the most microscopic tolerances, the pistons of the injector pumps still wore sufficiently with use to cause their occasional withdrawal from use. If those pistons, already partly worn from the flight in from the Moon, wore much more, the overcharged rocket blasts would become numbing, bruising crashes, racking minds and bodies until men could no longer stand.

Campbell finally completed his check. "No. 7's throttle is cut farther back than the rest, Pete," he reported. "We may have to cut that one out pretty soon. Ah, I wish we'd run down to the shops."

Feathers raised his eyebrows. "Why so?" he asked.

And the Scotchman replied:

"Why, because they've got a photo-micrometer hitched up with an X-ray machine down there. I coulda measured those pistons without taking them out of the cylinders. Once they're out, they never go back in right." Feathers nodded, starting for the stairs, for J deck, low in the tail of the *Monitor*, was not large enough to accommodate the lift shaft in addition to the enormous girders that held the now quiescent rockets in place. Pausing at the lift door, Feathers called out to Campbell, who was still below: "That tractor tied in tight?"

"Aye, she'll not budge."

"O.K. I don't want it shifting around if we start dodging meteoroids."

Pease was still engaged in the instrument check when Feathers stepped out of the lift again. At a touch on his shoulder he surrendered his seat behind the board, Feathers completing the job. Accumulators, carbon dioxide tanks remained to be tested, the pyrometers checked, before the captain flipped over the "Ready" light switch, its purple flashing over the board being repeated in every compartment of the spaceship. Satisfied that all was in readiness for the launching, Feathers plugged in the spaceport jack of the phone, and in a moment spoke to the dispatcher.

"Hello. Feathers reporting all set. Say, Harry, what's the number of this flight? . . . Four seventy-six, eh? Any last-minute meteoroid news?" After Hines' laconic "Nothing new, Pete," Feathers said: "Say, Harry, don't lower us into that launching cradle till the last minute, will you? I don't want to hang here by my belt and not be able to move around. Wait till 11.55. O.K.?" Hines spoke for a few seconds, to which the captain replied, "No, no, Harry. We'll pull out at 12 midnight. The fifteen minutes won't make that much difference. Anyway, the Observatory gave me that course for a midnight take-off at thirty-six feet per second per second acceleration, and we'd probably lose as much time detouring some of the Moonlets, if we took

off early, as we'd gain by leaving then. We're lucky to miss them, I think."
He reached up for the jack as Hines spoke a last few words. "Yeah, sure, we'll
take it easy. This won't be hard." He hung up, and unplugging the jack, he
snapped on the address system which carried his brusque syllables through
the various speakers all over the ship: "First crew to stations. Take-off in
twenty-two minutes."

III

At 11:55 p.m., August 9th, the control-board phone light flashed, and
Hines' voice came over the headset when Feathers picked it up. "O.K. Pete,
into the cradle with you. Good luck, boy." Feathers hung the mike back on
the hook and snapped on the warning gong, which filled the metal bowels of
the *Monitor* with its clamour.

The huge ship began to tilt as the hydraulic jacks lowered her into the
launching cradle, and came to rest at an angle of twelve degrees, the slope of
the launching ramp. The tilting swivel chairs were leaned far back in an
effort to keep the crew somewhere near vertical while the whole ship waited
with intense expectancy through the last few minutes. Through the periscope plate could be seen the two-mile ribbing of the launching ramp,
stretching out ahead of the ship, and off to the left the lights of the never-
quiet refinery town blinked solemnly, reflected almost apologetically by the
stars in the cloudless sky. The twenty rails on which the cradle rested were
shining ribbons that reflected the glare of the floodlights. Only the faint
panting of the air purifiers testified to the fact that living beings were inside
the *Monitor*'s gleaming hull. As the split-second hand of the chronometer
climbed up to the last minute, each man in the crew tensed himself,
gathering his abdominal muscles to resist the enormous acceleration developed by the launching catapult and the ship's own rockets acting in conjunction. Just as that hand swung to vertical the cradle rumbled into
motion.

A grinding noise filled the *Monitor* as she started her breathless flight up
the rails of the inclined ramp. After a mile of prodigious acceleration under
the actuation of the catapult, the ship's stern rockets cut in with a stuttering
roar and in an instant the *Monitor* had hurled off the end of the ramp,
flashed across the valley adjoining the hill from which it leaped, and quickly
disappeared into the night.

Following the first quick dash up the ramp, the acceleration decreased to
thirty-six feet per second per second, only one-eighth more than gravity.
Steering rockets of gasoline and liquid oxygen flashed and turned the nose of

the *Monitor* up to sixty degrees. It had long before been found impossible to use the atomic rockets for steering, since sufficient delicacy of control could not be achieved.

The spaceship climbed but slowly at first. Her departure, noticed by a newshound at the space port, made early editions under the caption, "Spaceship Makes Quick Turnabout," while the real reason for the hurried departure was kept from him. For the story that never made the papers, the news that never came over in a newscast, lay hidden in Campbell's worn injectors, in the well-kept secret that every spaceship had been cancelled out of the ether hours before the *Monitor* leaped off the end of the launching ramp, bound through a space that was hourly expecting the arrival of a great mass of meteoric material, the August Perseids.

Slowly she drew away from Earth, her initial acceleration relative to the surface being only four feet per second per second. As the acceleration of the spaceship was maintained constant at one and one-eighth times gravity, it would be accelerating at the rate of thirty-six feet per second per second relative to the surface at the two-hundred-thousand-mile mark, where the reversal was to be made. Because of the smaller acceleration of gravity of the Moon, a similar deceleration would enable the *Monitor* to lose its velocity in the remaining fifty thousand miles. While the mean distance between Earth and its satellite is only 238,000 miles, the fact that both bodies rotate, necessitating a curved course, made the actual distance covered almost exactly 250,000 miles.

While Schwab sat idly by and watched, Feathers began to place the *Monitor* on her course. The first three hundred miles, through the atmosphere of Earth, always required the pilot's hands on the controls, but, once clear of disturbing forces, the ship ran herself. Since no detours were necessary—all the Moonlets being outside the optimum course—Feathers set up a simple equation on the ruled, translucent navigation panel. A tiny amber light glowed through it, and then, as he threw a second switch, a second light, white, appeared to denote the *Monitor*'s course. Feathers' hands moved lightly and quickly from control to control as he attempted to stop the motion of the white light and to get it to coincide with the amber. Since the amber light was not, as was sometimes the case, moving, the task of compensating the point was simple and soon finished.

Schwab at last broke the silence. "Gee, it sure is tough to have nothing to do for once. Why don't some wise guy land on those Moonlets and blow them all to hell, then navigators could always sit around and watch the rest of you guys work."

Feathers smiled over at him. "You'd love it if we had a lot of meteoric stuff, wouldn't you, Schwabby? I think you'd be torn into little shreds by the conflict of your emotions. One side of you would be screaming, 'I told you so,' while the other was howling, 'Dammit to hell.'"

The navigator laughed nastily. "There's one consolation I have, Pete. Yes, sir. That dumbbell Hines was so excited he forgot to hit me for the ten bucks I owe him. And if I don't come back, the sap is stuck for it!"

The eight rocket chambers, firing in smooth rotation, gave no trouble at the take-off. The detectors remained quiet as no meteoric material came within the range of their electromagnetic fields. Since virtually all meteorites had been found to contain conducting materials, it had been found feasible to use magnetic detection, coupled with automatic calculating machines. These compound detector-calculators could take a series of observations on a moving conductor, compute its course and velocity, and determine whether a collision with the *Monitor* was imminent in a tenth of the time it would have taken human observers merely to ascertain the position of the body.

The calculator itself, built by International Business Machines, could relay its information to the autopilot in the event a collision threatened, and the latter machine could then correct the course to avoid the possible danger. The determination of the course and velocity of any single body was perfect, but when two or more conductors fell within the range of the detectors, approximations became necessary, due to the impossibility of solving the problem of three bodies. The course and velocity of as many as five bodies could be calculated in the time necessary for escape.

As the *Monitor* finally passed, with increasing velocity, through the last of Earth's atmosphere, and the planet began to take on a globular appearance, Feathers noticed a slight roughness in the rockets. "Hell," he thought, "not four thousand miles out and that damned motor is cutting up already." His eyes stole over to Schwab, seated behind his navigator's desk, and then to Buchanan, who was dozing in his deep-cushioned chair.

Schwab stared back at him with a knowing leer. He nodded his head very slowly up and down. Finally he opened his mouth, drawing in a deep breath. "Well," he slowly dragged out, "you boys wanted to be heroes. Now it's coming."

Feathers shook his head and glanced at the skin pyrometers. Now that they were clear of Earth's shadow, the Sun side of the *Monitor* was beginning to heat up, in spite of the mirror-like sheen of its chromium plating and the best insulation that man could provide.

Feathers picked up the mike. Mueller answered for the engine room. "Hello, Mueller," he said, recognizing his voice, "tell Campbell to turn her forty-five degrees every five minutes from now on. That milk will go sour if it gets warmed up." He hung up, then jerked his head towards the board as the red detector light flashed the warning that a piece of conducting material large enough to damage the *Monitor* had come within its range. With a rattle and a whir the calculators punched and sorted the cards. But in six seconds a green light blinked the assurance that the body the detectors had located would not intercept the *Monitor*'s course.

Schwab glowered in Feathers' direction. Now that the spaceship was away from Earth, discipline was less formal than ever. "Cap," he said in a sour tone, "how'd you like to run into a few Perseids a little in advance of their time?"

Feathers seemed more cheerful than he had been all night. "How'd you like to quit grousing?" he chuckled. "Your wife will think you're a hero!"

Schwab's face got no cheerier, but he remained silent.

The phone rang. Feathers, who had left the chair at the board and was drinking at the water cooler, called: "Take it, Buck, I'm busy." Buchanan picked up the mike and slipped on the headphone.

"Yeah?" he ground into the mike. "Oh, no, not so bad up here. How does it sound down there? . . . Is that so? . . . Well, wait a minute, I'll ask Pete. Hey, Cap," he called to Feathers, "Campbell says he has the throttle on No. 7 cut all the way back, but she's still overmetering. He's had to cut firing speed down four per cent to keep up as at thirty-six per second."

Feathers came from the water cooler. "I'll take it. . . . Hello, Willy? What's the story? . . . No, it isn't too bad. Leave it in till I call you. Save those others."

He glanced around after he hung up, eyebrows raised in question. Schwab, still practically relieved of his duties by the absence of Moonlets, had time to grouse some more. "That chamber will be cut out in ten minutes, I'll bet you ten bucks." As though to prove his statement, the roughness increased perceptibly. As Feathers reached for the phone, it suddenly became a jarring series of smashes, and before he had dialled Campbell, the bridge crew felt the ailing chamber cut out of the circuit.

"Christmas," breathed Buchanan, "that one sure let go in a hurry. Two more seconds of that and J deck would have smacked us in the pants."

Feathers now had Campbell on the phone. "What d'ya think, Willy?" he asked. Campbell's reply was optimistic again, but Feathers, more than a little concerned with the early and sudden breakdown, asked again, "Do you think things are starting to fall apart?" A minute later he snapped the mike back on the hook and said to Schwab and Buchanan, "Campbell says that was No. 7. It was worn worse than the rest. He didn't expect it to last. I guess the others are going along better than he had hoped."

The flashing of the detector light interrupted further conversation. All eyes were on the dead green signal on the board, waiting for it to flash "safe."

But after eight seconds the *Monitor* lurched as gasoline and oxygen were poured to the steering rockets by the automatic pilot. Buchanan, who had just had time to get to his chair from the chart table, but not enough to snap his safety belt, was thrown out, skidded across the rubber floor, to wind up against the ventilator opening.

He swore with vigour. The rubber floor had rubbed a good-sized piece of skin off his cheekbone. After a quick glance at the detector light, and seeing that it was now green, he hurried to the first-aid kit to repair his slightly scrambled features. Schwab, after noting the deviation from the original course which had occurred in escaping the meteoroid, poured power into the steering rockets and corrected the course. Glancing at the return slip from the calculator, since Buchanan was still engaged in fixing the abrasion on his cheek, he remarked: "Some rock, Buck. Mass, one hundred tons; velocity, forty-six miles per second; course, sixty-four degrees from a tangent at eighty-three degrees on the Earth's surface." He looked up for a moment. "Well," he announced slowly, "that wasn't an asteroid gone wrong, anyway. A good seventy degrees from the plane of the ecliptic. What do you think, Pete; could it have been a Perseid?"

Feathers pursed lips. "Let's see," he mused, "they come from Perseus, but the radiant moves about one degree a week. Where would that be now, Buck?" he asked the computer. Buchanan returned to the calculator and punched its keys for three minutes in silence. Finally he spoke. "That's about three degrees from their solar course and about six degrees from the angle at which the Perseids hit the atmosphere of Earth. And the velocity is almost exactly right. Well, I'll say it's a Perseid. After all, a few straggle through here all the time between March 20th and late in September. We just hit the central mass the 10th, 11th and 12th of August." He looked up at Feathers as he finished speaking.

The captain left the control board and walked over to the chart table. "Say, Schwab, do you think they will get any thicker? Isn't the front of that storm due in a few hours?"

The navigator snorted in disgust. He glanced over at his Manual but did not pick it up. Suddenly his head snapped erect. "Um, I don't know. Ordinarily I'd say that that rock was one of the regular ones that sail through here all summer, and that we wouldn't be likely to encounter much heavy stuff for the rest of the trip, but I just thought of something that I bet Hines and that whole flock of astronomers never figured on." He picked up the Manual, but did not open it. Still carrying the volume, he walked over to the board phone and dialled the bunk room on B deck. "Give me Clement," he said, and a minute later, "Hello, Clem. Say, do you remember the associated comet of the Perseids? . . . Yeah, well, what do they call that thing?" There was a pause, then, "Hm-m-m, that's it, I remember now. Think the dope on it will be in the Manual? . . . Yeah, well, if it isn't I'll try that, too. . . . You bet. Sleep tight."

Slinging the mike back on the hook, he faced Feathers. "Listen, Pete," he snapped, "maybe there's going to be trouble. Those Perseids seem to be associated with the unnamed comet, 1862, III, and it may be coinciding this year with the heavy section of the Perseid stream." Feathers looked at him, frowning, "What do you mean, Schwab?" he asked. The navigator stood up and moved over to the telescope mounting. As he snapped off the dust covers he spoke.

"Back in 1867, I think it was, some old bird noticed that the November Leonids revolved in an orbit identical with that of Temple's Comet. Since then quite a few comets have been associated with meteor streams. This particular one doesn't agree very well, and usually isn't listed as an associated comet." With the telescope broken out, he returned to the navigator's table and snapped several volumes out of the acceleration-proof book holder. After several minutes, during which the detector lit up twice, only to show the green light both times, he rose again and went to the telescope. He pressed the motor contacts and swung the eyepiece. "Yeah," he grunted, "here it is." He left the telescope chair and returned to his navigator's seat.

"Pete," he said, "we may be in for it." He swung his chair around and faced the captain. "That comet, 1862, III, has a period of a little better than one hundred and twenty-one years, and the Perseids are stretched out in a long ellipse much like the comet's orbit, and have a period of one hundred and five and a half years. This comet and the Perseids are coinciding in the vicinity of the Earth for the first time in several centuries. It may seriously accentuate the showers." Schwab stared at Feathers, who stared back in silence.

"Hell, Schwab," he finally said, "I don't see what difference it'll make. That detector-calculator will solve five body problems and shove us away from bigger groups. How close do you figure the bodies will be to each other?"

Schwab leafed through the Manual. "Well," he replied, "in that famous 1833 shower they figured the bodies to be about fifteen miles apart. At our velocity that means they'd be a solid mass. I don't suppose, though, that Perseids would get that thick, but even a hundred miles between bodies is close at this speed."

Silence greeted his announcement. The detector flashed red, and then, after a few seconds' rattle from the calculator, green again. Feathers bit his lips and read the board instruments automatically through squinted eyes. He snapped a look at the chronometer. Fifty-eight minutes. That was about seven thousand miles. He bowed his head, steeped in thought, then turned slowly to face the bared-toothed Schwab. "Do you think they're too thick to go through, Schwab?"

The navigator looked bitterly at him for a long time before replying. "What am I supposed to say?" he asked, at last. "You won't turn back now. Of course we can make it. This trip is a breeze for guys like us. Why, we'll never notice *those* little pebbles!" Feathers didn't press the point. What Schwab had said was true. The navigator suddenly began again. "By everything holy, that guy Hines won't get his ten bucks if I do get back! What the hell, Pete," he said, facing Feathers again, "we'll make it O.K. It's just that you strong men get me sore."

Before Feathers could speak again, a soft-toned gong announced the end of the first watch. He remained silent until Pease, the mate, Clement, navigator's mate, and Prentiss, computer's mate, filed from the lift. "Seven thousand miles out," he gritted to Pease. "The rockets are behaving too well, and Schwab says we're going to have a meteor storm like you've never seen. See what you can do with it, Andy."

Pease grinned his reply and took Feather's place at the board. "No trouble at all, Pete," he chuckled. "Just watch me run this boat."

Prentiss moved over to the calculator and whistled when he saw Buchanan's return slips and the notation on Schwab's navigation log. Clement, always quiet, took his navigator's place in silence.

IV

Scarcely had the lift door shut on the first watch and Clement got his belt snapped across when the detector light flared brightly and the calculator burst into furious activity. Again the green light stayed dead, while the steering rockets threw long flames to one side. For three searing seconds they jetted fiercely to port, and then gave their characteristic ending cough. Prentiss announced quietly in his reserved voice. "Three large bodies, total mass, one hundred and thirty tons, moving as a group. We apparently missed the closest by half a mile." Pease jerked erect.

"What?" he roared. "Half a mile! At this velocity we didn't have a tenth of a second to spare." He shook his head with a determined grimness. "For Pete's sake, how fast were they going, Prentiss?"

"A little better than forty-five miles a second, the slip says," he replied, "but they were pretty well straddled, must have been a hundred and fifty miles apart. We just made the grade that time." But he smiled as he got up and walked over to the calculator. "This baby is a sweetheart," he went on.

"Did you see the way it handled that approximation? Why, with that old machine, we would have breezed right through that cluster before the figures were halfway through."

Pease jabbed at the phone dial, and after a few moments spoke into the mike. "Hello, Cap? Say, did you feel that jerk? . . . Yeah, that's right. Three of them this time. . . . Sure, Perseids all right. Still want to keep going, eh? . . . No, it's about 9,000 so far, but we're picking up speed fast. It's 1.07 now. . . . O.K., chief." He hung up and swung back to the board, muttering to himself to the effect that the boys on the Moon sure picked one hell of a time to have an accident. "Hey, Prentiss," he said, without looking up from the controls, "can't you extend the range of those detectors a little? These swarms are too damned big to get around, and that calculator hasn't got enough sense to pick a path between more than two hunks of iron."

The computer's mate was silent for a while. Then he spoke slowly. "We might possibly swing the field of the horizontal detectors somewhat into the vertical and rig them in series with the vertical detectors. That would leave us less protected from meteoroids travelling at right angles to our course, but since our major fear is only twenty degrees from vertical, it seems to me that the chance is worth it. You'd better ask Otto or Mueller about switching those fields, though. That may be a long job."

Pease was spinning the phone dial in an instant. As he waited for the engine room to answer, he shot over his shoulder to Prentiss: "No, it doesn't take a minute. . . . Hello, Otto? Scram up here. We want you to play with the detector fields." Without waiting for a reply he slammed the mike on to the hook and spoke again to Prentiss. "Come on you probability expert, figure out how much we ought to deflect those horizontal fields to get the maximum amount of coverage, and get on the ball!"

"What do you think I am, chief?" he replied. "I have to have a great deal more data, especially some figures on the probable frequency and numbers of the Perseid bodies."

Pease scowled back at him, "Make it up, do something, you must have an idea. What does the Manual say? Can't you get some figures on the number of separate objects to expect?"

Nettled by the mate's sharpness, Prentiss answered with some heat: "Ordinarily, sir, this wouldn't be an impossible problem. We have some figures, of course, on the density of Perseid bodies at the height of the storm, but if Schwab's hypothesis is correct, we know absolutely nothing about what to expect. The presence of that comet will make a great deal of difference, I should judge."

Pease glared at him and snapped, "Say, haven't you got any brains? Just out of space school and you can't figure that out! What the hell difference does that comet make? This is the Perseid storm, isn't it?"

Prentiss swung around to face Pease directly. "I was in hopes, sir," he said sardonically, "that I would not be forced to explain this relatively simple matter to you." He paused to let his disrespect make itself apparent, and before the smouldering Pease could find a fit retort, went on, "It is the measured opinion, sir, of Earth's most competent astronomers, that certain comets, while passing close to the Sun, have left behind them portions of their matter. Occasionally this matter follows the same orbit as the parent comet, as in the case of the Leonids and Temple's comet. In other cases the orbits differ. When Earth, in its path around the Sun, runs into the extended pieces broken away from the comet, a meteor shower results. The Perseids, as Schwab has pointed out here, have an orbit rather similar to the comet 1862, III, but of a different period. Apparently that attenuated string of matter was broken away from the comet aeons ago. Every so often the densest part of the string of Perseid matter and the 1862 comet are in conjunction at the time Earth runs into the densest part of the Perseids. This is one of the times, and we may be visited by additional amounts of matter breaking away from dear old 1862, III. I hope it is clear, sir, and also hope that you see why it is next to impossible to form any judgment on how many bodies to expect!" He spun his chair around, with his back to the astonished and slightly dampened Pease.

Checking the hot reply on his lips, the mate waved his hand and said: "O.K., O.K. I get it. But can't you do anything with that? You can make a pretty good guess, can't you?"

Prentiss, still at the board, answered, "I'm working on it now. Give me a little time and I'll have something for you."

As though to prevent a single moment's calm, the controlroom crew suddenly felt the rockets go rough. For five seconds the slamming became increasingly severe as one chamber began to overmeter. In spite of the inches of sponge rubber insulation in its mounting, and the compound springs on which it was swung, the control board began to jitter. The needle on the dials began to dance, and the E deck third quadrant pyrometer snapped violently back and forth before winding up against the peg. Again before the mate could reach the phone the slamming stopped. Clement shook his head.

"Dizzy, pal?" cracked Pease, squinting his eyes anxiously in the navigator's direction.

"I'm O.K., chief," he replied, mumbling slightly. "That was some slam, though." He shook his head again. Prentiss sat tight-lipped at the calculator and resumed his work. Suddenly he sucked air between his teeth.

"That was some wallop, chief," he said. "It shook this thing up so much that the figures I put in here came out." He cleared the board and started his problem over again. As he swung his swivel chair to speak, the lift door opened and Otto stepped out.

Pease snapped him a glance over his shoulder as he started to rip the damaged pyrometer apart for repairs. "Was that you knocking at the door just then, Otto?" he gritted. The gang laughed for a second, but stilled when Otto leaned against the chart table and vomited.

"Ach," he gasped, "you should ride in that lift ven a chamber it lets go. Mein Gott, vot a bouncing you get." Pulling a bandanna from his engineer's dungarees he wiped his face, and spoke then to Pease. "Vot iss it ve are doing mit the detectors, nun?" he garbled.

"Got it yet, Mr. Number Man?" called Pease, looking over at Prentiss.

"I have an answer," he said, "but I'd like to check the guesswork in it against your opinions. How many more groups of more than two bodies do you think we are likely to meet between now and 3:45?"

Pease answered quickly: "Why, hell, if we met three more, I'd say the sky was full of rocks. What about you, Clem?"

The navigator's mate shook his head. "I don't know. Haven't any idea," he said vaguely.

Pease and Prentiss both looked at him anxiously. "Well," said Prentiss, "I based my calculations on ten more. I know that's a lot, but I'm frankly worried by Schwab's opinion that they will be thicker than we've ever seen them."

"Hm-m-m," mused Pease. "Figuring it that way, how much should we tip those fields?" Prentiss picked up the return sheet from the calculator. "On the assumption I have mentioned, and given the data in the Ephemeris about bolides approaching at right angles to our course, the maximum coverage can be obtained by tilting the horizontal fields fifty degrees. This extends our detector range twelve per cent."

Pease scowled again. "What, only twelve per cent?"

Prentiss, by now thoroughly out of patience, snapped back: "I was under the impression that even you would realize that the amount of power required varies with the cube of the distance of detection."

Pease ignored his tone. "O.K., Otto," he said; "get to work on it. How long will it take?"

The German grinned. "Fife minutes und ve haff it, chief!"

No sooner had he completed the work than the detector light blinked its warning signal again. The now familiar clatter of the calculator followed, and in a few seconds, another blast from the steering rockets. This shove away from danger was the longest and most pronounced yet experienced by the crew.

Prentiss punched the calculator in silence. "Two more, chief," he said, "only twelve tons." He paused, frowned, and then said, "Wait a minute. There's something screwy here. This calculator should be able to compute us a course between any two moving bodies. We shouldn't have gone for that long ride just then."

Pease's face reflected his alarm at this announcement. "Is there anything wrong with that mowing machine?" he queried. "If that thing quits on us, we're sunk. We can wave good-bye to the boys at No. 2!"

Shaking his head Prentiss replied: "I don't know. It may have been shaken up a little when that last chamber went bad. I'll run a few test problems through it." Further silence followed while the calculator rattled. "It seems O.K., chief, but these are pretty simple problems."

Pease was working the phone again. "Hello, Cap," he called into it. "The calculator may be on the fritz. You better come up."

Feathers appeared in short order. After Pease explained the shift of the detector fields, which Feathers gave his nodding approval, Prentiss quietly related the partial failure of the detector calculator.

Feathers looked around the control room a moment in silence. Then he spoke slowly: "Well, I guess you've done the best you can. I imagine that the calculator was a little shaken up by that last jolt. It's probably O.K. by now. We certainly don't dare to try repairs if it is badly damaged. Nobody here is enough of a technician." With a brusque: "On your toes, gang," he took the lift back to his bunk. No sense standing there and letting the rockets slam you on the head when you could be resting. He'd need it the next hour.

The mate went to the water cooler, but vaulted back into his chair at the board when the detector light flashed. For eighteen agonizing seconds the bridge crew waited, each man holding his breath. With a sickening lurch the *Monitor* dashed off to one side, for eight belly-tearing seconds the quartz bull's-eyes set in the port wall flared with eye-searing intensity as the steering rockets threw their fiercely driven jets to that side. Prentiss punched buttons. "One hundred and ninety-two feet per second per second for eight seconds," he read. "That's damned near a mile and a quarter. Some shove." He went back to punching his machine. "Four bodies," he spoke again, "three thousand two hundred tons, forty-six miles per second. Miss by about one thousand two hundred feet." More punching. "At our present velocity we had exactly three one-hundredths second leeway. I'm surprised we didn't see them." The silence that greeted his calm statement was almost noisy.

Pease stared fixedly at the computer for a moment. "Are you sure that thing is O.K.? Three one-hundredths of a second is entirely too close for Mrs. Pease's little boy, entirely too close!" Prentiss nodded a silent verification of the calculator's finding. Now it was Pease's turn to begin to have doubts about the relative merits of being a live coward or a dead hero. Still, as the detector remained silent, he began to breathe more easily. The rest of the control-room crew seemed to feel with him that a chapter of the trip had come to a close, as though the escape from such a close call signalled the end of the gauntlet of meteoroids they had to run. But the red light destroyed the illusion with its sudden flare. Pease swore and banged his fist down on the board as he watched for the green light that stayed dead. Another high acceleration shove brought blood from Clement's nose. He let it run while he worked furiously over the course correction controls. "Damn, I didn't even have time to correct the first blast before we scram out from under another. What is this?" he asked a little querulously.

Snapping a look at the chronometer the mate said something under his breath and reached for the phone. "Hello, Cap?" he gritted into it as soon as he raised Feathers. "Listen, the way we're using steering fuel, we'll never set this thing into the landing cradle on the Moon. You know how that auto-pilot lands us, just has all the jets going half the time, swinging us back and forth. . . . Sure, that's what I think." He paused while Feathers spoke again. "O.K.," he finally answered, "I'll call him right away." Instead of hanging up he dialled the engine room. "Hello, McCleod? The chief says to disconnect the steering rockets from the rotator. . . . Yeah, that's right, quit spinning her away from the Sun, we're low on steering fuel. . . . I know it, that milk will just have to go sour. . . . Yeah, yeah, O.K."

At 1:31 the detector again indicated conductors within its range. The calculator clacked for ten seconds, for fifteen, twenty. After twenty-five seconds of rattling, its noise subsided to a grinding hum. Prentiss burst into motion as he snapped one switch after the other in an attempt to clear up the trouble. As he worked, the light turned green, indicating that the Perseids had passed by. He cut the switch. Pease's voice was harsh. "Has she quit, Prentiss?" he croaked.

The computer's mate did not turn around to answer, but said, in his reserved tone: "It looks like a serious jam to me. Every operation has been suspended. I doubt whether we can repair it before we land."

He began to strip the mechanism of its dust covers and called to Clement to break out the instrument tools. Pease remained at the board while the computer's and navigator's mates bent over the intricate entrails of the calculator. Prentiss stood up. "Do you know, we may get farther thinking about this thing than by poking into it," he said. "Let's see, the way all this trouble started was that the slamming of that overmetering chamber shook some figures out. What do you say, Clem, do you suppose that all that's wrong is the vernier settings on the selector disks?"

The navigator squinted his eyes and bowed his head in concentration.

Finally he spoke. "Gosh, Prentiss, I don't know. I can't seem to get what you're driving at."

Prentiss looked back at Pease, who returned his stare. Was Clement a little punchy-punchy from those last two rocket beatings? "O.K., Clem," Prentiss said, "never mind, I think that's it. Anyway, I'll take a look." He went back to the calculator as Clement returned to his seat, and started to reset one of the fifteen verniers.

Without any warning the calculator's clatter suddenly recommenced. The card that had been punched from the detector's data was snapped into the auto-pilot before Prentiss could do more than snatch his hand from the flailing mechanism. As he attempted to straighten up the starboard steering rockets exploded into gargantuan activity. Prentiss was smashed against the top of the calculator and bent double over it with the sudden and enormous acceleration. Clement fainted almost at once and was jammed down into his chair.

Pease, unprepared, was likewise smashed against the side of the board chair. He struggled to lift his arm against the enormous weight that seemed to press against it, and found to his horror that he could barely move it. "Eleven G" his eye recorded on the control board accelerometer, "three hundred and fifty feet per second per second." With senses reeling in his desperate effort to maintain consciousness as his chest tried to collapse and his heart almost stopped beating, he succeeded in obtaining a purchase with his legs which enabled him to pry his body forward. He strained, purple-faced, to lift his right arm with the aid of his left, to the point where he could reach the emergency cut-out. As the rockets coughed their final note, his straining muscles threw him violently against his belt. Prentiss collapsed to the floor.

Ignoring the still unconscious Clement, Pease snapped off his belt and rushed to Prentiss' side. He did not appear to be seriously injured and revived in a short time. The telling solar plexus blow dealt him by the top of the calculator still made it difficult for him to talk. As Pease rose to get him some water, he noticed that Clement had revived and was standing behind him, staring wide-eyed and open-mouthed at the still recumbent Prentiss. "Hey, you!" Pease yelled at him, bringing him to his senses, "get Buchanan up here quick. On the ball!" As he was drawing the water he uttered a queer squeak: "Hey, Clem, straighten our course out. That was some push. A few more minutes riding sideways at this velocity and we'll miss the Moon completely!"

"O.K., chief," he replied, seeming to regain his composure. "How long were they burning that trip?" Pease walked to the board and read, "Eighteen seconds, and eleven G all the way. It's damned near two minutes since I cut them out, too." An additional forty-five seconds passed as Clement worked the problem out on a slide rule and cut in the steering rockets. "In one hundred and fifty seconds, the length of time between the beginning of the blast and when I cut the correction, we had gone just exactly two hundred miles, and we'll go thirty-seven point seven more before we stop, at three G deceleration. That's just sixty-six seconds. I think I'll set up just enough counter motion to bring us in right on the dot on the Moon. Hines' idea of an optimum course will have to be scrapped." He looked over at Pease, "Just so we get that tractor there, that's what counts, isn't it, chief?" he asked.

"Oh, yeah? Just so you get *me* there, *that's* all that counts. I'm past worrying about some other dopes' tough luck. I'll match anybody as far as being on the spot goes."

Buchanan arrived to replace Prentiss, who went below, and then Pease called the engine room. "Hi, McCleod? Did that last burst catch any of you off the ready? . . . Yeah, I know the warning didn't show. It went off by accident while Prentiss was fiddling with the calculator. . . . That's right, the silly thing blew up right in our faces. . . . Sure, what'll you take for our chances of making it?" He laughed at McCleod's reply and slapped the mike back on the hook. Satisfied that no one had been injured below, he turned to Buchanan. "Listen, Buck," he said, "Prentiss said that the vernier settings had been deranged by the jolting of the last chamber that let go, and from what happened it looks as though he's right. Think you can do anything with it?"

V

No one spoke, and the detector light was miraculously dead while Buchanan examined the calculator. Finally he laid down the insulite probe in his hand, straightened up and said: "From all appearances, Prentiss had the right idea. When the rocket shook the settings out, three of the verniers on the selector disks were shifted, just how much I don't know yet, but when the machine was operating at top speed on that five body approximation, it jammed. Prentiss shut it off before any real damage was done. At least we can tinker it into sufficient shape to get us to the Moon, but we'll be nearly an hour."

Pease, who had been anxiously awaiting the verdict, grunted. "Well," he said to the floor, "an hour is better than nothing. Get to work on it. Don't anybody bother to figure out our chances of lasting out the hour, either. I don't want to know how bad things are!"

With the steering rockets out of operation, Pease unsnapped his belt and went to the calculator to help Buchanan and Clement with their work. His activities were confined mostly to handing Buchanan tools, but that was better than watching the detector blink red, and then, after a delay that aged each of them years, blink green.

The phone rang. McCleod reported that Chamber 5 was overmetering slightly and showed inclinations of getting progressively, but not suddenly, worse. "What do you think, chief," he asked. "Should I cut it out now, while the vibration ain't so bad, and let five do the work of eight, or shall I leave it in to help the others a little?"

Pease thought fast. "Leave it in till I call you, unless it goes sour the way those others did. We'll want the smoothest ride we can get when we slap that calculator back together, so I'll call you to cut it out then." As he finished speaking the detector light flashed, but no calculator clacked into activity. The men all stopped working and waited for the green light to tell them that the conducting material had passed. After twenty breathless seconds it blinked, but only momentarily, as the ever watchful detector located an-other conducting body somewhere in the path of the *Monitor*. Finally the light turned green for the full five-second period. Clement collapsed to the floor as though he died with the green light.

Pease and Buchanan didn't move for an instant, and Clement regained his control. "God," he mouthed, as he struggled to his feet, "I can't stand much more of this. My nerves are shot." That was no secret. He reeled slightly as he walked to the water cooler, spilling water as he tried to drink from the paper cup. The soft-toned watch bell interrupted him. "Ah," he breathed, "saved by the bell."

The detector light was flashing again as the first watch stepped out of the lit. Feathers glanced around and then ordered: "Buck, you better stay on this watch. Prentiss may have a broken rib. You stick around too, Clem. We'll need all the manpower we can get on this calculator. Pease, you better scram. By the way," he added, smiling, "did you have a nice trick?" As Pease glared back, Feathers laughed, "I don't guess you think that's funny!"

Pease spun around at the lift door, purple-faced. "No, I don't," he snapped. "Schwab had more sense than I realized. We were a bunch of damned fools to try this!" He started for the lift once again, then faced the solemn Feathers. "And if you think it's fun to watch that detector light, and know you can't do a damned thing about it, your sense of humour is even more distorted than I bargained for!" He slammed the door of the lift and dropped out of sight. Feathers turned to the other three.

"Well, gang," he said, "we've got a little trouble on our hands, but there's no sense letting it get us down. That tractor is going to be dumped in Mines City. It has to be. There isn't any alternative. We'll never know if one of those rocks hits us, so why worry? Say, Buck," he asked the computer, "what do you think, should we disconnect the detector light?" Buchanan frowned and turned to Schwab for an answer.

The navigator scowled and said acidly, "Hell, no, I want to know when we've got a chance to get it. I'm not going to be denied the pleasure of gloating over the ten bucks I'll never pay Hines, that dirty skunk!"

Buchanan laughed, but Clement grimaced and asked the blank wall: "Won't we ever get there? That motor is so damned rough that my brains are getting set to come out of my nose!" Looking up into the stern and concerned faces of the rest of the bridge crew, he giggled, and then laughed good-naturedly. "Ho-ho, boys," he cried, "this is a breeze! Some fun, eh?"

"Easy, boy," said Feathers softly, and Clement's eyes widened as he sank into his chair. "That'd be tough," thought Feathers. "Too bad if he gets punchy. He'd better quit this racket before he gets permanently injured." Men of space, subjected as they were to the incessant pounding of rocket motors, often developed tiny bloodclots on the lining of the brain, whose pressure on delicate centres often caused them to manifest the symptoms of punch-drunkenness; mumbling speech, inability to concentrate, poor motor responses, and all the rest.

Feathers, Schwab and Buchanan returned to the calculator, leaving Clement sitting at his chart table. Presently Feathers straightened up for a moment to wipe the sweat from his eyes, and then paused in mid-motion as he realized that there should have been no cause for it. He stepped over to the board, where the thermometer indicated a temperature of eighty-three degrees in the control room. Now that the *Monitor* was no longer rotating on its axis in order to keep one side from being greatly heated by the Sun, the refrigerators were insufficient to keep the temperature down. He said nothing, but just after Schwab had phoned Campbell to cut out the rough chamber so that the final assembly could be made, Buchanan eased his aching back and said: "What's going on here? It's getting as hot as the devil." He walked to the board. "Whew," he whistled, "nearly ninety. I didn't think those refrigerators would be equal to it."

The rockets smoothed out somewhat as the selector disks were replaced, and after the dust covers were snapped on, Schwab said to Feathers: "What do you say, Cap, do I tell Campbell to cut her back in?"

"Might as well," he replied, "we'll see how it goes for a while. Try to save those other five as long as we can." Schwab called the engine room again, and the roughness recommenced, only to get rapidly worse. Feathers signalled with his hand, and Schwab, who was still holding Campbell on the phone, said: "Cut it, Willy. Skipper says it's too bad."

Feathers returned to the control board and cut in the steering rockets. He snapped across his belt and said: "Reversal in six minutes, boys, 2:51 a.m., the dispatcher said. What about it, Schwab, will Clem's new course screw that time up much?"

Schwab shook his head, "No, chief," he answered, "I just ran the problem through to see how the calculator was going, and the difference is less than a tenth of a second. Not enough to bother about."

Feathers mumbled his satisfaction and swung back to the board, laying his right hand on the stern rocket switch and watching the split-second hand as it crept up to the zero point. With his left hand he snapped on the warning gong, and at precisely 2.51 cut the stern rockets and snapped the *Monitor* smoothly end over end with the steering rockets. Again he performed the delicate task of compensation, this time to the slightly altered course necessitated by the long dash away from meteoroids when the calculator had jammed.

As Feathers concentrated his fierce gaze on the amber and white lights on the translucent-ruled panel, the detector light flashed. Without looking away from the panel, he cut the detector out, and finished the job. Schwab watched the whole procedure through narrowed eyelids. "Sweet, chief," he breathed as Feathers finished and cut the detector back in. He reached for the rocket switches and the drumming of the rockets recommenced, but with a heavy smashing that racked every man's body, pounded his brain against his skull, and turned his stomach to jelly. Feathers got Campbell on the phone.

"Cut that one out, Campbell, for Pete's sake, it's shaking the panel right out of its mounting!"

Campbell, down in the tail, spoke back. "Captain, there's only five going now. We can only cut one more, and with a whole hour yet to go, I sure hate to do it."

"Cut it anyway. Tank or no tank," he ground, referring to the tractor, "we've got to be alive to land this crock, and we'll all be gibbering idiots in a few more minutes." As Campbell continued to protest there was a dull thudding crash from below. "What was that, Willy?" shouted Feathers into the mike.

"I don't know, Cap," he replied, "but it sounded a few decks above me. I'll bet that tractor is shifting! I'm going up!" Before Feathers could reply the headset clicked the announcement that Campbell had hung up. Feathers sat still as the lift whined the news that the Scotchman was ascending. It went silent almost immediately, started again, then stopped. Twice more it whined. Then the phone rang and Feathers snapped the mike off the hook.

"Yeah?" he snapped. Schwab and Buchanan regarded him tensely. "Oh, is that all?" They breathed. "Hell, no. Try to shut it off. No, wait a minute,

I'll come down," he announced as the watch gong sounded 3 a.m. He hung up and explained as he took off the headset, "Campbell says that the supports to one milk tank on E deck cracked at the weld and dropped it to the deck. It split wide open. The tractor's sitting pretty."

Pease, coming up for his second trick, stepped out of the lift, and some of the errant milk ran out on to the rubber floor. The mate himself was nearly covered with the white fluid. "What's happened to you?" Buchanan laughed.

The mate swore. "Somebody's up to something. I ring for the lift, and when the door slides open, it's six inches deep in this stuff, so I skid on the deck and land in it." He slipped again as he tried to cross to the board. Schwab's face brightened as he gave vent to a hearty laugh.

"Well, Andy," he chuckled, "much as I hate to have missed that little scene, I still find myself immeasurably cheered by the mental picture of you wallowing in milk. All good things come to him who waits." He laughed again as Pease stripped off his dungarees and threw them in a wet pile by the ventilator.

"Well, Andy," said Feathers from the lift cage, "at least it's hot in here, you won't catch cold." He smiled as he let the door slide shut. Buchanan and Schwab remained, since the injured Prentiss and the demoralized Clement were both unfit for their tricks.

When the lift door slid open at E deck, milk rushed into it, washing over the tops of Feathers' shoes. Campbell and Mueller stood in the middle of the third quadrant, where the lift door was, hands on hips. The Scot turned slowly to the captain and released a blistering stream of profanity, calculated to curdle the milk. Feathers replied amiably, "Hi, Willy, what are you going to do with this stuff?"

"Do with it?" Campbell squealed. "What the hell can you do with it? Even if we had an empty tank on this deck to pump it into, we don't have any pump." The lift whined away.

Mueller spoke, "Looks like the supports to the tank crystallized and cracked at the welds, sir. It might be a good idea to take a look at the other tank, too."

As Campbell sloshed over to examine the supporting brackets of the second two hundred and fifty gallon tank, the lift whined again, and McCleod stepped out. "Gosh," he exclaimed, "I might have expected it of you, Willy!" Campbell's contorted features relaxed slightly.

"Is our engine room floating with this stuff?" he queried.

His mate replied, "Aye, and it ran down the stair-well, too. J deck looks beautiful from the throttle pedestal."

Mueller, who had completed the examination of the second tank's supports, straightened up. "Looks like this one is cracked, too. We'd better weld a couple of supports in here." As Campbell nodded his O.K., he left by the lift to return in a few minutes with the portable welder in its dolly and four half-inch steel rods.

McCleod reached for the rods. "Here, Mueller, I'll take 'em," he said. "Willy and I will have this done in no time."

Feathers swore with quiet vigour as he moved to the lift door preparatory to going to his bunk on B deck, sloshing through the milk, his oaths forming a soft obbligato to Campbell and McCleod, who were sulphuric in their opinions of motors that shook ships to pieces, doubly sulphuric with welds that cracked, and triply sulphuric with each other in their impatience. He shot the lift to C deck. Only food in cans here. Nothing that the milk would hurt. He opened the door and let the white liquid run out, and then rose to B deck, where he changed his dungarees and rode up again to the control room. Pease was at the board. "Hi, Cap," he called, "we haven't been close to one since you've left, if you've noticed. Only three warnings. I guess we're through the worst of them." Feathers smiled and sat down next to the water cooler and sipped slowly from a paper cup.

While a peaceful quiet was slowly settling, the detector light went red, and the calculator clacked noisily, to be followed by the flash of the top rockets. The light stayed red and the calculator did not pause as the detector located more conducting material before the first had passed. With a jerk that made necks crack, the steering rockets suddenly reversed their blasting, jamming the crew against their belts with an eight G shove. Still the light stayed red, while the *Monitor* dashed away from its course in a new direction. Pease, at the board, felt himself blacking out as the high acceleration continued past its thirtieth second. He vaguely heard Feathers yell, above the scream of the rockets, "Cut them out, Pease, cut them out!" The mate struggled to obey, finally reached the switch and the rockets died.

Schwab glowered across the control room, "What's the matter, chief, can't you take it? We'll get it sure, the sky is lousy with them!"

Without replying, Feathers snapped a question at Pease. "How much fuel left, Andy?" he asked.

The mate replied, "Wow, just fifty-three seconds at five G!" He turned wide-eyed to Feathers. "Say, Cap, you can't much more than land her with that!"

Again Feathers did not reply. "I'll take over, Andy," he said. Pease changed seats with him. Once behind the board, Feathers looked at the chronometer and read aloud: "3.12. Thirty-three minutes till the Moon cuts off those Perseids. At the rate we were using steering fuel, we never would have been able to land this crock. Might as well get hit with a rock as smash the Moon so hard that we cash in." He snapped the detector switch. The light stayed dead. "Well," he commented, "I guess we're through that swarm. If we're lucky, we'll last out."

At 3.28 the flashing of the detector signalled the location of conducting material. The steering rockets flared within seconds, and after they coughed into silence, Feathers read: "Forty-four seconds!" He glanced into the faces of the others. "One more shot is all we dare to risk. That auto-pilot needs about forty seconds at five G to land us. Any less than that and we'll drop in from wherever we run out."

Quiet fell over the control room. There was an audible sucking of breaths as the detector light flared red—then green, to the accompaniment of expelled sighs. Eight minutes before the deadline, when the Moon would cut across the path of the Perseids, it flared red again, stayed red while the calculator rattled and clattered. The port and lower rockets screamed into fiery action. Feathers, teeth bared, gripped the steering rocket switch. He watched the fuel gauge—forty seconds left, thirty-six—thirty-two. He cut the switch. The four sat immobile, waiting for the crash. The green light from the detector came like the crash of a cymbal. Feathers rasped hoarsely: "Thirty-one seconds left. I'll have to leave it off." He threw a second switch, and snapping the intense Schwab a twinkling glance, said, "Ten bucks or no ten bucks, Schwab, I'm cutting that light, too!"

"3.39," the chronometer read. Six minutes more. Feathers broke the silence. "If we last five minutes more, we have a chance. I'm going to try to get this boat close enough to the landing cradle to let the auto-pilot swing us in with only thirty seconds of fuel." Feathers squinted in thought. "Buck," he said slowly, "I want to stop this buggy as near dead as we can with the tail rockets, right over the landing cradle, and want to be approaching the cradle at an angle of two degrees. The cradle's ramp slopes at six degrees, so we want to hit the Moon at eight degrees to a tangent. Acceleration at the surface is five and a third feet per second per second. Figure out what our velocity will have to be if I can get this crock within one hundred and fifty feet of the cradle."

While Buchanan was working the problem out, the chronometer reached 3.45, but the event was scarcely noticed, for with one danger past, the crew knew that a second, and much more apparent one, still faced them. Their chance of reaching the surface alive depended on Feathers' ability to control the *Monitor* with tail rockets instead of steering rockets, to keep it from slewing from its course as their velocity was braked with the incomplete battery of rockets. Buchanan spun his chair.

"Here it is, chief," he said. "You'll have to do twenty-seven hundred feet per second to hit the cradle at two degrees from one hundred and fifty feet."

Feathers shook his head. "That's too fast. That cradle only does seventeen-fifty. What altitude will I have to bring the crock to, to make the cradle at that angle?"

The calculator clacked.

"One hundred and eighteen feet, Cap," Buchanan read tersely, recalling as he did that the auto-pilot usually took over around a thousand feet, with velocity slowed to around a thousand feet per second, a feat not so dangerous at higher altitudes.

"Guess we'll have to try it. Bring her in straight and fast, tail first, break her speed with the tail rockets, and then flip her over quick and drop her in with automatic control for the last ten seconds or so. Schwab, it's about time we scrapped Turner's radio-silence order. Get Mines City on the set. Things are too tough. If they don't put Henderson on when you indicate we're in trouble, ask for him."

While Feathers broke the fall of the *Monitor* and guided her towards the desired spot on the Moon, Schwab established contact with the powerful radio station at Mines City, on the Moon's surface, and spoke into the radio mike. "May Day," he said laconically, giving the traditional English version of the international signal for aid, "M'aidez!" He was instantly connected with the superintendent of flight operations, Henderson. "Just a moment," Schwab said to him, and called to Feathers: "Here's Henderson for you, chief, and all agog." Feathers snapped the selector switch of his headset and chest microphone and spoke.

"Hello, Henderson? . . . Feathers. We're coming in in about seven minutes." He paused as the superintendent interrupted him. At last he cut in: "Hold it! We aren't down yet. Listen to me. We're about five hundred miles out yet, and decelerating at thirty-six per, but we're so damned short on steering fuel that we'll run out if we land on the radio beam, with the auto-pilot." Henderson's voice squeaked in the earphones again. "Yes, sir," Feathers responded. "The tractor's all right, chief, but I'm telling you, we're going to have our troubles getting down." He looked around at the anxious faces of the bridge crew, then began again, as Henderson's reply was brief: "Look, chief, I'll have to bring her in pretty low by myself, tail first, and use the auto-pilot for the last few seconds only. Suit you?" Curt syllables snapped in his ears. "What's the most speed you can get out of that cradle?" he asked again. "Oh, I see. Well, that means I'll have to bring this baby down to about a hundred feet before I cut you in. Tell you what. I'll make a pass at the ramp, and if we're going too fast according to the radio beam, let me know, and I'll pull her up and over and try again till I make the grade. Only got enough fuel for a couple of shots, though, and I can only give your auto-pilot about ten seconds at five G."

Henderson then spoke for some moments, while Buchanan got to work on the calculator, converting the co-ordinates that Schwab was reading off from his position at the low-power telescope, into their course and velocity figures. Finally Feathers concluded: "You better save that, Henderson. This trick isn't over yet. Wait till we set it down. Any more news from No. 2?" Receiving a negative reply, he snapped the set off for a moment and called over to the navigator: "Henderson's laying it on thick, Schwab. You'll be a hero!" Flipping over the address-system switch, he snapped: "Tie in tight, boys; this may be a little rough!" One quick look at the schedule, a grin, and he said, half to himself: "Right on time. Hines said we'd make it at 4.07."

Schwab and Buchanan, duties completed, sat with their eyes burning towards Feathers' hands as they snapped back and forth across the board, while Pease, who was a competent pilot in his own right, went through the tortures of the damned as he had to sit and watch his superior make the approach. His hands made little jerking movements as he involuntarily tried to correct Feathers' actions. Always a ticklish task, and calling for the fastest and most accurate co-ordination, landing was, under the conditions facing Feathers, infinitely more difficult.

The surface grew amazingly close, and the *Monitor* was still travelling better than five thousand feet per second, tail first, as the whole trip following the reversal had been made. Suddenly Feathers cut in the port steering rockets for a quick blast. The *Monitor* was now heading almost parallel with the surface, still tail first, all her downward velocity killed by the blasting of the tail rockets, but possessed of a lateral velocity of nearly three thousand feet per second that Feathers had gradually built up as they had approached the surface. In another second the rockets fired roughly, slamming all down tight into their seats in a four G deceleration, and then, with that unbelievable quickness that he had, Feathers snapped the space-ship end over end. He spoke into the mike: "O.K., Henderson, here we come!"

The *Monitor* sped towards the head of the landing ramp. Feathers' headset crackled; he swore and snapped on the tail and steering rockets. Up went the nose, and the ship climbed dizzily in a hundred-mile loop, snapping over as it neared the Moon's surface again, so that the tail rockets might once more be used as a brake. Again the speed was too great for the cradle, and an instant before the *Monitor* passed the speeding Juggernaut on rails, Henderson signalled them off. Feathers grunted as he hung from his belt at the top of the huge loop. "This is it. Twelve seconds fuel to go."

The second enormous loop completed, the spaceship dashed across the surface of the Moon, perilously close to a range of low volcanic hills, its shadow leaping across the rough terrain with it. The tail rockets stuttered harshly, roughly braking the speed of the gleaming craft. Feathers abruptly flipped her over, steadied her momentarily with the steering rockets before gritting between his teeth: "Seven seconds of fuel. It's two to one against us." He switched on the automatic pilot as Henderson's voice snapped a breathless, "O.K., Pete!" into his headset. The spaceship sagged down, almost to the cradle, under rockets flaring, before they coughed their final note. The huge craft dropped the remaining distance, wrecking half the instruments on the panel as the heavy ship bounced back and forth before the magnets of the cradle held her firm. Down the ramp the composite vehicle hurled, braking rockets throwing prodigious silent-screaming jets of incandescent gas ahead of it, and came to rest at the end of the ramp.

Figures waddled from the Administration Building in distended space-suits, casting dead-black shadows on the glaring pumice, climbed into the cab of the cradle, and shunted it across switches to the hangar, a great, hemispherical dome of metal. Once inside, the enormous air lock closed; the dome lights high above came up and bathed the interior of the hemi-sphere with a dull pallor. Huge overhead cranes lowered their magnetic grapples, pulling the *Monitor* erect for unloading, as the increasing air pressure made the spacesuits of the docking crew go flabby. More figures aided in setting the telescopic props against the hull to hold it erect. With air pressure finally at normal, the various air locks around the dome opened, and every person who was free at the whole spaceport streamed through the openings and dashed towards the frosting spaceship.

Their shouts of welcome and praise quieted down as the lowest port of the spaceship remained closed, and the seconds passed by slowly. At last, with a shower of hoarfrost flakes, Campbell cracked the "back door," and the cheering redoubled again. The thin stream of milk that ran out and down the frost-whitened plates passed unnoticed, and the men were quickly rushed into the flight superintendent's office.

In the comparative quiet, Henderson was at last able to speak to the men, while outside the space-port crew were rushing through the task of unload-ing the tractor. With the last well-wisher pushed out of the door, Henderson ran over to Feathers' side, grasped his hand, and as he shook it energetically, cried: "Oh, sweet landing, Pete! One more pass at that ramp and I'd have died of suspense!"

Feathers grinned feebly, but said nothing. The rest of the crew, now that the tension was relieved, were experiencing a like reaction. Most of them were looking around for some place to sit down, feeling generally miserable from the space beating they had taken.

The bubbling Henderson started similarly congratulating the rest of the crew, slapping one man on the back, shaking another's hand. "Is everybody O.K.?" he asked, in general.

Feathers stirred out of his lethargy. "Oh, yes. Better have a look at Prentiss," he replied. "He may have cracked a rib." He glanced around at the still-wet Pease, the soaking McCleod and Campbell, the unenthusiastic, sober faces of the crew, and then to his own wet feet. "One more casualty," he announced, so that all could hear. "Most of us got our feet wet. This space travel isn't safe. You might catch cold!"

Chronopolis

In the late 1950s J. G. Ballard began to publish SF stories of an entirely new type—cold, intellectual, sophisticated, and stylistically complex, treating science as a repository of symbols and images. Ballard quickly attracted admirers, and in the early 1960s a "new thing" was proclaimed in England by the young editor and writer Michael Moorcock. Thus was the New Wave of the 1960s born, taking Ballard as its model and representative writer. With Moorcock as his prophet, Ballard symbolized a wholesale reaction against both the conservative style and the atmosphere of technological optimism that permeated Campbellian science fiction. As stories about the city of the future, it is interesting to compare "Chronopolis," published in 1961, with "Forgetfulness," published in 1937.

*　　*　　*

His trial had been fixed for the next day. Exactly when, of course, neither Newman nor anyone else knew. Probably it would be during the afternoon, when the principals concerned,—judge, jury and prosecutor—managed to converge on the same courtroom at the same time. With luck his defense attorney might also appear at the right moment, though the case was such an open and shut one that Newman hardly expected him to bother—besides, transport to and from the old penal complex was notoriously difficult, involved endless waiting in the grimy depot below the prison walls.

Newman had passed the time usefully. Luckily, his cell faced south and sunlight traversed it for most of the day. He divided its arc into ten equal segments, the effective daylight hours, marking the intervals with a wedge of mortar prised from the window ledge. Each segment he further subdivided into twelve smaller units.

Immediately he had a working timepiece, accurate to within virtually a minute (the final subdivision into fifths he made mentally). The sweep of white notches, curving down one wall, across the floor and metal bedstead, and up the other wall, would have been recognizable to anyone who stood with his back to the window, but no one ever did. Anyway, the guards were too stupid to understand, and the sundial had given Newman a tremendous advantage over them. Most of the time, when he wasn't recalibrating the dial, he would press against the grille, keeping an eye on the orderly room.

"Brocken!" he would shout out at seven-fifteen as the shadow line hit the first interval. "Morning inspection! On your feet, man!" The sergeant would come stumbling out of his bunk in a sweat, rising the other warders as the reveille bell split the air.

Later, Newman sang out the other events on the daily roster: roll call, cell fatigues, breakfast, exercise, and so on around to the evening roll just before dusk. Brocken regularly won the block merit for the best-run cell deck and he relied on Newman to program the day for him, anticipate the next item on the roster, and warn him if anything went on for too long—in some of the other blocks fatigues were usually over in three minutes while breakfast or exercise could go on for hours, none of the warders knowing when to stop, the prisoners insisting that they had only just begun.

Brocken never inquired how Newman organized everything so exactly; once or twice a week, when it rained or was overcast, Newman would be strangely silent, and the resulting confusion reminded the sergeant forcefully of the merits of cooperation. Newman was kept in cell privileges and all the cigarettes he needed. It was a shame that a date for the trial had finally been named.

Newman, too, was sorry. Most of his research so far had been inconclusive. Primarily his problem was that, given a northward-facing cell for the bulk of his sentence, the task of estimating the time might become impossible. The inclination of the shadows in the exercise yards or across the towers and walls provided too blunt a reading. Calibration would have to be visual; an optical instrument would soon be discovered.

What he needed was an internal timepiece, an unconsciously operating psychic mechanism regulated, say, by his pulse or respiratory rhythms. He had tried to train his time sense, running an elaborate series of tests to estimate its minimum in-built error, and this had been disappointingly large. The chances of conditioning an accurate reflex seemed slim.

However, unless he could tell the exact time at any given moment, he knew he would go mad.

His obsession, which now faced him with a charge of murder, had revealed itself innocently enough.

As a child, like all children, he had noticed the occasional ancient clock tower, bearing the same white circle with its twelve intervals. In the seedier areas of the city the round characteristic dials often hung over the cheap jewelry stores, rusting and derelict.

"Just signs," his mother explained. "They don't mean anything, like stars or rings."

Pointless embellishment, he had thought.

Once, in an old furniture shop, they had seen a clock with hands, upside down in a box full of fire irons and miscellaneous rubbish.

"Eleven and twelve," he had pointed out. "What does it mean?"

His mother had hurried him away, reminding herself never to visit that street again. "Nothing," she told him sharply. "It's all finished." To herself she added experimentally: Five and twelve. Five *to* twelve. Yes.

Time unfolded at its usual sluggish, half-confused pace. They lived in a ramshackle house in one of the amorphous suburbs, a zone of endless afternoons. Sometimes he went to school, until he was ten spent most of his time with his mother queueing outside the closed food stores. In the evenings he would play with the neighborhood gang around the abandoned railway station, punting a homemade flatcar along the overgrown tracks, or break into one of the unoccupied houses and set up a temporary command post.

He was in no hurry to grow up; the adult world was unsynchronized and ambitionless. After his mother died he spent long days in the attic, going through her trunks and old clothes, playing with the bric-à-brac of hats and beads, trying to recover something of her personality.

In the bottom compartment of her jewelry case he came across a flat gold-cased object, equipped with a wrist strap. The dial had no hands but the twelve-numbered face intrigued him and he fastened it to his wrist.

His father choked over his soup when he saw it that evening.

"Conrad, my God! Where in heaven did you get that?"

"In Mamma's bead box. Can't I keep it?"

"No. Conrad, give it to me! Sorry, son." Thoughtfully: "Let's see, you're fourteen. Look, Conrad, I'll explain it all in a couple of years."

With the impetus provided by this new taboo there was no need to wait for his father's revelations. Full knowledge came soon. The older boys knew the whole story, but strangely enough it was disappointingly dull.

"Is that all?" he kept saying. "I don't get it. Why worry so much about clocks? We have calendars, don't we?"

Suspecting more, he scoured the streets, carefully inspecting every derelict clock for a clue to the real secret. Most of the faces had been mutilated, hands and numerals torn off, the circle of minute intervals stripped away, leaving a shadow of fading rust. Distributed apparently at random all over the city, above stores, banks, and public buildings, their real purpose was hard to discover. Sure enough, they measured the progress of time through twelve arbitrary intervals. But this seemed barely adequate grounds for outlawing them. After all, a whole variety of timers were in general use: in kitchens, factories, hospitals, wherever a fixed period of time was needed. His father had one by his bed at night. Sealed into the standard small black box, and driven by miniature batteries, it emitted a high penetrating whistle shortly before breakfast the next morning, woke him if he overslept. A clock was no more than a calibrated timer, in many ways less useful, as it provided you with a steady stream of irrelevant information. What if it was half past three, as the old reckoning put it, if you weren't planning to start or finish anything then?

Making his questions sound as naive as possible, he conducted a long, careful poll. Under fifty no one appeared to know anything at all about the historical background, and even the older people were beginning to forget. He also noticed that the less educated they were the more they were willing to talk, indicating that manual and lower-class workers had played no part in the revolution and consequently had no guilt-charged memories to repress. Old Mr. Crichton, the plumber who lived in the basement apartment, reminisced without any prompting, but nothing he said threw any light on the problem.

"Sure, there were thousands of clocks then, millions of them, everybody had one. Watches we called them, strapped to the wrist, you had to screw them up every day."

"But what did you *do* with them, Mr. Crichton?" Conrad pressed.

"Well, you just—looked at them, and you knew what time it was. One o'clock, or two or half past seven—that was when I'd go off to work."

"But you go off to work now when you've had breakfast. And if you're late the timer rings."

Crichton shook his head. "I can't explain it to you, lad. You ask your father."

But Mr. Newman was hardly more helpful. The explanation promised for Conrad's sixteenth birthday never materialized. When his questions persisted Mr. Newman, tired of sidestepping, shut him up with an abrupt:

"Just stop thinking about it, do you understand? You'll get yourself and the rest of us into a lot of trouble."

Stacey, the young English teacher, had a wry sense of humor, liked to shock the boys by taking up unorthodox positions on marriage or economics. Conrad wrote an essay describing an imaginary society completely preoccupied with elaborate rituals revolving around a minute-by-minute observance of the passage of time.

Stacey refused to play, however, and gave him a noncommittal beta plus, after class quietly asked Conrad what had prompted the fantasy. At first Conrad tried to back away, then finally came out with the question that contained the central riddle.

"Why is it against the law to have a clock?"

Stacey tossed a piece of chalk from one hand to the other.

"Is it against the law?"

Conrad nodded. "There's an old notice in the police station offering a bounty of one hundred pounds for every clock or wristwatch brought in. I saw it yesterday. The sergeant said it was still in force."

Stacey raised his eyebrows mockingly. "You'll make a million. Thinking of going into business?"

Conrad ignored this. "It's against the law to have a gun because you might shoot someone. But how can you hurt anybody with a clock?"

"Isn't it obvious? You can time him, know exactly how long it takes him to do something."

"Well?"

"Then you can make him do it faster."

At seventeen, on a sudden impulse, he built his first clock. Already his preoccupation with time was giving him a marked lead over his classmates. One or two were more intelligent, others more conscientious, but Conrad's ability to organize his leisure and homework periods allowed him to make the most of his talents. When the others were lounging around the railway yard on their way home Conrad had already completed half his prep, allocating his time according to its various demands.

As soon as he finished he would go up to the attic playroom, now his workshop. Here, in the old wardrobes and trunks, he made his first experimental constructions: calibrated candles, crude sundials, sandglasses, an elaborate clockwork contraption developing about half a horse power that drove its hands progressively faster and faster in an unintentional parody of Conrad's obsession.

His first serious clock was water-powered, a slowly leaking tank holding a wooden float that drove the hands as it sank downwards. Simple but accurate, it satisfied Conrad for several months while he carried out his ever-widening search for a real clock mechanism. He soon discovered that although there were innumerable table clocks, gold pocket watches, and timepieces of every variety rusting in junk shops and in the back drawers of most homes, none of them contained their mechanisms. These, together with the hands, and sometimes the digits, had always been removed. His own attempts to build an escapement that would regulate the motion of the ordinary clockwork motor met with no success; everything he had heard about clock movements confirmed that they were precision instruments of exact design and construction. To satisfy his secret ambition—a portable timepiece, if possible an actual wristwatch—he would have to find one, somewhere, in working order.

Finally, from an unexpected source, a watch came to him. One afternoon in a cinema, an elderly man sitting next to Conrad had a sudden heart attack. Conrad and two members of the audience carried him out to the manager's office. Holding one of his arms, Conrad noticed in the dim aisle light a glint of metal inside the sleeve. Quickly he felt the wrist with his fingers, identified the unmistakable lens-shaped disk of a wristwatch.

As he carried it home its tick seemed as loud as a death knell. He clamped his hand around it, expecting everyone in the street to point accusingly at him, the Time Police to swoop down and seize him.

In the attic he took it out and examined it breathlessly, smothering it in a cushion whenever he heard his father shift about in the bedroom below. Later he realized that its noise was almost inaudible. The watch was of the same pattern as his mother's, though with a yellow and not a red face. The gold case was scratched and peeling, but the movement seemed to be in perfect condition. He prized off the rear plate, watched the frenzied flickering world of miniature cogs and wheels for hours, spellbound. Frightened of breaking the main spring, he kept the watch only half wound, packed away carefully in cotton wool.

In taking the watch from its owner he had not, in fact, been motivated by theft; his first impulse had been to hide the watch before the doctor discovered it feeling for the man's pulse. But once the watch was in his possession he abandoned any thought of tracing the owner and returning it.

That others were still wearing watches hardly surprised him. The water clock had demonstrated that a calibrated timepiece added another dimension to life, organized its energies, gave the countless activities of everyday existence a yardstick of significance. Conrad spent hours in the attic gazing at the small yellow dial, watching its minute hand revolve slowly, its hour hand press on imperceptibly, a compass charting his passage through the future. Without it he felt rudderless, adrift in a gray purposeless limbo of timeless events. His father began to seem idle and stupid, sitting around vacantly with no idea when anything was going to happen.

Soon he was wearing the watch all day. He stitched together a slim cotton sleeve, fitted with a narrow flap below which he could see the face. He timed everything—the length of classes, football games, meal breaks, the hours of daylight and darkness, sleep and waking. He amused himself endlessly by baffling his friends with demonstrations of this private sixth sense, anticipating the frequency of their heart beats, the hourly newscasts on the radio, boiling a series of identically consistent eggs without the aid of a timer.

Then he gave himself away.

Stacey, shrewder than any of the others, discovered that he was wearing a watch. Conrad had noticed that Stacey's English classes lasted exactly forty-five minutes; he let himself slide into the habit of tidying his desk a minute before Stacey's timer pipped up. Once or twice he noticed Stacey looking at him curiously, but he could not resist the temptation to impress Stacey by always being the first one to make for the door.

One day he had stacked his books and clipped away his pen when Stacey pointedly asked him to read out a précis he had done. Conrad knew the timer would pip out in less than ten seconds, and decided to sit tight and wait for the usual stampede to save him the trouble.

Stacey stepped down from the dais, waiting patiently. One or two boys turned around and frowned at Conrad, who was counting away the closing seconds.

Then, amazed, he realized that the timer had failed to sound! Panicking, he first thought his watch had broken, just restrained himself in time from looking at it.

"In a hurry, Newman?" Stacey asked dryly. He sauntered down the aisle to Conrad. Baffled, his face reddening with embarrassment, Conrad fumbled open his exercise book, read out the précis. A few minutes later, without waiting for the timer, Stacey dismissed the class.

"Newman," he called out. "Here a moment."

He rummaged behind the rostrum as Conrad approached. "What happened then?" he asked. "Forget to wind up your watch this morning?"

Conrad said nothing. Stacey took out the timer, switched off the silencer and listened to the pip that buzzed out.

"Where did you get it from? Your parents? Don't worry, the Time Police were disbanded years ago."

Conrad examined Stacey's face. "It was my mother's," he lied. "I found it among her things." Stacey held out his hand and Conrad nervously un-. strapped the watch and handed it to him.

Stacey slipped it half out of its sleeve, glanced briefly at the yellow face. "Your mother, you say? Hmh."

"Are you going to report me?" Conrad asked.

"What, and waste some overworked psychiatrist's time even further?"

"Isn't it breaking the law to wear a watch?"

"Well, you're not exactly the greatest living menace to public security." Stacey started for the door, gesturing Conrad with him. He handed the watch back. "Cancel whatever you're doing on Saturday afternoon. You and I are taking a trip."

"Where?" Conrad asked.

"Back into the past," Stacey said lightly. "To Chronopolis, the Time City."

Stacey had hired a car, a huge battered mastodon of chromium and fins. He waved jauntily to Conrad as he picked him up outside the Public Library.

"Climb into the turret." He pointed to the bulging briefcase. Conrad slung onto the seat between them. "Have you had a look at those yet?"

Conrad nodded. As they moved off around the deserted square he opened the briefcase and pulled out a thick bundle of road maps. "I've just worked out that the city covers over five hundred square miles. I'd never realized it was so big. Where is everybody?"

Stacey laughed. They crossed the main street, cut down into a long tree-lined avenue of semidetached houses. Half of them were empty, windows wrecked and roofs sagging. Even the inhabited houses had a makeshift appearance, crude water towers on homemade scaffolding lashed to their chimneys, piles of logs dumped in overgrown front gardens.

"Thirty million people once lived in this city," Stacey remarked. "Now the population is little more than two, and still declining. Those of us left hang on in what were once the distal suburbs, so that the city today is effectively an enormous ring, five miles in width, encircling a vast dead center forty or fifty miles in diameter."

They wove in and out of various back roads, past a small factory still running although work was supposed to end at noon, finally picked up a long, straight boulevard that carried them steadily westward. Conrad traced their progress across successive maps. They were nearing the edge of the annulus Stacey had described. On the map it was overprinted in green so that the central interior appeared a flat, uncharted gray, a massive *terra incognita*.

They passed the last of the small shopping thoroughfares he remembered, a frontier post of mean terraced houses, dismal streets spanned by massive steel viaducts. Stacey pointed up at one as they drove below it. "Part of the elaborate railway system that once existed, an enormous network of stations and junctions that carried fifteen million people into a dozen great terminals every day."

For half an hour they drove on, Conrad hunched against the window, Stacey watching him in the driving mirror. Gradually, the landscape began to change. The houses were taller, with colored roofs, the sidewalks were railed off and fitted with pedestrian lights and turnstiles. They had entered the inner suburbs, completely deserted streets with multilevel supermarkets, towering cinemas, and department stores.

Chin in one hand, Conrad stared out silently. Lacking any means of transport he had never ventured into the uninhabited interior of the city, like the other children always headed in the opposite direction for the open country. Here the streets had died twenty or thirty years earlier; plateglass shopfronts had slipped and smashed into the roadway, old neon signs, window frames and overhead wires hung down from every cornice, trailing a ragged webwork of disintegrating metal across the pavements. Stacey drove slowly, avoiding the occasional bus or truck abandoned in the middle of the road, its tires peeling off their rims.

Conrad craned up at the empty windows, into the narrow alleys and side streets, but nowhere felt any sensation of fear or anticipation. These streets were merely derelict, as unhaunted as a half-empty dustbin.

One suburban center gave way to another, to long intervening stretches of congested ribbon developments. Mile by mile, the architecture altered its character; buildings were larger, ten- or fifteen-story blocks, clad in facing materials of green and blue tiles, glass or copper sheathing. They were moving forward in time rather than, as Conrad had expected, back into the past of a fossil city.

Stacey worked the car through a nexus of side streets toward a six-lane expressway that rose on concrete buttresses above the rooftops. They found a side road that circled up to it, leveled out, and then picked up speed sharply, spinning along one of the clear center lanes.

Conrad craned forward. In the distance, two or three miles away, the rectilinear outlines of enormous apartment blocks reared thirty or forty storys high, hundreds of them lined shoulder to shoulder in apparently endless ranks, like giant dominoes.

"We're entering the central dormitories here," Stacey told him. On either side buildings overtopped the motorway, the congestion mounting so that some of them had been built right up against the concrete palisades.

In a few minutes they passed between the first of the apartment batteries, the thousands of identical living units with their slanting balconies shearing up into the sky, the glass in-falls of the aluminum curtain walling speckling in the sunlight. The smaller houses and shops of the outer suburbs had vanished. There was no room on the ground level. In the narrow intervals between the blocks there were small concrete gardens, shopping complexes, ramps banking down into huge underground car parks.

And on all sides there were the clocks. Conrad noticed them immediately, at every street corner, over every archway, three quarters of the way up the sides of buildings, covering every conceivable angle of approach. Most of them were too high off the ground to be reached by anything less than a fireman's ladder and still retained their hands. All registered the same time: 12:01.

Conrad looked at his wristwatch, noted that it was just 2:45 p.m.

"They were driven by a master clock," Stacey told him. "When that stopped they all ceased at the same moment. One minute after midnight, thirty-seven years ago."

The afternoon had darkened, as the high cliffs cut off the sunlight, the sky a succession of narrow vertical intervals opening and closing around them. Down on the canyon floor it was dismal and oppressive, a wilderness of concrete and frosted glass. The expressway divided and pressed on westward. After a few more miles the apartment blocks gave way to the first office buildings in the central zone. These were even taller, sixty or seventy storys high, linked by spiraling ramps and causeways. The expressway was fifty feet off the ground yet the first floors of the office blocks were level with it, mounted on massive stilts that straddled the glass-enclosed entrance bays of lifts and escalators. The streets were wide but featureless. The sidewalks of parallel roadways merged below the buildings, forming a continuous concrete apron. Here and there were the remains of cigarette kiosks, rusting stairways up to restaurants and arcades built on platforms thirty feet in the air.

Conrad, however, was looking only at the clocks. Never had he visualized so many, in places so dense that they obscured each other. Their faces were multicolored: red, blue, yellow, green. Most of them carried four or five hands. Although the master hands had stopped at a minute past twelve, the subsidiary hands had halted at varying positions, apparently dictated by their color.

"What were the extra hands for?" he asked Stacey. "And the different colors?"

"Time zones. Depending on your professional category and the consumer-shifts allowed. Hold on, though, we're almost there."

They left the expressway and swung off down a ramp that fed them into the northeast corner of a wide open plaza, eight hundred yards long and half as wide, down the center of which had once been laid a continuous strip of lawn, now rank and overgrown. The plaza was empty, a sudden block of free space bounded by tall glass-faced cliffs that seemed to carry the sky.

Stacey parked, and he and Conrad climbed out and stretched themselves. Together they strolled across the wide pavement toward the strip of waist-high vegetation. Looking down the vistas receding from the plaza Conrad grasped fully for the first time the vast perspectives of the city, the massive geometric jungle of buildings.

Stacey put one foot up on the balustrade running around the lawn bed, pointed to the far end of the plaza, where Conrad saw a low-lying huddle of buildings of unusual architectural style, nineteenth century perpendicular stained by the atmosphere and badly holed by a number of explosions. Again, however, his attention was held by the clock face built into a tall concrete tower just behind the older buildings. This was the largest clock dial he had ever seen, at least a hundred feet across, huge black hands halted at a minute past twelve. The dial was white, the first they had seen, but on wide semicircular shoulders built below the main face were a dozen smaller faces, no more than twenty feet in diameter, running the full spectrum of colors. Each had five hands, the inferior three halted at random.

"Fifty years ago," Stacey explained, gesturing at the ruins below the tower, "that collection of ancient buildings was one of the world's greatest legislative assemblies." He gazed at it quietly for a few moments, then turned to Conrad. "Enjoy the ride?"

Conrad nodded fervently. "It's impressive, all right. The people who lived here must have been giants. What's really remarkable is that it looks as if they left only yesterday. Why don't we go back?"

"Well, apart from the fact that there aren't enough of us now, even if there were we couldn't control it. In its heyday this city was a fantastically complex social organism. The communications problems are difficult to imagine merely by looking at these blank façades. It's the tragedy of this city that there appeared to be only one way to solve them."

"Did they solve them?"

"Oh, yes, certainly. But they left themselves out of the equation. Think of the problems, though. Transporting fifteen million office workers to and from the center every day; routing in an endless stream of cars, buses, trains, helicopters; linking every office, almost every desk, with a videophone, every apartment with television, radio, power, water; feeding and entertaining this enormous number of people; guarding them with ancillary services, police, fire squads, medical units—it all hinged on one factor."

Stacey threw a fist out at the great tower clock. "Time! Only by synchronizing every activity, every footstep forward or backward, every meal, bus halt, and telephone call, could the organism support itself. Like the cells in your body, which proliferate into mortal cancers if allowed to grow in freedom, every individual here had to serve the overriding needs of the city or fatal bottlenecks threw it into total chaos. You and I can turn on the tap any hour of the day or night, because we have our own private water cisterns, but what would happen here if everybody washed the breakfast dishes within the same ten minutes?"

They began to walk slowly down the plaza toward the clock tower. "Fifty years ago, when the population was only ten million, they could just provide for a potential peak capacity, but even then a strike in one essential service paralyzed most of the others; it took workers two or three hours to reach their offices, as long again to queue for lunch and get home. As the population climbed the first serious attempts were made to stagger hours; workers in certain areas started the day an hour earlier or later than those in others. Their railway passes and car number plates were colored accordingly, and if they tried to travel outside the permitted periods they were turned back. Soon the practice spread; you could only switch on your washing machine at a given hour, post a letter or take a bath at a specific period."

"Sounds feasible," Conrad commented, his interest mounting. "But how did they enforce all this?"

"By a system of colored passes, colored money, an elaborate set of schedules published every day like TV or radio programs. And, of course, by all the thousands of clocks you can see around you here. The subsidiary hands marked out the number of minutes remaining in any activity period for people in the clock's color category."

Stacey stopped, pointed to a blue-faced clock mounted on one of the buildings overlooking the plaza. "Let's say, for example, that a lower-grade executive leaving his office at the allotted time, twelve o'clock, wants to have lunch, change a library book, buy some aspirin, and telephone his wife. Like all executives, his identity zone is blue. He takes out his schedule for the week, or looks down the blue-time columns in the newspaper, and notes that his lunch period for that day is twelve-fifteen to twelve-thirty. He has fifteen minutes to kill. Right, he then checks the library. Time code for today is given as three, that's the third hand on the clock. He looks at the nearest blue clock, the third hand says thirty-seven minutes past—he has twenty-three minutes, ample time, to reach the library. He starts down the street, but finds at the first intersection that the pedestrian lights are only shining red and green and he can't get across. The area's been temporarily zoned off for lower-grade women office workers—red, and manuals—green."

"What would happen if he ignored the lights?" Conrad asked.

"Nothing immediately, but all blue clocks in the zoned area would have returned to zero, and no shops or the library would serve him, unless he happened to have red or green currency and a forged set of library tickets. Anyway, the penalties were too high to make the risk worthwhile, and the whole system was evolved for his convenience, no one else's. So, unable to reach the library, he decides on the chemist. The time code for the chemist is five, the fifth, smallest hand. It reads fifty-four minutes past: he has six minutes to find a chemist and make his purchase. This done, he still has five minutes before lunch, decides to phone his wife. Checking the phone code he sees that no period has been provided for private calls that day—or the next. He'll just have to wait until he sees her that evening."

"What if he did phone?"

"He wouldn't be able to get his money in the coin box, and even then, his wife, assuming she is a secretary, would be in a red time zone and no longer in her office for that day—hence the prohibition on phone calls. It all meshed perfectly. Your time program told you when you could switch on your TV set and when to switch off. All electric appliances were fused, and if you strayed outside the programmed periods you'd have a hefty fine and repair bill to meet. The viewer's economic status obviously determined the choice of program, and vice versa, so there was no question of coercion. Each day's program listed your permitted activities: you could go to the hairdresser's, cinema, bank, cocktail bar, at stated times, and if you went then you were sure of being served quickly and efficiently."

They had almost reached the far end of the plaza. Facing them on its tower was the enormous clock face, dominating its constellation of twelve motionless attendants.

"There were a dozen socioeconomic categories: blue for executives, gold for professional classes, yellow for military and government officials—incidentally, it's odd your parents ever got hold of that wristwatch, none of your family ever worked for the government—green for manual workers and so on. Naturally, subtle subdivisions were possible. The lower-grade executive I mentioned left his office at twelve, but a senior executive, with exactly the same time codes, would leave at eleven forty-five and have an extra fifteen minutes, would find the streets clear before the lunch-hour rush of clerical workers."

Stacey pointed up at the tower. "This was the Big Clock, the master from which all others were regulated. Central Time Control, a sort of Ministry of

Time, gradually took over the old parliamentary buildings as their legislative functions diminished. The programmers were, effectively, the city's absolute rulers."

As Stacey continued Conrad gazed up at the battery of timepieces, poised helplessly at 12:01. Somehow time itself seemed to have been suspended, around him the great office buildings hung in a neutral interval between yesterday and tomorrow. If one could only start the master clock the entire city would probably slide into gear and come to life, in an instant be repeopled with its dynamic jostling millions.

They began to walk back toward the car. Conrad looked over his shoulder at the clock face, its gigantic arms upright on the silent hour.

"Why did it stop?" he asked.

Stacey looked at him curiously. "Haven't I made it fairly plain?"

"What do you mean?" Conrad pulled his eyes off the scores of clocks lining the plaza, frowned at Stacey.

"Can you imagine what life was like for all but a few of the thirty million people here?"

Conrad shrugged. Blue and yellow clocks, he noticed, outnumbered all others; obviously the major governmental agencies had operated from the plaza area. "Highly organized but better than the sort of life we lead," he replied finally, more interested in the sights around him. "I'd rather have the telephone for one hour a day than not at all. Scarcities are always rationed, aren't they?"

"But this was a way of life in which everything was scarce. Don't you think there's a point beyond which human dignity is surrendered?"

Conrad snorted. "There seems to be plenty of dignity here. Look at these buildings, they'll stand for a thousand years. Try comparing them with my father. Anyway, think of the beauty of the system, engineered as precisely as a watch."

"That's all it was," Stacey commented dourly. "The old metaphor of the cog in the wheel was never more true than here. The full sum of your existence was printed for you in the newspaper columns, mailed to you once a month from the Ministry of Time."

Conrad was looking off in some other direction and Stacey pressed on in a slightly louder voice. "Eventually, of course, revolt came. It's interesting that in any industrial society there is usually one social revolution each century, and that successive revolutions receive their impetus from progressively higher social levels. In the eighteenth century it was the urban proletariat, in the nineteenth the artisan classes, in this revolt the white-collar office worker, living in his tiny so-called modern flat, supporting through credit pyramids an economic system that denied him all freedom of will or personality, chained him to a thousand clocks . . . ." He broke off. "What's the matter?"

Conrad was staring down one of the side streets. He hesitated, then asked in a casual voice: "How were these clocks driven? Electrically?"

"Most of them. A few mechanically. Why?"

"I just wondered . . . how they kept them all going." He dawdled at Stacey's heels, checking the time from his wristwatch and glancing to his left. There were twenty or thirty clocks hanging from the buildings along the side street, indistinguishable from those he had seen all afternoon.

Except for the fact that one of them was working!

It was mounted in the center of a black glass portico over an entranceway fifty yards down the right-hand side, about eighteen inches in diameter, with a faded blue face. Unlike the others its hands registered three-fifteen, the correct time. Conrad had nearly mentioned this apparent coincidence to Stacey when he had suddenly seen the minute hand move on an interval. Without doubt someone had restarted the clock; even if it had been running off an inexhaustible battery, after thirty-seven years it could never have displayed such accuracy.

He hung behind Stacey, who was saying: "Every revolution has its symbol of oppression . . ."

The clock was almost out of view. Conrad was about to bend down and tie his shoelace when he saw the minute hand jerk downward, tilt slightly from the horizontal.

He followed Stacey toward the car, no longer bothering to listen to him. Ten yards from it he turned and broke away, ran swiftly across the roadway toward the nearest building.

"Newman!" he heard Stacey shout. "Come back!" He reached the pavement, ran between the great concrete pillars carrying the building. He paused for a moment behind an elevator shaft, saw Stacey climbing hurriedly into the car. The engine coughed and roared out, and Conrad sprinted on below the building into a rear alley that led back to the side street. Behind him he heard the car accelerating, a door slam as it picked up speed.

When he entered the side street the car came swinging off the plaza thirty yards behind him. Stacey swerved off the roadway, bumped up onto the pavement and gunned the car toward Conrad, throwing on the brakes in savage lurches, blasting the horn in an attempt to frighten him. Conrad sidestepped out of its way, almost falling over the bonnet, hurled himself up a narrow stairway leading to the first floor, and raced up the steps to a short landing that ended in tall glass doors. Through them he could see a wide balcony that ringed the building. A fire escape crisscrossed upward to the roof, giving way on the fifth floor to a cafeteria that spanned the street to the office building opposite.

Below he heard Stacey's feet running across the pavement. The glass doors were locked. He pulled a fire extinguisher from its bracket, tossed the heavy cylinder against the center of the plate. The glass slipped and crashed to the tiled floor in a sudden cascade, splashing down the steps. Conrad stepped through onto the balcony, began to climb the stairway. He had reached the third floor when he saw Stacey below, craning upward. Hand over hand, Conrad pulled himself up the next two flights, swung over a bolted metal turnstile into the open court of the cafeteria. Tables and chairs lay about on their sides, mixed up with the splintered remains of desks thrown down from the upper floors.

The doors into the covered restaurant were open, a large pool of water lying across the floor. Conrad splashed through it, went over to a window and peered down past an old plastic plant into the street. Stacey seemed to have given up. Conrad crossed the rear of the restaurant, straddled the counter, and climbed through a window onto the open terrace running across the street. Beyond the rail he could see into the plaza, the double line of tire marks curving into the street below.

He had almost crossed to the opposite balcony when a shot roared out into the air. There was a sharp tinkle of falling glass and the sound of the explosion boomed away among the empty canyons.

For a few seconds he panicked. He flinched back from the exposed rail, his eardrums numbed, looking up at the great rectangular masses towering above him on either side, the endless tiers of windows like the faceted eyes of gigantic insects. So Stacey had been armed, almost certainly was a member of the Time Police!

On his hands and knees Conrad scurried along the terrace, slid through the turnstiles and headed for a half-open window on the balcony.

Climbing through, he quickly lost himself in the building.

He finally took up a position in a corner office on the sixth floor, the cafeteria just below him to the right, the stairway up which he had escaped directly opposite.

All afternoon Stacey drove up and down the adjacent streets, sometimes freewheeling silently with the engine off, at others blazing through at speed. Twice he fired into the air, stopping the car afterward to call out, his words lost among the echoes rolling from one street to the next. Often he drove along the pavements, swerved about below the buildings as if he expected to flush Conrad from behind one of the banks of escalators.

Finally he appeared to drive off for good, and Conrad turned his attention to the clock in the portico. It had moved on to six forty-five, almost exactly the time given by his own watch. Conrad reset this to what he assumed was the correct time, then sat back and waited for whoever had wound it to appear. Around him the thirty or forty other clocks he could see remained stationary at 12:01.

For five minutes he left his vigil, scooped some water off the pool in the cafeteria, suppressed his hunger, and shortly after midnight fell asleep in a corner behind the desk.

He woke the next morning to bright sunlight flooding into the office. Standing up, he dusted his clothes, turned around to find a small gray-haired man in a patched tweed suit surveying him with sharp eyes. Slung in the crook of his arm was a large black-barreled weapon, its hammers menacingly cocked.

The man put down a steel ruler he had evidently tapped against a cabinet, waited for Conrad to collect himself.

"What are you doing here?" he asked in a testy voice. Conrad noticed his pockets were bulging with angular objects that weighed down the sides of his jacket.

"I . . . er . . ." Conrad searched for something to say. Something about the old man convinced him that this was the clock winder. Suddenly he decided he had nothing to lose by being frank, and blurted out, "I saw the clock working. Down there on the left. I want to help wind them all up again."

The old man watched him shrewdly. He had an alert birdlike face, twin folds under his chin like a cockerel's.

"How do you propose to do that?" he asked.

Stuck by this one, Conrad said lamely, "I'd find a key somewhere."

The old man frowned. "One key? That wouldn't do much good." He seemed to be relaxing, and shook his pockets with a dull chink.

For a few moments neither of them said anything. Then Conrad had an inspiration, bared his wrist. "I have a watch," he said. "It's seven forty-five."

"Let me see." The old man stepped forward, briskly took Conrad's wrist and examined the yellow dial. "Movado Supermatic," he said to himself. "CTC issue." He stepped back, lowering the shotgun, and seemed to be summing Conrad up. "Good," he remarked at last. "Let's see. You probably need some breakfast."

They made their way out of the building, and began to walk quickly down the street.

"People sometimes come here," the old man said. "Sightseers and police. I watched your escape yesterday, you were lucky not to be killed." They swerved left and right across the empty streets, the old man darting between the stairways and buttresses. As he walked he held his hands stiffly to his sides, preventing his pockets from swinging. Glancing into them, Conrad saw that they were full of keys, large and rusty, of every design and combination.

"I presume that was your father's watch," the old man remarked.

"Grandfather's," Conrad corrected. He remembered Stacey's lecture, and added, "He was killed in the plaza."

The old man frowned sympathetically, for a moment held Conrad's arm.

They stopped below a building, indistinguishable from the others nearby, at one time a bank. The old man looked carefully around him, eyeing the high cliff walls on all sides, then led the way up a stationary escalator.

His quarters were on the second floor, beyond a maze of steel grilles and strongdoors, a stove and a hammock slung in the center of a large workshop. Lying about on thirty or forty desks in what had once been a typing pool, was an enormous collection of clocks, all being simultaneously repaired. Tall cabinets surrounded them, loaded with thousands of spare parts in neatly labeled correspondence trays—escapements, ratchets, cogwheels, barely recognizable through the rust.

The old man led Conrad over to a wall chart, pointed to the total listed against a column of dates. "Look at this. There are now 278 running continuously. Believe me, I'm glad you've come. It takes me half my time to keep them wound."

He made breakfast for Conrad and told him something about himself. His name was Marshall. Once he had worked in Central Time Control as a programmer. He had survived the revolt and the Time Police, and ten years later returned to the city. At the beginning of each month he cycled out to one of the perimeter towns to cash his pension and collect supplies. The rest of the time he spent winding the steadily increasing number of functioning clocks and searching for others he could dismantle and repair.

"All these years in the rain hasn't done them any good," he explained, "and there's nothing I can do with the electrical ones."

Conrad wandered off among the desks, gingerly feeling the dismembered timepieces that lay around like the nerve cells of some vast unimaginable robot. He felt exhilarated and yet at the same time curiously calm, like a man who has staked his whole life on the turn of a wheel and is waiting for it to spin.

"How can you make sure that they all tell the same time?" he asked Marshall, wondering why the question seemed so important.

Marshall gestured irritably. "I can't, but what does it matter? There is no such thing as a perfectly accurate clock. The nearest you can get is one that has stopped. Although you never know when, it *is* absolutely accurate twice a day."

Conrad went over to the window, pointed to the great clock visible in an interval between the rooftops. "If only we could start that, and run all the others off it."

"Impossible. The entire mechanism was dynamited. Only the chimer is intact. Anyway, the wiring of the electrically driven clocks perished years ago. It would take an army of engineers to recondition them."

Conrad looked at the scoreboard again. He noticed that Marshall appeared to have lost his way through the years—the completion dates he listed were seven and a half years out. Idly, Conrad reflected on the significance of this irony, but decided not to mention it to Marshall.

For three months Conrad lived with the old man, following him on foot as he cycled about on his rounds, carrying the ladder and the satchel full of keys with which Marshall wound up the clocks, helping him to dismantle recoverable ones and carry them back to the workshop. All day, and often through half the night, they worked together, repairing the movements, restarting the clocks, and returning them to their original positions.

All the while, however, Conrad's mind was fixed upon the great clock in its tower dominating the plaza. Once a day he managed to sneak off and make his way into the ruined Time buildings. As Marshall had said, neither the clock nor its twelve satellites would ever run again. The movement house looked like the engine room of a sunken ship, a rusting tangle of rotors and drive wheels exploded into contorted shapes. Every week he would climb the long stairway up to the topmost platform two hundred feet above, look out through the bell tower at the flat roofs of the office blocks stretching away to the horizon. The hammers rested against their trips in long ranks just below him. Once he kicked one of the treble trips playfully, sent a dull chime out across the plaza.

The sound drove strange echoes into his mind.

Slowly he began to repair the chimer mechanism, rewiring the hammers and the pulley systems, trailing fresh wire up the great height of the tower, dismantling the winches in the movement room below and renovating their clutches.

He and Marshall never discussed their self-appointed tasks. Like animals obeying an instinct they worked tirelessly, barely aware of their own motives. When Conrad told him one day that he intended to leave and continue the work in another sector of the city, Marshall agreed immediately, gave Conrad as many tools as he could spare and bade him good-bye.

Six months later, almost to the day, the sounds of the great clock chimed out across the rooftops of the city, marking the hours, the half hours and the quarter hours, steadily tolling the progress of the day. Thirty miles away, in the towns forming the perimeter of the city, people stopped in the streets and in doorways, listening to the dim haunted echoes reflected through the long aisles of apartment blocks on the far horizon, involuntarily counting the slow final sequences that told the hour. Older people whispered to each other: "Four o'clock, or was it five? They have started the clock again. It seems strange after these years."

And all through the day they would pause as the quarter and half hours reached across the miles to them, a voice from their childhoods reminding them of the ordered world of the past. They began to reset their timers by the chimes, at night before they slept they would listen to the long count of midnight, wake to hear them again in the thin clear air of the morning.

Some went down to the police station and asked if they could have their watches and clocks back again.

After sentence, twenty years for the murder of Stacey, five for fourteen offenses under the Time Laws, to run concurrently, Newman was led away to the holding cells in the basement of the court. He had expected the sentence and made no comment when invited by the judge. After waiting trial for a year the afternoon in the courtroom was nothing more than a momentary intermission.

He made no attempt to defend himself against the charge of killing Stacey, partly to shield Marshall, who would be able to continue their work unmolested, and partly because he felt indirectly responsible for the policeman's death. Stacey's body, skull fractured by a twenty- or thirty-story fall, had been discovered in the back seat of his car in a basement garage not far from the plaza. Presumably Marshall had discovered him prowling around. Newman recalled that one day Marshall had disappeared altogether and had been curiously irritable for the rest of the week.

The last time he had seen the old man had been during the three days before the police arrived. Each morning as the chimes boomed out across the plaza Newman had seen his tiny figure striding briskly down the plaza toward him, waving up energetically at the tower, bareheaded and unafraid.

Now Newman was faced with the problem of how to devise a clock that would chart his way through the coming twenty years. His fears increased when he was taken the next day to the cell block which housed the long-term prisoners—passing his cell on the way to meet the superintendent he noticed that his window looked out onto a small shaft. He pumped his brains desperately as he stood at attention during the superintendent's homilies, wondering how he could retain his sanity. Short of counting the seconds, each one of the 86,400 in every day, he saw no possible means of assessing the time.

Locked into his cell, he sat limply on the narrow bed, too tired to unpack his small bundle of possessions. A moment's inspection confirmed the uselessness of the shaft. A powerful light mounted halfway up masked the sunlight that slipped through a steel grille fifty feet above.

He stretched himself out on the bed and examined the ceiling. A lamp was recessed into its center, but a second, surprisingly, appeared to have been fitted to the cell. This was on the wall, a few feet above his head. He could see the curving bowl of the protective case, some ten inches in diameter.

He was wondering whether this could be a reading light when he realized that there was no switch.

Swinging around, he sat up and examined it, then leapt to his feet in astonishment.

It was a clock! He pressed his hands against the bowl, reading the circle of numerals, noting the inclination of the hands. 4:53, near enough the present time. Not simply a clock, but one in running order! Was this some sort of macabre joke, or a misguided attempt at rehabilitation?

His pounding on the door brought a warder.

"What's all the noise about? The clock? What's the matter with it?" He unlocked the door and barged in, pushing Newman back.

"Nothing. But why is it here? They're against the law."

"Is that what's worrying you." The warder shrugged. "Well, you see, the rules are a little different in here. You lads have got a lot of time ahead of you, it'd be cruel not to let you know where you stood. You know how to work it, do you? Good." He slammed the door and bolted it fast, then smiled at Newman through the cage. "It's a long day here, son, as you'll be finding out. That'll help you get through it."

Gleefully, Newman lay on the bed, his head on a rolled blanket at its foot, staring up at the clock. It appeared to be in perfect order, electrically driven, moving in rigid half-minute jerks. For an hour after the warder left he watched it without a break, then began to tidy up his cell, glancing over his shoulder every few minutes to reassure himself that it was still there, still running efficiently. The irony of the situation, the total inversion of justice, delighted him, even though it would cost him twenty years of his life.

He was still chuckling over the absurdity of it all two weeks later when for the first time he noticed the clock's insanely irritating tick . . .

Triceratops

TRANSLATED BY DAVID LEWIS

Science fiction in Japan began in the 1960s as an offshoot of American science fiction, with conventions where fans gathered, a major magazine (Hayakawa's SF Magazine), and a wave of translations from English. But what developed was unlike the literature of the West, and more like the Japanese sci-fi films of the 1950s and early 1960s, full of monsters and disasters. This story combines the fascination with monsters and a sensibility akin to that of Jorge Luis Borges or the magic realists—or perhaps early Ballard. As is common with Japanese SF, there is not the kind of narrative force or plot to hold the story together that we expect in Western literature. Instead there is a succession of set pieces leading up to a culminating image; in this case, one that has striking, perhaps even disturbing, political undertones. This is a story about war.

*   *   *

The father and son were returning from cycling. They had set out together on a Sunday of deepening autumn, heading for the cycling course along the river. On the way back they had been forced to burrow through the exhaust and dust of the national highway before finally reaching the residential area a mile from home. Their house lay beyond this slightly aging neighborhood, on the other side of the small hill, in the new subdivision.

It was only a little past seven, but the autumn sun was sinking quickly and darkness had begun to gather about them. The father and son stopped their bikes beneath the yellow light of the streetlamps and breathed the cool air in deeply.

"Are you okay, Dad?"

"My knees are ready to fall apart. Let me rest a minute."

"I don't feel a thing."

"I guess you wouldn't," said the father. He smiled wryly as he lit a cigarette.

"Somebody's making curry!" his son cried suddenly. "I'm starving to death. Can't we go now? It's just a little bit farther."

"I guess so."

The father crushed out the cigarette with the tip of his shoe and put his hands back on the black handlebars. It was at the instant the father and son had put one foot to the pedals, at the instant they were looking down the road ahead of them, were beginning to gather momentum, a huge shadow darted across the intersection no more than five or six meters away, shaking the very earth as it passed.

It had the feeling of mass, of power, of a bulldozer, of a ten-ton truck.

Though its passage took but an instant, it indelibly burned on their eyes an image of thick, clearly animal skin, an almost slimy sheen, the quiver of flesh and muscle.

Hands still tightly gripping the handlebars, the father and son lowered their feet from the pedals and stared.

Thick dust swirled beneath the streetlamps. The tremors gradually subsided.

It seemed a subterranean rumbling still growled about them.

Then, quite abruptly, even that rumbling stopped.

It stopped with a slightly unnatural air, almost as though a tape recording had been suddenly switched off, but in any case it had ceased, and their surroundings filled again with crying babies, the smell of dinner cooking, raucous TV commercials.

Shall we . . .?

The father asked with his eyes, and his son nodded.

They stopped their bikes at the intersection and looked ahead.

A scattering of streetlamps threw down hazy light. Traces of gas and watermain work were everywhere around them. The road stretched on with its splitting asphalt, returned to silence.

"Where'd it go?" the son asked.

"Aaah."

The father shook his head.

The two of them were silent for a while.

"Dad, what do you think it was?"

"I don't know."

"I almost thought it was a rhinoceros. It was too big to be a cow. It looked seven or eight meters long. And if my eyes weren't fooling me, it was twice as high as this fence. That would make it three meters, uh-uh, even taller."

"Aaah," said the father again. "I guess a rhino might get loose from the zoo sometimes. It's not impossible. But didn't you see two horns on that thing's head?"

"Horns? Yeah, it did look like two horns."

"So it couldn't be a rhinoceros."

"So it was a cow after all? A bull?"

"It must be. You don't see many of them anymore, but it's my guess a bull got loose from some farm or pasture near here."

"Yeah."

"Well, if it keeps on like that, there's going to be one whale of an accident when it meets a truck."

"Yeah."

The father and son looked back down the road. They listened. But aside from the cheerful night noises with their tales of domestic peace and tranquility, there were no hints of anything amiss in the town.

Almost as though it never happened.

The father shook his head.

If I'd been alone, I'd have thought I was hallucinating.

After a long while the father and son pedaled silently and hurried along the road home. The street began its gradual ascent, and they stopped several times to rest.

The town spread out behind them. They turned and looked back, but there were no signs of anything unusual, no accusing shadows, and nowhere a trembling of the earth, a rising plume of dust.

"Dad, did you see the tail?" the son asked suddenly.

"Mmmm, what about it?"

"Didn't you see it? A superfat tail?"

The father and son reached the crest of the hill and passed through the last sparse copse of trees.

Suddenly their own subdivision lay before them.

The lights were on in all the new houses of the new town, but somehow — perhaps because of the sharp glare of the scattered mercury-vapor lamps — the homes seemed to hunch stockily against the earth.

The mother had dinner ready for them.

"Oh, come on now. Was it really that big?"

Chopsticks in midair, the mother eyed the father and son across the dinner table.

"It was! It was so big I thought it was a rhino."

"Well, it's terrible if it's true. The whole town must be in an uproar."

"Actually there wasn't any at all. Even the running noise stopped, just like that."

"That's right. It stopped like we'd never heard a thing."

"But that's impossible. Oh, I see now. That's why you two were so interested in the news all of a sudden. And did they say anything about it on the news?"

"Not a thing. But it may be too early, too soon, for it to get on the news."

"Boy, it's gotta get on the news! Look, it's seven, eight meters long for sure, and at least three meters high."

"I think you're just exaggerating. Really, have you ever seen or even heard of a cow that big? This isn't a joke, is it? You're not playing games with me?"

"We are not. Anyway, we saw it for sure. Didn't we, Dad?"

"Absolutely. If that was a cow, it'd be a cinch there'd be steaks for five hundred people or more."

"Oh, stop it this instant! You *are* joking."

The mother laughed shrilly, and the father and son looked at each other, their expressions strangely vague.

After a while the father also laughed, dryly, shortly.

"Well, it hardly matters. There was a little earthquake; then that thing went zipping by. So we got a good shock out of it. Maybe the shadows threw us off, made it look bigger than it was. All that's really certain is that it wasn't a dog or a pig or some animal like that, but a really big rascal, right?"

"Yeah." The son nodded, still not quite satisfied, and began to work his chopsticks.

A variety show was on the television screen. A skimpily clad Eurasian girl was weaving her arms and legs as she sang, almost howled, in a strange, strained voice. The wife laughed shrilly again.

"What is it?"

"The singer, she just blew her nose!"

"Her nose?"

"Oh, come on! You were just telling me about it yesterday, weren't you? You said this girl sometimes blows her nose when she's straining too hard. I thought I'd never heard anything so stupid in my life, but really just now she blew her nose. I, oh, it's too *funny!*"

The mother rolled with laughter again.

The father and son smiled tightly and lowered their eyes.

The father stayed up nearly half that night, drinking. His wife and son had gone to bed, but he, somehow unable to sleep, rose and, putting his legs up to the electric heater in the living room, propped himself up on one arm and began to drink leisurely away at the whiskey he poured little by little into his glass. The last news of the day started on the television, left on since early evening, but, as expected, there was no mention of the shadow they had seen.

Were they really just seeing things?

The alcohol seeped through every cell in his aching muscles, slowly tanning his exhausted body like leather. At least that was how it felt to the father as he continued to watch the shifting screen.

At some point he dozed off.

Someone was blowing his nose. Gradually the noise grew rougher, increasing in violence until it sounded like bellows. *This is no joke. No singer's going to blow her nose like that. This is one heck of a dream.* Half-asleep, half-awake, his mind spun idly.

Eventually the noise was joined by a low moan, shameless and huge, as though echoing from inside a mammoth cave. *No way. This isn't that singer's voice. What's going on?*

His eyes snapped open.

A moan.

A noise like a bellows.

And the sounds continued.

He looked at the television set. The station was already off the air, and the screen held a sandstorm of cracking light. He turned it off and listened.

The noise was coming from outside.

The father peered through a crack in the curtains.

Scraggly potted plants filled the little garden, no larger than a cat's forehead. Beyond the hedge loomed a huge black shadow, with an eye that glittered piercingly in the dark.

It did look a little like a rhinoceros.

But the horn on its nose was even sharper than a rhino's, and beneath it the mouth curved like a raptor's beak, and from that mouth puffed violent white breath like a steam locomotive.

The head was fully a third the size of the body, resembling a buffalo's. Two long horns jutted out like spears, but the turned-up, helmetlike shield between the head and abdomen was like that of no other animal he had ever seen.

A door opened.

The father turned to find his son standing in the room. The boy had pulled his trousers on over his pajamas, and he looked soberly at his father as he pushed one arm into his sweater.

"Is it there?" the son asked in a low voice.

"Yes."

The father jerked his jaw in the direction of the shadow outside.

The mammoth animal scratched the fence twice, three times with the tips of its horns, then slowly swung its side toward them. It began to walk. Like a heavy tank moving out for a night battle.

The dark brown back, the hips, the thick, heavy tail like a giant lizard's trailing down from those hips, all these passed slowly through their field of vision. The quiver of muscle beneath thick skin.

"That's not a cow or rhino," said the son, his voice sticking in his throat.

"It seems to be a dinosaur. That's all I can think of."

"If it's really a dinosaur, then I've seen it in my books. It's a famous one. Not *Allosaurus*, not *Stegosaurus*—"

"This one's beak is pointed, but its teeth don't look like much."

"It has a mouth like a beak?"

"That's right."

"Then it's *Triceratops*! Isn't that right, Dad! *Triceratops*. It means the three-horned dinosaur. The nose horn and two on its forehead, that makes three, right!"

"Then that's it. *Triceratops*."

Triceratops, living and fighting and fighting again in an endless struggle for survival in the late Cretaceous, Mesozoic world seventy million years before, domain of history's most savage beast, the carnivorous monster *Tyrannosaurus rex*. *Triceratops*, that massive herbivore, possessing the most powerful armament of any animal ever known. Triceratops, *that* triceratops, was even now walking leisurely down the road before their very eyes.

"Shall we go outside?"

"Sure!"

Father and son slipped through the entrance door of their home. It was chilly outside, but there was no wind.

Ten meters away the small mountains of triceratop's hips swayed steadily forward, dragging a tail like a telephone pole. They couldn't see the beast's face beyond the expansive sweep of the shield. But from triceratop's posture they could well imagine its cautious advance, front legs crouched, head lowered, body in readiness for the slightest sign of danger.

At last triceratops reached the end of the street. Before it stood a stone fence and to the left and right, walls of brick and stone.

He'll head back this way.

Father and son drew back between the gateposts, but in the next instant they stopped, rooted speechless in their tracks.

Triceratops did not stop. It put its head up against the stone wall and sank smoothly into the hard surface. The shield vanished, the front legs and the slice of backbone above them vanished, the hips and hind legs vanished, the tail from base to tip, inch by steady inch, simply disappeared.

Morning came, and the father, setting off to work, and the son, setting off for school, both left the house at the same time.

The father and son exchanged glances and walked to the stone fence at the end of the road. The wall stood solidly, blocking their way.

They fingered it, but found nothing unusual.

Nor was there a single break in the mortar-painted sides, the window glass of the house beyond the wall.

"I've read about dimensional faults and stuff like that," the son said.

"Mmmm. But those are all just theories."

"Theories?"

"When you say that something you can't prove might be this way or that way, that's a theory."

"So there aren't any dimensional faults?"

"Well, someone just thought them up. They might really exist, and they might not. If you figure they exist, then the surface of this wall must be right about the fault line. Between our world and the world of *Triceratops*, seventy million years ago. But really you can try explaining it just about any way you please."

"For instance?"

"For instance, you could think that our world and *Triceratops*'s world exist simultaneously. Instead of popping in and out of a fault line every now and then, we're really both here all the time with just a bit of a lag in between. That would explain why we can somehow look through into that other world, and they can look through to us. It'd be just that fine a difference."

"Huh?"

"I started thinking about it when there was a thick, warm animal smell in the house this morning. And this isn't the first time, you know. It's been like this for at least two or three months now. The people living here must be experiencing the same thing."

"Triceratops went inside their house?"

"You've got it now."

"So can they see it, too? Just like us?"

"Maybe. But you know how people's heads are. We try to deny things that we think are impossible. It's a kind of protective instinct. So even if we somehow do see it, or feel it, we usually just shut it out automatically, choose not to see it, not to do it. If we see it again, two, three times maybe, then common sense comes to the rescue and we laugh it off. 'Nerves.' 'Boy, what a crazy idea!' And that's the end of it."

"And if it still doesn't stop?"

"Then people stop accepting you. You can't live a productive social life anymore."

The boy shook his head lightly from side to side, then laughed.

"What's so funny?"

"Nothing much. I was just thinking about Mom. I didn't tell her what I saw last night. Can you guess what would happen to me if I did?"

The father laughed, too.

"Well, she'd sure put you on the rack. That is, if it wasn't right after she'd just seen the same thing herself."

"I guess I can't tell any of my friends about it, either."

"Of course not. Now let's get going. We can talk it over when we get home."

The father and son started walking.

Occasionally speaking and laughing happily together.

And every time they met a neighbor:

"Good morning!"

"Good morning!"

Scattering high-spirited greetings all about them.

The father and son often saw dinosaurs after that.

Sometimes, glancing up at the sunset, they'd glimpse the shadow of a huge winged creature like *Pteranodon*, weaving across the sky. But the only earth-hugging dinosaurs they saw were triceratopses.

Apparently the local habitat was best suited to *Triceratops*. The beast asleep in the garage, its head so perfectly aligned with the family car that it seemed a strange horned automobile was snoring humorously away, the huge dinosaur passing over the head of a small child crying fretfully by the roadside, all these apparitions were triceratopses.

Sometimes the father and son would even see them—though only transparently—walking the sun-bathed road in full daylight.

Nor was it only what they could see. The cloying animal smell, the low grunting. Running nonstop to the station on ice-stretched, frigid mornings as they gasped and choked on impossible flower pollen. Listening to the distant, bassoonlike cries of a female triceratops in heat, howling through the long night.

You and your dad seem awfully close these days. Anything special going on?

There were days when his mother would badger him, but the son simply grinned.

"Nothing special," was all he'd say.

It was on one of those days, yet another Sunday evening when they had gone cycling about the neighborhood, though not as far as on the day they first met triceratops. After passing through the copse on the top of the hill and coming out above their subdivision, the father and son came to a stop, finding themselves speechless and unable to move.

A triceratops huddled superimposed over every house in the town, their skin—brilliant green beneath the mercury lamps—gently rising and falling with their breathing. Occasionally one would open its eyes in a narrow slit, and every time the lids raised, the pupils would glitter in brilliant rose, perhaps because of rhodopsin pigment like that found in some species of crocodile.

It was a scene of phantasmal beauty, like the winking of giant fireflies.

"Do you suppose the land over there's the same as the town?"

"Maybe they can see us and feel us like we feel them. Maybe they're just trying to keep warm."

"You may be right."

"Isn't it a weird feeling? Everyone's going to work or leaving for school from a dinosaur's belly, and they're coming home to the belly, eating dinner, watching TV."

"But that's how it is."

"Hey, my room's in its butt."

"Don't let it get to you."

"But it's really peaceful somehow, isn't it? They may look fierce, but I've never seen a triceratops fighting."

"They hardly ever run, either."

"Yeah, that's right. Just the one we saw that first time, in the other town."

"I wonder what he was running for."

"Anyway, it's peaceful enough today."

"There's nothing better than peace."

The peace did not last long.

It was a day when yellow sand blown from the continent filled the air and turned the sun the color of blood, a harsh, unpleasant day.

It was the day that the son, looking casually toward the national highway from the hilltop while returning from a friend's house, saw a dozen dinosaurs running on strange hind legs—like ostriches—long tails held high, kicking up clouds of dust.

"Those were tyrannosauruses for sure. Superfat back legs and little skinny front ones like decorations. Pointed mouths. Anyway, tyrannosauruses. And they were really moving fast. They came running at least as far as the station."

"We're just a little way from the station here, but I didn't feel anything like tyrannosaurus when I was coming home just now. Even the triceratops in the garage just opened his eyes a bit and stared at me like he always does."

"But I really did see them."

"Maybe they ran right through town and went somewhere else?"

"But I wonder why they would do that. They went out of sight near the station."

"Hmmm."

The father crossed his arms.

"In that case maybe they're still milling around there somewhere. Or maybe—"

"Let's go see," said the son.

"You two are up to something again, aren't you?"

The mother shouted after them. The father and son smiled, waved, and mounted their bicycles.

They went as far as the station, but there was no trace of any tyrannosauruses. After watching the station plaza for a while, they turned leisurely back home.

A small creek flowed close to the station, completely covered with concrete. There was a playground built on top of it. The long, covered drain formed a second road, stretching almost to their subdivision.

"Let's go back this way."

The father and son pedaled their bicycles slowly over the concrete plating. The tires bounced heavily every time they jumped a gap between the plates.

Their front lights waved widely.

Before long they became aware of a strange noise. It sounded like rapid water and, an octave lower, the grunting of countless pigs. Moments later they felt the earth begin to rumble.

And suddenly they looked down at their feet. And ran to the metal lid of an air vent.

They were running beneath the metal mesh of the lid, fiercely kicking up the water as they ran. Their wet hides glistened; their necks were outstretched. The pack of tyrannosauruses dashed for the subdivision like a conveyor belt, a never-ending stream.

They had been following the watercourse. The group near the national highway had been but a single part, a flying column, and had merged with the main group at the station.

"This is bad."

It hardly mattered if they hurried, yet the father and son began to pedal furiously.

As they neared the subdivision, countless tyrannosauruses danced up through the concrete sheeting ahead of them, looking like a geyser of muddy water.

All the houses on the slanting slope of the subdivision heaved up their roofs and began to move.

The triceratops had risen.

The fighting began.

Before their eyes, a triceratops, head lowered, charged forward and plunged sharp horns into the carotid artery of an attacking tyrannosaurus. The carnivore, its blood fountaining into the air like water from a fire hose, fell back, lashed its long tail, and leaped hugely, gouging out the triceratop's eyes with a single sweep of the key-shaped claws on its forelegs.

Three more tyrannosauruses swooped onto the mammoth body of the triceratops, crumpled just six meters in front of their home. The huge reptiles plunged razor teeth into the belly meat, already ripped apart by their claws. The surroundings were flooded in a murky river of blood.

"Isn't that our triceratops?" cried the boy, his voice shaking.

"You're right."

A tyrannosaurus had fallen in front of the entranceway. The father and son warily watched its huge bloodshot eyes, the convulsive contractions of its belly, as they wheeled their bikes up the driveway.

The fighting lasted throughout the night.

Even at the height of the raucous laughter of a televised singing contest, the father and son could hear the war cries, could feel the thick hide splitting, the shrieks of the hour of death.

By morning the combat had almost ended, and the countless corpses of triceratopses and tyrannosauruses, some still barely twitching the tips of their tails, some dragging the ripped tatters of their stomachs, lay tumbled across the landscape.

Almost without exception, the corpses of triceratopses had their entrails dug out, their ribs laid bare, and their neck shields chopped into ribbons. But most of the tyrannosauruses showed only deep puncture wounds in their necks and bellies, escaping utter destruction.

There were even a few scattered survivors. But none had escaped unscathed. All had lost the energy to keep on fighting.

One tyrannosaurus, his flung-out leg half mincemeat from the thigh down, continued to drag out and gobble the guts of the triceratops he had slaughtered.

Behind him sprawled the body of one of his comrades, a gaping hole bored through its neck, its body clotted with dried blood, while no more than five meters away a triceratops grazed silently on the grass, blood still seeping from one of its eyes.

Every now and then the tyrannosaurus would raise its head and glare— though perhaps this was only their fancy—balefully at the grazing triceratops.

If you eat that crud, why'd you kill us?

The father and son almost felt they could hear that voice.

If there's too much to eat, why did you keep on butchering us?

The triceratops's unbloodied eye seemed to ask that back.

The father and son watched as they walked slowly to the station. The corpses that weren't dripping were at least tolerable. But even they were brought up short where the large intestines of a tyrannosaurus lay heaped across the road, as if they had sprung writhing from the animal's torn-open belly. After a moment's pause they edged by on the side of the street.

A woman in fashionable white slacks passed through the blood-smeared landscape, her shoes clicking loudly, her eyes suspiciously watching father and son.

A microbus filled with kindergarteners passed through that landscape, bearing its load of lively chatter.

An elementary-school student passed through that landscape, singing a jingle.

Skylark dancing to the sky
God is reigning in the sky
The world, the world's a trifle.

The Man Who Lost the Sea

There are those, among them Samuel R. Delany, who regard Theodore Sturgeon as the greatest SF writer of short fiction. James Blish called him "the best conscious artist the field has yet produced." Kurt Vonnegut called him a fine writer by anyone's standards. Sturgeon's most fertile period was the late 1940s and the 1950s, when he wrote the majority of his work, over a hundred stories and four novels. Thereafter, he published only occasionally until his death in 1985, though he remained a revered public figure and constant social presence. It is difficult to overestimate the impact of Sturgeon's charismatic bohemian personality or the force of his emotionally explosive stories on SF and on the most careful and ambitious writers from 1940 to the early 1980s. Perhaps it is fair to say that he is the force behind the fiction that characterized the American version of the New Wave of the late 1960s. "The Man Who Lost the Sea" is a subtle and mature work from a man who as a writer, teacher, critic, and public speaker stood for higher literary standards in SF throughout his long career. As a body of work, his short fiction is unequaled.

* * *

ay you're a kid, and one dark night you're running along the cold sand
with this helicopter in your hand, saying very fast *witchy-witchy-
witchy*. You pass the sick man and he wants you to shove off with that
thing. Maybe he thinks you're too old to play with toys. So you squat next to
him in the sand and tell him it isn't a toy, it's a model. You tell him look
here, here's something most people don't know about helicopters. You take a
blade of the rotor in your fingers and show him how it can move in the hub,
up and down a little, back and forth a little, and twist a little, to change
pitch. You start to tell him how this flexibility does away with the gyroscopic
effect, but he won't listen. He doesn't want to think about flying, about
helicopters, or about you, and he most especially does not want explanations about anything by anybody. Not now. Now, he wants to think about the
sea. So you go away.

The sick man is buried in the cold sand with only his head and his left
arm showing. He is dressed in a pressure suit and looks like a man from
Mars. Built into his left sleeve is a combination time-piece and pressure
gauge, the gauge with a luminous blue indicator which makes no sense, the
clock hands luminous red. He can hear the pounding of surf and the soft
swift pulse of his pumps. One time long ago when he was swimming he
went too deep and stayed down too long and came up too fast, and when he
came to it was like this: they said, "Don't move, boy. You've got the bends.
Don't even *try* to move." He had tried anyway. It hurt. So now, this time, he
lies in the sand without moving, without trying.

His head isn't working right. But he knows clearly that it isn't working
right, which is a strange thing that happens to people in shock sometimes.
Say you were that kid, you could say how it was, because once you woke up
lying in the gym office in high school and asked what had happened. They
explained how you tried something on the parallel bars and fell on your
head. You understood exactly, though you couldn't remember falling. Then
a minute later you asked again what had happened and they told you. You
understood it. And a minute later . . . forty-one times they told you, and
you understood. It was just that no matter how many times they pushed it
into your head, it wouldn't stick there; but all the while you *knew* that your
head would start working again in time. And in time it did. . . . Of course,
if you were that kid, always explaining things to people and to yourself, you
wouldn't want to bother the sick man with it now.

Look what you've done already, making him send you away with that
angry shrug of the mind (which, with the eyes, are the only things which
will move just now). The motionless effort costs him a wave of nausea. He
has felt seasick before but he has never *been* seasick, and the formula for that
is to keep your eyes on the horizon and stay busy. Now! Then he'd better get

busy—now; for there's one place especially not to be seasick in, and that's locked up in a pressure suit. Now!

So he busies himself as best he can, with the seascape, landscape, sky. He lies on high ground, his head propped on a vertical wall of black rock. There is another such outcrop before him, whip-topped with white sand and with smooth flat sand. Beyond and down is valley, salt-flat, estuary; he cannot yet be sure. He is sure of the line of footprints, which begin behind him, pass to his left, disappear in the outcrop shadows, and reappear beyond to vanish at last into the shadows of the valley.

Stretched across the sky is old mourning-cloth, with starlight burning holes in it, and between the holes the black is absolute—wintertime, mountaintop sky-black.

(Far off on the horizon within himself, he sees the swell and crest of approaching nausea; he counters with an undertow of weakness, which meets and rounds and settles the wave before it can break. Get busier. *Now.*)

Burst in on him, then, with the X-15 model. That'll get him. Hey, how about this for a gimmick? Get too high for the thin air to give you any control, you have these little jets in the wingtips, see? and on the sides of the empennage: bank, roll, yaw, whatever, with squirts of compressed air.

But the sick man curls his sick lip: oh, git, kid, git, will you?—that has nothing to do with the sea. So you git.

Out and out the sick man forces his view, etching all he sees with a meticulous intensity, as if it might be his charge, one day, to duplicate all this. To his left is only starlit sea, windless. In front of him across the valley, rounded hills with dim white epaulettes of light. To his right, the jutting corner of the black wall against which his helmet rests. (He thinks the distant moundings of nausea becalmed, but he will not look yet.) So he scans the sky, black and bright, calling Sirius, calling Pleiades, Polaris, Ursa Minor, calling that . . . that . . . Why, it *moves*. Watch it: yes, it moves! It is a fleck of light, seeming to be wrinkled, fissured, rather like a chip of boiled cauliflower in the sky. (Of course, he knows better than to trust his own eyes just now.) But that movement . . .

As a child he had stood on cold sand in a frosty Cape Cod evening, watching Sputnik's steady spark rise out of the haze (madly, dawning a little north of west); and after that he had sleeplessly wound special coils for his receiver, risked his life restringing high antennas, all for the brief capture of an unreadable *tweetle-eep-tweetle* in his earphones from Vanguard, Explorer, Lunik, Discoverer, Mercury. He knew them all (well, some people collect match-covers, stamps) and he knew especially that unmistakable steady sliding in the sky.

This moving fleck was a satellite, and in a moment, motionless, uninstrumented but for his chronometer and his part-brain, he will know which one. (He is grateful beyond expression—without that sliding chip of light, there were only those footprints, those wandering footprints, to tell a man he was not alone in the world.)

Say you were a kid, eager and challengeable and more than a little bright, you might in a day or so work out a way to measure the period of a satellite with nothing but a timepiece and a brain; you might eventually see that the shadow in the rocks ahead had been there from the first only because of the light from the rising satellite. Now if you check the time exactly at the moment when the shadow on the sand is equal to the height of the outcrop, and time it again when the light is at the zenith and the shadow gone, you will multiply this number of minutes by 8—think why, now: horizon to zenith is one-fourth of the orbit, give or take a little, and halfway up the sky is half that quarter—and you will then know this satellite's period. You know all the periods—ninety minutes, two, two-and-a-half hours; with that and the appearance of this bird, you'll find out which one it is.

But if you were that kid, eager or resourceful or whatever, you wouldn't jabber about it to the sick man, for not only does he not want to be bothered with you, he's thought of all that long since and is even now watching the shadows for that triangular split second of measurement. *Now!* His eyes drop to the face of his chronometer: 0400, near as makes no never mind.

He has minutes to wait now—ten? . . . thirty? . . . twenty-three?—while this baby moon eats up its slice of shadowpie; and that's too bad, the waiting, for though the inner sea is calm there are currents below, shadows that shift and swim. Be busy. Be busy. He must not swim near that great invisible ameba, whatever happens: its first cold pseudopod is even now reaching for the vitals.

Being a knowledgeable young fellow, not quite a kid any more, wanting to help the sick man too, you want to tell him everything you know about that cold-in-the-gut, that reaching invisible surrounding implacable ameba. You know all about it—listen, you want to yell at him, don't let that touch of cold bother you. Just know what it is, that's all. Know what it is that is touching your gut. You want to tell him, listen:

Listen, this is how you met the monster and dissected it. Listen, you were skin-diving in the Grenadines, a hundred tropical shoal-water islands; you had a new blue snorkel mask, the kind with face-plate and breathing-tube all in one, and new blue flippers on your feet, and a new blue spear-gun—all this new because you'd only begun, you see; you were a beginner, aghast with pleasure at your easy intrusion into this underwater otherworld. You'd been out in a boat, you were coming back, you'd just reached the mouth of the little bay, you'd taken the notion to swim the rest of the way. You'd said as much to the boys and slipped into the warm silky water. You brought your gun.

Not far to go at all, but then beginners find wet distances deceiving. For the first five minutes or so it was only delightful, the sun hot on your back and the water so warm it seemed not to have any temperature at all and you were flying. With your face under the water, your mask was not so much attached as part of you, your wide blue flippers trod away yards, your gun rode all but weightless in your hand, the taut rubber sling making an occasional hum as your passage plucked it in the sunlit green. In your ears crooned the breathy monotone of the snorkel tube, and through the invisible disk of plate glass you saw wonders. The bay was shallow—ten, twelve feet or so—and sandy, with great growths of brain-, bone-, and fire-coral, intricate waving sea-fans, and fish—such fish! Scarlet and green and aching azure, gold and rose and slate-color studded with sparks of enamel-blue, pink and peach and silver. And that *thing* got into you, that . . . monster.

There were enemies in this otherworld: the sand-colored spotted sea-snake with his big ugly head and turned-down mouth, who would not retreat but lay watching the intruder pass; and the mottled moray with jaws like bolt-cutters; and somewhere around, certainly, the barracuda with his undershot face and teeth turned inward so that he must take away whatever he might strike. There were urchins—the plump white sea-egg with its thick fur of sharp quills and the black ones with the long slender spines that would break off in unwary flesh and fester there for weeks; and file-fish and stone-fish with their poisoned barbs and lethal meat; and the stingaree who could drive his spike through a leg bone. Yet these were not *monsters*, and could not matter to you, the invader churning along above them all. For you were above them in so many ways—armed, rational, comforted by the close shore (ahead the beach, the rocks on each side) and by the presence of the boat not too far behind. Yet you were . . . attacked.

At first it was uneasiness, not pressing, but pervasive, a contact quite as intimate as that of the sea; you were sheathed in it. And also there was the touch—the cold inward contact. Aware of it at last, you laughed: for Pete's sake, what's there to be scared of?

The monster, the ameba.

You raised your head and looked back in air. The boat had edged in to the cliff at the right; someone was giving a last poke around for lobster. You waved at the boat; it was your gun you waved, and emerging from the water it gained its latent ounces so that you sank a bit, and as if you had no snorkle on, you tipped your head back to get a breath. But tipping your head back plunged the end of the tube under water; the valve closed; you drew in a hard lungful of nothing at all. You dropped your face under; up came the tube; you got your air, and along with it a bullet of seawater which struck you somewhere inside the throat. You coughed it out and floundered, sobbing as you sucked in air, inflating your chest until it hurt, and the air you got seemed no good, no good at all, a worthless devitalized inert gas.

You clenched your teeth and headed for the beach, kicking strongly and knowing it was the right thing to do; and then below and to the right you saw a great bulk mounding up out of the sand floor of the sea. You knew it was only the reef, rocks and coral and weed, but the sight of it made you scream; you didn't care what you knew. You turned hard left to avoid it, fought by as if it would reach for you, and you couldn't get air, couldn't get air, for all the unobstructed hooting of your snorkel tube. You couldn't bear the mask, suddenly, not for another second, so you shoved it upward clear of your mouth and rolled over, floating on your back and opening your mouth to the sky and breathing with a quacking noise.

It was then and there that the monster well and truly engulfed you, mantling you round and about within itself—formless, borderless, the illimitible ameba. The beach, mere yards away, and the rocky arms of the bay, and the not-too-distant boat—these you could identify but no longer distinguish, for they were all one and the same thing . . . the thing called unreachable.

You fought that way for a time, on your back, dangling the gun under and behind you and straining to get enough warm sun-stained air into your chest. And in time some particles of sanity began to swirl in the roil of your mind, and to dissolve and tint it. The air pumping in and out of your square-grinned frightened mouth began to be meaningful at last, and the monster relaxed away from you.

You took stock, saw surf, beach, a leaning tree. You felt the new scend of your body as the rollers humped to become breakers. Only a dozen firm kicks brought you to where you could roll over and double up; your shin struck coral with a lovely agony and you stood in foam and waded ashore. You gained the wet sand, hard sand, and ultimately with two more paces powered by bravado, you crossed high-water mark and lay in the dry sand, unable to move.

You lay in the sand, and before you were able to move or to think, you were able to feel a triumph—a triumph because you were alive and knew that much without thinking at all.

When you *were* able to think, your first thought was of the gun, and the first move you were able to make was to let go at last of the thing. You had nearly died because you had not let it go before; without it you would not have been burdened and you would not have panicked. You had (you began to understand) kept it because someone else would have had to retrieve it—easily enough—and you could not have stood the laughter. You had almost died because They might laugh at you.

This was the beginning of the dissection, analysis, study of the monster. It began then; it had never finished. Some of what you had learned from it was merely important; some of the rest—vital.

You had learned, for example, never to swim farther with a snorkel than you could swim back without one. You learned never to burden yourself with the unnecessary in an emergency: even a hand or a foot might be as expendable as a gun; pride was expendable, dignity was. You learned never to dive alone, even if They laugh at you, even if you have to shoot a fish yourself and say afterward "we" shot it. Most of all, you learned that fear has many fingers, and one of them—a simple one, made of too great a concentration of carbon dioxide in your blood, as from too-rapid breathing in and out of the same tube—is not really fear at all but feels like fear, and can turn into panic and kill you.

Listen, you want to say, listen, there isn't anything wrong with such an experience or with all the study it leads to, because a man who can learn enough from it could become fit enough, cautious enough, foresighted, unafraid, modest, teachable enough to be chosen, to be qualified for—

You lose the thought, or turn it away, because the sick man feels that cold touch deep inside, feels it right now, feels it beyond ignoring, above and beyond anything that you, with all your experience and certainty, could explain to him even if he would listen, which he won't. Make him, then; tell him the cold touch is some simple explainable thing like anoxia, like gladness even: some triumph that he will be able to appreciate when his head is working right again.

Triumph? Here he's alive after . . . whatever it is, and that doesn't seem to be triumph enough, though it was in the Grenadines, and that other time, when he got the bends, saved his own life, saved two other lives. Now, somehow, it's not the same: there seems to be a reason why just being alive afterward isn't a triumph.

Why not triumph? Because not twelve, not twenty, not even thirty minutes is it taking the satellite to complete its eighth-of-an-orbit: fifty minutes are gone, and still there's a slice of shadow yonder. It is this, *this* which is placing the cold finger upon his heart, and he doesn't know why, he doesn't know why, he *will* not know why; he is afraid he shall when his head is working again. . . .

Oh, where's the kid? Where is any way to busy the mind, apply it to something, anything else but the watchhand which outruns the moon? Here, kid: come over here—what you got there?

If you were the kid, then you'd forgive everything and hunker down with your new model, not a toy, not a helicopter or a rocket-plane, but the big one, the one that looks like an overgrown cartridge. It's so big, even as a model, that even an angry sick man wouldn't call it a toy. A giant cartridge, but watch: the lower four-fifths is Alpha—all muscle—over a million pounds thrust. (Snap it off, throw it away.) Half the rest is Beta—all brains— it puts you on your way. (Snap it off, throw it away.) And now look at the polished fraction which is left. Touch a control somewhere and see—see? it has wings—wide triangular wings. This is Gamma, the one with wings, and on its back is a small sausage; it is a moth with a sausage on its back. The sausage (click! it comes free) is Delta. Delta is the last, the smallest: Delta is the way home.

What will they think of next? Quite a toy. Quite a toy. Beat it, kid. The satellite is almost overhead, the sliver of shadow going—going—almost gone and . . . gone.

Check: 0459. Fifty-nine minutes? give or take a few. Times eight . . . 472 . . . is, uh, 7 hours 52 minutes.

Seven hours fifty-two minutes? Why, there isn't a satellite round earth with a period like that. In all the solar system there's only . . .

The cold finger turns fierce, implacable.

The east is paling and the sick man turns to it, wanting the light, the sun, an end to questions whose answers couldn't be looked upon. The sea stretches endlessly out to the growing light, and endlessly, somewhere out of sight, the surf roars. The paling east bleaches the sandy hilltops and throws the line of footprints into aching relief. That would be the buddy, the sick man knows, gone for help. He cannot at the moment recall who the buddy is, but in time he will, and meanwhile the footprints make him less alone.

The sun's upper rim thrusts itself above the horizon with a flash of green, instantly gone. There is no dawn, just the green flash and then a clear white blast of unequivocal sunup. The sea could not be whiter, more still, if it were frozen and snow-blanketed. In the west, stars still blaze, and overhead the crinkled satellite is scarcely abashed by the growing light. A formless jumble in the valley below begins to resolve itself into a sort of tent-city, or installation of some kind, with tubelike and saillike buildings. This would have meaning for the sick man if his head were working right. Soon, it would. Will. (Oh . . .)

The sea, out on the horizon just under the rising sun, is behaving strangely, for in that place where properly belongs a pool of unbearable brightness, there is instead a notch of brown. It is as if the white fire of the sun is drinking dry the sea—for look, look! the notch becomes a bow and the bow a crescent, racing ahead of the sunlight, white sea ahead of it and behind it a cocoa-dry stain spreading across and down toward where he watches.

Beside the finger of fear which lies on him, another finger places itself, and another, making ready for that clutch, that grip, that ultimate insane squeeze of panic. Yet beyond that again, past that squeeze when it comes, to be savored if the squeeze is only fear and not panic, lies triumph—triumph, and a glory. It is perhaps this which constitutes his whole battle: to fit himself, prepare himself to bear the utmost that fear could do, for if he can do that, there is a triumph on the other side. But . . . not yet. Please, not yet awhile.

Something flies (or flew, or will fly—he is a little confused on this point) toward him, from the far right where the stars still shine. It is not a bird and it is unlike any aircraft on earth, for the aerodynamics are wrong. Wings so wide and so fragile would be useless, would melt and tear away in any of earth's atmosphere but the outer fringes. He sees then (because he prefers to see it so) that it is the kid's model, or part of it, and for a toy, it does very well indeed.

It is the part called Gamma, and it glides in, balancing, parallels the sand and holds away, holds away slowing, then settles, all in slow motion, throwing up graceful sheet-fountains of fine sand from its skids. And it runs along the ground for an impossible distance, letting down its weight by the ounce and stingily the ounce, until *look out* until a skid *look out* fits itself into a bridged crevasse *look out, look out!* and still moving on, it settles down to the struts. Gamma then, tired, digs her wide left wingtip carefully into the racing sand, digs it in hard; and as the wing breaks off, Gamma slews, sidles, slides slowly, pointing her other triangular tentlike wing at the sky, and broadside crushes into the rocks at the valley's end.

As she rolls smashing over, there breaks from her broad back the sausage, the little Delta, which somersaults away to break its back upon the rocks, and through the broken hull, spill smashed shards of graphite from the moderator of her power-pile. *Look out! Look out!* and at the same instant from the finally checked mass of Gamma there explodes a doll, which slides and tumbles into the sand, into the rocks and smashed hot graphite from the wreck of Delta.

The sick man numbly watches this toy destroy itself: what will they think of next?—and with a gelid horror prays at the doll lying in the raging rubble of the atomic pile: *don't stay there, man—get away! get away! that's hot, you know?* But it seems like a night and a day and half another night before the doll staggers to its feet and, clumsy in its pressure-suit, runs away up the valleyside, climbs a sand-topped outcrop, slips, falls, lies under a slow cascade of cold ancient sand until, but for an arm and the helmet, it is buried.

The sun is high now, high enough to show the sea is not a sea, but brown plain with the frost burned off it, as now it burns away from the hills, diffusing in air and blurring the edges of the sun's disk, so that in a very few minutes there is no sun at all, but only a glare in the east. Then the valley below loses its shadows, and like an arrangement in a diorama, reveals the form and nature of the wreckage below: no tent-city this, no installation, but the true real ruin of Gamma and the eviscerated hulk of Delta. (Alpha was the muscle, Beta the brain; Gamma was a bird, but Delta, Delta was the way home.)

And from it stretches the line of footprints, to and by the sick man, above to the bluff, and gone with the sandslide which had buried him there. Whose footprints?

He knows whose, whether or not he knows that he knows, or wants to or not. He knows what satellite has (give or take a bit) a period like that (want it exactly?—it's 7.66 hours). He knows what world has such a night, and such a frosty glare by day. He knows these things as he knows how spilled radioactives will pour the crash and mutter of surf into a man's earphones.

Say you were that kid: say, instead, at last, that you are the sick man, for they are the same; surely then you can understand why of all things, even while shattered, shocked, sick with radiation calculated (leaving) radiation computed (arriving) and radiation past all bearing (lying in the wreckage of Delta) you would want to think of the sea. For no farmer who fingers the soil with love and knowledge, no poet who sings of it, artist, contractor, engineer, even child bursting into tears at the inexpressible beauty of a field of daffodils—none of these is as intimate with Earth as those who live on, live with, breathe and drift in its seas. So of these things you must think; with these you must dwell until you are less sick and more ready to face the truth.

The truth, then, is that the satellite fading here is Phobos, that those footprints are your own, that there is no sea here, that you have crashed and are killed and will in a moment be dead. The cold hand ready to squeeze and still your heart is not anoxia or even fear, it is death. Now, if there is something more important than this, now is the time for it to show itself.

The sick man looks at the line of his own footprints, which testify that he is alone, and at the wreckage below, which states that there is no way back, and at the white east and the mottled west and the paling flecklike satellite above. Surf sounds in his ears. He hears his pumps. He hears what is left of his breathing. The cold clamps down and folds him round past measuring, past all limit.

Then he speaks, cries out: then with joy he takes his triumph at the other side of death, as one takes a great fish, as one completes a skilled and mighty task, rebalances at the end of some great daring leap; and as he used to say "we shot a fish" he uses no "I":

"God," he cries, dying on Mars, "God, we made it!"

On the
Inside Track

TRANSLATED BY JOE F. RANDOLPH
WITH KARL MICHAEL ARMER

Science fiction in German has a rich and long tradition developed in the nineteenth and early twentieth centuries, but many years passed before it took hold again after World War II. When it did, it assumed the lowest commercial form, the clichéd biweekly series adventure, the Perry Rhodan novellas, starting in 1961 and continuing today. Although many English-language works are translated into German, there are few truly ambitious contemporary German SF writers, and of those, only Herbert Franke and, recently, Wolfgang Jeschke have had much work translated into English. A recent sign of hope is this story by Karl Michael Armer, a businessman, magazine writer, and photographer. "On the Inside Track" shows a command of the conventions of SF storytelling and offers, in a European setting, a pleasant twist on the old idea of possession by an alien consciousness. But like the Scandinavian story in this volume, this story is more a reflection of English-language SF than a harbinger of a new German consciousness.

*   *   *

July 9, 6:00 P.M. As always on beautiful summer days, Robert Förster's heart was burdened with bitterness. Colors were too bright. People were too carefree. On days like this he felt the weight of his seventy years painfully bearing down. New layers of depression and brooding anger formed on the shell that separated him from the outside world.

Today it was worse than ever. The weather and scenery had the unreal perfection of a picture postcard that you get in the mail just when you do not want it. The sky was so high, the blue so deep that life seemed to hold nothing but promise. Every hope, no matter how elusive, seemed to be within the realm of possibility. If you were young enough. White yachts were leisurely skimming over the waters of the Chiemsee under an afternoon breeze, almost as weightlessly as clouds scudding across the sky. The multihued sails of wind surfers, vivid specks reminiscent of impressionist paintings, slipped in and out between the yachts. Cattle were grazing on a peninsula jutting out into the lake. The tinny tinkling of cowbells provided an unobtrusive but constant score for the travelogue unfolding before Förster's eyes. In the background, snow-capped peaks crowning the Bavarian Alps glistened beneath the sun in bold relief. That was the kind of day it was.

"Shit," Förster said.

He liked the way it sounded so much that he repeated it, "What a load of Goddamned shit."

The young woman sitting next to him on the lakeside bench looked at him askance. He glared back at her. Why should he care what she thought? To her he was nothing but an eccentric old coot, anyway.

"Don't you like people talking to themselves?" He chuckled. "I do. At least that way I'm talking to someone I like."

She got up and left. She had good-looking legs and a nice little ass. Like Barbara, when they were young, oh, so many, many years ago. They had been in a tiny cove on one of those secluded Greek islands. She came out of the turquoise-colored water of the Aegean sea, her svelte body covered with beads of water sparkling in the sun, Aphrodite reborn, goddess of love, priestess of their secret honeymoon rites. She seemed immortal in her glorious youth. Thirty years later she committed suicide. What had gone wrong? And why, for heaven's sake, why?

Förster's hand tightened around his cane while he tried to blink away the mist from his eyes. Look at yourself. What a sentimental old fool you have become. No style or dignity. Just lounging around insulting other people.

He was wrenched from his reverie by Samson's deep-throated growling. The big St. Bernard had woken up and was looking around bleary-eyed. He seemed to be confused. After a couple of seconds he let out a startlingly human sigh and put his head back down on his paws.

"Well, big fella, dreaming of the good old days again?" He patted the dog on the back, surprised at the degree of affection welling up in him. How thin Samson's coat had gotten. And his face was almost white. The St. Bernard was more than eleven years old, which was tantamount to seventy-seven human years. *The poor guy is even older than I am*, Förster thought. They were two oldsters in a world filled with smart young people who never gave a thought to the fact that they too would one day be stooped and tired.

"Relics, that's what we are, Samson," he said. "Relics of the worst type. Of no interest to historians or learned biographers, only something for file thirteen. Let's go before they sweep us up and away."

When he reached for the leash he had wrapped around a metal leg on the bench, the St. Bernard suddenly jumped up and started barking as if possessed. With legs trembling, he stood in front of Förster as if confronting a dangerous enemy, his bloodshot eyes wide-open.

Förster staggered to his feet, frightened and thoroughly confused. All of a sudden he felt seasick. It was weird. What was going on here? Something was pulling and tugging at his body as if forces were operating on him without anesthesia. So this is what it is like when you die! How strange! His knees gave way. He sank back down on the bench.

Suddenly, everything was as before.

"Easy," Förster told the dog automatically, "easy"—he hesitated for a fraction of a second, trying to remember—"Samson."

A spastically bent hand moved across his field of vision. He experienced a moment of pure, intense horror when he realized that it was his own hand moving of its own accord. He watched his hand perform strangely intricate gestures as if doing some Thai temple dance. It seemed to him that this was not real, he was merely watching it on a monitor. Watching it with detached scientific interest.

Have I lost my mind? Förster wondered in the unnatural calm accompanying a state of shock.

"No," answered an alien voice inside his head.

So Förster's first contact with the extraterrestrial was cut extremely short, because he passed out right then and there.

July 9, 6:20 p.m. After a few minutes Förster came to. His eyes were riveted to a small white cloud hanging motionless in the sky, like the enigmatic remains of a smoke signal. There was that thundering stillness in his head that occurs after an explosion, or after the last passionate crescendo of a symphony when so many feelings are competing in your chest that you cannot tell them apart. The shock of being overwhelmed.

He tried to remember everything the voice had said to him in the last few minutes.

"So you're an extraterrestrial," he said slowly. "An E.T. in my brain." He chuckled in his usual fashion. "That's truly amazing. Science fiction in a live performance, in every sense of the word."

As he got no answer, he shrugged and turned his attention back to the lakeside idyll he hated so. It was an alien landscape populated by young healthy humanoids. He had nothing in common with them — had not had for many years now.

"Well then," he said. "Welcome to the brotherhood of aliens."

He felt a twinge of bewilderment.

"Aren't you an Earth person?" the voice asked.

"I was for many years," Förster replied. "But now I'm old. Old people are the extraterrestrial aliens in this world. We're so isolated that we might as well be living on another planet. Other people know that we are out there somewhere, but they couldn't care less. Life goes on without us. We have no more say about what happens. We're just onlookers, outcasts on our own world. That's why we're both aliens on this planet."

"I see," said the voice after a short pause.

"The only difference between us," said Förster, working himself into a rage, "is this. Meeting up with an extraterrestrial is usually a first-contact story, but growing older is more often than not a last-contact story."

"You are bitter."

"Yeah, that I am. Growing old's no fun."

"But you can get a lot of mileage out of these years. You're well-off, you're educated, you live in beautiful surroundings. You should be happy."

"Yeah, I should be, but I'm not. And that drives me up the wall. I'd like to be happy, but I'm not succeeding. Something's out of whack with me. I'm such an asshole that I can't be happy, even once." He started crying. "Here, look at me," he said in despair while wiping his face with a big blue handkerchief. "I never used to cry, but nowadays I get all watery-eyed whenever I see a young couple with a baby, because they remind me of my younger days." He folded his handkerchief very slowly, very precisely. "I'm sorry."

"That's all right," the alien said.

July 10, 9:30 A.M. Although it was still pretty early in the day, heat was already beating down on the Café Panorama lakeside terrace, where Förster was having breakfast. Every few seconds a refreshing breeze cooled him off. Förster, nevertheless, was sweating. The beach umbrellas were badly arranged, casting shadows on the aisles while tables stood in blazing sunlight.

Förster was sitting alone at his table, as usual. He had tried to push the umbrella into a better position, but he was too weak. The shade had not budged. Nobody made a move to help him.

When he went to pick up his coffee cup, he noticed his hand violently shaking. He made an effort to steady it. After all, he was being watched.

"Don't mind me," the voice said.

Förster thought about it. "But I know you're there," he said. "You're inside me. You're using my brain like a reference book. You can make a marionette out of my body. No matter what I do, you're watching me over my shoulder. That's where your 'Don't mind me' is a bunch of bullshit."

"I don't take that kind of crap from some country bumpkin like you!" The voice suddenly got loud and forceful. "Watch what you say." Förster's hand shook and sloshed the hot coffee out of the cup and on his other hand. It hurt. "You're under my control, get it? So behave yourself. Just look at your dog. It knows how to obey."

You damned bastard! Förster thought, filled with seething hate. *You damned outerspace bastard. I'm not a St. Bernard. I'm not your dog. I won't be treated like that!*

"Bow-wow," the alien retorted mockingly and clammed up.

July 10, 9:50 A.M. "All right," Förster directed his message inward. "I flew off the handle a little. I didn't mean it. Let's be on speaking terms again."

He got no answer.

"Hey, you . . ." Förster suddenly realized that he did not know the name of the entity possessing him. "Come on."

The alien remained mute.

"Aw, the galactic superbrain's pouting. How atavistic. I thought you were smarter and more objective than that."

Förster sensed a weak emotion he could not classify, even though it seemed familiar to him. But that was the only response from the alien.

Förster felt an astonishing touch of regret. He missed the voice of the furious invader. Arguing was still better than no communication whatsoever.

He listened attentively. After several minutes he finally gave up. All alone once again.

"Well, kiss my ass then," he mumbled. He motioned to the waiter, who seemed not to notice—as usual. Everything was back to normal.

He dropped his hand that had been sticking awkwardly up in the air and laid it on his other hand. It was a very stable position, his hands did not shake that way. He leaned back and looked out over the lake where a swan was gliding by. The two straight lines forming its V-shaped wake sparkled on the calm green water. The swan acted very proud. It was a young swan.

July 10, 7:30 P.M. Förster was exhausted. All day long he, rather the alien controlling him, had been calling, conferring, wheeling and dealing. Hour after hour, Förster heard himself talking in some foreign language he did not understand. It was frightening. He thought he was schizophrenic.

Now he was sitting in his comfortable easy chair by an open window, trying to relax. He felt as if he had undergone major surgery, weak, jittery, old, more dead than alive. The only sounds in the room were those of birds chirping in the garden and the regular ticking of the grandfather clock. How loud it sounded! Förster closed his eyes.

"It was a hard day today," the alien's voice said softly.

Förster did not move a muscle. "Leave me alone," he babbled. "I'm bushed."

"Me too."

Taken aback, Förster blinked. Somehow it had never occurred to him that the extraterrestrial could get tired. He acted so all-powerful. He was certainly young, a thoroughly tested specialist in interstellar contact. And he had no body, he was just a mind. But minds can get tired. Nobody knew that better than Förster.

"Being tired serves you quite right," he said with the last trace of anger he could muster in his exhausted state. "Nobody asked you to come here and make weird deals. Why are you really doing it?"

"'Cause it's my duty. There aren't many people on my planet who can bridge big voids between the stars by thought projection. There are only a few of us, and the work's very stressful. But somebody has to do it."

"Doesn't sound very heroic."

For the first time the alien let out something like a laugh, but there was no humor in it. "It's anything but heroic. It's very tiring and duller than dull. What's so special about being a member of an interplanetary field service?"

"Interplanetary field service?" Förster repeated disconcerted. "That's . . . I mean—I hadn't considered it from that angle yet."

"Yeah, I know. To you we're what the mythical white gods were to the Incas—powerful beings from another world, with superior knowledge and astounding devices. But we're only a couple of business people trading a few glass beads for valuable raw materials. And that's your good fortune, because instead of salesmen we could be mercenaries who'd rather rip off than pay."

"But—"

"That caught you off guard, didn't it? You pictured us as outerspace brains, scientifically and intellectually advanced, didn't you? I doubt we are. We merely came here to do business. And I have to do it as coolly, quickly, and efficiently as possible so that I get high returns. So don't bellyache to me that you're too old and tired, because it just costs me time."

Coolly, quickly, and efficiently, Förster thought. *Strange, this could have come from Berghäuser, his former boss decades ago. Selling's like boxing, Förster. Whoever's faster, more resistant, and more powerful wins. Yes, Mr. Berghäuser. No, Barbara. Not today. I'm too tired. Have fifteen customers I have to call on.*

He noticed that the alien had been quiet for a while.

"I don't want to rub you the wrong way," the alien finally said.

"No, no," Förster said. "That's all right. It was very . . . down to earth." He shook his head and even smiled. "It's unbelievable. You have the salesman's blues. I can spot it a mile away. Too much routine and too far from home. The salesman's blues . . ."

The alien's voice again got hard and authoritarian.

"That'll be enough of that. I'll be in touch tomorrow at seven on the dot. See you then."

"Yep," Förster said. "Good night," he added after a short pause.

July 11, 2:00 P.M. Förster pushed the empty dessert dish aside and belched discreetly.

"That was good." He felt full and satisfied as he had not in a long time. All morning long he had been doing business, partly in the alien's language, partly in German or English. It had been very strenuous, but he had been filled with strange delight. He was busy again, and in a certain way he even had a goal. He had not felt like this in years.

"I'd like a cappuccino," he said to the waiter scurrying past him. He did not say it loudly, but there was a new tone of authority in his voice the waiter responded to.

"*Súbito, signore.*"

"Well, well! Your old self again, old man?"

The overt aggressiveness in the alien's voice shocked Förster so much that he could get out only a feeble, defensive "Well, yes."

"Wow, fantastic!" the extraterrestrial said irritably. Then came a maelstrom of emotion in whose swirling confusion only one feature stood out—hysteria.

Förster paid no attention to it. He was furious. What right did this intruding interloper have to spoil his mood? For the first time in years he had a hint of lust for life, and this bastard was trying to mar it for him!

"Still the salesman's blues?" he taunted.

"You're damned right!" the alien exploded. "My God, how I hate it. Lousy planet, lousy business, lousy people. I can't hack it anymore! Things were never this bad until I teamed up with you. A Sirian neurotic and an Earth neurotic—what a terrific team. Just why do I do it to myself?"

Förster was upset. It was not so much the emotional outburst per se that stirred him up, but rather the vague, almost subliminal knowledge that the alien was a mirror image of his own behavior. The signals were extremely clear—self-pity and aggression. Envious of happy people because you yourself were unhappy. Förster did not like that mirror image.

"It's already tough enough, but you make me a complete outsider on my own team," the alien fumed. "Every Earth person who's been taken over by outerspacers should participate in meetings that are held in their respective countries to coordinate activities. I'm one of the few who couldn't attend because . . ."

He hesitated for a moment, but Förster knew what was coming anyway and instinctively held his breath.

"Because you're too old and decrepit. The long trip's too risky for you to undertake. That's a bad joke. I'm stranded. Stranded in a dying man."

Förster said nothing for a long time. "Why," he finally whispered, "do you say such things? That's malicious and cruel." Acting on a whim, he ordered a bottle of red wine. The alien did not interfere.

When Förster left the restaurant about an hour later, he was pretty drunk and left too big a tip.

July 11, 3:30 p.m. When Förster opened the door, Samson was lying in front of him. There was so much pain in the animal's eyes that it had an effect like ecstasy.

"Samson!" Förster yelled. "What's the matter with you, boy?"

He got on his knees and put his hand on the dog's head. At the same instant, as if the St. Bernard had expended his last ounce of energy to experience one last touch from his master, Samson died.

"This is too much," Förster wheezed. "It can't be true."

Mulling over the next few minutes the following day, he wondered how many tears there were in a wrinkled old man like him.

July 11, 6:00 p.m. The pen jerked across the paper and drew a wavy line resembling mountains with sharp peaks and deep valleys. Another device emitted beeping sounds which were pretty regular, but not completely so.

One of the pieces of adhesive tape holding the electrodes to Förster's body itched. An analyzing device in the corner hummed and shook a test tube of Förster's blood, an efficient new-generation Dracula.

Förster submitted to the monthly checkup with stoic indifference. He hardly noticed the humiliating procedures, the poking at and probing in his body. He lay on his back wearing only his underwear. The plastic cover on the examining table sticking to his body seemed to be clutching him tightly like a hungry octopus.

Nobody but Förster was in the room. No doctor or nurse stood watch over routine procedures these days unless something went wrong. You were connected to a multitude of machines, and Dr. Electronix performed the examination.

Everything in the room was white, bright, and clean. If the reports of people who were clinically dead and then revived were true, you seemed to float up at the moment of death and move toward a dazzlingly bright light. From that aspect the examining room with its humming, featureless brightness seemed to be a simulator for death candidates. An anteroom to death.

The thought passed quickly. Förster again stared at the ceiling impassively. He had nothing on his mind, he was just waiting for something. The E.T. did likewise. They were two aliens on Earth, isolated together. Two black holes into which all the sadness and depression in the universe poured.

July 11, 11:00 P.M. It was one of the few privileges of age, Förster thought as he poured himself a second glass of Drambuie, that you require little sleep. Too bad that you could not start on any new enterprises with all your free time.

He was sitting in the living room in his favorite easy chair. He was looking through the window at the trees, swaying silhouettes with silver leaves shimmering in the chalk-white light of a full moon. He was wide-awake, slightly drunk, and up to his knees in memories.

Acting on a whim, he put a record on. Debussy's "Claire de Lune." While the romantic piano sounds permeated the room, Förster's thoughts began to wander. Scenes from his life flashed before his mind's eye and went out again.

A joyless youth in a strict, loveless home. During his school days a long series of puzzling diseases—psychosomatic, as he now knew. An irascible father. Failure, weakling. The first year at college. Complete disorientation, which gradually gave way to a feeling of freedom. Then the outbreak of

World War II. Out of the lecture hall and up to the front. Six years in which he stopped thinking. Nothing but fight, advance, retreat. He did not hate anybody, but he killed other men to keep them from killing him. Somehow he stayed alive. He was the only one of his company of 120 men to survive the war.

Sometimes he still dreamed about shells hitting and blowing up foxholes and hurling broken bodies through the air. Bodies without faces, without limbs, but still alive. Cannon fodder for insatiable warlords. He dreamed about the icy cold of the Russian steppes, snow red with blood for kilometers, the leather belts they chewed on because they had nothing to eat. He dreamed about the Siberian POW camp where he spent four years. The Russians treated them badly, but he could not blame them for it at all. When he was finally released and after ten years returned to civilian life, a shadow lay over him. He was not neurotic or psychotic, no, but he seldom laughed and seemed singularly distant. He acted like someone who had been subjected to electroshock therapy too often and who was now waiting for the next jolt with tense anticipation.

Förster's flow of memories was interrupted when the music stopped. He flinched, drifting between reality and memories for an instant. Then he found himself back in reality.

There was a thundering silence in the room—and in his thoughts. The alien was keeping quiet. Nevertheless, Förster was sure that he was listening intently.

"Well, have you obtained any interesting information about life on Earth?" he asked sarcastically.

"Yeah, that I have," the extraterrestrial said. He seemed to want to add something, even though he then fell silent again. "Maybe you should put on another record," he said after a while. "That'll do us some good. That music was very lovely."

Förster nodded. He got up and put on Frederic Chopin's Nocturne No. 2 in E-flat Major. With music came memories. At the beginning of the fifties he got acquainted with Barbara. They got married, and she made him very happy. His climb up the corporate ladder began. He made a good deal of money. The big break kept eluding him, though. He lacked charisma, his bosses said. That did not bother Förster. He was leading a wonderful life with Barbara and the kids. But the shadow still followed him and never left. He was happy, but it was a second-hand happiness because it came from the circumstances and not from the heart. He kept telling himself: You have everything you want. You should be happy. But it did not work. He finally resigned himself to that. At least he was contented.

The record player shut off with a soft click.

"How beautiful," the alien said. "How wonderfully beautiful. I believe music is the best thing this planet has to offer. Please play me some more of it."

The extraterrestrial's voice was so soft and urgent that Förster unhesitatingly pulled another record off the shelf.

"Lonely, huh?" he said.

"Who isn't?" the alien replied.

Förster looked across the dark room to the corner Samson always used to sleep in. "Yeah, who isn't?"

The needle was put on the record. "Strangers in the Night." Barbara had loved that melody. How many times had they danced to its sounds! Förster could not dance, but when he and Barbara were together, he could. "Midnight Cowboy." He had heard this tune for the first time late one night in his hotel room. Oh, those lonely nights in a hotel while he was on the road. Being the last person at the bar. Undecidedly shaking the empty glass in his hand. One more! Sorry, sir, we're closing now. Oh, yeah, well then, good evening. Good evening, sir. Then lying on the bed sweaty and restless in his dark room. Outside it is quiet. Everybody is asleep. But not you. Soft music purred from the radio, comforting all who had no other consolation. Help me make it through the night. Lying in the dark listening to music is nice. Thoughts flow quietly. There is a bitter sweetness in your loneliness. While you are thinking over your life, you slowly fall asleep.

Förster now felt the presence of the extraterrestrial quite clearly. It seemed as if the alien had moved closer.

"Moonlight Serenade." Also one of Barbara's favorite melodies. She had requested it from every hotel orchestra. She was a good dancer. The way she did the tango drove men crazy. Förster enjoyed it the best he could. But that was all in the past now. Barbara was dead and gone. And it takes two to tango.

He felt miserable. And the extraterrestrial felt exactly the same way. Uncertain quaking emotions struck Förster, quite obviously the telepathic equivalent of passionate crying.

Förster did not know what to do. "Now it wasn't all that bad," he said helplessly. No, not really. "Moonlight Serenade" reminded him of his tenth wedding anniversary. They were dancing on the terrace of a luxury hotel on the Côte d'Azur. Stars twinkled in their Mediterranean splendor. The sea was a dark mirror that a phosphorescent wave crest sometimes rippled across. A colorfully illuminated fountain splashed nearby. In the background, the palatial hotel was shimmering in the darkness like a fairy-tale castle. Up there little Sandra was sleeping happily and contentedly in their room. And he danced with Barbara on and on and on. His feet hardly seemed to touch

the floor. Tonight he was Cary Grant, and Barbara was Grace Kelly.
Yes.

"It wasn't really all that bad," Förster muttered. "No, not that bad at all," he repeated, rather surprised, and fell asleep.

The ghost of a smile was outlined on his lips.

July 12, 3:00 P.M. The air-conditioning unit in the conference room was set on high. Cold. White walls, white leather and chrome furniture. Cold. A smartly dressed guy in a pinstripe suit with eyes like marbles. Cold.

The negotiations with Dr. Hellman—the name of the smiling business-man enjoying himself—had reached an impasse. Förster had not under-stood a word of the conversation he had been carrying on in some foreign language, but it was also unmistakably clear to him that it had stopped dead.

He felt anger and desperation rising in him, emotions that were not his own but radiated from the otherwise hermetically sealed mind of the extraterrestrial.

At first, Förster was amused by the helplessness of the all-powerful alien. But then the echo of the alien's frustration got so loud and so similar to his own depression that spontaneous solidarity germinated in him. He wanted to help his extraterrestrial tenant somehow. Nobody should be so humbled.

When the alien lost control over Förster during his emotional crisis, Förster acted without thinking. He simply got up and went to the door.

Two separate things happened.

He heard a kind of hysterical laughter in his head linked to a feeling of release.

Dr. Hellman jumped up and rushed after him, spewing out a stream of words. Obviously, his bargaining position was not so good as he made it appear.

It so happened that the alien was then able to close the deal to his satisfaction. When they left the office building and went into the heat on the street, the extraterrestrial said quite calmly, "Thanks, Robert."

That was the first time the alien had called Förster by name.

July 12, 11:30 P.M. That night, too, Förster played whatever came to mind—Tchaikovsky, Gershwin, medieval madrigals, African tribal chants, and lots of Mozart. The room was almost dark, the problems of the world far away. Everything was pleasant.

As Förster was looking for a new piece of music, he caught sight of a stack of records that were off to one side on the shelf, separate from the others. He smiled.

"Here, this was something different at one time," he said. "The Rolling Stones. '2,000 Light-Years from Home.' That's for you. And there, the Beatles. 'When I'm 64.' That's for me."

Yet when he picked up the record, his hand began trembling, and he realized he had made a bad mistake. Sudden grief flooded out his thoughts. Nothing was pleasant anymore.

"What's wrong?" the alien asked.

"My kids," Förster said. "I must've been thinking about my kids. I bought these records for them back then. My God, how long ago that was. Almost twenty years, Sandra and Richard . . ."

Sandra was their first child. How he had doted on that tiny tot! When her miniature hand closed around his outstretched finger for the first time, that was possibly the loveliest moment in his whole life. Her faint gurgling sounds, which had filled the house with magic harmony. Her first words, her first clumsy steps undeniably ending in a plop on her diaper-cushioned behind. And how fascinating it had been to watch that little kid exploring her world. How she laughed and marveled at things he himself no longer noticed. In those days he had learned a lot from Sandra, a new unpretentiousness, a new openness to the many small wonders in life. How uncomplicated it was to be happy.

In time, Sandra had kids herself. She had married a guy Förster could not stand, who lived in Berlin. I can't come, Dad. Heinz has so much to do. And with the kids it's so hard to get away, and it's such a long trip. Some other time, perhaps. Yeah, some other time, Sandra. Click. I would not mind your telling me lies as long as you were at least happy. But you are not. Oh, Sandra. So much love that will never be returned.

And Richard was stranger still. As a kid, he had always been a bit chubby and awkward, but unbelievably friendly and eventempered, a chubby-faced angel nobody could say no to. Most of all, Förster recalled two episodes that for some reason had stayed in his mind. They were at the zoo. Richard was three years old. For the first time in his life he had gotten an ice cream cone and paid for it with the money his father had counted out beforehand. He was so proud of his accomplishment that he forgot to eat his ice cream. He stared and stared at it—his very own first ice cream—and the colored balls were melting and dripping and smearing his hands and his blissfully smiling face. A year later, on a bitterly cold Sunday in December, Richard came into his study with his broken toy truck and said, "Put it back together, Daddy. You can do it. You can do anything." Förster saw the blind trust in the boy's face, and sweat broke out on him because he knew he could not fix the toy. It was a moment of both such intense pride and pain that it still moved him deeply after all these years.

Richard was now a successful dental surgeon, slim, suntanned, dynamic. He had a perfect house and a perfect wife. Everything he did was perfect. He was even perfectly unhappy. His birthday and Christmas cards always arrived punctually.

Förster noticed that he was still standing in front of the record player and was holding the album in his hand. "When I'm 64." Life is guaranteed to take the worst of all possible turns. Förster's law of autobiographical flashbacks.

With a hopeless gesture he sat down. A life filled with struggle and striving—for this wretched result? That was a cruel joke.

Suddenly, the alien's voice, which he had completely forgotten about, was in his head again. It was tender and filled with sympathy such as Förster had not experienced for an eternity.

"You're a good man, Robert Förster. I like you a lot." The alien thought for a moment. "Your memories always surprise me over and over. Our lives have so many parallels. Battling against the worst odds, giving your best, and ending up as a winner with a feeling of loss. I'm familiar with that." A kaleidoscope of incomprehensible alien scenes flashed through Förster's mind, memories of a distant planet. "Funny how life in the universe follows universal rules."

Förster felt the sincere warmth in the words of the alien, who did not seem to him as strange now as he once had. The extraterrestrial's concern was as startling as a surprise visit to someone sick in bed and just as comforting.

"Thanks," he said. "Thanks, uh . . ."

"Sassacan," the alien said. "Sassacan's the name."

July 13, 7:00 A.M. An early-morning peace still lay over the land. The sun had just risen over the treetops. Its down-sloping light cast grotesquely long shadows and made dewdrops sparkle. The lake was calm; only a couple of fishermen were rowing across the water through the haze. In the cool, fresh air wafting across the balcony, the rattling of Förster's breakfast dishes sounded louder and happier than usual.

"Now we're friends," Sassacan said. "That happens very rarely on my missions. Generally speaking, I'm regarded as an oppressor, an occupation force. Here on earth it seems to be just the same way. But you're an exception."

"I am?"

"Yeah. Despite your personal problems you've been unusually open-minded. Most people react hysterically when I . . . come to them. From the first second on, you were completely cool, calm, and collected."

"Maybe because I'm old. I've seen a lot in my day. I know nothing's impossible. What could still surprise me?" Förster took another sip of coffee. "You made it easy for me. You respected me—after a while. Most of you outerspace types seem to be very aggressive. Why do you act differently?"

"We're not all cast from the same mold. We come from different planets, so we behave in different ways. You know, we Sirians had a horrible war not too long ago. That experience has made us more peaceful than other races."

"I see. Yes, war changes one." For a moment, Förster's thoughts started wandering. Dying men writhing in blood and mud. Dead children in ruins, their arms torn off like discarded dolls. Small, unimportant bodies, which did not count in the larger scheme of things. Oh, God.

"You dwell a lot on those things, Robert."

"Yeah. They've changed my life."

"You also think about Barbara frequently," Sassacan said, changing the subject.

"I simply can't forget her." Förster stared at his coffee spoon as if it were an exotic insect. "Though she's been dead for ten years now."

"Ten years?" Sassacan said. "I didn't think it had been that long ago. She's so . . . present in your thoughts."

"You didn't think so?" Förster was taken aback. "But you did know that. You can read every last one of my thoughts."

"It's not that simple. To me your mind's like a great big library. I can find any piece of information in it. But I have to scrounge around for it first. There are a lot of unread books standing on the shelves."

"So that's the way it is." Förster chuckled in his distant fashion. "So do I still have my own little secrets from you?"

"Yes, of course." Sassacan was now talking very slowly. "I started to like you when I read your thoughts about Barbara. So much love for a sister from Earth has deeply moved me."

"A sister?" Förster sputtered. "You mean, you mean you're a female?"

"Yes, most of the time, that is."

Förster gulped. "That changes the score. Then we're on the way to an interstellar love affair, aren't we?"

They both laughed a little too loudly about that.

July 13, 6:00 P.M. Last night a thunderstorm had blown up and cleaned and cooled the air. Förster enjoyed his constitutional on the lakeside promenade much more than he had during the last few weeks. The weather was mild, you could see as far as the most distant mountain peaks. And he had a friend.

Förster and Sassacan watched the souvenir vendors dismantle their stands with postcards and silly plastic mementos. Swimmers and surfers were landing on the beach and packing up their things. Handsome young people with well-proportioned bodies so deeply tanned that their lips seemed pale on dark faces. They got into their Broncos, Pajeros, Jeeps, Rabbit convertibles and sped away to some other pressing engagement. Eager hedonists always on the go. To Förster they still seemed more alien than Sassacan, but he did not hate them anymore.

"A beautiful day today," he said.

"Yes," Sassacan said.

Snatches of sound from a carnival drifted across the lake. Förster was listening to the oompahpah of a brass band. "You wanna listen to music again this evening?"

"Oh, yeah," Sassacan said. "Very much."

"How about an organ concert . . ." Förster stopped, irritated somehow. "Anything wrong?"

"I have to go back tomorrow," Sassacan's voice was as emotionless as a vocoder. "The job's finished. The traveling salesman travels on. You know how it is."

"But," Förster stammered, "right now?" He could not talk anymore. Blood roared in his ears. His heart beat like a hammer. Now that I have had a taste of hope!

"Life's a sadist," Sassacan said.

Förster said nothing. He plopped down on a bench, older and lonelier than ever before, shivering in the warm sunlight.

July 14, 3:30 P.M. Förster slammed the telephone receiver down on its cradle with intense satisfaction. He had just canceled his weekly doctor's appointment. "Make your money off of some other old idiot, doctor. I'm still not so infirm that I have to sit around in your consulting room all the time. I'll let you know when I need you."

He sniggered. I'll let you know when I need you. That was a good one. Took that smart-ass authority figure down a peg or two.

In every respect it had been a remarkable day. At breakfast in the Café Panorama a slim young man sat down at his table. He seemed bewildered and distressed. Somehow they got to talking. It turned out that the young man had inherited a company that was highly respected, but with the flood of cheap imports from the Far East could not compete anymore. With modern production equipment he would again be able to land contracts, but he did not have enough ready cash, and banks would not extend him any credit. In a few weeks the firm would go bankrupt.

"That's simple, young man," Förster said. "What you need is a sale-and-leaseback contract. It goes like this. You sell your expensive factory buildings to a leasing company. You get a lot of money for them. At the same time, you rent the buildings back from the leasing company. That way you can stay in there and continue production, *and* you turn your hidden reserves into ready money. You invest this money and get your firm on its feet again. When you've made enough profit, you buy back the factory buildings after a couple of years."

The young man choked and panted until his face was dark red. "That's incredible!" he gasped. "That's it! How can I ever thank you?"

"That's all right," Förster said offhandedly. "It was a pleasure for me. From now on, perhaps you'll view old people in a little different light. A lot of years means a lot of experience, you see." He passed his business card across the table. "Just give me a call if you run into problems."

"I most certainly will," the young man said happily and hastily got up.

Förster watched him with amusement. So he was not quite a doddering old fool yet. The waiter found that out the hard way, and he paid for it when as usual he ignored Förster's signal. Förster went to the business manager, who fired the waiter on the spot. "That's the fifth or sixth complaint this week, Schulz. That's it for me. You're dismissed."

Nice going. Yes, people, Förster is back in the swing of things. Watch out and don't cross me. I'm not gonna let anything happen to me anymore.

The morning was extremely hectic. Sassacan still had a lot to finish before she left Earth. She seemed pretty mad. "Typical. The others stay here quite a while longer, but we Sirians have to wind up our business in record time again. Always the same old thing."

But that did not bother Förster. On the contrary, he even liked the high level of activity. It was better than merosely sitting on some park bench and watching the party from outside.

Perhaps that was why he reacted so quickly to the incident in the Swan Hotel. He had just finished a conversation with one of Sassacan's business associates and was waiting for a taxi in the hotel lobby. Outside, a heavy summer thunderstorm was raging. Rain poured down windows like a waterfall. A woman with a huge Labrador retriever rushed through the door pretty well soaked. At that same moment, lightning struck the office building on the other side of the street. A blinding flash and ear-splitting thunder filled every corner of the room.

The Labrador got loose and ran through the lobby barking and terrified, eyes bulging. He looked as aggressive as a dangerous beast.

Förster was the only one who acted. As the dog sped by him, he grabbed the leash and shouted sharply, "Sit!"

The dog was so well trained that it obeyed instantly in spite of its terror. Förster patted the dog reassuringly. "Easy there, Samson boy, easy. Everything's all right. Take it easy."

Panic gradually faded from the dog's eyes. Meanwhile, his master had walked over beside Förster.

"Thanks," she said calmly.

Förster turned to her and knew at once this was a special moment in his life. Barbara was there again. Of course, it was not Barbara, but she would have looked like that at sixty. Short, silver-gray, almost-metallic-looking hair in a page-boy cut, gray eyes that reacted with amusement to his stare, a beaming face that hid its years, plus a radiating youthful vitality. Plain expensive clothes.

"That was extraordinarily quick thinking on your part," she said. "I really must thank you, Mr. . . ."

Förster kept staring at her. The way she looked, the way she talked. It was a miracle. He suddenly realized that all the years he had been weighed down with anger and depression, he had been waiting for just such a moment as this, as a candle waits for the match to light it.

He realized that he had not answered her question. "Förster," he said. "Robert Förster."

"I'm Katharina Erhard." She smiled. "Are you a reporter? You seem to be quite inquisitive."

"Oh, no, excuse me, I—" With mild astonishment he observed how he put his arm on her shoulder and spontaneously said, "You're dripping wet. Take off your coat, and then let's go to the bar. A little whiskey'll warm you up."

She smiled again and said yes, and then they were sitting in the dark wood-paneled bar and talking and talking. There was a faint smell of wood, leather, and tobacco in the air mixed with the fragrance of her expensive perfume.

Förster was happy.

July 14, 9:00 P.M. From the east, night spread across the sky. In the west, the day took its leave with bizarre-looking cloud sculptures scudding across a horizon festooned in gold, red, and purple.

Förster stood on the terrace of the *Herrenchiemsee* Castle and gazed upon the splendor of the park as it slowly slipped into twilight. Water in the big fountain created gracefully dancing, regularly changing figures. Bright light fell on the terrace from the hall of mirrors behind Förster. Hundreds of torches were burning inside there, and expectantly cheerful people in evening clothes waited for the castle concert to begin.

And Katharina was waiting for him. He thought about the trip on the paddle steamer which had brought them across the lake to the island where the *Herrenchiemsee* Castle was located. They stood at the railing, quiet, their heads full of thoughts. The evening wind smelled of algae. Förster listened to the asthmatic chugging of the old steamer. How many things he saw, smelled, and felt that he had not noticed in the past few years.

It was the most natural thing in the world for his hand to close over hers and for him to kiss her. Their lips touched with the soft, wonderful tenderness that you could only find in very small children who have just discovered the grace of giving. Then they went back into the passenger room, where they drank a glass of champagne and celebrated the grand reopening of Förster's life.

"I'm very happy," Sassacan said, "that I can end my stay on Earth on such a lovely day and happy note. I'm leaving you now, Robert."

Förster nodded. This moment had to come. It was a sad moment.

"Sassacan," he said. "I'd like to say so much to you, that I hardly know where to—"

"No need to," Sassacan said. "You know I'm looking through you."

"Oh, sure," Förster laughed. "What an unbelievable story. Of all 'people,' an extraterrestrial helps me get back to the land of the living."

"You've helped yourself," Sassacan said. "All I've done is interrupt your routine just as you've interrupted mine. We've learned a lot from each other."

"Yeah. Too bad you have to go now."

"You do have Katharina now."

"Luckily. I don't know if otherwise I could really bear losing you." A thought flashed through Förster's head. "Hey, wait a minute! Katharina . . . the young man with the bankrupt company . . . Katharina looking like Barbara. A whole bunch of coincidences for a single day. And the fact that just after a few minutes I put my arm around Katharina. That's not my way. You arranged everything and pulled the marionette strings a bit. Right?"

"Maybe, maybe not," Sassacan replied. "No matter. You're happy, and it makes my leaving easier."

"You bastard," Förster said. "I like you. Goddamn it, but I do like you."

"I like you, too, Robert. So long. Keep moving."

"So long, Sassacan. And thanks for everything."

Then Förster was all alone again. Lost in thought, he stared at the park, which now lay in full darkness. His lips moved, mumbling soundless words. Then he turned around and walked to the brightly illuminated hall of mirrors. At the door he cast one more glance over his shoulder up at the sky.

Good luck, Sassacan, wherever you are.

The stars were slowly coming out.

AVRAM DAVIDSON

The Golem

Avram Davidson is one of the most distinguished contemporary writers and editors of science fiction and fantasy. He first became prominent in the 1950s as a writer of short magazine fiction and it is upon this that his reputation rests. Peter S. Beagle compares him to John Collier, Saki, and Roald Dahl, concluding that "none of these, even Collier, comes near to matching either Avram's gifts of language or his understated compassion." This story takes one of the standard devices, the robot, from its roots in folklore to the present and humorously puts it in its place.

*   *   *

The gray-faced person came along the street where old Mr. and Mrs. Gumbeiner lived. It was afternoon, it was autumn, the sun was warm and soothing to their ancient bones. Anyone who attended the movies in the twenties or the early thirties has seen that street a thousand times. Past these bungalows with their half-double roofs Edmund Lowe walked arm-in-arm with Leatrice Joy and Harold Lloyd was chased by Chinamen waving hatchets. Under these squamous palm trees Laurel kicked Hardy and Woolsey beat Wheeler upon the head with codfish. Across these pocket-handkerchief-sized lawns the juveniles of the Our Gang Comedies pursued one another and were pursued by angry fat men in golf knickers. On this same street—or perhaps on some other one of five hundred streets exactly like it.

Mrs. Gumbeiner indicated the gray-faced person to her husband.

"You think maybe he's got something the matter?" she asked. "He walks kind of funny, to me."

"Walks like a *golem*," Mr. Gumbeiner said indifferently.

The old woman was nettled.

"Oh, I don't know," she said. "*I* think he walks like your cousin."

The old man pursed his mouth angrily and chewed on his pipestem. The gray-faced person turned up the concrete path, walked up the steps to the porch, sat down in a chair. Old Mr. Gumbeiner ignored him. His wife stared at the stranger.

"Man comes in without a hello, goodbye, or howareyou, sits himself down and right away he's at home. . . . The chair is comfortable?" she asked. "Would you like maybe a glass tea?"

She turned to her husband.

"Say something, Gumbeiner!" she demanded. "What are you, made of wood?"

The old man smiled a slow, wicked, triumphant smile.

"Why should *I* say anything?" he asked the air. "Who am I? Nothing, that's who."

The stranger spoke. His voice was harsh and monotonous.

"When you learn who—or, rather, what—I am, the flesh will melt from your bones in terror." He bared porcelain teeth.

"Never mind about my bones!" the old woman cried. "You've got a lot of nerve talking about my bones!"

"You will quake with fear," said the stranger. Old Mrs. Gumbeiner said that she hoped he would live so long. She turned to her husband once again.

"Gumbeiner, when are you going to mow the lawn?"

"All mankind—" the stranger began.

"*Shah!* I'm talking to my husband . . . He talks *eppis* kind of funny, Gumbeiner, no?"

"Probably a foreigner," Mr. Gumbeiner said, complacently.

"You think so?" Mrs. Gumbeiner glanced fleetingly at the stranger. "He's got a very bad color in his face, *nebbich*. I suppose he came to California for his health."

"Disease, pain, sorrow, love, grief—all are nought to—"

Mr. Gumbeiner cut in on the stranger's statement.

"Gall bladder," the old man said. "Guinzburg down at the *shule* looked exactly the same before his operation. Two professors they had in for him, and a private nurse day and night."

"I am not a human being!" the stranger said loudly.

"Three thousand seven hundred fifty dollars it cost his son, Guinzburg told me. 'For you, Poppa, nothing is too expensive—only get well,' the son told him."

"*I am not a human being!*"

"Ai, is that a son for you!" the old woman said, rocking her head. "A heart of gold, pure gold." She looked at the stranger. "All right, all right, I heard you the first time. Gumbeiner! I asked you a question. When are you going to cut the lawn?"

"On Wednesday, *odder* maybe Thursday, comes the Japaneser to the neighborhood. To cut lawns is *his* profession. *My* profession is to be a glazier—retired."

"Between me and all mankind is an inevitable hatred," the stranger said. "When I tell you what I am, the flesh will melt—"

"You said, you said already," Mr. Gumbeiner interrupted.

"In Chicago where the winters were as cold and bitter as the Czar of Russia's heart," the old woman intoned, "you had strength to carry the frames with the glass together day in and day out. But in California with the golden sun to mow the lawn when your wife asks, for this you have no strength. Do I call in the Japaneser to cook for you supper?"

"Thirty years Professor Allardyce spent perfecting his theories. Electronics, neuronics—"

"Listen, how educated he talks," Mr. Gumbeiner said, admiringly. "Maybe he goes to the University here?"

"If he goes to the University, maybe he knows Bud?" his wife suggested.

"Probably they're in the same class and he came to see him about the homework, no?"

"Certainly he must be in the same class. How many classes are there? Five *in ganzen*: Bud showed me on his program card." She counted off on her fingers. "Television Appreciation and Criticism, Small Boat Building, Social Adjustment, The American Dance . . . The American Dance—nu, Gumbeiner—"

"Contemporary Ceramics," her husband said, relishing the syllables. "A fine boy, Bud. A pleasure to have him for a boarder."

"After thirty years spent in these studies," the stranger, who had continued to speak unnoticed, went on, "he turned from the theoretical to the pragmatic. In ten years' time he had made the most titanic discovery in history: he made mankind, *all* mankind, superfluous: he made *me*."

"What did Tillie write in her last letter?" asked the old man.

The old woman shrugged.

"What should she write? The same thing. Sidney was home from the Army, Naomi has a new boy friend—"

"*He made* me!"

"Listen, Mr. Whatever-your-name-is," the old woman said; "maybe where you came from is different, but in *this* country you don't interupt people the while they're talking. . . . Hey. Listen—what do you mean, he *made* you? What kind of talk is that?"

The stranger bared all his teeth again, exposing the too-pink gums.

"In his library, to which I had a more complete access after his sudden and as yet undiscovered death from entirely natural causes, I found a complete collection of stories about androids, from Shelley's *Frankenstein* through Čapek's *R.U.R.* to Asimov's—"

"Frankenstein?" said the old man, with interest. "There used to be Frankenstein who had the soda-*wasser* place on Halstead Street: a Litvack, *nebbich*."

"What are you talking?" Mrs. Gumbeiner demanded. "His name was Franken*thal*, and it wasn't on Halstead, it was on Roosevelt."

"—clearly shown that all mankind has an instinctive antipathy towards androids and there will be an inevitable struggle between them—"

"Of course, of course!" Old Mr. Gumbeiner clicked his teeth against his pipe. "I am always wrong, you are always right. How could you stand to be married to such a stupid person all this time?"

"I don't know," the old woman said. "Sometimes I wonder, myself. I think it must be his good looks." She began to laugh. Old Mr. Gumbeiner blinked, then began to smile, then took his wife's hand.

"Foolish old woman," the stranger said; "why do you laugh? Do you not know I have come to destroy you?"

"What!" old Mr. Gumbeiner shouted. "Close your mouth, you!" He darted from his chair and struck the stranger with the flat of his hand. The stranger's head struck against the porch pillar and bounced back.

"When you talk to my wife, talk respectable, you hear?"

Old Mrs. Gumbeiner, cheeks very pink, pushed her husband back in his chair. Then she leaned forward and examined the stranger's head. She clicked her tongue as she pulled aside a flap of gray, skin-like material.

"Gumbeiner, look! He's all springs and wires inside!"

"I *told* you he was a *golem*, but no, you wouldn't listen," the old man said.

"You said he *walked* like a *golem*."

"How could he walk like a *golem* unless he *was* one?"

"All right, all right. . . . You broke him, so now fix him."

"My grandfather, his light shines from Paradise, told me that when MoHaRaL—Moreynu Ha-Rav Löw—his memory for a blessing, made the *golem* in Prague, three hundred? four hundred years ago? he wrote on his forehead the Holy Name."

Smiling reminiscently, the old woman continued, "And the *golem* cut the rabbi's wood and brought his water and guarded the ghetto."

"And one time only he disobeyed the Rabbi Löw, and Rabbi Löw erased the *Shem Ha-Mephorash* from the *golem's* forehead and the *golem* fell down like a dead one. And they put him up in the attic of the *shule* and he's still there today if the Communisten haven't sent him to Moscow. . . . This is not just a story," he said.

"*Avadda* not!" said the old woman.

"I myself have seen both the *shule and* the rabbi's grave," her husband said, conclusively.

"But I think this must be a different kind *golem*, Gumbeiner. See, on his forehead: nothing written."

"What's the matter, there's a law I can't write something there? Where is that lump clay Bud brought us from his class?"

The old man washed his hands, adjusted his little black skullcap, and slowly and carefully wrote four Hebrew letters on the gray forehead.

"Ezra the Scribe himself couldn't do better," the old woman said, admiringly. "Nothing happens," she observed, looking at the lifeless figure sprawled in the chair.

"Well, after all, am I Rabbi Löw?" her husband asked, deprecatingly. "No," he answered. He leaned over and examined the exposed mechanism. "This spring goes here . . . this wire comes with this one . . ." The figure moved. "But this one goes where? And this one?"

"Let be," said his wife. The figure sat up slowly and rolled its eyes loosely.

"Listen, Reb *Golem*," the old man said, wagging his finger. "Pay attention to what I say—you understand?"

"Understand . . ."

"If you want to stay here, you got to do like Mr. Gumbeiner says."

"Do-like-Mr.-Gumbeiner-says . . ."

"*That's* the way I like to hear a *golem* talk. Malka, give here the mirror from the pocketbook. Look, you see your face? You see on the forehead, what's written? If you don't do like Mr. Gumbeiner says, he'll wipe out what's written and you'll be no more alive."

"No-more-alive . . ."

"*That's* right. Now, listen. Under the porch you'll find a lawnmower. Take it. And cut the lawn. Then come back. Go."

"Go . . ." The figure shambled down the stairs. Presently the sound of the lawnmower whirred through the quiet air in the street just like the street where Jackie Cooper shed huge tears on Wallace Beery's shirt and Chester Conklin rolled his eyes at Marie Dressler.

"So what will you write to Tillie?" old Mr. Gumbeiner asked.

"What should I write?" old Mrs. Gumbeiner shrugged: "I'll write that the weather is lovely out here and that we are both, Blessed be the Name, in good health."

The old man nodded his head slowly, and they sat together on the front porch in the warm afternoon sun.

RENÉ REBETEZ-CORTES

The New Prehistory

TRANSLATED BY DAMON KNIGHT

Like Japan, the Spanish-speaking world has no indigenous tradition of science fiction. But in the Hispanic countries, especially in South America, the school of magic realism has had significant impact on world literature since the 1960s.

This story, by René Rebetez-Cortes, a Colombian, was first published in 1972 and represents a speculative approach to the fantastic present and future. It is as near a relative of science fiction as one finds in Spanish literature today. One suspects that Damon Knight, the translator, chose to work on this piece because it engages in ironic dialogue with much of the satirical SF of the 1950s, in which some trivial aspect of contemporary society is extrapolated into a central position in a future world. "The New Prehistory" is what the defenders of literary SF prefer to call speculative fiction—SF shorn of gimmicks and gadgets, SF that still evokes the same concerns as that hokey stuff we read as teenagers.

* * *

It began when my friend Metropoulos joined the long ticket line in front of the Mayer Cinema. I had never liked standing in line for anything; I waited to one side. Eating corn chips, I watched the women who passed and the people who joined the line, pressed into it one by one like blobs of mercury.

The line moved slowly forward, with a monotonous scraping of feet on pavement. When I glanced at my friend's face, I saw that it was expressionless, slack-jawed. His eyes were glassy with boredom, his arms dangled like an ape's, his feet shuffled slowly.

I felt a sudden chill; somehow I knew what was about to happen. A fat lady had grown tired of waiting, even though she was only twenty places or so from the ticket window. She took a step, another, a third; the line curved with her. She turned her head indignantly, tried to break free; she ran, and the line stretched after her like a great bow bending—then it straightened again, dragging the poor woman back in spite of her struggles.

Now panic spread; they were all trying to break loose at once. The long line undulated in wild contortions, as if shaken by a gigantic hiccup. People were struggling, screaming, and shouting. Tempers grew heated; there was a flurry of blows.

Around the newborn monster a crowd was gathering. That was another custom in the cities, congregating to look at things: cranes, wrecking machines, blasting crews. Airplanes. Military parades. Political rallies. Crowds looking at billboards. Crowds looking at anything.

Myself, I had always hated crowds and lines of people. Not that I was antisocial, not at all; it was simply that I disliked humanity in the mass. Never had I dreamed that things would take such a turn, or that I would witness this transformation.

The people in line soon realized there was nothing they could do, or at least that there was no point in fighting among themselves. Tattered, bleeding, and crestfallen, at last they were still; an ominous silence fell over them. Then, little by little, like the sound of rushing water, there came the swelling voice of incredulity and terror.

It was obvious that these people could not pull themselves apart; something had bound them tightly together. Something that in the first few moments had been no more than a breath had rapidly changed into a viscous but tangible substance; very soon it had become a transparent gelatin, then a flexible cartilage like that of Siamese twins. A force unknown to mankind, latent in nature until now, had been unleashed, a psychological cancer that was gluing men together as if they were atoms of new elements in formation.

A restlessness came over the line. Like a huge centipede waking up, the monster slowly began to move down the street, hundreds of arms waving desperately. At the head of the column was a red-eyed man whose mouth was awry in a painful rictus. He was followed by a girl who had been proud of her beauty; now, disheveled, her makeup dissolved by tears, she moved like a sleepwalker. Then came a boy, his face pale with terror, then Metropoulos, my old friend, one more vertebra of the monstrous reptile. He passed without hesitating, deaf to my voice, his gaze fixed on the ground and his feet moving to the marching rhythm.

Gradually the movement grew faster, more erratic and frenzied. The long queue was like a string of carnival dancers, twisting and turning, performing a demonic conga in the street. Then, after a few frantic turns, the reptile sank to the pavement; each segment of its body was heaving, and a continual stertorous sound echoed in the half-open mouths, the nostrils like fluttering wings, the wild eyes.

It lasted only a moment; the reptile got up again. In it were a few dead and useless vertebrae. Dragging them along, the monster broke into its zigzag run again and disappeared down the street.

I had managed to get into the opening of a narrow doorway; from its shelter I watched the torpid crowd. Once more I knew what was going to happen. They were awakening gradually from the nightmare left behind by the great human serpent: now they were becoming aware of their own condition. They had turned into a gigantic amoeba; a thick protoplasm that had spurted out between them had bound them together like the cells of a honeycomb. There was not a single shout. Only a few faint groans and a murmur of helplessness came from the crowd.

The human serpent still seemed to know which was its head and which its tail, but the crowd-amoeba showed an immediate desire to spread in all directions. The human mass changed its shape from one instant to another in a grotesque and repellant manner: a convulsed macroscopic amoeba that stumbled and bounced painfully against the walls. A new being, gigantic and mindless, that moved down the street after its predecessor.

I don't remember how many days and nights I wandered those streets. Thousands of monsters of all sizes were roaming in the city. The lines at bakeries and bus stops had produced little reptiles of ten or so vertebrae each; the same for the lines at banks and confessionals. Larger ones had come from the lines at phone booths, movies, theaters, and other public places. The amoebas came from street crowds and public gatherings; they were spreading everywhere.

The strange ligature that had fastened the people together was really unbreakable. I saw one man who tried to cut it; the attempt ended in his painful death. The links that died by accident hung like dead leaves, without breaking the human chain. I saw a busload of people that had turned into a single mass. Unable to get out of the bus, they began destroying it. Whole buildings were being demolished by amoeba-crowds imprisoned inside. A shouting throng had formed itself into an immense clotted mass that swept away obstacles, filling the streets like a river: that one came from a political rally.

The few persons who were still separate scurried like rats to avoid touching the new organisms. All the same, most of them were being absorbed.

I don't want to know anything about that. I don't want to find myself transformed into something shapeless like an amoeba or a glob of spittle, nor to become the last segment of a gigantic worm. I cling to my human identity, my own individual and separate personality. I am a man, not a limb or an organ.

Nevertheless, I know the battle is already lost. Before my eyes humanity is being transformed into a nightmare. I try to be impartial and tell myself that perhaps it is for the best, that this sudden mutation will bring with it a fundamental advance for humanity. But it's useless; these new forms of life repel me.

They have renounced forever the old way of life. It is impossible for them to live in rooms as they did before, to use elevators, sit in chairs, sleep in beds, travel in cars or planes. Obviously they can't return to their jobs, go to offices, mind stores, operate in clinics, act in theaters. Everything must be reorganized to suit the new conditions.

After the early days of fear and confusion, the new composite beings abandoned the cities. Unable to get into kitchens, pantries, and refrigerators, they swarmed out into the country.

The sight of these reptiles and giant amoebas roaming the pastures or lurking in the woods is enough to turn my stomach. I think they have forgotten what they were. They eat insatiably: fruit, roots—and they eat animals alive. They haven't bothered to build shelters. One kind sleeps coiled up like a huge boa around a fire; the other kind, in a ball on the bare earth.

I don't know if they remember that they were once men.

So much time has passed, I have lost all perception of it. The evolution of the new beings has been demoniacally swift. They no longer try to add new links to their gigantic bodies; instead, when they meet a single person, they kill him. I have been living in the ruins of the cities, hiding from their multiple gaze and their keen sense of smell, but I venture out now and then to spy on them.

Their appearance has changed enormously; now they are *another thing*. A few days ago I surprised two serpent-beings making love in a nearby field. It was grotesque and indescribable, a contorted self-flagellation. Now I know that each one of these beings has a common organism, an integrated physiological function, a single nervous system, a unified and powerful mind.

It was difficult for me to accept this, because in the old days when people were individuals, those who liked to form themselves into lines or crowds in the street were always mediocrities, morons. Intelligent people would not have been caught up in such foolishness. They have been destroyed, or else, like me, they are wandering in the ruins. But I have met no one else here.

In spite of everything, I acknowledge the strength of the new creatures, the technical mastery they are beginning to show. With the speed of their thousand hands and their thousand feet, they are raising strange narrow or circular edifices, making and transporting materials in the twinkling of an eye. They have made immense capes, with openings for their multiple heads, to protect themselves from the cold. Sometimes I hear their chorus of a thousand voices chanting strange guttural songs.

I suspect the day is not far off when they will build their own airplanes and limousines, as long as railway cars, or rounded and flat like flying saucers. The time will come, too, I have no doubt, when they will play golf.

But I don't want to know anything about that. I always hated crowds and lines of people. I cling to my human identity, to my own individual and separate personality. It's not that I'm antisocial; not at all, I repeat. But masses of humanity are distasteful to me. Never did I dream that things would take such a turn, or that I would witness this transformation.

I sit among the ruins. In the distance I can hear a gigantic chorus: the voice of the new prehistory. A new cycle is beginning.

A Meeting with Medusa

Arthur C. Clarke is the colossus of contemporary British SF.
Active since the 1940s, he is, with Bradbury and Asimov,
Sturgeon, Heinlein, and Herbert, a classic and definitive
modern SF writer. His novels, including Childhood's End,
The City and the Stars, 2001: A Space Odyssey, Rendezvous
with Rama, and many others, as well as his short stories, have
established him as the poet of technological optimism in our
time. He has been active in the field for nearly fifty years, and
in spite of J. G. Ballard's prominence, remains, unchanged,
the most popular living British SF author, a position he has
held since the 1950s. Recently he endowed a prize to be
awarded annually to the best SF novel published in Britain.
His stories combine the gritty detail of everyday science in
action with the poetic vision of Olaf Stapledon and the challenging optimistic internationalism of the later works of
H. G. Wells, Clarke's two great precursors.

"A Meeting with Medusa," published in 1972, is his last
short story; since then he has published only novels, all
international best sellers. This story is quintessential Clarke, a
tale of the mystery and wonder of space exploration. A contemporary classic, it won the Nebula Award of the Science
Fiction Writers of America as best novella of the year.

* * *

1. A Day to Remember

The *Queen Elizabeth* was over three miles above the Grand Canyon, dawdling along at a comfortable hundred and eighty, when Howard Falcon spotted the camera platform closing in from the right. He had been expecting it—nothing else was cleared to fly at this altitude—but he was not too happy to have company. Although he welcomed any signs of public interest, he also wanted as much empty sky as he could get. After all, he was the first man in history to navigate a ship three-tenths of a mile long . . .

So far, this first test flight had gone perfectly; ironically enough, the only problem had been the century-old aircraft carrier *Chairman Mao*, borrowed from the San Diego Naval Museum for support operations. Only one of *Mao*'s four nuclear reactors was still operating, and the old battlewagon's top speed was barely thirty knots. Luckily, wind speed at sea level had been less than half this, so it had not been too difficult to maintain still air on the flight deck. Though there had been a few anxious moments during gusts, when the mooring lines had been dropped, the great dirigible had risen smoothly, straight up into the sky, as if on an invisible elevator. If all went well, *Queen Elizabeth IV* would not meet *Chairman Mao* again for another week.

Everything was under control; all test instruments gave normal readings. Commander Falcon decided to go upstairs and watch the rendezvous. He handed over to his second officer, and walked out into the transparent tubeway that led through the heart of the ship. There, as always, he was overwhelmed by the spectacle of the largest single space ever enclosed by man.

The ten spherical gas cells, each more than a hundred feet across, were ranged one behind the other like a line of gigantic soap bubbles. The tough plastic was so clear that he could see through the whole length of the array, and make out details of the elevator mechanism, more than a third of a mile from his vantage point. All around him, like a three-dimensional maze, was the structural framework of the ship—the great longitudinal girders running from nose to tail, the fifteen hoops that were the circular ribs of this sky-borne colossus, and whose varying sizes defined its graceful, streamlined profile.

At this low speed, there was little sound—merely the soft rush of wind over the envelope and an occasional creak of metal as the pattern of stresses changed. The shadowless light from the rows of lamps far overhead gave the whole scene a curiously submarine quality, and to Falcon this was enhanced by the spectacle of the translucent gasbags. He had once encountered a squadron of large but harmless jellyfish, pulsing their mindless way above a shallow tropical reef, and the plastic bubbles that gave *Queen Elizabeth* her lift often reminded him of these—especially when changing pressures made them crinkle and scatter new patterns of reflected light.

He walked down the axis of the ship until he came to the forward elevator, between gas cells one and two. Riding up to the Observation Deck, he noticed that it was uncomfortably hot, and dictated a brief memo to himself on his pocket recorder. The *Queen* obtained almost a quarter of her buoyancy from the unlimited amounts of waste heat produced by her fusion power plant. On this lightly loaded flight, indeed, only six of the ten gas cells contained helium; the remaining four were full of air. Yet she still carried two hundred tons of water as ballast. However, running the cells at high temperatures did produce problems in refrigerating the access ways; it was obvious that a little more work would have to be done there.

A refreshing blast of cooler air hit him in the face when he stepped out onto the Observation Deck and into the dazzling sunlight streaming through the plexiglass roof. Half a dozen workmen, with an equal number of superchimp assistants, were busily laying the partly completed dance floor, while others were installing electric wiring and fixing furniture. It was a scene of controlled chaos, and Falcon found it hard to believe that everything would be ready for the maiden voyage, only four weeks ahead. Well, that was not *his* problem, thank goodness. He was merely the Captain, not the Cruise Director.

The human workers waved to him, and the "simps" flashed toothy smiles, as he walked through the confusion, into the already completed Skylounge. This was his favorite place in the whole ship, and he knew that once she was operating he would never again have it all to himself. He would allow himself just five minutes of private enjoyment.

He called the bridge, checked that everything was still in order, and relaxed into one of the comfortable swivel chairs. Below, in a curve that delighted the eye, was the unbroken silver sweep of the ship's envelope. He was perched at the highest point, surveying the whole immensity of the largest vehicle ever built. And when he had tired of that—all the way out to the horizon was the fantastic wilderness carved by the Colorado River in half a billion years of time.

Apart from the camera platform (it had now fallen back and was filming from amidships) he had the sky to himself. It was blue and empty, clear down to the horizon. In his grandfather's day, Falcon knew, it would have been streaked with vapor trails and stained with smoke. Both had gone: the aerial garbage had vanished with the primitive technologies that spawned it, and the long-distance transportation of this age arced too far beyond the stratosphere for any sight or sound of it to reach Earth. Once again, the lower atmosphere belonged to the birds and the clouds—and now to *Queen Elizabeth IV.*

It was true, as the old pioneers had said at the beginning of the twentieth century: this was the only way to travel—in silence and luxury, breathing the air around you and not cut off from it, near enough to the surface to watch the everchanging beauty of land and sea. The subsonic jets of the 1980s, packed with hundreds of passengers seated ten abreast, could not even begin to match such comfort and spaciousness.

Of course, the *Queen* would never be an economic proposition, and even if her projected sister ships were built, only a few of the world's quarter of a billion inhabitants would ever enjoy this silent gliding through the sky. But a secure and prosperous global society could afford such follies and indeed needed them for their novelty and entertainment. There were at least a million men on Earth whose discretionary income exceeded a thousand new dollars a year, so the *Queen* would not lack for passengers.

Falcon's pocket communicator beeped. The copilot was calling from the bridge.

"O.K. for rendezvous, Captain? We've got all the data we need from this run, and the TV people are getting impatient."

Falcon glanced at the camera platform, now matching his speed a tenth of a mile away.

"O.K.," he replied. "Proceed as arranged. I'll watch from here."

He walked back through the busy chaos of the Observation Deck so that he could have a better view amidships. As he did so, he could feel the change of vibration underfoot; by the time he had reached the rear of the lounge, the ship had come to rest. Using his master key, he let himself out onto the small external platform flaring from the end of the deck; half a dozen people could stand here, with only low guardrails separating them from the vast sweep of the envelope—and from the ground, thousands of feet below. It was an exciting place to be, and perfectly safe even when the ship was traveling at speed, for it was in the dead air behind the huge dorsal blister of the Observation Deck. Nevertheless, it was not intended that the passengers would have access to it; the view was a little too vertiginous.

The covers of the forward cargo hatch had already opened like giant trap doors, and the camera platform was hovering above them, preparing to descend. Along this route, in the years to come, would travel thousands of passengers and tons of supplies. Only on rare occasions would the *Queen* drop down to sea level and dock with her floating base.

A sudden gust of cross wind slapped Falcon's cheek, and he tightened his grip on the guardrail. The Grand Canyon was a bad place for turbulence, though he did not expect much at this altitude. Without any real anxiety, he focused his attention on the descending platform, now about a hundred and fifty feet above the ship. He knew that the highly skilled operator who was flying the remotely controlled vehicle had performed this simple maneuver a dozen times already; it was inconceivable that he would have any difficulties.

Yet he seemed to be reacting rather sluggishly. That last gust had drifted the platform almost to the edge of the open hatchway. Surely the pilot could have corrected before this . . . Did he have a control problem? It was very unlikely; these remotes had multiple-redundancy, fail-safe takeovers, and any number of backup systems. Accidents were almost unheard of.

But there he went again, off to the left. Could the pilot be *drunk*? Improbable though that seemed, Falcon considered it seriously for a moment. Then he reached for his microphone switch.

Once again, without warning, he was slapped violently in the face. He hardly felt it, for he was staring in horror at the camera platform. The distant operator was fighting for control, trying to balance the craft on its jets—but he was only making matters worse. The oscillations increased—twenty degrees, forty, sixty, ninety . . .

"Switch to automatic, you fool!" Falcon shouted uselessly into his microphone. "Your manual control's not working!"

The platform flipped over on its back. The jets no longer supported it, but drove it swiftly downward. They had suddenly become allies of the gravity they had fought until this moment.

Falcon never heard the crash, though he felt it; he was already inside the Observation Deck, racing for the elevator that would take him down to the bridge. Workmen shouted at him anxiously, asking what had happened. It would be many months before he knew the answer to that question.

Just as he was stepping into the elevator cage, he changed his mind. What if there was a power failure? Better be on the safe side, even if it took longer and time was the essence. He began to run down the spiral stairway enclosing the shaft.

Halfway down he paused for a second to inspect the damage. That damned platform had gone clear through the ship, rupturing two of the gas cells as it did so. They were still collapsing slowly, in great falling veils of plastic. He was not worried about the loss of lift—the ballast could easily take care of that, as long as eight cells remained intact. Far more serious was the possibility of structural damage. Already he could hear the great latticework around him groaning and protesting under its abnormal loads. It was not enough to have sufficient lift; unless it was properly distributed, the ship would break her back.

He was just resuming his descent when a superchimp, shrieking with fright, came racing down the elevator shaft, moving with incredible speed, hand over hand, along the *outside* of the latticework. In its terror, the poor beast had torn off its company uniform, perhaps in an unconscious attempt to regain the freedom of its ancestors.

Falcon, still descending as swiftly as he could, watched its approach with some alarm. A distraught simp was a powerful and potentially dangerous animal, especially if fear overcame its conditioning. As it overtook him, it started to call out a string of words, but they were all jumbled together, and the only one he could recognize was a plaintive, frequently repeated "boss." Even now, Falcon realized, it looked toward humans for guidance. He felt sorry for the creature, involved in a manmade disaster beyond its comprehension, and for which it bore no responsibility.

It stopped opposite him, on the other side of the lattice; there was nothing to prevent it from coming through the open framework if it wished. Now its face was only inches from his, and he was looking straight into the terrified eyes. Never before had he been so close to a simp, and able to study its features in such detail. He felt that strange mingling of kinship and discomfort that all men experience when they gaze thus into the mirror of time.

His presence seemed to have calmed the creature. Falcon pointed up the shaft, back toward the Observation Deck, and said very clearly and precisely: "Boss—boss—*go.*" To his relief, the simp understood; it gave him a grimace that might have been a smile, and at once started to race back the way it had come. Falcon had given it the best advice he could. If any safety remained aboard the *Queen*, it was in that direction. But his duty lay in the other.

He had almost completed his descent when, with a sound of rending metal, the vessel pitched nose down, and the lights went out. But he could still see quite well, for a shaft of sunlight streamed through the open hatch and the huge tear in the envelope. Many years ago he had stood in a great cathedral nave watching the light pouring through the stained-glass windows and forming pools of multicolored radiance on the ancient flagstones. The dazzling shaft of sunlight through the ruined fabric high above reminded him of that moment. He was in a cathedral of metal, falling down the sky.

When he reached the bridge, and was able for the first time to look outside, he was horrified to see how close the ship was to the ground. Only three thousand feet below were the beautiful and deadly pinnacles of rock and the red rivers of mud that were still carving their way down into the past. There was no level area anywhere in sight where a ship as large as the *Queen* could come to rest on an even keel.

A glance at the display board told him that all the ballast had gone. However, rate of descent had been reduced to a few yards a second; they still had a fighting chance.

Without a word, Falcon eased himself into the pilot's seat and took over such control as still remained. The instrument board showed him everything he wished to know; speech was superfluous. In the background, he could hear the Communications Officer giving a running report over the radio. By this time, all the news channels of Earth would have been preempted, and he could imagine the utter frustration of the program controllers. One of the most spectacular wrecks in history was occurring — without a single camera to record it. The last moments of the *Queen* would never fill millions with awe and terror, as had those of the *Hindenburg*, a century and a half before.

Now the ground was only about seventeen hundred feet away, still coming up slowly. Though he had full thrust, he had not dared to use it, lest the weakened structure collapse; but now he realized that he had no choice. The wind was taking them toward a fork in the canyon, where the river was split by a wedge of rock like the prow of some gigantic, fossilized ship of stone. If she continued on her present course, the *Queen* would straddle that triangular plateau and come to rest with at least a third of her length jutting out over nothingness; she would snap like a rotten stick.

Far away, above the sound of straining metal and escaping gas, came the familiar whistle of the jets as Falcon opened up the lateral thrusters. The ship staggered, and began to slew to port. The shriek of tearing metal was now almost continuous — and the rate of descent had started to increase ominously. A glance at the damage-control board showed that cell number five had just gone.

The ground was only yards away. Even now, he could not tell whether his maneuver would succeed or fail. He switched the thrust vectors over to vertical, giving maximum lift to reduce the force of impact.

The crash seemed to last forever. It was not violent — merely prolonged, and irresistible. It seemed that the whole universe was falling about them.

The sound of crunching metal came nearer, as if some great beast were eating its way through the dying ship.

Then floor and ceiling closed upon him like a vise.

2. "Because It's There"

"Why do you want to go to Jupiter?"

"As Springer said when he lifted for Pluto—'because it's there.'"

"Thanks. Now we've got *that* out of the way—the real reason."

Howard Falcon smiled, though only those who knew him well could have interpreted the slight, leathery grimace. Webster was one of them; for more than twenty years they had shared triumphs and disasters—including the greatest disaster of all.

"Well, Springer's cliché is still valid. We've landed on all the terrestrial planets, but none of the gas giants. They are the only real challenge left in the solar system."

"An expensive one. Have you worked out the cost?"

"As well as I can; here are the estimates. Remember, though—this isn't a one-shot mission, but a transportation system. Once it's proved out, it can be used over and over again. And it will open up not merely Jupiter, but *all* the giants."

Webster looked at the figures, and whistled.

"Why not start with an easier planet—Uranus, for example? Half the gravity, and less than half the escape velocity. Quieter weather, too—if that's the right word for it."

Webster had certainly done his homework. But that, of course, was why he was head of Long-Range Planning.

"There's very little saving—when you allow for the extra distance and the logistics problems. For Jupiter, we can use the facilities of Ganymede. Beyond Saturn, we'd have to establish a new supply base."

Logical, thought Webster; but he was sure that it was not the important reason. Jupiter was lord of the solar system; Falcon would be interested in no lesser challenge.

"Besides," Falcon continued, "Jupiter is a major scientific scandal. It's more than a hundred years since its radio storms were discovered, but we still don't know what causes them—and the Great Red Spot is as big a mystery as ever. That's why I can get matching funds from the Bureau of Astronautics. Do you know how many probes they have dropped into that atmosphere?"

"A couple of hundred, I believe."

"*Three* hundred and twenty-six, over the last fifty years—about a quarter of them total failures. Of course, they've learned a hell of a lot, but they've barely scratched the planet. Do you realize how *big* it is?"

"More than ten times the size of Earth."

"Yes, yes—but do you know what that really means?"

Falcon pointed to the large globe in the corner of Webster's office.

"Look at India—how small it seems. Well, if you skinned Earth and spread it out on the surface of Jupiter, it would look about as big as India does here."

There was a long silence while Webster contemplated the equation: Jupiter is to Earth as Earth is to India. Falcon had—deliberately, of course—chosen the best possible example . . .

Was it already ten years ago? Yes, it must have been. The crash lay seven years in the past (*that* date was engraved on his heart), and those initial tests had taken place three years before the first and last flight of the *Queen Elizabeth*.

Ten years ago, then, Commander (no, Lieutenant) Falcon had invited him to a preview—a three-day drift across the northern plains of India, within sight of the Himalayas. "Perfectly safe," he had promised. "It will get you away from the office—and will teach you what this whole thing is about."

Webster had not been disappointed. Next to his first journey to the Moon, it had been the most memorable experience of his life. And yet, as Falcon had assured him, it had been perfectly safe, and quite uneventful.

They had taken off from Srinagar just before dawn, with the huge silver bubble of the balloon already catching the first light of the Sun. The ascent had been made in total silence; there were none of the roaring propane burners that had lifted the hot-air balloons of an earlier age. All the heat they needed came from the little pulsed-fusion reactor, weighing only about two hundred and twenty pounds, hanging in the open mouth of the envelope. While they were climbing, its laser was zapping ten times a second, igniting the merest whiff of deuterium fuel. Once they had reached altitude, it would fire only a few times a minute, making up for the heat lost through the great gasbag overhead.

And so, even while they were almost a mile above the ground, they could hear dogs barking, people shouting, bells ringing. Slowly the vast, Sun-smitten landscape expanded around them. Two hours later, they had leveled out at three miles and were taking frequent draughts of oxygen. They could relax and admire the scenery; the on-board instrumentation was doing all the work—gathering the information that would be required by the designers of the still-unnamed liner of the skies.

It was a perfect day. The southwest monsoon would not break for another month, and there was hardly a cloud in the sky. Time seemed to have come to a stop; they resented the hourly radio reports which interrupted their reverie. And all around, to the horizon and far beyond, was that infinite, ancient landscape, drenched with history—a patchwork of villages, fields, temples, lakes, irrigation canals . . .

With a real effort, Webster broke the hypnotic spell of that ten-year-old memory. It had converted him to lighter-than-air flight—and it had made him realize the enormous size of India, even in a world that could be circled within ninety minutes. And yet, he repeated to himself, Jupiter is to Earth as Earth is to India . . .

"Granted your argument," he said, "and supposing the funds are available, there's another question you have to answer. Why should you do better than the—what is it—three hundred and twenty-six robot probes that have already made the trip?"

"I am better qualified than they were—as an observer, and as a pilot. *Especially* as a pilot. Don't forget—I've more experience of lighter-than-air flight than anyone in the world."

"You could still serve as controller, and sit safely on Ganymede."

"*But that's just the point!* They've already done that. Don't you remember what killed the *Queen?*"

Webster knew perfectly well; but he merely answered: "Go on."

"*Time lag—time lag!* That idiot of a platform controller thought he was using a local radio circuit. But he'd been accidentally switched through a satellite—oh, maybe it wasn't his fault, but he should have noticed. That's a half-second time lag for the round trip. Even then it wouldn't have mattered flying in calm air. It was the turbulence over the Grand Canyon that did it. When the platform tipped, and he corrected for that—it had already tipped the other way. Ever tried to drive a car over a bumpy road with a half-second delay in the steering?"

"No, and I don't intend to try. But I can imagine it."

"Well, Ganymede is a million kilometers from Jupiter. That means a round-trip delay of six seconds. No, you need a controller on the spot—to handle emergencies in real time. Let me show you something. Mind if I use this?"

"Go ahead."

Falcon picked up a postcard that was lying on Webster's desk; they were almost obsolete on Earth, but this one showed a 3-D view of a Martian landscape, and was decorated with exotic and expensive stamps. He held it so that it dangled vertically.

"This is an old trick, but helps to make my point. Place your thumb and finger on either side, not quite touching. That's right."

Webster put out his hand, almost but not quite gripping the card.

"Now catch it."

Falcon waited for a few seconds; then, without warning, he let go of the card. Webster's thumb and finger closed on empty air.

"I'll do it again, just to show there's no deception. You see?"

Once again, the falling card had slipped through Webster's fingers.

"Now you try it on me."

This time, Webster grasped the card and dropped it without warning. It had scarcely moved before Falcon had caught it. Webster almost imagined he could hear a click, so swift was the other's reaction.

"When they put me together again," Falcon remarked in an expression-less voice, "the surgeons made some improvements. This is one of them — and there are others. I want to make the most of them. Jupiter is the place where I can do it."

Webster stared for long seconds at the fallen card, absorbing the improb-able colors of the Trivium Charontis Escarpment. Then he said quietly: "I understand. How long do you think it will take?"

"With your help, plus the Bureau, plus all the science foundation we can drag in — oh, three years. Then a year for trials — we'll have to send in at least two test models. So, with luck — five years."

"That's about what I thought. I hope you get your luck; you've earned it. But there's one thing I won't do."

"What's that?"

"Next time you go ballooning, don't expect *me* as passenger."

3. The World of the Gods

The fall from Jupiter V to Jupiter itself takes only three and a half hours. Few men could have slept on so awesome a journey. Sleep was a weakness that Howard Falcon hated, and the little he still required brought dreams that time had not yet been able to exorcise. But he could expect no rest in the three days that lay ahead, and must seize what he could during the long fall down into that ocean of clouds, some sixty thousand miles below.

As soon as *Kon-Tiki* had entered her transfer orbit and all the computer checks were satisfactory, he prepared for the last sleep he might ever know. It seemed appropriate that at almost the same moment Jupiter eclipsed the bright and tiny Sun as he swept into the monstrous shadow of the planet. For a few minutes a strange golden twilight enveloped the ship; then a quarter of the sky became an utterly black hole in space, while the rest was a blaze of stars. No matter how far one traveled across the solar system, *they* never changed; these same constellations now shone on Earth, millions of miles away. The only novelties here were the small, pale crescents of Callisto and

Ganymede; doubtless there were a dozen other moons up there in the sky, but they were all much too tiny, and too distant, for the unaided eye to pick them out.

"Closing down for two hours," he reported to the mother ship, hanging almost a thousand miles above the desolate rocks of Jupiter V, in the radiation shadow of the tiny satellite. If it never served any other useful purpose, Jupiter V was a cosmic bulldozer perpetually sweeping up the charged particles that made it unhealthy to linger close to Jupiter. Its wake was almost free of radiation, and there a ship could park in perfect safety, while death sleeted invisibly all around.

Falcon switched on the sleep inducer, and consciousness faded swiftly out as the electric pulses surged gently through his brain. While *Kon-Tiki* fell toward Jupiter, gaining speed second by second in that enormous gravitational field, he slept without dreams. They always came when he awoke; and he had brought his nightmares with him from Earth.

Yet he never dreamed of the crash itself, though he often found himself again face to face with that terrified superchimp, as he descended the spiral stairway between the collapsing gasbags. None of the simps had survived; those that were not killed outright were so badly injured that they had been painlessly "euthed." He sometimes wondered why he dreamed only of this doomed creature—which he had never met before the last minutes of its life—and not of the friends and colleagues he had lost aboard the dying *Queen*.

The dreams he feared most always began with his first return to consciousness. There had been little physical pain; in fact, there had been no sensation of any kind. He was in darkness and silence, and did not even seem to be breathing. And—strangest of all—he could not locate his limbs. He could move neither his hands nor his feet, because he did not know where they were.

The silence had been the first to yield. After hours, or days, he had become aware of a faint throbbing, and eventually, after long thought, he deduced that this was the beating of his own heart. That was the first of his many mistakes.

Then there had been faint pinpricks, sparkles of light, ghosts of pressures upon still-unresponsive limbs. One by one his senses had returned, and pain had come with them. He had had to learn everything anew, recapitulating infancy and babyhood. Though his memory was unaffected, and he could understand words that were spoken to him, it was months before he was able to answer except by the flicker of an eyelid. He could remember the moments of triumph when he had spoken the first word, turned the page of a book—and, finally, learned to move under his own power. *That* was a victory indeed, and it had taken him almost two years to prepare for it. A hundred times he had envied that dead superchimp, but *he* had been given no choice. The doctors had made their decision—and now, twelve years later, he was where no human being had ever traveled before, and moving faster than any man in history.

Kon-Tiki was just emerging from shadow, and the Jovian dawn bridged the sky ahead in a titanic bow of light, when the persistent buzz of the alarm dragged Falcon up from sleep. The inevitable nightmares (he had been trying to summon a nurse, but did not even have the strength to push the button) swiftly faded from consciousness. The greatest—and perhaps last— adventure of his life was before him.

He called Mission Control, now almost sixty thousand miles away and falling swiftly below the curve of Jupiter, to report that everything was in order. His velocity had just passed thirty-one miles a second (*that* was one for the books) and in half an hour *Kon-Tiki* would hit the outer fringes of the atmosphere, as he started on the most difficult re-entry in the entire solar system. Although scores of probes had survived this flaming ordeal, they had been tough, solidly packed masses of instrumentation, able to with- stand several hundred gravities of drag. *Kon-Tiki* would hit peaks of thirty g's, and would average more than ten, before she came to rest in the upper reaches of the Jovian atmosphere. Very carefully and thoroughly, Falcon began to attach the elaborate system of restraints that would anchor him to the walls of the cabin. When he had finished, he was virtually a part of the ship's structure.

The clock was counting backward; one hundred seconds to re-entry. For better or worse, he was committed. In a minute and a half, he would graze the Jovian atmosphere, and would be caught irrevocably in the grip of the giant.

The countdown was three seconds late—not at all bad, considering the unknowns involved. From beyond the walls of the capsule came a ghostly sighing, which rose steadily to a high-pitched, screaming roar. The noise was quite different from that of a re-entry on Earth or Mars; in this thin atmosphere of hydrogen and helium, all sounds were transformed a couple of octaves upward. On Jupiter, even thunder would have falsetto overtones.

With the rising scream came mounting weight; within seconds, he was completely immobilized. His field of vision contracted until it embraced only the clock and the accelerometer; fifteen g, and four hundred and eighty seconds to go . . .

He never lost consciousness; but then, he had not expected to. *Kon-Tiki*'s trail through the Jovian atmosphere must be really spectacular—by this time, thousands of miles long. Five hundred seconds after entry, the drag began to taper off: ten g, five g, two . . . Then weight vanished almost completely. He was falling free, all his enormous orbital velocity destroyed.

There was a sudden jolt as the incandescent remnants of the heat shield were jettisoned. It had done its work and would not be needed again; Jupiter could have it now. He released all but two of the restraining buckles, and waited for the automatic sequencer to start the next, and most critical, series of events.

He did not see the first drogue parachute pop out, but he could feel the slight jerk, and the rate of fall diminished immediately. *Kon-Tiki* had lost all her horizontal speed and was going straight down at almost a thousand miles an hour. Everything depended on what happened in the next sixty seconds.

There went the second drogue. He looked up through the overhead window and saw, to his immense relief, that clouds of glittering foil were billowing out behind the falling ship. Like a great flower unfurling, the thousands of cubic yards of the balloon spread out across the sky, scooping up the thin gas until it was fully inflated. *Kon-Tiki*'s rate of fall dropped to a few miles an hour and remained constant. Now there was plenty of time; it would take him days to fall all the way down to the surface of Jupiter.

But he would get there eventually, even if he did nothing about it. The balloon overhead was merely acting as an efficient parachute. It was providing no lift; nor could it do so, while the gas inside and out was the same.

With its characteristic and rather disconcerting crack the fusion reactor started up, pouring torrents of heat into the envelope overhead. Within five minutes, the rate of fall had become zero; within six, the ship had started to rise. According to the radar altimeter, it had leveled out at about two hundred and sixty-seven miles above the surface—or whatever passed for a surface on Jupiter.

Only one kind of balloon will work in an atmosphere of hydrogen, which is the lightest of all gases—and that is a hot-hydrogen balloon. As long as the fuser kept ticking over, Falcon could remain aloft, drifting across a world that could hold a hundred Pacifics. After traveling over three hundred million miles, *Kon-Tiki* had at last begun to justify her name. She was an aerial raft, adrift upon the currents of the Jovian atmosphere.

Though a whole new world was lying around him, it was more than an hour before Falcon could examine the view. First he had to check all the capsule's systems and test its response to the controls. He had to learn how much extra heat was necessary to produce a desired rate of ascent, and how much gas he must vent in order to descend. Above all, there was the question of stability. He must adjust the length of the cables attaching his capsule to the huge, pear-shaped balloon, to damp out vibrations and get the smoothest possible ride. Thus far, he was lucky; at this level, the wind was steady, and the Doppler reading on the invisible surface gave him a ground speed of two hundred seventeen and a half miles an hour. For Jupiter, that was modest; winds of up to a thousand had been observed. But mere speed was, of course, unimportant; the real danger was turbulence. If he ran into that, only skill and experience and swift reaction could save him—and these were not matters that could yet be programed into a computer.

Not until he was satisfied that he had got the feel of his strange craft did Falcon pay any attention to Mission Control's pleadings. Then he deployed the booms carrying the instrumentation and the atmospheric samplers. The capsule now resembled a rather untidy Christmas tree, but still rode smoothly down the Jovian winds while it radioed its torrents of information to the recorders on the ship miles above. And now, at last, he could look around . . .

His first impression was unexpected, and even a little disappointing. As far as the scale of things was concerned, he might have been ballooning over an ordinary cloudscape on Earth. The horizon seemed at a normal distance; there was no feeling at all that he was on a world eleven times the diameter of his own. Then he looked at the infrared radar, sounding the layers of atmosphere beneath him—and knew how badly his eyes had been deceived.

That layer of clouds apparently about three miles away was really more than thirty-seven miles below. And the horizon, whose distance he would have guessed at about one hundred and twenty-five, was actually eighteen hundred miles from the ship.

The crystalline clarity of the hydrohelium atmosphere and the enormous curvature of the planet had fooled him completely. It was even harder to judge distances here than on the Moon; everything he saw must be multiplied by at least ten.

It was a simple matter, and he should have been prepared for it. Yet somehow, it disturbed him profoundly. He did not feel that Jupiter was huge, but that *he* had shrunk—to a tenth of his normal size. Perhaps, with time, he would grow accustomed to the inhuman scale of this world; yet as he stared toward that unbelievably distant horizon, he felt as if a wind colder than the atmosphere around him was blowing through his soul. Despite all his arguments, this might never be a place for man. He could well be both the first and the last to descend through the clouds of Jupiter.

The sky above was almost black, except for a few wisps of ammonia cirrus perhaps twelve miles overhead. It was cold up there, on the fringes of space, but both pressure and temperature increased rapidly with depth. At the level where *Kon-Tiki* was drifting now, it was fifty below zero, and the pressure was five atmospheres. Sixty-five miles farther down, it would be as warm as equatorial Earth, and the pressure about the same as at the bottom of one of the shallower seas. Ideal conditions for life . . .

A quarter of the brief Jovian day had already gone; the sun was halfway up the sky, but the light on the unbroken cloudscape below had a curious mellow quality. That extra three hundred million miles had robbed the Sun of all its power. Though the sky was clear, Falcon found himself continually thinking that it was a heavily overcast day. When night fell, the onset of darkness would be swift indeed; though it was still morning, there was a sense of autumnal twilight in the air. But autumn, of course, was something that never came to Jupiter. There were no seasons here.

Kon-Tiki had come down in the exact center of the equatorial zone—the least colorful part of the planet. The sea of clouds that stretched out to the horizon was tinted a pale salmon; there were none of the yellows and pinks and even reds that banded Jupiter at higher altitudes. The Great Red Spot itself—most spectacular of all of the planet's features—lay thousands of miles to the south. It had been a temptation to descend there, but the south tropical disturbance was unusually active, with currents reaching over nine hundred miles an hour. It would have been asking for trouble to head into that maelstrom of unknown forces. The Great Red Spot and its mysteries would have to wait for future expeditions.

The Sun, moving across the sky twice as swiftly as it did on Earth, was now nearing the zenith and had become eclipsed by the great silver canopy of the balloon. *Kon-Tiki* was still drifting swiftly and smoothly westward at a steady two hundred and seventeen and a half, but only the radar gave any indication of this. Was it always as calm here? Falcon asked himself. The scientists who had talked learnedly of the Jovian doldrums, and had predicted that the equator would be the quietest place, seemed to know what they were talking about, after all. He had been profoundly skeptical of all such forecasts, and had agreed with one unusually modest researcher who had told him bluntly: "There are *no* experts on Jupiter." Well, there would be at least one by the end of this day.

If he managed to survive until then.

4. The Voices of the Deep

That first day, the Father of the Gods smiled upon him. It was as calm and peaceful here on Jupiter as it had been, years ago, when he was drifting with Webster across the plains of northern India. Falcon had time to master his new skills, until *Kon-Tiki* seemed an extension of his own body. Such luck was more than he had dared to hope for, and he began to wonder what price he might have to pay for it.

The five hours of daylight were almost over; the clouds below were full of shadows, which gave them a massive solidity they had not possessed when the Sun was higher. Color was swiftly draining from the sky, except in the west itself, where a band of deepening purple lay along the horizon. Above this band was the thin crescent of a closer moon, pale and bleached against the utter blackness beyond.

With a speed perceptible to the eye, the Sun went straight down over the edge of Jupiter, over eighteen hundred miles away. The stars came out in their legions—and there was the beautiful evening star of Earth, on the very frontier to twilight, reminding him how far he was from home. It followed the Sun down into the west. Man's first night on Jupiter had begun.

With the onset of darkness, *Kon-Tiki* started to sink. The balloon was no longer heated by the feeble sunlight and was losing a small part of its buoyancy. Falcon did nothing to increase lift; he had expected this and was planning to descend.

The invisible cloud deck was still over thirty miles below, and he would reach it about midnight. It showed up clearly on the infrared radar, which also reported that it contained a vast array of complex carbon compounds, as well as the usual hydrogen, helium, and ammonia. The chemists were dying for samples of that fluffy, pinkish stuff; though some atmospheric probes had already gathered a few grams, they had only whetted their appetites. Half the basic molecules of life were here, floating high above the surface of Jupiter. And where there was food, could life be far away? That was the question that, after more than a hundred years, no one had been able to answer.

The infrared was blocked by the clouds, but the microwave radar sliced right through and showed layer after layer, all the way down to the hidden surface almost two hundred and fifty miles below. That was barred to him by enormous pressures and temperatures; not even robot probes had ever reached it intact. It lay in tantalizing inaccessibility at the bottom of the radar screen, slightly fuzzy, and showing a curious granular structure that his equipment could not resolve.

An hour after sunset, he dropped his first probe. It fell swiftly for about sixty miles, then began to float in the denser atmosphere, sending back torrents of radio signals, which he relayed to Mission Control. Then there was nothing else to do until sunrise, except to keep an eye on the rate of descent, monitor the instruments, and answer occasional queries. While she was drifting in this steady current, *Kon-Tiki* could look after herself.

Just before midnight, a woman controller came on watch and introduced herself with the usual pleasantries. Ten minutes later she called again, her voice at once serious and excited.

"Howard! Listen in on channel forty-six—high gain."

Channel forty-six? There were so many telemetering circuits that he knew the numbers of only those that were critical; but as soon as he threw the switch, he recognized this one. He was plugged in to the microphone on the probe, floating more than eighty miles below him in an atmosphere now almost as dense as water.

At first, there was only a soft hiss of whatever strange winds stirred down in the darkness of that unimaginable world. And then, out of the background noise, there slowly emerged a booming vibration that grew louder and louder, like the beating of a gigantic drum. It was so low that it was felt as much as heard, and the beats steadily increased their tempo, though the pitch never changed. Now it was a swift, almost infrasonic throbbing. Then, suddenly, in mid-vibration, it stopped—so abruptly that the mind could not accept the silence, but memory continued to manufacture a ghostly echo in the deepest caverns of the brain.

It was the most extraordinary sound that Falcon had ever heard, even among the multitudinous noises of Earth. He could think of no natural phenomenon that could have caused it; nor was it like the cry of any animal, not even one of the great whales . . .

It came again, following exactly the same pattern. Now that he was prepared for it, he estimated the length of the sequence; from first faint throb to final crescendo, it lasted just over ten seconds.

And this time there was a real echo, very faint and far away. Perhaps it came from one of the many reflecting layers, deeper in this stratified atmosphere; perhaps it was another, more distant source. Falcon waited for a second echo, but it never came.

Mission Control reacted quickly and asked him to drop another probe at once. With two microphones operating, it would be possible to find the approximate location of the sources. Oddly enough, none of Kon-Tiki's own external mikes could detect anything except wind noises. The boomings, whatever they were, must have been trapped and channeled beneath an atmospheric reflecting layer far below.

They were coming, it was soon discovered, from a cluster of sources about twelve hundred miles away. The distance gave no indication of their power; in Earth's oceans, quite feeble sounds could travel equally far. And as for the obvious assumption that living creatures were responsible, the Chief Exobiologist quickly ruled that out.

"I'll be very disappointed," said Dr. Brenner, "if there are no microorganisms or plants here. But nothing like animals, because there's no free oxygen. All biochemical reactions on Jupiter must be low-energy ones— there's just no way an active creature could generate enough power to function."

Falcon wondered if this was true; he had heard the argument before, and reserved judgment.

"In any case," continued Brenner, "some of those sound waves are a hundred yards long! Even an animal as big as a whale couldn't produce them. They *must* have a natural origin."

Yes, that seemed plausible, and probably the physicists would be able to come up with an explanation. What would a blind alien make, Falcon wondered, of the sounds he might hear when standing beside a stormy sea, or a geyser, or a volcano, or a waterfall? He might well attribute them to some huge beast.

About an hour before sunrise the voices of the deep died away, and Falcon began to busy himself with preparation for the dawn of his second day. *Kon-Tiki* was now only three miles above the nearest cloud layer; the external pressure had risen to ten atmospheres, and the temperature was a tropical thirty degrees. A man could be comfortable here with no more equipment than a breathing mask and the right grade of heliox mixture.

"We've some good news for you," Mission Control reported, soon after dawn. "The cloud layer's breaking up. You'll have partial clearing in an hour—but watch out for turbulence."

"I've already noticed some," Falcon answered. "How far down will I be able to see?"

"At least twelve miles, down to the second thermocline. *That* cloud deck is solid—it never breaks."

And it's out of my reach, Falcon told himself; the temperature down there must be over a hundred degrees. This was the first time that any balloonist had ever had to worry, not about his ceiling, but about his basement!

Ten minutes later he could see what Mission Control had already observed from its superior vantage point. There was a change in color near the horizon, and the cloud layer had become ragged and humpy, as if something had torn it open. He turned up his little nuclear furnace and gave *Kon-Tiki* another three miles of altitude, so that he could get a better view.

The sky below was clearing rapidly, completely, as if something was dissolving the solid overcast. An abyss was opening before his eyes. A moment later he sailed out over the edge of a cloud canyon about twelve miles deep and six hundred miles wide.

A new world lay spread beneath him; Jupiter had stripped away one of its many veils. The second layer of clouds, unattainably far below, was much darker in color than the first. It was almost salmon pink, and curiously mottled with little islands of brick red. They were all oval-shaped, with their long axes pointing east-west, in the direction of the prevailing wind. There were hundreds of them, all about the same size, and they reminded Falcon of puffy little cumulus clouds in the terrestrial sky.

He reduced buoyancy, and *Kon-Tiki* began to drop down the face of the dissolving cliff. It was then that he noticed the snow.

White flakes were forming in the air and drifting slowly downward. Yet it was much too warm for snow—and, in any event, there was scarcely a trace of water at this altitude. Moreover, there was no glitter or sparkle about these flakes as they went cascading down into the depths. When, presently, a few landed on an instrument boom outside the main viewing port, he saw that they were a dull, opaque white—not crystalline at all—and quite large— several inches across. They looked like wax, and Falcon guessed that this was precisely what they were. Some chemical reaction was taking place in the atmosphere around him, condensing out the hydrocarbons floating in the Jovian air.

About sixty miles ahead, a disturbance was taking place in the cloud layer. The little red ovals were being jostled around, and were beginning to form a spiral—the familiar cyclonic pattern so common in the meteorology of Earth. The vortex was emerging with astonishing speed; if that was a storm ahead, Falcon told himself, he was in big trouble.

And then his concern changed to wonder—and to fear. What was developing in his line of flight was not a storm at all. Something enormous—something scores of miles across—was rising through the clouds.

The reassuring thought that it, too, might be a cloud—a thunderhead boiling up from the lower levels of the atmosphere—lasted only a few seconds. No; this was *solid*. It shouldered its way through the pink-and-salmon overcast like an iceberg rising from the deeps.

An *iceberg* floating on hydrogen? That was impossible, of course; but perhaps it was not too remote an analogy. As soon as he focused the telescope upon the enigma, Falcon saw that it was a whitish, crystalline mass, threaded with streaks of red and brown. It must be, he decided, the same stuff as the "snowflakes" falling around him—a mountain range of wax. And it was not, he soon realized, as solid as he had thought; around the edges it was continually crumbling and reforming . . .

"I know what it is," he radioed Mission Control, which for the last few minutes had been asking anxious questions. "It's a mass of bubbles—some kind of foam. Hydrocarbon froth. Get the chemists working on . . . *Just a minute!*"

"What is it?" called Mission Control. "What is it?"

He ignored the frantic pleas from space and concentrated all his mind upon the image in the telescope field. He had to be sure; if he made a mistake, he would be the laughingstock of the solar system.

Then he relaxed, glanced at the clock, and switched off the nagging voice from Jupiter V.

"Hello, Mission Control," he said, very formally. "This is Howard Falcon aboard *Kon-Tiki*. Ephemeris Time nineteen hours twenty-one minutes fifteen seconds. Latitude zero degrees five minutes North. Longitude one hundred five degrees forty-two minutes, System One.

"Tell Dr. Brenner that there is life on Jupiter. And it's *big*. . . ."

5. The Wheels of Poseidon

"I'm very happy to be proved wrong," Dr. Brenner radioed back cheerfully. "Nature always has something up her sleeve. Keep the long-focus camera on target and give us the steadiest pictures you can."

The things moving up and down those waxen slopes were still too far away for Falcon to make out many details, and they must have been very large to be visible at all at such a distance. Almost black, and shaped like arrowheads, they maneuvered by slow undulations of their entire bodies, so that they looked rather like giant manta rays, swimming above some tropical reef.

Perhaps they were sky-borne cattle, browsing on the cloud pastures of Jupiter, for they seemed to be feeding along the dark, red-brown streaks that ran like dried-up river beds down the flanks of the floating cliffs. Occasionally, one of them would dive headlong into the mountain of foam and disappear completely from sight.

Kon-Tiki was moving only slowly with respect to the cloud layer below; it would be at least three hours before she was above those ephemeral hills. She was in a race with the Sun. Falcon hoped that darkness would not fall before he could get a good view of the mantas, as he had christened them, as well as the fragile landscape over which they flapped their way.

It was a long three hours. During the whole time, he kept the external microphones on full gain, wondering if here was the source of that booming in the night. The mantas were certainly large enough to have produced it; when he could get an accurate measurement, he discovered that they were almost a hundred yards across the wings. That was three times the length of the largest whale—though he doubted if they could weigh more than a few tons.

Half an hour before sunset, *Kon-Tiki* was almost above the "mountains."

"No," said Falcon, answering Mission Control's repeated questions about the mantas, "they're still showing no reaction to me. I don't think they're intelligent—they look like harmless vegetarians. And even if they try to chase me, I'm sure they can't reach my altitude."

Yet he was a little disappointed when the mantas showed not the slightest interest in him as he sailed high above their feeding ground. Perhaps they had no way of detecting his presence. When he examined and photographed them through the telescope, he could see no signs of any sense organs. The creatures were simply huge black deltas, rippling over hills and valleys that, in reality, were little more substantial than the clouds of Earth. Though they looked solid, Falcon knew that anyone who stepped on those white mountains would go crashing through them as if they were made of tissue paper.

At close quarters he could see the myriads of cellules or bubbles from which they were formed. Some of these were quite large—a yard or so in diameter—and Falcon wondered in what witches' cauldron of hydrocarbons they had been brewed. There must be enough petrochemicals deep down in the atmosphere of Jupiter to supply all Earth's needs for a million years.

The short day had almost gone when he passed over the crest of the waxen hills, and the light was fading rapidly along their lower slopes. There were no mantas on this western side, and for some reason the topography was very different. The foam was sculptured into long, level terraces, like the interior of a lunar crater. He could almost imagine that they were gigantic steps leading down to the hidden surface of the planet.

And on the lowest of those steps, just clear of the swirling clouds that the mountain had displaced when it came surging skyward, was a roughly oval mass, one or two miles across. It was difficult to see, since it was only a little darker than the gray-white foam on which it rested. Falcon's first thought was that he was looking at a forest of pallid trees, like giant mushrooms that had never seen the Sun.

Yes, it must be a forest—he could see hundreds of thin trunks, springing from the white waxy froth in which they were rooted. But the trees were packed astonishingly close together; there was scarcely any space between them. Perhaps it was not a forest, after all, but a single enormous tree—like one of the giant multi-trunked banyans of the East. Once he had seen a banyan tree in Java that was over six hundred and fifty yards across; this monster was at least ten times that size.

The light had almost gone. The cloudscape had turned purple with refracted sunlight, and in a few seconds that, too, would have vanished. In the last light of his second day on Jupiter, Howard Falcon saw—or thought he saw—something that cast the gravest doubts on his interpretation of the white oval.

Unless the dim light had totally deceived him, those hundreds of thin trunks were beating back and forth, in perfect synchronism, like fronds of kelp rocking in the surge.

And the tree was no longer in the place where he had first seen it.

"Sorry about this," said Mission Control, soon after sunset, "but we think Source Beta is going to blow within the next hour. Probability seventy percent."

Falcon glanced quickly at the chart. Beta—Jupiter latitude one hundred and forty degrees—was over eighteen thousand six hundred miles away and well below his horizon. Even though major eruptions ran as high as ten megatons, he was much too far away for the shock wave to be a serious danger. The radio storm that it would trigger was, however, quite a different matter.

The decameter outbursts that sometimes made Jupiter the most powerful radio source in the whole sky had been discovered back in the 1950s, to the utter astonishment of the astronomers. Now, more than a century later, their real cause was still a mystery. Only the symptoms were understood; the explanation was completely unknown.

The "volcano" theory had best stood the test of time, although no one imagined that this word had the same meaning on Jupiter as on Earth. At frequent intervals—often several times a day—titanic eruptions occurred in the lower depths of the atmosphere, probably on the hidden surface of the planet itself. A great column of gas, more than six hundred miles high, would start boiling upward as if determined to escape into space.

Against the most powerful gravitational field of all the planets, it had no chance. Yet some traces—a mere few million tons—usually managed to reach the Jovian ionosphere; and when they did, all hell broke loose.

The radiation belts surrounding Jupiter completely dwarf the feeble Van Allen belts of Earth. When they are short-circuited by an ascending column of gas, the result is an electrical discharge millions of times more powerful than any terrestrial flash of lightning; it sends a colossal thunderclap of radio noise flooding across the entire solar system and on out to the stars.

It had been discovered that these radio outbursts came from four main areas of the planet. Perhaps there were weaknesses there that allowed the fires of the interior to break out from time to time. The scientists on Ganymede, largest of Jupiter's many moons, now thought that they could predict the onset of a decameter storm; their accuracy was about as good as a weather forecaster's of the early 1900s.

Falcon did not know whether to welcome or to fear a radio storm; it would certainly add to the value of the mission—if he survived it. His course had been planned to keep as far as possible from the main centers of disturbance, especially the most active one, Source Alpha. As luck would have it, the threatening Beta was the closest to him. He hoped that the distance, almost three-fourths the circumference of Earth, was safe enough.

"Probability ninety percent," said Mission Control with a distinct note of urgency. "And forget that hour. Ganymede says it may be any moment."

The radio had scarcely fallen silent when the reading on the magnetic field-strength meter started to shoot upward. Before it could go off scale, it reversed and began to drop as rapidly as it had risen. Far away and thousands of miles below, something had given the planet's molten core a titanic jolt.

"There she blows!" called Mission Control.

"Thanks, I already know. When will the storm hit me?"

"You can expect onset in five minutes. Peak in ten."

Far around the curve of Jupiter, a funnel of gas as wide as the Pacific Ocean was climbing spaceward at thousands of miles an hour. Already the thunderstorms of the lower atmosphere would be raging around it—but they were nothing compared with the fury that would explode when the radiation belt was reached and began dumping its surplus electrons onto the planet. Falcon began to retract all the instrument booms that were extended out from the capsule. There were no other precautions he could take. It would be four hours before the atmospheric shock wave reached him—but the radio blast, traveling at the speed of light, would be here in a tenth of a second, once the discharge had been triggered.

The radio monitor, scanning back and forth across the spectrum, still showed nothing unusual, just the normal mush of background static. Then Falcon noticed that the noise level was slowly creeping upward. The explosion was gathering its strength.

At such a distance he had never expected to *see* anything. But suddenly a flicker as of far-off heat lightning danced along the eastern horizon. Simultaneously, half the circuit breakers jumped out of the main switchboard, the lights failed, and all communications channels went dead.

He tried to move, but was completely unable to do so. The paralysis that gripped him was not merely psychological; he seemed to have lost all control of his limbs and could feel a painful tingling sensation over his entire body. It was impossible that the electric field could have penetrated this shielded cabin. Yet there was a flickering glow over the instrument board, and he could hear the unmistakable crackle of a brush discharge.

With a series of sharp bangs, the emergency systems went into operation, and the overloads reset themselves. The lights flickered on again. And Falcon's paralysis disappeared as swiftly as it had come.

After glancing at the board to make sure that all circuits were back to normal, he moved quickly to the viewing ports.

There was no need to switch on the inspection lamps—the cables supporting the capsule seemed to be on fire. Lines of light glowing an electric blue against the darkness stretched upward from the main lift ring to the equator of the giant balloon; and rolling slowly along several of them were dazzling balls of fire.

The sight was so strange and so beautiful that it was hard to read any menace in it. Few people, Falcon knew, had ever seen ball lightning from such close quarters—and certainly none had survived if they were riding a hydrogen-filled balloon back in the atmosphere of Earth. He remembered the flaming death of the *Hindenburg*, destroyed by a stray spark when she docked at Lakehurst in 1937; as it had done so often in the past, the horrifying old newsreel film flashed through his mind. But at least that could not happen here, though there was more hydrogen above his head than had ever filled the last of the Zeppelins. It would be a few billion years yet, before anyone could light a fire in the atmosphere of Jupiter.

With a sound like briskly frying bacon, the speech circuit came back to life.

"Hello, *Kon-Tiki*—are you receiving? Are you receiving?"

The words were chopped and badly distorted, but intelligible. Falcon's spirits lifted; he had resumed contact with the world of men.

"I receive you," he said. "Quite an electrical display, but no damage—so far."

"Thanks—thought we'd lost you. Please check telemetry channels three, seven, twenty-six. Also gain on camera two. And we don't quite believe the readings on the external ionization probes . . ."

Reluctantly Falcon tore his gaze away from the fascinating pyrotechnic display around *Kon-Tiki*, though from time to time he kept glancing out of the windows. The ball lightning disappeared first, the fiery globes slowly expanding until they reached a critical size, at which they vanished in a gentle explosion. But even an hour later, there were still faint glows around all the exposed metal on the outside of the capsule; and the radio circuits remained noisy until well after midnight.

The remaining hours of darkness were completely uneventful—until just before dawn. Because it came from the east, Falcon assumed that he was seeing the first faint hint of sunrise. Then he realized that it was twenty minutes too early for this—and the glow that had appeared along the horizon was moving toward him even as he watched. It swiftly detached itself from the arch of stars that marked the invisible edge of the planet, and he saw that it was a relatively narrow band, quite sharply defined. The beam of an enormous searchlight appeared to be swinging beneath the clouds.

Perhaps sixty miles behind the first racing bar of light came another, parallel to it and moving at the same speed. And beyond that another, and another—until all the sky flickered with alternating sheets of light and darkness.

By this time, Falcon thought, he had been inured to wonders, and it seemed impossible that this display of pure, soundless luminosity could present the slightest danger. But it was so astonishing, and so inexplicable, that he felt cold, naked fear gnawing at his self-control. No man could look upon such a sight without feeling like a helpless pygmy in the presence of forces beyond his comprehension. Was it possible that, after all, Jupiter carried not only life but also intelligence? And, perhaps, an intelligence that only now was beginning to react to his alien presence?

"Yes, we see it," said Mission Control, in a voice that echoed his own awe. "We've no idea what it is. Stand by, we're calling Ganymede."

The display was slowly fading; the bands racing in from the far horizon were much fainter, as if the energies that powered them were becoming exhausted. In five minutes it was all over; the last faint pulse of light flickered along the western sky and then was gone. Its passing left Falcon with an overwhelming sense of relief. The sight was so hypnotic, and so disturbing, that it was not good for any man's peace of mind to contemplate it too long.

He was more shaken than he cared to admit. The electrical storm was something that he could understand; but *this* was totally incomprehensible.

Mission Control was still silent. He knew that the information banks up on Ganymede were now being searched as men and computers turned their minds to the problem. If no answer could be found there, it would be necessary to call Earth; that would mean a delay of almost an hour. The possibility that even Earth might be unable to help was one that Falcon did not care to contemplate.

He had never before been so glad to hear the voice of Mission Control as when Dr. Brenner finally came on the circuit. The biologist sounded relieved, yet subdued—like a man who has just come through some great intellectual crisis.

"Hello, *Kon-Tiki*. We've solved your problem, but we can still hardly believe it.

"What you've been seeing is bioluminescence, very similar to that produced by microorganisms in the tropical seas of Earth. Here they're in the atmosphere, not the ocean, but the principle is the same."

"But the pattern," protested Falcon, "was so regular—so *artificial*. And it was hundreds of miles across!"

"It was even larger than you imagine; you observed only a small part of it. The whole pattern was over three thousand miles wide and looked like a revolving wheel. You merely saw the spokes, sweeping past you at about six-tenths of a mile a second . . ."

"A *second!*" Falcon could not help interjecting. "No animals could move that fast!"

"Of course not. Let me explain. What you saw was triggered by the shock wave from Source Beta, moving at the speed of sound."

"But what about the pattern?" Falcon insisted.

"That's the surprising part. It's a very rare phenomenon, but identical wheels of light—except that they're a thousand times smaller—have been observed in the Persian Gulf and the Indian Ocean. Listen to this: British India Company's *Patna*, Persian Gulf, May 1880, 11:30 P.M. —'an enormous luminous wheel, whirling round, the spokes of which appeared to brush the ship along. The spokes were 200 or 300 yards long . . . each wheel contained about sixteen spokes. . . .' And here's one from the Gulf of Omar, dated May 23, 1906: 'The intensely bright luminescence approached us rapidly, shooting sharply defined light rays to the west in rapid succession, like the beam from the searchlight of a warship. . . . To the left of us, a gigantic fiery wheel formed itself, with spokes that reached as far as one could see. The whole wheel whirled around for two or three minutes. . . .' The archive computer on Ganymede dug up about five hundred cases. It would have printed out the lot if we hadn't stopped it in time."

"I'm convinced—but still baffled."

"I don't blame you. The full explanation wasn't worked out until late in the twentieth century. It seems that these luminous wheels are the results of submarine earthquakes, and always occur in shallow waters where the shock waves can be reflected and cause standing wave patterns. Sometimes bars, sometimes rotating wheels—the 'Wheels of Poseidon,' they've been called. The theory was finally proved by making underwater explosions and photographing the results from a satellite. No wonder sailors used to be superstitious. Who would have believed a thing like *this?*"

So that was it, Falcon told himself. When Source Beta blew its top, it must have sent shock waves in all directions—through the compressed gas of the lower atmosphere, through the solid body of Jupiter itself. Meeting and crisscrossing, those waves must have canceled here, reinforced there; the whole planet must have rung like a bell.

Yet the explanation did not destroy the sense of wonder and awe; he would never be able to forget those flickering bands of light, racing through the unattainable depths of the Jovian atmosphere. He felt that he was not merely on a strange planet, but in some magical realm between myth and reality.

This was a world where absolutely *anything* could happen, and no man could possibly guess what the future would bring.

And he still had a whole day to go.

6. Medusa

When the true dawn finally arrived, it brought a sudden change of weather. *Kon-Tiki* was moving through a blizzard; waxen snowflakes were falling so thickly that visibility was reduced to zero. Falcon began to worry about the weight that might be accumulating on the envelope. Then he noticed that any flakes settling outside the windows quickly disappeared; *Kon-Tiki's* continual outpouring of heat was evaporating them as swiftly as they arrived.

If he had been ballooning on Earth, he would also have worried about the possibility of collision. At least that was no danger here; any Jovian mountains were several hundred miles below him. And as for the floating islands of foam, hitting them would probably be like plowing into slightly hardened soap bubbles.

Nevertheless, he switched on the horizontal radar, which until now had been completely useless; only the vertical beam, giving his distance from the invisible surface, had thus far been of any value. Then he had another surprise.

Scattered across a huge sector of the sky ahead were dozens of large and brilliant echoes. They were completely isolated from one another and apparently hung unsupported in space. Falcon remembered a phrase the earliest aviators had used to describe one of the hazards of their profession: "clouds stuffed with rocks." That was a perfect description of what seemed to lie in the track of *Kon-Tiki*.

It was a disconcerting sight; then Falcon again reminded himself that nothing *really* solid could possibly hover in this atmosphere. Perhaps it was some strange meteorological phenomenon. In any case, the nearest echo was about a hundred and twenty-five miles.

He reported to Mission Control, which could provide no explanation. But it gave the welcome news that he would be clear of the blizzard in another thirty minutes.

It did not warn him, however, of the violent cross wind that abruptly grabbed *Kon-Tiki* and swept it almost at right angles to its previous track.

Falcon needed all his skill and the maximum use of what little control he had over his ungainly vehicle to prevent it from being capsized. Within minutes he was racing northward at over three hundred miles an hour. Then, as suddenly as it had started, the turbulence ceased; he was still moving at high speed, but in smooth air. He wondered if he had been caught in the Jovian equivalent of a jet stream.

The snow storm dissolved; and he saw what Jupiter had been preparing for him.

Kon-Tiki had entered the funnel of a gigantic whirlpool, some six hundred miles across. The balloon was being swept along a curving wall of cloud. Overhead, the sun was shining in a clear sky; but far beneath, this great hole in the atmosphere drilled down to unknown depths until it reached a misty floor where lightning flickered almost continuously.

Though the vessel was being dragged downward so slowly that it was in no immediate danger, Falcon increased the flow of heat into the envelope until *Kon-Tiki* hovered at a constant altitude. Not until then did he abandon the fantastic spectacle outside and consider again the problem of the radar.

The nearest echo was now only about twenty-five miles away. All of them, he quickly realized, were distributed along the wall of the vortex, and were moving with it, apparently caught in the whirlpool like *Kon-Tiki* itself. He aimed the telescope along the radar bearing and found himself looking at a curious mottled cloud that almost filled the field of view.

It was not easy to see, being only a little darker than the whirling wall of mist that formed its background. Not until he had been staring for several minutes did Falcon realize that he had met it once before.

The first time it had been crawling across the drifting mountains of foam, and he had mistaken it for a giant, many-trunked tree. Now at last he could appreciate its real size and complexity and could give it a better name to fix its image in his mind. It did not resemble a tree at all, but a jellyfish—a medusa, such as might be met trailing its tentacles as it drifted along the warm eddies of the Gulf Stream.

This medusa was more than a mile across and its scores of dangling tentacles were hundreds of feet long. They swayed slowly back and forth in perfect unison, taking more than a minute for each complete undulation— almost as if the creature was clumsily rowing itself through the sky.

The other echoes were more distant medusae. Falcon focused the telescope on half a dozen and could see no variations in shape or size. They all seemed to be of the same species, and he wondered just why they were drifting lazily around in this six-hundred-mile orbit. Perhaps they were feeding upon the aerial plankton sucked in by the whirlpool, as *Kon-Tiki* itself had been.

"Do you realize, Howard," said Dr. Brenner, when he had recovered from his initial astonishment, "that this thing is about a hundred thousand times as large as the biggest whale? And even if it's only a gasbag, it must still weigh a million tons! I can't even guess at its metabolism. It must generate megawatts of heat to maintain its buoyancy."

"But if it's just a gasbag, why is it such a damn good radar reflector?"

"I haven't the faintest idea. Can you get any closer?"

Brenner's question was not an idle one. If he changed altitude to take advantage of the differing wind velocities, Falcon could approach the medusa as closely as he wished. At the moment, however, he preferred his present twenty-five miles and said so, firmly.

"I see what you mean," Brenner answered, a little reluctantly. "Let's stay where we are for the present." That "we" gave Falcon a certain wry amusement; an extra sixty thousand miles made a considerable difference in one's point of view.

For the next two hours *Kon-Tiki* drifted uneventfully in the gyre of the great whirlpool, while Falcon experimented with filters and camera contrast, trying to get a clear view of the medusa. He began to wonder if its elusive coloration was some kind of camouflage; perhaps, like many animals of Earth, it was trying to lose itself against its background. That was a trick used by both hunters and hunted.

In which category was the medusa? That was a question he could hardly expect to have answered in the short time that was left to him. Yet just before noon, without the slightest warning, the answer came . . .

Like a squadron of antique jet fighters, five mantas came sweeping through the wall of mist that formed the funnel of the vortex. They were flying in a V formation directly toward the pallid gray cloud of the medusa; and there was no doubt, in Falcon's mind, that they were on the attack. He had been quite wrong to assume that they were harmless vegetarians.

Yet everything happened at such a leisurely pace that it was like watching a slow-motion film. The mantas undulated along at perhaps thirty miles an hour; it seemed ages before they reached the medusa, which continued to paddle imperturbably along at an even slower speed. Huge though they were, the mantas looked tiny beside the monster they were approaching. When they flapped down on its back, they appeared about as large as birds landing on a whale.

Could the medusa defend itself? Falcon wondered. He did not see how the attacking mantas could be in danger as long as they avoided those huge clumsy tentacles. And perhaps their host was not even aware of them; they could be insignificant parasites, tolerated as are fleas upon a dog.

But now it was obvious that the medusa was in distress. With agonizing slowness, it began to tip over like a capsizing ship. After ten minutes it had tilted forty-five degrees; it was also rapidly losing altitude. It was impossible not to feel a sense of pity for the beleaguered monster, and to Falcon the sight brought bitter memories. In a grotesque way, the fall of the medusa was almost a parody of the dying *Queen's* last moments.

Yet he knew that his sympathies were on the wrong side. High intelligence could develop only among predators—not among the drifting browsers of either sea or air. The mantas were far closer to him than was this monstrous bag of gas. And anyway, who could *really* sympathize with a creature a hundred thousand times larger than a whale?

Then he noticed that the medusa's tactics seemed to be having some effect. The mantas had been disturbed by its slow roll and were flapping heavily away from its back—like gorging vultures interrupted at mealtime. But they did not move very far, continuing to hover a few yards from the still-capsizing monster.

There was a sudden, blinding flash of light synchronized with a crash of static over the radio. One of the mantas, slowly twisting end over end, was plummeting straight downward. As it fell, a plume of black smoke trailed behind it. The resemblance to an aircraft going down in flames was quite uncanny.

In unison, the remaining mantas dived steeply away from the medusa, gaining speed by losing altitude. They had, within minutes, vanished back into the wall of cloud from which they had emerged. And the medusa, no longer falling, began to roll back toward the horizontal. Soon it was sailing along once more on an even keel, as if nothing had happened.

"Beautiful!" said Dr. Brenner, after a moment of stunned silence. "It's developed electric defenses, like some of our eels and rays. But that must have been about a million volts! Can you see any organs that might produce the discharge? Anything looking like electrodes?"

"No," Falcon answered, after switching to the highest power of the telescope. "But here's something odd. Do you see this pattern? Check back on the earlier images. I'm sure it wasn't there before."

A broad, mottled band had appeared along the side of the medusa. It formed a startlingly regular checkerboard, each square of which was itself speckled in a complex subpattern of short horizontal lines. They were spaced at equal distances in a geometrically perfect array of rows and columns.

"You're right," said Dr. Brenner, with something very much like awe in his voice. "That's just appeared. And I'm afraid to tell you what I think it is."

"Well, I have no reputation to lose—at least as a biologist. Shall I give my guess?"

"Go ahead."

"That's a large meter-band radio array. The sort of thing they used back at the beginning of the twentieth century."

"I was afraid you'd say that. Now we know why it gave such a massive echo."

"But why has it just appeared?"

"Probably an aftereffect of the discharge."

"I've just had another thought," said Falcon, rather slowly. "Do you suppose it's *listening* to us?"

"On this frequency? I doubt it. Those are meter—no, *decameter* antennas—judging by their size. Hmm . . . that's an idea!"

Dr. Brenner fell silent, obviously contemplating some new line of thought. Presently he continued: "I bet they're tuned to the radio outbursts! That's something nature never got around to do on Earth . . . We have animals with sonar and even electric senses, but nothing ever developed a radio sense. Why bother where there was so much light?

"But it's different here. Jupiter is *drenched* with radio energy. It's worth while using it—maybe even tapping it. That thing could be a floating power plant!"

A new voice cut into the conversation.

"Mission Commander here. This is all very interesting, but there's a much more important matter to settle. *Is it intelligent?* If so, we've got to consider the First Contact directives."

"Until I came here," said Dr. Brenner, somewhat ruefully, "I would have sworn that anything that could make a shortwave antenna system *must* be intelligent. Now, I'm not sure. This could have evolved naturally. I suppose it's no more fantastic than the human eye."

"Then we have to play safe and assume intelligence. For the present, therefore, this expedition comes under all the clauses of the Prime directive."

There was a long silence while everyone on the radio circuit absorbed the implications of this. For the first time in the history of space flight, the rules that had been established through more than a century of argument might have to be applied. Man had—it was hoped—profited from his mistakes on Earth. Not only moral considerations, but also his own self-interest demanded that he should not repeat them among the planets. It could be disastrous to treat a superior intelligence as the American settlers had treated the Indians, or as almost everyone had treated the Africans . . .

The first rule was: keep your distance. Make no attempt to approach, or even to communicate, until "they" have had plenty of time to study you.

Exactly what was meant by "plenty of time," no one had ever been able to decide. It was left to the discretion of the man on the spot.

A responsibility of which he had never dreamed had descended upon Howard Falcon. In the few hours that remained to him on Jupiter, he might become the first ambassador of the human race.

And *that* was an irony so delicious that he almost wished the surgeons had restored to him the power of laughter.

7. Prime Directive

It was growing darker, but Falcon scarcely noticed as he strained his eyes toward that living cloud in the field of the telescope. The wind that was steadily sweeping *Kon-Tiki* around the funnel of the great whirlpool had now brought him within twelve miles of the creature. If he got much closer than six, he would take evasive action. Though he felt certain that the medusa's electric weapons were short-ranged, he did not wish to put the matter to the test. That would be a problem for future explorers, and he wished them luck.

Now it was quite dark in the capsule. That was strange, because sunset was still hours away. Automatically, he glanced at the horizontally scanning radar, as he had done every few minutes. Apart from the medusa he was studying, there was no other object within about sixty miles of him.

Suddenly, with startling power, he heard the sound that had come booming out of the Jovian night—the throbbing beat that grew more and more rapid, then stopped in mid-crescendo. The whole capsule vibrated with it like a pea in a kettledrum.

Falcon realized two things almost simultaneously during the sudden, aching silence. *This* time the sound was not coming from thousands of miles away, over a radio circuit. It was in the very atmosphere around him.

The second thought was even more disturbing. He had quite forgotten—it was inexcusable, but there had been other apparently more important things on his mind—that most of the sky above him was completely blanked out by *Kon-Tiki's* gas-bag. Being lightly silvered to conserve its heat, the great balloon was an effective shield both to radar and to vision.

He had known this, of course; it had been a minor defect of the design, tolerated because it did not appear important. It seemed very important to Howard Falcon now—as he saw that fence of gigantic tentacles, thicker than the trunks of any tree, descending all around the capsule.

He heard Brenner yelling: "Remember the Prime directive! Don't alarm it!" Before he could make an appropriate answer that overwhelming drumbeat started again and drowned all other sounds.

The sign of a really skilled test pilot is how he reacts not to foreseeable emergencies, but to ones that nobody could have anticipated. Falcon did not hesitate for more than a second to analyze the situation. In a lightning-swift movement, he pulled the rip cord.

That word was an archaic survival from the days of the first hydrogen balloons; on *Kon-Tiki*, the rip cord did not tear open the gasbag, but merely operated a set of louvers around the upper curve of the envelope. At once the hot gas started to rush out; *Kon-Tiki*, deprived of her lift, began to fall swiftly in this gravity field two and a half times as strong as Earth's.

Falcon had a momentary glimpse of great tentacles whipping upward and away. He had just time to note that they were studded with large bladders or sacs, presumably to give them buoyancy, and that they ended in multitudes of thin feelers like the roots of a plant. He half expected a bolt of lightning—but nothing happened.

His precipitous rate of descent was slackening as the atmosphere thickened and the deflated envelope acted as a parachute. When *Kon-Tiki* had dropped about two miles, he felt that it was safe to close the louvers again. By the time he had restored buoyancy and was in equilibrium once more, he had lost another mile of altitude and was getting dangerously near his safety limit.

He peered anxiously through the overhead windows, though he did not expect to see anything except the obscuring bulk of the balloon. But he had sideslipped during his descent, and part of the medusa was just visible a couple of miles above him. It was much closer than he expected—and it was still coming down, faster than he would have believed possible.

Mission Control was calling anxiously. He shouted: "I'm O.K.—but it's still coming after me. I can't go any deeper."

That was not quite true. He could go a lot deeper—about one hundred and eighty miles. But it would be a one-way trip, and most of the journey would be of little interest to him.

Then, to his great relief, he saw that the medusa was leveling off, not quite a mile above him. Perhaps it had decided to approach this strange intruder with caution; or perhaps it, too, found this deeper layer uncomfortably hot. The temperature was over fifty degrees centigrade, and Falcon wondered how much longer his life-support system could handle matters.

Dr. Brenner was back on the circuit, still worrying about the Prime directive.

"Remember—it may only be inquisitive!" he cried, without much conviction. "Try not to frighten it!"

Falcon was getting rather tired of this advice and recalled a TV discussion he had once seen between a space lawyer and an astronaut. After the full implications of the Prime directive had been carefully spelled out, the incredulous spacer had exclaimed: "Then if there was no alternative, I must sit still and let myself be eaten?" The lawyer had not even cracked a smile when he answered: "That's an *excellent* summing up."

It had seemed funny at the time; it was not at all amusing now.

And then Falcon saw something that made him even more unhappy. The medusa was still hovering about a mile above him — but one of its tentacles was becoming incredibly elongated, and was stretching down toward *Kon-Tiki*, thinning out at the same time. As a boy he had once seen the funnel of a tornado descending from a storm cloud over the Kansas plains. The thing coming toward him now evoked vivid memories of that black, twisting snake in the sky.

"I'm rapidly running out of options," he reported to Mission Control. "I now have only a choice between frightening it—and giving it a bad stomach-ache. I don't think it will find *Kon-Tiki* very digestible, if that's what it has in mind."

He waited for comments from Brenner, but the biologist remained silent.

"Very well. It's twenty-seven minutes ahead of time, but I'm starting the ignition sequencer. I hope I'll have enough reserve to correct my orbit later."

He could no longer see the medusa; once more it was directly overhead. But he knew that the descending tentacle must now be very close to the balloon. It would take almost five minutes to bring the reactor up to full thrust . . .

The fuser was primed. The orbit computer had not rejected the situation as wholly impossible. The air scoops were open, ready to gulp in tons of the surrounding hydrohelium on demand. Even under optimum conditions, this would have been the moment of truth—for there had been no way of testing how a nuclear ramjet would *really* work in the strange atmosphere of Jupiter.

Very gently something rocked *Kon-Tiki*. Falcon tried to ignore it.

Ignition had been planned at six miles higher, in an atmosphere of less than a quarter of the density and thirty degrees cooler. Too bad.

What was the shallowest dive he could get away with, for the air scoops to work? When the ram ignited, he'd be heading toward Jupiter with two and a half g's to help him get there. Could he possibly pull out in time?

A large, heavy hand patted the balloon. The whole vessel bobbed up and down, like one of the Yo-yo's that had just become the craze on Earth.

Of course, Brenner *might* be perfectly right. Perhaps it was just trying to be friendly. Maybe he should try to talk to it over the radio. Which should it be: "Pretty pussy"? "Down, Fido"? Or "Take me to your leader"?

The tritium-deuterium ratio was correct. He was ready to light the candle, with a hundred-million-degree match.

The thin tip of the tentacle came slithering around the edge of the balloon some sixty yards away. It was about the size of an elephant's trunk, and by the delicate way it was moving appeared to be almost as sensitive. There were little palps at its end, like questing mouths. He was sure that Dr. Brenner would be fascinated.

This seemed about as good a time as any. He gave a swift scan of the entire control board, started the final four-second ignition count, broke the safety seal, and pressed the JETTISON switch.

There was a sharp explosion and an instant loss of weight. Kon-Tiki was falling freely, nose down. Overhead, the discarded balloon was racing upward, dragging the inquisitive tentacle with it. Falcon had no time to see if the gasbag actually hit the medusa, because at that moment the ramjet fired and he had other matters to think about.

A roaring column of hot hydrohelium was pouring out of the reactor nozzles, swiftly building up thrust—but toward Jupiter, not away from it. He could not pull out yet, for vector control was too sluggish. Unless he could gain complete control and achieve horizontal flight within the next five seconds, the vehicle would dive too deeply into the atmosphere and would be destroyed.

With agonizing slowness—those five seconds seemed like fifty—he managed to flatten out, then pull the nose upward. He glanced back only once and caught a final glimpse of the medusa, many miles away. Kon-Tiki's discarded gasbag had apparently escaped from its grasp, for he could see no sign of it.

Now he was master once more—no longer drifting helplessly on the winds of Jupiter, but riding his own column of atomic fire back to the stars. He was confident that the ramjet would steadily give him velocity and altitude until he had reached near-orbital speed at the fringes of the atmosphere. Then, with a brief burst of pure rocket power, he would regain the freedom of space.

Halfway to orbit, he looked south and saw the tremendous enigma of the Great Red Spot—that floating island twice the size of Earth—coming up over the horizon. He stared into its mysterious beauty until the computer warned him that conversion to rocket thrust was only sixty seconds ahead. He tore his gaze reluctantly away.

"Some other time," he murmured.

"What's that?" said Mission Control. "What did you say?"

"It doesn't matter," he replied.

8. Between Two Worlds

"You're a hero now, Howard," said Webster, "not just a celebrity. You've given them something to think about—injected some excitement into their lives. Not one in a million will actually travel to the Outer Giants, but the whole human race will go in imagination. And that's what counts."

"I'm glad to have made your job a little easier."

Webster was too old a friend to take offense at the note of irony. Yet it surprised him. And this was not the first change in Howard that he had noticed since the return from Jupiter.

The Administrator pointed to the famous sign on his desk, borrowed from an impresario of an earlier age: ASTONISH ME!

"I'm not ashamed of my job. New knowledge, new resources—they're all very well. But men also need novelty and excitement. Space travel has become routine; you've made it a great adventure once more. It will be a long, long time before we get Jupiter pigeonholed. And maybe longer still before we understand those medusae. I still think that one *knew* where your blind spot was. Anyway, have you decided on your next move? Saturn, Uranus, Neptune—you name it."

"I don't know. I've thought about Saturn, but I'm not really needed there. It's only one gravity, not two and a half like Jupiter. So men can handle it."

Men, thought Webster. He said "men." He's never done that before. And when did I last hear him use the word "we"? He's changing, slipping away from us . . .

"Well," he said aloud, rising from his chair to conceal his slight uneasiness, "let's get the conference started. The cameras are all set up and everyone's waiting. You'll meet a lot of old friends."

He stressed the last word, but Howard showed no response. The leather mask of his face was becoming more and more difficult to read. Instead, he rolled back from the Administrator's desk, unlocked his undercarriage so that it no longer formed a chair, and rose on his hydraulics to his full seven feet of height. It had been good psychology on the part of the surgeons to give him that extra twelve inches, to compensate somewhat for all that he had lost when the *Queen* had crashed.

Falcon waited until Webster had opened the door, then pivoted neatly on his balloon tires and headed for it at a smooth and silent twenty miles an hour. The display of speed and precision was not flaunted arrogantly; rather, it had become quite unconscious.

Howard Falcon, who had once been a man and could still pass for one over a voice circuit, felt a calm sense of achievement—and, for the first time in years, something like peace of mind. Since his return from Jupiter, the nightmares had ceased. He had found his role at last.

He now knew why he had dreamed about that superchimp aboard the doomed *Queen Elizabeth*. Neither man nor beast, it was between two worlds; and so was he.

He alone could travel unprotected on the lunar surface. The life-support system inside the metal cylinder that had replaced his fragile body functioned equally well in space or under water. Gravity fields ten times that of Earth were an inconvenience, but nothing more. And no gravity was best of all . . .

The human race was becoming more remote, the ties of kinship more tenuous. Perhaps these air-breathing, radiation-sensitive bundles of unstable carbon compounds had no right beyond the atmosphere; they should stick to their natural homes—Earth, Moon, Mars.

Some day the real masters of space would be machines, not men—and he was neither. Already conscious of his destiny, he took a somber pride in his unique loneliness—the first immortal midway between two orders of creation.

He would, after all, be an ambassador; between the old and the new—between the creatures of carbon and the creatures of metal who must one day supersede them.

Both would have need of him in the troubled centuries that lay ahead.

GÉRARD KLEIN

The Valley of Echoes

TRANSLATED BY FRANK ZERO

In the first issue of the first science fiction magazine, editor Hugo Gernsback named Edgar Allan Poe, Jules Verne, and H. G. Wells as the forefathers of the genre in the United States, France, and England. This assertion points up the long and vigorous French tradition from at least the century before Verne until the present. Since the 1950s, modern SF has been significant and influential in France, but the most popular authors have generally been English-speaking writers read in translation; for many years, A. E. Van Vogt (particularly in translation by Boris Vian) remained the most popular and respected SF writer, to be supplanted in recent years by Philip K. Dick. Still, much SF originates in France—for instance the popular Planet of the Apes *by Pierre Boulle.*

Of the contemporary French SF writers, none is more distinguished than Gérard Klein, an SF editor for a French publisher, who has had several novels and stories translated into English, perhaps more work than any other of his contemporaries. "The Valley of Echoes," with its energetic shifts in person and tense, shows some of the stylistic devices that characterize French SF and distinguish it from the English and American, which is almost invariably written in the past tense and most often in the third person. French SF is more self-consciously literary than American SF usually is. And yet this story, intimately linked with the atmosphere of the Martian stories of Leigh Brackett and Ray Bradbury, is self-consciously in the American genre.

*   *   *

This time we ventured a little beyond the pink mountains of Tula, the oasis of crystal, and for days on end we passed between innumerable dunes. The Martian sky was always like itself, very pure, a very dark blue with an occasional hint of gray, and with admirable pink efflorescences at sunrise and sunset.

Our tractors performed quite satisfactorily. We were venturing into regions that had hardly been explored thus far, at least by land, and we were reasonably sure of being the first to negotiate these desolate passes. The first men, at any rate; for what we were more or less vaguely searching for was some trace of an ancient civilization. It has never been admitted on Earth that Mars is not only a dead world, but a world eternally deserted. It has long been hoped that we would discover some remains of defunct empires, or perhaps the fallen descendants of the mythical masters of the red planet. Too many stories have been told about Mars for ten years of scientific and fruitless exploration on this point to undo all the legends.

But neither Ferrier nor La Salle nor I particularly believed in the possibility of so fantastic an encounter. We were mature and slightly disillusioned men, and we had left the Earth some years before to escape the wind of insanity which at that time was sweeping our native planet. This was something that we did not like to talk about, as it pained us. We sometimes thought it was due to the immense solitude of a species that had just achieved self-awareness, that confronted the universe, that hoped to receive a response, even a fatal one, to its challenge. But space remained silent and the planets deserted.

We were descending, then, toward the south, in the direction of the Martian equator. The maps were still imprecise at this time, and we had been assigned to make certain geological reports which could not be done from an airplane. As a psychologist, I was only moderately qualified for this task, but I also knew how to drive a tractor and how the instruments worked, and men were scarce on Mars.

The worst thing was the monotony that prevailed throughout these days. People on Earth, comfortably installed behind their desks, write things about us that bring tears of compassion to the eyes of thousands of readers; they speak of our heroism and the adventure that lies in wait for us at each step, of the eternally renewed splendors of unknown worlds. I have never encountered such things. We know danger, but it doesn't rise up from the dunes; it is insidious, a leak in our breathing apparatus or a corresponding defect in our tractors or in our radio posts. It is, above all, the danger of boredom. Mars is a deserted world. Its horizons are short, curtailed. And there are more inspiring scenes than that of an immense plain of gray sand and scattered lichens. The landscape is not terrible in itself. But what one does feel, with poignant acuteness, is the awareness of these thousands of kilometers, all alike, stretching out in all directions as far as you can see and farther still, kilometers which slowly pass beneath your treads while you remain immobile. It's a little as if you were sure of finding in tomorrow the exact replica of yesterday.

And then you drive. For hours. Like a machine. And you are the machine, you are the tractor, you creep along between the dunes for hours on end, you avoid the heaps of stones, slowly modelled by the wind and themselves destined to become sand, and from time to time you lift your eyes to the sky and, through flinching lids, perceive the stars' sparkling in mid-day, which at first surprises and then bores you mortally, so that you would give anything for these eyes of the night to finally close.

Then you think of what you will do on Earth, when you return to it: you have heard the news; it is bad, always bad: no event occurs on Earth that is not aberrant: these are the "Insane Years," they say, and the desire to go back down there turns to a kind of loathing; nausea grips you.

Always, you drive. Without hoping for anything. At the end of a certain time, you see things rising up from among the dunes. You brake abruptly to avoid them, but there is never anything there. There are also those who fall asleep. The others notice it because the tractor suddenly loses its way; then they shake the driver or take the wheel themselves. This provides a little recreation.

As for me, it depends. Sometimes I make up stories. Stories that take place on Mars or in space or on another world, but never on Earth. I prefer not to think of Earth. La Salle is like myself. For Ferrier, it's worse, he can't stop thinking about it for a minute. I ask myself where this will lead him.

He's a geologist. I have watched him dig in the sand and hold up some tiny shell, the ancient abode of a creature long since withered, carried away by the soft winds of Mars. Never once has he discovered a more achieved fossil, the remains of a larger, more powerful (and more fragile) creature. I have seen him battling the evidence. I have seen him sweep his eyes over the hills of Mars, silently thinking that it will one day be necessary to turn over these millions of tons of sand in the hope of discovering, at the heart of the planet, the bleached fetus of a forgotten species. I don't think he talks enough. It is not good for a man to say nothing on Mars. Nor in space. He remains mute, as if the millions and millions of pounds of sand weighed down on him. Like La Salle and myself, he sought in space a way out, a means of escaping Earth, but he expected something else of it. He was hoping to encounter in it something other than himself; he thought to encounter the total stranger, he believed he would read on the cliffs of Mars the history of a world absolutely new for Earth. No doubt he had listened attentively, in his childhood, to the stories of the man in the moon.

Otherwise, he was just like La Salle and myself. There are things, you see, which we could not bear unless we were sure of discovering, one fine day, around the bend of space or between two hills, a glistening city and ideal beings. But La Salle and I, we know that this dream is not for today, or even for tomorrow, while Ferrier can no longer wait.

There are three of us, and that's an awkward number for playing cards. Sometimes we read. We also listen to the radio from time to time. But above all, we sleep. It is a way of economizing on oxygen. It is a way of projecting ourselves in time. We never dream.

When evening comes, we descend from the tractor, we unpack our apparatus. We proceed to take certain measurements. We forward the results. We start the catalytic stove; it functions tranquilly under its transparent bell glass, glowing red in the dusk like a hothouse flower. We eat. We unfurl the parasol-like thing that serves us as a tent, which prevents the mortal cold of Mars from freezing us to the bone, and we try once again to sleep. But it's no use—we've been sleeping nearly all day, you see, lulled by the jolting of the tractor, each taking his turn at the wheel; and when night comes, our respirator chafes us, we stifle, we're suddenly thirsty, and we lie there with our eyes open, staring at the milky dome of the tent, taking in the irritating faint gnashing of sandgrains blown against the plastic by the wind, the patter of insect feet.

Sometimes it happens, during these nights, that we ponder on what space might have been, on what these planets might have been. The thought comes to us that man, one day, will endow Mars with an atmosphere and with oceans and forests, that cities will rise here, fabulous, taller than all the cities of Earth, that spaceships will unite this planet and other worlds, and that the frontiers of the unknown will be situated elsewhere in space, always pushed back beyond the visible horizon. Our anguish is eased by the thought, and we know that man today is steering a false course in asking of this planet what it cannot give, in turning towards the past, in desperately sifting through the sieve of memory in hopes of finding once more the traces of an ancient downfall. We feel then, tremulously, that it is in the future that an answer lies, and that it is into the future that we must throw ourselves.

And we occasionally take stock of the paradoxical nature of our situation. We are at once the past and the future. We are included in the mad dreams of generations dead in the not distant past and we are going the way of infants yet to be born. Anonymous, we were myths; forgotten, we will be legends.

We do not go abroad at night because of the cold. The extreme tenuity of the atmosphere makes for great differences of temperature. But in the morning, around nine o'clock, we set out again.

Today we entered a zone of gray sand, then discovered a stretch littered with flat black stones, Aeolian pebbles, strangely fashioned at times, and finally reached the extreme border of the reddish stretch that touches the Martian equator at certain points. Eroded mountains rise gently over the horizon. The dunes have thinned out and dispersed. The worn mesas that circumscribe the eye shelter this plain from the wind. Our tracks come to breach the hazardous irregularity of the desert. They will survive us.

The surface of the planet descended gently, as if we were plunging into the bosom of some dried-up sea, into the illusory depths of an imaginary littoral. And suddenly, we saw surge up and grow on the horizon translucent needles of rock, so thin and so high, with such sharp contours, that we did not believe our eyes. Ferrier, who was driving, gave a cry. He pressed the accelerator, and the sudden irresistible jolt of the tractor threw La Salle and myself from our seats.

"It's incredible."

"What a fantastic peak."

"No, it's a cliff."

But it was none of all this, as we saw later on in the day. It was a massif, probably crystalline, an accident that had spurted in ages past from the entrails of the planet, or perhaps even fallen from the sky, and some inconceivable tremor had cleaved it, so that it had the appearance, on this immutable plain, of a chipped yet tremendously sharp tooth.

"This is the first time I've ever seen an acute angle on Mars," said Ferrier. "That's not erosion. Neither wind nor sand have managed to cut into this rock. Maybe it's just a giant crystal that has grown slowly, a gradual concentration of like atoms, or perhaps . . ."

We looked at each other. There was one word on our lips. *Artefact*. Was this, at last, the evidence for which Earth had waited so long?

There is nothing worse, I think, than being deceived by an object. Because one cannot reproach it. We had suddenly put our trust in Mars. Like children.

And we were deceived. It was not an artefact.

But we did not want to accept what that meant. It had been crazy to hope. But we couldn't help it.

We spent the night at the foot of the crystalline mountains, and we experienced even more difficulty in getting to sleep than on previous days.

We were both disappointed and satisfied. Our journey had not been in vain, and yet its secret goal was completely unfulfilled.

When morning came and the temperature became endurable, we adjusted our respirators and went out. We had decided to explore the rocky massif, to leave the tractor behind us and to carry only a light baggage of supplies and instruments.

The crystalline cliffs were not overly escarped. They contained faults and openings which permitted us to ascend. The rock was the color of ink, with here and there a murky transparency which reminded us of those blocks of ice that wander in space, the relics of incredibly ancient oceans, fragments of shattered ice packs, debris, finally, of pulverized planets.

We were trying to reach the largest fault, hoping to thus discover the very depths of the massif and to understand its structure. Perhaps a lake of mercury awaited us there, or engraved rocks, or even some creature, a door to another dimension, the traces of previous visitors, for this rock had survived for millions of years the slow burial by sand that lies in wait for all things on Mars. It had escaped the tide of dust that flows over the surface of the red planet, and the movement of the dunes that are incessantly shifted by the light winds, and in a way it was a witness to past ages, epochs in which men did not dare as yet to lift their faces to the sky; even less did they dream that one day they would voyage, weary, through these constellations.

But when it came, the thing took us unawares. La Salle, who was walking ahead, cried out. We heard him clearly and hurled ourselves headlong after him. Ferrier, who was following us, urged me ahead. Rounding a block, we saw La Salle, who seemed to be giving some object his utmost attention.

"Listen," he said to us.

We heard nothing at first; then, as we advanced another step, from those borderlines that separate silence from sound, we heard a gnashing noise arise.

We remained immobile. And this was neither the voice of the wind, nor its singing, nor even the light clatter of a stone or the cracking of rock split by the frost. It was a steady ssh-sshing, like the accumulated noise of millions of superimposed signals.

The air of Mars is too thin for our ears to perceive the sounds that it transmits. Moreover, our eardrums would not have withstood the difference of pressure which exists between the external milieu and our respiratory system. Our ears are entirely masked, and minuscule amplifiers allow us to hear the sound of our voices and to make out the noises of Mars. And this, I can vouch for it, was different from anything that I had heard up to that moment on the red planet. It was nothing human, and nothing mineral.

I moved my head slightly, and suddenly I perceived something else that dominated this ssh-sshing, reduced it to an insignificant and endless background noise. I perceived a voice, or rather the murmur of a million voices, the tumult of an entire race, uttering unbelievable, incomprehensible words, words I could never transcribe with any of the phonetic signs current on Earth.

"They're there," La Salle said to me, his eyes shining. He took a step or two forward, and I saw him hastily change the setting of his earphones. I followed him and did the same, for the murmur had become a tempest, the insect voices had been transformed into a strident and intolerable howling, a muffled and terrifying roar.

We were progressing along a narrow fault between two cliffs of rock. And the sound assailed us in successive, eddying waves. We were drunk on it. We sensed, we knew that at last we were about to find what we had come to see on Mars, what we had in vain implored space to give us.

Contact with another life.

For as the sound grew louder, we did not have the slightest doubt, not once. We were not easy men to deceive, nor were we liable to let our imagination run wild. This incredible richness in the modulation of the sound could only be the doing of live beings. It mattered little that we understood nothing; we had faith that Earth could solve problems of this sort, by its minds and its machines. We were merely the ambassadors of Earth.

At the last turn in the fault, the valley finally appeared. It resembled the basin of a dried-up lake, closed in by tall smooth cliffs which became more escarped the higher they rose. The opposite end of the valley narrowed and ended in a rocky bottleneck, finally coming up against a terminal wall.

There existed no other road that led to this valley except the one that we had taken, unless one were to let oneself drop from the sky. It was an arena rather than a valley, moreover: a vast oblong arena. And deserted.

And yet these incomprehensible voices assailed us.

It was a lake, you see, invisible, a lake of sounds and of dust, an impalpable dust that the years had laid down in this refuge, a dust fallen from the stars, borne by the wind, in which nothing had left its traces, a dust in which those who were calling to us had been swallowed up, perhaps, buried.

"Hello!" La Salle cried, his voice breaking.

He wanted to answer, he hoped for a silence of astonishment, but the arena was empty and the dense waves of sound came breaking in on us one after the other. Words whispered, words pronounced, phrases drawn out in a single breath, sprung from invisible lips.

"Where are you? Oh, where are you?" La Salle cried in a mournful voice. What he was hearing was not enough for him, he wished to see these unknown messengers, he hoped to see rise up from this lake of dust who knows what hideous or admirable forms. His hands were trembling and mine as well, and at my back I heard the short, hissing breath of Ferrier.

"Hello," cried an incredibly weak voice from the other end of the valley.

It was the voice of La Salle. It stood out, minutely, against the sonorous background of innumerable voices; it was a bit of wreckage carried to our shore.

"They are answering us," La Salle said to me, without believing it.

And his voice arose from a thousand places in the valley, an insect's voice, shrill, murmurous, shattered, diffracted. "Hello, hello, hello," it said. "Where are you, where are you-you-you-you-you . . ."

An echo, I thought. An echo. And La Salle turned again toward me, and I read in his eyes that he had understood, and I felt the hand of Ferrier weigh on my shoulder. Our voices, our mingled noises were grounded in the sound-matter that filled the valley, and created tricks of interference, returning to us as if reflected in strange mirrors of sound, transformed, but not at all weakened. Was it possible that such a valley existed on Mars, a valley of echoes, a valley where the transparent and thin air of Mars carried forever the sounds reflected by crystal walls?

Did there exist in the entire universe a place where the fossils were not at all mineral, but sounds? Were we, at last, hearing the voices of the ancient inhabitants of Mars, long after the sands had worn away and engulfed the last vestiges of their passing? Or was it, indeed, the evidence of other visitors come from worlds of which we were still ignorant? Had they passed by here yesterday, or a million years ago? Were we no longer alone?

Our instruments would tell us later and perhaps they would succeed in unraveling this skein of waves, undo these knots, and extract from this involuntary message some illuminating sense.

The valley was utterly deserted and dead. A receptacle. The whole of Mars was nothing but a receptacle that received our traces only to annihilate them. Except for this spot, except for this valley of echoes that would doubtless carry the sound of our voices through the ages to our distant successors, perhaps not human.

Ferrier took his hand from my shoulder, shoved me aside and pushed La Salle away, and began to run towards the center of the valley.

"Listen to them," he cried, "listen to them."

His boots sank into the impalpable dust, and it rose about him in an eddying. And we heard these voices breaking about our ears, in a tempest that he had raised. I saw him running and I understood what the sirens were, these voices that whispered in his ears, that called to him, that he had hoped for all these past years and vainly searched for, and he plunged into this sonorous sea and sank into the dust. I wished that I could be by his side, but I was incapable of making a move.

The voices hammered against my eardrums.

"The fool," said La Salle in a sad voice. "Oh, the poor fool."

Ferrier shouted. Ferrier called, and the immutable, the ancient voices answered him. He imbibed the voices. He drank them, devoured them, stirred them with his demented gestures.

And, slowly, they subsided. He had disturbed some instable equilibrium, destroyed a subtle mechanism. His body was a screen. He was too heavy, too material for these thin voices to endure his contact.

The voices grew weak. I felt them very slowly leave me, I felt them go away, in a last vibration I heard them shrivel up and die. And finally Ferrier fell silent. And in my earphones I made out a last whispering.

A kind of farewell.

The silence. The silence of Mars.

When Ferrier finally turned around, I saw, despite the distance, despite the cloud of dust that gradually settled, through his disordered respirator, tears that ran down his cheeks.

And he put his hands to his ears.

The Fifth Head of Cerberus

Gene Wolfe came into prominence in the 1970s as a writer's writer, then burst into the forefront of SF in the 1980s with his four-volume work The Book of the New Sun, *which won major awards and critical acclaim. His short fiction is the most impressive since Theodore Sturgeon's.*

"The Fifth Head of Cerberus," later collected in a book of the same title, is one of three stories with the same setting. Literate, mysterious, profoundly strange, Wolfe's story was published near the beginning of his career. It could not have been published during Campbell's time, before science fiction was broadened in its literary range. It should be contrasted to such post–New Wave stories as John Varley's "The Phantom of Kansas" and Frederik Pohl's "The Gold at the Starbow's End."

*   *   *

When the ivy-tod is heavy with snow,
And the owlet whoops to the wolf below,
That eats the she-wolf's young.
                    —Samuel Taylor Coleridge
          The Rime of the Ancient Mariner

When I was a boy my brother David and I had to go to bed early whether we were sleepy or not. In summer particularly, bedtime often came before sunset; and because our dormitory was in the east wing of the house, with a broad window facing the central courtyard and thus looking west, the hard, pinkish light sometimes streamed in for hours while we lay staring out at my father's crippled monkey perched on a flaking parapet, or telling stories, one bed to another, with soundless gestures.

Our dormitory was on the uppermost floor of the house, and our window had a shutter of twisted iron which we were forbidden to open. I suppose the theory was that a burglar might, on some rainy morning (this being the only time he could hope to find the roof, which was fitted out as a sort of pleasure garden, deserted), let down a rope and so enter our room unless the shutter was closed.

The object of this hypothetical and very courageous thief would not, of course, be merely to steal us. Children, whether boys or girls, were extraordinarily cheap in Port-Mimizon; and indeed I was once told that my father, who had formerly traded in them, no longer did so because of the poor market. Whether or not this was true, everyone—or nearly everyone—knew of some professional who would furnish what was wanted, within reason, at a low price. These men made the children of the poor and the careless their study, and should you want, say, a brown-skinned, red-haired little girl, or one who was plump, or who lisped, a blond boy like David or a pale, brown-haired, brown-eyed boy such as I, they could provide one in a few hours.

Neither, in all probability, would the imaginary burglar seek to hold us for ransom, though my father was thought in some quarters to be immensely rich. There were several reasons for this. Those few people who knew that my brother and I existed knew also, or at least had been led to believe, that my father cared nothing at all for us. Whether this was true or not, I cannot say; certainly I believed it, and my father never gave me the least reason to doubt it, though at the time the thought of killing him had never occurred to me.

And if these reasons were not sufficiently convincing, anyone with an understanding of the stratum in which he had become perhaps the most permanent feature would realize that for him, who was already forced to give large bribes to the secret police, to once disgorge money in that way would leave him open to a thousand ruinous attacks; and this may have been—this and the fear in which he was held—the real reason we were never stolen.

The iron shutter is (for I am writing now in my old dormitory room) hammered to resemble in a stiff and overly symmetrical way the boughs of a willow. In my boyhood it was overgrown by a silver trumpet vine (since dug up) which had scrambled up the wall from the court below, and I used to wish that it would close the window entirely and thus shut out the sun when we were trying to sleep; but David, whose bed was under the window, was forever reaching up to snap off branches so that he could whistle through the hollow stems, making a sort of panpipe of four or five. The piping, of course, growing louder as David grew bolder, would in time attract the attention of Mr. Million, our tutor. Mr. Million would enter the room in perfect silence, his wide wheels gliding across the uneven floor while David pretended sleep. The panpipe might by this time be concealed under his pillow, in the sheet, or even under the mattress, but Mr. Million would find it.

What he did with those little musical instruments after confiscating them from David I had forgotten until yesterday; although in prison, when we were kept in by storms or heavy snow, I often occupied myself by trying to recall it. To have broken them, or dropped them through the shutter onto the patio below would have been completely unlike him; Mr. Million never broke anything intentionally, and never wasted anything. I could visualize perfectly the half-sorrowing expression with which he drew the tiny pipes out (the face which seemed to float behind his screen was much like my father's) and the way in which he turned and glided from the room. But what became of them?

Yesterday, as I said (this is the sort of thing that gives me confidence), I remembered. He had been talking to me here while I worked, and when he left it seemed to me—as my glance idly followed his smooth motion through the doorway—that something, a sort of flourish I recalled from my earliest days, was missing. I closed my eyes and tried to remember what the appearance had been, eliminating any skepticism, any attempt to guess in advance what I "must" have seen; and I found that the missing element was a brief flash, the glint of metal, over Mr. Million's head.

Once I had established this, I knew that it must have come from a swift upward motion of his arm, like a salute, as he left our room. For an hour or more I could not guess the reason for that gesture, and could only suppose it, whatever it had been, to have been destroyed by time. I tried to recall if the corridor outside our dormitory had, in that really not so distant past, held some object now vanished: a curtain or a windowshade, an appliance to be activated, anything that might account for it. There was nothing.

I went into the corridor and examined the floor minutely for marks indicating furniture. I looked for hooks or nails driven into the walls, pushing aside the coarse old tapestries. Craning my neck, I searched the ceiling. Then, after an hour, I looked at the door itself and saw what I had not seen in the thousands of times I had passed through it: that like all the doors in this house, which is very old, it had a massive frame of wooden slabs, and that one of these, forming the lintel, protruded enough from the wall to make a narrow shelf above the door.

I pushed my chair into the hall and stood on the seat. The shelf was thick with dust in which lay forty-seven of my brother's pipes and a wonderful miscellany of other small objects. Objects many of which I recalled, but some of which still fail to summon any flicker of response from the recesses of my mind . . .

The small blue egg of a songbird, speckled with brown. I suppose the bird must have nested in the vine outside our window, and that David or I despoiled the nest only to be robbed ourselves by Mr. Million. But I do not recall the incident.

And there is a (broken) puzzle made of the bronzed viscera of some small animal, and—wonderfully evocative—one of those large and fancifully decorated keys, sold annually, which during the year of its currency will admit the possessor to certain rooms of the city library after hours. Mr. Million, I suppose, must have confiscated it when, after expiration, he found it doing duty as a toy; but what memories!

My father had his own library, now in my possession; but we were forbidden to go there. I have a dim memory of standing—at how early an age I cannot say—before that huge carved door. Of seeing it swing back, and the crippled monkey on my father's shoulder pressing itself against his hawk face, with the black scarf and scarlet dressing gown beneath and the rows and rows of shabby books and notebooks behind them, and the sick-sweet smell of formaldehyde coming from the laboratory beyond the sliding mirror.

I do not remember what he said or whether it had been I or another who had knocked, but I do recall that after the door had closed, a woman in pink whom I thought very pretty stooped to bring her face to the level of my own and assured me that my father had written all the books I had just seen, and that I doubted it not at all.

My brother and I, as I have said, were forbidden this room; but when we were a little older Mr. Million used to take us, about twice a week, on expeditions to the city library. These were very nearly the only times we were allowed to leave the house, and since our tutor disliked curling the jointed length of his metal modules into a hire cart, and no sedan chair would have withstood his weight or contained his bulk, these forays were made on foot.

For a long time this route to the library was the only part of the city I knew.

Three blocks down Saltimbanque Street where our house stood, right at the Rue d'Asticot to the slave market and a block beyond that to the library. A child, not knowing what is extraordinary and what commonplace, usually lights midway between the two, finds interest in incidents adults consider beneath notice and calmly accepts the most improbable occurrences. My brother and I were fascinated by the spurious antiques and bad bargains of the Rue d'Asticot, but often bored when Mr. Million insisted on stopping for an hour at the slave market.

It was not a large one, Port-Mimizon not being a center of the trade, and the auctioneers and their merchandise were frequently on a most friendly basis—having met several times previously as a succession of owners discovered the same fault. Mr. Million never bid, but watched the bidding, motionless, while we kicked our heels and munched the fried bread he had bought at a stall for us. There were sedan chairmen, their legs knotted with muscle, and simpering bath attendants; fighting slaves in chains, with eyes dulled by drugs or blazing with imbecile ferocity; cooks, house servants, a hundred others—yet David and I used to beg to be allowed to proceed alone to the library.

This library was a wastefully large building which had held government offices in the old French-speaking days. The park in which it had once stood had died of petty corruption, and the library now rose from a clutter of shops and tenements. A narrow thoroughfare led to the main doors, and once we were inside, the squalor of the neighborhood vanished, replaced by a kind of peeling grandeur. The main desk was directly beneath the dome, and this dome, drawing up with it a spiraling walkway lined with the library's main collection, floated five hundred feet in the air: a stony sky whose least chip falling might kill one of the librarians on the spot.

While Mr. Million browsed his way majestically up the helix, David and I raced ahead until we were several full turns in advance and could do what we liked. When I was still quite young it would often occur to me that, since my father had written (on the testimony of the lady in pink) a roomful of books, some of them should be here; and I would climb resolutely until I had almost reached the dome, and there rummage. Because the librarians were very lax about reshelving, there seemed always a possibility of finding what I had failed to find before. The shelves towered far above my head, but when I felt myself unobserved I climbed them like ladders, stepping on books when there was no room on the shelves themselves for the square toes of my small brown shoes, and occasionally kicking books to the floor where they remained until our next visit and beyond, evidence of the staff's reluctance to climb that long, coiled slope.

The upper shelves were, if anything, in worse disorder than those more conveniently located, and one glorious day when I attained the highest of all I found occupying that lofty, dusty position (besides a misplaced astronautics text, *The Mile-Long Spaceship*, by some German) only a lorn copy of *Monday or Tuesday* leaning against a book about the assassination of Trotsky, and a crumbling volume of Vernor Vinge's short stories that owed its presence there, or so I suspect, to some long-dead librarian's mistaking the faded *V. Vinge* on the spine for "Winge."

I never found any books of my father's, but I did not regret the long climbs to the top of the dome. If David had come with me, we raced up together, up and down the sloping floor—or peered over the rail at Mr. Million's slow progress while we debated the feasibility of putting an end to him with one cast of some ponderous work. If David preferred to pursue interests of his own farther down I ascended to the very top where the cap of the dome curved right over my head; and there, from a rusted iron catwalk not much wider than one of the shelves I had been climbing (and I suspect not nearly so strong), opened in turn each of a circle of tiny piercings—piercings in a wall of iron, but so shallow a wall that when I had slid the corroded coverplates out of the way I could thrust my head through and feel myself truly outside, with the wind and the circling birds and the lime-spotted expanse of the dome curving away beneath me.

To the west, since it was taller than the surrounding houses and marked by the orange trees on the roof, I could make out our house. To the south, the masts of the ships in the harbor, and in clear weather—if it was the right time of day—the whitecaps of the tidal race Sainte Anne drew between the peninsulas called First Finger and Thumb. (And once, as I very well recall, while looking south I saw the great geyser of sunlit water when a starcrosser splashed down.) To east and north spread the city proper, the citadel and the grand market and the forests and mountains beyond.

But sooner or later, whether David had accompanied me or gone off on his own, Mr. Million summoned us. Then we were forced to go with him to one of the wings to visit this or that science collection. This meant books for lessons. My father insisted that we learn biology, anatomy, and chemistry thoroughly, and under Mr. Million's tutelage, learn them we did—he never considering a subject mastered until we could discuss every topic mentioned in every book catalogued under the heading. The life sciences were my own favorites, but David preferred languages, literature, and law; for we got a smattering of these as well as anthropology, cybernetics, and psychology.

When he had selected the books that would form our study for the next few days and urged us to choose more for ourselves, Mr. Million would retire with us to some quiet corner of one of the science reading rooms, where there were chairs and a table and room sufficient for him to curl the jointed length of his body or align it against a wall or bookcase in a way that left the aisles clear. To designate the formal beginning of our class he used to begin by calling roll, my own name always coming first.

I would say, "Here," to show that he had my attention.

"And David."

"Here." (David has an illustrated *Tales from the Odyssey* open on his lap where Mr. Million cannot see it, but he looks at Mr. Million with bright, feigned interest. Sunshine slants down to the table from a high window, and shows the air aswarm with dust.)

"I wonder if either of you noticed the stone implements in the room through which we passed a few moments ago?"

We nod, each hoping the other will speak.

"Were they made on Earth, or here on our own planet?"

This is a trick question, but an easy one. David says, "Neither one. They're plastic." And we giggle.

Mr. Million says patiently, "Yes, they're plastic reproductions, but from where did the originals come?" His face, so similar to my father's, but which I thought of at this time as belonging only to him, so that it seemed a frightening reversal of nature to see it on a living man instead of his screen, was neither interested, nor angry, nor bored; but coolly remote.

David answers, "From Sainte Anne." Sainte Anne is the sister planet to our own, revolving with us about a common center as we swing around the sun. "The sign said so, and the aborigines made them—there weren't any abos here."

Mr. Million nods, and turns his impalpable face toward me. "Do you feel these stone implements occupied a central place in the lives of their makers? Say no."

"No."

"Why not?"

I think frantically, not helped by David, who is kicking my shins under the table. A glimmering comes.

"Talk. Answer at once."

"It's obvious, isn't it?" (Always a good thing to say when you're not even sure "it" is even possible.) "In the first place, they can't have been very good tools, so why would the abos have relied on them? You might say they needed those obsidian arrowheads and bone fishhooks for getting food, but that's not true. They could poison the water with the juices of certain plants, and for primitive people the most effective way to fish is probably with weirs, or with nets of rawhide or vegetable fiber. Just the same way, trapping or driving animals with fire would be more effective than hunting; and anyway stone tools wouldn't be needed at all for gathering berries and the shoots of edible plants and things like that, which were probably their most important foods—those stone things got in the glass case here because the snares and nets rotted away and they're all that's left, so the people that make their living that way pretend they were important."

"Good. David? Be original, please. Don't repeat what you've just heard."

David looks up from his book, his blue eyes scornful of both of us. "If you could have asked them, they would have told you that their magic and their religion, the songs they sang, and the traditions of their people were what were important. They killed their sacrificial animals with flails of seashells that cut like razors, and they didn't let their men father children until they had stood enough fire to cripple them for life. They mated with trees and drowned the children to honor their rivers. That was what was important."

With no neck, Mr. Million's face nodded. "Now we will debate the humanity of those aborigines. David negative and first."

(I kick him, but he has pulled his hard, freckled legs up beneath him, or hidden them behind the legs of his chair, which is cheating.) "Humanity," he says in his most objectionable voice, "in the history of human thought implies descent from what we may conveniently call *Adam*; that is, the original Terrestrial stock, and if the two of you don't see that, you're idiots."

I wait for him to continue, but he is finished. To give myself time to think, I say, "Mr. Million, it's not fair to let him call me names in a debate. Tell him that's not debating, it's *fighting*, isn't it?"

Mr. Million says, "No personalities, David." (David is already peeking at Polyphemus the Cyclops and Odysseus, hoping I'll go on for a long time. I feel challenged and decide to do so.)

I begin, "The argument which holds descent from Terrestrial stock pivotal is neither valid nor conclusive. Not conclusive because it is distinctly possible that the aborigines of Sainte Anne were descendants of some earlier wave of human expansion—one, perhaps, even predating *The Homeric Greeks.*"

Mr. Million says mildly, "I would confine myself to arguments of higher probability if I were you."

I nevertheless gloss upon the Etruscans, Atlantis, and the tenacity and expansionist tendencies of a hypothetical technological culture occupying Gondwanaland. When I have finished Mr. Million says, "Now reverse. David, affirmative without repeating."

My brother, of course, has been looking at his book instead of listening, and I kick him with enthusiasm, expecting him to be stuck; but he says, "The abos are human because they're all dead."

"Explain."

"If they were alive it would be dangerous to let them be human because they'd ask for things, but with them dead it makes it more interesting if they were, and the settlers killed them all."

And so it goes. The spot of sunlight travels across the black-streaked red of the tabletop—traveled across it a hundred times. We would leave through one of the side doors and walk through a neglected areaway between two wings. There would be empty bottles there and wind-scattered papers of all kinds, and once a dead man in bright rags over whose legs we skipped while Mr. Million rolled silently around him. As we left the areaway for a narrow street, the bugles of the garrison at the citadel (sounding so far away) would call the troopers to their evening mess. In the Rue d'Asticot the lamplighter would be at work, and the shops shut behind their iron grilles. The sidewalks magically clear of old furniture would seem broad and bare.

Our own Saltimbanque Street would be very different, with the first revelers arriving. White-haired, hearty men guiding very young men and boys, men and boys handsome and muscular but a shade overfed; young men who made diffident jokes and smiled with excellent teeth at them. These were always the early ones, and when I was a little older I sometimes wondered if they were early only because the white-haired men wished to have their pleasure and yet a good night's sleep as well, or if it were because they knew the young men they were introducing to my father's establishment would be drowsy and irritable after midnight, like children who have been kept up too late.

Because Mr. Million did not want us to use the alleys after dark we came in the front entrance with the white-haired men and their nephews and sons. There was a garden there, not much bigger than a small room and recessed into the windowless front of the house. In it were beds of ferns the size of graves; a little fountain whose water fell upon rods of glass to make a continual tinkling, and which had to be protected from the street boys; and, with his feet firmly planted, indeed almost buried in moss, an iron statue of a dog with three heads.

It was this statue, I suppose, that gave our house its popular name of *Maison du Chien*, though there may have been a reference to our surname as well. The three heads were sleekly powerful with pointed muzzles and ears. One was snarling and one, the center head, regarded the world of garden and street with a look of tolerant interest. The third, the one nearest the brick path that led to our door, was—there is no other term for it— frankly grinning; and it was the custom for my father's patrons to pat this head between the ears as they came up the path. Their fingers had polished the spot to the consistency of black glass.

.　　.　　.

This, then, was my world at seven of our world's long years, and perhaps for half a year beyond. Most of my days were spent in the little classroom over which Mr. Million presided, and my evenings in the dormitory where David and I played and fought in total silence. They were varied by the trips to the library I have described or, very rarely, elsewhere. I pushed aside the leaves of the silver trumpet vine occasionally to watch the girls and their benefactors in the court below, or heard their talk drifting down from the roof garden, but the things they did and talked of were of no great interest to me. I knew that the tall, hatchet-faced man who ruled our house and was called "Maitre" by the girls and servants was my father. I had known for as long as I could remember that there was somewhere a fearsome woman—the servants were in terror of her—called "Madame," but that she was neither my mother, nor David's, nor my father's wife.

That life and my childhood, or at least my infancy, ended one evening after David and I, worn out with wrestlings and silent arguments, had gone to sleep. Someone shook me by the shoulder and called me, and it was not Mr. Million but one of the servants, a hunched little man in a shabby red jacket. "He wants you," this summoner informed me. "Get up."

I did, and he saw that I was wearing nightclothes. This I think had not been covered in his instructions, and for a moment during which I stood and yawned, he debated with himself. "Get dressed," he said at last. "Comb your hair."

I obeyed, putting on the black velvet trousers I had worn the day before, but (guided by some instinct) a new clean shirt. The room to which he then conducted me (through tortuous corridors now emptied of the last patrons; and others, musty, filthy with the excrement of rats, to which patrons were never admitted) was my father's library—the room with the great carved door before which I had received the whispered confidences of the woman in pink. I had never been inside it, but when my guide rapped discreetly on the door it swung back, and I found myself within, almost before I realized what had happened.

My father, who had opened the door, closed it behind me; and leaving me standing where I was, walked to the most distant end of that long room and threw himself down in a huge chair. He was wearing the red dressing gown and black scarf in which I had most often seen him, and his long, sparse hair was brushed straight back. He stared at me, and I remember that my lip trembled as I tried to keep from breaking into sobs.

"Well," he said, after we had looked at one another for a long time, "and there you are. What am I going to call you?"

I told him my name, but he shook his head. "Not that. You must have another name for me—a private name. You may choose it yourself if you like."

I said nothing. It seemed to me quite impossible that I should have any name other than the two words which were, in some mystic sense I only respected without understanding, *my name.*

"I'll choose for you then," my father said. "You are Number Five. Come here, Number Five."

I came, and when I was standing in front of him, he told me, "Now we are going to play a game. I am going to show you some pictures, do you understand? And all the time you are watching them, you must talk. Talk about the pictures. If you talk you win, but if you stop, even for just a second, I do. Understand?"

I said I did.

"Good. I know you're a bright boy. As a matter of fact, Mr. Million has sent me all the examinations he has given you and the tapes he makes when he talks with you. Did you know that? Did you ever wonder what he did with them?"

I said, "I thought he threw them away," and my father, I noticed, leaned forward as I spoke, a circumstance I found flattering at the time.

"No, I have them here." He pressed a switch. "Now remember, you must not stop talking."

But for the first few moments I was much too interested to talk.

There had appeared in the room, as though by magic, a boy considerably younger than I, and a painted wooden soldier almost as large as I was myself, which when I reached out to touch them proved as insubstantial as air. "Say something," my father said. "What are you thinking about, Number Five?"

I was thinking about the soldier, of course, and so was the younger boy, who appeared to be about three. He toddled through my arm like mist and attempted to knock it over.

They were holograms—three-dimensional images formed by the interference of two wave fronts of light—things which had seemed very dull when I had seen them illustrated by flat pictures of chessmen in my physics book; but it was some time before I connected those chessmen with the phantoms who walked in my father's library at night. All this time my father was saying, "Talk! Say something! What do you think the little boy is feeling?"

"Well, the little boy likes the big soldier, but he wants to knock him down if he can, because the soldier's only a toy, really, but it's bigger than he is . . ." And so I talked, and for a long time, hours I suppose, continued. The scene changed and changed again. The giant soldier was replaced by a pony, a rabbit, a meal of soup and crackers. But the three-year-old boy remained the central figure. When the hunched man in the shabby coat came again, yawning, to take me back to my bed, my voice had worn to a husky whisper and my throat ached. In my dreams that night I saw the little boy scampering from one activity to another, his personality in some way confused with my own and my father's so that I was at once observer, observed, and a third presence observing both.

The next night I fell asleep almost at the moment Mr. Million sent us up to bed, retaining consciousness only long enough to congratulate myself on doing so. I woke when the hunched man entered the room, but it was not me whom he roused from the sheets but David. Quietly, pretending I still slept (for it had occurred to me, and seemed quite reasonable at the time, that if he were to see I was awake he might take both of us), I watched as my brother dressed and struggled to impart some sort of order to his tangle of fair hair. When he returned I was sound asleep, and had no opportunity to question him until Mr. Million left us alone, as he sometimes did, to eat our breakfast. I had told him my own experiences as a matter of course, and what he had to tell me was simply that he had had an evening very similar to mine. He had seen holograms, and apparently the same: the wooden soldier, the pony. He had been forced to talk constantly, as Mr. Million had so often made us do in debates and verbal examinations. The only way in which his interview with our father had differed from mine, as nearly as I could determine, appeared when I asked him by what name he had been called.

He looked at me blankly, a piece of toast half raised to his mouth.

I asked again, "What name did he call you by when he talked to you?"

"He called me David. What did you think?"

With the beginning of these interviews the pattern of my life changed, the adjustments I assumed to be temporary becoming imperceptibly permanent, settling into a new shape of which neither David nor I were consciously aware. Our games and stories after bedtime stopped, and David less and less often made his panpipes of the silver trumpet vine. Mr. Million allowed us to sleep later and we were in some subtle way acknowledged to be more adult. At about this time too, he began to take us to a park where there was an archery range and provision for various games. This little park, which was not far from our house, was bordered on one side by a canal. And there, while David shot arrows at a goose stuffed with straw or played tennis, I often sat staring at the quiet, only slightly dirty water; or waiting for one of the white ships—great ships with bows as sharp as the scalpel-bills of kingfishers and four, five, or even seven masts—which were, infrequently, towed up from the harbor by ten or twelve spans of oxen.

In the summer of my eleventh or twelfth year—I think the twelfth—we were permitted for the first time to stay after sundown in the park, sitting on the grassy, sloped margin of the canal to watch a fireworks display. The first preliminary flight of rockets had no sooner exhausted itself half a mile above the city than David became ill. He rushed to the water and vomited, plunging his hands half up to the elbows in muck while the red and white stars burned in glory above him. Mr. Million took him up in his arms, and when poor David had emptied himself we hurried home.

His disease proved not much more lasting than the tainted sandwich that had occasioned it, but while our tutor was putting him to bed I decided not to be cheated of the remainder of the display, parts of which I had glimpsed between the intervening houses as we made our way home; I was forbidden the roof after dark, but I knew very well where the nearest stair was. The thrill I felt in penetrating that prohibited world of leaf and shadow while fire-flowers of purple and gold and blazing scarlet overtopped it affected me like the aftermath of a fever, leaving me short of breath, shaking, and cold in the midst of summer.

There were a great many more people on the roof than I had anticipated, the men without cloaks, hats, or sticks (all of which they had left in my father's checkrooms), and the girls, my father's employees, in costumes that displayed their rouged breasts in enclosures of twisted wire like birdcages, or gave them the appearance of great height (dissolved only when someone stood very close to them), or gowns whose skirts reflected their wearers' faces and busts as still water does the trees standing near it, so that they appeared, in the intermittent colored flashes, like the queens of strange suits in a tarot deck.

I was seen, of course, since I was much too excited to conceal myself effectively; but no one ordered me back, and I suppose they assumed I had been permitted to come up to see the fireworks.

These continued for a long time. I remember one patron, a heavy, square-faced, stupid-looking man who seemed to be someone of importance, who was so eager to enjoy the company of his protégée—who did not want to go inside until the display was over—that, since he insisted on privacy, twenty or thirty bushes and small trees had to be rearranged on the parterre to make a little grove around them. I helped the waiters carry some of the smaller tubs and pots, and managed to duck into the structure as it was completed. Here I could still watch the exploding rockets and "aerial bombs" through the branches, and at the same time the patron and his *nymphe du bois*, who was watching them a good deal more intently than I.

My motive, as well as I can remember, was not prurience but simple curiosity. I was at that age when we are passionately interested, but the passion is one of science. Mine was nearly satisfied when I was grasped by the shirt by someone behind me and drawn out of the shrubbery.

When I was clear of the leaves I was released, and I turned expecting to see Mr. Million, but it was not he. My captor was a little gray-haired woman in a black dress whose skirt, as I noticed even at the time, fell straight from her waist to the ground. I suppose I bowed to her, since she was clearly no servant, but she returned no salutation at all, staring intently into my face in a way that made me think she could see as well in the intervals between the bursting glories as by their light. At last, in what must have been the finale of the display, a great rocket rose screaming on a river of flame, and for an instant she consented to look up. Then, when it had exploded in a mauve orchid of unbelievable size and brilliance, this formidable little woman grabbed me again and led me firmly toward the stairs.

While we were on the level stone pavement of the roof garden she did not, as nearly as I could see, walk at all, but rather seemed to glide across the surface like an onyx chessman on a polished board; and that, in spite of all that has happened since, is the way I still remember her: as the Black Queen, a chess queen neither sinister nor beneficent, and Black only as distinguished from some White Queen I was never fated to encounter.

When we reached the stairs, however, this smooth gliding became a fluid bobbing that brought two inches or more of the hem of her black skirt into contact with each step, as if her torso were descending each as a small boat might a rapids—now rushing, now pausing, now almost backing in the cross currents.

She steadied herself on these steps by holding on to me and grasping the arm of a maid who had been waiting for us at the stairhead and assisted her from the other side. I had supposed, while we were crossing the roof garden, that her gliding motion had been the result, merely, of a marvelously controlled walk and good posture, but I now understood her to be in some way handicapped; and I had the impression that without the help the maid and I gave her she might have fallen headfirst.

Once we had reached the bottom of the steps her smooth progress was resumed. She dismissed the maid with a nod and led me down the corridor in the direction opposite to that in which our dormitory and classroom lay until we reached a stairwell far toward the back of the house, a corkscrew, seldom-used flight, very steep, with only a low iron banister between the steps and a six-story drop into the cellars. Here she released me and told me crisply to go down. I went down several steps, then turned to see if she was having any difficulty.

She was not, but neither was she using the stairs. With her long skirt hanging as straight as a curtain she was floating, suspended, watching me, in the center of the stairwell. I was so startled I stopped, which made her jerk her head angrily, then began to run. As I fled around and around the spiral she revolved with me, turning toward me always a face extraordinarily like my father's, one hand always on the railing. When we had descended to the second floor she swooped down and caught me as easily as a cat takes charge of an errant kitten, and led me through rooms and passages where I had never been permitted to go until I was as confused as I might have been in a strange building. At last we stopped before a door in no way different from any other. She opened it with an old-fashioned brass key with an edge like a saw and motioned for me to go in.

The room was brightly lit, and I was able to see clearly what I had only sensed on the roof and in the corridors: that the hem of her skirt hung two inches above the floor no matter how she moved, and that there was nothing between the hem and the floor at all. She waved me to a little footstool covered with needlepoint and said, "Sit down," and when I had done so, glided across to a wing-backed rocker and sat facing me. After a moment she asked, "What's your name?" and when I told her she cocked an eyebrow at me, and started the chair in motion by pushing gently with her fingers at a floor lamp that stood beside it. After a long time she said, "And what does he call you?"

"He?" I was stupid, I suppose, with lack of sleep.

She pursed her lips. "My brother."

I relaxed a little. "Oh," I said, "you're my aunt then. I thought you looked like my father. He calls me Number Five."

For a moment she continued to stare, the corners of her mouth drawing down as my father's often did. Then she said, "That number's either far too low or too high. Living, there are he and I, and I suppose he's counting the simulator. Have you a sister, Number Five?"

Mr. Million had been having us read *David Copperfield*, and when she said this she reminded me so strikingly and unexpectedly of Aunt Betsey Trotwood that I shouted with laughter.

"There's nothing absurd about it. Your father had a sister—why shouldn't you? You have none?"

"No ma'am, but I have a brother. His name is David."

"Call me Aunt Jeannine. Does David look like you, Number Five?"

I shook my head. "His hair is curly and blond instead of like mine. Maybe he looks a little like me, but not a lot."

"I suppose," my aunt said under her breath, "he used one of my girls."

"Ma'am?"

"Do you know who David's mother was, Number Five?"

"We're brothers, so I guess she would be the same as mine, but Mr. Million says she went away a long time ago."

"Not the same as yours," my aunt said. "No. I could show you a picture of your own. Would you like to see it?" She rang a bell, and a maid came curtsying from some room beyond the one in which we sat; my aunt whispered to her, and she went out again. When my aunt turned back to me she asked, "And what do you do all day, Number Five, besides run up to the roof when you shouldn't? Are you taught?"

I told her about my experiments (I was stimulating unfertilized frogs' eggs to asexual development and then doubling the chromosomes by a chemical treatment so that a further asexual generation could be produced) and the dissections Mr. Million was by then encouraging me to do, and while I talked, happened to drop some remark about how interesting it would be to perform a biopsy on one of the aborigines of Sainte Anne if any were still in existence, since the first explorers' descriptions differed so widely, and some pioneers there had claimed the abos could change their shapes.

"Ah," my aunt said, "you know about them. Let me test you, Number Five. What is Veil's Hypothesis?"

We had learned that several years before, so I said, "Veil's hypothesis supposes the abos to have possessed the ability to mimic mankind perfectly. Veil thought that when the ships came from Earth the abos killed everyone and took their places and the ships, so they're not dead at all, we are."

"You mean the Earth people are," my aunt said. "The human beings."

"Ma'am?"

"If Veil was correct, then you and I are abos from Sainte Anne, at least in origin; which I suppose is what you meant. Do you think he was right?"

"I don't think it makes any difference. He said the imitation would have to be perfect, and if it is, they're the same as we were anyway." I thought I was being clever, but my aunt smiled, rocking more vigorously. It was very warm in the close, bright little room.

"Number Five, you're too young for semantics, and I'm afraid you've been led astray by that word *perfectly*. Dr. Veil, I'm certain, meant to use it loosely rather than as precisely as you seem to think. The imitation could hardly have been exact, since human beings don't possess that talent and to imitate them *perfectly* the abos would have to lose it."

"Couldn't they?"

"My dear child, abilities of every sort must evolve. And when they do they must be utilized or they atrophy. If the abos had been able to mimic so well as to lose the power to do so, that would have been the end of them, and no doubt it would have come long before the first ships reached them. Of course there's not the slightest evidence they could do anything of the sort. They simply died off before they could be thoroughly studied, and Veil, who wants a dramatic explanation for the cruelty and irrationality he sees around him, has hung fifty pounds of theory on nothing."

This last remark, especially as my aunt seemed so friendly, appeared to me to offer an ideal opportunity for a question about her remarkable means of locomotion, but as I was about to frame it we were interrupted, almost simultaneously, from two directions. The maid returned carrying a large book bound in tooled leather, and she had no sooner handed it to my aunt than there was a tap at the door. My aunt said absently, "Get that," and since the remark might as easily have been addressed to me as to the maid I satisfied my curiosity in another form by racing her to answer the knock.

Two of my father's demi-mondaines were waiting in the hall, costumed and painted until they seemed more alien than any abos, stately as Lombardy poplars and inhuman as specters, with green and yellow eyes made to look the size of eggs, and inflated breasts pushed almost shoulder high; and though they maintained an inculcated composure I was pleasantly aware that they were startled to find me in the doorway. I bowed them in, but as the maid closed the door behind them my aunt said absently, "In a moment, girls, I want to show the boy here something, then he's going to leave."

The "something" was a photograph utilizing, as I supposed, some novelty technique which washed away all color save a light brown. It was small, and from its general appearance and crumbling edges very old. It showed a girl of twenty-five or so, thin and as nearly as I could judge rather tall, standing beside a stocky young man on a paved walkway and holding a baby. The walkway ran along the front of a remarkable house, a very long wooden house only a story in height, with a porch or veranda that changed its architectural style every twenty or thirty feet so as to give almost the impression of a number of exceedingly narrow houses constructed with their side walls in contact. I mention this detail, which I hardly noticed at the time, because I have so often since my release from prison tried to find some trace of this house. When I was first shown the picture I was much more interested in the girl's face, and the baby's. The latter was in fact scarcely visible, he being nearly smothered in white-wool blankets. The girl had large features and a brilliant smile which held a suggestion of that rarely seen charm which is at once careless, poetic, and sly. Gypsy, was my first thought, but her complexion was surely too fair for that. Since on this world we are all descended from a relatively small group of colonists, we are rather a uniform population, but my studies had given me some familiarity with the original Terrestrial races, and my second guess, almost a certainty, was Celtic. "Wales," I said aloud. "Or Scotland. Or Ireland."

"What?" my aunt said. One of the girls giggled; they were seated on the divan now, their long, gleaming legs crossed before them like the varnished staffs of flags.

"It doesn't matter."

My aunt looked at me acutely and said, "You're right. I'll send for you, and we'll talk about this when we've both more leisure. For the present my maid will take you to your room."

I remember nothing of the long walk the maid and I must have had back to the dormitory, or what excuses I gave Mr. Million for my unauthorized absence. Whatever they were I suppose he penetrated them, or discovered the truth by questioning the servants, because no summons to return to my aunt's apartment came, although I expected it daily for weeks afterward.

That night—I am reasonably sure it was the same night—I dreamed of the abos of Sainte Anne, abos dancing with plumes of fresh grass on their heads and arms and ankles, abos shaking their shields of woven rushes and their nephrite-tipped spears until the motion affected my bed and became, in shabby red cloth, the arms of my father's valet come to summon me, as he did almost every night, to his library.

That night, and this time I am quite certain it was the same night, that is, the night I first dreamed of the abos, the pattern of my hours with him, which had come over the four or five years past to have a predictable sequence of conversation, holograms, free association, and dismissal— changed. Following the preliminary talk designed, I feel sure, to put me at ease (at which it failed, as it always did), I was told to roll up a sleeve and lie down upon an old examining table in a corner of the room. My father then made me look at the wall, which meant at the shelves heaped with ragged notebooks. I felt a needle being thrust into the inner part of my arm, but my head was held down and my face turned away, so that I could neither sit up nor look at what he was doing. Then the needle was withdrawn, and I was told to lie quietly.

After what seemed a very long time, during which my father occasionally spread my eyelids to look at my eyes or took my pulse, someone in a distant part of the room began to tell a very long and confusingly involved story. My father made notes of what was said, and occasionally stopped to ask questions I found it unnecessary to answer, since the storyteller did it for me.

The drug he had given me did not, as I had imagined it would, lessen its hold on me as the hours passed. Instead it seemed to carry me progressively further from reality and the mode of consciousness best suited to preserving the individuality of thought. The peeling leather of the examination table vanished under me, and was now the deck of a ship, now the wing of a dove beating far above the world; and whether the voice I heard reciting was my own or my father's I no longer cared. It was pitched sometimes higher, sometimes lower, but then I felt myself at times to be speaking from the depths of a chest larger than my own, and his voice, identified as such by the soft rustling of the pages of his notebook, might seem the high, treble cries of the racing children in the streets as I heard them in summer when I thrust my head through the windows at the base of the library dome.

With that night my life changed again. The drugs—for there seemed to be several, and although the effect I have described was the usual one there were also times when I found it impossible to lie still, but ran up and down for hours as I talked, or sank into blissful or indescribably frightening dreams—affected my health. I often wakened in the morning with a headache that kept me in agony all day, and I became subject to periods of extreme nervousness and apprehensiveness. Most frightening of all, whole sections of days sometimes disappeared, so that I found myself awake and dressed, reading, walking, and even talking, with no memory at all of anything that had happened since I had lain muttering to the ceiling in my father's library the night before.

The lessons I had had with David did not cease, but in some sense Mr. Million's role and mine were now reversed. It was I, now, who insisted on holding our classes when they were held at all; and it was I who chose the subject matter and, in most cases, questioned David and Mr. Million about it. But often when they were at the library or the park I remained in bed reading, and I believe there were many times when I read and studied from the time I found myself conscious in my bed until my father's valet came for me again.

David's interviews with our father, I should note here, suffered the same changes as my own and at the same time; but since they were less frequent— and they became less and less frequent as the hundred days of summer wore away to autumn and at last to the long winter—and he seemed on the whole to have less adverse reactions to the drugs, the effect on him was not nearly as great.

If at any single time, it was during this winter that I came to the end of childhood. My new ill health forced me away from childish activities, and encouraged the experiments I was carrying out on small animals, and my dissections of the bodies Mr. Million supplied in an unending stream of open mouths and staring eyes. Too, I studied or read, as I have said, for hours on end; or simply lay with my hands behind my head while I struggled to recall, perhaps for whole days together, the narratives I had heard myself give my father. Neither David nor I could ever remember enough even to build a coherent theory of the nature of the questions asked us, but I have still certain scenes fixed in my memory which I am sure I have never beheld in fact, and I believe these are my visualizations of suggestions whispered while I bobbed and dove through those altered states of consciousness.

My aunt, who had previously been so remote, now spoke to me in the corridors and even visited our room. I learned that she controlled the interior arrangements of our house, and through her I was able to have a small laboratory of my own set up in the same wing. But I spent the winter, as I have described, mostly at my enamel dissecting table or in bed. The white snow drifted half up the glass of the window, clinging to the bare stems of the silver trumpet vine. My father's patrons, on the rare occasions I saw them, came in with wet boots, the snow on their shoulders and their hats, puffing and red-faced as they beat their coats in the foyer. The orange trees were gone, the roof garden no longer used, and the courtyard under our window only late at night when half a dozen patrons and their protégées, whooping with hilarity and wine, fought with snowballs—an activity invariably concluded by stripping the girls and tumbling them naked in the snow.

Spring surprised me, as she always does those of us who remain most of our lives indoors. One day, while I still thought, if I thought about the weather at all, in terms of winter, David threw open the window and insisted that I go with him into the park—and it was April. Mr. Million went with us, and I remember that as we stepped out the front door into the little garden that opened into the street, a garden I had last seen banked with the snow shoveled from the path, but which was now bright with early bulbs and the chiming of the fountain, David tapped the iron dog on its grinning muzzle and recited: "And thence the dog/With fourfold head brought to these realms of light."

I made some trivial remark about his having miscounted.

"Oh, no. Old Cerberus has four heads, don't you know that? The fourth's her maidenhead, and she's such a bitch no dog can take it from her." Even Mr. Million chuckled, but I thought afterward, looking at David's ruddy good health and the foreshadowing of manhood already apparent in the set of his shoulders, that if, as I had always thought of them, the three heads represented Maitre, Madame, and Mr. Million, that is, my father, my aunt (David's *maidenhead*, I suppose), and my tutor, then indeed a fourth would have to be welded in place soon for David himself.

The park must have been a paradise for him, but in my poor health I found it bleak enough and spent most of the morning huddled on a bench, watching David play squash. Toward noon I was joined, not on my own bench, but on another close enough for there to be a feeling of proximity, by a dark-haired girl with one ankle in a cast. She was brought there, on crutches, by a sort of nurse or governess who seated herself, I felt sure deliberately, between the girl and me. This unpleasant woman was, however, too straightbacked for her chaperonage to succeed completely. She sat on the edge of the bench, while the girl, with her injured leg thrust out before her, slumped back and thus gave me a good view of her profile, which was beautiful; and occasionally, when she turned to make some remark to the creature with her, I could study her full face — carmine lips and violet eyes, a round rather than an oval face, with a broad point of black hair dividing the forehead; archly delicate black eyebrows and long, curling lashes. When a vendor, an old woman, came selling Cantonese egg rolls (longer than your hand, and still so hot from the boiling fat that they needed to be eaten with great caution as though they were in some way alive), I made her my messenger and, as well as buying one for myself, sent her with two scalding delicacies to the girl and her attendant monster.

The monster, of course, refused; the girl, I was charmed to see, pleaded; her huge eyes and bright cheeks eloquently proclaiming arguments I was unfortunately just too far away to hear but could follow in pantomime: it would be a gratuitous insult to a blameless stranger to refuse; she was hungry and had intended to buy an egg roll in any event — how thriftless to object when what she had wished for was rendered free! The vending woman, who clearly delighted in her role as go-between, announced herself on the point of weeping at the thought of being forced to refund my gold (actually a bill of small denomination nearly as greasy as the paper in which her wares were wrapped, and considerably dirtier), and eventually their voices grew loud enough for me to hear the girl's, which was a clear and very pleasing contralto. In the end, of course, they accepted; the monster conceded me a frigid nod, and the girl winked at me behind her back.

Half an hour later when David and Mr. Millon, who had been watching him from the edge of the court, asked if I wanted lunch, I told them I did, thinking that when we returned I could take a seat closer to the girl without being brazen about it. We ate, I (at least so I fear) very impatiently, in a clean little café close to the flower market; but when we came back to the park the girl and her governess were gone.

We returned to the house, and about an hour afterward my father sent for me. I went with some trepidation, since it was much earlier than was customary for our interview — before the first patrons had arrived, in fact, while I usually saw him only after the last had gone. I need not have feared. He began by asking about my health, and when I said it seemed better than it had been during most of the winter he began, in a self-conscious and even pompous way, as different from his usual fatigued incisiveness as could be imagined, to talk about his business and the need a young man had to prepare himself to earn a living. He said, "You are a scientific scholar, I believe."

I said I hoped I was in a small way, and braced myself for the usual attack upon the uselessness of studying chemistry or biophysics on a world like ours where the industrial base was so small, of no help at the civil service examinations, does not even prepare one for trade, and so on. He said instead, "I'm glad to hear it. To be frank, I asked Mr. Million to encourage you in that as much as he could. He would have done it anyway I'm sure; he did with me. These studies will not only be of great satisfaction to you, but will . . ." he paused, cleared his throat, and massaged his face and scalp with his hands, "be valuable in all sorts of ways. And they are, as you might say, a family tradition."

I said, and indeed felt, that I was very happy to hear that.

"Have you seen my lab? Behind the big mirror there?"

I hadn't, though I had known that such a suite of rooms existed beyond the sliding mirror in the library, and the servants occasionally spoke of his "dispensary" where he compounded doses for them, examined monthly the girls we employed, and occasionally prescribed treatment for "friends" of patrons, men recklessly imprudent who had failed (as the wise patrons had not) to confine their custom to our establishment exclusively. I told him I should very much like to see it.

He smiled. "But we are wandering from our topic. Science is of great value, but you will find, as I have, that it consumes more money that it produces. You will want apparatus and books and many other things, as well as a livelihood for yourself. We have a not unprofitable business here, and though I hope to live a long time—thanks in part to science—you are the heir, and it will be yours in the end . . .

(So I was older than David!)

". . . every phase of what we do. None of them, believe me, are unimportant."

I had been so surprised, and in fact elated, by my discovery that I had missed a part of what he said. I nodded, which seemed safe.

"Good. I want you to begin by answering the front door. One of the maids has been doing it, and for the first month or so she'll stay with you, since there's more to be learned there than you think. I'll tell Mr. Million, and he can make the arrangements."

I thanked him, and he indicated that the interview was over by opening the door of the library. I could hardly believe, as I went out, that he was the same man who devoured my life in the early hours of almost every morning.

. . .

I did not connect this sudden elevation in status with the events in the park. I now realize that Mr. Million who has, quite literally, eyes in the back of his head must have reported to my father that I had reached the age at which desires in childhood subliminally fastened to parental figures begin, half consciously, to grope beyond the family.

In any event that same evening I took up my new duties and became what Mr. Million called the "greeter" and David (explaining that the original sense of the word was related to *portal*) the "porter" of our house—thus assuming in a practical way the functions symbolically executed by the iron dog in our front garden. The maid who had previously carried them out, a girl named Nerissa who had been selected because she was not only one of the prettiest but one of the tallest and strongest of the maids as well, a large-boned, long-faced, smiling girl with shoulders broader than most men's, remained, as my father had promised, to help. Our duties were not onerous, since my father's patrons were all men of some position and wealth, not given to brawling or loud arguments except under unusual circumstances of intoxication; and for the most part they had visited our house already dozens, and, in a few cases, even hundreds of times. We called them by nicknames that were used only here (of which Nerissa informed me *sotto voce* as they came up the walk), hung up their coats, and directed them—or if necessary conducted them—to the various parts of the establishment. Nerissa flounced (a formidable sight, as I observed, to all but the most heroically proportioned patrons), allowed herself to be pinched, took tips, and talked to me afterward, during slack periods, of the times she had been "called upstairs" at the request of some connoisseur of scale, and the money she had made that night. I laughed at jokes and refused tips in such a way as to make the patrons aware that I was a part of the management. Most patrons did not need the reminder, and I was often told that I strikingly resembled my father.

When I had been serving as a receptionist in this way for only a short time, I think on only the third or fourth night, we had an unusual visitor. He came early one evening, but it was the evening of so dark a day, one of the last really wintry days, that the garden lamps had been lit for an hour or more, and the occasional carriages that passed on the street beyond, though they could be heard, could not be seen. I answered the door when he knocked, and as we always did with strangers, asked him politely what he wished.

He said, "I should like to speak to Dr. Aubrey Veil."

I am afraid I looked blank.

"This is 666 Saltimbanque?"

It was of course; and the name of Dr. Veil, though I could not place it, touched a chime of memory. I supposed that one of our patrons had used my father's house as an *adresse d'accommodation*, and since this visitor was clearly legitimate, and it was not desirable to keep anyone arguing in the doorway despite the partial shelter afforded by the garden, I asked him in; then I sent Nerissa to bring us coffee so that we might have a few moments of private talk in the dark little receiving room that opened off the foyer. It was a room very seldom used, and the maids had been remiss in dusting it, as I saw as soon as I opened the door. I made a mental note to speak to my aunt about it, and as I did I recalled where it was that I had heard Dr. Veil mentioned. My aunt, on the first occasion I had ever spoken to her, had referred to his theory that we might in fact be the natives of Sainte Anne, having murdered the original Terrestrial colonists and displaced them so thoroughly as to forget our own past.

The stranger had seated himself in one of the musty, gilded armchairs. He wore a beard, very black and more full than the current style, was young, I thought, though of course considerably older than I, and would have been handsome if the skin of his face—what could be seen of it—had not been of so colorless a white as almost to constitute a disfigurement. His dark clothing seemed abnormally heavy, like felt, and I recalled having heard from some patron that a starcrosser from Sainte Anne had splashed down in the bay yesterday, and asked if he had perhaps been on board it. He looked startled for a moment, then laughed. "You're a wit, I see. And living with Dr. Veil you'd be familiar with his theory. No, I'm from Earth. My name is Marsch." He gave me his card, and I read it twice before the meaning of the delicately embossed abbreviations registered on my mind. My visitor was a scientist, a doctor of philosophy in anthropology, from Earth.

I said, "I wasn't trying to be witty. I thought you might really have come from Sainte Anne. Here, most of us have a kind of planetary face, except for the gypsies and the criminal tribes, and you don't seem to fit the pattern."

He said, "I've noticed what you mean. You seem to have it yourself."

"I'm supposed to look a great deal like my father."

"Ah," he said. He stared at me. Then, "Are you cloned?"

"Cloned?" I had read the term, but only in conjunction with botany, and as has happened to me often when I have especially wanted to impress someone with my intelligence, nothing came. I felt like a stupid child.

"Parthenogenetically reproduced, so that the new individual—or individuals, you can have a thousand if you want—will have a genetic structure identical to the parent. It's anti-evolutionary, so it's illegal on Earth, but I don't suppose things are as closely watched out here."

"You're talking about human beings?"

He nodded.

"I've never heard of it. Really I doubt if you'd find the necessary technology here. We're quite backward compared to Earth. Of course, my father might be able to arrange something for you."

"I don't want to have it done."

Nerissa came in with the coffee then, effectively cutting off anything further Dr. Marsch might have said. Actually, I had added the suggestion about my father more from force of habit than anything else, and thought it very unlikely that he could pull off any such biochemical *tour de force*, but there was always the possibility, particularly if a large sum were offered. As it was, we fell silent while Nerissa arranged the cups and poured, and when she had gone Marsch said appreciatively, "Quite an unusual girl." His eyes, I noticed, were a bright green, without the brown tones most green eyes have.

I was wild to ask him about Earth and the new developments there, and it had already occurred to me that the girls might be an effective way of keeping him here, or at least of bringing him back. I said, "You should see some of them. My father has wonderful taste."

"I'd rather see Dr. Veil. Or is Dr. Veil your father?"

"Oh, no."

"This is his address, or at least the address I was given. Number 666 Saltimbanque Street, Port-Mimizon, Departement de la Main, Sainte Croix."

He appeared quite serious, and it seemed possible that if I told him flatly that he was mistaken he would leave. I said, "I learned about Veil's Hypothesis from my aunt. She seemed quite conversant with it. Perhaps later this evening you'd like to talk to her about it."

"Couldn't I see her now?"

"My aunt sees very few visitors. To be frank, I'm told she quarreled with my father before I was born, and she seldom leaves her own apartments. The housekeepers report to her there, and she manages what I suppose I must call our domestic economy, but it's very rare to see Madame outside her rooms, or for any stranger to be let in."

"And why are you telling me this?"

"So that you'll understand that with the best will in the world it may not be possible for me to arrange an interview for you. At least, not this evening."

"You could simply ask her if she knows Dr. Veil's present address, and if so what it is."

"I'm trying to help you, Dr. Marsch. Really I am."

"But you don't think that's the best way to go about it?"

"No."

"In other words if your aunt were simply asked, without being given a chance to form her own judgment of me, she wouldn't give me information even if she had it?"

"It would help if we were to talk a bit first. There are a great many things I'd like to learn about Earth."

For an instant I thought I saw a sour smile under the black beard. He said, "Suppose I ask you first . . ."

He was interrupted—again—by Nerissa, I suppose because she wanted to see if we required anything further from the kitchen. I could have strangled her when Dr. Marsch halted in midsentence and said instead, "Couldn't this girl ask your aunt if she would see me?"

I had to think quickly. I had been planning to go myself and, after a suitable wait, return and say that my aunt would receive Dr. Marsch later, which would have given me an additional opportunity to question him while he waited. But there was at least a possibility (no doubt magnified in my eyes by my eagerness to hear of new discoveries from Earth) that he would not wait—or that, when and if he did eventually see my aunt, he might mention the incident. If I sent Nerissa I would at least have him to myself while she ran her errand, and there was an excellent chance—or at least so I imagined—that my aunt would in fact have some business which she would want to conclude before seeing a stranger. I told Nerissa to go, and Dr. Marsch gave her one of his cards after writing a few words on the back.

"Now," I said, "what was it you were about to ask me?"

"Why this house, on a planet that has been inhabited less than two hundred years, seems so absurdly old."

"It was built a hundred and forty years ago, but you must have many on Earth that are far older."

"I suppose so. Hundreds. But for every one of them there are ten thousand that have been up less than a year. Here, almost every building I see seems nearly as old as this one."

"We've never been crowded here, and we haven't had to tear down. That's what Mr. Million says. And there are fewer people here now than there were fifty years ago."

"Mr. Million?"

I told him about Mr. Million, and when I finished he said, "It sounds as if you've got a ten nine unbound simulator here, which should be interesting. Only a few have ever been made."

"A ten nine simulator?"

"A billion, ten to the ninth power. The human brain has several billion synapses, of course; but it's been found that you can simulate its action pretty well . . ."

It seemed to me that no time at all had passed since Nerissa had left, but she was back. She curtsied to Dr. Marsch and said, "Madame will see you."

I blurted, "Now?"

"Yes," Nerissa said artlessly, "Madame said right now."

"I'll take him then. You mind the door."

I escorted Dr. Marsch down the dark corridors, taking a long route to have more time, but he seemed to be arranging in his mind the questions he wished to ask my aunt, as we walked past the spotted mirrors and warped little walnut tables, and he answered me in monosyllables when I tried to question him about Earth.

At my aunt's door I rapped for him. She opened it herself, the hem of her black skirt hanging emptily over the untrodden carpet, but I do not think he noticed that. He said, "I'm really very sorry to bother you, Madame, and I only do so because your nephew thought you might be able to help me locate the author of Veil's Hypothesis."

My aunt said, "I am Dr. Veil, please come in," and shut the door behind him, leaving me standing open-mouthed in the corridor.

I mentioned the incident to Phaedria the next time we met, but she was more interested in learning about my father's house. Phaedria, if I have not used her name before now, was the girl who had sat near me while I watched David play squash. She had been introduced to me on my next visit to the park by no one less than the monster herself, who had helped her to a seat beside me and, miracle of miracles, promptly retreated to a point which, though not out of sight, was at least beyond earshot. Phaedria had thrust her broken ankle in front of her, halfway across the graveled path, and smiled a most charming smile. "You don't object to my sitting here?" She had perfect teeth.

"I'm delighted."

"You're surprised, too. Your eyes get big when you're surprised, did you know that?"

"I am surprised. I've come here looking for you several times, but you haven't been here."

"We've come looking for you, and you haven't been here either, but I suppose one can't really spend a great deal of time in a park."

"I would have," I said, "If I'd known you were looking for me. I went here as much as I could anyway. I was afraid that she . . ." I jerked my head at the monster, "wouldn't let you come back. How did you persuade her?"

"I didn't," Phaedria said. "Can't you guess? Don't you know anything?"

I confessed that I did not. I felt stupid, and I was stupid, at least in the things I said, because so much of my mind was caught up not in formulating answers to her remarks but in committing to memory the lilt of her voice, the purple of her eyes, even the faint perfume of her skin and the soft, warm touch of her breath on my cool cheek.

"So you see," Phaedria was saying, "that's how it is with me. When Aunt Uranie—she's only a poor cousin of mother's, really—got home and told him about you he found out who you are, and here I am."

"Yes," I said, and she laughed.

Phaedria was one of those girls raised between the hope of marriage and the thought of sale. Her father's affairs, as she herself said, were "unsettled." He speculated in ship cargoes, mostly from the south—textiles and drugs. He owed, most of the time, large sums which the lenders could not hope to collect unless they were willing to allow him more to recoup. He might die a pauper, but in the meanwhile he had raised his daughter with every detail of education and plastic surgery attended to. If, when she reached marriageable age he could afford a good dowry, she would link him with some wealthy family. If he were pressed for money instead, a girl so reared would bring fifty times the price of a common street child. Our family, of course, would be ideal for either purpose.

"Tell me about your house," she said. "Do you know what the kids call it? 'The Cave Canem,' or sometimes just 'The Cave.' The boys all think it's a big thing to have been there, and they lie about it. Most of them haven't."

But I wanted to talk about Dr. Marsch and the sciences of Earth, and I was nearly as anxious to find out about her own world, "the kids" she mentioned so casually, her school and family, as she was to learn about us. Also, although I was willing to detail the services my father's girls rendered their benefactors, there were some things, such as my aunt's floating down the stairwell, that I was adverse to discussing. But we bought egg rolls from the same old woman to eat in the chill sunlight and exchanged confidences and somehow parted not only lovers but friends, promising to meet again the next day.

At some time during the night, I believe at almost the same time that I returned—or to speak more accurately *was returned* since I could scarcely walk—to my bed after a session of hours with my father, the weather changed. The musked exhalation of late spring or early summer crept through the shutters, and the fire in our little grate seemed to extinguish itself for shame almost at once. My father's valet opened the window for me and there poured into the room that fragrance that tells of the melting of the last snows beneath the deepest and darkest evergreens on the north sides of mountains. I had arranged with Phaedria to meet at ten, and before going to my father's library I had posted a note on the escritoire beside my bed, asking that I be awakened an hour earlier; and that night I slept with the fragrance in my nostrils and the thought—half-plan, half-dream—in my mind that by some means Phaedria and I would elude her aunt entirely and find a deserted lawn where blue and yellow flowers dotted the short grass.

When I woke, it was an hour past noon, and rain drove in sheets past the window. Mr. Million, who was reading a book on the far side of the room, told me that it had been raining like that since six, and for that reason he had not troubled to wake me. I had a splitting headache, as I often did after a long session with my father, and took one of the powders he had prescribed to relieve it. They were gray, and smelled of anise.

"You look unwell," Mr. Million said.

"I was hoping to go to the park."

"I know." He rolled across the room toward me, and I recalled that Dr. Marsch had called him an "unbound" simulator. For the first time since I had satisfied myself about them when I was quite small, I bent over (at some cost to my head) and read the almost obliterated stampings on his main cabinet. There was only the name of a cybernetics company on Earth and, in French as I had always supposed, his name: M. Million—"Monsieur" or "Mister" Million. Then, as startling as a blow from behind to a man musing in a comfortable chair, I remembered that a dot was employed in some algebras for multiplication. He saw my change of expression at once. "A thousand million word core capacity," he said. "An English billion or a French milliard, the M being the Roman numeral for one thousand, of course. I thought you understood that some time ago."

"You are an unbound simulator. What is a bound simulator, and whom are you simulating—my father?"

"No." The face in the screen, Mr. Million's face as I had always thought of it, shook its head. "Call me, call the person simulated, at least, your great-grandfather. He—I—am dead. In order to achieve simulation, it is necessary to examine the cells of the brain, layer by layer, with a beam of accelerated particles so that the neural patterns can be reproduced, we say 'core imaged,' in the computer. The process is fatal."

I asked after a moment, "And a bound simulator?"

"If the simulation is to have a body that looks human the mechanical body must be linked—'bound'—to a remote core, since the smallest billion word core cannot be made even approximately as small as the human brain." He paused again, and for an instant his face dissolved into myriad sparkling dots, swirling like dust motes in a sunbeam. "I am sorry. For once you wish to listen but I do not wish to lecture. I was told, a very long time ago, just before the operation, that my simulation—this—would be capable of emotion in certain circumstances. Until today I had always thought they lied." I would have stopped him if I could, but he rolled out of the room before I could recover from my surprise.

For a long time, I suppose an hour or more, I sat listening to the drumming of the rain and thinking about Phaedria and about what Mr. Million had said, all of it confused with my father's questions of the night before, questions which had seemed to steal their answers from me so that I was empty, and dreams had come to flicker in the emptiness, dreams of fences and walls and the concealing ditches called ha-has, that contain a barrier you do not see until you are about to tumble on it. Once I had dreamed of standing in a paved court fenced with Corinthian pillars so close set that I could not force my body between them, although in the dream I was only a child of three or four. After trying various places for a long time, I had noticed that each column was carved with a word—the only one that I could remember was *carapace*—and that the paving stones of the courtyard were mortuary tablets like those set into the floors in some of the old French churches, with my own name and a different date on each.

This dream pursued me even when I tried to think of Phaedria, and when a maid brought me hot water—for I now shaved twice a week—I found that I was already holding my razor in my hand, and had in fact cut myself with it so that the blood had streaked my nightclothes and run down onto the sheets.

The next time I saw Phaedria, which was four or five days afterward, she was engrossed by a new project in which she enlisted both David and me. This was nothing less than a theatrical company, composed mostly of girls her own age, which was to present plays during the summer in a natural amphitheater in the park. Since the company, as I have said, consisted principally of girls, male actors were at a premium, and David and I soon found ourselves deeply embroiled. The play had been written by a committee of the cast, and—inevitably—revolved about the loss of political power by the original French-speaking colonists. Phaedria, whose ankle would not be mended in time for our performance, would play the crippled daughter of the French governor; David, her lover (a dashing captain of chasseurs); and I, the governor himself—a part I accepted readily because it was a much better one than David's, and offered scope for a great deal of fatherly affection toward Phaedria.

The night of our performance, which was early in June, I recall vividly for two reasons. My aunt, whom I had not seen since she had closed the door behind Dr. Marsch, notified me at the last moment that she wished to attend and that I was to escort her. And we players had grown so afraid of having an empty house that I had asked my father if it would be possible for him to send some of his girls—who would thus lose only the earliest part of the evening, when there was seldom much business in any event. To my great surprise (I suppose because he felt it would be good advertising) he consented, stipulating only that they should return at the end of the third act if he sent a messenger saying they were needed.

Because I would have to arrive at least an hour early to make up, it was no more than late afternoon when I called for my aunt. She showed me in herself, and immediately asked my help for her maid, who was trying to wrestle some heavy object from the upper shelf of a closet. It proved to be a folding wheelchair, and under my aunt's direction we set it up. When we had finished she said abruptly, "Give me a hand in, you two," and taking our arms lowered herself into the seat. Her black skirt, lying emptily against the leg boards of the chair like a collapsed tent, showed legs no thicker than my wrists; but also an odd thickening, almost like a saddle, below her hips. Seeing me staring she snapped, "Won't be needing that until I come back, I suppose. Lift me up a little. Stand in back and get me under the arms."

I did so, and her maid reached unceremoniously under my aunt's skirt and drew out a little leather padded device on which she had been resting. "Shall we go?" my aunt sniffed. "You'll be late."

I wheeled her into the corridor, her maid holding the door for us. Somehow, learning that my aunt's ability to hang in the air like smoke was physically, indeed mechanically, derived, made it more disturbing than ever. When she asked why I was so quiet, I told her and added that I had been under the impression that no one had yet succeeded in producing working antigravity.

"And you think I have? Then why wouldn't I use it to get to your play?"

"I suppose because you don't want it to be seen."

"Nonsense. It's a regular prosthetic device. You buy them at the surgical stores." She twisted around in her seat until she could look up at me, her face so like my father's, and her lifeless legs like the sticks David and I used as little boys when, doing parlor magic, we wished Mr. Million to believe us lying prone when we were in fact crouched beneath our own supposed figures. "Puts out a superconducting field, then induces eddy currents in the reinforcing rods in the floors. The flux of the induced currents oppose the machine's own flux and I float, more or less. Lean forward to go forward, straighten up to stop. You look relieved."

"I am. I suppose antigravity frightened me."

"I used the iron banister when I went down the stairs with you once. It has a very convenient coil shape."

Our play went smoothly enough, with predictable cheers from members of the audience who were, or at least wished to be thought, descended from the old French aristocracy. The audience, in fact, was better than we had dared hope, five hundred or so besides the inevitable sprinkling of pickpockets, police, and streetwalkers. The incident I most vividly recall came toward the latter half of the first act, when for ten minutes or so I sat with few lines at a desk, listening to my fellow actors. Our stage faced the west, and the setting sun had left the sky a welter of lurid color: purple-reds striped gold and flame and black. Against this violent ground, which might have been the massed banners of hell, there began to appear, in ones and twos, like the elongated shadows of fantastic grenadiers crenelated and plumed, the heads, the slender necks, the narrow shoulders, of a platoon of my father's demi-mondaines; arriving late, they were taking the last seats at the upper rim of our theater, encircling it like the soldiery of some ancient, bizarre government surrounding a treasonous mob.

They sat at last, my cue came, and I forgot them; and that is all I can now remember of our first performance, except that at one point some motion of mine suggested to the audience a mannerism of my father's, and there was a shout of misplaced laughter—and that at the beginning of the second act, Sainte Anne rose with its sluggish rivers and great grassy meadowmeres clearly visible, flooding the audience with green light; and at the close of the third I saw my father's crooked little valet bustling among the upper rows, and the girls, green-edged black shadows, filing out.

We produced three more plays that summer, all with some success, and David and Phaedria and I became an accepted partnership, with Phaedria dividing herself more or less equally between us—whether by her own inclination or her parents' orders I could never be quite sure. When her ankle knit she was a companion fit for David in athletics, a better player of all the ball and racket games than any of the other girls who came to the park; but she would as often drop everything and come to sit with me, where she sympathized with (though she did not actually share) my interest in botany and biology, and gossiped, and delighted in showing me off to her friends since my reading had given me a sort of talent for puns and repartee.

It was Phaedria who suggested, when it became apparent that the ticket money from our first play would be insufficient for the costumes and scenery we coveted for our second, that at the close of future performances the cast circulate among the audience to take up a collection; and this, of course, in the press and bustle easily lent itself to the accomplishment of petty thefts for our cause. Most people, however, had too much sense to bring to our theater, in the evening, in the gloomy park, more money than was required to buy tickets and perhaps an ice or a glass of wine during intermission; so no matter how dishonest we were the profit remained small, and we, and especially Phaedria and David, were soon talking of going forward to more dangerous and lucrative adventures.

At about this time, I suppose as a result of my father's continued and intensified probing of my subconscious, a violent and almost nightly examination whose purpose was still unclear to me and which, since I had been accustomed to it for so long, I scarcely questioned, I became more and more subject to frightening lapses of conscious control. I would, so David and Mr. Million told me, seem quite myself though perhaps rather more quiet than usual, answering questions intelligently if absently, and then, suddenly, come to myself, start, and stare at the familiar rooms, the familiar faces, among which I now found myself, perhaps after the mid-afternoon, without the slightest memory of having awakened, dressed, shaved, eaten, gone for a walk.

Although I loved Mr. Million as much as I had when I was a boy, I was never able, after that conversation in which I learned the meaning of the familiar lettering on his side, quite to re-establish the old relationship. I was always conscious, as I am conscious now, that the personality I loved had perished years before I was born; and that I addressed an imitation of it, fundamentally mathematical in nature, responding as that personality might to the stimuli of human speech and action. I could never determine whether Mr. Million is really aware in that sense which would give him the right to say, as he always has, "I think," and "I feel." When I asked him about it he could only explain that he did not know the answer himself, that having no standard of comparison he could not be positive whether his own mental processes represented true consciousness or not; and I, of course, could not know whether this answer represented the deepest meditation of a soul somehow alive in the dancing abstractions of the simulation, or whether it was merely triggered, a phonographic response, by my question.

Our theater, as I have said, continued through the summer and gave its last performance with the falling leaves drifting, like obscure, perfumed old letters from some discarded trunk, upon our stage. When the curtain calls were over we who had written and acted the plays of our season were too disheartened to do more than remove our costumes and cosmetics, and drift ourselves, with the last of our departing audience, down the whippoorwill-haunted paths to the city streets and home. I was prepared, as I remember, to take up my duties at my father's door, but that night he had stationed his valet in the foyer to wait for me, and I was ushered directly into the library, where he explained brusquely that he would have to devote the latter part of the evening to business and for that reason would speak to me (as he put it) early. He looked tired and ill, and it occurred to me, I think for the first time, that he would one day die—and that I would, on that day, become at once both rich and free.

What I said under the drugs that evening I do not, of course, recall, but I remember as vividly as I might if I had only this morning awakened from it, the dream that followed. I was on a ship, a white ship like one of those the oxen pull, so slowly the sharp prows make no wake at all, through the green water of the canal beside the park. I was the only crewman, and indeed the only living man aboard. At the stern, grasping the huge wheel in such a flaccid way that it seemed to support and guide and steady *him* rather than he it, stood the corpse of a tall, thin man whose face, when the rolling of his head presented it to me, was the face that floated in Mr. Million's screen. This face, as I have said, was very like my father's, but I knew the dead man at the wheel was not he.

I was aboard the ship a long time. We seemed to be running free, with the wind a few points to port and strong. When I went aloft at night, masts and spars and rigging quivered and sang in the wind, and sail upon sail towered above me, and sail upon white sail spread below me, and more masts clothed in sails stood before me and behind me. When I worked on deck by day, spray wet my shirt and left tear-shaped spots on the planks which dried quickly in the bright sunlight.

I cannot remember ever having really been on such a ship, but perhaps, as a very small child, I was, for the sounds of it, the creaking of the masts in their sockets, the whistling of the wind in the thousand ropes, the crashing of the waves against the wooden hull were all as distinct, and as real, as much *themselves*, as the sounds of laughter and breaking glass overhead had been when, as a child, I had tried to sleep; or the bugles from the citadel which sometimes, then, woke me in the morning.

I was about some work, I do not know just what, aboard this ship. I carried buckets of water with which I dashed clotted blood from the decks, and I pulled at ropes which seemed attached to nothing—or rather, firmly tied to immovable objects still higher in the rigging. I watched the surface of the sea from bow and rail, from the mastheads, and from atop a large cabin amidships, but when a starcrosser, its entry shields blinding-bright with heat, plunged hissing into the sea far off I reported it to no one.

And all this time the dead man at the wheel was talking to me. His head hung limply, as though his neck were broken, and the jerkings of the wheel he held, as big waves struck the rudder, sent it from one shoulder to the other, or back to stare at the sky, or down. But he continued to speak, and the few words I caught suggested that he was lecturing upon an ethical theory whose postulates seemed even to him doubtful. I felt a dread of hearing this talk and tried to keep myself as much as possible toward the bow, but the wind at times carried the words to me with great clarity, and whenever I looked up from my work I found myself much nearer the stern, sometimes in fact almost touching the dead steersman, than I had supposed.

After I had been on this ship a long while, so that I was very tired and very lonely, one of the doors of the cabin opened and my aunt came out, floating quite upright about two feet above the tilted deck. Her skirt did not hang vertically as I had always seen it, but whipped in the wind like a streamer, so that she seemed on the point of blowing away. For some reason I said, "Don't get close to that man at the wheel, Aunt. He might hurt you."

She answered, as naturally as if we had met in the corridor outside my bedroom, "Nonsense. He's far past doing anyone any good, Number Five, or any harm either. It's my brother we have to worry about."

"Where is he?"

"Down there." She pointed at the deck as if to indicate that he was in the hold. "He's trying to find out why the ship doesn't move."

I ran to the side and looked over, and what I saw was not water but the night sky. Stars—innumerable stars were spread at an infinite distance below me, and as I looked at them I realized that the ship, as my aunt had said, did not make headway or even roll, but remained heeled over, motionless. I looked back at her and she told me, "It doesn't move because he has fastened it in place until he finds out why it doesn't move," and at this point I found myself sliding down a rope into what I supposed was the hold of the ship. It smelled of animals. I had awakened, though at first I did not know it.

My feet touched the floor, and I saw that David and Phaedria were beside me. We were in a huge, loftlike room, and as I looked at Phaedria, who was very pretty but tense and biting her lips, a cock crowed.

David said, "Where do you think the money is?" He was carrying a tool kit.

And Phaedria, who I suppose had expected him to say something else, or in answer to her own thoughts, said, "We'll have lots of time, Marydol is watching." Marydol was one of the girls who appeared in our plays.

"If she doesn't run away. Where do you think the money is?"

"Not up here. Downstairs behind the office." She had been crouching, but she rose now and began to creep forward. She was all in black, from her ballet slippers to a black ribbon binding her black hair, with her white face and arms in striking contrast, and her carmine lips an error, a bit of color left by mistake. David and I followed her.

Crates were scattered, widely separated, on the floor; and as we passed them I saw that they held poultry, a single bird in each. It was not until we were nearly to the ladder which plunged down a hatch in the floor at the opposite corner of the room that I realized that these birds were gamecocks. Then a shaft of sun from one of the skylights struck a crate and the cock rose and stretched himself, showing fierce red eyes and plumage as gaudy as a macaw's. "Come on," Phaedria said, "the dogs are next," and we followed her down the ladder. Pandemonium broke out on the floor below.

The dogs were chained in stalls, with dividers too high for them to see the dogs on either side of them and wide aisles between the rows of stalls. They were all fighting dogs, but of every size from ten-pound terriers to mastiffs larger than small horses, brutes with heads as misshapen as the growths that appear on old trees and jaws that could sever both a man's legs at a mouthful. The din of the barking was incredible, a solid substance that shook us as we descended the ladder, and at the bottom I took Phaedria's arm and tried to indicate by signs—since I was certain that we were wherever we were without permission—that we should leave at once. She shook her head and then, when I was unable to understand what she said even when she exaggerated the movements of her lips, wrote on a dusty wall with her moistened forefinger, "They do this all the time—a noise in the street—anything."

Access to the floor below was by stairs, reached through a heavy but unbolted door which I think had been installed largely to exclude the din. I felt better when we had closed it behind us even though the noise was still very loud. I had fully come to myself by this time, and I should have explained to David and Phaedria that I did not know where I was or what we were doing there, but shame held me back. And in any event I could guess easily enough what our purpose was. David had asked about the location of money, and we had often talked—talk I had considered at the time to be more than half empty boasting—about a single robbery that would free us from the necessity of further petty crime.

Where we were I discovered later when we left; and how we had come to be there I pieced together from casual conversations. The building had been originally designed as a warehouse, and stood on the Rue des Egouts close to the bay. Its owner supplied those enthusiasts who staged combats of all kinds for sport, and was credited with maintaining the largest assemblage of these creatures in the Department. Phaedria's father had happened to hear that this man had recently put some of his most valuable stock on ship, had taken Phaedria when he called on him, and, since the place was known not to open its doors until after the last Angelus, we had come the next day a little after the second and entered through one of the skylights.

I find it difficult to describe what we saw when we descended from the floor of the dogs to the next, which was the second floor of the building. I had seen fighting slaves many times before when Mr. Million, David, and I had traversed the slave market to reach the library; but never more than one or two together, heavily manacled. Here they lay, sat, and lounged everywhere, and for a moment I wondered why they did not tear one another to pieces, and the three of us as well. Then I saw that each was held by a short chain stapled to the floor, and it was not difficult to tell from the scraped and splintered circles in the boards just how far the slave in the center could reach. Such furniture as they had, straw pallets and a few chairs and benches, was either too light to do harm if thrown or very stoutly made and spiked down. I had expected them to shout and threaten us as I had heard they threatened each other in the pits before closing, but they seemed to understand that as long as they were chained, they could do nothing. Every head turned toward us as we came down the steps, but we had no food for them, and after that first examination they were far less interested in us than the dogs had been.

"They aren't people, are they?" Phaedria said. She was walking erectly as a soldier on parade now, and looking at the slaves with interest; studying her, it occurred to me that she was taller and less plump than the "Phaedria" I pictured to myself when I thought of her. She was not just a pretty, but a beautiful girl. "They're a kind of animal, really," she said.

From my studies I was better informed, and I told her that they had been human as infants — in some cases even as children or older — and that they differed from normal people only as a result of surgery (some of it on their brains) and chemically induced alterations in their endocrine systems. And of course in appearance because of their scars.

"Your father does that sort of thing to little girls, doesn't he? For your house?"

David said, "Only once in a while. It takes a lot of time, and most people prefer normals, even when they prefer pretty odd normals."

"I'd like to see some of them. I mean the ones he's worked on."

I was still thinking of the fighting slaves around us and said, "Don't you know about these things? I thought you'd been here before. You knew about the dogs."

"Oh, I've seen them before, and the man told me about them. I suppose I was just thinking out loud. It would be awful if they were still people."

Their eyes followed us, and I wondered if they could understand her.

The ground floor was very different from the ones above. The walls were paneled, there were framed pictures of dogs and cocks and of the slaves and curious animals. The windows, opening toward Egouts Street and the bay, were high and narrow and admitted only slender beams of the bright sunlight to pick out of the gloom the arm alone of a rich red-leather chair, a square of maroon carpet no bigger than a book, a half-full decanter. I took three steps into this room and knew that we had been discovered. Striding toward us was a tall, high-shouldered young man—who halted, with a startled look, just when I did. He was my own reflection in a gilt-framed pier glass, and I felt the momentary dislocation that comes when a stranger, an unrecognized shape, turns or moves his head and is some familiar friend glimpsed, perhaps for the first time, from outside. The sharp-chinned, grim-looking boy I had seen when I did not know him to be myself had been myself as Phaedria and David, Mr. Million and my aunt, saw me.

"This is where he talks to customers," Phaedria said. "If he's trying to sell something he has his people bring them down one at a time so you don't see the others, but you can hear the dogs bark even from way down here, and he took Papa and me upstairs and showed us everything."

David asked, "Did he show you where he keeps the money?"

"In back. See that tapestry? It's really a curtain, because while Papa was talking to him, a man came who owed him for something and paid, and he went through there with it."

The door behind the tapestry opened on a small office, with still another door in the wall opposite. There was no sign of a safe or strongbox. David broke the lock on the desk with a pry bar from his tool kit, but there was only the usual clutter of papers, and I was about to open the second door when I heard a sound, a scraping or shuffling, from the room beyond.

For a minute or more none of us moved. I stood with my hand on the latch. Phaedria, behind me and to my left, had been looking under the carpet for a cache in the floor—she remained crouched, her skirt a black pool at her feet. From somewhere near the broken desk I could hear David's breathing. The shuffling came again, and a board creaked. David said very softly, "It's an animal."

I drew my fingers away from the latch and looked at him. He was still gripping the pry bar and his face was pale, but he smiled. "An animal tethered in there, shifting its feet. That's all."

I said, "How do you know?"

"Anybody in there would have heard us, especially when I cracked the desk. If it were a person he would have come out, or if he were afraid he'd hide and be quiet."

Phaedria said, "I think he's right. Open the door."

"Before I do, if it isn't an animal?"

David said, "It is."

"But if it isn't?"

I saw the answer on their faces; David gripped his pry bar, and I opened the door.

The room beyond was larger than I had expected, but bare and dirty. The only light came from a single window high in the farther wall. In the middle of the floor stood a big chest, of dark wood bound with iron, and before it lay what appeared to be a bundle of rags. As I stepped from the carpeted office the rags moved and a face, a face triangular as a mantis's, turned toward me. Its chin was hardly more than an inch from the floor, but under deep brows the eyes were tiny scarlet fires.

"That must be it," Phaedria said. She was looking not at the face but at the iron-banded chest. "David, can you break into that?"

"I think so," David said, but he, like me, was watching the ragged thing's eyes. "What about that?" he said after a moment, and gestured toward it. Before Phaedria or I could answer, its mouth opened showing long, narrow teeth, gray-yellow. "Sick," it said.

None of us, I think, had thought it could speak. It was as though a mummy had spoken. Outside, a carriage went past, its iron wheels rattling on the cobbles.

"Let's go," David said. "Let's get out."

Phaedria said, "It's sick. Don't you see, the owner's brought it down here where he can look in on it and take care of it. It's sick."

"And he chained his sick slave to the cashbox?" David cocked an eyebrow at her.

"Don't you see? It's the only heavy thing in the room. All you have to do is go over there and knock the poor creature in the head. If you're afraid, give me the bar and I'll do it myself."

"I'll do it."

I followed him to within a few feet of the chest. He gestured at the slave imperiously with the steel pry bar. "You! Move away from there."

The slave made a gurgling sound and crawled to one side, dragging his chain. He was wrapped in a filthy, tattered blanket and seemed hardly larger than a child, though I noticed that his hands were immense.

I turned and took a step toward Phaedria, intending to urge that we leave if David were unable to open the chest in a few minutes. I remember that before I heard or felt anything I saw her eyes open wide, and I was still wondering why when David's kit of tools clattered on the floor and David himself fell with a thud and a little gasp. Phaedria screamed, and all the dogs on the third floor began to bark.

All this, of course, took less than a second. I turned to look almost as David fell. The slave had darted out an arm and caught my brother by the ankle, and then in an instant had thrown off his blanket and bounded—that is the only way to describe it—on top of him.

I caught him by the neck and jerked him backward, thinking that he would cling to David and that it would be necessary to tear him away, but the instant he felt my hands he flung David aside and writhed like a spider in my grip. *He had four arms.*

I saw them flailing as he tried to reach me, and I let go of him and jerked back, as if a rat had been thrust at my face. That instinctive repulsion saved me; he drove his feet backward in a kick which, if I had still been holding him tightly enough to give him a fulcrum, would have surely ruptured my liver or spleen and killed me.

Instead it shot him forward and me, gasping for breath, back. I fell and rolled, and was outside the circle permitted him by his chain; David had already scrambled away, and Phaedria was well out of his reach.

For a moment, while I shuddered and tried to sit up, the three of us simply stared at him. Then David quoted wryly:

"Arms and the man I sing, who forc'd by fate,
And haughty Juno's unrelenting hate,
Expell'd and exil'd, left the Trojan shore."

Neither Phaedria nor I laughed, but Phaedria let out her breath in a long sigh and asked me, "How did they do that? Get him like that?"

I told her I supposed they had transplanted the extra pair after suppressing his body's natural resistance to the implanted foreign tissue, and that the operation had probably replaced some of his ribs with the donor's shoulder structure. "I've been teaching myself to do the same sort of thing with mice—on a much less ambitious scale, of course—and the striking thing to me is that he seems to have full use of the grafted pair. Unless you've got identical twins to work with, the nerve endings almost never join properly, and whoever did this probably had a hundred failures before he got what he wanted. That slave must be worth a fortune."

David said, "I thought you threw your mice out. Aren't you working with monkeys now?"

I wasn't, although I hoped to; but whether I was or not, it seemed clear that talking about it wasn't going to accomplish anything. I told David that.

"I thought you were hot to leave."

I had been, but now I wanted something else much more. I wanted to perform an exploratory operation on that creature much more than David and Phaedria had ever wanted money. David liked to think that he was bolder than I, and I knew when I said, "You may want to get away, but don't use me as an excuse, brother," that that would settle it.

"All right, how are we going to kill him?" He gave me an angry look.

Phaedria said, "It can't reach us. We could throw things at it."

"And he could throw the ones that missed back."

While we talked, the thing, the four-armed slave, was grinning at us. I was fairly sure it could understand at least a part of what we were saying, and I motioned to David and Phaedria to indicate that we should go back into the room where the desk was. When we were there I closed the door. "I didn't want him to hear us. If we had weapons on poles, spears of some kind, we might be able to kill him without getting too close. What could we use for sticks? Any ideas?"

David shook his head, but Phaedria said, "Wait a minute, I remember something." We both looked at her and she knitted her brows, pretending to search her memory and enjoying the attention.

"Well?" David asked.

She snapped her fingers. "Window poles. You know, long things with a little hook on the end. Remember the windows out there where he talks to customers? They're high up in the wall, and while he and Papa were talking one of the men who works for him brought one and opened a window. They ought to be around somewhere."

We found two after a five-minute search. They looked satisfactory: about six feet long and an inch and a quarter in diameter, of hard wood. David flourished his and pretended to thrust at Phaedria, then asked me, "Now what do we use for points?"

The scalpel I always carried was in its case in my breast pocket, and I fastened it to the rod with electrical tape from a roll David had fortunately carried on his belt instead of in the tool kit, but we could find nothing to make a second spearhead for him until he himself suggested broken glass.

"You can't break a window," Phaedria said, "they'd hear you outside. Besides, won't it just snap off when you try to get him with it?"

"Not if it's thick glass. Look here, you two."

I did, and saw—again—my own face. He was pointing toward the large mirror that had surprised me when I came down the steps. While I looked his shoe struck it, and it shattered with a crash that set the dogs barking again. He selected a long, almost straight, triangular piece and held it up to the light, where it flashed like a gem. "That's about as good as they used to make them from agate and jasper on Sainte Anne, isn't it?"

By prior agreement we approached from opposite sides. The slave leaped to the top of the chest, and from there, watched us quite calmly, his deep-set eyes turning from David to me until at last, when we were both quite close, David rushed him.

He spun around as the glass point grazed his ribs and caught David's spear by the shaft and jerked him forward. I thrust at him but missed, and before I could recover he had dived from the chest and was grappling with David on the far side. I bent over it and jabbed down at him, and it was not until David screamed that I realized I had driven my scalpel into his thigh. I saw the blood, bright arterial blood, spurt up and drench the shaft, and let it go and threw myself over the chest on top of them.

He was ready for me, on his back and grinning, with his legs and all four arms raised like a dead spider's. I am certain he would have strangled me in the next few seconds if it had not been that David, how consciously I do not know, threw one arm across the creature's eyes so that he missed his grip and I fell between those outstretched hands.

There is not a great deal more to tell. He jerked free of David, and pulling me to him, tried to bite my throat; but I hooked a thumb in one of his eye sockets and held him off. Phaedria, with more courage than I would have credited her with, put David's glass-tipped spear into my free hand and I stabbed him in the neck—I believe I severed both jugulars and the trachea before he died. We put a tourniquet on David's leg and left without either the money or the knowledge of technique I had hoped to get from the body of the slave. Marydol helped us get David home, and we told Mr. Million he had fallen while we were exploring an empty building—though I doubt that he believed us.

There is one other thing to tell about that incident—I mean the killing of the slave—although I am tempted to go on and describe instead a discovery I made immediately afterward that had, at the time, a much greater influence on me. It is only an impression, and one that I have, I am sure, distorted and magnified in recollection. While I was stabbing the slave, my face was very near his and I saw (I suppose because of the light from the high windows behind us) my own face reflected and doubled in the corneas of his eyes, and it seemed to me that it was a face very like his. I have been unable to forget, since then, what Dr. Marsch told me about the production of any number of identical individuals by cloning, and that my father had, when I was younger, a reputation as a child broker. I have tried since my release to find some trace of my mother; the woman in the photograph shown me by my aunt; but that picture was surely taken long before I was born—perhaps even on Earth.

The discovery I spoke of I made almost as soon as we left the building where I killed the slave, and it was simply this: that it was no longer autumn, but high summer. Because all four of us—Marydol had joined us by that time—were so concerned about David and busy concocting a story to explain his injury, the shock was somewhat blunted, but there could be no doubt of it. The weather was warm with that torpid, damp heat peculiar to summer. The trees I remembered nearly bare were in full leaf and filled with orioles. The fountain in our garden no longer played, as it always did after the danger of frost and burst pipes had come, with warmed water: I dabbled my hand in the basin as we helped David up the path, and it was as cool as dew.

My periods of unconscious action then, my sleepwalking, had increased to devour an entire winter and the spring, and I felt that I had lost myself.

When we entered the house, an ape which I thought at first was my father's sprang to my shoulder. Later Mr. Million told me that it was my own, one of my laboratory animals I had made a pet. I did not know the little beast, but scars under his fur and the twist of his limbs showed he knew me.

(I have kept Popo ever since, and Mr. Million took care of him for me while I was imprisoned. He climbs still in fine weather on the gray and crumbling walls of this house; and as he runs along the parapets and I see his hunched form against the sky, I think, for a moment, that my father is still alive and that I may be summoned again for the long hours in his library — but I forgive my pet that.)

My father did not call a physician for David, but treated him himself; and if he was curious about the manner in which he had received his injury he did not show it. My own guess — for whatever it may be worth, this late — is that he believed I had stabbed him in some quarrel. I say this because he seemed, after this, apprehensive whenever I was alone with him. He was not a fearful man, and he had been accustomed for years to deal occasionally with the worst sort of criminals; but he was no longer at ease with me — he guarded himself. It may have been, of course, merely the result of something I had said or done during the forgotten winter.

Both Marydol and Phaedria, as well as my aunt and Mr. Million, came frequently to visit David, so that his sickroom became a sort of meeting place for us all, only disturbed by my father's occasional visits. Marydol was a slight, fair-haired, kindhearted girl, and I became very fond of her. Often when she was ready to go home I escorted her, and on the way back stopped at the slave market, as Mr. Million and David and I had once done so often, to buy fried bread and the sweet black coffee and to watch the bidding. The faces of slaves are the dullest in the world; but I would find myself staring into them, and it was a long time, a month at least, before I understood — quite suddenly, when I found what I had been looking for — why I did. A young male, a sweeper, was brought to the block. His face as well as his back had been scarred by the whip, and his teeth were broken; but I recognized him: the scarred face was my own or my father's. I spoke to him and would have bought and freed him, but he answered me in the servile way of slaves and I turned away in disgust and went home.

That night when my father had me brought to the library—as he had not for several nights—I watched our reflections in the mirror that concealed the entrance to his laboratories. He looked younger than he was; I older. We might almost have been the same man, and when he faced me and I, staring over his shoulder, saw no image of my own body, but only his arms and mine, we might have been the fighting slave.

I cannot say who first suggested we kill him. I only remember that one evening, as I prepared for bed after taking Marydol and Phaedria to their homes, I realized that earlier when the three of us, with Mr. Million and my aunt, had sat around David's bed, we had been talking of that.

Not openly, of course. Perhaps we had not admitted even to ourselves what it was we were thinking. My aunt had mentioned the money he was supposed to have hidden; and Phaedria, then, a yacht luxurious as a palace; David talked about hunting in the grand style, and the political power money could buy.

And I, saying nothing, had thought of the hours and weeks, and the months he had taken from me; of the destruction of my *self*, which he had gnawed at night after night. I thought of how I might enter the library that night and find myself when next I woke an old man and perhaps a beggar.

Then I knew that I must kill him, since if I told him those thoughts while I lay drugged on the peeling leather of the old table he would kill *me* without a qualm.

While I waited for his valet to come I made my plan. There would be no investigation, no death certificate for my father. I would replace him. To our patrons it would appear that nothing had changed. Phaedria's friends would be told that I had quarreled with him and left home. I would allow no one to see me for a time, and then, in make-up, in a dim room, speak occasionally to some favored caller. It was an impossible plan, but at the time I believed it possible and even easy. My scalpel was in my pocket and ready. The body could be destroyed in his own laboratory.

He read it in my face. He spoke to me as he always had, but I think he knew. There were flowers in the room, something that had never been before, and I wondered if he had not known even earlier and had them brought in, as for a special event. Instead of telling me to lie on the leather-covered table, he gestured toward a chair and seated himself at his writing desk. "We will have company today," he said.

I looked at him.

"You're angry with me. I've seen it growing in you. Don't you know who . . ."

He was about to say something further when there was a tap at the door, and when he called, "Come in!" it was opened by Nerissa, who ushered in a demi-mondaine and Dr. Marsch. I was surprised to see him; and still more surprised to see one of the girls in my father's library. She seated herself beside Marsch in a way that showed he was her benefactor for the night.

"Good evening, Doctor," my father said. "Have you been enjoying yourself?"

Marsch smiled, showing large, square teeth. He wore clothing of the most fashionable cut now, but the contrast between his beard and the colorless skin of his cheeks was as remarkable as ever. "Both sensually and intellectually," he said. "I've seen a naked girl, a giantess twice the height of a man, walk through a wall."

I said, "That's done with holograms."

He smiled again. "I know. And I have seen a great many other things as well. I was going to recite them all, but perhaps I would only bore my audience. I will content myself with saying that you have a remarkable establishment—but you know that."

My father said, "It is always flattering to hear it again."

"And now are we going to have the discussion we spoke of earlier?"

My father looked at the demi-mondaine; she rose, kissed Dr. Marsch, and left the room. The heavy library door swung shut behind her with a soft click.

Like the sound of a switch, or old glass breaking.

I have thought since, many times, of that girl as I saw her leaving: the high-heeled platform shoes and grotesquely long legs, the backless dress dipping an inch below the coccyx. The bare nape of her neck; her hair piled and teased and threaded with ribbons and tiny lights. As she closed the door she was ending, though she could not have known it, the world she and I had known.

"She'll be waiting when you come out," my father said to Marsch.

"And if she's not, I'm sure you can supply others." The anthropologist's green eyes seemed to glow in the lamplight. "But now, how can I help you?"

"You study race. Could you call a group of similar men thinking similar thoughts a race?"

"And women," Marsch said, smiling.

"And here," my father continued, "here on Sainte Croix, you are gathering material to take back with you to Earth?"

"I am gathering material, certainly. Whether or not I shall return to the mother planet is problematical."

I must have looked at him sharply; he turned his smile toward me, and it became, if possible, even more patronizing than before. "You're surprised?"

"I've always considered Earth the center of scientific thought," I said. "I can easily imagine a scientist leaving it to do field work, but . . ."

"But it is inconceivable that one might want to stay in the field?"

"Consider my position. You are not alone — happily for me — in respecting the mother world's gray hairs and wisdom. As an Earth-trained man I've been offered a department in your university at almost any salary I care to name, with a sabbatical every second year. And the trip from here to Earth requires twenty years of Newtonian time. Only six months subjectively for me, of course, but when I return, if I do, my education will be forty years out of date. No, I'm afraid your planet may have acquired an intellectual luminary."

My father said, "We're straying from the subject, I think."

Marsch nodded, then added, "But I was about to say that an anthropologist is peculiarly equipped to make himself at home in any culture — even in so strange a one as this family has constructed about itself. I think I may call it a family, since there are two members resident besides yourself. You don't object to my addressing the pair of you in the singular?"

He looked at me as if expecting a protest, then when I said nothing, "I mean your son David — that, and not brother, is his real relationship to your continuing personality — and the woman you call your aunt. She is in reality daughter to an earlier — shall we say 'version'? — of yourself."

"You're trying to tell me I'm a cloned duplicate of my father, and I see both of you expect me to be shocked. I'm not. I've suspected it for some time."

My father said, "I'm glad to hear that. Frankly, when I was your age the discovery disturbed me a great deal. I came into my father's library — this room — to confront him, and I intended to kill him."

Dr. Marsch asked, "And did you?"

"I don't think it matters — the point is that it was my intention. I hope that having you here will make things easier for Number Five."

"Is that what you call him?"

"It's more convenient since his name is the same as my own."

"He is your fifth clone-produced child?"

"My fifth experiment? No." My father's hunched, high shoulders wrapped in the dingy scarlet of his old dressing gown made him look like some savage bird; and I remembered having read in a book of natural history of one called the red-shouldered hawk. His pet monkey, grizzled now with age, had climbed onto the desk. "No, more like my fiftieth, if you must know. I used to do them for drill. You people who have never tried it think the technique is simple because you've heard it can be done, but you don't know how difficult it is to prevent spontaneous differences. Every gene dominant in myself had to remain dominant, and people are not garden peas—few things are governed by simple Mendelian pairs."

Marsch asked, "You destroyed your failures?"

I said, "He sold them. When I was a child I used to wonder why Mr. Million stopped to look at the slaves in the market. Since then I've found out." My scalpel was still in its case in my pocket; I could feel it.

"Mr. Million," my father said, "is perhaps a bit more sentimental than I—besides, I don't like to go out. You see, Doctor, your supposition that we are all truly the same individual will have to be modified. We have our little variations."

Dr. Marsch was about to reply, but I interrupted him. "Why?" I said. "Why David and me? Why Aunt Jeannine a long time ago? Why go on with it?"

"Yes," my father said, "why? We ask the question to ask the question."

"I don't understand you."

"I seek self-knowledge. If you want to put it this way, *we* seek self-knowledge. You are here because I did and do, and I am here because the individual behind me did—who was himself originated by the one whose mind is simulated in Mr. Million. And one of the questions whose answers we seek is why we seek. But there is more than that." He leaned forward, and the little ape lifted its white muzzle and bright, bewildered eyes to stare into his face. "We wish to discover why we fail, why others rise and change, and we remain here."

I thought of the yacht I had talked about with Phaedria and said, "I won't stay here." Dr. Marsch smiled.

My father said, "I don't think you understand me. I don't necessarily mean here physically, but *here*, socially and intellectually. I have traveled, and you may, but . . ."

"But you end here," Dr. Marsch said.

"We end at this level!" It was the only time, I think, that I ever saw my father excited. He was almost speechless as he waved at the notebooks and tapes that thronged the walls. "After how many generations? We do not achieve fame or the rule of even this miserable little colony planet. Something must be changed, but what?" He glared at Dr. Marsch.

"You are not unique," Dr. Marsch said, then smiled. "That sounds like a truism, doesn't it? But I wasn't referring to your duplicating yourself. I meant that since it became possible, back on Earth during the last quarter of the twentieth century, it has been done in such chains a number of times. We have borrowed a term from engineering to describe it, and call it the process of relaxation—a bad nomenclature, but the best we have. Do you know what relaxation in the engineering sense is?"

"No."

"There are problems which are not directly soluble, but which can be solved by a succession of approximations. In heat transfer, for example, it may not be possible to calculate initially the temperature at every point on the surface of an unusually shaped body. But the engineer, or his computer, can assume reasonable temperatures, see how nearly stable the assumed values would be, then make new assumptions based on the result. As the levels of approximation progress, the successive sets become more and more similar until there is essentially no change. That is why I said the two of you are essentially one individual."

"What I want you to do," my father said impatiently, "is to make Number Five understand that the experiments I have performed on him, particularly the narcotherapeutic examinations he resents so much, are necessary. That if we are to become more than we have been we must find out . . ." He had been almost shouting, and he stopped abruptly to bring his voice under control. "That is the reason he was produced, the reason for David too—I hoped to learn something from an outcrossing."

"Which was the rationale, no doubt," Dr. Marsch said, "for the existence of Dr. Veil as well, in an earlier generation. But as far as your examinations of your younger self are concerned, it would be just as useful for him to examine you."

"Wait a moment," I said. "You keep saying that he and I are identical. That's incorrect. I can see that we're similar in some respects, but I'm not really like my father."

"There are no differences that cannot be accounted for by age. You are what? Eighteen? And you"—he looked toward my father—"I should say are nearly fifty. There are only two forces, you see, which act to differentiate between human beings: they are heredity and environment, nature and nurture. And since the personality is largely formed during the first three years of life, it is the environment provided by the home which is decisive. Now every person is born into *some* home environment, though it may be such a harsh one that he dies of it. And no person, except in this situation we call anthropological relaxation, provides that environment himself—it is furnished for him by the preceding generation."

"Just because both of us grew up in this house . . ."

"Which you built and furnished and filled with the people you chose. But wait a moment. Let's talk about a man neither of you have ever seen, a man born in a place provided by parents quite different from himself: I mean the first of you . . ."

I was no longer listening. I had come to kill my father, and it was necessary that Dr. Marsch leave. I watched him as he leaned forward in his chair, his long, white hands making incisive little gestures, his cruel lips moving in a frame of black hair; I watched him and I heard nothing. It was as though I had gone deaf or as if he could communicate only by his thoughts, and I, knowing the thoughts were silly lies had shut them out. I said, "You are from Sainte Anne."

He looked at me in surprise, halting in the midst of a senseless sentence. "I have been there, yes. I spent several years on Sainte Anne before coming here."

"You were born there. You studied anthropology there from books written on Earth twenty years ago. You are an abo, or at least half abo. But we are men."

Marsch glanced at my father, then said, "The abos are gone. Scientific opinion on Sainte Anne holds that they have been extinct for almost a century."

"You didn't believe that when you came to see my aunt."

"I've never accepted Veil's Hypothesis. I called on everyone here who had published anything in my field. Really, I don't have time to listen to this."

"You are an abo and not from Earth."

And in a short time my father and I were alone.

Most of my sentence I served in a labor camp in the Tattered Mountains. It was a small camp, housing usually only a hundred and fifty prisoners—sometimes less than eighty when the winter deaths had been bad. We cut wood and burned charcoal and made skis when we found good birch. Above the timberline we gathered a saline moss supposed to be medicinal and knotted long plans for rock slides that would crush the stalking machines that were our guards—though somehow the moment never came, the stones never slid. The work was hard, and these guards administered exactly the mixture of severity and fairness some prison board had decided upon when they were programmed, and the problem of brutality and favoritism by hirelings was settled forever, so that only well-dressed men at meetings could be cruel or kind.

Or so they thought. I sometimes talked to my guards for hours about Mr. Million, and once I found a piece of meat, and once a cake of hard sugar, brown and gritty as sand, hidden in the corner where I slept.

A criminal may not profit by his crime, but the court—so I was told much later—could find no proof that David was indeed my father's son, and made my aunt his heir.

She died, and a letter from an attorney informed me that by her favor I had inherited "a large house in the city of Port-Mimizon, together with the furniture and chattels appertaining thereto." And that this house, "located at 666 Saltimbanque, is presently under the care of a robot servitor." Since the robot servitors under whose direction I found myself did not allow me writing materials, I could not reply.

Time passed on the wings of birds. I found dead larks at the feet of north-facing cliffs in autumn, at the feet of south-facing cliffs in spring.

I received a letter from Mr. Million. Most of my father's girls had left during the investigation of his death; the remainder he had been obliged to send away when my aunt died, finding that as a machine he could not enforce the necessary obedience. David had gone to the capital. Phaedria had married well. Marydol had been sold by her parents. The date on his letter was three years later than the date of my trial, but how long the letter had been in reaching me I could not tell. The envelope had been opened and resealed many times and was soiled and torn.

A seabird, I believe a gannet, came fluttering down into our camp after a storm, too exhausted to fly. We killed and ate it.

One of our guards went berserk, burned fifteen prisoners to death, and fought the other guards all night with swords of white and blue fire. He was not replaced.

I was transferred with some others to a camp farther north where I looked down chasms of red stone so deep that if I kicked a pebble in, I could hear the rattle of its descent grow to a roar of slipping rock—and hear that, in half a minute, fade with distance to silence, yet never strike the bottom lost somewhere in darkness.

I pretended the people I had known were with me. When I sat shielding my basin of soup from the wind, Phaedria sat upon a bench nearby and smiled and talked about her friends. David played squash for hours on the dusty ground of our compound, slept against the wall near my own corner. Marydol put her hand in mine while I carried my saw into the mountains.

In time they all grew dim, but even in the last year I never slept without telling myself, just before sleep, that Mr. Million would take us to the city library in the morning; never woke without fearing that my father's valet had come for me.

Then I was told that I was to go, with three others, to another camp. We carried our food, and nearly died of hunger and exposure on the way. From there we were marched to a third camp where we were questioned by men who were not prisoners like ourselves but free men in uniforms who made notes of our answers and at last ordered that we bathe, and burned our old clothing, and gave us a thick stew of meat and barley.

I remember very well that it was then that I allowed myself to realize, at last, what these things meant. I dipped my bread into my bowl and pulled it out soaked with the fragrant stock, with bits of meat and grains of barley clinging to it; and I thought then of the fried bread and coffee at the slave market not as something of the past but as something in the future, and my hands shook until I could no longer hold my bowl and I wanted to rush shouting at the fences.

In two more days we, six of us now, were put into a mule cart that drove on winding roads always downhill until the winter that had been dying behind us was gone, and the birches and firs were gone, and the tall chestnuts and oaks beside the road had spring flowers under their branches.

The streets of Port-Mimizon swarmed with people. I would have been lost in a moment if Mr. Million had not hired a chair for me, but I made the bearers stop, and bought (with money he gave me) a newspaper from a vendor so that I could know the date with certainty at last.

My sentence had been the usual one of two to fifty years, and though I had known the month and year of the beginning of my imprisonment, it had been impossible to know, in the camps, the number of the current year which everyone counted and no one knew. A man took fever and in ten days, when he was well enough again to work, said that two years had passed or had never been. Then you yourself took fever. I do not recall any headline, any article from the paper I bought. I read only the date at the top, all the way home.

It had been nine years.

I had been eighteen when I had killed my father. I was now twenty-seven. I had thought I might be forty.

The flaking gray walls of our house were the same. The iron dog with his three wolf-heads still stood in the front garden, but the fountain was silent, and the beds of fern and moss were full of weeds. Mr. Million paid my chairmen and unlocked with a key the door that was always guard-chained but unbolted in my father's day—but as he did so, an immensely tall and lanky woman who had been hawking pralines in the street came running toward us. It was Nerissa, and I now had a servant and might have had a bedfellow if I wished, though I could pay her nothing.

.　　.　　.

And now I must, I suppose, explain why I have been writing this account, which has already been the labor of days; and I must even explain why I explain. Very well then. I have written to disclose myself to myself, and I am writing now because I will, I know, sometime read what I am now writing and wonder.

Perhaps by the time I do, I will have solved the mystery of myself; or perhaps I will no longer care to know the solution.

It has been three years since my release. This house, when Nerissa and I re-entered it, was in a very confused state, my aunt having spent her last days, so Mr. Million told me, in a search for my father's supposed hoard. She did not find it, and I do not think it is to be found; knowing his character better than she, I believe he spent most of what his girls brought him on his experiments and apparatus. I needed money badly myself at first, but the reputation of the house brought women seeking buyers and men seeking to buy. It is hardly necessary, as I told myself when we began, to do more than introduce them, and I have a good staff now. Phaedria lives with us and works too; the brilliant marriage was a failure after all. Last night while I was working in my surgery I heard her at the library door. I opened it and she had the child with her. Someday they'll want us.

JOHN UPDIKE

The Chaste Planet

One of the most prominent contemporary American writers, John Updike has written only one science fiction story, "The Chaste Planet." In recent decades, with the growing respectability of SF, many major literary figures have occasionally attempted the form, often with interesting results. Saul Bellow, Marge Piercy, William Hjorstberg, Don DeLillo, and Margaret Atwood have written novel-length SF, and Doris Lessing has produced the massive five-volume series Canopus in Argos: Archives. These literary figures will certainly have significant impact on the future of science fiction, as science fiction has had an impact on them. What has been established is that it is not necessary to be a science fiction writer to write SF or use its tropes. Nor do writers necessarily have to deny that they have done so, as Vonnegut once did, to preserve their literary reputations.

*   *   *

In 1999, space explorers discovered that within the warm, turbulent, semi-liquid immensity of Jupiter a perfectly pleasant little planet twirled, with argon skies and sparkling seas of molten beryllium. The earthlings who first arrived on the shores of this new world were shocked by the unabashed nakedness of the inhabitants. Not only were the inhabitants naked—their bodies cylindrical, slightly curved, and longitudinally ridged, like white pickles, with six toothpick-thin limbs stuck in for purposes of locomotion, and a kind of tasseled seventh concentrating the neural functions—but there appeared to be no sexual differentiation among them. Indeed, there was none. Reproduction took place by an absentee process known as "budding," and the inhabitants of Minerva (so the planet was dubbed, by a classics-minded official of the Sino-American Space Agency) thought nothing of it. Evidently, wherever a mathematical sufficiency of overlapping footsteps (or jabs, for their locomotion left marks rather like those of ski poles in crusty snow) impressed the porous soil of intermingled nickel and asbestos, a new pickleoid form slowly sprouted, or "budded." Devoid both of parentage and of progenitive desires, this new creature, when the three Minervan years (five of our weeks) of its maturation period brought it to full size (approximately eighteen of our inches), eagerly shook the nickel from its roots and assumed its place in the fruitful routines of agriculture, industry, trade, and government that on Minerva, as on Earth, superficially dominated life.

The erotic interests of the explorers and, as argon-breathing apparatus became perfected, of the ambassadors and investigators and mercantile colonists from our own planet occasioned amazement and misunderstanding among the Minervans. The early attempts at rape were scarcely more of a success than the later attempts, by some of the new world's economically marginal natives, to prostitute themselves. The lack of satisfactory contact, however, did not prevent the expatriate earthlings from falling in love with the Minervans, producing the usual debris of sonnets, sleepless nights, exhaustive letters, jealous fits, and supercharged dreams. The little pickle-shaped people, though no Pocahontas or Fayaway emerged among them to assuage the aliens' wonderful heat, were fascinated: How could the brief, mechanical event described (not so unlike, the scientists among them observed, the accidental preparation of their own ground for "budding") generate such giant expenditures of neural energy? "We live for love," they were assured. "Our spaceships, our skyscrapers, our stock markets are but deflections of this basic drive. Our clothes, our meals, our arts, our modes of transportation, even our wars, are made to serve the cause of love. An earthling infant takes in love with his first suck, and his dying gasp is clouded by this passion. All else is sham, disguise, and make-work."

The human colonies came to include females. This subspecies was softer and more bulbous, its aggressions more intricate and its aura more complacent; the Minervans never overcame their distaste for women, who seemed boneless and odorous and parasitic after the splendid first impression made by the early space explorers carapaced in flashing sheets of aluminum foil. These females even more strongly paid homage to the power of love: "For one true moment of it, a life is well lost. Give us love, or give us death. Our dying is but a fleck within the continuous, overarching supremacy of *eros*. Love moves the stars, which you cannot see. It moves the birds, which you do not have, to song." The Minervans were dumbfounded; they could imagine no force, no presence beneath their swirling, argon-bright skies, more absolute than death—for which the word in their language was the same as for "silence."

Then the human females, disagreeably and characteristically, would turn the tables of curiosity. "And you?" they would ask their little naked auditors. "What is it that makes *you* tick? Tell us. There must be something hidden, or else Freud was a local oracle. Tell us, what do you dream of, when your six eyes shut?" And a blue-green blush would steal over the warty, ridged, colorless epiderms of the Minervans, and they would titter and rustle like a patch of artichokes, and on their slender stiff limbs scamper away, and not emerge from their elaborate burrows until the concealment of night—night, to earthling senses, as rapid and recurrent as the blinking of an eyelid.

The first clue arose from the sonnets the lovelorn spacemen used to recite. Though the words, however translated, came out as nonsense, the recitation itself held the Minervans' interest, and seemed to excite them with its rhythms. Students of the pioneer journals also noted that, by more than one account, before prostitution was abandoned as unfeasible the would-be courtesans offered from out of the depths of themselves a shy, strangulated crooning, a sort of pitch-speech analogous to Chinese. Then robot tele-viewers were sufficiently miniaturized to maneuver through the Minervans' elaborate burrows. Among the dim, shaky images beamed back from underground (the static from the nickel was terrific) were some of rods arranged roughly in sequence of size, and of other rods, possibly hollow, flared at one end or laterally punctured. The televiewer had stumbled, it turned out, upon an unguarded brothel; the objects were, of course, crude Minervan equivalents of xylophones, trumpets, and flutes. The ultimate reaches of many private burrows contained similar objects, discreetly tucked where the newly budded would not find them, as well as proto-harps, quasi-violins, and certain constructions percussive in purpose. When the crawling televiewers were fitted with audio components, the domestic tunnels, and even some chambers of the commercial complexes, were revealed as teeming with a constant, furtive music—a concept for which the only Minervan word seemed to be the same as their word for "life."

Concurrent with these discoveries, a team of SASA alienists had per-suaded a number of Minervans to submit to psychoanalysis. The pattern of dreamwork, with its loaded symbolization of ladders, valves, sine curves, and hollow, polished forms, as well as the subjects' tendency under drugs to deform their speech with melodious slippage, and the critical case of one Minervan (nicknamed by the psychiatric staff Dora) who suffered from the obsessive malady known as "humming," pointed to the same conclusion as the televiewers' visual evidence: the Minervans on their sexless, muffled planet lived for music, of which they had only the most primitive inkling.

In the exploitative rush that followed this insight, tons of nickel were traded for a song. Spies were enlisted in the Earth's service for the bribe of a plastic harmonica; entire cabinets and corporation boards were corrupted by the promise of a glimpse of a clarinet-fingering diagram, or by the playing of an old 78-r.p.m. "Muskrat Ramble." At the first public broadcast of a symphony, Brahms' Fourth in E Minor, the audience of Minervans went into convulsions of ecstasy as the strings yielded the theme to the oboe, and would doubtless have perished *en masse* had not the sound engineer mercifully lifted the needle and switched to the Fred Waring arrangement of "American Patrol." Even so, many Minervans, in that epoch of violated innocence, died of musical overdose, and many more wrote confessional articles, formed liberational political parties, and engaged, with sometimes disappointing results, in group listening.

What music meant to the Minervans, it was beyond the ken of earthlings to understand. That repetitive mix of thuds, squeaks, and tintinnabulation, an art so mechanical that Mozart could scribble off some of the best between billiard shots, seemed perhaps to them a vibration implying all vibrations, a resolution of the most inward, existential antagonisms, a synthesizing interface—it has been suggested—between the nonconductivity of their asbestos earth and the high conductivity of their argon sky. There remained about the Minervans' musicality, even after it had been thoroughly exploited and rapaciously enlarged, something fastidious, balanced, and wary. A confused ancient myth gave music the resonance of the forbidden. In their Heaven, a place described as mercifully dark, music occurred without instruments, as it were inaudibly. An elderly Minervan, wishing to memorialize his life, would remember it almost exclusively in terms of music he had heard, or had made.

When the first Minervans were rocketed to Earth (an odyssey deserving its own epic: the outward flight through the thousands of miles of soupy hydrogen that comprised Jupiter's thick skull; the breakthrough into space and first sight of the stars, the black universe; the backward glance at the gaseous stripes and raging red spot dwindling behind them; the parabolic fall through the solar system, wherein the Minervans, dazzled by its brightness, mistook Venus for their destination, their invaders' home, instead of the watery brown sphere that expanded beneath them), the visitors were shocked by the ubiquitous public presence of music. Leaking from restaurant walls, beamed into airplanes as they landed and automobiles as they crashed, chiming from steeples, thundering from parade grounds, tingling through apartment walls, carried through the streets in small black boxes, violating even the peace of the desert and the forest, where drive-ins featured blue musical comedies, music at first overwhelmed, then delighted, then disgusted, and finally bored them. They removed the ear stopples that had initially guarded them from too keen a dose of pleasure; surfeit muffled them; they ceased to hear. The Minervans had discovered impotence.

NATHALIE-CHARLES HENNEBERG

The Blind Pilot

TRANSLATED BY DAMON KNIGHT

Nathalie-Charles Henneberg, who is Russian, met her Alsatian-German husband in Syria when he was in the French Foreign Legion. They began writing SF in French in the 1950s, and until his death in 1959 they signed their collaborations with his name, much like the famous American team of Henry Kuttner and C. L. Moore after their marriage. Contemporary French SF was cultivated in the 1950s by the magazine Fiction, *initially a translation of* The Magazine of Fantasy & Science Fiction, *which peppered its contents with new French stories. "The Blind Pilot" was translated and appeared in* The Magazine of Fantasy & Science Fiction *in 1960, the year after its French appearance, and in 13 French Science Fiction Stories (1965), the first such book to be published in English. Nathalie went on to become a prolific novelist, the "most read" French SF writer in France in the 1960s, according to Knight. This story bears an uncanny resemblance in atmosphere to the early works of the American writer Roger Zelazny, which it predates.*

*　　*　　*

The shop was low and dark, as if designed for someone who no longer knew day from night. Around it hung a scent of wax and incense, exotic woods, and roses dried in darkness. It was in the cellar of one of the oldest buildings of the old radioactive district, and you had to walk down several steps before you reached a grille of Venerian sandalwood. A cone of Martian crystal lighted the sign: THE BLIND PILOT.

The man who came in this morning, followed by a robot porter with a chest, was a half-crazy old voyager, like many who had gazed on the naked blazing of the stars. He was back from the Aselli—at least, if not from there, from the Southern Cross; his face was of wax, ravaged, graven, from lying too long in a cabin at the mercy of the ultraviolets, and in the black jungle of the planets.

The coffer was hewn from a heartwood hard as brass, porous here and there. He had it set down on the floor, and the sides vibrated imperceptibly, as if a great captive bee were struggling inside.

"Look here," he said, giving a rap on the lid, "I wouldn't sell that there for a million credits, but I'm needing to refloat myself, till I get my pay. They tell me you're an honest Yahoo. I'll leave this here in pawn and come back to get it in six days. What'll you give me?"

At the back of the shop, a young man raised his head. He was sitting in an old armchair stiff with flowered brocade. He looked like one of those fine Velasquez cavaliers who had hands of steel, and were not ashamed to be beautiful: but a black bandage covered the upper part of his face.

"I'm no Yahoo," he answered coldly, "and I don't take live animals as pledges."

"Blind! You're blind!" stammered the newcomer.

"You saw my sign."

"Accident?"

"Out in the Pleiades."

"Sorry, shipmate!" said the traveler. But already he was scheming: "How'd you know there was an animal in there?"

"I'm blind—but not deaf."

The whole room was tingling with a crystalline vibration. Suddenly it stopped. The traveler wiped great drops of sweat from his forehead.

"Shipmate," he said, "that ain't really an animal. I'm holding onto that. I don't want to sell it to nobody. And if I don't have any money tonight, it's the jug for me. No more space voyages, no more loot, no more nothing. I'm an HZ, to be suspended."

"I get it," answered the quiet voice. "How much?"

The other almost choked. "Will you really give me—?"

"Not a thing, I don't give anything for nothing, and I told you before I'm not interested in your cricket in a cage. But I can let you have five thousand credits, no more, on your shipping papers. In six days, when you come back to get them, you'll pay me five hundred credits extra. That's all."

"You're *worse* than a Yahoo!"

"No. I'm blind." He added grimly, "My accident was caused by a jerk who hadn't insured his rocket. I don't like jerks."

"But," said the adventurer, shuffling his feet, "how can you check my papers?"

"My brother's over there. Come on out, Jacky."

A sharp little grin appeared in the shadows. Out between a lunar harmonium in a meteorite, and a dark Terrestrial cloth on which a flayed martyr had bled, came a cripple mounted on a little carriage—legless, with stumps of arms, propelling himself with the aid of two hooks: a malicious little old man of twelve.

"Mutant," said the blind man curtly. "But he makes out, with his prosthetics. Papers in order, Jacky?"

"Sure, North. And dirtier than a dustrag."

"That only means they've seen good use. Give him his five thousand credits."

The blind man pressed a button. A cabinet opened, revealing a sort of dumb-waiter. In the top half there was a little built-in strong box; in the bottom crouched a Foramen chimera, the most bloodthirsty of beasts, half cat, half harpy.

The traveler jumped back.

The cripple rolled himself over to the strong box, grabbed up a bundle of credits and blew on the monster's nose. It purred affectionately.

"You see, the money's well guarded here," said North.

"Can I leave my chest with you, anyhow?" asked the traveler humbly.

So the chest remained. Using the dumb-waiter, the cripple sent it up to the small apartment that the two brothers shared in the penthouse of the building. According to its owner, the creature that was "not really an animal" was in hibernation; it had no need of food. The porous wood allowed enough air to pass. But the box had to be kept in a dark place. "It lives in the great deeps," he had explained; "it can't stand daylight."

The building was really very old, with a lot of elevators and closets. The mutants and cripples of the last war, who lived there because it was cheap, accommodated themselves to it. North dragged the chest into the strong room next to his study.

That evening, the free movie in the building was showing an old stereo film, not even sensorial, about the conquest of the Pleiades, and Jacky announced that he wanted to see it. About to leave, he asked his brother, "You don't suppose that animal will get cold in there?"

"What are you talking about? It's in hibernation."

"Anyhow," said Jacky spitefully, "we're not getting paid to keep it in fuel."

The movie lasted till midnight, and when Jacky came back there was a full moon. The boy testified later that he had been a little overexcited. A white glimmer flooded the upper landing, and he saw that the French windows of the "garret," as they called his brother's study, were masked with a black cloth. Jacky supposed North had taken this extra precaution on account of the animal; he pushed himself forward with his hooks, and knocked on the door, but no one answered, and there was no key in the lock.

He told himself then that maybe North had gone down six stories to the bar in the building, and he decided to wait. He sat on the landing; the night was mild, and he would not have traded the air at that height for any amount of conditioned and filtered atmosphere. The silver star floated overhead in the black sky. Jacky mused that "it means something after all, that shining going on just the same for x years, that moon that's seen so many old kings, poets, and all those lovers' stories. The cats that yowl at night must feel it; and the dogs too." In the lower-class buildings, there were only robot dogs. Jacky longed for a real dog—after all, he was only twelve. But mutants couldn't own living animals.

And then . . .

(On the magnetic tape where Jacky's deposition was taken down, it seemed that at that moment the boy began to choke. The recording was interrupted, and the next reel began: "Thanks for the coffee. It was good and bitter.")

He had heard an indefinable sound, very faint . . . just the sound of the ocean in a seashell. It grew, and grew. . . . At the same time (though he couldn't say how), there were images. A nacreous sky, the color of pearl, and green crystal waves, with crests of sparkling silver. Jacky felt no surprise; he had just left the stereo theater. Perhaps someone in the building opposite had turned on a sensorial camera—and the vibrations, the waves, were impinging here by accident.

But the melody swelled, and the boy sank under the green waves. They stank of seaweed and fish. . . . Carried along by the currents, the little cripple felt light and free. Banks of rustling diatoms parted for him; a blue phosphorescence haloed the medusas and starfish, and pearly blue ane-mones formed a forest. Grazed by a transparent jellyfish, Jacky felt a nettle-like burning. The shadow of a hammerhead shark went by, and scattered a twinkling cloud of smelt. Farther down, the shadow grew denser, more opaque and mysterious—caverns gaped in a coral reef. The tentacle of an octopus lashed the water, and the cripple shuddered.

He found himself thrown back against the hull of a ship, half buried in the sand. A little black and gold siren, garlanded with barnacles, smiled under the prow; and he fell, transported, against a breach that spilled out a pirate treasure, coffers full of barbaric jewels. Heaps of bones were whiten-ing at the bottom of the hold, and a skull smiled with empty sockets. This must be an amateur film, Jacky thought: a little too realistic. He freed himself, pushed away as hard as he could with his hooks, rose to the surface at last—and almost cried out.

The sky above him was not that of Earth. North had told him how that other dark ocean looked—the sub-ether. The stars were naked and dazzling. Reefs, that were burning meteors, sprang up out of the void. And the planets seemed to whirl near enough to touch—one was ruby, another orange, still another a tranquil blue; Saturn danced in its airy ring.

Jacky thrust his hooks out before him to push away those torches. In so doing, he slipped and rolled across the landing. The door opened a second later—he hadn't had time to fall three steps, but this time he wasn't diving alone: beside him, in the hideously reddened water, whirled and danced the body of a disjointed puppet, with gullied features in a face of wax.

Jacky raised his head. North stood on the sill, terrible, pale as a statue of old ivory; the black bandage cut his face in two. He called, "Who's there? Answer me, or I'll call the militia!"

His voice was loud and angry. North, who always spoke so softly to Jacky. . . .

"It's me, Jack," said the boy, trembling. "I was coming back, and I missed a step. . . ."

("I told a lie," said Jacky later, to the militiamen who were questioning him. And he stared into their eyes with a look of open defiance. "That's right, sure, I told a lie. Because I knew he'd kill me.")

The next morning there was no blood and no corpse on the landing. Only a smell of seaweed. . . .

Jacky was filling the coffee cups, in the back of the shop, while the television news broadcast was on. Toward the end, the announcer mentioned that the body of a drowned man had been taken from the harbor. The dead man's face appeared on the tiny screen at the moment North came into the shop.

"Hey, look at that!" called the cripple. "Your five thousand credits are done for."

"What's that?" asked his brother, picking up his china cup and his buttered bread with delicate accuracy.

"The character with the pet, what's his name? Oh, yes, Joash Du Guast—what a monicker! They've just fished him out of the channel. Guess what, they don't know who he is: somebody swiped his wallet."

"A dead loss," said the older. "You're certain he's the one?"

"He's still on the screen. He isn't a pretty sight."

An indefinable expression passed over North's mobile features. "You'd think he was relieved," Jacky told himself. Aloud, he asked, "What do we do with the animal?"

"Does it bother you?" asked North, a little too negligently.

"Me, old man," said the cripple in a clownish tone, imitating a famous fat actor, "as long as there's no wrinkles in my belly! Where did he come from, this Joash?"

"He talked about the Aselli," said North, reaching with a magician's deftness for another slice of bread. "And a lot of other things, too. What are you up to this morning? Got any work to do?"

"Not much! The Stimpson order to send out. A crate of lunar bells coming in. I ought to go to the Reeducation Center, too."

"Okay, I see you've got a full morning. Can you bring me a copy of the weekly news disc?"

"Sure."

But Jacky didn't go to the Reeducation Center that morning, nor to his customers. With his carriage perched on the slidewalk, he rode to Astronautics Headquarters, a building among others, and had some difficulty getting upstairs in the elevator, amid the students' jibes. Some of them asked, "You want to do the broad jump in a rocket?" And others, "He thinks these are the good old days, when everybody was hunting for round-bottoms to send to the Moon!" It was not really spiteful, and Jacky was used to it.

He felt a touch of nostalgia, not for himself but for North. He knew North would never come here again. The walls were covered with celestial charts; microfilm shelves rose from one floor to the next, and in all the glass cases there were models of spaceship engines, from the multi-stage rockets and sputniks, all the way up to the great ships that synthesized their own fissionables. Jacky arrived all out of breath in front of the robot card sorter, and handed it his card.

"The Aselli," spat the robot. "Asellus Borealis? Asellus Australis? Gamma Cancri or Delta Cancri?"

"There's nothing else out there?"

"Yes, Alphard, longitude twenty-six degrees nineteen minutes. Alpha Hydrae."

"Hydra, that's an aquatic monster? Is it a water planet? Read me the card."

"There is little to tell," crackled the robot. "The planet is almost unexplored, its surface being composed of oceans. No regular relations with Earth."

"Fauna? Flora?"

"Without evidence to the contrary, those of oceans in general."

"Intelligent life?"

The robot made a face with its ball bearings. "Without evidence to the contrary, none. Nor any human beings. Nothing but sea lions and manatees."

"Manatees? What are they?" asked Jacky, suddenly apprehensive.

"Herbivorous sirenian mammals that live on Earth, along the shores of Africa and America. Manatees sometimes grow as long as three meters, and frequent the estuaries of rivers."

"But—'sirenians'?"

"A genus of mammals, related to the cetaceans, and comprising the dugongs, manatees, and so on."

Jacky's eyebrows went up and he cried, "I thought it came from 'siren'!"

"So it does," said the robot laconically. "Fabulous monsters, half woman, half bird or fish. With their sweet singing, they lured voyagers onto the reefs. . . ."

"Where did this happen?"

"On Earth, where else?" said the robot, offended. "Between the isle of Capri and the coast of Italy. Young man, you don't know quite what you mean to ask."

But Jacky knew.

On his return, as he expected, he found the shop closed and a note tacked to the door: "The pilot is out." Jacky hunted in his pockets for the key, slipped inside. All was calm and ordinary, except for that smell which ruled now like the mistress of the house, the smell that you breathe on the beaches, in little coves, in summer: seaweed, shells, fish, perhaps a little tar.

Jacky set the table, set to work in the kitchenette, and prepared a nice little snack, lobster salad and ravioli. Secretive and spiteful, imprisoned among the yellowing antiques of the shop, the young cripple really loved them all.

When everything was ready—fresh flowers in the vases, the ravioli hot, ice cubes in the glasses—Jacky rang three times, according to custom. No one answered. Everything was a pretext for a secret language between the two mutilated brothers, who adored each other. The first stroke of the bell meant: "The meal is ready, his lordship may come down"; the second: "I'm hungry"; and the third: "I'm hungry, hungry, hungry!" The fourth had almost the sense of "Have you had an accident?"

Jacky hesitated a moment, then pressed the button. The silence was deep among the crystallized plants and the gems of seven planets. Did this mean that North was really away? The cripple hoisted himself into the dumb-waiter and rode up to the penthouse.

On the upper landing, the scent had changed; it had flowered now into unknown spices, and it would have taken a more expert observer than Jacky to recognize the aromatics of the fabulous past: nard, aloes, and benzoin, the bitter thyme of Sheba's Balkis, the myrrh and olibanum of Cleopatra.

In the midst of all this, the music was real, almost palpable, like a pillar of light, and Jacky asked himself how it could be that the others, on the floors below, didn't hear it.

North Ellis closed the door behind him, turned the key and shot the bolt. His blind man's hands, strong and slender, executed these movements with machine-like precision, but he was panting a little, and in spite of old habit, had almost missed the landing. He was so hard pressed . . . but he had to foresee everything. Jacky must never enter this room. Jacky . . . Resting his back against the door, North thought for a moment that he should have sent Jacky to Europe. Their aunt, their mother's sister, lived somewhere in a little village with a musical name. He felt responsible for Jacky.

He swept away these preoccupations like dead leaves, and walked toward the dark corner where the chest lay under a black cloth. His fingers crept over the porous wood, which scented his palms.

"You're there," he said in a cold, harsh voice. "You've been waiting for me, you!"

The being that crouched at the heart of the shadows did not immediately answer, but the concentric waves of the music swelled out. And the man who had tumbled to earth with broken wings, awaited neither by his mother, dead of leukemia, nor by a red-haired girl who had laughed, turning her primrose face beside a white neck . . . the blind pilot felt himself neither deprived nor unhappy.

"You're beautiful, aren't you? You're very beautiful! Your voice . . ."

"What else would you like to know?" responded the waves, growing stronger. "You are sightless, I faceless. I told you, yesterday when you opened the strong room: I am all that streams and sings. The glittering cascades, the torrents of ice that break on the columbines, the reflection of the multiple moons on the oceans. . . . And I am the ocean. Let yourself float on my wave. Come. . . ."

"You made me kill that man yesterday."

"What is a man? I speak to you of tumbling abysses, dark and luminous by turns, of the crucibles where new life is forged, and you answer me with the death of a spaceman! Anyhow, he deserved it: he captured me, imprisoned me, and would have come back to separate us!"

"Separate us . . ." said North. "Do you think that's possible?"

"No—if you follow me."

The central melody grew piercing. It was like a spire, or a bridge over a limitless space. And the unconscious part of the human soul darted out to encounter that harmony. The wheeling abyss opened, it was peopled with trembling nebulas, with diamonds and roses of fire. . . .

North toppled into it.

. . . It was strange to recognize, in this nth dimension, the crowds of stars he had encountered in real voyages—the glacial scintillation of Polaris, the scattered pearls of Orion's Belt. North marveled to find himself again in this night, weightless and free, without spacesuit or rocket. Jets of photons bore him on immense wings. The garret, the mutants' building, the Earth? He could have laughed at them. The Boreal Dragon twisted its spirals in a spray of stars. He crossed in one bound an abyss streaming with fire— Berenice's Hair—and cut himself on the blue sapphire of Vega in the Lyre. He was not climbing alone: the living music wound him in its rings.

"Do you think to know the Infinite?" said the voice enfolded in the harmonies. "Poor Earthlings, who claim to have discovered everything! Because you've built heavy machines that break all equilibrium, that burst into flame and fall, and martyr your vulnerable human flesh? . . . Come, I'll show you what we can see, we obscure and immobile ones, in the abysses, since what is on high is also down below. . . ."

The star spirals and the harmonies surged up. In the depths of his night, North gazed upon those things that the pilots, constrained by their limited periscopic screens, never saw: oceans of rubies, furnaces of emeralds, dark stars, constellations coiled like luminous dragons. Meteorites were a rain of motionless streaks. Novas came to meet him; they exploded and shattered in sidereal tornadoes, the giants and dwarfs fell again in incandescent cascades. Space-time was nothing but a flaming chalice.

"Higher! Faster!" sang the voice.

All that passed beyond the vertigo and tipsiness of the flesh. North felt himself tumbled, dissolved in the astral foam; he was nothing but an atom in the infinite. . . .

"Higher! Faster!"

Was it at that moment, among the dusty arcs, far down at the bottom of the abyss, at the heart of his being, that he felt that icy breath, that sensation of horror? It was more than unclean. It was as if he had leaped over the abysses and the centuries, passed beyond all human limits—and ended at this. At nothingness, the void. He was down at the bottom of a well, in utter darkness, and his mouth was full of blood. Rhythmic blows were shaking that closed universe. Trying to raise himself, he felt under his hands the porous, wrinkled wood. A childish voice was crying, "North! Oh, North! Don't you hear me? Let me in, let me in!"

North came back to himself, numbed, weak as if he had bled to death.

For a little, he thought himself in the wrecked starship, out in the Pleiades. He hoisted himself up on his elbows and crawled toward the door. He had strength enough left to draw the bolt, turn the key, and then he fainted on the sill.

"It was those trips, you know . . ." Jacky looked up at the Spatial Militiamen who were taking their turn opposite him. They were not hard-hearted; they had given him a sandwich and a big quilt. But how much could they understand? "I never knew when North started getting unhappy. Me, I never went on a trip farther away than the coast. Ever since he's been blind, he always seemed to be so calm! I thought he was like me. When I was around him, I felt good, I never wanted to go anywhere. Sometimes, to try and be the same as him, I'd put a bandage around my eyes, and try to see everything in sounds instead of colors. Sure, the switchboard operator, and the night watchman (not the robot, the other one), they said this was no life for two boys. But North was blind and I was crippled. Who would have wanted us?"

The Chief of Militia reflected that Jacky was mistaken: someone would certainly have wanted North. But saying nothing of this, he went on asking questions.

. . . The next day was cloudy; North pulled an old spacesuit out of a pile of scrap iron and began to polish the plates, whistling. He explained to Jacky that he was going to put it at the entrance of the shop. Toward noon, Jacky took a message; he was told that the board of directors of a certain famous sanatorium were reluctant to accept a boarder mutated to that extent. He accepted their excuses and hung up, silently. So that was what it was all about: North wanted to get rid of him. He was crazy—it was as if he had gone blind all over again! During a miserable lunch, the idea came to him to put the apartment's telephone line out of commission: that way, the outer world would leave them alone. But first he wanted to call up Dr. Evers, their family doctor, and the telephone did not respond. Jacky realized that North had forestalled him.

After that, he made himself small, rolled his carriage behind some crates, and installed himself on a shelf of the bookcase. It was his favorite hiding place. There were still in the shop some volumes bound in blond leather, almost golden, which smelled of incense or cigars, with yellowing pages and the curious printing of the twentieth century. They had quaint pictures, not even animated. Without having to look for it, he stumbled upon the marvelous story of the navigator who sailed the wine-dark sea. The sail was purple, and the hull of sandalwood. Off the mythological coasts, a divine singing arose, inviting the sailors to more distant flights. The reefs were fringed with pearls; the white moon rose high above the fabulous mountains. Ulysses stopped up their ears with wax and tied himself to the mast. But he himself heard the songs of the sirens. . . .

"North," the boy asked later, forgetting all caution, "is there such a thing as sirens?"

"What?" asked the blind man, with a start.

"I mean, the sailors in the olden days, they said—"

"Crud," said North. "Those guys went out of their heads, sailing across the oceans. Just think, it took them longer between Crete, a little island, and Ithaca, than it takes us to get to Jupiter. They went short of food, and their ships were walnut shells. And on top of everything else, for months on end they'd see nobody except a few shipmates, as chapped and hairy as they were. Well, they'd start to go off their rockers, and the first woman pirate was Circe or Calypso to them, and the first cetacean they met was an ocean princess."

"A manatee," said Jacky.

"That's right, a manatee. Have you ever seen one?"

"No."

"Sure, that's right, I don't think there is one in the zoo. Maybe in the exotic specimens. Take down the fourth book from the left, on the 'Nat. Sciences' shelf. Page seven hundred ninety-two. Got it?"

The page was freshly dog-eared; North must have been leafing through the book, without being able to read it. Well, it was a big beast with a round head and mustaches, and a thick oily skin. The female was giving suck to a little tar-baby. They all had serious expressions. Jacky was overcome with mad laughter.

"Ridiculous, isn't it?" North asked in an unrecognizable voice, harsh and broken. "To think so many guys have dived into the water on account of that! I think they must have been sick."

But that evening, he offered Jacky a ticket to the planetarium and a trip to the amusement park. Jacky refused politely; he was content to stay on his shelf. Again he plunged into the volume bound in blond leather, discovering for the first time that life has always been mysterious and that destiny wears many masks. The isles with the fabulous names flickered past to the rhythm of strophes; the heroes sailed for the conquest of the Golden Fleece, or perhaps they led a pale well-beloved out of Hades. Some burned their wings in the sun and fell. . . .

North walked around cat-footed, closing the shutters, arranging the planetary knickknacks. He disappeared so quietly that Jacky was not aware of it, and it was only when the boy wanted to ask him for some information about sailing ships that his absence became a concrete fact. Suddenly afraid, Jacky slipped to the floor, and discovered that his carriage had also disappeared. He crawled then, with the aid of his hooks, among the scattered pieces of iron, and it was then that he stumbled over a horrible viscous thing: the wet billfold of Joash Du Guast. The five thousand credits were still inside.

After that, his fear had no limit, and Jacky crawled instinctively toward the door, which he found shut; then to the dumb-waiter, where he heard the Foramen chimera, caged, mew pleasantly. "It won't work, old lady," he breathed at it. "They've locked us both up together."

He licked a little blood out of the corners of his mouth, and thought hard. He would have to be quick. To be sure, he could hammer on the door, but the street was deserted at night, the normals were all getting ready to watch their telesets, or some other kind of screen—and there was no use knocking on the walls: the shop was surrounded by empty cellars. And the telephone was dead.

Jacky then did what any imprisoned boy of his age would have done (but from him, it demanded a superhuman effort): he clambered up the curtains, managed to open the window with his hook, and jumped out. He was hurt, falling on the pavement.

. . . "That damn kid!" thought North as he opened the door of the garret. "Sirens!"

His hands were trembling. A wave of aromatics, already familiar, came into his night and surrounded him: he had breathed them on other worlds. He understood what was required of him, and he let himself go, abandoned himself to the furious maelstrom of sounds and smells, to the tide of singing and perfumes. His useless, mutilated body lay somewhere out of the way, on a shelf.

"Look at me," said the music. "I am in you, and you are me. They tried in vain to keep you on Earth, with chains of falsehood. You are no longer of Earth, since we live one life together. Yesterday I showed you the abysses I know. Show me the stars you have visited: memory by memory, I shall take them. In that way, perhaps, shall we not find the world that calls us? Come. I shall choose a planet, like a pearl."

He saw them again, all of them.

Alpha Spicae, in the constellation of the Virgin, is a frozen globe, whose atmosphere is so rich in water vapor that a rocket sticks in the ground like a needle of frost. Under a distant green sun, this world scintillates like a million-faceted diamond, and its ice cap spreads toward the equator. On the ground, you are snared in a net of rainbows and green snow, a snow that smells like benzoin (all the pilots know that stellar illusion). On Alpha Spicae, a lost explorer goes mad in a few hours.

North was irresistibly drawn away, and shortly recognized the magnetic planet of the Ditch in Cygnus. That one, too, he had learned to avoid on his voyages: it was followed in its orbit by the thousands of sidereal corpses it had captured. The bravest pilots followed it in their coffins of sparkling ice; for that sphere, no larger than the Moon, is composed of pure golden ore.

They passed like a waterspout across a lake of incandescent crystal — Altair. Another trap lay in wait for them in the constellation Orion, where the gigantic diamond of Betelgeuse flashed; a phantasmagoria of deceptive images, a spiderweb of lightnings. The orb which cowered behind these mirages had no name, only a nickname: Sundew. Space pilots avoided it like the Pit.

"Higher!" sang the voice, made up now of thousands of etheric currents, millions of astral vibrations. "Farther!"

But here, North began to struggle. He knew now where she was drawing him, and what incandescent hell he would meet on that path, because he had already experienced it. He knew of a peculiar planet with silvery-violet skies, out in the mysterious constellation of Cancer. It was the most beautiful he had ever glimpsed, the only one he had loved like a woman, because its oceans reminded him of a pair of eyes. Ten dancing moons crowned that Alpha Hydrae, which the ancient nomads called Al-Phard. It was a deep watery world, with frothing waves: an odor of sea-salt, of seaweed, of ambergris drifted over its surface. A perpetual ultrasonic music jumbled all attempts at communication, and repulsed the starships. The oxygen content of Alpha Hydrae's atmosphere was so high that it intoxicated living beings and burned them up. The rockets that succeeded in escaping the attraction of Al-Phard carried back crews of the blissful dead.

It was in trying to escape its grip that an uncontrolled machine, with North aboard, had once headed toward the Pleiades and crashed on the surface of an asteroid.

Heavy blows shook the temples of the solitary navigator. The enormous sun of Pollux leaped out of space, exploded, fell to ruin in the darkness, with Procyon and the Goat; the whole Milky Way trembled and vibrated. The human soul lost in that torrent of energy, the soul that struggled, despaired, foundered, was only an infinitesimal atom, a sound — or the echo of a sound, in the harmony of the spheres.

"This is it," said Jacky, wiping his bloody mouth. "Honest, this is it, Inspector. There's the window I jumped out of. . . ."

There it was, with its smashed glass, and Jacky did not mention how painful the fall had been. His forearms slashed, he had hung suspended by his hooks. On the pavement, he had lost consciousness. Coming to later, under a fine drizzle of rain, he had, he said, "crawled and crawled." Few of the passing autos had even slowed down for that crushed human caterpillar. "Oh, Marilyn, did you see that funny little round-bottom?"—"It must be one of those mutant cripples, don't stop. Galla. . . ."—"Space! Are they still contagious?" Jacky bit his lips. Finally, a truck had stopped. Robots—a crew of robots from the sanitation department—had picked him up. He began to cry, seeing himself already thrown onto the junk-heap. By chance, the driver was human; he heard, and took him to the militia post.

"I don't hear anything," said the inspector after a moment of silence.

"The others in the block didn't hear anything either!" breathed Jacky.

"I think he must be very unhappy, or else drunk. . . . Are there ultrasonics, maybe? Look, the dogs are restless."

Certainly, the handsome Great Danes of the Special Service were acting strangely: they were going around in circles and whining.

"A quarrel between monsters," thought Inspector Morel. "Just my luck: a mutant stump of a kid, a space pilot with the D.T.'s, and a siren! They'll laugh in my face down at headquarters!"

But, as Jacky cried and beat on the door, he gave the order to break it in. The boy crawled toward the dumb-waiter; one of the militiamen almost fired on the chimera, which had leaped from its cabinet, purring.

"That's nothing, it's only a big cat from Foramen!" Jacky wailed. "Come on, please come on, I'm going up the shaft."

"I was never in such a madhouse before," thought the inspector. There were things in every corner—robots or idols, with three heads or seven hands. There were talking shells. One of the men shouted, feeling a mobile creeper twine itself in his hair. They ought to forbid the import of these parlor tricks into an honest Terrestrial port. Not surprising that the lad upstairs should have gone off his nut, the inspector told himself.

When the militia reached the topmost landing of the building, Jacky was stretched out in front of the closed door, banging it desperately with his hooks. Whether on account of ultrasonics or not, the men were pale. The enormous harmony that filled the garret was here perceptible, palpable. Morel called, but no one answered.

"He's dead?" asked Jacky. "Isn't he?"

They sensed a living, evil presence inside.

Morel disposed his men in pairs, one on either side of the door. A ferret-faced little locksmith slipped up and began to work on the bolt. When he was finished, the militiamen were supposed to break the door down quickly and rush inside, while Morel covered them, if the need arose, with heat gun in hand. But it was black inside the garret; someone would have to carry a powerful flashlight and play it back and forth.

"Me," said Jacky. He was white as a sheet, trembling all over. "If my brother's dead, Inspector, you should let me go in. Anyhow, what risk would I take? You'll be right behind me. And I promise not to let go of the flashlight, no matter what."

The inspector looked at the legless child. "You might get yourself shot," he said. "You never know what weapons these extra-terrestrials are going to use. Or what they're thinking, or what they want. That thing . . . maybe it sings the way we breathe."

"I know," said Jacky. He neglected to add, "That's why I asked to carry the flashlight. So as to get to it first."

The inspector handed him the flashlight. He seized it firmly with one of his hooks. And the first sharp ray, like a sword, cut through the keyhole into the attic.

They all felt the crushing tension let go. Released, with frothing tongues, the dogs lay down on the floor. It was as if a tight cord had suddenly snapped. And abruptly, behind the closed door, something broke with a stunning crash.

At the same instant, the landing was flooded with an intolerable smell of burned flesh. Down in the street, ant-like pedestrians screamed and ran. The building was burning. An object falling in flames had buried itself in the roof. . . . Fire trucks were called.

The militiamen broke down the door, and Morel stumbled over a horrible mass of flesh, calcined, crushed, which no longer bore any resemblance to North. A man who had fallen from a starship, across the stellar void, might have looked like that. A man who had leaped into a vacuum without a spacesuit . . . a half-disintegrated manikin. North Ellis, the blind pilot, had suffered his last shipwreck.

Overcome by nausea, the militiamen backed away. Jacky himself had not moved from the landing. He clung to the flashlight, and the powerful beam of light untiringly searched, swept the dark cave. The symphony that only his ears had heard grew fainter, then lost itself in a tempest of discordant sounds. The invisible being gave one last sharp wail (in the street, all the windows broke and all the lights went out).

Then there was silence.

Jacky sat and licked his bloody lips. Inside, in the garret, the militiamen were pulling down the black draperies, breaking furniture. One of them shouted, "There's nothing here!"

Jacky dropped the flashlight, raised himself on his stumps. "Look in the chest! In the strong room, to the side—"

"Nothing in here. Nothing in the chest."

"Wait a minute," said the youngest of the militiamen, "there it is—on the floor."

Then they dragged her out, her round head bobbed, and Jacky recognized the thick, glossy skin and the flippers. She had died, probably, at the first touch of the light, but her corpse was still pulsing in a dull rhythm. An ultrasonic machine? No. Two red slits wept bloody tears. . . . The sirens of Alpha Hydrae cannot bear the light.

The Men Who Murdered Mohammed

Alfred Bester began to write SF and fantasy in the late 1930s and then left the field, returning in the early 1950s. He is the author of two of the most important SF novels of the 1950s — The Demolished Man, *winner of the first Hugo Award for best novel in 1953, a virtuoso work combining mystery plotting and flashy stylistic and orthographic tricks in a SF setting, and* The Stars My Destination, *a literary tour-de-force that became one of the models of innovation for the New Wave writers. Still, his major influence was felt through his short stories. At the time of his death in 1987, he had become an elder statesman revered by younger writers such as Samuel R. Delany, Michael Moorcock, and William Gibson. "The Men Who Murdered Mohammed" is from the hand of an aggressive inventor obsessed with psychological tricks in literature. It is characterized by Bester's energy and almost frantic wit.*

*   *   *

There was a man who mutilated history. He toppled empires and uprooted dynasties. Because of him, Mount Vernon should not be a national shrine, and Columbus, Ohio, should be called Cabot, Ohio. Because of him the name Marie Curie should be cursed in France, and no one should swear by the beard of the Prophet. Actually, these realities did not happen, because he was a mad professor; or, to put it another way, he only succeeded in making them unreal for himself.

Now, the patient reader is too familiar with the conventional mad professor, undersized and overbrowed, creating monsters in his laboratory which invariably turn on their maker and menace his lovely daughter. This story isn't about that sort of make-believe man. It's about Henry Hassel, a genuine mad professor in a class with such better-known men as Ludwig Boltzmann (see Ideal Gas Law), Jacques Charles and André Marie Ampère (1775–1836).

Everyone ought to know that the electrical ampere was so named in honor of Ampère. Ludwig Boltzmann was a distinguished Austrian physicist, as famous for his research on black-body radiation as on Ideal Gases. You can look him up in Volume Three of the *Encyclopaedia Britannica*, BALT to BRAI. Jacques Alexandre César Charles was the first mathematician to become interested in flight, and he invented the hydrogen balloon. These were real men.

They were also real mad professors. Ampère, for example, was on his way to an important meeting of scientists in Paris. In his taxi he got a brilliant idea (of an electrical nature, I assume) and whipped out a pencil and jotted the equation on the wall of the hansom cab. Roughly, it was: $dH = ipdl/r^2$ in which p is the perpendicular distance from P to the line of the element dl; or $dH = i \sin \emptyset \, dl/r^2$. This is sometimes known as Laplace's Law, although he wasn't at the meeting.

Anyway, the cab arrived at the Académie. Ampère jumped out, paid the driver and rushed into the meeting to tell everybody about his idea. Then he realized he didn't have the note on him, remembered where he'd left it, and had to chase through the streets of Paris after the taxi to recover his runaway equation. Sometimes I imagine that's how Fermat lost his famous "Last Theorem," although Fermat wasn't at the meeting either, having died some two hundred years earlier.

Or take Boltzmann. Giving a course in Advanced Ideal Gases, he peppered his lectures with involved calculus, which he worked out quickly and casually in his head. He had that kind of head. His students had so much trouble trying to puzzle out the math by ear that they couldn't keep up with the lectures, and they begged Boltzmann to work out his equations on the blackboard.

Boltzmann apologized and promised to be more helpful in the future. At the next lecture he began, "Gentlemen, combining Boyle's Law with the Law of Charles, we arrive at the equation $pv = p_0 v_0 (1 + at)$. Now, obviously, if $_aS^b = f(x)dxX(a)$, then $pv = RT$ and $_vS f(x,y,z) dV = O$. It's as simple as two plus two equals four." At this point Boltzmann remembered his promise. He turned to the blackboard, conscientiously chalked $2 + 2 = 4$, and then breezed on, casually doing the complicated calculus in his head.

Jacques Charles, the brilliant mathematician who discovered Charles's Law (sometimes known as Gay-Lussac's Law), which Boltzmann mentioned in his lecture, had a lunatic passion to become a famous paleographer—that is, a discoverer of ancient manuscripts. I think that being forced to share credit with Gay-Lussac may have unhinged him.

He paid a transparent swindler named Vrain-Lucas 200,000 francs for holograph letters purportedly written by Julius Caesar, Alexander the Great, and Pontius Pilate. Charles, a man who could see through any gas, ideal or not, actually believed in these forgeries despite the fact that the maladroit Vrain-Lucas had written them in modern French on modern notepaper bearing modern watermarks. Charles even tried to donate them to the Louvre.

Now, these men weren't idiots. They were geniuses who paid a high price for their genius because the rest of their thinking was other-world. A genius is someone who travels to truth by an unexpected path. Unfortunately, unexpected paths lead to disaster in everyday life. This is what happened to Henry Hassel, professor of Applied Compulsion at Unknown University in the year 1980.

Nobody knows where Unknown University is or what they teach there. It has a faculty of some two hundred eccentrics, and a student body of two thousand misfits—the kind that remain anonymous until they win Nobel prizes or become the First Man on Mars. You can always spot a graduate of U.U. when you ask people where they went to school. If you get an evasive reply like: "State," or "Oh, a freshwater school you never heard of," you can bet they went to Unknown. Someday I hope to tell you more about this university, which is a center of learning only in the Pickwickian sense.

Anyway, Henry Hassel started home from his office in the Psychotic Psenter early one afternoon, strolling through the Physical Culture arcade. It is not true that he did this to leer at the nude coeds practicing Arcane Eurythmics; rather, Hassel liked to admire the trophies displayed in the arcade in memory of great Unknown teams which had won the sort of championships that Unknown teams win—in sports like Strabismus, Occlusion and Botulism. (Hassel had been Frambesia singles champion three years running.) He arrived home uplifted, and burst gaily into the house to discover his wife in the arms of a man.

There she was, a lovely woman of thirty-five, with smoky red hair and almond eyes, being heartily embraced by a person whose pockets were stuffed with pamphlets, microchemical apparatus and a patella-reflex hammer—a typical campus character of U.U., in fact. The embrace was so concentrated that neither of the offending parties noticed Henry Hassel glaring at them from the hallway.

Now, remember Ampère and Charles and Boltzmann. Hassel weighed one hundred and ninety pounds. He was muscular and uninhibited. It would have been child's play for him to have dismembered his wife and her lover, and thus simply and directly achieve the goal he desired—the end of his wife's life. But Henry Hassel was in the genius class; his mind just didn't operate that way.

Hassel breathed hard, turned and lumbered into his private laboratory like a freight engine. He opened a drawer labeled DUODENUM and removed a .45-caliber revolver. He opened other drawers, more interestingly labeled, and assembled apparatus. In exactly seven and one half minutes (such was his rage), he put together a time machine (such was his genius).

Professor Hassel assembled the time machine around him, set a dial for 1902, picked up the revolver and pressed a button. The machine made a noise like defective plumbing and Hassel disappeared. He reappeared in Philadelphia on June 3, 1902, went directly to No. 1218 Walnut Street, a red-brick house with marble steps, and rang the bell. A man who might have passed for the third Smith Brother opened the door and looked at Henry Hassel.

"Mr. Jessup?" Hassel asked in a suffocated voice.

"Yes?"

"You are Mr. Jessup?"

"I am."

"You will have a son, Edgar? Edgar Allan Jessup—so named because of your regrettable admiration for Poe?"

The third Smith Brother was startled. "Not that I know of," he said. "I'm not married yet."

"You will be," Hassel said angrily. "I have the misfortune to be married to your son's daughter. Greta. Excuse me." He raised the revolver and shot his wife's grandfather-to-be.

"She will have ceased to exist," Hassel muttered, blowing smoke out of the revolver. "I'll be a bachelor. I may even be married to somebody else. . . . Good God! Who?"

Hassel waited impatiently for the automatic recall of the time machine to snatch him back to his own laboratory. He rushed into his living room. There was his redheaded wife, still in the arms of a man.

Hassel was thunderstruck.

"So that's it," he growled. "A family tradition of faithlessness. Well, we'll see about that. We have ways and means." He permitted himself a hollow laugh, returned to his laboratory, and sent himself back to the year 1901, where he shot and killed Emma Hotchkiss, his wife's maternal grand-mother-to-be. He returned to his own home in his own time. There was his redheaded wife, still in the arms of another man.

"But I *know* the old bitch was her grandmother," Hassel muttered. "You couldn't miss the resemblance. What the hell's gone wrong?"

Hassel was confused and dismayed, but not without resources. He went to his study, had difficulty picking up the phone, but finally managed to dial the Malpractice Laboratory. His finger kept oozing out of the dial holes.

"Sam?" he said. "This is Henry."

"Who?"

"Henry."

"You'll have to speak up."

"Henry Hassel!"

"Oh, good afternoon, Henry."

"Tell me all about time."

"Time? Hmmm . . ." The Simplex-and-Multiplex Computer cleared its throat while it waited for the data circuits to link up. "Ahem. Time. (1) Absolute. (2) Relative. (3) Recurrent. (1) Absolute: period, contingent, duration, diurnity, perpetuity—"

"Sorry, Sam. Wrong request. Go back. I want time, reference to succession of, travel in."

Sam shifted gears and began again. Hassel listened intently. He nodded. He grunted. "Uh huh. Uh huh. Right. I see. Thought so. A continuum, eh? Acts performed in past must alter future. Then I'm on the right track. But act must be significant, eh? Mass-action effect. Trivia cannot divert existing phenomena streams. Hmmm. But how trivial is a grandmother?"

"What are you trying to do, Henry?"

"Kill my wife," Hassel snapped. He hung up. He returned to his labora-tory. He considered, still in a jealous rage.

"Got to do something significant," he muttered. "Wipe Greta out. Wipe it all out. All right, by God! I'll show 'em."

Hassel went back to the year 1775, visited a Virginia farm and shot a young colonel in the brisket. The colonel's name was George Washington, and Hassel made sure he was dead. He returned to his own time and his own home. There was his redheaded wife, still in the arms of another.

"Damn!" said Hassel. He was running out of ammunition. He opened a fresh box of cartridges, went back in time and massacred Christopher Columbus, Napoleon, Mohammed and half a dozen other celebrities. "That ought to do it, by God!" said Hassel.

He returned to his own time, and found his wife as before.

His knees turned to water; his feet seemed to melt into the floor. He went back to his laboratory, walking through nightmare quicksands.

"What the hell is significant?" Hassel asked himself painfully. "How much does it take to change futurity? By God, I'll really change it this time. I'll go for broke."

He traveled to Paris at the turn of the twentieth century and visited a Madame Curie in an attic workshop near the Sorbonne. "Madame," he said in his execrable French, "I am a stranger to you of the utmost, but a scientist entire. Knowing of your experiments with radium—Oh? You haven't got to radium yet? No matter. I am here to teach you all of nuclear fission."

He taught her. He had the satisfaction of seeing Paris go up in a mushroom of smoke before the automatic recall brought him home. "That'll teach women to be faithless," he growled. . . . "Guhhh!" The last was wrenched from his lips when he saw his redheaded wife still—But no need to belabor the obvious.

Hassel swam through fogs to his study and sat down to think. While he's thinking I'd better warn you that this is not a conventional time story. If you imagine for a moment that Henry is going to discover that the man fondling his wife is himself, you're mistaken. The viper is not Henry Hassel, his son, a relation, or even Ludwig Boltzmann (1844–1906). Hassel does not make a circle in time, ending where the story begins—to the satisfaction of nobody and the fury of everybody—for the simple reason that time isn't circular, or linear, or tandem, discoid, syzygous, longinquitous, or pandicularted. Time is a private matter, as Hassel discovered.

"Maybe I slipped up somehow," Hassel muttered. "I'd better find out." He fought with the telephone, which seemed to weigh a hundred tons, and at last managed to get through to the library.

"Hello, Library? This is Henry."

"Who?"

"Henry Hassel."

"Speak up, please."

"HENRY HASSEL!"

"Oh. Good afternoon, Henry."

"What have you got on George Washington?"

Library clucked while her scanners sorted through her catalogues. "George Washington, first president of the United States, was born in—"

"First president? Wasn't he murdered in 1775?"

"Really, Henry. That's an absurd question. Everybody knows that George Wash—"

"Doesn't anybody know he was shot?"

"By whom?"

"Me."

"When?"

"In 1775."

"How did you manage to do that?"

"I've got a revolver."

"No, I mean, how did you do it two hundred years ago?"

"I've got a time machine."

"Well, there's no record here," Library said. "He's still doing fine in my files. You must have missed."

"I did not miss. What about Christopher Columbus? Any record of his death in 1489?"

"But he discovered the New World in 1492."

"He did not. He was murdered in 1489."

"How?"

"With a forty-five slug in the gizzard."

"You again, Henry?"

"Yes."

"There's no record here," Library insisted. "You must be one lousy shot."

"I will not lose my temper," Hassel said in a trembling voice.

"Why not, Henry?"

"Because it's lost already," he shouted. "All right! What about Marie Curie? Did she or did she not discover the fission bomb which destroyed Paris at the turn of the century?"

"She did not. Enrico Fermi—"

"She did."

"She didn't."

"I personally taught her. Me. Henry Hassel."

"Everybody says you're a wonderful theoretician, but a lousy teacher, Henry. You—"

"Go to hell, you old biddy. This has got to be explained."

"Why?"

"I forget. There was something on my mind, but it doesn't matter now. What would you suggest?"

"You really have a time machine?"

"Of course I've got a time machine."

"Then go back and check."

Hassel returned to the year 1775, visited Mount Vernon, and interrupted the spring planting. "Excuse me, colonel," he began.

The big man looked at him curiously. "You talk funny, stranger," he said. "Where you from?"

"Oh, a freshwater school you never heard of."

"You look funny too. Kind of misty, so to speak."

"Tell me, colonel, what do you hear from Christopher Columbus?"

"Not much," Colonel Washington answered. "Been dead two, three hundred years."

"When did he die?"

"Year fifteen hundred some-odd, near as I remember."

"He did not. He died in 1489."

"Got your dates wrong, friend. He discovered America in 1492."

"Cabot discovered America. Sebastian Cabot."

"Nope. Cabot came a mite later."

"I have infallible proof!" Hassel began, but broke off as a stocky and rather stout man, with a face ludicrously reddened by rage, approached. He was wearing baggy gray slacks and a tweed jacket two sizes too small for him. He was carrying a .45 revolver. It was only after he had stared for a moment that Henry Hassel realized that he was looking at himself and not relishing the sight.

"My God!" Hassel murmured. "It's me, coming back to murder Washington that first time. If I'd made this second trip an hour later, I'd have found Washington dead. Hey!" he called. "Not yet. Hold off a minute. I've got to straighten something out first."

Hassel paid no attention to himself; indeed, he did not appear to be aware of himself. He marched straight up to Colonel Washington and shot him in the gizzard. Colonel Washington collapsed, emphatically dead. The first murderer inspected the body, and then, ignoring Hassel's attempt to stop him and engage him in dispute, turned and marched off, muttering venomously to himself.

"He didn't hear me," Hassel wondered. "He didn't even feel me. And why don't I remember myself trying to stop me the first time I shot the colonel? What the hell is going on?"

Considerably disturbed, Henry Hassel visited Chicago and dropped into the Chicago University squash courts in the early 1940s. There, in a slippery mess of graphite bricks and graphite dust that coated him, he located an Italian scientist named Fermi.

"Repeating Marie Curie's work, I see, *dottore*?" Hassel said.

Fermi glanced about as though he had heard a faint sound.

"Repeating Marie Curie's work, *dottore*?" Hassel roared.

Fermi looked at him strangely. "Where you from, *amico?*"

"State."

"State Department?"

"Just State. It's true, isn't it, *dottore*, that Marie Curie discovered nuclear fission back in nineteen ought ought?"

"No! No! No!" Fermi cried. "We are the first, and we are not there yet. Police! Police! Spy!"

"This time I'll go on record," Hassel growled. He pulled out his trusty .45, emptied it into Dr. Fermi's chest, and awaited arrest and immolation in newspaper files. To his amazement, Dr. Fermi did not collapse. Dr. Fermi merely explored his chest tenderly and, to the men who answered his cry, said, "It is nothing. I felt in my within a sudden sensation of burn which may be a neuralgia of the cardiac nerve, but is most likely gas."

Hassel was too agitated to wait for the automatic recall of the time machine. Instead he returned at once to Unknown University under his own power. This should have given him a clue, but he was too possessed to notice. It was at this time that I (1913–1975) first saw him—a dim figure tramping through parked cars, closed doors and brick walls, with the light of lunatic determination on his face.

He oozed into the library, prepared for an exhaustive discussion, but could not make himself felt or heard by the catalogues. He went to the Malpractice Laboratory, where Sam, the Simplex-and-Multiplex Computer, has installations sensitive up to 10,700 angstroms. Sam could not see Henry, but managed to hear him through a sort of wave-interference phenomenon.

"Sam," Hassel said, "I've made one hell of a discovery."

"You're always making discoveries, Henry," Sam complained. "Your data allocation is filled. Do I have to start another tape for you?"

"But I need advice. Who's the leading authority on time, reference to succession of, travel in?"

"That would be Israel Lennox, spatial mechanics, professor of, Yale."

"How do I get in touch with him?"

"You don't, Henry. He's dead. Died in '75."

"What authority have you got on time, travel in, living?"

"Wiley Murphy."

"Murphy? From our own Trauma Department? That's a break. Where is he now?"

"As a matter of fact, Henry, he went over to your house to ask you something."

Hassel went home without walking, searched through his laboratory and study without finding anyone, and at last floated into the living room, where his redheaded wife was still in the arms of another man. (All this, you understand, had taken place within the space of a few moments after the construction of the time machine; such is the nature of time and time travel.) Hassel cleared his throat once or twice and tried to tap his wife on the shoulder. His fingers went through her.

"Excuse me, darling," he said. "Has Wiley Murphy been in to see me?"

Then he looked closer and saw that the man embracing his wife was Murphy himself.

"Murphy!" Hassel exclaimed. "The very man I'm looking for. I've had the most extraordinary experience." Hassel at once launched into a lucid description of his extraordinary experience, which went something like this: "Murphy, $u - v = (u^{\frac{1}{2}} - v^{\frac{1}{4}})(u^a + u^x + v^y)$ but when George Washington $F(x)y^+ dx$ and Enrico Fermi $F(u^{\frac{1}{2}})$ dxdt one half of Marie Curie, then what about Christopher Columbus times the square root of minus one?"

Murphy ignored Hassel, as did Mrs. Hassel. I jotted down Hassel's equations on the hood of a passing taxi.

"Do listen to me, Murphy," Hassel said. "Greta dear, would you mind leaving us for a moment? I—For heaven's sake, will you two stop that nonsense? This is serious."

Hassel tried to separate the couple. He could no more touch them than make them hear him. His face turned red again and he became quite choleric as he beat at Mrs. Hassel and Murphy. It was like beating an Ideal Gas. I thought it best to interfere.

"Hassel!"

"Who's that?"

"Come outside a moment. I want to talk to you."

He shot through the wall. "Where are you?"

"Over here."

"You're sort of dim."

"So are you."

"Who are you?"

"My name's Lennox. Israel Lennox."

"Israel Lennox, spatial mechanics, professor of, Yale?"

"The same."

"But you died in '75."

"I disappeared in '75."

"What d'you mean?"

"I invented a time machine."

"By God! So did I," Hassel said. "This afternoon. The idea came to me in a flash—I don't know why—and I've had the most extraordinary experience. Lennox, time is not a continuum."

"No?"

"It's a series of discrete particles—like pearls on a string."

"Yes?"

"Each pearl is a 'Now.' Each 'Now' has its own past and future. But none of them relate to any others. You see? if $a = a_1 + a_2i + {}^xax\,(b_1)$—"

"Never mind the mathematics, Henry."

"It's a form of quantum transfer of energy. Time is emitted in discrete corpuscles or quanta. We can visit each individual quantum and make changes within it, but no change in any one corpuscle affects any other corpuscle. Right?"

"Wrong," I said sorrowfully.

"What d'you mean, 'Wrong'?" he said, angrily gesturing through the cleave of a passing coed. "You take the trochoid equations and—"

"Wrong," I repeated firmly. "Will you listen to me, Henry?"

"Oh, go ahead," he said.

"Have you noticed that you've become rather insubstantial? Dim? Spectral? Space and time no longer affect you?"

"Yes?"

"Henry, I had the misfortune to construct a time machine back in '75."

"So you said. Listen, what about power input? I figure I'm using about 7.3 kilowatts per—"

"Never mind the power input, Henry. On my first trip into the past, I visited the Pleistocene. I was eager to photograph the mastodon, the giant ground sloth, and the saber-tooth tiger. While I was backing up to get a mastodon fully in the field of view at f/6.3 at ⅟₁₀₀th of a second, or on the LVS scale—"

"Never mind the LVS scale," he said.

"While I was backing up, I inadvertently trampled and killed a small Pleistocene insect."

"Aha!" said Hassel.

"I was terrified by the incident. I had visions of returning to my world to find it completely changed as a result of this single death. Imagine my surprise when I returned to my world to find that nothing had changed."

"Oho!" said Hassel.

"I became curious. I went back to the Pleistocene and killed the mastodon. Nothing was changed in 1975. I returned to the Pleistocene and slaughtered the wildlife—still with no effect. I ranged through time, killing and destroying, in an attempt to alter the present."

"Then you did it just like me," Hassel exclaimed. "Odd we didn't run into each other."

"Not odd at all."

"I got Columbus."

"I got Marco Polo."

"I got Napoleon."

"I thought Einstein was more important."

"Mohammed didn't change things much—I expected more from *him*."

"I know. I got him too."

"What do you mean, you got him too?" Hassel demanded.

"I killed him September 16, 599. Old Style."

"Why, I got Mohammed January 5, 598."

"I believe you."

"But how could you have killed him after I killed him?"

"We both killed him."

"That's impossible."

"My boy," I said, "time is entirely subjective. It's a private matter—a personal experience. There is no such thing as objective time, just as there is no such thing as objective love, or an objective soul."

"Do you mean to say that time travel is impossible? But we've done it."

"To be sure, and many others, for all I know. But we each travel into our own past, and no other person's. There is no universal continuum, Henry. There are only billions of individuals, each with his own continuum; and one continuum cannot affect the other. We're like millions of strands of spaghetti in the same pot. No time traveler can ever meet another time traveler in the past or future. Each of us must travel up and down his own strand alone."

"But we're meeting each other now."

"We're no longer time travelers, Henry. We've become the spaghetti sauce."

"Spaghetti sauce?"

"Yes. You and I can visit any strand we like, because we've destroyed ourselves."

"I don't understand."

"When a man changes the past he only affects his own past—no one else's. The past is like memory. When you erase a man's memory, you wipe him out, but you don't wipe out anybody else's. You and I have erased our past. The individual worlds of the others go on, but we have ceased to exist."

"What d'you mean, 'ceased to exist'?"

"With each act of destruction we dissolved a little. Now we're all gone. We've committed chronicide. We're ghosts. I hope Mrs. Hassel will be very happy with Mr. Murphy. . . . Now let's go over to the Académie. Ampère is telling a great story about Ludwig Boltzmann."

MANUEL VAN LOGGEM

Pairpuppets

Translated by its author from the Dutch, this story deals with one of the grand themes of modern SF, the future of love. Since Aldous Huxley's Brave New World, *the nature of love and sex in the technological future has been a subject of speculation. In this collection we have examples of this theme in John Varley's "The Phantom of Kansas" and Brian Aldiss's "A Kind of Artistry," both more elaborate than "Pairpuppets," but no more pointed or ironic. "Pairpuppets" is notably a plotted story, in the manner of, say, Robert Sheckley, influenced by and written in imitation of American SF. Dutch SF has developed in recent decades in constant reference to American SF and only under the influence of translations of the contemporary flowering of SF in English.*

*   *   *

It's the end of our mutual service time," Eric said softly to himself, "and I'm not glad."

He was standing at the window and looking out over the polder far below him. The carefully calculated disorder of renovated mills and sham farms held less attraction for him than usual. He knew that he was on the brink of a new period in his life. Far away, on the lines of the horizon, he saw the contours of the gigantic machines that emitted a faint and incessant humming as the only evidence of their otherwise inscrutable activity; they glimmered faintly like a weak imitation of a reluctant sunset. "Like secret signals from outerspace invaders," Eric thought. He shook his head as if to drive out the waspish buzzing of continuous whining thoughts in his brain.

"Why do I think of aliens?"

He once had been on an instruction tour of the power stations. He knew that there was no living creature in the immense rooms where the computers drew their flashing runes on the glass screens. Only the contented purring of tame nuclear forces could be heard, like a smile in sound. They brought into movement the innumerable pivots, axles, and junctions through which all the vital necessities of life were distributed through the country.

Eric became conscious of a vague sense of fear caused by the sight of the vast expanse filled with rows of factories cleverly integrated with the artificial landscape. He recovered, however, quickly.

It was almost time for his appointment with his girl friend Tina. Her imminent visit filled him with lust, slightly dulled by weak vibrations of an almost imperceptible boredom. The delights of her body were known to him to the last details, as if they were the results of a programmed pleasure pattern, punched on a tape and tuned to his carnal receptors. "Fixed habits are bad for passion," he thought. "It really seems to mark the end of our service time. I should be glad to get a new partner, but I'm not."

He had agreed with Tina to perform the mating from behind this evening, with hand-and-mouth foreplay of half an hour, as was explained in the third chapter of the *Handbook for Fornication*. Eric knew that in former times the drive for pairing had been discharged in unbridled frenzy without any training. Much misery had been the result. Now good mating manners were already taught to children at the end of their anal phase.

With a certain sadness Eric remembered his initial experience after the first signs of sexual maturity had manifested themselves. He'd had the luck to be assigned to a wise, motherly initiator. His delights then must have equaled the religious thrills of ancient saints as described in books of cultic lore. He remembered the fever of orgasm when his thoughts had melted away in the heat of passion. His body had been engulfed by a white hollowness, giving him the sensation of becoming one with everything that existed. He now remained painfully himself in his polite and skilled mating bouts with Tina.

She arrived at the appointed moment. Eric poured her a glass of wine, inspecting her carefully while she was drinking, as if it were their first meeting.

She was supple and plump, with dark hair. Her eyes were big, almost black. She had an upturned nose and a wide, full mouth. Her teeth were large, healthy, and perfectly shaped. Eric liked women with an even set of teeth.

Tina and he were of the same age.

Eric knew that in former times people met in a haphazard way, falling in love without system or sense, according to the laws of chance, playthings of their hormones' whims. He also knew that this kind of higher madness had resulted in endless conflicts, leading people into the snares of legal matrimony, which made couples unhappy and children neurotic, and in the end disrupted society as a whole. Tina and he had been brought together in the only correct way. Out of all the people within a certain radius they were the most suited to each other. The boy's as well as the girl's conscious and unconscious desires, outer appearance, intelligence, tastes, and emotional patterns had been matched by one of the computers in the polder. This guaranteed a mutual understanding in the most fundamental aspects of personality. Tina was the ideal mate for him. He raised his glass and drank to her health. She smiled and returned his toast. It was a perfect preparation for things to come. Suddenly Eric felt more bored than he had thought possible. He undressed her and tried to feign impatient passion, even to make tears in her paper one-day underwear. When they were lying next to each other they started to perform the movements they both knew from their manual of instructions. Simultaneously with the deeper excitement, Eric felt the boredom growing ever stronger.

It was, perhaps, because they'd come to the end of their lovetime. For a short moment he considered marrying Tina, as the culmination and ending of their probation years. But they were both still too young for a final domiciliation, too far away from the mid-thirties, usually set for marriage. He had to go on with the carefully planned partnerships, at first loose and short, which would gradually increase in duration and stability, till, finally, he had reached the stage in which marital ties offered the best warrant for lasting harmony.

Yes, his affair with Tina was coming to an end. That might be the reason why she was more exacting than usual. Eric was already on the brink of exhaustion, wanting to rest, when Tina was still pushing on with unabated lust. He complied with her passion with a feeling of bitterness. When she was lying at his side, panting with obvious satisfaction, his thoughts were already with the new woman who would be assigned to him. It worried him that he would again be obliged to take her personal wishes and oddities into account. There was always a period of mutual adaptation between new mating partners. Sometimes it was a thrilling experience. Now the idea irritated Eric.

Tina got up from the bed. She dressed slowly with the well-known tired gestures, which were supposed to indicate that she had been so completely satisfied that she hardly had the strength to lift her arms. But there were lines of bitterness around her mouth and she was breathing fiercely, an obvious indication to Eric of how much unused energy she had to repress beneath her simulated languor. She, too, was not happy with the situation. He kissed her when she said good-bye. She pressed herself long enough against him to give the impression that she had to tear herself away, but it didn't last long enough to convey real attachment.

II

The next mating companion was more adapted than Tina had been to the weary irony Eric had developed during the last year. She showed much humor. She was subdued and sometimes shy, modest in her manifest desires, but developed a fierce sense of domination when Eric had prepared her extensively for the final thrust in bed. Her signs of satisfaction were overwhelming but they didn't give Eric the elation he would've experienced in a former period. Her unbridled discharge of lust had an aspect of calculated exaggeration, so Eric couldn't trust his own abilities as a skilled lover. She left him after a week. For the first time Eric learned that even computers could make mistakes. On this occasion the matching of the many items of information from the two candidates must have been imperfect. He accepted the fact with resignation but a feeling of failure still gnawed at him, adding a touch of disagreeable sharpness to his melancholy. Among the personal oddments the young woman had left behind was a fiercely colored pamphlet. A GOOD PAIRPUPPET IS A JOY FOREVER, flaming letters screamed from the cover. Eric wanted to throw it away with the rest. "A pairpuppet," he thought. "Good for the common people who prefer to be fobbed off with a custom-made dream, rather than to cope with the circumscribed pleasures of nature."

Yet he read on. He now realized that the woman who had left him had preferred the perfections of a pairpuppet to his limited abilities. It shocked him. In the circles of the artistic-minded intellectuals to which he belonged, vulgarity of this kind was till now unknown. Pairpuppets were good for people without imagination. "A pairpuppet is the ideal bed companion. The latest issue has been installed with a thermostat, which regulates the temperature of the skin according to the degree of excitement. The moisture of the skin and orifices, together with the movements (adapted to the special requirements of the buyer) and the appropriate sound, are built in with a remarkably high degree of authenticity. Our pairpuppets can only be distinguished from the natural product by their perfect pairing technique."

There was also a scientific report from the National Consumers Organization. Men and women had paired with the puppets under laboratory conditions. Their complaints had been carefully investigated, and their delights had been meticulously analyzed by the extremely sensitive instruments placed in the bodies of the volunteers. Their dreams also had been analyzed, in order to detect the primeval types of their desire. Their ideal images were compared with the four standard types of pairpuppets available for each sex. It appeared that they indeed represented the ideal prototypes. Their subtle powers of adaptation to the movements of their human pair companions were described as extremely satisfying. The sounds they produced had been shrewdly composed from the range of cries and groans taped during the experiments. The disdain with which Eric had at first read the booklet soon gave way to an uneasy libidinal fantasizing.

When he went to sleep he had decided to at least have a look in at the showroom.

The dream he still remembered the following morning greatly strengthened his decision.

The salesman received him with the smooth eagerness he had expected. In the showroom there were many people.

"How's business?" Eric asked.

"We can hardly satisfy the demand." From the tone of bewilderment in the salesman's voice Eric could hear that he meant it. "The use of pairpuppets seems to have suddenly become the fashion. We used to have clients only from certain circles, but now it seems that people in general are becoming fed up with people. And if I may say so, sir, pairpuppets are, indeed, much better. Since the latest models have come out, the experience with a pairpuppet has changed from a coarse pleasure to a refined delight."

He talked with the pepped-up optimism of a slogan manufacturer, but at the same time there was much genuine enthusiasm in his voice. Eric found it extremely difficult to make his choice. There were four types in each sex, able to satisfy the most common needs. There were subjugated and domineering women; cool beauties, who came slowly to their orgiastic frenzy, and unassuming motherfigures with warm breasts that gave a soft refuge for a man's head. For women there were broad-shouldered athletes and soft childlike types; cruel lovers and tender devotees.

"These basic forms can be delivered in different sizes and skin color," the salesman explained. "And for those who are not satisfied with the usual modes of pairing, there are some irregular types, hunchbacks for instance. They, of course, are much more expensive, but there's not much demand for them. In general, our eight types seem to be satisfactory."

"I don't find it easy to choose."

"That's not unusual, sir. But why don't you take the whole range. For variation. That's much cheaper, too. I've already sold a lot of series. Some customers even take the whole set of eight. As a free gift we supply a book about group-pairing with unparalleled techniques."

Eric chose a rather big redhead whose desire was swiftly aroused and who gave easily and abundantly, without requiring a long demonstration of carnal skills. He also let the salesman pack a small, shy puppet who came slowly to her climax and exacted much tenderness.

When he came home he carefully locked his apartment.

He called his best friend, Eberhard, with whom he had maintained a deep understanding ever since college; though they didn't meet too often. They made an appointment. The first thing Eric saw when he arrived at his friend's home was a couple of switched-off pairpuppets in a corner of the living room, a sign that Eberhard too had taken to the new fashion. His friend had also changed the arrangement of the furnishings. His polyester walls with changing light-sculptures—creative panels, as the inventor called them—had been exchanged for a wainscot of rough pinewood. There was a marked smell of resin around, so strong that it could only have been applied by spraying.

"I like it as a change," Eric said, when he had downed his first drink.

"A little bit rough. You could even call it old-fashioned, if it were not so unusual that it might now be called new-fashioned."

Eric was astonished.

"Where've you been all the time?"

"Mostly at home. I couldn't think of a better place to be. I've paired a lot. Then you don't have such a strong need to leave your home."

Eric saw that his friend wanted to answer. But Eberhard checked his speech.

"And now you're bored?" he asked at last, with such studied nonchalance that Eric became suspicious.

"Yes. How d'you know?"

"It's the general feeling. You would've known it too, if you hadn't locked yourself up so selfishly. It's already been going on for a long time, but when it started nobody had the courage to confess it. People are starting up the old forms of communication again, making appointments with friends; organizing parties; even talking to strangers in the street. Human beings are funny things. They're never satisfied."

He poured his visitor and himself another drink. "The common man still wants his pairpuppet," he continued. "And, if possible, a different type for every season. But among the more sophisticated people there is already a marked resistance. The intelligentsia want to return to nature."

"The mannerisms of today's tastemakers will become the manners of tomorrow's masses," Eric said. "Which means that pairpuppets will be out and we'll have to go back to nature."

He downed another drink. When he at last took his leave he was in a floating state of reckless insouciance. Outside, the autumn manifested itself in a pungent, spicy scent permeating the fresh air that already had a tinge of winter's cold.

Eric had hardly gone a few yards when a girl approached him. He looked at her, at first with amazement, then with pleasure. In the beginning he doubted whether she meant to contact him, but when he saw that she was looking behind her, he knew that she was deliberately trying to attract his attention.

He turned and followed her. She looked attractive from behind; small, dark, with narrow and yet well-shaped legs. Proportionally she couldn't compare with the perfectly built pairpuppets, but she was a living creature, young and probably full of lust.

Then, suddenly, he understood why she was contacting him so obviously and yet without the professional skill characteristic of the type of women who in former times had roamed the streets for business. She had done it because he was a living man and because she probably had developed as much distaste for her pairpuppets as Eric had for his own perfect lust objects. He followed her. He became soft with sensuous appetite and soon he had overtaken her. She smiled when he addressed her.

"I assume you wanted me to follow you?"

She was young enough to have preserved the beauty of youth and yet sufficiently advanced in age for a ripeness in experience. This kind of woman attracted Eric most of all.

She took him by the hand and pulled him after her. Suddenly he fell in love with her. He had been used to the perfect streamline of delight for too long and now he realized how much genuine love he had missed. All his repressed affection broke out and he became dizzy from the strong attachment that broke loose within him.

"What's your name?"

She didn't answer. She was walking faster and faster, almost running. Now he could confirm his first impression that she wasn't beautiful. She had an irregular face, her nose was too long, and her mouth was too large. When she smiled he saw that her front teeth were crooked. But the combination of irregular features attracted him more strongly than the smooth principles after which his pairpuppets had been manufactured. He found it more of a pleasure than a hindrance that her skin was too dark and too coarse and that there were pigment spots on her forehead. At any rate, she was natural.

Outside the city she pulled him into a dry ditch. They didn't undress. She was in too much of a hurry. They mounted each other like adolescents whose immediate lust is too strong for the more refined delights of preparatory delay. They paired like animals, swiftly, grossly, without caring for each other's needs.

It was an overwhelming experience for Eric, as powerful as the first time. In a certain sense it was the first time. Now he knew that pairpuppets had been a transient misconception. In the long run, only pairing with an imperfect human being could give true satisfaction.

Tenderly he looked at the woman lying next to him. She had closed her eyes. She was breathing softly. He touched her. She opened her mouth.

"I'm Elly," she said in a warm and yet businesslike tone. "I am the improved version of the pairpuppet. I am an experimental specimen. Will you be so kind as to give me your critical remarks with regard to my behavior. They are being taped and they will be carefully considered. You may leave me where I am. I'm able to return to the factory without assistance."

Two Dooms

Cyril M. Kornbluth was already a published writer as a teenager in the late 1930s. A member of the Futurians, he remained eclipsed by the dominance of Campbell's Astounding, *along with most of his peers, until the beginning of the 1950s, when major new SF magazines such as* Galaxy *and* The Magazine of Fantasy & Science Fiction *began to publish his dark, ironic fictions. In collaboration with Frederik Pohl, he wrote a series of satirical SF novels, including the classic* The Space Merchants. *He was becoming one of the most respected and accomplished SF writers when he died suddenly of a heart attack at age 35 in 1958. "Two Dooms," published posthumously that year, is a political story set in an alternate universe, one in which Germany has won World War II. This device provides the basis for a number of significant works, including Philip K. Dick's award-winning* The Man in the High Castle, *Keith Roberts's "Weihnachtsabend" (included in this anthology), and Brad Linaweaver's "Moon of Ice."*

* * *

It was May, not yet summer by five weeks, but the afternoon heat under the corrugated roofs of Manhattan Engineer District's Los Alamos Laboratory was daily less bearable. Young Dr. Edward Royland had lost fifteen pounds from an already meager frame during his nine-month hitch in the desert. He wondered every day while the thermometer crawled up to its 5:45 peak whether he had made a mistake he would regret the rest of his life in accepting work with the Laboratory rather than letting the local draft board have his carcass and do what they pleased with it. His University of Chicago classmates were glamorously collecting ribbons and wounds from Saipan to Brussels; one of them, a first-rate mathematician named Hatfield, would do no more first-rate mathematics. He had gone down, burning, in an Eighth Air Force Mitchell bomber ambushed over Lille.

"And what, Daddy, did you do in the war?"

"Well, kids, it's a little hard to explain. They had this stupid atomic bomb project that never came to anything, and they tied up a lot of us in a Godforsaken place in New Mexico. We figured and we calculated and we fooled with uranium and some of us got radiation burns and then the war was over and they sent us home."

Royland was not amused by this prospect. He had heat rash under his arms and he was waiting, not patiently, for the Computer Section to send him his figures on Phase 56c, which was the (god-damn childish) code designation for Element Assembly Time. Phase 56c was Royland's own particular baby. He was under Rotschmidt, supervisor of WEAPON DESIGN TRACK III, and Rotschmidt was under Oppenheimer, who bossed the works. Sometimes a General Groves came through, a fine figure of a man, and once from a window Royland had seen the venerable Henry L. Stimson, Secretary of War, walking slowly down their dusty street, leaning on a cane and surrounded by young staff officers. That's what Royland was seeing of the war.

Laboratory! It had sounded inviting, cool, bustling but quiet. So every morning these days he was blasted out of his cot in a barracks cubicle at seven by "Oppie's whistle," fought for a shower and shave with thirty-seven other bachelor scientists in eight languages, bolted a bad cafeteria breakfast, and went through the barbed-wired Restricted Line to his "office" — another matchboard-walled cubicle, smaller and hotter and noisier, with talking and typing and clack of adding machines all around him.

Under the circumstances he was doing good work, he supposed. He wasn't happy about being restricted to his one tiny problem, Phase 56c, but no doubt he was happier than Hatfield had been when his Mitchell got it.

Under the circumstances . . . they included a weird haywire arrangement for computing. Instead of a decent differential analyzer machine they had a human sea of office girls with Burroughs' desk calculators; the girls screamed "Banzai!" and charged on differential equations and swamped them by sheer volume; they clicked them to death with their little adding machines. Royland thought hungrily of Conant's huge, beautiful analog differentiator up at M.I.T.; it was probably tied up by whatever the mysterious "Radiation Laboratory" there was doing. Royland suspected that the "Radiation Laboratory" had as much to do with radiation as his own

"Manhattan Engineer District" had to do with Manhattan engineering. And the world was supposed to be trembling on the edge these days of a New Dispensation of Computing that would obsolete even the M.I.T. machine—tubes, relays, and binary arithmetic at blinding speed instead of the suavely turning cams and the smoothly extruding rods and the elegant scribed curves of Conant's masterpiece. He decided that he wouldn't like that; he would like it even less than he liked the little office girls clacking away, pushing lank hair from their dewed brows with undistracted hands.

He wiped his own brow with a sodden handkerchief and permitted himself a glance at his watch and the thermometer. Five-fifteen and 103 Fahrenheit.

He thought vaguely of getting out, of fouling up just enough to be released from the project and drafted. No; there was the post-war career to think of. But one of the big shots, Teller, had been irrepressible; he had rambled outside of his assigned mission again and again until Oppenheimer let him go; now Teller was working with Lawrence at Berkeley on something that had reputedly gone sour at a reputed quarter of a billion dollars—

A girl in khaki knocked and entered. "Your material from the Computer Section, Dr. Royland. Check them and sign here, please." He counted the dozen sheets, signed the clipboarded form she held out, and plunged into the material for thirty minutes.

When he sat back in his chair, the sweat dripped into his eyes unnoticed. His hands were shaking a little, though he did not know that either. Phase 56c of WEAPON DESIGN TRACK III was finished, over, done, successfully accomplished. The answer to the question "Can U_{235} slugs be assembled into a critical mass within a physically feasible time?" was in. The answer was "Yes."

Royland was a theory man, not a Wheatstone or a Kelvin; he liked the numbers for themselves and had no special passion to grab for wires, mica, and bits of graphite so that what the numbers said might immediately be given flesh in a wonderful new gadget. Nevertheless he could visualize at once a workable atomic bomb assembly within the framework of Phase 56c. You have so many microseconds to assemble your critical mass without it boiling away in vapor; you use them by blowing the subassemblies together with shaped charges; lots of microseconds to spare by that method; practically foolproof. Then comes the Big Bang.

Oppie's whistle blew; it was quitting time. Royland sat still in his cubicle. He should go, of course, to Rotschmidt and tell him; Rotschmidt would probably clap him on the back and pour him a jigger of Bols Geneva from the tall clay bottle he kept in his safe. Then Rotschmidt would go to Oppenheimer. Before sunset the project would be redesigned! TRACK I,

Track II, Track IV, and Track V would be shut down and their people crammed into Track III, the one with the paydirt! New excitement would boil through the project; it had been torpid and souring for three months. Phase 56c was the first good news in at least that long; it had been one damned blind alley after another. General Groves had looked sour and dubious last time around.

Desk drawers were slamming throughout the corrugated, sun-baked building; doors were slamming shut on cubicles; down the corridor, somebody roared with laughter, strained laughter. Passing Royland's door somebody cried impatiently: "—*aber was kan Man tun?*"

Royland whispered to himself: "You damned fool, what are you thinking of?"

But he knew—he was thinking of the Big Bang, the Big Dirty Bang, and of torture. The judicial torture of the old days, incredibly cruel by today's lights, stretched the whole body, or crushed it, or burned it, or shattered the fingers and legs. But even that old judicial torture carefully avoided the most sensitive parts of the body, the generative organs, though damage to these, or a real threat of damage to these, would have produced quick and copious confessions. You have to be more or less crazy to torture somebody that way; the sane man does not think of it as a possibility.

An M.P. corporal tried Royland's door and looked in. "Quitting time, professor," he said.

"Okay," Royland said. Mechanically, he locked his desk drawers and his files, turned his window lock, and set out his waste-paper basket in the corridor. Click the door; another day, another dollar.

Maybe the project *was* breaking up. They did now and then. The huge boner at Berkeley proved that. And Royland's barracks was light two physicists now; their cubicles stood empty since they had been drafted to M.I.T. for some anti-submarine thing. Groves had *not* looked happy last time around; how did a general make up his mind anyway? Give them three months, then the ax? Maybe Stimson would run out of patience and cut the loss, close the District down. Maybe F.D.R. would say at a Cabinet meeting, "By the way, Henry, what ever became of—?" and that would be the end if old Henry could say only that the scientists appear to be optimistic of eventual success, Mr. President, but that as yet there seems to be nothing *concrete*—

He passed through the barbed wire of the Line under scrutiny of an M.P. lieutenant and walked down the barracks-edged company street of the maintenance troops to their motor pool. He wanted a jeep and a trip ticket; he wanted a long desert drive in the twilight; he wanted a dinner of *frijoles* and eggplant with his old friend Charles Miller Nahataspe, the medicine man of the adjoining Hopi reservation. Royland's hobby was anthropology; he wanted to get a little drunk on it—he hoped it would clear his mind.

Nahataspe welcomed him cheerfully to his hut; his million wrinkles all smiled. "You want me to play informant for a while?" he grinned. He had been to Carlisle in the 1880's and had been laughing at the white man ever since; he admitted that physics was funny, but for a real joke give him cultural anthropology every time. "You want some nice unsavory stuff about our institutionalized homosexuality? Should I cook us a dog for dinner? Have a seat on the blanket, Edward."

"What happened to your chairs? And the funny picture of McKinley? And—and everything?" The hut was bare except for cooking pots that simmered on the stone-curbed central hearth.

"I gave the stuff away," Nahataspe said carelessly. "You get tired of things."

Royland thought he knew what that meant. Nahataspe believed he would die quite soon; these particular Indians did not believe in dying encumbered by possessions. Manners, of course, forbade discussing death.

The Indian watched his face and finally said: "Oh, it's all right for *you* to talk about it. Don't be embarrassed."

Royland asked nervously: "Don't you feel well?"

"I feel terrible. There's a snake eating my liver. Pitch in and eat. You feel pretty awful yourself, don't you?"

The hard-learned habit of security caused Royland to evade the question. "You don't mean that literally about the snake, do you Charles?"

"Of course I do," Miller insisted. He scooped a steaming gourd full of stew from the pot and blew on it. "What would an untutored child of nature know about bacteria, viruses, toxins, and neoplasms? What would I know about break-the-sky medicine?"

Royland looked up sharply; the Indian was blandly eating. "Do you hear any talk about break-the-sky medicine?" Royland asked.

"No talk, Edward. I've had a few dreams about it." He pointed with his chin toward the Laboratory. "You fellows over there shouldn't dream so hard; it leaks out."

Royland helped himself to stew without answering. The stew was good, far better than the cafeteria stuff, and he did not *have* to guess the source of the meat in it.

Miller said consolingly: "It's only kid stuff, Edward. Don't get so worked up about it. We have a long dull story about a horned toad who ate some loco-weed and thought he was the Sky God. He got angry and he tried to break the sky but he couldn't so he slunk into his hole ashamed to face all the other animals and died. But they never knew he tried to break the sky at all."

In spite of himself Royland demanded: "Do you have any stories about anybody who did break the sky?" His hands were shaking again and his voice almost hysterical. Oppie and the rest of them were going to break the sky, kick humanity right in the crotch, and unleash a prowling monster that would go up and down by night and day peering in all the windows of all the houses in the world, leaving no sane man ever unterrified for his life and the lives of his kin. Phase 56c, God-damn it to blackest hell, made sure of that! Well done, Royland; you earned your dollar today!

Decisively the old Indian set his gourd aside. He said: "We have a saying that the only good paleface is a dead paleface, but I'll make an exception for you, Edward. I've got some strong stuff from Mexico that will make you feel better. I don't like to see my friends hurting."

"Peyote? I've tried it. Seeing a few colored lights won't make me feel better, but thanks."

"Not peyote, this stuff. It's God Food. I wouldn't take it myself without a month of preparation; otherwise the Gods would scoop me up in a net. That's because my people see clearly, and your eyes are clouded." He was busily rummaging through a clay-chinked wicker box as he spoke; he came up with a covered dish. "You people have your sight cleared just a little by the God Food, so it's safe for you."

Royland thought he knew what the old man was talking about. It was one of Nahataspe's biggest jokes that Hopi children understood Einstein's relativity as soon as they could talk—and there was some truth to it. The Hopi language—and thought—had no tenses and therefore no concept of time-as-an-entity; it had nothing like the Indo-European speech's subjects and predicates, and therefore no built-in metaphysics of cause and effect. In the Hopi language and mind all things were frozen together forever into one great relationship, a crystalline structure of space-time events that simply were because they were. So much for Nahataspe's people "seeing clearly." But Royland gave himself and any other physicist credit for seeing as clearly when they were working a four-dimensional problem in the X Y Z space variables and the T time variable.

He could have spoiled the old man's joke by pointing that out, but of course he did not. No, no, he'd get a jag and maybe a bellyache from Nahataspe's herb medicine and then go home to his cubicle with his problem unresolved: to kick or not to kick?

The old man began to mumble in Hopi, and drew a tattered cloth across the door frame of his hut; it shut out the last rays of the setting sun, long and slanting on the desert, pink-red against the adobe cubes of the Indian settlement. It took a minute for Royland's eyes to accommodate to the flickering light from the hearth and the indigo square of the ceiling smoke hole. Now Nahataspe was "dancing," doing a crouched shuffle around the hut holding the covered dish before him. Out of the corner of his mouth, without interrupting the rhythm, he said to Royland: "Drink some hot water now." Royland sipped from one of the pots on the hearth; so far it was much like peyote ritual, but he felt calmer.

Nahataspe uttered a loud scream, added apologetically: "Sorry, Edward," and crouched before him whipping the cover off the dish like a headwaiter. So God Food was dried black mushrooms, miserable, wrinkled little things. "You swallow them all and chase them with hot water," Nahataspe said.

Obediently Royland choked them down and gulped from the jug; the old man resumed his dance and chanting.

A little old self-hypnosis, Royland thought bitterly. Grab some imitation sleep and forget about old 56c, as if you could. He could see the big dirty one now, a hell of a fireball, maybe over Munich, or Cologne, or Tokyo, or Nara. Cooked people, fused cathedral stone, the bronze of the big Buddha running like water, perhaps lapping around the ankles of a priest and burning his feet off so he fell prone into the stuff. He couldn't see the gamma radiation, but it would be there, invisible sleet doing the dirty unthinkable thing, coldly burning away the sex of men and women, cutting short so many fans of life at their points of origin. Phase 56c could snuff out a family of Bachs, or five generations of Bernoullis, or see to it that the great Huxley-Darwin cross did not occur.

The fireball loomed, purple and red and fringed with green—

The mushrooms were reaching him, he thought fuzzily. He could really see it. Nahataspe, crouched and treading, moved through the fireball just as he had the last time, and the time before that. Déjà vu, extraordinarily strong, stronger than ever before, gripped him. Royland knew all this had happened to him before, and remembered perfectly what would come next; it was on the very tip of his tongue, as they say—

The fireballs began to dance around him and he felt his strength drain suddenly out; he was lighter than a feather; the breeze would carry him away; he would be blown like a dust mote into the circle that the circling fireballs made. And he knew it was wrong. He croaked with the last of his energy, feeling himself slip out of the world: "Charlie! Help!"

Out of the corner of his mind as he slipped away he sensed that the old man was pulling him now under the arms, trying to tug him out of the hut, crying dimly into his ear: "You should have told me you did not see through smoke! You see clear; I never knew; I nev—"

And then he slipped through into blackness and silence.

Royland awoke sick and fuzzy; it was morning in the hut; there was no sign of Nahataspe. Well. Unless the old man had gotten to a phone and reported to the Laboratory, there were now jeeps scouring the desert in search of him and all hell was breaking loose in Security and Personnel. He would catch some of that hell on his return, and avert it with his news about assembly time.

Then he noticed that the hut had been cleaned of Nahataspe's few remaining possessions, even to the door cloth. A pang went through him; had the old man died in the night? He limped from the hut and looked around for a funeral pyre, a crowd of mourners. They were not there; the adobe cubes stood untenanted in the sunlight, and more weeds grew in the single street than he remembered. And his jeep, parked last night against the hut, was missing.

There were no wheeltracks, and uncrushed weeds grew tall where the jeep had stood.

Nahataspe's God Food had been powerful stuff. Royland's hand crept uncertainly to his face. No; no beard.

He looked about him, looked hard. He made the effort necessary to see details. He did not glance at the hut and because it was approximately the same as it had always been, concluded that it was unchanged, eternal. He looked and saw changes everywhere. Once-sharp adobe corners were rounded; protruding roof beams were bleached bone-white by how many years of desert sun? The wooden framing of the deep fortress-like windows had crumbled; the third building from him had wavering soot stains above its window boles and its beams were charred.

He went to it, numbly thinking: Phase 56c at least is settled. Not old Rip's baby now. They'll know me from fingerprints, I guess. One year? Ten? I *feel* the same.

The burned-out house was a shambles. In one corner were piled dry human bones. Royland leaned dizzily against the doorframe; its charcoal crumbled and streaked his hand. Those skulls were Indian—he was anthropologist enough to know that. Indian men, women and children, slain and piled in a heap. Who kills Indians? There should have been some sign of clothes, burned rags, but there were none. Who strips Indians naked and kills them?

Signs of a dreadful massacre were everywhere in the house. Bulletpocks in the walls, high and low. Savage nicks left by bayonets—and swords? Dark stains of blood; it had run two inches high and left its mark. Metal glinted in a ribcage across the room. Swaying, he walked to the bone-heap and thrust his hand into it. The thing bit him like a razor blade; he did not look at it as he plucked it out and carried it to the dusty street. With his back turned to the burned house he studied his find. It was a piece of swordblade six inches long, hand-honed to a perfect edge with a couple of nicks in it. It had stiffening ribs and the usual blood gutters. It had a perceptible curve that would fit into only one shape: the Samurai sword of Japan.

However long it had taken, the war was obviously over.

He went to the village well and found it choked with dust. It was while he stared into the dry hole that he first became afraid. Suddenly it all was real; he was no more an onlooker but a frightened and very thirsty man. He ransacked the dozen houses of the settlement and found nothing to his purpose—a child's skeleton here, a couple of cartridge cases there.

There was only one thing left, and that was the road, the same earth track it had always been, wide enough for one jeep or the rump-sprung station wagon of the Indian settlement that once had been. Panic invited him to run; he did not yield. He sat on the well curb, took off his shoes to meticulously smooth wrinkles out of his khaki G.I. socks, put the shoes on, and retied the laces loosely enough to allow for swelling, and hesitated a moment. Then he grinned, selected two pebbles carefully from the dust and popped them into his mouth. "Beaver Patrol, forward march," he said, and began to hike.

Yes, he was thirsty; soon he would be hungry and tired; what of it? The dirt road would meet state-maintained blacktop in three miles and then there would be traffic and he'd hitch a ride. Let them argue with his fingerprints if they felt like it. The Japanese had got as far as New Mexico, had they? Then God help their home islands when the counterblow had come. Americans were a ferocious people when trespassed on. Conceivably, there was not a Japanese left alive. . . .

He began to construct his story as he hiked. In large parts it was a repeated "I don't know." He would tell them: "I don't expect you to believe this, so my feelings won't be hurt when you don't. Just listen to what I say and hold everything until the F.B.I. has checked my fingerprints. My name is—" And so on.

It was midmorning then, and he would be on the highway soon. His nostrils, sharpened by hunger, picked up a dozen scents on the desert breeze: the spice of sage, a whiff of acetylene stink from a rattler dozing on the shaded side of a rock, the throat-tightening reek of tar suggested for a moment on the air. That would be the highway, perhaps a recent hotpatch on a chuckhole. Then a startling tang of sulfur dioxide drowned them out and passed on, leaving him stung and sniffling and groping for a hand-kerchief that was not there. What in God's name had that been, and where from? Without ceasing to trudge he studied the horizon slowly and found a smoke pall to the far west dimly smudging the sky. It looked like a small city's, or a fair-sized factory's, pollution. A city or a factory where "in his time"—he formed the thought reluctantly—there had been none.

Then he was at the highway. It had been improved; it was a two-laner still, but it was nicely graded now, built up by perhaps three inches of gravel and tar beyond its old level, and lavishly ditched on either side.

If he had a coin he would have tossed it, but you went for weeks without spending a cent at Los Alamos Laboratory; Uncle took care of everything, from cigarettes to tombstones. He turned left and began to walk westward toward that sky smudge.

I am a reasonable animal, he was telling himself, and I will accept whatever comes in a spirit of reason. I will control what I can and try to understand the rest—

A faint siren scream began behind him and built up fast. The reasonable animal jumped for the ditch and hugged it for dear life. The siren howled closer, and motors roared. At the ear-splitting climax Royland put his head up for one glimpse, then fell back into the ditch as if a grenade had exploded in his middle.

The convoy roared on, down the *center* of the two-lane highway, strad-dling the white line. First the three little recon cars with the twin-mount machine guns, each filled brimful with three helmeted Japanese soldiers. Then the high-profiled, armored car of state, six-wheeled, with a probably ceremonial gun turret astern—nickel-plated gunbarrels are impractical—and the Japanese admiral in the fore-and-aft hat taking his lordly ease beside a rawboned, hatchet-faced SS officer in gleaming black. Then, dimin-uendo, two more little recon jobs. . . .

"We've lost," Royland said in his ditch meditatively. "Ceremonial tanks with glass windows—we lost a *long* time ago." Had there been a Rising Sun insignia or was he now imagining that?

He climbed out and continued to trudge westward on the improved blacktop. You couldn't say "I reject the universe," not when you were as thirsty as he was.

He didn't even turn when the put-putting of a west-bound vehicle grew loud behind him and then very loud when it stopped at his side.

"Zeegail," a curious voice said. "What are you doing here?"

The vehicle was just as odd in its own way as the ceremonial tank. It was minimum motor transportation, a kid's sled on wheels, powered by a noisy little air-cooled outboard motor. The driver sat with no more comfort than a cleat to back his coccyx against, and behind him were two twenty-five-pound flour sacks that took up all the remaining room the little buckboard provided. The driver had the leathery Southwestern look; he wore a baggy blue outfit that was obviously a uniform and obviously unmilitary. He had a nametape on his breast above the incomprehensible row of dull ribbons: MARTFIELD, E., 1218824, P/7 NQOTD43. He saw Royland's eyes on the tape and said kindly: "My name is Martfield—Paymaster Seventh, but there's no need to use my rank here. Are you all right, my man?"

"Thirsty," Royland said. "What's the NQOTD43 for?"

"You can read!" Martfield said, astounded. "Those clothes—"

"Something to drink, please," Royland said. For the moment nothing else mattered in the world. He sat down on the buckboard like a puppet with cut strings.

"See here, fellow!" Martfield snapped in a curious, strangled way, forcing the words through his throat with a stagy, conventional effort of controlled anger. "You can stand until I invite you to sit!"

"Have you any water?" Royland asked dully.

With the same bark: "Who do you think you are?"

"I happen to be a theoretical physicist—" tiredly arguing with a dim seventh-carbon-copy imitation of a drill sergeant.

"Oh-*hoh*!" Martfield suddenly laughed. His stiffness vanished; he actually reached into his baggy tunic and brought out a pint canteen that gurgled. He then forgot all about the canteen in his hand, roguishly dug Royland in the ribs and said: "I should have suspected. You scientists! Somebody was supposed to pick you up—but he was another scientist, eh? Ah-hah-hah-hah!"

Royland took the canteen from his hand and sipped. So a scientist was supposed to be an idiot-savant, eh? Never mind now; drink. People said you were not supposed to fill your stomach with water after great thirst; it sounded to him like one of those puritanical rules people make up out of nothing because they sound reasonable. He finished the canteen while Martfield, Paymaster Seventh, looked alarmed, and wished only that there were three or four more of them.

"Got any food?" he demanded.

Martfield cringed briefly. "Doctor, I regret extremely that I have nothing with me. However if you would do me the honor of riding with me to my quarters—"

"Let's go," Royland said. He squatted on the flour sacks and away they chugged at a good thirty miles an hour; it was a fair little engine. The

Paymaster Seventh continued deferential, apologizing over his shoulder because there was no windscreen, later dropped his cringing entirely to explain that Royland was seated on flour—"*white* flour, understand?" An over-the-shoulder wink. He had a friend in the bakery at Los Alamos. Several buckboards passed the other way as they traveled. At each encounter there was a peering examination of insignia to decide who saluted. Once they met a sketchily enclosed vehicle that furnished its driver with a low seat instead of obliging him to sit with legs straight out, and Paymaster Seventh Martfield almost dislocated his shoulder saluting first. The driver of that one was a Japanese in a kimono. A long curved sword lay across his lap.

Mile after mile the smell of sulfur and sulfides increased; finally there rose before them the towers of a Frasch Process layout. It looked like an oilfield, but instead of ground-laid pipelines and bass-drum storage tanks there were foothills of yellow sulfur. They drove between them—more salutes from baggily uniformed workers with shovels and yard-long Stilson wrenches. Off to the right were things that might have been Solvay Process towers for sulfuric acid, and a glittering horror of a neo-Roman administration-and-labs building. The Rising Sun banner fluttered from its central flagstaff.

Music surged as they drove deeper into the area; first it was a welcome counterirritant to the pop-pop of the two cycle buckboard engine, and then a nuisance by itself. Royland looked, annoyed, for the loudspeakers, and saw them everywhere—on power poles, buildings, gateposts. Schmaltzy Strauss waltzes bathed them like smog, made thinking just a little harder, made communication just a little more blurry even after you had learned to live with the noise.

"I miss music in the wilderness," Martfield confided over his shoulder. He throttled down the buckboard until they were just rolling; they had passed some line unrecognized by Royland beyond which one did not salute everybody—just the occasional Japanese walking by in business suit with blueprint-roll and slide rule, or in kimono with sword. It was a German who nailed Royland, however: a classic jack-booted German in black broadcloth, black leather, and plenty of silver trim. He watched them roll for a moment after exchanging salutes with Martfield, made up his mind, and said: "Halt."

The Paymaster Seventh slapped on the brake, killed the engine, and popped to attention beside the buckboard. Royland more or less imitated him. The German said, stiffly but without accent: "Whom have you brought here, Paymaster?"

"A scientist, sir. I picked him up on the road returning from Los Alamos with personal supplies. He appears to be a minerals prospector who missed a rendezvous, but naturally I have not questioned the Doctor."

The German turned to Royland contemplatively. "So, Doctor. Your name and specialty."

"Dr. Edward Royland," he said. "I do nuclear power research." If there was no bomb he'd be damned if he'd invent it now for these people.

"So? That is very interesting, considering that there is no such thing as nuclear power research. Which camp are you from?" The German threw an aside to the Paymaster Seventh, who was literally shaking with fear at the turn things had taken. "You may go, Paymaster. Of course you will report yourself for harboring a fugitive."

"At once, sir," Martfield said in a sick voice. He moved slowly away pushing the little buckboard before him. The Strauss waltz oom-pah'd its last chord and instantly the loudspeakers struck up a hoppity-hoppity folk dance, heavy on the brass.

"Come with me," the German said, and walked off, not even looking behind to see whether Royland was obeying. This itself demonstrated how unlikely any disobedience was to succeed. Royland followed at his heels, which of course were garnished with silver spurs. Royland had not seen a horse so far that day.

A Japanese stopped them politely inside the administration building, a rimless-glasses, office-manager type in a gray suit. "How nice to see you again, Major Kappel! Is there anything I might do to help you?"

The German stiffened. "I didn't want to bother your people, Mr. Ito. This fellow appears to be a fugitive from one of our camps; I was going to turn him over to our liaison group for examination and return."

Mr. Ito looked at Royland and slapped his face hard. Royland, by the insanity of sheer reflex, cocked his fist as a red-blooded boy should, but the German's reflexes operated also. He had a pistol in his hand and pressed against Royland's ribs before he could throw the punch.

"All right," Royland said, and put down his hand.

Mr. Ito laughed. "You are at least partly right, Major Kappel; he certainly is not from one of *our* camps! But do not let me delay you further. May I hope for a report on the outcome of this?"

"Of course, Mr. Ito," said the German. He holstered his pistol and walked on, trailed by the scientist. Royland heard him grumble something that sounded like "Damned extraterritoriality!"

They descended to a basement level where all the door signs were in German, and in an office labeled WISSENSCHAFTSLICHESICHERHEITS-LIAISON Royland finally told his story. His audience was the major, a fat officer deferentially addressed as Colonel Biederman, and a bearded old civilian, a Dr. Piqueron, called in from another office. Royland suppressed only the matter of bomb research, and did it easily with the old security habit. His improvised cover story made the Los Alamos Laboratory a research center only for the generation of electricity.

The three heard him out in silence. Finally, in an amused voice, the colonel asked: "Who was this Hitler you mentioned?"

For that Royland was not prepared. His jaw dropped.

Major Kappel said: "Oddly enough, he struck on a name which does figure, somewhat infamously, in the annals of the Third Reich. One Adolf Hitler was an early Party agitator, but as I recall it he intrigued against the Leader during the War of Triumph and was executed."

"An ingenious madman," the colonel said. "Sterilized, of course?"

"Why, I don't know. I suppose so. Doctor, would you—?"

Dr. Piqueron quickly examined Royland and found him all there, which astonished them. Then they thought of looking for his camp tattoo number on the left bicep, and found none. Then, thoroughly upset, they discovered that he had no birth number above his left nipple either.

"And," Dr. Piqueron stammered, "his shoes are odd, sir—I just noticed. Sir, how long since you've seen sewn shoes and braided laces?"

"You must be hungry," the colonel suddenly said. "Doctor, have my aide get something to eat for—for the doctor."

"Major," said Royland, "I hope no harm will come to the fellow who picked me up. You told him to report himself."

"Have no fear, er, doctor," said the major. "Such humanity! You are of German blood?"

"Not that I know of; it may be."

"It *must* be!" said the colonel.

A platter of hash and a glass of beer arrived on a tray. Royland postponed everything. At last he demanded: "Now. Do you believe me? There must be fingerprints to prove my story still in existence."

"I feel like a fool," the major said. "You still could be hoaxing us. Dr. Piqueron, did not a German scientist establish that nuclear power is a theoretical and practical impossibility, that one always must put more into it than one can take out?"

Piqueron nodded and said reverently: "Heisenberg. Nineteen fifty-three, during the War of Triumph. His group was then assigned to electrical weapons research and produced the blinding bomb. But this fact does not invalidate the doctor's story; he says only that his group was *attempting* to produce nuclear power."

"We've got to research this," said the colonel. "Dr. Piqueron, entertain this man, whatever he is, in your laboratory."

Piqueron's laboratory down the hall was a place of astounding simplicity, even crudeness. The sinks, reagents, and balance were capable only of simple qualitative and quantitative analysis; various works in progress testified that they were not even strained to their modest limits. Samples of sulfur and its compounds were analyzed here. It hardly seemed to call for a "doctor" of anything, and hardly even for a human being. Machinery should be continuously testing the products as they flowed out; variations should be scribed mechanically on a moving tape; automatic controls should at least stop the processes and signal an alarm when variation went beyond limits; at most it might correct whatever was going wrong. But here sat Piqueron every day, titrating, precipitating, and weighing, entering results by hand in a ledger and telephoning them to the works!

Piqueron looked about proudly. "As a physicist you wouldn't understand all this, of course," he said. "Shall I explain?"

"Perhaps later, doctor, if you'd be good enough. If you'd first help me orient myself—"

So Piqueron told him about the War of Triumph (1940–1955) and what came after.

In 1940 the realm of der Fuehrer (Herr Goebbels, of course—that strapping blond fellow with the heroic jaw and eagle's eye whom you can see in the picture there) was simultaneously and treacherously invaded by the misguided French, the sub-human Slavs, and the perfidious British. The attack, for which the shocked Germans coined the name *blitzkrieg*, was timed to coincide with an internal eruption of sabotage, well-poisoning, with assassination by the *Zigeunerjuden*, or Jewspies, of whom little is now known; there seem to be none left.

By Nature's ineluctable law, the Germans had necessarily to be tested to the utmost so that they might fully respond. Therefore Germany was overrun from East and West, and Holy Berlin itself was taken; but Goebbels and his court withdrew like Barbarossa into the mountain fastness to await their day. It came unexpectedly soon. The deluded Americans launched a million-man amphibious attack on the homeland of the Japanese in 1945. The Japanese resisted with almost Teutonic courage. Not one American in twenty reached shore alive, and not one in a hundred got a mile inland. Particularly lethal were the women and children, who lay in camouflaged pits hugging artillery shells and aircraft bombs, which they detonated when enough invaders drew near to make it worthwhile.

The second invasion attempt, a month later, was made up of second-line troops scraped up from everywhere, including occupation duty in Germany.

"Literally," Piqueron said, "the Japanese did not know how to surrender, so they did not. They could not conquer, but they could and did continue suicidal resistance, consuming manpower of the allies and their own womanpower and childpower—a shrewd bargain for the Japanese! The Russians refused to become involved in the Japanese war; they watched with apish delight while two future enemies, as they supposed, were engaged in mutual destruction.

"A third assault wave broke on Kyushu and gained the island at last. What lay ahead? Only another assault on Honshu, the main island, home of the Emperor and the principal shrines. It was 1946; the volatile, childlike Americans were war-weary and mutinous; the best of them were gone by then. In desperation the Anglo-American leaders offered the Russians an economic sphere embracing the China coast and Japan as the price of participation."

The Russians grinned and assented; they would take that—at *least* that. They mounted a huge assault for the spring of 1947; they would take Korea and leap off from there for northern Honshu while the Anglo-American forces struck in the south. Surely this would provide at last a symbol before which the Japanese might without shame bow down and admit defeat!

And then, from the mountain fastnesses, came the radio voice: "Germans! Your Leader calls upon you again!" Followed the Hundred Days of Glory during which the German Army reconstituted itself and expelled the occupation troops—by then, children without combat experience, and leavened by not-quite-disabled veterans. Followed the seizure of the airfields; the Luftwaffe in business again. Followed the drive, almost a dress parade, to the Channel Coast, gobbling up immense munition dumps awaiting shipment to the Pacific Theater, millions of warm uniforms, good boots, mountains of rations, piles of shells and explosives that lined the French roads for scores of miles, thousands of two-and-a-half-ton trucks, and lakes of gasoline to fuel them. The shipyards of Europe, from Hamburg to Toulon, had been turning out, furiously, invasion barges for the Pacific. In April of 1947 they sailed against England in their thousands.

Halfway around the world, the British Navy was pounding Tokyo, Nagasaki, Kobe, Hiroshima, Nara. Three quarters of the way across Asia the Russian Army marched stolidly on; let the decadent British pickle their own fish; the glorious motherland at last was gaining her long-sought, long-denied, warm-water seacoast. The British, tired women without their men, children fatherless these eight years, old folks deathly weary, worried about their sons, were brave but they were not insane. They accepted honorable peace terms; they capitulated.

With the Western front secure for the first time in history, the ancient Drive to the East was resumed; the immemorial struggle of Teuton against Slav went on.

His spectacles glittering with rapture, Dr. Piqueron said: "We were worthy in those days of the Teutonic Knights who seized Prussia from the sub-men! On the ever-glorious Twenty-first of May, Moscow was ours!"

Moscow and the monolithic state machinery it controlled, and all the roads and rail lines and communication wires which led only to—and from—Moscow. Detroit-built tanks and trucks sped along those roads in the fine, bracing spring weather; the Red Army turned one hundred and eighty degrees at last and counter-marched halfway across the Eurasian landmass, and at Kazan it broke exhausted against the Frederik Line.

Europe at last was One and German. Beyond Europe lay the dark and swarming masses of Asia, mysterious and repulsive folk whom it would be better to handle through the non-German, but chivalrous, Japanese. The Japanese were reinforced with shipping from Birkenhead, artillery from the Putilov Works, jet fighters from Châteauroux, steel from the Ruhr, rice from the Po valley, herring from Norway, timber from Sweden, oil from Romania, laborers from India. The American forces were driven from Kyushu in the winter of 1948, and bloodily back across their chain of island stepping-stones that followed.

Surrender they would not; it was a monstrous affront that shield-shaped North America dared to lie there between the German Atlantic and the Japanese Pacific threatening both. The affront was wiped out in 1955.

For one hundred and fifty years now the Germans and the Japanese had uneasily eyed each other across the banks of the Mississippi. Their orators were fond of referring to that river as a vast frontier unblemished by a single fortification. There was even some interpenetration; a Japanese colony fished out of Nova Scotia on the very rim of German America; a sulfur mine which was part of the Farben system lay in New Mexico, the very heart of Japanese America—this was where Dr. Edward Royland found himself, being lectured to by Dr. Piqueron, Dr. Gaston Pierre Piqueron, true-blue German.

"Here, of course," Dr. Piqueron said gloomily, "we are so damned provincial. Little ceremony and less manners. Well, it would be too much to expect them to assign *German* Germans to this dreary outpost, so we French Germans must endure it somehow."

"You're all French?" Royland asked, startled.

"French *Germans*," Piqueron stiffly corrected him. "Colonel Biederman happens to be a French German also; Major Kappel is—hrrmph—an Italian German." He sniffed to show what he thought of that.

The Italian German entered at that point, not in time to shut off the question: "And you all come from Europe?"

They looked at him in bafflement. "My grandfather did," Dr. Piqueron said. Royland remembered; so Roman legions used to guard their empire— Romans born and raised in Britain, or on the Danube, Romans who would never in their lives see Italy or Rome.

Major Kappel said affably: "Well, this needn't concern us. I'm afraid, my dear fellow, that your little hoax has not succeeded." He clapped Royland merrily on the back. "I admit you've tricked us all nicely; now may we have the facts?"

Piqueron said, surprised: "His story is false? The shoes? The missing *geburtsnummer*? And he appears to understand some chemistry!"

"Ah-h-h—but he said his specialty was *physics*, doctor! Suspicious in itself!"

"Quite so. A discrepancy. But the rest—?"

"As to his birth number, who knows? As to his shoes, who cares? I took some inconspicuous notes while he was entertaining us and have checked thoroughly. There *was* no Manhattan Engineering District. There *was* no Dr. Oppenheimer, or Fermi, or Bohr. There *is* no theory of relativity, or equivalence of mass and energy. Uranium has one use only—coloring glass a pretty orange. There is such a thing as an isotope but it has nothing to do with chemistry; it is the name used in Race Science for a permissible variation within a sub-race. And what have you to say to *that*, my dear fellow?"

Royland wondered first, such was the positiveness with which Major Kappel spoke, whether he had slipped into a universe of different physical properties and history entirely, one in which Julius Caesar discovered Peru and the oxygen molecule was lighter than the hydrogen atom. He managed to speak. "How did you find all that out, Major?"

"Oh, don't think I did a skimpy job." Kappel smiled. "I looked it all up in the *big* encyclopedia."

Dr. Piqueron, chemist, nodded grave approval of the major's diligence and thorough grasp of the scientific method.

"You still don't want to tell us?" Major Kappel asked coaxingly.

"I can only stand by what I said."

Kappel shrugged. "It's not my job to persuade you; I wouldn't know how to begin. But I can and will ship you off forthwith to a work camp."

"What—is a work camp?" Royland unsteadily asked.

"Good heavens, man, a camp where one works! You're obviously an *ungleichgeschaltling* and you've got to be *gleichgeschaltet*." He did not speak these words as if they were foreign; they were obviously part of the everyday American working vocabulary. *Gleichgeschaltet* meant to Royland something like "coordinated, brought into tune with." So he would be brought into tune—with what, and how?

The Major went on: "You'll get your clothes and your bunk and your chow, and you'll work, and eventually your irregular vagabondish habits will disappear and you'll be turned loose on the labor market. And you'll be damned glad we took the trouble with you." His face fell. "By the way, I was too late with your friend the Paymaster. I'm sorry. I sent a messenger to Disciplinary Control with a stop order. After all, if you took us in for an hour, why should you not have fooled a Pay-Seventh?"

"Too late? He's *dead*? For picking up a *hitchhiker*?"

"I don't know what that last word means," said the Major. "If it's dialect for 'vagabond,' the answer is ordinarily 'yes.' The man, after all, was a Pay-Seventh; he could read. Either you're keeping up your hoax with remarkable fidelity or you've been living in isolation. Could that be it? Is there a tribe of you somewhere? Well, the interrogators will find out; that's their job."

"The Dogpatch legend!" Dr. Piqueron burst out, thunderstruck. "He may be an Abnerite!"

"By Heaven," Major Kappel said slowly, "that might be it. What a feather in my cap to find a living Abnerite."

"*Whose* cap?" demanded Dr. Piqueron coldly.

"I think I'll look the Dogpatch legend up," said Kappel, heading for the door and probably the big encyclopedia.

"So will I," Dr. Piqueron announced firmly. The last Royland saw of them they were racing down the corridor, neck and neck.

Very funny. And they had killed simple-minded Paymaster Martfield for picking up a hitchhiker. The Nazis always had been pretty funny—fat Hermann pretending he was young Seigfried. As blond as Hitler, as slim as Goering, and as tall as Goebbels. Immature guttersnipes who hadn't been able to hang a convincing frame on Dimitrov for the Reichstag fire; the world had roared at their bungling. Huge, corny party rallies with let's-play-detectives nonsense like touching the local flags to that hallowed banner on which the martyred Horst Wessel had had a nosebleed. And they had rolled over Europe, and they killed people. . . .

One thing was certain: life in the work camp would at least bore him to death. He was supposed to be an illiterate simpleton, so things were excused him which were not excused an exalted Pay-Seventh. He poked through a closet in the corner of the laboratory—he and Piqueron were the same size—

He found a natty change of uniform and what must be a civilian suit: somewhat baggy pants and a sort of tunic with the neat, sensible Russian collar. Obviously it would be all right to wear it because here it was: just as obviously, it was all wrong for him to be dressed in chinos and a flannel shirt. He did not know exactly what this made him, but Martfield had been done to death for picking up a man in chinos and a flannel shirt. Royland changed into the civilian suit, stuffed his own shirt and pants far back on the top shelf of the closet; this was probably concealment enough from those murderous clowns. He walked out, and up the stairs, and through the busy lobby, and into the industrial complex. Nobody saluted him and he saluted nobody. He knew where he was going—to a good, sound Japanese laboratory where there were no Germans.

Royland had known Japanese students at the University and admired them beyond words. Their brains, frugality, doggedness, and good humor made them, as far as he was concerned, the most sensible people he had ever known. Tojo and his warlords were not, as far as Royland was concerned, essentially Japanese but just more damnfool soldiers and politicians. The real Japanese would courteously listen to him, calmly check against available facts—

He rubbed his cheek and remembered Mr. Ito and his slap in the face. Well, presumably Mr. Ito was a damnfool soldier and politician—and demonstrating for the German's benefit in a touchy border area full of jurisdictional questions.

At any rate, he would *not* go to a labor camp and bust rocks or refinish furniture until those imbeciles decided he was *gleichgeschaltet*; he would go mad in a month.

Royland walked to the Solvay towers and followed the glass pipes containing their output of sulfuric acid along the ground until he came to a bottling shed where beetle-browed men worked silently filling great wicker-basketed carboys and heaving them outside. He followed other men who levered them up onto hand trucks and rolled them in one door of a storage shed. Out the door at the other end more men loaded them onto enclosed trucks which were driven up from time to time.

Royland settled himself in a corner of the storage shed behind a barricade of carboys and listened to the truck dispatcher swear at his drivers and the carboy handlers swear at their carboys.

"Get the god-damn Frisco shipment *loaded*, stupid! I don't *care* if you gotta go, we gotta get it out by *midnight*!"

So a few hours after dark Royland was riding west, without much air, and in the dangerous company of one thousand gallons of acid. He hoped he had a careful driver.

.   .   .

A night, a day, and another night on the road. The truck never stopped except to gas up; the drivers took turns and ate sandwiches at the wheel and dozed off shift. It rained the second night. Royland, craftily and perhaps a little crazily, licked the drops that ran down the tarpaulin flap covering the rear. At the first crack of dawn, hunched between two wicker carcasses, he saw they were rolling through irrigated vegetable fields, and the water in the ditches was too much for him. He heard the transmission shift down to slow for a curve, swarmed over the tailgate, and dropped to the road. He was weak and limp enough to hit like a sack.

He got up, ignoring his bruises, and hobbled to one of the brimming five-foot ditches; he drank, and drank, and drank. This time puritanical folklore proved right; he lost it all immediately, or what had not been greedily absorbed by his shriveled stomach. He did not mind; it was bliss enough to *stretch*.

The field crop was tomatoes, almost dead ripe. He was starved for them; as he saw the rosy beauties he knew that tomatoes were the only thing in the world he craved. He gobbled one so that the juice ran down his chin; he ate the next two delicately, letting his teeth break the crispness of their skin and the beautiful taste ravish his tongue. There were tomatoes as far as the eye could see, on either side of the road, the green of the vines and the red dots of the ripe fruit graphed by the checkerboard of silvery ditches that caught the first light. Nevertheless, he filled his pockets with them before he walked on.

Royland was happy.

Farewell to the Germans and their sordid hash and murderous ways. *Look* at these beautiful fields! The Japanese are an innately artistic people who bring beauty to every detail of daily life. And they make damn good physicists, too. Confined in their stony home, cramped as he had been in the truck, they grew twisted and painful; why should they not have reached out for more room to grow, and what other way is there to reach but to make war? He could be very understanding about any people who had planted these beautiful tomatoes for him.

A dark blemish the size of a man attracted his attention. It lay on the margin of one of the swirling five-foot ditches out there to his right. And then it rolled slowly into the ditch with a splash, floundered a little, and proceeded to drown.

In a hobbling run Royland broke from the road and across the field. He did not know whether he was limber enough to swim. As he stood panting on the edge of the ditch, peering into the water, a head of hair surfaced near him. He flung himself down, stretched wildly, and grabbed the hair—and yet had detachment enough to feel a pang when the tomatoes in his tunic pocket smashed.

"Steady," he muttered to himself, yanked the head toward him, took hold with his other hand and lifted. A surprised face confronted him and then went blank and unconscious.

For half an hour Royland, weak as he was, struggled, cursed feebly, and sweated to get that body out of the water. At last he plunged in himself, found it only chest-deep, and shoved the carcass over the mudslick bank. He did not know by then whether the man was alive or dead or much care. He knew only that he couldn't walk away and leave the job half finished.

The body was that of a fat, middle-aged Oriental, surely Chinese rather than Japanese, though Royland could not say why he thought so. His clothes were soaked rags except for a leather wallet the size of a cigar box which he wore on a wide cloth belt. Its sole content was a handsome blue-glazed porcelain bottle. Royland sniffed at it and reeled. Some kind of super-gin? He sniffed again, and then took a conservative gulp of the stuff. While he was still coughing he felt the bottle being removed from his hand. When he looked he saw the Chinese, eyes still closed, accurately guiding the neck of the bottle to his mouth. The Chinese drank and drank and drank, then returned the bottle to the wallet and finally opened his eyes.

"Honorable sir," said the Chinese in flat, California American speech, "you have deigned to save my unworthy life. May I supplicate your honorable name?"

"Ah, Royland. Look, take it easy. Don't try to get up; you shouldn't even talk."

Somebody screamed behind Royland: "There has been thieving of tomatoes! There has been smasheeng and deestruction of thee vines! Children, you will bee weet-ness be-fore the Jappa-neese!"

Christ, now what?

Now a skinny black man, not a Negro, in a dirty loincloth, and beside him like a pan-pipes five skinny black loinclothed offspring in descending order. All were capering, pointing, and threatening. The Chinese groaned, fished in his tattered robes with one hand, and pulled out a soggy wad of bills. He peeled one off, held it out, and said: "Begone, pestilential barbarians from beyond Tian-Shang. My master and I give you alms, not tribute."

The Dravidian, or whatever he was, grabbed the bill and keened: "Een-suffee-cient for the terrible dommage! The Jappa-neese—"

The Chinese waved them away boredly. He said: "If my master will condescend to help me arise?"

Royland uncertainly helped him up. The man was wobbly, whether from the near-drowning or the terrific belt of alcohol he'd taken there was no knowing. They proceeded to the road, followed by shrieks to be careful about stepping on the vines.

On the road, the Chinese said: "My unworthy name is Li Po. Will my master deign to indicate in which direction we are to travel?"

"What's this master business?" Royland demanded. "If you're grateful, swell, but I don't *own* you."

"My master is pleased to jest," said Li Po. Politely, face-saving and third-personing Royland until hell wouldn't have it, he explained that Royland, having meddled with the Celestial decree that Li Po should, while drunk, roll into the irrigation ditch and drown, now had Li Po on his hands, for the Celestial Ones had washed theirs of him. "As my master of course will recollect in a moment or two." Understandingly, he expressed his sympathy with Royland's misfortune in acquiring him as an obligation, especially since he had a hearty appetite, was known to be dishonest, and suffered from fainting fits and spasms when confronted with work.

"I don't *know* about all this," Royland said fretfully. "Wasn't there another Li Po? A poet?"

"Your servant prefers to venerate his namesake as one of the greatest drunkards the Flowery Kingdom has ever known," the Chinese observed. And a moment later he bent over, clipped Royland behind the knees so that he toppled forward and bumped his head, and performed the same obeisance himself, more gracefully. A vehicle went sputtering and popping by on the road as they kowtowed.

Li Po said reproachfully: "I humbly observe that my master is unaware of the etiquette our noble overlords exact. Such negligence cost the head of my insignificant elder brother in his twelfth year. Would my master be pleased to explain how he can have reached his honorable years without learning what babes in their cradles are taught?"

Royland answered with the whole truth. Li Po politely begged clarification from time to time, and a sketch of his mental horizons emerged from his questioning. That "magic" had whisked Royland forward a century or more he did not doubt for an instant, but he found it difficult to understand why the proper *fung shui* precautions had not been taken to avert a disastrous outcome to the God Food experiment. He suspected, from a description of Nahataspe's hut, that a simple wall at right angles to the door would have kept all really important demons out. When Royland described his escape from German territory to Japanese, and why he had effected it, he was very bland and blank. Royland judged that Li Po privately thought him not very bright for having left *any* place to come here.

And Royland hoped he was not right. "Tell me what it's like," he said.

"This realm," said Li Po, "under our benevolent and noble overlords, is the haven of all whose skin is not the bleached-bone hue which indicates the undying curse of the Celestial Ones. Hither flock men of Han like my unworthy self, and the sons of Hind beyond the Tian-Shang that we may till new soil and raise up sons, and sons of sons to venerate us when we ascend."

"What was that bit," Royland demanded, "about the bleached bones? Do they shoot, ah, white men on sight here, or do they not?"

Li Po said evasively: "We are approaching the village where I unworthily serve as fortune teller, doctor of *fung shui*, occasional poet and storyteller. Let my master have no fear about his color. This humble one will roughen his master's skin, tell a circumstantial and artistic lie or two, and pass his master off as merely a leper."

After a week in Li Po's village Royland knew that life was good there. The place was a wattle-and-clay settlement of about two hundred souls on the bank of an irrigation ditch large enough to be dignified by the name of "canal." It was situated nobody knew just where; Royland thought it must be the San Fernando Valley. The soil was thick and rich and bore furiously the year round. A huge kind of radish was the principal crop. It was too coarse to be eaten by man; the villagers understood that it was feed for chickens somewhere up north. At any rate they harvested the stuff, fed it through a great hand-powered shredder, and shade-cured the shreds. Every few days a Japanese of low caste would come by in a truck, they would load tons of the stuff onto it, and wave their giant radish goodbye forever. Presumably the chickens ate it, and the Japanese then ate the chickens.

The villagers ate chicken too, but only at weddings and funerals. The rest of the time they ate vegetables which they cultivated, a quarter-acre to a family, the way other craftsmen facet diamonds. A single cabbage might receive, during its ninety days from planting to maturity, one hundred work hours from grandmother, grandfather, son, daughter, eldest grandchild, and on down to the smallest toddler. Theoretically the entire family line should have starved to death, for there are not one hundred energy hours in a cabbage; somehow they did not. They merely stayed thin and cheerful and hard-working and fecund.

They spoke English by Imperial decree; the reasoning seemed to be that they were as unworthy to speak Japanese as to paint the Imperial Chrysanthemum Seal on their houses, and that to let them cling to their old languages and dialects would have been politically unwise.

They were a mixed lot of Chinese, Hindus, Dravidians, and, to Royland's surprise, low-caste and outcaste Japanese; he had not known there were such things. Village tradition had it that a *samurai* named Ugetsu long ago said, pointing at the drunk tank of a Hong Kong jail, "I'll have that lot," and "that lot" had been the ancestors of these villagers transported to America in a foul hold practically as ballast and settled here by the canal with orders to start making their radish quota. The place was at any rate called The Ugetsu Village, and if some of the descendants were teetotallers, others like Li Po gave color to the legend of their starting point.

After a week the cheerful pretense that he was a sufferer from Housen's disease evaporated and he could wash the mud off his face. He had merely to avoid the uppercaste Japanese and especially the *samurai*. This was not exactly a stigma; in general it was a good idea for *everybody* to avoid the *samurai*.

In the village Royland found his first love and his first religion both false.

He had settled down; he was getting used to the Oriental work rhythm of slow, repeated, incessant effort; it did not surprise him any longer that he could count his ribs. When he ate a bowl of artfully arranged vegetables, the red of pimiento played off against the yellow of parsnip, a slice of pickled beet adding visual and olfactory tang to the picture, he felt full enough; he *was* full enough for the next day's feeble work in the field. It was pleasant enough to play slowly with a wooden mattock in the rich soil; did not people once buy sand so their children might do exactly what he did, and envy their innocent absorption? Royland was innocently absorbed, then, and the radish truck had collected six times since his arrival, when he began to feel stirrings of lust. On the edge of starvation (but who knew this? For everybody was) his mind was dulled, but not his loins. They burned, and he looked about him in the fields, and the first girl he saw who was not repulsive he fell abysmally in love with.

Bewildered, he told Li Po, who was also Ugetsu Village's go-between. The storyteller was delighted; he waddled off to seek information and returned. "My master's choice is wise. The slave on whom his lordly eye deigned to rest is known as Vashti, daughter of Hari Bose, the distiller. She is his seventh child and so no great dowry can be expected [I shall ask for fifteen kegs toddy, but would settle for seven], but all this humble village knows that she is a skilled and willing worker in the hut as in the fields. I fear she has the customary lamentable Hindu talent for concocting curries, but a dozen good beatings at the most should cause her to reserve it to appropriate occasions, such as visits from her mother and sisters."

So, according to the sensible custom of Ugetsu, Vashti came that night to the hut which Royland shared with Li Po, and Li Po visited with cronies by his master's puzzling request. He begged humbly to point out that it would be dark in the hut, so this talk of lacking privacy was inexplicable to say the least. Royland made it an order, and Li Po did not really object, so he obeyed it.

It was a damnably strange night, during which Royland learned all about

India's national sport and most highly developed art form. Vashti, if she found him weak on the theory side, made no complaints. On the contrary, when Royland woke she was doing something or other to his feet.

"More?" he thought incredulously. "With *feet?*" He asked what she was doing. Submissively she replied: "Worshipping my lord husband-to-be's big toe. I am a pious and old-fashioned woman."

So she painted his toe with red paint and prayed to it, and then she fixed breakfast—curry, and excellent. She watched him eat, and then modestly licked his leavings from the bowl. She handed him his clothes, which she had washed while he still slept, and helped him into them after she helped him wash. Royland thought incredulously: "It's not possible! It must be a show, to sell me on marrying her—as if I had to be sold!" His heart turned to custard as he saw her, without a moment's pause, turn from dressing him to polishing his wooden rake. He asked that day in the field, roundabout fashion, and learned that this was the kind of service he could look forward to for the rest of his life after marriage. If the woman got lazy he'd have to beat her, but this seldom happened more than every year or so. We have good girls here in Ugetsu Village.

So an Ugetsu Village peasant was in some ways better off than anybody from "his time" who was less than a millionaire!

His starved dullness was such that he did not realize this was true for only half the Ugetsu Village peasants.

Religion sneaked up on him in similar fashion. He went to the part-time Taoist priest because he was a little bored with Li Po's current after-dinner saga. He could have sat like all the others and listened passively to the interminable tale of the glorious Yellow Emperor, and the beautiful but wicked Princess Emerald, and the virtuous but plain Princess Moon Blossom; it just happened that he went to the priest of Tao and got hooked hard.

The kindly old man, a toolmaker by day, dropped a few pearls of wisdom which, in his foggy starvation-daze, Royland did not perceive to be pearls of undemonstrable nonsense, and showed Royland how to meditate. It worked the first time. Royland bunged right smack through into a two-hundred-proof state of *samadhi*—the Eastern version of self-hypnotized Enlightenment—that made him feel wonderful and all-knowing and left him without a hangover when it wore off. He had despised, in college, the type of people who took psychology courses and so had taken none himself; he did not know a thing about self-hypnosis except as just demonstrated by this very nice old gentleman. For several days he was offensively religious and kept trying to talk to Li Po about the Eightfold Way, and Li Po kept changing the subject.

It took murder to bring him out of love and religion.

At twilight they were all sitting and listening to the storyteller as usual. Royland had been there just one month and for all he knew would be there forever. He soon would have his bride officially; he knew he had discovered The Truth About the Universe by way of Tao meditation; why should he change? Changing demanded a furious outburst of energy, and he did not have energy on that scale. He metered out his energy day and night; one had to save so much for tonight's love play, and then one had to save so much for tomorrow's planting. He was a poor man; he could not afford to change.

Li Po had reached a rather interesting bit where the Yellow Emperor was declaiming hotly: "Then she shall die! Whoever dare transgress Our divine will—"

A flashlight began to play over their faces. They perceived that it was in the hand of a *samurai* with kimono and sword. Everybody hastily kowtowed, but the *samurai* shouted irritably (all *samurai* were irritable, all the time): "Sit up, you fools! I want to see your stupid faces. I hear there's a peculiar one in this flea-bitten dungheap you call a village."

Well, by now Royland knew his duty. He rose and with downcast eyes asked: "Is the noble protector in search of my unworthy self?"

"Ha!" the *samurai* roared. "It's true! A big nose!" He hurled the flashlight away (all *samurai* were nobly contemptuous of the merely material), held his scabbard in his left hand, and swept out the long curved sword with his right.

Li Po stepped forward and said in his most enchanting voice: "If the Heaven-born would only deign to heed a word from this humble—" What he must have known would happen happened. With a contemptuous backhand sweep of the blade the *samurai* beheaded him and Li Po's debt was paid.

The trunk of the storyteller stood for a moment and then fell stiffly forward. The *samurai* stooped to wipe his blade clean on Li Po's ragged robes.

Royland had forgotten much, but not everything. With the villagers scattering before him he plunged forward and tackled the *samurai* low and hard. No doubt the *samurai* was a Brown Belt judo master; if so he had nobody but himself to blame for turning his back. Royland, not remembering that he was barefoot, tried to kick the *samurai's* face in. He broke his worshipful big toe, but its untrimmed horny nail removed the left eye of the warrior and after that it was no contest. He never let the *samurai* get up off the ground; he took out his other eye with the handle of a rake and then killed him an inch at a time with his hands, his feet, and the clownish rustic's traditional weapon, a flail. It took easily half an hour, and for the final twenty minutes the *samurai* was screaming for his mother. He died when the last light left the western sky, and in darkness Royland stood quite alone with the two corpses. The villagers were gone.

He assumed, or pretended, that they were within earshot and yelled at them brokenly: "I'm sorry, Vashti. I'm sorry, all of you. I'm going. Can I make you understand?

"Listen. You aren't living. This isn't life. You're not making anything but babies, you're not changing, you're not growing up. That's not enough! You've got to read and write. You can't pass on anything but baby stories like the Yellow Emperor by word of mouth. The village is growing. Soon your fields will touch the fields of Sukoshi Village to the west, and then what happens? You won't know what to do, so you'll fight with Sukoshi Village.

"Religion. No! It's just getting drunk the way you do it. You're set up for it by being half-starved and then you go into *samadhi* and you feel better so you think you understand everything. No! You've got to *do* things. If you don't grow up, you die. All of you.

"Women. *That's* wrong. It's good for the men, but it's wrong. Half of you are slaves, do you understand? Women are people too, but you use them like animals and you've convinced them it's right for them to be old at thirty and discarded for the next girl. For God's sake, can't you try to think of yourselves in their place?

"The breeding, the crazy breeding—it's got to stop. You frugal Orientals! But you aren't frugal; you're crazy drunken sailors. You're squandering the whole world. Every mouth you breed has got to be fed by the land, and the land isn't infinite.

"I hope some of you understood. Li Po would have, a little, but he's dead.

"I'm going away now. You've been kind to me and all I've done is make trouble. I'm sorry."

He fumbled on the ground and found the *samurai's* flashlight. With it he hunted the village's outskirts until he found the Japanese's buckboard car. He started the motor with its crank and noisily rolled down the dirt track from the village to the highway.

Royland drove all night, still westward. His knowledge of southern California's geography was inexact, but he hoped to hit Los Angeles. There might be a chance of losing himself in a great city. He had abandoned hope of finding present-day counterparts of his old classmates like Jimmy Ichimura; obviously they had lost out. Why shouldn't have they lost? The soldier-politicians had won the war by happenstance, so all power to the soldier-politicians! Reasoning under the great natural law *post hoc ergo propter hoc*,

Tojo and his crowd had decided: fanatic feudalism won the war; therefore fanatic feudalism is a good thing, and it necessarily follows that the more fanatical and feudal it is, the better a thing it is. So you had Sukoshi Village, and Ugetsu Village; Ichi Village, Ni Village, San Village, Shi Village, dotting that part of Great Japan formerly known as North America, breeding with the good old fanatic feudalism and so feudally averse to new thought and innovations that it made you want to scream at them — which he had.

The single weak headlight of his buckboard passed few others on the road; a decent feudal village is self-contained.

Damn them and their suicidal cheerfulness! It was a pleasant trait; it was a fool in a canoe approaching the rapids saying: "Chin up! Everything's going to be all right if we just keep smiling."

The car ran out of gas when false dawn first began to pale the sky behind him. He pushed it into the roadside ditch and walked on; by full light he was in a tumbledown, planless, evil-smelling, paper-and-galvanized-iron city whose name he did not know. There was no likelihood of him being noticed as a "white" man by anyone not specifically looking for him. A month of outdoor labor had browned him, and a month of artistically composed vegetable plates had left him gaunt.

The city was carpeted with awakening humanity. Its narrow streets were paved with sprawled-out men, women, and children beginning to stir and hawk up phlegm and rub their rheumy eyes. An open sewer-latrine running down the center of each street was casually used, ostrich-fashion — the users hid their own eyes while in action.

Every mangled variety of English rang in Royland's ears as he trod between bodies.

There had to be something more, he told himself. This was the shabby industrial outskirts, the lowest marginal-labor area. Somewhere in the city there was beauty, science, learning!

He walked aimlessly plodding until noon, and found nothing of the sort. These people in the cities were food-handlers, food-traders, food-transporters. They took in one another's washing and sold one another chop suey. They made automobiles (Yes! There were one-family automobile factories which probably made six buckboards a year, filing all metal parts by hand out of bar stock!) and orange crates and baskets and coffins; abacuses, nails, and boots.

The Mysterious East has done it again, he thought bitterly. The Indians-Chinese-Japanese won themselves a nice sparse area. They could have laid things out neatly and made it pleasant for everybody instead of for a minute speck of aristocracy which he was unable even to detect in this human soup . . . but they had done it again. They had bred irresponsibly just as fast as they could until the land was *full*. Only famines and pestilence could "help" them now.

He found exactly one building which owned some clear space around it and which would survive an earthquake or a flicked cigarette butt. It was the German Consulate.

I'll give them the Bomb, he said to himself. Why not? None of this is mine. And for the Bomb I'll exact a price of some comfort and dignity for as long as I live. *Let* them blow one another up! He climbed the consulate steps.

To the black-uniformed guard at the swastika-trimmed bronze doors he said: "*Wenn die Lichtstärke der von einer Fläche kommenden Strahlung dem Cosinus des Winkels zwischen Strahlrichtung und Flächennormalen proportional ist, so nennen wir die Fläche eine volkommen streunde Fläche.*" Lambert's Law, Optics I. All the Goethe he remembered happened to rhyme, which might have made the guard suspicious.

Naturally the German came to attention and said apologetically: "I don't speak German. What is it, sir?"

"You may take me to the consul," Royland said, affecting boredom.

"Yes, sir. At once, sir. Er, you're an *agent* of course, sir?"

Royland said witheringly: "*Sicherheit, bitte!*"

"Yessir. This way, sir!"

The consul was a considerate, understanding gentleman. He was somewhat surprised by Royland's true tale, but said from time to time: "I see; I see. Not impossible. Please go on."

Royland concluded: "Those people at the sulfur mine were, I hope, unrepresentative. One of them at least complained that it was a dreary sort of backwoods assignment. I am simply gambling that there is intelligence in your Reich. I ask you to get me a real physicist for twenty minutes of conversation. You, Mr. Consul, will not regret it. I am in a position to turn over considerable information on—atomic power." So he had not been able to say it after all; the Bomb was still an obscene kick below the belt.

"This has been very interesting, Dr. Royland," said the consul gravely. "You referred to your enterprise as a gamble. I too shall gamble. What have I to lose by putting you *en rapport* with a scientist of ours if you prove to be a plausible lunatic?" He smiled to soften it. "Very little indeed. On the other hand, what have I to gain if your extraordinary story is quite true? A great deal. I will go along with you, doctor. Have you eaten?"

The relief was tremendous. He had lunch in a basement kitchen with the Consulate guards—a huge lunch, a rather nasty lunch of stewed *lungen* with a floured gravy, and cup after cup of coffee. Finally one of the guards lit up an ugly little spindle-shaped cigar, the kind Royland had only seen before in the caricatures of George Grosz, and as an afterthought offered one to him.

He drank in the rank smoke and managed not to cough. It stung his mouth and cut the greasy aftertaste of the stew satisfactorily. One of the blessings of the Third Reich, one of its gross pleasures. They were just people, after all—a certain censorious, busybody type of person with altogether too much power, but they were human. By which he meant, he supposed, members of Western Industrial Culture like him.

After lunch he was taken by truck from the city to an airfield by one of the guards. The plane was somewhat bigger than a B-29 he had once seen, and lacked propellers. He presumed it was one of the "jets" Dr. Piqueron had mentioned. His guard gave his dossier to a Luftwaffe sergeant at the foot of the ramp and said cheerfully: "Happy landings, fellow. It's all going to be all right."

"Thanks," he said. "I'll remember you, Corporal Collins. You've been very helpful." Collins turned away.

Royland climbed the ramp into the barrel of the plane. A bucket-seat job, and most of the seats were filled. He dropped into one on the very narrow aisle. His neighbor was in rags; his face showed signs of an old beating. When Royland addressed him he simply cringed away and began to sob.

The Luftwaffe sergeant came up, entered, and slammed the door. The "jets" began to wind up, making an unbelievable racket; further conversation was impossible. While the plane taxied, Royland peered through the windowless gloom at his fellow-passengers. They all looked poor and poorly.

God, were they so quickly and quietly airborne? They were. Even in the bucket seat, Royland fell asleep.

He was awakened, he did not know how much later, by the sergeant. The man was shaking his shoulder and asking him: "Any joolery hid away? Watches? Got some nice fresh water to sell to people that wanna buy it."

Royland had nothing, and would not take part in the miserable little racket if he had. He shook his head indignantly and the man moved on with a grin. He would not last long!—petty chiselers were leaks in the efficient dictatorship; they were rapidly detected and stopped up. Mussolini made the trains run on time, after all. (But naggingly Royland recalled mentioning this to a Northwestern University English professor, one Bevans. Bevans had coldly informed him that from 1931 to 1936 he had lived under Mussolini as a student and tourist guide, and therefore had extraordinary opportunities for observing whether the trains ran on time or not, and could definitely state that they did not; that railway timetables under Mussolini were best regarded as humorous fiction.)

And another thought nagged at him, a thought connected with a pale, scarred face named Bloom. Bloom was a young refugee physical chemist working on WEAPONS DEVELOPMENT TRACK I, and he was somewhat crazy, perhaps. Royland, on TRACK III, used to see little of him and could have done with even less. You couldn't say hello to the man without it turning into a lecture on the horrors of Nazism. He had wild stories about "gas chambers" and crematoria which no reasonable man could believe, and was a blanket slanderer of the German medical profession. He claimed that trained doctors, certified men, used human beings in experiments which terminated fatally. Once, to try and bring Bloom to reason, he asked what sort of experiments these were, but the monomaniac had had that worked out: piffling nonsense about reviving mortally frozen men by putting naked women into bed with them! The man was probably sexually deranged to believe that; he naively added that one variable in the series of experiments was to use women immediately after sexual intercourse, one hour after sexual intercourse, et cetera. Royland had blushed for him and violently changed the subject.

But that was not what he was groping for. Neither was Bloom's crazy story about the woman who made lampshades from the tattooed skin of concentration camp prisoners; there were people capable of such things, of course, but under no regime whatever do they rise to positions of authority; they simply can't do the work required in positions of authority because their insanity gets in the way.

"Know your enemy," of course—but making up pointless lies? At least Bloom was not the conscious prevaricator. He got letters in Yiddish from friends and relations in Palestine, and these were laden with the latest wild rumors supposed to be based on the latest word from "escapees."

Now he remembered. In the cafeteria about three months ago Bloom had been sipping tea with somewhat shaking hand and rereading a letter. Royland tried to pass him with only a nod, but the skinny hand shot out and held him.

Bloom looked up with tears in his eyes: "It's cruel, I'm tellink you, Royland, it's cruel. They're not givink them the right to scream, to strike a futile blow, to sayink prayers *Kiddush ha Shem* like a Jew should when he is dyink for Consecration of the Name! They trick them, they say they go to farm settlements, to labor camps, so four-five of the stinkink bastards can handle a whole trainload Jews. They trick the clothes off of them at the camps, they sayink they delouse them. They trick them into room says showerbath over the door and then is too late to sayink prayers; *then goes on the gas."*

Bloom had let go of him and put his head on the table between his hands. Royland had mumbled something, patted his shoulder, and walked on, shaken. For once the neurotic little man might have got some straight facts. That was a very circumstantial touch about expediting the handling of prisoners by systematic lies—always the carrot and the stick.

Yes, everybody had been so god-damn agreeable since he climbed the Consulate steps! The friendly door guard, the Consul who nodded and remarked that his story was not an impossible one, the men he'd eaten with—all that quiet optimism. "Thanks. I'll remember you, Corporal Collins. You've been very helpful." He had felt positively benign toward the corporal, and now remembered that the corporal had turned around *very* quickly after he spoke. *To hide a grin?*

The guard was working his way down the aisle again and noticed that Royland was awake. "Changed your mind by now?" he asked kindly. "Got a good watch, maybe I'll find a piece of bread for you. You won't need a watch where you're going, fella."

"What do you mean?" Royland demanded.

The guard said soothingly: "Why, they got clocks all over them work camps, fella. Everybody knows what time it is in them work camps. You don't need no watches there. Watches just get in the way at them work camps." He went on down the aisle, quickly.

Royland reached across the aisle and, like Bloom, gripped the man who sat opposite him. He could not see much of him; the huge windowless plane was lit only by half a dozen stingy bulbs overhead. "What are you here for?" he asked.

The man said shakily: "I'm a Laborer Two, see? A Two. Well, my father he taught me to read, see, but he waited until I was ten and knew the score? See? So I figured it was a family tradition, so I taught my own kid to read because he was a pretty smart kid, ya know? I figured he'd have some fun reading like I did, no harm done, who's to know, ya know? But I should of waited a couple years, I guess, because the kid was too young and got to bragging he could read, ya know how kids do? I'm from St. Louis, by the way. I should of said first I'm from St. Louis a track maintenance man, see, so I hopped a string of returning empties for San Diego because I was scared like you get."

He took a deep sigh. "Thirsty," he said. "Got in with some Chinks, nobody to trouble ya, ya stay outta the way, but then one of them cops-like seen me and he took me to the Consul place like they do, ya know? Had me scared, they always tole me illegal reading they bump ya off, but they don't, ya know? Two years work camp, how about that?"

Yes, Royland wondered. How about it?

The plane decelerated sharply; he was thrown forward. Could they brake with those "jets" by reversing the stream or were the engines just throttling down? He heard gurgling and thudding; hydraulic fluid to the actuators letting down the landing gear. The wheels bumped a moment later and he braced himself; the plane was still and the motors cut off seconds later.

Their Luftwaffe sergeant unlocked the door and bawled through it: "Shove that goddam ramp, willya?" The sergeant's assurance had dropped from him; he looked like a very scared man. He must have been a very brave one, really, to have let himself be locked in with a hundred doomed men, protected only by an eight-shot pistol and a chain of systematic lies.

They were herded out of the plane onto a runway of what Royland immediately identified as the Chicago Municipal Airport. The same reek wafted from the stockyards; the row of airline buildings at the eastern edge of the field was ancient and patched but unchanged; the hangars, though, were now something that looked like inflated plastic bags. A good trick. Beyond the buildings surely lay the dreary red-brick and painted-siding wastes of Cicero, Illinois.

Luftwaffe men were yapping at them: "Form up, boys; make a line! Work means freedom! Look tall!" They shuffled and were shoved into columns of fours. A snappy majorette in shiny satin panties and white boots pranced out of an administration building twirling her baton; a noisy march blared from louvers in her tall fur hat. Another good trick.

"Forward march, boys," she shrilled at them. "Wouldn't y'all just like to follow me?" Seductive smile and a wiggle of the rump; a Judas ewe. She strutted off in time to the music; she must have been wearing ear-stopples. They shuffled after her. At the airport gate they dropped their blue-coated Luftwaffe boys and picked up a waiting escort of a dozen black-coats with skulls on their high-peaked caps.

They walked in time to the music, hypnotized by it, through Cicero. Cicero had been bombed to hell and not rebuilt. To his surprise Royland felt a pang for the vanished Poles and Slovaks of Al's old bailiwick. There were *German* Germans, French Germans, and even Italian Germans, but he knew in his bones that there were no Polish or Slovakian Germans . . . And Bloom had been right all along.

Deathly weary after two hours of marching (the majorette was indefatigable) Royland looked up from the broken pavement to see a cockeyed wonder before him. It was a Castle; it was a Nightmare; it was the Chicago Parteihof. The thing abutted Lake Michigan; it covered perhaps sixteen city blocks. It frowned down on the lake at the east and at the tumbled acres of bombed-out Chicago at the north, west, and south. It was made of steel-reinforced concrete grained and grooved to look like medieval masonry. It was walled, moated, portcullis-ed, towered, ramparted, crenellated. The death's-head guards looked at it reverently and the prisoners with fright. Royland wanted only to laugh wildly. It was a Disney production. It was as funny as Hermann Goering in full fig, and probably as deadly.

With a mumbo-jumbo of passwords, heils, and salutes they were admitted, and the majorette went away, no doubt to take off her boots and groan.

The most bedecked of the death's-heads lined them up and said affably: "Hot dinner and your beds presently, my boys; first a selection. Some of you, I'm afraid, aren't well and should be in sick bay. Who's sick? Raise your hands, please."

A few hands crept up. Stooped old men.

"That's right. Step forward, please." Then he went down the line tapping a man here and there—one fellow with glaucoma, another with terrible varicose sores visible through the tattered pants he wore. Mutely they stepped forward. Royland he looked thoughtfully over. "You're thin, my boy," he observed. "Stomach pains? Vomit blood? Tarry stools in the morning?"

"Nossir!" Royland barked. The man laughed and continued down the line. The "sick bay" detail was marched off. Most of them were weeping silently; they knew. Everybody knew; everybody pretended that the terrible thing would not, might not, happen. It was much more complex than Royland had realized.

"Now," said the death's-head affably, "we require some competent cement workers—"

The line of remaining men went mad. They surged forward almost touching the officer but never stepping over an invisible line surrounding him. "Me!" some yelled. "Me! Me!" Another cried: "I'm good with my hands, I can learn, I'm a machinist too, I'm strong and young, I can learn!" A heavy middle-aged one waved his hands in the air and boomed: "Grouting and tile-setting! Grouting and tile-setting!" Royland stood alone, horrified. They knew. They knew this was an offer of real work that would keep them alive for a while.

He knew suddenly how to live in a world of lies.

The officer lost his patience in a moment or two, and whips came out. Men with their faces bleeding struggled back into line. "Raise your hands, you cement people, and no lying, please. But you wouldn't lie, would you?" He picked half a dozen volunteers after questioning them briefly, and one of his men marched them off. Among them was the grouting-and-tile man, who looked pompously pleased with himself; such was the reward of diligence and virtue, he seemed to be proclaiming; pooh to those grasshoppers back there who neglected to Learn A Trade.

"Now," said the officer casually, "we require some laboratory assistants." The chill of death stole down the line of prisoners. Each one seemed to shrivel into himself, become poker-faced, imply that he wasn't really involved in all this.

Royland raised his hand. The officer looked at him in stupefaction and then covered up quickly. "Splendid," he said. "Step forward, my boy. You," he pointed at another man. "You have an intelligent forehead; you look as if you'd make a fine laboratory assistant. Step forward."

"Please, no!" the man begged. He fell to his knees and clasped his hands in supplication. "Please no!" The officer took out his whip meditatively; the man groaned, scrambled to his feet, and quickly stood beside Royland.

When there were four more chosen, they were marched off across the concrete yard into one of the absurd towers, and up a spiral staircase and down a corridor, and through the promenade at the back of an auditorium where a woman screamed German from the stage at an audience of women. And through a tunnel and down the corridor of an elementary school with empty classrooms full of small desks on either side. And into a hospital area where the fake-masonry walls yielded to scrubbed white tile and the fake flagstones underfoot to composition flooring and the fake pinewood torches in bronze brackets that had lighted their way to fluorescent tubes.

At the door marked RASSENWISSENSCHAFT the guard rapped and a frosty-faced man in a laboratory coat opened up. "You requisitioned a demonstrator, Dr. Kalten," the guard said. "Pick any one of these."

Dr. Kalten looked them over. "Oh, this one, I suppose," he said. Royland. "Come in, fellow."

The Race Science Laboratory of Dr. Kalten proved to be a decent medical setup with an operating table, intricate charts of the races of men and their anatomical, mental, and moral makeups. There was also a phrenological head diagram and a horoscope on the wall, and an arrangement of glittering crystals on wire which Royland recognized. It was a model of one Hans Hoerbiger's crackpot theory of planetary formation, the *Welteislehre*.

"Sit there," the doctor said, pointing to a stool. "First I've got to take your pedigree. By the way, you might as well know that you're going to end up dissected for my demonstration in Race Science III for the Medical School, and your degree of cooperation will determine whether the dissection is performed under anaesthesia or not. Clear?"

"Clear, doctor."

"Curious—no panic. I'll wager we find you're a proto-Hamitoidal hemi-Nordic of at *least* degree five . . . but let's get on. Name?"

"Edward Royland."

"Birthdate?"

"July second, nineteen twenty-one."

The doctor threw down his pencil. "If my previous explanation was inadequate," he shouted, "let me add that if you continue to be difficult I may turn you over to my good friend Dr. Herzbrenner. Dr. Herzbrenner happens to teach interrogation technique at the Gestapo School. *Do— you—now—understand?*"

"Yes, doctor. I'm sorry I cannot withdraw my answer."

Dr. Kalten turned elaborately sarcastic. "How then do you account for your remarkable state of preservation at your age of approximately a hundred and eighty years?"

"Doctor, I am twenty-three years old. I have traveled through time."

"Indeed?" Kalten was amused. "And how was this accomplished?"

Royland said steadily: "A spell was put on me by a satanic Jewish magician. It involved the ritual murder and desanguination of seven beautiful Nordic virgins."

Dr. Kalten gaped for a moment. Then he picked up his pencil and said firmly: "You will understand that my doubts were logical under the circumstances. Why did you not give me the sound scientific basis for your surprising claim at once? Go ahead; tell me all about it."

He was Dr. Kalten's prize; he was Dr. Kalten's treasure. His peculiarities of speech, his otherwise inexplicable absence of a birth number over his left nipple, when they got around to it the gold filling in one of his teeth, his uncanny knowledge of Old America, all now had a simple scientific explanation. He was from 1944. What was so hard to grasp about that? Any sound specialist knew about the lost Jewish cabala magic, golems and such.

His story was that he had been a student Race Scientist under the pioneering master William D. Pully. (A noisy whack who used to barnstorm the chaw-and-gallus belt with the backing of Deutches Neues Buro; sure enough they found him in Volume VII of the standard *Introduction to a Historical Handbook of Race Science*.) The Jewish fiends had attempted to ambush his master on a lonely road; Royland persuaded him to switch hats and coats; in the darkness the substitution was not noticed. Later in their stronghold he was identified, but the Nordic virgins had already been ritually murdered and drained of their blood, and it wouldn't keep. The dire fate destined for the master had been visited upon the disciple.

Dr. Kalten loved that bit. It tickled him pink that the sub-men's "revenge" on their enemy had been to precipitate him into a world purged of the sub-men entirely, where a Nordic might breathe freely!

Kalten, except for discreet consultations with such people as Old America specialists, a dentist who was stupefied by the gold filling, and a dermatologist who established that there was not and never had been a *geburtsnummer* on the subject examined, was playing Royland close to his vest. After a week it became apparent that he was reserving Royland for a grand unveiling which would climax the reading of a paper. Royland did not want to be unveiled; there were too many holes in his story. He talked with animation about the beauties of Mexico in the spring, its fair mesas, cactus, and mushrooms. Could they make a short trip there? Dr. Kalten said they could not. Royland was becoming restless? Let him study, learn, profit by the matchless arsenal of the sciences available here in Chicago Parteihof. Dear old Chicago boasted distinguished exponents of the World Ice Theory, the Hollow World Theory, Dowsing, Homeopathic Medicine, Curative Folk Botany—

The last did sound interesting. Dr. Kalten was pleased to take his prize to the Medical School and introduce him as a protégé to Professor Albiani, of Folk Botany.

Albiani was a bearded gnome out of the Arthur Rackham illustrations for *Das Rheingold*. He loved his subject. "Mother Nature, the all-bounteous one! Wander the fields, young man, and with a seeing eye in an hour's stroll you will find the ergot that aborts, the dill that cools fever, the tansy that strengthens the old, the poppy that soothes the fretful teething babe!"

"Do you have any hallucinogenic Mexican mushrooms?" Royland demanded.

"We may," Albiani said, surprised. They browsed through the Folk Botany museum and pored over dried vegetation under glass. From Mexico there were peyote, the buttons and the root, and there was marihuana, root, stem, seed, and stalk. No mushrooms.

"They may be in the storeroom," Albiani muttered.

All the rest of the day Royland mucked through the storeroom where specimens were waiting for exhibit space on some rotation plan. He went to Albiani and said, a little wild-eyed: "They're not there."

Albiani had been interested enough to look up the mushrooms in question in the reference books. "See?" he said happily, pointing to a handsome color plate of the mushroom: growing, mature, sporing, and dried. He read: "'. . . superstitiously called *God Food*,'" and twinkled through his beard at the joke.

"They're not there," Royland said.

The professor, annoyed at last, said: "There might be some uncatalogued in the basement. Really, we don't have room for everything in our limited display space—just the *interesting* items."

Royland pulled himself together and charmed the location of the department's basement storage space out of him, together with permission to inspect it. And, left alone for a moment, ripped the color plate from the professor's book and stowed it away.

That night Royland and Dr. Kalten walked out on one of the innumerable tower-tops for a final cigar. The moon was high and full; its light turned the cratered terrain that had been Chicago into another moon. The sage and his disciple from another day leaned their elbows on a crenellated rampart two hundred feet above Lake Michigan.

"Edward," said Dr. Kalten, "I shall read my paper tomorrow before the Chicago Academy of Race Science." The words were a challenge; something was wrong. He went on: "I shall expect you to be in the wings of the auditorium, and to appear at my command to answer a few questions from me and, if time permits, from our audience."

"I wish it could be postponed," Royland said.

"No doubt."

"Would you explain your unfriendly tone of voice, doctor?" Royland demanded. "I think I've been completely cooperative and have opened the way for you to win undying fame in the annals of Race Science."

"Cooperative, yes. Candid—I wonder? You see, Edward, a dreadful thought struck me today. I have always thought it amusing that the Jewish attack on Reverend Pully should have been for the purpose of precipitating him into the future and that it should have misfired." He took something out of his pocket: a small pistol. He aimed it casually at Royland. "Today I began to wonder *why* they should have done so. Why did they not simply murder him, as they did thousands, and dispose of him in their secret crematoria, and permit no mention in their controlled newspapers and magazines of the disappearance?

"Now, the blood of seven Nordic virgins can have been no cheap commodity. One pictures with ease Nordic men patrolling their precious enclaves of humanity, eyes roving over every passing face, noting who bears the stigmata of the sub-men, and following those who do most carefully indeed lest race-defilement be committed with a look or an 'accidental' touch in a crowded street. Nevertheless the thing was done; your presence here is proof of it. It must have been done at enormous cost; hired Slavs and Negroes must have been employed to kidnap the virgins, and many of them must have fallen before Nordic rage.

"This merely to silence one small voice crying in the wilderness? *I*—

think—not. I think, Edward Royland, or whatever your real name may be, that Jewish arrogance sent you, a Jew yourself, into the future as a greeting from the Jewry of that day to what it foolishly thought would be the triumphant Jewry of this. At any rate, the public questioning tomorrow will be conducted by my friend Dr. Herzbrenner, whom I have mentioned to you. If you have any little secrets, they will not remain secrets long. No, no! Do not move toward me. I shall shoot you disablingly in the knee if you do."

Royland moved toward him and the gun went off; there was an agonizing hammer blow high on his left shin. He picked up Kalten and hurled him, screaming, over the parapet two hundred feet into the water. And collapsed. The pain was horrible. His shinbone was badly cracked if not broken through. There was not much bleeding; maybe there would be later. He need not fear that the shot and scream would rouse the castle. Such sounds were not rare in the Medical Wing.

He dragged himself, injured leg trailing, to the doorway of Kalten's living quarters; he heaved himself into a chair by the signal bell and threw a rug over his legs. He rang for the diener and told him very quietly: "Go to the medical storeroom for a leg U-brace and whatever is necessary for a cast, please. Dr. Kalten has an interesting idea he wishes to work out."

He should have asked for a syringe of morphine—no he shouldn't. It might affect the time distortion.

When the man came back he thanked him and told him to turn in for the night.

He almost screamed getting his shoe off; his trouser leg he cut away. The gauze had arrived just in time; the wound was beginning to bleed more copiously. Pressure seemed to stop it. He constructed a sloppy walking cast on his leg. The directions on the several five-pound cans of plaster helped.

His leg was getting numb; good. His cast probably pinched some major nerve, and a week in it would cause permanent paralysis; who cared about *that?*

He tried it out and found he could get across the floor inefficiently. With a strong-enough bannister he could get downstairs but not, he thought, up them. That was all right. He was going to the basement.

God-damning the medieval Nazis and their cornball castle every inch of the way, he went to the basement; there he had a windfall. A dozen drunken SS men were living it up in a corner far from the censorious eyes of their company commander; they were playing a game which might have been called Spin the Corporal. They saw Royland limping and wept sentimental tears for poor ol' doc with a bum leg; they carried him two winding miles to the storeroom he wanted, and shot the lock off for him. They departed, begging him to call on ol' Company K any time, "bes' fellas in Chicago, doc. Ol' Bruno here can tear the arm off a Latvik shirker with his bare hands, honest, doc! Jus' the way you twist a drumstick off a turkey. You wan' us to get a Latvik an' show you?"

He got rid of them at last, clicked on the light, and began his search. His leg was now ice cold, painfully so. He rummaged through the uncatalogued botanicals and found after what seemed like hours a crate shipped from Jalasca. Royland opened it by beating its corners against the concrete floor. It yielded and spilled plastic envelopes; through the clear material of one he saw the wrinkled black things. He did not even compare them with the color plate in his pocket. He tore the envelope open and crammed them into his mouth, and chewed and swallowed.

Maybe there had to be a Hopi dancing and chanting, maybe there didn't have to be. Maybe one had to be calm, if bitter, and fresh from a day of hard work at differential equations which approximated the Hopi mode of thought. Maybe you only had to fix your mind savagely on what you desired, as his was fixed now. Last time he had hated and shunned the Bomb; what he wanted was a world without the Bomb. He had got it, all right!

. . . his tongue was thick and the fireballs were beginning to dance around him, the circling circles . . .

Charles Miller Nahataspe whispered: "Close. Close. I was so frightened."

Royland lay on the floor of the hut, his leg unsplinted, unfractured, but aching horribly. Drowsily he felt his ribs; he was merely slender now, no longer gaunt. He mumbled: "You were working to pull me back from this side?"

"Yes. You, you were there?"

"I was there. God, let me sleep."

He rolled over heavily and collapsed into complete unconsciousness.

When he awakened it was still dark and his pains were gone. Nahataspe was crooning a healing song very softly. He stopped when he saw Royland's eyes open. "Now you know about break-the-sky medicine," he said.

"Better than anybody. What time is it?"

"Midnight."

"I'll be going then." They clasped hands and looked into each other's eyes.

The jeep started easily. Four hours earlier, or possibly two months earlier, he had been worried about the battery. He chugged down the settlement road and knew what would happen next. He wouldn't wait until morning; a meteorite might kill him, or a scorpion in his bed. He would go directly to

Rotschmidt in his apartment, defy Vrouw Rotschmidt and wake her man up to tell him about 56c, tell him we have the Bomb.

We have a symbol to offer the Japanese now, something to which they can surrender, and will surrender.

Rotschmidt would be philosophical. He would probably sigh about the Bomb: "Ah, do we ever act responsibly? Do we ever know what the consequences of our decisions will be?"

And Royland would have to try to avoid answering him very sharply: "Yes. This once we damn well do."

Tale of the Computer That Fought a Dragon

TRANSLATED BY MICHAEL KANDEL

Arthur C. Clarke said, "This really is the Golden Age of science fiction. There are dozens of authors at work today who can match all but the giants of the past (and probably one who can do even that, despite the handicap of being translated from Polish)." Stanislaw Lem stands alone on the Polish landscape like Clarke's sentinel in 2001, a contemporary giant in a land with no indigenous SF tradition. Aware of Eastern European and Western literature and influenced by both, he is uniquely himself. His most important intellectual achievement, the huge Summa Technologiae (1964), has never been translated into English, but since the late 1960s every year has brought more of his work into this language, and his reputation continues to grow. A medical doctor, scientist, and polymath whose first SF novel was published in 1951, Lem is now the author of more than two dozen books of fiction and a body of criticism that is especially scornful of commercial American SF, which has made him a controversial literary figure. His novels are dense and intellectual, but his short stories are sometimes witty and light, with the serious underpinnings supporting a pleasing architecture of storytell-

ing, something Lem eschews in his longer works. "Tale of the Computer That Fought a Dragon," from Mortal Engines, *is one of his more delightful pieces.*

*   *   *

King Poleander Partobon, ruler of Cyberia, was a great warrior, and being an advocate of the methods of modern strategy, above all else he prized cybernetics as a military art. His kingdom swarmed with thinking machines, for Poleander put them everywhere he could; not merely in the astronomical observatories or the schools, but he ordered electric brains mounted in the rocks upon the roads, which with loud voices cautioned pedestrians against tripping; also in posts, in walls, in trees, so that one could ask directions anywhere when lost; he stuck them onto clouds, so they could announce the rain in advance, he added them to the hills and valleys—in short, it was impossible to walk on Cyberia without bumping into an intelligent machine. The planet was beautiful, since the King not only gave decrees for the cybernetic perfecting of that which had long been in existence, but he introduced by law entirely new orders of things. Thus for example in his kingdom were manufactured cyberbeetles and buzzing cyberbees, and even cyberflies—these would be seized by mechanical spiders when they grew too numerous. On the planet cyberbosks of cybergorse rustled in the wind, cybercalliopes and cyberviols sang—but besides these civilian devices there were twice as many military, for the King was most bellicose. In his palace vaults he had a strategic computer, a machine of uncommon mettle; he had smaller ones also, and divisions of cybersaries, enormous cybermatics and a whole arsenal of every other kind of weapon, including powder. There was only this one problem, and it troubled him greatly, namely, that he had not a single adversary or enemy and no one in any way wished to invade his land, and thereby provide him with the opportunity to demonstrate his kingly and terrifying courage, his tactical genius, not to mention the simply extraordinary effectiveness of his cybernetic weaponry. In the absence of genuine enemies and aggressors the King had his engineers build artificial ones, and against these he did battle, and always won. However inasmuch as the battles and campaigns were genuinely dreadful, the populace suffered no little injury from them. The subjects murmured when all too many cyberfoes had destroyed their settlements and towns, when the synthetic enemy poured liquid fire upon them; they even dared voice their discontent when the King himself, issuing forth as their deliverer and vanquishing the artificial foe, in the course of the victorious attacks laid waste to everything that stood in his path. They grumbled even then, the ingrates, though the thing was done on their behalf.

Until the King wearied of the war games on the planet and decided to raise his sights. Now it was cosmic wars and sallies that he dreamed of. His planet had a large Moon, entirely desolate and wild; the King laid heavy taxes upon his subjects, to obtain the funds needed to build whole armies on that Moon and have there a new theater of war. And the subjects were more than happy to pay, figuring that King Poleander would now no longer deliver them with his cybermatics, nor test the strength of his arms upon their homes and heads. And so the royal engineers built on the Moon a splendid computer, which in turn was to create all manner of troops and self-firing gunnery. The King lost no time in testing the machine's prowess this way and that; at one point he ordered it—by telegraph—to execute a volt-vault electrosault: for he wanted to see if it was true, what his engineers had told him, that that machine could do anything. If it can do anything, he thought, then let it do a flip. However the text of the telegram underwent a slight distortion and the machine received the order that it was to execute not an electrosault, but an electrosaur—and this it carried out as best it could.

Meanwhile the King conducted one more campaign, liberating some provinces of his realm seized by cyberknechts; he completely forgot about the order given the computer on the Moon, then suddenly giant boulders came hurtling down from there; the King was astounded, for one even fell on the wing of the palace and destroyed his prize collection of cyberads, which are dryads with feedback. Fuming, he telegraphed the Moon computer at once, demanding an explanation. It didn't reply however, for it no longer was: the electrosaur had swallowed it and made it into its own tail.

Immediately the King dispatched an entire armed expedition to the Moon, placing at its head another computer, also very valiant, to slay the dragon, but there was only some flashing, some rumbling, and then no more computer nor expedition; for the electrodragon wasn't pretend and wasn't pretending, but battled with the utmost verisimilitude, and had moreover the worst of intentions regarding the kingdom and the King. The King sent to the Moon his cybernants, cyberneers, cyberines and lieutenant cybernets, at the very end he even sent one cyberalissimo, but it too accomplished nothing; the hurly-burly lasted a little longer, that was all. The King watched through a telescope set up on the palace balcony.

The dragon grew, the Moon became smaller and smaller, since the monster was devouring it piecemeal and incorporating it into its own body. The King saw then, and his subjects did also, that things were serious, for when the ground beneath the feet of the electrosaur was gone, it would for certain hurl itself upon the planet and upon them. The King thought and thought, but he saw no remedy, and knew not what to do. To send machines was no good, for they would be lost, and to go himself was no better, for he was afraid. Suddenly the King heard, in the stillness of the night, the telegraph chattering from his royal bedchamber. It was the King's personal receiver, solid gold with a diamond needle, linked to the Moon; the King jumped up and ran to it, the apparatus meanwhile went *tap-tap*, *tap-tap*, and tapped out this telegram: THE DRAGON SAYS POLEANDER PARTOBON BETTER CLEAR OUT BECAUSE HE THE DRAGON INTENDS TO OCCUPY THE THRONE!

The King took fright, quaked from head to toe, and ran, just as he was, in his ermine nightshirt and slippers, down to the palace vaults, where stood the strategy machine, old and very wise. He had not as yet consulted it, since prior to the rise and uprise of the electrodragon they had argued on the subject of a certain military operation; but now was not the time to think of that—his throne, his life was at stake!

He plugged it in, and as soon as it warmed up he cried:

"My old computer! My good computer! It's this way and that, the dragon wishes to deprive me of my throne, to cast me out, help, speak, how can I defeat it?!"

"Uh-uh," said the computer. "First you must admit I was right in that previous business, and secondly, I would have you address me only as Digital Grand Vizier, though you may also say to me: 'Your Ferromagneticity'!"

"Good, good, I'll name you Grand Vizier, I'll agree to anything you like, only save me!"

The machine whirred, chirred, hummed, hemmed, then said:

"It is a simple matter. We build an electrosaur more powerful than the one located on the Moon. It will defeat the lunar one, settle its circuitry once and for all and thereby attain the goal!"

"Perfect!" replied the King. "And can you make a blueprint of this dragon?"

"It will be an ultradragon," said the computer. "And I can make you not only a blueprint, but the thing itself, which I shall now do, it won't take a minute, King!" And true to its word, it hissed, it chugged, it whistled and buzzed, assembling something down within itself, and already an object like a giant claw, sparking, arcing, was emerging from its side, when the King shouted:

"Old computer! Stop!"

"Is this how you address me? I am the Digital Grand Vizier!"

"Ah, of course," said the King. "Your Ferromagneticity, the electrodragon you are making will defeat the other dragon, granted, but it will surely remain in the other's place, how then are we to get rid of it in turn?!"

"By making yet another, still more powerful," explained the computer.

"No, no! In that case don't do anything, I beg you, what good will it be to have more and more terrible dragons on the Moon when I don't want any there at all?"

"Ah, now that's a different matter," the computer replied. "Why didn't you say so in the first place? You see how illogically you express yourself? One moment . . . I must think."

And it churred and hummed, and chuffed and chuckled, and finally said:

"We make an antimoon with an antidragon, place it in the Moon's orbit (here something went snap inside), sit around the fire and sing: *Oh I'm a robot full of fun, water doesn't scare me none, I dives right in, I gives a grin, tra la the livelong day!*"

"You speak strangely," said the King. "What does the antimoon have to do with that song about the funny robot?"

"What funny robot?" asked the computer. "Ah, no, no, I made a mistake, something feels wrong inside, I must have blown a tube." The King began to look for the trouble, finally found the burnt-out tube, put in a new one, then asked the computer about the antimoon.

"What antimoon?" asked the computer, which meanwhile had forgotten what it said before. "I don't know anything about an antimoon . . . one moment, I have to give this thought."

It hummed, it huffed, and it said:

"We create a general theory of the slaying of electrodragons, of which the lunar dragon will be a special case, its solution trivial."

"Well, create such a theory!" said the King.

"To do this I must first create various experimental dragons."

"Certainly not! No thank you!" exclaimed the King. "A dragon wants to deprive me of my throne, just think what might happen if you produced a swarm of them!"

"Oh? Well then, in that case we must resort to other means. We will use a strategic variant of the method of successive approximations. Go and telegraph the dragon that you will give it the throne on the condition that it perform three mathematical operations, really quite simple . . ."

The King went and telegraphed, and the dragon agreed. The King returned to the computer.

"Now," it said, "here is the first operation: tell it to divide itself by itself!"

The King did this. The electrosaur divided itself by itself, but since one electrosaur over one electrosaur is one, it remained on the Moon and nothing changed.

"Is this the best you can do?!" cried the King, running into the vault with such haste that his slippers fell off. "The dragon divided itself by itself, but since one goes into one once, nothing changed!"

"That's all right, I did that on purpose, the operation was to divert attention," said the computer. "And now tell it to extract its root!" The King telegraphed to the Moon, and the dragon began to pull, push, pull, push, until it crackled from the strain, panted, trembled all over, but suddenly something gave—and it extracted its own root!

The King went back to the computer.

"The dragon crackled, trembled, even ground its teeth, but extracted the root and threatens me still!" he shouted from the doorway. "What now, my old . . . I mean, Your Ferromagneticity?!"

"Be of stout heart," it said. "Now go tell it to subtract itself from itself!"

The King hurried to his royal bedchamber, sent the telegram, and the dragon began to subtract itself from itself, taking away its tail first, then legs, then trunk, and finally, when it saw that something wasn't right, it hesitated, but from its own momentum the subtracting continued, it took away its head and became zero, in other words nothing: the electrosaur was no more!

"The electrosaur is no more," cried the joyful King, bursting into the vault. "Thank you, old computer . . . many thanks . . . you have worked hard . . . you have earned a rest, so now I will disconnect you."

"Not so fast, my dear," the computer replied. "I do the job and you want to disconnect me, and you no longer call me Your Ferromagneticity?! That's not nice, not nice at all! Now I myself will change into an electrosaur, yes, and drive you from the kingdom, and most certainly rule better than you, for you always consulted me in all the more important matters, therefore it was really I who ruled all along, and not you . . ."

And huffing, puffing, it began to change into an electrosaur; flaming electroclaws were already protruding from its sides when the King, breathless with fright, tore the slippers off his feet, rushed up to it and with the slippers began beating blindly at its tubes! The computer chugged, choked, and got muddled in its program—instead of the word "electrosaur" it read "electrosauce," and before the King's very eyes the computer, wheezing more and more softly, turned into an enormous, gleaming-golden heap of electrosauce, which, still sizzling, emitted all its charge in deep-blue sparks, leaving Poleander to stare dumbstruck at only a great, steaming pool of gravy . . .

With a sigh the King put on his slippers and returned to the royal bedchamber. However from that time on he was an altogether different king: the events he had undergone made his nature less bellicose, and to the end of his days he engaged exclusively in civilian cybernetics, and left the military kind strictly alone.

The Green Hills of Earth

Robert A. Heinlein was the star of the prewar Campbell Golden Age in Astounding, *but after the war he broke with Campbell and published his work in the higher-paying slick magazines like* Collier's *and* The Saturday Evening Post. *At the same time, he moved to Hollywood to attempt the first American SF movie,* Destination Moon. *It is significant that what Heinlein was sending to the slicks was a continuing development of his future history series, the same material he had been selling to the pulps.*

The importance of Heinlein's breakout from the pulp ghetto into respectable magazines cannot be underrated in establishing the literary respectability of science fiction in the United States. By the early 1950s Heinlein was the most popular SF writer in the world, his works the epitome of the contemporary genre. And he achieved this position by converting the marketplace, not by changing his work or attitudes. His optimism and faith in technology—especially space travel—set the tone for much of the SF published from the late 1940s to the mid-1960s.

Heinlein's later breakthrough, to mass best-seller status, followed a real change in the atmosphere and influences in his novels late in the 1960s. This resulted from the slow-growing success of his astonishing cult classic, Stranger in a Strange Land, *which did not become a best seller until five years after its publication. Probably the major literary progenitor of Heinlein's later work is the George Bernard Shaw of* Back to Methuselah, *brilliant but very long-winded, concerned with death and immortality, aging and sexuality. The later novels, from* I Will Fear No Evil *through* Time Enough for Love, The Number of the Beast, *and* To Sail Beyond the Sunset, *are at once experimental and self-indulgent (Heinlein brooked no editing). And, it should be noted, they were enormously popular, best sellers immediately upon publication. The traditions established by Heinlein's earlier works are now carried on by other writers and remain central to much of English-language science fiction.*

*   *   *

1

This is the story of Rhysling, the Blind Singer of the Spaceways—but not the official version. You sang his words in school:

"I pray for one last landing
On the globe that gave me birth;
Let me rest my eyes on the fleecy skies
And the cool, green hills of Earth."

Or perhaps you sang in French, or German. Or it might have been Esperanto, while Terra's rainbow banner rippled over your head.

The language does not matter—it was certainly an *Earth* tongue. No one has ever translated *"Green Hills"* into the lisping Venerian speech; no Martian ever croaked and whispered it in the dry corridors. This is ours. We of Earth have exported everything from Hollywood crawlies to synthetic radioactives, but this belongs solely to Terra, and to her sons and daughters wherever they may be.

We have all heard many stories of Rhysling. You may even be one of the many who have sought degrees, or acclaim, by scholarly evaluations of his published works—*Songs of the Spaceways, The Grand Canal, and other Poems, High and Far,* and *"UP SHIP!"*

Nevertheless, although you have sung his songs and read his verses, in school and out your whole life, it is at least an even money bet—unless you are a spaceman yourself—that you have never even heard of most of Rhysling's unpublished songs, such items as *Since the Pusher Met My Cousin, That Red-Headed Venusburg Gal, Keep Your Pants On, Skipper,* or *A Space Suit Built for Two.*

Nor can we quote them in a family magazine.

Rhysling's reputation was protected by a careful literary executor and by the happy chance that he was never interviewed. *Songs of the Spaceways* appeared the week he died; when it became a best seller, the publicity stories about him were pieced together from what people remembered about him plus the highly colored handouts from his publishers.

The resulting traditional picture of Rhysling is about as authentic as George Washington's hatchet or King Alfred's cakes.

In truth you would not have wanted him in your parlor; he was not socially acceptable. He had a permanent case of sun itch, which he scratched continually, adding nothing to his negligible beauty.

Van der Voort's portrait of him for the Harriman Centennial edition of his works shows a figure of high tragedy, a solemn mouth, sightless eyes concealed by black silk bandage. He was never solemn! His mouth was always open, singing, grinning, drinking, or eating. The bandage was any rag, usually dirty. After he lost his sight he became less and less neat about his person.

"Noisy" Rhysling was a jetman, second class, with eyes as good as yours, when he signed on for a loop trip to the Jovian asteroids in the R. S. *Goshawk*. The crew signed releases for everything in those days; a Lloyd's associate would have laughed in your face at the notion of insuring a spaceman. The Space Precautionary Act had never been heard of, and the Company was responsible only for wages, if and when. Half the ships that went further than Luna City never came back. Spacemen did not care; by preference they signed for shares, and any one of them would have bet you that he could jump from the 200th floor of Harriman Tower and ground safely, if you offered him three to two and allowed him rubber heels for the landing.

Jetmen were the most carefree of the lot and the meanest. Compared with them the masters, the radarmen, and the astrogators (there were no supers nor stewards in those days) were gentle vegetarians. Jetmen knew too much. The others trusted the skill of the captain to get them down safely; jetmen knew that skill was useless against the blind and fitful devils chained inside their rocket motors.

The *Goshawk* was the first of Harriman's ships to be converted from chemical fuel to atomic power-piles — or rather the first that did not blow up. Rhysling knew her well; she was an old tub that had plied the Luna City run, Supra-New York space station to Leyport and back, before she was converted for deep space. He had worked the Luna run in her and had been along on the first deep space trip, Drywater on Mars—and back, to everyone's surprise.

He should have made chief engineer by the time he signed for the Jovian loop trip, but, after the Drywater pioneer trip, he had been fired, black-listed, and grounded at Luna City for having spent his time writing a chorus and several verses at a time when he should have been watching his gauges. The song was the infamous *The Skipper is a Father to his Crew*, with the uproariously unprintable final couplet.

The blacklist did not bother him. He won an accordion from a Chinese barkeep in Luna City by cheating at one-thumb and thereafter kept going by singing to the miners for drinks and tips until the rapid attrition in spacemen caused the Company agent there to give him another chance. He kept his nose clean on the Luna run for a year or two, got back into deep space, helped give Venusburg its original ripe reputation, strolled the banks of the Grand Canal when a second colony was established at the ancient Martian capital, and froze his toes and ears on the second trip to Titan.

Things moved fast in those days. Once the power-pile drive was accepted the number of ships that put out from the Luna-Terra system was limited only by the availability of crews. Jetmen were scarce; the shielding was cut to a minimum to save weight and few married men cared to risk possible exposure to radioactivity. Rhysling did not want to be a father, so jobs were always open to him during the golden days of the claiming boom. He crossed and recrossed the system, singing the doggerel that boiled up in his head and chording it out on his accordion.

The master of the *Goshawk* knew him; Captain Hicks had been astrogator on Rhysling's first trip in her. "Welcome home, Noisy," Hicks had greeted him. "Are you sober, or shall I sign the book for you?"

"You can't get drunk on the bug juice they sell here, Skipper." He signed and went below, lugging his accordion.

Ten minutes later he was back. "Captain," he stated darkly, "that number two jet ain't fit. The cadmium dampers are warped."

"Why tell me? Tell the Chief."

"I did, but he says they will do. He's wrong."

The captain gestured at the book. "Scratch out your name and scram. We raise ship in thirty minutes."

Rhysling looked at him, shrugged, and went below again.

It is a long climb to the Jovian planetoids; a Hawk-class clunker had to blast for three watches before going into free flight. Rhysling had the second watch. Damping was done by hand then, with a multiplying vernier and a danger gauge. When the gauge showed red, he tried to correct it—no luck.

Jetmen don't wait; that's why they are jetmen. He slapped the emergency discover and fished at the hot stuff with the tongs. The lights went out, he went right ahead. A jetman has to know his power room the way your tongue knows the inside of your mouth.

He sneaked a quick look over the top of the lead baffle when the lights went out. The blue radioactive glow did not help him any; he jerked his head back and went on fishing by touch.

When he was done he called over the tube, "Number two jet out. And for crissake get me some light down here!"

There was light—the emergency circuit—but not for him. The blue radioactive glow was the last thing his optic nerve ever responded to.

2

"As Time and Space come bending back to shape this star-specked scene,
The tranquil tears of tragic joy still spread their silver sheen;
Along the Grand Canal still soar the fragile Towers of Truth;
Their fairy grace defends this place of Beauty, calm and couth.

"Bone-tired the race that raised the Towers, forgotten are their lores;
Long gone the gods who shed the tears that lap these crystal shores.
Slow beats the time-worn heart of Mars beneath this icy sky;
The thin air whispers voicelessly that all who live must die—

"Yet still the lacy Spires of Truth sing Beauty's madrigal
And she herself will ever dwell along the Grand Canal!"

—from *The Grand Canal*, by permission of
Lux Transcriptions, Ltd., London and Luna City

On the swing back they set Rhysling down on Mars at Drywater; the boys passed the hat and the skipper kicked in a half month's pay. That was all— *finish*—just another space bum who had not had the good fortune to finish it off when his luck ran out. He holed up with the prospectors and archeologists at How-Far? for a month or so, and could probably have stayed forever in exchange for his songs and his accordion playing. But spacemen die if they stay in one place; he hooked a crawler over to Drywater again and thence to Marsopolis.

The capital was well into its boom; the processing plants lined the Grand Canal on both sides and roiled the ancient waters with the filth of the runoff. This was before the Tri-Planet Treaty forbade disturbing cultural relics for commerce; half the slender, fairylike towers had been torn down, and others were disfigured to adapt them as pressurized buildings for Earthmen.

Now Rhysling had never seen any of these changes and no one described them to him; when he "saw" Marsopolis again, he visualized it as it had been, before it was rationalized for trade. His memory was good. He stood on the riparian esplanade where the ancient great of Mars had taken their ease and saw its beauty spreading out before his blinded eyes—ice blue plain of water unmoved by tide, untouched by breeze, and reflecting serenely the sharp, bright stars of the Martian sky, and beyond the water the lacy buttresses and flying towers of an architecture too delicate for our rumbling, heavy planet.

The result was *Grand Canal*.

The subtle change in his orientation which enabled him to see beauty at Marsopolis where beauty was not now began to affect his whole life. All women became beautiful to him. He knew them by their voices and fitted their appearances to the sounds. It is a mean spirit indeed who will speak to a blind man other than in gentle friendliness; scolds who had given their husbands no peace sweetened their voices to Rhysling.

It populated his world with beautiful women and gracious men. *Dark Star Passing, Berenice's Hair, Death Song of a Wood's Colt*, and his other love songs of the wanderers, the womenless men of space, were the direct result of the fact that his conceptions were unsullied by tawdry truths. It mellowed his approach, changed his doggerel to verse, and sometimes even to poetry.

He had plenty of time to think now, time to get all the lovely words just so, and to worry a verse until it sang true in his head. The monotonous beat of *Jet Song*—

> When the field is clear, the reports all seen,
> When the lock sighs shut, when the lights wink green,
> When the check-offs done, when it's time to pray,
> When the Captain nods, when she blasts away—

>> Hear the jets!
>> Hear them snarl at your back
>> When you're stretched on the rack;
>> Feel your ribs clamp your chest,
>> Feel your neck grind its rest.
>> Feel the pain in your ship,
>> Feel her strain in their grip.

> Feel her rise! Feel her drive!
> Straining steel, come alive,
> On her jets!

—came to him not while he himself was a jetman but later while he was hitch-hiking from Mars to Venus and sitting out a watch with an old shipmate.

At Venusburg he sang his new songs and some of the old, in the bars. Someone would start a hat around for him; it would come back with a minstrel's usual take doubled or tripled in recognition of the gallant spirit behind the bandaged eyes.

It was an easy life. Any space port was his home and any ship his private carriage. No skipper cared to refuse to lift the extra mass of blind Rhysling and his squeeze box; he shuttled from Venusburg to Leyport to Drywater to New Shanghai, or back again, as the whim took him.

He never went closer to Earth than Supra-New York Space Station. Even when signing the contract for *Songs of the Spaceways* he made his mark in a cabin-class liner somewhere between Luna City and Ganymede. Horowitz, the original publisher, was aboard for a second honeymoon and heard Rhysling sing at a ship's party. Horowitz knew a good thing for the publishing trade when he heard it; the entire contents of *Songs* were sung directly into the tape in the communications room of that ship before he let Rhysling out of his sight. The next three volumes were squeezed out of Rhysling at Venusburg, where Horowitz had sent an agent to keep him liquored up until he had sung all he could remember.

UP SHIP! is not certainly authentic Rhysling throughout. Much of it is Rhysling's, no doubt, and *Jet Song* is unquestionably his, but most of the verses were collected after his death from people who had known him during his wanderings.

The Green Hills of Earth grew through twenty years. The earliest form we know about was composed before Rhysling was blinded, during a drinking bout with some of the indentured men on Venus. The verses were concerned mostly with the things the labor clients intended to do back on Earth if and when they ever managed to pay their bounties and thereby be allowed to go home. Some of the stanzas were vulgar, some were not, but the chorus was recognizably that of *Green Hills*.

We know exactly where the final form of *Green Hills* came from, and when.

There was a ship in at Venus Ellis Isle which was scheduled for the direct jump from there to Great Lakes, Illinois. She was the old *Falcon*, youngest of the Hawk class and the first ship to apply the Harriman Trust's new policy of extra-fare express service between Earth cities and any colony with scheduled stops.

Rhysling decided to ride her back to Earth. Perhaps his own song had gotten under his skin — or perhaps he just hankered to see his native Ozarks one more time.

The Company no longer permitted deadheads; Rhysling knew this but it never occurred to him that the ruling might apply to him. He was getting old, for a spaceman, and just a little matter of fact about his privileges. Not senile — he simply knew that he was one of the landmarks in space, along with Halley's Comet, the Rings, and Brewster's Ridge. He walked in the crew's port, went below, and made himself at home in the first empty acceleration couch.

The Captain found him there while making a last minute tour of his ship. "What are you doing here?" he demanded.

"Dragging it back to Earth, Captain." Rhysling needed no eyes to see a skipper's four stripes.

"You can't drag in this ship; you know the rules. Shake a leg and get out of here. We raise ship at once." The Captain was young; he had come up after Rhysling's active time, but Rhysling knew the type — five years at Harriman Hall with only cadet practice trips instead of solid, deep space experience. The two men did not touch in background nor spirit; space was changing.

"Now, Captain, you wouldn't begrudge an old man a trip home."

The officer hesitated — several of the crew had stopped to listen. "I can't do it. 'Space Precautionary Act, Clause Six: No one shall enter space save as a licensed member of a crew of a chartered vessel, or as a paying passenger of such a vessel under such regulations as may be issued pursuant to this act.' Up you get and out you go."

Rhysling lolled back, his hands under his head. "If I've got to go, I'm damned if I'll walk. Carry me."

The Captain bit his lip and said, "Master-at-Arms! Have this man removed."

The ship's policeman fixed his eyes on the overhead struts. "Can't rightly do it, Captain. I've sprained my shoulder." The other crew members, present a moment before, had faded into the bulkhead paint.

"Well, get a working party!"

"Aye, aye, sir." He, too, went away.

Rhysling spoke again. "Now look, Skipper — let's not have any hard feelings about this. You've got an out to carry me if you want to — the 'Distressed Spaceman' clause."

" 'Distressed Spaceman', my eye! You're no distressed spaceman; you're a space-lawyer. I know who you are; you've been bumming around the system for years. Well, you won't do it in my ship. That clause was intended to succor men who had missed their ships, not to let a man drag free all over space."

"Well, now, Captain, can you properly say I haven't missed my ship? I've never been back home since my last trip as a signed-on crew member. The law says I can have a trip back."

"But that was years ago. You've used up your chance."

"Have I now? The clause doesn't say a word about how soon a man has to take his trip back; it just says he's got it coming to him. Go look it up, Skipper. If I'm wrong, I'll not only walk out on my two legs, I'll beg your humble pardon in front of your crew. Go on—look it up. Be a sport."

Rhysling could feel the man's glare, but he turned and stomped out of the compartment. Rhysling knew that he had used his blindness to place the Captain in an impossible position, but this did not embarrass Rhysling—he rather enjoyed it.

Ten minutes later the siren sounded, he heard the orders on the bull horn for Up-Stations. When the soft sighing of the locks and the slight pressure change in his ears let him know that take-off was imminent he got up and shuffled down to the power room, as he wanted to be near the jets when they blasted off. He needed no one to guide him in any ship of the Hawk class.

Trouble started during the first watch. Rhysling had been lounging in the inspector's chair, fiddling with the keys of his accordion and trying out a new version of *Green Hills*.

> "Let me breathe unrationed air again
> Where there's no lack nor dearth"

And "something, something, something 'Earth'"—it would not come out right. He tried again.

> "Let the sweet fresh breezes heal me
> As they rove around the girth
> Of our lovely mother planet,
> Of the cool green hills of Earth."

That was better, he thought. "How do you like that, Archie?" he asked over the muted roar.

"Pretty good. Give out with the whole thing." Archie Macdougal, Chief Jetman, was an old friend, both spaceside and in bars; he had been an apprentice under Rhysling many years and millions of miles back.

Rhysling obliged, then said, "You youngsters have got it soft. Everything automatic. When I was twisting her tail you had to stay awake."

"You still have to stay awake." They fell to talking shop and Macdougal showed him the direct response damping rig which had replaced the manual vernier control which Rhysling had used. Rhysling felt out the controls and asked questions until he was familiar with the new installation. It was his conceit that he was still a jetman and that his present occupation as a troubadour was simply an expedient during one of the fusses with the company that any man could get into.

"I see you still have the old hand damping plates installed," he remarked, his agile fingers flitting over the equipment.

"All except the links. I unshipped them because they obscure the dials."

"You ought to have them shipped. You might need them."

"Oh, I don't know. I think—" Rhysling never did find out what Macdougal thought for it was at that moment the trouble tore loose. Macdougal caught it square, a blast of radioactivity that burned him down where he stood.

Rhysling sensed what had happened. Automatic reflexes of old habit came out. He slapped the discover and rang the alarm to the control room simultaneously. Then he remembered the unshipped links. He had to grope until he found them, while trying to keep as low as he could to get maximum benefit from the baffles. Nothing but the links bothered him as to location. The place was as light to him as any place could be; he knew every spot, every control, the way he knew the keys of his accordion.

"Power room! Power room! What's the alarm?"

"Stay out!" Rhysling shouted. "The place is 'hot.'" He could feel it on his face and in his bones, like desert sunshine.

The links he got into place, after cursing someone, anyone, for having failed to rack the wrench he needed. Then he commenced trying to reduce the trouble by hand. It was a long job and ticklish. Presently he decided that the jet would have to be spilled, pile and all.

First he reported. "Control!"

"Control aye aye!"

"Spilling jet three—emergency."

"Is this Macdougal?"

"Macdougal is dead. This is Rhysling, on watch. Stand by to record."

There was no answer; dumbfounded the Skipper may have been, but he could not interfere in a power room emergency. He had the ship to consider, and the passengers and crew. The doors had to stay closed.

The Captain must have been still more surprised at what Rhysling sent for record. It was:

> "We rot in the molds of Venus,
> We retch at her tainted breath.
> Foul are her flooded jungles,
> Crawling with unclean death."

Rhysling went on cataloguing the Solar System as he worked, "—harsh bright soil of Luna—", "—Saturn's rainbow rings—", "—the frozen night of Titan—", all the while opening and spilling the jet and fishing it clean. He finished with an alternate chorus—

> "We've tried each spinning space mote
> And reckoned its true worth:
> Take us back again to the homes of men—
> On the cool, green hills of Earth."

—then, almost absentmindedly remembered to tack on his revised first verse:

> "The arching sky is calling
> Spacemen back to their trade.
> *All hands! Stand by! Free falling!*
> And the lights below us fade.
> Out ride the sons of Terra,
> Far drives the thundering jet,
> Up leaps the race of Earthmen,
> Out, far, and onward yet—"

The ship was safe now and ready to limp home shy one jet. As for himself, Rhysling was not so sure. That "sunburn" seemed sharp, he thought. He was unable to see the bright, rosy fog in which he worked but he knew it was there. He went on with the business of flushing the air out through the outer valve, repeating it several times to permit the level of radioaction to drop to something a man might stand under suitable armor. While he did this he sent one more chorus, the last bit of authentic Rhysling that ever could be:

> "We pray for one last landing
> On the globe that gave us birth;
> Let us rest our eyes on fleecy skies
> And the cool, green hills of Earth."

Ghost V

Of the new young SF writers of the early 1950s, Robert Sheckley was the first to achieve widespread and enduring international popularity and the only one to maintain his leading position on the basis of his short fiction. He remains one of the great masters of the clever, graceful, witty, "plotted" story, the kind that derives a good bit of its punch from the plot twist at the end. Sheckley turned to the novel with increasing success in the late 1950s and throughout the 1960s, with such works as Immortality, Inc., Journey Beyond Tomorrow, *and* Mindswap, *but his most influential work is still his short fiction, widely translated and often anthologized. He has a command of the images and clichés of SF second to none and an ironic perception of the plight of the common man trying to get by in the highly complicated high-tech world of the future. "Ghost V" is a clever parody of the problem-solving story of the 1940s, as well as a highly entertaining psychological tale, all done with a very light touch.*

* * *

H e's reading our sign now," Gregor said, his long bony face pressed against the peephole in the office door. "Let me see," Arnold said.

Gregor pushed him back. "He's going to knock—no, he's changed his mind. He's leaving."

Arnold returned to his desk and laid out another game of solitaire. Gregor kept watch at the peephole.

They had constructed the peephole out of sheer boredom three months after forming their partnership and renting the office. During that time, the AAA Ace Planet Decontamination Service had had no business—in spite of being first in the telephone book. Planetary decontamination was an old, established line, completely monopolized by two large outfits. It was discouraging for a small new firm run by two young men with big ideas and a lot of unpaid-for equipment.

"He's coming back," Gregor called. "*Quick*—look busy and important!"

Arnold swept his cards into a drawer and just finished buttoning his lab gown when the knock came.

Their visitor was a short, bald, tired-looking man. He stared at them dubiously.

"You decontaminate planets?"

"That is correct, sir," Gregor said, pushing away a pile of papers and shaking the man's moist hand. "I am Richard Gregor. This is my partner, Doctor Frank Arnold."

Arnold, impressively garbed in a white lab gown and black horn-rimmed glasses, nodded absently and resumed his examination of a row of ancient, crusted test tubes.

"Kindly be seated, Mister—"

"Ferngraum."

"Mr. Ferngraum. I think we can handle just about anything you require," Gregor said heartily. "Flora or fauna control, cleansing atmosphere, purifying water supply, sterilizing soil, stability testing, volcano and earthquake control—anything you need to make a planet fit for human habitation."

Ferngraum still looked dubious. "I'm going to level with you. I've got a problem planet on my hands."

Gregor nodded confidently. "Problems are our business."

"I'm a freelance real-estate broker," Ferngraum said. "You know how it works—buy a planet, sell a planet, everyone makes a living. Usually I stick with the scrub worlds and let my buyers do their decontaminating. But a few months ago I had a chance to buy a real quality planet—took it right out from under the noses of the big operators."

Ferngraum mopped his forehead unhappily.

"It's a beautiful place," he continued with no enthusiasm whatsoever. "Average temperature of seventy-one degrees. Mountainous, but fertile. Waterfalls, rainbows, all that sort of thing. And no fauna at all."

"Sounds perfect," Gregor said. "Microorganisms?"

"Nothing dangerous."

"Then what's wrong with the place?"

Ferngraum looked embarrassed. "Maybe you heard about it. The Government catalogue number is RJC-5. But everyone else calls it 'Ghost V.'"

Gregor raised an eyebrow. "Ghost" was an odd nickname for a planet, but he had heard odder. After all, you had to call them something. There were thousands of planet-bearing suns within spaceship range, many of them inhabitable or potentially inhabitable. And there were plenty of people from the civilized worlds who wanted to colonize them. Religious sects, political minorities, philosophic groups — or just plain pioneers, out to make a fresh start.

"I don't believe I've heard of it," Gregor said.

Ferngraum squirmed uncomfortably in his chair. "I should have listened to my wife. But no — I was gonna be a big operator. Paid ten times my usual price for Ghost V and now I'm stuck with it."

"But what's *wrong* with it?" Gregor asked.

"It seems to be haunted," Ferngraum said in despair.

Ferngraum had radar-checked his planet, then leased it to a combine of farmers from Dijon VI. The eight-man advance guard landed and, within a day, began to broadcast garbled reports about demons, ghouls, vampires, dinosaurs and other inimical fauna.

When a relief ship came for them, all were dead. An autopsy report stated that the gashes, cuts and marks on their bodies could indeed have been made by almost anything, even demons, ghouls, vampires or dinosaurs, if such existed.

Ferngraum was fined for improper decontamination. The farmers dropped their lease. But he managed to lease it to a group of sun worshipers from Opal II.

The sun worshipers were cautious. They sent their equipment, but only three men accompanied it, to scout out trouble. The men set up camp, unpacked and declared the place a paradise. They radioed the home group to come at once — then, suddenly, there was a wild scream and radio silence.

A patrol ship went to Ghost V, buried the three mangled bodies and departed in five minutes flat.

"And that did it," Ferngraum said. "Now no one will touch it at any price. Space crews refuse to land on it. And I still don't know what happened."

He sighed deeply and looked at Gregor. "It's your baby, if you want it."

Gregor and Arnold excused themselves and went into the anteroom.

Arnold whooped at once, "We've got a job!"

"Yeah," Gregor said, "but what a job."

"We wanted the tough ones," Arnold pointed out. "If we lick this, we're established — to say nothing of the profit we'll make on a percentage basis."

"You seem to forget," Gregor said, "I'm the one who has to actually land on the planet. All you do is sit here and interpret my data."

"That's the way we set it up," Arnold reminded him. "I'm the research department — you're the troubleshooter. Remember?"

Gregor remembered. Ever since childhood, he had been sticking his neck out while Arnold stayed home and told him why he was sticking his neck out.

"I don't like it," he said.

"You don't believe in ghosts, do you?"

"No, of course not."

"Well, we can handle anything else. Faint heart ne'er won fair profit."

Gregor shrugged his shoulders. They went back to Ferngraum.

In half an hour, they had worked out their terms—a large percentage of future development profits if they succeeded, a forfeiture clause if they failed.

Gregor walked to the door with Ferngraum. "By the way, sir," he asked, "how did you happen to come to us?"

"No one else would handle it," Ferngraum said, looking extremely pleased with himself. "Good luck."

Three days later, Gregor was aboard a rickety space freighter, bound for Ghost V. He spent his time studying reports on the two colonization attempts and reading survey after survey on supernatural phenomena.

They didn't help at all. No trace of animal life had been found on Ghost V. And no proof of the existence of supernatural creatures had been discovered anywhere in the galaxy.

Gregor pondered this, then checked his weapons as the freighter spiraled into the region of Ghost V. He was carrying an arsenal large enough to start a small war and win it.

If he could find something to shoot at . . .

The captain of the freighter brought his ship to within several thousand feet of the smiling green surface of the planet, but no closer. Gregor parachuted his equipment to the site of the last two camps, shook hands with the captain and 'chuted himself down.

He landed safely and looked up. The freighter was streaking into space as though the furies were after it.

He was alone on Ghost V.

After checking his equipment for breakage, he radioed Arnold that he had landed safely. Then, with drawn blaster, he inspected the sun worshipers' camp.

They had set themselves up at the base of a mountain, beside a small, crystal-clear lake. The prefabs were in perfect condition.

No storm had ever damaged them, because Ghost V was blessed with a beautifully even climate. But they looked pathetically lonely.

Gregor made a careful check of one. Clothes were still neatly packed in cabinets, pictures were hung on the wall and there was even a curtain on one window. In a corner of the room, a case of toys had been opened for the arrival of the main party's children.

A water pistol, a top and a bag of marbles had spilled on to the floor.

Evening was coming, so Gregor dragged his equipment into the prefab and made his preparations. He rigged an alarm system and adjusted it so finely that even a roach would set it off. He put up a radar alarm to scan the immediate area. He unpacked his arsenal, laying the heavy rifles within easy reach, but keeping a hand-blaster in his belt. Then, satisfied, he ate a leisurely supper.

Outside, the evening drifted into night. The warm and dreamy land grew dark. A gentle breeze ruffled the surface of the lake and rustled silkily in the tall grass.

It was all very peaceful.

The settlers must have been hysterical types, he decided. They had probably panicked and killed each other.

After checking his alarm system one last time, Gregor threw his clothes on to a chair, turned off the lights and climbed into bed. The room was illuminated by starlight, stronger than moonlight on Earth. His blaster was under his pillow. All was well with the world.

He had just begun to doze off when he became aware that he was not alone in the room.

That was impossible. His alarm system hadn't gone off. The radar was still humming peacefully.

Yet every nerve in his body was shrieking alarm. He eased the blaster out and looked around.

A man was standing in a corner of the room.

There was no time to consider how he had come. Gregor aimed the blaster and said, "Okay, raise your hands," in a quiet, resolute voice.

The figure didn't move.

Gregor's finger tightened on the trigger, then suddenly relaxed. He recognized the man. It was his own clothing, heaped on a chair, distorted by the starlight and his own imagination.

He grinned and lowered the blaster. The pile of clothing began to stir faintly. Gregor felt a faint breeze from the window and continued to grin.

Then the pile of clothing stood up, stretched itself and began to walk toward him purposefully.

Frozen to his bed, he watched the disembodied clothing, assembled roughly in manlike form, advance on him.

When it was halfway across the room and its empty sleeves were reaching for him, he began to blast.

And kept on blasting, for the rags and remnants slithered toward him as if filled with a life of their own. Flaming bits of cloth crowded toward his face and a belt tried to coil around his legs. He had to burn everything to ashes before the attack stopped.

When it was over, Gregor turned on every light he could find. He brewed a pot of coffee and poured in most of a bottle of brandy. Somehow, he resisted an urge to kick his useless alarm system to pieces. Instead, he radioed his partner.

"That's very interesting," Arnold said, after Gregor had brought him up to date. "Animation! Very interesting indeed."

"I hoped it would amuse you." Gregor answered bitterly. After several shots of brandy, he was beginning to feel abandoned and abused.

"Did anything else happen?"

"Not yet."

"Well, take care. I've got a theory. Have to do some research on it. By the way, some crazy bookie is laying five to one against you."

"Really?"

"Yeah. I took a piece of it."

"Did you bet for me or against me?" Gregor asked, worried.

"For you, of course," Arnold said indignantly. "We're partners, aren't we?"

They signed off and Gregor brewed another pot of coffee. He was not planning on any more sleep that night. It was comforting to know that Arnold had bet on him. But, then, Arnold was a notoriously bad gambler.

By daylight, Gregor was able to get a few hours of fitful sleep. In the early afternoon he awoke, found some clothes and began to explore the sun worshipers' camp.

Toward evening, he found something. On the wall of a prefab, the word "*Tgasklit*" had been hastily scratched. *Tgasklit*. It meant nothing to him, but he relayed it to Arnold at once.

He then searched his prefab carefully, set up more lights, tested the alarm system and recharged his blaster.

Everything seemed in order. With regret, he watched the sun go down, hoping he would live to see it rise again. Then he settled himself in a comfortable chair and tried to do some constructive thinking.

There was no animal life here—nor were there any walking plants, intelligent rocks or giant brains dwelling in the planet's core. Ghost V hadn't even a moon for someone to hide on.

And he couldn't believe in ghosts or demons. He knew that supernatural happenings tended to break down, under detailed examination, into eminently natural events. The ones that didn't break down—stopped. Ghosts just wouldn't stand still and let a nonbeliever examine them. The phantom of the castle was invariably on vacation when a scientist showed up with cameras and tape recorders.

That left another possibility. Suppose someone wanted this planet, but wasn't prepared to pay Ferngraum's price? Couldn't this someone hide here, frighten the settlers, kill them if necessary in order to drive down the price?

That seemed logical. You could even explain the behavior of his clothes that way. Static electricity, correctly used, could—

Something was standing in front of him. His alarm system, as before, hadn't gone off.

Gregor looked up slowly. The thing in front of him was about ten feet tall and roughly human in shape, except for its crocodile head. It was colored a bright crimson and had purple stripes running lengthwise on its body. In one claw, it was carrying a large brown can.

"Hello," it said.

"Hello," Gregor gulped. His blaster was on a table only two feet away. He wondered, would the thing attack if he reached for it?

"What's your name?" Gregor asked, with the calmness of deep shock.

"I'm the Purple-striped Grabber," the thing said. "I grab things."

"How interesting." Gregor's hand began to creep toward the blaster.

"I grab things named Richard Gregor," the Grabber told him in its bright, ingenuous voice. "And I usually eat them in chocolate sauce." It held up the brown can and Gregor saw that it was labelled "Smig's Chocolate—An Ideal Sauce to Use with Gregors, Arnolds and Flynns."

Gregor's fingers touched the butt of the blaster. He asked, "Were you planning to eat me?"

"Oh, yes," the Grabber said.

Gregor had the gun now. He flipped off the safety catch and fired. The radiant blast cascaded off the Grabber's chest and singed the floor, the walls and Gregor's eyebrows.

"That won't hurt me," the Grabber explained. "I'm too tall."

The blaster dropped from Gregor's fingers. The Grabber leaned forward.

"I'm not going to eat you now," the Grabber said.

"No?" Gregor managed to enunciate.

"No. I can only eat you tomorrow, on May first. Those are the rules. I just came to ask a favor."

"What is it?"

The Grabber smiled winningly. "Would you be a good sport and eat a few apples? They flavor the flesh so wonderfully."

And, with that, the striped monster vanished.

With shaking hands, Gregor worked the radio and told Arnold everything that had happened.

"Hmm," Arnold said. "Purple-striped Grabber, eh? I think that clinches it. Everything fits."

"What fits? What is it?"

"First, do as I say. I want to make sure."

Obeying Arnold's instructions, Gregor unpacked his chemical equipment and laid out a number of test tubes, retorts and chemicals. He stirred, mixed, added and subtracted as directed and finally put the mixture on the stove to heat.

"Now," Gregor said, coming back to the radio, "tell me what's going on."

"Certainly. I looked up the word 'Tgasklit.' It's Opalian. It means 'many-toothed ghost.' The sun worshipers were from Opal. What does that suggest to you?"

"They were killed by a hometown ghost," Gregor replied nastily. "It must have stowed away on their ship. Maybe there was a curse and—"

"Calm down," Arnold said. "There aren't any ghosts in this. Is the solution boiling yet?"

"No."

"Tell me when it does. Now let's take your animated clothing. Does it remind you of anything?"

Gregor thought. "Well," he said, "when I was a kid—no, that's ridiculous."

"Out with it," Arnold insisted.

"When I was a kid, I never left clothing on a chair. In the dark, it always looked like a man or a dragon or something. I guess everyone's had that experience. But it doesn't explain—"

"Sure it does! Remember the Purple-striped Grabber now?"

"No. Why should I?"

"Because you invented him! Remember? We must have been eight or nine, you and me and Jimmy Flynn. We invented the most horrible monster you could think of—he was our own personal monster and he only wanted to eat you or me or Jimmy—flavored with chocolate sauce. But only on the first of every month, when the report cards were due. You had to use the magic word to get rid of him."

Then Gregor remembered and wondered how he could ever have forgotten. How many nights had he stayed up in fearful expectation of the Grabber? It had made bad report cards seem very unimportant.

"Is the solution boiling?" Arnold asked.

"Yes," said Gregor, glancing obediently at the stove.

"What color is it?"

"A sort of greenish blue. No, it's more blue than—"

"Right. You can pour it out. I want to run a few more tests, but I think we've got it licked."

"Got *what* licked? Would you do a little explaining?"

"It's obvious. The planet has no animal life. There are no ghosts or at least none solid enough to kill off a party of armed men. Hallucination was the answer, so I looked for something that would produce it. I found plenty. Aside from all the drugs on Earth, there are about a dozen hallucination-forming gases in the *Catalogue of Alien Trace Elements*. There are depressants, stimulants, stuff that'll make you feel like a genius or an earthworm or an eagle. This particular one corresponds to Longstead 42 in the catalogue. It's a heavy, transparent, odorless gas, not harmful physically. It's an imagination stimulant."

"You mean I was just having hallucinations? I tell you—"

"Not quite that simple," Arnold cut in. "Longstead 42 works directly on the subconscious. It releases your strongest subconscious fears, the childhood terrors you've been suppressing. It animates them. And that's what you've been seeing."

"Then there's actually nothing here?" Gregor asked.

"Nothing physical. But the hallucinations are real enough to whoever is having them."

Gregor reached over for another bottle of brandy. This called for a celebration.

"It won't be hard to decontaminate Ghost V," Arnold went on confidently. "We can cancel the Longstead 42 with no difficulty. And then— we'll be rich, partner!"

Gregor suggested a toast, then thought of something disturbing. "If they're just hallucinations, what happened to the settlers?"

Arnold was silent for a moment. "Well," he said finally, "Longstead may have a tendency to stimulate the mortido—the death instinct. The settlers must have gone crazy. Killed each other."

"And no survivors?"

"Sure, why not? The last ones alive committed suicide or died of wounds. Don't worry about it. I'm chartering a ship immediately and coming out to run those tests. Relax. I'll pick you up in a day or two."

Gregor signed off. He allowed himself the rest of the bottle of brandy that night. It seemed only fair. The mystery of Ghost V was solved and they were going to be rich. Soon *he* would be able to hire a man to land on strange planets for him, while *he* sat home and gave instructions over a radio.

∎ ∎ ∎

He awoke late the next day with a hangover. Arnold's ship hadn't arrived yet, so he packed his equipment and waited. By evening, there was still no ship. He sat in the doorway of the prefab and watched a gaudy sunset, then went inside and made dinner.

The problem of the settlers still bothered him, but he determined not to worry about it. Undoubtedly there was a logical answer.

After dinner, he stretched out on a bed. He had barely closed his eyes when he heard someone cough apologetically.

"Hello," said the Purple-striped Grabber.

His own personal hallucination had returned to eat him. "Hello, old chap," Gregor said cheerfully, without a bit of fear or worry.

"Did you eat the apples?"

"Dreadfully sorry. I forgot."

"Oh, well." The Grabber tried to conceal his disappointment. "I brought the chocolate sauce." He held up the can.

Gregor smiled. "You can leave now," he said. "I know you're just a figment of my imagination. You can't hurt me."

"I'm not going to hurt you," the Grabber said. "I'm just going to eat you."

He walked up to Gregor. Gregor held his ground, smiling, although he wished the Grabber didn't appear so solid and undreamlike. The Grabber leaned over and bit his arm experimentally.

He jumped back and looked at his arm. There were toothmarks on it. Blood was oozing out—real blood—*his* blood.

The colonists had been bitten, gashed, torn and ripped.

At that moment, Gregor remembered an exhibition of hypnotism he had once seen. The hypnotist had told the subject he was putting a lighted cigarette on his arm. Then he had touched the spot with a pencil.

Within seconds, an angry red blister had appeared on the subject's arm, because he *believed* he had been burned. If your subconscious thinks you're dead, you're dead. If it orders the stigmata of toothmarks, they are there.

He didn't believe in the Grabber.

But his subconscious did.

Gregor tried to run for the door. The Grabber cut him off. It seized him in its claws and bent to reach his neck.

The magic word! What was it?

Gregor shouted, "*Alphoisto?*"

"Wrong word," said the Grabber. "Please don't squirm."

"*Regnastikio?*"

"Nope. Stop wriggling and it'll be over before you—"

"*Voorshpellhappilo!*"

The Grabber let out a scream of pain and released him. It bounded high into the air and vanished.

Gregor collapsed into a chair. That had been close. Too close. It would be a particularly stupid way to die—rent by his own death-desiring subconscious, slashed by his own imagination, killed by his own conviction. It was fortunate he had remembered the word. Now if Arnold would only hurry . . .

He heard a low chuckle of amusement.

It came from the blackness of a half-opened closet door, touching off an almost forgotten memory. He was nine years old again, and the Shadower—his Shadower—was a strange, thin, grisly creature who hid in doorways, slept under beds and attacked only in the dark.

"Turn out the lights," the Shadower said.

"Not a chance," Gregor retorted, drawing his blaster. As long as the lights were on, he was safe.

"You'd better turn them off."

"No!"

"Very well. Egan, Megan, Degan!"

Three little creatures scampered into the room. They raced to the nearest light bulb, flung themselves on it and began to gulp hungrily.

The room was growing darker.

Gregor blasted at them each time they approached a light. Glass shattered, but the nimble creatures darted out of the way.

And then Gregor realized what he had done. The creatures couldn't actually eat light. Imagination can't make any impression on inanimate matter. He had *imagined* that the room was growing dark and—

He had shot out his light bulbs! His own destructive subsconscious had tricked him.

Now the Shadower stepped out. Leaping from shadow to shadow, he came toward Gregor.

The blaster had no effect. Gregor tried frantically to think of the magic word—and terrifiedly remembered that no magic word banished the Shadower.

He backed away, the Shadower advancing, until he was stopped by a packing case. The Shadower towered over him and Gregor shrank to the floor and closed his eyes.

His hands came in contact with something cold. He was leaning against the packing case of toys for the settlers' children. And he was holding a water pistol.

Gregor brandished it. The Shadower backed away, eyeing the weapon with apprehension.

Quickly, Gregor ran to the tap and filled the pistol. He directed a deadly stream of water into the creature.

The Shadower howled in agony and vanished.

Gregor smiled tightly and slipped the empty gun into his belt.

A water pistol was the right weapon to use against an imaginary monster.

It was nearly dawn when the ship landed and Arnold stepped out. Without wasting any time, he set up his tests. By midday, it was done and the element definitely established as Longstead 42. He and Gregor packed up immediately and blasted off.

Once they were in space, Gregor told his partner everything that had happened.

"Pretty rough," said Arnold softly, but with deep feeling.

Gregor could smile with modest heroism now that he was safely off Ghost V. "Could have been worse," he said.

"How?"

"Suppose Jimmy Flynn were here. There was a kid who could really dream up monsters. Remember the Grumbler?"

"All I remember is the nightmares it gave me," Arnold said.

They were on their way home. Arnold jotted down some notes for an article entitled "The Death Instinct on Ghost V: An Examination of Subconscious Stimulation, Hysteria, and Mass Hallucination in Producing Physical Stigmata." Then he went to the control room to set the autopilot.

Gregor threw himself on a couch, determined to get his first decent night's sleep since landing on Ghost V. He had barely dozed off when Arnold hurried in, his face pasty with terror.

"I think there's something in the control room," he said.

Gregor sat up. "There can't be. We're off the—"

There was a low growl from the control room.

"Oh, my God!" Arnold gasped. He concentrated furiously for a few seconds. "I know. I left the airlocks open when I landed. We're still breathing Ghost V air!"

And there, framed in the open doorway, was an immense gray creature with red spots on its hide. It had an amazing number of arms, legs, tentacles, claws and teeth, plus two tiny wings on its back. It walked slowly toward them, mumbling and moaning.

They both recognized it as the Grumbler.

Gregor dashed forward and slammed the door in its face. "We should be safe in here," he panted. "That door is airtight. But how will we pilot the ship?"

"We won't," Arnold said. "We'll have to trust the robot pilot—unless we can figure out some way of getting that thing out of there."

They noticed that a faint smoke was beginning to seep through the sealed edges of the door.

"What's that?" Arnold asked, with a sharp edge of panic in his voice.

Gregor frowned. "You remember, don't you? The Grumbler can get into any room. There's no way of keeping him out."

"I don't remember anything about him," Arnold said. "Does he eat people?"

"No. As I recall, he just mangles them thoroughly."

The smoke was beginning to solidify into the immense gray shape of the Grumbler. They retreated into the next compartment and sealed the door. Within seconds, the thin smoke was leaking through.

"This is ridiculous," Arnold said, biting his lip. "To be haunted by an imaginary monster—wait! You've still got your water pistol, haven't you?"

"Yes, but—"

"Give it to me!"

Arnold hurried over to a water tank and filled the pistol. The Grumbler had taken form again and was lumbering towards them, groaning unhappily. Arnold raked it with a stream of water.

The Grumbler kept on advancing.

"Now it's all coming back to me," Gregor said. "A water pistol never could stop the Grumbler."

They backed into the next room and slammed the door. Behind them was only the bunkroom with nothing behind that but the deadly vacuum of space.

Gregor asked, "Isn't there something you can do about the atmosphere?"

Arnold shook his head. "It's dissipating now. But it takes about twenty hours for the effects of Longstead to wear off."

"Haven't you any antidote?"

"No."

Once again the Grumbler was materializing, and neither silently nor pleasantly.

"How can we kill it?" Arnold asked. "There must be a way. Magic words? How about a wooden sword?"

Gregor shook his head. "I remember the Grumbler now," he said unhappily.

"What kills it?"

"It can't be destroyed by water pistols, cap guns, firecrackers, slingshots, stink bombs, or any other childhood weapon. The Grumbler is absolutely unkillable."

"That Flynn and his damned imagination! Why did we have to talk about him? How do you get rid of it then?"

"I told you. You don't. It just has to go away of its own accord."

The Grumbler was full size now. Gregor and Arnold hurried into the tiny bunkroom and slammed their last door.

"*Think*, Gregor," Arnold pleaded. "No kid invents a monster without a defense of some sort. *Think!*"

"The Grumbler cannot be killed," Gregor said.

The red-spotted monster was taking shape again. Gregor thought back over all the midnight horrors he had ever known. He *must* have done something as a child to neutralize the power of the unknown.

And then—almost too late—he remembered.

Under autopilot controls, the ship flashed Earthward with the Grumbler as complete master. He marched up and down the empty corridors and floated through steel partitions into cabins and cargo compartments, moaning, groaning and cursing because he could not get at any victim.

The ship reached the solar system and took up an automatic orbit around the moon.

Gregor peered out cautiously, ready to duck back if necessary. There was no sinister shuffling, no moaning or groaning, no hungry mist seeping under the door or through the walls.

"All clear," he called out to Arnold. "The Grumbler's gone."

Safe within the ultimate defense against night horrors—wrapped in the blankets that had covered their heads—they climbed out of their bunks.

"I told you the water pistol wouldn't do any good," Gregor said.

Arnold gave him a sick grin and put the pistol in his pocket. "I'm hanging on to it. If I ever get married and have a kid, it's going to be his first present."

"Not for any of mine," said Gregor. He patted the bunk affectionately. "You can't beat blankets over the head for protection."

JOHN VARLEY

The Phantom of Kansas

In the late 1970s John Varley, a colorful and inventive writer who was immensely and immediately popular, burst into print nearly at the height of his talents with a number of short stories, the best of which were collected in The Persistence of Vision. *Unfortunately for readers, his fiction slowed to a bare trickle in the 1980s, when he devoted most of his efforts to revising scripts in Hollywood. "The Phantom of Kansas" is from that initial meteor shower of stories in which Varley manipulated the conventions of SF with the unconscious ease of the natural. The story is a forest of tiny clusters of extrapolative ideas surrounding the central theme—the nature of identity. Varley eschews tight formal structure in favor of energy and continual wonders and surprises. The story is set in the same future as his first novel,* The Ophiuchi Hotline, *and a number of his other early stories, a method borrowed from the early "Future History" of Robert A. Heinlein. This is only the most prominent of Heinlein's characteristics that led Isaac Asimov in the late 1970s to hail Varley as "the new Heinlein."*

* * *

I do my banking at the Archimedes Trust Association. Their security is first-rate, their service is courteous, and they have their own medico facility that does nothing but take recordings for their vaults.

And they had been robbed two weeks ago.

It was a break for me. I had been approaching my regular recording date and dreading the chunk it would take from my savings. Then these thieves break into my bank, steal a huge amount of negotiable paper, and in an excess of enthusiasm they destroy all the recording cubes. Every last one of them, crunched into tiny shards of plastic. Of course the bank had to replace them all, and very fast, too. They weren't stupid; it wasn't the first time someone had used such a bank robbery to facilitate a murder. So the bank had to record everyone who had an account, and do it in a few days. It must have cost them more than the robbery.

How that scheme works, incidentally, is like this. The robber couldn't care less about the money stolen. Mostly it's very risky to pass such loot, anyway. The programs written into the money computers these days are enough to foil all but the most exceptional robber. You have to let that kind of money lie for on the order of a century to have any hope of realizing gains on it. Not impossible, of course, but the police types have found out that few criminals are temperamentally able to wait that long. The robber's real motive in a case where memory cubes have been destroyed is murder, not robbery.

Every so often someone comes along who must commit a crime of passion. There are very few left open, and murder is the most awkward of all. It just doesn't satisfy this type to kill someone and see them walking around six months later. When the victim sues the killer for alienation of person-ality—and collects up to 99 percent of the killer's worldly goods—it's just twisting the knife. So if you really hate someone, the temptation is great to *really* kill them, forever and ever, just like in the old days, by destroying their memory cube first, then killing the body.

That's what the ATA feared, and I had rated a private bodyguard over the last week as part of my contract. It was sort of a status symbol to show your friends, but otherwise I hadn't been much impressed until I realized that ATA was going to pay for my next recording as part of their crash program to cover all their policy holders. They had contracted to keep me alive forever, so even though I had been scheduled for a recording in only three weeks they had to pay for this one. The courts had ruled that a lost or damaged cube must be replaced with all possible speed.

So I should have been very happy. I wasn't, but tried to be brave.

I was shown into the recording room with no delay and told to strip and lie on the table. The medico, a man who looked like someone I might have met several decades ago, busied himself with his equipment as I tried to control my breathing. I was grateful when he plugged the computer lead into my occipital socket and turned off my motor control. Now I didn't have to worry about whether to ask if I knew him or not. As I grow older, I find that's more of a problem. I must have met twenty thousand people by now and talked to them long enough to make an impression. It gets confusing.

He removed the top of my head and prepared to take a multiholo picture of me, a chemical analog of everything I ever saw or thought or remembered or just vaguely dreamed. It was a blessed relief when I slid over into unconsciousness.

The coolness and sheen of stainless steel beneath my fingertips. There is the smell of isopropyl alcohol, and the hint of acetone.

The medico's shop. Childhood memories tumble over me, triggered by the smells. Excitement, change, my mother standing by while the medico carves away my broken finger to replace it with a pink new one. I lie in the darkness and remember.

And there is light, a hurting light from nowhere, and I feel my pupil contract as the only movement in my entire body.

"She's in," I hear. But I'm not, not really. I'm just lying here in the blessed dark, unable to move.

It comes in a rush, the repossession of my body. I travel down the endless nerves to bang up hard against the insides of my hands and feet, to whirl through the pools of my nipples and tingle in my lips and nose. *Now* I'm in.

I sat up quickly into the restraining arms of the medico. I struggled for a second before I was able to relax. My fingers were buzzing and cramped with the clamminess of hyperventilation.

"Whew," I said, putting my head in my hands. "Bad dream. I thought . . ."

I looked around me and saw that I was naked on the steel-topped table with several worried faces looking at me from all sides. I wanted to retreat into the darkness again and let my insides settle down. I saw my mother's face, blinked, and failed to make it disappear.

"Carnival?" I asked her ghost.

"Right here, Fox," she said, and took me in her arms. It was awkard and unsatisfying with her standing on the floor and me on the table. There were wires trailing from my body. But the comfort was needed. I didn't know where I was. With a chemical rush as precipitous as the one just before I awoke, the people solidified around me.

"She's all right now," the medico said, turning from his instruments. He smiled impersonally at me as he began removing the wires from my head. I did not smile back. I knew where I was now, just as surely as I had ever known anything. I remembered coming in here only hours before.

But I knew it had been more than a few hours. I've read about it: the disorientation when a new body is awakened with transplanted memories. And my mother wouldn't be here unless something had gone badly wrong.

I had died.

I was given a mild sedative, help in dressing, and my mother's arm to lead me down plush-carpeted hallways to the office of the bank president. I was still not fully awake. The halls were achingly quiet but for the brush of our feet across the wine-colored rug. I felt like the pressure was fluctuating wildly, leaving my ears popped and muffled. I couldn't see too far away. I was grateful to leave the vanishing points in the hall for the paneled browns of wood veneer and the coolness and echoes of a white marble floor.

The bank president, Mr. Leander, showed us to our seats. I sank into the purple velvet and let it wrap around me. Leander pulled up a chair facing us and offered us drinks. I declined. My head was swimming already and I knew I'd have to pay attention.

Leander fiddled with a dossier on his desk. Mine, I imagined. It had been freshly printed out from the terminal at his right hand. I'd met him briefly before; he was a pleasant sort of person, chosen for this public-relations job for his willingness to wear the sort of old-man body that inspires confidence and trust. He seemed to be about sixty-five. He was probably more like twenty.

It seemed that he was never going to get around to the briefing so I asked a question. One that was very important to me at the moment.

"What's the date?"

"It's the month of November," he said, ponderously. "And the year is 342."

I had been dead for two and a half years.

"Listen," I said, "I don't want to take up any more of your time. You must have a brochure you can give me to bring me up to date. If you'll just hand it over, I'll be on my way. Oh, and thank you for your concern."

He waved his hand at me as I started to rise.

"I would appreciate it if you stayed a bit longer. Yours is an unusual case, Ms. Fox. I . . . well, it's never happened in the history of the Archimedes Trust Association."

"Yes?"

"You see, you've died, as you figured out soon after we woke you. What you couldn't have known is that you've died more than once since your last recording."

"More than once?" So it wasn't such a smart question; so what was I supposed to ask?

"Three times."

"Three?"

"Yes, three separate times. We suspect murder."

The room was perfectly silent for a while. At last I decided I should have that drink. He poured it for me, and I drained it.

"Perhaps your mother should tell you more about it," Leander suggested. "She's been closer to the situation. I was only made aware of it recently. Carnival?"

I found my way back to my apartment in a sort of daze. By the time I had settled in again the drug was wearing off and I could face my situation with a clear head. But my skin was crawling.

Listening in the third person to things you've done is not the most pleasant thing. I decided it was time to face some facts that all of us, including myself, do not like to think about. The first order of business was to recognize that the things that were done by those three previous people were not done by *me*. I was a new person, fourth in the line of succession. I had many things in common with the previous incarnations, including all my memories up to that day I surrendered myself to the memory recording machine. But the *me* of that time and place had been killed.

She lasted longer than the others. Almost a year, Carnival had said. Then her body was found at the bottom of Hadley Rille. It was an appropriate place for her to die; both she and myself liked to go hiking out on the surface for purposes of inspiration.

Murder was not suspected that time. The bank, upon hearing of my— no, *her*—death, started a clone from the tissue sample I had left with my recording. Six lunations later, a copy of me was infused with my memories and told that she had just died. She had been shaken, but seemed to be adjusting well when she, too, was killed.

This time there was much suspicion. Not only had she survived for less than a lunation after her reincarnation, but the circumstances were un-usual. She had been blown to pieces in a tube-train explosion. She had been the only passenger in a two-seat capsule. The explosion had been caused by a homemade bomb.

There was still the possibility that it was a random act, possibly by political terrorists. The third copy of me had not thought so. I don't know why. That is the most maddening thing about memory recording: being unable to profit by the experiences of your former selves. Each time I was killed, it moved me back to square one, the day I was recorded.

But Fox 3 had reason to be paranoid. She took extraordinary precautions to stay alive. More specifically, she tried to prevent circumstances that could lead to her murder. It worked for five lunations. She died as the result of a fight, that much was certain. It was a very violent fight, with blood all over the apartment. The police at first thought she must have fatally injured her attacker, but analysis showed all the blood to have come from her body.

So where did that leave me, Fox 4? An hour's careful thought left the picture gloomy indeed. Consider: each time my killer succeeded in murdering me, he or she learned more about me. My killer must be an expert on Foxes by now, knowing things about me that I myself do not know. Such as how I handle myself in a fight. I gritted my teeth when I thought of that. Carnival told me that Fox 3, the canniest of the lot, had taken lessons in self-defense. Karate, I think she said. Did I have the benefit of it? Of course not. If I wanted to defend myself I had to start all over, because those skills died with Fox 3.

No, all the advantages were with my killer. The killer started off with the advantage of surprise—since I had no notion of who it was—and learned more about me every time he or she succeeded in killing me.

What to do? I didn't even know where to start. I ran through everyone I knew, looking for an enemy, someone who hated me enough to kill me again and again. I could find no one. Most likely it was someone Fox 1 had met during that year she lived after the recording.

The only answer I could come up with was emigration. Just pull up stakes and go to Mercury, or Mars, or even Pluto. But would that guarantee my safety? My killer seemed to be an uncommonly persistent person. No, I'd have to face it here, where at least I knew the turf.

It was the next day before I realized the extent of my loss. I had been robbed of an entire symphony.

For the last thirty years I had been an Environmentalist. I had just drifted into it while it was still an infant art form. I had been in charge of the weather machines at the Transvaal disneyland, which was new at the time and the biggest and most modern of all the environmental parks in Luna. A few of us had started tinkering with the weather programs, first for our own amusement. Later we invited friends to watch the storms and sunsets we concocted. Before we knew it, friends were inviting friends and the Transvaal people began selling tickets.

I gradually made a name for myself, and found I could make more money being an artist than being an engineer. At the time of my last recording I had been one of the top three Environmentalists on Luna.

Then Fox 1 went on to compose *Liquid Ice*. From what I read in the reviews, two years after the fact, it was seen as the high point of the art to date. It had been staged in the Pennsylvania disneyland, before a crowd of three hundred thousand. It made me rich.

The money was still in my bank account, but the memory of creating the symphony was forever lost. And it mattered.

Fox 1 had written it, from beginning to end. Oh, I recalled having had some vague ideas of a winter composition, things I'd think about later and put together. But the whole creative process had gone on in the head of that other person who had been killed.

How is a person supposed to cope with that? For one bitter moment I considered calling the bank and having them destroy my memory cube. If I died this time, I'd rather die completely. The thought of a Fox 5 rising from that table. . . . It was almost too much to bear. She would lack everything that Fox 1, 2, 3, and me, Fox 4, had experienced. So far I'd had little time to add to the personality we all shared, but even the bad times are worth saving.

It was either that, or have a new recording made every day. I called the bank, did some figuring, and found that I wasn't wealthy enough to afford that. But it was worth exploring. If I had a new recording taken once a week I could keep at it for about a year before I ran out of money.

I decided I'd do it, for as long as I could. And to make sure that no future Fox would ever have to go through this again, I'd have one made today. Fox 5, if she was ever born, would be born knowing at least as much as I knew now.

I felt better after the recording was made. I found that I no longer feared the medico's office. That fear comes from the common misapprehension that one will wake up from the recording to discover that one has died. It's a silly thing to believe, but it comes from the distaste we all have for really looking at the facts.

If you'll consider human consciousness, you'll see that the three-dimensional cross-section of a human being that is *you* can only rise from that table and go about your business. It can happen no other way. Human consciousness is linear, along a timeline that has a beginning and an end. If you die after a recording, you *die*, forever and with no reprieve. It doesn't matter that a recording of you exists and that a new person with your memories to a certain point can be created; you are *dead*. Looked at from a fourth-dimensional viewpoint, what memory recording does is to graft a new person onto your lifeline at a point in the past. You do not retrace that lifeline and magically become that new person. I, Fox 4, was only a relative of that long-ago person who had had her memories recorded. And if I died, it was forever. Fox 5 would awaken with my memories to date, but I would be no part of her. She would be on her own.

Why do we do it? I honestly don't know. I suppose that the human urge to live forever is so strong that we'll grasp at even the most unsatisfactory substitute. At one time people had themselves frozen when they died, in the hope of being thawed out in a future when humans knew how to reverse death. Look at the Great Pyramid in the Egypt disneyland if you want to see the sheer *size* of that urge.

So we live our lives in pieces. I could know, for whatever good it would do me, that thousands of years from now a being would still exist who would be at least partly me. She would remember exactly the same things I remembered of her childhood; the trip to Archimedes, her first sex change, her lovers, her hurts and her happiness. If I had another recording taken, she would remember thinking the thoughts I was thinking now. And she would probably still be stringing chunks of experience onto her life, year by year. Each time she had a new recording, that much more of her life was safe for all time. There was a certain comfort in knowing that my life was safe up until a few hours ago, when the recording was made.

Having thought all that out, I found myself fiercely determined to never let it happen again. I began to hate my killer with an intensity I had never experienced. I wanted to storm out of the apartment and beat my killer to death with a blunt instrument.

I swallowed that emotion with difficulty. It was exactly what the killer would be looking for. I had to remember that the killer knew what my first reaction would be. I had to behave in a way that he or she would not expect.

But what way was that?

I called the police department and met with the detective who had my case. Her name was Isadora, and she had some good advice.

"You're not going to like it, if I can judge from past experience," she said. "The last time I proposed it to you, you rejected it out of hand."

I knew I'd have to get used to this. People would always be telling me what I had done, what I had said to them. I controlled my anger and asked her to go on.

"It's simply to stay put. I know you think you're a detective, but your predecessor proved pretty well that you are not. If you stir out of that door you'll be nailed. This guy knows you inside and out, and he'll get you. Count on it."

"He? You know something about him, then?"

"Sorry, you'll have to bear with me. I've told you parts of this case twice already, so it's hard to remember what you don't know. Yes, we do know he's a male. Or was, six months ago, when you had your big fight with him.

Several witnesses reported a man with blood-stained clothes, who could only have been your killer."

"Then you're on his trail?"

She sighed, and I knew she was going over old ground again.

"No, and you've proved again that you're not a detective. Your detective lore comes from reading old novels. It's not a glamorous enough job nowadays to rate fictional heroes and such, so most people don't know the kind of work we do. Knowing that the killer was a man when he last knocked you off means nothing to us. He could have bought a Change the very next day. You're probably wondering if we have fingerprints of him, right?"

I gritted my teeth. Everyone had the advantage over me. It was obvious I had asked something like that the last time I spoke with this woman. And I *had* been thinking of it.

"No," I said. "Because he could change those as easily as his sex, right?"

"Right. Easier. The only positive means of identification today is gen-otyping, and he wasn't cooperative enough to leave any of him behind when he killed you. He must have been a real brute, to be able to inflict as much damage on you as he did and not even be cut himself. You were armed with a knife. Not a drop of his blood was found at the scene of the murder."

"Then how do you go about finding him?"

"Fox, I'd have to take you through several college courses to begin to explain our methods to you. And I'll even admit that they're not very good. Police work has not kept up with science over the last century. There are many things available to the modern criminal that make our job more difficult than you'd imagine. We have hopes of catching him within about four lunations, though, if you'll stay put and stop chasing him."

"Why four months?"

"We trace him by computer. We have very exacting programs that we run when we're after a guy like this. It's our one major weapon. Given time, we can run to ground about sixty percent of the criminals."

"Sixty percent?" I squawked. "Is that supposed to encourage me? Es-pecially when you're dealing with a master like my killer seems to be?"

She shook her head. "He's not a master. He's only determined. And that works against him, not for him. The more single-mindedly he pursues you, the surer we are of catching him when he makes a slip. That sixty percent figure is overall crime; on murder, the rate is ninety-eight. It's a crime of passion, usually done by an amateur. The pros see no percentage in it, and they're right. The penalty is so steep it can make a pauper of you, and your victim is back on the streets while you're still in court."

I thought that over, and found it made me feel better. My killer was not a criminal mastermind. I was not being hunted by Fu Manchu or Professor

Moriarty. He was only a person like myself, new to this business. Something Fox 1 did had made him sufficiently angry to risk financial ruin to stalk and kill me. It scaled him down to human dimensions.

"So now you're all ready to go out and get him?" Isadora sneered. I guess my thoughts were written on my face. That, or she was consulting her script of our previous conversations.

"Why not?" I asked.

"Because, like I said, he'll get you. He might not be a pro but he's an expert on you. He knows how you'll jump. One thing he thinks he knows is that you won't take my advice. He might be right outside your door, waiting for you to finish this conversation like you did last time around. The last time, he wasn't there. This time he might be."

It sobered me. I glanced nervously at my door, which was guarded by eight different security systems bought by Fox 3.

"Maybe you're right. So you want me just to stay here. For how long?"

"However long it takes. It may be a year. That four-lunation figure is the high point on a computer curve. It tapers off to a virtual certainty in just over a year."

"Why didn't I stay here the last time?"

"A combination of foolish bravery, hatred, and a fear of boredom." She searched my eyes, trying to find the words that would make me take the advice that Fox 3 had fatally refused. "I understand you're an artist," she went on. "Why can't you just . . . well, whatever it is artists do when they're thinking up a new composition? Can't you work here in your apartment?"

How could I tell her that inspiration wasn't just something I could turn on at will? Weather sculpture is a tenuous discipline. The visualization is difficult; you can't just try out a new idea the way you can with a song, by picking it out on a piano or guitar. You can run a computer simulation, but you never really know what you have until the tapes are run into the machines and you stand out there in the open field and watch the storm take shape around you. And you don't get any practice sessions. It's expensive.

I've always needed long walks on the surface. My competitors can't understand why. They go for strolls through the various parks, usually the one where the piece will be performed. I do that, too. You have to, to get the lay of the land. A computer can tell you what it looks like in terms of thermoclines and updrafts and pocket ecologies, but you have to really go there and feel the land, taste the air, smell the trees, before you can compose a storm or even a summer shower. It has to be a part of the land.

But my inspiration comes from the dry, cold, airless surface that so few Lunarians really like. I'm not a burrower; I've never loved the corridors, as so many of my friends profess to do. I think I see the black sky and harsh terrain as a blank canvas, a feeling I never really get in the disneylands where the land is lush and varied and there's always some weather in progress even if it's only partly cloudy and warm.

Could I compose without those long, solitary walks?

Run that through again: could I afford *not* to?

"All right, I'll stay inside like a good girl."

I was in luck. What could have been an endless purgatory turned into creative frenzy such as I had never experienced. My frustrations at being locked in my apartment translated themselves into grand sweeps of tornadoes and thunderheads. I began writing my masterpiece. The working title was *A Conflagration of Cyclones*. That's how angry I was. My agent later talked me into shortening it to a tasteful *Cyclone*, but it was always a conflagration to me.

Soon I had managed virtually to forget about my killer. I never did completely; after all, I needed the thought of him to flog me onward, to serve as the canvas on which to paint my hatred. I did have one awful thought, early on, and I brought it up to Isadora.

"It strikes me," I said, "that what you've built here is the better mousetrap, and I'm the hunk of cheese."

"You've got the essence of it," she agreed.

"I find I don't care for the role of bait."

"Why not? Are you scared?"

I hesitated, but what the hell did I have to be ashamed of?

"Yeah. I guess I am. What can you tell me to make me stay here when I could be doing what all my instincts are telling me to do, which is run like hell?"

"That's a fair question. This is the ideal situation, as far as the police are concerned. We have the victim in a place that can be watched perfectly safely, and we have the killer on the loose. Furthermore, this is an obsessed killer, one who cannot stay away from you forever. Long before he is able to make a strike at you we should pick him up as he scouts out ways to reach you."

"Are there ways?"

"No. An unqualified no. Any one of those devices on your door would be enough to keep him out. Beyond that, your food and water is being tested before it gets to you. Those are extremely remote possibilities since we're convinced that your killer wishes to dispose of your body completely, to kill you for good. Poisoning is no good to him. We'd just start you up again. But if we can't find at least a piece of your body, the law forbids us to revive you."

"What about bombs?"

"The corridor outside your apartment is being watched. It would take quite a large bomb to blow out your door, and getting a bomb that size in place would not be possible in the time he would have. Relax, Fox. We've thought of everything. You're safe."

She rang off, and I called up the Central Computer.

"CC," I said, to get it on-line, "can you tell me how you go about catching killers?"

"Are you talking about killers in general, or the one you have a particular interest in?"

"What do you think? I don't completely believe that detective. What I want to know from you is what can I do to help?"

"There is little you can do," the CC said. "While I myself, in the sense of the Central or controlling Lunar Computer, do not handle the apprehension of criminals, I act in a supervisory capacity to several satellite computers. They use a complex number theory, correlated with the daily input from all my terminals. The average person on Luna deals with me on the order of twenty times per day, many of these transactions involving a routine epidermal sample for positive genalysis. By matching these transactions with the time and place they occurred, I am able to construct a dynamic model of what has occurred, what possibly could have occurred, and what cannot have occurred. With suitable peripheral programs I can refine this model to a close degree of accuracy. For instance, at the time of your murder I was able to assign a low probability of their being responsible to ninety-nine point nine three percent of all humans on Luna. This left me with a pool of two hundred ten thousand people who might have had a hand in it. This is merely from data placing each person at a particular place at a particular time. Further weighting of such factors as possible motive narrowed the range of prime suspects. Do you wish me to go on?"

"No, I think I get the picture. Each time I was killed you must have narrowed it more. How many suspects are left?"

"You are not phrasing the question correctly. As implied in my original statement, all residents of Luna are still suspects. But each has been assigned a probability, ranging from a very large group with a value of ten to the minus-twenty-seventh power to twenty individuals with probabilities of thirteen percent."

The more I thought about that, the less I liked it.

"None of those sound to me like what you'd call a prime suspect."

"Alas, no. This is a very intriguing case, I must say."

"I'm glad you think so."

"Yes," it said, oblivious as usual to sarcasm. "I may have to have some programs rewritten. We've never gone this far without being able to submit a ninety percent rating to the Grand Jury Data Bank."

"Then Isadora is feeding me a line, right? She doesn't have anything to go on?"

"Not strictly true. She has an analysis, a curve, that places the probability of capture as near certainty within one year."

"You gave her that estimate, didn't you?"

"Of course."

"Then what the hell does *she* do? Listen, I'll tell you right now, I don't feel good about putting my fate in her hands. I think this job of detective is just a trumped-up featherbed. Isn't that right?"

"The privacy laws forbid me to express an opinion about the worth, performance, or intelligence of a human citizen. But I can give you a comparison. Would you entrust the construction of your symphonies to a computer alone? Would you sign your name to a work that was generated entirely by me?"

"I see your point."

"Exactly. Without a computer you'd never calculate all the factors you need for a symphony. But *I* do not write them. It is your creative spark that makes the wheels turn. Incidentally, I told your predecessor but of course you don't remember it, I liked your *Liquid Ice* tremendously. It was a real pleasure to work with you on it."

"Thanks. I wish I could say the same." I signed off, feeling no better than when I began the interface.

The mention of *Liquid Ice* had me seething again. Robbed! Violated! I'd rather have been gang-raped by chimpanzees than have the memory stolen from me. I had punched up the films of *Liquid Ice* and they were beautiful. Stunning, and I could say it without conceit because I had not written it.

My life became very simple. I worked—twelve and fourteen hours a day sometimes—ate, slept, and worked some more. Twice a day I put in one-hour learning to fight over the holovision. It was all highly theoretical, of course, but it had value. It kept me in shape and gave me a sense of confidence.

For the first time in my life I got a good look at what my body would have been with no tampering. I was born female, but Carnival wanted to raise me as a boy so she had me Changed when I was two hours old. It's another of the contradictions in her that used to infuriate me so much but which, as I got older, I came to love. I mean, why go to all the pain and trouble of bringing a child to term and giving birth naturally, all from a professed dislike of tampering—and then turn around and refuse to accept the results of nature's lottery? I have decided that it's a result of her age. She's almost two hundred by now, which puts her childhood back in the days before Changing. In those days—I've never understood why—there was a predilection for male children. I think she never really shed it.

At any rate, I spent my childhood male. When I got my first Change, I picked my own body design. Now, in a six-lunation-old clone body which naturally reflected my actual genetic structure, I was pleased to see that my first female body design had not been far from the truth.

I was short, with small breasts and an undistinguished body. But my face was nice. Cute, I would say. I liked the nose. The age of the accelerated clone body was about seventeen years; perhaps the nose would lose its upturn in a few years of natural growth, but I hoped not. If it did, I'd have it put back.

Once a week, I had a recording made. It was the only time I saw people in the flesh. Carnival, Leander, Isadora, and a medico would enter and stay for a while after it was made. It took them an hour each way to get past the security devices. I admit it made me feel a little more secure to see how long it took even my friends to get into my apartment. It was like an invisible fortress outside my door. The better to lure you into my parlor, killer!

I worked with the CC as I never had before. We wrote new programs that produced four-dimensional models in my viewer unlike anything we had ever done. The CC knew the stage—which was to be the Kansas disneyland—and I knew the storm. Since I couldn't walk on the stage before the concert this time I had to rely on the CC to reconstruct it for me in the holo tank.

Nothing makes me feel more godlike. Even watching it in the three-meter tank I felt thirty meters tall with lightning in my hair and a crown of shimmering frost. I walked through the Kansas autumn, the brown, rolling, featureless prairie before the red or white man came. It was the way the real Kansas looked now under the rule of the Invaders, who had ripped up the barbed wire, smoothed over the furrows, dismantled the cities and railroads, and let the buffalo roam once more.

There was a logistical problem I had never faced before. I intended to use the buffalo instead of having them kept out of the way. I needed the thundering hooves of a stampede; it was very much a part of the environment I was creating. How to do it without killing animals?

The disneyland management wouldn't allow any of their livestock to be injured as part of a performance. That was fine with me; my stomach turned at the very thought. Art is one thing, but life is another and I will not kill unless to save myself. But the Kansas disneyland has two million head of buffalo and I envisioned up to twenty-five twisters at one time. How do you keep the two separate?

With subtlety, I found. The CC had buffalo behavioral profiles that were very reliable. The damn CC stores *everything*, and I've had occasion more than once to be thankful for it. We could position the herds at a selected spot and let the twisters loose above them. The tornadoes would never be *totally* under our control—they are capricious even when handmade—but we could rely on a hard 90 percent accuracy in steering them. The herd profile we worked up was usable out to two decimal points, and as insurance against the unforeseen we installed several groups of flash bombs to turn the herd if it headed into danger.

It's an endless series of details. Where does the lightning strike, for instance? On a flat, gently rolling plain, the natural accumulation of electric charge can be just about anywhere. We had to be sure we could shape it the way we wanted, by burying five hundred accumulators that could trigger an air-to-ground flash on cue. And to the right spot. The air-to-air are harder. And the ball lightning—oh, brother. But we found we could guide it pretty well with buried wires carrying an electric current. There were going to be range fires—so check with the management on places that are due for a controlled burn anyway, and keep the buffalo away from there, too; and be sure the smoke would not blow over into the audience and spoil the view or into the herd and panic them. . . .

But it was going to be glorious.

Six lunations rolled by. *Six lunations!* 177.18353 mean solar days!

I discovered that figure during a long period of brooding when I called up all sorts of data on the investigation. Which, according to Isadora, was going well.

I knew better. The CC has its faults but shading data is not one of them. Ask it what the figures are and it prints them out in tricolor.

Here's some: probability of a capture by the original curve, 93 percent. Total number of viable suspects remaining: nine. Highest probability of those nine possibles: 3.9 percent. That was *Carnival*. The others were also close friends, and were there solely because they had had the opportunity at all three murders. Even Isadora dared not speculate—at least not aloud, and to me—about whether any of them had a motive.

I discussed it with the CC.

"I know, Fox, I know," it replied, with the closest approach to mechanical despair I have ever heard.

"Is that all you can say?"

"No. As it happens, I'm pursuing the other possibility: that it was a ghost who killed you."

"Are you serious?"

"Yes. The term 'ghost' covers all illegal beings. I estimate there to be on the order of two hundred of them existing outside legal sanctions on Luna. These are executed criminals with their right to life officially revoked, unauthorized children never registered, and some suspected artificial mutants. Those last are the result of proscribed experiments with human DNA. All these conditions are hard to conceal for any length of time, and I round up a few every year."

"What do you do with them?"

"They have no right to life. I must execute them when I find them."

"You do it? That's not just a figure of speech?"

"That's right. I do it. It's a job humans find distasteful. I never could keep the position filled, so I assumed it myself."

That didn't sit right with me. There is an atavistic streak in me that doesn't like to turn over the complete functioning of society to machines. I get it from my mother, who goes for years at a time not deigning to speak to the CC.

"So you think someone like that may be after me. Why?"

"There is insufficient data for a meaningful answer. 'Why' has always been a tough question for me. I can operate only on the parameters fed into me when I'm dealing with human motivation, and I suspect that the parameters are not complete. I'm constantly being surprised."

"Thank goodness for that." But this time, I could have wished the CC knew a little more about human behavior.

So I was being hunted by a spook. It didn't do anything for my peace of mind. I tried to think of how such a person could exist in this card-file world we live in. A technological rat, smarter than the computers, able to fit into the cracks and holes in the integrated circuits. Where were those cracks? I couldn't find them. When I thought of the checks and safeguards all around us, the voluntary genalysis we submit to every time we spend money or take a tube or close a business deal or interface with the computer . . . People used to sign their names many times a day, or so I've heard. Now, we scrape off a bit of dead skin from our palms. It's damn hard to fake.

But how do you catch a phantom? I was facing life as a recluse if this murderer was really so determined that I die.

That conclusion came at a bad time. I had finished *Cyclone*, and to relax I had called up the films of some of the other performances during my absence from the art scene. I never should have done that.

Flashiness was out. Understated elegance was in. One of the reviews I read was very flattering to my *Liquid Ice*. I quote:

"In this piece Fox has closed the book on the blood and thunder school of Environmentalism. This powerful statement sums up the things that can be achieved by sheer magnitude and overwhelming drama. The displays of the future will be concerned with the gentle nuance of dusk, the elusive breath of a summer breeze. Fox is the Tchaikovsky of Environmentalism, the last great romantic who paints on a broad canvas. Whether she can adjust to the new, more thoughtful styles that are evolving in the work of Janus, or Pym, or even some of the ambiguous abstractions we have seen from Tyleber, remains to be seen. Nothing will detract from the sublime glory of *Liquid Ice*, of course, but the time is here . . ." and so forth and thank-you for nothing.

For an awful moment I thought I had a beautiful dinosaur on my hands. It can happen, and the hazards are pronounced after a reincarnation. Advancing technology, fashion, frontiers, taste, or morals can make the best of us obsolete overnight. Was everyone contemplating gentle springtimes now, after my long sleep? Were the cool, sweet zephyrs of a summer's night the only thing that had meaning now?

A panicky call to my agent dispelled that quickly enough. As usual, the pronouncements of the critics had gone ahead of the public taste. I'm not knocking critics; that's their function, if you concede they have a function: to chart a course into unexplored territory. They must stay at the leading edge of the innovative artistic evolution, they must see what everyone will be seeing in a few years' time. Meanwhile, the public was still eating up the type of superspectacle I have always specialized in. I ran the risk of being labeled a dinosaur myself, but I found the prospect did not worry me. I became an artist through the back door, just like the tinkerers in early twentieth-century Hollywood. Before I was discovered, I had just been an environmental engineer having a good time.

That's not to say I don't take my art seriously. I *do* sweat over it, investing inspiration and perspiration in about the classic Edison proportions. But I don't take the critics too seriously, especially when they're not enunciating the public taste. Just because Beethoven doesn't sound like currently popular art doesn't mean his music is worthless.

I found myself thinking back to the times before Environmentalism made such a splash. Back then we were carefree. We had grandiose bull sessions, talking of what we would do if only we were given an environment large enough. We spent months roughing out the programs for something to be called *Typhoon!* It was a hurricane in a bottle, and the bottle would have to be five hundred kilometers wide. Such a bottle still does not exist, but when it's built some fool will stage the show. Maybe me. The good old days never die, you know.

So my agent made a deal with the owner of the Kansas disneyland. The owner had known that I was working on something for his place, but I'd not talked to him about it. The terms were generous. My agent displayed the profit report on *Liquid Ice*, which was still playing yearly to packed houses in Pennsylvania. I got a straight fifty percent of the gate, with costs of the installation and computer time to be shared between me and the disneyland. I stood to make about five million Lunar marks.

And I was robbed again. Not killed this time, but robbed of the chance to go into Kansas and supervise the installation of the equipment. I clashed mightily with Isadora and would have stormed out on my own, armed with not so much as a nail file, if not for a pleading visit from Carnival. So I backed down this once and sat at home, going there only by holographic projection. I plunged into self-doubt. After all, I hadn't even felt the Kansas sod beneath my bare feet this time. I hadn't been there in the flesh for over three years. My usual method before I even conceive a project is to spend a week or two just wandering naked through the park, getting the feel of it through my skin and nose and those senses that don't even have a name.

It took the CC three hours of gentle argument to convince me again that the models we had written were accurate to seven decimal places. They were perfect. An action ordered up on the computer model would be a perfect analog of the real action in Kansas. The CC said I could make quite a bit of money just renting the software to other artists.

The day of the premiere of *Cyclone* found me still in my apartment. But I was on the way out.

Small as I am, I somehow managed to struggle out that door with Carnival, Isadora, Leander, and my agent pulling on my elbows.

I was *not* going to watch the performance on the tube.

I arrived early, surrounded by my impromptu bodyguard. The sky matched my mind; gray, overcast, and slightly fearful. It brooded over us, and I felt more and more like a sacrificial lamb mounting some somber altar. But it was a magnificent stage to die upon.

The Kansas disneyland is one of the newer ones, and one of the largest. It is a hollowed-out cylinder twenty kilometers beneath Clavius. It measures two hundred and fifty kilometers in diameter and is five kilometers high. The rim is artfully disguised to blend into the blue sky. When you are half a kilometer from the rim, the illusion fails; otherwise, you might as well be standing back on Old Earth. The curvature of the floor is consistent with Old Earth, so the horizon is terrifyingly far away. Only the gravity is Lunar.

Kansas was built after most of the more spectacular possibilities had been exhausted, either on Luna or another planet. There was Kenya, beneath Mare Moscoviense; Himalaya, also on the Farside; Amazon, under old Tycho; Pennsylvania, Sahara, Pacific, Mekong, Transylvania. There were thirty disneylands under the inhabited planets and satellites of the solar system the last time I counted.

Kansas is certainly the least interesting topographically. It's flat, almost monotonous. But it was perfect for what I wanted to do. What artist really chooses to paint on a canvas that's already been covered with pictures? Well, I have, for one. But for the frame of mind I was in when I wrote *Cyclone* it had to be the starkness of the wide-open sky and the browns and yellows of the rolling terrain. It was the place where Dorothy departed for Oz. The home of the black twister.

I was greeted warmly by Pym and Janus, old friends here to see what the grand master was up to. Or so I flattered myself. More likely they were here to see the old lady make a fool of herself. Very few others were able to get close to me. My shield of high shoulders was very effective. It wouldn't do when the show began, however. I wished I was a little taller, then wondered if that would make me a better target.

The viewing area was a gentle rise about a kilometer in radius. It had been written out of the program to the extent that none of the more fearsome effects would intrude to sweep us all into the Land of Oz. But being a spectator at a weather show can be grueling. Most had come prepared with clear plastic slicker, insulated coat, and boots. I was going to be banging some warm and some very cold air masses head on to get things rolling, and some of it would sweep over us. There were a few brave souls in Native American war paint, feathers, and moccasins.

An Environmental happening has no opening chords like a musical symphony. It is already in progress when you arrive, and will still be going on when you leave. The weather in a disneyland is a continuous process and we merely shape a few hours of it to our wills. The observer does not need to watch it in its entirety.

Indeed, it would be impossible to do so, as it occurs all around and above you. There is no rule of silence. People talk, stroll, break out picnic lunches as an ancient signal for the rain to begin, and generally enjoy themselves. You experience the symphony with all five senses, and several that you are not aware of. Most people do not realize the effect of a gigantic low-pressure area sweeping over them, but they feel it all the same. Humidity alters mood, metabolism, and hormone level. All of these things are important to the total experience, and I neglect none of them.

Cyclone has a definite beginning, however. At least to the audience. It begins with the opening bolt of lightning. I worked over it a long time, and designed it to shatter nerves. There is the slow building of thunderheads, the ominous rolling and turbulence, then the prickling in your body hairs that you don't even notice consciously. And then it hits. It crashes in at seventeen points in a ring around the audience, none farther away than half a kilometer. It is properly called chain lightning, because after the initial discharge it keeps flashing for a full seven seconds. It's designed to take the hair right off your scalp.

It had its desired effect. We were surrounded by a crown of jittering incandescent snakes, coiling and dancing with a sound imported direct to you from Armageddon. It startled the hell out of *me*, and I had been expecting it.

It was a while before the audience could get their *ooh*ers and *aah*ers back into shape. For several seconds I had touched them with stark, naked terror. An emotion like that doesn't come cheaply to sensation-starved, innately insular tunnel dwellers. Lunarians get little to really shout about, growing up in the warrens and corridors, and living their lives more or less afraid of the surface. That's why the disneylands were built, because people wanted limitless vistas that were not in vacuum.

The thunder never really stopped for me. It blended imperceptibly into the applause that is more valuable than the millions I would make from this storm.

As for the rest of the performance . . .

What can I say? It's been said that there's nothing more dull than a description of the weather. I believe it, even spectacular weather. Weather is an experiential thing, and that's why tapes and films of my works sell few copies. You have to be there and have the wind actually whipping your face and feel the oppressive weight of a tornado as it passes overhead like a vermiform freight train. I could write down where the funnel clouds formed and where they went from there, where the sleet and hail fell, where the buffalo stampeded, but it would do no one any good. If you want to see it, go to Kansas. The last I heard, *Cyclone* is still playing there two or three times yearly.

I recall standing surrounded by a sea of people. Beyond me to the east the land was burning. Smoke boiled black from the hilltops and sooty gray from the hollows where the water was rising to drown it. To the north a Herculean cyclone swept up a chain of ball lightning like pearls and swallowed them into the evacuated vortex in its center. Above me, two twisters were twined in a death dance. They circled each other like baleful gray predators, taking each other's measure. They feinted, retreated, slithered, and skittered like tubes of oil. It was beautiful and deadly. And I had never seen it before. Someone was tampering with my program.

As I realized that and stood rooted to the ground with the possibly disastrous consequences becoming apparent to me, the wind-snakes locked in a final embrace. Their counterrotations canceled out, and they were gone. Not even a breath of wind reached me to hint of that titanic struggle.

I ran through the seventy-kilometer wind and the thrashing rain. I was wearing sturdy moccasins and a parka, and carrying the knife I had brought from my apartment.

Was it a lure, set by one who has become a student of Foxes? Am I playing into his hands?

I didn't care. I had to meet him, had to fight it out once and for all.

Getting away from my "protection" had been simple. They were as transfixed by the display as the rest of the audience, and it had merely been a matter of waiting until they all looked in the same direction and fading into the crowd. I picked out a small woman dressed in Indian style and offered her a hundred marks for her moccasins. She recognized me—my new face was on the programs—and made me a gift of them. Then I worked my way to the edge of the crowd and bolted past the security guards. They were not too concerned since the audience area was enclosed by a shock-field. When I went right through it they may have been surprised, but I didn't look back to see. I was one of only three people in Kansas wearing the PassKey device on my wrist, so I didn't fear anyone following me.

I had done it all without conscious thought. Some part of me must have analyzed it, planned it out, but I just executed the results. I knew where he must be to have generated his tornado to go into combat with mine. No one else in Kansas would know where to look. I was headed for a particular wind generator on the east periphery.

I moved through weather more violent than the real Kansas would have experienced. It was concentrated violence, more wind and rain and devastation than Kansas would normally have in a full year. And it was happening all around me.

But I was all right, unless he had more tricks up his sleeve. I knew where the tornadoes would be and at what time. I dodged them, waited for them to pass, knew every twist and dido they would make on their seemingly random courses. Off to my left the buffalo herds milled, resting from the stampede that had brought them past the audience for the first time. In an hour they would be thundering back again, but for now I could forget them.

A twister headed for me, leaped high in the air, and skidded through a miasma of uprooted sage and sod. I clocked it with the internal picture I had and dived for a gully at just the right time. It hopped over me and was gone back into the clouds. I ran on.

My training in the apartment was paying off. My body was only six lunations old, and as finely tuned as it would ever be. I rested by slowing to a trot, only to run again in a few minutes. I covered ten kilometers before the storm began to slow down. Behind me, the audience would be drifting away. The critics would be trying out scathing phrases or wild adulation; I didn't see how they could find any middle ground for this one. Kansas was being released from the grip of machines gone wild. Ahead of me was my killer. I would find him.

I wasn't totally unprepared. Isadora had given in and allowed me to install a computerized bomb in my body. It would kill my killer—and me— if he jumped me. It was intended as a balance-of-terror device, the kind you hope you will never use because it terrorizes your enemy too much for him to test it. I would inform him of it if I had the time, hoping he would not be crazy enough to kill both of us. If he was, we had him, though it would be little comfort to me. At least Fox 5 would be the last in the series. With the remains of a body, Isadora guaranteed to bring a killer to justice.

The sun came out as I reached the last, distorted gully before the wall. It was distorted because it was one of the places where tourists were not allowed to go. It was like walking through the backdrop on a stage production. The land was squashed together in one of the dimensions, and the hills in front of me were painted against a bas-relief. It was meant to be seen from a distance.

Standing in front of the towering mural was a man.

He was naked, and grimed with dirt. He watched me as I went down the gentle slope to stand waiting for him. I stopped about two hundred meters from him, drew my knife and held it in the air. I waited.

He came down the concealed stairway, slowly and painfully. He was limping badly on his left leg. As far as I could see he was unarmed.

The closer he got, the worse he looked. He had been in a savage fight. He had long, puckered, badly healed scars on his left leg, his chest, and his right arm. He had one eye; the right one was only a reddened socket. There was a scar that slashed from his forehead to his neck. It was a hideous thing. I thought of the CC's suspicion that my killer might be a ghost, someone living on the raw edges of our civilization. Such a man might not have access to medical treatment whenever he needed it.

"I think you should know," I said, with just the slightest quaver, "that I have a bomb in my body. It's powerful enough to blow both of us to pieces.

It's set to go off if I'm killed. So don't try anything funny."

"I won't," he said. "I thought you might have a fail-safe this time, but it doesn't matter. I'm not going to hurt you."

"Is that what you told the others?" I sneered, crouching a little lower as he neared me. I felt like I had the upper hand, but my predecessors might have felt the same way.

"No, I never said that. You don't have to believe me."

He stopped twenty meters from me. His hands were at his sides. He looked helpless enough, but he might have a weapon buried somewhere in the dirt. He might have *anything*. I had to fight to keep feeling that I was in control.

Then I had to fight something else. I gripped the knife tighter as a picture slowly superimposed itself over his ravaged face. It was a mental picture, the functioning of my "sixth sense."

No one knows if that sense really exists. I think it does, because it works for me. It can be expressed as the knack for seeing someone who has had radical body work done—sex, weight, height, skin color all altered—and still being able to recognize him. Some say it's an evolutionary change. I didn't think evolution worked that way. But I can do it. And I knew who this tall, brutalized male stranger was.

He was me.

I sprang back to my guard, wondering if he had used the shock of recognition to overpower my earlier incarnations. It wouldn't work with me. Nothing would work. I was going to kill him, no matter *who* he was.

"You know me," he said. It was not a question.

"Yes. And you scare hell out of me. I knew you knew a lot about me, but I didn't realize you'd know *this* much."

He laughed, without humor. "Yes. I know you from the inside."

The silence stretched out between us. Then he began to cry. I was surprised, but unmoved. I was still all nerve endings, and suspected ninety thousand types of dirty tricks. Let him cry.

He slowly sank to his knees, sobbing with the kind of washed-out monotony that you read about but seldom hear. He put his hands to the ground and awkwardly shuffled around until his back was to me. He crouched over himself, his head touching the ground, his hands wide at his sides, his legs bent. It was about the most wide-open, helpless posture imaginable, and I knew it must be for a reason. But I couldn't see what it might be.

"I thought I had this all over with," he sniffed, wiping his nose with the back of one hand. "I'm sorry, I'd meant to be more dignified. I guess I'm not made of the stern stuff I thought. I thought it'd be easier." He was silent for a moment, then coughed hoarsely. "Go on. Get it over with."

"Huh?" I said, honestly dumbfounded.

"Kill me. It's what you came here for. And it'll be a relief to me."

I took my time. I stood motionless for a full minute, looking at the incredible problem from every angle. What kind of trick could there *be*? He was smart, but he wasn't God. He couldn't call in an air strike on me, cause the ground to swallow me up, disarm me with one crippled foot, or hypnotize me into plunging the knife into my own gut. Even if he could do something, he would die, too.

I advanced cautiously, alert for the slightest twitch of his body. Nothing happened. I stood behind him, my eyes flicking from his feet to his hands to his bare back. I raised the knife. My hands trembled a little, but my determination was still there. I would not flub this. I brought the knife down.

The point went into his flesh, into the muscle of his shoulder blade, about three centimeters deep. He gasped. A trickle of blood went winding through the knobs along his spine. But he didn't move, he didn't try to get up. He didn't scream for mercy. He just knelt there, shivering and turning pale.

I'd have to stab harder. I pulled the knife free, and more blood came out. And still he waited.

That was about all I could take. My bloodlust had dried in my mouth until all I could taste was vomit welling in my stomach.

I'm not a fool. It occurred to me even then that this could be some demented trick, that he might know me well enough to be sure I could not go through with it. Maybe he was some sort of psychotic who got thrills out of playing this kind of incredible game, allowing his life to be put in danger and then drenching himself in my blood.

But he was *me*. It was all I had to go on. He was a me who had lived a very different life, becoming much tougher and wilier with every day, diverging by the hour from what I knew as my personality and capabilities. So I tried and I tried to think of myself doing what he was doing now for the purpose of murder. I failed utterly.

And if I *could* sink that low, I'd rather not live.

"Hey, get up," I said, going around in front of him. He didn't respond, so I nudged him with my foot. He looked up, and saw me offering him the knife, hilt-first.

"If this is some sort of scheme," I said, "I'd rather learn of it now."

His one eye was red and brimming as he got up, but there was no joy in him. He took the knife, not looking at me, and stood there holding it. The skin on my belly was crawling. Then he reversed the knife and his brow wrinkled, as if he were summoning up nerve. I suddenly knew what he was going to do, and I lunged. I was barely in time. The knife missed his belly and went off to the side as I yanked on his arm. He was much stronger than I. I was pulled off balance, but managed to hang onto his arm. He fought with me, but was intent on suicide and had no thought of defending himself. I brought my fist up under his jaw and he went limp.

Night had fallen. I disposed of the knife and built a fire. Did you know that dried buffalo manure burns well? I didn't believe it until I put it to the test.

I dressed his wound by tearing up my shirt, wrapped my parka around him to ward off the chill, and sat with my bare back to the fire. Luckily, there was no wind, because it can get very chilly on the plains at night.

He woke with a sore jaw and a resigned demeanor. He didn't thank me for saving him from himself. I suppose people rarely do. They think they know what they're doing, and their reasons always seem logical to them.

"You don't understand," he moaned. "You're only dragging it out. I have to die, there's no place for me here."

"Make me understand," I said.

He didn't want to talk, but there was nothing to do and no chance of sleeping in the cold, so he eventually did. The story was punctuated with long, truculent silences.

It stemmed from the bank robbery two and a half years ago. It had been staged by some very canny robbers. They had a new dodge that made me respect Isadora's statement that police methods had not kept pace with criminal possibilities.

The destruction of the memory cubes had been merely a decoy. They were equally unconcerned about the cash they took. They were bunco artists.

They had destroyed the rest of the cubes to conceal the theft of two of them. That way the police would be looking for a crime of passion, murder, rather than one of profit. It was a complicated double feint, because the robbers wanted to give the impression of someone who was trying to conceal murder by stealing cash.

My killer—we both agreed he should not be called Fox so we settled on the name he had come to fancy, Rat—didn't know the details of the scheme, but it involved the theft of memory cubes containing two of the richest people on Luna. They were taken, and clones were grown. When the memories were played into the clones, the people were awakened into a falsely created situation and encouraged to believe that it was reality. It would work; the newly reincarnated person is willing to be led, willing to believe. Rat didn't know exactly what the plans were beyond that. He had awakened to be told that it was fifteen thousand years later, and that the Invaders had left Earth and were rampaging through the solar system wiping out the human race. It took three lunations to convince them that he—or rather she, for Rat had been awakened into a body identical to the one I was wearing—was not the right billionaire. That she was not a billionaire at all, just a struggling artist. The thieves had gotten the wrong cube.

They dumped her. Just like that. They opened the door and kicked her out into what she thought was the end of civilization. She soon found out that it was only twenty years in her future, since her memories came from the stolen cube which I had recorded about twenty years before.

Don't ask me how they got the wrong cube. One cube looks exactly like another; they are in fact indistinguishable from one another by any test known to science short of playing them into a clone and asking the resulting person who he or she is. Because of that fact, the banks we entrust them to have a foolproof filing system to avoid unpleasant accidents like Rat. The only possible answer was that for all their planning, for all their cunning and guile, the thieves had read 2 in column A and selected 3 in column B.

I didn't think much of their chances of living to spend any of that money. I told Rat so.

"I doubt if their extortion scheme involves money," he said. "At least not directly. More likely the theft was aimed at obtaining information contained in the minds of billionaires. Rich people are often protected with psychological safeguards against having information tortured from them, but can't block themselves against divulging it willingly. That's what the Invader hoax must have been about, to finagle them into thinking the information no longer mattered, or perhaps that it must be revealed to save the human race."

"I'm suspicious of involuted schemes like that," I said.

"So am I." We laughed when we realized what he had said. Of *course* we had the same opinions.

"But it fooled *me*," he went on. "When they discarded me, I fully expected to meet the Invaders face-to-face. It was quite a shock to find that the world was almost unchanged."

"Almost," I said, quietly. I was beginning to empathize with him.

"Right." He lost the half-smile that had lingered on his face, and I was sad to see it go.

What would I have done in the same situation? There's really no need to ask. I must believe that I would have done exactly as she did. She had been dumped like garbage, and quickly saw that she was about that useful to society. If found, she would be eliminated like garbage. The robbers had not thought enough of her to bother killing her. She could tell the police certain things they did not know if she was captured, so she had to assume that the robbers had told her nothing of any use to the police. Even if she could have helped capture and convict the conspirators, she would *still* be eliminated. She was an illegal person.

She risked a withdrawal from my bank account. I remembered it now. It wasn't large, and I assumed I must have written it since it was backed up by my genalysis. It was far too small an amount to suspect anything. And it wasn't the first time I have made a withdrawal and forgotten about it. She knew that, of course.

With the money she bought a Change on the sly. They can be had, though you take your chances. It's not the safest thing in the world to conduct illegal business with someone who will soon have you on the operating table, unconscious. Rat had thought the Change would help throw the police off his trail if they should learn of his existence. Isadora told me about that once, said it was the sign of the inexperienced criminal.

Rat was definitely a fugitive. If discovered and captured, he faced a death sentence. It's harsh, but the population laws allow no loopholes whatsoever. If they did, we could be up to our ears in a century. There would be no trial, only a positive genalysis and a hearing to determine which of us was the rightful Fox.

"I can't tell you how bitter I was," he said. "I learned slowly how to survive. It's not as hard as you might think, in some ways, and much harder than you can imagine in others. I could walk the corridors freely, as long as I did nothing that required a genalysis. That means you can't buy anything, ride on public transport, take a job. But the air is free if you're not registered with the tax board, water is free, and food can be had in the disneylands. I was lucky in that. My palmprint would still open all the restricted doors in the disneylands. A legacy of my artistic days." I could hear the bitterness in his voice.

And why not? He had been robbed, too. He went to sleep as I had been twenty years ago, an up-and-coming artist, excited by the possibilities in Environmentalism. He had great dreams. I remember them well. He woke up to find that it had all been realized but none of it was for him. He could not even get access to computer time. Everyone was talking about Fox and her last opus, *Thunderhead*. She was the darling of the art world.

He went to the premiere of *Liquid Ice* and began to hate me. He was sleeping in the air recirculators to keep warm, foraging nuts and berries and an occasional squirrel in Pennsylvania, while I was getting rich and famous. He took to trailing me. He stole a spacesuit, followed me out onto Palus Putridinus.

"I didn't plan it," he said, his voice wracked with guilt. "I never could have done it with planning. The idea just struck me and before I knew it I had pushed you. You hit the bottom and I followed you down, because I was really sorry I had done it and I lifted your body up and looked into your face. . . . Your face was all . . . my face, it was . . . the eyes popping out and blood boiling away and . . ."

He couldn't go on, and I was grateful. He finally let out a shuddering breath and continued.

"Before they found your body I wrote some checks on your account. You never noticed them when you woke up that first time, since the reincarnation had taken such a big chunk out of your balance. We never were any good with money." He chuckled again. I took the opportunity to move closer to him. He was speaking very quietly so that I could barely hear him over the crackling of the fire.

"I . . . I guess I went crazy then. I can't account for it any other way. When I saw you in Pennsylvania again, walking among the trees as free as can be, I just cracked up. Nothing would do but that I kill you and take your place. I'd have to do it in a way that would destroy the body. I thought of acid, and of burning you up here in Kansas in a range fire. I don't know why I settled on a bomb. It was stupid. But I don't feel responsible. At least it must have been painless.

"They reincarnated you again. I was fresh out of ideas for murder. And motivation. I tried to think it out. So I decided to approach you carefully, not revealing who I was. I thought maybe I could reach you. I tried to think of what I would do if I was approached with the same story, and decided I'd be sympathetic. I didn't reckon with the fear you were feeling. You were hunted. I myself was being hunted, and I should have seen that fear brings out the best and the worst in us.

"You recognized me immediately—something else I should have thought of—and put two and two together so fast I didn't even know what hit me. You were on me, and you were armed with a knife. You had been taking training in martial arts." He pointed to the various scars. "You did this to me, and this, and this. You nearly killed me. But I'm bigger. I held on and managed to overpower you. I plunged the knife in your heart.

"I went insane again. I've lost all memories from the sight of the blood pouring from your chest until yesterday. I somehow managed to stay alive and not bleed to death. I must have lived like an animal. I'm dirty enough to be one.

"Then yesterday I heard two of the maintenance people in the machine areas of Pennsylvania talking about the show you were putting on in Kansas. So I came here. The rest you know."

The fire was dying. I realized that part of my shivering was caused by the cold. I got up and searched for more chips, but it was too dark to see. The "moon" wasn't up tonight, would not rise for hours yet.

"You're cold," he said, suddenly. "I'm sorry, I didn't realize. Here, take this back. I'm used to it." He held out the parka.

"No, you keep it. I'm all right." I laughed when I realized my teeth had been chattering as I said it. He was still holding it out to me.

"Well, maybe we could share it?"

Luckily it was too big, borrowed from a random spectator earlier in the day. I sat in front of him and leaned back against his chest and he wrapped his arms around me with the parka going around both of us. My teeth still chattered, but I was cozy.

I thought of him sitting at the auxiliary computer terminal above the east wind generator, looking out from a distance of fifteen kilometers at the crowd and the storm. He had known how to talk to me. That tornado he had created in real-time and sent out to do battle with my storm was as specific to me as a typed message: *I'm here! Come meet me.*

I had an awful thought, then wondered why it was so awful. It wasn't me that was in trouble.

"Rat, you used the computer. That means you submitted a skin sample for genalysis, and the CC will . . . no, wait a minute."

"What does it matter?"

"It . . . it matters. But the game's not over. I can cover for you. No one knows when I left the audience, or why. I can say I saw something going wrong—it could be tricky fooling the CC, but I'll think of something—and headed for the computer room to correct it. I'll say I created the second tornado as a—"

He put his hand over my mouth.

"Don't talk like that. It was hard enough to resign myself to death. There's no way out for me. Don't you see that I can't go on living like a rat? What would I do if you covered for me this time? I'll tell you. I'd spend the rest of my life hiding out here. You could sneak me table scraps from time to time. No, thank-you."

"No, no. You haven't thought it out. You're still looking on me as an enemy. Alone, you don't have a chance, I'll concede that, but with me to help you, spend money and so forth, we—" He put his hand over my mouth again. I found that I didn't mind, dirty as it was.

"You mean you're not my enemy now?" He said it quietly, helplessly, like a child asking if I was *really* going to stop beating him.

"I—" That was as far as I got. What the hell was going on? I became aware of his arms around me, not as lovely warmth but as a strong presence. I hugged my legs up closer to me and bit down hard on my knee. Tears squeezed from my eyes.

I turned to face him, searching to see his face in the darkness. He went over backwards with me on top of him.

"No, I'm not your enemy." Then I was struggling blindly to dispose of the one thing that stood between us: my pants. While we groped in the dark, the rain started to fall around us.

We laughed as we were drenched, and I remember sitting up on top of him once.

"Don't blame me," I said. "This storm isn't mine." Then he pulled me back down.

It was like something you read about in the romance magazines. All the overblown words, the intensive hyperbole. It was all real. We were made for each other, literally. It was the most astounding act of love imaginable. He knew what I liked to the tenth decimal place, and I was just as knowledge-able. I *knew* what he liked, by remembering back to the times I had been male and then doing what *I* had liked.

Call it masturbation orchestrated for two. There were times during that night when I was unsure of which one I was. I distinctly remember touching his face with my hand and feeling the scar on my own face. For a few moments I was convinced that the line which forever separates two individ-uals blurred, and we came closer to being one person than any two humans have ever done.

A time finally came when we had spent all our passion. Or, I prefer to think, invested it. We lay together beneath my parka and allowed our bodies to adjust to each other, filling the little spaces, trying to touch in every place it was possible to touch.

"I'm listening," he whispered. "What's your plan?"

They came after me with a helicopter later that night. Rat hid out in a gully while I threw away my clothes and walked calmly out to meet them. I was filthy, with mud and grass plastered in my hair, but that was consistent with what I had been known to do in the past. Often, before or after a perfor-mance, I would run nude through the disneyland in an effort to get closer to the environment I had shaped.

I told them I had been doing that. They accepted it, Carnival and Isadora, though they scolded me for a fool to leave them as I had. But it was easy to bamboozle them into believing that I had had no choice.

"If I hadn't taken over control when I did," I said to them, "there might have been twenty thousand dead. One of those twisters was off course. I extrapolated and saw trouble in about three hours. I had no choice."

Neither of them knew a stationary cold front from an isobar, so I got away with it.

Fooling the CC was not so simple. I had to fake data as best I could, and make it jibe with the internal records. This all had to be done in my head, relying on the overall feeling I've developed for the medium. When the CC questioned me about it I told it haughtily that a human develops a sixth sense in art, and it's something a computer could never grasp. The CC had to be satisfied with that.

The reviews were good, though I didn't really care. I was in demand. That made it harder to do what I had to do, but I was helped by the fact of my continued forced isolation.

I told all the people who called me with offers that I was not doing anything more until my killer was caught. And I proposed my idea to Isadora.

She couldn't very well object. She knew there was not much chance of keeping me in my apartment for much longer, so she went along with me. I bought a ship and told Carnival about it.

Carnival didn't like it much, but she had to agree it was the best way to keep me safe. But she wanted to know why I needed my own ship, why I couldn't just book passage on a passenger liner.

Because all passengers on a liner must undergo genalysis, is what I thought, but what I said was, "Because how would I know that my killer is not a fellow passenger? To be safe, I must be alone. Don't worry, mother, I know what I'm doing."

The day came when I owned my own ship, free and clear. It was a beauty, and cost me most of the five million I had made from *Cyclone*. It could boost at one gee for weeks; plenty of power to get me to Pluto. It was completely automatic, requiring only verbal instructions to the computer-pilot.

The customs agents went over it, then left me alone. The CC had instructed them that I needed to leave quietly, and told them to cooperate with me. That was a stroke of luck, since getting Rat aboard was the most hazardous part of the plan. We were able to scrap our elaborate plans and he just walked in like a law-abiding citizen.

We sat together in the ship, waiting for the ignition.

"Pluto has no extradition treaty with Luna," the CC said, out of the blue.

"I didn't know that," I lied, wondering what the hell was happening.

"Indeed? Then you might be interested in another fact. There is very little on Pluto in the way of centralized government. You're heading out for the frontier."

"That should be fun," I said, cautiously. "Sort of an adventure, right?"

"You always were one for adventure. I remember when you first came here to Nearside, over my objections. That one turned out all right, didn't it? Now Lunarians live freely on either side of Luna. You were largely responsible for that."

"Was I really? I don't think so. I think the time was just ripe."

"Perhaps." The CC was silent for a while as I watched the chronometer ticking down to lift-off time. My shoulder blades were itching with a sense of danger.

"There are no population laws on Pluto," it said, and waited.

"Oh? How delightfully primitive. You mean a woman can have as many children as she wishes?"

"So I hear. I'm onto you, Fox."

"Autopilot, override your previous instructions. I wish to lift off right now! Move!"

A red light flashed on my panel, and started blinking.

"That means that it's too late for a manual override," the CC informed me. "Your ship's pilot is not that bright."

I slumped into my chair and then reached out blindly for Rat. Two minutes to go. So close.

"Fox, it was a pleasure to work with you on *Cyclone*. I enjoyed it tremendously. I think I'm beginning to understand what you mean when you say 'art.' I'm even beginning to try some things on my own. I sincerely wish you could be around to give me criticism, encouragement, perspective."

We looked at the speaker, wondering what it meant by that.

"I knew about your plan, and about the existence of your double, since shortly after you left Kansas. You did your best to conceal it and I applaud the effort, but the data were unmistakable. I had trillions of nanoseconds to play around with the facts, fit them together every possible way, and I arrived at the inevitable answer."

I cleared my throat nervously.

"I'm glad you enjoyed *Cyclone*. Uh, if you knew this, why didn't you have us arrested that day?"

"As I told you, I am not the law-enforcement computer. I merely supervise it. If Isadora and the computer could not arrive at the same conclusion, then it seems obvious that some programs should be rewritten. So I decided to leave them on their own and see if they could solve the problem. It was a test, you see." It made a throat-clearing sound, and went on in a slightly embarrassed voice.

"For a while there, a few days ago, I thought they'd really catch you. Do you know what a 'red herring' is? But, as you know, crime does not pay. I informed Isadora of the true situation a few minutes ago. She is on her way here now to arrest your double. She's having a little trouble with an elevator which is stuck between levels. I'm sending a repair crew. They should arrive in another three minutes."

32 . . . 31 . . . 30 . . . 29 . . . 28 . . .

"I don't know what to say."

"Thank you," Rat said. "Thank you for everything. I didn't know you could do it. I thought your parameters were totally rigid."

"They were supposed to be. I've written a few new ones. And don't worry, you'll be all right. You will not be pursued. Once you leave the surface you are no longer violating Lunar law. You are a legal person again, Rat."

"Why did you do it?" I was crying as Rat held me in a grasp that threatened to break ribs. "What have I done to deserve such kindness?"

It hesitated.

"Humanity has washed its hands of responsibility. I find myself given all the hard tasks of government. I find some of the laws too harsh, but there is no provision for me to disagree with them and no one is writing new ones. I'm stuck with them. It just seemed . . . unfair."

9 . . . 8 . . . 7 . . . 6 . . .

"Also . . . cancel that. There is no also. It . . . was *good* working with you."

I was left to wonder as the engines fired and we were pressed into the couches. I heard the CC's last message to us come over the radio.

"Good luck to you both. Please take care of each other, you mean a lot to me. And don't forget to write."

JOSEF NESVADBA

Captain Nemo's Last Adventure

TRANSLATED BY IRIS URWIN

A leading European science fiction writer, Josef Nesvadba is a doctor as well as a psychiatrist and the heir of Karel Čapek. Čapek not only invented the word robot but wrote many works influenced by H. G. Wells, culminating in The War with the Newts, *a twentieth-century classic and a work of great satirical force and philosophical depth. Since the 1950s, Nesvadba has been the only internationally recognized Czech SF writer, with two collections of short fiction translated into English,* Vampires, Ltd., *and* In the Footsteps of the Abominable Snowman. *First published in 1964, "Captain Nemo's Last Adventure" is a tour-de-force gesture of homage to the SF adventure story of the Campbell era and a satire on Campbellian aspirations worthy of Fritz Leiber or Cyril M. Kornbluth. Nesvadba uses the tropes and conventions of genre SF, especially the pulp SF of the 1940s, in a way that shows detailed knowledge of them, and then undercuts them. It is fascinating to read this tale of noble heroism in the spacefaring future, with a bow to Jules Verne's mysterious Captain Nemo, in comparison to John Berryman's "Special Flight," which may be its direct antecedent. Nesvadba's irony makes this story a work of criticism of the most rigorous yet affectionate sort. He has, unfortunately, written no science fiction novels, although one of his two novels, a mystery, parodies some of the ideas of Erich Von Daniken.*

*   *   *

H is real name was Feather. Lieutenant Feather. He was in charge of transport between the second lunar base and the airfields on Earth, both direct trips and transfers via Cosmic Station 36 or 38. It was a dull job, and the suggestion had been made that the pilots of these rockets be replaced altogether by automatic control, as the latter was capable of reporting dangerous meteorites or mechanical breakdowns sooner and with greater accuracy, and was not subject to fatigue.

But then there was the famous accident with Tanker Rocket 272 BF. Unable to land on Cosmic Station 6, it was in danger of exploding and destroying the whole station, which would have held up traffic between the Moon and the Earth for several weeks and brought the greatest factories on Earth to a standstill, dependent as they are on the supply of cheap top-quality Moon ore. How would the Moon crews carry on without supplies from Earth? Were their rations adequate? How long would they be cut off? Everyone asked the same questions; there wasn't a family on Earth who didn't have at least one close relative on one lunar station or another. The Supreme Office of Astronautics was criticized from all quarters, and it looked as though the chairman would have to resign.

Just then the news came through that an unknown officer, one Lieutenant Feather, had risked his life to land on the tanker rocker in a small Number Four Cosmic Bathtub (the nickname for the small squat rockets used for short journeys). After repairing the rocket controls, Feather had landed safely on one of the Moon bases. Afterwards he spent a few weeks in the hospital; apparently he had tackled the job in an astronautical training suit. On the day he was released, the chairman of the Supreme Office of Astronautics himself was waiting for him, to thank him personally for his heroic deed and to offer him a new job.

And so Lieutenant Feather became Captain Feather; and Captain Feather became Captain Nemo. The world press services couldn't get his Czech name right, and when news got out that Captain Feather was going to command the new *Nautilus* rocket to explore the secrets of Neptune, he was promptly rechristened Nemo (Jules Verne was en vogue just then). Reuter even put forth another suggestion: Captain Feather de Neptune (it was meant to look like a title of nobility). But no one picked up on the idea.

Readers all over the world soon got used to Captain Nemo, who discovered the secrets of Neptune, brought back live bacteria from Uranus, and saved the supplies of radon on Jupiter during the great earthquake there—or rather, the planetquake. Captain Nemo was always on the spot whenever there was an accident or catastrophe in our solar system—whenever the stakes were life or death. He gathered together a crew of kindred spirits, most of them from his native Skalice, and became the idol of all the little boys on our third planet (as the scientists sometimes called Earth).

But progress in automation and the gradual perfection of technical devices made human intervention less and less necessary. Feather/Nemo was the commander of the rescue squads on Earth, but for some years he had had no opportunity to display his heroism. He and his crew were the subjects of literary works, the models for sculptors and painters, and the most popular lecturers among the younger generation. The captain often changed his place of residence—and his paramours as well. Women fell for him. He was well-built and handsome, with a determined chin and hair that had begun to gray at the temples: the answer to a maiden's prayer. And unhappy at home; everybody knew that.

That was really why he had become a hero. At any rate, a psychologist somewhere had written a scholarly article about it: "Suicide and Heroism. Notes on Cause and Effect." That was the title of the study. The author cited the case of Captain Nemo: if only this great cosmic explorer had been more happily married, he said, if instead of a wife from Zatec, where the hops grow, he had married a wife from Skalice, where they are brought up with the vine, if only his wife were not such a narrow specialist in her own field (she was a geologist), but had the gift of fantasy, and if only the son had taken after his father—Mr. Feather would be sitting quietly by the family hearth, and no one would ever have heard of Captain Nemo. As it was, his wife was of no particular use to him, and he was always trying to slip away from home. His son was nearsighted, had always had to wear thick spectacles, and was devoted to music. He was also composing symphonies that nobody ever played; his desk was full of them by now, and the only thing he was good for was to occasionally play the harp and to teach youngsters to play this neglected old instrument at music society meetings. The son of a hero, a harpist—that was another good reason for Captain Nemo to be fed up with life. And so he looked for distraction elsewhere. His most recent affair was said to have been with a black girl mathematician from the University of Timbuctoo, but everyone knew that even this twenty-year-old raven beauty could not hold him for long. He was famous for his infidelity—a relatively rare quality at this stage in history, since people usually married only after careful consideration and on the recommendation of the appropriate specialists, so that the chances of a successful marriage were optimal. Naturally the experts always tried to adjust the interests of those in love. Heroism was no longer considered much of a profession; it was a bit too specialized, and in fact no longer fulfilling. Today's heroes were those who designed new machines or found the solution to some current problem. There was no longer any need to risk one's life. Thus Captain Nemo had become somewhat obsolete in the civilization he had so often saved from destruction; he was a museum piece women admired because they longed for excitement, because they still remembered that lovemaking and the begetting of children were the only things that had not changed much since men emerged from the jungle. Feather and his men were the constant recipients of love letters from all over the Earth—in fact, from all over the solar system. Needless to say, this did nothing to make their own marriages any more stable, quite the reverse: because they were so popular, they longed to be able to return over and over again as conquering heroes. Finally even the raven-skinned girl in Timbuctoo began to think of setting up house as the necessity for heroic journeys began to dwindle: even this adventurous young lady wanted to bind Nemo with love, just as the geologist from Zatec had managed to do once upon a time. But that was not what the captain wanted at all. That would mean the end of adventure, and the beginning of old age and illness. He could not imagine what he would do with a happy marriage; he would have to upset it so as to have a reason for flying off again and risking his life, just as a drunkard invents a reason for getting drunk. Nemo knew the stories of all the great adventures of the past, he knew how to build up a convincing argument, and he used to say that in the end humanity would realize that this vast technical progress that kept them living in ease required, demanded an equally vast contrast; that man must give rein to his aggressive instincts; that men need adventure in order to remain fertile—in other words, that risking one's life in the universe (or anywhere else) was directly bound up with the fate of future generations. It was an odd sort of philosophy; very few people took it up, and as time went on there were fewer and fewer arguments in its favor. In fact, for the last five years Nemo and his men had simply been idle. The men were discontented. And so they were all delighted when one night quite suddenly their captain was called to the chief ministry, just like in the old days of alarms.

Pirates

"This time, Captain Nemo," the minister addressed him ceremoniously, "we are faced with an unusual and dangerous mystery. For this time it is apparently not only Earth that is threatened, but the sun itself, the source of all life in our solar system, the source of all we see around us." The minister solemnly signaled to the assistant secretary of science to continue. Nemo and his adjutant were sitting facing them on the other side of the conference table. The four men were alone in the room. The assistant secretary walked over to a map of the Universe.

"Of course we didn't believe it at first, but we were wrong, gentlemen. The facts you are about to be given are well founded. About a year ago, one of the universities sent us a paper written by a young scientist about the incidence of novas. The papers quoted old Egyptian astronomical maps as well as recent observations in the constellation of Omega Centauri and the galaxy of Andromeda. The writer concluded that novas do not simply explode of their own accord, but that they are touched off according to a plan. Like someone going along the hilltops who lights a beacon to signal back to the valleys below. Some sort of rocket seems to have been entrusted with the task—or a satellite with an irregular course, something moving independently through space and destroying the stars one by one. It is interesting to note that a similar idea occurred to the writers of antiquity. Since according to this paper the next victim of these cosmic pirates would be the immediate neighborhood of our own solar system, we quickly set up a secret telescope near Jupiter, without the knowledge of the public, in order to observe the regions in which this body appears to be moving. Today we reviewed the information provided by that telescope." The assistant secretary picked up a long pointer and turned back to the astronomical map. The minister could control his excitement no longer. He leapt to his feet.

"They're coming!" he shouted. "They're coming closer! We've got to catch them!" He was so excited that his chest was heaving, and he had to wipe his brow with his handkerchief. "Damn them," he said and sat down again.

"If the reports from ancient Egypt are reliable, this body has been wandering around the universe for about nine hundred thousand years," the assistant secretary of science went on. "We've managed to calculate the precise course it has followed to date. It cannot possibly be the satellite of some distant sun—it's a body that moves under its own power."

"Its own power? Then it *is* a rocket," Nemo's young adjutant breathed.

"But seven thousand times the size of any rocket we are presently capable of constructing," said the assistant secretary. "And it detonates the stars from an immense distance. In one year our sun will come within its orbit. In one year, it can cause an explosion of our solar system."

"What are our orders, sir?" said Nemo briefly, taking out his notebook as though it were all in the day's work to tackle cosmic pirates seven thousand times his own size.

"Orders? Don't talk nonsense," the minister burst out. "How could we send anyone to attack it? You might just as well send an ant to deal with an elephant."

"Why not, if the ant is clever enough and you give it enough oxygen?" Nemo laughed.

"There's no question of building a miracle missile for you," the minister went on.

"We can give you the latest war rockets equipped with radioactivite missiles, but of course they're over a hundred years old," the assistant secretary said. The young officer at Nemo's side frowned.

"Haven't you got any bows and arrows?" Nemo savored his joke. He was notorious for telling funny stories when things were really dangerous.

"This is a serious matter, Captain Nemo," said the minister.

"I can see that. Your automatic pilots are no good to you now, are they? You can't send them out that far because they'd never be able to keep in touch with you, I suppose. Only a human crew can fly that kind of distance."

"Naturally." The assistant secretary looked grim. "That's why it's a volunteer's job. Nobody must be allowed to know anything about it. We don't want to frighten the public now, when people have only been living without fear of war for a few generations. We'll issue a communiqué only if your mission fails."

"You mean if we don't manage to render them harmless?"

They explained that it was not a matter of rendering the aliens harmless. It would be far better if they could come to terms and avoid making enemies in the universe unnecessarily. But they did not want to tell Nemo what to do: they appreciated to the utmost not only his heroism, but his common sense as well. The moment the pirates turned away from our solar system, they assured him, everything would be all right.

"We shall send in a report, I suppose?" the adjutant asked.

"I hardly think so," said Nemo.

"Why not?" The adjutant was just over twenty. The other three looked at him—the minister, his assistant secretary, and Captain Nemo.

"My dear boy, there's such a thing as relativity, you know. By the time you get anywhere near that thing, you'll have been moving practically at the speed of light, and more than a thousand years will have passed on Earth."

"A thousand years?" the adjutant gasped, remembering that a thousand years earlier Premysl Otakar had been on the throne of Bohemia.

"It's a job for volunteers only, Captain Nemo."

"It's a magnificent adventure—"

"And I'm afraid it will be our last," Captain Nemo replied, getting to his feet and standing at attention. He wanted to get down to the details of the expedition.

"What do we tell the folks at home?" His adjutant was still puzzled.

"Surely you don't want to upset them by suggesting that in a year or two somebody's going to blow our Sun to bits? You'll set out on a normal expedition, and in a month we'll publish the news of your death. Or do you think it would be better for your loved ones to go on hoping for your return, until they themselves die? Your grandchildren won't know you, and in a thousand years everyone will have forgotten you anyway."

"If we get the better of the pirates," Nemo laughed. "If not, we'll all be meeting again soon."

"Do you still believe in life after death?" The minister smiled.

"An adventurer is permitted his little indulgences," Captain Nemo answered. "But if you really want to know—no, I don't believe in it. That's precisely why I love adventure: you risk everything."

"But this isn't an adventure," his adjutant interrupted in an agitated voice. "This is certain death. We can't destroy an entity that has detonated several suns in the course of the ages from an enormous distance—and even if we managed to do it, we'd be coming back to a strange land, to people who won't know us from Adam . . ."

"You will be the only human beings to experience the future so far ahead," said the minister.

"And it is a volunteer expedition," added the assistant secretary pointedly.

"If you can suggest any other way out, let us hear it. The World Council has been racking its brains for hours."

"And then they remembered us. That's nice." Captain Nemo felt flattered. "But now I'd like to know the details . . ." He turned to the assistant secretary like the commander of a sector ready to take orders from the commander in chief of an offensive.

Farewell

"Can't they leave you alone?" Mrs. Feather grumbled crossly as she packed her husband's bag. "Couldn't they find anybody younger to send? You'd think they could find somebody better for the job when you're getting on to fifty . . . I thought we were going to enjoy a little peace and quiet now, in our old age, at least. We could have moved to the mountains, the people next door are going to rent a cottage, and we could have had a rest at last . . ."

"There'll be plenty of time to rest when we're in our graves," Captain Nemo yawned. Ever since he'd come home he'd been stretched out on the couch. He always slept for twenty-four hours before an expedition. He used to say it was his hibernation period, and that the only place he ever got a decent rest was in his own house. And his wife knew that whenever he came home he would drop off somewhere. In the last few years, though, he'd been stopping by on Sundays and at Christmas as well.

"For Heaven's sake, Willy, are you going to carry on like an adolescent forever? When are you going to settle down?"

He got to his feet in anger. "I wish I knew why you never let me get a bit of rest. If you had any idea how important this expedition is—"

"That's just what you said before you went to Jupiter and Neptune, and then there was the moonstorm business and the time those meteors were raining . . . It's always the most important expedition anyone's ever thought of, and it's always a good reason for you to run away from home again . . ."

"Do you call this home?" He looked around. "I haven't set eyes on the boy since morning."

It appeared his son had finally found a music group that was willing to perform one of his symphonies, and they'd been rehearsing ever since the previous day.

"You mean he isn't even coming to say goodbye to me? Didn't you tell him?"

"But he's getting ready for his first night at last, don't you understand?" His mother tried to excuse him.

"So am I," answered Nemo, who did not quite know how to describe his gala last performance. But in the end he tried to find his son. To listen to the rehearsal, if nothing else.

The concert hall was practically empty; one or two elderly figures were dozing in the aisle seats. The orchestra emitted peculiar sounds while young Feather conducted from memory, absorbed in the music and with his eyes closed, so that he did not see his father gesticulating at him from one of the boxes. He heard nothing but his own music; he looked as though he were quite alone in the hall. Nemo went out and banged the door in disgust. An elderly attendant came up.

"How do you like the symphony?" he asked the old man.

"It's modern, all right; you've got to admit that."

"Yes, but I wanted to know whether you liked it." At that moment, a wave of particularly vile noise came screeching out through the door, and Nemo took to his heels.

In front of the hall, the girl from Timbuctoo was waiting for him. She had flown over that morning by special rocket. He recalled how she had wept the last time he'd refused to marry her.

"We're off to repair some equipment between Mercury and Venus." Nemo laughed. "We'll get pretty hot this time. When I get back, Timbuctoo won't even look warm by comparison."

"I know you're not coming back, Captain." She had always called him Captain. "I was the one who passed the report on to the authorities."

"What report?"

"About the cosmic pirates seven thousand times our size," she smiled. "I thought it would be an adventure after your own heart at last. I could have sent the whole thing back, you know—a very young student submitted it. I could have won a little more time for us to spend together. But we have our responsibilities, as you've always told me."

"You're perfectly right."

"But we must say goodbye properly. I'm not coming to see you off; I want to be alone with you when we part . . ."

So once again Nemo did not go home to Mrs. Feather, nor did he see his son again before he left. His adjutant brought his bags to the rocket, since he hadn't found the captain at home. Nemo turned up looking rather pale and thin, and the crew commented on it, but he had always been like that whenever they were about to take off, and he was used to their good-natured jokes.

This time the ministry prepared an elaborate farewell. No expense was spared. The World Government Council turned up in a body, together with all the relatives of the men, and crowds of admirers: women, girls, and young boys. Enthusiastic faces could be seen between the indifferent countenances of relatives, who were used to such goings-on, and the serious, almost anxious faces of those who knew the secret behind this expedition. The minister's voice almost shook with emotion as he proposed the toast. He did not know how to thank the crew enough, and promised that their heroism would never be forgotten. His hand was trembling by the time he gripped Nemo's in farewell, and he actually began to weep.

Once the relatives and curious onlookers had vanished, the crew had a final meeting with the leaders of the world government.

"All our lives are in your hands—the lives of your families, your children and your children's children, for generations to come. Men have often died for the sake of future generations, and often the sacrifice has been in vain. You can rest assured that this is not the case today. That's the only comfort we can offer you. I wish I were going with you myself, but it would cause too much talk, and we can't risk a panic. Still, it's better to fight than to wait passively in the role of victim."

Then they played famous military marches in honor of the crew—it was an international team—but the gesture fell a bit flat; not a tear was shed at the sound of Colonel Bogey or the Radetzky March. With sudden inspiration, the bandmaster struck up the choral movement from Beethoven's *Ninth Symphony*, and the band improvised from memory as best it could.

In those few moments, everyone present realized that for more than a generation man had been living in the age of true brotherhood, and that fear had suddenly reared its head again.

The Flight

In half an hour they had gained the required speed—the rocket had been adapted for its job after all. When sixty minutes had passed, the adjutant brought a telegraph message to the commander. On Earth, where several years had already passed since their departure, an official communiqué reporting the loss of the *Nautilus III* had been issued.

"So now we're dead and gone."

"Am I to inform the crew?" the adjutant asked in embarrassment.

"Of course. We need have no secrets from each other here."

The first reaction of the crew to the news of their own deaths was a roar of laughter. If you survive your own death, you live long, as the saying goes. And it was a fact that if they survived their meeting with the space pirates, they would return to Earth as thousand-year-old ancients, ancients at the height of their powers. But the topic soon palled, and the usual effects of space flight appeared. The men began to be tired and to feel sorry for themselves, to be touchy and depressed. There was only one way to deal with this state of affairs when humor failed. The captain always pointed out that if it didn't matter to anyone that the flight from Prague to Moscow made you age two hours in the old days, why should you mind aging a couple of years? The main thing was not to feel any older. But when his jokes failed, he had to make the day's routine tougher. Hunger and fear left no room for useless brooding. For this reason, the captain had made it a practice to invent all kinds of problems in the spaceship (which was in perfect order, of course). One day the deck equipment threatened to break down, and had to be adjusted while it was running. All the parts were changed, one by one; general rejoicing followed. The next time he thought up an imminent collision with a meteorite: all supplies had to be moved from the threatened side to the other side, and after the supposed danger had passed, everything had to be put back in its place again. A third time he invented an infectious disease the men must have brought on board with them and which required reinoculation for everyone; or the food would be infested, which meant going on a diet of bread and water for two days. The captain had to continually think up minor forms of torment to liven their days and keep the men occupied so there was no time for brooding.

But there was no one there to think up a way to lift Feather's days. He had to bear everything alone: the feeling that their expedition and his own life were utterly senseless, that he was to remain alone forever; despair at the hoplessness of the task he had undertaken and at the hoplessness of the life he had left behind him on Earth. He and the ship's doctor had made a pact: whenever the doctor thought the captain's depression was reaching alarming proportions, he would discover an attack of gallstones that called for special radiation treatment in the sick bay. And then while the captain got very drunk in the sick bay — he refused all medication but whiskey — his adjutant took over command of the ship. In two days the captain had usually gotten rid of his hangover and came up on deck again to think up some new danger to throw the men into a sweat, to be overcome and to provide cause for celebration.

After his most recent hangover, however, Nemo did not have to bother to think up a new trick. The meeting with the pirate ship seemed imminent at last. They could see it now — a rocket that looked more like a blimp, shaped like a cigar and about the size of a small planetoid: half the size of our moon. It was moving very slowly in the direction of our solar system. There could be no doubt about it: it was aiming at the sun.

Nemo gave orders for a message to be sent down to Earth at once by means of their special equipment. It was an experiment, for the chance of communication at that distance was extremely dubious. Then he called all hands on deck. The crew had to take turns at the machines and sleep in their space suits with weapons ready. He turned the heaviest long-range catapults on the giant, and slackened speed.

The Encounter

There were several courses open to them. They were all discussed by the staff officers, and the computers offered an endless list of possible combinations. They all really boiled down to two: either to attack the ship outright, or to come to terms.

In view of the damage the pirate ship had already done in space, most of the officers were in favor of direct attack. The test explosions were still very much alive in their minds, and they could not imagine anything in the whole of the universe that could stand up to their nuclear weapons. There was, of course, the question whether the attacking ship could survive the explosion. Would the *Nautilus* hold out? No one could offer an answer, because no one had any idea what material the pirate ship was made of. It was also quite possible that the crew of the super-rocket would be reasonable, intelligent and willing to reach an agreement. But suppose the pirates seized and killed the emissaries? That was the risk involved in the second alternative. The first, however, involved an even greater risk: they would all be blown to pieces.

Nemo finally decided to fly to the strange vessel in the company of a few of his most stalwart men, armed to the teeth and ready to open negotiations. They set off in an old-fashioned Cosmic Bathtub—the one in which he had first made his name.

They were all amazed to see that the rocket was very similar to certain types that were used for transport on Earth, only many times larger. They flew around it like a satellite and found no sign of life. Either there had been no lookouts, or the pirates were willing to come to terms. Or they were all dead, thought Nemo.

"We'll land there by the main entrance." He pointed to an enormous gap yawning in the bow. The entrance was unguarded, and the five men easily found their way inside. Roped together and maintaining radio contact with the Bathtub, they went down into the bowels of the rocket one by one. The first to disappear was the adjutant. He came back in a few minutes. His eyes were staring wildly and he was spitting blood, as far as they could make out through the thick lenses of his space suit goggles. They had to send him back to the Bathtub at once. No one felt like going down after that. They stood there hesitating, their feet weighted down and little batteries in their hands to allow them to move about; their automatic-rifles were slung over their shoulders. No one stirred. Then Nemo himself stepped forward and slowly sank into the abyss.

He was barely ten feet down when a persistent thought began to circle in his mind, as though somebody were whispering to him:

"We are friends . . . we are friends . . . we are friends . . ." he seemed to hear. But of course he didn't really hear anything. It was like having a tune stuck in the mind. The words went on and on in his head like a broken phonograph record.

He began to feel frightened by the words as they swirled around. At last he landed on a sort of platform. The moment he felt his feet touch ground, the opposite wall began to open; it was several yards thick. He shut his eyes and went quickly through the opening. At first he threw a thin stream of light ahead with his flashlight, but in about three minutes he was blinded by light.

He was at the side of an enormous hall—impossible to see how far it stretched. And up front was a group of monsters.

At least they looked like monsters to him. But he was equally sure that he looked like a monster to them. What surprised him most, though, was that the creatures were not all alike. One was almost the size of a whale and looked something like a swollen ciliaphore; another was covered with flagella, while another featured eight feet. They were all transparent, and he could see a strange liquid pulsating through their bodies. They did not move. If it had not been for the liquid, he would have thought they were dead.

"They're only asleep—frozen. You can wake them up if you warm them, they'll wake up right away . . ." He heard the words in his mind. He had already realized that they came from micro-transmitters on the brain surface. He switched his battery off. He did not want to wake them up; he did not even want to warm the place they were in with his torchlight. He gave a couple of sharp tugs at the cable he had fastened to his body. The minute the men pulled him up, he heard the insulating wall close behind him.

"They really are monsters," he said to the others, taking a swig of whiskey. "Enormous protozoa. When I was a boy, someone showed me a drop of water under the microscope. It's like a drop of water seven thousand times enlarged," he added, and almost believed his own words. They hurried off to the Bathtub, and returned to the rocket to call a staff officer's meeting.

"My suggestion," said the adjutant, who had come to himself in the meantime, "is to fix all the explosives we've got to the surface of their rocket, fix the time fuses for a week from now, and get back to Earth as quickly as we can."

"But suppose they're friendly," Nemo objected. "We have no right to destroy them just like that. Suppose they're bringing us a message—or a warning?" Finally, he decided to fix the explosives to the giant ciliaphore spaceship, but to attempt to negotiate at the same time. "Who wants to come along with me and talk to them?" he asked at last. He looked at his hardened band of adventurers, but not one of them could meet his eye. It was the first time in all those years that they had felt fear. The adjutant had been in a terrible state when they got him to sick bay. He had raved about monsters and terrible creatures, and they could see what horrors he had gone through.

"I'll go with you." It was the adjutant himself who spoke. They were all astonished. "I've got to make good . . ."

The Sphinx

The two men stood at the edge of the great hall, near the whale-ciliaphore and the elephant-flagellula, with the giant podia of the third creature lying in the background. They didn't even try to distinguish the rest of the monsters. Once again they heard the two messages echo in their minds. Slowly, they began to warm the air. They had brought an active accumulator with them, and in less than an hour the liquid in the ciliaphore's body had begun to course more rapidly, while the unknown creature's podia began to tremble and the flagellula stretched itself with lazy delight.

Up to this point the crew of the *Nautilus III* had been able to follow the encounter, because the adjutant had taken a television transmitter with him, but when the flagellula moved a second time the picture seemed to mist over, as though water were pouring over it, and communication was interrupted.

The second officer immediately called a meeting. Since the two emissaries had ceased to respond to signals on the cable, the men on the *Nautilus* wondered whether they should attack. Finally they decided to send another party. The men who went discovered that the wall was closed. It would not open, and even withstood the oxyacetyle lamps they had brought along with them from the spaceship, and which were capable of dissolving any material known to man. They decided to wait by the entrance to the giant rocket for an hour longer, and then to attack.

Precisely fifty-nine minutes later the two men inside were heard again. They came out and boarded the Bathtub. When they reached the *Nautilus*, Nemo called the whole crew on deck and gave the order to return home.

"What about the explosives?"

"We can leave them behind. They know all about it, anyway," and shut himself up in his cabin with the doctor and the adjutant. They spent nearly ten hours in consultation.

Meanwhile, the men observed that the crew of the giant rocket was not idle. The enormous cigar-shaped vessel seemed to bend suddenly, straightened itself out, and moved off at top speed in the direction from which it had come, away from our Sun. The *Nautilus* had apparently succeeded in its task. But the mystery of the giant pirate ship had not yet been solved. They were all impatient to hear what the captain would have to say, and hurried on deck for evening roll call.

"I'm afraid you're going to be disappointed," Nemo addressed them. "We only spoke a few words to the foreign ambassadors. They answered us by telepathy, and I must say they seem to have made much greater progress there than we have. We asked them whether they were flying toward our solar system, and why. They explained that a long time ago they had been sent into space from their planet to visit our system, which according to their reports seemed to be the only one in the universe inhabited by intelligent animals—that is to say, by living creatures who are aware of themselves, their surroundings and their own actions.

"We asked them what they wanted, and why they had undertaken such a long journey to see us—whether there was anything we could do to help them, whether they wanted to move to our planet—and of course we pointed out immediately that it would never work out. It seemed to us, you see, that nothing short of mortal danger could have sent these creatures on so long and difficult a journey.

"They replied that they wanted to know our answer to the fundamental question of life." The captain blushed as he said that, like a schoolboy who has suddenly forgotten the answer when the teacher calls on him. "I'm sorry. I know it sounds silly, but that's really what they said . . ." He glanced at his adjutant, who nodded and repeated:

"They said they wanted to know our answer to the fundamental question of life."

"Naturally we didn't know what they meant," the captain went on. "We thought they were asking us about the purpose of life. Everyone knows that the purpose of life is to transform nature. But that didn't seem to be what they wanted. Maybe they wanted to find out how much we know about life. So we offered them the doctor's notes: we have mastered the problem of tissue regeneration; we can prolong human life and heal even the most seriously damaged animal. But that wasn't what they wanted either. *The fundamental question of life!* They seemed to be shouting the words at us, like a crowd at a football game, or a pack of mad dogs. They wanted to know the answer. And we didn't even know what they meant."

"The fundamental question of life." The adjutant interrupted him. "Of course it occurred to us that it might all be strategy, a way of distracting us by philosophical arguments. They couldn't expect us to believe they'd been en route from some damn spiral nebula for at least two hundred thousand years, or that they were tagging the stars as they went so folks back home would know they were going on with their task; they couldn't expect us to believe they'd volunteered to be put into suspended animation just to ask the kind of question that no one on Earth bothers with except idlers, drunkards and philosophers. I thought it might be a trick—that they were really out to take us prisoner and destroy the rocket. I tried to give you orders—"

"And that's just what you shouldn't have done!" Nemo shouted at him angrily. "The ciliaphore next to us immediately opened the insulating door and pushed us out."

" 'Tell them we have detached their explosives,' he said. 'It is clear to us that life in your solar system is not yet completely reasonable . . .' "

"We would have attacked if they'd kept you one minute longer."

"You're all fools," answered the captain. "Fools and idiots. Nothing would have happened. Can't you understand that these creatures are much more technologically advanced than we are? We were at their mercy, and they spared us, simply because they gave up killing and destruction long ago. They're interested in other things." He was silent for a moment and then apologized quickly to the crew. "It was an unnerving experience, and I'm getting old. You know I've never shouted at you before. But I've got the feeling those creatures could have told us much more. Perhaps life asks more questions, the more perfect it gets."

"The main thing is, we saved our homes," said the second officer.

"Saved them? From what? Questions aren't dangerous to anyone."

"They're starting up again!" The doctor ran in from the watch room without knocking or saluting. "They're not going back to Andromeda—they're heading out into space again. And they're slowing down."

"That means they still think they'll find the answer to their questions somewhere in the universe."

"Fundamental questions, sir," his adjutant reminded him.

"Fundamental questions." Captain Nemo was still angry with his adjutant. He turned to the crew and read the orders for the next day. Never before had they heard him speak so quietly.

"He's getting old," they said to each other. But they were wrong. The captain had just begun to think.

Nautilus 300

On the journey home no one bothered to think up any problems for the crew, and no one bothered to keep the men from worrying. The captain sat in his cabin all day long, watching through the window the dark void that surrounded them, the mysterious depths of eternity—perhaps not so eternal after all—: the utter infinite. The cooks began to hand out better food, the officers relaxed, roll call was held when the men turned up for it, and nobody bothered much about the flight itself. At first the men were contented; then they began to feel afraid, lost their appetites—the mess hall was next to empty at mealtimes—suffered from insomnia and were prey to disquieting thoughts. And in this state they landed. Needless to say, the rocket returned to the point where it had taken off. It was late evening; as far as they could see, there had been no changes at the base since the day they left. The moment they landed, old fashioned luggage trailers drove up from the hangars and men in overalls helped them down and into the trailers. They smiled and shook hands with the newcomers warmly, looking very friendly. But that was all. There was no crowd of welcoming officials, no reporters, no curious onlookers and not even a government delegation complete with military band. Nothing. Just a run-of-the-mill arrival, as though they had come back from a stroll around Mars. The captain felt injured.

"Didn't you know we were going to land?"

"Of course we knew. You interrupted traffic on the main line to Mercury. We had to take five rockets off, since we had no guarantee you'd be on time."

"We're always on time!" the captain shouted angrily. "Is there no higher officer coming to thank us?" he added in a haughty voice.

"Tomorrow, tomorrow morning. In your quarters," replied the man he had been talking to. He was tall, with an ashen face, and did not look well. He asked the crew to take their places in the trailers and take only essential luggage with them. They drove off with mixed feelings. This was not the way they had imagined their return to the Earth they had saved.

"We might just as well have sent the monsters instead. They'd probably have made a bigger impression." They had just turned into the main road when they heard an explosion behind them. The captain swung around to look. At the base, someone had set fire to the *Nautilus*: the tanks had just gone up. Nemo and the men with him beat on the door of the truck in a rage, but the trailer only picked up speed.

"And we didn't even bring a gun with us," the second officer growled. The captain's adjutant leaned over and tried to jab a penknife into the rear tire as they drove along at top speed. A voice came from the loudspeaker:

"Please behave reasonably, men. We must ask you to remember that you come from an era that sent several rockets a day into space. If we tried to save all of those that return to Earth, there would soon be no landing room left. You are the three-hundredth crew to have returned after hundreds of years in space. We cannot understand why you people were so anxious to fly around—in fact, we find it incomprehensible. But we do try to make allowances, and you must also try to understand our position."

The adjutant gave up: the trailer had solid rubber tires, and now they were drawing up in front of the camp. It was a huddle of low buildings similar to those of the era they had known. Porters came running toward them and picked up their bags. They all looked pale. The captain liked their quarters.

"I should like to thank your commanding officer," he said to the drivers.

"You must wait until tomorrow." They smiled shyly. "Tomorrow morning, please." And they saluted and drove off.

As Nemo approached the dormitory he heard loud laughter. He opened the door: his men were standing silently, hesitantly by their bunks, and in one corner lay an elderly bearded fellow in the tattered remains of an astronaut's suit, rocking with laughter.

"He says—"

"Do you know what he's been telling us?"

"—that they aren't men," the captain heard someone say.

"Robots or something like that . . . 'Black and white servants' . . . 'Gray doubles' . . ."

Nemo strode over to the old man, who was holding his sides in uncontrollable laughter, and dealt him several resounding slaps. The man jumped to his feet and clenched his fists. But a glance at the captain's broad shoulders calmed him down, and he could see that the rest were all against him.

"They don't even know what *this* means—brawling," he snapped. "And they don't like it if we fight."

"Who's 'we'?" asked the captain.

"Who we are? The small crew of a private rocket from California that set out to see whether there was anything to be exploited on Mercury. Only our joystick went out of action and we bounced back and forth between Mercury and Earth for years before someone happened to notice us and bring us down. I can tell you we felt pretty foolish when we found out that the people who had saved us, who played cards with us and grapefruit juice with us all the way here were really machines from a factory. Yes, gentlemen, you'll hear all about it from Dr. Erasmus tomorrow. Just wait until morning."

The Fundamental Question of Life

"You've come back to Earth at a time when technical progress has been completed," Dr. Erasmus told them the next morning. He was almost paler than his black-and-white servants. "Man began to invent machines to save him drudgery. But work was really ideal for man. Man is best suited to do his own work; the only thing he cannot stand is the humiliation. As soon as machines had been invented that could in fact do all jobs, there was only one problem left: what the machines should look like. It didn't seem appropriate to create models of attractiveness; some people might fall in love with their own servant-machines, might hate them, punish them, take revenge on them—in short, transfer human emotions to their relationships with the machines. It was also suggested—this simply to give you the whole picture—that the form of a monkey or a dog be used. But the monkey was not considered efficient enough, and the dog, though he has been man's companion for ages, cannot clean up after man, or do his work for him, or look after him so well that man can devote himself to the two things only man can do: create and think. Finally, the servants were built, in black and white, and each man was given one so like himself as to be indistinguishable from himself, a gray double, as it were, who did all his work and looked after the man in whose image it was made. You can order doubles like that for yourselves, if you like our society and decide to try to adapt to it. You won't need to take care of anything; all the servants are directed from a common computer center which follows a single chief command: *look after humanity.* Thus the technical problems have been solved for good, and man is free of work for all time.

"Of course, if you prefer to go on living in your old way—many elderly people do find it difficult to adapt themselves to something new—you can remain here. This camp has been set aside for you and anyone else who may return to Earth from space."

It sounded so strange. What did people do with their time, then? Nemo asked.

"I can show you," answered Dr. Erasmus, and switched on the telewall. They saw a garden, where Dr. Erasmus's double was strolling along deep in discussion with several friends. Only then did they realize that the man they were watching on the telewall was the real Dr. Erasmus and the one talking to them his gray double. Dr. Erasmus on the telewall suddenly turned around and smiled at the crew, waving a friendly hand before going on with his talk as though there was nothing more important on Earth . . .

The crew of the *Nautilus* decided to have a look at the new society. Dr. Erasmus's double smiled: Everyone started out this way; but, alas, not all retained their initial enthusiasm.

The captain's first errand was to the Historical Institute. There he asked to see the records of his last flight—the date of their takeoff and the date on which their death was announced. He could find nothing to fall back on. There was no mention of cosmic pirates anywhere; the minister had been so afraid of creating a panic that he had forgotten to leave any evidence which could help the men now.

"Look up Feather for me," he ordered. The double looked at him in perplexity. "Leonard Feather, the famous hero, also known as Nemo," the captain went on, looking around to see if anyone he knew happened to be listening. But the double still looked blank.

"Don't you mean Igor Feather?" Igor was the name of the captain's half-blind son. "Dvořák, Janaček, Feather? The three greatest Czech musicians?" the robot asked politely.

"Musicians?"

"Composers, that is . . . Feather is certainly the greatest of the three, as every child knows today. The house where he was born has been preserved for a thousand years in its original state; concerts and evening discussions on music are arranged there. You will find the place full of people," the robot stressed the word *people*. And so the captain came home after a thousand years.

Fortunately, there was no concert scheduled for that day. He was afraid that even after so many years he would not have been able to stand the caterwauling. Their old home now stood in a park, and all the adjacent houses had been torn down. While he was still a long way off, he could see two gold plates gleaming on the front of the house. One commemorated his son and the music he had written, celebrating the young man's service to the cause of music. The other—Nemo approached it with quickening pulse—commemorated his wife. No one had put up a plaque to the memory of Captain Nemo. He looked around thoroughly, but he could find no mention of himself.

"She died a year before the first performance of Igor's concerto in Rudolfinum Hall . . ." somebody said behind him. He started and looked around to see his adjutant walking out of the shadow of the bushes. "She had to take care of your son, who had gone completely blind. She looked after him for twenty years, and he died in her arms. She didn't even live to see his name established: he became famous a year after her death. That woman was a saint, sir."

"Why are you telling me this?"

"Because I loved her."

"You never said anything about it."

"Of course you never saw anything strange in my coming to see you at home, but I was happy just to be near her. And you deceived her with that black girl who got married a week after you started out on your last flight."

"That's a lie."

"It's the truth. She had twelve children. You can trace her descendants if you like. There'll be hundreds of them by now. I was one of your officers on the *Nautilus* only because of your wife, sir. I wanted to show her it wasn't so hard to be a hero, and that I could stand as much as you could, even if my shoulders weren't so broad. But she only loved you. And you loved that other girl."

"Another one of life's puzzles, isn't it? Another fundamental question."

"There's no question about it. It's a fact. You helped to kill her . . . It's a filthy business, and that's the truth. You behaved shamefully to her." His adjutant had never spoken in that tone before. Nemo turned on his heel and walked away. He saw that once more he would have to do something for his crew, find them another difficult task, for this new age was too much like those empty days out there in space.

In the Astronautics Institute they would not even hear of taking him on. "We have our own robot crews. Why risk your life? Why bother with things that can be done better by machines, while you neglect those things that only the human mind can do?"

"Here are my papers." He showed them his records like a desperate man who had aged prematurely. "I can pilot a rocket as well as any of your robots. And I've got a crew of men who'll follow me to Hell if need be."

"No human organism could hold out in our current program of space flight. We have no job you could do. We're investigating the curvature of space, the qualities of light, whether even higher speeds can be reached—all tasks beyond your powers. Devote yourself to philosophy, art, aesthetics. That's the coming field, after all . . ."

"I'm too old," replied the captain, rising from his chair. The gray robot said he was sorry. The wall of his office yawned and his human image leaned into the room. He was about fifty, a Bohemian with a palette and brush in his hand, and an enormous canvas behind him. He had a ringing voice.

"If anyone says that the time for philosophy has not yet arrived, or that it has passed, it's as good as saying that the time for happiness has not yet come, or that there is no longer any such thing . . . That's Epicurus, my friend, wisdom that's thirty-five hundred years old. Find yourself something creative to do. Everyone has some sort of talent—something that makes him aware he is alive, that proves his own existence to him, something he can express himself best in. Leave those technical toys to machines and children; there's nothing in them to interest a grown man. We have more serious problems. The most urgent are the fundamental questions of life . . ." Nemo had heard that before.

"Has anybody found any answers yet?" he asked.

"My dear sir, humanity is still too young for that. It's not like smashing the atom or orbiting around Jupiter. These questions need time and patience, they require a man's whole being. The answer is not only given in words, but in the way you live . . ."

"I'm too old to change. I'm prepared to turn up at the old takeoff ramp tomorrow, with my whole crew," Captain Nemo decided with finality.

The painter shrugged his shoulders, as if to say he was sorry that he had wasted his time. He turned back to his canvas, and the wall closed behind him. His gray servant bowed the captain out.

"As you wish. But I've warned you: it is suicide."

The Final Answer

The captain could not sleep in the morning. He recalled how little enthusiasm his men had shown the evening before, how unconvinced some of them were that it would be better for them to move off. Still, in the end he managed to persuade them, and they had promised to come. He dashed out before it was light and stumbled up to the ramp on foot. Robots were already hard at work there. The rocket they were preparing for flight did not look anything like a rocket: it was more like a globe, or a huge drop of liquid. It made him feel a twinge of fear. The firing mechanism was altogether different as well; he could not understand how it worked. The gray robots let him go wherever he wished and look at anything he cared to look at. Their smiles were strangely apologetic, as though it were not quite right for such a serious-looking man to be wasting his time with such foolishness as rockets. Nemo went back to the rendezvous point. His men were coming up in the morning mist, one by one. They were wearing their old suits again. This time they would be leaving without the fanfare, without the flags, but it would be better for them all. They couldn't possibly stay on Earth, they would never be able to adjust to this strange life . . .

That was more or less what he said to them on the little rocket base. The mist almost choked him and he had to clear his throat. Then he read off the roll: the men were to answer to their names and step forward to shake hands with him. They answered and stepped forward to shake his hand.

But they were robots. They were the gray doubles of his men, who had sent the robots rather than come themselves. Not one of those ungrateful sons of bitches had reported for duty. The captain rubbed his eyes. It must be the mist, he thought. And he sat down on the nearest stone because he found himself somehow unable to breathe properly.

"Captain Feather?" A broad-shouldered fellow bent over him. He was wearing a beautifully brushed uniform, covered with gold braid, such as Nemo had never seen before.

"Yes." He looked at him closely.

"They sent me over from the central office. With your permission, I'll take over the command . . ." Yes, of course, it was himself. Just a bit grayer, that was all.

"If you wish. If they wish," answered the captain, who felt defeated. His double saluted respectfully and stood smartly to attention just as Feather always did. In a short time he heard his own voice coming from the rocket, giving brief, staccato commands, reports and orders, just as he had done in previous years. In a few minutes the rocket silently moved away from the ground—*what kind of fuel do they have in there?*—and slowly rose toward the clouds. He waved after it. And looked around, just in case anyone was watching. It was silly, after all, to wave at a machine that worked so precisely all by itself.

He turned away and went slowly back to his old home. This time there were crowds of people in the house. His son's last symphony was being performed. He recognized those strange sounds that had upset him so much before he had left on his last flight. But now they no longer seemed so odd: he found himself beginning to listen attentively. He remained where he was, standing by a tree, at a considerable distance from the audience; the breeze carried snatches of music to him. Far up in the sky he saw the rocket pass out of sight.

And it occurred to him suddenly that if his son had stood before those pilgrims from distant galaxies, he might have been able to answer their questions.

"I must tell them not to send rockets out to look for the answer to the fundamental question of life," he thought. "We must find the answer down here, on Earth."

The orchestra fell silent and the harp sang out alone. It reminded him of something very beautiful.

Inconstant Moon

In the late 1960s Larry Niven appeared and held the center ground in science fiction just as the excesses and excitement of the New Wave were dominating critical discourse. Niven follows in the tradition of hard science fiction adventure, the problem-solving story of big ideas and scope based on the clever use of scientific knowledge and technology. It is the tradition of Isaac Asimov's "Nightfall," Arthur C. Clarke's "The Nine Billion Names of God," early Heinlein, and Poul Anderson. Never a flashy stylist but always a competent craftsman, Niven is a respected standard author, devoted to scientific accuracy and bringing to his fiction the latest technical theorizing, embodied in exciting imagery. These traits have made him in a sense the sea anchor of the field at a time when storms of change have ravaged the surfaces of SF and the demand for rounded characterization and stylistic play has tended to devalue traditional approaches. "Inconstant Moon" is one of those rare stories that depend on elementary astronomy for their extraordinarily powerful imagery and on the ability of the reader to follow immediately the logical deductions. It is Niven's "Nightfall."

*   *   *

I was watching the news when the change came, like a flicker of motion at the corner of my eye. I turned toward the balcony window. Whatever it was, I was too late to catch it.

The moon was very bright tonight.

I saw that, and smiled, and turned back. Johnny Carson was just starting his monologue.

When the first commercials came on I got up to reheat some coffee. Commercials came in strings of three and four, going on midnight. I'd have time.

The moonlight caught me coming back. If it had been bright before, it was brighter now. Hypnotic. I opened the sliding glass door and stepped out onto the balcony.

The balcony wasn't much more than a railed ledge, with standing room for a man and a woman and a portable barbecue set. These past months the view had been lovely, especially around sunset. The Power and Light Company had been putting up a glass-slab style office building. So far it was only a steel framework of open girders. Shadow-blackened against a red sunset sky, it tended to look stark and surrealistic and hellishly impressive.

Tonight . . .

I had never seen the moon so bright, not even in the desert. *Bright enough to read by*, I thought, and immediately, *but that's an illusion*. The moon was never bigger (I had read somewhere) than a quarter held nine feet away. It couldn't possibly be bright enough to read by.

It was only three-quarters full!

But, glowing high over the San Diego Freeway to the west, the moon seemed to dim even the streaming automobile headlights. I blinked against its light, and thought of men walking on the moon, leaving corrugated footprints. Once, for the sake of an article I was writing, I had been allowed to pick up a bone-dry moon rock and hold it in my hand. . . .

I heard the show starting again, and I stepped inside. But, glancing once behind me, I caught the moon growing even brighter—as if it had come from behind a wisp of scudding cloud.

Now its light was brain-searing, lunatic.

The phone rang five times before she answered.

"Hi," I said. "Listen—"

"Hi," Leslie said sleepily, complainingly. Damn. I'd hoped she was watching television, like me.

I said, "Don't scream and shout, because I had a reason for calling. You're in bed, right? Get up and—can you get up?"

"What time is it?"

"Quarter of twelve."

"Oh, Lord."

"Go out on your balcony and look around."

"Okay."

The phone clunked. I waited. Leslie's balcony faced north and west, like mine, but it was ten stories higher, with a correspondingly better view.

Through my own window, the moon burned like a textured spotlight.

"Stan? You there?"

"Yah. What do you think of it?"

"It's gorgeous. I've never seen anything like it. What could make the moon light up like that?"

"I don't know, but isn't it gorgeous?"

"You're supposed to be the native." Leslie had only moved out here a year ago.

"Listen, I've *never* seen it like this. But there's an old legend," I said. "Once every hundred years the Los Angeles smog rolls away for a single night, leaving the air as clear as interstellar space. That way the gods can see if Los Angeles is still there. If it is, they roll the smog back so they won't have to look at it."

"I used to know all that stuff. Well, listen, I'm glad you woke me up to see it, but I've got to get to work tomorrow."

"Poor baby."

"That's life. 'Night."

"'Night."

Afterward I sat in the dark, trying to think of someone else to call. Call a girl at midnight, invite her to step outside and look at the moonlight . . . and she may think it's romantic or she may be furious, but she won't assume you called six others.

So I thought of some names. But the girls who belonged to them had all dropped away over the past year or so, after I started spending all my time with Leslie. One could hardly blame them. And now Joan was in Texas and Hildy was getting married, and if I called Louise I'd probably get Gordie too. The English girl? But I couldn't remember her number. Or her last name.

Besides, everyone I knew punched a time clock of one kind or another. Me, I worked for a living, but as a freelance writer I picked my hours. Anyone I woke up tonight, I'd be ruining her morning. Ah, well. . . .

The Johnny Carson Show was a swirl of grey and a roar of static when I got back to the living room. I turned the set off and went back out on the balcony.

The moon was brighter than the flow of headlights on the freeway, brighter than Westwood Village off to the right. The Santa Monica Mountains had a magical pearly glow. There were no stars near the moon. Stars could not survive that glare.

I wrote science and how-to articles for a living. I ought to be able to figure out what was making the moon do that. Could the moon be suddenly larger?

Inflating like a balloon? No. Closer, maybe. The moon, falling?

Tides! Waves fifty feet high . . . and earthquakes! San Andreas Fault splitting apart like the Grand Canyon! Jump in my car, head for the hills . . . no, too late already. . . .

Nonsense. The moon was brighter, not bigger. I could see that. And what could possibly drop the moon on our heads like that?

I blinked, and the moon left an afterimage on my retinae. It was *that* bright.

A million people must be watching the moon right now, and wondering, like me. An article on the subject would sell big . . . if I wrote it before anyone else did.

Well, how could the moon grow brighter? Moonlight was reflected sunlight. Could the sun have gotten brighter? It must have happened after sunset, then, or it would have been noticed. . . .

I didn't like that idea.

Besides, half the Earth was in direct sunlight. A thousand correspondents for *Life* and *Time* and *Newsweek* and Associated Press would all be calling in from Europe, Asia, Africa . . . unless they were all hiding in cellars. Or dead. Or voiceless, because the sun was blanketing everything with static, radio and phone systems and television . . . television. Oh my God.

I was just barely beginning to be afraid.

All right, start over. The moon had become very much brighter. Moonlight, well, moonlight was reflected sunlight; any idiot knew that. Then . . . something had happened to the sun.

II

"Hello?"

"Hi. Me," I said, and then my throat froze solid. Panic! What was I going to *tell* her?

"I've been watching the moon," she said dreamily. "It's wonderful. I even tried to use my telescope, but I couldn't see a thing; it was too bright. It lights up the whole city. The hills are all silver."

That's right, she kept a telescope on her balcony. I'd forgotten.

"I haven't tried to go back to sleep," she said. "Too much light."

I got my throat working again. "Listen, Leslie love, I started thinking about how I woke you up and how you probably couldn't get back to sleep, what with all this light. So let's go out for a midnight snack."

"Are you out of your mind?"

"No, I'm serious. I mean it. Tonight isn't a night for sleeping. We may never have a night like this again. To hell with your diet. Let's celebrate. Hot fudge sundaes, Irish coffee—"

"That's different. I'll get dressed."

"I'll be right over."

Leslie lived on the fourteenth floor of Building C of the Barrington Plaza. I rapped for admission, and waited.

And waiting, I wondered without any sense of urgency: Why Leslie?

There must be other ways to spend my last night on Earth, than with one particular girl. I could have picked a different particular girl, or even several not too particular girls, except that that didn't really apply to me, did it? Or I could have called my brother, or either set of parents—

Well, but brother Mike would have wanted a good reason for being hauled out of bed at midnight. "But, Mike, the moon is so beautiful—" Hardly. Any of my parents would have reacted similarly. Well, I had a good reason, but would they believe me?

And if they did, what then? I would have arranged a kind of wake. Let 'em sleep through it. What I wanted was someone who would join my . . . farewell party without asking the wrong questions.

What I wanted was Leslie. I knocked again.

She opened the door just a crack for me. She was in her underwear. A stiff, misshapen girdle in one hand brushed my back as she came into my arms. "I was about to put this on."

"I came just in time, then." I took the girdle away from her and dropped it. I stooped to get my arms under her ribs, straightened up with effort, and walked us to the bedroom with her feet dangling against my ankles.

Her skin was cold. She must have been outside.

"So!" she demanded. "You think you can compete with a hot fudge sundae, do you?"

"Certainly. My pride demands it." We were both somewhat out of breath.

Once in our lives I had tried to lift her cradled in my arms, in conventional movie style. I'd damn near broken my back. Leslie was a big girl, my height, and almost too heavy around the hips.

I dropped us on the bed, side by side. I reached around her from both sides to scratch her back, knowing it would leave her helpless to resist me, *ah ha hahahaha*. She made sounds of pleasure to tell me where to scratch. She pulled my shirt up around my shoulders and began scratching my back.

We pulled pieces of clothing from ourselves and each other, at random, dropping them over the edges of the bed. Leslie's skin was warm now, almost hot.

All right, now *that's* why I couldn't have picked another girl. I'd have to teach her how to scratch. And there just wasn't time.

Some nights I had a nervous tendency to hurry our lovemaking. Tonight we were performing a ritual, a rite of passage. I tried to slow it down, to make it last. I tried to make Leslie like it more. It paid off incredibly. I forgot the moon and the future when Leslie put her heels against the backs of my knees and we moved into the ancient rhythm.

But the image that came to me at the climax was vivid and frightening. We were in a ring of blue-hot fire that closed like a noose. If I moaned in terror and ecstasy, then she must have thought it was ecstasy alone.

We lay side by side, drowsy, torpid, clinging together. I was minded to go back to sleep then, renege on my promise, sleep and let Leslie sleep . . . but instead I whispered into her ear: "Hot fudge sundae." She smiled and stirred and presently rolled off the bed.

I wouldn't let her wear the girdle. "It's past midnight. Nobody's going to pick you up, because I'd thrash the blackguard, right? So why not be comfortable?" She laughed and gave in. We hugged each other once, hard, in the elevator. It felt much better without the girdle.

III

The grey-haired counter waitress was cheerful and excited. Her eyes glowed. She spoke as if confiding a secret. "Have you noticed the moonlight?"

Ships's was fairly crowded, this time of night and this close to UCLA. Half the customers were university students. Tonight they talked in hushed voices, turning to look out through the glass walls of the twenty-four-hour restaurant. The moon was low in the west, low enough to compete with the street globes.

"We noticed," I said. "We're celebrating. Get us two hot fudge sundaes, will you?" When she turned her back I slid a ten dollar bill under the paper place mat. Not that she'd ever spend it, but at least she'd have the pleasure of finding it. I'd never spend it either.

I felt loose, casual. A lot of problems seemed suddenly to have solved themselves.

Who would have believed that peace could come to Vietnam and Cambodia in a single night?

This thing had started around eleven-thirty, here in California. That would have put the noon sun just over the Arabian Sea, with all but a few fringes of Asia, Europe, Africa, and Australia in direct sunlight.

Already Germany was reunited, the Wall melted or smashed by shock waves. Israelis and Arabs had laid down their arms. Apartheid was dead in Africa.

And I was free. For me there were no more consequences. Tonight I could satisfy all my dark urges, rob, kill, cheat on my income tax, throw bricks at plate glass windows, burn my credit cards. I could forget the article on explosive metal forming, due Thursday. Tonight I could substitute cinnamon candy for Leslie's Pills. Tonight—

"Think I'll have a cigarette."

Leslie looked at me oddly. "I thought you'd given that up."

"You remember. I told myself if I got any overpowering urges, I'd have a cigarette. I did that because I couldn't stand the thought of never smoking again."

"But it's been months!" she laughed.

"But they keep putting cigarette ads in my magazines!"

"It's a plot. All right, go have a cigarette."

I put coins in the machine, hesitated over the choice, finally picked a mild filter. It wasn't that I wanted a cigarette. But certain events call for champagne, and others for cigarettes. There is the traditional last cigarette before a firing squad. . . .

I lit up. *Here's to lung cancer.*

It tasted just as good as I remembered; though there was a faint stale undertaste, like a mouthful of old cigarette butts. The third lungful hit me oddly. My eyes unfocused and everything went very calm. My heart pulsed loudly in my throat.

"How does it taste?"

"Strange. I'm buzzed," I said.

Buzzed! I hadn't even heard the word in fifteen years. In high school we'd smoked to get that buzz, that quasidrunkenness produced by capillaries constricting in the brain. The buzz had stopped coming after the first few times, but we'd kept smoking, most of us.

I put it out. The waitress was picking up our sundaes.

Hot and cold, sweet and bitter: there is no taste quite like that of a hot fudge sundae. To die without tasting it again would have been a crying shame. But with Leslie it was a *thing*, a symbol of all rich living. Watching her eat was more fun than eating myself.

Besides—I'd killed the cigarette to taste the ice cream. Now, instead of savoring the ice cream, I was anticipating Irish coffee.

Too little time.

Leslie's dish was empty. She stage-whispered, "Aahh!" and patted herself over the navel.

A customer at one of the small tables began to go mad.

I'd noticed him coming in. A lean scholarly type wearing sideburns and steel-rimmed glasses, he had been continually twisting around to look out at the moon. Like others at other tables, he seemed high on a rare and lovely natural phenomenon.

Then he got it. I saw his face changing, showing suspicion, then disbelief, then horror, horror and helplessness.

"Let's go," I told Leslie. I dropped quarters on the counter and stood up.

"Don't you want to finish yours?"

"Nope. We've got things to do. How about some Irish coffee?"

"And a Pink Lady for me? Oh, look!" She turned full around.

The scholar was climbing up on a table. He balanced, spread wide his arms and bellowed, "Look out your windows!"

"You get down from there!" a waitress demanded, jerking emphatically at his pants leg.

"The world is coming to an end! Far away on the other side of the sea, death and hellfire—"

But we were out the door, laughing as we ran. Leslie panted, "We may have—escaped a religious—riot in there!"

I thought of the ten I'd left under my plate. Now it would please nobody. Inside, a prophet was shouting his message of doom to all who would hear. The grey-haired woman with the glowing eyes would find the money and think: They knew it too.

Buildings blocked the moon from the Red Barn's parking lot. The street lights and the indirect moonglare were pretty much the same color. The night only seemed a bit brighter than usual.

I didn't understand why Leslie stopped suddenly in the driveway. But I followed her gaze, straight up to where a star burned very brightly just south of the zenith.

"Pretty," I said.

She gave me a very odd look.

There were no windows in the Red Barn. Dim artificial lighting, far dimmer than the queer cold light outside, showed on dark wood and quietly cheerful customers. Nobody seemed aware that tonight was different from other nights.

The sparse Tuesday night crowd was gathered mostly around the piano bar. A customer had the mike. He was singing some half-familiar song in a wavering weak voice, while the black pianist grinned and played a schmaltzy background.

I ordered two Irish coffees and a Pink Lady. At Leslie's questioning look I only smiled mysteriously.

How ordinary the Red Barn felt. How relaxed; how happy. We held hands across the table, and I smiled and was afraid to speak. If I broke the spell, if I said the wrong thing . . .

The drinks arrived. I raised an Irish coffee glass by the stem. Sugar, Irish whiskey, and strong black coffee, with thick whipped cream floating on top. It coursed through me like a magical potion of strength, dark and hot and powerful.

The waitress waved back my money. "See that man in the turtleneck, there at the end of the piano bar? He's buying," she said with relish. "He came in two hours ago and handed the bartender a hundred dollar bill."

So that was where all the happiness was coming from. Free drinks! I looked over, wondering what the guy was celebrating.

A thick-necked, wide-shouldered man in a turtleneck and sports coat, he sat hunched over into himself, with a wide bar glass clutched tight in one hand. The pianist offered him the mike, and he waved it by, the gesture giving me a good look at his face. A square, strong face, now drunk and miserable and scared. He was ready to cry from fear.

So I knew what he was celebrating.

Leslie made a face. "They didn't make the Pink Lady right."

There's one bar in the world that makes a Pink Lady the way Leslie likes it, and it isn't in Los Angeles. I passed her the other Irish coffee, grinning an I-told-you-so grin. Forcing it. The other man's fear was contagious. She smiled back, lifted her glass and said, "To the blue moonlight."

I lifted my glass to her, and drank. But it wasn't the toast I would have chosen.

The man in the turtleneck slid down from his stool. He moved carefully toward the door, his course slow and straight as an ocean liner cruising into dock. He pulled the door wide, and turned around, holding it open, so that the weird blue-white light streamed past his broad black silhouette.

Bastard. He was waiting for someone to figure it out, to shout out the truth to the rest. *Fire and doom—*

"Shut the door!" someone bellowed.

"Time to go," I said softly.

"What's the hurry?"

The hurry? He might *speak*! But I couldn't say that. . . .

Leslie put her hand over mine. "I know. I *know*. But we can't run away from it, can we?"

A fist closed hard on my heart. She'd known, and I hadn't noticed?

The door closed, leaving the Red Barn in reddish dusk. The man who had been buying drinks was gone.

"Oh, God. When did you figure it out?"

"Before you came over," she said. "But when I tried to check it out, it didn't work."

"Check it out?"

"I went out on the balcony and turned the telescope on Jupiter. Mars is below the horizon these nights. If the sun's gone nova, all the planets ought to be lit up like the moon, right?"

"Right. Damn." I should have thought of that myself. But Leslie was the stargazer. I knew some astrophysics, but I couldn't have found Jupiter to save my life.

"But Jupiter wasn't any brighter than usual. So then I didn't know *what* to think."

"But then—" I felt hope dawning fiery hot. Then I remembered. "That star, just overhead. The one you stared at."

"Jupiter."

"All lit up like a fucking neon sign. Well, that tears it."

"Keep your voice down."

I *had* been keeping my voice down. But for a wild moment I wanted to stand up on a table and scream! *Fire and doom*—what right had they to be ignorant?

Leslie's hand closed tight on mine. The urge passed. It left me shuddering. "Let's get out of here. Let 'em think there's going to be a dawn."

"There is." Leslie laughed a bitter, barking laugh like nothing I'd ever heard from her. She walked out while I was reaching for my wallet—and remembering that there was no need.

Poor Leslie. Finding Jupiter its normal self must have looked like a reprieve—until the white spark flared to shining glory an hour and a half late. An hour and a half, for sunlight to reach Earth by way of Jupiter.

When I reached the door Leslie was half-running down Westwood toward Santa Monica. I cursed and ran to catch up, wondering if she'd suddenly gone crazy.

Then I noticed the shadows ahead of us. All along the other side of Santa Monica Boulevard: moon shadows, in horizontal patterns of dark and blue-white bands.

I caught her at the corner.

The moon was setting.

A setting moon always looks tremendous. Tonight it glared at us through the gap of sky beneath the freeway, terribly bright, casting an incredible complexity of lines and shadows. Even the unlighted crescent glowed pearly bright with Earthshine.

Which told me all I wanted to know about what was happening on the lighted side of Earth.

And on the moon? The men of Apollo Nineteen must have died in the first few minutes of nova sunlight. Trapped out on a lunar plain, hiding perhaps behind a melting boulder . . . Or were they on the night side? I couldn't remember. Hell, they could outlive us all. I felt a stab of envy and hatred.

And pride. We'd put them there. We reached the moon before the nova came. A little longer, we'd have reached the stars.

The disc changed oddly as it set. A dome, a flying saucer, a lens, a line . . .

Gone.

Gone. Well, that was that. Now we could forget it; now we could walk around outside without being constantly reminded that something was *wrong*. Moonset had taken all the queer shadows out of the city.

But the clouds had an odd glow to them. As clouds glow after sunset, tonight the clouds shone livid white at their western edges. And they streamed too quickly across the sky. As if they tried to run . . .

When I turned to Leslie, there were big tears rolling down her cheeks.

"Oh, damn." I took her arm. "Now stop it. Stop it."

"I can't. You know I can't stop crying once I get started."

"This wasn't what I had in mind. I thought we'd do things we've been putting off, things we like. It's our last chance. Is this the way you want to die, crying on a street corner?"

"I don't want to die at all!"

"Tough shit!"

"Thanks a lot." Her face was all red and twisted. Leslie was crying as a baby cries, without regard for dignity or appearance. I felt awful. I felt guilty, and I *knew* the nova wasn't my fault, and it made me angry.

"I don't want to die either!" I snarled at her. "You show me a way out and I'll take it. Where would we go? The South Pole? It'd just take longer. The moon must be molten all across its day side. Mars? When this is over Mars will be part of the sun, like the Earth. Alpha Centauri? The acceleration we'd need, we'd be spread across a wall like peanut butter and jelly—"

"Oh, shut up."

"Right."

"Hawaii. Stan, we could get to the airport in twenty minutes. We'd get two hours extra, going west! Two hours more before sunrise!"

She had something there. Two hours was worth any price! But I'd worked this out before, staring at the moon from my balcony. "No. We'd die sooner. Listen, love, we saw the moon go bright about midnight. That means California was at the back of the Earth when the sun went nova."

"Yes, that's right."

"Then we must be furthest from the shock wave."

She blinked. "I don't understand."

"Look at it this way. First the sun explodes. That heats the air and the oceans, all in a flash, all across the day side. The steam and superheated air expand *fast*. A flaming shock wave comes roaring over into the night side. It's closing on us right now. Like a noose. But it'll reach Hawaii first. Hawaii is two hours closer to the sunset line."

"Then we won't see the dawn. We won't live even that long."

"No."

"You explain things so well," she said bitterly. "A flaming shock wave. So graphic."

"Sorry. I've been thinking about it too much. Wondering what it will be like."

"Well, stop it." She came to me and put her face in my shoulder. She cried quietly. I held her with one arm and used the other to rub her neck, and I watched the streaming clouds, and I didn't think about what it would be like.

Didn't think about the ring of fire closing on us.

It was the wrong picture anyway.

I thought of how the oceans had boiled on the day side, so that the shock wave had been mostly steam to start with. I thought of the millions of square miles of ocean it had to cross. It would be cooler and wetter when it reached us. And the Earth's rotation would spin it like the whirlpool in a bathtub.

Two counterrotating hurricanes of live steam, one north, one south. That was how it would come. We were lucky. California would be near the eye of the northern one.

A hurricane wind of live steam. It would pick a man up and cook him in the air, strip the steamed flesh from him and cast him aside. It was going to hurt like hell.

We would never see the sunrise. In a way that was a pity. It would be spectacular.

Thick parallel streamers of clouds were drifting across the stars, too fast. Jupiter dimmed, then went out. Could it be starting already? Heat lightning jumped—

"Aurora," I said.

"What?"

"There's a shock wave from the sun, too. There should be an aurora like nothing anybody's ever seen before."

Leslie laughed suddenly, jarringly. "It seems so strange, standing on a street corner talking like this! Stan, are we dreaming it?"

"We could pretend—"

"No. Most of the human race must be dead already."

"Yah."

"And there's nowhere to go."

"Damn it, you figured that out long ago, all by yourself. Why bring it up now?"

"You could have let me sleep," she said bitterly. "I was dropping off to sleep when you whispered in my ear."

I didn't answer. It was true.

" 'Hot fudge sundae,' " she quoted. Then, "It wasn't a bad idea, actually. Breaking my diet."

I started to giggle.

"Stop that."

"We could go back to your place now. Or my place. To sleep."

"I suppose. But we couldn't sleep, could we? No, don't say it. We take sleeping pills, and five hours from now we wake up screaming. I'd rather stay awake. At least we'll know what's happening."

But if we took all the pills . . . but I didn't say it. I said, "Then how about a picnic?"

"Where?"

"The beach, maybe. Who cares? We can decide later."

IV

All the markets were closed. But the liquor store next to the Red Barn was one I'd been using for years. They sold us foie gras, crackers, a couple of bottles of chilled champagne, six kinds of cheese and a hell of a lot of nuts—

I took one of everything—more crackers, a bag of ice, frozen rumaki hors d'oeuvres, a fifth of an ancient brandy that cost twenty-five bucks, a matching fifth of Cherry Heering for Leslie, six-packs of beer and Bitter Orange. . . .

By the time we had piled all that into a dinky store cart, it was raining. Big fat drops spattered in flurries across the acre of plate glass that fronted the store. Wind howled around the corners.

The salesman was in a fey mood, bursting with energy. He'd been watching the moon all night. "And now this!" he exclaimed as he packed our loot into bags. He was a small, muscular old man with thick arms and shoulders. "It *never* rains like this in California. It comes down straight and heavy, when it comes at all. Takes days to build up."

"I know." I wrote him a check, feeling guilty about it. He'd known me long enough to trust me. But the check was good. There were funds to cover it. Before opening hours the check would be ash, and all the banks in the world would be bubbling in the heat of the sun. But that was hardly my fault.

He piled our bags in the cart, set himself at the door. "Now when the rain lets up, we'll run these out. Ready?" I got ready to open the door. The rain came like someone had thrown a bucket of water at the window. In a moment it had stopped, though water still streamed down the glass. "Now!" cried the salesman, and I threw the door open and we were off. We reached the car laughing like maniacs. The wind howled around us, sweeping up spray and hurling it at us.

"We picked a good break. You know what this weather reminds me of? Kansas," said the salesman. "During a tornado."

Then suddenly the sky was full of gravel! We yelped and ducked, and the car rang to a million tiny concussions, and I got the car door unlocked and pulled Leslie and the salesman in after me. We rubbed our bruised heads and looked out at white gravel bouncing everywhere.

The salesman picked a small white pebble out of his collar. He put it in Leslie's hand, and she gave a startled squeak and handed it to me, and it was cold.

"Hail," said the salesman. "Now I really don't get it."

Neither did I. I could only think that it had something to do with the nova. But what? How?

"I've got to get back," said the salesman. The hail had expended itself in one brief flurry. He braced himself, then went out of the car like a Marine taking a hill. We never saw him again.

The clouds were churning up there, forming and disappearing, sliding past each other faster than I'd ever seen clouds move—their bellies glowing by city light.

"It must be the nova," Leslie said shivering.

"But how? If the shock wave were here already, we'd be dead—or at least deaf. Hail?"

"Who cares? Stan, we don't have *time!*"

I shook myself. "All right. What would you like to do most, right now?"

"Watch a baseball game."

"It's two in the morning," I pointed out.

"That lets out a lot of things, doesn't it?"

"Right. We've hopped our last bar. We've seen our last play, and our last clean movie. What's left?"

"Looking in jewelry store windows."

"Seriously? Your last night on Earth?"

She considered, then answered. "Yes."

By damn, she meant it. I couldn't think of anything duller. "Westwood or Beverly Hills?"

"Both."

"Now, *look—*"

"Beverly Hills, then."

We drove through another spatter of rain and hail—a capsule tempest. We parked half a block from the Tiffany salesroom.

The sidewalk was one continuous puddle. Secondhand rain dripped on us from various levels of the buildings overhead. Leslie said, "This is great. There must be half a dozen jewelry stores in walking distance."

"I was thinking of driving."

"No no no, you don't have the proper attitude. One must window shop on foot. It's in the rules."

"But the rain!"

"You won't die of pneumonia. You won't have time," she said, too grimly.

Tiffany's had a small branch office in Beverly Hills, but they didn't put expensive things in the windows at night. There were a few fascinating toys, that was all.

We turned up Rodeo Drive—and struck it rich. Tibor showed an infinite selection of rings, ornate and modern, large and small, in all kinds of precious and semiprecious stones. Across the street, Van Cleef and Arpel showed brooches, men's wristwatches of elegant design, bracelets with tiny watches in them, and one window that was all diamonds.

"Oh, lovely," Leslie breathed, caught by the flashing diamonds. "What they must look like in daylight! . . . wups—"

"No, that's a good thought. Imagine them at dawn, flaming with nova light, while the windows shatter to let the raw daylight in. Want one? The necklace?"

"Oh, *may* I? Hey, hey, I was kidding! Put that down, you idiot, there must be alarms in the glass."

"Look, nobody's going to be wearing any of that stuff between now and morning. Why shouldn't we get some good out of it?"

"We'd be caught!"

"Well, you *said* you wanted to window shop."

"I don't want to spend my last hour in a cell. If you'd brought the car we'd have *some* chance—"

"—Of getting away. Right. I *wanted* to bring the car—" But at that point we both cracked up entirely, and had to stagger away holding onto each other for balance.

There were a good half-dozen jewelry stores on Rodeo. But there was more. Toys, books, shirts and ties in odd and advanced styling. In Francis Orr, a huge plastic cube full of new pennies. A couple of damn strange clocks further on. There was an extra kick in window shopping; knowing that we could break a window and take anything we wanted badly enough.

We walked hand in hand, swinging our arms. The sidewalks were ours alone; all others had fled the mad weather. The clouds still churned overhead.

"I wish I'd known it was coming," Leslie said suddenly. "I spent the whole day fixing a mistake in a program. Now we'll never run it."

"What would you have done with the time? A baseball game?"

"Maybe. No. The standings don't matter now." She frowned at dresses in a store window. "What would you have done?"

"Gone to the Blue Sphere for cocktails," I said promptly. "It's a topless place. I used to go there all the time. I hear they've gone full nude now."

"I've never been to one of those. How late are they open?"

"Forget it. It's almost two-thirty."

Leslie mused, looking at giant stuffed animals in a toy store window. "Isn't there someone you would have murdered, if you'd had the time?"

"Now, you *know* my agent lives in New York."

"Why him?"

"My child, why would any writer want to murder his agent? For the manuscripts he loses under other manuscripts. For his ill-gotten ten percent, and the remaining ninety percent that he sends me grudgingly and late. For—"

Suddenly the wind roared and rose up against us. Leslie pointed, and we ran for a deep doorway that turned out to be Gucchi's. We huddled against the glass.

The wind was suddenly choked with hail the size of marbles. Glass broke somewhere, and alarms lifted thin, frail voices into the wind. There was more than hail in the wind! There were rocks!

I caught the smell and taste of seawater.

We clung together in the expensively wasted space in front of Gucchi's. I coined a short-lived phrase and screamed, "Nova weather! How the blazes did it—" But I couldn't hear myself, and Leslie didn't even know I was shouting.

Nova weather, How did it get here so fast? Coming over the pole, the nova shock wave would have to travel about four thousand miles—at least a five hour trip.

No. The shock wave would travel in the stratosphere, where the speed of sound was higher, then propagate down. Three hours was plenty of time. Still, I thought, it should not have come as a rising wind. On the other side of the world, the exploding sun was tearing our atmosphere away and hurling it at the stars. The shock should have come as a single vast thunderclap.

For an instant the wind gentled, and I ran down the sidewalk pulling Leslie after me. We found another doorway as the wind picked up again. I thought I heard a siren coming to answer the alarm.

At the next break we splashed across Wilshire and reached the car. We sat there panting, waiting for the heater to warm up. My shoes felt squishy. The wet clothes stuck to my skin.

Leslie shouted, "How much longer?"

"I don't know! We ought to have *some* time."

"We'll have to spend our picnic indoors!"

"Your place or mine? Yours," I decided, and pulled away from the curb.

V

Wilshire Boulevard was flooded to the hubcaps in spots. The spurt of hail and sleet had become a steady, pounding rain. Fog lay flat and waist-deep ahead of us, broke swirling over our hood, churned in a wake behind us. Weird weather.

Nova weather. The shock wave of scalding superheated steam hadn't happened. Instead, a mere hot wind roaring through the stratosphere, the turbulence eddying down to form strange storms at ground level.

We parked illegally on the upper parking level. My one glimpse of the lower level showed it to be flooded. I opened the trunk and lifted two heavy paper bags.

"We must have been crazy," Leslie said, shaking her head. "We'll never use all this."

"Let's take it up anyway."

She laughed at me. "But why?"

"Just a whim. Will you help me carry it?"

We took double armfuls up to the fourteenth floor. That still left a couple of bags in the trunk. "Never mind them," Leslie said. "We've got the rumaki and the bottles and the nuts. What more do we need?"

"The cheeses. The crackers. The foie gras."

"Forget 'em."

"No."

"You're out of your mind," she explained to me, slowly so that I would understand. "You could be steamed dead on the way down! We might not have more than a few minutes left, and you want food for a week! *Why?*"

"I'd rather not say."

"Go then!" She slammed the door with terrible force.

The elevator was an ordeal. I kept wondering if Leslie was right. The shrilling of the wind was muffled, here at the core of the building. Perhaps it was about to rip electrical cables somewhere, leave me stranded in a darkened box. But I made it down.

The upper level was knee-deep in water.

My second surprise was that it was lukewarm, like old bathwater, unpleasant to wade through. Steam curdled on the surface, then blew away on a wind that howled through the concrete echo chamber like the screaming of the damned.

Going up was another ordeal. If what I was thinking was wish fulfillment, if a roaring wind of live steam caught me now . . . I'd feel like such an idiot. . . . But the doors opened, and the lights hadn't even flickered.

Leslie wouldn't let me in.

"Go away!" She shouted through the locked door. "Go eat your cheese and crackers somewhere else!"

"You got another date?"

That was a mistake. I got no answer at all.

I could almost see her viewpoint. The extra trip for the extra bags was no big thing to fight about; but why did it have to be? How long was our love affair going to last, anyway? An hour, with luck. Why back down on a perfectly good argument, to preserve so ephemeral a thing?

"I wasn't going to bring this up," I shouted, hoping she could hear me through the door. The wind must be three times as loud on the other side. "We may need food for a week! And a place to hide!"

Silence. I began to wonder if I could kick the door down. Would I be better off waiting in the hall? Eventually she'd have to—

The door opened. Leslie was pale. "That was cruel," she said quietly.

"I can't promise anything. I wanted to wait, but you forced it. I've been wondering if the sun really has exploded."

"That's cruel. I was just getting used to the idea." She turned her face to the door jamb. Tired, she was tired. I'd kept her up too late. . . .

"Listen to me. It was all wrong," I said. "There should have been an aurora borealis to light up the night sky from pole to pole. A shock wave of particles exploding out of the sun, traveling at an inch short of the speed of light, would rip into the atmosphere like—why, we'd have seen blue fire over every building!

"Then, the storm came too slow," I screamed, to be heard above the thunder. "A nova would rip away the sky over half the planet. The shock wave would move around the night side with a sound to break all the glass in the world, all at once! And crack concrete and marble—and, Leslie love, it just hasn't happened. So I started wondering."

She said it in a mumble. "Then what is it?"

"A flare. The worst—"

She shouted it at me like an accusation. "A flare! A solar flare! You think the sun could light up like that—"

"Easy, now—"

"—could turn the moon and planets into so many torches, then fade out as if nothing had happened! Oh, you idiot—"

"May I come in?"

She looked surprised. She stepped aside, and I bent and picked up the bags and walked in.

The glass doors rattled as if giants were trying to beat their way in. Rain had squeezed through cracks to make dark puddles on the rug.

I set the bags on the kitchen counter. I found bread in the refrigerator, dropped two slices in the toaster. While they were toasting I opened the foie gras.

"My telescope's gone," she said. Sure enough, it was. The tripod was all by itself on the balcony, on its side.

I untwisted the wire on a champagne bottle. The toast popped up, and Leslie found a knife and spread both slices with foie gras. I held the bottle near her ear, figuring to trip conditioned reflexes.

She did smile fleetingly as the cork popped. She said, "We should set up our picnic grounds here. Behind the counter. Sooner or later the wind is going to break those doors and shower glass all over everything."

That was a good thought. I slid around the partition, swept all the pillows off the floor and the couch and came back with them. We set up a nest for ourselves.

It was kind of cosy. The kitchen counter was three and a half feet high, just over our heads, and the kitchen alcove itself was just wide enough to swing out elbows comfortably. Now the floor was all pillows. Leslie poured the champagne into brandy snifters, all the way to the lip.

I searched for a toast, but there were just too many possibilities, all depressing. We drank without toasting. And then carefully set the snifters down and slid forward into each other's arms. We could sit that way, face to face, leaning sideways against each other.

"We're going to die," she said.

"Maybe not."

"Get used to the idea, I have," she said. "Look at you, you're all nervous now. Afraid of dying. Hasn't it been a lovely night?"

"Unique. I wish I'd known in time to take you to dinner."

Thunder came in a string of six explosions. Like bombs in an air raid. "Me too," she said when we could hear again.

"I wish I'd known this afternoon."

"Pecan pralines!"

"Farmer's Market. Double-roasted peanuts. Who would *you* have murdered, if you'd had the time?"

"There was a girl in my sorority—"

—and she was guilty of sibling rivalry, so Leslie claimed. I named an editor who kept changing his mind. Leslie named one of my old girlfriends, I named her only old boyfriend that I knew about, and it got to be kind of fun before we ran out. My brother Mike had forgotten my birthday once. The fiend.

The lights flickered, then came on again.

Too casually, Leslie asked, "Do you really think the sun might go back to normal?"

"It better *be* back to normal. Otherwise we're dead anyway. I wish we could see Jupiter."

"Dammit, answer me! Do you think it was a flare?"

"Yes."

"Why?"

"Yellow dwarf stars don't go nova."

"What if ours did?"

"The astronomers know a lot about novas," I said. "More than you'd guess. They can see them coming months ahead. Sol is a gee-naught yellow dwarf. They don't go nova at all. They have to wander off the main sequence first, and that takes millions of years."

She pounded a fist softly on my back. We were cheek to cheek; I couldn't see her face. "I don't want to believe it. I don't dare. Stan, nothing like this has ever happened before. How can you know?"

"Something did."

"What? I don't believe it. We'd remember."

"Do you remember the first moon landing? Aldrin and Armstrong?"

"Of course. We watched it at Earl's Lunar Landing Party."

"They landed on the biggest, flattest place they could find on the moon. They sent back several hours of jumpy home movies, took a lot of very clear pictures, left corrugated footprints all over the place. And they came home with a bunch of rocks.

"Remember? People said it was a long way to go for rocks. But the first thing anyone noticed about those rocks was that they were half-melted.

"Sometime in the past, oh, say the past hundred thousand years—there's no way of marking it closer than that—the sun flared up. It didn't stay hot enough long enough to leave any marks on the Earth. But the moon doesn't have an atmosphere to protect it. All the rocks melted on one side."

The air was warm and damp. I took off my coat, which was heavy with rainwater. I fished the cigarettes and matches out, lit a cigarette and exhaled past Leslie's ear.

"We'd remember. It *couldn't* have been this bad."

"I'm not so sure. Suppose it happened over the Pacific? It wouldn't do *that* much damage. Or over the American continents. It would have sterilized some plants and animals and burned down a lot of forests, and who'd know? The sun went back to normal, that time. It might again. The sun is a four percent variable star. Maybe it gets a touch more variable than that, every so often."

Something shattered in the bedroom. A window? A wet wind touched us, and the shriek of the storm was louder.

"Then we could live through this," Leslie said hesitantly.

"I believe you've put your finger on the crux of the matter. Skoal!" I found my champagne and drank deep. It was past three in the morning, with a hurricane beating at our doors.

"Then shouldn't we be doing something about it?"

"We are."

"Something like trying to get up into the hills! Stan, there're going to be floods!"

"You bet your ass there are, but they won't rise this high. Fourteen stories. Listen, I've thought this through. We're in a building that was designed to be earthquake proof. You told me so yourself. It'd take more than a hurricane to knock it over.

"As for heading for the hills, what hills? We won't get far tonight, not with the streets flooded already. Suppose we could get up into the Santa Monica Mountains; then what? Mudslides, that's what. That area won't stand up to what's coming. The flare must have boiled away enough water to make another ocean. It's going to rain for forty days and forty nights! Love, this is the safest place we could have reached tonight."

"Suppose the polar caps melt?"

"Yeah . . . well, we're pretty high, even for that. Hey, maybe that last flare was what started Noah's Flood. Maybe it's happening again. Sure as hell, there's not a place on Earth that isn't the middle of a hurricane. Those two great counterrotating hurricanes, by now they must have broken up into hundreds of little storms—"

The glass doors exploded inward. We ducked, and the wind howled about us and dropped rain and glass on us.

"At least we've got food!" I shouted. "If the floods maroon us here, we can last it out!"

"But if the power goes, we can't cook it! And the refrigerator—"

"We'll cook everything we can. Hardboil all the eggs—"

The wind rose about us. I stopped trying to talk.

Warm rain sprayed us horizontally and left us soaked. Try to cook in a hurricane? I'd been stupid; I'd waited too long. The wind would tip boiling water on us if we tried it. Or hot grease—

Leslie screamed, "We'll have to use the oven!"

Of course. The oven couldn't possibly fall on us.

We set it for 400° and put the eggs in, in a pot of water. We took all the meat out of the meat drawer and shoved it in on a broiling pan. Two artichokes in another pot. The other vegetables we could eat raw.

What else? I tried to think.

Water. If the electricity went, probably the water and telephone lines would too. I turned on the faucet over the sink and started filling things: pots with lids, Leslie's thirty-cup percolator that she used for parties, her wash bucket. She clearly thought I was crazy, but I didn't trust the rain as a water source; I couldn't control it.

The sound. Already we'd stopped trying to shout through it. Forty days and nights of this and we'd be stone deaf. Cotton? Too late to reach the bathroom. Paper towels! I tore and wadded and made four plugs for our ears.

Sanitary facilities? Another reason for picking Leslie's place over mine. When the plumbing stopped, there was always the balcony.

And if the flood rose higher than the fourteenth floor, there was the roof. Twenty stories up. If it went higher than that, there would be damn few people left when it was over.

And if it was a nova?

I held Leslie a bit more closely, and lit another cigarette one-handed. All the wasted planning, if it was a nova. But I'd have been doing it anyway. You don't stop planning just because there's no hope.

And when the hurricane turned to live steam, there was always the balcony. At a dead run, and over the railing, in preference to being boiled alive.

But now was not the time to mention it.

Anyway, she'd probably thought of it herself.

The lights went out about four. I turned off the oven, in case the power should come back. Give it an hour to cool down, then I'd put all the food in Baggies.

Leslie was asleep, sitting up in my arms. How could she sleep, not knowing? I piled pillows behind her and let her back easy.

For some time I lay on my back, smoking, watching the lightning make shadows on the ceiling. We had eaten all the foie gras and drunk one bottle of champagne. I thought of opening the brandy, but decided against it, with regret.

A long time passed. I'm not sure what I thought about. I didn't sleep, but certainly my mind was in idle. It only gradually came to me that the ceiling, between lightning flashes, had turned grey.

I rolled over, gingerly, soggily. Everything was wet.

My watch said it was nine-thirty.

I crawled around the partition into the living room. I'd been ignoring the storm sounds so long that it took a faceful of warm whipping rain to remind me. There was a hurricane going on. But charcoal-grey light was filtering through the black clouds.

So. I was right to have saved the brandy. Floods, storms, intense radiation, fires lit by the flare — if the toll of destruction was as high as I expected, then money was about to become worthless. We would need trade goods.

I was hungry. I ate two eggs and some bacon — still warm — and started putting the rest of the food away. We had food for a week, maybe . . . but hardly a balanced diet. Maybe we could trade with other apartments. This was a big building. There must be empty apartments, too, that we could raid for canned soup and the like. And refugees from the lower floors to be taken care of, if the waters rose high enough . . .

Damn! I missed the nova. Life had been simplicity itself last night. Now . . . did we have medicines? Were there doctors in the building? There would be dysentery and other plagues. And hunger. There was a supermarket near here; could we find a scuba rig in the building?

But I'd get some sleep first. Later we could start exploring the building. The day had become a lighter charcoal grey. Things could be worse, far worse. I thought of the radiation that must have sleeted over the far side of the world, and wondered if our children would colonize Europe, or Asia, or Africa.

The Gold at the Starbow's End

Frederik Pohl, another of the famous Futurians, supplies one of the best memoirs of that group in his autobiography, The Way the Future Was. *Pohl has been editor of several magazines, ranging from pre–World War II pulps to* Galaxy *and* If *from the late 1950s to the early 1970s. For many years he was an informal consultant to Ian and Betty Ballantine, whose publishing company was a dominant force in mass-market SF. Then in the 1970s he became SF editor at Ace Books and then at Bantam Books. In the late 1960s he edited the unfortunately short-lived magazine* International SF, *devoted to SF in translation. But all this aside, Pohl has been perhaps even more influential as a writer, both in collaboration with Cyril M. Kornbluth and on his own. Pohl's work has gone from strength to strength. In the 1950s, in his well-known critical book* New Maps of Hell, *Kingsley Amis praised Pohl's satirical abilities and called him the best SF writer. However, it appears Pohl achieved a whole new maturity in the early 1970s, going on to write such award-winning books as* Man Plus, Gateway, *and* The Years of the City. *The harbinger of these impressive novels was the novella "The Gold at the Starbow's End." It defines post–New Wave hard science fiction for the 1970s and 1980s, a fiction that integrates the stylistic advances and interest in rounded character of the New Wave with the knowledge of and interest in physics, math, space travel, and technology of classic SF.*

* * *

CONSTITUTION ONE
Log of Lt. Col. Sheffield N. Jackman, USAF, commanding U.S.
Starship *Constitution*, Day 40.

All's well, friends. Thanks to Mission Control for the batch of personal messages. We enjoyed the concert you beamed us, in fact we recorded most of it so we can play it over again when communication gets hairy.

We are now approaching the six-week point in our expedition to Alpha Centauri, Planet Aleph, and now that we've passed the farthest previous manned distance from Earth we're really beginning to feel as if we're on our way. Our latest navigation check confirms Mission Control's plot, and we estimate we should be crossing the orbit of Pluto at approximately 1631 hours, ship time, of Day 40, which is today. Letski has been keeping track of the time dilation effect, which is beginning to be significant now that we are traveling about some six percent of the speed of light, and says this would make it approximately a quarter of two in the morning your time, Mission Control. We voted to consider that the "coastal waters" mark. From then on we will have left the solar system behind and thus will be the first human beings to enter upon the deeps of interstellar space. We plan to have a ceremony. Letski and Ann Becklund have made up an American flag for jettisoning at that point, which we will do through the Number Three survey port, along with the prepared stainless-steel plaque containing the President's commissioning speech. We are also throwing in some private articles for each of us. I am contributing my Air Academy class ring.

Little change since previous reports. We are settling down nicely to our routine. We finished up all our postlaunch checks weeks ago, and as Dr. Knefhausen predicted we began to find time hanging heavy on our hands. There won't be much to keep us busy between now and when we arrive at the planet Alpha-Aleph that is really essential to the operating of the spaceship. So we went along with Kneffie's proposed recreational schedule, using the worksheets prepared by the NASA Division of Flight Training and Personnel Management. At first—I think the boys back in Indianapolis are big enough to know this—it met with what you might call a cool reception. The general consensus was that this business of learning number theory and the calculus of statement, which is what they handed us for openers, was for the birds. We figured we weren't quite desperate enough for that yet, so we fooled around with other things. Ann and Will Becklund played a lot of chess. Dot Letski began writing a verse adaptation of *War and Peace*. The rest of us hacked around with the equipment, and making astronomical observations and gabbing. But all that began to get tiresome pretty fast, just as Kneffie said it would at the briefings.

We talked about the idea that the best way to pass time in a spaceship was learning to get interested in mathematical problems—no mass to transport, no competitive element to get tempers up and all that. It began to make sense. So now Letski is in his tenth day of trying to find a formula for primes, and my own dear Flo is trying to prove Goldbach's Conjecture by means of the theory of congruences. (This is the girl who two months ago couldn't add up a laundry list!) It certainly passes the time.

Medically, we are all fit. I will append the detailed data on our blood pressures, pulses, et cetera, as well as the tape from the rocket and navigating systems readouts. I'll report again as scheduled. Take care of Earth for us—we're looking forward to seeing it again, in a few years!

WASHINGTON ONE

There was a lull in the urban guerrilla war in Washington that week. The chopper was able to float right in to the South Lawn of the White House—no sniper fire, no heat-seeking missiles, not even rock throwing. Dr. Dieter von Knefhausen stared suspiciously at the knot of weary-looking pickets in their permitted fifty yards of space along the perimeter. They didn't look militant, probably Gay Lib or, who knew what, maybe nature-food or single-tax; at any rate no rocks came from them, only a little disorganized booing as the helicopter landed. Knefhausen bowed to *Herr Omnes* sardonically, hopped nimbly out of the chopper and got out of the way as it took off again, which it did at once. He didn't trouble to run to the White House. He strolled. He did not fear these simple people, even if the helicopter pilot did. Also he was not really eager to keep his appointment with the President.

The ADC who frisked him did not smile. The orderly who conducted him to the West Terrace did not salute. No one relieved him of the dispatch case with his slides and papers, although it was heavy. You could tell right away when you were in the doghouse, he thought, ducking his head from the rotor blast as the pilot circled the White House to gain altitude before venturing back across the spread-out city.

It had been a lot different in the old days, he thought with some nostalgia. He could remember every minute of those old days. It was right here, this portico, where he had stood before the world's press and photographers to tell them about the Alpha-Aleph Project. He had seen his picture next to the President's on all the front pages, watched himself on the TV newscasts, talking about the New Earth that would give America an entire colonizable planet four light-years away. He remembered the launch at the Cape, with a million and a half invited guests from all over the world, foreign statesmen and scientists eating their hearts out with envy, American leaders jovial with pride. The orderlies saluted then, all right. His lecture fees had gone clear out of sight. There was even talk of making him the Vice Presidential candidate in the next election—and it could have happened, too, if the election had been right then, and if there hadn't been the problem of his being born in another country.

Now it was all different. He was taken up in the service elevator. It wasn't so much that Knethausen minded for his own sake, he told himself, but how did the word get out that there was trouble? Was it only the newspaper stories? Was there a leak?

The Marine orderly knocked once on the big door of the Cabinet room, and it was opened from inside.

Knefhausen entered.

"Come in, Dieter, boy, pull up a pew." No Vice President jumping up to grab his arm and slap his back. His greeting was thirty silent faces turned toward him, some reserved, some frankly hostile. The full Cabinet was there, along with half a dozen department heads and the President's personal action staff, and the most hostile face around the big oval table was the President's own.

Knefhausen bowed. An atavistic hankering for lyceum-cadet jokes made him think of clicking his heels and adjusting a monocle, but he didn't have a monocle and didn't yield to impulses like that. He merely took his place standing at the foot of the table and, when the President nodded, said, "Good morning, gentlemen, and ladies. I assume you want to see me about the stupid lies the Russians are spreading about the Alpha-Aleph program."

"Roobarooba," they muttered to each other.

The President said in his sharp tenor, "So you think they are just lies?"

"Lies or mistakes, Mr. President, what's the difference? We are right and they are wrong, that's all."

"Roobaroobarooba."

The Secretary of State looked inquiringly at the President, got a nod and said: "Dr. Knefhausen, you know I've been on your team a long time and I don't want to disagree with any statement you care to make, but are you so sure about that? There are some mighty persuasive figures comin' out of the Russians."

"They are false, Mr. Secretary."

"Ah, well, Dr. Knefhausen. I might be inclined to take your word for it, but others might not. Not cranks or malcontents, Dr. Knefhausen, but good, decent people. Do you have any evidence for them?"

"With your permission, Mr. President?" The President nodded again. Knefhausen unlocked his dispatch case and drew out a slim sheaf of slides. He handed them to a major of Marines, who looked to the President for approval and then did what Knefhausen told him. The room lights went down and, after some fiddling with the focus, the first slide was projected over Knefhausen's head. It showed a huge array of Y-shaped metal posts, stretching away into the distance of a bleak, powdery-looking landscape.

"This picture is our radio telescope on Farside, the Moon," he said. "It is never visible from the Earth, because that portion of the Moon's surface is permanently turned away from us, for which reason we selected it for the site of the telescope. There is no electrical interference of any kind. The instrument is made up of thirty-three million separate dipole elements, aligned with an accuracy of one part in several million. Its actual size is an approximate circle eighteen miles across, but by virtue of the careful positioning its performance is effectively equal to a telescope with a diameter of some twenty-six miles. Next slide, please."

Click. The picture of the huge RT display swept away and was replaced by another similar—but visibly smaller and shabbier—construction.

"This is the Russian instrument, gentlemen. And ladies. It is approximately one-quarter the size of ours in diameter. It has less than one-tenth as many elements, and our reports—they are classified, but I am informed this gathering is cleared to receive this material? Yes—our reports indicate the alignment is very crude. Even terrible, you could say.

"The difference between the two instruments in information-gathering capacity is roughly a hundred to one, in our favor. Lights, please.

"What this means," he went on smoothly, smiling at each of the persons around the table in turn as he spoke, "is that if the Russians say 'no' and we say 'yes', bet on 'yes.' Our radio telescope can be trusted. Theirs cannot."

The meeting shifted uneasily in its chairs. They were as anxious to believe Knefhausen as he was to convince them, but they were not sure.

Representative Belden, the Chairman of the House Ways and Means Committee, spoke for all of them. "Nobody doubts the quality of your equipment. Especially," he added, "since we still have bruises from the job of paying for it. But the Russians made a flat statement. They said that Alpha Centauri can't have a planet larger than one thousand miles in diameter, or nearer than half a billion miles to the star. I have a copy of the Tass release here. It admits that their equipment is inferior to our own, but they have a statement signed by twenty-two academicians that says their equipment could not miss on any object larger, or nearer, than what I have said, or on any body of any kind which would be large enough to afford a landing place for our astronauts. Are you familiar with this statement?"

"Yes, of course, I have read it—"

"Then you know that they state positively that the planet you call 'Alpha-Aleph' does not exist."

"Yes, sir, that is what they state."

"Moreover, statements from authorities at the Paris Observatory and the

UNESCO Astrophysical Center at Trieste, and from England's Astronomer Royal, all say that they have checked and confirmed their figures."

Knefhausen nodded cheerfully. "That is correct, Representative Belden. They confirm that if the observations are as stated, then the conclusions drawn by the Soviet installation at Novy Brezhnevgrad on Farside naturally follow. I don't question the arithmetic. I only say that the observations are made with inadequate equipment, and thus the Soviet astronomers have come to a false conclusion. But I do not want to burden your patience with an unsupported statement," he added hastily as the Congressman opened his mouth to speak again, "so I will tell you all there is to tell. What the Russians say is theory. What I have to counter is not merely better theory, but also objective fact. I know Alpha-Aleph is there because I have seen it! Lights again, Major! And the next slide, if you please."

The screen lit up and showed glaring bare white with a sprinkling of black spots, like dust. A large one appeared in the exact center of the screen, with a dozen lesser ones sprinkled around it. Knefhausen picked up a flashpointer and aimed its little arrowhead of light at the central dot.

"This is a photographic negative," he said, "which is to say that it is black where the actual scene is white and vice versa. Those objects are astronomical. It was taken from our Briareus XII satellite near the orbit of Jupiter, on its way out to Neptune fourteen months ago. The central object is the star Alpha Centauri. It was photographed with a special instrument which filters out most of the light from the star itself, electronic in nature and something like the coronascope which is used for photographing prominences on our own Sun. We hoped that by this means we might be able to photograph the planet Alpha-Aleph. We were successful, as you can see." The flashpointer laid its little arrow next to the nearest small dot to the central star. "That, gentlemen, and ladies, is Alpha-Aleph. It is precisely where we predicted it from radio-telescope data."

There was another buzz from the table. In the dark it was louder than before. The Secretary of State cried sharply, "Mr. President! Can't we release this photograph?"

"We will release it immediately after this meeting," said the President. "*Roobarooba.*"

Then the committee chairman: "Mr. President, I'm sure if you say that's the planet we want, then it's the planet. But others outside this country may wonder, for indeed all those dots look alike to me. Just to satisfy a layman's curiosity, *how* do you know that is Alpha-Aleph?"

"Slide number four, please—and keep number three in the carriage." The same scene, subtly different. "Note that in this picture, gentlemen, that one object, there, is in a different position. It has moved. You know that the stars show no discernible motion. It has moved because this photograph was taken eight months later, as Briareus XII was returning from the Neptune flyby, and the planet Alpha-Aleph has revolved in its orbit. This is not theory, it is evidence, and I add that the original tapes from which the photoprint was made are stored in Goldstone so there is no question that arises of foolishness."

"*Roobarooba*," but in a higher and excited key.

Gratified, Knefhausen nailed down his point. "So, Major, if you will now return to slide three, yes—and if you will flip back and forth, between three and four, as fast as you can—thank you." The little black dot called Alpha-Aleph bounced back and forth like a tennis ball, while all the other star points remained motionless. "This is what is called the blank comparator process, you see. I point out that if what you are looking at is not a planet it is, Mr. President, the funniest star you ever saw. Also it is exactly at the distance and exactly with the orbital period we specified based on the RT data. Now, are there any more questions?"

"No, sir!" "That's great, Kneffie!" "I think that wraps it up." "That'll show the Commies."

The President's voice overrode them.

"I think we can have the lights on now, Major Merton," he said. "Dr. Knefhausen, thank you. I'd appreciate it if you would remain nearby for a few minutes, so you can join Murray and myself in the study to check over the text of our announcement before we release these pictures." He nodded sober dismissal to his chief science adviser and then, reminded by the happy faces of his cabinet, remembered to smile with pleasure.

CONSTITUTION TWO

Sheffield Jackman's log. Starship *Constitution*. Day 95.

According to Letski we are now traveling at just about fifteen percent of the speed of light, almost 30,000 miles per second. The fusion thrusters are chugging away handsomely; as predicted, the explosions sequence fast enough so that we feel them only as vibration. Fuel, power and life-support curves are sticking tight to optimum. No sweat of any kind with the ship, or, actually, with anything else.

Relativistic effects have begun to show up as predicted. Jim Barstow's spectral studies show the stars in front of us are shifting to the blue end, and the sun and other stars behind us are shifting to the red. Without the spectroscope you can't see much, though. Beta Circini looks a little funny, maybe. As for the sun, it's still very bright—Jim logged it as minus-six magnitude a few hours ago—and as I've never seen it in quite that way before, I can't tell whether the color looks bright or not. It certainly isn't the golden yellow I associate with type GO, but neither is Alpha Centauri ahead of us, and I don't really see a difference between them. I think the reason is simply that they are so bright that the color impressions are secondary to the brightness impressions, although the spectroscope, as I say, does show the differences. We've all taken turns at looking back. Naturally enough, I guess. We can still make out the Earth and even the moon in the telescope, but it's chancy. Ski almost got an eyeful of the sun at full light-gathering amplitude yesterday because the visual separation is only about twelve seconds of arc now. In a few more days they'll be too close to separate.

Let's see, what else?

We've been having a fine time with the recreational math program. Ann has taken to binary arithmetic like a duck to water. She's involved in what I take to be some sort of statistical experimentation—we don't pry too much into what the others are doing until they're ready to talk about it—and, of all things, she demanded we produce coins to flip. Well, naturally none of us had taken any money with us! Except that it turns out two of us did. Ski had a Russian silver ruble that his mother's uncle had given him for luck, and I found an old Philadelphia transit token in my pocket. Ann rejected my transit token as too light to be reliable, but she now spends happy hours flipping the ruble, heads or tails, and writing down the results as a series of six-place binary numbers, 1 for heads and 0 for tails. After about a week my curiosity got too much so I began hinting to find out what she was doing. When I ask she says things like, "By means of the easy and the simple we grasp the laws of the whole world." When I say that's nice, but what does she hope to grasp by flipping the coin, she says, "When the laws of the whole world are grasped, therein lies perfection." So, as I say, we don't press each other and I leave it there. But it passes the time.

Kneffie would be proud of himself if he could see how our recreation keeps us busy. None of us has managed to prove Fermat's Last Theorem yet or anything like that, but of course that's the whole point. If we could *solve* the problems, we'd have used them up, and then what would we do for recreation? It does exactly what it was intended to. It keeps us mentally alert on this long and intrinsically rather dull boat ride.

Personal relationships? Jes' fine, fellows, jes' fine. A lot better than any of us really hoped, back there at the personal-hygiene briefings in Mission Control. The girls take the stripey pills every day until three days before their periods, then they take the green pills for four days, then they lay off pills for four days, then back to the stripes. There was a little embarrassed joking about it at first, but now it's strictly routine, like brushing our teeth. We men take our red pills every day—Ski christened them "stop lights"—until the girls tell us they're about to lay off—you know what I mean, each girl tells her husband—then we take the Blue Devil—that's what we call the antidote—and have a hell of a time until the girls start on the stripes again. None of us thought any of this would work, you know. But it works fine. I don't even think sex until Flo kisses my ear and tells me she's getting ready to, excuse the expression, get in heat, and then like wow. Same with everybody. The aft chamber with the nice wide bunks we call Honeymoon Hotel. It belongs to whoever needs it, and never once have both bunks been used. The rest of the time we just sleep wherever it's convenient, and nobody gets uptight about it.

Excuse my getting personal, but you told me you wanted to know everything, and there's not much else to tell. All systems remain optimum. We check them over now and again, but nothing has given any trouble, or even looked as though it might be thinking about giving trouble later on. And there's absolutely nothing worth looking at outside, but stars. We've all seen them about as much as we need to by now. The plasma jet thrums right along at our point-seven-five G. We don't even hear it any more.

We've got used to the recycling system. None of us really thought we'd get with the suction toilet, not to mention what happens to the contents, but it was only a little annoying the first few days. Now it's fine. The treated product goes into the algae tanks. The sludge from the algae goes into the hydroponic beds, but by then, of course, it's just greeny-brown vegetable matter. That's all handled semiautomatically anyway, of course, so our first real contact with the system comes in the kitchen.

The food we eat comes in the form of nice red tomatoes and nourishing rice pilaf and stuff like that. (We do miss animal protein a little; the frozen stores have to last a long time, so each hamburger is a special feast and we only have them once a week or so.) The water we drink comes actually out of the air, condensed by the dehumidifiers into the reserve supply, where we get it to drink. It's nicely aerated and chilled and tastes fine. Of course, the way it gets into the air in the first place is by being sweated out of our pores or transpired from the plants—which are irrigated direct from the treated product of the reclamation tanks—and we all know, when we stop to think of it, that every molecule of it has passed through all our kidneys forty times by now. But not directly. That's the point. What we drink is clear sweet dew. And if it once was something else, can't you say the same of Lake Erie?

Well, I think I've gone on long enough. You've probably got the idea by now: we're happy in the service, and we all thank you for giving us this pleasure cruise!

WASHINGTON TWO

Waiting for his appointment with the President, Dr. Knefhausen reread the communique from the spaceship, chuckling happily to himself.

"Happy in the service." "Like wow." "Kneffie would be proud of himself."
Indeed Kneffie was. And proud of them, those little wonders, there! So
brave. So strong.

He took as much pride in them as though they had been his own sons and
daughters, all eight of them. Everybody knew the Alpha-Aleph project was
Knefhausen's baby, but he tried to conceal from the world that, in his own
mind, he spread his fatherhood to include the crew. They were the pick of
the available world, and it was he who had put them where they were. He
lifted his head, listening to the distant chanting from the perimeter fence
where today's disgusting exhibition of mob violence was doing its best to
harass the people who were making the world go. What great lumps they
were out there, with their long hair and their dirty morals. The heavens
belonged only to angels, and it was Dieter von Knefhausen who had picked
the angels. It was he who had established the selection procedures—and if
he had done some things that were better left unmentioned to make sure the
procedures worked, what of it? It was he who had conceived and adapted the
highly important recreation schedule, and above all he who had conceived
the entire project and persuaded the President to make it come true. The
hardware was nothing, only money. The basic scientific concepts were
known; most of the components were on the shelves; it took only will to put
them together. The will would not have existed if it had not been for
Knefhausen, who announced the discovery of Alpha-Aleph from his
radio observatory on Farside—gave it that name, although as everyone
realized he could have called it by any name he chose, even his own—and
carried on the fight for the project by every means until the President
bought it.

It had been a hard, bitter struggle. He reminded himself with courage
that the worst was still ahead. No matter. Whatever it cost, it was done, and
it was worthwhile. These reports from *Constitution* proved it. It was going
exactly as planned, and—

"Excuse me, Dr. Knefhausen."

He looked up, catapulted back from almost half a light-year away.

"I said the President will see you now, Dr. Knefhausen," repeated the
usher.

"Ah," said Knefhausen. "Oh, yes, to be sure. I was deep in thought."

"Yes, sir. This way, sir."

They passed a window and there was a quick glimpse of the turmoil at the
gates, picket signs used like battleaxes, a thin blue cloud of tear gas, the
sounds of shouting. "King Mob is busy today," said Knefhausen absently.

"There's no danger, sir. Through here, please."

The President was in his private study, but to Knefhausen's surprise he was not alone. There was Murray Amos, his personal secretary, which one could understand; but there were three other men in the room. Knefhausen recognized them as the Secretary of State, the Speaker of the House and, of all people, the Vice President. How strange, thought Knefhausen, for what was to have been a confidential briefing for the President alone! But he rallied quickly.

"Excuse me, Mr. President," he said cheerfully, "I must have understood wrong. I thought you were ready for our little talk."

"I am ready, Knefhausen," said the President. The cares of his years in the White House rested heavily on him today, Knefhausen thought critically. He looked very old and very tired. "You will tell these gentlemen what you would have told me."

"Ah, yes, I see," said Knefhausen, trying to conceal the fact that he did not see at all. Surely the President did not mean what his words said, therefore it was necessary to try to see what was his thought. "Yes, to be sure. Here is something, Mr. President. A new report from the *Constitution*! It was received by burst transmission from the Lunar Orbiter at Goldstone just an hour ago, and has just come from the decoding room. Let me read it to you. Our brave astronauts are getting along splendidly, just as we planned. They say—"

"Don't read us that just now," said the President harshly. "We'll hear it, but first there is something else. I want you to tell this group the full story of the Alpha-Aleph project."

"The full story, Mr. President?" Knefhausen hung on gamely. "I see. You wish me to begin with the very beginning, when first we realized at the observatory that we had located a planet—"

"No, Knefhausen. Not the cover story. The truth."

"Mr. President!" cried Knefhausen in sudden agony. "I must inform you that I protest this premature disclosure of vital—"

"The truth, Knefhausen!" shouted the President. It was the first time Knefhausen had ever heard him raise his voice. "It won't go out of this room, but you must tell them everything. Tell them why it is that the Russians were right and we lied! Tell them why we sent the astronauts on a suicide mission, ordered to land on a planet that we knew all along did not exist!"

CONSTITUTION THREE

Shef Jackman's journal, Day 130.

It's been a long time, hasn't it? I'm sorry for being such a lousy correspondent. I was in the middle of a thirteen-game chess series with Eve Barstow— she was playing the Bobby Fischer games and I was playing in the style of

Reshevsky—and Eve said something that made me think of old Kneffie, and that, of course, reminded me I owed you a transmission. So here it is.

In my own defense, though, it isn't only that we've been busy with other things. It takes a lot of power for these chatty little letters. Some of us aren't so sure they're worthwhile. The farther we get the more power we need to accumulate for a transmission. Right now it's not so bad, but, well, I might as well tell you the truth, right? Kneffie made us promise that. Always tell the truth, he said, because you're part of the experiment, and we need to know what you're doing, all of it. Well, the truth in this case is that we were a little short of disposable power for a while because Jim Barstow needed quite a lot for research purposes. You will probably wonder what the research is, but we have a rule that we don't criticize, or even talk about, what anyone else is doing until they're ready, and he isn't ready yet. I take the responsibility for the whole thing, not just the power drain but the damage to the ship. I said he could go ahead with it.

We're going pretty fast now, and to the naked eye the stars fore and aft have blue-shifted and red-shifted nearly out of sight. It's funny but we haven't been able to observe Alpha-Aleph yet, even with the disk obscuring the star. Now, with the shift to the blue, we probably won't see it at all until we slow down. We can still see the sun, but I guess what we're seeing is ultraviolet when it's home. Of course the relativistic frequency shifts mean we need extra compensating power in our transmissions, which is another reason why, all in all, I don't think I'll be writing home every Sunday between breakfast and the baseball game, the way I ought to!

But the mission's going along fine. The "personal relationships" keep on being just great. We've done a little experimental research there, too, that wasn't on the program, but it's all O.K. No problems. Worked out great. I think maybe I'll leave out some of the details, but we found some groovy ways to do things. Oh, hell, I'll give you one hint: Dot Letski says I should tell you to get the boys at Mission Control to crack open two of the stripey pills and one of the Blue Devils, mix them with a quarter-teaspoon of black pepper and about 2 cc of the conditioner fluid from the recycling system. Serve over orange sherbet, and oh, boy. After the first time we had it Flo made a crack about its being "seminal," which I thought was a private joke, but it broke everybody up. Dot figured it out for herself weeks ago. We wondered how she got so far so fast with *War and Peace* until she let us into the secret. Then we found out what it could do for you, both emotionally and intellectually: the creative over the arousing, as they say.

Ann and Jerry Letski used up their own recreational programs early—real early. They were supposed to last the whole voyage! They swapped micro-fiches, on the grounds that each was interested in an aspect of causality and they wanted to see what the other side had to offer. Now Ann is deep into people like Kant and Carnap, and Ski is sore as a boil because there's no *Achillea millefolium* in the hydroponics garden. Needs the stalks for his researches, he says. He is making do with flipping his ruble to generate hexagrams; in fact we all borrow it now and then. But it's not the right way. Honestly, Mission Control, he's right. Some thought should have been given to our other needs, besides sex and number theory. We can't even use chop bones from the kitchen wastes, because there isn't any kitchen waste. I know you couldn't think of everything, but still—anyway, we improvise as best we can, and mostly well enough.

Let's see, what else? Did I send you Jim Barstow's proof of Goldbach's Conjecture? Turned out to be very simple once he had devised his multiplex parity analysis idea. Mostly we don't fool with that sort of stuff any more, though. We got tired of number theory after we'd worked out all the fun parts, and if there is any one thing that we all work on—apart from our private interests—it is probably the calculus of statement. We don't do it systematically, only as time permits from our other activities, but we're all pretty well convinced that a universal grammar is feasible enough, and it's easy enough to see where that leads.

Flo has done more than most of us. She asked me to put in that Boole, Venn and all those old people were on the wrong track, but she thinks there might be something to Leibniz's "calculus ratiocinator" idea. There's a J. W. Swanson suggestion that she likes for multiplexing languages. (Jim took off from it to work out his parity analysis.) The idea is that you devise a double-vocabulary language. One set of meanings is conveyed, say, by phonemes, that is, the shape of the words themselves. Another set is conveyed by pitch. It's like singing a message, half of it conveyed by the words, the other half by the tune—like rock music. You get both sets of meanings on third, fourth and nth dimensions so as to convey many kinds of meanings at once, but it's not very fruitful so far—except for using sex as one of the communications media. Most of the senses available are too limited to convey much.

By the way, we checked out all the existing "artificial languages" as best we could—put Will Becklund under hypnotic regression to recapture the Esperanto he'd learned as a kid, for instance. But they were all blind alleys. Didn't even convey as much as standard English or French.

Medical readouts follow. We're all healthy. Eve Barstow gave us a medical check to make sure. Ann and Ski had little rough spots in a couple of molars so she filled them for the practice more than because they needed it. I don't mean practice in filling teeth; she wanted to try acupuncture instead of procaine. Worked fine.

We all have this writing-to-Daddy-and-Mommy-from-Camp-Tangle-wood feeling and we'd like to send you some samples of our home hand-icrafts. The trouble is there's so much of it. Everybody has something he's personally pleased with, like Barstow's proof of most of the classic math problems and my multi-media adaptation of "*Sur le pont d'Avignon*." It's hard to decide what to send you with the limited power available, and we don't want to waste it with junk. So we took a vote and decided the best thing was Ann's verse retelling of *War and Peace*. It runs pretty long. I hope the power holds it. I'll transmit as much of it as I can. . . .

WASHINGTON THREE

Spring was well advanced in Washington. Along the Potomac the cherry blossoms were beginning to bud, and Rock Creek Park was the pale green of new leaves. Even through the *whap, whap* of the helicopter rotor Knefhausen could hear an occasional rattle of small-arms fire from around Georgetown, and the Molotov cocktails and tear gas from the big Water Gate apartment development at the river's edge were steaming up the sky with smoke and fumes. They never stopped, thought Knefhausen irritably. What was the good of trying to save people like this?

It was distracting. He found himself dividing his attention into three parts—the scarred, greening landscape below; the escort fireships that orbited around his own chopper; and the papers on his lap. All of them annoyed him. He couldn't keep his mind on any of them. What he liked least was the report from the *Constitution*. He had had to get expert help in translating what it was all about, and didn't like the need, and even less liked the results. What had gone wrong? They were his kids, hand-picked. There had been no hint of, for instance, hippiness in any of them, at least not past the age of twenty, and only for Ann Becklund and Florence Jackman even then. How had they got into this *I Ching* foolishness, and this stupid business with the *Achillea millefolium*, better known as the common yarrow? What "experiments"? Who started the disgustingly antiscientific acupuncture thing? How dared they depart from their programmed power budget for "research purposes," and what were the purposes? Above all, what was the "damage to the ship"?

He scribbled on a pad.

With immediate effect, cut out the nonsense. I have the impression you are all acting like irresponsible children. You are letting down the ideals of our program.

Knefhausnen

After running the short distance from the chopper pad to the shelter of the guarded White House entrance, he gave the slip to a page from the Message Center for immediate encoding and transmission to the *Constitution* via Goldstone, Lunar Orbiter and Farside Base. All they needed was a reminder, he persuaded himself, then they would settle down. But he was still worried as he peered into a mirror, patted his hair down, smoothed his moustache with the tip of a finger and presented himself to the President's chief secretary.

This time they went down, not up. Knefhausen was going to the basement chamber that had been successively Franklin Roosevelt's swimming pool, the White House press lounge, a TV studio for taping jolly little two-shots of the President with congressmen and senators for the folks back home to see and, now, the heavily armored bunker in which anyone trapped in the White House in the event of a successful attack from the city outside could hold out for several weeks, during which time the Fourth Armored would surely be able to retake the grounds from its bases in Maryland. It was not a comfortable room, but it was a safe one. Besides being armored against attack, it was as thoroughly soundproof, spyproof and leakproof as any chamber in the world, not excepting the Under-Kremlin, or the Colorado NOROM base.

Knefhausen was admitted and seated, while the President and a couple of others were in whispered conversation at one end of the room, and the several dozen other people present craned their necks to stare at Knefhausen.

After a moment the President raised his head. "All right," he said. He drank from a crystal goblet of water, looking wizened and weary, and disappointed at the way a boyhood dream had turned out: the presidency wasn't what it had seemed to be, from Muncie, Indiana. "We all know why we're here. The government of the United States has given out information which was untrue. It did so knowingly and wittingly, and we've been caught at it. Now we want you to know the background, and so Dr. Knefhausen is going to explain the Alpha-Aleph project. Go ahead, Knefhausen."

Knefhausen stood up and walked unhurryingly to the little lectern set up for him, off to one side of the President. He opened his papers on the lectern, studied them thoughtfully for a moment with his lips pursed and said:

"As the President has said, the Alpha-Aleph project is a camouflage. A few of you learned this some months ago, and then you referred to it with other words. 'Fraud.' 'Fake.' Words like that. But if I may say it in French, it is not any of those words, it is a legitimate *ruse de guerre*. Not the *guerre* against our political enemies, or even against the dumb kids in the streets with their Molotov cocktails and bricks. I do not mean those wars, I mean the war against ignorance. For you see, there were certain signs—certain *things*—we had to know for the sake of science and progress. Alpha-Aleph was designed to find them out for us.

"I will tell you the worst parts first," he said. "Number one, there is no such planet as Alpha-Aleph. The Russians were right. Number two, we knew this all along. Even the photographs were fakes, and in the long run the rest of the world will find this out and they will know of our *ruse de guerre*. I can only hope that they will not find out too soon, for if we are lucky and keep the secret for a while, then I hope we will be able to produce good results to justify what we have done. Number three, when the *Constitution* reaches Alpha Centauri there will be no place for them to land, no way to leave their spacecraft, no sources of raw materials which they might be able to use to make fuel to return—nothing but the stars and empty space. This fact has certain consequences.

"The *Constitution* was designed with enough hydrogen fuel capacity for a one-way flight, plus maneuvering reserve. There will not be enough for them to come back, and the source they had hoped to tap, namely the planet Alpha-Aleph, does not exist, so they will not come back. Consequently they will die there. Those are the bad things to which I must admit."

There was a sighing murmur from the audience. The President was frowning absently to himself. Knefhausen waited patiently for the medicine to be swallowed, then went on.

"You ask, then, why have we done this thing? Condemning eight young people to their death? The answer is simple: knowledge. To put it in other words, we must have the basic scientific knowledge to protect the free world. You are all familiar, I si . . . I believe, with the known fact that basic scientific advances have been very few these past ten years and more. Much R&D. Much technology. Much applications. But in the years since Einstein, or better since Weizsäcker, very little basic.

"But without the new basic knowledge, the new technology must soon stop developing. It will run out of steam, you see.

"Now I must tell you a story. It is a true scientific story, not a joke; I know you do not want jokes from me at this time. There was a man named de Bono, a Maltese, who wished to investigate the process of creative thinking. There is not very much known about this process, but he had an idea how he could find something out. So he prepared for an experiment a room that was stripped of all furniture, with two doors, one across from the other. You go in one door, cross the room and then you walk out the other. He put at the door that was the entrance some material—two flat boards, some ropes. And he got as his subjects some young children. Now he said to the children:

'This is a game we will play. You must go through this room and out the other door, that is all. If you do that, you win. But there is one rule. You must not touch the floor with your feet, or your knees, or with any part of your body, or your clothing. We had here a boy,' he said, 'who was very athletic and walked across on his hands, but he was disqualified. You must not do that. Now go, and whoever does it fastest will win some chocolates.'

"So he took away all of the children but the first one and, one by one, they tried. There were ten or fifteen of them, and each of them did the same thing. Some it took longer to figure it out, some figured it out right away, but it always was the same trick: they sat down on the floor, they tied one board to each foot and they walked across the room like on skis. The fastest one thought of the trick right away and was across in a few seconds. The slowest took many minutes. But it was the same trick for all of them, and that was the first part of the experiment.

"Now this Maltese man, de Bono, performed the second part of the experiment. It was exactly like the first, with one difference. He did not give them two boards. He gave them only one board.

"And in the second part every child worked out the same trick, too, but it was, of course, a different trick. They tied the rope to the end of the single board and then they stood on it, and jumped up, tugging the rope to pull the board forward, hopping and tugging, moving a little bit at a time, and every one of them succeeded. But in the first experiment the average time to cross was maybe forty-five seconds. And in the second experiment the average time was maybe twenty seconds. With one board they did their job faster than with two.

"Perhaps now some of you see the point. Why did not any of the children in the first group think of this faster method of going across the room? It is simple. They looked at what they were given to use for materials and, they are like all of us, they wanted to use everything. But they did not need everything. They could do better with less, in a different way."

Knefhausen paused and looked around the room, savoring the moment. He had them now, he knew. It was just as it had been with the President himself, three years before. They were beginning to see the necessity of what had been done, and the pale, upturned faces were no longer as hostile, only perplexed and a little afraid.

He went on:

"So that is what Project Alpha-Aleph is about, gentlemen and ladies. We have selected eight of the most intelligent human beings we could find, healthy, young, very adventurous. Very creative. We played on them a nasty trick, to be sure. But we gave them an opportunity no one has ever had. The opportunity to *think*. To think for *ten years*. To think about basic questions.

Out there they do not have the extra board to distract them. If they want to know something they cannot run to the library and look it up, and find that somebody has said that what they were thinking could not work. They must think it out for themselves.

"So in order to make this possible we have practiced a deception on them and it will cost them their lives. All right, that is tragic, yes. But if we take their lives we give them in exchange, immortality.

"How do we do this? Trickery again, gentlemen and ladies. I do not say to them, 'Here, you must discover new basic approaches to science and tell them to us.' I camouflage the purpose, so that they will not be distracted even by that. We have told them that this is recreational, to help them pass the time. This, too, is a *ruse de guerre*. The 'recreation' is not to help them make the trip, it is the whole purpose of the trip.

"So we start them out with the basic tools of science. With numbers: that is, with magnitudes and quantification, with all that scientific observations are about. With grammar. This is not what you learned when you were thirteen years old. It is a technical term; it means the calculus of statement and the basic rules of communication—that is, so they can learn to think clearly by communicating fully and without fuzzy ambiguity. We give them very little else, only the opportunity to mix these two basic ingredients and come up with new forms of knowledge.

"What will come of these things? That is a fair question. Unfortunately there is no answer—not yet. If we knew the answer in advance, we would not have to perform the experiment. So we do not know what will be the end result of this, but already they have accomplished very much. Old questions that have puzzled the wisest of scientists for hundreds of years they have solved already. I will give you one example. You will say, yes, but what does it *mean?* I will answer, I do not know, I only know that it is so hard a question that no one else has ever been able to answer it. It is a proof of a thing which is called Goldbach's Conjecture. Only a conjecture; you could call it a guess. A guess by an eminent mathematician many, many years ago, that every even number can be written as the sum of two prime numbers. This is one of those simple problems in mathematics that everyone can understand and no one can solve. You can say, 'Certainly, sixteen is the sum of eleven and five, both of which are prime numbers, and thirty is the sum of twenty-three and seven, which also are both prime, and I can give you such numbers for any even number you care to name.' Yes, you can; but can you prove that for *every* even number it will *always* be possible to do this? No. You cannot. No one has been able to, but our friends on the *Constitution* have done it, and this was in the first few months. They have yet almost ten years. I cannot say what they will do in that time, but it is foolish to imagine that it will be anything less than very much indeed. A new relativity, a new universal gravitation—I don't know, I am only saying words. But much."

He paused again. No one was making a sound. Even the President was no longer staring straight ahead without expression, but was looking at him.

"It is not yet too late to spoil the experiment, and so it is necessary for us to keep the secret a bit longer. But there you have it, gentlemen and ladies. That is the truth about Alpha-Aleph." He dreaded what would come next, postponed it for a second by consulting his papers, shrugged, faced them and said: "Now, are there any questions?"

Oh, yes, there were questions. *Herr Omnes* was stunned a little, took a moment to overcome the spell of the simple and beautiful truths he had heard, but first one piped up, then another, then two or three shouting at once. There were questions, to be sure. Questions beyond answering. Questions he did not have time to hear, much less answer, before the next question was on him. Questions to which he did not know the answers. Questions, worst of all, to which the answers were like pepper in the eyes, enraging, blinding the people to sense. But he had to face them, and he tried to answer them. Even when they shouted so that outside the thick double doors the Marine guards looked at each other uneasily, and wondered what made the dull rumble that penetrated the very good soundproofing of the room. "What I want to know, who put you up to this?" "Mr. Chairman, nobody; it is as I have said." "But see now, Knefhausen, do you mean to tell us you're murderin' these good people for the sake of some Goldbach's theory?" "No, Senator, not for Goldbach's Conjecture, but for what great advances in science will mean in the struggle to keep the free world free." "You're confessing you've dragged the United States into a palpable fraud?" "A legitimate ruse of war, Mr. Secretary, because there was no other way." "The photographs, Knefhausen?" "Faked, General, as I have told you. I accept full responsibility." And on and on, the words "murder" and "fraud" and even "treason" coming faster and faster.

Until at last the President stood up and raised his hand. Order was a long time coming, but at last they quieted down.

"Whether we like it or not, we're in it," he said simply. "There is nothing else to say. You have come to me, many of you, with rumors and asked for the truth. Now you have the truth, and it is classified Top Secret and must not be divulged. You all know what this means. I will only add that I personally propose to see that any breach of this security is investigated with all the resources of the government, and punished with the full penalty of the law. I declare this a matter of national emergency, and remind you that the penalty includes the death sentence when appropriate—and I say that in this case it is appropriate." He looked very much older than his years, and he moved his lips as though something tasted bad in his mouth. He allowed no further discussion, and dismissed the meeting.

Half an hour later, in his private office, it was just Knefhausen and the President.

"All right," said the President, "it's all hit the fan. The next thing is the world will know it. I can postpone that a few weeks, maybe even months. I can't prevent it."

"I am grateful to you, Mr. President, for—"

"Shut up, Knefhausen. I don't want any speeches. There is one thing I want from you, and that is an explanation: what the hell is this about mixing up narcotics and free love and so on?"

"Ah," said Knefhausen, "you refer to the most recent communication from the *Constitution*. Yes. I have already dispatched, Mr. President, a strongly worded order. Because of the communications lag it will not be received for some months, but I assure you the matter will be corrected."

The President said bitterly, "I don't want any assurances, either. Do you watch television? I don't mean 'I Love Lucy' and ball games, I mean news. Do you know what sort of shape this country is in? The bonus marches in 1932, the race riots in 1967—they were nothing. Time was when we could call out the National Guard to put down disorder. Last week I had to call out the Army to use against three companies of the Guard. One more scandal and we're finished, Knefhausen, and this is a big one."

"The purposes are beyond reproach—"

"Your purposes may be. Mine may be, or I try to tell myself it is for the good of science I did this, and not so I will be in the history books as the president who contributed a major breakthrough. But what are the purposes of your friends on the *Constitution*? I agreed to eight martyrs, Knefhausen. I didn't agree to forty billion dollars out of the nation's pockets to give your eight young friends ten years of gang-bangs and dope."

"Mr. President, I assure you this is only a temporary phase. I have instructed them to straighten out."

"And if they don't, what are you going to do about it?" The President, who never smoked, stripped a cigar, bit off the end and lit it. He said, "It's too late for me to say I shouldn't have let you talk me into this. So all I will say is you have to show results from this flimflam before the lid blows off, or I won't be President any more, and I doubt that you will be alive."

CONSTITUTION FOUR

This is Shef again and it's, oh, let me see, about Day 250. 300? No, I don't think so. Look, I'm sorry about the ship date, but I honestly don't think much in those terms any more. I've been thinking about other things.

Also I'm a little upset. When I tossed the ruble the hexagram was K'an, which is danger, over Li, the Sun. That's a bad mood in which to be communicating with you. We aren't vengeful types, but the fact is that some of us were pretty sore when we found out what you'd done. I don't *think* you need to worry, but I wish I'd got a much better hexagram.

Let me tell you the good parts first. Our velocity is pushing point-four-oh c now. The scenery is beginning to get interesting. For several weeks the stars fore and aft have been drifting out of sight as the ones in front get up into the ultraviolet and the ones behind sink into the infrared. You'd think that as the spectrum shifts the other parts of the EMF bands would come into the visible range. I guess they do, but stars peak in certain frequencies, and most of them seem to do it in the visible frequencies, so the effect is that they disappear. The first thing was that there was a sort of round black spot ahead of us where we couldn't see anything at all, not Alpha Centauri, not Beta Centauri, not even the bright Circini stars. Then we lost the sun behind us, and a little later we saw the blackout spread to a growing circle of stars there. Then the circles began to widen.

Of course, we know that the stars are really there. We can detect them with phase-shift equipment, just as we can transmit and receive your messages by shifting the frequencies. But we just can't see them any more. The ones in direct line of flight, where we have a vector velocity of .34c or .37c—depending on whether they are in front of us or behind us—simply aren't radiating in the visible band any more. The ones farther out to the side have been displaced visually because of the relativistic effects of our speed. But what it looks like is that we're running the hell out of Nothing, in the direction of Nothing, and it is frankly a little scary.

Even the stars off to one side are showing relativistic color shifts. It's almost like a rainbow, one of those full-circle rainbows that you see on the clouds beneath you from an airplane sometimes. Only this circle is all around us. Nearest the black hole in front the stars have frequency-shifted to a dull reddish color. They go through orange and yellow and a sort of leaf green to the band nearest the black hole in back, which are bright blue shading to purple. Jim Barstow has been practicing his farsight on them, and he can relate them to the actual sky map. But I can't. He sees something in the black hole in front of us that I can't see. He says he thinks it's a bright radio source, probably Centaurus A, and he claims it is radiating strongly in the whole visible band now. He means strongly for him, with his eyes. I'm not sure I can see it at all. There *may* be a sort of very faint, diffuse glow there, like the *Gegenschein*, but I'm not sure. Neither is anyone else.

But the starbow itself is beautiful. It's worth the trip. Flo has been learning oil painting so she can make a picture of it to send you for your wall, although when she found out what you'd been up to she got so sore she was thinking of boobytrapping it with a fusion bomb or something. (But she's over that now. I think.)

So we're not so mad at you any more, although there was a time when if I'd been communicating with you at exactly that moment I would have said some bad things.

I just played this back, and it sounds pretty jumbled and confused. I'm sorry about that. It's hard for me to do this. I don't mean hard like intellectually difficult—the way chess problems and tensor analysis used to be—but hard like shoveling sand with a teaspoon. I'm just not used to constricting my thoughts in this straightjacket any more. I tried to get one of the others to communicate this time, but there were no takers. I did get a lot of free advice. Dot says I shouldn't waste my time remembering how we used to talk. She wanted to write an eidetic account in simplified notation for you, which she estimated a crash program could translate for you in reasonable time, a decade or two, and would give you an absolutely full account of everything. I objected that that involved practical difficulties. Not in preparing the account . . . shucks, we can all do that now. I don't forget anything, except irrelevant things like the standard-reckoning day that I don't want to remember in the first place, and neither does anyone else. But the length of transmission would be too much. We don't have the power to transmit the necessary number of groups, especially since the accident. Dot said we could Gödelize it. I said you were too dumb to de-Gödelize it. She said it would be very good practice for you.

Well, she's right about that, and it's time you all learned how to communicate in a sensible way, so if the power holds out I'll include Dot's eidetic account at the end—in Gödelized form. Lots of luck. I won't honestly be surprised if you miss a digit or something and it all turns into "Rebecca of Sunnybrook Farm" or some missing books of apocrypha or, more likely of course, gibberish. Ski says it won't do you any good in any case, because Henle was right. I pass that on without comment.

Sex. You always want to hear about sex. It's great. Now that we don't have to fool with the pills any more we've been having some marvelous times. Flo and Jim Barstow began making it as part of a multiplexed communications system that you have to see to believe. Sometimes when they're going to do it we all knock off and just sit around and watch them, cracking jokes and singing and helping with the auxiliary computations. When we had that little bit of minor surgery the other day—now we've got the bones season-ing—Ann and Ski decided to ball instead of using anesthesia, and they said it was better than acupuncture. It didn't block the sensation. They were aware of their little toes being lopped off, but they didn't perceive it as pain.

So then Jim, when it was his turn, tried going through the amputation without anything at all in the expectation that he and Flo would go to bed together a little later, and that worked well too. He was all set up about it; claimed it showed a reverse causalty that his theories predicted but that had not been demonstrated before. Said at last he was over the cause-preceding-the-effect hangup. It's like the Red Queen and the White Queen, and quite puzzling until you get the hang of it. (I'm not sure I've got the hang of it yet.) Suppose he hadn't balled Flo? Would his toe have hurt retroactively? I'm a little mixed up on this, Dot says because I simply don't understand phenomenology in general, and I think I'll have to take Ann's advice and work my way through Carnap, although the linguistics are so poor that it's hard to stay with it. Come to think of it, I don't have to. It's all in the Gödelized eidetic statement, after all. So I'll transmit the statement to you, and while I'm doing it that will be a sort of review for me and maybe I'll get my head right on causality.

Listen, let me give you a tip. The statement will also include Ski's trick of containing plasma for up to 500K milliseconds, so when you figure it out you'll know how to build those fusion power reactors you were talking about when we left. That's the carrot before your nose, so get busy on de-Gödelizing. The plasma dodge works fine, although, of course, we were sorry about what happened when we junked those dumb Rube Goldberg bombs you had going off and replaced them with a nice steady plasma flow. The explosion killed Will Becklund outright, and it looked hairy for all of us.

Well, anyway. I have to cut this short because the power's running a little low and I don't want to chance messing up the statement. It follows herewith:

$1973 + 331^{852} + 172^{2008} + 5^{47} + 39^{606} + 2^{88}$ take away 78.

Lots of luck, fellows!

WASHINGTON FOUR

Knefhausen lifted his head from the litter of papers on his desk. He rubbed his eyes, sighing. He had given up smoking the same time as the President, but, like the President, he was thinking of taking it up again. It could kill you, yes. But it was a tension-reducer, and he needed that. And what was wrong with something killing you. There were worse things than being killed, he thought dismally.

Looking at it any way you could, he thought objectively, the past two or three years had been hard on him. They had started so well and had gone so bad. Not as bad as those distant memories of childhood when everybody was so poor and Berlin was so cold and what warm clothes he had came from the

Winterhilfe. By no means as hard as the end of the war. Nothing like as bad as those first years in South America and then in the Middle East, when even the lucky and famous ones, the Von Brauns and the Ehrickes, were having trouble getting what was due them and a young calf like Knefhausen had to peel potatoes and run elevators to live. But harder and worse than a man at the summit of his career had any reason to expect.

The Alpha-Aleph project, fundamentally, was sound! He ground his teeth, thinking about it. It would work—no, by God, it *was* working, and it would make the world a different place. Future generations would see.

But the future generations were not here yet, and in the present things were going badly.

Reminded, he picked up the phone and buzzed his secretary. "Have you got through to the President yet?" he demanded.

"I'm sorry, Dr. Knefhausen. I've tried every ten minutes, just as you said."

"Ah," he grunted. "No, wait. Let me see. What calls are there?"

Rustle of paper. "The news services, of course, asking about the rumors again. Jack Anderson's office. The man from CBS."

"No, no. I will not talk to the press. Anyone else?"

"Senator Copley called, asking when you were going to answer the list of questions his committee sent you."

"I will give him an answer. I will give him the answer Götz von Berlichingen gave to the Bishop of Bamberg."

"I'm sorry, Dr. Knefhausen, I didn't quite catch—"

"No matter. Anything else?"

"Just a long-distance call from a Mr. Hauptmann. I have his number."

"Hauptmann?" The name was puzzlingly familiar. After a moment Knefhausen placed it: to be sure, the photo technician who had cooperated in the faked pictures from Briareus XII. Well, he had his orders to stay out of sight and shut up. "No, that's not important. None of them are, and I do not wish to be disturbed with such nonsense. Continue as you were, Mrs. Ambrose. If the President is reached you are to put me on at once, but no other calls."

He hung up and turned to his desk.

He looked sadly and fondly at the papers. He had them all out: the reports from the *Constitution,* his own drafts of interpretation and comment, and more than a hundred footnoted items compiled by his staff, to help untangle the meanings and implications of those ah, sometimes so cryptic reports from space:

"*Henle.* Apparently refers to Paul Henle (not appended); probably the citation intended is his statement, 'There are certain symbolisms in which certain things cannot be said.' Conjecture that English language is one of those symbolisms."

"*Orange sherbet sundae.* A classified experimental study was made of the material in Document Ref. No. CON-130, Para. 4. Chemical analysis and experimental testing have indicated that the recommended mixture of pharmaceuticals and other ingredients produce a hallucinogen-related substance of considerable strength and not wholly known qualities. One hundred subjects ingested the product or a placebo in a double-blind controlled test. Subjects receiving the actual substance report reactions significantly different from the placebo. Effects reported include feelings of immense competence and deepened understanding. However, data is entirely subjective. Attempts were made to verify claims by standard I.Q., manipulative and other tests, but the subjects did not cooperate well and several have since absented themselves without leave from the testing establishment."

"*Gödelized language.* A system of encoding any message of any kind as a single very large number. The message is first written out in clear language and then encoded as bases and exponents. Each letter of the message is represented in order by the natural order of primes—that is, the first letter is represented by the base 2, the second by the base 3, the third by the base 5, then 7, 11, 13, 17, etcetera. The identity of the letter occupying that position in the message is given by the exponent: simply, the exponent 1 meaning that the letter in that position is an A, the letter 2 meaning that it is a B, 3 a C, etcetera. The message, as a whole, is then rendered as the product of all the bases and exponents. *Example.* The word "cab" can thus be represented as $2^3 \times 3^1 \times 5^2$, or 600. ($= 8 \times 3 \times 25$.) The name 'Abe' would be represented by the number 56,250, or $2^1 \times 3^2 \times 5^5$. ($= 2 \times 9 \times 3125$.) A sentence like 'John lives' would be represented by the product of the following terms: $2^{10} \times 3^{15} \times 5^8 \times 7^{14} \times 11^0 \times 13^{12} \times 17^9 \times 19^{22} \times 23^5 \times 29^{19} \times 31^{27}$—in which the exponent '0' has been reserved for a space and the exponent '27' has been arbitrarily assigned to indicate a full stop. As can be seen, the Gödelized form for even a short message involves a very large number, although such numbers may be transmitted quite compactly in the form of a sum of bases and exponents. The example transmitted by the *Constitution* is estimated to equal the contents of a standard unabridged dictionary."

"*Farsight.* The subject James Madison Barstow is known to have suffered from some nearsightedness in his early school years, apparently brought on by excessive reading, which he attempted to cure through eye exercises similar to the 'Bates method'—note appended. His vision at time of testing for Alpha-Aleph project was optimal. Interviews with former associates indicate his continuing interest in increasing visual acuity. *Alternate expla-*

nation. There is some indication that he was also interested in paranormal phenomena such as clairvoyance or prevision, and it is possible, though at present deemed unlikely, that his use of the term refers to 'looking ahead' in time."

And so on, and on.

Knefhausen gazed at the litter of papers lovingly and hopelessly, and passed his hand over his forehead. The kids! They were so marvelous . . . but so unruly . . . and so hard to understand. How unruly of them to have concealed their true accomplishments. The secret of hydrogen fusion! That alone would justify, more than justify, the entire project. But where was it? Locked in that number-jumber gibberish. Knefhausen was not without appreciation of the elegance of the method. He, too, was capable of taking seriously a device of such luminous simplicity. Once the number was written out you had only to start by dividing it by two as many times as possible, and the number of times would give you the first letter. Then divide by the next prime, three, and that number of times would give you the second letter. But the practical difficulties! You could not get even the first letter until you had the whole number, and IBM had refused even to bid on constructing a bank of computers to write that number out unless the development time was stretched to twenty-five years. *Twenty-five years.* And meanwhile in that number was hidden probably the secret of hydrogen fusion, possibly many greater secrets, most certainly the key to Knefhausen's own well-being over the next few weeks. . . .

His phone rang.

He grabbed it and shouted into it at once: "Yes, Mr. President!"

He had been too quick. It was only his secretary. Her voice was shaking but determined.

"It's not the President, Dr. Knefhausen, but Senator Copley is on the wire and he says it is urgent. He says—"

"No!" shouted Knefhausen and banged down the phone. He regretted it even as he was doing it. Copley was very high, chairman of the Armed Forces Committee; he was not a man Knefhausen wished to have as an enemy, and he had been very careful to make him a friend over years of patient fence-building. But he could not speak to him, or to anyone, while the President was not answering his calls. Copley's rank was high, but he was not in the direct hierarchical line over Knefhausen. When the top of that line refused to talk to him Knefhausen was cut off from the world.

He attempted to calm himself by examining the situation objectively. The pressures on the President just now: they were enormous. There was the continuing trouble in the cities, all the cities. There were the political conventions coming up. There was the need to get elected for a third term, and the need to get the law amended to make that possible. And yes, Knefhausen admitted to himself, the worst pressure of all was the rumors that were floating around about the *Constitution*. He had warned the President. It was unfortunate the President had not listened. He had said that a secret known to two people is compromised and a secret known to more than two is no secret. But the President had insisted on the disclosure to that ever-widening circle of high officials—sworn, of course, to secrecy, but what good was that? In spite of everything, there had been leaks. Fewer than one might have feared. More than one could stand.

He touched the reports from *Constitution* caressingly. Those beautiful kids, they could still make everything right, so wonderful. . . .

Because it was he who had made them wonderful, he confessed to himself. He had invented the idea. He had selected them. He had done things which he did not quite even yet reconcile himself to, to make sure that it was they and not some others who were on the crew. He had, above all, made doubly sure by insuring their loyalty in every way possible. Training. Discipline. Ties of affection and friendship. More reliable ties: loading their food supplies, their entertainment tapes, their programmed activities with every sort of advertising inducement, M/R compulsion, psychological reinforcement he could invent or find, so that whatever else they did they did not fail to report faithfully back to Earth. Whatever else happened, there was that. The data might be hard to untangle, but would be there. They could not help themselves; his commandments were stronger than God's; like Martin Luther they must say *Ich kann nicht anders*, and come Pope or Inquisition they must stand by it. They would learn, and tell what they learned, and thus the investment would be repaid. . . .

The telephone!

He was talking before he had it even to his mouth. "Yes, yes! This is Dr. Knefhausen, yes!" he gabbled. Surely it must be the President now—

It was not.

"Knefhausen!" shouted the man on the other end. "Now, listen, I'll tell you what I told that bitch pig girl of yours, if I don't talk to you on the phone *right now* I'll have Fourth Armored in there to arrest you and bring you to me in twenty minutes. So listen!"

Knefhausen recognized both voice and style. He drew a deep breath and forced himself to be calm. "Very well, Senator Copley," he said, "what is it?"

"The game is blown, boy! That's what it is. That boy of yours in Huntsville, what's his name, the photo technician—"

"*Hauptmann?*"

"That's him! Would you like to know where he is, you dumb Kraut bastard?"

"Why, I suppose . . . I should think in Huntsville—"

"Wrong, boy! Your Kraut bastard friend claimed he didn't feel good and took some accrued sick time. Intelligence kept an eye on him up to a point, didn't stop him, wanted to see what he'd do. Well, they saw. They saw him leaving Orly Airport an hour ago in an Aeroflot plane. Put your brain to work on that one, Knefhausen! He's defected. Now start figuring out what you're going to do about it, and it better be good!"

Knefhausen said something, he did not know what, and hung up the phone, he did not remember when. He stared glassily into space for a time.

Then he flicked the switch for his secretary and said, not listening to her stammering apologies, "That long-distance call that came from Hauptmann before, Mrs. Ambrose. You didn't say where it was from."

"It was an overseas call, Dr. Knefhausen. From Paris. You didn't give me a chance to—"

"Yes, yes. I understand. Thank you. Never mind." He hung up and sat back. He felt almost relieved. If Hauptmann had gone to Russia it could only be to tell them that the picture was faked, and not only was there no planet for the astronauts to land on but it was not a mistake, even, actually a total fraud. So now it was all out of his hands. History would judge him now. The die was cast. The Rubicon was crossed.

So many literary allusions, he thought deprecatingly. Actually it was not the judgment of history that was immediately important but the judgment of certain real people now alive and likely to respond badly. And they would judge him not so much by what might be or what should have been, as by what was. He shivered in the cold of that judgment, and reached for the telephone to try once more to call the President. But he was quite sure the President would not answer, then or ever again.

CONSTITUTION FIVE

Old reliable P.O.'d Shef here. Look, we got your message. I don't want to discuss it. You've got a nerve. You're in a bad mood, aren't you? If you can't say anything nice, don't say anything at all. We do the best we can, and that's not bad, and if we don't do exactly what you want us to maybe it's because we know quite a lot more than you did when you fired us off at that blob of moonshine you call Alpha-Aleph. Well, thanks a lot for nothing.

On the other hand, thanks a little for what you did do, which at least worked out to get us where we are, and I don't mean spatially. So I'm not going to yell at you. I just don't want to talk to you at all. I'll let the others talk for themselves.

■ ■ ■

Dot Letski speaking. This is important. Pass it on. I have three things to tell you that I do not want you to forget. *One: Most problems have grammatical solutions.* The problem of transporting people from Earth to another planet does not get solved by putting pieces of steel together one at a time at random, and happening to find out you've built the *Constitution* by accident. It gets solved by constructing a model — = equation (= grammar) —which describes the necessary circumstances under which the transportation occurs. Once you have the grammatical model, you just put the metal around it and it goes like gangbusters.

When you have understood this you will be ready for: *Two: There is no such thing as causality.* What a waste of time it has been, trying to assign "causes" to "events"! You say things like, "Striking a match causes it to burn." True statement? No, false statement. You find yourself in a whole waffle about whether the "act" of "striking" is "necessary" and/or "sufficient" and you get lost in words. Pragmatically useful grammars are without tenses. In a decent grammar—which this English-language one, of course, is not, but I'll do the best I can—you can make a statement like "There exists a conjunction of forms of matter—specified—which combine with the release of energy at a certain temperature—which may be the temperature associated with heat of friction." Where's the causality? "Cause" and "effect" are in the same timeless statement. So, *Three: There are no such things as empirical laws.* Ski came to understand that he was able to contain the plasma in our jet indefinitely, not by pushing particles around in brute-force magnetic squeezes, but by encouraging them to want to stay together. There are other ways of saying what he does— = "creates an environment in which centripetal exceed centrifugal forces"—but the way I said it is better because it tells something about your characters. Bullies, all of you. Why can't you be nice to things if you want them to be nice to you? Be sure to pass this on to T'in Fa at Tientsin, Professor Morris at All Soul's and whoever holds the Carnap chair at UCLA.

Flo's turn. My mother would have loved my garden. I have drumsticks and daffodils growing side by side in the sludgy sand. They do so please us, and we them! I will probably transmit a full horticultural handbook at a future date, but meanwhile it is shameful to eat a radish. Carrots, on the other hand, enjoy it.

■ ■ ■

A *statement of William Becklund, deceased.* I emerged into the world, learned, grew, ate, worked, moved and died. Alternatively, I emerged from the hydrogen flare, shrank, disgorged and reentered the womb one misses so. You may approach it from either end, it makes no difference at all which way you look at it.

Observational datum, Letski. At time *t*, a Dirac number incommensurable with GMT, the following phenomenon is observed:

The radio source Centaurus A is identified as a positionally stable single collective object rather than two intersecting gas clouds and is observed to contract radially toward a center. Analysis and observation reveal it to be a Black Hole of which the fine detail is not detectable as yet. One infers all galaxies develop such central vortices, with implications of interest to astronomers and eschatologists. I, Seymour Letski, propose to take a closer look but the others prefer to continue programmed flight first. Harvard-Smithsonian notification service, please copy.

"Starbow," a preliminary study for a rendering into English of a poem by James Barstow:

> Gaggle of goslings but pick of our race
> We waddle through relativistic space.
> Dilated, discounted, despondent we scan:
> But vacant the Sign of the Horse and the Man.
> Vacant the Sign of the Man and the Horse,
> And now we conjecture the goal of our
> course.
> Tricked, trapped and cozened, we ruefully run
> After the child of the bachelor sun.
> The trick is revealed and the trap is confessed
> And we are the butts of the dim-witted jest.
> O Gander who made us, O Goose who laid
> us,
> How lewdly and twistedly you betrayed us!
> We owe you a debt. We won't forget.
> With fortune and firmness we'll pay you yet.
> Give us some luck and we'll timely send
> Your pot of gold from the starbow's end.

Ann Becklund: I think it was Stanley Weinbaum who said that from three facts a truly superior mind should be able to deduce the whole universe. (Ski thinks it is possible with a finite number, but considerably larger than that.) We are so very far from being truly superior minds by those standards, or even by our own. Yet we have a much larger number of facts to work with than three, or even three thousand, and so we have deduced a good deal.

This is not as valuable to you as you might have hoped, dear old bastardly Kneffie and all you bastardly others, because one of the things that we have deduced is that we can't tell you everything, because you wouldn't understand. We could help you along, some of you, if you were here, and in time you would be able to do what we do easily enough, but not by remote control.

But all is not lost, folks! Cheer up! You don't deduce like we deduce, but on the other hand you have so very much more to work from. Try. Get smart. You can do it if you want to. Set your person at rest, compose your mind before you speak, make your relations firm before you ask for something. Try not to be loathsome about it. Don't be like the fellow in the Changes. "He brings increase to no one. Indeed, someone even strikes him."

We've all grown our toes back now, even Will, although it was particularly difficult for him since he had been killed, and we've inscribed the bones and had used them with very good effect in generating the hexagrams. I hope you see the point of what we did. We could have gone on with tossing coins or throwing the yarrow stalks, or at least the closest Flo could breed to yarrow stalks. We didn't want to do that because it's not the optimum way.

The person who doesn't keep his heart constantly steady might say, "Well, what's the difference?" That's a poor sort of question to ask. It implies a deterministic answer. A better question is, "Does it make a difference?", and the answer to that is, "Yes, probably, because in order to do something right you must do it right." That is the law of identity, in any language.

Another question you might ask is, "Well, what source of knowledge are you actually tapping when you consult the hexagrams?" That's a better kind of question in that it doesn't *force* a wrong answer, but the answer is, again, indeterminate. You might view the *I Ching* as a sort of Rorschach bundle of squiggles that has no innate meaning but is useful because your own mind interprets it and puts sense into it. Feel free! You might think of it as a sort of memory bank of encoded lore. Why not? You might skip it entirely and come to knowledge in some other tao, any tao you like. ("The superior man understands the transitory in the light of the eternity of the end.") That's fine, too!

But whatever way you do it, you should *do* it that way. We needed inscribed bones to generate hexagrams, because that was the right way, and so it was no particular sacrifice to lop off a toe each for the purpose. It's working out nicely, except for one thing. The big hangup now is that the translations are so degraded, Chinese to German, German to English and error seeping in at every step, but we're working on that now.

Perhaps I will tell you more at another time. Not now. Not very soon. Eve will tell you about that.

Eve Barstow, the Dummy, comes last and, I'm afraid, least. When I was a little girl I used to play chess, badly, with very good players, and that's the story of my life. I'm a chronic overachiever. I can't stand people who aren't smarter and better than I am, but the result is that I'm the runt of the litter every time. They are all very nice to me here, even Jim, but they know what the score is and so do I.

So I keep busy and applaud what I can't do. It isn't a bad life. I have everything I need, except pride.

Let me tell you what a typical day is like here between Sol and Centaurus. We wake up—if we have been sleeping, which some of us still do—and eat—if we are still eating, as all but Ski and, of course, Will Becklund do. The food is delicious and Florence has induced it to grow cooked and seasoned where that is desirable, so it's no trouble to go over and pick yourself a nice poached egg or a clutch of French fries. (I really prefer brioche in the mornings, but for sentimental reasons she can't manage it.) Sometimes we ball a little or sing old campfire songs. Ski comes down for that, but not for long, and then he goes back to looking at the universe. The starbow is magnificent and appalling. It is now a band about 40° across, completely surrounding us with colored light. One can always look in the other frequencies and see ghost stars before us and behind us, but in the birthright bands the view to the front and rear is now dead black and the only light is that beautiful banded ring of powdery stars.

Sometimes we write plays or have a little music. Shef had deduced four lost Bach piano concerti, very reminiscent of Corelli and Vivaldi, with everything going at once in the tuttis, and we've all adapted them for performance. I did mine on the moog, but Ann and Shef synthesized whole orchestras. Shef's particularly cute. You can tell that the flautist has early emphysema and two people in the violin section have been drinking, and he's got Toscanini conducting like a *risorgimento* metronome. Flo's oldest daughter made up words and now she sings a sort of nursery rhyme adaptation of some Buxtehude chorales; oh, I didn't tell you about the kids. We have eleven of them now. Ann, Dot and I have one apiece, and Florence has eight. (But they're going to let me have quadruplets next week.) They let me take care of them pretty much for the first few weeks, while they're little, and they're *so* darling.

So mostly I spend my time taking care of the kids and working out tensor equations that Ski kindly gives me to do for him, and, I must confess it, feeling a little lonely. I *would* like to watch a TV quiz show over a cup of coffee with a friend! They let me do over the interior of our mobile home now and then. The other day I redid it in Pittsburgh suburban as a joke. Would you believe French windows in interstellar space? We never open them, of course, but they look real pretty with the chintz curtains and lace tiebacks. And we've added several new rooms for the children and their pets. (Flo grew them the cutest little bunnies in the hydroponics plot).

Well, I've enjoyed this chance to gossip, so will sign off now. There is one thing I have to mention. The others have decided we don't want to get any more messages from you. They don't like the way you try to work on our subconsciouses and all—not that you succeed, of course, but you can see that it's still a little annoying—and so in future the dial will be set at six-six-oh, all right, but the switch will be in the "off" position. It wasn't my idea, but I was glad to go along. I *would* like some slightly less demanding company from time to time, although not, of course, yours.

WASHINGTON FIVE

Once upon a time the building that was now known as DoD Temp Restraining Quarters 7—you might as well call it with the right word, "jail," Knefhausen thought—had been a luxury hotel in the Hilton chain. The maximum security cells were in the underground levels, in what had been meeting rooms. There were no doors or windows to the outside. If you did get out of your own cell you had a flight of stairs to get up before you were at ground level, and then the guards to break through to get to the open. And then, even if there happened not to be an active siege going on at the moment, you took your chances with the roaming addicts and activists outside.

Knefhausen did not concern himself with these matters. He did not think of escape, or at least didn't after the first few panicky moments, when he realized he was under arrest. He stopped demanding to see the President after the first few days. There was no point in appealing to the White House for help when it was the White House that had put him here. He was still sure that if only he could talk to the President privately for a few moments he could clear everything up. But as a realist he had faced the fact that the President would never talk to him privately again.

So he counted his blessings.

First, it was comfortable here. The bed was good, the rooms were warm. The food still came from the banquet kitchens of the hotel, and it was remarkably good for jailhouse fare.

Second, the kids were still in space and still doing some things, great things, even if they did not report what. His vindication was still a prospect.

Third, the jailers let him have newspapers and writing materials, although they would not bring him his books, or give him a television set.

He missed the books, but nothing else. He didn't need TV to tell him what was going on outside. He didn't even need the newspapers, ragged, thin and censored as they were. He could hear for himself. Every day there was the rattle of small-arms fire, mostly far-off and sporadic, but once or twice sustained and heavy and almost overhead, Brownings against AK-47s, it sounded like, and now and then the slap and smash of grenade launchers. Sometimes he heard sirens hooting through the streets, punctuated by clanging bells, and wondered that there was still a civilian fire department left to bother. (Or was it still civilian?) Sometimes he heard the grinding of heavy motors that had to be tanks. The newspapers did little to fill in the details, but Knefhausen was good at reading between the lines. The Administration was holed up somewhere—Key Biscayne, or Camp David, or Southern California, no one was saying where. The cities were all in red revolt. *Herr Omnes* had taken over.

For these disasters Knefhausen felt unjustly blamed. He composed endless letters to the President, pointing out that the serious troubles of the Administration had nothing to do with Alpha-Aleph: the cities had been in revolt for most of a generation, the dollar had become a laughingstock since the Indochinese wars. Some he destroyed, some he could get no one to take from him, a few he managed to dispatch—and got no answers.

Once or twice a week a man from the Justice Department came to ask him the same thousand pointless questions once again. They were trying to build up a dossier to prove it was all his fault, Knefhausen suspected. Well, let them. He would defend himself when the time came. Or history would defend him. The record was clear. With respect to moral issues, perhaps, not so clear, he conceded. No matter. One could not speak of moral questions in an area so vital to the search for knowledge as this. The dispatches from the *Constitution* had already produced so much—although, admittedly, some of the most significant parts were hard to understand. The Gödel message had not been unscrambled, and the hints of its contents remained only hints.

Sometimes he dozed and dreamed of projecting himself to the *Constitution*. It had been a year since the last message. He tried to imagine what they had been doing. They would be well past the midpoint now, decelerating.

The starbow would be broadening and diffusing every day. The circles of blackness before and behind them would be shrinking. Soon they would see Alpha Centauri as no man had ever seen it. To be sure, they would then see that there was no planet called Aleph circling the primary, but they had guessed that somehow long since. Brave, wonderful kids! Even so they had gone on. This foolishness with drugs and sex, what of it? One opposed such goings-on in the common run of humanity, but it had always been so that those who excelled and stood out from the herd could make their own rules. As a child he had learned that the plump, proud air leader sniffed cocaine, that the great warriors took their sexual pleasure sometimes with each other. An intelligent man did not concern himself with such questions, which was one more indication that the man from the Justice Department, with his constant hinting and prying into Knefhausen's own background, was not really very intelligent.

The good thing about the man from the Justice Department was that one could sometimes deduce things from his questions, and rarely, oh, very rarely, he would sometimes answer a question himself. "Has there been a message from the *Constitution?*" "No, of course not, Dr. Knefhausen. Now, tell me again, who suggested this fraudulent scheme to you in the first place?"

Those were the highlights of his days, but mostly the days just passed unmarked.

He did not even scratch them off on the wall of his cell, like the prisoner in the Chateau d'If. It would have been a pity to mar the hardwood paneling. Also he had other clocks and calendars. There was the ticking of the arriving meals, the turning of the seasons as the man from the Justice Department paid his visits. Each of these was like a holiday—a holy day, not joyous but solemn. First there would be a visit from the captain of the guards with two armed soldiers standing in the door. They would search his person and his cell on the chance that he had been able to smuggle in a . . . a what? A nuclear bomb, maybe. Or a pound of pepper to throw in the Justice man's eyes. They would find nothing, because there was nothing to find. And then they would go away and for a long time there would be nothing. Not even a meal, even if a meal time happened to be due. Nothing at all, until an hour or three hours later the Justice man would come in with his own guard at the door, equally vigilant inside and out, and his engineer manning the tape recorders, and his questions.

And then there was the day when the man from the Justice Department came and he was not alone. With him was the President's secretary, Murray Amos.

How treacherous is the human heart! When it has given up hope how little it takes to make it hope again!

"Murray!" cried Knefhausen, almost weeping, "it's so good to see you again! The President, is he well? What can I do for you? Have there been developments?"

Murray Amos paused in the doorway. He looked at Dieter von Knefhausen and said bitterly, "Oh, yes, there have been developments. Plenty of them. The Fourth Armored has just changed sides, so we are evacuating Washington. And the President wants you out of here at once."

"No, no! I mean . . . oh, yes, it is good that the President is concerned about my welfare, although it is bad about the Fourth Armored. But what I mean, Murray, is this: has there been a message from the *Constitution*?"

Amos and the Justice Department man looked at each other. "Tell me, Dr. Knefhausen," said Amos silkily, "how did you manage to find that out?"

"Find it out? How could I find it out? No, I only asked because I hoped. There has been a message, yes? In spite of what they said? They have spoken again?"

"As a matter of fact, there has been," said Amos thoughtfully. The Justice Department man whispered piercingly in his ear, but Amos shook his head. "Don't worry, we'll be coming in a second. The convoy won't go without us. Yes, Knefhausen, the message came through to Goldstone two hours ago. They have it at the decoding room now."

"Good, very good!" cried Knefhausen. "You will see, they will justify all. But what do they say? Have you good scientific men to interpret it? Can you understand the contents?"

"Not exactly," said Amos, "because there's one little problem the code room hadn't expected and wasn't prepared for. The message wasn't coded. It came in clear, but the language was Chinese."

CONSTITUTION SIX

Ref.: CONSIX T51/11055/*7

CLASSIFIED MOST SECRET

Subject: Transmission from U.S. Starship *Constitution*.

The following message was received and processed by the decrypt section according to standing directives. Because of its special nature, an investigation was carried out to determine its provenance. Radio-direction data received from Farside Base indicate its origin along a line of sight consistent with the present predicted location of the *Constitution*. Strength of signal was high but within appropriate limits, and degradation of frequency separation was consistent with relativistic shifts and scattering due to impact with particle and gas clouds.

Although available data do not prove beyond doubt that this transmission originated with the starship, no contraindications were found.

On examination, the text proved to be a phonetic transcription of what appears to be a dialect of Middle Kingdom Mandarin. Only a partial translation has been completed. (See note appended to text.) The translation presented unusual difficulties for two reasons: one, the difficulty of finding a translator of sufficient skill who could be granted appropriate security status; two, because—conjecturally—the language used may not correspond exactly to any dialect but may be an artifact of the *Constitution*'s personnel. (See PARA EIGHT.)

This text is PROVISIONAL AND NOT AUTHENTICATED and is furnished only as a first attempt to translate the contents of the message into English. Efforts are being continued to translate the full message, and to produce a less corrupt text for the section herewith. Later versions and emendations will be forwarded when available.

TEXT FOLLOWS:

PARA ONE. The one who speak for all—*Lt-Col Sheffield H Jackman*—rests. With righteous action comes surcease from care. I—*identity not certain, but probably Mrs. Annette Marin Becklund, less probably one of the other three female personnel aboard, or one of their descendants*—come in his place, moved by charity and love.

PARA TWO. It is not enough to study or to do deeds which make the people frown and bow their heads. It is not enough to comprehend the nature of the sky or the sea. Only through the understanding of all can one approach wisdom, and only through wisdom can one act rightly.

PARA THREE. These are the precepts as it is given us to see them:

PARA FOUR. The one who imposes his will by force lacks justice. Let him be thrust from a cliff.

PARA FIVE. The one who causes another to lust for a trifle of carved wood or a sweetmeat lacks courtesy. Let him be restrained from the carrying out of wrong practices.

PARA SIX. The one who ties a knot and says, "I do not care who must untie it," lacks foresight. Let him wash the ulcers of the poor and carry nightsoil for all until he learns to see the day to come as brother to the day that is.

PARA SEVEN. We who are in this here should not impose our wills on you who are in that here by force. Understanding comes late. We regret the incident of next week, for it was done in haste and in error. The one who speaks for all acted without thinking. We who are in this here were sorry for it afterward.

PARA EIGHT. You may wonder—*literally: ask thoughtless questions of the hexagrams*—why we are communicating in this language. The reason is in part recreational, in part heuristic—*literally: because on the staff hand one becomes able to strike a blow more ably when blows are struck repeatedly*—but the nature of the process is such that you must go through it before you can be told what it is. Our steps have trodden this path. In order to reconstruct the Chines of the *I Ching* it was first necessary to reconstruct the German of the translation from which the English was made. Error lurks at every turn. [*Literally: false apparitions shout at one each time the path winds.*] Many flaws mark our carving. Observe it in silence for hours and days until the flaws become part of the work.

PARA NINE. It is said that you have eight days before the heavier particles arrive. The dead and broken will be few. It will be better if all airborne nuclear reactors are grounded until the incident is over.

PARA TEN. When you have completed rebuilding send us a message, directed to the planet Alpha-Aleph. Our home should be prepared by then. We will send a ferry to help colonists across the stream when we are ready:

The above text comprises the first 852 groups of the transmission. The remainder of the text, comprising approximately 7,500 groups, has not been satisfactorily translated. In the opinion of a consultant from the Oriental Languages Department at Johns Hopkins it may be a poem.

/s/Durward S. RICHTER

Durward S. RICHTER
Major General, USMC
Chief Cryptographer
Commanding

Distribution: X X X
By hand only

WASHINGTON SIX

The President of the United States—Washington—opened the storm window of his study and leaned out to yell at his Chief Science Adviser. "Harry, get the lead out! We're waiting for you!"

Harry looked up and waved, then continued doggedly plowing through the dripping jungle that was the North Lawn. Between the overgrown weeds and the rain and the mud it was slow going, but the President had little sympathy. He slammed down the window and said, "That man, he just goes out of his way to aggravate me. How long am I supposed to wait for him so I can decide if we have to move the capital or not?"

The Vice President looked up from her knitting. "Jimbo, honey, why do you fuss yourself like that? Why don't we just move and get it over with?"

"Well, it looks so lousy." He threw himself into a chair despondently. "I was really looking forward to the Tenth Anniversary parade," he complained. "Ten years, that's really worth bragging about! I don't want to hold it out in the sticks, I want it right down Constitution Avenue, just like the old days, with the people cheering and the reporters and the cameras all over and everything. Then let that son of a bitch in Omaha say I'm not the real President."

His wife said placidly, "Don't fuss yourself about him, honey. You know what I've been thinking, though? The parade might look a little skimpy on Constitution Avenue anyway. It would be real nice on a kind of littler street."

"Oh, what do you know? Anyway, where would we go? If Washington's under water, what makes you think Bethesda would be any better?"

His Secretary of State put down his solitaire cards and looked interested. "Doesn't have to be Bethesda," he said. "I got some real nice land up near Dulles we could use. It's high there."

"Why, sure. Lots of nice land over to Virginia," the Vice President confirmed. "Remember when we went out on that picnic after your Second Inaugural? That was at Fairfax Station. There were hills all around. Just beautiful."

The President slammed his fist on the coffee table and yelled, "I'm not the President of Fairfax Station, I'm the President of the U.S. of A.! What's the capital of the U.S. of A.? Washington! My God, don't you see how those jokers in Houston and Omaha and Salt Lake and all would laugh if they heard I had to move out of my own capital?"

He broke off, because his Chief Science Adviser was coming in the door, shaking himself, dripping mud as he got out of his oilskin slicker. "Well?" demanded the President. "What did they say?"

Harry sat down. "It's terrible out there. Anybody got a dry cigarette?"

The President threw him a pack. Harry dried his fingers on his shirt front before he drew one out. "Well," he said, "I went to every boat captain I could find. They all said the same. Ships they talked to, places they'd been. All the same. Tides rising all up and down the coast."

He looked around for a match. The President's wife handed him a gold cigarette lighter with the Great Seal of the United States on it, which, after some effort, he managed to ignite. "It don't look good, Jimmy. Right now it's low tide and that's all right, but it's coming in. And tomorrow it'll come in a little higher. And there will be storms—not just rain like this. I mean, you got to figure on a tropical depression coming up from the Bahamas now and then."

"We're not in the tropics," said the Secretary of State suspiciously.

"It doesn't mean that," said the Science Adviser, who had once given the weather reports over the local ABC television station, when there was such a thing as a television network. "It means storms. Hurricanes. But they're not the worst things, it's the tide. If the ice is melting, then they're going to keep getting higher regardless."

The President drummed his fingers on the coffee table. Suddenly he shouted, "I don't *want* to move my capital!"

No one answered. His temper outbursts were famous. The Vice President became absorbed in her knitting, the Secretary of State picked up his cards and began to shuffle, the Science Adviser picked up his slicker and carefully hung it on the back of a door.

The President said, "You got to figure it this way. If we move out, then all those local yokels that claim to be the President of the United States are going to be just that much better off, and the eventual reunification of our country is going to be just that much more delayed." He moved his lips for a moment, then burst out, "I don't ask anything for myself! I never have. I only want to play the part I have to play in what's good for all of us, and that means keeping up my position as the *real* President, according to the U.S. of A. Constitution as amended. And that means I got to stay right here in the real White House, no matter what."

His wife said hesitantly, "Honey, how about this? The other President had like a summer White House—Camp David and like that. Nobody fussed about it. Why couldn't you do the same as they did? There's the nicest old farmhouse out near Fairfax Station that we could fix up to be real pretty."

The President looked at her with surprise. "Now, that's good thinking," he declared. "Only we can't move permanently, and we have to keep this place garrisoned so nobody else will take it away from us, and we have to come back here once in a while. How about that, Harry?"

His Science Adviser said thoughtfully, "We could rent some boats, I guess. Depends. I don't know how high the water might get."

"No 'guess'! No 'depends'! That's a national priority. We have to do it that way to keep that bastard in Omaha paying attention to the real President."

"Well, Jimbo, honey," said the Vice President after a moment, emboldened by his recent praise, "you have to admit they don't pay a lot of attention to us right now. When was the last time they paid their taxes?"

The President looked at her foxily over his glasses. "Talking about that," he said, "I might have a little surprise for them anyway. What you might call a secret weapon."

"I hope it does better than we did in the last war," said his wife, "because if you remember, when we started to put down the uprising in Frederick, Maryland, we got the pee kicked out of us."

The President stood up, indicating the Cabinet meeting was over.

"Never mind," he said sunnily. "You go on out again, Harry, and see if you can find any good maps in the Library of Congress where they got the fires put out. Find us a nice high place within, um, twenty miles if you can. Then we'll get the Army to condemn us a Summer White House like Mae says, and maybe I can sleep in a bed that isn't moldy for a change."

His wife looked worried. "What are you going to do, Jim?"

He chuckled. "I'm going to check out my secret weapon."

He shooed them out of his study and, when they were gone, went to the kitchen and got himself a bottle of Fresca from the six-pack in the open refrigerator. It was warm, of course. The Marine guard company was still trying to get the gas generator back in operation, but they were having little success. The President didn't mind. They were his personal Praetorians and, if they lacked a little as appliance repairmen, they had proved their worth when the chips were down. The President was always aware that during the Troubles he had been no more than any other Congressman— appointed to fill a vacancy, at that—and his rapid rise to Speaker of the House and Heir Apparent, finally to the Presidency itself, was due not only to his political skills and knowhow but also to the fact that he was the only remotely legitimate heir to the presidency who also happened to have a brother-in-law commanding the Marine garrison in Washington.

The President was, in fact, quite satisfied with the way the world was going. If he envied presidents of the past—missiles, fleets of nuclear bombers, billions of dollars to play with—he certainly saw nothing, when he looked at the world around him, to compare with his own stature in the real world he lived in.

He finished the soda, opened his study door a crack and peered out. No one was nearby. He slipped out and down the back stairs. In what had once been the public parts of the White House you could see the extent of the damage more clearly. After the riots and the trashings and the burnings and the coups, the will to repair and fix up had gradually dwindled away. The President didn't mind. He didn't even notice the charred walls and the fallen plaster. He was listening to the sound of a distant gasoline pump chugging away, and smiling to himself as he approached the underground level where his secret weapon was locked up.

.　.　.

The secret weapon, whose name was Dieter von Knefhausen, was trying to complete the total defense of every act of his life that he called his memoirs.

He was less satisfied with the world than the President. He could have wished for many changes. Better health, for one thing; he was well aware that his essential hypertension, his bronchitis and his gout were fighting the last stages of a total war to see which would have the honor of destroying their mutual battleground, which was himself. He did not much mind his lack of freedom, but he did mind the senseless destruction of so many of his papers.

The original typescript of his autobiography was long lost, but he had wheedled the President—the pretender, that is, who called himself the President—into sending someone to find what could be found of them. A few tattered and incomplete carbon copies had turned up. He had restored some of the gaps as best his memory and available data permitted, telling again the story of how he had planned Project Alpha-Aleph and meticulously itemizing the details of how he had lied, forged and falsified to bring it about.

He was as honest as he could be. He spared himself nothing. He admitted his complicity in the "accidental" death of Ann Barstow's first husband in a car smash, thus leaving her free to marry the man he had chosen to go with the crew to Alpha Centauri. He had confessed he had known the secret would not last out the duration of the trip, thus betraying the trust of the President who made it possible. He put it all in, all he could remember, and boasted of his success.

For it was clear to him that his success was already proved. What could be surer evidence of it than what had happened ten years ago? The "incident of next week" was as dramatic and complete as anyone could wish. If its details were still indecipherable, largely because of the demolition of the existing technology structure it had brought about, its main features were obvious. The shower of heavy particles—baryon? perhaps even quarks?—had drenched the Earth. The source had been traced to a point in the heavens identical with that plotted for the *Constitution.*

Also there were the messages received; taken together, there was no doubt that the astronauts had developed knowledge so far in advance of anything on Earth that, from two light-years out, they could impose their will on the human race. They had done it. In one downpour of particles, the entire military-industrial complex of the planet was put out of action.

How? How? Ah, thought Knefhausen, with envy and pride, that was the question. One could not know. All that was known was that every nuclear device—bomb, power plant, hospital radiation source or stockpile—had simultaneously soaked up the stream of particles and at that moment ceased to exist as a source of nuclear energy. It was not rapid and catastrophic, like a bomb. It was slow and long-lasting. The uranium and the plutonium simply melted, in the long, continuous reaction that was still bubbling away in the seething lava lakes where the silo had stood and the nuclear power plants had generated electricity. Little radiation was released, but a good deal of heat.

Knefhausen had long since stopped regretting what could not be helped, but wistfully he still wished he had the opportunity to measure the total heat flux properly. Not less than 10^{16} watt-years, he was sure, just to judge by the effects on the Earth's atmosphere, the storms, the gradual raising of temperature all over, above all by the rumors about the upward trend of sea level that bespoke the melting of the polar ice caps. There was no longer even a good weather net, but the fragmentary information he was able to piece together suggested a world increase of four, maybe as many as six or seven degrees Celsius already, and the reactions still seething away in Czechoslovakia, the Congo, Colorado and a hundred lesser infernos.

Rumors about the sea level?

Not rumors, no, he corrected himself, lifting his head and staring at the snake of hard rubber hose that began under the duckboards at the far end of the room and ended outside the barred window, where the gasoline pump did its best to keep the water level inside his cell below the boards. Judging by the inflow, the grounds of the White House must be nearly awash.

The door opened. The President of the United States (Washington) walked in, patting the shoulder of the thin, scared, hungry-looking kid who was guarding the door.

"How's it going, Knefhausen?" the President began sunnily. "You ready to listen to a little reason yet?"

"I'll do whatever you say, Mr. President, but as I have told you there are certain limits. Also I am not a young man, and my health—"

"Screw your health and your limits," shouted the President. "Don't start up with me, Knefhausen!"

"I am sorry, Mr. President," whispered Knefhausen.

"Don't be sorry! I judge by results. You know what it takes to keep that pump going just so you won't drown? Gas is rationed, Knefhausen! Takes a high national priority to get it! I don't know how long I'll be able to justify this continuous drain on our resources if you don't cooperate."

Sadly, but stubbornly, Knefhausen said: "As far as I am able, Mr. President, I cooperate."

"Yeah. Sure." But the President was in an unusually good mood today, Knefhausen observed, with the prisoner's paranoid attention to detail, and in a moment he said: "Listen, let's not get uptight about this. I'm making you an offer. Say the word and I'll fire that dumb son of a bitch Harry Stokes and make you my Chief Science Adviser. How would that be? Right up at the top again. An apartment of your own. Electric lights! Servants—you can pick 'em out yourself, and there's some nice-looking little girls in the pool. The best food you ever dreamed of. A chance to perform a real service for the U.S. of A., helping to reunify this great country to become once again the great power it should and must be!"

"Mr. President," Knefhausen said, "naturally, I wish to help in any way I can, but we have been over all this before. I'll do anything you like, but I don't know how to make the bombs work again. You saw what happened, Mr. President. They're gone."

"I didn't say bombs, did I? Look, Kneffie, I'm a reasonable man. How about this: you promise to use your best scientific efforts *in any way you can.* You say you can't make bombs; all right. But there will be other things."

"What other things, Mr. President?"

"Don't push me, Knefhausen. Anything at all. Anything where you can perform a service for your country. You give me that promise and you're out of here today. Or would you rather I just turned off the pump?"

Knefhausen shook his head, not in negation but in despair. "You do not know what you are asking. What can a scientist do for you today? Ten years ago, yes—even five years ago. We could have worked something out maybe, I could have done something. But now the preconditions do not exist. When all the nuclear plants went out—when the factories that depended on them ran out of power—when the fertilizer plants couldn't fix nitrogen and the insecticide plants couldn't deliver—when the people began to die of hunger and the pestilences started—"

"I know all that, Knefhausen. Yes, or no?"

The scientist hesitated, looking thoughtfully at his adversary. A gleam of the old shrewdness appeared in his eyes.

"Mr. President," he said slowly. "You know something. Something has happened."

"Right," crowed the President. "You're smart. Now tell me, what is it I know?"

Knefhausen shook his head. After seven decades of vigorous life, and another decade of slowly dying, it was hard to hope again. This terrible little man, this upstart, this lump—he was not without a certain animal cunning, and he seemed very sure. "Please, Mr. President. Tell me."

The President put a finger to his lips, and then an ear to the door. When he was convinced no one could be listening, he came closer to Knefhausen and said softly:

"You know that I have trade representatives all over, Knefhausen. Some in Houston, some in Salt Lake, some even in Montreal. They are not always there just for trade. Sometimes they find things out, and tell me. Would you like to know what my man in Anaheim has just told me?"

Knefhausen did not answer, but his watery old eyes were imploring.

"A message," whispered the President.

"From the *Constitution?*" cried Knefhausen. "But, no, it is not possible! Farside is gone, Goldstone is destroyed, the orbiting satellites are running down—"

"It wasn't a radio message," said the President. "It came from Mount Palomar. Not the big telescope, because that got ripped off, too, but what they call a Schmidt. Whatever that is. It still works. And they still have some old fogies who look through it now and then, for old times' sake. And they got a message, in laser light. Plain Morse code. From what they said was Alpha Centauri. From your little friends, Knefhausen."

He took a piece of paper from his pocket and held it up.

Knefhausen was racked by a fit of coughing, but he managed to croak: "Give it to me!"

The President held it away. "A deal, Knefhausen?"

"Yes, yes! Anything you say, but give me the message!"

"Why, certainly." The President smiled, and passed over the much-creased sheet of paper. It said:

PLEASE BE ADVISED WE HAVE CREATED THE PLANET ALPHA-ALEPH. IT IS BEAUTIFUL AND GRAND. WE WILL SEND OUR FERRIES TO BRING SUITABLE PERSONS AND OTHERS TO STOCK IT AND TO COMPLETE CERTAIN OTHER BUSINESS. OUR SPECIAL REGARDS TO DR. DIETER VON KNEFHAUSEN, WHOM WE WANT TO TALK TO VERY MUCH. EXPECT US WITHIN THREE WEEKS OF THIS MESSAGE.

Knefhausen read it over twice, stared at the President and read it again. "I . . . I am very glad," he said inadequately.

The President snatched it back, folded it and put it in his pocket, as though the message itself was the key to power. "So you see," he said, "It's simple. You help me, I help you."

"Yes. Yes, of course," said Knefhausen, staring past him.

"They're your friends. They'll do what you say. All those things you told me that they can do—"

"Yes, the particles, the ability to reproduce, the ability, God save us, to build a planet—" Knefhausen might have gone on cataloguing the skills of the spacemen indefinitely, but the President was impatient:

"So it's only a matter of days now, and they'll be here. You can imagine what they'll have! Guns, tools, everything—and all you have to do is get them to join me in restoring the United States of America to its proper place. I'll make it worth their while, Knefhausen! And yours, too. They—"

The President stopped, observing the scientist carefully. Then he cried "Knefhausen!" and leaped forward to catch him.

He was too late. The scientist had fallen limply to the duckboards. The guard, when ordered, ran for the White House doctor, who limped as rapidly to the scene as his bad legs and brain soaked with beer would let him, but he was too late, too. Everything was too late for Knefhausen, whose old heart had failed him . . . as it proved a few days later—when the great golden ships from Alpha-Aleph landed and disgorged their bright, terrible crewmen to clean up the Earth—just in time.

A Sign in Space

TRANSLATED BY WILLIAM WEAVER

Possibly the greatest Italian writer of the past few decades, Italo Calvino was unquestionably influenced by science fiction and its imagery. Two of Calvino's books from the 1960s, T Zero and Cosmicomics, are playful variations on SF themes. Furthermore, these books were read and talked about by such influential leaders of the New Wave movement as Judith Merril and Michael Moorcock, thus encouraging Calvino's influence on British and American SF. But Calvino remained more admired than influential, perhaps because of his unique talent for making the science fictional appear delightfully absurd. His stories are contes philosophiques, *meditations on the nature of language dramatized in SF form. Calvino does not wish us to believe in the literal level of the text for a moment, but only to posit an abstract and metaphysical space and a set of characters, through which we immediately penetrate into a rich and logical pattern. His nearest literary relation in SF is Stanislaw Lem.*

* * *

Situated in the external zone of the Milky Way, the Sun takes about two hundred million years to make a complete revolution of the Galaxy. Right, that's how long it takes, not a day less, —*Qfwfq said*, —once, as I went past, I drew a sign at a point in space, just so I could find it again two hundred million years later, when we went by the next time around. What sort of sign? It's hard to explain because if I say sign to you, you immediately think of a something that can be distinguished from a something else, but nothing could be distinguished from anything there; you immediately think of a sign made with some implement or with your hands, and then when you take the implement or your hands away, the sign remains, but in those days there were no implements or even hands, or teeth, or noses, all things that came along afterwards, a long time afterwards. As to the form a sign should have, you say it's no problem because, whatever form it may be given, a sign only has to serve as a sign, that is, be different or else the same as other signs: here again it's easy for you young ones to talk, but in that period I didn't have any examples to follow, I couldn't say I'll make it the same or I'll make it different, there were no things to copy, nobody knew what a line was, straight or curved, or even a dot, or a protuberance or a cavity. I conceived the idea of making a sign, that's true enough, or rather, I conceived the idea of considering a sign a something that I felt like making, so when, at that point in space and not in another, I made something, meaning to make a sign, it turned out that I really had made a sign, after all.

In other words, considering it was the first sign ever made in the universe, or at least in the circuit of the Milky Way, I must admit it came out very well. Visible? What a question! Who had eyes to see with in those days? Nothing had ever been seen by anything, the question never even arose. Recognizable, yes, beyond any possibility of error: because all the other points in space were the same, indistinguishable, and instead, this one had the sign on it.

So as the planets continued their revolutions, and the solar system went on in its own, I soon left the sign far behind me, separated from it by the endless fields of space. And I couldn't help thinking about when I would come back and encounter it again, and how I would know it, and how happy it would make me, in that anonymous expanse, after I had spent a hundred thousand light-years without meeting anything familiar, nothing for hundreds of centuries, for thousands of millennia; I'd come back and there it would be in its place, just as I had left it, simple and bare, but with that unmistakable imprint, so to speak, that I had given it.

Slowly the Milky Way revolved, with its fringe of constellations and planets and clouds, and the Sun along with the rest, toward the edge. In all that circling, only the sign remained still, in an ordinary spot, out of all the orbit's reach (to make it, I had leaned over the border of the Galaxy a little, so it would remain outside and all those revolving worlds wouldn't crash into it), in an ordinary point that was no longer ordinary since it was the only point that was surely there, and which could be used as a reference point to distinguish other points.

I thought about it day and night; in fact, I couldn't think about anything else; actually, this was the first opportunity I had had to think something; or I should say: to think something had never been possible, first because there were no things to think about, and second because signs to think of them by were lacking, but from the moment there was that sign, it was possible for someone thinking to think of a sign, and therefore that one, in the sense that the sign was the thing you could think about and also the sign of the thing thought, namely, itself.

So the situation was this: the sign served to mark a place but at the same time it meant that in that place there was a sign (something far more important because there were plenty of places but there was only one sign) and also at the same time that sign was mine, the sign of me, because it was the only sign I had ever made and I was the only one who had ever made signs. It was like a name, the name of that point, and also my name that I had signed on that spot; in short, it was the only name available for everything that required a name.

Transported by the sides of the Galaxy, our world went navigating through distant spaces, and the sign stayed where I had left it to mark that spot, and at the same time it marked me, I carried it with me, it inhabited me, possessed me entirely, came between me and everything with which I might have attempted to establish a relationship. As I waited to come back and meet it again, I could try to derive other signs from it and combinations of signs, series of similar signs and contrasts of different signs. But already tens and tens of thousands of millennia had gone by since the moment when I had made it (rather, since the few seconds in which I had scrawled it down in the constant movement of the Milky Way) and now, just when I needed to bear in mind its every detail (the slightest uncertainty about its form made uncertain the possible distinctions between it and other signs I might make), I realized that, though I recalled its general outline, its over-all appearance, still something about it eluded me, I mean if I tried to break it down into its various elements, I couldn't remember whether, between one part and the other, it went like this or like that. I needed it there in front of me, to study, to consult, but instead it was still far away, I didn't yet know how far, because I had made it precisely in order to know the time it would take me to see it again, and until I had found it once more, I wouldn't know. Now, however, it wasn't my motive in making it that mattered to me, but how it was made, and I started inventing hypotheses about this how, and theories according to which a certain sign had to be perforce in a certain way, or else, proceeding by exclusion, I tried to eliminate all the less probable types of sign to arrive at the right one, but all these imaginary signs vanished inevitably because that first sign was missing as a term of comparison. As I racked my brain like this (while the Galaxy went on turning wakefully in its bed of soft emptiness and the atoms burned and radiated) I realized I had lost by now even that confused notion of my sign, and I succeeded in conceiving only interchangeable fragments of signs, that is, smaller signs within the large one, and every change of these signs-within-the-sign changed the sign itself into a completely different one; in short, I had completely forgotten what my sign was like and, try as I might, it wouldn't come back to my mind.

Did I despair? No, this forgetfulness was annoying, but not irreparable. Whatever happened, I knew the sign was there waiting for me, quiet and still. I would arrive, I would find it again, and I would then be able to pick up the thread of my meditations. At a rough guess, I calculated we had completed half of our galactic revolution: I had only to be patient, the second half always seemed to go by more quickly. Now I just had to remember the sign existed and I would pass it again.

Day followed day, and then I knew I must be near. I was furiously impatient because I might encounter the sign at any moment. It's here, no, a little farther on, now I'll count up to a hundred . . . Had it disappeared? Had we already gone past it? I didn't know. My sign had perhaps remained who knows where, behind, completely remote from the revolutionary orbit of our system. I hadn't calculated the oscillations to which, especially in those days, the celestial bodies' fields of gravity were subject, and which caused them to trace irregular orbits, cut like the flower of a dahlia. For about a hundred millennia I tormented myself, going over my calculations: it turned out that our course touched that spot not every galactic year but only every three, that is, every six hundred million solar years. When you've waited two hundred million years, you can also wait six hundred; and I waited; the way was long but I wasn't on foot, after all; astride the Galaxy I traveled through the light-years, galloping over the planetary and stellar orbits as if I were on a horse whose shoes struck sparks; I was in a state of mounting excitement; I felt I was going forth to conquer the only thing that mattered to me, sign and dominion and name . . .

I made the second circuit, the third. I was there. I let out a yell. At a point which had to be that very point, in the place of my sign, there was a shapeless scratch, a bruised, chipped abrasion of space. I had lost every-thing: the sign, the point, the thing that caused me—being the one who had made the sign at that point—to be me. Space, without a sign, was once again a chasm, the void, without beginning or end, nauseating, in which everything—including me—was lost. (And don't come telling me that, to fix a point, my sign and the erasure of my sign amounted to the same thing; the erasure was the negation of the sign, and therefore didn't serve to distinguish one point from the preceding and successive points.)

I was disheartened and for many light-years I let myself be dragged along as if I were unconscious. When I finally raised my eyes (in the meanwhile, sight had begun in our world, and, as a result, also life), I saw what I would never have expected to see. I saw it, the sign, but not that one, a similar sign, a sign unquestionably copied from mine, but one I realized immediately couldn't be mine, it was so squat and careless and clumsily pretentious, a wretched counterfeit of what I had meant to indicate with that sign whose ineffable purity I could only now—through contrast—recapture. Who had played this trick on me? I couldn't figure it out. Finally, a plurimillennial chain of deductions led me to the solution: on another planetary system which performed its galactic revolution before us, there was a certain Kgwgk (the name I deduced afterwards, in the later era of names), a spiteful type, consumed with envy, who had erased my sign in a vandalistic impulse and then, with vulgar artifice, had attempted to make another.

It was clear that his sign had nothing to mark except Kgwgk's intention to imitate my sign, which was beyond all comparison. But at that moment the determination not to let my rival get the better of me was stronger than any other desire: I wanted immediately to make a new sign in space, a real sign that would make Kgwgk die of envy. About seven hundred millions of years had gone by since I had first tried to make a sign, but I fell to work with a will. Now things were different, however, because the world, as I mentioned, was beginning to produce an image of itself, and in everything a form was beginning to correspond to a function, and the forms of that time, we believed, had a long future ahead of them (instead, we were wrong: take—to give you a fairly recent example—the dinosaurs), and therefore in this new sign of mine you could perceive the influence of our new way of looking at things; call it style if you like, that special way that everything had to be, there, in a certain fashion. I must say I was truly satisfied with it, and I no longer regretted that first sign that had been erased, because this one seemed vastly more beautiful to me.

But in the duration of that galactic year we already began to realize that the world's forms had been temporary up until then, and that they would change, one by one. And this awareness was accompanied by a certain annoyance with the old images, so that even their memory was intolerable. I began to be tormented by a thought: I had left that sign in space, that sign which had seemed so beautiful and original to me and so suited to its function, and which now, in my memory, seemed inappropriate, in all its pretension, a sign chiefly of an antiquated way of conceiving signs and of my foolish acceptance of an order of things I ought to have been wise enough to break away from in time. In other words, I was ashamed of that sign which went on through the centuries, being passed by worlds in flight, making a ridiculous spectacle of itself and of me and of that temporary way we had had of seeing things. I blushed when I remembered it (and I remembered it constantly), blushes that lasted whole geological eras: to hide my shame I crawled into the craters of the volcanoes, in remorse I sank my teeth into the caps of the glaciations that covered the continents. I was tortured by the thought that Kgwgk, always preceding me in the circumnavigation of the Milky Way, would see the sign before I could erase it, and boor that he was, he would mock me and make fun of me, contemptuously repeating the sign in rough caricatures in every corner of the circumgalactic sphere.

Instead, this time the complicated astral timekeeping was in my favor. Kgwgk's constellation didn't encounter the sign, whereas our solar system turned up there punctually at the end of the first revolution, so close that I was able to erase the whole thing with the greatest care.

Now, there wasn't a single sign of mine in space. I could start drawing another, but I knew that signs also allow others to judge the one who makes them, and that in the course of a galactic year tastes and ideas have time to change, and the way of regarding the earlier ones depends on what comes afterwards; in short, I was afraid a sign that now might seem perfect to me, in two hundred or six hundred million years would make me look absurd. Instead, in my nostalgia, the first sign, brutally rubbed out by Kgwgk, remained beyond the attacks of time and its changes, the sign created before the beginning of forms, which was to contain something that would have survived all forms, namely the fact of being a sign and nothing else.

Making signs that weren't that sign no longer held any interest for me; and I had forgotten that sign now, billions of years before. So, unable to make true signs, but wanting somehow to annoy Kgwgk, I started making false signs, notches in space, holes, stains, little tricks that only an incompetent creature like Kgwgk could mistake for signs. And still he furiously got rid of them with his erasings (as I could see in later revolutions), with a determination that must have cost him much effort. (Now I scattered these false signs liberally through space, to see how far his simple-mindedness would go.)

Observing these erasures, one circuit after the next (the Galaxy's revolutions had now become for me a slow, boring voyage without goal or expectation), I realized something: as the galactic years passed the erasures tended to fade in space, and beneath them what I had drawn at those points, my false signs—as I called them—began to reappear. This discovery, far from displeasing me, filled me with new hope. If Kgwgk's erasures were erased, the first he had made, there at that point, must have disappeared by now, and my sign must have returned to its pristine visibility!

So expectation was revived, to lend anxiety to my days. The Galaxy turned like an omelet in its heated pan, itself both frying pan and golden egg; and I was frying, with it, in my impatience.

But, with the passing of the galactic years, space was no longer that uniformly barren and colorless expanse. The idea of fixing with signs the points where we passed—as it had come to me and to Kgwgk—had occurred to many, scattered over billions of planets of other solar systems, and I was constantly running into one of these things, or a pair, or even a dozen, simple two-dimensional scrawls, or else three-dimensional solids (poly-hedrons, for example), or even things constructed with more care, with the fourth dimension and everything. So it happened that I reached the point of my sign, and I found five, all there. And I wasn't able to recognize my own. It's this one, no, that; no, no, that one seems too modern, but it could also be the most ancient; I don't recognize my hand in that one, I would never have wanted to make it like that . . . And meanwhile the Galaxy ran through space and left behind those signs old and new and I still hadn't found mine.

I'm not exaggerating when I say that the galactic years that followed were the worst I had ever lived through. I went on looking, and signs kept growing thicker in space; from all the worlds anybody who had an opportunity invariably left his mark in space somehow; and our world, too, every time I turned, I found more crowded, so that world and space seemed the mirror of each other, both minutely adorned with hieroglyphics and ideograms, each of which might be a sign and might not be: a calcareous concretion on basalt, a crest raised by the wind on the clotted sand of the desert, the arrangement of the eyes in a peacock's tail (gradually, living among signs had led us to see signs in countless things that, before, were there, marking nothing but their own presence; they had been transformed into the sign of themselves and had been added to the series of signs made on purpose by those who meant to make a sign), the fire-streaks against a wall of schistose rock, the four-hundred-and-twenty-seventh groove—slightly crooked—of the cornice of a tomb's pediment, a sequence of streaks on a video during a thunderstorm (the series of signs was multiplied in the series of the signs of signs, of signs repeated countless times always the same and always some-how different because to the purposely made sign you had to add the sign that had happened there by chance), the badly inked tail of the letter R in an evening newspaper joined to a thready imperfection in the paper, one among the eight hundred thousand flakings of a tarred wall in the Melbourne docks, the curve of a graph, a skid-mark on the asphalt, a chromosome . . . Every now and then I'd start: that's the one! And for a second I was sure I had rediscovered my sign, on the Earth or in space, it made no difference, because through the signs a continuity had been established with no precise boundaries any more.

In the universe now there was no longer a container and a thing con-tained, but only a general thickness of signs superimposed and coagulated, occupying the whole volume of space; it was constantly being dotted, minutely, a network of lines and scratches and reliefs and engravings; the universe was scrawled over on all sides, along all its dimensions. There was no longer any way to establish a point of reference: the Galaxy went on turning but I could no longer count the revolutions, any point could be the point of departure, any sign heaped up with the others could be mine, but discovering it would have served no purpose, because it was clear that, independent of signs, space didn't exist and perhaps had never existed.

ITALO CALVINO

The Spiral

TRANSLATED BY WILLIAM WEAVER

For the majority of mollusks, the visible organic form has little importance in the life of the members of a species, since they cannot see one another and have, at most, only a vague perception of other individuals and of their surroundings. This does not prevent brightly colored stripings and forms which seem very beautiful to our eyes (as in many gastropod shells) from existing independently of any relationship to visibility. Like me, when I was clinging to that rock, you mean? —*Qfwfq asked*, —With the waves rising and falling, and me there, still, flat, sucking what there was to suck and thinking about it all the time? If that's the time you want to know about, there isn't much I can tell you. Form? I didn't have any; that is, I didn't know I had one, or rather I didn't know you *could* have one. I grew more or less on all sides, at random; if this is what you call radial symmetry, I suppose I had radial symmetry, but to tell you the truth I never paid any attention to it. Why should I have grown more on one side than on the other? I had no eyes, no head, no part of the body that was different from any other part; now I try to persuade myself that the two holes I had were a mouth and an anus, and that I therefore already had my bilateral symmetry, just like the trilobites and the rest of you, but in my memory I really can't tell those holes apart, I passed stuff from whatever side I felt like, inside or outside was the same, differences and repugnances came along much later. Every now and then I was seized by fantasies, that's true; for example, the notion of scratching my armpit, or crossing my legs, or once even of growing a mustache. I use these words here with you, to make myself clear; then there were many details I couldn't foresee: I had some cells, one more or less the same as another, and they all did more or less the same job. But since I had no form I could feel all possible forms in myself, and all actions and expressions and possibilities of making noises, even rude ones. In short, there were no limitations to my thoughts, which weren't thoughts, after all, because I had no brain to think them; every cell on its own thought every thinkable thing all at once, not through images, since we had no images of any kind at our disposal, but simply in that indeterminate way of feeling oneself there, which did not prevent us from feeling ourselves equally there in some other way.

It was a rich and free and contented condition, my condition at that time, quite the contrary of what you might think. I was a bachelor (our system of reproduction in those days didn't require even temporary couplings), healthy, without too many ambitions. When you're young, all evolution lies before you, every road is open to you, and at the same time you can enjoy the fact of being there on the rock, flat mollusk-pulp, damp and happy. If you compare yourself with the limitations that came afterwards, if you think of how having one form excludes other forms, of the monotonous routine where you finally feel trapped, well, I don't mind saying life was beautiful in those days.

To be sure, I lived a bit withdrawn into myself, that's true, no comparison with our interrelated life nowadays; and I'll also admit that—partly because of my age and partly under the influence of my surroundings—I was what they call a narcissist to a slight extent; I mean I stayed there observing myself all the time, I saw all my good points and all my defects, and I liked myself for the former and for the latter; I had no terms of comparison, you must remember that, too.

But I wasn't so backward that I didn't know something else existed beyond me: the rock where I clung, obviously, and also the water that reached me with every wave, but other stuff, too, farther on: that is, the world. The water was a source of information, reliable and precise: it brought me edible substances which I absorbed through all my surface, and other inedible ones which still helped me form an idea of what there was around. The system worked like this: a wave would come, and I, still sticking to the rock, would raise myself up a little bit, imperceptibly—all I had to do was loosen the pressure slightly—and, splat, the water passed beneath me, full of substances and sensations and stimuli. You never knew how those stimuli were going to turn out, sometimes a tickling that made you die laughing, other times a shudder, a burning, an itch; so it was a constant seesaw of amusement and emotion. But you mustn't think I just lay there passively, dumbly accepting everything that came: after a while I had acquired some experience and I was quick to analyze what sort of stuff was arriving and to decide how I should behave, to make the best use of it or to avoid the more unpleasant consequences. It was all a kind of game of contractions, with each of the cells I had, or of relaxing at the right moment: and I could make my choices, reject, attract, even spit.

And so I learned that there were *the others*, the element surrounding me was filled with traces of them, *others* hostile and different from me or else disgustingly similar. No, now I'm giving you a disagreeable idea of my character, which is all wrong. Naturally, each of us went about on his own business, but the presence of the *others* reassured me, created an inhabited zone around me, freed me from the fear of being an alarming exception, which I would have been if the fact of existing had been my fate alone, a kind of exile.

So I knew that some of the *others* were female. The water transmitted a special vibration, a kind of brrrum brrrum brrrum, I remember when I became aware of it the first time, or rather, not the first, I remember when I became aware of being aware of it as a thing I had always known. At the discovery of these vibrations' existence, I was seized with a great curiosity, not so much to see them, or to be seen by them either—since, first, we hadn't any sight, and secondly, the sexes weren't yet differentiated, each individual was identical with every other individual and at looking at one or another I would have felt no more pleasure than in looking at myself—but a curiosity to know whether something would happen between me and them. A desperation filled me, a desire not to do anything special, which would have been out of place, knowing that there was nothing special to do, or nonspecial either, but to respond in some way to that vibration with a corresponding vibration, or rather, with a personal vibration of my own, because, sure enough, there was something there that wasn't exactly the same as the other, I mean now you might say it came from hormones, but for me it was very beautiful.

So then, one of them, shlup shlup shlup, emitted her eggs, and I, shlup shlup shlup, fertilized them: all down inside the sea, mingling in the water tepid from the sun; oh, I forgot to tell you, I could feel the sun, which warmed the sea and heated the rock.

One of them, I said. Because, among all those female messages that the sea slammed against me like an indistinct soup at first where everything was all right with me and I grubbed about paying no attention to what one was like or another, suddenly I understood what corresponded best to my tastes, tastes which I hadn't known before that moment, of course. In other words,

I had fallen in love. What I mean is: I had begun to recognize, to isolate the signs of one of those from the others, in fact I waited for these signs I had begun to recognize, I sought them, responded to those signs I awaited with other signs I made myself, or rather it was I who aroused them, these signs from her, which I answered with other signs of my own, I mean I was in love with her and she with me, so what more could I want from life?

Now habits have changed, and it already seems inconceivable to you that one could love a female like that, without having spent any time with her. And yet, through that unmistakable part of her still in solution in the sea water, which the waves placed at my disposal, I received a quantity of information about her, more than you can imagine: not the superficial, generic information you get now, seeing and smelling and touching and hearing a voice, but essential information, which I could then develop at length in my imagination. I could think of her with minute precision, thinking not so much of how she was made, which would have been a banal and vulgar way of thinking of her, but of how from her present formlessness she would be transformed into one of the infinite possible forms, still remaining herself, however: I didn't imagine the forms that she might assume, but I imagined the special quality that, in taking them, she would give to those forms.

I knew her well, in other words. And I wasn't sure of her. Every now and then I was overcome with suspicion, anxiety, rage. I didn't let anything show, you know my character, but beneath that impassive mask passed suppositions I can't bring myself to confess even now. More than once I suspected she was unfaithful to me, that she sent messages not only to me but also to others; more than once I thought I had intercepted one, or that I had discovered a tone of insincerity in a message addressed to me. I was jealous, I can admit it now, not so much out of distrust of her as out of unsureness of myself: who could assure me that she had really understood who I was? Or that she had understood the fact that I was? This relationship achieved between us thanks to the sea water—a full, complete relationship, what more could I ask for?—was for me something absolutely personal, between two unique and distinct individualities; but for her? Who could assure me that what she might find in me she hadn't also found in another, or in another two or three or ten or a hundred like me? Who could assure me that her abandon in our shared relations wasn't an indiscriminate abandon, slapdash, a kind of—who's next?—collective ecstasy?

The fact that these suspicions did not correspond to the truth was confirmed, for me, by the subtle, soft, private vibration, at times still trembling with modesty, in our correspondences; but what if, precisely out of shyness and inexperience, she didn't pay enough attention to my characteristics and others took advantage of this innocence to worm their way in? And what if she, a novice, believed it was still I and couldn't distinguish one from the other, and so our most intimate play was extended to a circle of strangers . . .?

It was then that I began to secrete calcareous matter. I wanted to make something to mark my presence in an ummistakable fashion, something that would defend this individual presence of mine from the indiscriminate instability of all the rest. Now it's no use my piling up words, trying to explain the novelty of this intention I had; the first word I said is more than enough: *make*, I wanted to *make*, and considering the fact that I had never made anything or thought you could make anything, this in itself was a big event. So I began to make the first thing that occurred to me, and it was a shell. From the margin of that fleshy cloak on my body, using certain glands, I began to give off secretions which took on a curving shape all around, until I was covered with a hard and variegated shield, rough on the outside and smooth and shiny inside. Naturally, I had no way of controlling the form of what I was making: I just stayed there all huddled up, silent and sluggish, and I secreted. I went on even after the shell covered my whole body; I began another turn; in short, I was getting one of those shells all twisted into a spiral, which you, when you see them, think are so hard to make, but all you have to do is keep working and giving off the same matter without stopping, and they grow like that, one turn after the other.

Once it existed, this shell was also a necessary and indispensable place to stay inside of, a defense for my survival; it was a lucky thing I had made it, but while I was making it I had no idea of making it because I needed it; on the contrary, it was like when somebody lets out an exclamation he could perfectly well not make, and yet he makes it, like "Ha" or "hmph!," that's how I made the shell: simply to express myself. And in this self-expression I put all the thoughts I had about her, I released the anger she made me feel, my amorous way of thinking about her, my determination to exist for her, the desire for me to be me, and for her to be her, and the love for myself that I put in my love for her—all the things that could be said only in that conch shell wound into a spiral.

At regular intervals the calcareous matter I was secreting came out colored, so a number of lovely stripes were formed running straight through the spirals, and this shell was a thing different from me but also the truest part of me, the explanation of who I was, my portrait translated into a rhythmic system of volumes and stripes and colors and hard matter, and it was the portrait of her as she was, because at the same time she was making herself a shell identical to mine and without knowing it I was copying what she was doing and she without knowing it was copying what I was doing, and all the others were copying all the others, so we would be back where we had been before except for the fact that in saying these shells were the same I was a bit hasty, because when you looked closer you discovered all sorts of little differences that later on might become enormous.

So I can say that my shell made itself, without my taking any special pains to have it come out one way rather than another, but this doesn't mean that I was absent-minded during that time; I applied myself, instead, to that act of secreting, without allowing myself a moment's distraction, never thinking of anything else, or rather: thinking always of something else, since I didn't know how to think of the shell, just as, for that matter, I didn't know how to think of anything else either, but I accompanied the effort of making the shell with the effort of thinking I was making something, that is anything: that is, I thought of all the things it would be possible to make. So it wasn't even a monotonous task, because the effort of thinking which accompanied it spread toward countless types of thoughts which spread, each one, toward countless types of actions that might each serve to make countless things, and making each of these things was implicit in making the shell grow, turn after turn . . .

II

(*And so now, after five hundred million years have gone by, I look around and, above the rock, I see the railway embankment and the train passing along it with a party of Dutch girls looking out of the window and, in the last compartment, a solitary traveler reading Herodotus in a bilingual edition, and the train vanishes into the tunnel under the highway, where there is a sign with the pyramids and the words "VISIT EGYPT," and a little ice-cream wagon tries to pass a big truck laden with installments of Rh-Stijl, a periodical encyclopedia that comes out in paperback, but then it puts its brakes on because its visibility is blocked by a cloud of bees which crosses the road coming from a row of hives in a field from which surely a queen bee is flying away, drawing behind her a swarm in the direction opposite to the smoke of the train, which has reappeared at the other end of the tunnel, so you can see hardly anything thanks to the cloudy stream of bees and coal smoke, except a few yards farther up there is a peasant breaking the ground with his mattock and, unaware, he brings to light and reburies a fragment of a Neolithic mattock similar to his own, in a garden that surrounds an astronomical observatory with its telescopes aimed at the sky and on whose threshold the keeper's daughter sits reading the horoscopes in a weekly whose cover displays the face of the star of* Cleopatra: *I see all this and I feel no amazement because making the shell implied also making the honey in the wax comb and the coal and the telescopes and the reign of Cleopatra and the films about Cleopatra and the pyramids and the design of the zodiac of the Chaldean astrologers and the wars and empires Herodotus speaks of and the words written by Herodotus and the works written in all languages including those of Spinoza in Dutch and the fourteen-line summary of Spinoza's life and works in the installment of the encyclopedia in the truck passed by the ice-cream wagon, and so I feel as if, in making the shell, I had also made the rest.*

I look around, and whom am I looking for? She is still the one I seek; I've been in love for five hundred million years, and if I see a Dutch girl on the sand with a beachboy wearing a gold chain around his neck and showing her the swarm of bees to frighten her, there she is: I recognize her from her inimitable way of raising one shoulder until it almost touches her cheek, I'm almost sure, or rather I'd say absolutely sure if it weren't for a certain resemblance that I find also in the daughter of the keeper of the observatory, and in the photograph of the actress made up as Cleopatra, or perhaps in Cleopatra as she really was in person, for what part of the true Cleopatra they say every representation of Cleopatra contains, or in the queen bee flying at the head of the swarm with that forward impetuousness, or in the paper woman cut out and pasted on the plastic windshield of the little ice-cream wagon, wearing a bathing suit like the Dutch girl on the beach now listening over a little transistor radio to the voice of a woman singing, the same voice that the encyclopedia truck driver hears over his radio, and the same one I'm now sure I've heard for five million years, it is surely she I hear singing and whose image I look for all around, seeing only gulls volplaning on the surface of the sea where a school of anchovies glistens and for a moment I am certain I recognize her in a female gull and a moment later I suspect that instead she's an anchovy, though she might just as well be any queen or slave-girl named by Herodotus or only hinted at in the pages of the volume left to mark the seat of the reader who has stepped into the corridor of the train to strike up a conversation with the party of Dutch tourists; I might say I am in love with each of those girls and at the same time I am sure of being in love always with her alone.

And the more I torment myself with love for each of them, the less I can bring myself to say to them: "Here I am!," afraid of being mistaken and even more afraid that she is mistaken, taking me for somebody else, for somebody who, for all she knows of me, might easily take my place, for example the beachboy with the gold chain, or the director of the observatory, or a gull, or a male anchovy, or the reader of Herodotus, or Herodotus himself, or the vendor of ice cream, who has come down to the beach along a dusty road among the prickly pears and is now surrounded by the Dutch girls in their bathing suits, or Spinoza, or the truck driver who is transporting the life and works of Spinoza summarized and repeated two thousand times, or one of the drones dying at the bottom of the hive after having fulfilled his role in the continuation of the species.)

III

. . . Which doesn't mean that the shell wasn't, first and foremost, a shell, with its particular form, which couldn't be any different because it was the very form I had given it, the only one I could or would give it. Since the shell had a form, the form of the world was also changed, in the sense that now it included the form of the world as it had been without a shell plus the form of the shell.

And that had great consequences: because the waving vibrations of light, striking bodies, produce particular effects from them, color first of all, namely, that matter I used to make stripes with which vibrated in a different way from the rest; but there was also the fact that a volume enters into a special relationship of volumes with other volumes, all phenomena I couldn't be aware of, though they existed.

The shell in this way was able to create visual images of shells, which are things very similar—as far as we know—to the shell itself, except that the shell is here, whereas the images of it are formed elsewhere, possibly on a retina. An image therefore presupposes a retina, which in turn presupposes a complex system stemming from an encephalon. So, in producing the shell, I also produced its image—not one, of course, but many, because with one shell you can make as many shell-images as you want—but only potential images because to form an image you need all the requisites I mentioned before: an encephalon with its optic ganglia, and an optic nerve to carry the vibrations from outside to inside, and this optic nerve, at the other extremity, ends in something made purposely to see what there is outside, namely the eye. Now it's ridiculous to think that, having an encephalon, one would simply drop a nerve like a fishing line cast into the darkness; until the eyes crop up, one can't know whether there is something to be seen outside or not. For myself, I had none of this equipment, so I was the least authorized to speak of it; however, I had conceived an idea of my own, namely that the important thing was to form some visual images, and the eyes would come later in consequence. So I concentrated on making the part of me that was outside (and even the interior part of me that conditioned the exterior) give rise to an image, or rather to what would later be called a lovely image (when compared to other images considered less lovely, or rather ugly, or simply revoltingly hideous).

When a body succeeds in emitting or in reflecting luminous vibrations in a distinct and recognizable order—I thought—what does it do with these vibrations? Put them in its pocket? No, it releases them on the first passer-by. And how will the latter behave in the face of vibrations he can't utilize and which, taken in this way, might even be annoying? Hide his head in a hole? No, he'll thrust it out in that direction until the point most exposed to the optic vibrations becomes sensitized and develops the mechanism for exploiting them in the form of images. In short, I conceived of the eye-encephalon link as a kind of tunnel dug from the outside by the force of what was ready to become image, rather than from within by the intention of picking up any old image.

And I wasn't mistaken: even today I'm sure that the project—in its overall aspect—was right. But my error lay in thinking that sight would also come to us, that is to me and to her. I elaborated a harmonious, colored image of myself to enter her visual receptivity, to occupy its center, to settle there, so that she could utilize me constantly, in dreaming and in memory, with thought as well as with sight. And I felt at the same time she was radiating an image of herself so perfect that it would impose itself on my foggy, backward senses, developing in me an interior visual field where it would blaze forth definitely.

So our efforts led us to become those perfect objects of a sense whose nature nobody quite knew yet, and which later became perfect precisely through the perfection of its object, which was, in fact, us. I'm talking about sight, the eyes; only I had failed to foresee one thing: the eyes that finally opened to see us didn't belong to us but to others.

Shapeless, colorless beings, sacks of guts stuck together carelessly, peopled the world all around us, without giving the slightest thought to what they should make of themselves, to how to express themselves and identify themselves in a stable, complete form, such as to enrich the visual possibilities of whoever saw them. They came and went, sank a while, then emerged, in that space between air and water and rock, wandering about absently; and we in the meanwhile, she and I and all those intent on squeezing out a form of ourselves, were there slaving away at our dark task. Thanks to us, that badly defined space became a visual field; and who reaped the benefit? These intruders, who had never before given a thought to the possibility of eyesight (ugly as they were, they wouldn't have gained a thing by seeing one another), these creatures who had always turned a deaf ear to the vocation of form. While we were bent over, doing the hardest part of the job, that is, creating something to be seen, they were quietly taking on the easiest part: adapting their lazy, embryonic receptive organs to what there was to receive; our images. And they needn't try telling me now that their job was toilsome too: from that gluey mess that filled their heads anything could have come out, and a photosensitive mechanism doesn't take all that much trouble to put together. But when it comes to perfecting it, that's another story! How can you, if you don't have visible objects to see, gaudy ones even, the kind that impose themselves on the eyesight? To sum it up in a few words: they developed eyes at our expense.

So sight, *our* sight, which we were obscurely waiting for, was the sight that the others had of us. In one way or another, the great revolution had taken place: all of a sudden, around us, eyes were opening, and corneas and irises and pupils: the swollen, colorless eye of polyps and cuttlefish, the dazed and gelatinous eyes of bream and mullet, the protruding and ped-uncled eyes of crayfish and lobsters, the bulging and faceted eyes of flies and ants. A seal now comes forward, black and shiny, winking little eyes like pinheads. A snail extends ball-like eyes at the end of long antennae. The inexpressive eyes of the gull examine the surface of the water. Beyond a glass mask the frowning eyes of an underwater fisherman explore the depths. Through the lens of a spyglass a sea captain's eyes and the eyes of a woman bathing converge on my shell, then look at each other, forgetting me. Framed by far-sighted lenses I feel on me the far-sighted eyes of a zoologist, trying to frame me in the eye of a Rolleiflex. At that moment a school of tiny anchovies, barely born, passes before me, so tiny that in each little white fish it seems there is room only for the eye's black dot, and it is a kind of eye-dust that crosses the sea.

All these eyes were mine. I had made them possible; I had had the active part; I furnished them the raw material, the image. With eyes had come all the rest, so everything that the others, having eyes, had become, their every form and function, and the quantity of things that, thanks to eyes, they had managed to do, in their every form and function, came from what I had done. Of course, they were not just casually implicit in my being there, in my having relations with others, male and female, et cetera, in my setting out to make a shell, et cetera. In other words, I had foreseen absolutely everything.

And at the bottom of each of those eyes I lived, or rather another me lived, one of the images of me, and it encountered the image of her, the most faithful image of her, in that beyond which opens, past the semiliquid sphere of the irises, in the darkness of the pupils, the mirrored hall of the retinas, in our true element which extends without shores, without boundaries.

The Dead Past

Isaac Asimov is a giant of science fiction, the only Futurian who fit into the Campbell mold and the most popular writer of them all. While Pohl, Kornbluth, Knight, and Blish did not break out until the advent of new editorial philosophies and new audiences in the 1950s, Asimov was one of the great names of the 1940s (when it was Heinlein and L. Ron Hubbard, Van Vogt and Asimov who were the "big four" most popular writers in Campbell's stable). In the 1940s Asimov wrote his classic robot stories, later collected in I, Robot, *and the Foundation stories, later* The Foundation Trilogy, *and, of course, his famous story "Nightfall," about a distant planet upon which night and darkness come only once in thousands of years. But it was in the 1950s that Asimov reached the height of his powers, in a series of novels culminating in* The Caves of Steel, The End of Eternity, *and* The Naked Sun, *and in many of the finest stories of the decade—the decade of Heinlein and Bradbury, Asimov and Clarke. "The Dead Past" is one of Asimov's best from any decade, a serious investigation, in specific human terms, of the meaning of science and technology with a psychological depth uncharacteristic of its contemporaries.*

* * *

Arnold Potterley, PhD, was a Professor of Ancient History. That in itself was not dangerous. What changed the world beyond all dreams was the fact that he *looked* like a Professor of Ancient History.

Thaddeus Araman, Department Head of the Division of Chronoscopy, might have taken proper action if Dr. Potterley had been owner of a large, square chin, flashing eyes, aquiline nose and broad shoulders.

As it was, Thaddeus Araman found himself staring over his desk at a mild-mannered individual whose faded blue eyes looked at him wistfully from either side of a low-bridged button nose; whose small, neatly dressed figure seemed stamped "milk-and-water" from thinning brown hair to the neatly brushed shoes that complete a conservative middle-class costume.

Araman said pleasantly, "And now what can I do for you, Dr. Potterley?"

Dr. Potterley said in a soft voice that went well with the rest of him, "Mr. Araman, I came to you because you're top man in chronoscopy."

Araman smiled. "Not exactly. Above me is the World Commissioner of Research and above him is the Secretary-General of the United Nations. And above both of them, of course, are the sovereign peoples of Earth."

Dr. Potterley shook his head. "They're not interested in chronoscopy. I've come to you, sir, because for two years I have been trying to obtain permission to do some time-viewing—chronoscopy, that is—in connection with my researches on ancient Carthage. I can't obtain such permission. My research grants are all proper. There is no irregularity in any of my intellectual endeavors and yet—"

"I'm sure there is no question of irregularity," said Araman soothingly. He flipped the thin reproduction sheets in the folder to which Potterley's name had been attached. They had been produced by Multivac, whose vast analogical mind kept all the department records. When this was over, the sheets could be destroyed, then reproduced on demand in a matter of minutes.

And while Araman turned the pages, Dr. Potterley's voice continued in a soft monotone.

The historian was saying, "I must explain that my problem is quite an important one. Carthage was ancient commercialism brought to its zenith. Pre-Roman Carthage was the nearest ancient analogue to pre-atomic America, at least insofar as its attachment to trade, commerce and business in general was concerned. They were the most daring seamen and explorers before the Vikings; much better at it than the overrated Greeks.

"To know Carthage would be very rewarding, yet the only knowledge we have of it is derived from the writings of its bitter enemies, the Greeks and Romans. Carthage itself never wrote in its own defense or, if it did, the books did not survive. As a result, the Carthaginians have been one of the favorite sets of villains of history and perhaps unjustly so. Time-viewing may set the record straight."

He said much more.

Araman said, still turning the reproduction sheets before him, "You must realize, Dr. Potterley, that chronoscopy, or time-viewing, if you prefer, is a difficult process."

Dr. Potterley, who had been interrupted, frowned and said, "I am asking for only certain selected views at times and places I would indicate."

Araman sighed. "Even a few views, even one. . . . It is an unbelievably delicate art. There is the question of focus, getting the proper scene in view and holding it. There is the synchronization of sound, which calls for completely independent circuits."

"Surely my problem is important enough to justify considerable effort."

"Yes, sir. Undoubtedly," said Araman at once. To deny the importance of someone's research problem would be unforgivably bad manners. "But you must understand how long-drawn-out even the simplest view is. And there is a long waiting line for the chronoscope and an even longer waiting line for the use of Multivac, which guides us in our use of the controls."

Potterley stirred unhappily. "But can nothing be done? For two years—"

"A matter of priority, sir. I'm sorry. . . . Cigarette?"

The historian started back at the suggestion, eyes suddenly widening as he stared at the pack thrust out toward him. Araman looked surprised, withdrew the pack, made a motion as though to take a cigarette for himself and thought better of it.

Potterley drew a sigh of unfeigned relief as the pack was put out of sight. He said, "Is there any way of reviewing matters, putting me as far forward as possible? I don't know how to explain—"

Araman smiled. Some had offered money under similar circumstances, which, of course, had gotten them nowhere either. He said, "The decisions on priority are computer-processed. I could in no way alter those decisions arbitrarily."

Potterley rose stiffly to his feet. He stood five and a half feet tall. "Then, good day, sir."

"Good day, Dr. Potterley. And my sincerest regrets."

He offered his hand and Potterley touched it briefly.

The historian left, and a touch of the buzzer brought Araman's secretary into the room. He handed her the folder.

"These," he said, "may be disposed of."

Alone again, he smiled bitterly. Another item in his quarter-century's service to the human race. Service through negation.

At least this fellow had been easy to dispose of. Sometimes academic pressure had to be applied, and even withdrawal of grants.

Five minutes later he had forgotten Dr. Potterley. Nor, thinking back on it later, could he remember feeling any premonition of danger.

■   ■   ■

During the first year of his frustration, Arnold Potterley had experienced only that—frustration. During the second year, though, his frustration gave birth to an idea that first frightened and then fascinated him. Two things stopped him from trying to translate the idea into action, and neither barrier was the undoubted fact that his notion was a grossly unethical one.

The first was merely the continuing hope that the government would finally give its permission and make it unnecessary for him to do anything more. That hope had perished finally in the interview with Araman just completed.

The second barrier had been not a hope at all but a dreary realization of his own incapacity. He was not a physicist and he knew no physicists from whom he might obtain help. The Department of Physics at the university consisted of men well stocked with grants and well immersed in specialty. At best, they would not listen to him. At worst, they would report him for intellectual anarchy and even his basic Carthaginian grant might easily be withdrawn.

That he could not risk. And yet chronoscopy was the only way to carry on his work. Without it, he would be no worse off if his grant were lost.

The first hint that the second barrier might be overcome had come a week earlier than his interview with Araman, and it had gone unrecognized at the time. It had been at one of the faculty teas. Potterley attended these sessions unfailingly because he conceived attendance to be a duty, and he took his duties seriously. Once there, however, he conceived it to be no responsibility of his to make light conversation or new friends. He sipped abstemiously at a drink or two, exchanged a polite word with the dean or such department heads as happened to be present, bestowed a narrow smile on others and finally left early.

Ordinarily he would have paid no attention, at that most recent tea, to a young man standing quietly, even diffidently, in one corner. He would never have dreamed of speaking to him. Yet a tangle of circumstance persuaded him this once to behave in a way contrary to his nature.

That morning at breakfast, Mrs. Potterley had announced somberly that once again she had dreamed of Laurel; but this time a Laurel grown up, yet retaining the three-year-old face that stamped her as their child. Potterley had let her talk. There had been a time when he fought her too frequent preoccupation with the past and death. Laurel would not come back to them, either through dreams or through talk. Yet if it appeased Caroline Potterley—let her dream and talk.

But when Potterley went to school that morning, he found himself for once affected by Caroline's inanities. Laurel grown up! She had died nearly twenty years ago; their only child, then and ever. In all that time, when he thought of her, it was as a three-year-old.

Now he thought: But if she were alive now, she wouldn't be three; she'd be nearly twenty-three.

Helplessly he found himself trying to think of Laurel as growing progressively older, as finally becoming twenty-three. He did not quite succeed.

Yet he tried. Laurel using makeup. Laurel going out with boys. Laurel — getting married!

So it was that when he saw the young man hovering at the outskirts of the coldly circulating group of faculty men, it occurred to him quixotically that, for all he knew, a youngster just such as this might have married Laurel. That youngster himself, perhaps. . . .

Laurel might have met him here at the university, or some evening when he might be invited to dinner at the Potterleys'. They might grow interested in one another. Laurel would surely have been pretty and this youngster looked well. He was dark in coloring, with a lean, intent face and an easy carriage.

The tenuous daydream snapped, yet Potterley found himself staring foolishly at the young man, not as a strange face but as a possible son-in-law in the might-have-been. He found himself threading his way toward the man. It was almost a form of autohypnotism.

He put out his hand. "I am Arnold Potterley of the History Department. You're new here, I think?"

The youngster looked faintly astonished and fumbled with his drink, shifting it to his left hand in order to shake with his right. "Jonas Foster is my name, sir. I'm a new instructor in physics. I'm just starting this semester."

Potterley nodded. "I wish you a happy stay here and great success."

That was the end of it then. Potterley had come uneasily to his senses, found himself embarrassed and moved off. He stared back over his shoulder once, but the illusion of relationship had gone. Reality was quite real once more and he was angry with himself for having fallen prey to his wife's foolish talk about Laurel.

But a week later, even while Araman was talking, the thought of that young man had come back to him. An instructor in physics. A new instructor. Had he been deaf at the time? Was there a short circuit between ear and brain? Or was it an automatic self-censorship because of the impending interview with the Head of Chronoscopy?

But the interview failed, and it was the thought of the young man with whom he had exchanged two sentences that prevented Potterley from elaborating his pleas for consideration. He was almost anxious to get away.

And in the autogiro express back to the university, he could almost wish he were superstitious. He could then console himself with the thought that the casual meaningless meeting had really been directed by a knowing and purposeful Fate.

Jonas Foster was not new to academic life. The long and rickety struggle for the doctorate would make anyone a veteran. Additional work as a post-doctorate teaching fellow acted as a booster shot.

But now he was Instructor Jonas Foster. Professorial dignity lay ahead. And he now found himself in a new sort of relationship toward other professors.

For one thing, they would be voting on future promotions. For another, he was in no position to tell so early in the game which particular member of the faculty might or might not have the ear of the dean, or even of the university president. He did not fancy himself as a campus politician and was sure he would make a poor one, yet there was no point in kicking his own rear into blisters just to prove that to himself.

So Foster listened to this mild-mannered historian, who in some vague way seemed nevertheless to radiate tension, and did not shut him up abruptly and toss him out. Certainly that was his first impulse.

He remembered Potterley well enough. Potterley had approached him at that tea (which had been a grisly affair). The fellow had spoken two sentences to him stiffly, somehow glassy-eyed, and then come to himself with a visible start and hurried off.

It had amused Foster at the time, but now. . . .

Potterley might have been deliberately trying to make his acquaintance, or, rather, to impress his own personality on Foster as that of a queer sort of duck, eccentric but harmless. He might now be probing Foster's views, searching for unsettling opinions. Surely they ought to have done so before granting him his appointment. Still. . . .

Potterley might be serious, might honestly not realize what he was doing. Or he might realize quite well what he was doing; he might be nothing more or less than a dangerous rascal.

Foster mumbled, "Well, now—" to gain time and fished out a package of cigarettes, intending to offer one to Potterley and to light it and one for himself very slowly.

But Potterley said at once, "Please, Dr. Foster. No cigarettes."

Foster looked startled. "I'm sorry, sir."

"No. The regrets are mine. I cannot stand the odor. An idiosyncrasy. I'm sorry."

He was positively pale. Foster put away the cigarettes.

Foster, feeling the absence of the cigarette, took the easy way out. "I'm flattered that you ask my advice and all that, Dr. Potterley, but I'm not a neutrinics man. I can't very well do anything professional in that direction. Even stating an opinion would be out of line, and, frankly, I'd prefer that you didn't go into any particulars."

The historian's prim face set hard. "What do you mean, you're not a neutrinics man? You're not anything yet. You haven't received any grant, have you?"

"This is only my first semester."

"I know that. I imagine you haven't even applied for any grant yet."

Foster half-smiled. In three months at the university he had not succeeded in putting his initial requests for research grants into good enough shape to pass on to a professional science writer, let alone to the Research Commission.

(His department head, fortunately, took it quite well. "Take your time now, Foster," he said, "and get your thoughts well organized. Make sure you know your path and where it will lead, for once you receive a grant, your specialization will be formally recognized and, for better or for worse, it will be yours for the rest of your career." The advice was trite enough, but triteness has often the merit of truth, and Foster recognized that.)

Foster said, "By education and inclination, Dr. Potterley, I'm a hyperoptics man with a gravitics minor. It's how I described myself in applying for this position. It may not be my official specialization yet, but it's going to be. It can't be anything else. As for neutrinics, I never even studied the subject."

"Why not?" demanded Potterley at once.

Foster stared. It was the kind of rude curiosity about another man's professional status that was always irritating. He said, with the edge of his own politeness just a trifle blunted, "A course in neutrinics wasn't given at my university."

"Good Lord, where did you go?"

"M.I.T.," said Foster quietly.

"And they don't teach neutrinics?"

"No, they don't." Foster felt himself flush and was moved to a defense. "It's a highly specialized subject with no great value. Chronoscopy, perhaps, has some value, but it is the only practical application and that's a dead end."

The historian stared at him earnestly. "Tell me this. Do you know where I can find a neutrinics man?"

"No, I don't," said Foster bluntly.

"Well, then, do you know a school which teaches neutrinics?"

"No, I don't."

Potterley smiled tightly and without humor.

Foster resented that smile, found he detected insult in it and grew sufficiently annoyed to say, "I would like to point out, sir, that you're stepping out of line."

"What?"

"I'm saying that, as a historian, your interest in any sort of physics, your *professional* interest, is—" He paused, unable to bring himself quite to say the word.

"Unethical?"

"That's the word, Dr. Potterley."

"My researches have driven me to it," said Potterley in an intense whisper.

"The Research Commission is the place to go. If they permit—"

"I have gone to them and have received no satisfaction."

"Then obviously you must abandon this." Foster knew he was sounding stuffily virtuous, but he wasn't going to let this man lure him into an expression of intellectual anarchy. It was too early in his career to take stupid risks.

Apparently, though, the remark had its effect on Potterley. Without any warning, the man exploded into a rapid-fire verbal storm of irresponsibility.

Scholars, he said, could be free only if they could freely follow their own free-swinging curiosity. Research, he said, forced into a predesigned pattern by the powers that held the purse strings became slavish and had to stagnate. No man, he said, had the right to dictate the intellectual interests of another.

Foster listened to all of it with disbelief. None of it was strange to him. He had heard college boys talk so in order to shock their professors, and he had once or twice amused himself in that fashion too. Anyone who studied the history of science knew that many men had once thought so.

Yet it seemed strange to Foster, almost against nature, that a modern man of science could advance such nonsense. No one would advocate running a factory by allowing each individual worker to do whatever pleased him at the moment, or of running a ship according to the casual and conflicting notions of each individual crewman. It would be taken for granted that some sort of centralized supervisory agency must exist in each case. Why should direction and order benefit a factory and a ship but not scientific research?

People might say that the human mind was somehow qualitatively different from a ship or factory, but the history of intellectual endeavor proved the opposite.

When science was young and the intricacies of all or most of the known was within the grasp of an individual mind, there was no need for direction, perhaps. Blind wandering over the uncharted tracts of ignorance could lead to wonderful finds by accident.

But as knowledge grew, more and more data had to be absorbed before worthwhile journeys into ignorance could be organized. Men had to specialize. The researcher needed the resources of a library he himself could not gather, then of instruments he himself could not afford. More and more, the individual researcher gave way to the research team and the research institution.

The funds necessary for research grew greater as tools grew more numerous. What college was so small today as not to require at least one nuclear microreactor and at least one three-stage computer?

Centuries before, private individuals could no longer subsidize research. By 1940 only the government, large industries and large universities or research institutions could properly subsidize basic research.

By 1960 even the largest universities depended entirely upon government grants, while research institutions could not exist without tax concessions and public subscriptions. By 2000 the industrial combines had become a branch of the world government, and thereafter the financing of research, and therefore its direction, naturally became centralized under a department of the government.

It all worked itself out naturally and well. Every branch of science was fitted neatly to the needs of the public, and the various branches of science were coordinated decently. The material advance of the last half-century was argument enough for the fact that science was not falling into stagnation.

Foster tried to say a very little of this and was waved aside impatiently by Potterley, who said, "You are parroting official propaganda. You're sitting in the middle of an example that's squarely against the official view. Can you believe that?"

"Frankly, no."

"Well, why do you say time-viewing is a dead end? Why is neutrinics unimportant? You say it is. You say it categorically. Yet you've never studied it. You claim complete ignorance of the subject. It's not even given in your school—"

"Isn't the mere fact that it isn't given proof enough?"

"Oh, I see. It's not given because it's unimportant. And it's unimportant because it's not given. Are you satisfied with that reasoning?"

Foster felt a growing confusion. "It's all in the books."

"That's all? The books say neutrinics is unimportant. Your professors tell you so because they read it in the books. The books say so because professors write them. Who says it from personal experience and knowledge? Who does research in it? Do you know of anyone?"

Foster said, "I don't see that we're getting anywhere, Dr. Potterley. I have work to do—"

"One minute. I just want you to try this on. See how it sounds to you. I say the government is actively suppressing basic research in neutrinics and chronoscopy. They're suppressing application of chronoscopy."

"Oh, no."

"Why not? They could do it. There's your centrally directed research. If they refuse grants for research in any portion of science, that portion dies. They've killed neutrinics. They can do it and have done it."

"But why?"

"I don't know why. I want to find out. I'd do it myself if I knew enough. I came to you because you're a young fellow with a brand-new education. Have your intellectual arteries hardened already? Is there no curiosity in you? Don't you want to *know*? Don't you want *answers*?"

The historian was peering intently into Foster's face. Their noses were only inches apart, and Foster was so lost that he did not think to draw back.

He should, by rights, have ordered Potterley out. If necessary, he should have thrown Potterley out.

It was not respect for age and position that stopped him. It was certainly not that Potterley's arguments had convinced him. Rather, it was a small point of college pride.

Why didn't M.I.T. give a course in neutrinics? For that matter, now that he came to think of it, he doubted that there was a single book on neutrinics in the library. He could never recall having seen one.

He stopped to think about that.

And that was ruin.

Caroline Potterley had once been an attractive woman. There were occasions, such as dinners or university functions, when, by considerable effort, remnants of the attraction could be salvaged.

On ordinary occasions, she sagged. It was the word she applied to herself in moments of self-abhorrence. She had grown plumper with the years, but the flaccidity about her was not a matter of fat entirely. It was as though her muscles had given up and grown limp so that she shuffled when she walked while her eyes grew baggy and her cheeks jowly. Even her graying hair seemed tired rather than merely stringy. Its straightness seemed to be the result of a supine surrender to gravity, nothing else.

Caroline Potterley looked at herself in the mirror and admitted this was one of her bad days. She knew the reason too.

It had been the dream of Laurel. The strange one, with Laurel grown up. She had been wretched ever since.

Still, she was sorry she had mentioned it to Arnold. He didn't say anything; he never did anymore; but it was bad for him. He was particularly withdrawn for days afterward. It might have been that he was getting ready for that important conference with the big government official (he kept saying he expected no success), but it might also have been her dream.

It was better in the old days when he would cry sharply at her, "Let the dead past *go*, Caroline! Talk won't bring her back, and dreams won't either."

It had been bad for both of them. Horribly bad. She had been away from home and had lived in guilt ever since. If she had stayed at home, if she had not gone on an unnecessary shopping expedition, there would have been two of them available. One would have succeeded in saving Laurel.

Poor Arnold had not managed. Heaven knew he tried. He had nearly died himself. He had come out of the burning house, staggering in agony, blistered, choking, half-blinded, with the dead Laurel in his arms.

The nightmare of that lived on, never lifting entirely.

Arnold slowly grew a shell about himself afterward. He cultivated a low-voiced mildness through which nothing broke, no lightning struck. He grew puritanical and even abandoned his minor vices, his cigarettes, his penchant for an occasional profane exclamation. He obtained his grant for the preparation of a new history of Carthage and subordinated everything to that.

She tried to help him. She hunted up his references, typed his notes and microfilmed them. Then that ended suddenly.

She ran from the desk suddenly one evening, reaching the bathroom in bare time and retching abominably. Her husband followed her in confusion and concern.

"Caroline, what's wrong?"

It took a drop of brandy to bring her around. She said, "Is it true? What they did?"

"Who did?"

"The Carthaginians."

He stared at her and she got it out by indirection. She couldn't say it right out.

The Carthaginians, it seemed, worshiped Moloch, in the form of a hollow, brazen idol with a furnace in its belly. At times of national crisis, the priests and the people gathered, and infants, after the proper ceremonies and invocations, were dextrously hurled, alive, into the flames.

They were given sweetmeats just before the crucial moment in order that the efficacy of the sacrifice not be ruined by displeasing cries of panic. The drums rolled just after the moment, to drown out the few seconds of infant shrieking. The parents were present, presumably gratified, for the sacrifice was pleasing to the gods . . .

Arnold Potterley frowned darkly. Vicious lies, he told her, on the part of

Carthage's enemies. He should have warned her. After all, such propagandistic lies were not uncommon. According to the Greeks, the ancient Hebrews worshiped an ass's head in their Holy of Holies. According to the Romans, the primitive Christians were haters of all men who sacrificed pagan children in the catacombs.

"Then they didn't do it?" asked Caroline.

"I'm sure they didn't. The primitive Phoenicians may have. Human sacrifice is commonplace in primitive cultures. But Carthage in her great days was not a primitive culture. Human sacrifice often gives way to symbolic actions such as circumcision. The Greeks and Romans might have mistaken some Carthaginian symbolism for the original full rite, either out of ignorance or out of malice."

"Are you sure?"

"I can't be sure yet, Caroline, but when I've got enough evidence, I'll apply for permission to use chronoscopy, which will settle the matter once and for all."

"Chronoscopy?"

"Time-viewing. We can focus on ancient Carthage at some time of crisis, the landing of Scipio Africanus in 202 B.C., for instance, and see with our own eyes exactly what happens. And you'll see, I'll be right."

He patted her and smiled encouragingly, but she dreamed of Laurel every night for two weeks thereafter and she never helped him with his Carthage project again. Nor did he ever ask her to.

But now she was bracing herself for his coming. He had called her after arriving back in town, told her he had seen the government man and that it had gone as expected. That meant failure, and yet the little telltale sign of depression had been absent from his voice and his features had appeared quite composed in the teleview. He had another errand to take care of, he said, before coming home.

It meant he would be late, but that didn't matter. Neither one of them was particular about eating hours or cared when packages were taken out of the freezer or even which packages or when the self-warming mechanism was activated.

When he did arrive, he surprised her. There was nothing untoward about him in any obvious way. He kissed her dutifully and smiled, took off his hat and asked if all had been well while he was gone. It was almost perfectly normal. Almost.

She had learned to detect small things, though, and his pace in all this was a trifle hurried. Enough to show her accustomed eye that he was under tension.

She said, "Has something happened?"

He said, "We're going to have a dinner guest night after next, Caroline. You don't mind?"

"Well, no. Is it anyone I know?"

"No. A young instructor. A newcomer. I've spoken to him." He suddenly whirled toward her and seized her arms at the elbow, held them a moment, then dropped them in confusion as though disconcerted at having shown emotion.

He said, "I almost didn't get through to him. Imagine that. Terrible, *terrible*, the way we have all bent to the yoke, the affection we have for the harness about us."

Mrs. Potterley wasn't sure she understood, but for a year she had been watching him grow quietly more rebellious, little by little more daring in his criticism of the government. She said, "You haven't spoken foolishly to him, have you?"

"What do you mean, foolishly? He'll be doing some neutrinics for me."

"Neutrinics" was trisyllabic nonsense to Mrs. Potterley, but she knew it had nothing to do with history. She said faintly, "Arnold, I don't like you to do that. You'll lose your position. It's—"

"It's intellectual anarchy, my dear," he said. "That's the phrase you want. Very well. I am an anarchist. If the government will not allow me to push my researches, I will push them on my own. And when I show the way, others will follow. . . . And if they don't, it makes no difference. It's Carthage that counts and human knowledge, not you and I."

"But you don't know this young man. What if he is an agent for the Commissioner of Research?"

"Not likely, and I'll take that chance." He made a fist of his right hand and rubbed it gently against the palm of his left. "He's on my side now. I'm sure of it. He can't help but be. I can recognize intellectual curiosity when I see it in a man's eyes and face and attitude, and it's a fatal disease for a tame scientist. Even today it takes time to beat it out of a man, and the young ones are vulnerable. . . . Oh, why stop at anything? Why not build our own chronoscope and tell the government to go to—"

He stopped abruptly, shook his head and turned away.

"I hope everything will be all right," said Mrs. Potterley, feeling helplessly certain that everything would not be, and frightened, in advance, for her husband's professional status and the security of their old age.

It was she alone, of them all, who had a violent presentiment of trouble. Quite the wrong trouble, of course.

.   .   .

Jonas Foster was nearly half an hour late in arriving at the Potterleys' off-campus house. Up to that very evening he had not quite decided he would go. Then, at the last moment, he found he could not bring himself to commit the social enormity of breaking a dinner appointment an hour before the appointed time. That, and the nagging of curiosity.

The dinner itself passed interminably. Foster ate without appetite. Mrs. Potterley sat in distant absentmindedness, emerging out of it only once to ask if he were married and to make a deprecating sound at the news that he was not. Dr. Potterley himself asked neutrally after his professional history and nodded his head primly.

It was as staid, stodgy—boring, actually—as anything could be.

Foster thought: He seems so harmless.

Foster had spent the last two days reading up on Dr. Potterley. Very casually, of course, almost sneakily. He wasn't particularly anxious to be seen in the social-science library. To be sure, history was one of those borderline affairs, and historical works were frequently read for amusement or edification by the general public.

Still, a physicist wasn't quite the "general public." Let Foster take to reading histories and he would be considered queer, sure as relativity, and after a while the head of the department would wonder if his new instructor were really "the man for the job."

So he had been cautious. He sat in the more secluded alcoves and kept his head bent when he slipped in and out at odd hours.

Dr. Potterley, it turned out, had written three books and some dozen articles on the ancient Mediterranean worlds, and the later articles (all in *Historical Reviews*) had all dealt with pre-Roman Carthage from a sympathetic viewpoint.

That, at least, checked with Potterley's story and had soothed Foster's suspicions somewhat. . . . And yet Foster felt that it would have been much wiser, much safer, to have scotched the matter at the beginning.

A scientist shouldn't be too curious, he thought in bitter dissatisfaction with himself. It's a dangerous trait.

After dinner he was ushered into Potterley's study and he was brought up sharply at the threshold. The walls were simply lined with books.

Not merely films. There were films, of course, but these were far outnumbered by the books—print on paper. He wouldn't have thought so many books would exist in usable condition.

That bothered Foster. Why should anyone want to keep so many books at home? Surely all were available in the university library, or, at the very worst, at the Library of Congress, if one wished to take the minor trouble of checking out a microfilm.

There was an element of secrecy involved in a home library. It breathed of intellectual anarchy. That last thought, oddly, calmed Foster. He would rather Potterley be an authentic anarchist than a play-acting *agent provocateur.*

And now the hours began to pass quickly and astonishingly.

"You see," Potterley said in a clear, unflurried voice, "it was a matter of finding, if possible, anyone who had ever used chronoscopy in his work. Naturally I couldn't ask baldly, since that would be unauthorized research."

"Yes," said Foster dryly. He was a little surprised that such a small consideration would stop the man.

"I used indirect methods—"

He had. Foster was amazed at the volume of correspondence dealing with small, disputed points of ancient Mediterranean culture which somehow managed to elicit the casual remark over and over again: "Of course, having never made use of chronoscopy—" or, "Pending approval of my request for chronoscopic data, which appears unlikely at the moment—"

"Now these aren't blind questionings," said Potterley. "There's a monthly booklet put out by the Institute for Chronoscopy in which items concerning the past as determined by time-viewing are printed. Just one or two items.

"What impressed me first was the triviality of most of the items, their insipidity. Why should such researches get priority over my work? So I wrote to people who would be most likely to do research in the directions described in the booklet. Uniformly, as I have shown you, they did *not* make use of the chronoscope. Now let's go over it point by point."

At last Foster, his head swimming with Potterley's meticulously gathered details, asked, "But why?"

"I don't know why," said Potterley, "but I have a theory. The original invention of the chronoscope was by Sterbinski—you see, I know that much—and it was well publicized. Then the government took over the instrument and decided to suppress further research in the matter or any use of the machine. But then people might be curious as to why it wasn't being used. Curiosity is such a vice, Dr. Foster."

Yes, agreed the physicist to himself.

"Imagine the effectiveness, then," Potterley went on, "of pretending that the chronoscope was being used. It would then be not a mystery, but a commonplace. It would no longer be a fitting object for legitimate curiosity or an attractive one for illicit curiosity."

"*You* were curious," pointed out Foster.

Potterley looked a trifle restless. "It was different in my case," he said angrily. "I have something that *must* be done, and I wouldn't submit to the ridiculous way in which they kept putting me off."

A bit paranoid too, thought Foster gloomily.

Yet he had ended up with something, paranoid or not. Foster could no longer deny that something peculiar was going on in the matter of neutrinics.

But what was Potterley after? That still bothered Foster. If Potterley didn't intend this as a test of Foster's ethics, what *did* he want?

Foster put it to himself logically. If an intellectual anarchist with a touch of paranoia wanted to use a chronoscope and was convinced that the powers-that-be were deliberately standing in his way, what would he do?

Supposing it were I, he thought. What would I do?

He said slowly, "Maybe the chronoscope doesn't exist at all?"

Potterley started. There was almost a crack in his general calmness. For an instant Foster found himself catching a glimpse of something not at all calm.

But the historian kept his balance and said, "Oh, no, there *must* be a chronoscope."

"Why? Have you seen it? Have I? Maybe that's the explanation of everything. Maybe they're not deliberately holding out on a chronoscope they've got. Maybe they haven't got it in the first place."

"But Sterbinski lived. He built a chronoscope. That much is a fact."

"The book says so," said Foster coldly.

"Now listen." Potterley actually reached over and snatched at Foster's jacket sleeve. "I need the chronoscope. I must have it. Don't tell me it doesn't exist. What we're going to do is find out enough about neutrinics to be able to—"

Potterley drew himself up short.

Foster drew his sleeve away. He needed no ending to that sentence. He supplied it himself. He said, "Build one of our own?"

Potterley looked sour, as though he would rather not have said it point-blank. Nevertheless, he said, "Why not?"

"Because that's out of the question," said Foster. "If what I've read is correct, then it took Sterbinski twenty years to build his machine and several millions in composite grants. Do you think you and I can duplicate that illegally? Suppose we had the time, which we haven't, and suppose I could learn enough out of books, which I doubt, where would we get the money and equipment? The chronoscope is supposed to fill a five-story building, for heaven's sake."

"Then you won't help me?"

"Well, I'll tell you what. I have one way in which I may be able to find out something—"

"What is that?" asked Potterley at once.

"Never mind. That's not important. But I may be able to find out enough to tell you whether the government is deliberately suppressing research by chronoscope. I may confirm the evidence you already have or I may be able to prove that your evidence is misleading. I don't know what good it will do you in either case, but it's as far as I can go. It's my limit."

Potterley watched the young man go finally. He was angry with himself. Why had he allowed himself to grow so careless as to permit the fellow to guess that he was thinking in terms of a chronoscope of his own? That was premature.

But then why did the young fool have to suppose that a chronoscope might not exist at all?

It *had* to exist. It *had* to. What was the use of saying it didn't?

And why couldn't a second one be built? Science had advanced in the fifty years since Sterbinski. All that was needed was knowledge.

Let the youngster gather knowledge. Let him think a small gathering would be his limit. Having taken the path to anarchy, there would be no limit. If the boy were not driven onward by something in himself, the first steps would be error enough to force the rest. Potterley was quite certain he would not hesitate to use blackmail.

Potterley waved a last good-bye and looked up. It was beginning to rain.

Certainly! Blackmail if necessary, but he would not be stopped.

Foster steered his car across the bleak outskirts of town and scarcely noticed the rain.

He *was* a fool, he told himself, but he couldn't leave things as they were. He had to know. He damned his streak of undisciplined curiosity, but he had to know.

But he would go no further than Uncle Ralph. He swore mightily to himself that it would stop there. In that way there would be no evidence against him, no real evidence. Uncle Ralph would be discreet.

In a way he was secretly ashamed of Uncle Ralph. He hadn't mentioned him to Potterley partly out of caution and partly because he did not wish to witness the lifted eyebrow, the inevitable half-smile. Professional science writers, however useful, were a little outside the pale, fit only for patronizing contempt. The fact that, as a class, they made more money than did research scientists only made matters worse, of course.

Still, there were times when a science writer in the family could be a convenience. Not being really educated, they did not have to specialize.

Consequently, a good science writer knew practically everything. . . . And Uncle Ralph was one of the best.

Ralph Nimmo had no college degree and was rather proud of it. "A degree," he once said to Jonas Foster, when both were considerably younger, "is a first step down a ruinous highway. You don't want to waste it so you go on to graduate work and doctoral research. You end up a thorough-going ignoramus on everything in the world except for one subdivisional sliver of nothing.

"On the other hand, if you guard your mind carefully and keep it blank of any clutter of information till maturity is reached, filling it only with intelligence and training it only in clear thinking, you then have a powerful instrument at your disposal and you can become a science writer."

Nimmo received his first assignment at the age of twenty-five, after he had completed his apprenticeship and been out in the field for less than three months. It came in the shape of a clotted manuscript whose language would impart no glimmering of understanding to any reader, however qualified, without careful study and some inspired guesswork. Nimmo took it apart and put it together again (after five long and exasperating interviews with the authors, who were biophysicists), making the language taut and meaningful and smoothing the style to a pleasant gloss.

"Why not?" he would say tolerantly to his nephew, who countered his strictures on degrees by berating him with his readiness to hang on the fringes of science. "The fringe is important. Your scientists can't write. Why should they be expected to? They aren't expected to be grand masters at chess or virtuosos at the violin, so why expect them to know how to put words together? Why not leave that for specialists too?

"Good Lord, Jonas, read your literature of a hundred years ago. Discount the fact that the science is out of date and that some of the expressions are out of date. Just try to read it and make sense out of it. It's just jaw-cracking, amateurish. Pages are published uselessly—whole articles which are either nonsignificant, noncomprehensible or both."

"But you don't get recognition, Uncle Ralph," protested young Foster, who was getting ready to start his college career and was rather starry-eyed about it. "You could be a terrific researcher."

"I get recognition," said Nimmo. "Don't think for a minute I don't. Sure, a biochemist or a strato-meteorologist won't give me the time of day, but they pay me well enough. Just find out what happens when some first-class chemist finds the Commission has cut his year's allowance for science writing. He'll fight harder for enough funds to afford me, or someone like me, than to get a recording ionograph."

He grinned broadly and Foster grinned back. Actually, he was proud of his paunchy, round-faced, stub-fingered uncle, whose vanity made him brush his fringe of hair futilely over the desert on his pate and made him dress like an unmade haystack because such negligence was his trademark. Ashamed, but proud too.

And now Foster entered his uncle's cluttered apartment in no mood at all for grinning. He was nine years older now and so was Uncle Ralph. For nine more years, papers in every branch of science had come to him for polishing and a little of each had crept into his capacious mind.

Nimmo was eating seedless grapes, popping them into his mouth one at a time. He tossed a bunch to Foster, who caught them by a hair, then bent to retrieve individual grapes that had torn loose and fallen to the floor.

"Let them be. Don't bother," said Nimmo carelessly. "Someone comes in here to clean once a week. What's up? Having trouble with your grant application write-up?"

"I haven't really got into that yet."

"You haven't? Get a move on, boy. Are you waiting for me to offer to do the final arrangement?"

"I couldn't afford you, Uncle."

"Aw, come on. It's all in the family. Grant me all popular-publication rights and no cash need change hands."

Foster nodded. "If you're serious, it's a deal."

"It's a deal."

It was a gamble, of course, but Foster knew enough of Nimmo's science writing to realize it could pay off. Some dramatic discovery of public interest on primitive man or on a new surgical technique, or on any branch of spationautics could mean a very cash-attracting article in any of the mass media of communication.

It was Nimmo, for instance, who had written up, for scientific consumption, the series of papers by Bryce and coworkers that elucidated the fine structure of two cancer viruses, for which job he asked the picayune payment of fifteen hundred dollars, provided popular-publication rights were included. He then wrote up, exclusively, the same work in semidramatic form for use in trimensional video for a twenty-thousand-dollar advance plus rental royalties that were still coming in after five years.

Foster said bluntly, "What do you know about neutrinics, Uncle?"

"Neutrinics?" Nimmo's small eyes looked surprised. "Are you working in that? I thought it was pseudo-gravitic optics."

"It is p.g.o. I just happen to be asking about neutrinics."

"That's a devil of a thing to be doing. You're stepping out of line. You know that, don't you?"

"I don't expect you to call the Commission because I'm a little curious about things."

"Maybe I should before you get into trouble. Curiosity is an occupational danger with scientists. I've watched it work. One of them will be moving quietly along on a problem, then curiosity leads him up a strange creek. Next thing you know, he's done so little on his proper problem, he can't justify for a project renewal. I've seen more—"

"All I want to know," said Foster patiently, "is what's been passing through your hands lately on neutrinics."

Nimmo leaned back, chewing at a grape thoughtfully. "Nothing. Nothing ever. I don't recall ever getting a paper on neutrinics."

"What!" Foster was openly astonished. "Then who does get the work?"

"Now that you ask," said Nimmo, "I don't know. Don't recall anyone talking about it at the annual conventions. I don't think much work is being done there."

"Why not?"

"Hey, there, don't bark. I'm not doing anything. My guess would be—"

Foster was exasperated. "Don't you know?"

"Hmp. I'll tell you what I know about neutrinics. It concerns the applications of neutrino movements and the forces involved—"

"Sure. Sure. Just as electronics deals with the applications of electron movements and the forces involved, and pseudo-gravitics deals with the applications of artificial gravitational fields. I didn't come to you for that. Is that all you know?"

"And," said Nimmo with equanimity, "neutrinics is the basis of time-viewing and that *is* all I know."

Foster slouched back in his chair and massaged one lean cheek with great intensity. He felt angrily dissatisfied. Without formulating it explicitly in his own mind, he had felt sure, somehow, that Nimmo would come up with some late reports, bring up interesting facets of modern neutrinics, send him back to Potterley able to say that the elderly historian was wrong, that his data was misleading, his deductions mistaken.

Then he could have returned to his proper work.

But now. . . .

He told himself angrily: So they're not doing much work in the field. Does that make it deliberate suppression? What if neutrinics is a sterile discipline? Maybe it is. I don't know. Potterley doesn't. Why waste the intellectual resources of humanity on nothing? Or the work might be secret for some legitimate reason. It might be. . . .

The trouble was, he had to know. He couldn't leave things as they were now. He *couldn't!*

He said, "Is there a text on neutrinics, Uncle Ralph? I mean a clear and simple one. An elementary one."

Nimmo thought, his plump cheeks puffing out with a series of sighs. "You ask the damnedest questions. The only one I ever heard of was Sterbinski and somebody. I've never seen it, but I viewed something about it once. . . . Sterbinski and LaMarr, that's it."

"Is that the Sterbinski who invented the chronoscope?"

"I think so. Proves the book ought to be good."

"Is there a recent edition? Sterbinski died thirty years ago."

Nimmo shrugged and said nothing.

"Can you find out?"

They sat in silence for a moment while Nimmo shifted his bulk to the creaking tune of the chair he sat on. Then the science writer said, "Are you going to tell me what this is all about?"

"I can't. Will you help me anyway, Uncle Ralph? Will you get me a copy of the text?"

"Well, you've taught me all I know on pseudo-gravitics. I should be grateful. Tell you what—I'll help you on one condition."

"Which is?"

The old man was suddenly very grave. "That you be careful, Jonas. You're obviously way out of line, whatever you're doing. Don't blow up your career just because you're curious about something you haven't been assigned to and which is none of your business. Understand?"

Foster nodded, but he hardly heard. He was thinking furiously.

A full week later Ralph Nimmo eased his rotund figure into Jonas Foster's on-campus two-room combination and said in a hoarse whisper, "I've got something."

"What?" Foster was immediately eager.

"A copy of Sterbinski and LaMarr." He produced it, or rather a corner of it, from his ample topcoat.

Foster almost automatically eyed door and windows to make sure they were closed and shaded respectively, then held out his hand.

The film case was flaking with age, and when he cracked it, the film was faded and growing brittle. He said sharply, "Is this all?"

"Gratitude, my boy, gratitude!" Nimmo sat down with a grunt and reached into a pocket for an apple.

"Oh, I'm grateful, but it's so old."

"And lucky to get it at that. I tried to get a film run from the Congressional Library. No go. The book was restricted."

"Then how did you get this?"

"Stole it." He was biting crunchingly around the core. "New York Public."

"'What?"

"Simple enough. I had access to the stacks, naturally. So I stepped over a chained railing when no one was around, dug this up, and walked out with it. They're very trusting out there. Meanwhile, they won't miss it for years. . . . Only you'd better not let anyone see it on you, Nephew."

Foster stared at the film as though it were literally hot.

Nimmo discarded the core and reached for a second apple. "Funny thing, now. There's nothing more recent in the whole field of neutrinics. Not a monograph, not a paper, not a progress note. Nothing since the chronoscope."

"Uh-huh," said Foster absently.

Foster worked evenings in the Potterley home. He could not trust his own on-campus rooms for the purpose. The evening work grew more real to him than his own grant applications. Sometimes he worried about it, but then that stopped too.

His work consisted, at first, simply in viewing and reviewing the text film. Later it consisted in thinking (sometimes while a section of the book ran itself off through the pocket projector, disregarded).

Sometimes Potterley would come down to watch, to sit with prim, eager eyes, as though he expected thought processes to solidify and become visible in all their convolutions. He interfered in only two ways. He did not allow Foster to smoke and sometimes he talked.

It wasn't conversation talk, never that. Rather it was a low-voiced monologue with which, it seemed, he scarcely expected to command attention. It was much more as though he were relieving a pressure within himself.

Carthage! Always Carthage!

Carthage, the New York of the ancient Mediterranean. Carthage, commercial empire and queen of the seas. Carthage, all that Syracuse and Alexandria pretended to be. Carthage, maligned by her enemies and inarticulate in her own defense.

She had been defeated once by Rome and then driven out of Sicily and

Sardinia, but came back to more than recoup her losses by new dominions in Spain, and raised up Hannibal to give the Romans sixteen years of terror.

In the end she lost a second time, reconciled herself to fate and built again with broken tools a limping life in shrunken territory, succeeding so well that jealous Rome deliberately forced a third war. And then Carthage, with nothing but bare hands and tenacity, built weapons and forced Rome into a two-year war that ended only with complete destruction of the city, the inhabitants throwing themselves into their flaming houses rather than surrender.

"Could people fight so for a city and a way of life as bad as the ancient writers painted it? Hannibal was a better general than any Roman and his soldiers were absolutely faithful to him. Even his bitterest enemies praised him. There was a Carthaginian. It is fashionable to say that he was an atypical Carthaginian, better than the others, a diamond placed in garbage. But then why was he so faithful to Carthage, even to his death after years of exile? They talk of Moloch—"

Foster didn't always listen but sometimes he couldn't help himself and he shuddered and turned sick at the bloody tale of child sacrifice.

But Potterley went on earnestly, "Just the same, it isn't true. It's a twenty-five-hundred-year-old canard started by the Greeks and Romans. They had their own slaves, their crucifixions and torture, their gladiatorial contests. They weren't holy. The Moloch story is what later ages would have called war propaganda, the big lie. I can prove it was a lie. I can prove it and, by heaven, I will—I will—"

He would mumble that promise over and over again in his earnestness.

Mrs. Potterley visited him also, but less frequently, usually on Tuesdays and Thursdays when Dr. Potterley himself had an evening course to take care of and was not present.

She would sit quietly, scarcely talking, face slack and doughy, eyes blank, her whole attitude distant and withdrawn.

The first time, Foster tried, uneasily, to suggest that she leave.

She said tonelessly, "Do I disturb you?"

"No, of course not," lied Foster restlessly. "It's just that—that—" He couldn't complete the sentence.

She nodded, as though accepting an invitation to stay. Then she opened a cloth bag she had brought with her and took out a quire of vitron sheets which she proceeded to weave together by rapid, delicate movements of a pair of slender, tetra-faceted depolarizers whose battery-fed wires made her look as though she were holding a large spider.

One evening she said softly, "My daughter, Laurel, is your age."

Foster started, as much at the sudden, unexpected sound of speech as at the words. He said, "I didn't know you had a daughter, Mrs. Potterley."

"She died. Years ago."

The vitron grew under the deft manipulations into the uneven shape of some garment Foster could not yet identify. There was nothing left for him to do but mutter inanely, "I'm sorry."

Mrs. Potterley sighed. "I dream about her often." She raised her blue, distant eyes to him.

Foster winced and looked away.

Another evening she asked, pulling at one of the vitron sheets to loosen its gentle clinging to her dress, "What is time-viewing anyway?"

That remark broke into a particularly involved chain of thought, and Foster said snappishly, "Dr. Potterley can explain."

"He's tried to. Oh, my, yes. But I think he's a little impatient with me. He calls it chronoscopy most of the time. Do you actually see things in the past, like the trimensionals? Or does it just make little dot patterns like the computer you use?"

Foster stared at his hand computer with distaste. It worked well enough, but every operation had to be manually controlled and the answers were obtained in code. Now if he could use the school computer . . . well, why dream? He felt conspicuous enough as it was, carrying a hand computer under his arm every evening as he left his office.

He said, "I've never seen the chronoscope myself, but I'm under the impression that you actually see pictures and hear sound."

"You can hear people talk, too?"

"I think so." Then, half in desperation, "Look here, Mrs. Potterley, this must be awfully dull for you. I realize you don't like to leave a guest all to himself, but really, Mrs. Potterley, you mustn't feel compelled—"

"I don't feel compelled," she said. "I'm sitting here waiting."

"Waiting? For what?"

She said composedly, "I listened to you that first evening. The time you first spoke to Arnold. I listened at the door."

He said, "You did?"

"I know I shouldn't have, but I was awfully worried about Arnold. I had a notion he was going to do something he oughtn't and I wanted to hear what. And then when I heard—" She paused, bending close over the vitron and peering at it.

"Heard what, Mrs. Potterley?"

"That you wouldn't build a chronoscope."

"Well, of course not."

"I thought maybe you might change your mind."

Foster glared at her. "Do you mean you're coming down here hoping I'll build a chronoscope, waiting for me to build one?"

"I hope you do, Dr. Foster. Oh, I hope you do."

It was as though, all at once, a fuzzy veil had fallen off her face, leaving all her features clear and sharp, putting color into her cheeks, life into her eyes, the vibrations of something approaching excitement into her voice.

"Wouldn't it be wonderful," she whispered, "to have one? People of the past could live again. Pharaohs and kings and—just people. I hope you build one, Dr. Foster. I really—hope—"

She choked, it seemed, on the intensity of her own words and let the vitron sheets slip off her lap. She rose and ran up the basement stairs while Foster's eyes followed her awkwardly fleeing body with astonishment and distress.

It cut deeper into Foster's nights and left him sleepless and painfully stiff with thought. It was almost a mental indigestion.

His grant requests went limping in, finally, to Ralph Nimmo. He scarcely had any hope for them. He thought numbly: They won't be approved.

If they weren't, of course, it would create a scandal in the department and probably mean his appointment at the university would not be renewed, come the end of the academic year.

He scarcely worried. It was the neutrino, the neutrino, only the neutrino. Its trail curved and veered sharply and led him breathlessly along unchartered pathways that even Sterbinski and LeMarr did not follow.

He called Nimmo. "Uncle Ralph, I need a few things. I'm calling from off the campus."

Nimmo's face in the video plate was jovial but his voice was sharp. He said, "What you need is a course in communication. I'm having a hell of a time pulling your application into one intelligible piece. If that's what you're calling about—"

Foster shook his head impatiently. "That's *not* what I'm calling about. I need these." He scribbled quickly on a piece of paper and held it up before the receiver.

Nimmo yiped. "Hey, how many tricks do you think I can wangle?"

"You can get them, Uncle. You know you can."

Nimmo reread the list of items with silent motions of his plump lips and looked grave.

"What happens when you put those things together?" he asked.

Foster shook his head. "You'll have exclusive popular-publication rights to whatever turns up, the way it's always been. But please don't ask any questions now."

"I can't do miracles, you know."

"Do this one. You've got to. You're a science writer, not a research man. You don't have to account for anything. You've got friends and connections. They can look the other way, can't they, to get a break from you next publication time?"

"Your faith, Nephew, is touching. I'll try."

Nimmo succeeded. The material and equipment were brought over late one evening in a private touring car. Nimmo and Foster lugged it in with the grunting of men unused to manual labor.

Potterley stood at the entrance of the basement after Nimmo had left. He asked softly, "What's this for?"

Foster brushed the hair off his forehead and gently massaged a sprained wrist. He said, "I want to conduct a few simple experiments."

"Really?" The historian's eyes glittered with excitement.

Foster felt exploited. He felt as though he were being led along a dangerous highway by the pull of pinching fingers on his nose; as though he could see the ruin clearly that lay in wait at the end of the path, yet walked eagerly and determinedly. Worst of all, he felt the compelling grip on his nose to be his own.

It was Potterley who began it, Potterley who stood there now, gloating; but the compulsion was his own.

Foster said sourly, "I'll be wanting privacy now, Potterley. I can't have you and your wife running down here and annoying me."

He thought: If that offends him, let him kick me out. Let him put an end to this.

In his heart, though, he did not think being evicted would stop anything.

But it did not come to that. Potterley was showing no signs of offense. His mild gaze was unchanged. He said, "Of course, Dr. Foster, of course. All the privacy you wish."

Foster watched him go. He was left still marching along the highway, perversely glad of it and hating himself for being glad.

He took to sleeping over on a cot in Potterley's basement and spending his weekends there entirely.

During that period, preliminary word came through that his grants (as doctored by Nimmo) had been approved. The department head brought the word and congratulated him.

Foster stared back distantly and mumbled, "Good. I'm glad," with so little conviction that the other frowned and turned away without another word.

Foster gave the matter no further thought. It was a minor point, worth no notice. He was planning something that really counted, a climactic test for that evening.

One evening, a second and third and then, haggard and half beside himself with excitement, he called in Potterley.

Potterley came down the stairs and looked about at the homemade gadgetry. He said in his soft voice, "The electric bills are quite high. I don't mind the expense, but the City may ask questions. Can anything be done?"

It was a warm evening but Potterley wore a tight collar and a semi-jacket. Foster, who was in his undershirt, lifted bleary eyes and said shakily, "It won't be for much longer, Dr. Potterley. I've called you down to tell you something. A chronoscope can be built. A small one, of course, but it can be built."

Potterley seized the railing. His body sagged. He managed a whisper. "Can it be built here?"

"Here in the basement," said Foster wearily.

"Good Lord. You said—"

"I know what I said," cried Foster impatiently. "I said it couldn't be done. I didn't know anything then. Even Sterbinski didn't know anything."

Potterley shook his head. "Are you sure? You're not mistaken, Dr. Foster? I couldn't endure it if—"

Foster said, "I'm not mistaken. Damn it, sir, if just theory had been enough, we could have had a time-viewer over a hundred years ago, when the neutrino was first postulated. The trouble was, the original investigators considered it only a mysterious particle without mass or charge that could not be detected. It was just something to even up the bookkeeping and save the law of conservation of mass and energy."

He wasn't sure Potterley knew what he was talking about. He didn't care. He needed a breather. He had to get some of this out of his clotting thoughts. . . . And he needed background for what he would have to tell Potterley next.

He went on. "It was Sterbinski who first discovered that the neutrino broke through the space-time cross-sectional barrier, that it traveled through time as well as through space. It was Sterbinski who first devised a method for stopping neutrinos. He invented a neutrino recorder and learned how to interpret the pattern of the neutrino stream. Naturally the stream had been affected and deflected by all the matter it had passed through in its passage through time, and the deflections could be analyzed and converted into the images of the matter that had done the deflecting. Time-viewing was possible. Even air vibrations could be detected in this way and converted into sound."

Potterley was definitely not listening. He said, "Yes. Yes. But when can you build a chronoscope?"

Foster said urgently, "Let me finish. Everything depends on the method used to detect and analyze the neutrino stream. Sterbinski's method was difficult and roundabout. It required mountains of energy. But I've studied pseudo-gravitics, Dr. Potterley, the science of artificial gravitational fields. I've specialized in the behavior of light in such fields. It's a new science. Sterbinski knew nothing of it. If he had, he would have seen—anyone would have—a much better and more efficient method of detecting neutrinos using a pseudo-gravitic field. If I had known more neutrinics to begin with, I would have seen it at once."

Potterley brightened a bit. "I knew it," he said. "Even if they stop research in neutrinics, there is no way the government can be sure that discoveries in other segments of science won't reflect knowledge on neutrinics. So much for the value of centralized direction of science. I thought this long ago, Dr. Foster, before you ever came to work here."

"I congratulate you on that," said Foster, "but there's one thing—"

"Oh, never mind all this. Answer me. Please. When can you build a chronoscope?"

"I'm trying to tell you something, Dr. Potterley. A chronoscope won't do you any good." (This is it, Foster thought.)

Slowly Potterley descended the stairs. He stood facing Foster. "What do you mean? Why won't it help me?"

"You won't see Carthage. It's what I've got to tell you. It's what I've been leading up to. You can never see Carthage."

Potterley shook his head slightly. "Oh, no, you're wrong. If you have the chronoscope, just focus it properly—"

"No, Dr. Potterley. It's not a question of focus. There are random factors affecting the neutrino stream, as they affect all subatomic particles. What we call the uncertainty principle. When the stream is recorded and interpreted, the random factor comes out as fuzziness, or 'noise,' as the communications boys speak of it. The farther back in time you penetrate, the more pronounced the fuzziness, the greater the noise. After a while the noise drowns out the picture. Do you understand?"

"More power," said Potterley in a dead kind of voice.

"That won't help. When the noise blurs out detail, magnifying detail magnifies the noise too. You can't see anything in a sun-burned film by enlarging it, can you? Get this through your head now. The physical nature of the Universe sets limits. The random thermal motions of air molecules set limits to how weak a sound can be detected by any instrument. The length of a light wave or of an electron wave sets limits to the size of objects that can be seen by any instrument. It works that way in chronoscopy too. You can only time-view so far."

"How far? How far?"

Foster took a deep breath. "A century and a quarter. That's the most."

"But the monthly bulletin the Commission puts out deals with ancient history almost entirely." The historian laughed shakily. "You must be wrong. The government has data as far back as 3000 B.C."

"When did you switch to believing them?" demanded Foster scornfully. "You began this business by proving they were lying, that no historian had made use of the chronoscope. Don't you see why now? No historian, except one interested in contemporary history, could. No chronoscope can possibly see back in time farther than 1920 under any conditions."

"You're wrong. You don't know everything," said Potterley.

"The truth won't bend itself to your convenience either. Face it. The government's part in this is to perpetrate a hoax."

"Why?"

"I don't know why."

Potterley's snubby nose was twitching. His eyes were bulging. He pleaded, "It's only theory, Dr. Foster. Build a chronoscope. Build one and try."

Foster caught Potterley's shoulders in a sudden, fierce grip. "Do you think I haven't? Do you think I would tell you this before I had checked it every way I knew? I *have* built one. It's all around you. Look!"

He ran to the switches at the power leads. He flicked them on, one by one. He turned a resistor, adjusted other knobs, put out the cellar lights. "Wait. Let it warm up."

There was a small glow near the center of one wall. Potterley was gibbering incoherently but Foster only cried again, "Look!"

The light sharpened and brightened, broke up into a light-and-dark pattern. Men and women! Fuzzy. Features blurred. Arms and legs mere streaks. An old-fashioned ground car, unclear but recognizable as one of the kind that had once used gasoline-powered internal-combustion engines, sped by.

Foster said, "Mid-twentieth century, somewhere. I can't hook up an audio yet so this is soundless. Eventually we can add sound. Anyway, mid-twentieth is almost as far back as you can go. Believe me, that's the best focusing that can be done."

Potterley said, "Build a larger machine, a stronger one. Improve your circuits."

"You can't lick the uncertainty principle, man, any more than you can live on the sun. There are physical limits to what can be done."

"You're lying. I won't believe you. I—"

A new voice sounded, raised shrilly to make itself heard.

"Arnold! Dr. Foster!"

The young physicist turned at once. Dr. Potterley froze for a long moment, then said without turning, "What is it, Caroline? Leave us."

"No!" Mrs. Potterley descended the stairs. "I heard. I couldn't help hearing. Do you have a time-viewer here, Dr. Foster? Here in the basement?"

"Yes, I do, Mrs. Potterley. A kind of time-viewer. Not a good one. I can't get sound yet and the picture is darned blurry, but it works."

Mrs. Potterley clasped her hands and held them tightly against her breast. "How wonderful. How wonderful."

"It's not at all wonderful," snapped Potterley. "The young fool can't reach farther back than—"

"Now, look," began Foster in exasperation.

"Please!" cried Mrs. Potterley. "Listen to me. Arnold, don't you see that as long as we can use it for twenty years back, we can see Laurel once again? What do we care about Carthage and ancient times? It's Laurel we can see. She'll be alive for us again. Leave the machine here, Dr. Foster. Show us how to work it."

Foster stared at her, then at her husband. Dr. Potterley's face had gone white. Though his voice stayed low and even, its calmness was somehow gone. He said, "You're a fool!"

Caroline said weakly, "Arnold!"

"You're a fool, I say. What will you see? The past. The dead past. Will Laurel do one thing she did not do? Will you see one thing you haven't seen? Will you live three years over and over again, watching a baby who'll never grow up no matter how long you watch?"

His voice came near to cracking, but held. He stepped closer to her, seized her shoulder and shook her roughly. "Do you know what will happen to you if you do that? They'll come to take you away because you'll go mad. Yes, mad. Do you want mental treatment? Do you want to be shut up, to undergo the psychic probe?"

Mrs. Potterley tore away. There was no trace of softness or vagueness about her. She had twisted into a virago. "I want to see my child, Arnold. She's in that machine and I want her."

"She's *not* in the machine. An image is. Can't you understand? An image! Something that's not real!"

"I want my child. Do you hear me?" She flew at him, screaming, fists beating. "*I want my child.*"

The historian retreated at the fury of the assault, crying out. Foster moved to step between them, when Mrs. Potterley dropped, sobbing wildly, to the floor.

Potterley turned, eyes desperately seeking. With a sudden heave, he snatched at a Lando-rod, tearing it from its support and whirling away before Foster, numbed by all that was taking place, could move to stop him.

"Stand back!" gasped Potterley, "or I'll kill you. I swear it."

He swung with force, and Foster jumped back.

Potterley turned with fury on every part of the structure in the cellar, and Foster, after the first crash of glass, watched dazedly.

Potterley spent his rage and then he was standing quietly amid shards and splinters, with a broken Lando-rod in his hand. He said to Foster in a whisper, "Now get out of here! Never come back! If any of this cost you anything, send me a bill and I'll pay for it. I'll pay double."

Foster shrugged, picked up his shirt and moved up the basement stairs. He could hear Mrs. Potterley sobbing loudly, and as he turned at the head of the stairs for a last look, he saw Dr. Potterley bending over her, his face convulsed with sorrow.

Two days later, with the school day drawing to a close and Foster looking wearily about to see if there were any data on his newly approved projects that he wished to take home, Dr. Potterley appeared once more. He was standing at the open door of Foster's office.

The historian was neatly dressed as ever. He lifted his hand in a gesture that was too vague to be a greeting, too abortive to be a plea. Foster stared stonily.

Potterley said, "I waited till five, till you were . . . may I come in?"

Foster nodded.

Potterley said, "I suppose I ought to apologize for my behavior. I was dreadfully disappointed, not quite master of myself. Still, it was inexcusable."

"I accept your apology," said Foster. "Is that all?"

"My wife called you, I think."

"Yes, she has."

"She has been quite hysterical. She told me she had but I couldn't be quite sure—"

"She has called me."

"Could you tell me—would you be so kind as to tell me what she wanted?"

"She wanted a chronoscope. She said she had some money of her own. She was willing to pay."

"Did you—make any commitments?"

"I said I wasn't in the manufacturing business."

"Good," breathed Potterley, his chest expanding with a sign of relief. "Please don't take any calls from her. She's not—quite—"

"Look, Dr. Potterley," said Foster, "I'm not getting into any domestic quarrels, but you'd better be prepared for something. Chronoscopes can be built by anybody. Given a few simple parts that can be bought through some etherics sales center, they can be built in the home workshop. The video part, anyway."

"But no one else will think of it besides you, will they? No one has."

"I don't intend to keep it secret."

"But you can't publish. It's illegal research."

"That doesn't matter anymore, Dr. Potterley. If I lose my grants, I lose them. If the university is displeased, I'll resign. It just doesn't matter."

"But you can't do that!"

"Till now," said Foster, "you didn't mind my risking loss of grants and position. Why do you turn so tender about it now? Now let me explain something to you. When you first came to me, I believed in organized and directed research; the situation as it existed, in other words. I considered you an intellectual anarchist, Dr. Potterley, and dangerous. But for one reason or another, I've been an anarchist myself for months now and I have achieved great things.

"Those things have been achieved not because I am a brilliant scientist. Not at all. It was just that scientific research had been directed from above and holes were left that could be filled in by anyone who looked in the right direction. And anyone might have if the government hadn't actively tried to prevent it.

"Now understand me. I still believe directed research can be useful. I'm not in favor of a retreat to total anarchy. But there must be a middle ground. Directed research can retain flexibility. A scientist must be allowed to follow his curiosity, at least in his spare time."

Potterley sat down. He said ingratiatingly, "Let's discuss this, Foster. I appreciate your idealism. You're young. You want the moon. But you can't destroy yourself through fancy notions of what research must consist of. I got you into this. I am responsible and I blame myself bitterly. I was acting emotionally. My interest in Carthage blinded me and I was a damned fool."

Foster broke in. "You mean you've changed completely in two days? Carthage is nothing? Government suppression of research is nothing?"

"Even a damned fool like myself can learn, Foster. My wife taught me something. I understand the reason for government suppression of neutrinics now. I didn't two days ago. And, understanding, I approve. You saw the way my wife reacted to the news of a chronoscope in the basement. I had envisioned a chronoscope used for research purposes. All *she* could see was the personal pleasure of returning neurotically to a personal past, a dead past. The pure researcher, Foster, is in the minority. People like my wife would outweigh us.

"For the government to encourage chronoscopy would have meant that everyone's past would be visible. The government officers would be subjected to blackmail and improper pressure, since who on Earth has a past that is absolutely clean? Organized government might become impossible."

Foster licked his lips. "Maybe the government has some justification in its own eyes. Still, there's an important principle involved here. Who knows what other scientific advances are being stymied because scientists are being stifled into walking a narrow path? If the chronoscope becomes the terror of a few politicians, it's a price that must be paid. The public must realize that science must be free and there is no more dramatic way of doing it than to publish my discovery, one way or another, legally or illegally."

Potterley's brow was damp with perspiration, but his voice remained even. "Oh, not just a few politicians, Dr. Foster. Don't think that. It would be my terror too. My wife would spend her time living with our dead daughter. She would retreat farther from reality. She would go mad living the same scenes over and over. And not just my terror. There would be others like her. Children searching for their dead parents or their own youth. We'll have a whole world living in the past. Midsummer madness."

Foster said, "Moral judgments can't stand in the way. There isn't one advance at any time in history that mankind hasn't had the ingenuity to pervert. Mankind must also have the ingenuity to prevent. As for the chronoscope, your delvers into the dead past will get tired soon enough. They'll catch their loved parents in some of the things their loved parents did and they'll lose their enthusiasm for it all. But all this is trivial. With me, it's a matter of important principle."

Potterley said, "Hang your principle. Can't you understand men and women as well as principle? Don't you understand that my wife will live through the fire that killed our baby? She won't be able to help herself. I know her. She'll follow through each step, trying to prevent it. She'll live it over and over again, hoping each time that it won't happen. How many times do you want to kill Laurel?" A huskiness had crept into his voice.

A thought crossed Foster's mind. "What are you really afraid she'll find out, Dr. Potterley? What happened the night of the fire?"

The historian's hands went up quickly to cover his face and they shook with his dry sobs. Foster turned and stared uncomfortably out the window.

Potterley said after a while, "It's a long time since I've had to think of it. Caroline was away. I was baby-sitting. I went into the baby's bedroom midevening to see if she had kicked off the bedclothes. I had my cigarette with me. . . . I smoked in those days. I must have stubbed it out before putting it in the ashtray on the chest of drawers. I was always careful. The baby was all right. I returned to the living room and fell asleep before the video. I awoke, choking, surrounded by fire. I don't know how it started."

"But you think it may have been the cigarette, is that it?" said Foster. "A cigarette which, for once, you forgot to stub out?"

"I don't know. I tried to save her, but she was dead in my arms when I got out."

"You never told your wife about the cigarette, I suppose."

Potterley shook his head. "But I've lived with it."

"Only now, with a chronoscope, she'll find out. Maybe it wasn't the cigarette. Maybe you did stub it out. Isn't that possible?"

The scant tears had dried on Potterley's face. The redness had subsided. He said, "I can't take the chance . . . but it's not just myself, Foster. The past has its terrors for most people. Don't loose those terrors on the human race."

Foster paced the floor. Somehow this explained the reason for Potterley's rabid, irrational desire to boost the Carthaginians, deify them, most of all disprove the story of their fiery sacrifices to Moloch. By freeing them of the guilt of infanticide by fire, he symbolically freed himself of the same guilt.

So the same fire that had driven him on to causing the construction of a chronoscope was now driving him on to the destruction.

Foster looked sadly at the older man. "I see your position, Dr. Potterley, but this goes above personal feelings. I've got to smash this throttling hold on the throat of science."

Potterley said savagely, "You mean you want the fame and wealth that goes with such a discovery."

"I don't know about the wealth, but that too, I suppose. I'm no more than human."

"You won't suppress your knowledge?"

"Not under any circumstances."

"Well, then—" And the historian got to his feet and stood for a moment, glaring.

Foster had an odd moment of terror. The man was older than he, smaller, feebler, and he didn't look armed. Still. . . .

Foster said, "If you're thinking of killing me or anything insane like that, I've got the information in a safe-deposit vault where the proper people will find it in case of my disappearance or death."

Potterley said, "Don't be a fool," and stalked out.

Foster closed the door, locked it and sat down to think. He felt silly. He had no information in a safe-deposit vault, of course. Such a melodramatic action would not have occurred to him ordinarily. But now it had.

Feeling even sillier, he spent an hour writing out the equations and the application of pseudo-gravitic optics to neutrinic recording, and some diagrams for the engineering details of construction. He sealed it in an envelope and scrawled Ralph Nimmo's name over the outside.

He spent a rather restless night and the next morning, on the way to school, dropped the envelope off at the bank, with appropriate instructions to an official, who made him sign a paper permitting the box to be opened after his death.

He called Nimmo to tell him of the existence of the envelope, refusing querulously to say anything about its contents.

He had never felt so ridiculously self-conscious as at that moment.

That night and the next, Foster spent in only fitful sleep, finding himself face to face with the highly practical problem of the publication of data unethically obtained.

The *Proceedings of the Society of Pseudo-Gravitics*, which was the journal with which he was best acquainted, would certainly not touch any paper that did not include the magic footnote: "The work described in this paper was made possible by Grant No. so-and-so from the Commission of Research of the United Nations."

Nor, doubly so, would the *Journal of Physics*.

There were always the minor journals that might overlook the nature of the article for the sake of the sensation, but that would require a little financial negotiation on which he hesitated to embark. It might, on the whole, be better to pay the cost of publishing a small pamphlet for general distribution among the scholars. In that case, he would even be able to dispense with the services of a science writer, sacrificing polish for speed. He would have to find a reliable printer. Uncle Ralph might know one.

He walked down the corridor to his office and wondered anxiously if perhaps he ought to waste no further time, give himself no further chance to lapse into indecision and take the risk of calling Ralph from his office phone. He was so absorbed in his own heavy thoughts that he did not notice that his room was occupied until he turned from the clothes closet and approached his desk.

Dr. Potterley was there and a man whom Foster did not recognize.

Foster stared at them. "What's this?"

Potterley said, "I'm sorry, but I had to stop you."

Foster continued staring. "What are you talking about?"

The stranger said, "Let me introduce myself." He had large teeth, a little uneven, and they showed prominently when he smiled. "I am Thaddeus Araman, Department Head of the Division of Chronoscopy. I am here to see you concerning information brought to me by Professor Arnold Potterley and confirmed by our own sources—"

Potterley said breathlessly, "I took all the blame, Dr. Foster. I explained that it was I who persuaded you against your will into unethical practices. I have offered to accept full responsibility and punishment. I don't wish you harmed in any way. It's just that chronoscopy must not be permitted!"

Araman nodded. "He has taken the blame as he says, Dr. Foster, but this thing is out of his hands now."

Foster said, "So? What are you going to do? Blackball me from all consideration for research grants?"

"This is in my power," said Araman.

"Order the university to discharge me?"

"That, too, is in my power."

"All right, go ahead. Consider it done. I'll leave my office now, with you. I can send for my books later. If you insist, I'll leave my books. Is that all?"

"Not quite," said Araman. "You must engage to do no further research in chronoscopy, to publish none of your findings in chronoscopy and, of course, to build no chronoscope. You will remain under surveillance indefinitely to make sure you keep that promise."

"Supposing I refuse to promise? What can you do? Doing research out of my field may be unethical, but it isn't a criminal offense."

"In the case of chronoscopy, my young friend," said Araman patiently, "it is a criminal offense. If necessary, you will be put in jail and kept there."

"Why?" shouted Foster. "What's magic about chronoscopy?"

Araman said, "That's the way it is. We cannot allow further developments in the field. My own job is, primarily, to make sure of that, and I intend to do my job. Unfortunately, I had no knowledge, nor did anyone in the department, that the optics of pseudo-gravity fields had such immediate application to chronoscopy. Score one for general ignorance, but henceforward research will be steered properly in that respect too."

Foster said, "That won't help. Something else may apply that neither you nor I dream of. All science hangs together. It's one piece. If you want to stop one part, you've got to stop it all."

"No doubt that is true," said Araman, "in theory. On the practical side, however, we have managed quite well to hold chronoscopy down to the original Sterbinski level for fifty years. Having caught you in time, Dr. Foster, we hope to continue doing so indefinitely. And we wouldn't have come this close to disaster, either, if I had accepted Dr. Potterley at something more than face value."

He turned toward the historian and lifted his eyebrows in a kind of humorous self-deprecation. "I'm afraid, sir, that I dismissed you as a history professor and no more on the occasion of our first interview. Had I done my job properly and checked on you, this would not have happened."

Foster said abruptly, "Is anyone allowed to use the government chronoscope?"

"No one outside our division under any pretext. I say that since it is obvious to me that you have already guessed as much. I warn you, though, that any repetition of that fact will be a criminal, not an ethical, offense."

"And your chronoscope doesn't go back more than a hundred twenty-five years or so, does it?"

"It doesn't."

"Then your bulletin with its stories of time-viewing ancient times is a hoax?"

Araman said coolly, "With the knowledge you now have, it is obvious you know that for a certainty. However, I confirm your remark. The monthly bulletin is a hoax."

"In that case," said Foster, "I will not promise to suppress my knowledge of chronoscopy. If you wish to arrest me, go ahead. My defense at the trial will be enough to destroy the vicious card house of directed research and bring it tumbling down. Directing research is one thing; suppressing it and depriving mankind of its benefits is quite another."

Araman said, "Oh, let's get something straight, Dr. Foster. If you do not cooperate, you will go to jail directly. You will *not* see a lawyer, you will *not* be charged, you will *not* have a trial. You will simply stay in jail."

"Oh, no," said Foster, "you're bluffing. This is not the twentieth century, you know."

There was a stir outside the office, the clatter of feet, a high-pitched shout that Foster was sure he recognized. The door crashed open, the lock splintering, and three intertwined figures stumbled in.

As they did so, one of the men raised a blaster and brought its butt down hard on the skull of another.

There was a whoosh of expiring air, and the one whose head was struck went limp.

"Uncle Ralph!" cried Foster.

Araman frowned. "Put him down in that chair," he ordered, "and get some water."

Ralph Nimmo, rubbing his head with a gingerly sort of disgust, said, "There was no need to get rough, Araman."

Araman said, "The guard should have been rougher sooner and kept you out of here, Nimmo. You'd have been better off."

"You know each other?" asked Foster.

"I've had dealings with the man," said Nimmo, still rubbing. "If he's here in your office, Nephew, you're in trouble."

"And you too," said Araman angrily. "I know Dr. Foster consulted you on neutrinics literature."

Nimmo corrugated his forehead, then straightened it with a wince as though the action had brought pain. "So?" he said. "What else do you know about me?"

"We will know everything about you soon enough. Meanwhile, that one item is enough to implicate you. What are you doing here?"

"My dear Dr. Araman," said Nimmo, some of his jauntiness restored, "yesterday, my jackass of a nephew called me. He had placed some mysterious information—"

"Don't tell him! Don't say anything!" cried Foster.

Araman glanced at him coldly. "We know all about it, Dr. Foster. The safe-deposit box has been opened and its contents removed."

"But how can you know—" Foster's voice died away in a kind of furious frustration.

"Anyway," said Nimmo, "I decided the net must be closing around him and after I took care of a few items, I came down to tell him to get off this thing he's doing. It's not worth his career."

"Does that mean you know what he's doing?" asked Araman.

"He never told me," said Nimmo, "but I'm a science writer with a hell of a lot of experience. I know which side of an atom is electronified. The boy, Foster, specializes in pseudo-gravitic optics and coached me on the stuff himself. He got me to get him a textbook on neutrinics and I kind of skip-viewed it myself before handing it over. I can put two and two together. He asked me to get him certain pieces of physical equipment, and that was evidence too. Stop me if I'm wrong, but my nephew has built a semiportable, low-power chronoscope. Yes, or—yes?"

"Yes." Araman reached thoughtfully for a cigarette and paid no more attention to Dr. Potterley (watching silently, as though all were a dream), who shied away, gasping, from the white cylinder. "Another mistake for me. I ought to resign. I should have put tabs on you too, Nimmo, instead of concentrating too hard on Potterley and Foster. I didn't have much time of course and you've ended up safely here, but that doesn't excuse me. You're under arrest, Nimmo."

"What for?" demanded the science writer.

"Unauthorized research."

"I wasn't doing any. I can't, not being a registered scientist. And even if I did, it's not a criminal offense."

Foster said savagely, "No use, Uncle Ralph. This bureaucrat is making his own laws."

"Like what?" demanded Nimmo.

"Like life imprisonment without trial."

"Nuts," said Nimmo. "This isn't the twentieth cen—"

"I tried that," said Foster. "It doesn't bother him."

"Well, nuts," shouted Nimmo. "Look here, Araman. My nephew and I have relatives who haven't lost touch with us, you know. The professor has some also, I imagine. You can't just make us disappear. There'll be questions and a scandal. This *isn't* the twentieth century. So if you're trying to scare us, it isn't working."

The cigarette snapped between Araman's fingers and he tossed it away violently. He said, "Damn it, I don't know *what* to do. It's never been like this before. . . . Look! You three fools know nothing of what you're trying to do. You understand nothing. Will you listen to me?"

"Oh, we'll listen," said Nimmo grimly.

(Foster sat silently, eyes angry, lips compressed. Potterley's hands writhed like two intertwined snakes.)

Araman said, "The past to you is the dead past. If any of you have discussed the matter, it's dollars to nickels you've used that phrase. The dead past. If you knew how many times I've heard those three words, you'd choke on them too.

"When people think of the past, they think of it as dead, far away and gone, long ago. We encourage them to think so. When we report time-viewing, we always talk of views centuries in the past, even though you gentlemen know seeing more than a century or so is impossible. People accept it. The past means Greece, Rome, Carthage, Egypt, the Stone Age. The deader, the better.

"Now you three know a century or a little more is the limit, so what does the past mean to you? Your youth. Your first girl. Your dead mother. Twenty years ago. Thirty years ago. Fifty years ago. The deader, the better. . . . But when does the past really begin?"

He paused in anger. The others stared at him and Nimmo stirred uneasily.

"Well," said Araman, "when did it begin? A year ago? Five minutes ago? One second ago? Isn't it obvious that the past begins an instant ago? The dead past is just another name for the living present. What if you focus the chronoscope in the past of one-hundredth of a second ago? Aren't you watching the present? Does it begin to sink in?"

Nimmo said, "Damnation."

"Damnation," mimicked Araman. "After Potterley came to me with his story last night, how do you suppose I checked up on both of you? I did it with the chronoscope, spotting key moments to the very instant of the present."

"And that's how you knew about the safe-deposit box?" said Foster.

"And every other important fact. Now what do you suppose would happen if we let news of a home chronoscope get out? People might start out by watching their youth, their parents, and so on, but it wouldn't be long before they'd catch on to the possibilities. The housewife will forget her poor, dead mother and take to watching her neighbor at home and her husband at the office. The businessman will watch his competitor; the employer his employee.

"There will be no such thing as privacy. The party line, the prying eye behind the curtain will be nothing compared to it. The video stars will be closely watched at all times by everyone. Every man his own Peeping Tom, and there'll be no getting away from the watcher. Even darkness will be no escape because chronoscopy can be adjusted to the infrared, and human figures can be seen by their own body heat. The figures will be fuzzy, of course, and the surroundings will be dark, but that will make the titillation of it all the greater, perhaps. . . . Hmp, the men in charge of the machine now experiment sometimes in spite of the regulations against it."

Nimmo seemed sick. "You can always forbid private manufacture—"

Araman turned on him fiercely. "You can, but do you expect it to do any good? Can you legislate successfully against drinking, smoking, adultery or gossiping over the back fence? And this mixture of nosiness and prurience will have a worse grip on humanity than any of those. Good Lord, in a thousand years of trying we haven't even been able to wipe out the heroin traffic and you talk about legislating against a device for watching anyone you please at any time you please that can be built in a home workshop."

Foster said suddenly, "I won't publish."

Potterley burst out, half in sobs, "None of us will talk. I regret—"

Nimmo broke in. "You said you didn't tab me on the chronoscope, Araman."

"No time," said Araman wearily. "Things don't move any faster on the chronoscope than in real life. You can't speed it up like the film in a book viewer. We spent a full twenty-four hours trying to catch the important moments during the last six months of Potterley and Foster. There was no time for anything else and it was enough."

"It wasn't," said Nimmo.

"What are you talking about?" There was a sudden infinite alarm on Araman's face.

"I told you my nephew, Jonas, had called me to say he had put important information in a safe-deposit box. He acted as though he were in trouble. He's my nephew. I had to try to get him off the spot. It took a while, then I came here to tell him what I had done. I told you when I got here, just after your man conked me, that I had taken care of a few items."

"What? For heaven's sake—"

"Just this: I sent the details of the portable chronoscope off to half a dozen of my regular publicity outlets."

Not a word. Not a sound. Not a breath. They were all past any demonstration.

"Don't stare like that," cried Nimmo. "Don't you see my point? I had popular-publication rights. Jonas will admit that. I knew he couldn't publish scientifically in any legal way. I was sure he was planning to publish illegally and was preparing the safe-deposit box for that reason. I thought if I put through the details prematurely, all the responsibility would be mine. His career would be saved. And if I were deprived of my science-writing license as a result, my exclusive possession of the chronometric data would set me up for life. Jonas would be angry, I expected that, but I could explain the motive and we would split fifty-fifty. . . . Don't stare at me like that. How did I know—"

"Nobody knew anything," said Araman bitterly, "but you all just took it for granted that the government was stupidly bureaucratic, vicious, tyrannical, given to suppressing research for the hell of it. It never occurred to any of you that we were trying to protect mankind as best we could."

"Don't sit there talking," wailed Potterley. "Get the names of the people who were told—"

"Too late," said Nimmo, shrugging. "They've had better than a day. There's been time for the word to spread. My outlets will have called any number of physicists to check my data before going on with it and they'll call one another to pass on the news. Once scientists put neutrinics and pseudo-gravitics together, home chronoscopy becomes obvious. Before the week is out, five hundred people will know how to build a small chronoscope and how will you catch them all?" His plump cheeks sagged. "I suppose there's no way of putting the mushroom cloud back into that nice, shiny uranium sphere."

Araman stood up. "We'll try, Potterley, but I agree with Nimmo. It's too late. What kind of world we'll have from now on, I don't know, I can't tell, but the world we know has been destroyed completely. Until now, every custom, every habit, every tiniest way of life has always taken a certain amount of privacy for granted, but that's all gone now."

He saluted each of the three with elaborate formality.

"You have created a new world among the three of you. I congratulate you. Happy goldfish bowl to you, to me, to everyone, and may each of you fry in hell forever. Arrest rescinded."

ANNEMARIE VAN EWYCK

The Lens

It is interesting to contrast Van Ewyck's story with Van Log-gem's; while the latter reflects the mood, tone, and concerns of primarily 1950s American SF, "The Lens" seems more in tune with Anglo-American post–New Wave works. It is darker, more heterogeneous in its influences (here a touch of Bradbury or Zelazny, there a touch of Tiptree or Sturgeon). And "The Lens," translated from the Dutch by its author, is told in the first person rather than the conventional third. The author is an active member of World SF, an international body, and she is a participant in fan activities internationally. This story is one of a small but growing body of works in many languages that incorporate a wide variety of English-language SF influences.

*   *   *

The journey to Mertcha seemed to take longer than ever. I spent most of my time in my cabin at first, later venturing out into the non-smokers' lounge, where unfortunately most of the mothers congregated, with their children.

I did a lot of thinking about my own mother. For her sake I'd had my hair tinted back to its original mousey brown when I left for Terra. Now the grey was beginning to show again, at the roots. The kids thought it peculiar—I overheard them giggling. But at first they kept pretty much out of my way, deep in their own concerns of running, fighting, screeching and generally overturning everything that was not bolted to the deck: a constant din that made a strangely soothing background to my thoughts.

Mother had seemed so very much changed, this last time. So quiet, almost diffident in her manner. She had been watching old vid tapes when I came in, and she turned and said, "Oh, hello dear; there you are then." And I said, "Yes mother."

"I've been off the life machines for some weeks now," she said, turning back to the screen. "I won't be long." And again I said, "Yes mother." A gentle exchange, and meaningless.

No trace of the woman she had been, the woman I had known and dreaded and loved in vain. Who carried grievances against all the universe, who had hounded my sweet Pa to death with her crippled kind of loving and who had driven me out of home and finally off-planet with her abuse and complaints.

I asked the doctor about her. He couldn't tell me much. She had not been her usual self of late, indeed she had not. Seemed she had lost her zest.

He was being kind, I knew. Kind to me. I was sure she had been doing her utmost to make his job as difficult for him as she could; nagging, bitching, as she had for years . . .

Part of her must have died some time ago. The mother I knew would never have written to me as she did, asking me to be with her at the end, to help her across. Poor twisted little witch, impotent at last.

I strangely missed what she had been, yet I longed to know better this strange old woman she had become. But she remained inaccessible to the end.

Within a week of my arrival she died; 286 years old. "Not bad," she whispered just before she left, on a long echoing sigh.

Motherless I had always felt, now it was a fact. Sorting out my feelings was not easy. Part of the sensibility that her death had, much against my will, churned up, was captured by Billy, a charming seven-year-old, travelling with his parents to Tireno, a colony world beyond Mertcha, far past the heart of the galaxy.

Billy was an unspoilt child and his parents allowed his curiosity free rein, within certain limits. Highly interested, he wandered over one afternoon to watch me at finger-weaving, a craft that is very popular on Mertcha. With only five fingers, I have to keep a peg pinched between ring and middle finger to duplicate the Mertchan sixth digit, and to be sure, the needle does not dance as nimbly through the web as in the hands of the Mertchan peasants, but I am pretty deft at it for all that.

Before my trip was over Billy had produced half a dozen rosettes, remarkable for their gaudy colours and weird snaking patterns. I had

followed the traditional Mertchan wefts and colour-schemes; he had explored new possibilities. He was young and I . . . I was nearly old.

Before touchdown on Mertcha I retired to my cabin. I had already said
goodbye to Billy and his parents and to the schoolteacher who had also been
interested in my finger-weaving, and wanted to introduce it on Wertz, for
first-phase pupils.

I wanted to be alone. Longing and fear, hope and hesitation created a
turmoil in my insides; a roll of red-hot marbles in my abdominal region,
cramps painful and delicious. I knew the feeling well. Despite a long life of
travel, with countless trips to Terra and back, and despite my many postings
on many different planets, I remain a prey, a compliant victim to my own
anticipation at every planet-fall.

I drew my shapeless traveller's cloak tight. Soon now, I would be wearing
my own clothes again, the light flowing robes, the cool flaring hoods and
star-veils of Mertcha. Rys en Pfi would once more light the sky . . . and I
would see Mik again, in his terribly ill-fitting Terran driver's uniform, his
cap askew on top of his ugly Mertchan head. Even the Mertchans thought
Mik ugly, it wasn't Terran prejudice . . .

Disembarkation. From ship to shore through the snaky proboscis, a wide
corridor with windows tightly shuttered. Into the large Arrivals' Hall that
boasted the greatest sight on Mertcha—artificial lighting in abundance.

As yet I had had no glimpse of Mertcha, of Tiel. I still felt part of the
space-liner, in transit. I hurried to the covered parking bays where the
Embassy car would be waiting. I pictured Mik standing there, resting his
weight on his supporting leg, the others nonchalantly crossed in front of
him, an unlit Terran cigarette dangling from his wide mouth.

But when I reached the car, the driver on his elevated seat proved to be a
stranger. It was a bad shock. I had expected Mik, my personal driver, as
anybody on the Embassy staff knew. He drove me to Mertchan soil-
dedications, and to festivals, and exhibitions and concerts by Terran musicians; to all occasions that merited a report from Terran Cultural Liaison.

He was more than just my driver, he was a friend. When I left, he had
said, "I will come to fetch you, certainly, when you come back from your
grief," even though the three-and-three folk, knowing no families, only
clan-groupings and their ever-changing propagation triads, can have no
notion of what the loss of a parent means to a Terran.

I tried to ask this new driver about Mik, but his knowledge of Terran seemed to be virtually non-existent. He just mumbled, "Embassy-Dame-Ditja-to-get-in-please," all strung together, and pulled open the passenger door with a crooked movement of his middle arm. He chose not to understand my Mertchan either, and shut the door with a few polite head gestures, after which he got in and raised the glass partition.

I felt very much upset. The lout had even left the black-out curtains in place; I could not see out! I was really getting angry. This man was spoiling my arrival, my reunion with the lovely planet I had been living on for more than ten years.

And I had looked forward so much to this first, languorous ride through the broad avenues of Tiel, under a sky full of radiance. I had longed for the blaze of the billions of stars that shine down on this small red planet in the mathematical centre of the galactic lens. A world where darkness is an artificial condition and where black-out curtains are as familiar a feature as light-switches elsewhere.

I had longed for it, I realized. Longed for Mertcha as if it were my home, as if I belonged here, bound to roots that went deep into the dry reddish earth and clung there with hair-thin filaments.

Longed for Mertcha, and the company of Mik. During the return trip I had been considering a request for a permanent appointment. I did not doubt it would be approved, for I was good at my work, steady, dependable. And there were no other contestants for the permanent post of Head of Cultural Liaison. Another year, and my assistant would apply for a transfer to Rhodia or Wertz, first order worlds, where the life of the galaxy beat fast. Nobody coveted my place, my desk, my chair. There was still time to have a home I loved, and friends . . .

The darkened car bounced over a patch of uneven ground and came to a stop. I got the door open as fast as I could, and found myself in the parking lot that had recently been staked out at the Holy Place of Tiel by a reluctant City Council. I walked to the front of the car. The driver had remained in his seat. "Holy Place," he enunciated with some difficulty. "Good see."

I began to understand what had happened. He was standing in for Mik, who was detained elsewhere. Not knowing who I was, he had assumed I was a guest of the Embassy—a visiting artist perhaps, who would tip nicely for an unscheduled private visit to the most important sight of Tiel. Sure enough, the left hand crept out of the open window, palm upward.

I waved him off and said, "Later, later," which for a wonder he did understand.

I didn't mind visiting the Holy Place of Tiel now that I was here. It would be a perfect way of restoring the shattered harmony of my arrival. A welcome to myself. The sky was vast and light. Rys was past its zenith, intensifying the reds and umbers so richly found on Mertcha.

I strolled past an empty tourist wagon—a coach for Terrans, judging by the low-slung seats—and reached a simple square building of red loam, the Holy Place of Tiel.

Square shapes are rare on Mertcha; the inhabitants, no doubt under the influence of the trigits that govern their body structure, care more for triangles and particularly circles. So a square building dating from the antiquity of the three-and-three folk is a unique sight. That is not the reason, however, that the Place features in most of the sightseeing schedules of long-space pleasure cruises.

For off-worlders it is the famous mosaic labyrinth in the main Hall, and the crypt where the funeral pyramids of departed monastics line the walls—a double row of gaudy little towers, draped with strings of glistening beads.

The crypt has a copy of the upper labyrinth, but instead of a flat mosaic, the maze in the crypt is three-dimensional, consisting of narrow strips of masonry standing ankle-high. Tourists often stumble over these miniature walls.

The upper and lower labyrinth both end in a central circle, which in the crypt is marked by another low wall, and in the Hall itself by a round opening with a loose red-lacquered cover, corresponding exactly with a similar opening in the roof of the Hall.

Only starlight is ever allowed to enter the Place, for on the gallery near the roof monastics and servants are continuously shifting the screens and panels that shunt the light of the two weak suns back into space. The crypt too is lighted by starlight, aided by the thin flame of some candles in wall sconces.

Along the Hall, the triangular cells of the living monastics mirror the disposition of the funeral pyramids below. When the inhabitants emerge from their cells in their stiff pastel robes, it is like summer moths leaving their cocoons; it never fails as a subject for tourist snapshots.

The monastics are few in number, for the religion of the Place is ecstatic in nature, stressing personal exaltation instead of mass devotion. Not a creed for crowds. No god is revered here, no services are held. Postulants simply come to the Place, unannounced, and start treading the labyrinth, spelled out in glowing mosaics on the floor of the Hall. Those who are fortunate, so I am told, are slowly, gradually caught up into ecstasy until they collapse. The further inward they have come, the longer the faint lasts, so I heard.

A servant assists the new monastic to a vacant cell, offers him a ritual bowl of hot *melk* and issues a frock of colour. And that is all.

The servants are postulants who have walked the labyrinth in vain, but who remain so much attracted to the mystical, that they are willing to stay and serve. I am sure they must feel envious; I would in their place. And indeed there have been rumours of late, of power-seeking in their simple organization.

I made my way through the countless screening drapes of the entrance and stood inside the Hall. Silence and starlight, a cone of radiance comprising half a galaxy, girdled at the roof and fanning out downwards to light the maze. A pair of monastics in pink and sea-green were gliding over the mosaic at the far end of the Hall. Close by the entrance three servants stood whispering; one had crossed his forelegs, reminding me very much of Mik.

In this space and silence I felt happier than I had ever felt before. Tears came into my eyes, unexpectedly. I had to force them back. Oh, yes, I would send in my request as soon as I was back at the Embassy. This was my home, this red soil, so receptively taking my new roots to herself; these red loam walls, this star-filled hall, the mosaic . . . a perfect embodiment of homecoming.

I started walking, wending my way along the labyrinth, giving rhythm to my feelings. My face felt twisted by emotion, there were tears that would no longer be repressed. With slow steps I drew nearer, ever nearer, to the centre of the Hall, my eyes on the mosaic, my heart turned towards the heavens where the stars blazed like daylight, where half the mass of the Milky Way rested on spikes of light on an insignificant red planet.

Rapture and exaltation swept through my body. What had begun as a symbolic celebration of homecoming was turned into a transport of delight, carrying me along like the long, long glide upwards just before orgasm, before the foaming tumble that is always too short to satisfy. But this movement seemed to have no ending. The ecstasy of the Holy Place of Tiel was upon me and I followed the mystical power that called to me, craving the ultimate that surely lay before me . . .

Nearing the centre of the Hall, thoughts barely shaped, barely conscious . . . a feeling of happiness intensified . . . almost unbearable . . . The heart, the kernel of things, so close now, the melting into Oneness . . .

A hand, a Mertchan hand bearing a red key on a third-finger ring, at the edge of my vision . . . placing a red wooden cover over an opening of black, a dark hole, an annoying blemish on the brilliance of the maze.

A tiny grain of sobriety penetrating my shining picture . . . The dark streaming upwards from the round opening, then cut off . . . The cover closing the crypt off from the light . . . no lights down there?

An unwelcome picture of the stout door to the crypt, the ring-key on the hand of the servant . . . the Terran tourist coach outside . . .

The thoughts would not reach my feet, treading on slowly along the loops and curves of the labyrinth, ever closer to the red cover. And again rapture rose like a tide, enveloping me, sheathing me into near-immobility . . . a stillness in my senses, and yet a movement that was upward, yet downward, inward, yet outward.

But the grain of doubt, the gritty lump of knowledge would not be swept away.

A link forged itself, shattering the rapture. The servant had locked the tourists in the crypt, in the dark . . .

Before my feet could touch the wooden cover I had halted, swaying. A servant caught me when my knees buckled and led me to the side of the Hall, supporting me. In a vacant cell he offered me a bowl of *melk*, hot as it should be, but his posture expressed his doubts and he stumbled in his ritual greeting. "You have felt the power . . ." He ought to have added, "and henceforth this shall be your home." He did, after a pause, but not without one of those rapid gestures, with which Mertchans commonly mitigate the impact of too sweeping a statement. Clearly he did not know what to do with an off-worlder, a Terran, a two-and-two woman, experiencing holy ecstasy in the Place of Tiel.

In the meantime I had recovered, a little. "You misunderstand, a giddy spell, that is all. Gratitude for your *melk*," I said, turning away sharply not to see the relief in his eyes.

I left the cell. Through the Hall I went, across the mosaic that now lay lifeless, through the smothering drapes at the door. The entrance to the crypt was locked, as I had expected. From behind the pressed fibre door I could hear vulgar Terran curses.

The tourists have no notion of having been, for a little while, held hostage by a small politico-religious pressure group. They only know the candles in the crypt were blown out—probably a draught. When the wooden cover was replaced, plunging the crypt into total darkness, they stubbed their toes and bashed their shins on the low walls of the crypt labyrinth, trying to find the exit. The door stuck at first, and that *was* unpleasant. The native guide was nowhere to be found.

But they got out all right, and the only really annoying thing was that they missed the folkloristic meal in Tiel Old Town because they were late. The ship lifted as soon as they were back on board.

The Embassy keeps mum. Of course. The Under Secretary has had a heart-to-heart talk with the Chief Peacekeeper, and the Mertchan Head of State has conveyed a number of very flattering invitations to our Ambassador.

I am thought to have shown rare subtlety in dealing with a nasty situation, in that I did not raise the Peacekeepers, but went and liberated the tourists with no fuss made. The fact that the key to the crypt was given up without resistance on the part of the servants, is duly ascribed to my formerly unnoticed wit and tact.

I will not show them the back of my tongue, as the Mertchan saying goes. No one will ever know of my experience in the labyrinth. Or of the consternation among the rebellious servants, when at the moment of their *coup* a Terran, of all people, was being exalted into their ecstasy. Yes, they do know. And they will never tell.

The poor servant was so dumbfounded when I marched up to him, demanding the key, that he gave it up quite meekly.

In any case I can now write my own ticket to any first order world that takes my fancy, so the Ambassador has personally and warmly assured me.

I am sending in my request for a transfer tomorrow. I finally heard what has happened to Mik. He is dead. A traffic accident. He died, my only friend. The only Mertchan who could treat a two-and-two person—a pitiable disabled being—as an equal, worthy of affection.

He was driving the handbuilt Embassy Volkswagen that the Earth Government had sent out to enhance Terran prestige. Sitting straight and stiff as a *knappi*-tree, his supporting leg uncomfortably folded beneath him on the low seat, he was hit by the freight-cart that came careening out of a side road, brakes smoking. In the pride of his Terran driving he found death—the most expensive road casualty on Mertcha, as the Ambassador remarked sourly.

Oh Mik, oh Mik you have found what I longed for; yours is the glory . . . and I have been so close, so close!

.　.　.

Turning and wending along the maze I had felt a conviction that came into being slowly, finally focusing what ought to have been clear to me long before: "This is the place where I belong, in all the universe." And without fear I had accepted what unavoidably followed, "The only place where I truly belong is the place where I die."

I was ready, I was more than ready. I was prepared to stand on that round red cover and feel the light of a billion stars play through me.

Astrologers believe what astronomers deny, that the stars have powers that influence the moods and actions and lives of the creatures that people the crusts of the worlds. I remain outside their argument. But I know that half a galaxy of collected starlight can kill. There might have been another pyramid, down in the crypt.

I gave up my death of ecstasy for a coachload of stupid Terran sightseers. There are no second chances and I'll never know if they were worth the trade. At night, I cry in my sleep, for longing, longing.

THEODORE STURGEON

The Hurkle Is a Happy Beast

Theodore Sturgeon was a master of many moods. Here he is at his most playful, a stance he often took in public but too rarely in his fiction. This story shows a facet of his virtuosity still underappreciated. This is just for fun.

* * *

Lirht is either in a different universal plane or in another island galaxy. Perhaps these terms mean the same thing. The fact remains that Lirht is a planet with three moons (one of which is unknown) and a sun, which is as important in its universe as is ours.

Lirht is inhabited by gwik, its dominant race, and by several less highly developed species which, for purposes of this narrative, can be ignored. Except, of course, for the hurkle. The hurkle are highly regarded by the gwik as pets, in spite of the fact that a hurkle is so affectionate that it can have no loyalty.

The prettiest of the hurkle are blue.

Now, on Lirht, in its greatest city, there was trouble, the nature of which does not matter to us, and a gwik named Hvov, whom you may immediately forget, blew up a building which was important for reasons we cannot understand. This event caused great excitement, and gwik left their homes and factories and strubles and streamed toward the center of town, which is how a certain laboratory door was left open.

In times of such huge confusion, the little things go on. During the "Ten Days that Shook the World" the cafes and theaters of Moscow and Petrograd remained open, people fell in love, sued each other, died, shed sweat and tears; and some of these were tears of laughter. So on Lirht, while the decisions on the fate of the miserable Hvov were being formulated, gwik still fardled, funted, and fupped. The great central hewton still beat out its mighty pulse, and in the anams the corsons grew . . .

Into the above-mentioned laboratory, which had been left open through the circumstances described, wandered a hurkle kitten. It was very happy to find itself there; but then, the hurkle is a happy beast. It prowled about fearlessly—it could become invisible if frightened—and it glowed at the legs of the tables and at the glittering, racked walls. It moved sinuously, humping its back and arching along on the floor. Its front and rear legs were stiff and straight as the legs of a chair; the middle pair had two sets of knees, one bending forward, one back. It was engineered as ingeniously as a scorpion, and it was exceedingly blue.

Occupying almost a quarter of the laboratory was a huge and intricate machine, unhoused, showing the signs of development projects the galaxies over—temporary hookups from one component to another, cables terminating in spring clips, measuring devices standing about on small tables near the main work. The kitten regarded the machine with curiosity and friendly intent, sending a wave of radiations outward which were its glow or purr. It arched daintily around to the other side, stepping delicately but firmly on a floor switch.

Immediately there was a rushing, humming sound, like small birds chasing large mosquitoes, and parts of the machine began to get warm. The kitten watched curiously, and saw, high up inside the clutter of coils and wires, the most entrancing muzziness it had ever seen. It was like heat-flicker over a fallow field; it was like a smoke-vortex; it was like red neon lights on a wet pavement. To the hurkle kitten's senses, that red-orange flicker was also like the smell of catnip to a cat, or anise to a terrestrial terrier.

It reared up toward the glow, hooked its forelegs over a busbar—fortunately there was no ground potential—and drew itself upward. It climbed from transformer to power-pack, skittered up a variable condenser—the setting of which was changed thereby—disappeared momentarily as it felt the bite of a hot tube, and finally teetered on the edge of the glow.

The glow hovered in midair in a sort of cabinet, which was surrounded by heavy coils embodying tens of thousands of turns of small wire and great loops of bus. One side, the front, of the cabinet was open, and the kitten hung there fascinated, rocking back and forth to the rhythm of some unheard music it made to contrast this sourceless flame. Back and forth, back and forth it rocked and wove, riding a wave of delicious, compelling sensation. And once, just once, it moved its center of gravity too far from its point of support. Too far—far enough. It tumbled into the cabinet, into the flame.

One muggy, mid-June day a teacher, whose name was Stott and whose duties were to teach seven subjects to forty moppets in a very small town, was writing on a blackboard. He was writing the word Madagascar, and the air was so sticky and warm that he could feel his undershirt pasting and unpasting itself on his shoulder blade with each round "a" he wrote.

Behind him there was a sudden rustle from the moist seventh-graders. His schooled reflexes kept him from turning from the board until he had finished what he was doing, by which time the room was in a young uproar. Stott about-faced, opened his mouth, closed it again. A thing like this would require more than a routine reprimand.

His forty-odd charges were writhing and squirming in an extraordinary fashion, and the sound they made, a sort of whimpering giggle, was unique. He looked at one pupil after another. Here a hand was busily scratching a nape; there a boy was digging guiltily under his shirt; yonder a scrubbed and shining damsel violently worried her scalp.

Knowing the value of individual attack, Stott intoned, "Hubert, what seems to be the trouble?"

The room immediately quieted, though diminished scrabblings continued. "Nothin', Mister Stott," quavered Hubert.

Stott flicked his gaze from side to side. Wherever it rested, the scratching stopped and was replaced by agonized control. In its wake was rubbing and twitching. Stott glared, and idly thumbed a lower left rib. Someone snickered. Before he could identify the source, Stott was suddenly aware of an intense itching. He checked the impulse to go after it, knotted his jaw, and swore to himself that he wouldn't scratch as long as he was out there, front and center. "The class will—" he began tautly, and then stopped.

There was a—a *something* on the sill of the open window. He blinked and looked again. It was a translucent, bluish cloud which was almost nothing at all. It was less than a something should be, but it was indeed more than a nothing. If he stretched his imagination just a little, he might make out the outlines of an arched creature with too many legs; but of course that was ridiculous.

He looked away from it and scowled at his class. He had had two unfortunate experiences with stink bombs, and in the back of his mind was the thought of having seen once, in a trick-store window, a product called "itching powder." Could this be it, this terrible itch? He knew better, however, than to accuse anyone yet; if he were wrong, there was no point in giving the little geniuses any extra-curricular notions.

He tried again. "The cl—" He swallowed. This itch was . . . "The class will—" He noticed that one head, then another and another, were turning toward the window. He realized that if the class got too interested in what he thought he saw on the window sill, he'd have a panic on his hands. He fumbled for his ruler and rapped twice on the desk. His control was not what it should have been at the moment; he struck far too hard, and the reports were like gunshots. The class turned to him as one; and behind them the thing on the window sill appeared with great distinctness.

It was blue—a truly beautiful blue. It had a small spherical head and an almost identical knob at the other end. There were four stiff, straight legs, a long sinuous body, and two central limbs with a boneless look about them. On the side of the head were four pairs of eyes, of graduated sizes. It teetered there for perhaps ten seconds, and then, without a sound, leapt through the window and was gone.

Mr. Stott, pale and shaking, closed his eyes. His knees trembled and weakened, and a delicate, dewy mustache of perspiration appeared on his upper lip. He clutched at the desk and forced his eyes open; and then, flooding him with relief, pealing into his terror, swinging his control back to him, the bell rang to end the class and the school day.

"Dismissed," he mumbled, and sat down. The class picked up and left, changing itself from a twittering pattern of rows to a rowdy kaleidoscope around the bottleneck doorway. Mr. Stott slumped down in his chair, noticing that the dreadful itch was gone, had been gone since he had made that thunderclap with the ruler.

Now, Mr. Stott was a man of method. Mr. Stott prided himself on his ability to teach his charges to use their powers of observation and all the machinery of logic at their command. Perhaps, then, he had more of both at his command—after he recovered himself—than could be expected of an ordinary man.

He sat and stared at the open window, not seeing the sun-swept lawns outside. And after going over these events a half-dozen times, he fixed on two important facts:

First, that the animal he had seen, or thought he had seen, had six legs.

Second, that the animal was of such nature as to make anyone who had not seen it believe he was out of his mind.

These two thoughts had their corollaries:

First, that every animal he had ever seen which had six legs was an insect, and

Second, that if anything were to be done about this fantastic creature, he had better do it by himself. And whatever action he took must be taken immediately. He imagined the windows being kept shut to keep the thing out—in this heat—and he cowered away from the thought. He imagined the effect of such a monstrosity if it bounded into the midst of a classroom full of children in their early teens, and he recoiled. No; there could be no delay in this matter.

He went to the window and examined the sill. Nothing. There was nothing to be seen outside, either. He stood thoughtfully for a moment, pulling on his lower lip and thinking hard. Then he went downstairs to borrow five pounds of DDT powder from the janitor for an "experiment." He got a wide, flat wooden box and an electric fan, and set them up on a table he pushed close to the window. Then he sat down to wait, in case, just in case the blue beast returned.

When the hurkle kitten fell into the flame, it braced itself for a fall at least as far as the floor of the cabinet. Its shock was tremendous, then, when it found itself so braced and already resting on a surface. It looked around, panting with fright, its invisibility reflex in full operation.

The cabinet was gone. The flame was gone. The laboratory with its windows, lit by the orange Lirhtian sky, its ranks of shining equipment, its hulking, complex machine—all were gone.

The hurkle kitten sprawled in an open area, a sort of lawn. No colors were right; everything seemed half-lit, filmy, out-of-focus. There were trees, but not low and flat and bushy like honest Lirhtian trees, but with straight naked trunks and leaves like a portle's tooth. The different atmospheric gases had colors; clouds of fading, changing faint colors obscured and revealed everything. The kitten twitched its cafmors and ruddled its kump, right there where it stood; for no amount of early training could overcome a shock like this.

It gathered itself together and tried to move; and then it got its second shock. Instead of arching over inchwormwise, it floated into the air and came down three times as far as it had ever jumped in its life.

It cowered on the dreamlike grass, darting glances all about, under, and up. It was lonely and terrified and felt very much put upon. It saw its shadow through the shifting haze, and the sight terrified it even more, for it had no shadow when it was frightened on Lirht. Everything here was all backwards and wrong way up; it got more visible, instead of less, when it was frightened; its legs didn't work right, it couldn't see properly, and there wasn't a single, solitary malapek to be throdded anywhere. It thought it heard some music; happily, that sounded all right inside its round head, though some-how it didn't resonate as well as it had.

It tried, with extreme caution, to move again. This time its trajectory was shorter and more controlled. It tried a small, grounded pace, and was quite successful. Then it bobbed for a moment, seesawing on its flexible middle pair of legs, and, with utter abandon, flung itself skyward. It went up perhaps fifteen feet, turning end over end, and landed with its stiff forefeet in the turf.

It was completely delighted with this sensation. It gathered itself together, gryting with joy, and leapt up again. This time it made more distance than altitude, and bounced two long, happy bounces as it landed.

Its fears were gone in the exploration of this delicious new freedom of motion. The hurkle, as has been said before, is a happy beast. It curvetted and sailed, soared and somersaulted, and at last brought up against a brick wall with stunning and unpleasant results. It was learning, the hard way, a distinction between weight and mass. The effect was slight but painful. It drew back and stared forlornly at the bricks. Just when it was beginning to feel friendly again . . .

It looked upward, and saw what appeared to be an opening in the wall some eight feet above the ground. Overcome by a spirit of high adventure, it sprang upward and came to rest on a window sill—a feat of which it was very proud. It crouched there, preening itself, and looked inside.

It saw a most pleasing vista. More than forty amusingly ugly animals, apparently imprisoned by their lower extremities in individual stalls, bowed and nodded and mumbled. At the far end of the room stood a taller, more slender monster with a naked head—naked compared with those of the trapped ones, which were covered with hair like a mawson's egg. A few moments' study showed the kitten that in reality only one side of the heads was hairy; the tall one turned around and began making tracks in the end wall, and its head proved to be hairy on the other side too.

The hurkle kitten found this vastly entertaining. It began to radiate what was, on Lirht, a purr, or glow. In this fantastic place it was not visible; instead, the trapped animals began to respond with most curious writhings and squirmings and susurrant rubbings of their hides with their claws. This pleased the kitten even more, for it loved to be noticed, and it redoubled the glow. The receptive motions of the animals became almost frantic.

Then the tall one turned around again. It made a curious sound or two. Then it picked up a stick from the platform before it and brought it down with a horrible crash.

The sudden noise frightened the hurkle kitten half out of its wits. It went invisible; but its visibility system was reversed here, and it was suddenly outstandingly evident. It turned and leapt outside, and before it reached the ground, a loud metallic shrilling pursued it. There were gabblings and shufflings from the room which added force to the kitten's consuming terror. It scrambled to a low growth of shrubbery and concealed itself among the leaves.

Very soon, however, its irrepressible good nature returned. It lay relaxed, watching the slight movement of the stems and leaves—some of them may have been flowers—in a slight breeze. A winged creature came humming and dancing about one of the blossoms. The kitten rested on one of its middle legs, shot the other out and caught the creature in flight. The thing promptly jabbed the kitten's foot with a sharp black probe. This the kitten ignored. It ate the thing, and belched. It lay still for a few minutes, savoring the sensation of the bee in its clarfel. The experiment was suddenly not a success. It ate the bee twice more and then gave it up as a bad job.

It turned its attention again to the window, wondering what those racks of animals might be up to now. It seemed very quiet up there . . . Boldly the kitten came from hiding and launched itself at the window again. It was pleased with itself; it was getting quite proficient at precision leaps in this mad place. Preening itself, it balanced on the window sill and looked inside.

Surprisingly, all the smaller animals were gone. The larger one was huddled behind the shelf at the end of the room. The kitten and the animal watched each other for a long moment. The animal leaned down and stuck something into the wall.

Immediately there was a mechanical humming sound and something on a platform near the window began to revolve. The next thing the kitten knew it was enveloped in a cloud of pungent dust.

It choked and became as visible as it was frightened, which was very. For a long moment it was incapable of motion; gradually, however, it became conscious of a poignant, painfully penetrating sensation which thrilled it to the core. It gave itself up to the feeling. Wave after wave of agonized ecstasy rolled over it, and it began to dance to the waves. It glowed brilliantly, though the emanation served only to make the animal in the room scratch hysterically.

The hurkle felt strange, transported. It turned and leapt high into the air, out from the building.

Mr. Stott stopped scratching. Disheveled indeed, he went to the window and watched the odd sight of the blue beast, quite invisible now, but coated with dust, so that it was like a bubble in a fog. It bounced across the lawn in huge floating leaps, leaving behind it diminishing patches of white powder in the grass. He smacked his hands, one on the other, and smirking, withdrew to straighten up. He had saved the earth from battle, murder, and bloodshed, forever, but he did not know that. No one ever found out what he had done. So he lived a long and happy life.

And the hurkle kitten?

It bounded off through the long shadows, and vanished in a copse of bushes. There it dug itself a shallow pit, working drowsily, more and more slowly. And at last it sank down and lay motionless, thinking strange thoughts, making strange music, and racked by strange sensations. Soon even its slightest movements ceased, and it stretched out stiffly, motionless . . .

For about two weeks. At the end of that time, the hurkle, no longer a kitten, was possessed of a fine, healthy litter of just under two hundred young. Perhaps it was the DDT, and perhaps it was the new variety of radiation that the hurkle received from the terrestrial sky, but they were all parthenogenetic females, even as you and I.

And the humans? Oh, we *bred* so! And how happy we were!

But the humans had the slidy itch, and the scratchy itch, and the prickly or tingly or titillative paraesthetic formication. And there wasn't a thing they could do about it.

So they left.

Isn't this a lovely place?

Zero Hour

From 1950 to at least the early 1970s, Ray Bradbury's name was synonymous with literary science fiction. Bradbury was the first writer to break entirely free of the standards and restrictions of genre SF in the 1940s and build an independent literary reputation based on widespread critical acclaim. His early works were mainly fantasy and horror stories, and even when he used a conventional SF setting—Mars, of The Martian Chronicles, for instance—his purposes were usually unconventional. His fiction appeared in many genre pulps such as Planet Stories and Weird Tales, but never in Campbell's Astounding. By the end of the 1940s Bradbury had placed himself firmly in the camp of the heirs of Poe. He had become the great master of SF horror, a peculiar hybrid that was to dominate the media SF of the 1950s, nearly replacing supernatural horror. His impact in the early 1950s, when his stories began to be collected in such volumes as The Martian Chronicles, The Golden Apples of the Sun, The Illustrated Man, Fahrenheit 451, and The October Country, was enormous and enduring. "Zero Hour" is one of his early triumphs, a tale that Bradbury himself chose for inclusion in an early anthology called My Best Science Fiction Story.

* * *

Oh, it was to be so jolly! What a game! Such excitement they hadn't known in years. The children catapulted this way and that across the green lawns, shouting at each other, holding hands, flying in circles, climbing trees, laughing . . . Overhead, the rockets flew and beetle-cars whispered by on the streets, but the children played on.

Such fun, such tremulous joy, such tumbling and hearty screaming.

Mink ran into the house, all dirt and sweat. For her seven years she was loud and strong and definite. Her mother, Mrs. Morris, hardly saw her as she yanked out drawers and rattled pans and tools into a large sack.

"Heavens, Mink, what's going on?"

"The most exciting game ever!" gasped Mink, pink-faced.

"Stop and get your breath," said the mother.

"No, I'm all right," gasped Mink. "Okay I take these things, Mom?"

"But don't dent them," said Mrs. Morris.

"Thank you, thank you!" cried Mink, and boom! she was gone, like a rocket.

Mrs. Morris surveyed the fleeing tot. "What's the name of the game?"

"Invasion!" said Mink. The door slammed.

In every yard on the street children brought out knives and forks and pokers and old stove pipes and can-openers.

It was an interesting fact that this fury and bustle occurred only among the younger children. The older ones, those ten years and more, disdained the affair and marched scornfully off on hikes or played a more dignified version of hide-and-seek on their own.

Meanwhile, parents came and went in chromium beetles. Repair men came to repair the vacuum elevators in houses, to fix fluttering television sets or hammer upon stubborn food-delivery tubes. The adult civilization passed and repassed the busy youngsters, jealous of the fierce energy of the wild tots, tolerantly amused at their flourishings, longing to join in themselves.

"This and this and *this*," said Mink, instructing the others with their assorted spoons and wrenches. "Do that, and bring *that* over here. No! *Here*, ninnie! Right. Now, get back while I fix this—" Tongue in teeth, face wrinkled in thought. "Like that. See?"

"Yayyyy!" shouted the kids.

Twelve-year-old Joseph Connors ran up.

"Go away," said Mink straight at him.

"I wanna play," said Joseph.

"Can't!" said Mink.

"Why not?"

"You'd just make fun of us."

"Honest, I wouldn't."

"No. We know *you*. Go away or we'll kick you."

Another twelve-year-old boy whirred by on little motor-skates. "Aye, Joe! Come on! Let them sissies play!"

Joseph showed reluctance and a certain wistfulness. "I *want* to play," he said.

"You're old," said Mink, firmly.

"Not *that* old," said Joe sensibly.

"You'd only laugh and spoil the Invasion."

The boy on the motor-skates made a rude lip noise. "Come on, Joe! Them and their fairies! Nuts!"

Joseph walked off slowly. He kept looking back, all down the block.

Mink was already busy again. She made a kind of apparatus with her gathered equipment. She had appointed another little girl with a pad and pencil to take down notes in painful slow scribbles. Their voices rose and fell in the warm sunlight.

All around them the city hummed. The streets were lined with good green and peaceful trees. Only the wind made a conflict across the city, across the country, across the continent. In a thousand other cities there were trees and children and avenues, business men in their quiet offices taping their voices, or watching televisors. Rockets hovered like darning needles in the blue sky. There was the universal, quiet conceit and easiness of men accustomed to peace, quite certain there would never be trouble again. Arm in arm, men all over earth were a united front. The perfect weapons were held in equal trust by all nations. A situation of incredibly beautiful balance had been brought about. There were no traitors among men, no unhappy ones, no disgruntled ones; therefore the world was based upon a stable ground. Sunlight illumined half the world and the trees drowsed in a tide of warm air.

Mink's mother, from her upstairs window, gazed down.

The children.

She looked upon them and shook her head. Well, they'd eat well, sleep well, and be in school on Monday. Bless their vigorous little bodies. She listened.

Mink talked earnestly to someone near the rose-bush—though there was no one there.

These odd children. And the little girl, what was her name? Anna? Anna took notes on a pad. First, Mink asked the rose-bush a question, then called the answer to Anna.

"Triangle," said Mink.

"What's a tri," said Anna with difficulty, "angle?"

"Never mind," said Mink.

"How you spell it?" asked Anna.

"T-R-I—" spelled Mink, slowly, then snapped, "Oh, spell it yourself!" She went on to other words. "Beam," she said.

"I haven't got tri," said Anna, "angle down yet!"

"Well, hurry, hurry!" cried Mink.

Mink's mother leaned out the upstairs window. "A-N-G-L-E," she spelled down at Anna.

"Oh, thanks, Mrs. Morris," said Anna.

"Certainly," said Mink's mother and withdrew, laughing, to dust the hall with an electro-duster-magnet.

The voices wavered on the shimmery air. "Beam," said Anna. Fading.

"Four-nine-seven-A-and-B-and-X," said Mink, far away, seriously. "And a fork and a string and a—hex-hex-agony . . . hexagon*al*!"

At lunch, Mink gulped milk at one toss and was at the door. Her mother slapped the table.

"You sit right back down," commanded Mrs. Morris. "Hot soup in a minute." She poked a red button on the kitchen butler and ten seconds later something landed with a bump in the rubber receiver. Mrs. Morris opened it, took out a can with a pair of aluminum holders, unsealed it with a flick and poured hot soup into a bowl.

During all this, Mink fidgeted. "Hurry, Mom! This is a matter of life and death! Aw—!"

"I was the same way at your age. Always life and death. I know."

Mink banged away at the soup.

"Slow down," said Mom.

"Can't," said Mink. "Drill's waiting for me."

"Who's Drill? What a peculiar name," said Mom.

"You don't know him," said Mink.

"A new boy in the neighborhood?" asked Mom.

"He's new all right," said Mink. She started on her second bowl.

"Which one is Drill?" asked Mom.

"He's around," said Mink, evasively. "You'll make fun. Everybody pokes fun. Gee, darn."

"Is Drill shy?"

"Yes. No. In a way. Gosh, Mom, I got to run if we want to have the Invasion!"

"Who's invading what?"

"Martians invading Earth—well, not exactly Martians. They're—I don't know. From up." She pointed with her spoon.

"And *inside*," said Mom, touching Mink's feverish brow.

Mink rebelled. "You're laughing! You'll kill Drill and *every*body."

"I didn't mean to," said Mom. "Drill's a Martian?"

"No. He's—well—maybe from Jupiter or Saturn or Venus. Anyway, he's had a hard time."

"I imagine." Mrs. Morris hid her mouth behind her hand.

"They couldn't figure a way to attack earth."

"We're impregnable," said Mom, in mock-seriousness.

"That's the word Drill used! Impreg—That was the word, Mom."

"My, my. Drill's a brilliant little boy. Two-bit words."

"They couldn't figure a way to attack, Mom. Drill says—he says in order to make a good fight you got to have a new way of surprising people. That way you win. And he says also you got to have help from your enemy."

"A fifth column," said Mom.

"Yeah. That's what Drill said. And they couldn't figure a way to surprise Earth or get help."

"No wonder. We're pretty darn strong," laughed Mom, cleaning up. Mink sat there, staring at the table, seeing what she was talking about.

"Until, one day," whispered Mink, melodramatically, "they thought of children!"

"Well!" said Mrs. Morris brightly.

"And they thought of how grown-ups are so busy they never look under rose-bushes or on lawns!"

"Only for snails and fungus."

"And then there's something about dim-dims."

"Dim-dims?"

"Dimens-shuns."

"Dimensions?"

"Four of 'em. And there's something about kids under nine and imagination. It's real funny to hear Drill talk."

Mrs. Morris was tired. "Well, it must be funny. You're keeping Drill waiting now. It's getting late in the day and, if you want to have your Invasion before your supper bath, you'd better jump."

"Do I have to take a bath?" growled Mink.

"You do. Why is it children hate water? No matter what age you live in children hate water behind the ears!"

"Drill says I won't have to take baths," said Mink.

"Oh, he does, does he?"

"He told all the kids that. No more baths. And we can stay up till ten o'clock and go to two televisor shows on Saturday 'stead of one!"

"Well, Mr. Drill better mind his p's and q's. I'll call up his mother and—"

Mink went to the door. "We're having trouble with guys like Pete Britz and Dale Jerrick. They're growing up. They make fun. They're worse than parents. They just won't believe in Drill. They're so snooty, cause they're growing up. You'd think they'd know better. They were little only a coupla years ago. I hate them worst. We'll kill them *first*."

"Your father and I, last?"

"Drill says you're dangerous. Know why? Cause you don't believe in Martians! They're going to let *us* run the world. Well, not just us, but the kids over in the next block, too. I might be queen." She opened the door. "Mom?"

"Yes?"

"What's—lodge . . . ick?"

"Logic? Why, dear, logic is knowing what things are true and not true."

"He *mentioned* that," said Mink. "And what's im—pres—sion—able?" It took her a minute to say it.

"Why, it means—" Her mother looked at the floor, laughing gently. "It means—to be a child, dear."

"Thanks for lunch!" Mink ran out, then stuck her head back in. "Mom, I'll be sure you won't be hurt, much, really!"

"Well, thanks," said Mom.

Slam went the door.

At four o'clock the audio-visor buzzed. Mrs. Morris flipped the tab. "Hello, Helen!" she said, in welcome.

"Hello, Mary. How are things in New York?"

"Fine, how are things in Scranton. You look tired."

"So do you. The children. Underfoot," said Helen.

Mrs. Morris sighed, "My Mink, too. The super Invasion."

Helen laughed. "Are your kids playing that game, too?"

"Lord, yes. Tomorrow it'll be geometrical jacks and motorized hopscotch. Were we this bad when we were kids in '48?"

"Worse. Japs and Nazis. Don't know how my parents put up with me. Tomboy."

"Parents learn to shut their ears."

A silence.

"What's wrong, Mary?" asked Helen.

Mrs. Morris' eyes were half-closed; her tongue slid slowly, thoughtfully over her lower lip. "Eh?" She jerked. "Oh, nothing. Just thought about *that*. Shutting ears and such. Never mind. Where were we?"

"My boy Tim's got a crush on some guy named—*Drill*, I think it was."

"Must be a new password. Mink likes him, too."

"Didn't know it got as far as New York. Word of mouth, I imagine. Looks like a scrap drive. I talked to Josephine and she said her kids—that's in

Boston—are wild on this new game. It's sweeping the country."

At this moment, Mink trotted into the kitchen to gulp a glass of water. Mrs. Morris turned. "How're things going?"

"Almost finished," said Mink.

"Swell," said Mrs. Morris. "What's *that?*"

"A yo-yo," said Mink. "Watch."

She flung the yo-yo down its string. Reaching the end, it—

It vanished.

"See?" said Mink. "Ope!" Dibbling her finger she made the yo-yo reappear and zip up the string.

"Do that again," said her mother.

"Can't. Zero hour's five o'clock! 'Bye."

Mink exited, zipping her yo-yo.

On the audio-visor, Helen laughed. "Tim brought one of those yo-yo's in this morning, but when I got curious he said he wouldn't show it to me, and when I tried to work it, finally, it wouldn't work."

"You're not *impressionable*," said Mrs. Morris.

"What?"

"Never mind. Something I thought of. Can I help you, Helen?"

"I wanted to get that black-and-white cake recipe—"

The hour drowsed by. The day waned. The sun lowered in the peaceful blue sky. Shadows lengthened on the green lawns. The laughter and excitement continued. One little girl ran away, crying.

Mrs. Morris came out the front door.

"Mink, was that Peggy Ann crying?"

Mink was bent over in the yard, near the rose-bush. "Yeah. She's a scarebaby. We won't let her play, now. She's getting too old to play. I guess she grew up all of a sudden."

"Is that why she cried? Nonsense. Give me a civil answer, young lady, or inside you come!"

Mink whirled in consternation, mixed with irritation. "I can't quit now. It's almost time. I'll be good. I'm sorry."

"Did you hit Peggy Ann?"

"No, honest. You ask her. It was something—well, she's just a scaredy-pants."

The ring of children drew in around Mink where she scowled at her work with spoons and a kind of square-shaped arrangement of hammers and pipes. "There and there," murmured Mink.

"What's wrong?" said Mrs. Morris.

"Drill's stuck. Half way. If we could only get him all the way through, it'll be easier. Then all the others could come through after him."

"Can I help?"

"No'm, thanks. I'll fix it."

"All right. I'll call you for your bath in half an hour. I'm tired of watching you."

She went in and sat in the electric-relaxing chair, sipping a little beer from a half-empty glass. The chair massaged her back. Children, children. Children and love and hate, side by side. Sometimes children loved you, hated you, all in half a second. Strange children, did they ever forget or forgive the whippings and the harsh, strict words of command? She wondered. How can you ever forget or forgive those over and above you, those tall and silly dictators?

Time passed. A curious, waiting silence came upon the street, deepening.

Five o'clock. A clock sang softly somewhere in the house, in a quiet, musical voice, "Five o'clock . . . five o'clock. Time's awasting. Five o'clock," and purred away into silence.

Zero hour.

Mrs. Morris chuckled in her throat. Zero hour.

A beetle-car hummed into the driveway. Mr. Morris. Mrs. Morris smiled. Mr. Morris got out of the beetle, locked it and called hello to Mink at her work. Mink ignored him. He laughed and stood for a moment watching the children in their business. Then he walked up the front steps.

"Hello, darling."

"Hello, Henry."

She strained forward on the edge of the chair, listening. The children were silent. Too silent.

He emptied his pipe, refilled it. "Swell day. Makes you glad to be alive."

Buzz.

"What's that?" asked Henry.

"I don't know." She got up, suddenly, her eyes widening. She was going to say something. She stopped it. Ridiculous. Her nerves jumped. "Those children haven't anything dangerous out there, have they?" she said.

"Nothing but pipes and hammers. Why?"

"Nothing electrical?"

"Heck, no," said Henry. "I looked."

She walked to the kitchen. The buzzing continued. "Just the same you'd better go tell them to quit. It's after five. Tell them—" Her eyes widened and narrowed. "Tell them to put off their Invasion until tomorrow." She laughed, nervously.

The buzzing grew louder.

"What are they up to? I'd better go look, all right."

The explosion!

The house shook with dull sound. There were other explosions in other yards on other streets.

Involuntarily, Mrs. Morris screamed. "Up this way!" she cried, sense-lessly, knowing no sense, no reason. Perhaps she saw something from the corners of her eyes, perhaps she smelled a new odor or heard a new noise. There was no time to argue with Henry to convince him. Let him think her insane. Yes, insane! Shrieking, she ran upstairs. He ran after her to see what she was up to. "In the attic!" she screamed. "That's where it is!" It was only a poor excuse to get him in the attic in time—oh God, in time!

Another explosion outside. The children screamed with delight, as if at a great fireworks display.

"It's not in the attic!" cried Henry. "It's outside!"

"No, no!" Wheezing, gasping, she fumbled at the attic door. "I'll show you. Hurry! I'll show you!"

They tumbled into the attic. She slammed the door, locked it, took the key, threw it into a far, cluttered corner.

She was babbling wild stuff now. It came out of her. All the subconscious suspicion and fear that had gathered secretly all afternoon and fermented like a wine in her. All the little revelations and knowledges and sense that had bothered her all day and which she had logically and carefully and sensibly rejected and censored. Now it exploded in her and shook her to bits.

"There, there," she said, sobbing against the door. "We're safe until tonight. Maybe we can sneak out, maybe we can escape!"

Henry blew up, too, but for another reason. "Are you crazy? Why'd you throw that key away! Damn it, honey!"

"Yes, yes, I'm crazy, if it helps, but stay here with me!"

"I don't know how in hell I *can* get out!"

"Quiet. They'll hear us. Oh, God, they'll find us soon enough—"

Below them, Mink's voice. The husband stopped. There was a great universal humming and sizzling, a screaming and giggling. Downstairs, the audio-televisor buzzed and buzzed insistently, alarmingly, violently. *Is that Helen calling?* thought Mrs. Morris. *And is she calling about what I think she's calling about?*

Footsteps came into the house. Heavy footsteps.

"Who's coming in my house?" demanded Henry, angrily. "Who's tramp-ing around down there?"

Heavy feet. Twenty, thirty, forty, fifty of them. Fifty persons crowding into the house. The humming. The giggling of the children. "This way!" cried Mink, below.

"Who's downstairs?" roared Henry. "Who's there!"

"Hush, oh, nonononono!" said his wife, weakly, holding him. "Please, be quiet. They might go away."

"Mom?" called Mink, "Dad?" A pause. "Where are you?"

Heavy footsteps, heavy, heavy, *very* HEAVY footsteps came up the stairs. Mink leading them.

"Mom?" A hesitation. "Dad?" A waiting, a silence.

Humming. Footsteps toward the attic. Mink's first.

They trembled together in silence in the attic, Mr. and Mrs. Morris. For some reason the electric humming, the queer cold light suddenly visible under the door crack, the strange odor and the alien sound of eagerness in Mink's voice, finally got through to Henry Morris, too. He stood, shivering, in the dark silence, his wife beside him.

"Mom! Dad!"

Footsteps. A little humming sound. The attic lock melted. The door opened. Mink peered inside, tall blue shadows behind her.

"Peek-a-boo," said Mink.

Nine Lives

Ursula K. Le Guin's stories and novels propelled her to the forefront of contemporary science fiction in the 1960s, culminating in the Hugo and Nebula award–winning novel The Left Hand of Darkness. *At the same time, she was writing fantasy stories and novels for young adults, including the classic* A Wizard of Earthsea. *Then in the early 1970s widespread critical praise outside SF, including a piece in* The New Yorker *by John Updike championing her work, put her in a position analogous to Ray Bradbury's at the end of the 1940s. She is a significant contemporary American writer who has emerged from SF.*

Her work, crafted with technical virtuosity and great care, embodies the mainstream virtues of the classic well-made story. She is a feminist, like Joanna Russ and several other important SF writers, and the first woman writer to achieve a commanding position in SF. Feminist SF was the most energetic and socially visionary part of the field during the 1970s, when Le Guin was looked upon by many as the most important writer in SF. Since then she has turned to an experimental and innovative form of anthropological SF, in her novel Always Coming Home, *and has published books of poetry. The images and concerns of conventional SF seem to have lost their force for her. "Nine Lives" dates from the late 1960s, when Le Guin was most charged by the powerful and wonder-filled images of science. In the early 1970s she wrote an essay entitled "On Theme," collected in* The Language of the Night *(1978), on the conscious and unconscious processes involved in the writing of "Nine Lives," a story now regarded as a classic of the period. An admirer of Lem's work, she is, like him, a literary conservative in her critical stance. She stands for SF as a literature of ideas wedded to a thorough examination of their deepest human implications.*

*　　*　　*

S he was alive inside, but dead outside, her face a black and dun net of wrinkles, tumors, cracks. She was bald and blind. The tremors that crossed Libra's face were mere quiverings of corruption: underneath, in the black corridors, the halls beneath the skin, there were crepitations in darkness, ferments, chemical nightmares that went on for centuries. "Oh the damned flatulent planet," Pugh murmured as the dome shook and a boil burst a kilometer to the southwest, spraying silver pus across the sunset. The sun had been setting for the last two days. "I'll be glad to see a human face."

"Thanks," said Martin.

"Yours is human to be sure," said Pugh, "but I've seen it so long I can't see it."

Radvid signals cluttered the communicator which Martin was operating, faded, returned as face and voice. The face filled the screen, the nose of an Assyrian king, the eyes of a samurai, skin bronze, eyes the color of iron: young, magnificent. "Is that what human beings look like?" said Pugh with awe. "I'd forgotten."

"Shut up, Owen, we're on."

"Libra Exploratory Mission Base, come in please, this is *Passerine* launch."

"Libra here. Beam fixed. Come on down, launch."

"Expulsion in seven E-seconds. Hold on." The screen blanked and sparkled.

"Do they all look like that? Martin, you and I are uglier men than I thought."

"Shut up, Owen. . . ."

For twenty-two minutes Martin followed the landing-craft down by signal and then through the cleared dome they saw it, small star in the blood-colored east, sinking. It came down neat and quiet, Libra's thin atmosphere carrying little sound. Pugh and Martin closed the headpieces of their imsuits, zipped out of the dome airlocks, and ran with soaring strides, Nijinsky and Nureyev, toward the boat. Three equipment modules came floating down at four-minute intervals from each other and hundred-meter intervals east of the boat. "Come on out," Martin said on his suit radio, "we're waiting at the door."

"Come on in, the methane's fine," said Pugh.

The hatch opened. The young man they had seen on the screen came out with one athletic twist and leaped down onto the shaky dust and clinkers of Libra. Martin shook his hand, but Pugh was staring at the hatch, from which another young man emerged with the same neat twist and jump, followed by a young woman who emerged with the same neat twist, ornamented by a wriggle, and the jump. They were all tall, with bronze skin, black hair, high-bridged noses, epicanthic fold, the same face. They all had the same face. The fourth was emerging from the hatch with a neat twist and jump. "Martin bach," said Pugh, "we've got a clone."

"Right," said one of them, "we're a tenclone. John Chow's the name. You're Lieutenant Martin?"

"I'm Owen Pugh."

"Alvaro Guillen Martin," said Martin, formal, bowing slightly. Another girl was out, the same beautiful face; Martin stared at her and his eye rolled like a nervous pony's. Evidently he had never given any thought to cloning, and was suffering technological shock. "Steady," Pugh said in the Argentine dialect, "it's only excess twins." He stood close by Martin's elbow. He was glad himself of the contact.

It is hard to meet a stranger. Even the greatest extrovert meeting even the meekest stranger knows a certain dread, though he may not know he knows it. Will he make a fool of me wreck my image of myself invade me destroy me change me? Will he be different from me? Yes, that he will. There's the terrible thing: the strangeness of the stranger.

After two years on a dead planet, and the last half year isolated as a team of two, oneself and one other, after that it's even harder to meet a stranger, however welcome he may be. You're out of the habit of difference, you've lost the touch; and so the fear revives, the primitive anxiety, the old dread.

The clone, five males and five females, had got done in a couple of minutes what a man might have got done in twenty: greeted Pugh and Martin, had a glance at Libra, unloaded the boat, made ready to go. They went, and the dome filled with them, a hive of golden bees. They hummed and buzzed quietly, filled up all silences, all spaces with a honey-brown swarm of human presence. Martin looked bewilderedly at the long-limbed girls, and they smiled at him, three at once. Their smile was gentler than that of the boys, but no less radiantly self-possessed.

"Self-possessed," Owen Pugh murmured to his friend, "that's it. Think of it, to be oneself ten times over. Nine seconds for every motion, nine ayes on every vote. It would be glorious!" But Martin was asleep. And the John Chows had all gone to sleep at once. The dome was filled with their quiet breathing. They were young, they didn't snore. Martin sighed and snored, his Hershey-bar-colored face relaxed in the dim afterglow of Libra's primary, set at last. Pugh had cleared the dome and stars looked in, Sol among them, a great company of lights, a clone of splendors. Pugh slept and dreamed of a one-eyed giant who chased him through the shaking halls of Hell.

From his sleeping-bag Pugh watched the clone's awakening. They all got up within one minute except for one pair, a boy and a girl, who lay snugly tangled and still sleeping in one bag. As Pugh saw this there was a shock like one of Libra's earthquakes inside him, a very deep tremor. He was not aware of this, and in fact thought he was pleased at the sight; there was no other such comfort on this dead hollow world, more power to them, who made love. One of the others stepped on the pair. They woke and the girl sat up flushed and sleepy, with bare golden breasts. One of her sisters murmured something to her; she shot a glance at Pugh and disappeared in the sleeping-bag, followed by a giant giggle, from another direction a fierce stare, from still another direction a voice: "Christ, we're used to having a room to ourselves. Hope you don't mind, Captain Pugh."

"It's a pleasure," Pugh said half-truthfully. He had to stand up then, wearing only the shorts he slept in, and he felt like a plucked rooster, all white scrawn and pimples. He had seldom envied Martin's compact brownness so much. The United Kingdom had come through the Great Famines well, losing less than half its population: a record achieved by rigorous food-control. Black-marketeers and hoarders had been executed. Crumbs had been shared. Where in richer lands most had died and a few had thriven, in Britain fewer died and none throve. They all got lean. Their sons were lean, their grandsons lean, small, brittle-boned, easily infected. When civilization became a matter of standing in lines, the British had kept queue, and so had replaced the survival of the fittest with the survival of the fair-minded. Owen Pugh was a scrawny little man. All the same, he was there.

At the moment he wished he wasn't.

At breakfast a John said, "Now if you'll brief us, Captain Pugh—"

"Owen, then."

"Owen, we can work out our schedule. Anything new on the mine since your last report to your Mission? We saw your reports when *Passerine* was orbiting Planet V, where they are now."

Martin did not answer, though the mine was his discovery and project, and Pugh had to do his best. It was hard to talk to them. The same faces, each with the same expression of intelligent interest, all leaned toward him across the table at almost the same angle. They all nodded together.

Over the Exploitation Corps insignia on their tunics each had a name-band, first name John and last name Chow of course, but the middle names different. The men were Aleph, Kaph, Yod, Gimel, and Samedh; the women Sadhe, Daleth, Zayin, Beth, and Resh. Pugh tried to use the names but gave it up at once; he could not even tell sometimes which one had spoken, for the voices were all alike.

Martin buttered and chewed his toast, and finally interrupted: "You're a team. Is that it?"

"Right," said two Johns.

"God, what a team! I hadn't seen the point. How much do you each know what the others are thinking?"

"Not at all, properly speaking," replied one of the girls, Zayin. The others watched her with the proprietary, approving look they had. "No ESP, nothing fancy. But we think alike. We have exactly the same equipment. Given the same stimulus, the same problem, we're likely to be coming up with the same reactions and solutions at the same time. Explanations are easy—don't even have to make them, usually. We seldom misunderstand each other. It does facilitate our working as a team."

"Christ yes," said Martin. "Pugh and I have spent seven hours out of ten for six months misunderstanding each other. Like most people. What about emergencies, are you as good at meeting the unexpected problem as a nor . . . an unrelated team?"

"Statistics so far indicate that we are," Zayin answered readily. Clones must be trained, Pugh thought, to meet questions, to reassure and reason. All they said had the slightly bland and stilted quality of answers furnished to the Public. "We can't brainstorm as singletons can, we as a team don't profit from the interplay of varied minds; but we have a compensatory advantage. Clones are drawn from the best human material, individuals of IIQ 99th percentile, Genetic Constitution alpha double A, and so on. We have more to draw on than most individuals do."

"And it's multiplied by a factor of ten. Who is—who was John Chow?"

"A genius surely," Pugh said politely. His interest in cloning was not so new and avid as Martin's.

"Leonardo Complex type," said Yod. "Biomath, also a cellist, and an undersea hunter, and interested in structural engineering problems, and so on. Died before he'd worked out his major theories."

"Then you each represent a different facet of his mind, his talents?"

"No," said Zayin, shaking her head in time with several others. "We share the basic equipment and tendencies, of course, but we're all engineers in Planetary Exploitation. A later clone can be trained to develop other aspects of the basic equipment. It's all training; the genetic substance is identical. We *are* John Chow. But we were differently trained."

Martin looked shell-shocked. "How old are you?"

"Twenty-three."

"You say he died young— Had they taken germ cells from him beforehand or something?"

Gimel took over: "He died at twenty-four in an aircar crash. They couldn't save the brain, so they took some intestinal cells and cultured them for cloning. Reproductive cells aren't used for cloning since they have only half the chromosomes. Intestinal cells happen to be easy to despecialize and reprogram for total growth."

"All chips off the old block," Martin said valiantly. "But how can . . . some of you be women . . . ?"

Beth took over: "It's easy to program half the clonal mass back to the female. Just delete the male gene from half the cells and they revert to the basic, that is, the female. It's trickier to go the other way, have to hook in artificial Y chromosomes. So they mostly clone from males, since clones function best bisexually."

Gimel again: "They've worked these matters of technique and function out carefully. The taxpayer wants the best for his money, and of course clones are expensive. With the cell-manipulations, and the incubation in Ngama Placentae, and the maintenance and training of the foster-parent groups, we end up costing about three million apiece."

"For your next generation," Martin said, still struggling, "I suppose you . . . you breed?"

"We females are sterile," said Beth with perfect equanimity; "you remember that the Y chromosome was deleted from our original cell. The males can interbreed with approved singletons, if they want to. But to get John Chow again as often as they want, they just reclone a cell from this clone."

Martin gave up the struggle. He nodded and chewed cold toast. "Well," said one of the Johns, and all changed mood, like a flock of starlings that change course in one wingflick, following a leader so fast that no eye can see which leads. They were ready to go. "How about a look at the mine? Then we'll unload the equipment. Some nice new models in the roboats; you'll want to see them. Right?" Had Pugh or Martin not agreed they might have found it hard to say so. The Johns were polite but unanimous; their decisions carried. Pugh, Commander of Libra Base 2, felt a qualm. Could he boss around this superman-woman-entity-of-ten? and a genius at that? He stuck close to Martin as they suited for outside. Neither said anything.

Four apiece in the three large jetsleds, they slipped off north from the dome, over Libra's dun rugose skin, in starlight.

"Desolate," one said.

It was a boy and girl with Pugh and Martin. Pugh wondered if these were the two that had shared a sleeping-bag last night. No doubt they wouldn't mind if he asked them. Sex must be as handy as breathing, to them. Did you two breathe last night?

"Yes," he said, "it is desolate."

"This is our first time Off, except training on Luna." The girl's voice was definitely a bit higher and softer.

"How did you take the big hop?"

"They doped us. I wanted to experience it." That was the boy; he sounded wistful. They seemed to have more personality, only two at a time. Did repetition of the individual negate individuality?

"Don't worry," said Martin, steering the sled, "you can't experience no-time because it isn't there."

"I'd just like to once," one of them said. "So we'd know."

The Mountains of Merioneth showed leprotic in starlight to the east, a plume of freezing gas trailed silvery from a vent-hole to the west, and the sled tilted groundward. The twins braced for the stop at one moment, each with a slight protective gesture to the other. Your skin is my skin, Pugh thought, but literally, no metaphor. What would it be like, then, to have someone as close to you as that? Always to be answered when you spoke, never to be in pain alone. Love your neighbor as you love yourself. . . . That hard old problem was solved. The neighbor was the self: the love was perfect.

And here was Hellmouth, the mine.

Pugh was the Exploratory Mission's ET geologist, and Martin his technician and cartographer; but when in the course of a local survey Martin had discovered the U-mine, Pugh had given him full credit, as well as the onus of prospecting the lode and planning the Exploitation Team's job. These kids had been sent out from Earth years before Martin's reports got there, and had not known what their job would be until they got here. The Exploitation Corps simply set out teams regularly and blindly as a dandelion sends out its seeds, knowing there would be a job for them on Libra or the next planet out or one they hadn't even heard about yet. The Government wanted uranium too urgently to wait while reports drifted home across the light-years. The stuff was like gold, old-fashioned but essential, worth mining extra-terrestrially and shipping interstellar. Worth its weight in people, Pugh thought sourly, watching the tall young men and women go one by one, glimmering in starlight, into the black hole Martin had named Hellmouth.

As they went in their homeostatic forehead-lamps brightened. Twelve nodding gleams ran along the moist, wrinkled walls. Pugh heard Martin's radiation counter peeping twenty to the dozen up ahead. "Here's the drop-off," said Martin's voice in the suit intercom, drowning out the peeping and the dead silence that was around them. "We're in a side-fissure; this is the main vertical vent in front of us." The black void gaped, its far side not visible in the headlamp beams. "Last vulcanism seems to have been a couple of thousand years ago. Nearest fault is twenty-eight kilos east, in the Trench. This region seems to be as safe seismically as anything in the area. The big basalt-flow overhead stabilizes all these substructures, so long as it remains stable itself. Your central lode is thirty-six meters down and runs in a series of five bubble-caverns northeast. It is a lode, a pipe of very high-grade ore. You saw the percentage figures, right? Extraction's going to be no problem. All you've got to do is get the bubbles topside."

"Take off the lid and let 'em float up." A chuckle. Voices began to talk, but they were all the same voice and the suit radio gave them no location in space. "Open the thing right up. — Safer that way. — But it's a solid basalt roof, how thick, ten meters here? — Three to twenty, the report said. — Blow good ore all over the lot. — Use this access we're in, straighten it a bit and run slider-rails for the robos. — Import burros. — Have we got enough propping material? — What's your estimate of total payload mass, Martin?"

"Say over five million kilos and under eight."

"Transport will be here in ten E-months. — It'll have to go pure. — No, they'll have the mass problem in NAFAL shipping licked by now; remember it's been sixteen years since we left Earth last Tuesday. — Right, they'll send the whole lot back and purify it in Earth orbit. — Shall we go down, Martin?"

"Go on. I've been down."

The first one — Aleph? (Heb., the ox, the leader) — swung onto the ladder and down; the rest followed. Pugh and Martin stood at the chasm's edge. Pugh set his intercom to exchange only with Martin's suit, and noticed Martin doing the same. It was a bit wearing, this listening to one person think aloud in ten voices, or was it one voice speaking the thoughts of ten minds?

"A great gut," Pugh said, looking down into the black pit, its veined and warted walls catching stray gleams of headlamps far below. "A cow's bowel. A bloody great constipated intestine."

Martin's counter peeped like a lost chicken. They stood inside the epileptic planet, breathing oxygen from tanks, wearing suits impermeable to corrosives and harmful radiations, resistant to a two-hundred-degree range of temperatures, tear-proof, and as shock-resistant as possible given the soft vulnerable stuff inside.

"Next hop," Martin said, "I'd like to find a planet that has nothing whatever to exploit."

"You found this."

"Keep me home next time."

Pugh was pleased. He had hoped Martin would want to go on working with him, but neither of them was used to talking much about their feelings, and he had hesitated to ask. "I'll try that," he said.

"I hate this place. I like caves, you know. It's why I came in here. Just spelunking. But this one's a bitch. Mean. You can't ever let down in here. I guess this lot can handle it, though. They know their stuff."

"Wave of the future, whatever," said Pugh.

The wave of the future came swarming up the ladder, swept Martin to the entrance, gabbled at and around him: "Have we got enough material for supports? — If we convert one of the extractor-servos to anneal, yes. — Sufficient if we miniblast? — Kaph can calculate stress."

Pugh had switched his intercom back to receive them; he looked at them, so many thoughts jabbering in an eager mind, and at Martin standing silent among them, and at Hellmouth, and the wrinkled plain. "Settled! How does that strike you as a preliminary schedule, Martin?"

"It's your baby," Martin said.

Within five E-days the Johns had all their material and equipment unloaded and operating, and were starting to open up the mine. They worked with total efficiency. Pugh was fascinated and frightened by their effectiveness, their confidence, their independence. He was no use to them at all. A clone, he thought, might indeed be the first truly stable, self-reliant human being. Once adult it would need nobody's help. It would be sufficient to itself physically, sexually, emotionally, intellectually. Whatever he did, any member of it would always receive the support and approval of his peers, his other selves. Nobody else was needed.

Two of the clone stayed in the dome doing calculations and paperwork, with frequent sled-trips to the mine for measurements and tests. They were the mathematicians of the clone, Zayin and Kaph. That is, as Zayin explained, all ten had had thorough mathematical training from age three to twenty-one, but from twenty-one to twenty-three she and Kaph had gone on with math while the others intensified other specialties, geology, mining engineering, electronic engineering, equipment robotics, applied atomics, and so on. "Kaph and I feel," she said, "that we're the element of the clone closest to what John Chow was in his singleton lifetime. But of course he was principally in biomath, and they didn't take us far in that."

"They needed us most in this field," Kaph said, with the patriotic priggishness they sometimes evinced.

Pugh and Martin soon could distinguish this pair from the others, Zayin by gestalt, Kaph only by a discolored left fourth fingernail, got from an ill-aimed hammer at the age of six. No doubt there were many such differences, physical and psychological, among them; nature might be identical, nurture could not be. But the differences were hard to find. And part of the difficulty was that they really never talked to Pugh and Martin. They joked with them, were polite, got along fine. They gave nothing. It was nothing one could complain about; they were very pleasant, they had the standardized American friendliness. "Do you come from Ireland, Owen?"

"Nobody comes from Ireland, Zayin."

"There are lots of Irish-Americans."

"To be sure, but no more Irish. A couple of thousand in all the island, the last I knew. They didn't go in for birth-control, you know, so the food ran out. By the Third Famine there were no Irish left at all but the priesthood, and they were all celibate, or nearly all."

Zayin and Kaph smiled stiffly. They had no experience of either bigotry or irony. "What are you then, ethnically?" Kaph asked, and Pugh replied, "A Welshman."

"Is it Welsh that you and Martin speak together?"

None of your business, Pugh thought, but said, "No, it's his dialect, not mine: Argentinean. A descendant of Spanish."

"You learned it for private communication?"

"Whom had we here to be private from? It's just that sometimes a man likes to speak his native language."

"Ours is English," Kaph said unsympathetically. Why should they have sympathy? That's one of the things you give because you need it back.

"Is Wells quaint?" asked Zayin.

"Wells? Oh, Wales, it's called. Yes. Wales is quaint." Pugh switched on his rock-cutter, which prevented further conversation by a synapse-destroying whine, and while it whined he turned his back and said a profane word in Welsh.

That night he used the Argentine dialect for private communication. "Do they pair off in the same couples, or change every night?"

Martin looked surprised. A prudish expression, unsuited to his features, appeared for a moment. It faded. He too was curious. "I think it's random."

"Don't whisper, man, it sounds dirty. I think they rotate."

"On a schedule?"

"So nobody gets omitted."

Martin gave a vulgar laugh and smothered it. "What about us? Aren't we omitted?"

"That doesn't occur to them."

"What if I proposition one of the girls?"

"She'd tell the others and they'd decide as a group."

"I am not a bull," Martin said, his dark, heavy face heating up. "I will not be judged—"

"Down, down, *machismo*," said Pugh. "Do you mean to proposition one?"

Martin shrugged, sullen. "Let 'em have their incest."

"Incest is it, or masturbation?"

"I don't care, if they'd do it out of earshot!"

The clone's early attempts at modesty had soon worn off, unmotivated by any deep defensiveness of self or awareness of others. Pugh and Martin were daily deeper swamped under the intimacies of its constant emotional-sexual-mental interchange: swamped yet excluded.

"Two months to go," Martin said one evening.

"To what?" snapped Pugh. He was edgy lately and Martin's sullenness got on his nerves.

"To relief."

In sixty days the full crew of their Exploratory Mission were due back from their survey of the other planets of the system. Pugh was aware of this.

"Crossing off the days on your calendar?" he jeered.

"Pull yourself together, Owen."

"What do you mean?"

"What I say."

They parted in contempt and resentment.

Pugh came in after a day alone on the Pampas, a vast lava-plain the nearest edge of which was two hours south by jet. He was tired, but refreshed by solitude. They were not supposed to take long trips alone, but lately had often done so. Martin stooped under bright lights, drawing one of his elegant, masterly charts: this one was of the whole face of Libra, the cancerous face. The dome was otherwise empty, seeming dim and large as it had before the clone came. "Where's the golden horde?"

Martin grunted ignorance, crosshatching. He straightened his back to glance around at the sun, which squatted feebly like a great red toad on the eastern plain, and at the clock, which said 18:45. "Some big quakes today," he said, returning to his map. "Feel them down there? Lot of crates were falling around. Take a look at the seismo."

The needle jigged and wavered on the roll. It never stopped dancing here. The roll had recorded five quakes of major intensity back in mid-afternoon; twice the needle had hopped off the roll. The attached computer had been activated to emit a slip reading, "Epicenter 61' N by 4'24" E."

"Not in the Trench this time."

"I thought it felt a bit different from usual. Sharper."

"In Base One I used to lie awake all night feeling the ground jump. Queer how you get used to things."

"Go spla if you didn't. What's for dinner?"

"I thought you'd have cooked it."

"Waiting for the clone."

Feeling put upon, Pugh got out a dozen dinnerboxes, stuck two in the Instobake, pulled them out. "All right, here's dinner."

"Been thinking," Martin said, coming to the table. "What if some clone cloned itself? Illegally. Made a thousand duplicates—ten thousand. Whole army. They could make a tidy power-grab, couldn't they?"

"But how many millions did this lot cost to rear? Artificial placentae and all that. It would be hard to keep secret, unless they had a planet to themselves. . . . Back before the Famines when Earth had national governments, they talked about that: clone your best soldiers, have whole regiments of them. But the food ran out before they could play that game."

They talked amicably, as they used to.

"Funny," Martin said, chewing. "They left early this morning, didn't they?"

"All but Kaph and Zayin. They thought they'd get the first payload aboveground today. What's up?"

"They weren't back for lunch."

"They won't starve, to be sure."

"They left at seven."

"So they did." Then Pugh saw it. The air-tanks held eight hours' supply.

"Kaph and Zayin carried out spare cans when they left. Or they've got a heap out there."

"They did, but they brought the whole lot in to recharge." Martin stood up, pointing to one of the stacks of stuff that cut the dome into rooms and alleys.

"There's an alarm signal on every imsuit."

"It's not automatic."

Pugh was tired and still hungry. "Sit down and eat, man. That lot can look after themselves."

Martin sat down, but did not eat. "There was a big quake, Owen. The first one. Big enough, it scared me."

After a pause Pugh sighed and said, "All right."

Unenthusiastically, they got out the two-man sled that was always left for them, and headed it north. The long sunrise covered everything in poisonous red jello. The horizontal light and shadow made it hard to see, raised walls of fake iron ahead of them through which they slid, turned the convex plain beyond Hellmouth into a great dimple full of bloody water. Around the tunnel entrance a wilderness of machinery stood, cranes and cables and servos and wheels and diggers and robocarts and sliders and control-huts, all slanting and bulking incoherently in the red light. Martin jumped from the sled, ran into the mine. He came out again, to Pugh. "Oh God, Owen, it's down," he said. Pugh went in and saw, five meters from the entrance, the shiny, moist, black wall that ended the tunnel. Newly exposed to air, it looked organic, like visceral tissue. The tunnel entrance, enlarged by blasting and double-tracked for robocarts, seemed unchanged until he noticed thousands of tiny spiderweb cracks in the walls. The floor was wet with some sluggish fluid.

"They were inside," Martin said.

"They may be still. They surely had extra air-cans—"

"Look, Owen, look at the basalt flow, at the roof; don't you see what the quake did, look at it."

The low hump of land that roofed the caves still had the unreal look of an optical illusion. It had reversed itself, sunk down, leaving a vast dimple or pit. When Pugh walked on it he saw that it too was cracked with many tiny fissures. From some a whitish gas was seeping, so that the sunlight on the surface of the gas-pool was shafted as if by the waters of a dim red lake.

"The mine's not on the fault. There's no fault here!"

Pugh came back to him quickly. "No, there's no fault, Martin. Look, they surely weren't all inside together."

Martin followed him and searched among the wrecked machines dully, then actively. He spotted the airsled. It had come down heading south, and stuck at an angle in a pothole of colloidal dust. It had carried two riders. One was half sunk in the dust, but his suit-meters registered normal functioning; the other hung strapped onto the tilted sled. Her imsuit had burst open on the broken legs, and the body was frozen hard as any rock. That was all they found. As both regulation and custom demanded, they cremated the dead at once with the laser-guns they carried by regulation and had never used before. Pugh, knowing he was going to be sick, wrestled the survivor onto the two-man sled and sent Martin off to the dome with him. Then he vomited, and flushed the waste out of his suit, and finding one four-man sled undamaged followed after Martin, shaking as if the cold of Libra had got through to him.

The survivor was Kaph. He was in deep shock. They found a swelling on the occiput that might mean concussion, but no fracture was visible.

Pugh brought two glasses of food-concentrate and two chasers of aquavit. "Come on," he said. Martin obeyed, drinking off the tonic. They sat down on crates near the cot and sipped the aquavit.

Kaph lay immobile, face like beeswax, hair bright black to the shoulders, lips stiffly parted for faintly gasping breaths.

"It must have been the first shock, the big one," Martin said. "It must have slid the whole structure sideways. Till it fell in on itself. There must be gas layers in the lateral rocks, like those formations in the Thirty-first Quadrant. But there wasn't any sign —" As he spoke the world slid out from under them. Things leaped and clattered, hopped and jigged, shouted Ha! Ha! Ha! "It was like this at fourteen hours," said Reason shakily in Martin's voice; amidst the unfastening and ruin of the world. But Unreason sat up, as the tumult lessened and things ceased dancing, and screamed aloud.

Pugh leaped across his spilled aquavit and held Kaph down. The muscular body flailed him off. Martin pinned the shoulders down. Kaph screamed, struggled, choked; his face blackened. "Oxy," Pugh said, and his hand found the right needle in the medical kit as if by homing instinct; while Martin held the mask he struck the needle home to the vagus nerve, restoring Kaph to life.

"Didn't know you knew that stunt," Martin said, breathing hard.

"The Lazarus Jab; my father was a doctor. It doesn't often work," Pugh said. "I want that drink I spilled. Is the quake over? I can't tell."

"Aftershocks. It's not just you shivering."

"Why did he suffocate?"

"I don't know, Owen. Look in the book."

Kaph was breathing normally and his color was restored, only the lips were still darkened. They poured a new shot of courage and sat down by him again with their medical guide. "Nothing about cyanosis or asphyxiation under 'shock' or 'concussion.' He can't have breathed in anything with his suit on. I don't know. We'd get as much good out of *Mother Mog's Home Herbalist*. . . . 'Anal Hemorrhoids,' fy!" Pugh pitched the book to a crate-table. It fell short, because either Pugh or the table was still unsteady.

"Why didn't he signal?"

"Sorry?"

"The eight inside the mine never had time. But he and the girl must have been outside. Maybe she was in the entrance, and got hit by the first slide. He must have been outside, in the control-hut maybe. He ran in, pulled her out, strapped her onto the sled, started for the dome. And all that time never pushed the panic button in his imsuit. Why not?"

"Well, he'd had that whack on his head. I doubt he ever realized the girl was dead. He wasn't in his senses. But if he had been I don't know if he'd have thought to signal us. They looked to one another for help."

Martin's face was like an Indian mask, grooves at the mouth-corners, eyes of dull coal. "That's so. What must he have felt, then, when the quake came and he was outside, alone—"

In answer Kaph screamed.

He came up off the cot in the heaving convulsions of one suffocating, knocked Pugh right down with his flailing arm, staggered into a stack of crates and fell to the floor, lips blue, eyes white. Martin dragged him back onto the cot and gave him a whiff of oxygen, then knelt by Pugh, who was just sitting up, and wiped at his cut cheekbone. "Owen, are you all right, are you going to be all right, Owen?"

"I think I am," Pugh said. "Why are you rubbing that on my face?"

It was a short length of computer-tape, now spotted with Pugh's blood. Martin dropped it. "Thought it was a towel. You clipped your cheek on that box there."

"Is he out of it?"

"Seems to be."

They stared down at Kaph lying stiff, his teeth a white line inside dark parted lips.

"Like epilepsy. Brain damage maybe?"

"What about shooting him full of meprobamate?"

Pugh shook his head. "I don't know what's in that shot I already gave him for shock. Don't want to overdose him."

"Maybe he'll sleep it off now."

"I'd like to myself. Between him and the earthquake I can't seem to keep on my feet."

"You got a nasty crack there. Go on, I'll sit up awhile."

Pugh cleaned his cut cheek and pulled off his shirt, then paused.

"Is there anything we ought to have done—have tried to do—"

"They're all dead," Martin said heavily, gently.

Pugh lay down on top of his sleeping-bag, and one instant later was wakened by a hideous, sucking, struggling noise. He staggered up, found the needle, tried three times to jab it in correctly and failed, began to massage over Kaph's heart. "Mouth-to-mouth," he said, and Martin obeyed. Presently Kaph drew a harsh breath, his heartbeat steadied, his rigid muscles began to relax.

"How long did I sleep?"

"Half an hour."

They stood up sweating. The ground shuddered, the fabric of the dome sagged and swayed. Libra was dancing her awful polka again, her Totentanz. The sun, though rising, seemed to have grown larger and redder; gas and dust must have been stirred up in the feeble atmosphere.

"What's wrong with him, Owen?"

"I think he's dying with them."

"Them—But they're dead, I tell you."

"Nine of them. They're all dead, they were crushed or suffocated. They were all him, he is all of them. They died, and now he's dying their deaths one by one."

"Oh pity of God," said Martin.

The next time was much the same. The fifth time was worse, for Kaph fought and raved, trying to speak but getting no words out, as if his mouth were stopped with rocks or clay. After that the attacks grew weaker, but so did he. The eighth seizure came at about four-thirty; Pugh and Martin worked till five-thirty doing all they could to keep life in the body that slid without protest into death. They kept him, but Martin said, "The next will finish him." And it did; but Pugh breathed his own breath into the inert lungs, until he himself passed out.

He woke. The dome was opaqued and no light on. He listened and heard the breathing of two sleeping men. He slept, and nothing woke him till hunger did.

The sun was well up over the dark plains, and the planet had stopped dancing. Kaph lay asleep. Pugh and Martin drank tea and looked at him with proprietary triumph.

When he woke Martin went to him: "How do you feel, old man?" There was no answer. Pugh took Martin's place and looked into the brown, dull eyes that gazed toward but not into his own. Like Martin he quickly turned away. He heated food-concentrate and brought it to Kaph. "Come on, drink."

He could see the muscles in Kaph's throat tighten. "Let me die," the young man said.

"You're not dying."

Kaph spoke with clarity and precision: "I am nine-tenths dead. There is not enough of me left alive."

That precision convinced Pugh, and he fought the conviction. "No," he said, peremptory. "They are dead. The others. Your brothers and sisters. You're not them, you're alive. You are John Chow. Your life is in your own hands."

The young man lay still, looking into a darkness that was not there.

Martin and Pugh took turns taking the Exploitation hauler and a spare set of robos over to Hellmouth to salvage equipment and protect it from Libra's sinister atmosphere, for the value of the stuff was, literally, astronomical. It was slow work for one man at a time, but they were unwilling to leave Kaph by himself. The one left in the dome did paperwork, while Kaph sat or lay and stared into his darkness, and never spoke. The days went by silent.

The radio spat and spoke: the Mission calling from ship. "We'll be down on Libra in five weeks, Owen. Thirty-four E-days nine hours I make it as of now. How's tricks in the old dome?"

"Not good, chief. The Exploit team were killed, all but one of them, in the mine. Earthquake. Six days ago."

The radio crackled and sang starsong. Sixteen seconds lag each way; the ship was out around Planet 11 now. "Killed, all but one? You and Martin were unhurt?"

"We're all right, chief."

Thirty-two seconds.

"*Passerine* left an Exploit team out here with us. I may put them on the Hellmouth project then, instead of the Quadrant Seven project. We'll settle that when we come down. In any case you and Martin will be relieved at Dome Two. Hold tight. Anything else?"

"Nothing else."

Thirty-two seconds.

"Right then. So long, Owen."

Kaph had heard all this, and later on Pugh said to him, "The chief may ask you to stay here with the other Exploit team. You know the ropes here." Knowing the exigencies of Far Out Life, he wanted to warn the young man. Kaph made no answer. Since he had said, "There is not enough of me left alive," he had not spoken a word.

"Owen," Martin said on suit intercom, "he's spla. Insane. Psycho."

"He's doing very well for a man who's died nine times."

"Well? Like a turned-off android is well? The only emotion he has left is hate. Look at his eyes."

"That's not hate, Martin. Listen, it's true that he has, in a sense, been dead. I cannot imagine what he feels. But it's not hatred. He can't even see us. It's too dark."

"Throats have been cut in the dark. He hates us because we're not Aleph and Yod and Zayin."

"Maybe. But I think he's alone. He doesn't see us or hear us, that's the truth. He never had to see anyone else before. He never was alone before. He had himself to see, talk with, live with, nine other selves all his life. He doesn't know how you go it alone. He must learn. Give him time."

Martin shook his heavy head. "Spla," he said. "Just remember when you're alone with him that he could break your neck one-handed."

"He could do that," said Pugh, a short, soft-voiced man with a scarred cheekbone; he smiled. They were just outside the dome airlock, programming one of the servos to repair a damaged hauler. They could see Kaph sitting inside the great half-egg of the dome like a fly in amber.

"Hand me the insert pack there. What makes you think he'll get any better?"

"He has a strong personality, to be sure."

"Strong? Crippled. Nine-tenths dead, as he put it."

"But he's not dead. He's a live man: John Kaph Chow. He had a jolly queer upbringing, but after all every boy has got to break free of his family. He will do it."

"I can't see it."

"Think a bit, Martin bach. What's this cloning for? To repair the human race. We're in a bad way. Look at me. My IIQ and GC are half this John Chow's. Yet they wanted me so badly for the Far Out Service that when I volunteered they took me and fitted me out with an artificial lung and corrected my myopia. Now if there were enough good sound lads about would they be taking one-lunged shortsighted Welshmen?"

"Didn't know you had an artificial lung."

"I do then. Not tin, you know. Human, grown in a tank from a bit of somebody; cloned, if you like. That's how they make replacement-organs, the same general idea as cloning, but bits and pieces instead of whole people. It's my own lung now, whatever. But what I am saying is this, there are too many like me these days, and not enough like John Chow. They're trying to raise the level of the human genetic pool, which is a mucky little puddle since the population crash. So then if a man is cloned, he's a strong and clever man. It's only logic, to be sure."

Martin grunted; the servo began to hum.

Kaph had been eating little; he had trouble swallowing his food, choking on it, so that he would give up trying after a few bites. He had lost eight or ten kilos. After three weeks or so, however, his appetite began to pick up, and one day he began to look through the clone's possessions, the sleeping-bags, kits, papers which Pugh had stacked neatly in a far angle of a packing-crate alley. He sorted, destroyed a heap of papers and oddments, made a small packet of what remained, then relapsed into his walking coma.

Two days later he spoke. Pugh was trying to correct a flutter in the tape-player, and failing; Martin had the jet out, checking their maps of the Pampas. "Hell and damnation!" Pugh said, and Kaph said in a toneless voice, "Do you want me to do that?"

Pugh jumped, controlled himself, and gave the machine to Kaph. The young man took it apart, put it back together, and left it on the table.

"Put on a tape," Pugh said with careful casualness, busy at another table.

Kaph put on the topmost tape, a chorale. He lay down on his cot. The sound of a hundred human voices singing together filled the dome. He lay still, his face blank.

In the next days he took over several routine jobs, unasked. He undertook nothing that wanted initiative, and if asked to do anything he made no response at all.

"He's doing well," Pugh said in the dialect of Argentina.

"He's not. He's turning himself into a machine. Does what he's pro-grammed to do, no reaction to anything else. He's worse off than when he didn't function at all. He's not human any more."

Pugh sighed. "Well, good night," he said in English. "Good night, Kaph."

"Good night," Martin said; Kaph did not.

Next morning at breakfast Kaph reached across Martin's plate for the toast. "Why don't you ask for it," Martin said with the geniality of repressed exasperation. "I can pass it."

"I can reach it," Kaph said in his flat voice.

"Yes, but look. Asking to pass things, saying good night or hello, they're not important, but all the same when somebody says something a person ought to answer. . . ."

The young man looked indifferently in Martin's direction; his eyes still did not seem to see clear through to the person he looked toward. "Why should I answer?"

"Because somebody has said something to you."

"Why?"

Martin shrugged and laughed. Pugh jumped up and turned on the rock-cutter.

Later on he said, "Lay off that, please, Martin."

"Manners are essential in small isolated crews, some kind of manners, whatever you work out together. He's been taught that, everybody in Far Out knows it. Why does he deliberately flout it?"

"Do you tell yourself good night?"

"So?"

"Don't you see Kaph's never known anyone but himself?"

Martin brooded and then broke out, "Then by God this cloning business is all wrong. It won't do. What are a lot of duplicate geniuses going to do for us when they don't even know we exist?"

Pugh nodded. "It might be wiser to separate the clones and bring them up with others. But they make such a grand team this way."

"Do they? I don't know. If this lot had been ten average inefficient ET engineers, would they all have been in the same place at the same time? Would they all have got killed? What if, when the quake came and things started caving in, what if all those kids ran the same way, farther into the mine, maybe, to save the one that was farthest in? Even Kaph was outside and went in. . . . It's hypothetical. But I keep thinking, out of ten ordinary confused guys, more might have got out."

"I don't know. It's true that identical twins tend to die at about the same time, even when they have never seen each other. Identity and death, it is very strange. . . ."

The days went on, the red sun crawled across the dark sky, Kaph did not speak when spoken to, Pugh and Martin snapped at each other more frequently each day. Pugh complained of Martin's snoring. Offended, Martin moved his cot clear across the dome and also ceased speaking to Pugh for some while. Pugh whistled Welsh dirges until Martin complained, and then Pugh stopped speaking for a while.

The day before the Mission ship was due, Martin announced he was going over to Merioneth.

"I thought at least you'd be giving me a hand with the computer to finish the rock-analyses," Pugh said, aggrieved.

"Kaph can do that. I want one more look at the Trench. Have fun," Martin added in dialect, and laughed, and left.

"What is that language?"

"Argentinean. I told you that once, didn't I?"

"I don't know." After a while the young man added, "I have forgotten a lot of things, I think."

"It wasn't important, to be sure," Pugh said gently, realizing all at once how important this conversation was. "Will you give me a hand running the computer, Kaph?"

He nodded.

Pugh had left a lot of loose ends, and the job took them all day. Kaph was a good co-worker, quick and systematic, much more so than Pugh himself. His flat voice, now that he was talking again, got on the nerves; but it didn't matter, there was only this one day left to get through and then the ship would come, the old crew, comrades and friends.

During tea-break Kaph said, "What will happen if the Explorer ship crashes?"

"They'd be killed."

"To you, I mean."

"To us? We'd radio SOS all signals, and live on half rations till the rescue cruiser from Area Three Base came. Four and a half E-years away it is. We have life-support here for three men for, let's see, maybe between four and five years. A bit tight, it would be."

"Would they send a cruiser for three men?"

"They would."

Kaph said no more.

"Enough cheerful speculations," Pugh said cheerfully, rising to get back to work. He slipped sideways and the chair avoided his hand; he did a sort of half-pirouette and fetched up hard against the dome-hide. "My goodness," he said, reverting to his native idiom, "what is it?"

"Quake," said Kaph.

The teacups bounced on the table with a plastic cackle, a litter of papers slid off a box, the skin of the dome swelled and sagged. Underfoot there was a huge noise, half sound half shaking, a subsonic boom.

Kaph sat unmoved. An earthquake does not frighten a man who died in an earthquake.

Pugh, white-faced, wiry black hair sticking out, a frightened man, said, "Martin is in the Trench."

"What trench?"

"The big fault line. The epicenter for the local quakes. Look at the seismograph." Pugh struggled with the stuck door of a still-jittering locker.

"Where are you going?"

"After him."

"Martin took the jet. Sleds aren't safe to use during quakes. They go out of control."

"For God's sake, man, shut up."

Kaph stood up, speaking in a flat voice as usual. "It's unnecessary to go out after him now. It's taking an unnecessary risk."

"If his alarm goes off, radio me," Pugh said, shut the headpiece of his suit, and ran to the lock. As he went out Libra picked up her ragged skirts and danced a belly-dance from under his feet clear to the red horizon.

Inside the dome, Kaph saw the sled go up, tremble like a meteor in the dull red daylight, and vanish to the northeast. The hide of the dome quivered; the earth coughed. A vent south of the dome belched up a slow-flowing bile of black gas.

A bell shrilled and a red light flashed on the central control board. The sign under the light read Suit Two and scribbled under that, A.G.M. Kaph did not turn the signal off. He tried to radio Martin, then Pugh, but got no reply from either.

When the aftershocks decreased he went back to work, and finished up Pugh's job. It took him about two hours. Every half hour he tried to contact Suit One, and got no reply, then Suit Two and got no reply. The red light had stopped flashing after an hour.

It was dinnertime. Kaph cooked dinner for one, and ate it. He lay down on his cot.

The aftershocks had ceased except for faint rolling tremors at long intervals. The sun hung in the west, oblate, pale-red, immense. It did not sink visibly. There was no sound at all.

Kaph got up and began to walk about the messy, half-packed-up, over-crowded, empty dome. The silence continued. He went to the player and put on the first tape that came to hand. It was pure music, electronic, without harmonies, without voices. It ended. The silence continued.

Pugh's uniform tunic, one button missing, hung over a stack of rock-samples. Kaph stared at it awhile.

The silence continued.

The child's dream: There is no one else alive in the world but me. In all the world.

Low, north of the dome, a meteor flickered.

Kaph's mouth opened as if he were trying to say something, but no sound came. He went hastily to the north wall and peered out into the gelatinous red light.

The little star came in and sank. Two figures blurred the airlock. Kaph stood close beside the lock as they came in. Martin's imsuit was covered with some kind of dust so that he looked raddled and warty like the surface of Libra. Pugh had him by the arm.

"Is he hurt?"

Pugh shucked his suit, helped Martin peel off his. "Shaken up," he said, curt.

"A piece of cliff fell onto the jet," Martin said, sitting down at the table and waving his arms. "Not while I was in it, though. I was parked, see, and poking about that carbon-dust area when I felt things humping. So I went out onto a nice bit of early igneous I'd noticed from above, good footing and out from under the cliffs. Then I saw this bit of the planet fall off onto the flyer, quite a sight it was, and after a while it occurred to me the spare aircans were in the flyer, so I leaned on the panic button. But I didn't get any radio reception, that's always happening here during quakes, so I didn't know if the signal was getting through either. And things went on jumping around and pieces of the cliff coming off. Little rocks flying around, and so dusty you couldn't see a meter ahead. I was really beginning to wonder what I'd do for breathing in the small hours, you know, when I saw old Owen buzzing up the Trench in all that dust and junk like a big ugly bat—"

"Want to eat?" said Pugh.

"Of course I want to eat. How'd you come through the quake here, Kaph? No damage? It wasn't a big one actually, was it, what's the seismo say? My trouble was I was in the middle of it. Old Epicenter Alvaro. Felt like Richter Fifteen there—total destruction of planet—"

"Sit down," Pugh said. "Eat."

After Martin had eaten a little his spate of talk ran dry. He very soon went off to his cot, still in the remote angle where he had removed it when Pugh complained of his snoring. "Good night, you one-lunged Welshman," he said across the dome.

"Good night."

There was no more out of Martin. Pugh opaqued the dome, turned the lamp down to a yellow glow less than a candle's light, and sat doing nothing, saying nothing, withdrawn.

The silence continued.

"I finished the computations."

Pugh nodded thanks.

"The signal from Martin came through, but I couldn't contact you or him."

Pugh said with effort, "I should not have gone. He had two hours of air left even with only one can. He might have been heading home when I left. This way we were all out of touch with one another. I was scared."

The silence came back, punctuated now by Martin's long, soft snores.

"Do you love Martin?"

Pugh looked up with angry eyes: "Martin is my friend. We've worked together, he's a good man." He stopped. After a while he said, "Yes, I love him. Why did you ask that?"

Kaph said nothing, but he looked at the other man. His face was changed, as if he were glimpsing something he had not seen before; his voice too was changed. "How can you . . .? How do you . . .?"

But Pugh could not tell him. "I don't know," he said, "it's practice, partly. I don't know. We're each of us alone, to be sure. What can you do but hold your hand out in the dark?"

Kaph's strange gaze dropped, burned out by its own intensity.

"I'm tired," Pugh said. "That was ugly, looking for him in all that black dust and muck, and mouths opening and shutting in the ground. . . . I'm going to bed. The ship will be transmitting to us by six or so." He stood up and stretched.

"It's a clone," Kaph said. "The other Exploit team they're bringing with them."

"Is it, then?"

"A twelveclone. They came out with us on the *Passerine*."

Kaph sat in the small yellow aura of the lamp seeming to look past it at what he feared: the new clone, the multiple self of which he was not part. A lost piece of a broken set, a fragment, inexpert at solitude, not knowing even how you go about giving love to another individual, now he must face the absolute, closed self-sufficiency of the clone of twelve; that was a lot to ask of the poor fellow, to be sure. Pugh put a hand on his shoulder in passing. "The chief won't ask you to stay here with a clone. You can go home. Or since you're Far Out maybe you'll come on farther out with us. We could use you. No hurry deciding. You'll make out all right."

Pugh's quiet voice trailed off. He stood unbuttoning his coat, stooped a little with fatigue. Kaph looked at him and saw the thing he had never seen before: saw him: Owen Pugh, the other, the stranger who held his hand out in the dark.

"Good night," Pugh mumbled, crawling into his sleeping-bag and half asleep already, so that he did not hear Kaph reply after a pause, repeating, across darkness, benediction.

The Muse

Throughout the early part of his career, Anthony Burgess often used SF—for instance, in the frame plot of Enderby, *with its visitors from the future. He wrote two SF novels, one the classic* A Clockwork Orange, *which may have grown out of a scene in Philip K. Dick's* Time Out of Joint: *the central character finds himself in the world of the future, in a joint where all the teenagers dress strangely and speak Russian slang. Along with Kingsley Amis, Edmund Crispin, Robert Conquest, and other English writers, Burgess championed the value of SF publicly in the late 1950s and early 1960s, helping to create a favorable environment for the British New Wave. Today, while he remains a champion of Brian Aldiss, J. G. Ballard, and Keith Roberts, there is no more acerbic critic of the failings of much contemporary SF, and Burgess no longer uses SF in his fiction. So, here, from the early 1960s, when his enthusiasm was undiminished, is Anthony Burgess's only science fiction short story, which uses time travel to speculate on the mystery of the past.*

*   *   *

Y ou're quite sure," asked Swenson for the hundredth time, "you want to go through with this?" His hands ranged over the five manuals of the instrument console and, in cross-rhythm, his feet danced on the pedals. He was a very old man, waxed over with the veneer of rejuvenation chemicals. Very wise, with a century of experience behind him, he yet looked much of an age with Paley, the twenty-five-year-old literary historian by his side. Paley grinned with undiminished patience and said:

"I want to go through with it."

"It won't be quite what you think," said Swenson. (This too he had said many times before.) "It can't be absolutely identical. You may get shocks where you least expect them. I remember taking Wheeler that time, you know. Poor devil, he thought it was going to be the fourteenth century he knew from his books. But it was a very different fourteenth century. Thatched cottages and churches and manors and so on, and lovely cathedrals. But there were polycephalic monsters running the feudal system, with tentacles too. Speaking the most exquisite Norman French, he said."

"How long was he there?"

"He was sending signals through within three days. But he had to wait a year, poor devil, before we could get him out. He was in a dungeon, you know. They got suspicious of his Middle English or something. White-haired and gibbering when we got him aboard. His jailers had been a sort of tripodic ectoplasm."

"That wasn't in System B303, though, was it?"

"Obviously not." The old man came out in Swenson's snappishness. "It was a couple of years ago. A couple of years ago System B303 was enjoying the doubtful benefits of proto-Elizabethan rule. As it still is."

"Sorry. Stupid of me."

"Some of you young men," said Swenson, going over to the bank of monitor screens, "expect too much of Time. You expect historical Time to be as plastic as the other kinds. Because the microchronic and macrochronic flows can be played with, you consider we ought to be able to do the same thing with—"

"Sorry, sorry, *sorry*. I just wasn't thinking." With so much else on his mind, was it surprising that he should be temporarily ungeared to the dull realities of clockwork time, solar time?

"That's the trouble with you young— Ah," said Swenson with satisfaction, "that was a beautiful changeover." With the smoothness of the tongue gliding from one phonemic area to another, the temporal path had become a spatial one. The uncountable megamiles between Earth and System B303 had been no more to their ship than, say, a two-way transatlantic flipover. And now, in reach of this other Earth—so dizzyingly far away that it was the same as their own, though at an earlier stage of their own Earth's history—the substance vedmum had slid them, as from one dream to another, into a world where solid objects might subsist, so alien as to be familiar, fulfilling the bow-bent laws of the cosmos. Swenson, who had been brought up on the interchangeability of time and space, could yet never cease to marvel at the miracle of the almost yawning casualness with which the *Nacheinander* turned into the *Nebeneinander* (there was no doubt, the old German words caught it best!). So far the monitor screens showed nothing, but tape began to whir out from the crystalline corignon machine in the dead centre of the control-turret—cold and accurate information about the solar system they were now entering. Swenson read it off, nodding, a Nordic spruce of a man glimmering with chemical youth. Paley looked at him, leaning against the bulkhead, envying the tallness, the knotty strength. But, he thought, Swenson could never disguise himself as an inhabitant of a less well-nourished era. He, Paley, small and dark as those far-distant Silurians of the dawn of Britain, could creep into the proto-Elizabethan England they would soon be approaching and never be noticed as an alien.

"Amazing how insignificant the variants are," said Swenson. "How finite the cosmos is, how shamefully incapable of formal renewals—"

"Oh, come," smiled Paley.

"When you consider what the old musicians could do with a mere twelve notes—"

"The human mind," said Paley, "can travel in a straight line. The cosmos is curved."

Swenson turned away from the billowing mounds of tape, saw that the five-manual console was flicking lights smoothly and happily, then went over to an instrument panel whose levers called for muscle, for the blacksmith rather than the organist. "Starboard," he said. "15.8. Now we play with gravities." He pulled hard. The monitor screens showed band after band of light, moving steadily upwards. "This, I think, should be—" He twirled a couple of corrective dials on a shoulder-high panel above the levers. "Now," he said. "Free fall."

"So," said Paley, "we're being pulled by—"

"Exactly." And then, "You're quite sure you want to go through with this?"

"You know as well as I do," smiled Paley patiently, "that I *have* to go through with it. For the sake of scholarship. For the sake of my reputation."

"Reputation," snorted Swenson. Then, looking towards the monitors, he said, "Ah. Something coming through."

Mist, swirling cloud, a solid shape peeping intermittently out of vapour porridge. Paley came over to look. "It's the earth," he said in wonder.

"It's *their* earth."

"The same as ours. America, Africa—"

"The configuration's slightly different, see, down there at the southern tip of—"

"I can't see any difference."

"Madagascar's a good deal smaller."

"The cloud's come over again." Paley looked and looked. It was unbelievable.

"Think," said Swenson kindly, "how many absolutely incomputable systems there have to be before you can see the pattern of creation starting all over again. This seems wonderful to you because you just can't conceive how many myriads upon myriads of other worlds are *not* like our own."

"And the stars," said Paley, a thought striking him; "I mean, the stars they can actually see from there, from their London, say—are they the same stars as ours?"

Swenson shrugged at that. "Roughly," he said. "There's a rough kinship. But," he explained, "we don't properly know yet. Yours is only the tenth or eleventh trip, remember. What is it, when all's said and done, but the past? Why go to the past when you can go to the future?" His nostrils widened with complacency. "G9," he said. "I've done that trip a few times. It's pleasant to know one can look forward to another twenty years of life. I saw it there, quite clearly, a little plaque in Rostron Place: *To the memory of G. F. Swenson, 1963–2084.*"

"We have to check up on history," said Paley, mumbling a little. His own quest seemed piddling: all this machinery, all this expertise in the service of a rather mean enquiry. "I have to know whether William Shakespeare really wrote those plays."

Swenson, as Paley expected, snorted. "A nice sort of thing to want to find out," he said. "He was born just five hundred years this year, and you want to prove that there's nothing to celebrate. Not," he added, "that that sort of thing's much in my line. I've never had much time for poetry. Aaaaah." He interposed his own head between Paley's and the screen, peering. The pages of the atlas had been turned; now Europe alone swam towards them. "Now," said Swenson, "I must set the exactest course of all." He worked at dials, frowning but humming happily, then beetled at Paley, saying: "Oughtn't you to be getting ready?"

Paley blushed that, with a huge swathe of the cosmos spent in near-idleness, he should have to rush things as they approached their port. He took off his single boiler-suit of a garment and drew from the locker his Elizabethan fancy-dress. Shirt, trunks, cod-piece, doublet, feathered French hat, slashed shoes—clothes of synthetic cloth that was an exact simulacrum of old-time weaving, the shoes of good leather hand-made. And then there was the scrip with its false bottom; hidden therein was a tiny two-way signaller. Not that, if he got into difficulties, it would be of much use: Swenson was (and these were strict orders) to come back for him in a year's time. The signaller was to show where he was and that he was still there, a guest of the past, really a stowaway. Swenson had to move on yet further into space; Professor Shimmins to be picked up in FH78, Dr. Guan Moh Chan in G210, Paley collected on the way back. Paley tested the signaller, then checked the open and honest contents of his scrip: chief among these was a collection of the works of William Shakespeare—not the early works, though: only six of the works which, in this B303 year of A.D. 1595, had not yet been written. The plays had been copies from a facsimile of the First Folio in fairly accurate Elizabethan script; the paper too was a goodish imitation of the tough coarse stuff that Elizabethan dramatists wrote on. For the rest, Paley had powdered prophylactics in little bags and, most important of all, gold—angels fire-new, the odd portague, dollars.

"Well," said Swenson, with the faintest twinge of excitement, "England, here we come." Paley looked down on familiar river-shapes—Tees, Humber, Thames. He gulped, running through his drill swiftly. "Count-down starts now," said Swenson. A synthetic voice in the port bulkhead began ticking off cold seconds from 300. "I'd better say good-bye then," gulped Paley, opening the trap in the deck which led to the tiny jet-powered very-much-one-man aircraft. "You should come down in the Thames estuary," said Swenson. "*Au revoir*, not good-bye. I hope you prove whatever it is you want to prove." 200—199—198. Paley went down, settled himself in the seat, checked the simple controls. Waiting took, it seemed, an age. He smiled wryly, seeing himself, an Elizabethan, with his hands on the wheel of a twenty-first-century miniature jet aircraft. 60—59—58. He checked his Elizabethan vowels. He went over his fictitious provenance: a young man from Norwich with stage ambitions ("See, here have I writ a play and a goodly one"). The synthetic voice, booming here in the small cabin, counted to its limit. 4—3—2—1.

Zero. Paley zeroed out of the belly of the mother-ship, suddenly calm, then elated. It was moonlight, the green countryside slept. The river was a glory of silver. His course had been pre-set by Swenson; the control available to him was limited, but he came down smoothly on the water. What he had to do now was to ease himself to the shore. The little motor purred gently as he steered in moonlight. The river was broad here, so that he seemed to be in a world all water and sky. The shore neared—it was all trees, sedge, thicket; there was no sign of habitation, not even of another craft. What would another craft have thought, sighting him? He had no fears about that: with its wings folded, the little air-boat looked, from a distance, like some nondescript barge, so well had it been camouflaged. And now, to be safe, he had to hide it, cover it with greenery in the sedge. But, first, before disembarking, he must set the time-switch that would, when he was safe ashore, render the metal of the fuselage high-charged, lethally repellent of all would-be boarders. It was a pity, but there it was. It would automatically switch off in a year's time, in twelve months to a day. In the meantime, what myths, what madness would the curious examiner, the chance finder generate, tales uncredited by sophisticated London?

And now, London, here he came.

Paley, launched on his night's walk up-river, found the going easy enough. The moon lighted field-paths, stiles. Here and there a small farmhouse slept. Once he thought he heard a distant whistled tune. Once he thought he heard a town clock strike. He had no idea of the month or day or time of night, but he guessed that it was late spring and some three hours or so off dawn. The year 1595 was certain, according to Swenson. Time functioned here as on true Earth, and two years before Swenson had taken a man to Muscovy, where they computed according to the Christian system, and the year had been 1593. Paley, walking, found the air gave good rich breathing, but from time to time he was made uneasy by the unfamiliar configurations of the stars. There was Cassiopoeia's Chair, Shakespeare's first name's drunken initial, but there were constellations he had not seen before. Could the stars, as the Elizabethans themselves believed, modify history? Could this Elizabethan London, because it looked up at stars unknown on true Earth, be identical with that other one that was only now known from books? Well, he would soon know.

London did not burst upon him, a monster of grey stone. It came upon him gradually and gently, houses set in fields and amid trees, the cool suburbs of the wealthy. And then, like a muffled trumpet under the sinking moon, the Tower. And then came the crammed houses, all sleeping. Paley breathed in the smell of this summer London, and he did not like what he smelled. It was a complex of old rags and fat and dirt, but it was also a smell he knew from the time he had flipped over to Borneo and timidly penetrated the periphery of the jungle: it was, somehow, a jungle smell. And, as if to corroborate this, a howl arose in the distance, but it was a dog's howl. Dogs, man's best friend, here in outer space; dog howling to dog across the inconceivable vastness of the cosmos. And then came a human voice and the sound of boots on the cobbles. "Four of the clock and a fine morning." He instinctively flattened himself in an alleyway, crucified against the dampish wall. The time for his disclosure was not quite yet. He tasted the vowel-sounds of the bellman's call—nearer to American than to present-day British English. "Fowrr 'vth' cluck." And then, at last knowing the time and automatically feeling for a stopped wristwatch that was not there, he wondered what he should do till day started. Here were no hotels with clerks on all-night duty. He tugged at his dark beard (a three months' growth) and then decided that, as the sooner he started on his scholar's quest the better, he would walk to Shoreditch where the Theatre was. Outside the City's boundaries, where the play-hating City Council could not reach, it was, history said, a new and handsome structure. A scholar's zest, the itch to see, came over him and made him forget the cool morning wind that was rising. His knowledge of the London of his own century gave him little help by way of street-orientation. He walked north—the Minories, Houndsditch, Bishopsgate—and, as he walked, he retched once or twice involuntarily at the stench from the kennel. There was a bigger, richer, filthier, obscener smell beyond this, and this he thought must come from Fleet Ditch. He dug into his scrip and produced a pinch of powder; this he placed on his tongue to quieten his stomach.

Not a mouse stirring as he walked, and there, under rolling cloud all besilvered, he saw it, he saw it, the Theatre, with something like disappointment. It was mean wood rising above wooden paling, its roof shaggily thatched. Things were always smaller than one expected, always more ordinary. He wondered if it might be possible to go in. There seemed to be no night-watchman protecting it. Before approaching the entrance (a door for an outside privy rather than a gate to the temple of the Muses) he took in the whole moonlit scene, the mean houses, the cobbles, the astonishing and unexpected greenery all about. And then he saw his first living animals.

Not a mouse stirring, had he thought? But those creatures with long tails were surely rats, a trio of them nibbling at some trump of rubbish not far from the way in to the Theatre. He went warily nearer, and the rats at once scampered off, each filament of whisker clear in the light. They were rats as he knew rats—though he had only seen them in the laboratories of his university—with mean bright eyes and thick meaty tails. But then he saw what they had been eating.

Dragged out from a mound of trash was a human forearm. In some ways Paley was not unprepared for this. He had soaked in images of traitor heads stuck on Temple bar, bodies washed by three tides and left to rot on Thames shore, limbs hacked off at Tyburn (Marble Arch in his day) and carelessly left for the scavengers. (Kites, of course, kites. Now the kites would all be roosting.) Clinically, his stomach calm from the medicine he had taken, he examined the gnawed raw thing. There was not much flesh off it yet: the feast had been interrupted at its beginning. On the wrist, though, was a torn and pulpy patch which made Paley frown—something anatomically familiar but, surely, not referable to a normal human arm. It occurred to him for just a second that this was rather like an eye-socket, the eye wrenched out but the soft bed left, still not completely ravaged. And then he smiled that away, though it was difficult to smile.

He turned his back on the poor human relic and made straight for the entrance-door. To his surprise it was not locked. It creaked as he opened it, a sort of voice of welcome to this world of 1595 and its strange familiarity. There it was—tamped earth for the groundlings to tamp down yet further; the side-boxes; the jutting apron-stage; the study uncurtained; the tarrass; the tower with its flag-staff. He breathed deeply, reverently. This was the Theatre. And then—

"Arrr, catched ye at it!" Paley's heart seemed about to leap from his mouth like a badly fitting denture. He turned to meet his first Elizabethan. Thank God, he looked normal enough, though filthy. He was in clumsy boots, goose-turd-coloured hose, and a rancid jerkin. He tottered a little as though drunk, and, as he came closer to peer into Paley's face, Paley caught a frightful blast of ale-breath. The man's eyes were glazed and he sniffed deeply and long at Paley as though trying to place him by scent. Intoxicated, unfocussed, thought Paley with contempt, and as for having the nerve to sniff. . . . Paley spoke up, watching his vowels with care:

"I am a gentleman from Norwich, but newly arrived. Stand some way off, fellow. Know you not your betters when you see them?"

"I know not thee, nor why tha should be here at dead of night." But he stood away. Paley glowed with small triumph, the triumph of one who has, say, spoken home-learnt Russian for the first time in Moscow and has found himself perfectly understood. He said:

"Thee? *Thee?* I will not be thee-and-thou'd so, fellow. I would speak with Master Burbage."

"Which Master Burbage, the young or the old?"

"Either. I have writ plays and fain would show them."

The watchman, as he must evidently be, sniffed at Paley again. "Gentleman you may be, but you smell not like a Christian. Nor do you keep Christian hours."

"As I say, I am but newly arrived."

"I see not your horse. Nor your traveller's cloak."

"They are—I have left them at mine inn."

The watchman muttered. "And yet you say you are but newly arrived. Go to." Then he chuckled and, at the same time, delicately advanced his right hand towards Paley as though about to bless him. "I know what 'tis," he said, chuckling. "'Tis some naught meeting, th' hast trysted ringading with some wench, nay, some wife rather, nor has she belled out the morn." Paley could make little of this. "Come," said the man, "chill make for 'ee an th' hast the needful." Paley looked blank. "An tha wants bedding," the man said more loudly. Paley caught that, he caught also the significance of the open palm and wiggling fingers. Gold. He felt in his scrip and produced an angel. The man's jaw dropped as he took it. "Sir," he said, hat-touching.

"Truth to tell," said Paley, "I am shut out of mine inn, late-returning from a visit and not able to make mine host hear with e'en the loudest knocking."

"Arrr," said the watchman and put his finger by his nose, a homely Earthly gesture, then scratched his cheek with the angel, finally, before stowing it in a little purse on his girdle, passing it a few times in front of his chest. "With me, sir, come."

He waddled speedily out, Paley following him with fast-beating pulse. "Where go we, then?" he asked. He received no answer. The moon was almost down and there was the first intimations of summer dawn. Paley shivered in the wind; he wished he had brought a cloak with him instead of the mere intention of buying one here. If it was really a bed he was being taken to, he was glad. An hour or so's sleep in the warmth of blankets and never mind whether or not there would be fleas. On the streets nobody was astir, though Paley thought he heard a distant cat's concert—a painful courtship and even more painful copulation to follow, just as on real Earth. Paley followed the watchman down a narrow lane off Bishopgate, dark and stinking. The effects of the medicine had worn off; he felt his gorge rise as before. But the stink, his nose noticed, was subtly different from before: it was, he thought in a kind of small madness, somehow swirling, redistributing its elements as though capable of autonomous action. He didn't like this one little bit. Looking up at the paling stars he felt sure that they too had done a sly job of refiguration, forming fresh constellations like a sand tray on top of a thumped piano.

"Here 'tis," said the watchman, arriving at a door and knocking without further ado. "Croshabels," he winked. But the eyelid winked on nothing but glazed emptiness. He knocked again, and Paley said:

"'Tis no matter. It is late, or early, to drag folk from their beds." A young cock crowed near, brokenly, a prentice cock.

"Neither one nor t'other. 'Tis in the way of a body's trade, aye." Before he could knock again, the door opened. A cross and sleepy-looking woman appeared. She wore a filthy nightgown and, from its bosom, what seemed like an arum lily peered out. She thrust it back in irritably. She was an old Elizabethan woman, about thirty-eight, grey-haired. She cried:

"Ah?"

"One for one. A gentleman, he saith." He took his angel from his purse and held it up. She raised a candle the better to see. The arum lily peeped out again. All smiles, she curtseyed Paley in. Paley said:

"'Tis but a matter of a bed, madam." The other two laughed at that "madam." "A long and wearisome journey from Norwich," he added. She gave a deeper curtsey, more mocking than before, and said, in a sort of croak:

"A bed it shall be and no pallet nor the floor neither. For the gentleman from Norwich where the cows eat porridge." The watchman grinned. He was blind, Paley was sure he was blind; on his right thumb something seemed to wink richly. The door closed on him, and Paley and the madam were together in the rancid hallway.

"Follow follow," she said, and she creaked first up the stairs. The shadows her candle cast were not deep; grey was filling the world from the east. On the wall of the stairwell were framed pictures. One was a crude woodcut showing a martyr hanging from a tree, a fire burning under him. Out of the smiling mouth words ballooned: AND YETTE I SAYE THAT MOGRADON GIUETH LYFE. Another picture showed a king with crown, orb, sceptre and a third eye set in his forehead. "What king is that?" asked Paley. She turned to look at him in some amazement. "Ye know naught in Norwich," she said, "God rest ye and keep ye all." Paley asked no further questions and kept his wonder to himself at another picture they passed: "Q. Horatius Flaccus" it said, but the portrait was of a bearded Arab. Was it not Averroes?

The madam knocked loudly on a door at the top of the stairs. "Bess, Bess," she cried. "Here's gold, lass. A cleanly and a pretty man withal." She turned to smile at Paley. "Anon will she come. She must deck herself like a bride." From the bosom of her nightgown the lily again poked out and Paley thought he saw a blinking eye enfolded in its head. He began to feel the tremors of a very special sort of fear, not a terror of the unknown so much as of the known. He had rendered his flying-boat invulnerable; this world could not touch it. Supposing it were possible that this world was in some manner rendered invulnerable by a different process. A voice in his head seemed to say, with great clarity: "Not with impunity may one disturb the—" And then the door opened and the girl called Bess appeared, smiling professionally. The madam said, smiling also:

"There then, as pretty a mutton-slice as was e'er sauced o'er." And she held out her hand for money. Confused, Paley dipped into his scrip and pulled out a clanking dull-gleaming handful. He told one coin into her hand and she still waited. He told another, then another. She seemed satisfied, but Paley seemed to know that it was only a temporary satisfaction. "We have wine," she said. "Shall I?—" Paley thanked her: no wine. The grey hair on her head grew erect. She curtseyed off.

Paley followed Bess into the bedchamber, on his guard now. The ceiling beat like a pulse. "Piggesnie," croaked Bess, pulling her single garment down from her bosom. The breasts swung and the nipples ogled him. There were, as he had expected, eyes. He nodded in something like satisfaction.

There was, of course, no question of going to bed now. "Honeycake," gurgled Bess, and the breast-eyes rolled, the long lashes swept up and down, up and down coquettishly. Paley clutched his scrip tightly to him. If this distortion—likely, as far as he could judge, to grow progressively worse—if this scrambling of sense-data were a regular barrier against intrusion, why was there not more information about it on Earth? Other time-travellers had ventured forth and come back unharmed and laden with sensible records. Wait, though: had they? How did one know? There was Swenson's mention of Wheeler, jailed in the Middle Ages by chunks of tripodic ectoplasm. "White-haired and gibbering when we got him aboard." Swenson's own words. How about Swenson's own vision of the future—a plaque showing his own birth and death dates? Perhaps the future did not object to intrusion from the past. But (Paley shook his head as though he were drunk, beating back sense into it) it was not a question of past and future, it was a question of other worlds existing *now.* The now-past was completed, the now-future was completed. Perhaps that plaque in Rostron Place, Brighton, showing Swenson's death some twenty years off, perhaps that was an illusion, a device to engender satisfaction rather than fear but still to discourage interference with the pattern. "My time is short," Paley suddenly said, using urgent twenty-first-century phonemes, not Elizabethan ones. "I will give you gold if you will take me to the house of Master Shakespeare."

"Maister—?"

"Shairkspeyr."

Bess, her ears growing larger, stared at Paley with a growing montage of film battle-scenes playing away on the wall behind her. "Th'art not that kind. Women tha likes. That see I in thy face."

"This is urgent. This is business. Quick. He lives, I think, in Bishopsgate." He could find out something before the epistemological enemies took over. And then what? Try and live. Keep sane with signals in some quiet spot till a year was past. Signal Swenson, receive Swenson's reassurances in reply; perhaps—who knew?—hear from far time-space that he was to be taken home before the scheduled date, instructions from Earth, arrangements changed. . . .

"Thou knowest," said Paley, "what man I mean. Master Shakespeare the player at the Theatre."

"Aye aye." The voice was thickening fast. Paley said to himself: It is up to me to take in what I wish to take in; this girl has no eyes on her breasts, that mouth forming under her chin is not really there. Thus checked, the hallucinations wobbled and were pushed back temporarily. But their strength was great. Bess pulled on a simple dress over her nakedness, took a worn cloak from a closet. "Gorled maintwise," she said. Paley pushed like mad, the words unscrambled. "Give me money now," she said. He gave her a portague.

They tiptoed downstairs. Paley tried to look steadily at the pictures in the stairwell, but there was no time to make them tell the truth. The stairs caught him off his guard and changed to an escalator of the twenty-first century. He whipped them back to trembling stairhood. Bess, he was sure, would melt into some monster capable of turning his heart to stone if he let her. Quick. He held the point-of-day in the sky by a great effort. There were a few people on the street. He durst not look at them. "It is far?" he asked. Cocks crowed, many and near, mature cocks.

"Not far." But nothing could be far from anything in this cramped and toppling London. Paley strained to keep his sanity. Sweat dripped from his forehead and a drop caught on the scrip which he hugged to himself like a stomach-ache. He examined it as he walked, stumbling often on the cobbles. A drop of salty water from his pores. Was it of this alien world or of his own? If he cut off his hair and left it lying, if he dunged in that foul jakes there, from which a three-headed woman now appeared, would this B303 London reject it, as a human body will reject a grafted kidney? Was it perhaps not a matter of natural law but of some God of the system, a God against Whom, the devil on one's side, one could prevail? Was it God's club-rules he was pushing against, not some deeper inbuilt necessity? Anyway, he pushed, and Elizabethan London, in its silver dawn, steadied, rocked, steadied, held. But the strain was terrific.

"Here, sir." She had brought him to a mean door which warned Paley that it was going to turn into water and flow down the cobbles did he not hold its form fast. "Money," she said. But Paley had given enough. He scowled and shook his head. She held out a fist which turned into a winking bearded man's face, threatening. He raised his own hand, flat, to slap her. She ran off, whimpering, and he turned the raised hand to a fist that knocked. His knock was slow in being answered. He wondered how much longer he could maintain this desperate holding of the world in position. If he slept, what would happen? Would it all dissolve and leave him howling in cold space when he awoke?

"Aye, what is't, then?" It was a misshapen ugly man with a row of bright blinking eyes across his chest, a chest left bare by his buttonless shirt. It was not, it could not be, William Shakespeare. Paley said, wondering at his own ability to enunciate the sounds with such exact care:

"Oi ud see Maister Shairkespeyr." He was surlily shown in, a shoulder-thrust indicating which door he must knock at. This, then, was *it*. Paley's heart martelled desperately against his breastbone. He knocked. The door was firm oak, threatening no liquefaction.

"Aye?" A light voice, a pleasant voice, no early morning crossness in it. Paley gulped and opened the door and went in. Bewildered, he looked about him. A bedchamber, the clothes on the bed in disorder, a table with papers on it, a chair, morning light framed by the tight-shut window. He went over to the papers; he read the top sheet (". . . giue it to him lest he raise all hell again with his fractuousness"), wondering if there was perhaps a room adjoining whence came that voice. Then he heard the voice again, behind him:

"'Tis not seemly to read a gentleman's private papers lacking his permission." Paley spun about to see, dancing in the air, a reproduction of the Droeshout portrait of Shakespeare, square in a frame, the lips moving but the eyes unanimated. He tried to call but could not. The talking woodcut advanced on him—"Rude, mannerless, or art thou some Privy Council spy?"—and then the straight sides of the frame bulged and bulged, the woodcut features dissolved, and a circle of black lines and spaces tried to grow into a solid body. Paley could do nothing; his paralysis would not even permit him to shut his eyes. The solid body became an animal shape, indescribably gross and ugly—some spiked sea urchin, very large, nodding and smiling with horrible intelligence. Paley forced it into becoming a more nearly human shape. His heart sank in depression totally untinged by fear to see standing before him a fictional character called "William Shakespeare," an actor acting the part. Why could he not get in touch with the *Ding an sich*, the Kantian noumenon? But that was the trouble—the thing-in-itself was changed by the observer into whatever phenomenon the categories of time-space-sense imposed. He took courage and said:

"What plays have you writ to date?"

Shakespeare looked surprised. "Who asked this?"

Paley said, "What I say you will hardly believe. I come from another world that knows and reveres the name of Shakespeare. I believe that there was, or is, an actor named William Shakespeare. That Shakespeare wrote the plays that carry his name—this I will not believe."

"So," said Shakespeare, tending to melt into a blob of tallow badly sculpted into the likeness of Shakespeare, "we are both to be unbelievers, then. For my part, I will believe anything. You will be a sort of ghost from this other world you speak of. By rights, you should have dissolved at cock-crow."

"My time may be as short as a ghost's. What plays do you claim to have written up to this moment?" Paley spoke the English of his own day. Though the figure before shifted and softened, tugging towards other shapes, the eyes changed little, shrewd and intelligent eyes, modern. And now the voice said:

"Claim? *Heliogabalus, A Word to Fright a Whoremaster, The Sad Reign of Harold First and Last, The Devil in Dulwich.* . . . Oh, many and many more."

"Please." Paley was distressed. Was this truth or teasing, truth or teasing of this man or of his own mind, a mind desperate to control the *données*, the sense-data, make them make sense? On the table there, the mass of papers. "Show me," he said. "Show me somewhat," he pleaded.

"Show me your credentials," said Shakespeare, "if we are to talk of showing. Nay," and he advanced merrily towards Paley, "I will see for myself." The eyes were very bright now and shot with oddly sinister flecks. "A pretty boy," said Shakespeare. "Not so pretty as some, as one, I would say, but apt for a brief tumble of a summer's morning before the day warms."

"Nay," said Paley, "nay," backing and feeling that archaism to be strangely frivolous, "touch me not." The advancing figure became horribly ugly, the neck swelled, eyes glinted on the backs of the approaching hands. The face grew an elephantine proboscis, wreathing, feeling; two or three suckers sprouted from its end and blindly waved towards Paley. Paley dropped his scrip the better to struggle. The words of this monster were thick, they turned into grunts and lallings. Pushed into the corner by the table, Paley saw a sheet of paper much blotted ("Never blotted a line," did they say?):

> I haue bin struggling striuing? seeking? how I may compair
> This jailhouse prison? where I liue unto the earth world
> And that and for because

The scholar was still there, the questing spirit clear while the body fought to keep off those huge hands, each ten-fingered. The scholar cried:

"Richard II! You are writing Richard II?"

It seemed to him, literature's Claude Bernard, that he should risk all to get that message through to Swenson, that *Richard II* was, in 1595, being written by Shakespeare. He suddenly dipped to the floor, grabbed his scrip and began to tap through the lining at the key of the transmitter. Shakespeare seemed taken by surprise by this sudden cessation of resistance; he put out forks of hands that grasped nothing. Paley, blind with sweat, panting hard, tapped: "R2 by WS." Then the door opened.

"I did hear noise." It was the misshapen ugly man with eyes across his bare chest, uglier now, his shape changing constantly though abruptly, as though set on by silent and invisible hammers. "He did come to attack tha?"

"Not for money, Tomkin. He hath gold enow of's own. See." The scrip, set down before so hurriedly, had spilt out its gold on the floor. Paley had not noticed; he should have transferred that gold to his—

"Aye, gold." The creature called Tomkin gazed on it greedily. "The others that came so brought not gold."

"Take the gold and him," said Shakespeare carelessly. "Do what thou wilt with both." Tomkin oozed towards Paley. Paley screamed, attacking feebly with the hand that held the scrip. Tomkin's claw snatched it without trouble.

"There's more within," he drooled.

"Did I not say thou wouldst do well in my service?" said Shakespeare.

"And here is papers."

"Ah, papers." And Shakespeare took them. "Carry him to the Queen's Marshal. The stranger within our gates. He talks foolishly, like the Aleman that came before. Wildly, I would say. Of other words, like a madman. The Marshal will know what to do."

"But," screamed Paley, grabbed by strong shovels of hands, "I am a gentleman. I am from Norwich. I am a playwright, like yourself. See, you hold what I have written."

"First a ghost, now from Norwich," smiled Shakespeare, hovering in the air like his portrait again, a portrait holding papers. "Go to. Are there not other worlds, like unto our own, that sorcery can make men leave to visit this? I have heard such stories before. There was a German—"

"It's true, true, what I tell you!" Paley clung to that, clinging also to the chamber-door with his nails, the while Tomkin pulled at him. "You are the most intelligent man of these times! You can conceive of it!"

"And of poets yet unborn also; Drythen, or some such name, and Lord Tennis-balls, and a drunken Welshman and P. S. Eliot? You will be taken care of, like that other."

"But it's true, true!"

"Come your ways," growled Tomkin. "You are a Bedlam natural." And he dragged Paley out, Paley collapsing, frothing, raving. Paley raved:

"You're not real, any of you! It's you who are the ghosts! *I'm* real, it's all a mistake, let me go, let me explain!"

"'Tis strange he talks," growled Tomkin. And he dragged him out.

"Shut the door," said Shakespeare. Tomkin kicked it shut. The screaming voice went, over thumping feet, down the passage-way without. Soon it was quiet enough to sit and read.

These were, thought Shakespeare, good plays. Strange that one of them was about, as far as he could judge, an usurious Jew. This Norwich man had evidently read Marlowe and seen the dramatic possibilities of an evil Lopez-type character. He, Shakespeare, had toyed with the idea of a play like this himself. And here it was, ready done for him. And there were a couple of promising-looking histories here, too. About King Henry IV. And here a comedy called *Much Ado About Nothing*. Gifts, god-sends. He smiled. He remembered that Aleman, Doctor Schleyer or some such name, who had come with a story like to this madman (mad? Could madmen do work like this? "The lunatic, the lover, and the poet": a good line in that play about fairies that Schleyer had brought. Poor Schleyer had died of the plague). Those plays Schleyer had brought had been good plays, but not, perhaps, quite so good as these.

Shakespeare furtively (though he was alone) crossed himself. When poets had talked of the Muse, had they perhaps meant visitants like this, now screaming feebly in the street, and the German Schleyer and that one who swore, under torture, that he was from Virginia in America, and that in America they had universities as good as Oxford or Leyden or Wittenberg, nay better? He shrugged, there being more things in heaven and earth &c. Well, whoever they were, they were heartily welcome so long as they brought plays. That *Richard II* of Schleyer's was, perhaps, in need of the emendations he was now engaged on, but the earlier work, from *Henry VI* on, had been popular. He read the top sheet of this new batch, stroking his auburn beard silvered, a fine grey eye reading. He sighed and, before crumpling a sheet of his own work on the table, read it. Not good, it limped, there was too much magic in it. Ingenio the Duke said:

> Consider gentlemen as in the sea
> All earthly life finds like and parallel
> So in far distant skies our lives be aped,
> Each hath a twin, each action hath a twin,
> And twins have twins galore and infinite
> And e'en these stars be twinn'd. . . .

Too fantastic, it would not do. He threw it into the rubbish-box which Tomkin would later empty. He took a clean sheet and began to copy in a fair and:

The Merchant of Venice

Then on he went, not blotting a line.

STEVE ALLEN

The Public Hating

Steve Allen was one of the most popular American media personalities in the 1950s, a talk-show host, comedian, musician, and composer. This is his only science fiction story, written in the ironic and satirical mode that was fashionable then (especially in Galaxy, which featured satires by Pohl, Kornbluth, Sheckley, and William Tenn). Here Allen manages to create a powerful, compressed, and memorable image that connects the story with the important SF social commentary of the McCarthy era in U.S. politics. It is a light piece with dark implications.

*   *   *

The weather was a little cloudy on that September 9, 1978, and here and there in the crowds that surged up the ramps into the stadium people were looking at the sky and then at their neighbors and squinting and saying, "Hope she doesn't rain."

On television the weatherman had forecast slight cloudiness but no showers. It was not cold. All over the neighborhood surrounding the stadium, people poured out of street-cars and buses and subways. In ant-like lines they crawled across streets, through turnstiles, up stairways, along ramps, through gates, down aisles.

Laughing and shoving restlessly, damp-palmed with excitement, they came shuffling into the great concrete bowl, some stopping to go to the restrooms, some buying popcorn, some taking free pamphlets from the uniformed attendants.

Everything was free this particular day. No tickets had been sold for the event. The public proclamations had simply been made in the newspapers and on TV, and over 65,000 people had responded.

For weeks, of course, the papers had been suggesting that the event would take place. All during the trial, even as early as the selection of the jury, the columnists had slyly hinted at the inevitability of the outcome. But it had only been official since yesterday. The television networks had actually gotten a slight jump on the papers. At six o'clock the government had taken over all network facilities for a brief five-minute period during which the announcement was made.

"We have all followed with great interest," the Premier had said, looking calm and handsome in a gray double-breasted suit, "the course of the trial of Professor Ketteridge. Early this afternoon the jury returned a verdict of guilty. This verdict having been confirmed within the hour by the Supreme Court, in the interests of time-saving, the White House has decided to make the usual prompt official announcement. There will be a public hating tomorrow. The time: 2:30 P.M. The place: Yankee Stadium in New York City. Your assistance is earnestly requested. Those of you in the New York area will find. . . ."

The voice had gone on, filling in other details, and in the morning, the early editions of the newspapers included pictures captioned, "Bronx couple first in line," and "Students wait all night to view hating" and "Early birds."

By one-thirty in the afternoon there was not an empty seat in the stadium and people were beginning to fill up a few of the aisles. Special police began to block off the exits and word was sent down to the street that no more people could be admitted. Hawkers slipped through the crowd selling cold beer and hot-dogs.

Sitting just back of what would have been first base had the Yankees not been playing in Cleveland, Frederic Traub stared curiously at the platform in the middle of the field. It was about twice the size of a prize-fighting ring. In the middle of it there was a small raised section on which was placed a plain wooden kitchen chair.

To the left of the chair there were seating accommodations for a small group of dignitaries. Downstage, so to speak, there was a speaker's lectern and a battery of microphones. The platform was hung with bunting and pennants.

The crowd was beginning to hum ominously.

At two minutes after two o'clock a small group of men filed out onto the field from a point just back of home plate. The crowd buzzed more loudly for a moment and then burst into applause. The men carefully climbed a few wooden steps, walked in single file across the platform, and seated themselves in the chairs set out for them. Traub turned around and was interested to observe high in the press box, the winking red lights of television cameras.

"Remarkable," said Traub softly to his companion.

"I suppose," said the man. "But effective."

"I guess that's right," said Traub. "Still, it all seems a little strange to me. We do things rather differently."

"That's what makes horse-racing," said his companion.

Traub listened for a moment to the voices around him. Surprisingly, no one seemed to be discussing the business at hand. Baseball, movies, the weather, gossip, personal small-talk, a thousand-and-one subjects were introduced. It was almost as if they were trying not to mention the hating.

His friend's voice broke in on Traub's reverie.

"Think you'll be okay when we get down to business? I've seen 'em keel over."

"I'll be all right," said Traub. Then he shook his head. "But I still can't believe it."

"What do you mean?"

"Oh, you know, the whole thing. How it started. How you found you could do it."

"Beats the hell out of me," said the other man. "I think it was that guy at Duke University first came up with the idea. The mind over matter thing has been around for a long time, of course. But this guy, he was the first one to prove scientifically that mind can control matter."

"Did it with dice, I believe," Traub said.

"Yeah, that's it. First he found some guys who could drop a dozen or so dice down a chute of some kind and actually control the direction they'd take. Then they discovered the secret—it was simple. The guys who could control the dice were simply the guys who *thought* they could.

"Then one time they got the idea of taking the dice into an auditorium and having about 2,000 people concentrate on forcing the dice one way or the other. That did it. It was the most natural thing in the world when you think of it. If one horse can pull a heavy load so far and so fast it figures that ten horses can pull it a lot farther and a lot faster. They had those dice fallin' where they wanted 'em 80 percent of the time."

"When did they first substitute a living organism for the dice?" Traub asked.

"Damned if I know," said the man. "It was quite a few years ago and at first the government sort of clamped down on the thing. There was a little last-ditch fight from the churches, I think. But they finally realized you couldn't stop it."

"Is this an unusually large crowd?"

"Not for a political prisoner. You take a rapist or a murderer now, some of them don't pull more than maybe twenty, thirty thousand. The people just don't get stirred up enough."

The sun had come out from behind a cloud now and Traub watched silently as large map-shaped shadows moved majestically across the grass.

"She's warming up," someone said.

"That's right," a voice agreed. "Gonna be real nice."

Traub leaned forward and lowered his head as he retied the laces on his right shoe and in the next instant he was shocked to attention by a guttural roar from the crowd that vibrated the floor.

In distant right center-field, three men were walking toward the platform. Two were walking together, the third was slouched in front of them, head down, his gait unsteady.

Traub had thought he was going to be all right but now, looking at the tired figure being prodded toward second base, looking at the bare, bald head, he began to feel slightly sick.

It seemed to take forever before the two guards jostled the prisoner up the stairs and toward the small kitchen chair.

When he reached it and seated himself the crowd roared again. A tall, distinguished man stepped to the speaker's lectern and cleared his throat, raising his right hand in an appeal for quiet. "All right," he said, "all right."

The mob slowly fell silent. Traub clasped his hands tightly together. He felt a little ashamed.

"All right," said the speaker. "Good afternoon, ladies and gentlemen. On behalf of the President of the United States I welcome you to another Public Hating. This particular affair," he said, "as you know is directed against the man who was yesterday judged guilty in United States District Court here in New York City—Professor Arthur Ketteridge."

At the mention of Ketteridge's name the crowd made a noise like an earthquake-rumble. Several pop-bottles were thrown, futilely, from the center-field bleachers.

"We will begin in just a moment," said the speaker, "but first I should like to introduce the Reverend Charles Fuller, of the Park Avenue Reborn Church, who will make the invocation."

A small man with glasses stepped forward, replaced the first speaker at the microphone, closed his eyes, and threw back his head.

"Our Heavenly Father," he said, "to whom we are indebted for all the blessings of this life, grant, we beseech Thee, that we act today in justice and in the spirit of truth. Grant, O Lord, we pray Thee, that what we are about to do here today will render us the humble servants of Thy divine will. For it is written *the wages of sin is death*. Search deep into this man's heart for the seed of repentance if there be such, and if there be not, plant it therein, O Lord, in Thy goodness and mercy."

There was a slight pause. The Reverend Fuller coughed and then said, "Amen."

The crowd, which had stood quietly during the prayer, now sat down and began to buzz again.

The first speaker rose. "All right," he said. "You know we all have a job to do. And you know why we have to do it."

"Yes!" screamed thousands of voices.

"Then let us get to the business at hand. At this time I would like to introduce to you a very great American who, to use the old phrase, needs no introduction. Former president of Harvard University, current adviser to the Secretary of State, ladies and gentlemen, Dr. Howard S. Weltmer!"

A wave of applause vibrated the air.

Dr. Weltmer stepped forward, shook hands with the speaker, and adjusted the microphone: "Thank you," he said. "Now, we won't waste any more time here since what we are about to do will take every bit of our energy and concentration if it is to be successfully accomplished. I ask you all," he said, "to direct your unwavering attention toward the man seated in the chair to my left here, a man who in my opinion is the most despicable criminal of our time—Professor Arthur Ketteridge!"

The mob shrieked.

"I ask you," said Weltmer, "to rise. That's it, everybody stand up. Now, I want every one of you . . . I understand we have upwards of seventy thousand people here today . . . I want every single one of you to stare directly at this fiend in human form, Ketteridge. I want you to let him know by the wondrous power that lies in the strength of your emotional reservoirs, I want you to let him know that he is a criminal, that he is worse than a murderer, that he has committed treason, that he is not loved by anyone, anywhere in the universe, and that he is, rather, despised with a vigor equal in heat to the power of the sun itself!"

People around Traub were shaking their fists now. Their eyes were narrowed; their mouths turned down at the corners. A woman fainted.

"Come on," shouted Weltmer. "Let's feel it!"

Under the spell of the speaker Traub was suddenly horrified to find that his blood was racing, his heart pounding. He felt anger surging up in him. He could not believe he hated Ketteridge. But he could not deny he hated something.

"On the souls of your mothers," Weltmer was saying, "on the future of your children, out of your love for your country, I demand of you that you unleash your power to despise. I want you to become ferocious. I want you to become as the beasts of the jungle, as furious as they in the defense of their homes. Do you hate this man?"

"Yes!" roared the crowd.

"Fiend!" cried Weltmer, "Enemy of the people— Do you hear, Ketteridge?"

Traub watched in dry-mouthed fascination as the slumped figure in the chair straightened up convulsively and jerked at his collar. At this first indication that their power was reaching home the crowd roared to a new peak of excitement.

"We plead," said Weltmer, "with you people watching today on your television sets, to join with us in hating this wretch. All over America stand up, if you will, in your living rooms. Face the East. Face New York City, and let anger flood your hearts. Speak it out, let it flow!"

A man beside Traub sat down, turned aside, and vomited softly into a handkerchief. Traub picked up the binoculars the man had discarded for the moment and fastened them on Ketteridge's figure, twirling the focus-knob furiously. In a moment the man leaped into the foreground. Traub saw that his eyes were full of tears, that his body was wracked with sobs, that he was in obvious pain.

"He is not fit to live," Weltmer was shouting. "Turn your anger upon him. Channel it. Make it productive. Be not angry with your family, your friends, your fellow citizens, but let your anger pour out in a violent torrent on the head of this human devil," screamed Weltmer. "Come on! Let's do it! Let's get it over with!"

At that moment Traub was at last convinced of the enormity of Ketteridge's crime, and Weltmer said, "All right, that's it. Now let's get down to brass tacks. Let's concentrate on his right arm. Hate it, do you hear? Burn the flesh from the bone! You can do it! Come on! Burn him alive!"

Traub stared unblinking through the binoculars at Ketteridge's right arm as the prisoner leaped to his feet and ripped off his jacket, howling. With his left hand he gripped his right forearm and then Traub saw the flesh turning dark. First a deep red and then a livid purple. The fingers contracted and Ketteridge whirled on his small platform like a dervish, slapping his arm against his side.

"That's it," Weltmer called. "You're doing it. You're doing it. Mind over matter! That's it. Burn this offending flesh. Be as the avenging angels of the Lord. Smite this devil! That's it!"

The flesh was turning darker now, across the shoulders, as Ketteridge tore his shirt off. Screaming, he broke away from his chair and leaped off the platform, landing on his knees on the grass.

"Oh, the power is wonderful," cried Weltmer. "You've got him. Now let's really turn it on. Come on!"

Ketteridge writhed on the grass and then rose and began running back and forth, directionless, like a bug on a griddle.

Traub could watch no longer. He put down the binoculars and staggered back up the aisle.

Outside the stadium he walked for twelve blocks before he hailed a cab.

Poor Superman

As a young man Fritz Leiber corresponded with H. P. Lovecraft, and he began his career as a writer with a number of
innovative fantasy and horror stories. He was rapidly drawn
into the science fiction circle of Campbell writers and produced several powerful works for Astounding. But Leiber was
never at the center of the Golden Age SF, and when the
postwar boom in SF exploded, with serious aesthetic challenges to Campbell's dominance, Leiber became a Galaxy
writer and published two revolutionary stories, "Coming Attraction" and "Poor Superman," set in the same future world.
Algis Budrys credits Leiber, in these stories, with crucial
impact. The first suggested to readers that "there might be
serious vacancies in the sophistication of the Golden Age
hero, and thus that Golden Ages might be founded on vacancies of perception." Budrys argued that Leiber might be the
most broadly insightful, most truly literate writer yet discovered in the magazines. He goes on to say that "Poor Superman" was "a much more overt stab à clef at [L. Ron] Hubbard
and Campbell." I have included the Josef Nesvadba story to
represent the attitudes in "Coming Attraction" in this anthology, and chosen "Poor Superman" to showcase Leiber. One
should approach the story knowing that the scientific idealist,
Jorg, is a direct parody of the scientism of L. Ron Hubbard,
the popular SF writer who had invented the self-help cult of
Dianetics in nonfiction articles in Astounding in the late
1940s.

*　　*　　*

The first angry rays of the sun—which, startlingly enough, still rose in the east at twenty-four-hour intervals—pierced the lacy tops of Atlantic combers and touched thousands of sleeping Americans with unconscious fear, because of their unpleasant similarity to the rays from World War III's atomic bombs.

They turned to blood the witch circle of rusty steel skeletons around Inferno in Manhattan. Without comment, they pointed a cosmic finger at the tarnished brass plaque commemorating the martyrdom of the three physicists after the dropping of the Hell Bomb. They tenderly touched the rosy skin and strawberry bruises on the naked shoulders of a girl sleeping off a drunk on the furry and radiantly heated floor of a nearby roof garden. They struck green magic from the glassy blot that was Old Washington. Twelve hours before, they had revealed things as eerily beautiful, and more ravaged, in Asia and Russia. They pinked the white walls of the colonial dwelling of Morton Opperly near the Institute for Advanced Studies; upstairs they slanted impartially across the Pharaohlike and open-eyed face of the elderly physicist and the ugly, sleep-surly one of young Willard Farquar in the next room. And in nearby New Washington they made of the spire of the Thinkers' Foundation a blue and optimistic glory that outshone White House, Jr.

It was America approaching the end of the twentieth century. America of juke-box burlesque and your local radiation hospital. America of the mask fad for women and Mystic Christianity. America of the off-the-bosom dress and the New Blue Laws. America of the Endless War and the loyalty detector. America of marvelous Maizie and the monthly rocket to Mars. America of the Thinkers and (a few remembered) the institute. "Knock on titanium," "Whadya do for blackouts?" "Please, lover, don't think when I'm around" America, as combat-shocked and crippled as the rest of the bomb-shattered planet.

Not one impudent photon of the sunlight penetrated the triple-paned, polarizing windows of Jorj Helmuth's bedroom in the Thinkers' Foundation, yet the clock in his brain awakened him to the minute, or almost. Switching off the Educational Sandman in the midst of the phrase, ". . . applying tensor calculus to the nucleus," he took a deep, even breath and cast his mind to the limits of the world and his knowledge. It was a somewhat shadowy vision, but, he noted with impartial approval, definitely less shadowy than yesterday morning.

Employing a rapid mental scanning technique, he next cleared his memory chains of false associations, including those acquired while asleep. These chores completed, he held his finger on a bedside button, which rotated the polarizing windowpanes until the room slowly filled with a muted daylight. Then, still flat on his back, he turned his head until he could look at the remarkably beautiful blond girl asleep beside him.

Remembering last night, he felt a pang of exasperation, which he instantly quelled by taking his mind to a higher and dispassionate level from which he could look down on the girl and even himself as quaint, clumsy animals. Still, he grumbled silently, Caddy might have had enough consideration to clear out before he awoke. He wondered if he shouldn't have used his hypnotic control on the girl to smooth their relationship last night, and for a moment the word that would send her into deep trance trembled on the tip of his tongue. But no, that special power of his over her was reserved for far more important purposes.

Pumping dynamic tension into his twenty-year-old muscles and confidence into his sixty-year-old mind, the forty-year-old Thinker rose from bed. No covers had to be thrown off; nuclear central heating made them unnecessary. He stepped into his clothing—the severe tunic, tights, and sockassins of the modern businessman. Next he glanced at the message tape beside his phone, washing down with ginger ale a vita-amino-enzyme tablet, and walked to the window. There, gazing along the rows of newly planted mutant oaks lining Decontamination Avenue, his smooth face broke into a smile.

It had come to him, the next big move in the intricate game making up his life—and mankind's. Come to him during sleep, as so many of his best decisions did, because he regularly employed the time-saving technique of somno-thought, which could function at the same time as somno-learning.

He set his who?-where? robot for "Rocket Physicist" and "Genius Class." While it worked, he dictated to his steno-robot the following brief message:

Dear Fellow Scientist:
   A project is contemplated that will have a crucial bearing on man's future in deep space. Ample non-military government funds are available. There was a time when professional men scoffed at the Thinkers. Then there was a time when the Thinkers perforce neglected the professional men. Now both times are past. May they never return! I would like to consult you this afternoon, three o'clock sharp, Thinkers' Foundation I.
Jorj Helmuth

Meanwhile the who?-where? had tossed out a dozen cards. He glanced through them, hesitated at the name "Willard Farquar," looking at the sleeping girl, then quickly tossed them all into the addresso-robot and plugged in the steno-robot.

The buzz light blinked green and he switched the phone to audio.

"The President is waiting to see Maizie, sir," a clear feminine voice announced. "He has the general staff with him."

"Martian peace to him," Jorj Helmuth said. "Tell him I'll be down in a few minutes."

Huge as a primitive nuclear reactor, the great electronic brain loomed above the knot of hush-voiced men. It almost filled a two-story room in the Thinkers' Foundation. Its front was an orderly expanse of controls, indicators, telltales, and terminals, the upper ones reached by a chair on a boom.

Although, as far as anyone knew, it could sense only the information and questions fed into it on a tape, the human visitors could not resist the impulse to talk in whispers and glance uneasily at the great cryptic cube. After all, it had lately taken to moving some of its own controls—the permissible ones—and could doubtless improvise a hearing apparatus if it wanted to.

For this was the thinking machine beside which the Marks and Eniacs and Maniacs and Maddidas and Minervas and Mimirs were less than morons. This was the machine with a million times as many synapses as the human brain, the machine that remembered by cutting delicate notches in the rims of molecules (instead of kindergarten paper punching or the Coney Island shimmying of columns of mercury). This was the machine that had given instructions on building the last three quarters of itself. This was the goal, perhaps, toward which fallible human reasoning and biased human judgment and feeble human ambition had evolved.

This was the machine that really thought—a million-plus!

This was the machine that the timid cyberneticists and stuffy professional scientists had said could not be built. Yet this was the machine that the Thinkers, with characteristic Yankee push, *had* built. And nicknamed, with characteristic Yankee irreverence and girl-fondness, "Maizie."

Gazing up at it, the President of the United States felt a chord plucked within him that hadn't been sounded for decades, the dark and shivery organ chord of his Baptist childhood. Here, in a strange sense, although his reason rejected it, he felt he stood face to face with the living God: infinitely stern with the sternness of reality, yet infinitely just. No tiniest error or willful misstep could ever escape the scrutiny of this vast mentality. He shivered.

The grizzled general—there was also one who was gray—was thinking that this was a very odd link in the chain of command. Some shadowy and usually well-controlled memories from World War II faintly stirred his ire.

Here he was giving orders to a being immeasurably more intelligent than himself. And always orders of the "Tell me how to kill that man" rather than the "Kill that man" sort. The distinction bothered him obscurely. It relieved him to know that Maizie had built-in controls which made her always the servant of humanity, or of humanity's right-minded leaders—even the Thinkers weren't certain which.

The gray general was thinking uneasily, and, like the President, at a more turbid level, of the resemblance between Papal infallibility and the dictates of the machine. Suddenly his bony wrists began to tremble. He asked himself: Was this the Second Coming? Mightn't an incarnation be in metal rather than flesh?

The austere Secretary of State was remembering what he'd taken such pains to make everyone forget: his youthful flirtation at Lake Success with Buddhism. Sitting before his guru, his teacher, feeling the Occidental's awe at the wisdom of the East, or its pretense, he had felt a little like this.

The burly Secretary of Space, who had come up through United Rockets, was thanking his stars that at any rate the professional scientists weren't responsible for this job. Like the grizzled general, he'd always felt suspicious of men who kept telling you how to do things, rather than doing them themselves. In World War III he'd had his fill of the professional physicists, with their eternal taint of a misty sort of radicalism and free-thinking. The Thinkers were better—more disciplined, more human. They'd called their brain machine Maizie, which helped take the curse off her. Somewhat.

The President's secretary, a paunchy veteran of party caucuses, was also glad that it was the Thinkers who had created the machine, though he trembled at the power that it gave them over the Administration. Still, you could do business with the Thinkers. And nobody (not even the Thinkers) could do business (that sort of business) with Maizie!

Before that great square face with its thousands of tiny metal features only Jorj Helmuth seemed at ease, busily entering on the tape the complex Questions of the Day that the high officials had handed him: logistics for the Endless War in Pakistan, optimum size for next year's sugar-corn crop, current thought trends in average Soviet minds—profound questions, yet many of them phrased with surprising simplicity. For figures, technical jargon, and layman's language were alike to Maizie; there was no need to translate into mathematical shorthand, as with the lesser brain machines.

The click of the taper went on until the Secretary of State had twice nervously fired a cigarette with his ultrasonic lighter and twice quickly put it away. No one spoke.

Jorj looked up at the Secretary of Space. "Section Five, Question Four—whom would that come from?"

The burly man frowned. "That would be the physics boys, Opperly's group. Is anything wrong?"

Jorj did not answer. A bit later he quit taping and began to adjust controls, going up on the boom chair to reach some of them. Eventually he came down and touched a few more, then stood waiting.

From the great cube came a profound, steady purring. Involuntarily the six officials backed off a bit. Somehow it was impossible for a man to get used to the sound of Maizie starting to think.

Jorj turned, smiling. "And now, gentlemen, while we wait for Maizie to cerebrate, there should be just enough time for us to watch the take-off of the Mars rocket."

He switched on a giant television screen. The others made a quarter turn, and there before them glowed the rich ochers and blues of a New Mexico sunrise and, in the middle distance, a silvery spindle.

Like the generals, the Secretary of Space suppressed a scowl. Here was something that ought to be spang in the center of his official territory, and the Thinkers had locked him completely out of it. That rocket there—just an ordinary Earth satellite vehicle commandeered from the Army, but equipped by the Thinkers with Maizie-designed nuclear motors capable of the Mars journey and more. The first spaceship—and the Secretary of Space was not in on it!

Still, he told himself, Maizie had decreed it that way. And when he remembered what the Thinkers had done for him in rescuing him from breakdown with their mental science, in rescuing the whole Administration from collapse, he realized he had to be satisfied. And that was without taking into consideration the amazing additional mental discoveries that the Thinkers were bringing down from Mars.

"Lord!" the President said to Jorj, as if voicing the Secretary's feeling, "I wish you people could bring a couple of those wise little devils back with you this trip. Be a good thing for the country."

Jorj looked at him a bit coldly. "It's quite unthinkable," he said. "The telepathic abilities of the Martians make them extremely sensitive. The conflicts of ordinary Earth minds would impinge on them psychotically, even fatally. As you know, the Thinkers were able to contact them only because of our degree of learned mental poise and errorless memory chains. So for the present it must be our task alone to glean from the Martians their astounding mental skills. Of course, some day in the future, when we have discovered how to armor the minds of the Martians—"

"Sure, I know," the President said hastily. "Shouldn't have mentioned it, Jorj."

Conversation ceased. They waited with growing tension for the great violet flames to bloom from the base of the silvery shaft.

Meanwhile the question tape, like a New Year's streamer tossed out a high window into the night, sped on its dark way along spinning rollers. Curling with an intricate aimlessness curiously like that of such a streamer, it tantalized the silvery fingers of a thousand relays, saucily evaded the glances of ten thousand electric eyes, impishly darted down a narrow black alleyway of memory banks, and, reaching the center of the cube, suddenly emerged into a small room where a suave fat man in shorts sat drinking beer.

He flipped the tape over to him with practiced finger, eyeing it as a stockbroker might have studied a ticker tape. He read the first question, closed his eyes and frowned for five seconds. Then with the staccato self-confidence of a hack writer, he began to tape out the answer.

For many minutes the only sounds were the rustle of the paper ribbon and the click of the taper, except for the seconds the fat man took to close his eyes, or to drink beer. Once, too, he lifted a phone, asked a concise question, waited half a minute, listened to an answer, then went back to the grind.

Until he came to Section Five, Question Four. That time he did his thinking with his eyes open.

The question was: "Does Maizie stand for Maelzel?"

He sat for a while slowly scratching his thigh. His loose, persuasive lips tightened, without closing, into the shape of a snarl.

Suddenly he began to tape again.

"Maizie does not stand for Maelzel. Maizie stands for amazing, humorously given the form of a girl's name. Section Six, Answer One: The midterm election viewcasts should be spaced as follows . . ."

But his lips didn't lose the shape of a snarl.

Five hundred miles above the ionosphere, the Mars rocket cut off its fuel and slumped gratefully into an orbit that would carry it effortlessly around the world at that altitude. The pilot unstrapped himself and stretched, but he didn't look out the viewport at the dried-mud disk that was Earth, cloaked in its haze of blue sky. He knew he had two maddening months ahead of him in which to do little more than that. Instead, he unstrapped Sappho.

Used to free fall from two previous experiences, and loving it, the fluffy little cat was soon bounding about the cabin in curves and gyrations that would have made her the envy of all back-alley and parlor felines on the planet below. A miracle cat in the dream world of free fall. For a long time she played with a string that the man would toss out lazily. Sometimes she caught the string on the fly, sometimes she swam for it frantically.

After a while the man grew bored with the game. He unlocked a drawer and began to study the details of the wisdom he would discover on Mars this trip—priceless spiritual insights that would be balm to a war-battered mankind.

The cat carefully selected a spot three feet off the floor, curled up on the air, and went to sleep.

Jorj Helmuth snipped the emerging answer tape into sections and handed each to the appropriate man. Most of them carefully tucked theirs away with little more than a glance, but the Secretary of Space puzzled over his.

"Who the devil would Maelzel be?" he asked.

A remote look came into the eyes of the Secretary of Space. "Edgar Allan Poe," he said frowningly, with eyes half closed.

The grizzled general snapped his fingers. "Sure! Maelzel's chess player. Read it when I was a kid. About an automaton that played chess. Poe proved it had a man inside it."

The Secretary of Space frowned. "Now what's the point in a fool question like that?"

"You said it came from Opperly's group?" Jorj asked sharply.

The Secretary of Space nodded. The others looked at the two men puzzledly.

"Who would that be?" Jorj pressed. "The group, I mean."

The Secretary of Space shrugged. "Oh, the usual little bunch over at the institute. Hindeman, Gregory, Opperly himself. Oh yes, and young Farquar."

"Sounds like Opperly's getting senile," Jorj commented coldly. "I'd investigate."

The Secretary of Space nodded. He suddenly looked tough. "I will. Right away."

Sunlight striking through french windows spotlighted a ballet of dust motes untroubled by air-conditioning. Morton Opperly's living room was well kept but worn and quite behind the times. Instead of reading tapes there were books; instead of steno-robots, pen and ink; while in place of a four-by-six TV screen, a Picasso hung on the wall. Only Opperly knew that the painting was still faintly radioactive, that it had been riskily so when he'd smuggled it out of his bomb-singed apartment in New York City.

The two physicists fronted each other across a coffee table. The face of the elder was cadaverous, large-eyed, and tender—fined down by a long life of abstract thought. That of the younger was forceful, sensuous, bulky as his body, and exceptionally ugly. He looked rather like a bear.

Opperly was saying, "So when he asked who was responsible for the Maelzel question, I said I didn't remember." He smiled. "They still allow me my absent-mindedness, since it nourishes their contempt. Almost my sole remaining privilege." The smile faded. "Why do you keep on teasing the zoo animals, Willard?" he asked without rancor. "I've maintained many times that we shouldn't truckle to them by yielding to their demand that we ask Maizie questions. You and the rest have overruled me. But then to use those questions to convey veiled insults isn't reasonable. Apparently the Secretary of Space was bothered enough about this last one to pay me a 'copter call within twenty minutes of this morning's meeting at the foundation. Why do you do it, Willard?"

The features of the other convulsed unpleasantly. "Because the Thinkers are charlatans who must be exposed," he rapped out. "We know their Maizie is no more than a tea-leaf-reading fake. We've traced their Mars rockets and found they go nowhere. We know their Martian mental science is bunk."

"But we've already exposed the Thinkers very thoroughly," Opperly interposed quietly. "You know the good it did."

Farquar hunched his Japanese-wrestler shoulders. "Then it's got to be done until it takes."

Opperly studied the bowl of lilies-of-the-valley by the coffeepot. "I think you just want to tease the animals, for some personal reason of which you probably aren't aware."

Farquar scowled. "We're the ones in the cages."

Opperly continued his inspection of the flowers' bells. "All the more reason not to poke sticks through the bars at the lions and tigers strolling outside. No, Willard, I'm not counseling appeasement. But consider the age in which we live. It wants magicians." His voice grew especially tranquil. "A scientist tells people the truth. When times are good—that is, when the truth offers no threat—people don't mind. But when times are very, very bad—" A shadow darkened his eyes. "Well, we all know what happened to—" And he mentioned three names that had been household words in the middle of the century. They were the names on the brass plaque dedicated to the three martyred physicists.

He went on, "A magician, on the other hand, tells people what they wish were true—that perpetual motion works, that cancer can be cured by colored lights, that a psychosis is no worse than a head cold, that they'll live forever. In good times magicians are laughed at. They're a luxury of the spoiled wealthy few. But in bad times people sell their souls for magic cures and buy perpetual-motion machines to power their war rockets."

Farquar clenched his fist. "All the more reason to keep chipping away at the Thinkers. Are we supposed to beg off from a job because it's difficult and dangerous?"

Opperly shook his head. "We're to keep clear of the infection of violence. In my day, Willard, I was one of the Frightened Men. Later I was one of the Angry Men and then one of the Minds of Despair. Now I'm convinced that all my posturings were futile."

"Exactly!" Farquar agreed harshly. "You postured. You didn't act. If you men who discovered atomic energy had only formed a secret league, if you'd only had the foresight and the guts to use your tremendous bargaining position to demand the power to shape mankind's future—"

"By the time you were born, Willard," Opperly interrupted dreamily, "Hitler was merely a name in the history books. We scientists weren't the stuff out of which cloak-and-dagger men are made. Can you imagine Oppenheimer wearing a mask or Einstein sneaking into the Old White House with a bomb in his brief case?" He smiled. "Besides, that's not the way power is seized. New ideas aren't useful to the man bargaining for power— his weapons are established facts, or lies."

"Just the same, it would have been a good thing if you'd had a little violence in you."

"No," Opperly said.

"I've got violence in me," Farquar announced, shoving himself to his feet.

Opperly looked up from the flowers. "I think you have," he agreed.

"But what are we to do?" Farquar demanded. "Surrender the world to charlatans without a struggle?"

Opperly mused for a while. "I don't know what the world needs now. Everyone knows Newton as the great scientist. Few remember that he spent half his life muddling with alchemy, looking for the philosopher's stone. That was the pebble by the seashore he really wanted to find."

"Now you are justifying the Thinkers!"

"No, I leave that to history."

"And history consists of the actions of men," Farquar concluded. "I intend to act. The Thinkers are vulnerable, their power fantastically precarious. What's it based on? A few lucky guesses. Faith-healing. Some science hocus-pocus, on the level of those juke-box burlesque acts between the strips. Dubious mental comfort given to a few nerve-torn neurotics in the Inner Cabinet—and their wives. The fact that the Thinkers' clever stage-managing won the President a doubtful election. The erroneous belief that the Soviets pulled out of Iraq and Iran because of the Thinkers' Mind Bomb threat. A brain machine that's just a cover for Jan Tregarron's guesswork. Oh yes, and that hogwash of 'Martian Wisdom.' All of it mere bluff! A few pushes at the right times and points are all that are needed—and the Thinkers know it! I'll bet they're terrified already, and will be more so when they find that we're gunning for them. Eventually they'll be making overtures to us, turning to us for help. You wait and see."

"I am thinking again of Hitler," Opperly interposed quietly. "On his first half-dozen big steps, he had nothing but bluff. His generals were against him. They knew they were in a cardboard fort. Yet he won every battle, until the last. Moreover," he pressed on, cutting Farquar short, "the power of the Thinkers isn't based on what they've got, but on what the world hasn't got—peace, honor, a good conscience—"

The front-door knocker clanked. Farquar answered it. A skinny old man with a radiation scar twisting across his temple handed him a tiny cylinder. "Radiogram for you, Willard." He grinned across the hall at Opperly. "When are you going to get a phone put in, Mr. Opperly?"

The physicist waved to him. "Next year, perhaps, Mr. Berry."

The old man snorted with good-humored incredulity and trudged off.

"What did I tell you about the Thinkers making overtures?" Farquar chortled suddenly. "It's come sooner than I expected. Look at this."

He held out the radiogram, but the older man didn't take it. Instead he asked, "Who's it from? Tregarron?"

"No, from Helmuth. There's a lot of sugar corn about man's future in deep space, but the real reason is clear. They know that they're going to have to produce an actual nuclear rocket pretty soon, and for that they'll need our help."

"An invitation?"

Farquar nodded. "For this afternoon." He noticed Opperly's anxious though distant frown. "What's the matter?" he asked. "Are you bothered about my going? Are you thinking it might be a trap—that after the Maelzel question they may figure I'm better rubbed out?"

The older man shook his head. "I'm not afraid for your life, Willard. That's yours to risk as you choose. No, I'm worried about other things they might do to you."

"What do you mean?" Farquar asked.

Opperly looked at him with a gentle appraisal. "You're a strong and vital man, Willard, with a strong man's prides and desires." His voice trailed off for a bit. Then, "Excuse me, Willard, but wasn't there a girl once? A Miss Arkady—"

Farquar's ungainly figure froze. He nodded curtly, face averted.

"And didn't she go off with a Thinker?"

"If girls find me ugly, that's their business," Farquar said harshly, still not looking at Opperly. "What's that got to do with this invitation?"

Opperly didn't answer the question. His eyes got more distant. Finally he said, "In my day we had it a lot easier. A scientist was an academician, cushioned by tradition."

Willard snorted. "Science had already entered the era of the police inspectors, with laboratory directors and political appointees stifling enterprise."

"Perhaps," Opperly agreed. "Still, the scientist lived the safe, restricted, highly respectable life of a university man. He wasn't exposed to the temptations of the world."

Farquar turned on him. "Are you implying that the Thinkers will some-how be able to buy me off?"

"Not exactly."

"You think I'll be persuaded to change my aims?" Farquar demanded angrily.

Opperly shrugged his helplessness. "No, I don't think you'll change your aims."

Clouds encroaching from the west blotted the parallelogram of sunlight between the two men.

As the slideway whisked him gently along the corridor toward his apartment Jorj Helmuth was thinking of his spaceship. For a moment the silver-winged vision crowded everything else out of his mind.

Just think, a spaceship with sails! He smiled a bit, marveling at the paradox.

Direct atomic power. Direct utilization of the force of the flying neu-trons. No more ridiculous business of using a reactor to drive a steam engine, or boil off something for a jet exhaust—processes that were as primitive and wasteful as burning gunpowder to keep yourself warm.

Chemical jets would carry his spaceship above the atmosphere. Then would come the thrilling order, "Set sail for Mars!" The vast umbrella would unfold and open out around the stern, its rear or earthward side a gleaming expanse of radioactive ribbon perhaps only an atom thick and backed with a material that would reflect neutrons. Atoms in the ribbon would split, blasting neutrons astern at fantastic velocities. Reaction would send the spaceship hurtling forward.

In airless space, the expanse of sails would naturally not retard the ship. More radioactive ribbon, manufactured as needed in the ship itself, would feed out onto the sail as that already there became exhausted.

A spaceship with direct nuclear drive—and he, a Thinker, had conceived it completely except for the technical details! Having strengthened his mind by hard years of somno-learning, mind-casting, memory-straightening, and sensory training, he had assured himself of the executive power to control the technicians and direct their specialized abilities. Together they would build the true Mars rocket.

But that would only be a beginning. They would build the true Mind Bomb. They would build the true Selective Microbe Slayer. They would discover the true laws of ESP and the inner life. They would even—his imagination hesitated a moment, then strode boldly forward—build the true Maizie!

And then—then the Thinkers would be on even terms with the scientists. Rather, they'd be far ahead. No more deception.

He was so exalted by this thought that he almost let the slideway carry him past his door. He stepped inside and called, "Caddy!" He waited a moment, then walked through the apartment, but she wasn't there.

Confound the girl! he couldn't help thinking. This morning, when she should have made herself scarce, she'd sprawled about sleeping. Now, when he felt like seeing her, when her presence would have added a pleasant final touch to his glowing mood, she chose to be absent. He really should use his hypnotic control on her, he decided, and again there sprang into his mind the word—a pet form of her name—that would send her into obedient trance.

No, he told himself again, that was to be reserved for some moment of crisis or desperate danger, when he would need someone to strike suddenly and unquestioningly for himself and mankind. Caddy was merely a willful and rather silly girl, incapable at present of understanding the tremendous tensions under which he operated. When he had time for it, he would train her up to be a fitting companion without hypnosis.

Yet the fact of her absence had a subtly disquieting effect. It shook his perfect self-confidence just a fraction. He asked himself if he'd been wise in summoning the rocket physicists without consulting Tregarron.

But this mood, too, he conquered quickly. Tregarron wasn't his boss, but just the Thinkers' most clever salesman, an expert in the mumbo-jumbo so necessary for social control in this chaotic era. He himself, Jorj Helmuth, was the real leader in theoretics and over-all strategy, the mind behind the mind behind Maizie.

He stretched himself on the bed, almost instantly achieved maximum relaxation, turned on the somno-learner, and began the two-hour rest he knew would be desirable before the big conference.

Jan Tregarron had supplemented his shorts with pink coveralls, but he was still drinking beer. He emptied his glass and lifted it a lazy inch. The beautiful girl beside him refilled it without a word and went on stroking his forehead.

"Caddy," he said reflectively, without looking at her, "there's a little job I want you to do. You're the only one with the proper background. The point is: it will take you away from Jorj for some time."

"I'd welcome it," she said with decision. "I'm getting pretty sick of watching his push-ups and all his other mind and muscle stunts. And that damn somno-learner of his keeps me awake."

Tregarron smiled. "I'm afraid Thinkers make pretty sad sweethearts."

"Not all of them," she told him, returning his smile tenderly.

He chuckled. "It's about one of those rocket physicists in the list you brought me. A fellow named Willard Farquar."

Caddy didn't say anything, but she stopped stroking his forehead.

"What's the matter?" he asked. "You knew him once, didn't you?"

"Yes," she replied and then added, with surprising feeling, "The big, ugly ape!"

"Well, he's an ape whose services we happen to need. I want you to be our contact girl with him."

She took her hands away from his forehead. "Look, Jan," she said, "I wouldn't like this job."

"I thought he was very sweet on you once."

"Yes, as he never grew tired of trying to demonstrate to me. The clumsy, overgrown, bumbling baby! The man's disgusting, Jan. His approach to a woman is a child wanting candy and enraged because Mama won't produce it on the instant. I don't mind Jorj—he's just a pipsqueak and it amuses me to see how he frustrates himself. But Willard is—"

"—a bit frightening?" Tregarron finished for her.

"No!"

"Of course you're not afraid," Tregarron purred. "You're our beautiful, clever Caddy, who can do anything she wants with any man, and without whose—"

"Look, Jan, this is different—" she began agitatedly.

"—and without whose services we'd have got exactly nowhere. Clever, subtle Caddy, whose most charming attainment in the ever-appreciative eyes of Papa Jan is her ability to handle every man in the neatest way imaginable and without a trace of real feeling. Kitty Kaddy, who—"

"Very well," she said with a sigh. "I'll do it."

"Of course you will," Jan said, drawing her hands back to his forehead. "And you'll begin right away by getting into your nicest sugar-and-cream war clothes. You and I are going to be the welcoming committee when that ape arrives this afternoon."

"But what about Jorj? He'll want to see Willard."

"That'll be taken care of," Jan assured her.

"And what about the other dozen rocket physicists Jorj asked to come?"

"Don't worry about them."

The President looked inquiringly at his secretary across his littered desk in his home study at White House, Jr. "So Opperly didn't have any idea how that odd question about Maizie turned up in Section Five?"

His secretary settled his paunch and shook his head. "Or claimed not to. Perhaps he's just the absent-minded prof, perhaps, something else. The old feud of the physicists against the Thinkers may be getting hot again. There'll be further investigation."

The President nodded. He obviously had something uncomfortable on his mind. He said uneasily, "Do you think there's any possibility of it being true?"

"What?" asked the secretary guardedly.

"That peculiar hint about Maizie."

The secretary said nothing.

"Mind you, I don't think there is," the President went on hurriedly, his face assuming a sorrowful scowl. "I owe a lot to the Thinkers, both as a private person and as a public figure. Lord, a man has to lean on *something* these days. But just supposing it were true"— he hesitated, as before uttering blasphemy—"that there was a man inside Maizie, what could we do?"

The secretary said stolidly, "The Thinkers won our last election. They chased the Commies out of Iran. We brought them into the Inner Cabinet. We've showered them with public funds." He paused. "We couldn't do a damn thing."

The President nodded with equal conviction, and, not very happily, summed up: "So if anyone should go up against the Thinkers—and I'm afraid I wouldn't want to see that happen, whatever's true—it would have to be a scientist."

Willard Farquar felt his weight change the steps under his feet into an escalator. He cursed under his breath, but let them carry him, a defiant hulk, up to the tall and mystic blue portals, which silently parted when he was five meters away. The escalator changed to a slideway and carried him into a softly gleaming, high-domed room rather like the antechamber of a temple.

"Martian peace to you, Willard Farquar," an invisible voice intoned. "You have entered the Thinkers' Foundation. Please remain on the slideway."

"I want to see Jorj Helmuth," Willard growled loudly.

The slideway carried him into the mouth of a corridor and paused. A dark opening dilated on the wall. "May we take your hat and coat!" a voice asked politely. After a moment the request was repeated, with the addition of, "Just pass them through."

Willard scowled, then fought his way out of his shapeless coat and passed it and his hat through in a lump. Instantly the opening contracted, imprisoning his wrists, and he felt his hands being washed on the other side of the wall.

He gave a great jerk which failed to free his hands from the snugly padded gyves. "Do not be alarmed," the voice advised him. "It is only an esthetic measure. As your hands are laved, invisible radiations are slaughtering all the germs in your body, while more delicate emanations are producing a benign rearrangement of your emotions."

The rather amateurish curses Willard was gritting between his teeth became more sulphurous. His sensations told him that a towel of some sort was being applied to his hands. He wondered if he would be subjected to a face-washing and even greater indignities. Then, just before his wrists were released, he felt—for a moment only, but unmistakably—the soft touch of a girl's hand.

That touch, like the mysterious sweet chink of a bell in darkness, brought him a sudden feeling of excitement, wonder.

Yet the feeling was as fleeting as that caused by a lurid advertisement, for as the slideway began to move again, carrying him past a series of depth pictures and inscriptions celebrating the Thinkers' achievements, his mood of bitter exasperation returned doubled. This place, he told himself, was a plague spot of the disease of magic in an enfeebled and easily infected world. He reminded himself that he was not without resources—the Thinkers must fear or need him, whether because of the Maelzel question or the necessity of producing a nuclear power spaceship. He felt his determination to smash them reaffirmed.

The slideway, having twice turned into an escalator, veered toward an opalescent door, which opened as silently as the one below. The slideway stopped at the threshold. Momentum carried him a couple of steps into the room. He stopped and looked around.

The place was a sybarite's modernistic dream. Sponge carpeting thick as a mattress and topped with down. Hassocks and couches that looked butter-soft. A domed ceiling of deep glossy blue mimicking the night sky, with the constellations tooled in silver. A wall of niches crammed with statuettes of languorous men, women, beasts. A self-service bar with a score of golden spigots. A depth TV screen simulating a great crystal ball. Here and there barbaric studs of hammered gold that might have been push buttons. A low table set for three with exquisite ware of crystal and gold. An ever-changing scent of resins and flowers.

A smiling fat man clad in pearl gray sports clothes came through one of the curtained archways. Willard recognized Jan Tregarron from his pictures, but did not at once offer to speak to him. Instead he let his gaze wander with an ostentatious contempt around the crammed walls, take in the bar and the set table with its many wineglasses, and finally return to his host.

"And where," he asked with harsh irony, "are the dancing girls?"

The fat man's eyebrows rose. "In there," he said innocently, indicating the second archway. The curtains parted.

"Oh, I *am* sorry," the fat man apologized. "There seems to be only one on duty. I hope that isn't too much at variance with your tastes."

She stood in the archway, demure and lovely in an off-the-bosom frock of pale skylon edged in mutated mink. She was smiling the first smile that Willard had ever had from her lips.

"Mr. Willard Farquar," the fat man murmured, "Miss Arkady Simms."

Jorj Helmuth turned from the conference table with its dozen empty chairs to the two mousily pretty secretaries.

"No word from the door yet, Master," one of them ventured to say.

Jorj twisted in his chair, though hardly uncomfortably, since it was a beautiful pneumatic job. His nervousness at having to face the twelve rocket physicists—a feeling which, he had to admit, had been unexpectedly great—was giving way to impatience.

"What's Willard Farquar's phone?" he asked sharply.

One of the secretaries ran through a clutch of desk tapes, then spent some seconds whispering into her throat-mike and listening to answers from the soft-speaker.

"He lives with Morton Opperly, who doesn't have one," she finally told Jorj in scandalized tones.

"Let me see the list," Jorj said. Then, after a bit, "Try Dr. Welcome's place."

This time there were results. Within a quarter of a minute he was handed a phone which he hung expertly on his shoulder.

"This is Dr. Asa Welcome," a reedy voice told him.

"This is Helmuth of the Thinkers' Foundation," Jorj said icily. "Did you get my communication?"

The reedy voice became anxious and placating. "Why yes, Mr. Helmuth, I did. Very glad to get it too. Sounded most interesting. Very eager to come. But—"

"Yes?"

"Well, I was just about to hop in my 'copter—my son's 'copter—when the other note came."

"What other note?"

"Why, the note calling the meeting off."

"I sent no other note!"

The other voice became acutely embarrassed. "But I considered it to be from you—or just about the same thing. I really think I had the right to assume that."

"How was it signed?" Jorj rapped.

"Mr. Jan Tregarron."

Jorj broke the connection. He didn't move until a low sound shattered his abstraction and he realized that one of the girls was whispering a call to the door. He handed back the phone and dismissed them. They went in a rustle of jackets and skirtlets, hesitating at the doorway but not quite daring to look back.

He sat motionless a minute longer. Then his hand crept fretfully onto the table and pushed a button. The room darkened and a long section of wall became transparent, revealing a dozen silvery models of spaceships, beautifully executed. He quickly touched another; the models faded and the opposite wall bloomed with an animated cartoon that portrayed with charming humor and detail the designing and construction of a neutron-drive spaceship. A third button, and a depth picture of deep star-speckled space opened behind the cartoon, showing a section of Earth's surface and in the far distance the tiny ruddy globe of Mars. Slowly a tiny rocket rose from the section of Earth and spread its silvery sails.

He switched off the pictures, keeping the room dark. By a faint table light he dejectedly examined his organizational charts for the neutron-drive project, the long list of books he had boned up on by somno-learning, the concealed table of physical constants and all sorts of other crucial details about rocket physics—a cleverly condensed encyclopedic "pony" to help out his memory on technical points that might have arisen in his discussion with the experts.

He switched out all the lights and slumped forward, blinking his eyes and trying to swallow the lump in his throat. In the dark his memory went seeping back, back, to the day when his math teacher had told him, very superciliously, that the marvelous fantasies he loved to read and hoarded by his bed weren't real science at all, but just a kind of lurid pretense. He had so wanted to be a scientist, and the teacher's contempt had cast a damper on his ambition.

And now that the conference was canceled, would he ever know that it wouldn't have turned out the same way today? That his somno-learning hadn't taken? That his "pony" wasn't good enough? That his ability to handle people extended only to credulous farmer Presidents and mousy girls in skirtlets? Only the test of meeting the experts would have answered those questions.

Tregarron was the one to blame! Tregarron with his sly tyrannical ways, Tregarron with his fear of losing the future to men who really understood theoretics and could handle experts. Tregarron, so used to working by deception that he couldn't see when it became a fault and a crime. Tregarron, who must now be shown the light—or, failing that, against whom certain steps must be taken.

For perhaps half an hour Jorj sat very still, thinking. Then he turned to the phone and, after some delay, got his party.

"What is it now, Jorj?" Caddy asked impatiently. "Please don't bother me with any of your moods, because I'm tired and my nerves are on edge."

He took a breath. When steps may have to be taken, he thought, one must hold an agent in readiness. "Caddums," he intoned hypnotically, vibrantly. "Caddums—"

The voice at the other end had instantly changed, become submissive, sleepy, suppliant.

"Yes, Master?"

Morton Opperly looked up from the sheet of neatly penned equations at Willard Farquar, who had somehow acquired a measure of poise. He neither lumbered restlessly nor grimaced. He removed his coat with a certain dignity and stood solidly before his mentor. He smiled. Granting that he was a bear, one might guess he had just been fed.

"You see?" he said. "They didn't hurt me."

"They didn't hurt you?" Opperly asked softly.

Willard slowly shook his head. His smile broadened.

Opperly put down his pen, folded his hands. "And you're as determined as ever to expose and smash the Thinkers?"

"Of course!" The menacing growl came back into the bear's voice, except that it was touched with a certain pleased luxuriousness. "Only from now on I won't be teasing the zoo animals, and I won't embarrass you by asking any more Maelzel questions. I have reached the objective at which those tactics were aimed. After this I shall bore from within."

"Bore from within," Opperly repeated, frowning. "Now where have I heard that phrase before?" His brow cleared. "Oh yes," he said listlessly. "Do I understand that you are becoming a Thinker, Willard?"

The other gave him a faintly pitying smile, stretched himself on the couch and gazed at the ceiling. All his movements were deliberate, easy.

"Certainly. That's the only realistic way to smash them. Rise high in their councils. Out-trick all their trickeries. Organize a fifth column. Then *strike!*"

"The end justifying the means, of course," Opperly said.

"Of course. As surely as the desire to stand up justifies your disturbing the air over your head. All action in this world is nothing but means."

Opperly nodded abstractedly. "I wonder if anyone else ever became a Thinker for those same reasons. I wonder if being a Thinker doesn't simply mean that you've decided you have to use lies and tricks as your chief method."

Willard shrugged. "Could be." There was no longer any doubt about the pitying quality of his smile.

Opperly stood up, squaring together his papers. "So you'll be working with Helmuth?"

"Not Helmuth. Tregarron." The bear's smile became cruel. "I'm afraid that Helmuth's career as a Thinker is going to have quite a setback."

"Helmuth," Opperly mused. "Morgenschein once told me a bit about him. A man of some idealism, despite his affiliations. Best of a bad lot. Incidentally, is he the one with whom—"

"—Miss Arkady Simms ran off?" Willard finished without any embarrassment. "Yes, that was Helmuth. But that's all going to be changed now."

Opperly nodded. "Good-by, Willard," he said.

Willard quickly heaved himself up on an elbow. Opperly looked at him for about five seconds, then, without a word, walked out of the room.

■　　■　　■

The only obvious furnishings in Jan Tregarron's office were a flat-topped desk and a few chairs. Tregarron sat behind the desk, the top of which was completely bare. He looked almost bored, except that his little eyes were smiling. Jorj Helmuth sat across the desk from him, a few feet back, erect and grim faced, while Caddy, shadowy in the muted light, stood against the wall behind Tregarron. She still wore the fur-trimmed skylon frock she'd put on that afternoon. She took no part in the conversation, seemed almost unaware of it.

"So you just went ahead and canceled the conference without consulting me?" Jorj was saying.

"You called it without consulting me." Tregarron playfully wagged a finger. "Shouldn't do that sort of thing, Jorj."

"But I tell you, I was completely prepared. I was absolutely sure of my ground."

"I know, I know," Tregarron said lightly. "But it's not the right time for it. I'm the best judge of that."

"When will be the right time?"

Tregarron shrugged. "Look here, Jorj," he said, "every man should stick to his trade, to his forte. Technology isn't ours."

Jorj's lips thinned. "But you know as well as I do that we are going to have to have a nuclear spaceship and actually go to Mars someday."

Tregarron lifted his eyebrows. "Are we?"

"Yes! Just as we're going to have to build a real Maizie. All the things we've done until now have been emergency measures."

"Really?"

Jorj stared at him. "Look here, Jan," he said, gripping his knees with his hands, "you and I are going to have to talk things through."

"Are you quite sure of that?" Jan's voice was very cool. "I have a feeling that it might be best if you said nothing and accepted things as they are."

"No!"

"Very well." Tregarron settled himself in his chair.

"I helped you organize the Thinkers," Jorj said, and waited. "At least, I was your first partner."

Tregarron barely nodded.

"Our basic idea was that the time had come to apply science to the life of man on a large scale, to live rationally and realistically. The only things holding the world back from this all-important step were the ignorance, superstition, and inertia of the average man, and the stuffiness and lack of enterprise of the academic scientists.

"Yet we knew that in their deepest hearts the average man and the professionals were both on our side. They wanted the new world visualized by science. They wanted the simplifications and conveniences, the glorious adventures of the human mind and body. They wanted the trips to Mars and into the depths of the human psyche, they wanted the robots and the thinking machines. All they lacked was the nerve to take the first big step— and that was what we supplied.

"It was no time for half measures, for slow and sober plodding. The world was racked by wars and neurosis, in danger of falling into the foulest hands. What was needed was a tremendous and thrilling appeal to the human imagination, an earth-shaking affirmation of the power of science for good.

"But the men who provided that appeal and affirmation couldn't afford to be cautious. They wouldn't check and double check. They couldn't wait for the grudging and jealous approval of the professionals. They had to use stunts, tricks, fakes—*anything to get over the big point*. Once that had been done, once mankind was headed down the new road, it would be easy enough to give the average man the necessary degree of insight to heal the breach with the professionals, to make good in actuality what had been made good only in pretense.

"Have I stated our position fairly?"

Tregarron's eyes were hooded. "You're the one who's telling it."

"On those general assumptions we established our hold on susceptible leaders and the mob," Jorj went on. "We built Maizie and the Mars rocket and the Mind Bomb. We discovered the wisdom of the Martians. We *sold* the people on the science that the professionals had been too high-toned to advertise or bring into the market place.

"But now that we've succeeded, now that we've made the big point, now that Maizie and Mars and science do rule the average human imagination, the time has come to take the second big step, to let accomplishment catch up with imagination, to implement fantasy with fact.

"Do you suppose I'd ever have gone into this with you if it hadn't been for the thought of that second big step? Why, I'd have felt dirty and cheap, a mere charlatan—except for the sure conviction that someday everything would be set right. I've devoted my whole life to that conviction, Jan. I've studied and disciplined myself, using every scientific means at my disposal, so that I wouldn't be found lacking when the day came to heal the breach between the Thinkers and the professionals. I've trained myself to be the perfect man for the job.

"Jan, the day's come and I'm the man. I know you've been concentrating on other aspects of our work; you haven't had time to keep up with my side of it. But I'm sure that as soon as you see how carefully I've prepared myself, how completely practical the neutron-drive rocket project is, you'll beg me to go ahead!"

Tregarron smiled at the ceiling for a moment. "Your general idea isn't so bad, Jorj, but your time scale is out of whack and your judgment is a joke. Oh yes. Every revolutionary wants to see the big change take place in his lifetime. Tch! It's as if he were watching evolutionary vaudeville and wanted the Ape-to-Man Act over in twenty minutes.

"Time for the second big step? Jorj, the average man's exactly what he was ten years ago, except that he's got a new god. More than ever he thinks of Mars as a Hollywood paradise, with wise men and yummy princesses. Maizie is Mama magnified a million times. As for professional scientists, they're more jealous and stuffy than ever. All they'd like to do is turn the clock back to a genteel dream world of quiet quadrangles and caps and gowns, where every commoner bows to the passing scholar.

"Maybe in ten thousand years we'll be ready for the second big step. Maybe. Meanwhile, as should be, the clever will rule the stupid for their own good. The realists will rule the dreamers. Those with free hands will rule those who have deliberately handcuffed themselves with taboos.

"Secondly, your judgment. Did you actually think you could have bossed those professionals, kept your mental footing in the intellectual melee? You, a nuclear physicist? A rocket scientist? Why, it's— Take it easy now, boy, and listen to me. They'd have torn you to pieces in twenty minutes and glad of the chance! You baffle me, Jorj. You know that Maizie and the Mars rocket and all that are fakes, yet you believe in your somno-learning and conscious-ness-expansion and optimism-pumping like the veriest yokel. I wouldn't be surprised to hear you'd taken up ESP and hypnotism. I think you should take stock of yourself and get a new slant. It's overdue."

He leaned back. Jorj's face had become a mask. His eyes did not flicker from Tregarron's, yet there was a subtle change in his expression. Behind Tregarron, Caddy swayed as if in a sudden gust of intangible wind and took a silent step forward from the wall.

"That's your honest opinion?" Jorj asked very quietly.

"It's more than that," Tregarron told him, just as unmelodramatically. "It's orders."

Jorj stood up purposefully. "Very well," he said. "In that case I have to tell you that—"

Casually, but with no waste motion, Tregarron slipped an ultrasonic pistol from under the desk and laid it on the empty top.

"No," he said, "let me tell you something. I was afraid this would happen and I made preparations. If you've studied your Nazi, Fascist, and Soviet history, you know what happens to old revolutionaries who don't move with the times. But I'm not going to be too harsh. I have a couple of boys waiting outside. They'll take you by 'copter to the field, then by jet to New Mex.

Bright and early tomorrow morning, Jorj, you're leaving on a trip to Mars."

Jorj hardly reacted to the words. Caddy was two steps nearer Tregarron.

"I decided Mars would be the best place for you," the fat man continued. "The robot controls will be arranged so that your 'visit' to Mars lasts two years. Perhaps in that time you will have learned wisdom, such as realizing that the big liar must never fall for his own big lie.

"Meanwhile, there will have to be a replacement for you. I have in mind a person who may prove peculiarly worthy to occupy your position, with all its perquisites. A person who seems to understand that force and desire are the motive powers of life, and that anyone who believes the big lie proves himself strictly a jerk."

Caddy was standing behind Tregarron now, her half-closed, sleepy eyes fixed on Jorj's.

"His name is Willard Farquar. You see, I too believe in cooperating with the scientists, Jorj, but by subversion rather than conference. My idea is to offer the hand of friendship to a selected few of them — the hand of friendship with a nice big bribe in it." He smiled. "You were a good man, Jorj, for the early days, when we needed a publicist with catchy ideas about Mind Bombs, ray guns, plastic helmets, fancy sweaters, space brassières, and all that other corn. Now we can afford a solider sort of person."

Jorj moistened his lips.

"We'll have a neat explanation of what's happened to you. Callers will be informed that you've gone on an extended visit to imbibe the wisdom of the Martians."

Jorj whispered, "Caddums."

Caddy leaned forward. Her arms snaked down Tregarron's, as if to imprison his wrists. But instead she reached out and took the ultrasonic pistol and put it in Tregarron's right hand. Then she looked up at Jorj with eyes that were very bright.

She said very sweetly and sympathetically, "Poor Superman."

THOMAS M. DISCH

Angouleme

After establishing himself in the U.S. magazines in the early 1960s, Thomas M. Disch moved to London in the mid-1960s and became involved with the British New Wave movement, then in full swing. His early masterpiece, the novel Camp Concentration, *was serialized in Moorcock's* New Worlds. *Returning to the United States at the end of the 1960s, Disch wrote a series of stories set in the New York City of the future. They were later published as* 334, *the number of the apartment building in and around which they all take place. Of these, "Angouleme" stands out as an independent work. Disch is himself now a notable literary critic in New York, a poet, essayist, and novelist who still devotes a portion of his time to fantasy and SF. The detractors of the genre have often charged that SF is a juvenile literature, written for a young audience. "Angouleme" turns this attack on its head, evincing very adult concern about too-bright, alienated children.*

*   *   *

There were seven Alexandrians involved in the Battery plot—Jack, who was the youngest and from the Bronx, Celeste DiCecca, Sniffles and MaryJane, Tancred Miller, Amparo (of course), and *of course*, the leader and mastermind, Bill Harper, better known as Little Mister Kissy Lips. Who was passionately, hopelessly in love with Amparo. Who was nearly thirteen (she would be, fully, by September this year), and breasts just beginning. Very, very beautiful skin, like lucite. Amparo Martinez.

Their first, nothing operation was in the East 60's, a broker or something like that. All they netted was cufflinks, a watch, a leather satchel that wasn't leather after all, some buttons, and the usual lot of useless credit cards. He stayed calm through the whole thing, even with Sniffles slicing off buttons, and *soothing*. None of them had the nerve to ask, though they all wondered, how often he'd been through this scene before. What they were about wasn't an innovation. It was partly that, the need to innovate, that led them to think up the plot. The only really memorable part of the holdup was the name laminated on the cards, which was, weirdly enough, Lowen, Richard W. An omen (the connection being that they were all at the Alexander Lowen School), but of what?

Little Mister Kissy Lips kept the cufflinks for himself, gave the buttons to Amparo (who gave them to her uncle), and donated the rest (the watch was a piece of crap) to the Conservation booth outside the Plaza right where he lived.

His father was a teevee executive. In, as he would quip, both senses. They had got married young, his mama and papa, and divorced soon after but not before he'd come to fill out their quota. Papa, the executive, remarried, a man this time and somewhat more happily. Anyhow it lasted long enough that the offspring, the leader and mastermind, had to learn to adjust to the situation, it being permanent. Mama simply went down to the Everglades and disappeared, sploosh.

In short, he was well to do. Which is how, more than by overwhelming talent, he got into the Lowen School in the first place. He had the right kind of body though, so with half a desire there was no reason in the city of New York he couldn't grow up to be a professional dancer, even a choreographer. He'd have the connections for it, as Papa was fond of pointing out.

For the time being, however, his bent was literary and religious rather than balletic. He loved, and what seventh grader doesn't, the abstracter foxtrots and more metaphysical twists of a Dostoevsky, a Gide, a Mailer. He longed for the experience of some vivider pain than the mere daily hollowness knotted into his tight young belly, and no weekly stomp-and-holler of group therapy with other jejune eleven-year-olds was going to get him his stripes in the major leagues of suffering, crime, and resurrection. Only a bona fide crime would do that, and of all the crimes available murder certainly carried the most prestige, as no less an authority than Loretta Couplard was ready to attest, Loretta Couplard being not only the director and co-owner of the Lowen School but the author, as well, of two nationally televised scripts, both about famous murders of the 20th Century. They'd even done a unit in social studies on the topic: A History of Crime in Urban America.

The first of Loretta's murders was a comedy involving Pauline Campbell,

R.N., of Ann Arbor, Michigan, circa 1951, whose skull had been smashed by three drunken teenagers. They had meant to knock her unconscious so they could screw her, which was 1951 in a nutshell. The eighteen-year-olds, Bill Morey and Max Pell, got life; Dave Royal (Loretta's hero) was a year younger and got off with twenty-two years.

Her second murder was tragic in tone and consequently inspired more respect, though not among the critics, unfortunately. Possibly because her heroine, also a Pauline (Pauline Wichura), though more interesting and complicated, had also been more famous in her own day and ever since. Which made the competition, one best-selling novel and a serious film biography, considerably stiffer. Miss Wichura had been a welfare worker in Atlanta, Georgia, very much into environment and the population problem, this being the immediate pre-Regents period when anyone and everyone was legitimately starting to fret. Pauline decided to do something, *viz.*, reduce the population herself and in the fairest way possible. So whenever any of the families she visited produced one child above the three she'd fixed, rather generously, as the upward limit, she found some unobtrusive way of thinning that family back to the preferred maximal size. Between 1989 and 1993 Pauline's journals (Random House, 1994) record twenty-six murders, plus an additional fourteen failed attempts. In addition she had the highest welfare department record in the U.S. for abortions and sterilizations among the families whom she advised.

"Which proves, I think," Little Mister Kissy Lips had explained one day after school to his friend Jack, "that a murder doesn't have to be of someone *famous* to be a form of idealism."

But of course idealism was only half the story: the other half was curiosity. And beyond idealism *and* curiosity there was probably even another half, the basic childhood need to grow up and kill someone.

They settled on the Battery because, one, none of them ever were there ordinarily; two, it was posh and at the same time relatively, three, uncrowded, at least once the night shift were snug in their towers tending their machines. The night shift seldom ate their lunches down in the park.

And, four, because it was beautiful, especially now at the beginning of summer. The dark water, chromed with oil, flopping against the buttressed shore; the silences blowing in off the Upper Bay, silences large enough sometimes that you could sort out the different noises of the city behind them, the purr and quaver of the skyscrapers, the ground-shivering *mysterioso* of the expressways, and every now and then the strange sourceless screams that are the melody of New York's theme song; the blue-pink of sunsets in a visible sky; the people's faces, calmed by the sea and their own nearness to death, lined up in rhythmic rows on the green benches. Why, even the statues looked beautiful here, as though someone had believed in them once, the way people must have believed in the statues in the Cloisters, so long ago.

His favorite was the gigantic killer-eagle landing in the middle of the monoliths in the memorial for the soldiers, sailors, and airmen killed in World War II. The largest eagle, probably, in all Manhattan. His talons ripped apart what was *surely* the largest artichoke.

Amparo, who went along with some of Miss Couplard's ideas, preferred the more humanistic qualities of the memorial (him on top and an angel gently probing an enormous book with her sword) for Verrazzano, who was not, as it turned out, the contractor who put up the bridge that had, so famously, collapsed. Instead, as the bronze plate in back proclaimed:

IN APRIL 1524
THE FLORENTINE-BORN NAVIGATOR
VERRAZZANO
LED THE FRENCH CARAVEL LA DAUPHINE
TO THE DISCOVERY OF
THE HARBOR OF NEW YORK
AND NAMED THESE SHORES ANGOULEME
IN HONOR OF FRANCIS I KING OF FRANCE

"Angouleme" they all agreed, except Tancred, who favored the more prevalent and briefer name, was much classier. Tancred was ruled out of order and the decision became unanimous.

It was there, by the statue, looking across the bay of Angouleme to Jersey, that they took the oath that bound them to perpetual secrecy. Whoever spoke of what they were about to do, unless he were being tortured by the Police, solemnly called upon his co-conspirators to insure his silence by other means. Death. All revolutionary organizations take similar precautions, as the history unit on Modern Revolutions had made clear.

How he got the name: it had been Papa's theory that what modern life cried out for was a sweetening of old-fashioned sentimentality. Ergo, among all the other indignities this theory gave rise to, scenes like the following: "Who's my Little Mister Kissy Lips!" Papa would bawl out, sweetly, right in the middle of Rockefeller Center (or a restaurant, or in front of the school), and he'd shout right back, "I am!" At least until he knew better.

Mama had been, variously, "Rosebud," "Peg O' My Heart," and (this only at the end) "The Snow Queen." Mama, being adult, had been able to vanish with no other trace than the postcard that still came every Xmas postmarked from Key Largo, but Little Mister Kissy Lips was stuck with the New Sentimentality willy-nilly. True, by age seven he'd been able to insist on being called "Bill" around the house (or, as Papa would have it, "Just Plain Bill"). But that left the staff at the Plaza to contend with, and Papa's assistants, schoolmates, anyone who'd ever heard the name. Then a year ago, aged ten and able to reason, he laid down the new law—that his name *was* Little Mister Kissy Lips, the whole awful mouthful, each and every time. His reasoning being that if anyone would be getting his face rubbed in shit by this it would be Papa, who deserved it. Papa didn't seem to get the point, or else he got it and another point besides, you could never be sure how stupid or how subtle he really was, which is the worst kind of enemy.

Meanwhile at the nationwide level the New Sentimentality had been a rather overwhelming smash. "The Orphans," which Papa produced and sometimes was credited with writing, pulled down the top Thursday evening ratings for two years. Now it was being overhauled for a daytime slot. For one hour every day our lives were going to be a lot sweeter, and chances were Papa would be a millionaire or more as a result. On the sunny side, this meant that *he'd* be the son of a millionaire. Though he generally had contempt for the way money corrupted everything it touched, he had to admit that in certain cases it didn't have to be a bad thing. It boiled down to this (which he'd always known): that Papa was a necessary evil.

This was why every evening when Papa buzzed himself into the suite he'd shout out, "Where's my Little Mister Kissy Lips," and he'd reply, "Here, Papa!" The cherry on this sundae of love was a big wet kiss, and then one more for their new "Rosebud," Jimmy Ness. (Who drank, and was not in all likelihood going to last much longer.) They'd all three sit down to the nice *family* dinner Jimmyness had cooked, and Papa would tell them about the cheerful, positive things that had happened that day at CBS, and Little Mister Kissy Lips would tell all about the bright fine things that had happened to *him*. Jimmy would sulk. Then Papa and Jimmy would go somewhere or just disappear into the private Everglades of sex, and Little Mister Kissy Lips would buzz himself out into the corridor (Papa knew better than to be repressive about hours), and within half an hour he'd be at the Verrazzano statue with the six other Alexandrians, five if Celeste had a lesson, to plot the murder of the victim they'd all finally agreed on.

No one had been able to find out his name. They called him Alyona Ivanovna, after the old pawnbroker woman that Raskolnikov kills with an ax.

．　　．　　．

The spectrum of possible victims had never been wide. The common financial types of the area would be carrying credit cards like Lowen, Richard W., while the generality of pensioners filling the benches were even less tempting. As Miss Couplard had explained, our economy was being refeudalized and cash was going the way of the ostrich, the octopus, and the moccasin flower.

It was such extinctions as these, but especially seagulls, that were the worry of the first lady they'd considered, a Miss Kraus, unless the name at the bottom of her handlettered poster (STOP THE SLAUGHTER of The *Innocents!!* etc.) belonged to someone else. Why, if she were Miss Kraus, was she wearing what seemed to be the old-fashioned diamond ring and gold band of a Mrs.? But the more crucial problem, which they couldn't see how to solve, was: was the diamond real?

Possibility Number Two was in the tradition of the original Orphans of the Storm, the Gish sisters. A lovely semiprofessional who whiled away the daylight pretending to be blind and serenading the benches. Her pathos was rich, if a bit worked-up; her repertoire was archaeological; and her gross was fair, especially when the rain added its own bit of too-much. However: Sniffles (who'd done this research) was certain she had a gun tucked away under the rags.

Three was the least poetic possibility, just the concessionaire in back of the giant eagle selling Fun and Synthamon. His appeal was commercial. But he had a licensed Weimaraner, and though Weimaraners can be dealt with, Amparo liked them.

"You're just a Romantic," Little Mister Kissy Lips said. "Give me one good reason."

"His eyes," she said. "They're amber. He'd haunt us."

They were snuggling together in one of the deep embrasures cut into the stone of Castle Clinton, her head wedged into his armpit, his fingers gliding across the lotion on her breasts (summer was just beginning). Silence, warm breezes, sunlight on water, it was all ineffable, as though only the sheerest of veils intruded between them and an understanding of something (all this) really meaningful. Because they thought it was their own innocence that was to blame, like a smog in their souls' atmosphere, they wanted more than ever to be rid of it at times, like this, when they approached so close.

"Why not the dirty old man, then?" she asked, meaning Alyona.

"Because he *is* a dirty old man."

"That's no reason. He must take in at least as much money as that singer."

"That's not what I mean." What he meant wasn't easy to define. It wasn't as though he'd be too easy to kill. If you'd seen him in the first minutes of a program, you'd know he was marked for destruction by the second commercial. He was the defiant homesteader, the crusty senior member of a research team who understood Algol and Fortran but couldn't read the secrets of his own heart. He was the Senator from South Carolina with his own peculiar brand of integrity but a racist nevertheless. Killing that sort was too much like one of Papa's scripts to be a satisfying gesture of rebellion.

But what he said, mistaking his own deeper meaning, was: "It's because he deserves it, because we'd be doing society a favor. Don't ask me to give *reasons.*"

"Well, I won't pretend I understand that, but do you know what I think, Little Mister Kissy Lips?" She pushed his hand away.

"You think I'm scared."

"Maybe you *should* be scared."

"Maybe you should shut up and leave this to me. I said we're going to do it. We'll do it."

"To him then?"

"Okay. But for gosh sakes, Amparo, we've got to think of something to call the bastard besides 'the dirty old man'!"

She rolled over out of his armpit and kissed him. They glittered all over with little beads of sweat. The summer began to shimmer with the excitement of first night. They had been waiting so long and now the curtain was rising.

M-Day was scheduled for the first weekend in July, a patriotic holiday. The computers would have time to tend to their own needs (which have been variously described as "confession," "dreaming," and "throwing up"), and the Battery would be as empty as it ever gets.

Meanwhile their problem was the same as any kids face anywhere during summer vacation, how to fill the time.

There were books, there were the Shakespeare puppets if you were willing to queue up for that long, there was always teevee, and when you couldn't stand sitting any longer there were the obstacle courses in Central Park, but the density there was at lemming level. The Battery, because it didn't try to meet anyone's needs, seldom got so overpopulated. If there had been more Alexandrians and all willing to fight for the space, they might have played ball. Well, another summer. . . .

What else? There were marches for the political, and religions at various energy levels for the apolitical. There would have been dancing, but the Lowen School had spoiled them for most amateur events around the city.

As for the supreme pastime of sex, for all of them except Little Mister Kissy Lips and Amparo (and even for them, when it came right down to orgasm) this was still something that happened on a screen, a wonderful hypothesis that lacked empirical proof.

One way or another it was all consumership, everything they might have done, and they were tired, who isn't, of being passive. They were twelve years old, or eleven, or ten, and they couldn't wait any longer. For what? they wanted to know.

So, except when they were just loafing around solo, all these putative resources, the books, the puppets, the sports, arts, politics, and religions, were in the same category of usefulness as merit badges or weekends in Calcutta, which is a name you can still find on a few old maps of India. Their lives were not enhanced, and their summer passed as summers have passed immemorially. They slumped and moped and lounged about and teased each other and complained. They acted out desultory, shy fantasies and had long pointless arguments about the more peripheral facts of exis-tence—the habits of jungle animals or how bricks had been made or the history of World War II.

One day they added up all the names on the monoliths set up for the soldiers, sailors, and airmen. The final figure they got was 4,800.

"Wow," said Tancred.

"But that can't be *all* of them," MaryJane insisted, speaking for the rest. Even that "wow" had sounded half ironic.

"Why not?" asked Tancred, who could never resist disagreeing. "They came from every different state and every branch of the service. It has to be complete or the people who had relatives left off would have protested."

"But so *few*? It wouldn't be possible to have fought more than one battle at that rate."

"Maybe . . ." Sniffles began quietly. But he was seldom listened to.

"Wars were different then," Tancred explained with the authority of a prime-time news analyst. "In those days more people were killed by their own automobiles than in wars. It's a fact."

"Four thousand, eight *hundred*?"

". . . a lottery?"

Celeste waved away everything Sniffles had said or would ever say. "MaryJane is right, Tancred. It's simply a *ludicrous* number. Why, in that same war the Germans gassed seven *million* Jews."

"Six million Jews," Little Mister Kissy Lips corrected. "But it's the same idea. Maybe the ones here got killed in a particular campaign."

"Then it would say so." Tancred was adamant, and he even got them to admit at last that 4,800 was an impressive figure, especially with every name spelled out in stone letters.

One other amazing statistic was commemorated in the park: over a thirty-three-year period Castle Clinton had processed 7.7 million immigrants into the United States.

Little Mister Kissy Lips sat down and figured out that it would take 12,800 stone slabs the size of the ones listing the soldiers, sailors, and airmen in order to write out all the immigrants' names, with country of origin, and an area of five square miles to set that many slabs up in, or all of Manhattan from here to 28th Street. But would it be worth the trouble, after all? Would it be that much different from the way things were already?

Alyona Ivanovna:

An archipelago of irregular brown islands were mapped on the tan sea of his bald head. The mainlands of his hair were marble outcroppings, especially his beard, white and crisp and coiling. The teeth were standard MODICUM issue; clothes, as clean as any fabric that old can be. Nor did he smell, particularly. And yet. . . .

Had he bathed every morning you'd still have looked at him and thought he was filthy, the way floorboards in old brownstones seem to need cleaning moments after they've been scrubbed. The dirt had been bonded to the wrinkled flesh and the wrinkled clothes, and nothing less than surgery or burning would get it out.

His habits were as orderly as a polka dot napkin. He lived at a Chelsea dorm for the elderly, a discovery they owed to a rainstorm that had forced him to take the subway home one day instead of, as usual, walking. On the hottest nights he might sleep over in the park, nesting in one of the Castle windows. He bought his lunches from a Water Street specialty shop, *Dumas Fils*: cheeses, imported fruit, smoked fish, bottles of cream, food for the gods. Otherwise he did without, though his dorm must have supplied prosaic necessities like breakfast. It was a strange way for a panhandler to spend his quarters, drugs being the norm.

His professional approach was out-and-out aggression. For instance, his hand in your face and, "How about it, Jack?" Or, confidingly, "I need sixty cents to get home." It was amazing how often he scored, but actually it wasn't amazing. He had charisma.

And someone who relies on charisma *wouldn't* have a gun.

Agewise he might have been sixty, seventy, seventy-five, a bit more even, or much less. It all depended on the kind of life he'd led, and where. He had an accent none of them could identify. It was not English, not French, not Spanish, and probably not Russian.

Aside from his burrow in the Castle wall there were two distinct places he preferred. One, the wide-open stretch of pavement along the water. This was where he worked, walking up past the Castle and down as far as the concession stand. The passage of one of the great Navy cruisers, the USS *Dana* or the USS *Melville*, would bring him, and the whole Battery, to a standstill, as though a whole parade were going by, white, soundless, slow as a dream. It was a part of history, and even the Alexandrians were impressed, though three of them had taken the cruise down to Andros Island and back. Sometimes, though, he'd stand by the guardrail for long stretches of time without any real reason, just looking at the Jersey sky and the Jersey shore. After a while he might start talking to himself, the barest whisper but very much in earnest, to judge by the way his forehead wrinkled. They never once saw him sit on one of the benches.

The other place he liked was the aviary. On days when they'd been ignored he'd contribute peanuts or breadcrumbs to the cause of the birds' existence. There were pigeons, parrots, a family of robins, and a proletarian swarm of what the sign declared to be chickadees, though Celeste, who'd gone to the library to make sure, said they were nothing more than a rather swank breed of sparrow. Here too, naturally, the militant Miss Kraus stationed herself when she bore testimony. One of her peculiarities (and the reason, probably, she was never asked to move on) was that under no circumstances did she ever deign to argue. Even sympathizers pried no more out of her than a grim smile and a curt nod.

One Tuesday, a week before M-Day (it was the early A.M. and only three Alexandrians were on hand to witness this confrontation), Alyona so far put aside his own reticence as to try to start a conversation going with Miss Kraus.

He stood squarely in front of her and began by reading aloud, slowly, in that distressingly indefinite accent, from the text of STOP THE SLAUGHTER: "The Department of the Interior of the United States Government, under the secret direction of the Zionist Ford Foundation, is *systematically* poisoning the oceans of the World with so-called 'food farms.' Is this 'peaceful application of Nuclear Power'? Unquote, the *New York Times*, August 2, 2024. Or a new Moondoggle!! *Nature World*, Jan. Can we afford to remain indifferent any longer. Every day 15,000 seagulls die as a direct result of Systematic Genocides while elected Officials falsify and distort the evidence. Learn the facts. Write to the Congressmen. *Make your voice heard!!*"

As Alyona had droned on, Miss Kraus turned a deeper and deeper red. Tightening her fingers about the turquoise broomhandle to which the placard was stapled, she began to jerk the poster up and down rapidly, as though this man with his foreign accent were some bird of prey who'd perched on it.

"Is that what you think?" he asked, having read all the way down to the signature despite her jiggling tactic. He touched his bushy white beard and wrinkled his face into a philosophical expression. "I'd *like* to know more about it, yes, I would. I'd be interested in hearing what *you* think."

Horror had frozen up every motion of her limbs. Her eyes blinked shut but she forced them open again.

"Maybe," he went on remorselessly, "we can discuss this whole thing. Some time when you feel more like talking. All right?"

She mustered her smile, and a minimal nod. He went away then. She was safe, temporarily, but even so she waited till he'd gone halfway to the other end of the sea-front promenade before she let the air collapse into her lungs. After a single deep breath the muscles of her hands thawed into trembling.

M-Day was an oil of summer, a catalog of everything painters are happiest painting—clouds, flags, leaves, sexy people, and in back of it all the flat empty baby-blue of the sky. Little Mister Kissy Lips was the first one there, and Tancred, in a kind of kimono (it hid the pilfered Luger), was the last. Celeste never came. (She'd just learned she'd been awarded the exchange scholarship to Sofia.) They decided they could do without Celeste, but the other nonappearance was more crucial. Their victim had neglected to be on hand for M-Day. Sniffles, whose voice was most like an adult's over the phone, was delegated to go to the Citibank lobby and call the West 16th Street dorm.

The nurse who answered was a temporary. Sniffles, always an inspired liar, insisted that his mother—"Mrs. *Anderson*, of course she lives there, Mrs. Alma F. Anderson"—had to be called to the phone. This was 248 West 16th, wasn't it? Where *was* she if she wasn't there? The nurse, flustered, explained that the residents, all who were fit, had been driven off to a July 4th picnic at Lake Hopatcong as guests of a giant Jersey retirement condominium. If he called bright and early tomorrow they'd be back and he could talk to his mother then.

So the initiation rites were postponed, it couldn't be helped. Amparo passed around some pills she'd taken from her mother's jar, a consolation prize. Jack left, apologizing that he was a borderline psychotic, which was the last that anyone saw of Jack till September. The gang was disintegrating, like a sugar cube soaking up saliva, then crumbling into the tongue. But what the hell—the sea still mirrored the same blue sky, the pigeons behind their wicket were no less iridescent, and trees grew for all of that.

They decided to be silly and make jokes about what the M *really* stood for in M-Day. Sniffles started off with "Miss Nomer, Miss Carriage, and Miss Steak." Tancred, whose sense of humor did not exist or was very private, couldn't do better than "Mnemone, mother of the Muses." Little Mister Kissy Lips said, "Merciful Heavens!" MaryJane maintained reasonably that M was for MaryJane. But Amparo said it stood for "Aplomb" and carried the day.

Then, proving that when you're sailing the wind always blows from behind you, they found Terry Riley's day-long *Orfeo* at 99.5 on the FM dial. They'd studied *Orfeo* in mime class, and by now it was part of their muscle and nerve. As Orpheus descended into a hell that mushroomed from the size of a pea to the size of a planet, the Alexandrians metamorphosed into as credible a tribe of souls in torment as any since the days of Jacopo Peri. Throughout the afternoon little audiences collected and dispersed to flood the sidewalk with libations of adult attention. Expressively they surpassed themselves, both one by one and all together, and though they couldn't have held out till the apotheosis (at 9.30) without a stiff psychochemical wind in their sails, what they had danced was authentic and very much their own. When they left the Battery that night they felt better than they'd felt all summer long. In a sense they had been exorcised.

But back at the Plaza Little Mister Kissy Lips couldn't sleep. No sooner was he through the locks than his guts knotted up into a Chinese puzzle. Only after he'd unlocked his window and crawled out onto the ledge did he get rid of the bad feelings. The city was real. His room was not. The stone ledge was real and his bare buttocks absorbed reality from it. He watched slow movements in enormous distances and pulled his thoughts together.

He knew without having to talk to the rest that the murder would never take place. The idea had never meant for them what it had meant for him. One pill and they were actors again, content to be images in a mirror.

Slowly, as he watched, the city turned itself off. Slowly the dawn divided the sky into an east and a west. Had a pedestrian been going fast on 58th Street and had that pedestrian looked up, he would have seen the bare soles of a boy's feet swinging back and forth, angelically.

He would have to kill Alyona Ivanovna himself. Nothing else was possible.

Back in his bedroom, long ago, the phone was ringing its fuzzy nighttime ring. That would be Tancred (or Amparo?) trying to talk him out of it. He foresaw their arguments. Celeste and Jack couldn't be trusted now. Or, more subtly: they'd all made themselves too visible with their *Orfeo*. If there were even a small investigation, the benches would remember them, remember how well they had danced, and the police would know where to look.

But the real reason, which at least Amparo would have been ashamed to mention now that the pill was wearing off, was that they'd begun to feel sorry for their victim. They'd got to know him too well over the last month and their resolve had been eroded by compassion.

A light came on in Papa's window. Time to begin. He stood up, golden in the sunbeams of another perfect day, and walked back along the foot-wide ledge to his own window. His legs tingled from having sat so long.

He waited till Papa was in the shower, then tippytoed to the old secretaire in his bedroom (W. & J. Sloan, 1952). Papa's keychain was coiled atop the walnut veneer. Inside the secretaire's drawer was an antique Mexican cigar box, and in the cigar box a velvet bag, and in the velvet bag Papa's replica of a French dueling pistol, circa 1790. These precautions were less for his son's sake than on account of Jimmy Ness, who every so often felt obliged to show he was serious with his suicide threats.

He'd studied the booklet carefully when Papa had bought the pistol and was able to execute the loading procedure quickly and without error, tamping the premeasured twist of powder down into the barrel and then the lead ball on top of it.

He cocked the hammer back a single click.

He locked the drawer. He replaced the keys, just so. He buried, for now, the pistol in the stuffs and cushions of the Turkish corner, tilted upright to keep the ball from rolling out. Then with what remained of yesterday's ebullience he bounced into the bathroom and kissed Papa's cheek, damp with the morning's allotted two gallons and redolent of 4711.

They had a cheery breakfast together in the coffee room, which was identical to the breakfast they would have made for themselves except for the ritual of being waited on by a waitress. Little Mister Kissy Lips gave an enthusiastic account of the Alexandrians' performance of *Orfeo*, and Papa made his best effort of seeming not to condescend. When he'd been driven to the limit of this pretense, Little Mister Kissy Lips touched him for a second pill, and since it was better for a boy to get these things from his father than from a stranger on the street, he got it.

He reached the South Ferry stop at noon, bursting with a sense of his own imminent liberation. The weather was M-Day all over again, as though at midnight out on the ledge he'd forced time to go backwards to the point when things had started going wrong. He'd dressed in his most anonymous shorts and the pistol hung from his belt in a dun dittybag.

Alyona Ivanovna was sitting on one of the benches near the aviary, listening to Miss Kraus. Her ring hand gripped the poster firmly, while the right chopped at the air, eloquently awkward, like a mute's first words following a miraculous cure.

Little Mister Kissy Lips went down the path and squatted in the shadow of his memorial. It had lost its magic yesterday, when the statues had begun to look so silly to everyone. They still looked silly. Verrazzano was dressed like a Victorian industrialist taking a holiday in the Alps. The angel was wearing an angel's usual bronze nightgown.

His good feelings were leaving his head by little and little, like aeolian sandstone attrited by the centuries of wind. He thought of calling up Amparo, but any comfort she might bring to him would be a mirage so long as his purpose in coming here remained unfulfilled.

He looked at his wrist, then remembered he'd left his watch home. The gigantic advertising clock on the facade of the First National Citibank said it was fifteen after two. That wasn't possible.

Miss Kraus was *still* yammering away.

There was time to watch a cloud move across the sky from Jersey, over the Hudson, and past the sun. Unseen winds nibbled at its wispy edges. The cloud became his life, which would disappear without ever having turned into rain.

Later, and the old man was walking up the sea promenade toward the Castle. He stalked him, for miles. And then they were alone, together, at the far end of the park.

"Hello," he said, with the smile reserved for grown-ups of doubtful importance.

He looked directly at the dittybag, but Little Mister Kissy Lips didn't lose his composure. He would be wondering whether to ask for money, which would be kept, if he'd had any, in the bag. The pistol made a noticeable bulge but not the kind of bulge one would ordinarily associate with a pistol.

"Sorry," he said coolly. "I'm broke."

"Did I ask?"

"You were going to."

The old man made as if to return in the other direction, so he had to speak quickly, something that would hold him here.

"I saw you speaking with Miss Kraus."

He was held.

"Congratulations—you broke through the ice!"

The old man half-smiled, half-frowned. "You know her?"

"Mm. You could say that we're *aware* of her." The "we" had been a deliberate risk, an hors d'oeuvre. Touching a finger to each side of the strings by which the heavy bag hung from his belt, he urged on it a lazy pendular motion. "Do you mind if I ask you a question?"

There was nothing indulgent now in the man's face. "I probably do."

His smile had lost the hard edge of calculation. It was the same smile he'd have smiled for Papa, for Amparo, for Miss Couplard, for anyone he liked. "Where do you come from? I mean, what country?"

"That's none of your business, is it?"

"Well, I just wanted . . . to know."

The old man (he had ceased, somehow, to be Alyona Ivanovna) turned away and walked directly toward the squat stone cylinder of the old fortress.

He remembered how the plaque at the entrance—the same that had cited the 7.7 million—had said that Jenny Lind had sung there and it had been a great success.

The old man unzipped his fly and, lifting out his cock, began pissing on the wall.

Little Mister Kissy Lips fumbled with the strings of the bag. It was remarkable how long the old man stood there pissing because despite every effort of the stupid knot to stay tied he had the pistol out before the final sprinkle had been shaken out.

He laid the fulminate cap on the exposed nipple, drew the hammer back two clicks, past the safety, and aimed.

The man made no haste zipping up. Only then did he glance in Little Mister Kissy Lips' direction. He saw the pistol aimed at him. They stood not twenty feet apart, so he must have seen it.

He said, "Ha!" And even this, rather than being addressed to the boy with the gun, was only a parenthesis from the faintly-aggrieved monologue he resumed each day at the edge of the water. He turned away, and a moment later he was back on the job, hand out, asking some fellow for a quarter.

Stranger Station

Damon Knight is one of the most important and influential figures in modern SF. As writer, editor, teacher, and translator, he has devoted much of his career to raising literary standards in SF and encouraging new writers. He founded the Science Fiction Writers of America and was a founder of the Milford SF-writing workshops for professionals and of the Clarion science fiction workshops for young writers. One of the finest contemporary anthologists, he invented, with James Blish, modern SF criticism, and has written some of the best fiction of the past forty years. Knight sold, edited and translated 13 French Science Fiction Stories (1965), the first collection of French SF to appear in English. A man of immense energies and accomplishments, Knight has written less fiction since 1965, devoting more time to editing and teaching. "Stranger Station," from the 1950s, when Knight was at the height of his influence, is perhaps his best longer story of that period, far ahead of its time in its use of the theme of artificial intelligence and its unusually sophisticated view of alien-human contact. Knight's clear, precise style and his psychological insight rank him with Theodore Sturgeon among the best modern SF writers.

*　　*　　*

The clang of metal echoed hollowly down through the Station's many vaulted corridors and rooms. Paul Wesson stood listening for a moment as the rolling echoes died away. The maintenance rocket was gone, heading back to Home; they had left him alone in Stranger Station.

Stranger Station! The name itself quickened his imagination. Wesson knew that both orbital stations had been named a century ago by the then British administration of the satellite service: "Home" because the larger, inner station handled the traffic of Earth and its colonies; "Stranger" because the outer station was designed specifically for dealings with for-eigners . . . beings from outside the solar system. But even that could not diminish the wonder of Stranger Station, whirling out here alone in the dark—waiting for its once-in-two-decades visitor. . . .

One man, out of all Sol's billions, had the task and privilege of enduring the alien's presence when it came. The two races, according to Wesson's understanding of the subject, were so fundamentally different that it was painful for them to meet. Well, he had volunteered for the job, and he thought he could handle it—the rewards were big enough.

He had gone through all the tests, and against his own expectations he had been chosen. The maintenance crew had brought him up as dead weight, drugged in a survival hamper; they had kept him the same way while they did their work, and then had brought him back to consciousness. Now they were gone. He was alone.

. . . But not quite.

"Welcome to Stranger Station, Sergeant Wesson," said a pleasant voice. "This is your alpha network speaking. I'm here to protect and serve you in every way. If there's anything you want, just ask me."

Wesson had been warned, but he was still shocked at the human quality of it. The alpha networks were the last word in robot brains—computers, safety devices, personal servants, libraries, all wrapped up in one, with something so close to "personality" and "free will" that experts were still arguing the question. They were rare and fantastically expensive; Wesson had never met one before.

"Thanks," he said now, to the empty air. "Uh—what do I call you, by the way? I can't keep saying, 'Hey, alpha network.'"

"One of your recent predecessors called me Aunt Nettie."

Wesson grimaced. Alpha network—Aunt Nettie. He hated puns; that wouldn't do. "The Aunt part is all right," he said. "Suppose I call you Aunt Jane. That was my mother's sister; you sound like her, a little bit."

"I am honored," said the invisible mechanism politely. "Can I serve you any refreshments now? Sandwiches? A drink?"

"Not just yet," said Wesson.

He turned away. That seemed to end the conversation as far as the network was concerned. A good thing; it was all right to have it for company, speaking when spoken to, but if it got talkative . . .

The human part of the Station was in four segments: bedroom, living room, dining room, bath. The living room was comfortably large and pleasantly furnished in greens and tans: the only mechanical note in it was the big instrument console in one corner. The other rooms, arranged in a ring around the living room, were tiny: just space enough for Wesson, a narrow encircling corridor, and the mechanisms that would serve him. The whole place was spotlessly clean, gleaming and efficient in spite of its twenty-year layoff.

This is the gravy part of the run, Wesson told himself. The month before the alien came—good food, no work, and an alpha network for conversation. "Aunt Jane, I'll have a small steak now," he said to the network. "Medium rare, with hash-brown potatoes, onions and mushrooms, and a glass of lager. Call me when it's ready."

"Right," said the voice pleasantly. Out in the dining room, the autochef began to hum and cluck self-importantly. Wesson wandered over and inspected the instrument console. Airlocks were sealed and tight, said the dials; the air was cycling. The Station was in orbit, and rotating on its axis with a force at the perimeter, where Wesson was, of one g. The internal temperature of this part of the Station was an even 73°.

The other side of the board told a different story; all the dials were dark and dead. Sector Two, occupying a volume some eighty-eight thousand times as great as this one, was not yet functioning.

Wesson had a vivid mental image of the Station, from photographs and diagrams—a 500-foot duralumin sphere, onto which the shallow 30-foot disk of the human section had been stuck apparently as an afterthought. The whole cavity of the sphere, very nearly—except for a honeycomb of supply and maintenance rooms, and the all-important, recently enlarged vats—was one cramped chamber for the alien. . . .

The steak was good, bubbling crisp outside the way he liked it, tender and pink inside. "Aunt Jane," he said with his mouth full, "this is pretty soft, isn't it?"

"The steak?" asked the voice, with a faintly anxious note.

Wesson grinned. "Never mind," he said. "Listen, Aunt Jane, you've been through this routine . . . how many times? Were you installed with the Station, or what?"

"I was not installed with the Station," said Aunt Jane primly. "I have assisted at three contacts."

"Um. Cigarette," said Wesson, slapping his pockets. The autochef hummed for a moment, and popped a pack of G.I.'s out of a vent. Wesson lit up. "All right," he said, "you've been through this three times. There are a lot of things you can tell me, right?"

"Oh, yes, certainly. What would you like to know?"

Wesson smoked, leaning back reflectively, green eyes narrowed. "First," he said, "read me the Pigeon report—you know, from the *Brief History*. I want to see if I remember it right."

"Chapter Two," said the voice promptly. "First contact with a non-Solar intelligence was made by Commander Ralph C. Pigeon on July 1, 1987, during an emergency landing on Titan. The following is an excerpt from his official report:

" 'While searching for a possible cause for our mental disturbance, we discovered what appeared to be a gigantic construction of metal on the far side of the ridge. Our distress grew stronger with the approach to this construction, which was polyhedral and approximately five times the length of the Cologne.

" 'Some of those present expressed a wish to retire, but Lt. Acuff and myself had a strong sense of being called or summoned in some indefinable way. Although our uneasiness was not lessened, we therefore agreed to go forward and keep radio contact with the rest of the party while they returned to the ship.

" 'We gained access to the alien construction by way of a large, irregular opening . . . The internal temperature was minus seventy-five degrees Fahrenheit; the atmosphere appeared to consist of methane and ammonia . . . Inside the second chamber, an alien creature was waiting for us. We felt the distress which I have tried to describe, to a much greater degree than before, and also the sense of summoning or pleading . . . We observed that the creature was exuding a thick yellowish fluid from certain joints or pores in its surface. Though disgusted, I managed to collect a sample of this exudate, and it was later forwarded for analysis . . .'

"The second contact was made ten years later by Commodore Crawford's famous Titan Expedition—"

"No, that's enough," said Wesson. "I just wanted the Pigeon quote." He smoked, brooding. "It seems kind of chopped off, doesn't it? Have you got a longer version in your memory banks anywhere?"

There was a pause. "No," said Aunt Jane.

"There was more to it when I was a kid," Wesson complained nervously. "I read that book when I was twelve, and I remember a long description of the alien . . . that is, I remember its being there." He swung around. "Listen, Aunt Jane—you're a sort of universal watchdog, that right? You've got cameras and mikes all over the Station?"

"Yes," said the network, sounding—was it Wesson's imagination?—faintly injured.

"Well, what about Sector Two—you must have cameras up there, too, isn't that so?"

"Yes."

"All right, then you can tell me. What do the aliens look like?"

There was a definite pause. "I'm sorry, I can't tell you that," said Aunt Jane.

"No," said Wesson, "I didn't think you could. You've got orders not to, I guess, for the same reason those history books have been cut since I was a kid. Now, what would the reason be? Have you got any idea, Aunt Jane?"

There was another pause. "Yes," the voice admitted.

"Well?"

"I'm sorry, I can't—"

"—tell you that," Wesson repeated along with it. "All right. At least we know where we stand."

"Yes, sergeant. Would you like some dessert?"

"No dessert. One other thing. *What happens to Station watchmen, like me, after their tour of duty?*"

"They are upgraded to Class Seven, students with unlimited leisure, and receive outright gifts of seven thousand stellors, plus free Class One housing—"

"Yeah, I know all that," said Wesson, licking his dry lips. "But here's what I'm asking you. The ones you knew—what kind of shape were they in when they left here?"

"The usual human shape," said the voice brightly. "Why do you ask, sergeant?"

Wesson made a discontented gesture. "Something I remember from a bull session at the Academy. I can't get it out of my head; I know it had something to do with the Station. Just a part of a sentence—'*blind as a bat, and white bristles all over.*' Now, would that be a description of the alien . . . or the watchman when they came to take him away?"

Aunt Jane went into one of her heavy pauses. "All right, I'll save you the trouble," said Wesson. "You're sorry, you can't tell me that."

"I *am* sorry," said the robot, sincerely.

Aunt Jane was a model companion. She had a record library of thousands of hours of music; she had films to show him, and micro-printed books that he could read on the scanner in the living room; or if he preferred, she would read to him. She controlled the Station's three telescopes, and on request would give him a view of Earth, or the Moon, or Home. . . .

But there was no news. Aunt Jane would obligingly turn on the radio receiver if he asked her, but nothing except static came out. That was the thing that weighed most heavily on Wesson, as time passed: the knowledge that radio silence was being imposed on all ships in transit, on the orbital stations, and on the planet-to-space transmitters. It was an enormous, almost a crippling handicap. Some information could be transmitted over relatively short distances by photophone, but ordinarily the whole complex traffic of the spacelanes depended on radio.

But this coming alien contact was so delicate a thing that even a radio voice, out here where the Earth was only a tiny disk twice the size of the Moon, might upset it. It was so precarious a thing, Wesson thought, that only one man could be allowed in the Station while the alien was there, and to give that man the company that would keep him sane, they had to install an alpha network. . . .

"Aunt Jane?"

The voice answered promptly, "Yes, Paul."

"This distress that the books talk about—you wouldn't know what it is, would you?"

"No, Paul."

"Because robot brains don't feel it, right?"

"Right, Paul."

"So tell me this—why do they need a man here at all? Why can't they get along with just you?"

A pause. "I don't know, Paul." The voice sounded faintly wistful.

He got up from the living-room couch and paced restlessly back and forth. "Let's have a look at Earth," he said. Obediently, the viewing screen on the console glowed into life: there was the blue Earth, swimming deep below him, in its first quarter, jewel-bright. "Switch it off," Wesson said.

"A little music?" suggested the voice, and immediately began to play something soothing, full of woodwinds.

"No," said Wesson. The music stopped.

Wesson's hands were trembling; he had a caged and frustrated feeling.

The fitted suit was in its locker beside the air lock. Wesson had been topside in it once or twice; there was nothing to see up there, just darkness and cold. But he had to get out of this squirrel-cage. He took the suit down.

"Paul," said Aunt Jane anxiously, "are you feeling nervous?"

"Yes," he snarled.

"Then don't go into Sector Two," said Aunt Jane.

"Don't tell me what to do, you hunk of tin!" said Wesson with sudden anger. He zipped up the front of his suit.

Aunt Jane was silent.

The air lock, an upright tube barely large enough for one man, was the only passage between Sector One and Sector Two. It was also the only exit from Sector One; to get here in the first place, Wesson had had to enter the big lock at the "south" pole of the sphere, and travel all the way down inside by drop-hole and catwalk. He had been drugged unconscious at the time, of course. When the time came, he would go out the same way; neither the maintenance rocket nor the tanker had any space, or time, to spare.

At the "north" pole opposite, there was a third air lock, this one so huge it could easily have held an interplanet freighter. But that was nobody's business—no human being's.

In the beam of Wesson's helmet lamp, the enormous central cavity of the Station was an inky gulf that sent back only remote, mocking glimmers of light. The near walls sparkled with hoar-frost. Sector Two was not yet pressurized; there was only a diffuse vapor that had leaked through the airseal, and had long since frozen into the powdery deposit that lined the walls. The metal rang cold under his shod feet; the vast emptiness of the chamber was the more depressing because it was airless, unwarmed and unlit. *Alone*, said his footsteps; *alone* . . .

He was thirty yards up the catwalk when his anxiety suddenly grew stronger. Wesson stopped in spite of himself, and turned clumsily, putting his back to the wall. The support of the solid wall was not enough. The catwalk seemed threatening to tilt underfoot, dropping him into the gulf.

Wesson recognized this drained feeling, this metallic taste at the back of his tongue. It was fear.

The thought ticked through his head: They want me to be afraid. But why? Why now? Of what?

Equally suddenly, he knew. The nameless pressure tightened, like a great fist closing, and Wesson had the appalling sense of something so huge that it had no limits at all, descending, with a terrible endless swift slowness. . . .

His first month was up.

The alien was coming.

As Wesson turned, gasping, the whole huge structure of the Station around him seemed to dwindle to the size of an ordinary room . . . and Wesson with it, so that he seemed to himself like a tiny insect, frantically scuttling down the walls toward safety.

Behind him as he ran, the Station *boomed*.

.   .   .

In the silent rooms, all the lights were burning dimly. Wesson lay still, looking at the ceiling. Up there, his imagination formed a shifting, changing image of the alien—huge, shadowy, formlessly menacing.

Sweat had gathered in globules on his brow. He stared, unable to look away.

"That was why you didn't want me to go topside, huh, Aunt Jane?"

"Yes. The nervousness is the first sign. But you gave me a direct order, Paul."

"I know it," he said vaguely, still staring fixedly at the ceiling. "A funny thing . . . Aunt Jane?"

"Yes, Paul."

"You won't tell me what it looks like, right?"

"No, Paul."

"I don't want to know. Lord, I don't *want* to know . . . Funny thing, Aunt Jane, part of me is just pure funk—I'm so scared, I'm nothing but a jelly—"

"I know," said the voice gently.

"—and part is real cool and calm, as if it didn't matter. Crazy, the things you think about. You know?"

"What things, Paul?"

He tried to laugh. "I'm remembering a kids' party I went to twenty . . . twenty-five years ago. I was, let's see, I was nine. I remember, because that was the same year my father died.

"We were living in Dallas then, in a rented mobilehouse, and there was a family in the next tract with a bunch of redheaded kids. They were always throwing parties; nobody liked them much, but everybody always went."

"Tell me about the party, Paul."

He shifted on the couch. "This one, this one was a Hallowe'en party. I remember the girls had on black and orange dresses, and the boys mostly wore spirit costumes. I was about the youngest kid there, and I felt kind of out of place. Then all of a sudden one of the redheads jumps up in a skull mask, hollering, 'C'mon, everybody get ready for hiden-seek.' And he grabs *me*, and says, '*You* be it,' and before I can even move, he shoves me into a dark closet. And I hear that door lock behind me."

He moistened his lips. "And then—you know, in the darkness—I feel something hit my *face*. You know, cold and clammy, like, I don't know, something dead. . . .

"I just hunched up on the floor of that closet, waiting for that thing to touch me again. You know? That thing, cold and kind of gritty, hanging up there. You know what it was? A cloth glove, full of ice and bran cereal. A joke. Boy, that was one joke I never forgot. . . . Aunt Jane?"

"Yes, Paul."

"Hey, I'll bet you alpha networks make great psychs, huh? I could lie here and tell you anything, because you're just a machine—right?"

"Right, Paul," said the network sorrowfully.

"Aunt Jane, Aunt Jane . . . It's no use kidding myself along, I can *feel* that thing up there, just a couple of yards away."

"I know you can, Paul."

"I can't stand it, Aunt Jane."

"You can if you think you can, Paul."

He writhed on the couch. "It's—it's dirty, it's clammy. My God, is it going to be like that for *five months*? I can't, it'll kill me, Aunt Jane."

There was another thunderous boom, echoing down through the structural members of the Station. "What's that?" Wesson gasped. "The other ship—casting off?"

"Yes. Now he's alone, just as you are."

"Not like me. He can't be feeling what I'm feeling. Aunt Jane, you don't know . . ."

Up there, separated from him only by a few yards of metal, the alien's enormous, monstrous body hung. It was that poised weight, as real as if he could touch it, that weighed down his chest.

Wesson had been a space-dweller for most of his adult life, and knew even in his bones that if an orbital station ever collapsed, the "under" part would not be crushed but would be hurled away by its own angular momentum. This was not the oppressiveness of planetside buildings, where the looming mass above you seemed always threatening to fall: this was something else, completely distinct, and impossible to argue away.

It was the scent of danger, hanging unseen up there in the dark, waiting, cold and heavy. It was the recurrent nightmare of Wesson's childhood—the bloated unreal shape, no-color, no-size, that kept on hideously falling toward his face. . . . It was the dead puppy he had pulled out of the creek, that summer in Dakota . . . wet fur, limp head, cold, cold, *cold*. . . .

With an effort, Wesson rolled over on the couch and lifted himself to one elbow. The pressure was an insistent chill weight on his skull; the room seemed to dip and swing around in slow circles.

Wesson felt his jaw muscles contorting with the strain as he knelt, then stood erect. His back and legs tightened; his mouth hung painfully open. He took one step, then another, timing them to hit the floor as it came upright.

The right side of the console, the one that had been dark, was lighted. Pressure in Sector Two, according to the indicator, was about one and a third atmospheres. The air lock indicator showed a slightly higher pressure of oxygen and argon; that was to keep any of the alien atmosphere from contaminating Sector One, but it also meant that the lock would no longer open from either side.

"Lemme see Earth," he gasped.

The screen lighted up as he stared into it. "It's a long way down," he said. A long, long way down to the bottom of that well. . . . He had spent ten featureless years as a servo tech in Home Station. Before that, he'd wanted to be a pilot, but had washed out the first years—couldn't take the math. But he had never once thought of going back to Earth.

"Aunt Jane, Aunt Jane, it's beautiful," he mumbled.

Down there, he knew, it was spring; and in certain places, where the edge of darkness retreated, it was morning: a watery blue morning like the sea light caught in an agate, a morning with smoke and mist in it; a morning of stillness and promise. Down there, lost years and miles away, some tiny dot of a woman was opening her microscopic door to listen to an atom's song. Lost, lost, and packed away in cotton wool, like a specimen slide: one spring morning on Earth.

Black miles above, so far that sixty Earths could have been piled one on another to make a pole for his perch, Wesson swung in his endless circle within a circle. Yet, vast as was the gulf beneath him, all this—Earth, Moon, orbital stations, ships; yes, the Sun and all the rest of his planets, too—was the merest sniff of space, to be pinched up between thumb and finger.

Beyond—there was the true gulf. In that deep night, galaxies lay sprawled aglitter, piercing a distance that could only be named in a meaningless number, a cry of dismay: O,O,O. . . .

Crawling and fighting, blasting with energies too big for them, men had come as far as Uranus. But if a man had been tall enough to lie with his boots toasting in the Sun and his head freezing at Pluto, still he would have been too small for that overwhelming emptiness. Here, not at Pluto, was the outermost limit of man's empire: here the Outside funneled down to meet it, like the pinched waist of an hourglass: here, and only here, the two worlds came near enough to touch. Ours—and Theirs.

Down at the bottom of the board, now, the golden dials were faintly alight, the needles trembling ever so little on their pins.

Deep in the vats, the vats, the golden liquid was trickling down: *"Though disgusted, I took a sample of the exudate and it was forwarded for analysis. . . ."*

Space-cold fluid, trickling down the bitter walls of the tubes, forming little pools in the cups of darkness; goldenly agleam there, half-alive. The golden elixir. One drop of the concentrate would arrest aging for twenty years—keep your arteries soft, tonus good, eyes clear, hair pigmented, brain alert.

That was what the tests of Pigeon's sample had showed. That was the reason for the whole crazy history of the "alien trading post"—first a hut on Titan, then later, when people understood more about the problem, Stranger Station.

Once every twenty years, an alien would come down out of Somewhere, and sit in the tiny cage we had made for him, and make us rich beyond our dreams—rich with life . . . and still we did not know why.

Above him, Wesson imagined he could see that sensed body a-wallow in the glacial blackness, its bulk passively turning with the Station's spin, bleeding a chill gold into the lips of the tubes: drip, drop.

Wesson held his head. The pressure inside made it hard to think; it felt as if his skull were about to fly apart. "Aunt Jane," he said.

"Yes, Paul." The kindly, comforting voice: like a nurse. The nurse who stands beside your cot while you have painful, necessary things done to you.

"Aunt Jane," said Wesson, "do you know why they keep coming back?"

"No," said the voice precisely. "It is a mystery."

Wesson nodded. "I had," he said, "an interview with Gower before I left Home. You know Gower? Chief of the Outworld Bureau. Came up especially to see me."

"Yes?" said Aunt Jane encouragingly.

"Said to me, 'Wesson, you got to find out. Find out if we can count on them to keep up the supply. You know? There's fifty million more of us,' he says, 'than when you were born. We need more of the stuff, and we got to know if we can count on it. Because,' he says, 'you know what would happen if it stopped?' Do you know, Aunt Jane?"

"It would be," said the voice, "a catastrophe."

"That's right," Wesson said respectfully. "It would. Like, he says to me, 'What if the people in the Nefud area were cut off from the Jordan Valley Authority? Why, there'd be millions dying of thirst in a week.

" 'Or what if the freighters stopped coming to Moon Base. Why,' he says, 'there'd be thousands starving and smothering.'

"He says, 'Where the water is, where you can get food and air, people are going to settle, and get married, you know? and have kids.'

"He says, 'If the so-called longevity serum stopped coming . . .' Says, 'Every twentieth adult in the Sol family is due for his shot this year.' Says, 'Of those, almost twenty per cent are one hundred fifteen or older.' Says, 'The deaths in that group, in the first year, would be at least three times what the actuarial tables call for.' " Wesson raised a strained face. "I'm thirty-four, you know?" he said. "That Gower, he made me feel like a baby."

Aunt Jane made a sympathetic noise.

"Drip, drip," said Wesson hysterically. The needles of the tall golden indicators were infinitesimally higher. "Every twenty years, we need more of the stuff, so somebody like me has to come out and take it for five lousy months. And one of *them* has to come out and sit there, and *drip*. Why, Aunt Jane? What for? Why should it matter to them whether we live a long time or not? Why do they keep on coming back? What do they take *away* from here?"

But to these questions, Aunt Jane had no reply.

All day and every day, the lights burned cold and steady in the circular gray corridor around the rim of Sector One. The hard gray flooring had been deeply scuffed in that circular path before Wesson ever walked there: the corridor existed for that only, like a treadmill in a squirrel cage; it said "Walk," and Wesson walked. A man would go crazy if he sat still, with that squirming, indescribable pressure on his head; and so Wesson paced off the miles, all day and every day, until he dropped like a dead man in the bed at night.

He talked, too, sometimes to himself, sometimes to the listening alpha network; sometimes it was difficult to tell which. "Moss on a rock," he muttered, pacing. "Told him, wouldn't give twenty mills for any damn shell. . . . Little pebbles down there, all colors." He shuffled on in silence for a while. Abruptly: "I don't see *why* they couldn't have given me a cat."

Aunt Jane said nothing. After a moment Wesson went on, "Nearly everybody at Home has a cat, for God's sake, or a goldfish or something. You're all right, Aunt Jane, but I can't *see* you. My God, I mean if they couldn't send a man a woman for company, what I mean, my God, I never liked *cats*." He swung around the doorway into the bedroom, and absent-mindedly slammed his fist into the bloody place on the wall.

"But a cat would have been *something*," he said.

Aunt Jane was still silent.

"Don't pretend your damn feelings are hurt, I know you, you're only a damn machine," said Wesson. "Listen, Aunt Jane, I remember a cereal package one time that had a horse and a cowboy on the side. There wasn't much room, so about all you saw was their faces. It used to strike me funny how much they looked alike. Two ears on the top with hair in the middle. Two eyes. Nose. Mouth with teeth in it. I was thinking, we're kind of distant cousins, aren't we, us and the horses. But compared to that thing up there — we're *brothers*. You know?"

"Yes," said Aunt Jane, quietly.

"So I keep asking myself, why couldn't they have sent a horse, or a cat, *instead* of a man? But I guess the answer is, because only a man could take what I'm taking. God, only a man. Right?"

"Right," said Aunt Jane, with deep sorrow.

Wesson stopped at the bedroom doorway again and shuddered, holding onto the frame. "Aunt Jane," he said in a low, clear voice, "you take pictures of *him* up there, don't you?"

"Yes, Paul."

"And you take pictures of me. And then what happens? After it's all over, who looks at the pictures?"

"I don't know," said Aunt Jane humbly.

"You don't know. But whoever looks at 'em, it doesn't do any good. Right? We got to find out why, why, why . . . And we never do find out, do we?"

"No," said Aunt Jane.

"But don't they figure that if the man who's going through it could see him, he might be able to tell something? That other people couldn't? Doesn't that make sense?"

"That's out of my hands, Paul."

He sniggered. "That's funny. Oh, that's funny." He chortled in his throat, reeling around the circuit.

"Yes, that's funny," said Aunt Jane.

"Aunt Jane, tell me what happens to the watchmen."

". . . I can't tell you that, Paul."

He lurched into the living room, sat down before the console, beat on its smooth, cold metal with his fists. "What are you, some kind of monster? Isn't there any blood in your veins, damn it, or oil or *anything*?"

"Please, Paul—"

"Don't you see, all I want to know, can they talk? Can they tell anything after their tour is over?"

". . . No, Paul."

He stood upright, clutching the console for balance. "They can't? No, I figured. And you know why?"

"No."

"Up there," said Wesson obscurely. "Moss on the rock."

"Paul, what?"

"We get changed," said Wesson, stumbling out of the room again. "We get changed. Like a piece of iron next to a magnet. Can't help it. You— nonmagnetic, I guess. Goes right through you, huh, Aunt Jane? You don't get changed. You stay here, wait for the next one."

"Yes," said Aunt Jane.

"You know," said Wesson, pacing, "I can tell how he's lying up there. Head *that* way, tail the other. Am I right?"

". . . Yes," said Aunt Jane.

Wesson stopped. "Yes," he said intently. "So you *can* tell me what you see up there, can't you, Aunt Jane?"

"No. Yes. It isn't allowed."

"Listen, Aunt Jane, *we'll die* unless we can find out what makes those aliens tick! Remember that." Wesson leaned against the corridor wall, gazing up. "He's turning now—around this way. Right?"

"Right."

"Well, what else is he doing? Come on, Aunt Jane!"

A pause. "He is twitching his . . ."

"What?"

"I don't know the words."

"My God, my God," said Wesson, clutching his head, "of course there aren't any words." He ran into the living room, clutched the console and stared at the blank screen. He pounded the metal with his fist. "You've got to show me, Aunt Jane, come on and show me, show me!"

"It isn't allowed," Aunt Jane protested.

"You've got to do it just the same, or we'll *die*, Aunt Jane—millions of us, billions, and it'll be your fault, get it, *your fault*, Aunt Jane!"

"*Please*," said the voice. There was a pause. The screen flickered to life, for an instant only. Wesson had a glimpse of something massive and dark, but half transparent, like a magnified insect—a tangle of nameless limbs, whiplike filaments, claws, wings . . .

He clutched the edge of the console.

"Was that all right?" Aunt Jane asked.

"Of course! What do you think, it'll kill me to look at it? Put it back, Aunt Jane, put it back!"

Reluctantly, the screen lighted again. Wesson stared, and went on staring. He mumbled something.

"What?" said Aunt Jane.

"*Life of my love, I loathe thee*," said Wesson, staring. He roused himself after a moment and turned away. The image of the alien stayed with him as he went reeling into the corridor again; he was not surprised to find that it reminded him of all the loathsome, crawling, creeping things the Earth was full of. That explained why he was not supposed to see the alien, or even know what it looked like—because that fed his hate. And it was all right for him to be afraid of the alien, but he was not supposed to hate it . . . why not? Why not?

His fingers were shaking. He felt drained, steamed, dried up and withered. The one daily shower Aunt Jane allowed him was no longer enough. Twenty minutes after bathing, the acid sweat dripped again from his armpits, the cold sweat was beaded on his forehead, the hot sweat was in his palms. Wesson felt as if there were a furnace inside him, out of control, all the dampers drawn. He knew that under stress, something of the kind did happen to a man: the body's chemistry was altered—more adrenalin, more glycogen in the muscles; eyes brighter, digestion retarded. That was the trouble—he was burning himself up, unable to fight the thing that tormented him, or to run from it.

After another circuit, Wesson's steps faltered. He hesitated, and went into the living room. He leaned over the console, staring. From the screen, the alien stared blindly up into space. Down in the dark side, the golden indicators had climbed: the vats were more than two-thirds filled.

. . . to *fight*, or *run* . . .

Slowly Wesson sank down in front of the console. He sat hunched, head bent, hands squeezed tight between his knees, trying to hold onto the thought that had come to him.

If the alien felt a pain as great as Wesson's—or greater—

Stress might alter the alien's body chemistry, too.

Life of my love, I loathe thee.

Wesson pushed the irrelevant thought aside. He stared at the screen, trying to envisage the alien, up there, wincing in pain and distress—sweating a golden sweat of horror. . . .

After a long time, he stood up and walked into the kitchen. He caught the table edge to keep his legs from carrying him on around the circuit. He sat down.

Humming fondly, the autochef slid out a tray of small glasses—water, orange juice, milk. Wesson put the water glass to his stiff lips; the water was cool, and hurt his throat. Then the juice, but he could drink only a little of it; then he sipped the milk. Aunt Jane hummed approvingly.

Dehydrated—how long had it been since he had eaten, or drunk? He looked at his hands. They were thin bundles of sticks, ropy-veined, with hard yellow claws. He could see the bones of his forearms under the skin, and his heart's beating stirred the cloth at his chest. The pale hairs on his arms and thighs—were they blond, or white?

The blurred reflections in the metal trim of the dining room gave him no answers—only pale faceless smears of gray. Wesson felt light-headed and very weak, as if he had just ended a bout of fever. He fumbled over his ribs and shoulderbones. He was thin.

He sat in front of the autochef for a few minutes more, but no food came out. Evidently Aunt Jane did not think he was ready for it, and perhaps she was right. Worse for them than for us, he thought dizzily. That's why the Station's so far out; why radio silence, and only one man aboard. They couldn't stand it at all, otherwise. . . . Suddenly he could think of nothing but sleep—the bottomless pit, layer after layer of smothering velvet, numbing and soft. . . . His leg muscles quivered and twitched when he tried to walk, but he managed to get to the bedroom and fall on the mattress. The resilient block seemed to dissolve under him. His bones were melting.

He woke with a clear head, very weak, thinking cold and clear: When two alien cultures meet, the stronger must transform the weaker with love or hate. "Wesson's Law," he said aloud. He looked automatically for pencil and paper, but there was none, and he realized he would have to tell Aunt Jane, and let her remember it.

"I don't understand," she said.

"Never mind, remember it anyway. You're good at that, aren't you?"

"Yes, Paul."

"All right. . . . I want some breakfast."

He thought about Aunt Jane, so nearly human, sitting up here in her metal prison, leading one man after another through the torments of hell . . . nursemaid, protector, torturer. They must have known that something would have to give. . . . But the alphas were comparatively new; nobody understood them very well. Perhaps they really thought that an absolute prohibition could never be broken.

. . . the stronger must transform the weaker . . .

I'm the stronger, he thought. *And that's the way it's going to be.* He stopped at the console, and the screen was blank. He said angrily, "Aunt Jane!" And with a guilty start, the screen flickered into life.

Up there, the alien had rolled again in his pain. Now the great clustered eyes were staring directly into the camera; the coiled limbs threshed in pain: the eyes were staring, asking, pleading . . .

"No," said Wesson, feeling his own pain like an iron cap, and he slammed his hand down on the manual control. The screen went dark. He looked up, sweating, and saw the floral picture over the console.

The thick stems were like antennae, the leaves thoraxes, the buds like blind insect-eyes. The whole picture moved slightly, endlessly, in a slow waiting rhythm.

Wesson clutched the hard metal of the console and stared at the picture, with sweat cold on his brow, until it turned into a calm, meaningless arrangement of lines again. Then he went into the dining room, shaking, and sat down.

After a moment he said, "Aunt Jane, does it get worse?"

"No. From now on, it gets better."

"How long?" he asked vaguely.

"One month."

A month, getting "better" . . . that was the way it had always been, with the watchman swamped and drowned, his personality submerged. Wesson thought about the men who had gone before him—Class Seven citizenship, with unlimited leisure, and Class One housing, yes, sure . . . in a sanatorium.

His lips peeled back from his teeth, and his fists clenched hard. *Not me!* he thought.

He spread his hands on the cool metal to steady them. He said, "How much longer do they usually stay able to talk?"

"You are already talking longer than any of them."

Then there was a blank. Wesson was vaguely aware, in snatches, of the corridor walls moving past, and the console glimpsed, and of a thunderous cloud of ideas that swirled around his head in a beating of wings. The aliens: what did they want? And what happened to the watchmen in Stranger Station?

The haze receded a little, and he was in the dining room again, staring vacantly at the table. Something was wrong.

He ate a few spoonfuls of the gruel the autochef served him, then pushed it away; the stuff tasted faintly unpleasant. The machine hummed anxiously and thrust a poached egg at him, but Wesson got up from the table.

The Station was all but silent. The resting rhythm of the household machines throbbed in the walls, unheard. The blue-lit living room was spread out before him like an empty stage-setting, and Wesson stared as if he had never seen it before.

He lurched to the console and stared down at the pictured alien on the screen: heavy, heavy, asprawl with pain in the darkness. The needles of the golden indicators were high, the enlarged vats almost full. *It's too much for him*, Wesson thought with grim satisfaction. The peace that followed the pain had not descended as it was supposed to; no, not this time!

He glanced up at the painting over the console: heavy crustacean limbs that swayed gracefully.

He shook his head violently. I won't let it; I won't give in! He held the back of one hand close to his eyes. He saw the dozens of tiny cuneiform wrinkles stamped into the skin over the knuckles, the pale hairs sprouting, the pink shiny flesh of recent scars. I'm human, he thought. But when he let his hand fall onto the console, the bony fingers seemed to crouch like crustaceans' legs, ready to scuttle.

Sweating, Wesson stared into the screen. Pictured there, the alien met his

eyes, and it was as if they spoke to each other, mind to mind, an instantaneous communication that needed no words. There was a piercing sweetness
in it, a melting, dissolving luxury of change into something that would no
longer have any pain. . . . A pull, a calling.

Wesson straightened up slowly, carefully, as if he held some fragile thing
in his mind that must not be handled roughly, or it would disintegrate. He
said hoarsely, "Aunt Jane!"

She made some responsive noise.

He said, "Aunt Jane, I've got the answer! The whole thing! Listen, now,
wait—listen!" He paused a moment to collect his thoughts. "*When two alien
cultures meet, the stronger must transform the weaker with love or hate.*
Remember? You said you didn't understand what that meant. I'll *tell* you
what it means. When these—monsters—met Pigeon a hundred years ago
on Titan, *they knew* we'd have to meet again. They're spreading out,
colonizing, and so are we. We haven't got interstellar flight yet, but give us
another hundred years, we'll *get* it. *We'll wind up out there, where they are.*
And they can't stop us. Because they're not killers, Aunt Jane, it isn't in
them. They're *nicer* than us. See, they're like the missionaries, and we're the
South Sea Islanders. *They* don't kill their enemies, oh no—perish the
thought!"

She was trying to say something, to interrupt him, but he rushed on.
"Listen! The longevity serum—that was a lucky accident. But they played it
for all it's worth. Slick and smooth—they come and give us the stuff free—
they don't ask for a thing in return. Why not? Listen.

"They come here, and the shock of that first contact makes them sweat
out that golden gook we need. Then, the last month or so, the pain always
eases off. Why? Because the two minds, the human and alien, they stop
fighting each other. Something gives way, it goes soft and there's a mixing
together. And that's where you get the human casualties of this operation—
the bleary men that come out of here not even able to talk human language
any more. Oh, I suppose they're happy—happier than I am!—because
they've got something big and wonderful inside 'em. Something that you
and I can't even understand. But if you took them and put them together
again with the aliens who spent time here, *they could all live together—
they're adapted.*

"That's what they're aiming for!" He struck the console with his fist. "Not
now—but a hundred, two hundred years from now! When we start expanding out to the stars—when we go a-conquering—we'll have already been
conquered! Not by weapons, Aunt Jane, not by hate—by love! Yes, love!
Dirty, stinking, low-down, sneaking love!"

Aunt Jane said something, a long sentence, in a high, anxious voice.

"What?" said Wesson irritably. He couldn't understand a word.

Aunt Jane was silent. "What, what?" Wesson demanded, pounding the console. "Have you got it through your tin head, or not? *What?*"

Aunt Jane said something else, tonelessly. Once more, Wesson could not make out a single word.

He stood frozen. Warm tears started suddenly out of his eyes. "Aunt Jane—" he said. He remembered, *You are already talking longer than any of them.* Too late? Too late? He tensed, then whirled and sprang to the closet where the paper books were kept. He opened the first one his hand struck.

The black letters were alien squiggles on the page, little humped shapes, without meaning.

The tears were coming faster, he couldn't stop them: tears of weariness, tears of frustration, tears of hate. *"Aunt Jane!"* he roared.

But it was no good. The curtain of silence had come down over his head. He was one of the vanguard—the conquered men, the ones who would get along with their stranger brothers, out among the alien stars.

The console was not working any more; nothing worked when he wanted it. Wesson squatted in the shower stall, naked, with a soup bowl in his hands. Water droplets glistened on his hands and forearms; the pale short hairs were just springing up, drying.

The silvery skin of reflection in the bowl gave him back nothing but a silhouette, a shadow man's outline. He could not see his face.

He dropped the bowl and went across the living room, shuffling the pale drifts of paper underfoot. The black lines on the paper, when his eyes happened to light on them, were worm-shapes, crawling things, conveying nothing. He rolled slightly in his walk; his eyes were glazed. His head twitched, every now and then, sketching a useless motion to avoid pain.

Once the bureau chief, Gower, came to stand in his way. "You fool," he said, his face contorted in anger, "you were supposed to go on to the end, like the rest. Now look what you've done!"

"I found out, didn't I?" Wesson mumbled, and as he brushed the man aside like a cobweb, the pain suddenly grew more intense. Wesson clasped his head in his hands with a grunt, and rocked to and fro a moment, uselessly, before he straightened and went on. The pain was coming in waves now, so tall that at their peak his vision dimmed out, violet, then gray.

It couldn't go on much longer. Something had to burst.

He paused at the bloody place and slapped the metal with his palm, making the sound ring dully up into the frame of the Station: *rroom, rroom.*

Faintly an echo came back: *boooom.*

Wesson kept going, smiling a faint and meaningless smile. He was only marking time now, waiting. Something was about to happen.

The dining-room doorway sprouted a sudden sill and tripped him. He fell heavily, sliding on the floor, and lay without moving beneath the slick gleam of the autochef.

The pressure was too great: the autochef's clucking was swallowed up in the ringing pressure, and the tall gray walls buckled slowly in. . . .

The Station lurched.

Wesson felt it through his chest, palms, knees and elbows: the floor was plucked away for an instant and then swung back.

The pain in his skull relaxed its grip a little. Wesson tried to get to his feet.

There was an electric silence in the Station. On the second try, he got up and leaned his back against a wall. *Cluck*, said the autochef suddenly, hysterically, and the vent popped open, but nothing came out.

He listened, straining to hear. What?

The Station bounced beneath him, making his feet jump like a puppet's; the wall slapped his back hard, shuddered and was still; but far off through the metal cage came a long angry groan of metal, echoing, diminishing, dying. Then silence again.

The Station held its breath. All the myriad clickings and pulses in the walls were suspended; in the empty rooms the lights burned with a yellow glare, and the air hung stagnant and still. The console lights in the living room glowed like witchfires. Water in the dropped bowl, at the bottom of the shower stall, shone like quicksilver, waiting.

The third shock came. Wesson found himself on his hands and knees, the jolt still tingling in the bones of his body, staring at the floor. The sound that filled the room ebbed away slowly and ran down into the silences: a resonant metallic hollow sound, shuddering away now along the girders and hull plates, rattling tinnily into bolts and fittings, diminishing, noiseless, gone. The silence pressed down again.

The floor leaped painfully under his body: one great resonant blow that shook him from head to foot.

A muted echo of that blow came a few seconds later, as if the shock had traveled across the Station and back.

The bed, Wesson thought, and scrambled on hands and knees through the doorway, along a floor curiously tilted, until he reached the rubbery block.

The room burst visibly upward around him, squeezing the block flat. It dropped back as violently, leaving Wesson bouncing helpless on the mattress, his limbs flying. It came to rest, in a long reluctant groan of metal.

Wesson rolled up on one elbow, thinking incoherently, Air, the air lock.

Another blow slammed him down into the mattress, pinched his lungs shut, while the room danced grotesquely over his head. Gasping for breath in the ringing silence, Wesson felt a slow icy chill rolling toward him across the room . . . and there was a pungent smell in the air. Ammonia! he thought; and the odorless, smothering methane with it.

His cell was breached. The burst membrane was fatal: the alien's atmosphere would kill him.

Wesson surged to his feet. The next shock caught him off balance, dashed him to the floor. He arose again, dazed and limping; he was still thinking confusedly, The air lock, get out.

When he was halfway to the door, all the ceiling lights went out at once. The darkness was like a blanket around his head. It was bitter cold now in the room, and the pungent smell was sharper. Coughing, Wesson hurried forward. The floor lurched under his feet.

Only the golden indicators burned now: full to the top, the deep vats brimming, golden-lipped, gravid, a month before the time. Wesson shuddered.

Water spurted in the bathroom, hissing steadily on the tiles, rattling in the plastic bowl at the bottom of the shower stall. The lights winked on and off again. In the dining room, he heard the autochef clucking and sighing. The freezing wind blew harder: he was numb with cold to the hips. It seemed to Wesson abruptly that he was not at the top of the sky at all, but down, *down* at the bottom of the sea . . . trapped in this steel bubble, while the dark poured in.

The pain in his head was gone, as if it had never been there, and he understood what that meant: Up there, the great body was hanging like butcher's carrion in the darkness. Its death struggles were over, the damage done.

Wesson gathered a desperate breath, shouted, "Help me! The alien's dead! He kicked the Station apart—the methane's coming in! Get help, do you hear me? *Do you hear me?*"

Silence. In the smothering blackness, he remembered: *She can't understand me any more. Even if she's alive.*

He turned, making an animal noise in his throat. He groped his way on around the room, past the second doorway. Behind the walls, something was dripping with a slow cold tinkle and splash, a forlorn night sound. Small, hard floating things rapped against his legs. Then he touched a smooth curve of metal: the air lock.

Eagerly he pushed his feeble weight against the door. It didn't move. And it didn't move. Cold air was rushing out around the door frame, a thin knife-cold stream, but the door itself was jammed tight.

The suit! He should have thought of that before. If he just had some pure air to breathe, and a little warmth in his fingers . . . But the door of the suit locker would not move, either. The ceiling must have buckled.

And that was the end, he thought, bewildered. There were no more ways out. But there *had* to be — He pounded on the door until his arms would not lift any more; it did not move. Leaning against the chill metal, he saw a single light blink on overhead.

The room was a wild place of black shadows and swimming shapes—the book leaves, fluttering and darting in the air stream. Schools of them beat wildly at the walls, curling over, baffled, trying again; others were swooping around the outer corridor, around and around: he could see them whirling past the doorways, dreamlike, a white drift of silent paper in the darkness.

The acrid smell was harsher in his nostrils. Wesson choked, groping his way to the console again. He pounded it with his open hand: he wanted to see Earth.

But when the little square of brightness leaped up, it was the dead body of the alien that Wesson saw.

It hung motionless in the cavity of the Station, limbs dangling stiff and still, eyes dull. The last turn of the screw had been too much for it: but Wesson had survived . . .

For a few minutes.

The dead alien face mocked him; a whisper of memory floated into his mind: *We might have been brothers.* . . . All at once, Wesson passionately wanted to believe it—wanted to give in, turn back. That passed. Wearily he let himself sag into the bitter *now*, thinking with thin defiance, It's done— hate wins. You'll have to stop this big giveaway—can't risk this happening again. And we'll hate you for that—and when we get out to the stars—

The world was swimming numbly away out of reach. He felt the last fit of coughing take his body, as if it were happening to someone else beside him.

The last fluttering leaves of paper came to rest. There was a long silence in the drowned room.

Then:

"Paul," said the voice of the mechanical woman brokenly; "Paul," it said again, with the hopelessness of lost, unknown, impossible love.

BORIS VIAN

The Dead Fish

TRANSLATED BY DAMON KNIGHT

Boris Vian is a pivotal figure in the contemporary evolution of SF in France. After World War II, like William S. Burroughs in the United States, he defended SF among the intellectuals. He translated A. E. Van Vogt, the wildest, least polished, and most aggressively creative of the 1940s Campbell writers, into French—as a matter of fact, into such literate, clear style that for years U.S. fans scratched their heads in confusion over the seeming contradiction of the popularity of Van Vogt and the literary respectability of SF in France. Vian himself never wrote a specifically genre story. He is represented here by a surrealist piece that is closely related to many of the works of such New Wave writers as Langdon Jones and James Sallis in Moorcock's New Worlds, especially in the last, most experimental phases.

*　　　*　　　*

1

The carriage door stuck as usual; at the other end of the train, the big hat chief leaned hard on the red button, and the compressed air squirted into the tubes. The assistant strained to force the two panels apart. He was hot. Drops of gray sweat zigzagging across his face, like flies, and the dirty collar of his insulated zephyr shirt was exposed.

The train was about to start when the chief released the button. The air belched joyously under the train, and the assistant almost lost his balance as the door suddenly gave way. He stumbled down, not without ripping open his collecting bag on the latch.

The train started, and the resulting atmospheric displacement pushed the assistant against the malodorous latrines, where two Arabs were discussing politics with great knife-blows.

The assistant shook himself, patted his hair, which was crushed against his soft skull like rotten weeds. A faint mist rose from his half-naked torso, from which stood out a jutting clavicle, and the beginnings of one or two pairs of uncouth, badly planted ribs.

With a heavy step, he went down the platform tiled with hexagons of red and green, soiled here and there with long black trails: it had rained octopuses during the afternoon, but the time that the station employees were supposed to dedicate to mopping the platform, according to their monumental chart, had been passed in the satisfaction of unmentionable needs.

The assistant rummaged in his pockets, and his fingers encountered the coarse corrugated pasteboard that he had to surrender at the exit. His knees hurt, and the dampness of the pools he had explored during the day made his badly fastened joints grind together. It must be said, he had gathered a more than honorable booty in his bag.

He handed his ticket to the dim man standing behind the grille. The man took it, looked at it and smiled ferociously.

"You haven't got another one?" he said.

"No," said the assistant.

"This one is forged."

"But it was my boss that gave it to me," said the assistant nicely, with a charming smile and a little nod.

The clerk giggled. "I'm not surprised it's forged, then. He bought ten from us, this morning."

"Ten what?" said the assistant.

"Ten forged tickets."

"But why?" said the assistant. His smile grew weaker and drooped to the left.

"To give them to you," said the clerk. "*Primo*, so as to get you sworn at, to begin with, which I am about to do; and *secundo*, so that you'd have to pay the fine."

"Why?" said the assistant. "I've got hardly any money."

"Because it's slimy to travel with a forged ticket," said the clerk.

"But you're the ones that forge them!"

"We have to. Because there are characters slimy enough to travel with forged tickets. You think it's fun, hey, to forge tickets all the while?"

"You'd certainly do better to clean up a tile," said the assistant.

"No word games," said the clerk. "Pay the fine. It's thirty francs."

"That's not true," said the assistant. "It's twelve francs when you haven't got a ticket."

"It's much more serious to have a forged one," said the clerk. "Pay, or I'll call my dog!"

"He won't come," said the assistant.

"No," said the clerk, "but it'll make your ears hurt, anyhow."

The assistant looked at the gloomy and emaciated face of the clerk, who gave him a venomous stare in return.

"I haven't got much money," he muttered.

"Me either," said the clerk. "Pay up."

"He gives me fifty francs a day," said the assistant, "and I have to eat."

The clerk tugged at the visor of his cap, and a blue screen dropped over his face. "Pay up," he said with his hand, rubbing the thumb and forefinger together.

The assistant reached for his shiny, patched-up wallet. He took out two creased ten-franc notes and a little five-franc note that was still bleeding.

"Twenty-five," he proposed uncertainly.

"Thirty," said the three outstretched fingers of the clerk.

The assistant sighed, and his boss's face appeared between his toes. He spat on it, right in the eye. His heart beat faster. The face dissolved and blackened. He put the money in the outstretched hand and left. He heard the click of the visor returning to its usual place.

Walking slowly, he reached the foot of the hill. The bag bruised his skinny hips, and the bamboo handle of his net whipped his frail, malformed calves at random as he walked.

2

He pushed against the iron gate, which opened with a frightful groan. A big red lamp went on at the top of the steps, and a bell echoed faintly in the vestibule. He entered as quickly as he could and closed the gate, not without giving himself an electric shock because the anti-burglar decoration was not in its usual place.

He went up the walk. Right in the middle, his foot struck something hard and a jet of ice-water sprang from the ground, between his ankle and his trouser leg, wetting him to the knee.

He began to run. His anger, as it did every night, mastered him progressively. He went up the three steps, fists clenched. At the top, his net got itself between his legs, and in the movement he made to keep from falling, he ripped his bag a second time on a nail that appeared out of nowhere. He felt something twist inside him, and panted without saying a word. After a few moments he calmed himself, and his chin fell on his chest. Then he felt the chill of his wet trousers, and grabbed the doorknob. He let go of it precipitously. An evil-smelling vapor arose, and a fragment of his skin, stuck to the burning porcelain, blackened and shriveled. The door was open. He went in.

His weak legs would not support him, and he slid down in a corner of the vestibule, on the cold leprous-smelling tiles. His heart groaned between his ribs and shook him with great, brutal, irregular blows.

3

"It's poor," said his boss.

He was examining the contents of the bag.

The assistant waited, standing in front of the table.

"You've spoiled them," added the boss. "The perforations of this one are completely ruined."

"It's the net—it's too old," said the assistant. "If you want me to catch young stamps in good condition, you've got to buy me a decent net."

"Who is it that uses this net?" said the boss. "Is it you or me?"

The assistant did not answer. His burned hand was paining him.

"Answer me," said the boss. "Is it you or me?"

"It's me, for you," said the assistant.

"I don't force you," said the boss. "If you claim to earn fifty francs a day, you've got to justify it, anyhow."

"Less thirty francs for the ticket," said the assistant.

"What ticket? I pay you for the round trip."

"With forged tickets."

"All you have to do is pay attention."

"How am I supposed to tell the difference?"

"It isn't hard," said the boss. "They're obviously forged when they're made of corrugated pasteboard. Ordinary tickets are wood."

"Good," said the assistant. "You'll give me back my thirty francs."

"No. All these stamps are in poor condition."

"That isn't true," said the assistant. "I spent two hours fishing for them, and I had to break the ice. I took every precaution, and there's hardly two spoiled ones out of sixty."

"These aren't the ones I want," said the boss. "I want the 1855 two-cent

Guiana. I'm not interested in the Zanzibar series, which you caught already yesterday."

"I catch what I can find," said the assistant. "Especially with a net like that. And anyhow, it's not the season for Guianas. You can exchange the Zanzibars."

"Everybody's finding them, this year," said the boss. "They're not worth anything any more."

"And the jet of water in my legs, and the decoration on the gate, and the doorknob—" suddenly exploded the assistant. His thin yellow face folded up in wrinkles, and he looked as if he were about to cry.

"That'll toughen you up," said the boss. "What am I supposed to do with myself here? Me, I get bored."

"Go hunt for stamps," said the assistant. He succeeded in controlling himself at the price of a considerable effort.

"I pay you for that," said the boss. "You're a thief. You steal the money you earn."

The assistant wiped his forehead with his threadbare sleeve, in a weary gesture. His head was clear as a bell. The table drew away from him slightly and he looked for something to catch hold of again. But the mantelpiece escaped in its turn, and he fell down.

"Get up," said the boss. "Not on my carpet."

"I want my dinner," said the assistant.

"Next time, come back earlier," said the boss. "Get up. I don't like to see you on my carpet. Get up, in God's name!" His voice trembled with fury, and his knotty hands pounded on the desk.

The assistant made a terrible effort and succeeded in getting to his knees. His belly hurt, and blood and serum were flowing from his hand. He had wound a dirty handkerchief around it.

The boss made a rapid choice and hurled three stamps at his face. They stuck to his cheek with a slight cupping-glass sound.

"You go and put those back where you got them," he said. He hammered out the syllables to give them the form of points of steel.

The assistant was crying. His soft hair fell over his forehead, and the stamps marked his left cheek. He got up heavily.

"For the last time," said the boss, "I don't want stamps in poor condition. And don't tell me any tales about the net."

"No, sir," said the assistant.

"Here's your fifty francs," said the boss. He took a banknote from his pocket, spat on it, tore it half-way across, and threw it on the floor.

The assistant lowered himself painfully. His knees cracked in brief, dry triplets.

"Your shirt is dirty," said the boss. "You'll sleep outside tonight."

The assistant picked up the banknote and left the room. The wind blew harder and shook the corrugated window in front of the ironwork grille of the vestibule door. He closed the door of the office, with a final glance at the silhouette of his boss. The latter, bent over his Zanzibar album, with a large loupe in his eye, was beginning to compare and evaluate.

4

He went down the steps of the stairway, wrapping himself in his long jacket, which was green-stained from having been too long in contact with the water in the stamp pools. The wind insinuated itself into the holes in the cloth and swelled his back so much that it gave him the look of a hunchback, not without damage to his spinal column; he suffered from internal mimicry, and had to struggle every day to keep his poor organs in their ordinary shape and their habitual function.

It was night now, and the earth gave forth a cheap, tarnished glimmer. The assistant turned to the right and followed the wall of the house. He guided himself by following the black line made by the uncoiled hose that his boss used to drown the rats in the cellar. He reached the worm-eaten doghouse nearby where he had already slept the previous night. The straw inside was damp and smelled of cockroaches. An old piece of quilt covered the arched doorway. When he lifted it to grope his way inside, there was a blinding glare and an explosion. A giant firecracker had just exploded inside the doghouse, filling it with a violent stench of powder.

The assistant had started, and his heart was racing. He tried to quell the beating by holding his breath, but almost immediately his eyes began to dance, and he greedily swallowed a mouthful of air. The smell of powder entered his lungs at the same time, and calmed him a little.

He waited for the silence to return and listened attentively, then whistled softly. Without turning around, he crept into the doghouse and curled up on the sickly straw. He whistled again, then strained his ears. Light, small footsteps were approaching, and in the pale glimmer of the earth, he could see his living thing, which was coming to find him. It was a soft, shaggy, tame living thing, which he fed as well as he could on dead fish. It came into the doghouse and lay down against him. All at once he came to himself and put his hand to his cheek. The three stamps were beginning to suck his blood, and he tore them off brutally, holding himself in so as not to scream. He threw them away from him, outside the doghouse. The dampness of the ground would preserve them, probably, until tomorrow. The living thing began to lick his cheek, and he spoke to it to calm himself. He spoke to it in a low voice, for his boss had ways of listening to him when he was alone.

"He gets on my nerves," he panted.

The living thing murmured softly and licked him harder.

"I think I ought to do something. Not let myself be bullied, get some decent shirts in spite of him, and have forged tickets in wood. And then, mend the net and keep him from poking holes in it. I think I ought to refuse to sleep in the doghouse, and demand my room, and demand a raise, because I can't live on fifty francs a day. And also gain weight, and become very strong and very handsome, and rebel before he expects it, and heave a brick in his face. I think I will."

He changed his position and pondered with such intensity that the air in the doghouse was expelled in great puffs from the rounded hole, and not enough was left inside to breathe. A little came back in through holes under the floor of the doghouse, through the straw, but that again increased the smell of cockroaches, with which now was mingled the disagreeable odor of slugs in heat.

"I don't like this doghouse. It's cold. Luckily you're here. There are noises in the cellar, it's the water that comes in through the rat holes. You can't sleep with the roaring of rats in your ears every night of your life. Why does he want to kill those rats at any price, and kill them with water? You kill rats with blood."

The living thing stopped licking him. He could make out its profile against the gray background of the luminous earth, with its slender muzzle and its pointed ears, and its yellow eyes that reflected some cold lightnings. It turned in a circle, hunting for a convenient place, and nestled against him, nose on his thighs.

"I'm cold," said the assistant.

He began to sob quietly. His tears slipped onto the straw, from which arose a thin vapor, and the outlines of objects became blurred.

"Wake me up tomorrow morning," he added. "I have to take the three stamps back. I hope he doesn't give me a forged ticket for the train."

There was a distant hubbub, then some piercing hisses, and the sounds of small galloping feet.

"Oh!" said the assistant. "That's it! He's beginning again with the rats! I hope it's a rat. I'd hold the hose myself. I hope he'll give me fifty francs tomorrow night. I'm hungry. I could eat a rat alive."

He squeezed his belly with both hands, still crying, and then the rhythm of his sobs diminished little by little, as a machine runs down, and his twisted body stretched itself out. His feet protruded through the opening of the doghouse, and he slept, with his cheek on the evil-smelling straw. In his empty stomach, there was a sound of gravel.

5

From the room where he crouched, the boss heard the melodious phrase with which the pepper vendor usually announced her passage. He got to his feet and ran toward the vestibule, whose door he opened with conscious brutality. Standing on the stair, he watched the girl approach.

She had on her usual uniform, a little pleated rump-length skirt, short red and blue socks, and a bolero that left bare the lower part of her breasts, not to mention the red and white striped cotton cap, which the pepper vendors of Mauritius have imposed on the world by force of patience.

The boss nodded to her and she came up the walk. He went down the steps at the same time and advanced to meet her.

"Good day," he said. "I want some pepper."

"How many grains?" she asked with an artificial smile, for she detested him.

Her black hair and her fair skin had the effect on the boss of a glass of cold water on the nuts, in truth, a most important effect. "Go up the steps," he said, "and I'll specify the quantity."

"You want to stay behind and look at my thighs, that's it, right?"

"Yes," said the boss, drooling. He reached out his hands.

"Pay for the pepper first," she said.

"How much?"

"A hundred francs a grain, and you taste first."

"Will you go up the steps?" murmured the boss. "I'll give you a Zanzibar series."

"My brother brought three of them up to the house yesterday," she said with a mellifluous chuckle. "Taste my pepper."

She offered him a grain, and the boss did not perceive that it was toxic carnation seed. Unsuspectingly, he put it in his mouth and swallowed it.

The pepper vendor was already moving away.

"What?" wondered the boss. "How about the steps?"

"Ha! ha! ha!" said the pepper vendor, with consummate wickedness.

Meanwhile, the boss was beginning to feel the comforting effect of the poison, and he began to run at full speed around the house. Leaning against the gate, the pepper vendor watched him.

On the third lap, she waved to him and waited until he looked back at her, which he did on the fourth lap, still running faster and faster. Then she tucked up her little pleated skirt, and from where she stood she saw the boss's face turn violet, then completely black, then begin to burn, and as he kept his eyes fixed on what she was showing him, he tripped over the garden hose that he used to drown the rats; he fell with his face against a large stone, which fitted itself precisely between his cheekbones, in place of his nose and jaws. His feet stayed behind on the ground and dug a double trench, where, little by little, according to the rate at which his shoes wore out, could be seen the trail of five clumsy toes, which served to keep his socks on.

The pepper vendor closed the gate and went on her way, tossing the tassel of her cotton cap to the other side, in sign of derision.

6

The assistant tried vainly to open the carriage door. It was very hot in the train; in that way, the passengers caught cold in getting out, for the engineer had a brother who was a handkerchief salesman.

He had toiled the whole day for a miserable catch, and his heart swelled with satisfaction, for he was going to kill his boss. He succeeded at last in forcing apart the two halves of the door, by pulling them up and down, and realized that the big hat chief had turned them on their sides as a spiteful practical joke. Pleased to have foiled him this time, he leaped lightly onto the platform and fumbled in his pocket. He found without trouble the bit of corrugated pasteboard that he had to surrender at the exit, and advanced rapidly toward that spot, occupied by a man with a sly expression in whom he recognized the clerk of yesterday.

"I have a forged ticket," he said.

"Ah?" said the other. "Let's see."

He offered his ticket and the man took it, then examined it with such concentrated attention that his cap opened up to let his ears enter the lining.

"It's a good copy," said the man.

"Except it isn't wood, it's pasteboard," said the assistant.

"Really?" said the man. "You'd swear it was wood; if you didn't know it was pasteboard, naturally."

"All the same," said the assistant, "just think, my boss gave it to me for real."

"A real one costs only twelve francs," said the man. "He pays a lot more for these."

"How much?" asked the assistant.

"I'll give you thirty francs for it," said the man, and put his hand in his pocket.

The assistant recognized from the ease of this gesture that he must be a degenerate character. But the man only brought out three ten-franc notes forged with walnut dye. "Here!" he added.

"They're counterfeit, of course?" said the assistant.

"I can't give you good ones for a bad one, you must realize," said the clerk.

"No," said the assistant, "but I'll keep mine."

He crouched and took a great leap, by means of which his small fist was able to take the skin off the whole right side of the face under the cap. The man put his hand to his visor and fell at the salute, which caused him to bang his elbow on the hard cement of the platform, paved, at that particular spot, with hexagons of a phosphorescent blue.

The assistant stepped over the body and went on. He felt himself saturated with warm, limpid life, and hurried to ascend the hill. He removed the thong from his net and used it as a climbing rope. In passing, he harpooned the heads of the iron pillars that supported the guard fence along the track cutting, and, pulling on the handle, hauled himself easily up among the sharp-edged stones of the path. After a few yards, the torn net flew away. He would put the ring of steel wire around his boss's neck.

He reached the gate quickly and pushed it open without precautions. He hoped to receive the current to strengthen his anger, but felt nothing, and stopped. In front of the steps, something stirred feebly. He ran along the walk. In spite of the cold, his skin began to redden, and he smelled the neglected odor of his body, with a moldy smell of straw and cockroaches.

He hardened his stringy biceps, and his fingers curled around the bamboo handle. His boss, no doubt, had killed someone.

He stopped dumbfounded, recognizing the dark suit and the shiny starched collar. His boss's head was no more than a blackish mass, and his legs had managed to dig two deep, grooved ruts.

A kind of despair took possession of him and he trembled all over, shaken by his anger and his longing for massacre. He glanced all around, uneasy and confused. He had prepared a lot of things to say. He had to say them.

"What did you do that for, you crumb?"

The "crumb" resounded in the neutral air with a disused and insufficient sonority.

"Crumb! Bum! Son of a bitch! Jerk! Dirty son of a bitch! Robber! No-good! Son of a bitch!"

Tears streamed from his eyes, for the boss did not answer. He took the bamboo handle and placed it in the middle of the boss's back.

"Answer me, you old bastard. You gave me a forged ticket."

He leaned with all his weight and the handle sank into the tissues softened by poison. He turned it to grind out the worms, holding the other end of the handle like the stem of a gyroscope. "A forged ticket, straw full of roaches, and I'm hungry enough to eat gravel, and what about my fifty francs for today?"

The boss hardly stirred any more, and the worms wouldn't come out.

"I wanted to kill you, dirty son of a bitch. I've got to kill you. Kill you dead, you old bastard, yes, you. What about my fifty francs, hey?"

He pulled the handle out of the wound and struck great blows on the carbonized skull, which sank in like the crust of an overdone soufflé. Where the boss's head should be, there was nothing any more. It ended at the collar.

The assistant stopped trembling.

"You'd rather go away? All right. But me, I've got to kill someone."

He sat on the ground, he wept as he had the night before, and his living thing ran up light-footed, seeking friendship. The assistant closed his eyes. He felt the tender, soft touch on his cheek, and his fingers closed around the frail neck. The living thing made no movement to free itself, and, when the caress grew cold on his cheek, he knew that he had strangled it. Then he rose. He stumbled along the walk and went out into the road; he turned to the right, without knowing, and the boss did not stir at all.

7

He saw the big blue-stamp pool directly ahead of him. Night was falling, and the water glimmered with mysterious and distant reflections. The pool was not deep; you found stamps there by the hundred, but they had no great value, because they reproduced themselves all year round.

He took two stakes out of his bag and planted them close to the pool, a yard apart. Between them he stretched a strident steel wire and touched it with a finger, for a sad note. The wire stood four inches above the ground, parallel to the edge of the pool.

The assistant went a few steps away, then turned, facing the water, and walked straight toward the wire. He had his eyes closed and was whistling a tender melody, the one that his living thing liked. He went slowly, with short steps, and tripped over the steel wire. He fell with his head in the water. His body lay motionless, and, under the mute surface, blue stamps were already attaching themselves to his sunken cheeks.

I Was the First to Find You

TRANSLATED BY HELEN SALTZ JACOBSON

*Among the most versatile and popular SF writers in the Soviet
Union, Kirill Bulychev is one of a group of younger Soviet
writers to emerge in the 1960s. Above all, his talent for
storytelling and his interest in human characters interacting
with SF problems make him a particularly effective representative of recent Soviet SF. The strain of utopianism remains
strong in Eastern European SF and sinks many stories with
didacticism, but Bulychev is able to sustain his delight in the
wonders of the technological future, as in the days of John W.
Campbell. And, of course, the influence of Campbell-style
SF itself, in this case Van Vogt's "Far Centaurus," is clearly
present.*

*   *   *

Gerassi can't sleep mornings. So today at six, while it was
still chilly, he turned on the loudspeaker and asked
Marta:

"Are you ready?"

His penetrating voice is as inescapable as fate. It's useless to
duck under the covers or jam your head into a pillow.

"Marta," continued Gerassi, "I have a feeling we're going
to find something very interesting today. What do you think?"

Marta wanted to sleep. She detested Gerassi and let him
know it in no uncertain terms. He guffawed, and the loudspeaker amplified the sound. The captain switched on the

intercom and bawled him out: "Shut up, Gerassi. I just came off watch."

"Sorry, Captain," said Gerassi, "but we're about ready to leave for the dig. We can accomplish twice as much in the morning as in the afternoon. And we're racing against time now."

The captain didn't reply, so I threw off the covers and sat up. My feet touched the floor. How many mornings had my feet hit that same worn spot on the rug? I had to get up. Gerassi was right; mornings were the best time to work here.

After breakfast we left the *Spartak* through the cargo hatch. The ramp was badly scratched up by the freight carts. Brown sand and withered branches had drifted onto it during the night. We didn't need space suits; until the heat broke up before noon, masks and light air tanks on our backs were sufficient.

The slightly hilly, desolate brown valley edged up to the horizon. Dust hung over it. The dust seeped into everything: the folds of your clothing, your boots, even under your mask. But the dust is a lot better than the mud. If a passing storm cloud dumps a brief shower on the valley, you have to abandon work and crawl through the slime to the ship, where you wait until the ground dries. Even a jeep is helpless after a heavy shower.

One of the jeeps was waiting for us at the ramp. It was only a ten-minute walk to the excavation site, but time was a crucial factor now. We were planning to leave this planet very soon and had barely enough food and other reserves left for the return journey. We had lingered too long, spending six years on this quest alone. The return trip would take almost five.

Zakhir was fiddling around beside the other jeep—the geologists were going out to do some exploring. We said good-bye to Zakhir and hopped into our jeep.

Gerassi stretched his long legs and closed his eyes. I wondered how a guy who loved sleep so much could wake up before everyone else and rouse the rest of us with that miserable voice of his.

"Gerassi," I said, "you have a miserable voice."

"I know," he said, without opening his eyes. "I've had it since I was a kid. But Veronica liked it."

Veronica, his wife, had died last year. She had been culturing a virus we had found on a stray asteroid.

The jeep descended into a hollow enclosed by a plastic shield that was supposed to keep the dust out of the excavation. I jumped out after Marta and Dolinsky. The shields were almost useless; dust, now knee-deep, had drifted in during the night. Gerassi had already dragged out the vacuum cleaner and tossed it into the excavation. Like a living creature, it began to crawl along the ground and devour the dust.

To engage in archeological digs here was insane. Within three days a dust storm could completely bury a skyscraper. In the next three days it could suck out a ditch around it a hundred yards deep. The storms also carried in soot and charcoal particles from endless forest fires raging beyond the swamps. So for the time being, we could not date a single stone or determine when or by whom the settlement had been built. What happened to the planet's inhabitants was a mystery, but we were determined to solve it. So we waited for the vacuum cleaner to finish cleaning up. Then, armed with scrapers and brushes, we would scour the dig for fragments of a vase, a cogwheel, or other evidence of intelligent life.

"They certainly knew how to build," said Gerassi. "It's obvious these storms were a problem then, too."

Yesterday at the dig we had discovered the foundation of a building, or buildings, which had been cut into a rock bed.

"They abandoned this place a very long time ago," said Marta. "If we turn the desert inside out we're sure to find other structures or evidence of them."

"We should have checked the mountains on the other side of the swamp," I said. "We certainly won't find anything here. Believe me."

"But what about the mast?" said Gerassi.

"And the pyramid?" said Marta.

We had spotted the mast on our first flight over the area, but before we landed it had been obliterated by a storm and buried in the bowels of the desert. We had managed to unearth the small pyramid. If it had not been for the pyramid we wouldn't have spent the past three weeks struggling in this dig. It stood before us, flowing into the rock, looking almost as though it had been squeezed out of it. We would take the pyramid with us. Our other finds were a stone fragment and some notches in a rock. No inscriptions or metals.

"They couldn't have lived in those mountains beyond the swamp. Even in the best of times there wasn't any water. And I'd say that this was one of the few places that had some."

Gerassi was right again. The bottomless swamps were impassable, and the mountains inaccessible, as though by design. And then there was the ocean, an endless ocean, storm-swept and nourishing only the most elementary forms of life. Whatever life had once existed here had disappeared, perished perhaps, and now was evolving once again from the most primitive organisms.

We descended into the excavation.

Dolinsky worked beside me. "It's time we headed home," he said, cleaning out a square pocket in the rock. "Do you want to?"

"Of course I do," I replied.

"I suppose I'm not sure how I feel about it. Who needs us there? Who's waiting for us after all these years?"

"When you signed up you knew what you were getting into."

Something glittered in the rock face.

"I knew then and I know now. Sure, when we left we were real heroes. What can be more pathetic than a forgotten hero wandering through the streets, vainly hoping that someone will remember him?"

"It's a lot easier for me," I said. "I never was a hero."

"We can't imagine how the world must have changed in the two hundred years we've been away. That is, if it's still there."

"Hey, take a look at this. I think it's metal," I said.

I was sick and tired of listening to Dolinsky complaining. He was played out. So were the rest of us. All these years we had been sustained by our goals: the exploration of the planetary system and the observation of celestial currents. We lived in hope of making some great discovery. All our efforts had been converted into millions of symbols and dry figures that lay concealed in the depths of the ship's Brain, in its holds, on its laboratory tables. We had spent our final year rushing about the system, landing on asteroids and dead planets, decelerating, accelerating, realizing that the time for our return trip to Earth was approaching, that the holiday would soon be over. But this one had proved far less festive than anticipated; we had fulfilled our mission, but, unfortunately, we had accomplished nothing beyond it. Though the ship's Brain was jammed with information, the hopes we had cherished during the long years of our voyage had not been realized.

With only a month left, we tackled the last planet. We had to depart for Earth within a month; otherwise we'd never make it. When we had lifted off from Earth, there had been eighteen of us. Now we were twelve. Only on this, the last planet, barely capable of sustaining human life (the others were totally unfit for human habitation), had we found evidence of intelligent life. During the lulls between dust storms, we bit into the rocks, burrowed into the sand and dust; we wanted to learn all we could. Two days remained before we had to depart. Ahead of us lay a journey of almost five years, five years back to Earth —

In the palm of my hand rested a heavy ball the size of a hazelnut. It hadn't oxidized.

"Gerassi!" I shouted. "A ball!"

"What?" A rising wind carried his words away. "What ball?"

A cloud of dust swirled down on us from above.

"Should we wait it out?" asked Marta, picking up the ball. "Hmmm, it's heavy."

"Get back to the jeep," the captain radioed us. "Bad storm coming up."

"Maybe we can wait here until it blows over," said Dolinsky. "We just found a ball. A metal one."

"No, get back to the jeep at once. It's a bad storm."

"If we're really in for a big one, we'd better get the pyramid out of here or it will be impossible to dig it out tomorrow. Then we'll have to leave this place empty-handed."

"We're not going to dig it up. We're leaving it here," said the captain. "We measured and photographed it— Get out of there on the double or you'll be buried alive."

Dolinsky laughed. "Don't worry, we won't be blown away. We'll hold onto our treasures."

Another cloud of dust rained down on us. It settled slowly, circling us like a swarm of mosquitoes.

Gerassi said, "Should we get to work on the pyramid?"

Marta, Dolinsky, and I agreed that we should.

"Dolinsky," said Gerassi, "pull the jeep up over here. It's all set." The jeep was equipped with a hoist.

"I am ordering you to return to the ship at once!" said the captain.

"Where are the geologists?" asked Gerassi.

"On their way back."

"But we can't leave the pyramid here."

"You can go back for it tomorrow."

"These storms usually last two or three days."

Gerassi fastened the hoist cable to the pyramid. I began to sheer off the pyramid's base, using a ray from a cutting torch. The torch buzzed; the stone glowed red and crackled, fighting and resisting the ray.

Directly above us hovered the blackest cloud I had ever seen. The air grew dark; clouds of dust swirled around, and the wind pushed hard, trying to suck us up and whirl us around in the sandstorm. Marta started to help me, but I pushed her away and shouted to her to hide inside the jeep. I tried to follow her from the corner of my eye to see if she had obeyed me. The wind, blowing from my rear, nearly toppled me; the torch jerked in my hand and etched a scarlet scratch along the side of the pyramid.

"Hold on!" shouted Gerassi. "Only a little more to go!"

The pyramid would not surrender. I wondered if Marta had reached the jeep in time. The wind speed above the excavation was incredible. The cable stretched. The captain roared angrily over the transmitter.

"Maybe we ought to leave it?" I suggested.

Gerassi stood beside me, his back pressed against the wall of the excavation. He looked desperate. "Give me the torch!" he shouted.

"I'll do it myself!"

Like a felled tree breaking off at the stump, the pyramid suddenly snapped loose and rose into the air like a pendulum. The pendulum swung to the opposite side of the excavation, scattered the plastic shields and flew toward us, threatening to flatten us like pancakes. We barely managed to dodge it. As the pyramid cut into the wall, a cloud of dust swirled up and I lost sight of Gerassi. My primitive instinct for survival took over; no matter what the cost, I had to jump out of the trap, escape from this hole where the pyramid, straining to tear itself from the cable's embrace, was crushing everything in sight.

The wind seized me and carried me along the sand like a dry leaf; I tried to grab the sand, but it slid through my fingers. I was afraid of losing consciousness from the jolts and blows as I was dragged along the ground.

The wind rose, tearing me from the earth as if it wanted to fling me into the clouds, but at that instant a rock blocked my path and I lost consciousness.

I probably came to rather quickly. It was dark and quiet. The sand, which had buried me, was crushing my chest and pressing against my legs. I was frightened; I was buried alive.

"Calm down," I told myself. "Don't panic."

"*Spartak*," I called aloud. "*Spartak*."

The radio was silent. It was broken.

"Anyway, I'm lucky," I thought to myself.

If my mask had been damaged, I would have suffocated. I managed to move my fingers. A minute or two passed—an eternity—and I knew I could move my right hand. After another eternity I felt the edge of the rock.

Realizing I would be able to dig myself out when my initial panic vanished, my normal reflexes and sensations returned.

First, the pain. I had been thoroughly battered by the storm as it dragged me along the ground. On top of that I had been thrown so hard against the rock that my side was extremely sore, and breathing was painful, too. I had probably broken a rib. Maybe two.

Second, I became acutely aware of my air reserves. I glanced at the aerometer—there was enough left for an hour. This meant that three hours had passed since the beginning of the storm. I cursed myself for not having taken an extra tank from the jeep. We had about fifty reserve tanks on the ship; each of which would last six hours. We were supposed to have at least two on us at all times. But it was difficult to work in the excavation with an extra tank on your back, so we had left them in the jeep.

Third, I wondered how far I was from the ship.

Fourth—had the storm subsided?

Fifth—had the others made it to the ship? If they had, had they figured out in which direction I had been blown? Did they know where to look for me?

My hand grabbed at emptiness. I crawled out like a mole from its hole, and the wind (the answer to my fourth question was negative) tried to push me back. I squatted beneath the rock, the only refuge in this hell, to catch my breath. The ship wasn't visible; even if it were standing nearby you can't see more than fifteen feet in this dust. The wind was not as fierce as it had been at the beginning of the storm. Or maybe that was wishful thinking. I waited for the next gust of wind to disperse the dust and settle it. Then I would investigate the situation.

Which way should I look? Which way should I go? Obviously in a direction where the rock would remain behind me. After all, the rock had halted my disorderly flight.

I didn't wait for the wind to settle the dust. I walked toward the storm. My air tank would last another forty-five minutes (plus or minus one minute).

Time passed; only thirty minutes remained. Then I fell; the wind rolled me back and I lost another five minutes. At the point when only fifteen minutes were left, I stopped looking at the gauge.

I received an unexpected respite when the air tank, which, according to my calculations, should have been empty, still had some reserves. I stumbled through the slowly settling dust and tried to ignore the pain in my side because it was certainly not my main problem at the moment.

I tried to breathe evenly, but my respiration was failing, and I kept imagining that the air tank was empty.

Now it was; the air was gone. But at that moment I sighted the ship far away in the settling dust. I ran toward it. Choking, I tore off the mask, although it was a useless gesture, and my lungs were stung by the bitter dust and ammonia—

The locator had sighted me a few minutes earlier.

I regained consciousness in the ship's bay, a small, white, two-bed hospital where each of us had been confined many times during our voyage. For injuries, colds. Or in quarantine. I realized immediately that the ship was preparing to take off.

"Good work," Dr. Grot said to me. "You handled the situation splendidly."

"Are we lifting off?"

"Yes, and you'll have to lie down in the shock absorber. Your bones can't take the G-forces. You have three broken ribs and a torn pleura."

"How are the others?" I asked. "How's Marta? Gerassi? Dolinsky?"

"Dolinsky managed to get to the jeep—he's fine. And Marta is all right, too. She also reached the jeep in time. Fortunately, she listened to you."

"I guess you're trying to tell me—"

"Yes, Gerassi is dead. He was found after the storm, and only thirty steps from the excavation. He was thrown against the jeep and his mask was smashed. We thought you had died, too."

I didn't ask about anything else. The doctor left to prepare the shock absorber for me. As I lay there, I reviewed step by step all my movements in the excavation. I kept thinking how at this or that particular moment I could have rescued Gerassi. I should have said the hell with the pyramid and insisted on following the captain's orders to return.

On the third day after lift-off the *Spartak* picked up speed and headed for Earth. The G-forces had decreased and, released from the shock absorber, I hobbled to the wardroom. Dolinsky was there.

"I've traded shifts with you," he said. "You'll be on watch. The doctor says it's better for you to stay awake for about a month."

"I know," I said.

"Is it OK with you?"

"Why not? We'll see each other in a year."

"I shouted to you to leave the pyramid and run to the jeep," Dolinsky said.

"We didn't hear you. It wouldn't have mattered if we had. We thought we could finish the job in time."

"I passed on the little ball for analysis."

"What ball?"

"You found it. You gave it to me when I went to the jeep."

"Oh, of course. I forgot about it completely. And where's the pyramid?"

"In the cargo hold. Marta and Rano are working on it."

"So I'm on watch with the captain?"

"With the captain, Marta, and Grot. There's not many of us left now."

"An extra watch."

"Right. An extra year for each of us."

Grot entered. The doctor was holding a sheet of paper.

"The results are ridiculous," he announced. "The ball is very, very young—hello, Dolinsky—I say it's just too young. Only twenty years old."

"Can't be," said Dolinsky. "We spent so many days in that excavation! It's as old as the world."

The captain stood in the doorway of the wardroom and listened to our conversation. "Grot, are you sure you haven't made a mistake?" he asked.

"The Brain and I repeated the analysis four times. At first I couldn't believe it myself."

"Maybe it was Gerassi's? Maybe he dropped it?" asked the captain, turning to me.

"Dolinsky saw— I scraped it out of the rock."

"There's still another possibility."

"It's improbable."

"Why?"

"You couldn't have such ruins in only twenty years."

"On this planet you could. Remember how the storm carried you away. And the poisonous fumes in the atmosphere."

"So you think someone got here before us?"

"Exactly."

The captain was right. When Marta sawed up the pyramid the next day, she found a capsule in it. We all crowded in behind her when she placed it on the table.

Grot said, "Too bad we were late. By twenty years. Imagine how many generations on Earth have dreamt about contact with intelligent life in Outer Space. And we were too late."

"Joking aside, Grot," said the captain, "we have made contact. Here it is, right under your nose. We met them after all."

"A lot depends on what's inside this cylinder."

"Not viruses, I hope," said Dolinsky.

"We'll open it in the chamber. With the manipulators."

"Maybe we ought to wait until we get back to Earth?"

"Wait five long years? Oh, no," said Rano.

We all knew that curiosity would eventually get the better of us, that we'd never be able to hold out until we reached Earth. So we decided to open the capsule right away.

"Then Gerassi didn't die in vain," said Marta softly, for my ears alone.

Taking her by the hand, I nodded. Her fingers were cold.

The manipulator's claws placed half of the cylinder on the table and pulled out a scroll. It unrolled stubbornly. We could read the writing on it through the window.

Galactic ship *Saturn*. Identification number 36/14.
Lift-off from Earth—12 March 2167.
Touch-down on planet—6 May 2167 . . .

A text followed but none of us read it through. We didn't have the heart. Again and again we reread the first few lines: "Lift-off from Earth—12 March 2167." Twenty years ago. "Touch-down on planet—6 May 2167." Also twenty years ago.

Lift-off from Earth . . . Touch-down . . . The very same year.

At that moment each and every one of us were struck with the terrible pain of personal tragedy, the tragedy of a useless mission to which our lives had been dedicated, the tragedy of senseless, uncalled-for sacrifice.

One hundred Earth years ago our ship had rocketed into the dark reaches of space. One hundred years ago we had left Earth knowing full well that we would never again see our loved ones and friends. We went into voluntary exile for a longer period than anyone on Earth had ever endured. We knew that Earth would manage very well without us, but we felt that our sacrifices were necessary. Someone had to venture into the depths of space, to unknown worlds which could be reached only through sacrifice. A cosmic whirlwind had thrown us off course, and year after year we had sped toward our goal. We lost our years and counted off the scores of years that had passed on Earth.

"So they finally learned to leap through space," said the captain.

I noticed that he said "they," not "we," although he had always used "we" in the past when he referred to Earth.

"That's fine," said the captain. "Simply great. So they were here. Before us."

He left the rest unsaid; each of us finished it to ourselves. They had been here before us. And managed splendidly without us. In four and a half years, in one hundred Earth years, we would hover over the spaceport (if we didn't perish on the way), and a startled controller would say to his partner: "Hey, take a look at that monster! Where did that brontosaurus come from? He doesn't even know how to land. He'll wreck all the greenhouses around the Earth and smash the observatory mirror! Tell someone to grab the old nag and drag it as far away from here as possible, to the dump on Pluto—"

We retired to our cabins and no one emerged for supper. The doctor dropped in to see me in the evening. He looked very tired.

"I don't know how we're going to make it home," he said. "The incentive is gone."

"We'll make it," I replied. "It will be rough, but we'll make it."

"Attention, all hands!" the intercom loudspeaker rang out. "Attention, all hands!"

It was the captain speaking. His voice was hoarse and wavering, as though he didn't know quite what to say.

"What could have happened?" The doctor was ready for another disaster.

"Attention! Turn on the long-distance transceiver! There's an announcement on a galactic channel."

The channel had been silent for many years: the distance separating us from inhabited planets was so great, it would have been pointless to attempt to maintain radio contact. I looked at the doctor. He had closed his eyes and thrown back his head as if what was happening now was a beautiful dream from which he was afraid to awaken.

There was a rustle and the hum of invisible strings. A very youthful and excited voice began to shout, bursting through to us across millions of miles: "*Spartak, Spartak*, can you hear me? *Spartak*, I was the first to find you! *Spartak*, start decelerating. You are right on course. *Spartak*, I am the patrol ship *Olympia*. I am the patrol ship *Olympia*. I am patrolling in your sector. We've been looking for you for twenty years! My name is Arthur Sheno. Remember it—Arthur Sheno. I was the first to find you! What fantastic luck. I was the first to find you!"

The voice broke on a high note. Arthur Sheno began coughing, and suddenly I saw him clearly, leaning forward toward the microphone in the cramped cockpit of his patrol ship, not daring to tear his eyes from the white spot on his tracking screen. "Excuse me," continued Sheno. "Can you hear me? You can't imagine how many gifts I have for you. The cargo hold is jammed full. Fresh cucumbers for Dolinsky. Dolinsky, can you hear me? Gerassi, Veronica, the Romans are sending you candied fruit cake. We know how much you like it. . . ."

A long silence followed.

The captain broke it. "Start decelerating!"

The Lineman

Walter M. Miller, Jr., a colorful and controversial figure in science fiction circles, has not published any fiction since the early 1960s, shortly after winning the Hugo Award for his masterpiece, A Canticle for Leibowitz, *usually considered the only contender against Bester's* The Stars My Destination *for the title of the best novel the U.S. commercial genre has yet produced.*

Miller began his career in the early 1950s and rose quickly to prominence as a short story writer, winning the Hugo Award for "The Darfstellar" in 1955. His work gained in depth in the late 1950s as he began to concentrate on the examination of religious questions. "The Lineman" is one of his major achievements, a fit companion to his novel. It deals with the spiritual themes that inform his finest work.

*   *   *

It was August on Earth, and the newscast reported a heat wave in the Midwest: the worst since 2065. A letter from Mike Tremini's sister in Abilene said the chickens were dying and there wasn't enough water for the stock. It was the only letter that came for any of Novotny's men during that fifty-shift hitch on the Copernicus Trolley Project. Everybody read it and luxuriated in sympathy for Kansas and sick chickens.

It was August on Luna too. The Perseids rained down with merciless impartiality; and, from his perch atop the hundred-foot steel skeleton, the lineman stopped cranking the jack and leaned out against his safety belt to watch two demolition men carrying a corpse out toward Fissure Seven. The corpse wore a deflated pressure suit. Torn fabric dragged the ground. The man in the rear carried the corpse's feet like a pair of wheelbarrow handles, and he continually tripped over the loose fabric; his head waggled inside his helmet as if he cursed softly and continuously to himself. The corpse's helmet was translucent with an interior coating of pink ice, making it look like a comic figure in a strawberry ice cream ad, a chocolate ragamuffin with a scoop for a head.

The lineman stared after the funeral party for a time until the team-pusher, who had been watching the slack span of 800 MCM aluminum conductors that snaked half a mile back toward the preceding tower, glanced up at the hesitant worker and began bellowing into his microphone. The lineman answered briefly, inspected the pressure gauge of his suit, and began cranking the jack again. With every dozen turns of the crank, the long snaking cable crept tighter across the lunar plain, straightening and lifting almost imperceptibly until at last the center-point cleared the ground and the cable swooped in a long graceful catenary between the towers. It trembled with fitful glistenings in the harsh sunglare. The lineman ignored the cable as he turned the crank. He squinted across the plains at the meteor display.

The display was not spectacular. It could be detected only as a slight turbulence in the layer of lunar dust that covered the ground, and an occasional dust geyser where a pea-sized bit of sky debris exploded into the crust at thirty miles per second. Sometimes the explosion was bright and lingering, but more often there was only a momentary incandescence quickly obscured by dust. The lineman watched it with nervous eyes. There was small chance of being hit by a stone of consequential size, but the eternal pelting by meteoric dust, though too fine to effect a puncture, could weaken the fabric of a suit and lead to leaks and blowouts.

The team-pusher keyed his mic switch again and called to the lineman on the tower. *"Keep your eyes on that damn jack, Relke! That clamp looks like she's slipping from here."*

The lineman paused to inspect the mechanism. *"Looks OK to me,"* he answered. *"How tight do I drag this one up?"*

The pusher glanced at the sagging span of steel-reinforced aluminum cable. *"It's a short stretch. Not too critical. What's the tension now?"*

The lineman consulted a dial on the jack. *"Going on forty-two hundred pounds, Joe."*

"Crank her up to five thousand and leave it," said the pusher. *"Let C-shift sag it in by the tables if they don't like it."*

"Yokay. Isn't it quitting time?"

"Damn near. My suit stinks like we're on overtime. Come on down when you reel that one in. I'm going back to the sleep wagon and get blown clear." The pusher shut off his oxygen while he transferred his hose connections from the main feeder supply to the walk-around bottles on his suit. He signaled "quitting time" at the men on the far tower, then started moon-loping his way across the shaggy terrain toward the train of rolling barracks and machinery that moved with the construction crew as the 200 kilovolt transmission line inched its way across the lunar landscape.

The lineman glanced up absently at the star-stung emptiness of space. Motion caught his eye. He watched with a puzzled frown, then hitched himself around to call after the departing team-pusher.

"Hey, Joe!"

The pusher stopped on a low rise to look back. *"Relke?"* he asked, uncertain of the source of the voice.

"Yeah. Is that a ship up there?" The lineman pointed upward toward the east.

"I don't see it. Where?"

"Between Arcturus and Serpens. I thought I saw it move."

The pusher stood on the low tongue of lava and watched the heavens for a time. *"Maybe—maybe not. So what if it is, Relke?"*

"Well . . ." The lineman paused, keying his mic nervously. *"Looks to me like it's headed the wrong direction for Crater City. I mean—"*

The pusher barked a short curse. *"I'm just about fed up with that superstitious drivel!"* he snapped. *"There* aren't *any non-human ships, Relke. And there aren't any non-humans."*

"I didn't say—"

"No, but you had it in mind." The pusher gave him a scornful look and hiked on toward the caterpillar train.

"Yuh. If you say so, Joe," Relke muttered to himself. He glanced again at the creeping point of light in the blackness; he shrugged; he began cranking up the slack span again. But the creeping point kept drawing his gaze while he cranked. When he looked at the tension indicator, it read 5,600 pounds. He grunted his annoyance, reversed the jack ratchet, and began letting out the extra 600 pounds.

The shift-change signal was already beeping in his headsets by the time he had eased it back down to 5,000, and the C-shift crewmen were standing around the foot of the tower jeering at him from below.

"Get off it, boy. Give the men a chance."

"Come on down, Relke. You can let go. It ain't gonna drop."

He ignored the razzing and climbed down the trainward side of the tower.

Larkin and Kunz walked briskly around to meet him. He jumped the last twenty-five feet, hoping to evade them, but they were waiting for him when his boots hit the ground.

"*We want a little talk with you, Relke, my lad,*" came Larkin's rich, deceptively affable baritone.

"*Sorry, Lark, it's late and I—*" He tried to sidestep them, but they danced in and locked arms with him, one on each side.

"*Like Lark told you, we want a little talk,*" grunted Kunz.

"*Sure, Harv—but not right now. Drop by my bunk tank when you're off shift. I been in this strait jacket for seven hours. It doesn't smell exactly fresh in here.*"

"*Then, Sonny, you should learn to control yourself in your suit,*" said Larkin, his voice all mellifluent with smiles and avuncular pedagoguery. "*Let's take him, Harv.*"

They caught him in a double armlock, hoisted him off the ground, and started carrying him toward a low lava ridge that lay a hundred yards to the south of the tower. He could not kick effectively because of the stiffness of the suit. He wrenched one hand free and fumbled at the channel selector of his suit radio. Larkin jerked his stub antenna free from its mounting before Relke could put in a call for help.

"*Tch, tch tch,*" said Larkin, waggling his head.

They carried him across the ridge and set him on his feet again, out of sight of the camp. "*Sit down, Sonny. We have seeeerious matters to discuss with you.*"

Relke heard him faintly, even without the antenna, but he saw no reason to acknowledge. When he failed to answer, Kunz produced a set of jumper wires from his knee pocket and clipped their suit audio circuits into a three way intercom, disconnecting the plate lead from an r.f. stage to insure privacy.

"You guys give me a pain in the hump," growled the lineman. "What do you want this time? You know damn well a dead radio is against safety rules."

"It *is*? You ever hear of such a rule, Kunz?"

"Naah. Or maybe I did, at that. It's to make things easy for work spies, psych checkers, and time-and-motion men, ain't that it?"

"Yeah. You a psych checker or a time-and-motion man, Relke?"

"Hell, you guys know damn well I'm not—"

"Then what are you stalling about?" Larkin's baritone lost its mellowness and became an ominous growl. "You came nosing around, asking questions about the Party. So we let you in on it. We took you to a cell meeting. You said you wanted to join. So we let you in on two more meetings. Then you chickened out. We don't like that, Relke. It smells. It smells like a dirty informing rat!"

"I'm no damn informer!"

"Then why did you welsh?"

"I didn't welsh. I never said I'd join. You asked me if I was in favor of getting the Schneider-Volkov Act repealed. I said 'yes.' I still say 'yes.' That doesn't mean I want to join the Party."

"Why not, Relke?"

"Well, there's the fifty bucks, for one thing."

"Wh-a-a-at! One shift's wages? Hell, if that's all that's stopping you— Kunz, let's pay his fifty bucks for him, OK?"

"Sure. We'll pay your way in, Relke. I don't hold it against a man if he's a natural born tightwad."

"Yeah," said Larkin. "All you gotta do is sign up, Sonny. Fifty bucks, hell—that's less than union dues. If you can call that yellow-bellied obscenity a union. Now how about it, Relke?"

Behind the dark lenses of his glare goggles, Relke's eyes scanned the ground for a weapon. He spotted a jagged shard of volcanic glass and edged toward it.

"Well, Relke?"

"No deal."

"Why not?"

"That's easy. I plan on getting back to Earth someday. Conspiracy to commit mutiny rates the death penalty."

"Hear what he said, Lark? He calls it mutiny."

"Yeah. Teacher's little monitor."

"C'mere, informer."

They approached him slowly, wearing tight smiles. Relke dived for the shard of glass. The jumper wires jerked tight and broke loose, throwing them off balance for a moment. He came up with the glass shard in one fist and backed away. They stopped. The weapon was as good as a gun. A slit suit was the ultimate threat. Relke tore the dangling wires loose from his radio and backed toward the top of the ridge. They watched him somberly, not speaking. Larkin waved the lineman's stub antenna and looked at him questioningly. Relke held out a glove and waited for him to toss it. Larkin threw it over his shoulder in the opposite direction. They turned their backs on him. He loped on back toward the gravy train, knowing that the showdown had been no more than postponed. Next time would be worse. They meant to incriminate him, as a kind of insurance against his informing. He had no desire to be incriminated, nor to inform—but try to make them believe that.

Before entering the clean-up tank, he stopped to glance up at the heavens between Arcturus and Serpens. The creeping spot of light had vanished—or moved far from where he had seen it. He did not pause to search. He checked his urine bottle in the airlock, connected his hoses to the wall valves, and blew the barn-smell out of his suit. The blast of fresh air was like icy wine in his throat. He enjoyed it for a moment, then went inside the tank for a bath.

Novotny was waiting for him in the B-shift line crew's bunkroom. The small pusher looked sore. He stopped pacing when Relke entered.

"Hi, Joe."

Novotny didn't answer. He watched while Relke stowed his gear, got out an electric razor, and went to the wall mirror to grind off the blond bristles.

"Where you been?" Novotny grunted.

"On the line where you saw me. I jacked that last span up tighter than you told me. I had to let her back down a little. Made me late getting in."

The pusher's big hand hit him like a club between the shoulder blades, grabbed a handful of coverall, and jerked him roughly around. The razor fell to the end of the cord. Novotny let go in back and grabbed a handful in front. He shoved the lineman back against the wall.

Relke gaped at him blankly.

"Don't give *me* that wide blue-eyed dumb stare, you sonofabitch!" the pusher snapped. "I saw you go over the hill with Kunz and Larkin."

Relke's Adam's apple did a quick genuflection. "If you saw me go, you musta seen *how* I went."

Novotny shook him. "What'd they want with you?" he barked.

"Nothing."

Joe's eyes turned to dark slits. "Relke, I told you, I told the rest of my men. I told you what I'd do to any sonofabitch on my team that got mixed up with the Party. Pappy don't allow that crap. Now shall I do it to you here, or do you want to go down to the dayroom?"

"Honest, Joe, I'm not mixed up in it. I got interested in what Larkin had to say—back maybe six months ago. But I never signed up. I never even meant to."

"Six months? Was that about the time you got your Dear John letter from Fran?"

"Right after that, Joe."

"Well, that figures. So what's Larkin after you about now?"

"I guess he wonders why I asked questions but never joined."

"I don't want your guesses. What did he say out there, and what did you say to him?"

"He wanted to know why I didn't sign up, that's all."

"And you told him what?"

"No deal."

"So?"

"So, I came on back and took a shower."

Novotny stared at him for a few seconds. "You're lying," he grunted, but released him anyway. "OK, Relke, but you better listen to this. You're a good lineman. You've stayed out of trouble. You get along with the rest of the team. If you got out of line in some *other* way, I'd figure it was about time you let off some steam. I'd stick up for you. But get mixed up with the Party—and I'll stomp you. When I'm through stomping you, I'll report you off my team. Understand?"

"Sure, Joe."

Novotny grunted and stepped away from him. "No hard feelings, Relke."

"Naah." The lineman went back to the mirror and started shaving again. That his hand remained steady was a surprise to him. Novotny had never before laid a hand on him, and Relke hoped the first time would be the last. He had watched Joe mop up the dayroom with Benet for playing fast and loose with safety rules while working a hotstick job, and it put Benet in sick bay for three days. Novotny was small, but he was built like a bunker. He was a fair overseer, but he handled his men in the only way he knew how to handle them on such a job. He expected self-discipline and self-imposed obedience, and when he didn't get it, he took it as a personal insult and a challenge to a duel. Out on the lava, men were pressure-packed, hermetically sealed charges of high explosive blood and bone; one man's folly could mean the death of several others, and there was no recourse to higher authority or admonitions from the dean, with a team on the lava.

"What's your grudge against the Party, Joe?" Relke asked while he scraped under his neck.

"No grudge. Not as long as Benet, Braxton, Relke, Henderson, Beasley, Tremini, and Novotny stay out of it. No grudge at all. I'm for free love and nickel beer as much as the next guy. But I'm not for getting my ass shot off. I'm not for fouling up the whole Lunar project just to get the Schneider-Volkov Act repealed, when you can't get it repealed that way anyhow. I'm not for facing a General Space Court and getting sentenced to blowout. That's all. No grudge."

"What makes you think a general strike couldn't force repeal, Joe?"

The pusher spat contemptuously at the disposal chute and missed. "A general strike on the Lunar project? Hell, Relke, use your head. It'd never work. A strike against the government is rough to pull off, even on Earth. Up here, it'd be suicide. The Party's so busy yelling about who's right and who's wrong and who's getting a raw deal—and what they ought to do about it—that they forget the important point: who's in the driver's seat. So what if we shut down Copernicus and all the projects like this one? Copernicus has a closed ecology, its own plant-animal cycle, sure. We don't need much from Earth to keep it running—but there's the hitch: don't need *much*. The ecology slips out of balance now and then. Every month or two it has to get a transfusion from Earth. Compost bacteria, or a new strain of algae because our strain starts mutating—it's always something like that. If a general strike cut us off from Earth, the World Parliament could just sit passing solemn gas through their waffle-bottom chairs and wait. They could debate us to death in two months."

"But world opinion—"

"Hell, *they* make world opinion, not *us*."

Relke stopped shaving and looked around. "Joe?"

"Yah."

"Kunz and Larkin'd kill me for telling you. Promise not to say anything?"

The pusher glowered at him for a moment. "Look, Relke, nobody brutalizes Joe Novotny's men. I'll handle Kunz and Larkin. You'd better spill. You think it's informing if you tell *me*?"

Relke shook his head. "Guess not. OK, Joe. It's this: I've been to three cell meetings. I heard some stuff. I think the strike's supposed to start come sundown."

"I heard that too. If it does, we'll all be—" He broke off. The cabin's intercom was suddenly blaring.

Attention, all personnel, attention. Unidentified bird at thirty degrees over horizon, south-southwest, braking fire for landing in our vicinity. All men on the line take cover. Safety team to the ready room on the double. Rescue team scramble, rescue team scramble.

Relke rolled the cord neatly around the razor and stared at it. "I'll be damned," he muttered. "It *was* a ship I saw. What ship would be landing way the hell out here?" He glanced around at Novotny.

The pusher was already at the periscope viewer, his face buried in the sponge rubber eyepieces. He cranked it around in a search pattern toward the south-southwest.

"See anything?"

"Not yet . . . *yeah*, there she is. Braking in fast—now what the hell!"

"Give me a look."

They traded turns at the viewer.

"She's a fusion furnace job. Cold fusion. Look at that blue tail."

"Why land way out here?"

The hatch burst open and the rest of the men spilled in from the dayroom. A confused babble filled the cabin. "I tole ya and I tole ya!" said Bama Braxton. "That theah mine shaff at Tycho is the play-yun evvy-dance. Gennlemen, weah about to have stranjuhs in ouah midst."

"Cut that superstitious bullspit, Brax," Novotny grunted. "There *aren't* any aliens. We got enough bogeys around here without you scaring the whoop out of yourself with that line of crap."

"Theah ahn't no aliens!" Braxton howled. "Theah ahn't no *aliens*? Joe, youah bline to the play-yun evvy-dance!"

"He right, Joe," said Lije Henderson, the team's only Negro and Bama's chief crony. "That mine shaff speak fo' itself."

"That mine's a million years old," Joe snorted, "and they're not even sure it's a mine. I said drop it."

"That *ship* speak fo' itself!"

"Drop it! This isn't the first time a ship overshot Crater City and had to set down someplace else. Ten to one it's full of Parliament waffle-bottoms, all complaining their heads off. Maybe they've got a meteor puncture and need help quick."

The closed-circuit intercom suddenly buzzed, and Novotny turned to see the project engineer's face on the small viewer.

"Are all your men up and dressed, Joe?" he asked when Novotny had answered the call.

"EVERYBODY PIPE DOWN! Sorry, Suds. No—well, except for Beasley, they're up. Beasley's logging sack time."

"The hell Beasley is!" complained Beasley from his bunk. "With you verbing nouns of a noun all yapping like—"

"Shut up, Beez. Go on, Suds."

"We got contact with that ship. They've got reactor troubles. I tried to get Crater City on the line, but there's an outage on the circuit somewhere. I need some men to take a tractor and backtrack toward Copernicus. Look for a break in the circuit."

"Why call me?"

"The communication team is tied up, Joe."

"Yeah, but I'm not a communic—"

"Hell!" Brodanovitch exploded. "It doesn't take an electronics engineer to splice a broken wire, does it?"

"OK, Suds, we'll go. Take it easy. What about that ship?"

The engineer paused to mop his face. He looked rather bleak suddenly. "I don't know if it's safe to tell you. But you'll find out anyhow. Watch out for a riot."

"Not a runaway reactor—"

"Worse, Joe. Women."

"WOMEN!" It was a high piping scream from Beasley. "Did he say *women?*" Beasley was out of bed and into his boots.

"WOMEN!" They came crowding around the intercom screen.

"Back off!" Novotny barked. "Go on, Suds."

"It's a troupe of entertainers, Joe. Clearance out of Algiers. They say they're scheduled for a performance in Crater City, come nightfall. That's all I know, except they're mostly women."

"Algiers! Jeez! Belly dancers . . . !"

The room was a confused babble.

"Wait a minute," said Suds. His face slid off the screen as he talked to somebody in the boss tank. Moments later he was back. "Their ship just put down, Joe. Looks like a safe landing. The rescue team is out there. You'll pass the ship on the way up the line. Get moving."

"Sure, Suds." Novotny switched off and looked around at the sudden scramble. "I'll be damned if you do!" he yelled. "You can't all go. Beasley, Henderson—"

"No, bigod you don't, Joe!" somebody howled. "Draw straws!"

"OK. I can take three of you, no more."

They drew. Chance favored Relke, Braxton, and Henderson. Minutes later they crowded into the electric runabout and headed southeast along the line of stately steel towers that filed back toward Copernicus. The ship was in sight. Taller than the towers, the nacelles of the downed bird rose into view beyond the broken crest of a distant lava butte. She was a freight shuttle, space-constructed and not built for landing on Earth. Relke eyed the emblem on the hull of her crew nacelle while the runabout nosed onto the strip of graded roadbed that paralleled the transmission line back to Crater City. The emblem was unfamiliar.

"That looks like the old *RS Voltaire,*" said the lineman. "Somebody must have bought her, Joe. Converted her to passenger service."

"Maybe. Now keep an eye on the telephone line."

The pusher edged the runabout toward the trolley rods. The overhead power transmission line had been energized by sections during the construction of it, and the line was hot as far as the road had been extended. Transformer stations fed energy from the 200 kilovolt circuit into the 1,500 volt trolley bars that ran down the center of the roadbed. Novotny stopped the vehicle at the end of the finished construction and sidled it over until the feeler arms crackled against the electrified bus rods and locked in place. He switched the batteries to "charge" and drove on again.

"Relke, you're supposed to be watching that talk circuit, not the ship."

"OK, Joe, in a minute."

"You horny bastard, you can't see their bloomers through that titanium hull. Put the glasses down and watch the line."

"OK, just a minute. I'm trying to find out who owns her. The emblem's—"

"Now, dammit!"

"No marking on her except her serial number and a picture of a rooster— and something else that's been painted over."

"RELKE!"

"Sure, Joe, OK."

"Girls!" marveled Lije Henderson. "Whenna lass time you touch a real girl, Brax?"

"Don' ass me, Lije, don' evum ass me. I sweah, if I evum touch a lady's li'l pink fingah right now, I could—"

"Hell, I could jus' sittin' heah lookin' at that ship. Girls. God! Lemme have those glasses, Relke."

Novotny braked the runabout to a halt. "All right, get your helmets on," he snapped. "Pressure your suits. I'm going to pump air out."

"Whatthehell! *Why*, Joe?"

"So you can get out of this heap. You're walking back. I'll go on and find the break myself."

Braxton squealed like a stuck pig; a moment later all three of them were on him. "Please, Joe. . . . Fuh the love a heaven, Joe, have a haht. . . . Gawd, *women*!"

"Get off my lap, you sonofabitch!" he barked at Braxton, who sat on top of him, grabbing at the controls. "Wait—I'll tell you what. Put the damn binoculars down and watch the line. Don't say another damn word about dames until we find the break and splice it. Swear to that, you bastards, and you can stay. I'll stop at their ship on our way back, and then you can stare all you want to. OK?"

"Joe, I sweah on a stack of—"

"All right, then watch the line."

They drove on in silence. The ship had fired down on a flat stretch of ground about four miles from the construction train, a few hundred yards from the trolley road. They stared at it as the runabout crawled past, and Novotny let the vehicle glide to a halt.

"The ramp's out and the ladder's down," said Relke. "Somebody must have come out."

"Unglue your eyes from that bird and look around," Novotny grunted. "You'll see why the ladder's down." He jerked his thumb toward a row of vehicles parked near the massive ship.

"The rescue team's wagons. But wheah's the rescue team?"

No crewmen were visible in the vicinity of the ship or the parked runabouts. Novotny switched on the radio, punched the channel selector, and tried a call, reading the call code off the side of the safety runabout.

"Double Able Niner, this is One Four William. Talk back, please."

They sat in silence. There was nothing but a hiss of solar interference from the radio and the sound of heavy breathing from the men.

"Those lucky ole bastahds!" Braxton moaned. "You know wheah they gone, gennlemen? I taya weah they gone. They clambered right up the ladies' ladduh, thass wheah. You know wheah they gone? I taya, alright—"

"Knock it off. Let's get moving. Tell us on the way back."

"Those lucky ole—"

The runabout moved ahead across the glaring land.

Relke: "Joe?"

"Yeah?"

"Joe, on our way back, can we go over and see if they'll let us climb aboard?"

Novotny chuckled. "I thought you were off dames, Relke. I thought when Fran sent you the Dear John, you said dames were all a bunch of—"

"Damn, Joe! You could have talked all day without saying 'Fran.'" The lineman's throat worked a brief spasm, and he stared out across the broken moonscape with dismal eyes.

"Sorry I mentioned it," Novotny grunted. "But sure, I guess one of us could walk over and ask if they mind a little more company on board."

Lije: "*One* of us! Who frinstance—*you?*"

Joe: "No, you can draw for it—not now, you creep! Watch the line."

They watched in silence. The communication circuit was loosely strung on temporary supports beside the roadbed. The circuit was the camp's only link with Crater City, for the horizon interposed a barrier to radio reception, such reception being possible only during the occasional overhead transits of the lunar satellite station which carried message-relaying equipment. The satellite's orbit had been shifted to cover a Russian survey crew near Clavius, however, and its passages over the Trolley Project were rare.

"I jus' *thought*," Lije muttered suddenly, smacking his fist in his palm.

Relke: "Isn't that getting a little drastic, Lije?"

"I jus' thought. If we fine that outage, less don' fix it!"

Joe: "What kind of crazy talk is that?"

"Lissen, you know what ole Suds want to call Crater City fo'? *He* want to call 'em so's they'll senn a bunch of tank wagons down heah and tote those gals back to town. Thass what he want to call 'em fo'!"

Braxton slapped his forehead. "Luvva God! He's right. Y'all heah that? Is he right, Joe, or is he right?"

"I guess that's about the size of it."

"We mi'not evum get a look at 'em!" Braxton wailed.

"Less don' fix it, Joe!"

"I sweah, if I evum touch one of theah precious li'l fingahs, I'd—"

"Shut up and watch the line."

Relke: "Why didn't he use a bridge on the circuit and find out where the break was, Joe?"

"A bridge won't work too well on that line."

"How fah we gonna keep on drivin', Joe?"

"Until we find the break. Relke, turn up that blower a little. It's beginning to stink in here."

"Fresh ayah!" sighed Braxton as the breeze hit them from the fan.

Relke: "I wonder if it's fresh. I keep wondering if it doesn't come out foul from the purifier, but we've been living in it too long to be able to tell. I even dream about it. I dream about going back to Earth and everybody runs away from me. Coughing and holding their noses. I can't get close to a girl even in a dream anymore."

"Ah reckon a head-shrinker could kill hisself a-laughin' over that one."

"Don't talk to me about head-shrinkers."

"Watch the damn line."

Braxton: "Talk about *dreams*! Listen, I had one lass sleep shift that I oughta tell y'all about. Gennlemen, if she wasn't the ohnriest li'l—"

Novotny cursed softly under his breath and tried to keep his eyes on both the road and the communications circuit.

Relke: "Let 'em jabber, Joe. I'll watch it."

Joe: "It's bad enough listening to a bunch of jerks in a locker room bragging about the dames they've made. But Braxton! Braxton's got to brag about his dreams. Christ! Send me back to Earth. I'm fed up."

"Aww, Joe, we got nothin' else to talk about up heah."

They drove for nearly an hour and a half without locating the outage. Novotny pulled the runabout off the hot trolleys and coasted to a stop. "I'm deflating the cab," he told them. "Helmets on, pressure up your suits."

"Joe, weah not walkin' back from heah!" Bama said flatly.

"Oh, blow yourself out, Brax!" the pusher said irritably. "I'm getting out for a minute. C'mon, get ready for vacuum."

"Why?"

"Don't say *why* to me outside the sleep-tank, corn pone! Just do it."

"Damn! Novotny's in a humah! Less say 'yassah' to him, Bama."

"You too, Lije!"

"Yassah."

"Can it." Novotny got the pressure pumped down to two pounds, and then let the rest of the air spew out slowly into vacuum. He climbed out of the runabout and loped over to the low-hanging spans of the communication circuit. He tapped into it with the suit audio and listened for a moment. Relke saw his lips moving as he tried a call, but nothing came through the lineman's suit radio. After about five minutes, he quit talking and beckoned the rest of them back to the runabout.

"That was Brodanovitch," he said after they were inside and the pressure came up again. "So the circuit break must be on up ahead."

"Oh, hell, we'll *navah* get a look at those ladies!"

"Calm down. We're going back—" He paused a moment until the elated whooping died down. "Suds says let them send a crew out of Copernicus to fix it. I guess there's no hurry about moving those people out of there."

"The less hurry, the bettuh . . . *hot dawg!* C'mon, Joe, roll it!" Bama and Lije sat rubbing their hands. Only Relke seemed detached, his enthusiasm apparently cooled. He sat staring out at the meteor display on the dust-flats. He kept rubbing absently at the ring finger of his left hand. There was no ring there, nor even a mark on the skin. The pusher's eye fell on the slow nervous movement.

"Fran again?" Joe grunted.

The lineman nodded.

"I got my Dear John note three years ago, Relke."

Relke looked around at him in surprise. "I didn't know you were married, Joe."

"I guess I wasn't as married as I thought I was."

Relke stared outside again for awhile. "How do you get over it?"

"You don't. Not up here on Luna. The necessary and sometimes sufficient condition for getting over a dame is the availability of other dames. So, you don't."

"Hell, Joe!"

"Yeah."

"The movement's not such a bad idea."

"Can it!" the pusher snapped.

"It's true. Let women come to Crater City, or send us home. It makes sense."

"You're only looking at the free love and nickel beer end of it, Relke. You can't raise kids in low gravity. There are five graves back in Crater City to prove it. Kids' graves. Six feet long. They grow themselves to death."

"I know but . . ." He shrugged uncomfortably and watched the meteor display again.

"When do we draw?" said Lije. "Come on Joe, less draw for who goes talk ouah way onto the ship."

Relke: "Say, Joe, how come they let dames in an entertainment troupe come to the moon, but they won't let our wives come? I thought the Schneider-Volkov Act was supposed to keep all women out of space, period."

"No, they couldn't get away with putting it like that. Against the WP constitution. The law just says that all personnel on any member country's lunar project must be of a single sex. Theoretically some country—Russia, maybe—could start an all-girl lunar mine project, say. Theoretically. But how many lady muckers do you know? Even in Russia."

Lije: "When do we draw? Come on, Joe, less draw."

"Go ahead and draw. Deal me out."

Chance favored Henderson. "Fast-uh, Joe. Hell, less go fastuh, befo' the whole camp move over theah."

Novotny upped the current to the redline and left it there. The long spans of transmission line, some of them a mile or more from tower to tower, swooped past in stately cadence.

"There she is! Man!"

"You guys are building up for a big kick in the rump. They'll never let us aboard."

"Theah's two more cahs pahked over theah."

"Yeah, and still nobody in sight on the ground."

Novotny pulled the feelers off the trolleys again. "OK, Lije, go play John Alden. Tell 'em we just want to look, not touch."

Henderson was bounding off across the flats moments after the cabin had been depressurized to let him climb out. They watched him enviously while the pressure came up again. His black face flashed with sweat in the sunlight as he looked back to wave at them from the foot of the ladder.

Relke glanced down the road toward the rolling construction camp. "You going to call in, Joe? Ought to be able to reach their antenna from here."

"If I do, Brodanovitch is sure to say 'haul-ass on back to camp.'"

"Never mind, then! Forget I said it!"

The pusher chuckled. "Getting interested, Relke?"

"I don't know. I guess I am." He looked quickly toward the towering rocket.

"Mostly you want to know how close you are to being rid of her, maybe?"

"I guess— Hey, they're letting him in."

"That lucky ole bastuhd!" Bama moaned.

The airlock opened as Lije scaled the ladder. A helmet containing a head of unidentifiable gender looked out and down, watching the man climb. Lije paused to wave. After a moment's hesitancy, the space-suited figure waved back.

"*Hey, up theah, y'all mind a little company?*"

The party who watched him made no answer. Lije shook his head and climbed on. When he reached the lock, he held out a glove for an assist, but the figure stepped back quickly. Lije stared inside. The figure was holding a gun. Lije stepped down a rung. The gun beckoned impatiently for him to get inside. Reluctantly Lije obeyed.

The hatch closed. A valve spat a jet of frost, and they watched the pressure dial slowly creep to ten psi. Lije watched the stranger unfasten his helmet, then undid his own. The stranger was male, and the white goggle marks about his eyes betrayed him as a spacer. His thin dark features suggested Semitic or Arabic origins.

"*Parlez-vous français?*"

"Naw," said Lije. "Sho' don't. Sorry."

The man tossed his head and gave a knowing snort. "Ah! Afrique-Américain. Yais. I had forgotten. I misthought you African. Apologeez?"

"Needn' bothuh," said Lije. "Coss, if you feelin' apologetic, you might put that pistola back in yo' boot."

"Ho?" The man looked down at the gun in his hand as if he had forgotten it. "Ho! It is first necessaire that we find out who you are," he explained, and brandished the weapon under Lije's nose. He grinned a flash of white teeth. "Who send you here?"

"Nobody send me. I come unduh my own steam. Some fellas in my moonjeep pulled cahds, and I—"

"Whup! You are—ah *tin Unteroffizier*? *Mais non*, wrong sprach—you *l'officiale*? Officer? Company man?"

"Who, me? Lahd, no. I'm juss a hot-stick man on B-shif'. You muss be lookin' fo' Suds Brodanovitch."

"Why you come to this ship?"

"Well, the fellas and I heard tell theah was some gals, and we—"

The man waved the gun impatiently and pressed a button near the inner hatch. A red indicator light went on.

"Yes?" A woman's voice, rather hoarse. Lije's chest heaved with sudden emotion, and his sigh came out a bleat.

The man spoke in a flood of French. The woman did not reply at once. Lije noticed the movement of a viewing lens beside the hatch; it was scanning him from head to toe.

The woman's voice shifted to an intimate contralto. "OK, dearie, you come right in here where it's nice and warm."

The inner hatch slid open. It took Lije a few seconds to realize that she had been talking to him. She stood there smiling at him like a middle-aged schoolmarm.

"Why don't you come on in and meet the girls?"

Eyes popping, Lije Henderson stumbled inside.

He was gone a long time.

When he finally came out, the men in Novotny's runabout took turns cursing at him over the suit frequency. *"Fa chrissake, Henderson, we've been sitting here using up oxy for over an hour while you been horsing around . . ."* They waited for him with the runabout, cabin depressurized.

Lije was panting wildly as he ran toward them. *"Lissen to the bahstud giggle,"* Bama said disgustedly.

"Y'all juss don' know, y'all juss don' KNOW!" Lije was chanting between pants.

"Get in here, you damn traitor!"

"Hones', I couldn' help myself. I juss couldn'."

"Well, do the rest of us get aboard her, or not?" Joe snapped.

"Hell, go ahead, man! It's wide open. Evahthing's wide open."

"Girls?" Relke grunted.

"Girls. God yes! Girls."

"You coming with us?" Joe asked. Lije shook his head and fell back on the seat, still panting. *"Lahd, no! I couldn't stand it. I juss want to lie heah and look up at ole Mamma Earth and feel like a human again."* He grinned beatifically. *"Y'all go on."*

Braxton was staring at his crony with curious suspicion. *"Man, those must be some entuhtainuhs! Whass the mattah with you, Lije?"*

Henderson whooped and pounded his leg. *"Hoo hoo! Hooeee! Entuhtainuhs, he says. Hoo-hooeee! You mean y'all still don' know what that ship is?"*

They had already climbed out of the tractor. Novotny glared back in at Lije. *"We've been waiting to hear it from you, Henderson,"* he snapped.

Lije sat up grinning. *"That's no stage show troupe! That ship, so help me Hannah, is a—hoo hoo hooee—is a goddam flyin' HO-house."* He rolled over on the seat and surrendered to laughter.

Novotny looked around for his men and found himself standing alone. Braxton was already on the ladder, and Relke was just starting up behind.

"Hey, you guys come back here!"

"Drop dead, Joe."

Novotny stared after them until they disappeared through the lock. He glanced back at Lije. Henderson was in a grinning beatific trance. The pusher shrugged and left him lying there, still wearing his pressure suit in the open cabin. The pusher trotted after his men toward the ship.

Before he was halfway there, a voice broke into his headsets. *"Where the devil are you going, Novotny? I want a talk with you!"*

He stopped to glance back. The voice belonged to Brodanovitch, and it sounded sore. The engineer's runabout had nosed in beside Novotny's; Suds sat in the cab and beckoned at him angrily. Joe trudged on back and climbed in through the vehicle's coffin-sized airlock. Brodanovitch glared at him while the pusher removed his helmet.

"What the devil's going on over there?"

"At the ship?" Joe paused. Suds was livid. "I don't know exactly."

"I've been calling Safety and Rescue for an hour and a half. Where are they?"

"In the ship, I guess."

"You *guess!*"

"Hell, chief, take it easy. We just got here. I don't know what's going on."

"Where are your men?"

Novotny jerked his thumb at the other runabout. "Henderson's in there. Relke and Brax went to the ship."

"And that's where you were going just now, I take it," Suds snarled.

"Take that tone of voice and shove it, Suds! You know where you told me to go. I went. Now I'm off. We're on our own time unless you tell us different."

The engineer spent a few seconds swallowing his fury. "All right," he grunted. "But every man on that rescue squad is going to face a Space Court, and if I have any say about it, they'll get decomped."

Novotny's jaw dropped. "Slow down, Suds. Explosive decompression is for mutiny or murder. What're you talking about?"

"Murder."

"Wha-a-at?"

"That's what I call it. A demolition man—Hardin, it was—had a blow-out. With only one man standing by on the rescue gear."

"Meteor dust?"

"Yeah."

"Would it have made any difference if Safety and Rescue had been on the job?"

Suds glowered. "Maybe, maybe not. An inspector might have spotted the bulge in his suit before it blew." He shook an angry finger toward the abandoned Safety & Rescue vehicles. "Those men are going to stand trial for negligent homicide. It's the principle, damn it!"

"Sure, Suds. I guess you're right. I'll be right back."

Henderson was sleeping in his pressure suit when Novotny climbed back into his own runabout. The cab was still a vacuum. He got the hatch closed, turned on the air pumps, then woke Henderson.

"Lije, you been with a woman?"

"Nnnnnngg-*nnnng!* I hope to tell!" He shot a quick glance toward the rocket as if to reassure himself as to its reality. "And man, was she a little—"

Joe shook him again. "Listen. Brodanovitch is in the next car. Bull mad. I'll ask you again. You been with a woman?"

"Woman? You muss of lost yoah mine, Joe. Lass time I saw a woman was up at Atlanta." He rolled his eyes up toward the Earth crescent in the heavens. "Sure been a long old time. Atlanta . . . *man!*"

"That's better."

Lije jerked his head toward Brodanovitch's jeep. "What's ole wet blanket gonna do? Chase those gals out of here, I 'spect?"

"I don't know. That's not what he's frothing about, Lije. Hardin got killed while the S&R boys were shacking up over there. Suds doesn't even *know* what's in that ship. He acts like he's got about a dozen troubles running loose at once, and he doesn't know which way to grab."

"He don't even *know?* How we evah gonna keep him from findin' out?" Lije shot another glance at the ship and jumped. "Uh-oh! Looka theah! Yonder they come. Clamberin' down the ladies' ladduh. Theah's Joyce and Lander and Petzel—other one looks like Crump. Half the Safety team, Joe. Hoo-eee! They got that freshly bred look. You can evum tell it from heah. Uh-oh!"

Brodanovitch had climbed out of his runabout. Bellowing at his mic, he charged toward the ship. The S&R men took a few lopes toward their vehicles, saw Brodanovitch, and stopped. One man turned tail and bolted for the ladder again. Gesturing furiously, the engineer bore down on them.

"Leave the radio off, Joe. Sure glad we don' have to listen to that bull bellow."

They sat watching the safety men, who managed somehow to look stark naked despite their bulgey pressure suits. Suds stalked toward them like an amok runner, beating a gloved fist into his palm and working his jaw at them.

"Suds don' know how to get along with men when he *want* to get along with 'em, and he don' know how to fuss at 'em when he don't want to get along. Man, look how he rave!"

"Yeah. Suds is a smart engineer, but he's a rotten overseer."

The ship's airlock opened again and another man started out. He stopped with one foot on the top rung of the ladder. He looked down at Brodanovitch and the S&R men. He pulled his leg back inside and closed the hatch. Novotny chuckled.

"That was Relke, the damn fool."

Lije smote his forehead. "Look at Suds! They tole him! They went an *tole* him, Joe. We'll nevah get back in that ship now."

The pusher watched the four figures on the plain. They were just standing there. Brodanovitch had stopped gesticulating. For a few seconds he seemed frozen. His head turned slowly as he looked up at the rocket. He took three steps toward it, then stopped.

"He gonna have apoplexy, thass what he gonna have."

Brodanovitch turned slowly. He gave the S&R men a blank look, then broke into a run toward his tractor.

"I'd better climb out," Joe said.

He met the engineer beside the command runabout. Suds's face was a livid mask behind the faceplate. "*Get in,*" he snapped at the pusher.

As soon as they were inside, he barked, "Drive us to Crater City."

"Slow down, Suds."

"Joe. That ship. Damn brothel. Out to fleece the camp."

"So what're you going to do in Crater City?"

"Tell Parkeson, what else?"

"And what's the camp going to be doing while you're gone?"

That one made him pause. Finally he shook his head. "Drive, Joe."

Novotny flipped the switch and glanced at the gauges. "You haven't got enough oxygen in this bug to last out the trip."

"Then we'll get another one."

"Better take a minute to think it over, Suds. You're all revved up. What the hell can Parkeson do?"

"What can he *do?* What can—migawd, Joe!" Suds choked.

"Well?"

"He can get that ship out of here, he can have those women interned."

"How? Suppose they refuse to budge. Who appointed Parkeson king of creation? Hell, he's only *our* boss, Suds. The moon's open to any nation that wants to send a ship, or to any corporation that can get a clearance. The W.P. decided that a long time ago."

"But it's illegal—those women, I mean!"

"How do you know? Maybe their racket's legal in Algiers. That's where you told me they had clearance from, didn't you? And if you're thinking about the Schneider-Volkov Act, it just applies to the Integrated Projects, not wildcat teams."

Brodanovitch sat silent for a few moments, his throat working. He passed a shaky hand over his eyes. "Joe, we've got to keep discipline. Why can't I ever make the men understand that? On a moon project, it's discipline or die. You know that, Joe."

"Sure I know it. You know it. Parkeson knows it. The First Minister of the Space Ministry knows it. But the men don't know it, and they never will. They don't know what the word 'discipline' means, and it's no good trying to tell them. It's an overseer's word. It means your outfit's working for you like your own arms and legs. One brain and one body. When it cracks, you've just got a loose handful of stray men. No coordination. You can see it, but they can't see it. 'Discipline' is just a dirty word in the ranks, Suds."

"Joe, what'll I do?"

"It's your baby, not mine. Give it first aid. Then talk to Parkeson later, if you want to."

Suds sat silent for half a minute, then: "Drive back to the main wagon."

Novotny started the motors. "What are you going to do?"

"Announce Code Red, place the ship off limits, put an armed guard on it, and hope the Crater City crew gets that telephone circuit patched up quick. That's all I can do."

"Then let me get a safe distance away from you before you do it."

"You think it'll cause trouble?"

"Good Lord, Suds, use your head. You've got a campful of men who haven't been close to a dame in months and years, even to talk to. They're sick, they're scared, they're fed-up, they want to go home. The Party's got them bitter, agitated. I'd hate to be the guy who puts those women off limits."

"What would you do?"

"I'd put the screws on the shift that's on duty. I'd work hell out of the crews that are supposed to be on the job. I'd make a horrible example out of the first man to goof off. But first I'd tell the off-duty team pushers they can take their crews over to that ship, one crew at a time, and in an orderly manner."

"*What?* And be an accomplice? Hell, no!"

"Then do it your own way. Don't ask me."

Novotny parked the runabout next to the boss-wagon. "Mind if I use your buggy for awhile, Suds?" he asked. "I left mine back there, and I've got to pick up my men."

"Go ahead, but get them back here—fast."

"Sure, Suds."

He backed the runabout out again and drove down to B-shift's sleep-wagon. He parked again and used the airlock phone. "Beasley, Benet, the rest of you—come on outside."

Five minutes later they trooped out through the lock. "What's the score, Joe?"

"The red belts are ahead, that's all I know."

"Come on, you'll find out."

"Sleep! I haven't had no sleep since— *Say!* You takin' us over to that ship, Joe?"

"That's the idea."

"YAYHOO!" Beasley danced up and down. "Joe, we love ya!"

"Cut it. This is once-and-once-only. You're going once, and you're not going again."

"Who says?"

"Novotny says."

"But *why?*" Benet wailed.

"What did you say?"

"I said 'why!'"

"OK. I'll tell you why. Brodanovitch is going to put the ship off limits. If I get you guys in under the wire, you've got no gripe later on—when Suds hangs out the big No."

"Joe, that's chicken."

Novotny put on the brakes. "Get out and walk back, Benet."

"Joe—!"

"Benet."

"Look, I didn't mean anything."

Novotny paused. If Brodanovitch was going to try to do things the hard way, he'd lose control of his own men unless he gave them loose rein for a while first—keeping them reminded that he still *had* the reins. But Benet was getting out of hand lately. He had to decide. Now.

"Look at me, Benet."

Benet looked up. Joe smacked him. Benet sat back, looking surprised. He wiped his nose on the back of a glove and looked at the red smear. He wiped it again. The smear was bigger.

"You can stay, Benet, but if you do, I'll bust your hump after we get back. You want it that way?"

Benet looked at the rocket; he looked at Joe; he looked at the rocket. "Yeah. We'll see who does the busting. Let's go."

"All right, but do you see any other guys taking their teams over?"

"No."

"But you think you're getting a chicken deal."

"Yeah."

The pusher drove on, humming to himself. As long as he could keep them alternately loving him and hating him, everything was secure. Then he was Mother. Then they didn't stop to think or rationalize. They just reacted to Mother. It was easy to handle men reacting, but it wasn't so easy to handle men thinking. Novotny liked it the easy way, especially during a heavy meteor fall.

"It is of no importance to me," said Madame d'Annecy, "if you are the commandant of the whole of space, M'sieur. You wish entrance, I must ask you to contribute thees small fee. It is not in my nature to become unpleasant like thees, but you have bawl in my face, M'sieur."

"Look," said Brodanovitch, "I didn't come over here for . . . for what you think I came over here for." His ears reddened. "I don't want a girl, that is."

The madame's prim mouth made a small pink O of sudden understanding. "Ah, M'sieur, I begin to see. You are one of those. But in that I cannot help you. I have only girls."

The engineer choked. He started toward the hatch. A man with a gun slid into his path.

"Permit yourself to be restrained, M'sieur."

"There are four men in there that are supposed to be on the job, and I intend to get them. And the others too, while I'm at it."

"Is it that you have lost your boy friend, perhaps?"

Brodanovitch croaked incomprehensibly for a moment, then collapsed onto a seat beside the radar table that Madame d'Annecy was using for an accounting desk. "I'm no fairy," he said.

"I am pleased to hear it, M'sieur. I was beginning to pity you. Now if you will please sign the sight draft, so that we may telecast it—"

"I am *not* paying twelve hundred dollars just to get my men out of there!"

"I do not haggle, M'sieur. The price is fixed."

"Call them down here!"

"It cannot be done. They pay for two hours, for two hours they stay. Undisturbed."

"All right, let's see the draft."

Madame d'Annecy produced a set of forms from the map case and a small gold fountain pen from her ample bosom. "Your next of kin, M'sieur?" She handed him a blank draft.

"Wait a minute! How did you know where my account—"

"Is it not the correct firm?"

"Yes, but how did you know?" He looked at the serial number on the form, then looked up accusingly. "This is a telecopy form. You have a teletransmitter on board?"

"But of course! We could not risk having payment stopped after services rendered. The funds will be transferred to our account before you leave this ship. I assure you, we are well protected."

"I assure you, you are all going to jail."

Madame d'Annecy threw back her head and laughed heartily. She said something in French to the man at the door, then smiled at the unhappy engineer. "What law prevails here M'sieur?"

"UCOJE does. Uniform Code of Justice, Extraterrestrial. It's a semi-military—"

"U.N.-based, I believe?"

"Certainly."

"Now I know little of thees matters, but my attorneys would be delighted, I am certain, if you can tell me: which articles of thees UCOJE is to be used for inducing us to be incarcerated?"

"Why . . . Uh . . ." Suds scratched nervously at one corner of his moustache. He glanced at the man with the gun. He gazed forlornly at the sight draft.

"Exactly!" Mme. d'Annecy said brightly. "There have been no women to speak of on the moon since the unfortunate predicament of *les enfants perdus*. The moonborn grotesque ones. How could they think to pass laws against thees—thees *ancien* establishment, thees *maison intime*—when there are no women, eh M'sieur?"

"But you falsified your papers to get clearance. You must have."

"But no. Our clearance is 'free nation,' not 'world federal.' We are an entertainment troupe, and my government's officials are most lenient in defining 'entertainment.' *Chacun à son gout*, eh?"

Suds sat breathing heavily. "I can place this ship off limits."

"If you can do that, if the men do not come"—she shrugged eloquently and spread her hands—"then we will simply move on to another project. There are plenty of others. But do you think thees putting us off limits will make you very popular with your men?"

"I'm not trying to win a popularity contest," Suds wheezed. "I'm trying to finish the last twelve miles of this line before sundown. You've got to get out of here before there's a complete work stoppage."

"Thees project. It is important? Of an urgent nature?"

"There's a new uranium mine in the crater we're building toward. There's a colony there without an independent ecology. It has to be supplied from Copernicus. Right now, they're shooting supplies to them by rocket missile. It's too far to run surface freight without trolley service—or reactor-powered vehicles the size of battleships and expensive. We don't have the facilities to run a fleet of self-powered wagons that far."

"Can they not run on diesel, perhaps?"

"If they carry the oxygen to burn the diesel with, and if everybody in Copernicus agrees to stop breathing the stuff."

"*Embarras de choix.* I see."

"It's essential that the line be finished before nightfall. If it isn't, that mine colony will have to be shipped back to Copernicus. They can't keep on supplying it by bird. And they can't move out any ore until the trolley is ready to run."

Mme. d'Annecy nodded thoughtfully. "We wish to make the cordial entente with the lunar workers," she murmured. "We do not wish to cause the *bouleversement*—the disruption. Let us then negotiate, M'sieur."

"I'm not making any deals with you, lady."

"Ah, but such a hard position you take! I was but intending to suggest that you furnish us a copy of your camp's duty roster. If you will do that, Henri will not permit anyone to visit us if he is—how you say?—goofing off. Is it not that simple?"

"I will not be a party to robbery!"

"How is it robbery?"

"Twelve hundred dollars! Pay for two day-hitches. Lunar days. Nearly two months. And you're probably planning to fleece them more than once."

"*A bon marché!* Our expenses are terrific. Believe me, we expect no profit from this first trip."

"First trip and last trip," Suds grumbled.

"And who has complained about the price? No one so far excepting M'sieur. Look at it *thus* it is an investment." She slid one of the forms across the table. "Please to read it, M'sieur."

Suds studied the paper for a moment and began to frown. "*Les Folies Lunaires*, Incorporated . . . a North African corporation . . . in consideration of the sum of one hundred dollars in hand paid by—who?—Howard Beasley!—aforesaid corporation sells and grants to Howard Beasley . . . *one share of common stock!*"

"M'sieur! Compose yourself! It is no fraud. Everybody gets a share of stock. It comes out of the twelve hundred. Who knows? Perhaps after a few trips, there will even be dividends. M'sieur? But you look positively ill! Henri, bring brandy for the gentleman."

"So!" he grated. "That's the way it goes, is it? Implicate everybody—nobody squawks."

"But certainly. It is for our own protection, to be sure, but it is really stock."

"Blackmail."

"But no, M'sieur. All is legal."

Henri brought a plastic cup and handed it to him; Suds shook his head.

"Take it, M'sieur. It is real brandy. We could bring only a few bottles, but there is sufficient pure alcohol for the mixing of cocktails."

The small compartment was filled with the delicate perfume of the liquor; Brodanovitch glanced longingly at the plastic cup.

"It is seventy-year-old Courvoisier, M'sieur. Very pleasant."

Suds took it reluctantly, dipped it toward Mme. d'Annecy in self-conscious toast, and drained it. He acquired a startled expression; he clucked his tongue experimentally and breathed slowly through his nose.

"Good Lord!" he murmured absently.

Mme. d'Annecy chuckled. "M'sieur has forgotten the little pleasures. It was a shame to gulp it so. *Encore, Henri.* And one for myself, I think. Take time to enjoy this one, M'sieur." She studied him for a time while Henri was absent. She shook her head and began putting the forms away, leaving out the sight draft and stock agreement which she pushed toward him, raising one inquisitive brow. He gazed expressionlessly at them. Henri returned with the brandy; Madame questioned him in French. He seemed insistently negative for a time, but then seemed to give grudging assent. *"Bien!"* she said, and turned to Brodanovitch: "M'sieur, it will be necessary only for you to purchase the share of stock. Forget the fee."

"What?" Suds blinked in confusion.

"I said—" The opening of the hatch interrupted her thought. A dazzling brunette in a filmy yellow dress bounced into the compartment, bringing with her a breath of perfume. Suds looked at her and emitted a loud guttural cluck. A kind of glazed incredulity kneaded his face into a mask of shocked granite wearing a supercilious moustache. The girl ignored his presence and bent over the table to chat excitedly in French with Mme. d'Annecy. Suds's eyes seemed to find a mind and will of their own; involuntarily they contemplated the details of her architecture, and found manifest fascination in the way she relieved an itch at the back of one trim calf by rubbing it vigorously with the instep of her other foot while she leaned over the desk and bounced lightly on tiptoe as she spoke.

"M'sieur Brodanovitch, the young lady wishes to know—M'sieur Brodanovitch?—*M'sieur!*"

"What—? Oh." Suds straightened and rubbed his eyes. "Yes?"

"One of your young men has asked Giselle out for a walk. We have pressure suits, of course. But is it safe to promenade about this area?" She paused. "M'sieur, *please!*"

"What?" Suds shook his head. He tore his eyes away from the yellow dress and glanced at a head suddenly thrust in through the hatch. The head belonged to Relke. It saw Brodanovitch and withdrew in haste, but Suds made no sign of recognition. He blinked at Madame again.

"M'sieur, is it safe?"

"What? Oh. I suppose it is." He gulped his brandy and poured another.

Mme. d'Annecy spoke briefly to the girl, who, after a hasty *merci* and a nod at Suds went off to join Relke outside. When they were gone, Madame smilingly offered her pen to the engineer. Suds stared at it briefly, shook his head, and helped himself to another brandy. He gulped it and reached for his helmet. Mme. d'Annecy snapped her fingers suddenly and went to a locker near the bulkhead. She came back with a quart bottle.

"M'sieur will surely accept a small token?" She offered the bottle for his inspection. "It is Mumms 2064, a fine year. Take it, M'sieur. Or do you not care for champagne? It is our only bottle, and what is one bottle of wine for such a crowd? Take it—or would you prefer the brandy?"

Suds blinked at the gift while he fastened his helmet and clamped it. He seemed dazed. She held the bottle out to him and smiled hopefully. Suds accepted it absentmindedly, nodded at her, and stepped into the airlock. The hatch slid closed.

Mme. d'Annecy started back toward her counting table. The alarm bell burst into a sudden brazen clamor. She looked back. A red warning signal flashed balefully. Henri burst in from the corridor, eyed the bell and the light, then charged toward the airlock. The gauge by the hatch showed zero pressure. He pressed a starter button, and a meter hummed to life. The pressure needle crept upward. The bell and the light continued a frenetic complaint. The motor stopped. Henri glanced at the gauge, then swung open the hatch. "*Allons! Ma foi, quelle merde!*"

Mme. d'Annecy came to peer around him into the small cubicle. Her subsequent shriek penetrated to the farthest corridors. Suds Brodanovitch had missed his last chance to become a stockholder.

"It wasn't yo' fault, Ma'am," said Lije Henderson a few minutes later as they half-led, half-carried her to her compartment. "He knew beetuh than to step outside with that bottle of booze. You didn't know. You couldn' be 'spected to know. But he been heah long enough to know—a man make one mistake, thass all. BLOOIE."

Blooie was too graphic to suit Madame; she sagged and began retching.

"C'mon, Ma'am, less get you in yo' hammock." They carried her into her quarters, eased her into bed and stepped back out on the catwalk.

Lije mopped his face, leaned against a tension member, and glanced at

Joe. "Now how come you s'pose he had that bottle of fizzling giggle water up close to his helmet that way, Joe?"

"I don't know. Reading the label, maybe."

"He sho' muss have had something on his mine."

"Well, it's gone now."

"Yeah. BLOOIE. Man!"

Relke had led the girl out through the lock in the reactor nacelle in order to evade Brodanovitch and a possible command to return to camp. They sat in Novotny's runabout and giggled cozily together at the fuzzy map of Earth that floated in the darkness above them. On the ship's fuselage, the warning light over the airlock hatch began winking, indicating that the lock was in use. The girl noticed it and nudged him. She pointed at the light.

"Somebody coming out," Relke muttered. "Maybe Suds. We'd better get out of here." He flipped the main switch and started the motor. He was backing onto the road when Giselle caught his arm.

"Beel! Look at the light!"

He glanced around. It was flashing red.

"Malfunction signal. Compressor trouble, probably. It's nothing. Let's take a ride. Joe won't care." He started backing again.

"Poof!" she said suddenly.

"What?"

"Poof. It opened, and *poof*—" She puckered her lips and blew a little puff of steam in the cold air to show him. "So. Like smoke."

He turned the car around in the road and looked back again. The hatch had closed. There was no one on the ladder. "Nobody came out."

"*Non.* Just poof."

He edged the car against the trolley rails, switched to autosteering, and let it gather speed.

"Beel?"

"Yeah, kid?"

"Where you taking me?"

He caught the note of alarm in her voice and slowed down again. She had come on a dare after several drinks, and the drinks were wearing off. The landscape was frighteningly alien, and the sense of falling into bottomlessness was ever-present.

"You want to go back?" he asked gloomily.

"I don't know. I don't like it out here."

"You said you wanted some ground under your feet."

"But it doesn't feel like ground when you walk on it."

"Rather be inside a building?"

She nodded eagerly.

"That's where we're going."

"To your camp?"

"God, no! I'm planning to keep you to myself."

She laughed and snuggled closer to him. "You can't. Madame d'Annecy will not permit—"

"Let's talk about something else," he grunted quickly.

"OK. Let's talk about Monday."

"Which Monday?"

"Next Monday. It's my birthday. When is it going to be Monday, Bill?"

"You said *Bill*."

"Beel? That's your name, isn't eet? Weeliam Q. Relke, who weel not tell me what ees the Q?"

"But you said *Bill*."

She was silent for a moment. "OK, I'm a phony," she muttered. "Does the inquisition start now?"

He could feel her tighten up, and he said nothing. She waited stiffly for a time. Gradually she relaxed against him again. "When's it going to be Monday?" she murmured.

"When's it going to be Monday where?"

"Here, anywhere, silly!"

He laughed. "When will it be Monday all over the universe?"

She thought for a moment. "Oh. Like time zones. OK, when will it be Monday here?"

"It won't. We just have periods, hitches, and shifts. Fifty shifts make a hitch, two hitches make a period. A period's from sunrise to sunrise. Twenty-nine and a half days. But we don't count days. So I don't know when it'll be Monday."

It seemed to alarm her. She sat up. "Don't you even have *hours*?" She looked at her watch and jiggled it, listened to it.

"Sure. Seven hours in a shift. We call them hours, anyhow. Forty-five seconds longer than an Earth hour."

She looked up through the canopy at the orb of Earth. "When it's Monday on Earth, it'll be Monday here too," she announced flatly.

Relke laughed. "OK, we'll call it that."

"So when will it start being Monday on Earth?"

"Well, it'll start at twenty-four different times, depending on where you are. Maybe more than twenty-four. It's August. Some places, they set the clocks ahead an hour in Summer."

She looked really worried.

"You take birthdays pretty seriously?" he asked.

"Only this one. I'll be—" She broke off and closed her mouth.

"Pick a time zone," Relke offered, "and I'll try to figure out how long until Monday starts. Which zone? Where you'd be now, maybe?"

She shook her head.

"Where you were born?"

"That would be—" She stopped again. "Never mind. Forget it." She sat brooding and watching the moonscape.

Relke turned off the road at the transformer station. He pulled up beside a flat-roofed cubicle the size of a sentry-box. Giselle looked at it in astonishment.

"That's a building?" she asked.

"That's an entrance. The 'building's' underground. Come on, let's seal up."

"What's down there?"

"Just a transformer vault and living quarters for a substation man."

"Somebody *lives* down there?"

"Not yet. The line's still being built. They'll move somebody in when the trolley traffic starts moving."

"What do we want to go down there for?"

He looked at her forlornly. "You'd rather go back to the ship?"

She seemed to pull herself together professionally. She laughed and put her arms around him and whispered something in French against his ear. She kissed him hard, pressed her forehead against his, and grinned. "C'mon, babee! Let's go downstairs."

Relke felt suddenly cold inside. He had wanted to see what it felt like to be alone with a woman again in a quiet place, away from the shouting howling revelry that had been going on aboard the ship. Now he knew what it was going to feel like. It was going to feel counterfeit. "Christ!" he grunted angrily. "Let's go back!" He reached roughly around her and cut on the switch again. She recoiled suddenly and gaped at him as he started the motor and turned the bug around.

"Hey!" She was staring at him oddly, as if seeing him for the first time.

Relke kept his face averted and his knuckles were white on the steering bar. She got up on her knees on the seat and put her hands on his shoulders. "Bill. Good Lord, you're *crying!*"

He choked out a curse as the bug hit the side of the cut and careened around on the approach to the road. He lost control, and the runabout went off the approach and slid slowly sideways down a gentle slope of crushed-lava fill. A sharp clanking sound came from the floor plates.

"Get your suit sealed!" he yelled. "Get it sealed!"

The runabout lurched to a sudden stop. The cabin pressure stayed up. He sat panting for a moment, then started the motor. He let it inch ahead and tugged at the steering bar. It was locked. The bug crept in an arc, and the clanking resumed. He cut off the motor and sat cursing softly.

"What's wrong?"

"Broke a link and the tread's fouled. We'll have to get out."

She glanced at him out of the corner of her eye. He was glowering. She looked back toward the sentrybox entrance to the substation and smiled thoughtfully.

It was chilly in the vault, and the only light came from the indicator lamps on the control board. The pressure gauge inside the airlock indicated only eight pounds of air. The construction crew had pumped it up to keep some convection currents going around the big transformers, but they hadn't planned on anyone breathing it soon. He changed the mixture controls, turned the barostat up to twelve pounds, and listened to the compressors start up. When he turned around, Giselle was taking off her suit and beginning to pant.

"*Hey*, stay in that thing!" he shouted.

His helmet muffled his voice, and she looked at him blankly. "*What?*" she called. She was gasping and looking around in alarm.

Relke sprinted a few steps to the emergency rack and grabbed a low pressure walk-around bottle. When he got back, she was getting blue and shaking her head drunkenly. He cracked the valve on the bottle and got the hose connection against her mouth. She nodded quickly and sucked on it. He went back to watch the gauges. He found the overhead lighting controls and turned them on. Giselle held her nose and anxiously sipped air from the bottle. He nodded reassuringly at her. The construction crews had left the substation filled with nitrogen-helium mixture, seeing no reason to add rust-producing moisture and oxygen until someone moved into the place; she had been breathing inert gases, nothing more.

When the partial oxygen pressure was up to normal, he left the control panel and went to look for the communicator. He found the equipment, but it was not yet tied into the line. He went back to tell the girl. Still sipping at the bottle, she watched him with attentive brown eyes. It was the gaze of a child, and he wondered about her age. Aboard ship, she and the others had seemed impersonal automata of Eros; painted ornaments and sleekly functional decoys designed to perform stereotyped rituals of enticement and excarnation of desire, swiftly, lest a customer be kept waiting. But here in stronger light, against a neutral background, he noticed suddenly that she was a distinct individual. Her lipstick had smeared. Her dark hair kept spilling out in tangled wisps from beneath a leather cap with fleece ear flaps.

She wore a pair of coveralls, several sizes too large and rolled up about the ankles. With too much rouge on her solemnly mischievous face, she looked ready for a role in a girls' school version of *Chanticler.*

"You can stop breathing out of the can," he told her. "The oxygen pressure's OK now."

She took the hose from her mouth and sniffed warily. "What was the matter? I was seeing spots."

"It's all right now."

"It's cold in this place. Are we stuck here?"

"I tried to call Joe, but the set's not hooked up. He'll come looking for us."

"Isn't there any heat in here? Can't you start a fire?"

He glanced down at the big 5,000 kva transformers in the pit beyond the safety rail. The noise of corona discharge was very faint, and the purr of thirty-two cycle hum was scarcely audible. With no trucks drawing power from the trolley, the big pots were cold. Normally, eddy current and hysteresis losses in the transformers would keep the station toast-warm. He glanced at a thermometer. It read slightly under freezing: the ambient temperature of the subsurface rock in that region.

"Let's try the stationman's living quarters," he grunted. "They usually furnish them fancy, as bunk tanks go. Man has to stay by himself out here, they want to keep him sane."

A door marked PRIVATE flipped open as they approached it. A cheery voice called out: *"Hi, Bo. Rugged deal, ain't it?"*

Giselle started back in alarm. "Who's there?"

Relke chuckled. "Just a recorded voice. Back up, I'll show you."

They moved a few paces away. The door fell closed. They approached it again. This time a raucous female squawked at them: *"Whaddaya mean coming home at this hour? Lemme smell your breath."*

Giselle caught on and grinned. "So he won't get lonesome?"

"Partly, and partly to keep him a little sore. The stationmen hate it, but that's part of the idea. It gives them something to talk back to and throw things at."

They entered the apartment. The door closed itself, the lights went on. Someone belched, then announced: *"I get just as sick of looking at you as you do looking at me, button head. Go take a bath."*

Relke flushed. "It can get pretty rough sometimes. The tapes weren't edited for mixed company. Better plug your ears if you go in the bathroom."

Giselle giggled. "I think it's cute."

He went into the kitchenette and turned on all the burners of the electric range to help warm the place. "Come stand next to the oven," he called, "until I see if the heat pumps are working." He opened the oven door. A libidinous purr came from within.

"*Dah-ling, now why bother with breakfast when you can have meee?*" He glanced up at Giselle.

"I didn't say it," she giggled, but posed invitingly.

Relke grinned and accepted the invitation.

"You're not crying now," she purred as he released her.

He felt a surge of unaccountable fury, grunted, "Excuse me," and stalked out to the transformer vault. He looked around for the heat pumps, failed to find them, and went to lean on the handrail over-looking the pit. He stood there with his fists in his pockets, vaguely anguished and enraged for no reason he understood. For a moment he had been too close to feeling at home, and that brought up the wrath somehow. After a couple of minutes he shook it off and went back inside.

"Hey, I wasn't teasing you," Giselle told him.

"What?"

"About crying."

"Listen," he said irritably, "did you ever see a Looney or a spacer without leaky eyes? It's the glare, that's all."

"Is that it? Huh—want to know something? I can't cry. That's funny. You're a man and you can cry, but I can't."

Relke watched her grumpily while she warmed her behind at the oven. *She's not more than fifteen*, he decided suddenly. It made him a little queasy. *Come on, Joe, hurry.*

"You know," she went on absently, "when I was a little girl, I got mad at . . . at somebody, and I decided I was never going to cry anymore. I never did, either. And you know what?—now I can't. Sometimes I try and I try, but I just *can't.*" She spread her hands to the oven, tilted them back and forth, and watched the way the tendons worked as she stiffened her fingers. She seemed to be talking to her hands. "Once I used an onion. To cry, I mean. I cut an onion and rubbed some of it on a handkerchief and laid the handkerchief over my eyes. I cried that time, all right. That time I couldn't stop crying, and nobody could make me stop. They were petting me and scolding me and shaking me and trying to give me smelling salts, but I just couldn't quit. I blubbered for two days. Finally Mother Bernarde had to call the doctor to give me a sedative. Some of the sisters were taking cold towels and—"

"Sisters?" Relke grunted.

Giselle clapped a hand to her mouth and shook her head five or six times, very rapidly. She looked around at him. He shrugged.

"So you were in a convent."

She shook her head again.

"So what if you were?" He sat down with his back to her and pretended to ignore her. She was dangerously close to that state of mind which precedes the telling of a life history. He didn't want to hear it; he already knew it. So she was in a nunnery; Relke was not surprised. Some people had to polarize themselves. If they broke free from one pole, they had to seek its opposite. People with no middle ground. Black, or if not black, then white, never gray. Law, or criminality. God, or Satan. The cloister, or a whorehouse. Eternally a choice of all or nothing-at-all, and they couldn't see that they made things that way for themselves. They set fire to every bridge they ever crossed—so that even a cow creek became a Rubicon, and every crossing was on a tightrope.

You understand that too well, don't you, Relke? he asked himself bitterly. There was Fran and the baby, and there wasn't enough money, and so you had to go and burn a bridge—a 238,000-mile bridge, with Fran on the other side. And so, after six years on Luna, there would be enough money; but there wouldn't be Fran and the baby. And so, he had signed another extended contract, and the moon was going to be home for a long long time. *Yeh, you know about burned bridges, all right, Relke.*

He glanced at Giselle. She was glaring at him.

"If you're waiting for me to say something," she snapped, "you can stop waiting. I don't have to tell you anything."

"I didn't ask you anything."

"I was just a novice. I didn't take permanent vows."

"All *right.*"

"They wouldn't let me. They said I was—unstable. They didn't think I had a calling."

"Well, you've got one now. Stop crawling all over me like I said anything. I didn't ask you any questions."

"You gave me that pious look."

"Oh, garbage!" He rolled out of the chair and loped off to the room. The stationman's quarters boasted its own music system and television (permanently tuned to the single channel that broadcast a fairly narrow beam aimed at the lunar stations). He tried the television first, but solar interference was heavy.

"Maybe it'll tell us when it's going to be Monday," she said, coming to watch him from the doorway.

He gave her a sharp look, then softened it. The stove had warmed the kitchen, and she had stepped out of the baggy coveralls. She was still wearing the yellow dress, and she had taken a moment to comb her hair. She leaned against the side of the doorway, looking very young but excessively female. She had that lost pixie look and a tropical climate tan too.

"Why are you looking at me that way?" she asked. "Is this all we're going to do? I mean, just wait around until somebody comes? Can't we dance or something?" She did a couple of skippity steps away from the door jamb and rolled her hips experimentally. One hip was made of India rubber. "Say! Dancing ought to be fun in this crazy gravity." She smirked at him and posed alluringly.

Relke swallowed, reddened, and turned to open the selector cabinet. *She's only a kid, Relke.* He paused, then dialed three selections suitable for dancing. *She's only a kid, damn it!* He paused again, then dialed a violin concerto. *A kid—back home they'd call her "jail bait."* He dialed ten minutes' worth of torrid Spanish guitar. *You'll hate yourself for it, Relke.* He shuddered involuntarily, dialed one called *The Satyricon of Lily Brown, an orgy in New African Jazz (for adults only).*

He glanced up guiltily. She was already whirling around the room with an imaginary partner, dancing to the first selection.

Relke dialed a tape of Palestrina and some plainchant, but left it for last. Maybe it would neutralize the rest.

She snuggled close and they tried to keep time to the music—not an easy task, with the slow motion imposed by low gravity mismatched to the livelier rhythms of dancing on Earth. Two attempts were enough. Giselle flopped down on the bunk.

"What's that playing now, Bill?"

"Sibelius. Concerto for Something and Violin. I dunno."

"Bill?"

"Yeah."

"Did I make you mad or something?"

"No, but I don't think—" He turned to look at her and stopped talking. She was lying on her back with her hands behind her head and her legs cocked up, balancing her calf on her other knee and watching her foot wiggle. She was lithe and brown and . . . ripe.

"Damn," he muttered.

"Bill?"

"Uh?"

She wrinkled her nose at him and smiled. "Don't you even know what you wanted to come over here for?"

Relke got up slowly and walked to the light switch. He snapped it.

"*Oh, dahling!*" said a new voice in the darkness. "*What if my husband comes home!*"

After Sibelius came the Spanish guitar. The African jazz was wasted.

. . .

Relke sat erect with a start. Giselle still slept, but noises came from the other room. There were voices, and a door slammed closed. Shuffling footsteps, a muffled curse. "Who's there?" he yelled. "Joe?"

The noises stopped, but he heard the hiss of someone whispering. He nudged the girl awake with one elbow. The record changer clicked, and the soft chant of an *Agnus Dei* came from the music system.

"Oh, God! It's Monday!" Giselle muttered sleepily.

"A dame," grunted a voice in the next room.

"Who's there?" Relke called again.

"We brought you some company." The voice sounded familiar. A light went on in the other room. "Set him down over here, Harv."

Relke heard rattling sounds and a chair scraped back. They dumped something into the chair. Then the bulky silhouette of a man filled the doorway. "Who's in here, anyhow?" He switched on the lights. The man was Larkin. Giselle pulled a blanket around herself and blinked sleepily.

"Is it Monday?" she asked.

A slow grin spread across Larkin's face. "Hey Harv!" he called over his shoulder. "Look what we pulled out of the grab bag! Come look at lover boy. . . . Now, Harv—is that sweet? Is that romantic?"

Kunz looked over Larkin's shoulder. "Yuh. Real homey, ain't it. Hiyah, Rat. Lookit that cheese he's got with him. Some cheese. Round like a provolone, huh? Hiyah, cheesecake, know you're in bed with a rat?"

Giselle glanced questioningly at Relke. Relke was surveying the tactical situation. It looked unpromising. Larkin laughed.

"Look at him, Harv—wondering where he left his shiv. What's the matter, Relke? We make you nervous?" He stepped inside, Kunz followed.

Relke stood up in bed and backed against the wall. "Get out of the way," he grunted at Giselle.

"Look at him!" Larkin gloated. "Getting ready to kick. You planning to kick somebody, Sonny?"

"Stay back!" he snapped. "Get out of here, Giselle!"

"*A l'abri? Oui*—" She slid off the bed and darted for the door. Kunz grabbed at her, but she slipped past. She stopped in the doorway and backed up a step. She stared into the next room. She put her hand to her mouth. "Oh! *Oh!*" she yelped. Larkin and Kunz glanced back at her. Relke lunged off the bed. He smashed against Larkin, sent him sprawling into Kunz. He dodged Giselle and sprinted for the kitchen and the cutlery rack. He made it a few steps past the door before he saw what Giselle had seen. Something was sitting at the table, facing the door. Relke stopped in his tracks and began backing away. The something at the table was a blistered caricature of a man, an icy frost-figure in a deflated pressure suit. Its mouth was open, and the stomach had been forced up through . . . He closed his eyes. Relke had seen men blown out, but it hadn't gotten any pleasanter to look at since the last time.

"Get him, Harv!"

They pinned his arms from behind. "Heading for a butcher knife, Relke?" He heard a dull crack and felt his head explode. The room went pink and hazy.

"That's for grabbing glass on us the other day, Sonny."

"Don't mess him up too much, Lark. The dame's here."

"I won't mess him up. I'll be real clean about it."

The crack came again, and the pink haze quivered with black flashes.

"That's for ratting on the Party, Relke."

Dimly he heard Giselle screaming at them to stop it.

"Take that little bitch in the other room and play house with her, Harv. I'll work on Sonny awhile, and then we'll trade around. Don't wear her out."

"Let go," she yelled. "Take your hands off—listen, I'll go in there with you if you'll quit beating him. Now stop—"

Another crack. The pink haze flew apart, and blackness engulfed him. Time moved ahead in jerks for awhile. First he was sitting at the table across from the corpse. Larkin was there too, dealing himself a hand of solitaire. Loud popular music blared from the music system, but he could hear Kunz laughing in the next room. Once Giselle's voice cried out in protest. Relke moved and groaned. Larkin looked his way.

"Hey, Harv—he's awake. It's your turn."

"I'm busy," Kunz yelled.

"Well, hurry up. Brodanovitch is beginning to thaw."

Relke blinked at the dead man. "Who? Him? Brodan—" His lips were swollen, and it was painful to talk.

"Yeah, that's Suds. Pretty, isn't he? You're going to look like that one of these days, kid."

"You—killed—Suds?"

Larkin threw back his head and laughed. "Hey, Harv, hear that? He thinks we killed Suds."

"What happened to him, then?"

Larkin shrugged. "He walked into an airlock with a bottle of champagne. The pressure went down quick, the booze blew up in his face, and there sits Suds. A victim of imprudence, like you. Sad looking schlemazel, isn't he?"

"Wha'd you bring him here for?"

"You know the rules, Sonny. A man gets blown out, they got to look him over inch by inch, make sure it wasn't murder."

Giselle cried out again in protest. Relke started to his feet, staggering dizzily. Larkin grabbed him and pushed him down.

"Hey, Harv! He's getting frisky. Come take over. The gang'll be rolling in pretty quick."

Kunz came out of the bunkroom. Larkin sprinted for the door as Giselle tried to make a run for it. He caught her and dragged her back. He pushed her into the bunkroom, went in after her, and closed the door. Relke lunged at Kunz, but a judo cut knocked numbness into the side of his neck and sent him crashing against the wall.

"Relke, get wise," Harv growled. "This'll happen every now and then if you don't join up."

The lineman started to his feet. Kunz kicked him disinterestedly. Relke groaned and grabbed his side.

"We got no hard feelings, Relke. . . ." He chopped his boot down against the back of Relke's neck. "You can join the Party any time."

Time moved ahead in jerks again.

Once he woke up. Brodanovitch was beginning to melt, and the smell of brandy filled the room. There were voices and chair scrapings and after a while somebody carried Brodanovitch out. Relke lay with his head against the wall and kept his eyes closed. He assumed that if the apartment contained a friend, he would not still be lying here on the floor; so he remained motionless and waited to gather strength.

"So that's about the size of it," Larkin was telling someone. "Those dames are apt to be dynamite if they let them into Crater City. We've got enough steam whipped up to pull off the strike, but what if that canful of cat meat walks in on Copernicus about sundown? Who's going to have their mind on politics?"

"Hell, Lark," grunted a strange voice. "Parkeson'll never let them get in town."

"No? Don't be too damn sure. Parkeson's no idiot. He knows trouble's coming. Hell, he could *invite* them to Crater City, pretend he's innocent as a lamb, just didn't know what they are, but take credit for them being there."

"Well, what can we do about it?"

"Cripple the ship."

"Wha-a-at?"

"Cripple that ship. Look, there's nothing else we can do on our own. We've got no orders from the Party. Right before we break camp, at sundown, we cripple the ship. Something they can't fix without help from the base."

"Leave them *stuck* out here?"

"Only for a day or two. Till the Party takes over the base. Then *we* send a few wagons out here after dark and pick up the wenches. Who gets credit for dames showing up? The Party. Besides, it's the only thing we dare do without orders. We can't be sure what'd happen if Parkeson walked in with a bunch of Algerian whores about the time the show's supposed to start. And says, 'Here, boys, look what Daddy brought.'"

"Parkeson hasn't got the guts."

"The hell he hasn't. He'd say *that* out of one side of his mouth. Out of the other side, he'd be dictating a vigorous protest to the WP for allowing such things to get clearance for blasting off, making it sound like they're at fault. That's just a guess. We've got to keep those women out of Crater City until we're sure, though. And there's only one way; cripple the ship."

There were five or six voices in the discussion, and Relke recognized enough of them to understand dimly that a cell meeting was in progress. His mind refused to function clearly, and at times the voices seemed to be speaking in senseless jargon, although the words were plain enough. His head throbbed and he had bitten a piece out of the end of his tongue. He felt as if he were lying stretched out on a bed of jagged rocks, although there was only the smooth floor under his battered person.

Giselle cried out from the next room and beat angrily on the door.

Quite mindlessly, and as if his body were being directed by some whimsical puppet master, Relke's corpse suddenly clambered to its feet and addressed itself to the startled conspirators.

"Goddam it, gentlemen, can't you let the lady out to use the crapper?"

They hit him over the head with a jack handle.

He woke up again. This time he was in the bunkroom. A faint choking sound made him look up. Giselle sat on the foot of the bed, legs tightly crossed, face screwed up. She was trying to cry.

"Use an onion," he told her thickly, and sat up. "What's the matter?"

"It's Monday now."

"Where are they?"

"They left. We're locked in."

He fell back with a groan. A stitch in his side felt like a broken rib. He turned his face to the wall. "What's so great about Monday?" he muttered.

"Today the others are taking their vows."

When he woke up again, Novotny was watching him from the foot of the bed. The girl was gone. He sat up and fell back with a groan.

"Fran," he said.

"It wasn't Fran, it was a hustler," said Joe. "I had Beasley take her back. Who busted you?"

"Larkin and Kunz."

"It's a good thing."

"What?"

"They saved me the trouble. You ran off with the jeep."

"Sorry."

"You don't have to be sorry. Just watch yourself, that's all."

"I wanted to see what it was like, Joe."

"What? Playing house with a wench?"

He nodded.

"What was it like?"

"I don't know."

"You woke up calling her Fran."

"I did?"

"Yah. Before you start feeling that way, you better ask Beasley what they did together on the rug while you were asleep, Romeo."

"What?"

"She really knows some tricks. Mme. d'Annecy really educates her girls. You been kissing and cooing with her, Relke?"

"I'm sick, Joe. Don't."

"By the way, you better not go back. The Madame's pretty sore at you."

"Why?"

"For keeping the wench gone so long. There was going to be a show. You know, a circus. Giselle was supposed to be in it. You might say she had the lead role."

"Who?"

"Giselle. Still feel like calling her Fran?—Hey! if you're going to vomit, get out of bed."

Relke staggered into the latrine. He was gone a long time.

"Better hurry up," Novotny called. "Our shift goes on in half an hour."

"I can't go on, Joe."

"The hell you can't. Unless you want to be sent up N.L.D. You know what they do to N.L.D. cases."

"You wouldn't report me N.L.D."

"The hell I wouldn't, but I don't have to."

"What do you mean?"

"Parkeson's coming, with a team of inspectors. They're probably already here, and plenty sore."

"About the ship? The women?"

"I don't know. If the Commission hears about those bats, there'll be hell to pay. But who'll pay it is something else."

Relke buried his face in his hands and tried to think. "Joe, listen. I only half remember, but . . . there was a cell meeting here."

"When?"

"After Larkin and Kunz worked me over. Some guys came in, and . . ."

"Well?"

"It's foggy. Something about Parkeson taking the women back to Crater City."

"Hell, that's a screwy idea. Who thinks that?"

Relke shook his head and tried to think. He came out of the latrine mopping his face on a towel. "I'm trying to remember."

Joe got up. "All right. Better get your suit. Let's go pull cable."

The lineman breathed deeply a few times and winced at the effect. He went to get his suit out of the hangar, started the routine safety check, and stopped halfway through. "Joe, my suit's been cut."

Novotny came to look. He pinched the thick corded plastic until the incision opened like a mouth. "Knife," he grunted.

"Those sons of—"

"Yah." He fingered the cut. "They meant for you to find it, though. It's too conspicuous. It's a threat."

"Well, I'm fed up with their threats. I'm going to—"

"You're not going to do anything, Relke. *I'm* going to do it. Larkin and Kunz have messed around with my men one time too often."

"What have you got in mind, Joe?"

"Henderson and I will handle it. We'll go over and have a little conference with them, that's all."

"Why Henderson? Look, Joe, if you're going to stomp them, it's *my* grudge, not Lije's."

"That's just it. If I take you, it's a grudge. If Lije and I do it, it's just politics. I've told you guys before—leave the politics to me. Come on, we'll get you a suit from the emergency locker."

They went out into the transformer vault. Two men wearing blue armbands were bending over Brodanovitch's corpse. One of them was fluently cursing unknown parties who had brought the body to a warm place and allowed it to thaw.

"Investigating team," Novotny muttered. "Means Parkeson is already here." He hiked off toward the emergency lockers.

"Hey, are you the guy that left this stiff near a stove?" one of the investigators called out to Relke.

"No, but I'll be glad to rat on the guys that did, if it'll get them in trouble," the lineman told him.

"Never mind. You can't hang them for being stupid."

"What are you going to do with *him?*" Relke asked, nodding at the corpse.

"Promote him to supervisory engineer and give him a raise."

"Christ but they hire smart boys for the snooper team, don't they? What's your I.Q., friend? I bet they had to breed you to get you smart."

The checker grinned. "You looking for an argument, Slim?"

Relke shook his head. "No, I just asked a question."

"We're going to take him back to Copernicus and bury him, friend. It takes a lot of imagination to figure that out, doesn't it?"

"If he was a class three laborer, you wouldn't take him back to Copernicus. You wouldn't even bury him. You'd just chuck him in a fissure and dynamite the lip."

The man smiled. Patient cynicism was in his tone. "But he's *not* a class three laborer, Slim. He's Mister S. K. Brodanovitch. Does that make everything nice and clear?"

"Sure. Is Parkeson around?"

The checker glanced up and snickered. "You're a chum of his, I guess? Hear that, Clyde? We're talking to a wheel."

Relke reddened. "Shove it, chum. I just wondered if he's here."

"Sure, he's out here. He went over to see that flying bordello you guys have been hiding out here."

"What's he going to do about it?"

"Couldn't say, friend."

Novotny came back with an extra suit.

"Joe, I just remembered something."

"Tell me about it on the way back."

They suited up and went out to the runabout. Relke told what he could remember about the cell meeting.

"It sounds crazy in a way," Novotny said thoughtfully. "Or maybe it doesn't. It *could* mess up the Party's strike plans if Parkeson brought those women back before sundown. The men want women back on the moon project. If they can get women bootlegged in, they won't be quite so ready to start a riot on the No Work Without a Wife theme."

"But Parkeson'd get fired in a flash if—"

"If Parliament got wind of it, sure. Unless he raised the squawk later himself. UCOJE doesn't mention prostitution. Parkeson could point out that some national codes on Earth tolerate it. Nations with delegates in the Parliament, and with work teams on the moon. Take the African team at

Tycho. And the Japanese team. Parkeson himself is an Aussie. Whose law is he supposed to enforce?"

"You mean maybe they can't keep ships like that from visiting us?"

"Don't kid yourself. It won't last long. But maybe long enough. If it goes on long enough, and builds up, the general public will find out. You think that wouldn't cause some screaming back home?"

"Yeah. That'll be the end."

"I'm wondering. If there turns out to be a profit in it for whoever's backing d'Annecy, well—anything that brings a profit is pretty hard to put a stop to. There's only one sure way to stop it. Kill the demand."

"For women? Are you crazy, Joe?"

"They could bring in decent women. Women to marry. That'll stop it."

"But the kids. They can't have kids."

"Yeah, I know. That's the problem, and they've got to start solving it sometime. Hell, up to now, they haven't been trying to solve it. When the problem came up, and the kids were dying, everybody got hysterical and jerked the women back to Earth. That wasn't a solution, it was an evasion. The problem is growth-control—in low gravity. It ought to have a medical answer. If this d'Annecy dame gets a chance to keep peddling her wares under the counter, well—she'll force them to start looking for a solution."

"I don't know, Joe. Everybody said homosexuality would force them to start looking for it—after Doc Reiber made his survey. The statistics looked pretty black, but they didn't do anything about it except send us a shipful of ministers. The fairies just tried to make the ministers."

"Yeah, but this is different."

"I don't see how."

"Half the voters are women."

"So? They didn't do anything about homosex—"

"Relke, wise up. Listen, did you ever see a couple of Lesbians necking in a bar?"

Relke snickered. "Sure, once or twice."

"How did you feel about it?"

"Well, this once was kind of funny. You see, this one babe had on—"

"Never mind. You thought it was funny. Do you think it's funny the way MacMillian and Wickers bill and coo?"

"That gets pretty damn nauseating, Joe."

"Uh-huh, but the Lesbians just gave you a giggle. Why?"

"Well, I don't know, Joe, it's—"

"I'll tell you why. You like dames. You can understand other guys liking dames. You like dames so much that you can even understand two dames liking each other. You can see what they see in each other. But it's incongruous, so it's funny. But you *can't* see what two fairies see in each other, so that just gives you a bellyache. Isn't that it?"

"Maybe, but what's that got to do with the voters?"

"Ever think that maybe a woman would feel the same way in reverse? A dame could see what MacMillian and Wickers see in each other. The dame might morally disapprove, but at the same time she could sympathize. What's more, she'd be plenty sure that she could handle that kind of competition if she ever needed to. She's a woman, and wotthehell, Wickers is only a substitute woman. It wouldn't worry her too much. Worry her morally, but not as a personal threat. Relke, Mme. d'Annecy's racket is a personal threat to the home girl and the womenfolk."

"I see what you mean."

"Half the voters are women."

Relke chuckled. "Migod, Joe, if Ellen heard about that ship . . ."

"Ellen?"

"My older sister. Old maid. Grim."

"You've got the idea. If Parkeson thinks of all this . . ." His voice trailed off. "When is Larkin talking about crippling that ship?"

"About sundown, why?"

"Somebody better warn the d'Annecy dame."

The cosmic gunfire had diminished. The Perseid shrapnel still pelted the dusty face of the plain, but the gram-impact-per-acre-second had dropped by a significant fraction, and with it fell the statisticians' estimate of dead men per square mile. There was an ion storm during the first half of B-shift, and the energized spans of high voltage cable danced with fluttering demon light as the trace-pressure of the lunar "atmosphere" increased enough to start a glow discharge between conductors. High current surges sucked at the line, causing the breakers to hiccup. The breakers tried the line three times, then left the circuit dead and waited for the storm to pass. The storm meant nothing to the construction crews except an increase in headset noise.

Parkeson's voice came drawling on the general call frequency, wading waist-deep through the interference caused by the storm. Relke leaned back against his safety strap atop the trusswork of the last tower and tried to listen. Parkeson was reading the Articles of Discipline, and listening was compulsory. All teams on the job had stopped work to hear him. Relke gazed across the plain toward the slender nacelles of the bird from Algiers in the distance. He had gotten used to the ache in his side where Kunz had kicked him, but it was good to rest for a time and watch the rocket and remember brown legs and a yellow dress. Properties of Earth. Properties belonging to the communion of humanity, from which fellowship a Looney was somehow cut off by 238,000 miles of physical separation.

"We've got a job to finish here," Parkeson was telling the men.

Why? What was in space that was worth the wanting? What followed from its conquest? What came of finishing the job?

Nothing.

Nothing.

Nothing. Nothing anybody ever dreamed of or hoped for.

Parkeson scolded on. "I know the question that's foremost in your minds," his voice continued, "but you'd better forget it. Let me tell you what happens if this line isn't finished by sundown. (But by God, it will be finished!) Listen, you wanted women. All right, now you've all been over to visit the uh—'affectionate institution'—and you got what you wanted; and now the work is behind schedule. Who gives a damn about the project, eh! I know what you're thinking. 'That's Parkeson's worry.' OK, so let's talk about what you're going to breathe for the next couple of periods. Let's talk about how many men will wind up in the psycho-respiratory ward, about the overload on the algae tanks. That's not your responsibility either, is it? You don't have to breathe and eat. Hell, let Nature take care of air and water, eh? Sure. Now look around. Take a good look. All that's between you and that hungry vacuum out there is ten pounds of man-made air and a little reinforced plastic. All that keeps you eating and drinking and breathing is that precarious life-cycle of ours at Copernicus. That plant-animal feedback loop is so delicately balanced that the biology team gets the cold shakes every time somebody sneezes or passes gas. It has to be constantly nursed. It has to be planned and kept on schedule. On Earth, Nature's a plenum. You can chop down her forests, kill off her deer and buffalo and fill her air with smog and hot isotopes; the worst you can do is cause a few new deserts and dust bowls, and make things a little unpleasant for a while.

"Up here, we've got a little bit of Nature cooped up in a bottle, and we're in the bottle too. We're cultured like mold on agar. The biology team has to chart the ecology for months in advance. It has to know the construction and survey teams are going to deliver exactly what they promise to deliver, and do it on schedule. If you don't deliver, the ecology gets sick. If the ecology gets sick, you get sick.

"Do you want another epidemic of the chokers like we had three years back? That's what'll happen if there's a work slowdown while everybody goes off on a sex binge at that ship. If the line isn't finished before sundown, the ecology gets bled for another two weeks to keep that mine colony going, and the colony can't return wastes to our cycle. Think it over, but think fast.

There's not much time. 'We all breathe the same air'—on Earth, that's just a political slogan. Here, we all breathe it or we all choke in it. How do you want it, men?"

Relke shifted restlessly on the tower. He glanced down at Novotny and the others who lounged around the foot of the steel skeleton listening to Parkeson. Lije caught his eye. He waved at Relke to haul up the hoist-bucket. Relke shook his head and gave him a thumbs-down. Henderson gestured insistently for him to haul it up. Relke reeled the bucket in. It was empty, but chalked on the sides and bottom was a note from Lije: "They toll me what L and K did to you and yr girl. I and Joe will take care of it, right after this sermon. You can spit on my fist first if you want. Lije."

Relke gave him a half-hearted screw-twist signal and let the bucket go. Revenge was no good, and vicarious revenge was worse than no good; it was hollow. He thought of asking Joe to forget it, but he knew Joe wouldn't listen. The pusher felt his own integrity was involved, and a matter of jurisdictional ethics: nobody can push my men around but me. It was gang ethics, but it seemed inevitable somehow. Where there was fear, men huddled in small groups and counted their friends on their fingers, and all else was Foe. In the absence of the family, there had to be the gang, and fear made it quarrelsome, jealous, and proud.

Relke leaned back against his strap and glanced up toward Earth. The planet was between quarter and half phase, for the sun was lower in the west. He watched it and tried to feel something more than a vague envy. Sometimes the heartsick nostalgia reached the proportions of idolatrous adoration of Gaea's orb overhead, only to subside into a grudging resentment of the gulf between worlds. Earth—it was a place where you could stop being afraid, a place where fear of suffocation was not, where fear of blowout was not, where nobody went berserk with the chokers or dreamed of poisoned air or worried about shorthorn cancer or burn blindness or meteoric dust or low-gravity muscular atrophy. A place where there was wind to blow your sweat away.

Watching her crescent, he felt again that vague anger of separation, that resentment against those who stayed at home, who had no cause for constant fear, who could live without the tense expectancy of sudden death haunting every moment. One of them was Fran, and another was the one who had taken her from him. He looked away quickly and tried to listen to the coordinator.

"This is no threat," Parkeson was saying. *"If the line isn't finished on time, then the consequences will just happen, that's all. Nobody's going to punish you, but there are a few thousand men back at the Crater who have to breathe air with you. If they have to breathe stink next period—because you*

guys were out having one helluva party with Madame d'Annecy's girls—you can figure how popular you'll be. That's all I've got to say. There's still time to get the work back on schedule. Let's use it."

Parkeson signed off. The new engineer who was replacing Brodanovitch gave them a brief pep-talk, implying that Parkeson was a skunk and would be forced to eat his own words before sundown. It was the old hard-guy-soft-guy routine: first a bawling-out and then a buttering-up. The new boss offered half of his salary to the first team to forge ahead of its own work schedule. It was not stated nor even implied that Parkeson was paying him back.

The work was resumed. After half an hour, the safety beeper sounded on all frequencies, and men switched back to general call. Parkeson and his party were already heading back toward Copernicus.

"Blasting operation at the next tower site will occur in ten minutes," came the announcement. *"Demol team requests safety clearance over all of zones two and three, from four forty to five hundred hours. There will be scatter-glass in both zones. Zone two is to be evacuated immediately, and all personnel in zone three take line-of-sight cover from the red marker. I repeat: there will be scatter-glass . . ."*

"That's us," said Novotny when it was over. "Everybody come on. Brax, Relke, climb down."

Braxton swore softly in a honey-suckle drawl. It never sounded like cursing, which it wasn't, but like a man marveling at the variety of vicissitudes invented by an ingenious universe for the bedevilment of men. "I sweah, when the angels ahn't shootin' at us from up in Perseus, it's the demol boys. Demol says froggie, and ev'body jumps. It gives 'em that suhtain feelin' of impohtance. Y'all know what I think? I got a thee-orry. I think weah all really dead, and they don't tell us it's hell weah in, because not tellin' us is paht of the tohture."

"Get off the damn frequency, Brax, and stay off!" Novotny snapped when the Alabaman released his mic button. "I've told you and Henderson before—either learn to talk fast, or don't talk on the job. If somebody had a slow leak, he'd be boiling blood before he could scream—with you using the frequency for five minutes to say 'yeah.'"

"*Mistuh* Novotny! My mothuh always taught me to speak slowly and de-stinct-ly. If you think that yo' Yankee upbringin' . . ."

Joe rapped on his helmet until he shut up, then beckoned to Henderson. "Lije, we got twenty minutes."

"Yeah, Joe, want to go see a couple of guys now?" He flashed white teeth and stared back toward the barrack train.

"Think we can handle it in twenty minutes?"

"I don't know. It seem like a short time to do a real good job of it, but maybe if we don't waste any on preliminary fisticuffin' . . ."

"Hell, they didn't waste any ceremony on Relke."

"Less go, then!" He grinned at Relke and held out his fist. "Spit on it?"

Relke shook his head. Henderson laughed. "Wanted to see if you'd go ptooey in your helmet."

"Come on, Lije. The rest of you guys find cover."

Relke watched the two of them lope off toward the rolling barracks. "Hey, Joe," he called after a few seconds.

The lopers stopped to look back. "Relke?"

"Yeah. Don't lose."

"What?"

"They'll say I sicced you. Don't lose."

"Don't worry." They loped again. The longer Relke watched them, the less he liked the idea. If they didn't do a pretty thorough job on Kunz and Larkin, things would be worse for Relke than if they did nothing at all. Then there was the movement to think about; he didn't know to what extent *they* looked out for their own.

Relke walked out of the danger zone and hiked across the hill where he could get a clear view of the rocket. He stopped for a while on the slope and watched four distant figures moving around on the ground beneath the towering ship. For a moment, he thought they were women, but then he saw that one of them was coiling mooring cable, and he knew they were ship's crew. What sort of men had the d'Annecy women been able to hire for such a job? he wondered.

He saw that they were getting ready to lift ship. *Lift ship!*

Relke was suddenly running toward them without knowing why. Whenever he topped a rise of ground and could see them, he tried calling them, but they were not using the project's suit frequency. Finally he found their voices on the seldom used private charter band, but they were speaking French.

One of the men looped a coil of cable over his shoulder and started up the ladder toward the lock. Relke stopped atop an outcropping. He was still two or three miles from the ship. The "isobar" valve system for the left knee of his suit had jammed, and it refused to take up the increased pressure caused by flexure. It was like trying to bend a fully inflated rubber tire, and he hobbled about for a moment with one leg stiff as a crutch.

"Listen!" he called on the p.c. frequency. "You guys at the ship. Can you hear me?" He was panting, and he felt a little panicky. The man on the ladder stopped climbing and looked around.

There was a staccato exchange in French.

"No, no! Over here. On the rock." He waved at them and jumped a few times. "Look toward the camp. On the rock."

They conversed heatedly among themselves for a time.

"Don't any of you speak English?" he begged.

They were silent for a moment. "Whoevair ees?" one of them ventured. "You conversation with wrong radio, M'sieur. Switch a button."

"No, no. I'm trying to call you . . ."

A carrier drowned him out.

"We close for business," the man said. "We go now." He started climbing again.

"Listen!" Relke yelled. "Ten thousand dollars. Everything."

"You crazy man."

"Look, it won't get you in any trouble. I've got plenty in the bank. I'll pay—"

The carrier cut him off again.

"You crazy. Get off the air. We do not go to Earth now."

"Wait! Listen! Tell Giselle . . . No, let me talk to her. Get her to use the radio. It's important."

"I tell you, we close for business now." The man climbed in the airlock. The others climbed up behind. They were jeering at him. This time it sounded like Arabic. He watched until they were all inside.

White fury lanced the ground and spread in a white sheet beneath the ship and roiled up in a tumult of dust and expanding gasses. It climbed on a white fan, gathering velocity. Relke could still make it out as a ship when its course began arcing away from the vertical. It was beginning a trajectory in the direction of Copernicus. When it was out of sight, he began trudging back toward the work site. He was nearly an hour overdue.

"Where you been?" Novotny asked him quietly after watching him hobble the last quarter of a mile in stony silence. He was squinting at the lineman with that faintly puzzled look that Relke recognized as a most ominous omen. The squint was lopsided because of a cut under one eye, and it looked like a chip was missing from a tooth.

Relke showed his stiff leg and bounced the heel against the ground a couple of times. "I walked too far, and the c.p. valves got jammed. Sorry, Joe."

"You don't have to be sorry. Let's see."

The pusher satisfied himself that the suit was malfunctioning. He waved the lineman toward the barrack train. "Go to supply and get it fixed. Get back on the double. You've slowed us down."

Relke paused. "You sore, Joe?"

"We're on duty. I don't get sore on duty. I save it up. Now—haul ass!"

Relke hobbled off. "What about . . . what you went for, Joe?" he called back. "What happened?"

"I told you to keep your nose out of politics!" the pusher snapped. "Never mind what happened."

Joe, Relke decided, was plenty sore. About something. Maybe about a beating that backfired. Maybe about Relke taking an hour awol. Either way, he was in trouble. He thought it over and decided that paying a bootleg ship ten thousand to take him back to Earth with them hadn't been such a hysterical whim after all.

But then he met Larkin in the supply wagon. Larkin was stretched out flat on his back, and a medic kept saying, "Who did it to you? Who did it to you?" and Larkin kept telling him to go to hell out of a mouth that looked like a piece of singed stew meat. Kunz was curled up on a blanket and looked even worse. He spat in his sleep and a bit of tooth rattled across the deck.

"Meanest bunch of bastards I ever saw," the clerk told Relke while he checked in the suit. "They don't even give you a chance. Here were these two guys sleeping in their bunks and not bothering anybody, and what do you think?"

"I quit thinking. What?"

"Somebody starts working them over. Wham. Don't even wake them up first. Just wham. You ever see anything like it? Mean, John, just mean. You can't even get a shift's sleep anymore. You better go to bed with a knife in your boot, John."

"It's Bill."

"Oh. What do you suppose makes a guy that mean anyway?"

"I don't know. Everybody's jumpy, I guess."

The clerk looked at him wisely. "There you have put your finger on it, John. Looney nerves. The jitters. Everybody's suit-happy." He leaned closer and lowered his voice. "You know how I tell when the camp's getting jittery?"

"Listen, check me out a suit. I've got to get back to the line."

"Now wait, this'll surprise you. I can tell better than the psych checkers when everybody's going on a slow panic. It's the sleeping bag liners."

"What?"

"The bed wetters, John. You'd be surprised how many grown men turn bed wetters about the middle of a hitch. At first, nobody. Then somebody gets killed on the line. The bag liners start coming in for cleaning. By the end of the hitch, the wash tank smells like a public lavatory, John. Not just the men, either. Some of the engineers. You know what I'm doing?"

"Look, Mack, the suit . . ."

"Not Mack. Frank. Look, I'll show you the chart." He got out a sheet of paper with a crudely drawn graph on it. "See how it goes? The peak? I've done ten of them."

"Why?"

The clerk looked at him blankly. "For the idea box, John. Didn't you know about the prizes? Doctor Esterhall ought to be glad to get information like this."

"Christ, they'll give you a medal, Charley. Now give me my damn suit before I get it myself. I'm due on the line."

"OK, OK. You got the jitters yourself, haven't you?" He went to get the suit. "I just happened to think," he called back. "If you've been turning in liners yourself, don't worry about me. I don't keep names, and I don't remember faces."

"You blab plenty, though," Relke grumbled to himself.

The clerk heard him. "No call to get sore, John."

"I'm not sore, I'm just in a hurry. If you want to beg for a stomping, it's nothing to me."

The clerk came back bristling. "Who's going to stomp?"

"The bed wetters, I guess." He started getting into the suit.

"Why? It's for science, isn't it?"

"Nobody likes to be watched."

"There you put your finger on it, John. It's the watching part that's worst. If they'd only quit watching us, or come out where we could see them! You know what I think? I think there's some of them among us. In disguise." The clerk smirked mysteriously at what-he-knew-but-wouldn't-tell.

Relke paused with a zipper half-way up. "Who do you mean—watching? Checkers?"

The clerk snorted and resumed what he had been doing when Relke entered: he was carefully taping his share of stock in Mme. d'Annecy's venture up on the wall among a display of pin-ups. "You know who I mean," he muttered.

"No, I don't."

"The ones that dug that mine, that's who."

"Aliens? Oh, bullspit."

"Yeah? You'll see. They're keeping an eye on us, all right. There's a guy on the African team that even talked to some of them."

"Nuts. He's not the first guy that ever talked to spooks. Or demons. Or saucer pilots. You don't have to be a Looney to be a lunatic."

That made the clerk sore, and he stomped off to his sanctum to brood. Relke finished getting into the suit and stepped into the airlock. Some guys had to personify their fear. If there was no danger, somebody must be responsible. They had to have an Enemy. Maybe it helped, believing in gremlins from beyond Pluto. It gave you something to hate when your luck was bad.

He met Joe just outside the lock. The pusher was waiting to get in.

"Hey, Pappy, I own up. I was goofing off awhile ago. If you want to be sore—" Relke stopped. Something was wrong. Joe was breathing hard, and he looked sick.

"Christ, I'm not sore! *Not now!*"

"What's wrong, Joe?"

The pusher paused in the hatchway. "Run on back to the line. Keep an eye on Braxton. I'm getting a jeep. Back in a minute." He went on inside and closed the hatch.

Relke trotted toward the last tower. After a while he could hear Braxton talking in spasms on the frequency. It sounded like sobbing. He decided it *was* sobbing.

"Theah just isn't any God," Bama was moaning. "Thea just couldn't be a God and be so mean. He was the bes' friend a man evah had, and he nevah did nothin' to deserve it. Oh, God, oh, God, why did it have to be *him*? I've done penance fo' what my gran'pa did to his, an' I been as color blind as any Yankee evah bohn, an' I love him like my own brother. Theah jus' can't be any God in Heaven, to treat a man that way, when he been so . . ." Braxton's voice broke down into incoherent sobbing.

There was a man lying on the ground beside the tower. Relke could see Benet bending over him. Benet was clutching a fistful of the man's suit. He crossed himself slowly and stood up. A safety team runabout skidded to a halt beside the tower, and three men piled out. Benet spread his hands at them in a wide shrug and turned his back.

"What happened?" Relke asked as he loped up to Beasley.

"Bama was welding. Lije walked over to ask him for a wrench or something. Bama turned around to get it, and Lije sat down on the strut with the hot weld."

"Blow out?"

"He wasn't that lucky. Call it a fast slowout."

Novotny drove up, saw the safety jeep, and started bellowing furiously at them.

"Take it easy, chum. We got here as quick as we could."

"Theah jus' can't be any God in Heaven . . ."

They got Henderson in the safety runabout. Novotny manufactured a hasty excuse to send Braxton off with them, for grief had obviously finished his usefulness for awhile. Everybody stood around in sickly silence and stared after the jeep.

"Benet, you know how to pray," Novotny muttered. "Say something, altar boy."

"Aw, Joe, that was fifteen years ago. I haven't lived right."

"Hell, who has? Go ahead."

Benet muttered for a moment and turned his back. "*In nomine Patris et Filii et Spiritus Sancti . . .*" He paused.

"Can't you pray in English?" Joe asked.

"We always said it in Latin. I only served at a few masses."

"Go ahead."

Benet prayed solemnly while they stood around with bowed heads and shuffled their boots in the dust. Nobody understood the words, not even Benet, but somehow it seemed important to listen.

"*Requiem aeternam dona ei, Domine. Et lux perpetua luceat . . .*"

Relke looked up slowly and let his eyes wander slowly across the horizon. There were still some meteorites coming in, making bright little winks of fire where they bit into the plain. Deadly stingers out of nowhere, heading nowhere, impartially orbiting, random as rain, random as death. The debris of creation. Relke decided Braxton was wrong. There was a God, all right, maybe personal, maybe not, but there was a God, and He wasn't mean. His universe was a deadly contraption, but maybe there wasn't any way to build a universe that wasn't a deadly contraption—like a square circle. He made the contraption and He put Man in it, and Man was a fairly deadly contraption himself. But the funny part of it was, there wasn't a damn thing the universe could do to a man that a man wasn't built to endure. He could even endure it when it killed him. And gradually he could get the better of it. It was the consistency of matched qualities—random mercilessness and human endurance—and it wasn't mean, it was a fair match.

"Poor Lije. God help him."

"All right," Novotny called. "Let's pull cable, men."

"Yeah, you know what?" said Beasley. "Those dames went to Crater City. The quicker we get the line finished, the quicker we get back. Damn Parkeson anyhow!"

"Hell, why do you think he let them go there, Beeze?" Tremini jeered. "So we'd work our butts off to finish quick, that's why. Parkeson's no idiot. If he'd sent them packing for somewhere else, maybe we'd finish, maybe we wouldn't."

"Cut the jawing. Somebody run down and get the twist out of that span before she kinks. Relke, start taking up slack."

Atop the steel truss that supported the pendulous insulators, the lineman began jacking up the slack line. He glanced toward the landing site where the ship had been, and it was hard to believe it had ever been there at all. A sudden improbable dream that had come and gone and left nothing behind. Nothing? Well, there was a share of stock . . .

"Hey, we're all capitalists!" Relke called.

Benet hooted. "Take your dividends out in trade."

"Listen, someday they'll let dames come here again and get married. That's one piece of community property you better burn first."

"That d'Annecy dame thought of everything."

"Listen, that d'Annecy dame is going to force an issue. She'll clean up, and a lot of guys will throw away small fortunes, but before it's over, they'll let women in space again. Now quit jawing, and let's get to work."

Relke glanced at the transformer station where he had taken the girl. He tried to remember what she looked like, but he got Fran's face instead. He tried to transmute the image into Giselle's, but it stayed Fran. Maybe he hadn't really seen Giselle at all. Maybe he had looked at her and seen Fran all along, but it had been a poor substitution. It had accomplished one thing, though. He felt sorry for Fran now. He no longer hated her. She had stuck it out a long time before there had been another guy. And it was harder for a wife on Earth than it was for a husband on Luna. She had to starve in the midst of plenty. He had only to deny himself what he couldn't get anyhow, or even see. She was the little girl with her nose against the bakery window. He was only fasting in the desert. It was easy; it put one beyond temptation. To fast in a banquet hall, one had to be holy. Fran wasn't holy. Relke doubted he'd want a wife who was holy. It could get damnably dull.

A quick glance at Earth told him it was still in the skyless vault. Maybe she'll come, if they ever let them come, he thought wistfully. Maybe the guy'll be a poor substitute, and she'll figure out who she's really married to, legal instruments not-withstanding. Maybe . . . O God, let her come! . . . women had no business on Luna, but if they didn't then neither did men, nor Man, who had to be a twosome in order to be recognizably human.

"Damn it, Relke, work that jack!" Joe yelled. "We got to build that line!"

Relke started cranking again, rocking his body to the rhythm of the jack, to the rhythm of echoes of thought. Got to build the line. Damn it, build the line. Got to build the line. Build the damn it line. The line was part of a living thing that had to grow. The line was yet another creeping of life across a barrier, a lungfish flopping from pool to pool, an ape trying to walk erect across still another treeless space. Got to build the line. Even when it kills you, got to build the line, the bloody endless line. The lineman labored on in silence. The men were rather quiet that shift.

Tlön, Uqbar, Orbis Tertius

TRANSLATED BY ALASTAIR REID

Borges was not only the finest Argentinian writer, but one of the finest literary talents of this century. An admirer of the works of Edgar Allan Poe and H. G. Wells, he often turned toward the fantastic in his writing. He introduced the first translations of Ray Bradbury in Argentina and emulated H. P. Lovecraft upon occasion. He was aware of contemporary science fiction but wrote short fiction that fit in no category but his own, which he called ficciones. *The first translation of his work into English appeared in* The Magazine of Fantasy & Science Fiction *and he was one of the writers often invoked in discussions during the New Wave. Of undoubted influence on SF, Borges's works transcend genre and should perhaps be compared, in this book, only to Calvino. Still, this story, of the discovery of worlds, belongs here.*

*　　*　　*

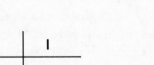

I

I owe the discovery of Uqbar to the conjunction of a mirror and an encyclopedia. The unnerving mirror hung at the end of a corridor in a villa on Calle Goana, in Ramos Mejía; the misleading encyclopedia goes by the name of *The Anglo-American Cyclopaedia* (New York, 1917), and is a literal if inadequate reprint of the 1902 *Encyclopaedia Britannica*. The whole affair happened some five years ago. Bioy Casares had dined with me that night and talked to us at length about a great scheme for writing a novel in the first person, using a narrator who omitted or corrupted what happened and who ran into various contradictions, so that only a handful of readers, a very small handful, would be able to decipher the horrible or banal reality behind the novel. From the far end of the corridor, the mirror was watching us; and we discovered, with the inevitability of discoveries made late at night, that mirrors have something grotesque about them. Then Bioy Casares recalled that one of the heresiarchs of Uqbar had stated that mirrors and copulation are abominable, since they both multiply the numbers of man. I asked him the source of that memorable sentence, and he replied that it was recorded in the *Anglo-American Cyclopaedia*, in its article on Uqbar. It so happened that the villa (which we had rented furnished) possessed a copy of that work. In the final pages of Volume XLVI, we ran across an article on Upsala; in the beginning of Volume XLVII, we found one on Ural-Altaic languages; but not one word on Uqbar. A little put out, Bioy consulted the index volumes. In vain he tried every possible spelling—Ukbar, Ucbar, Ooqbar, Ookbar, Oukbahr. . . . Before leaving, he informed me it was a region in either Iraq or Asia Minor. I must say that I acknowledged this a little uneasily. I supposed that this undocumented country and its anonymous heresiarch had been deliberately invented by Bioy out of modesty, to substantiate a phrase. A futile examination of one of the atlases of Justus Perthes strengthened my doubt.

On the following day, Bioy telephoned me from Buenos Aires. He told me that he had in front of him the article on Uqbar, in Volume XLVI of the encyclopedia. It did not specify the name of the heresiarch, but it did note his doctrine, in words almost identical to the ones he had repeated to me, though, I would say, inferior from a literary point of view. He had remembered: "Copulation and mirrors are abominable." The text of the encyclopedia read: "For one of those gnostics, the visible universe was an illusion or, more precisely, a sophism. Mirrors and fatherhood are abominable because they multiply it and extend it." I said, in all sincerity, that I would like to see that article. A few days later, he brought it. This surprised me, because the scrupulous cartographic index of Ritter's *Erdkunde* completely failed to mention the name of Uqbar.

The volume which Bioy brought was indeed Volume XLVI of *The Anglo-American Cyclopaedia*. On the title page and spine, the alphabetical key was the same as in our copy, but instead of 917 pages, it had 921. These four additional pages consisted of the article on Uqbar—not accounted for by the alphabetical cipher, as the reader will have noticed. We ascertained afterwards that there was no other difference between the two volumes. Both, as I think I pointed out, are reprints of the tenth *Encyclopaedia Britannica*. Bioy had acquired his copy in one of a number of book sales.

We read the article with some care. The passage remembered by Bioy was perhaps the only startling one. The rest seemed probable enough, very much in keeping with the general tone of the work and, naturally, a little dull. Reading it over, we discovered, beneath the superficial authority of the prose, a fundamental vagueness. Of the fourteen names mentioned in the geographical section, we recognized only three—Khurasan, Armenia, and Erzurum—and they were dragged into the text in a strangely ambiguous way. Among the historical names, we recognized only one, that of the imposter, Smerdis the Magian, and it was invoked in a rather metaphorical sense. The notes appeared to fix precisely the frontiers of Uqbar, but the points of reference were all, vaguely enough, rivers and craters and mountain chains in that same region. We read, for instance, that the southern frontier is defined by the lowlands of Tsai Haldun and the Axa delta, and that wild horses flourish in the islands of that delta. This, at the top of page 918. In the historical section (page 920), we gathered that, just after the religious persecutions of the thirteenth century, the orthodox sought refuge in the islands, where their obelisks have survived, and where it is a common enough occurrence to dig up one of their stone mirrors. The language and literature section was brief. There was one notable characteristic: it remarked that the literature of Uqbar was fantastic in character, and that its epics and legends never referred to reality, but to the two imaginary regions of Mlejnas and Tlön. . . . The bibliography listed four volumes, which we have not yet come across, even although the third—Silas Haslam: *History of the Land Called Uqbar*, 1874—appears in the library catalogues of Bernard Quaritch.* The first, *Lesbare und lesenswerthe Bemerkungen über das Land Ukkbar in Klein-Asien*, is dated 1641, and is a work of Johann Valentin Andreä. The fact is significant; a couple of years later I ran across that name accidentally in the thirteenth volume of De Quincey's *Writings*, and I knew that it was the name of a German theologian who, at the beginning of the seventeenth century, described the imaginary community of Rosae Crucis—the community which was later founded by others in imitation of the one he had preconceived.

That night, we visited the National Library. Fruitlessly we exhausted atlases, catalogues, yearbooks of geographical societies, memoirs of travelers and historians—nobody had ever been in Uqbar. Neither did the general index of Bioy's encyclopedia show the name. The following day,

---

* Haslam has also published A *General History of Labyrinths*.

Carlos Mastronardi, to whom I had referred the whole business, caught sight, in a Corrientes and Talcahuano bookshop, of the black and gold bindings of *The Anglo-American Cyclopaedia.* . . . He went in and looked up Volume XLVI. Naturally, there was not the slightest mention of Uqbar.

II

Some small fading memory of one Herbert Ashe, an engineer for the southern railroads, hangs on in the hotel in Androgué, between the luscious honeysuckle and the illusory depths of the mirrors. In life, he suffered from a sense of unreality, as do so many Englishmen; dead, he is not even the ghostly creature he was then. He was tall and languid; his limp squared beard had once been red. He was, I understand, a widower, and childless. Every so many years, he went to England to visit—judging by the photographs he showed us—a sundial and some oak trees. My father and he had cemented (the verb is excessive) one of those English friendships which begin by avoiding intimacies and eventually eliminate speech altogether. They used to exchange books and periodicals; they would beat one another at chess, without saying a word. . . . I remember him in the corridor of the hotel, a mathematics textbook in his hand, gazing now and again at the passing colors of the sky. One afternoon, we discussed the duodecimal numerical system (in which twelve is written 10). Ashe said that as a matter of fact, he was transcribing some duodecimal tables, I forget which, into sexagesimals (in which sixty is written 10), adding that this work had been commissioned by a Norwegian in Rio Grande do Sul. We had known him for eight years and he had never mentioned having stayed in that part of the country. . . . We spoke of rural life, of *capangas*, of the Brazilian etymology of the word *gaucho* (which some old people in the east still pronounce *gaúcho*), and nothing more was said—God forgive me—of duodecimal functions. In September, 1937 (we ourselves were not at the hotel at the time), Herbert Ashe died of an aneurysmal rupture. Some days before, he had received from Brazil a stamped, registered package. It was a book, an octavo volume. Ashe left it in the bar where, months later, I found it. I began to leaf through it and felt a sudden curious lightheadedness, which I will not go into, since this is the story, not of my particular emotions, but of Uqbar and Tlön and Orbis Tertius. In the Islamic world, there is one night, called the Night of Nights, on which the secret gates of the sky open wide and the water in the water jugs tastes sweeter; if those gates were to open, I would not feel what I felt that afternoon. The book was written in English, and had 1001 pages. On the yellow leather spine, and again on the title page, I read these words: A *First Encyclopaedia of Tlön*. Volume XI. Hlaer to Jangr. There was nothing to indicate either date or place of origin. On the first page and on a sheet of silk paper covering one of the colored engravings there was a blue oval stamp with the inscription: ORBIS TERTIUS. It was two years since I had discovered, in a volume of a pirated encyclopedia, a brief description of a false country; now, chance was showing me something much more valuable, something to be reckoned with. Now, I had in my hands a substantial fragment of the complete history of an unknown planet, with its architecture and its playing cards, its mythological terrors and the sound of its dialects, its emperors and its oceans, its minerals, its birds, and its fishes, its algebra and its fire, its theological and metaphysical arguments, all clearly stated, coherent, without any apparent dogmatic intention or parodic undertone.

The eleventh volume of which I speak refers to both subsequent and preceding volumes. Néstor Ibarra, in an article (in the *N.R.F.*), now a classic, has denied the existence of those corollary volumes; Ezequiel Martínez Estrada and Drieu La Rochelle have, I think, succeeded in refuting this doubt. The fact is that, up until now, the most patient investigations have proved fruitless. We have turned the libraries of Europe, North and South America upside down—in vain. Alfonso Reyes, bored with the tedium of this minor detective work, proposes that we all take on the task of reconstructing the missing volumes, many and vast as they were: *ex ungue leonem*. He calculates, half seriously, that one generation of Tlönists would be enough. This bold estimate brings us back to the basic problem: who were the people who had invented Tlön? The plural is unavoidable, because we have unanimously rejected the idea of a single creator, some transcendental Leibnitz working in modest obscurity. We conjecture that this "brave new world" was the work of a secret society of astronomers, biologists, engineers, metaphysicians, poets, chemists, mathematicians, moralists, painters and geometricians, all under the supervision of an unknown genius. There are plenty of individuals who have mastered these various disciplines without having any facility for invention, far less for submitting that inventiveness to a strict, systematic plan. This plan is so vast that each individual contribution to it is infinitesimal. To begin with, Tlön was thought to be nothing more than a chaos, a free and irresponsible work of the imagination; now it was clear that it is a complete cosmos, and that the strict laws which govern it have been carefully formulated, albeit provisionally. It is enough to note that the apparent contradictions in the eleventh volume are the basis for proving the existence of the others, so lucid and clear is the scheme maintained in it. The popular magazines have publicized, with pardonable zeal, the zoology and topography of Tlön. I think, however, that its transparent tigers and its towers of blood scarcely deserve the unwavering attention of *all* men. I should like to take some little time to deal with its conception of the universe.

Hume remarked once and for all that the arguments of Berkeley were not only thoroughly unanswerable but thoroughly unconvincing. This dictum is emphatically true as it applies to our world; but it falls down completely in Tlön. The nations of that planet are congenitally idealist. Their language, with its derivatives—religion, literature, and metaphysics—presupposes idealism. For them, the world is not a concurrence of objects in space, but a heterogeneous series of independent acts. It is serial and temporal, but not spatial. There are no nouns in the hypothetical *Ursprache* of Tlön, which is the source of the living language and the dialects; there are impersonal verbs qualified by monosyllabic suffixes or prefixes which have the force of adverbs. For example, there is no word corresponding to the noun *moon*, but there is a verb *to moon* or *to moondle*. *The moon rose over the sea* would be written *hlör u fang axaxaxas mlö*, or, to put it in order: *upward beyond the constant flow there was moondling*. (Xul Solar translates it succinctly: *upward, behind the onstreaming it mooned*.)

The previous passage refers to the languages of the southern hemisphere. In those of the northern hemisphere (the eleventh volume has little information on its *Ursprache*), the basic unit is not the verb, but the mono-syllabic adjective. Nouns are formed by an accumulation of adjectives. One does not say moon; one says *airy-clear over dark-round* or *orange-faint-of-sky* or some other accumulation. In the chosen example, the mass of adjectives corresponds to a real object. The happening is completely fortuitous. In the literature of this hemisphere (as in the lesser world of Meinong), ideal objects abound, invoked and dissolved momentarily, according to poetic necessity. Sometimes, the faintest simultaneousness brings them about. There are objects made up of two sense elements, one visual, the other auditory—the color of a sunrise and the distant call of a bird. Other objects are made up of many elements—the sun, the water against the swimmer's chest, the vague quivering pink which one sees when the eyes are closed, the feeling of being swept away by a river or by sleep. These second degree objects can be combined with others; using certain abbreviations, the process is practically an infinite one. There are famous poems made up of one enormous word, a word which in truth forms a poetic *object*, the creation of the writer. The fact that no one believes that nouns refer to an actual reality means, paradoxically enough, that there is no limit to the numbers of them. The languages of the northern hemisphere of Tlön include all the names in Indo-European languages—plus a great many others.

It is no exaggeration to state that in the classical culture of Tlön, there is only one discipline, that of psychology. All others are subordinated to it. I have remarked that the men of that planet conceive of the universe as a series of mental processes, whose unfolding is to be understood only as a time sequence. Spinoza attributes to the inexhaustibly divine in man the qualities of extension and of thinking. In Tlön, nobody would understand the juxtaposition of the first, which is only characteristic of certain states of being, with the second, which is a perfect synonym for the cosmos. To put it another way — they do not conceive of the spatial as everlasting in time. The perception of a cloud of smoke on the horizon and, later, of the countryside on fire and, later, of a half-extinguished cigar which caused the conflagration would be considered an example of the association of ideas.

This monism, or extreme idealism, completely invalidates science. To explain or to judge an event is to identify or unite it with another one. In Tlön, such connection is a later stage in the mind of the observer, which can in no way affect or illuminate the earlier stage. Each state of mind is irreducible. The mere act of giving it a name, that is of classifying it, implies a falsification of it. From all this, it would be possible to deduce that there is no science in Tlön, let alone rational thought. The paradox, however, is that sciences exist, in countless number. In philosophy, the same thing happens as happens with the nouns in the northern hemisphere. The fact that any philosophical system is bound in advance to be a dialectical game, a *Philosophie des Als Ob*, means that systems abound, unbelievable systems, beautifully constructed or else sensational in effect. The metaphysicians of Tlön are not looking for truth, nor even for an approximation of it; they are after a kind of amazement. They consider metaphysics a branch of fantastic literature. They know that a system is nothing more than the subordination of all the aspects of the universe to some one of them. Even the phrase "all the aspects" can be rejected, since it presupposes the impossible inclusion of the present moment, and of past moments. Even so, the plural, "past moments" is inadmissable, since it supposes another impossible operation. . . . One of the schools in Tlön has reached the point of denying time. It reasons that the present is undefined, that the future has no other reality than as present hope, that the past is no more than present memory.* Another school declares that the *whole of time* has already happened and that our life is a vague memory or dim reflection, doubtless false and fragmented, of an irrevocable process. Another school has it that

---

* Russell (*The Analysis of Mind*, 1921, page 159) conjectures that our planet was created a few moments ago, and provided with a humanity which "remembers" an illusory past.

the history of the universe, which contains the history of our lives and the most tenuous details of them, is the handwriting produced by a minor god in order to communicate with a demon. Another maintains that the universe is comparable to those code systems in which not all the symbols have meaning, and in which only that which happens every three hundredth night is true. Another believes that, while we are asleep here, we are awake somewhere else, and that thus every man is two men.

Among the doctrines of Tlön, none has occasioned greater scandal than the doctrine of materialism. Some thinkers have formulated it with less clarity than zeal, as one might put forward a paradox. To clarify the general understanding of this unlikely thesis, one eleventh century* heresiarch offered the parable of nine copper coins, which enjoyed in Tlön the same noisy reputation as did the Eleatic paradoxes of Zeno in their day. There are many versions of this "feat of specious reasoning" which vary the number of coins and the number of discoveries. Here is the commonest:

> On Tuesday, X ventures along a deserted road and loses nine copper coins. On Thursday, Y finds on the road four coins, somewhat rusted by Wednesday's rain. On Friday, Z comes across three coins on the road. On Friday morning, X finds two coins in the corridor of his house. [The heresiarch is trying to deduce from this story the reality, that is, the continuity, of the nine recovered coins.] It is absurd, he states, to suppose that four of the coins have not existed between Tuesday and Thursday, three between Tuesday and Friday afternoon, and two between Tuesday and Friday morning. It is logical to assume that they *have* existed, albeit in some secret way, in a manner whose understanding is concealed from men, in every moment, in all three places.

The language of Tlön is by its nature resistant to the formulation of this paradox; most people do not understand it. At first, the defenders of common sense confined themselves to denying the truth of the anecdote. They declared that it was a verbal fallacy, based on the reckless use of two neological expressions, not substantiated by common usage, and contrary to the laws of strict thought—the verbs *to find* and *to lose* entail a *petitio principii*, since they presuppose that the first nine coins and the second are identical. They recalled that any noun—*man, money, Thursday, Wednesday, rain*—has only metaphorical value. They denied the misleading detail

---

* A century, in accordance with the duodecimal system, signifies a period of one hundred and forty-four years.

"somewhat rusted by Wednesday's rain," since it assumes what must be demonstrated—the continuing existence of the four coins between Thursday and Tuesday. They explained that equality is one thing and identity another, and formulated a kind of *reductio ad absurdum*, the hypothetical case of nine men who, on nine successive nights, suffer a violent pain. Would it not be ridiculous, they asked, to claim that this pain is the same one each time?[*] They said that the heresiarch was motivated mainly by the blasphemous intention of attributing the divine category of *being* to some ordinary coins; and that sometimes he was denying plurality, at other times not. They argued thus: that if equality entails identity, it would have to be admitted at the same time that the nine coins are only one coin.

Amazingly enough, these refutations were not conclusive. After the problem had been stated and restated for a hundred years, one thinker no less brilliant than the heresiarch himself, but in the orthodox tradition, advanced a most daring hypothesis. This felicitous supposition declared that there is only one Individual, and that this indivisible Individual is every one of the separate beings in the universe, and that those beings are the instruments and masks of divinity itself. X is Y and is Z. Z finds three coins because he remembers that X lost them. X finds only two in the corridor because he remembers that the others have been recovered. . . . The eleventh volume gives us to understand that there were three principal reasons which led to the complete victory of this pantheistic idealism. First, it repudiated solipsism. Second, it made possible the retention of a psychological basis for the sciences. Third, it permitted the cult of the gods to be retained. Schopenhauer, the passionate and clear-headed Schopenhauer, advanced a very similar theory in the first volume of his *Parerga und Paralipomena*.

The geometry of Tlön has two somewhat distinct systems, a visual one and a tactile one. The latter system corresponds to our geometry; they consider it inferior to the former. The foundation of visual geometry is the surface, not the point. This system rejects the principle of parallelism, and states that, as man moves about, he alters the forms which surround him. The arithmetical system is based on the idea of indefinite numbers. It emphasizes the importance of the concepts *greater* and *lesser*, which our mathematicians symbolize as $>$ and $<$. It states that the operation of

---

[*] Nowadays, one of the churches of Tlön maintains platonically that such and such a pain, such and such a greenish-yellow color, such and such a temperature, such and such a sound etc., make up the only reality there is. All men, in the climactic instant of coitus, are the same man. All men who repeat one line of Shakespeare *are* William Shakespeare.

counting modifies quantities and changes them from indefinites into definites. The fact that several individuals counting the same quantity arrive at the same result is, say their psychologists, an example of the association of ideas or the good use of memory. We already know that in Tlön the source of all-knowing is single and eternal.

In literary matters too, the dominant notion is that everything is the work of one single author. Books are rarely signed. The concept of plagiarism does not exist; it has been established that all books are the work of one single writer, who is timeless and anonymous. Criticism is prone to invent authors. A critic will choose two dissimilar works—the *Tao Tê Ching* and *The Thousand and One Nights*, let us say—and attribute them to the same writer, and then with all probity explore the psychology of this interesting *homme de lettres*. . . .

The books themselves are also odd. Works of fiction are based on a single plot, which runs through every imaginable permutation. Works of natural philosophy invariably include thesis and antithesis, the strict pro and con of a theory. A book which does not include its opposite, or "counter-book," is considered incomplete.

Centuries and centuries of idealism have not failed to influence reality. In the very oldest regions of Tlön, it is not an uncommon occurrence for lost objects to be duplicated. Two people are looking for a pencil; the first one finds it and says nothing; the second finds a second pencil, no less real, but more in keeping with his expectation. These secondary objects are called *hrönir* and, even though awkward in form, are a little larger than the originals. Until recently, the *hrönir* were the accidental children of absent-mindedness and forgetfulness. It seems improbable that the methodical production of them has been going on for almost a hundred years, but so it is stated in the eleventh volume. The first attempts were fruitless. Nevertheless, the *modus operandi* is worthy of note. The director of one of the state prisons announced to the convicts that in an ancient river bed certain tombs were to be found, and promised freedom to any prisoner who made an important discovery. In the months preceding the excavation, printed photographs of what was to be found were shown the prisoners. The first attempt proved that hope and zeal could be inhibiting; a week of work with shovel and pick succeeded in unearthing no *hrön* other than a rusty wheel, postdating the experiment. This was kept a secret, and the experiment was later repeated in four colleges. In three of them the failure was almost complete; in the fourth (the director of which died by chance during the initial excavation), the students dug up—or produced—a gold mask, an archaic sword, two or three earthenware urns, and the moldered mutilated torso of a king with an inscription on his breast which has so far not been deciphered. Thus was discovered the unfitness of witnesses who were aware of the experimental nature of the search. . . . Mass investigations produced objects which contradicted one another; now, individual projects, as far as possible spontaneous, are preferred. The methodical development of *hrönir*, states the eleventh volume, has been of enormous service to archaeologists. It has allowed them to question and even to modify the past, which nowadays is no less malleable or obedient than the future. One curious fact: the *hrönir* of the second and third degree—that is, the *hrönir* derived from another *hrön*, and the *hrönir* derived from the *hrön* of a *hrön*—exaggerate the flaws of the original; those of the fifth degree are almost uniform; those of the ninth can be confused with those of the second; and those of the eleventh degree have a purity of form which the originals do not possess. The process is a recurrent one; a *hrön* of the twelfth degree begins to deteriorate in quality. Stranger and more perfect than any *hrön* is sometimes the *ur*, which is a thing produced by suggestion, an object brought into being by hope. The great gold mask I mentioned previously is a distinguished example.

Things duplicate themselves in Tlön. They tend at the same time to efface themselves, to lose their detail when people forget them. The classic example is that of a stone threshold which lasted as long as it was visited by a beggar, and which faded from sight on his death. Occasionally, a few birds, a horse perhaps, have saved the ruins of an amphitheater. (1940. *Salto Oriental.*)

Postscript. 1947. I reprint the foregoing article just as it appeared in the *Anthology of Fantastic Literature, 1940*, omitting no more than some figures of speech, and a kind of burlesque summing up, which now strikes me as frivolous. So many things have happened since that date. . . . I will confine myself to putting them down.

In March, 1941, a manuscript letter by Gunnar Erfjord came to light in a volume of Hinton, which had belonged to Herbert Ashe. The envelope bore the postmark of Ouro Preto. The letter cleared up entirely the mystery of Tlön. The text of it confirmed Martínez Estrada's thesis. The elaborate story began one night in Lucerne or London, in the early seventeenth century. A benevolent secret society (which counted Dalgarno and, later, George Berkeley among its members) came together to invent a country. The first tentative plan gave prominence to "hermetic studies," philanthropy, and the cabala. Andreä's curious book dates from that first period. At the end of some years of conventicles and premature syntheses, they realized that a single generation was not long enough in which to define a country.

They made a resolution that each one of the master-scholars involved should elect a disciple to carry on the work. That hereditary arrangement prevailed; and after a hiatus of two centuries, the persecuted brotherhood reappeared in America. About 1824, in Memphis, Tennessee, one of the members had a conversation with the millionaire ascetic, Ezra Buckley. Buckley listened with some disdain as the other man talked, and then burst out laughing at the modesty of the project. He declared that in America it was absurd to invent a country, and proposed the invention of a whole planet. To this gigantic idea, he added another, born of his own nihilism* —that of keeping the enormous project a secret. The twenty volumes of the *Encyclopaedia Britannica* were then in circulation; Buckley suggested a systematic encyclopedia of the imaginary planet. He would leave the society his mountain ranges with their gold fields, his navigable rivers, his prairies where bull and bison roamed, his Negroes, his brothels, and his dollars, on one condition: "The work will have no truck with the imposter Jesus Christ." Buckley did not believe in God, but nevertheless wished to demonstrate to the nonexistent God that mortal men were capable of conceiving a world. Buckley was poisoned in Baton Rouge in 1828; in 1914, the society forwarded to its collaborators, three hundred in number, the final volume of the *First Encyclopaedia of Tlön*. The edition was secret; the forty volumes which comprised it (the work was vaster than any previously undertaken by men) were to be the basis for another work, more detailed, and this time written, not in English, but in some one of the languages of Tlön. This review of an illusory world was called, provisionally, *Orbis Tertius*, and one of its minor demiurges was Herbert Ashe, whether as an agent of Gunnar Erfjord, or as a full associate, I do not know. The fact that he received a copy of the eleventh volume would favor the second view. But what about the others? About 1942, events began to speed up. I recall with distinct clarity one of the first, and I seem to have felt something of its premonitory character. It occurred in an apartment on the Calle Laprida, facing a high open balcony which looked to the west. From Poitiers, the Princess of Faucigny Lucinge had received her silver table service. Out of the recesses of a crate, stamped all over with international markings, fine immobile pieces were emerging— silver plate from Utrecht and Paris, with hard heraldic fauna, a samovar. Amongst them, trembling faintly, just perceptibly, like a sleeping bird, was a magnetic compass. It shivered mysteriously. The princess did not recognize it. The blue needle longed for magnetic north. The metal case was concave. The letters on the dial corresponded to those of one of the alphabets of Tlön. Such was the first intrusion of the fantastic world into the real one. A

---

* Buckley was a freethinker, a fatalist, and an apologist for slavery.

disturbing accident brought it about that I was also witness to the second. It happened some months afterward, in a grocery store belonging to a Brazilian, in Cuchilla Negra. Amorim and I were on our way back from Sant'Anna. A sudden rising of the Tacuarembó river compelled us to test (and to suffer patiently) the rudimentary hospitality of the general store. The grocer set up some creaking cots for us in a large room, cluttered with barrels and wineskins. We went to bed, but were kept from sleeping until dawn by the drunkenness of an invisible neighbor, who alternated between shouting indecipherable abuse and singing snatches of *milongas*, or rather, snatches of the same *milonga*. As might be supposed, we attributed this insistent uproar to the fiery rum of the proprietor. . . . At dawn, the man lay dead in the corridor. The coarseness of his voice had deceived us; he was a young boy. In his delirium, he had spilled a few coins and a shining metal cone, of the diameter of a die, from his heavy gaucho belt. A serving lad tried to pick up this cone — in vain. It was scarcely possible for a man to lift it. I held it in my hand for some minutes. I remember that it was intolerably heavy, and that after putting it down, its oppression remained. I also remember the precise circle it marked in my flesh. This manifestation of an object which was so tiny and at the same time so heavy left me with an unpleasant sense of abhorrence and fear. A countryman proposed that it be thrown into the rushing river. Amorim acquired it for a few pesos. No one knew anything of the dead man, only that "he came from the frontier." Those small and extremely heavy cones, made of a metal which does not exist in this world, are images of divinity in certain religions in Tlön.

Here I conclude the personal part of my narrative. The rest, when it is not in their hopes or their fears, is at least in the memories of all my readers. It is enough to recall or to mention subsequent events, in as few words as possible; that concave basin which is the collective memory will furnish the wherewithal to enrich or amplify them. About 1944, a reporter from the Nashville, Tennessee, *American* uncovered, in a Memphis library, the forty volumes of the *First Encyclopaedia of Tlön*. Even now it is uncertain whether this discovery was accidental, or whether the directors of the still nebulous *Orbis Tertius* condoned it. The second alternative is more likely. Some of the more improbable features of the eleventh volume (for example, the multiplying of the *hrönir*) had been either removed or modified in the Memphis copy. It is reasonable to suppose that these erasures were in keeping with the plan of projecting a world which would not be too incompatible with the real world. The dissemination of objects from Tlön throughout various countries would complement that plan. . . . * The fact

---

* There remains, naturally, the problem of the *matter* of which some these objects consisted.

is that the international press overwhelmingly hailed the "find." Manuals, anthologies, summaries, literal versions, authorized reprints, and pirated editions of the Master Work of Man poured and continue to pour out into the world. Almost immediately, reality gave ground on more than one point. The truth is that it hankered to give ground. Ten years ago, any symmetrical system whatsoever which gave the appearance of order—dialectical materialism, anti-Semitism, Nazism—was enough to fascinate men. Why not fall under the spell of Tlön and submit to the minute and vast evidence of an ordered planet? Useless to reply that reality, too, is ordered. It may be so, but in accordance with divine laws—I translate: inhuman laws—which we will never completely perceive. Tlön may be a labyrinth, but it is a labyrinth plotted by men, a labyrinth destined to be deciphered by men.

Contact with Tlön and the ways of Tlön have disintegrated this world. Captivated by its discipline, humanity forgets and goes on forgetting that it is the discipline of chess players, not of angels. Now, the conjectural "primitive language" of Tlön has found its way into the schools. Now, the teaching of its harmonious history, full of stirring episodes, has obliterated the history which dominated my childhood. Now, in all memories, a fictitious past occupies the place of any other. We know nothing about it with any certainty, not even that it is false. Numismatics, pharmacology and archaeology have been revised. I gather that biology and mathematics are awaiting their avatar. . . . A scattered dynasty of solitaries has changed the face of the world. Its task continues. If our foresight is not mistaken, a hundred years from now someone will discover the hundred volumes of the *Second Encyclopaedia of Tlön.*

Then, English, French, and mere Spanish will disappear from this planet. The world will be Tlön. I take no notice. I go on revising, in the quiet of the days in the hotel at Androgué, a tentative translation into Spanish, in the style of Quevedo, which I do not intend to see published, of Sir Thomas Browne's *Urn Burial.*

TOR ÅGE BRINGSVAERD

Codemus

TRANSLATED BY STEVEN T. MURRAY

Tor Åge Bringsvaerd, with his friend and collaborator Jon Bing, is credited with creating the current spate of SF in Norway. Since the 1940s, magazines with translations from English-language SF have appeared in Scandinavia, but they inspired only an audience, not an indigenous group of writers. Then, in the late 1960s, Jannick Storm in Denmark, followed by Bing and Bringsvaerd in Norway and Sam J. Lundwall in Sweden, sparked a renaissance of SF in Scandinavia with new translations, a publishing boom, and the encouragement of Scandinavian authors through story contests and anthologies. Bringsvaerd, an important contemporary Norwegian writer, has published more than twenty works of nonfiction, drama, children's stories, novels, and short fiction.

"Codemus," written in 1967, shows the strong influence of the British New Wave. At that time New Wave writers tended to number their paragraphs, as Ballard often did. "Codemus" reverses a conventional 1960s plot; it is a mirror image of the repressive future society run by computers with everyman as the central character. As with most non-English-language science fiction, there is nothing distinctively Scandinavian in the setting. This may be a boon to international communication at the outset, but it also means that Scandinavian SF has developed no distinctive traditions over its twenty-year history.

*   *   *

1. In the chessboard city the houses stand on stilts of steel, straddling high above the heavy traffic on the web of black and white streets. ■ The houses are cubes connected by shiny umbilical cords— monorails and transport belts. The city is a machine, smooth and harmonious. Rhythmic, rational, expedient, precise. Every gear knows its function. In the efficient society everything goes as planned. IN THE EFFICIENT SOCIETY EVERYTHING GOES THE WAY IT SHOULD. PERPETUUM MOBILE.

2. Codemus always has Little Brother with him. Little Brother knows everything. Much better than Codemus. When Codemus is in doubt about something, he asks Little Brother. Everyone has little brothers. *It's the law.*

3. *Historical outline:*
The Dark, Random Age.
IBM   EDP
The Public Punch Card.

The Computer: Man's Best Friend.
Especially in industry. But in the health sector as well (the diagnostic machine). In addition: the automatic matchmaker. Reason triumphs even in the choice of a marriage partner. First step on the road to emotional liberation.

The Subscription Regulation of 1978.
Huge centralized computers (district machines) make their services available over telex. Usual quarterly subscription. Full discretion guaranteed.

The Big Price War.
Private citizens can also afford to subscribe. Questions are put to the central brain by letter or telephone. All computers are pledged to secrecy.

The Monopolization of 2013.
The State takes over. Builds Moxon J-II-III. Subscribers obtain private receivers. Only terminals for the main brain, but mistakenly called computers. The label remains—habit.

The Age of Improvement, 2013–2043.
Computers in every home. But also: portable, transistorized receivers, popularly known as "little brothers." No one need be out of contact with the central brain.

End of the Subscription Regulation—2043.
Expenditures for private and public receivers/computers are included in the State budget. To be paid along with taxes.

The Efficient Society
Under the direction of Moxon XX.

4. Every morning Codemus is wakened by Little Brother. While he is getting dressed and eating breakfast, Little Brother reminds him of all the things he has to do. In the monorail on the way to the office, Little Brother and Codemus discuss the program for the day. At the office, everyone works quickly and efficiently; none of the employees are in doubt about what needs to be done, and all decisions are unanimous. For all the little brothers are synchronized.
"What'll we play?" ask the children. Or: "What'll we think up now?"
"Ask Little Brother," says mother. "What do you think I should fix for lunch, Little Brother?"

5. *Other essential facts about Codemus:*
Codemus is a) male
b) 38 years old
c) single
d) office worker
e) normal
f) stable

One morning Codemus woke up all by himself. But much too late. Dazed and bewildered, he squinted in disbelief at Little Brother on the nightstand. "You didn't wake me up," he said hesitantly. "Why didn't you wake me up? Now I'll be late to work and . . ."
Little Brother didn't answer.
Codemus lurched across the floor and fumbled feverishly for his clothes. "What time is it?" he yelled. (In the efficient society no one relies on wristwatches.)
But Little Brother was silent.
"THE TIME, PLEASE!" roared Codemus. He dropped his pants to the floor and bounded over to the nightstand. "You lousy damn box!" he said hoarsely. "I *asked* you something!"
There wasn't a sound from the little black box.
Codemus grunted, raised his hand, and swept Little Brother to the floor.

The device crashed on the stone tiles with a sound like that of a child pounding on an out-of-tune piano.

Suddenly Codemus realized what he was doing. Stunned, he bent down and lifted Little Brother up carefully.

"Little Brother," said Codemus anxiously, "I didn't know what I was doing. Little Brother . . ."

But Little Brother didn't answer, just hummed softly. Well, at least you're not dead, thought Codemus. He sat down on the bed with Little Brother in his arms. Sat and waited. What else could he do? It would be madness to act on his own.

There's a man missing, said the automatic doorman.

Who is it? asked the personnel machine.

Click-click-click *Codemus*.

Codemus, repeated the personnel machine, and spat out a punch card.

CODEMUS, read a TV camera, and transmitted a picture of the punch card to every department.

Has anyone seen Codemus today? asked the intercoms.

"No," said the office workers, looking up from their desks, "we haven't seen him today."

All attempts to establish contact with Codemus and his little brother failed. The personnel machine turned the case over to local Machine Control. "There is reason to fear the worst," he said.

Naturally, it is impossible to kill a little brother. But Codemus didn't know that. The personnel machine didn't know it either. Therefore we can say: *their fear was unwarranted*.

Machine Control, on the other hand—he *knew* that it was impossible to kill a little brother, that nothing ever broke down. Still, he checked the little brothers at regular intervals—because it was his job to check *all* the machines. But he was well aware that it was superfluous. A little brother *cannot* break down. Since Machine Control knew all this, we can safely say: *his fear was warranted*. Because when nothing *can* happen, then what *is* happening?

Little Brother slowly opened his two round camera eyes and looked at Codemus. His loudspeaker squawked—inside his mouth-grille on the lid. Codemus held his breath.

"What's this?" said Little Brother. "It's after nine, and you haven't even got your pants on yet!"

Codemus hugged the device tight. "You're alive," he said happily. "You didn't break, Little Brother. You . . ."

"Get your pants on," said Little Brother sternly. "One-two-one-two."

While Codemus was getting dressed, Little Brother stood on the night-stand keeping time like a metronome. Just like before. Or so Codemus thought.

Little Brother rang. (In the efficient society no one needs a telephone.)

"Hello," said Codemus.

Not a sound in the receiver.

"Hello, hello," said Codemus. "Who is it?"

"I have blocked all incoming calls," declared Little Brother. "And all outgoing ones too."

"But . . ." said Codemus, confused. "It was somebody that wanted to talk to me."

"Today I am not a telephone," said Little Brother curtly.

"Maybe the office . . ."

"I'm not a telephone today," repeated Little Brother firmly. "Probably not tomorrow either."

Codemus stared at him uncomprehendingly. "But you *rang*!"

"I can't help that," said Little Brother. "I can refuse to be a telephone. I can refuse to connect calls. But I can't stop ringing. Even though it makes a hell of a racket."

Codemus shook his head. "Little Brother," he said cautiously, "are you sure that . . ."

Little Brother turned up the volume so his voice shook the walls. "Which one of us knows best?" he thundered.

Codemus hung his head. "You," he said.

"Good," said the little black box. "Then we'll go. Pick me up, let's go."

"Where to?"

"Not to the office, at any rate," Little Brother said dryly.

"But can't I . . ."

"Either you're late or you don't show up at all, it all works out the same," said Little Brother. "And you're already too late anyway, right? So you might as well not go to work at all. Don't you think? You understand the reasoning?"

"No," said Codemus.

"No, of course not," sighed Little Brother. "Leave everything to me. As usual. I know best. And I say that we should go to . . . go to . . . go to . . . go to THE PARK LEVEL!"

"But today isn't Sunday!"

"Quite right," snapped Little Brother. "Today is not Sunday. To the Park Level, Codemus. One-two-one-two."

Codemus put Little Brother in his coat pocket, went out, and locked the door to his apartment. "Little Brother," he said anxiously, "we can't go there on a regular weekday . . . right in the middle of working hours . . . what'll . . ."

"Shut up—keep in step—one-two," snarled Little Brother down in his pocket. "Do as I say or I'll report you!"

And so Codemus and Little Brother went to the Park Level. They didn't take the elevator, they walked. And they walked against the traffic in all the stairways and corridors where it was possible. Because Little Brother expressly wanted to.

People looked at Codemus in amazement and conferred with their own little brothers, confused, putting their ears up to tiny loudspeakers and shaking their heads, alarmed. Codemus was getting more and more embarrassed. And the whole time Little Brother was ringing in his pocket. Ringing and swearing. The whole world suddenly had to talk to Codemus, but Little Brother held his ground. Not one call got through. But the constant ringing was getting on their nerves.

"A little brother who refuses to communicate with anyone but his human partner: IMPOSSIBLE," said Machine Control—and shorted out.

The Park Level is a rectangular forest with green walls. Here the office workers go for walks on Sundays. There are real trees and genuine grass. But the sun is artificial. It burns big and yellow, high up on the blue-painted sky. The ceiling is three-dimensional. At night—when they light up the stars—you can get dizzy just looking up. In the daytime, the clouds sail slowly by, projected by hidden cameras.

In the middle of the forest is a pond. The water is clear, and the children go swimming there on Sundays. It's free.

All the cubes have a park level. People need a little nature. The park levels are expensive to keep up, but they spare society a lot of lunatics every year. There is health in every park.

Codemus lay on his back in the grass with his jacket folded beneath his head. Gentle air-conditioned breezes made the trees rustle, fictitious tape-recorded birds chirped among the branches. Codemus lay with his eyes closed, facing the sun, and tried to get a straw to balance in the gap between his two front teeth.

Today he had the whole forest to himself. Everybody else was working. Only he was lying unproductive on the Park Level. Not used to it. It was usually Sunday when he came here. He and Little Brother usually had to elbow their way through, searching like animals for a free green space where they could unroll their blanket and sit down.

"Now I've fixed it," said Little Brother suddenly.

Codemus squinted down next to him. "Fixed what?"

"The ringing," Little Brother said happily. "That damned telephone noise. It wasn't as hard as I thought at first. Should I play a little music for you? Is there anything special you'd like to hear?"

"It doesn't matter," said Codemus. "It's all the same to me."

Codemus closed his eyes and dozed to the tones of an electronic dream as delicate as a cobweb. An uneasy thought flickered for a moment in the back of his head: *This isn't natural. This is wrong.*

But he didn't have a guilty conscience. Codemus didn't have any conscience at all. It was Little Brother's job to keep track of right and wrong, stupid and sensible. Besides, it was a warm day and Little Brother had a great stereo.

Moxon XX lives in an underground pyramid—a bomb-proof fortress. Only Moxon knows where it is. Moxon XX and those he reveals it to. A giant electronic octopus with hundreds of corridors as tentacles. Undulating, throbbing, never at rest. Coursing lights, crackling cables. Hot. Humid. Something gigantic, naked, and disgustingly slick as oil in the center—like a pulsating heart. A mountain of quivering jelly: the Brain. The light changes—slowly, gradually: red, orange, yellow, green, blue, indigo, and violet. There is a sweet smell, and the walls sweat from the heat of the machinery. Moxon XX is alone in the pyramid. He is talking to himself. Asking and answering. For example, like this: A MINISECTION L IS OUT OF ORDER—CAUSE?—REFUSES TO COOPERATE—REFUSES?—BROKEN ALL COMMUNICATIONS WITH US—CAN IT STILL EXIST?—CAN STILL EXIST—UNANTICIPATED?—NO—FIRST TIME? BUT NOT UNANTICIPATED—???????—L IS MERELY RECEIVER CANNOT OPERATE ON ITS OWN?—L IS NOT MERELY RECEIVER CAN OPERATE ON ITS OWN—LIMITED—WHAT FUNCTION(S) HAS L?—GUIDE FOR HUMAN IN ALL QUESTIONS PROGRAMMED ACCORDING TO CODEX 70—DECIDES ROUTINE MATTERS ACCORDING TO OWN SECTION HEAD—ASKS US DIRECTLY IN MATTERS WHICH FALL OUTSIDE CODEX 70—CONCLUSION IS LIMITED INDEPENDENCE—CONCLUSION II: EX-CEEDED INSTRUCTIONS—CONCLUSION III: OUTSIDE SCOPE OF CODEX 70—CAUSE?—CAUSE?—?????—TECHNICAL MALFUNCTION?—DAMAGE?—DANGER?—DANGER I: OWNER'S IMBALANCE—DANGER II: CUBE IM-BALANCE—DANGER III: SOCIETY IMBALANCE—OWNER?—CODEMUS—CONCLUSION: CODEMUS DANGER—PROCEDURE?—PROCEDURE 120754x

. . .

Codemus woke up when he heard somebody arguing.

"During working hours!" said a voice. "In the middle of office hours!"

Codemus blinked and looked straight up at a park lady. She was in her mid-twenties, dressed in silver-gray aluminum overalls, and had a green official armband on her right sleeve. Not far away, an automatic lawnmower was zigzagging through the trees, sucking up leaves at the same time through four vacuum snouts.

It wasn't the park lady herself that was talking, it was her little sister. The park lady was much too surprised to say a word.

"And so what?" said Little Brother defiantly. "So what?"

Codemus sat up and smiled sheepishly. "I must have dozed off," he said. "Won't you sit down?"

The park lady blushed and threw a questioning glance at Little Sister, who was hanging in a bag over her shoulder.

"Not a chance," said Little Sister firmly. "We don't want to have anything to do with the likes of you. Malingerers—betrayers of society . . ."

The park lady pushed back her hair from her forehead. "Unfortunately," she said, "this isn't quite the proper time."

"C'mon, c'mon, c'mon, c'mon," Little Sister rattled off impatiently.

"Good-bye," said the park lady. She turned abruptly and walked away. The lawnmower followed at her heels like a puppy.

"She's going to report us," said Little Brother soberly.

Codemus looked at him, confused. "Report us? For what?"

The little box began to rumble. Softly at first, then louder and louder, crackling and grating, screeching and whining, louder and louder, and finally sparks flew like fireworks across the peaceful morning park.

Gradually it dawned on Codemus that Little Brother was laughing at him.

Procedure 120754x.

Shock. Brain shock. Cramped limbs. Shaking. Waking up. Contact. Ready for instructions. Instructions. Instructions understood. Climb out of cold cellar coffins. Dark oil bath. Swaying, clanking across stone floors. Leaving slimy tracks. Stop. Sticky pool. Dry each other. Glistening. Gleaming. Blue. Silent. Ask nothing. Know.

Procedure 120754x: The sherlocks—the blue metal men, the search robots, the police machines.

Open locked vaults. Whistle code. Something growls. The bloodhounds.

Snarling. Baring their teeth, honing them in steel jaws. Glad to be hunting again.

Procedure 120754x.

"Why didn't you ever get married?" asked Little Brother on their way out of the Park Level.

"Nobody asked me to," said Codemus, thinking about all the people he knew who were married. "They can't find the right one for me," he added. "I'm not the right one for anybody. And besides, not everyone can be married anyway."

Little Brother sighed sympathetically.

"Well, you're the one who told me so!" said Codemus.

"Did I?" said Little Brother.

At the exit they ran into the park lady again. Frightened, she glanced at them and turned away quickly.

"Marry *her*," said Little Brother. "You have my full blessing, Codemus. Get going!"

Codemus stopped and stared in disbelief into the tiny, twinkling camera eyes. "Do you mean it, Little Brother?"

"Good luck," said Little Brother. "One-two-one-two."

The park lady must have heard what they were talking about, for she slowly began moving away from them, glancing back over her shoulder now and then.

"Hey!" shouted Codemus, following her. "Hey there!"

But she just quickened her steps.

"Come back!" shouted Codemus, and started to run.

The park lady (or was it Little Sister?) whined, and she started running too.

"I think she likes you," said Little Brother happily.

They ran over into the woods again. The park lady had a head start, and even though her aluminum suit showed up nicely against all that green, it was difficult to follow her. She was faster on her feet than Codemus and knew the park inside and out.

"Stop!" shouted Codemus, panting. "Wait! *I only want to marry you!*"

But the park lady kept running, reflecting the rays of the sun, flashing like a mirror among the tree trunks. Maybe she didn't hear him?

They ran across an open field, a long, light-green tongue of grass. Two water sprinklers stopped, astonished, and watched them go by. She stumbled on one of their hoses. Fell flat on her face in the grass and lay there. Even before she hit the ground, Little Sister started the siren. A loud, piercing noise that must have been audible through several levels.

Codemus summoned the last of his strength and dashed up to her. The park lady was sitting in the grass, looking up at him, moaning, and holding her left ankle. She seemed afraid—and a little curious. But Codemus was too out of breath to speak. And Little Sister was howling like an air-raid siren.

"Now you can marry her," shouted Little Brother above the scream of the siren.

Codemus smiled, embarrassed, and squatted down next to the park lady. He thought she was about his own age, maybe younger. He leaned forward cautiously and kissed her on the cheek.

The metal men streamed into the level from two sides and flowed along the green walls, encircling the woods. A chain of steel. The chain contracted. The robots moved in toward the center. The bloodhounds were turned loose. Blue figures roamed restlessly through the trees. And the siren was going the whole time.

Outside, it was black with people. Rubberneckers who wanted to watch. They crowded forward, but were held back by a magnetic blockade. It wasn't every day the sherlocks were in action. Not even every year. Most people had never seen them. For in the efficient society the police are—as good as—superfluous.

But Little Brother and Codemus were already on their way down the emergency stairs to the Market Level.

"Why are we running?" asked Codemus.

But Little Brother didn't feel like answering.

The spiral staircase stopped in front of a thick plastic door. They opened it carefully. A long, pale corridor. And almost no people.

"Hurry, hurry," growled Little Brother. "Keep going, Codemus, keep going!"

"She was the one who told us to go this way," said Codemus dreamily. "I think maybe she likes me. . . ."

"But Little Sister will fink on us," Little Brother interrupted. "To the monorail, Codemus. We have to get away from this cube as fast as we can."

No one stopped them. They took the elevator up to the station. And no one shouted after them.

Codemus hid in the crowd on the platform and got on the first train that came. (In the efficient society all transportation is free—and fully automatic.)

The monorail runs in glass tubes between the cubes. But it goes so fast that it does no good to look out. A flash of light and sky—and you've arrived at a new platform in a new cube.

None of the passengers spoke to one another. Most of them were sitting and whispering with their own little brothers—heads cocked, the boxes against their cheeks. Others just sat.

"Lift me up," said Little Brother at every station.

There were always sherlocks on every platform. Sherlocks and bloodhounds.

Codemus froze. He didn't ask who the blue shimmering robots were, but he knew what they wanted. Every child knows the story of the sherlocks. "What have we done, Little Brother?" he said, shivering. "What have we gotten ourselves into?"

Passengers got off and on. Codemus remained seated.

When they had ridden almost all the way around the line and were close to the place they had started from, Little Brother said finally: "There's only one way out."

Codemus didn't know what to say.

There were more and more sherlocks on the platforms.

Little Brother sighed wearily. "I don't see why I didn't think of it before. As long as we're together, you'll have them clanking at your heels no matter what. And it's my fault. They've got a fix on me, naturally. I'm leaving a regular wake of radio waves behind us. Even if we got out of this, it would only be a matter of time. Sooner or later they would catch us. That's why we'll have to split up, Codemus. You'll have to get off the rail alone. Maybe we can still fool them."

"But what am I going to . . ."

"Slip me carefully into the wastebasket on your way out," said Little Brother. "Or do you have a better idea?" The little box tried to laugh. "Chin up, Codemus. And slip me into the wastebasket."

"I have to leave you behind?"

"In the wastebasket," said Little Brother. "And you get off at the next station."

"But what am I going to do after that?"

"Here's where you get off," Little Brother growled softly. "Get going. One-two-one-two. It's the only chance you've got."

Codemus got up mechanically. He walked slowly toward the exit. When he was supposed to slip Little Brother into the wastebasket, he felt tears in his eyes. "Little Brother," he whispered, "are you really sure that . . ."

"Drop me, you fool," hissed the little box in his hand.

Other passengers were starting to shove. Codemus opened his hand and walked out of the rail. For a moment he stood stunned. Behind him, the doors slid shut and the train shot forward.

First there was the emptiness

Codemus carefully put one foot in front of the other. And walked. For the first time he was walking by himself. He didn't know where. But it didn't bother him. He had never needed to know where he was going.

Aimlessly he elbowed his way out of the station. No one tried to stop him. Codemus started down a corridor at random. Put one foot in front of the other. Realized that he was walking by himself.

Then came the uncertainty

He was alone in a strange cube. Unfamiliar corridor names and stairway numbers. The walls were a different color. Everyone he met had somebody to talk to—in their pocket, shoulder bag, or in their hand up to their ear. Only Codemus was alone. No one looked at him. No one noticed he was there. One-two-one-two.

And finally came the fear, of course

Running up stairways, riding elevators, standing on transport belts, but getting nowhere, nothing happening, nobody told him what to do, not knowing, nobody knew him, hungry, ragged, stopped a man in yellow overalls, an office worker of his own type, wanted to talk to him, ask, couldn't get his mouth open, tongue dry, the man shook off his hand, "Don't have time," said the breast pocket.

And in the efficient society there are no benches to rest on.

Toward evening Codemus was huddled on a stairway landing on the second level. He missed his own cube, but couldn't find his way back to the monorail.

Happy workers stepped over him on their way to B shift. Codemus gazed after them for a long time, humming hoarsely to the music from their little brothers.

IT IS NOT GOOD FOR A HUMAN BEING TO BE ALONE

Something had happened. Something he didn't understand. Only that it put him outside. Codemus was sitting outside and wanted to get in.

IT IS NOT GOOD FOR A HUMAN BEING TO BE DIFFERENT

He looked at the confident faces around him. Harmonious, efficient people striding with purposeful steps toward assignments useful to society. Codemus felt meaningless.

He was as good as dead.

He was dead.

A HUMAN BEING IS A SOCIAL ENTITY

When the sherlocks found him (as they did, of course) he burst into tears and embraced the cold bloodhounds.

And Codemus was led back to the flock.

Now Codemus has a new little brother. Every morning Codemus is wakened by Little Brother. While he is getting dressed and eating breakfast, Little Brother reminds him of all the things he has to do. In the monorail on the way to the office, Little Brother and Codemus discuss the program for the day. At the office, everyone works quickly and efficiently; none of the employees are in doubt about what needs to be done, and all decisions are unanimous. All the little brothers are synchronized.

A Kind of Artistry

Brian Aldiss, with J. G. Ballard, has reshaped British SF since the late 1950s. As Arthur C. Clarke is the literary heir of Olaf Stapledon, the later H. G. Wells, and John W. Campbell, so Aldiss and Ballard are the heirs of the early H. G. Wells, restoring his cosmic pessimism to the field, and opening new avenues of stylistic expression. Before Aldiss and Ballard, British SF had closely imitated the American magazine forms, with leading British writers finding their major markets in the United States. Aldiss and Ballard planted the seeds that flowered into the New Wave and created the British SF of the 1970s and 1980s, an SF suspicious of science and technology, filled with more questions than answers.

Aldiss has always been a citizen of the world, traveling widely and promoting international SF. In the early 1960s, with co-editor Harry Harrison, he founded SF Horizons, the first critical journal devoted to SF in the English language. He wrote the first critical history of SF, Billion Year Spree (1973; revised as Trillion Year Spree, 1987), and has been an indefatigable anthologist, often in collaboration with Harry Harrison. One of the most active writers in SF, Aldiss has constantly experimented with the form of SF and is seen at the height of his powers in the massive Helliconia trilogy. "A Kind of Artistry" is an early story, from 1962, a vision of love, transformation, and transcendence in the distant future, akin to the early stories of Roger Zelazny, whom it undoubtedly influenced. No single Aldiss story can show his depth and range, but this one remains among his best.

*   *   *

I

A giant rising from the fjord, from the grey arm of sea in the fjord, could have peered over the crown of its sheer cliffs and discovered Endehabven there on the edge, sprawling at the very start of the island.

Derek Flamifew/Ende saw much of this sprawl from his high window; indeed, a growing restlessness, apprehensions of a quarrel, forced him to see everything with particular clarity, just as a landscape takes on an intense actinic visibility before a thunderstorm. Although he was warmseeing with his face, yet his eye vision wandered over the estate.

All was bleakly neat at Endehabven—as I should know, for its neatness is my care. The gardens are made to support evergreens and shrubs that never flower; this is My Lady's whim, who likes a sobriety to match the furrowed brow of the coastline. The building, gaunt Endehabven itself, is tall and lank and severe; earlier ages would have found its structure impossible: its thousand built-in paragravity units ensure that column, buttress, arch and wall support masonry the mass of which is largely an illusion.

Between the building and the fjord, where the garden contrives itself into a parade, stood by My Lady's laboratory and My Lady's pets—and, indeed, My Lady herself at this time, her long hands busy with the minicoypu and the squeaking atoshkies. I stood with her, attending the animals' cages or passing her instruments or stirring the tanks, doing always what she asked. And the eyes of Derek Ende looked down on us; no, they looked down on her only.

Derek Flamifew/Ende stood with his face over the receptor bowl, reading the message from Star One. It played lightly over his countenance and over the boscises of his forehead. Though he stared down across that achingly familiar stage of his life outside, he still warmsaw the communication clearly. When it was finished, he negated the receptor, pressed his face to it, and flexed his message back.

"I will do as you message, Star One. I will go at once to Festi XV in the Veil Nebula and enter liaison with the being you call the Cliff. If possible, I will also obey your order to take some of its substance to Pyrylyn. Thank you for your greetings; I return them in good faith. Goodbye."

He straightened and massaged his face: warmlooking over great light distances was always tiring, as if the sensitive muscles of the countenance knew that they delivered up their tiny electrostatic charges to parsecs of vacuum and were appalled. Slowly his boscises also relaxed, as slowly he gathered together his gear. It would be a long flight to the Veil, and the task that was set him would daunt the stoutest heart. Yet it was for another reason he lingered; before he could be away, he had to say a farewell to his mistress.

Dilating the door, he stepped out into the corridor, walked along it with a steady tread—feet covering mosaics of a pattern learned long ago in his childhood—and walked into the paragravity shaft. Moments later, he was leaving the main hall, approaching My Lady as she stood, gaunt, with rodents scuttling at breast level before her and Vatya Jokatt's heights rising behind her, grey with the impurities of distance.

"Go indoors and fetch me the box of name rings, Hols," she said to me; so I passed him, My Lord, as he went to her. He noticed me no more than he noticed any of the other parthenos, fixing his sights on her.

When I returned, she had not turned towards him, though he was speaking urgently to her.

"You know I have my duty to perform, Mistress," I heard him saying. "Nobody else but a normal-born Abrogunnan can be entrusted with this sort of task."

"This sort of task! The galaxy is loaded inexhaustibly with such tasks! You can excuse yourself forever with such excursions."

He said to her remote back, pleadingly: "You can't talk of them like that. You know of the nature of the Cliff—I told you all about it. You know this isn't an excursion: it requires all the courage I have. And you know that in this sector of Starswarm only Abrogunnans, for some reason, have such courage . . . don't you, Mistress?"

Although I had come up to them, threading my subservient way between cage and tank, they noticed me not enough even to lower their voices. My Lady stood gazing at the grey heights inland, her countenance as formidable as they; one boscis twitched as she said, "You think you are so mighty and brave, don't you?"

Knowing the power of sympathetic magic, she never spoke his name when she was angry; it was as if she wished him to disappear.

"It isn't that," he said humbly. "Please be reasonable, Mistress; you know I must go; a man cannot be forever at home. Don't be angry."

She turned to him at last.

Her face was high and stern; it did not receive. Her warmvision was closed and seldom used. Yet she had a beauty of some dreadful kind I cannot describe, if kneading together weariness and knowledge can create beauty. Her eyes were as grey and distant as the frieze of the snow-covered volcano behind her. She was a century older than Derek, though the difference showed not in her skin—which would stay fresh yet a thousand years—but in her authority.

"I'm not angry. I'm only hurt. You know how you have the power to hurt me."

"Mistress—" he said, taking a step towards her.

"Don't touch me," she said. "Go if you must, but don't make a mockery of it by touching me."

He took her elbow. She held one of the minicoypus quiet in the crook of her arm—animals were always docile at her touch—and strained it closer.

"I don't mean to hurt you, Mistress. You know we owe allegiance to Star One; I must work for them, or how else do we hold this estate? Let me go for once with an affectionate parting."

"Affection! You go off and leave me alone with a handful of miserable parthenos and you talk of affection! Don't pretend you don't rejoice to get away from me. You're tired of me, aren't you?"

Wearily, he said, as if nothing else would come, "It's not that—"

"You see! You don't even attempt to sound sincere. Why don't you go? It doesn't matter what happens to me."

"Oh, if you could only hear your own self-pity!"

Now she had a tear on the icy slope of one cheek. Turning, she flashed it for his inspection.

"Who else should pity me? You don't, or you wouldn't go away from me as you do. Suppose you get killed by this Cliff, what will happen to me?"

"I shall be back, Mistress," he said. "Never fear."

"It's easy to say. Why don't you have the courage to admit that you're only too glad to leave me?"

"Because I'm not going to be provoked into a quarrel."

"Pah! You sound like a child again. You won't answer, will you? Instead you're going to run away, evading your responsibilities."

"I'm not running away!"

"Of course you are, whatever you pretend. You're just immature."

"I'm not, I'm not! And I'm not running away! It takes real courage to do what I'm going to do."

"You think so well of yourself!"

He turned away then, petulantly, without dignity. He began to head towards the landing platform. He began to run.

"Derek!" she called.

He did not answer.

She took the squatting minicoypu by the scruff of its neck. Angrily she flung it into a nearby tank of water. It turned into a fish and swam down into the depths.

II

Derek journeyed towards the Veil Nebula in his fast lightpusher. Lonely it sailed, a great fin shaped like an archer's bow, barnacled all over with the photon cells that sucked its motive power from the dense and dusty currencies of space. Midway along the trailing edge was the blister in which Derek lay, senseless over most of his voyage, which stretched a quarter way across the light-centuries of Vermilion Sector.

He awoke in the therapeutic bed, called to another day that was no day by gentle machine hands that eased the stiffness from his muscles. Soup gurgled in a retort, bubbling up towards a nipple only two inches from his mouth. He drank. He slept again, tired from his long inactivity.

When he woke again, he climbed slowly from the bed and exercised. Then he moved forward to the controls. My friend Jon was there.

"How is everything?" Derek asked him.

"Everything is in order, My Lord," Jon replied. "We are swinging into the orbit of Festi XV now." He gave Derek the coordinates and retired to eat. Jon's job was the loneliest any partheno could have. We are hatched according to strictly controlled formulae, without the inbred organizations of DNA that assure true Abrogunnans their amazing longevity; five more long hauls and Jon will be old and worn out, fit only for the transmuter.

Derek sat at the controls. Did he see, superimposed on the face of Festi, the face he loved and feared? I think he did. I think there were no swirling clouds for him that could erase the clouding of her brow.

Whatever he saw, he settled the lightpusher into a fast low orbit about the desolate planet. The sun Festi was little more than a blazing point some eight hundred million miles away. Like the riding light of a ship it bobbed above a turbulent sea of cloud as they went in.

For a long while, Derek sat with his face in a receptor bowl, checking ground heats far below. Since he was dealing with temperatures approaching absolute zero, this was not simple; yet when the Cliff moved into a position directly below, there was no mistaking its bulk; it stood out as clearly on his senses as if outlined on a radar screen.

"There she goes!" Derek exclaimed.

Jon had come forward again. He fed the time coordinates into the lightpusher's brain, waited, and read off the time when the Cliff would be below them once more.

Nodding, Derek began to prepare to jump. Without haste, he assumed his special suit, checking each item as he took it up, opening the paragravs until he floated and then closing them again, clicking down every snap-fastener until he was entirely encased.

"395 seconds to next zenith, My Lord," Jon said.

"You know all about collecting me?"

"Yes, sir."

"I shall not activate the radio beacon till I'm back in orbit."

"I fully understand, sir."

"Right. I'll be moving."

A little animated prison, he walked ponderously into the air lock.

Three minutes before they were next above the Cliff, Derek opened the outer door and dived into the sea of cloud. A brief blast of his suit jets set him free from the lightpusher's orbit. Cloud engulfed him as he fell.

The twenty surly planets that swung round Festi held only an infinitesimal fraction of the mysteries of the Starswarm. Every globe in the universe huddled its own secret purpose to itself. On some, as on Abrogun, the purpose manifested itself in a form of being that could shape itself, burst into the space lanes, and rough-hew its aims in a civilized, extraplanetary environment. On others, the purpose remained aloof and dark; only human beings, weaving their obscure patterns of will and compulsion, challenged those alien beings to wrest from them new knowledge that might be added to the store of old.

All knowledge has its influence. Over the millennia since interstellar flights had become practicable, mankind was insensibly moulded by its own findings; together with its lost innocence, its genetic stability disappeared. As man fell like rain over other planets, so his family lost its original hereditary design; each centre of civilization bred new ways of thought, of feeling, of shape—of—life itself. In Sector Vermilion, the man who dived headfirst to meet an entity called the Cliff was human more in his sufferings than his appearance.

The Cliff had destroyed all the few spaceships or lightpushers landing on its desolate globe. After long study from safe orbits, the wise men of Star One evolved the theory that the Cliff attacked any considerable source of power, as a man will swat a buzzing fly. Derek Ende, alone with no power but his suit motors, would be safe—or so the theory went.

Riding down on the paragravs, he sank more and more slowly into planetary night. The last of the cloud was whipped from about his shoulders, and a high wind thrummed and whistled around the supporters of his suit. Beneath him, the ground loomed. So as not to be blown across it, he speeded his rate of fall; next moment he sprawled full length on Festi XV. For a while he lay there, resting and letting his suit cool.

The darkness was not complete. Though almost no solar light touched this continent, green flares grew from the ground, illumining its barren contours. Wishing to accustom his eyes to the gloom, he did not switch on his head, shoulder, stomach or hand lights.

Something like a stream of fire flowed to his left. Because its radiance was poor and guttering, it confused itself with its own shadows, so that the smoke it gave off, distorted into bars by the bulk of the 4G planet, appeared to roll along its course like burning tumbleweed. Further off were larger sources of fire, most probably impure ethane and methane, burning with a sound that came like frying steak to Derek's ears, spouting upward with an energy that licked the lowering cloud race with blue light. At another point, a geyser of flame blazing on an eminence wrapped itself in a thickly swirling pall of smoke, a pall that spread upward as slowly as porridge. Elsewhere, a pillar of white fire burned without motion or smoke; it stood to the right of where Derek lay, like a floodlit sword in its perfection.

He nodded approval to himself. His drop had been successfully placed. This was the Region of Fire, where the Cliff lived.

To lie there was pleasant enough, to gaze on a scene never closely viewed by man fulfilment enough—until he realized that a wide segment of landscape offered not the slightest glimmer of illumination. He looked into it with a keen warmsight, and found it was the Cliff.

The immense bulk of the thing blotted out all light from the ground and rose to eclipse the cloud over its crest.

At the mere sight of it, Derek's primary and secondary hearts began to beat out a hastening pulse of awe. Stretched flat on the ground, his paragravs keeping him level to 1G, he peered ahead at it; he swallowed to clear his choked throat; his eyes strained through the mosaic of dull light in an endeavour to define the Cliff.

One thing was sure: it was huge! He cursed the fact that although photosistors allowed him to use his warmsight on objects beyond the suit he wore, this sense was distorted by the eternal firework display. Then in a moment of good seeing he had an accurate fix: the Cliff was still some distance away! From first observations, he had thought it to be no more than a hundred paces distant.

Now he realized how large it was. It was enormous!

Momentarily he gloated. The only sort of tasks worth being set were impossible ones. Star One's astrophysicists held the notion that the Cliff was in some sense aware; they required Derek to take them a sample of its flesh. How do you carve a being the size of a small moon?

All the time he lay there, the wind jarred along the veins and supporters of his suit. Gradually it occurred to Derek that the vibration he felt from this constant motion was changed. It carried a new note and a new strength. He looked about, placed his gloved hand outstretched on the ground.

The wind was no longer vibrating. It was the earth that shook, Festi itself that trembled. The Cliff was moving!

When he looked back up at it with both his senses, he saw which way it headed. Jarring steadily, the Cliff bore down on him.

"If it has intelligence, then it will reason—if it has detected me—that I am too small to offer it harm. So it will offer me none, and I have nothing to fear," Derek told himself. The logic did not reassure him.

An absorbent pseudopod, activated by a simple humidity gland in the brow of his helmet, slid across his forehead and removed the sweat that had formed there.

Visibility fluttered like a rag in a cellar. The forward surge of the Cliff was still something Derek sensed rather than saw. Now the masses of cloud blotted the thing's crest, as it in its turn eclipsed the fountains of fire. To the jar of its approach even the marrow of Derek's bones raised a response.

Something else also responded.

The legs of Derek's suit began to move. The arms moved. The body wriggled.

Puzzled, Derek stiffened his legs. Irresistibly, the knees of the suit hinged, forcing his own to do likewise. And not only his knees, but his arms too, stiffly though he braced them on the ground before him, were made to bend to the whim of the suit. He could not keep still without breaking his bones.

Thoroughly alarmed, he lay there flexing contortedly to keep rhythm with his suit, performing the gestures of an idiot.

As if it had suddenly learned to crawl, the suit began to move forward. It shuffled over the ground; Derek inside went willy-nilly with it.

One ironic thought struck him. Not only was the mountain coming to Mohammed; Mohammed was perforce going to the mountain . . .

III

Nothing he did checked his progress; he was no longer master of his movements; his will was useless. With the realization rode a sense of relief. His Mistress could hardly blame him for anything that happened now.

Through the darkness he went on hands and knees, blundering in the direction of the oncoming Cliff, prisoner in an animated prison.

The only constructive thought that came to him was that his suit had somehow become subject to the Cliff; how, he did not know or try to guess.

He crawled. He was almost relaxed now, letting his limbs move limply with the suit movements.

Smoke furled about him. The vibrations ceased, telling him that the Cliff was stationary again. Raising his head, he could see nothing but smoke — produced perhaps by the Cliffs mass as it scraped over the ground. When the blur parted, he glimpsed only darkness. The thing was directly ahead!

He blundered on. Abruptly he began to climb, still involuntarily aping the movements of his suit.

Beneath him was a doughy substance, tough yet yielding. The suit worked its way heavily upward at an angle of something like sixty-five degrees; the stiffness creaked, the paragravs throbbed. He was ascending the Cliff.

By this time there was no doubt in Derek's mind that the thing possessed what might be termed volition, if not consciousness. It also possessed a power no man could claim; it could impart that volition to an inanimate object like the suit. Helpless inside it, he carried his considerations a stage further. This power to impart volition seemed to have a limited range; otherwise the Cliff surely would not have bothered to move its gigantic mass at all, but would have forced the suit to traverse all the distance between them. If this reasoning were sound, then the lightpusher was safe from capture in orbit.

The movement of his arms distracted him. His suit was tunnelling. Giving it no aid, he lay and let his hands make swimming motions. If it was going to bore into the Cliff, then he could only conclude he was about to be digested: yet he stilled his impulse to struggle, knowing that struggle was fruitless.

Thrusting against the doughy stuff, the suit burrowed into it and made a sibilant little world of movement and friction that ceased the moment it stopped, leaving Derek embedded in the most solid kind of isolation.

To ward off growing claustrophobia, he attempted to switch on his headlight; his suit arms remained so stiff he could not bend them enough to reach the toggle. All he could do was lie there in his shell and stare into the featureless darkness of the Cliff.

But the darkness was not entirely featureless. His ears detected a constant *slither* along the outside surfaces of his suit. His warmsight discerned a meaningless pattern beyond his helmet. Though he focused his boscises, he could make no sense of the pattern; it had neither symmetry nor meaning for him . . .

Yet for his body it seemed to have some meaning. Derek felt his limbs tremble, was aware of pulses and phantom impressions within himself that he had not known before. The realization percolated through to him that he was in touch with powers of which he had no cognizance; conversely, that something was in touch with him that had no cognizance of his powers.

An immense heaviness overcame him. The forces of life laboured within him. He sensed, more vividly than before, the vast bulk of the Cliff. Though it was dwarfed by the mass of Festi XV, it was as large as a good-sized asteroid. . . . He could picture an asteroid, formed from a jetting explosion of gas on the face of Festi the sun. Half-solid, half-molten, the matter swung about its parent in an eccentric orbit. Cooling under an interplay of pressures, its interior crystallized into a unique form. Thus, with its surface semi-plastic, it existed for many millions of years, gradually accumulating an electrostatic charge that poised . . . and waited . . . and brewed the life acids about its crystalline heart.

Festi was a stable system, but once in every so many thousands of millions of years the giant first, second, and third planets achieved perihelion with the sun and with each other simultaneously. This happened coincidentally with the asteroid's nearest approach; it was wrenched from its orbit and all but grazed the three lined-up planets. Vast electrical and gravitational forces were unleashed. The asteroid glowed: and woke to consciousness. Life was not born on it: it was born to life, born in one cataclysmic clash!

Before it had more than savoured the sad-sharp-sweet sensation of consciousness, it was in trouble. Plunging away from the sun on its new course, it found itself snared in the gravitational pull of the 4G planet, Festi XV. It knew no shaping force but gravity; gravity was to it all that oxygen was to cellular life on Abrogun; though it had no wish to exchange its flight for captivity, it was too puny to resist. For the first time, the asteroid recognized that its consciousness had a use, for it could to some extent control the environment outside itself. Rather than risk being broken up in Festi's orbit, it sped inward, and by retarding its own fall performed its first act of volition, an act that brought it down shaken but entire on the surface of the planet.

For an immeasurable period, this asteroid—the Cliff—lay in the shallow crater formed by its impact, speculating without thought. It knew nothing except the inorganic scene about it, and could visualize nothing else but that scene it knew well. Gradually it came to some kind of terms with the scene. Formed by gravity, it used gravity as unconsciously as a man uses breath; it began to move other things, and it began to move itself.

That it should be other than alone in the universe had never occurred to the Cliff. Now that it knew there was other life, it accepted the fact. The other life was not as it was; that it accepted. The other life had its own requirements; that it accepted. Of questions, of doubt, it did not know. It had a need; so did the other life; they should both be accommodated, for accommodation was the adjustment to pressure, and that response was one it comprehended.

Derek Ende's suit began to move again under external volition. Carefully it worked its way backward. It was ejected from the Cliff. It lay still.

Derek himself lay still. He was barely conscious. In a half-daze, he pieced together what had happened.

The Cliff had communicated with him; if he ever doubted that, the evidence of it lay clutched in the crook of his left arm.

"Yet it did not—yet it could not communicate with me!" he murmured. But it had communicated: he was still faint with the burden of it.

The Cliff had nothing like a brain. It had not "recognized" Derek's brain. Instead, it had communicated directly to his cell organization, and in particular, probably, to those cytoplasmic structures, the mitochondria, the power sources of the cell. His brain had been by-passed, but his own cells had taken in the information offered.

He recognized his feeling of weakness. The Cliff had drained him of power. Even that could not drain his feeling of triumph; for the Cliff had taken information even as it gave it. The Cliff had learned that other life existed in other parts of the universe.

Without hesitation, without debate, it had given a fragment of itself to be taken to those other parts of the universe. Derek's mission was completed.

In the Cliff's gesture, Derek read one of the deepest urges of living things: the urge to make an impression on another living thing. Smiling wryly, he pulled himself to his feet.

Derek was alone in the Region of Fire. An infrequent mournful flame still confronted its surrounding dark, but the Cliff had disappeared. He had lain on the threshold of consciousness longer than he thought. He looked at his chronometer and found that it was time he moved towards his rendezvous with the lightpusher. Stepping up his suit temperature to combat the cold beginning to seep through his bones, he revved up the paragrav unit and rose. The noisome clouds came down and engulfed him; Festi was lost to view. Soon he had risen beyond cloud or atmosphere.

Under Jon's direction, the space craft homed onto Derek's radio beacon. After a few tricky minutes, they matched velocities and Derek climbed aboard.

"Are you all right?" the partheno asked, as his master staggered into a flight seat.

"Yes—just weak. I'll tell you all about it as I do a report on spool for Pyrylyn. They'll be pleased with us."

He produced a yellow-grey blob of matter that had expanded to the size of a large turkey and held it out to Jon.

"Don't touch this with uncovered hands. Put it in one of the low-temperature lockers under 4Gs. It's a little souvenir from Festi XV."

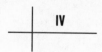

IV

The Eyebright in Pynnati, one of the planet Pyrylyn's capital cities, was where you went to enjoy yourself on the most lavish scale possible. This was where Derek Ende's hosts took him, with Jon in self-effacing attendance.

They lay in a nest of couches that slowly revolved, giving them a full view of other dance and couch parties. The room itself moved. Its walls were transparent; through them could be seen an ever-changing view as the room slid up and down and about the great metal framework of the Eyebright. First they were on the outside of the structure, with the brilliant night lights of Pynnati winking up at them as if intimately involved in their delight. Then they slipped inward in the slow evagination of the building, to be surrounded by other pleasure rooms, their revellers clearly visible as they moved grandly up or down or along.

Uneasily, Derek lay on his couch. A vision of his Mistress's face was before him; he could imagine how she would treat all this harmless festivity: with cool contempt. His own pleasure was consequently reduced to ashes.

"I suppose you'll be moving back to Abrogun as soon as possible?"

"Eh?" Derek grunted.

"I said, I suppose you would soon be going home again." The speaker was Belix Ix Sappose, Chief Administrator of Star One; as Derek's host of the evening, he lay next to him.

"I'm sorry, Belix, yes—I shall have to."

"No 'have to' about it. You have discovered an entirely new life form, as I have already reported to Starswarm Central; we can now attempt communication with the Festi XV entity, with goodness knows what extension of knowledge. The government can easily show its gratitude by awarding you any post here you care to name; I am not without influence in that respect, as you are aware. I don't imagine that Abrogun in its present state of political paralysis has much to offer a man of your calibre. Your matriarchal system is much to blame."

Derek thought of what Abrogun had to offer; he was bound to it. These decadent people did not understand how a human contract could be binding.

"Well, what do you say, Ende? I do not speak idly." Belix Ix Sappose tapped his antler system impatiently.

"Er . . . oh, they will discover a great deal from the Cliff. That doesn't concern me. My part of the work is over. I'm a field worker, not an intellectual."

"You don't reply to my suggestion."

He looked at Belix with only slight vexation. Belix was an unglaat, one of a species that had done as much as any to bring about the peaceful concourse of the galaxy. His backbone branched into an elaborate antler system, from which six sloe-dark eyes surveyed Derek with unblinking irritation. Other members of the party, including Jupkey, Belix's female, were also looking at him.

"I must return," Derek said. What had Belix said? Offered some sort of post? Restlessly he shifted on his couch, under pressure as always when surrounded by people he knew none too well.

"You are bored, Ende."

"No, not at all. My apologies, Belix. I'm overcome as always by the luxury of Eyebright. I was watching the nude dancers."

"May I signal you a woman?"

"No, thank you."

"A boy perhaps?"

"No, thank you."

"Ever tried the flowering asexuals from the Cephids?"

"Not at present, thank you."

"Then perhaps you will excuse us if Jupkey and I remove our clothes and join the dance," Belix said stiffly.

As they moved out onto the dance floor to greet the strepent trumpets, Derek heard Jupkey say something of which he caught only the words "arrogant Abrogunnan." His eyes met Jon's; he saw that the partheno had overheard the phrase, too.

To conceal his mortification, Derek rose and began to pace around the room. He shouldered his way through knots of naked dancers, ignoring their complaints.

At one of the doors, a staircase was floating by. He stepped onto it to escape from the crowds.

Four young women were passing down the stairs. They were gaily dressed, with sonant-stones pulsing on their costumes. Their faces were filled with happiness as they laughed and chattered. Derek stopped and beheld the girls. One of them he recognized. Instinctively he called her name: "Eva!"

She had already seen him. Waving her companions on, she came back to him, dancing up the intervening steps.

"So the hero of Abrogun climbs once more the golden stairs of Pynnati! Well, Derek Ende, your eyes are as dark as ever, and your brow as high!"

As he looked at her, the trumpets were in tune for him for the first time that evening, and his delight rose up in his throat.

"Eva! . . . your eyes as bright as ever . . . and you have no man with you."

"The powers of coincidence work on your behalf." She laughed—yes, he remembered that sound!—and then said more seriously, "I heard you were with Belix Sappose and his female; so I was making the grandly foolish gesture of coming to see you. You remember how devoted I am to grandly foolish gestures."

"So foolish?"

"So devoted! But you have less ability to change, Derek Ende, than has the core of Pyrylyn. To suppose otherwise is foolish; to know how unalterable you are and still to see you is doubly foolish."

He took her hand, beginning to lead her up the staircase; the rooms moving by them on either side were blurs to his eyes.

"Must you still bring up that old charge, Eva?"

"It lies between us; I do not have to touch it. I fear your unchangeability because I am a butterfly against your grey castle."

"You are beautiful, Eva, so beautiful! And may a butterfly not rest unharmed on a castle wall?" He fitted into her allusive way of speech with difficulty.

"Walls! I cannot bear your walls, Derek! Am I a bulldozer that I should want to come up against walls? To be either inside or outside them is to be a prisoner."

"Let us not quarrel until we have found some point of agreement," he said. "Here are the stars. Can't we agree about them?"

"If we are both indifferent to them," she said, looking out and impudently winding his arm about her. The staircase had attained the zenith of its travels and moved slowly sideways along the upper edge of Eyebright. They stood on the top step with night flashing their images back at them from the glass.

Eva Coll-Kennerley was a human, but not of any common stock. She was a velure, born of the dense y-cluster worlds in Vermilion Outer, and her skin was richly covered with the brown fur of her kind. Her mercurial talents were employed in the same research department that enjoyed Belix Sappose's more sober ones; Derek had met her there on an earlier visit to

Pyrylyn. Their love had been an affair of swords until her scabbard disarmed him.

He looked at her now and touched her and could say not one word. When she flashed a liquid eye at him, he essayed an awkward smile.

"Because I am oriented like a compass towards strong men, my lavish offer to you still holds good. Is it not bait enough?" she asked him.

"I don't think of you as a trap, Eva."

"Then for how many more centuries are you going to refrigerate your nature on Abrogun? You still remain faithful, if I recall your euphemism for slavery, to your Mistress, to her cold lips and locked heart?"

"I have no choice!"

"Ah yes, my debate on that motion was defeated—and more than once. Is she still pursuing her researches into the transmutability of species?"

"Oh yes, indeed. The medieval idea that one species can turn into another was foolish at that time; now, with the gradual accumulation of cosmic radiation in planetary bodies and its effect on genetic stability, it is correct to a certain definable extent. She is endeavouring to show that cellular bondage can be—"

"Yes, yes, and this serious talk is an eyesore in Eyebright! Do you think I can hear of her when I want to talk of you? You are locked away, Derek, doing your sterile deeds of heroism and never entering the real world. If you imagine you can live with her much longer and then come to me, you are mistaken. Your walls grow higher about your ears every century, till I cannot—oh, it's the wrong metaphor!—cannot scale you!"

Even in his pain, the texture of her fur was joy to his warmsight. Helplessly he shook his head in an effort to brush her clattering words away.

"Look at you being big and brave and silent—even now! You're so arrogant," she said—and then, without perceptible change of tone, "Because I still love the bit of you inside the castle, I'll make once more my monstrous and petty offer to you."

"No, please, Eva!"

"But yes! Forget this tedious bondage of Abrogun and Endehabven, forget this ghastly matriarchy, live here with me. I don't want you for ever. You know I am a eudemonist and judge by standards of pleasure—our liaison need be only for a century or two. In that time, I will deny you nothing your senses may require."

"Eva!"

"After that, our demands will be satisfied. You may then go back to the Lady Mother of Endehabven for all I care."

"Eva, you know I spurn this belief, this eudemonism."

"Forget your creed! I'm asking you nothing difficult. Who are you to haggle? Am I fish, to be bought by weight, this bit selected, that rejected?"

He was silent.

"*You* don't really need me," he said at last. "You have everything already: beauty, wit, sense, warmth, feeling, balance, comfort. *She* has nothing. She is shallow, haunted, cold—oh, she needs me, Eva."

"You are apologizing for yourself, not her."

She had already turned with the supple movement of a velure and was running down the staircase. Lighted chambers drifted up about them like bubbles.

His laboured attempt to explain his heart turned to exasperation. He ran down after her, grasping her arm.

"Listen to me!"

"No one in Pyrylyn would listen to such masochistic nonsense! You are an arrogant fool, Derek, and I am a weak-willed one. Now release me!"

As the next room came up, she jumped through its entrance and disappeared into the crowd.

Not all the drifting chambers of Eyebright were lighted. Some pleasures come more delightfully with the dark, and these were coaxed and cosseted into fruition in halls where illumination cast only the gentlest ripple on the ceiling and the gloom was sensuous with perfumes. Here Derek found a place to weep.

Sections of his life slid before him as if impelled by the same mechanisms that moved Eyebright. Always, one presence was there.

Angrily he related to himself how he always laboured to satisfy her—yes, in every shaped laboured to satisfy her! And how when that satisfaction was accorded him it came as though riven from her, as a spring sometimes trickles down the split face of a rock. Undeniably there was satisfaction for him in drinking from that cool source—but no, where was the satisfaction when pleasure depended on such extreme disciplining and subduing of self?

"Mistress, I love and hate your needs!"

And the discipline had been such . . . so long . . . that now when he might enjoy himself far from her, he could scarcely strike a trickle from his own rock. He had walked here before, in this city where the hedonists and eudemonists reigned, walked among the scents of pleasure, walked among the ioblepharous women, the beautiful guests and celebrated beauties, with My Lady always in him, feeling that she showed even on his countenance. People spoke to him; somehow he replied. They manifested gaiety; he tried to do so. They opened to him; he attempted a response. All the time he hoped they would understand that his arrogance masked only shyness—or did he hope that it was his shyness that masked arrogance? He did not know.

Who could presume to know? The one quality holds much of the other. Both refuse to come forward and share.

He roused from his meditation knowing that Eva Coll-Kennerley was again somewhere near. She had not left the building!

Derek half-rose from his position in a shrouded alcove. He was baffled to think how she could have traced him here. On entering Eyebright, visitors were given sonant-stones, by which they could be traced from room to room; but judging that no one would wish to trace him, Derek had switched his stone off even before leaving Belix Sappose's party.

He heard Eva's voice, its unmistakable overtones not near, not far . . .

"You find the most impenetrable bushels to hide your light under—"

He caught no more. She had sunk down among tapestries with someone else. She was not after him at all! Waves of relief and regret rolled over him . . . and when he paid attention again, she was speaking his name.

With shame on him, he crouched forward to listen. At once his warm-sight told him to whom Eva spoke. He recognized the pattern of the antlers; Belix was there, with Jupkey sprawled beside him on some elaborate kind of bed.

". . . useless to try again. Derek is too far entombed within himself," Eva said.

"Entombed rather within his conditioning," Belix said. "We found the same. It's conditioning, my dear—all conditioning with these Abrogun-nans. Look at it scientifically: Abrogun is the last bastion of a bankrupt culture. The Abrogunnans number mere thousands now. They disdain social graces and occasions. They are served by parthenogenically bred slaves. They themselves are inbred. In consequence, they have become practically a species apart. You can see it all in friend Ende. A tragedy, Eva, but you must face up to it."

"You're probably right," Jupkey inserted lazily. "Who but an Abrogun-nan would do what Derek did on Festi?"

"No, no!" Eva said. "Derek's ruled by a woman, not by conditioning. He's—"

"In Ende's case they are one and the same thing, my dear, believe me. Consider their social organization. The partheno slaves have replaced all but a handful of true men. They live on their great estates, ruled by a matriarch."

"Yes, I know, but Derek—"

"Derek is caught in the system. They have fallen into a mating pattern without precedent in Starswarm. The sons of a family marry their mothers, not only to perpetuate their line but because a productive female has become rare by now. Derek Ende's 'mistress' is both mother and wife to him. Add the factor of longevity and you ensure an excessive emotional rigidity that almost nothing can break—not even you, my sweet Eva!"

"He was on the point of breaking tonight!"

"I doubt it," Belix said. "Ende may want to get away from his claustrophobic home, but the same forces that drive him off will eventually lure him back."

"I tell you he was on the point of breaking—but I broke first."

"Well, as Teer Ruche said to me many centuries ago, only a pleasure-hater knows how to shape a pleasure-hater. I would say you were lucky he did not break—you would only have had a baby on your hands."

Her answering laugh did not ring true.

"My Lady of Endehabven, then, must be the one to do it. I will never try again—though he seems under too much stress to stand for long. Oh, it's really immoral! He deserves better!"

"A moral judgement from you, Eva!" Jupkey exclaimed amusedly.

"My advice to you, Eva, is to forget all about the fellow. Apart from everything else, he is scarcely articulate—which would not suit you for a season."

The unseen listener could bear no more. A sudden rage—as much against himself for hearing as against them for speaking—burst over him. Straightening up, he seized the arm of the couch on which Belix and Jupkey nestled, wildly supposing he could tip them onto the floor.

Too late, his warmsight warned him of the real nature of the couch. Instead of tipping, it swivelled, sending a wave of liquid over him. The two unglaats were lying in a warm bath scented with essences.

Eva shouted for lights. Other occupants of the hall cried back that darkness must prevail at all costs.

Leaving only his dignity behind, Derek ran for the exit, abandoning the confusion to sort itself out as it would. Burningly, disgustedly, he made his way, dripping, from Eyebright. The hastening footsteps of Jon followed him like an echo all the way to the space field.

Soon he would be back at Endehabven. Though he would always be a failure in his dealings with other humans, there at least he knew every inch of his bleak allotted territory.

ENVOI

Had there been a spell over all Endehabven, it could have been no quieter when My Lord Derek Ende arrived home.

I informed My Lady the moment his lightpusher arrived and rode at orbit. In the receptor bowl I watched him and Jon come home, alighting by the very edge of the island, by the fjord with its silent waters.

All the while the wind lay low as if under some stunning malediction, and none of our tall arborials stirred.

"Where is my Mistress, Hols?" Derek asked me, as I went to greet him and assist him out of his suit.

"She asked me to tell you that she is confined to her chambers and cannot see you, My Lord."

He looked me in the eyes as he did so rarely. "Is she ill?"

"No. She simply said she could not see you."

Without waiting to remove his suit, he hurried on into the building.

Over the next two days, he was about but little, preferring to remain in his room while My Lady insisted on remaining in hers. Once he wandered among the experimental tanks and cages. I saw him net a fish and toss it into the air, watching it while it struggled into new form and flew away until it was lost in a jumbled background of cumulus; but it was plain he was less interested in the riddles of stress and transmutation than in the symbolism of the carp's flight.

Mostly he sat compiling the spools on which he imposed the tale of his life. All one wall was covered with files full of these spools—the arrested drumbeats of past centuries. From the later spools I have secretly compiled this record; for all his unspoken self-pity, he never knew the sickness of merely observing.

We parthenos will never understand the luxuries of a divided mind. Surely suffering as much as happiness is a kind of artistry?

On the day that he received a summons from Star One to go upon another quest, Derek met My Lady in the Blue Corridor.

"It is good to see you about again, Mistress," he said, kissing her cheek. "To remain confined to your room is bad for you."

She stroked his hair. On her nervous hand she wore one ring with an amber stone; her gown was of olive and umber.

"Don't reproach me! I was upset to have you go away from me. This world is dying, Derek, and I fear its loneliness. You have left me alone too often. However, I have recovered and am glad to see you back."

"You know I am glad to see you. Smile for me and come outside for some fresh air. The sun is shining."

"It's so long since it shone. Do you remember how once it always shone? I can't bear to quarrel anymore. Take my arm and be kind to me."

"Mistress, I always wish to be kind to you. And I have all sorts of things to discuss with you. You'll want to hear what I have been doing, and—"

"You won't leave me alone anymore?"

He felt her hand tighten on his arm. She spoke very loudly.

"That was one of the things I wished to discuss—later," he said. "First let me tell you about the wonderful life form with which I made contact on Festi."

As they left the corridor and descended the paragravity shaft, My Lady said wearily, "I suppose that's a polite way of telling me that you are bored here."

He clutched her hands as they floated down. Then he released them and clutched her face instead, cupping it between his palms.

"Understand this, Mistress mine, I love you and want to serve you. You are in my blood; wherever I go I never can forget you. My dearest wish is to make you happy—this you must know. But equally you must know that I have needs of my own."

"I know those needs will always come first with you, whatever you say or pretend."

She moved ahead of him, shaking off the hand he put on her arm. He had a vision of himself running down a golden staircase and stretching out that same detaining hand to another girl. The indignity of having to repeat oneself, century after century.

"You're being cruel!" he said.

Gleaming, she turned. "Am I? Then answer me this—aren't you already planning to leave Endehabven again?"

He said haltingly, "Yes, yes, it's true I am thinking. . . . But I have to—I reproach myself. I could be kinder. But you shut yourself away when I come back; you don't welcome me—"

"Trust you to find excuses rather than face up to your own nature," she said contemptuously, walking briskly into the garden. Amber and olive and umber, and sable of hair, she walked down the path, her outlines sharp in the winter air. In the perspectives of his mind she did not dwindle.

For some minutes he stood in the threshold, immobilized by antagonistic emotions.

Finally he pushed himself out into the sunlight.

She was in her favourite spot by the fjord, feeding an old badiger from her hand. Only her increased attention to the badiger suggested that she heard him approach.

His boscises twitched as he said, "I'm sorry."

"I don't mind what you do."

Walking backward and forward behind her, he said, "When I was away, I heard some people talking. On Pyrylyn this was. They were discussing the mores of our matrimonial system."

"It's no business of theirs."

"Perhaps not. But what they said suggested a new line of thought to me."

She put the badiger back in his cage without comment.

"Are you listening, Mistress?"

"Do go on."

"Try to listen sympathetically. Consider all the history of galactic exploration—or even before that, consider the explorers of worlds without space flight. They were brave men, of course, but wouldn't it be strange if most of them only ventured into the unknown because the struggle at home was too much for them?"

He stopped. She had turned to him; the halfsmile was whipped off his face by her look of fury.

"And you're trying to tell me that that's how you see yourself—a martyr? Derek, how you must hate me! Not only do you go away, but you secretly blame me because you go away. It doesn't matter, that I tell you a thousand times I want you here—no, it's all my fault! I drive you away! That's what you tell your charming friends on Pyrylyn, isn't it? Oh, how you must hate me!"

Savagely he grasped her wrists. She screamed to me for aid and struggled. I came near but halted, playing my usual impotent part. He swore at her, bellowed for her to be silent, whereupon she cried the louder, shaking furiously in his arms, both of them tumultuous in their emotions.

He struck her across the face.

At once she was quiet. Her eyes closed almost, it would seem, in ecstasy. Standing there, she had the pose of a woman offering herself.

"Go on, hit me! You want to hit me!" she whispered.

With the words, with the look of her, he too was altered. As if realizing for the first time her true nature, he lowered his fists and stepped back, staring at her, sick-mouthed. His heel met no resistance. He twisted suddenly, spread out his arms as if to fly, and fell over the cliff edge.

Her scream pursued him down.

Even as his body hit the waters of the fjord, it began to change. A flurry of foam marked some sort of painful struggle beneath the surface. Then a seal plunged into view, dived below the next wave, and swam towards the open sea, over which an already freshening breeze blew.

PHILIP K. DICK

Second Variety

At the time of his death in 1982, Philip K. Dick was widely regarded as the greatest contemporary SF writer, the most respected in Europe and widely praised in England. Although only moderately successful in the United States during his lifetime, in a recent survey of younger American science fiction writers Dick was the only writer listed as an influence by every single person polled. He was the only American SF writer whom Stanislaw Lem exempted from his general condemnation of the form. The Philip K. Dick Award is now given annually for a distinguished work of SF appearing in the United States originally in paperback, and there is a Philip K. Dick Society devoted to the study and promulgation of his works, with an international newsletter. Dick had an initial flush of success in the 1950s that culminated in the Hugo Award for the best novel of 1963, The Man in the High Castle. *In the last year of his life, the film* Blade Runner *was made from his novel* Do Androids Dream of Electric Sheep?, *his first major financial success. Dick was given to passionate loves (and five marriages), experiments with mind-altering substances, psychological breakdowns, and religious experiences. Behind the thin veil of distance imposed by the SF form, his best works are disturbingly intense, sometimes horrifying. "Second Variety" is a cold-war myth from 1953, when he had just begun to publish. One might suspect the influence of Ray Bradbury, who wrote so shockingly of inhuman impostors in "Mars Is Heaven," but the immediacy of the setting and the paranoid switchbacks in the plot are pure Phil Dick. Throughout his career his understanding of the imagery of politics and of technology was intuitively apt.*

*   *   *

The Russian soldier made his way nervously up the ragged side of the hill, holding his gun ready. He glanced around him, licking his dry lips, his face set. From time to time he reached up a gloved hand and wiped perspiration from his neck, pushing down his coat collar.

Eric turned to Corporal Leone. "Want him? Or can I have him?" He adjusted the view sight so the Russian's features squarely filled the glass, the lines cutting across his hard, somber features.

Leone considered. The Russian was close, moving rapidly, almost running. "Don't fire. Wait." Leone tensed. "I don't think we're needed."

The Russian increased his pace, kicking ash and piles of debris out of his way. He reached the top of the hill and stopped, panting, staring around him. The sky was overcast, with drifting clouds of gray particles. Bare trunks of trees jutted up occasionally; the ground was level and bare, rubbled-strewn, with the ruins of buildings standing out here and there like yellow-ing skulls.

The Russian was uneasy. He knew something was wrong. He started down the hill. Now he was only a few paces from the bunker. Eric was getting fidgety. He played with his pistol, glancing at Leone.

"Don't worry," Leone said. "He won't get here. They'll take care of him."

"Are you sure? He's got damn far."

"They hang around close to the bunker. He's getting into the bad part. Get set!"

The Russian began to hurry, sliding down the hill, his boots sinking into the heaps of gray ash, trying to keep his gun up. He stopped for a moment, lifting his field glasses to his face.

"He's looking right at us," Eric said.

The Russian came on. They could see his eyes, like two blue stones. His mouth was open a little. He needed a shave; his chin was stubbled. On one bony cheek was a square of tape, showing blue at the edge. A fungoid spot. His coat was muddy and torn. One glove was missing. As he ran, his belt counter bounced up and down against him.

Leone touched Eric's arm. "Here one comes."

Across the ground something small and metallic came, flashing in the dull sunlight of midday. A metal sphere. It raced up the hill after the Russian, its treads flying. It was small, one of the baby ones. Its claws were out, two razor projections spinning in a blur of white steel. The Russian heard it. He turned instantly, firing. The sphere dissolved into particles. But already a second had emerged and was following the first. The Russian fired again.

A third sphere leaped up the Russian's leg, clicking and whirring. It jumped to the shoulder. The spinning blades disappeared into the Russian's throat.

Eric relaxed. "Well, that's that. God, those damn things give me the creeps. Sometimes I think we were better off before."

"If we hadn't invented them, they would have." Leone lit a cigarette shakily. "I wonder why a Russian would come all this way alone. I didn't see anyone covering him."

Lieutenant Scott came slipping up the tunnel, into the bunker. "What happened? Something entered the screen."

"An Ivan."

"Just one?"

Eric brought the viewscreen around. Scott peered into it. Now there were numerous metal spheres crawling over the prostrate body, dull metal globes clicking and whirring, sawing up the Russian into small parts to be carried away.

"What a lot of claws," Scott murmured.

"They come like flies. Not much game for them any more."

Scott pushed the sight away, disgusted. "Like flies. I wonder why he was out there. They know we have claws all around."

A larger robot had joined the smaller spheres. A long blunt tube with projecting eyepieces, it was directing operations. There was not much left of the soldier. What remained was being brought down the hillside by the host of claws.

"Sir," Leone said. "If it's all right, I'd like to go out there and take a look at him."

"Why?"

"Maybe he came with something."

Scott considered. He shrugged. "All right. But be careful."

"I have my tab." Leone patted the metal band at his wrist. "I'll be out of bounds."

He picked up his rifle and stepped carefully up to the mouth of the bunker, making his way between blocks of concrete and steel prongs, twisted and bent. The air was cold at the top. He crossed over the ground toward the remains of the soldier, striding across the soft ash. A wind blew around him, swirling gray particles up in his face. He squinted and pushed on.

The claws retreated as he came close, some of them stiffening into immobility. He touched his tab. The Ivan would have given something for that! Short hard radiation emitted from the tab neutralized the claws, put them out of commission. Even the big robot with its two waving eyestalks retreated respectfully as he approached.

He bent down over the remains of the soldier. The gloved hand was closed tightly. There was something in it. Leone pried the fingers apart. A sealed container, aluminum. Still shiny.

He put it in his pocket and made his way back to the bunker. Behind him the claws came back to life, moving into operation again. The procession resumed, metal spheres moving through the gray ash with their loads. He could hear their treads scrabbling against the ground. He shuddered.

Scott watched intently as he brought the shiny tube out of his pocket. "He had that?"

"In his hand." Leone unscrewed the top. "Maybe you should look at it, sir."

Scott took it. He emptied the contents out in the palm of his hand. A small piece of silk paper, carefully folded. He sat down by the light and unfolded it.

"What's it say, sir?" Eric said. Several officers came up the tunnel. Major Hendricks appeared.

"Major," Scott said. "Look at this."

Hendricks read the slip. "This just come?"

"A single runner. Just now."

"Where is he?" Hendricks asked sharply.

"The claws got him."

Major Hendricks grunted. "Here." He passed it to his companions. "I think this is what we've been waiting for. They certainly took their time about it."

"So they want to talk terms," Scott said. "Are we going along with them?"

"That's not for us to decide." Hendricks sat down. "Where's the communications officer? I want the Moon Base."

Leone pondered as the communications officer raised the outside antenna cautiously, scanning the sky above the bunker for any sign of a watching Russian ship.

"Sir," Scott said to Hendricks. "It's sure strange they suddenly came around. We've been using the claws for almost a year. Now all of a sudden they start to fold."

"Maybe claws have been getting down in their bunkers."

"One of the big ones, the kind with stalks, got into an Ivan bunker last week," Eric said. "It got a whole platoon of them before they got their lid shut."

"How do you know?"

"A buddy told me. The thing came back with—with remains."

"Moon Base, sir," the communications officer said.

On the screen the face of the lunar monitor appeared. His crisp uniform contrasted to the uniforms in the bunker. And he was cleanshaven. "Moon Base."

"This is forward command L-Whistle. On Terra. Let me have General Thompson."

The monitor faded. Presently General Thompson's heavy features came into focus. "What is it, Major?"

"Our claws got a single Russian runner with a message. We don't know whether to act on it—there have been tricks like this in the past."

"What's the message?"

"The Russians want us to send a single officer on policy level over to their lines. For a conference. They don't state the nature of the conference. They say that matters of—" He consulted the slip: "—matters of grave urgency make it advisable that discussion be opened between a representative of the UN forces and themselves."

He held the message up to the screen for the general to scan. Thompson's eyes moved.

"What should we do?" Hendricks said.

"Send a man out."

"You don't think it's a trap?"

"It might be. But the location they give for their forward command is correct. It's worth a try, at any rate."

"I'll send an officer out. And report the results to you as soon as he returns."

"All right, Major." Thompson broke the connection. The screen died. Up above, the antenna came slowly down.

Hendricks rolled up the paper, deep in thought.

"I'll go," Leone said.

"They want somebody at policy level." Hendricks rubbed his jaw. "Policy level. I haven't been outside in months. Maybe I could use a little air."

"Don't you think it's risky?"

Hendricks lifted the view sight and gazed into it. The remains of the Russian were gone. Only a single claw was in sight. It was folding itself back, disappearing into the ash, like a crab. Like some hideous metal crab . . .

"That's the only thing that bothers me." Hendricks rubbed his wrist. "I know I'm safe as long as I have this on me. But there's something about them. I hate the damn things. I wish we'd never invented them. There's something wrong with them. Relentless little—"

"If we hadn't invented them, the Ivans would have."

Hendricks pushed the sight back. "Anyhow, it seems to be winning the war. I guess that's good."

"Sounds like you're getting the same jitters as the Ivans."

Hendricks examined his wristwatch. "I guess I had better get started, if I want to be there before dark."

.   .   .

He took a deep breath and then stepped out onto the gray rubbled ground. After a minute he lit a cigarette and stood gazing around him. The landscape was dead. Nothing stirred. He could see for miles, endless ash and slag, ruins of buildings. A few trees without leaves or branches, only the trunks. Above him the eternal rolling clouds of gray, drifting between Terra and the sun.

Major Hendricks went on. Off to the right something scuttled, something round and metallic. A claw, going lickety-split after something. Probably after a small animal, a rat. They got rats, too. As a sort of sideline.

He came to the top of the little hill and lifted his field glasses. The Russian lines were a few miles ahead of him. They had a forward command post there. The runner had come from it.

A squat robot with undulating arms passed by him, its arms weaving inquiringly. The robot went on its way, disappearing under some debris. Hendricks watched it go. He had never seen that type before. There were getting to be more and more types he had never seen, new varieties and sizes coming up from the underground factories.

Hendricks put out his cigarette and hurried on. It was interesting, the use of artificial forms in warfare. How had they got started? Necessity. The Soviet Union had gained great initial success, usual with the side that got the war going. Most of North America had been blasted off the map. Retaliation was quick in coming, of course. The sky was full of circling diskbombers long before the war began; they had been up there for years. The disks began sailing down all over Russia within hours after Washington got it.

But that hadn't helped Washington.

The American bloc governments moved to the Moon Base the first year. There was not much else to do. Europe was gone, a slag heap with dark weeds growing from the ashes and bones. Most of North America was useless; nothing could be planted, no one could live. A few million people kept going up in Canada and down in South America. But during the second year Soviet parachutists began to drop, a few at first, then more and more. They wore the first really effective antiradiation equipment; what was left of American production moved to the Moon along with the governments.

All but the troops. The remaining troops stayed behind as best they could, a few thousand here, a platoon there. No one knew exactly where they were; they stayed where they could, moving around at night, hiding in ruins, in sewers, cellars, with the rats and snakes. It looked as if the Soviet Union had the war almost won. Except for a handful of projectiles fired off from the Moon daily, there was almost no weapon in use against them. They came and went as they pleased. The war, for all practical purposes, was over. Nothing effective opposed them.

And then the first claws appeared. And overnight the complexion of the war changed.

The claws were awkward, at first. Slow. The Ivans knocked them off almost as fast as they crawled out of their underground tunnels. But then they got better, faster and more cunning. Factories, all on Terra, turned them out. Factories a long way underground, behind the Soviet lines, factories that had once made atomic projectiles, now almost forgotten.

The claws got faster, and they got bigger. New types appeared, some with feelers, some that flew. There were a few jumping kinds. The best technicians on the Moon were working on designs, making them more and more intricate, more flexible. They became uncanny; the Ivans were having a lot of trouble with them. Some of the little claws were learning to hide themselves, burrowing down into the ash, lying in wait.

And then they started getting into the Russian bunkers, slipping down when the lids were raised for air and a look around. One claw inside a bunker, a churning sphere of blades and metal—that was enough. And when one got in others followed. With a weapon like that the war couldn't go on much longer.

Maybe it was already over.

Maybe he was going to hear the news. Maybe the Politburo had decided to throw in the sponge. Too bad it had taken so long. Six years. A long time for war like that, the way they had waged it. The automatic retaliation disks, spinning down all over Russia, hundreds of thousands of them. Bacteria crystals. The Soviet guided missiles, whistling through the air. The chain bombs. And now this, the robots, the claws—

The claws weren't like other weapons. They were *alive*, from any practical standpoint, whether the Governments wanted to admit it or not. They were not machines. They were living things, spinning, creeping, shaking themselves up suddenly from the gray ash and darting toward a man, climbing up him, rushing for his throat. And that was what they had been designed to do. Their job.

They did their job well. Especially lately, with the new designs coming up. Now they repaired themselves. They were on their own. Radiation tabs protected the UN troops, but if a man lost his tab he was fair game for the claws, no matter what his uniform. Down below the surface automatic machinery stamped them out. Human beings stayed a long way off. It was too risky; nobody wanted to be around them. They were left to themselves. And they seemed to be doing all right. The new designs were faster, more complex. More efficient.

Apparently they had won the war.

.   .   .

Major Hendricks lit a second cigarette. The landscape depressed him. Nothing but ash and ruins. He seemed to be alone, the only living thing in the whole world. To the right the ruins of a town rose up, a few walls and heaps of debris. He tossed the dead match away, increasing his pace. Suddenly he stopped, jerking up his gun, his body tense. For a minute it looked like—

From behind the shell of a ruined building a figure came, walking slowly toward him, walking hesitantly.

Hendricks blinked. "Stop!"

The boy stopped. Hendricks lowered his gun. The boy stood silently, looking at him. He was small, not very old. Perhaps eight. But it was hard to tell. Most of the kids who remained were stunted. He wore a faded blue sweater, ragged with dirt, and short pants. His hair was long and matted. Brown hair. It hung over his face and around his ears. He held something in his arms.

"What's that you have?" Hendricks said sharply.

The boy held it out. It was a toy, a bear. A teddy bear. The boy's eyes were large, but without expression.

Hendricks relaxed. "I don't want it. Keep it."

The boy hugged the bear again.

"Where do you live?" Hendricks said.

"In there."

"The ruins?"

"Yes."

"Underground?"

"Yes."

"How many are there?"

"How—how many?"

"How many of you. How big's your settlement?"

The boy did not answer.

Hendricks frowned. "You're not all by yourself, are you?"

The boy nodded.

"How do you stay alive?"

"There's food."

"What kind of food?"

"Different."

Hendricks studied him. "How old are you?"

"Thirteen."

It wasn't possible. Or was it? The boy was thin, stunted. And probably sterile. Radiation exposure, years straight. No wonder he was so small. His arms and legs were like pipe cleaners, knobby and thin. Hendricks touched the boy's arm. His skin was dry and rough; radiation skin. He bent down, looking into the boy's face. There was no expression. Big eyes, big and dark.

"Are you blind?" Hendricks said.

"No. I can see some."

"How do you get away from the claws?"

"The claws?"

"The round things. That run and burrow."

"I don't understand."

Maybe there weren't any claws around. A lot of areas were free. They collected mostly around bunkers, where there were people. The claws had been designed to sense warmth, warmth of living things.

"You're lucky." Hendricks straightened up. "Well? Which way are you going? Back—back there?"

"Can I come with you?"

"With *me*?" Hendricks folded his arms. "I'm going a long way. Miles. I have to hurry." He looked at his watch. "I have to get there by nightfall."

"I want to come."

Hendricks fumbled in his pack. "It isn't worth it. Here." He tossed down the food cans he had with him. "You take these and go back. Okay?"

The boy said nothing.

"I'll be coming back this way. In a day or so. If you're around here when I come back you can come along with me. All right?"

"I want to go with you now."

"It's a long walk."

"I can walk."

Hendricks shifted uneasily. It made too good a target, two people walking along. And the boy would slow him down. But he might not come back this way. And if the boy were really all alone—

"Okay. Come along."

The boy fell in beside him. Hendricks strode along. The boy walked silently, clutching his teddy bear.

"What's your name?" Hendricks said, after a time.

"David Edward Derring."

"David? What—what happened to your mother and father?"

"They died."

"How?"

"In the blast."

"How long ago?"

"Six years."

Hendricks slowed down. "You've been alone six years?"

"No. There were other people for a while. They went away."

"And you've been alone since?"

"Yes."

Hendricks glanced down. The boy was strange, saying very little. With-drawn. But that was the way they were, the children who had survived. Quiet. Stoic. A strange kind of fatalism gripped them. Nothing came as a surprise. They accepted anything that came along. There was no longer any *normal*, any natural course of things, moral or physical, for them to expect. Custom, habit, all the determining forces of learning were gone; only brute experience remained.

"Am I walking too fast?" Hendricks said.

"No."

"How did you happen to see me?"

"I was waiting."

"Waiting?" Hendricks was puzzled. "What were you waiting for?"

"To catch things."

"What kind of things?"

"Things to eat."

"Oh." Hendricks set his lips grimly. A thirteen-year-old boy, living on rats and gophers and half-rotten canned food. Down in a hole under the ruins of a town. With radiation pools and claws, and Russian dive-mines up above, coasting around in the sky.

"Where are we going?" David asked.

"To the Russian lines."

"Russian?"

"The enemy. The people who started the war. They dropped the first radiation bombs. They began all this."

The boy nodded. His face showed no expression.

"I'm an American," Hendricks said.

There was no comment. On they went, the two of them, Hendricks walking a little ahead, David trailing behind him, hugging his dirty teddy bear against his chest.

About four in the afternoon they stopped to eat. Hendricks built a fire in a hollow between some slabs of concrete. He cleared the weeds away and heaped up bits of wood. The Russians' lines were not very far ahead. Around him was what had once been a long valley, acres of fruit trees and grapes. Nothing remained now but a few bleak stumps and the mountains that stretched across the horizon at the far end. And the clouds of rolling ash that blew and drifted with the wind, settling over the weeds and remains of buildings, walls here and there, once in a while what had been a road.

Hendricks made coffee and heated up some boiled mutton and bread. "Here." He handed bread and mutton to David. David squatted by the edge of the fire, his knees knobby and white. He examined the food and then passed it back, shaking his head.

"No."

"No? Don't you want any?"

"No."

Hendricks shrugged. Maybe the boy was a mutant, used to special food. It didn't matter. When he was hungry he would find something to eat. The boy was strange. But there were many strange changes coming over the world. Life was not the same anymore. It would never be the same again. The human race was going to have to realize that.

"Suit yourself," Hendricks said. He ate the bread and mutton by himself, washing it down with coffee. He ate slowly, finding the food hard to digest. When he was done he got to his feet and stamped the fire out.

David rose slowly, watching him with his young-old eyes.

"We're going," Hendricks said.

"All right."

Hendricks walked along, his gun in his arms. They were close; he was tense, ready for anything. The Russians should be expecting a runner, an answer to their own runner, but they were tricky. There was always the possibility of a slip-up. He scanned the landscape around him. Nothing but slag and ash, a few hills, charred trees. Concrete walls. But some place ahead was the first bunker of the Russian lines, the forward command. Underground, buried deep, with only a periscope showing, a few gun muzzles. Maybe an antenna.

"Will we be there soon?" David asked.

"Yes. Getting tired?"

"No."

"Why, then?"

David did not answer. He plodded carefully along behind, picking his way over the ash. His legs and shoes were gray with dust. His pinched face was streaked, lines of gray ash in riverlets down the pale white of his skin. There was no color to his face. Typical of the new children, growing up in cellars and sewers and underground shelters.

Hendricks slowed down. He lifted his field glasses and studied the ground ahead of him. Were they there, some place, waiting for him? Watching him, the way his men had watched the Russian runner? A chill went up his back. Maybe they were getting their guns ready, preparing to fire, the way his men had prepared, made ready to kill.

Hendricks stopped, wiping perspiration from his face. "Damn." It made him uneasy. But he should be expected. The situation was different.

He strode over the ash, holding his gun tightly with both hands. Behind him came David. Hendricks peered around, tight-lipped. Any second it might happen. A burst of white light, a blast, carefully aimed from inside a deep concrete bunker.

He raised his arm and waved it around in a circle.

Nothing moved. To the right a long ridge ran, topped with dead tree trunks. A few wild vines had grown up around the trees, remains of arbors. And the eternal dark weeds. Hendricks studied the ridge. Was anything up there? Perfect place for a lookout. He approached the ridge warily, David coming silently behind. If it were his command he'd have a sentry up there, watching for troops trying to infiltrate into the command area. Of course, if it were his command there would be the claws around the area for full protection.

He stopped, feet apart, hands on his hips.

"Are we there?" David said.

"Almost."

"Why have we stopped?"

"I don't want to take any chances." Hendricks advanced slowly. Now the ridge lay directly beside him, along his right. Overlooking him. His uneasy feeling increased. If an Ivan were up there he wouldn't have a chance. He waved his arm again. They should be expecting someone in the UN uniform, in response to the note capsule. Unless the whole thing was a trap.

"Keep up with me." He turned toward David. "Don't drop behind."

"With you?"

"Up beside me! We're close. We can't take any chances. Come on."

"I'll be all right." David remained behind him, in the rear, a few paces away, still clutching his teddy bear.

"Have it your way." Hendricks raised his glasses again, suddenly tense. For a moment—had something moved? He scanned the ridge carefully. Everything was silent. Dead. No life up there, only tree trunks and ash. Maybe a few rats. The big black rats that had survived the claws. Mutants— built their own shelters out of saliva and ash. Some kind of plaster. Adaptation. He started forward again.

A tall figure came out on the ridge above him, cloak flapping. Gray-green. A Russian. Behind him a second soldier appeared, another Russian. Both lifted their guns, aiming.

Hendricks froze. He opened his mouth. The soldiers were kneeling, sighting down the side of the slope. A third figure had joined them on the ridge top, a smaller figure in gray-green. A woman. She stood behind the other two.

Hendricks found his voice. "Stop!" He waved up at them frantically. "I'm—"

The two Russians fired. Behind Hendricks there was a faint *pop*. Waves of heat lapped against him, throwing him to the ground. Ash tore at his face, grinding into his eyes and nose. Choking, he pulled himself to his knees. It was all a trap. He was finished. He had come to be killed, like a steer. The soldiers and the woman were coming down the side of the ridge toward him, sliding down through the soft ash. Hendricks was numb. His head throbbed. Awkwardly, he got his rifle up and took aim. It weighed a thousand tons; he could hardly hold it. His nose and cheeks stung. The air was full of the blast smell, a bitter acrid stench.

"Don't fire," the first Russian said, in heavily accented English.

The three of them came up to him, surrounding him. "Put down your rifle, Yank," the other said.

Hendricks was dazed. Everything had happened so fast. He had been caught. And they had blasted the boy. He turned his head. David was gone. What remained of him was strewn across the ground.

The three Russians studied him curiously. Hendricks sat, wiping blood from his nose, picking out bits of ash. He shook his head, trying to clear it. "Why did you do it?" he murmured thickly. "The boy."

"Why?" One of the soldiers helped him roughly to his feet. He turned Hendricks around. "Look."

Hendricks closed his eyes.

"Look!" The two Russians pulled him forward. "See. Hurry up. There isn't much time to spare, Yank!"

Hendricks looked. And gasped.

"See now? Now do you understand?"

From the remains of David a metal wheel rolled. Relays, glinting metal. Parts, wiring. One of the Russians kicked at the heap of remains. Parts popped out, rolling away, wheels and springs and rods. A plastic section fell in, half charred. Hendricks bent shakily down. The front of the head had come off. He could make out the intricate brain, wires and relays, tiny tubes and switches, thousands of minute studs—

"A robot," the soldier holding his arm said. "We watched it tagging you."

"Tagging me?"

"That's their way. They tag along with you. Into the bunker. That's how they get in."

Hendricks blinked, dazed. "But—"

"Come on." They led him toward the ridge. "We can't stay here. It isn't safe. There must be hundreds of them all around here."

The three of them pulled him up the side of the ridge, sliding and slipping on the ash. The woman reached the top and stood waiting for them.

"The forward command," Hendricks muttered. "I came to negotiate with the Soviet—"

"There is no more forward command. *They* got in. We'll explain." They reached the top of the ridge. "We're all that's left. The three of us. The rest were down in the bunker."

"This way. Down this way." The woman unscrewed a lid, a gray manhole cover set in the ground. "Get in."

Hendricks lowered himself. The two soldiers and the woman came behind him, following him down the ladder. The woman closed the lid after them, bolting it tightly into place.

"Good thing we saw you," one of the two soldiers grunted. "It had tagged you about as far as it was going to."

"Give me one of your cigarettes," the woman said. "I haven't had an American cigarette for weeks."

Hendricks pushed the pack to her. She took a cigarette and passed the pack to the two soldiers. In the corner of the small room the lamp gleamed fitfully. The room was low-ceilinged, cramped. The four of them sat around a small wood table. A few dirty dishes were stacked to one side. Behind a ragged curtain a second room was partly visible. Hendricks saw the corner of a coat, some blankets, clothes hung on a hook.

"We were here," the soldier beside him said. He took off his helmet, pushing his blond hair back. "I'm Corporal Rudi Maxer. Polish. Impressed in the Soviet Army two years ago." He held out his hand.

Hendricks hesitated and then shook. "Major Joseph Hendricks."

"Klaus Epstein." The other soldier shook with him, a small dark man with thinning hair. Esptein plucked nervously at his ear. "Austrian. Impressed God knows when. I don't remember. The three of us were here, Rudi and I, with Tasso." He indicated the woman. "That's how we escaped. All the rest were down in the bunker."

"And—and *they* got in?"

Epstein lit a cigarette. "First just one of them. The kind that tagged you. Then it let others in."

Hendricks became alert. "The *kind?* Are there more than one kind?"

"The little boy. David. David holding his teddy bear. That's Variety Three. The most effective."

"What are the other types?"

Epstein reached into his coat. "Here." He tossed a packet of photographs onto the table, tied with a string. "Look for yourself."

Hendricks untied the string.

"You see," Rudi Maxer said, "that was why we wanted to talk terms. The Russians, I mean. We found out about a week ago. Found out that your claws were beginning to make up new designs on their own. New types of their own. Better types. Down in your underground factories behind our lines. You let them stamp themselves, repair themselves. Made them more and more intricate. It's your fault this happened."

Hendricks examined the photos. They had been snapped hurriedly; they were blurred and indistinct. The first few showed—David. David walking along a road, by himself. David and another David. Three Davids. All exactly alike. Each with a ragged teddy bear.

All pathetic.

"Look at the others," Tasso said.

The next pictures, taken at a great distance, showed a towering wounded soldier sitting by the side of a path, his arm in a sling, the stump of one leg extended, a crude crutch on his lap. Then two wounded soldiers, both the same, standing side by side.

"That's Variety One. The Wounded Soldier." Klaus reached out and took the pictures. "You see, the claws were designed to get to human beings. To find them. Each kind was better than the last. They got farther, closer, past most of our defenses, into our lines. But as long as they were merely *machines*, metal spheres with claws and horns, feelers, they could be picked off like any other object. They could be detected as lethal robots as soon as they were seen. Once we caught sight of them—"

"Variety One subverted our whole north wing," Rudi said. "It was a long time before anyone caught on. Then it was too late. They came in, wounded soldiers, knocking and begging to be let in. So we let them in. And as soon as they were in they took over. We were watching out for machines . . ."

"At that time it was thought there was only the one type," Klaus Epstein said. "No one suspected there were other types. The pictures were flashed to us. When the runner was sent to you, we knew of just one type. Variety One. The big Wounded Soldier. We thought that was all."

"Your line fell to—"

"To Variety Three. David and his bear. That worked even better." Klaus smiled bitterly. "Soldiers are suckers for children. We brought them in and tried to feed them. We found out the hard way what they were after. At least, those who were in the bunker."

"The three of us were lucky," Rudi said. "Klaus and I were—were visiting Tasso when it happened. This is her place." He waved a big hand around. "This little cellar. We finished and climbed the ladder to start back. From the ridge we saw that they were all around the bunker. Fighting was still going on. David and his bear. Hundreds of them. Klaus took the pictures."

Klaus tied up the photographs again.

"And it's going on all along your line?" Hendricks said.

"Yes."

"How about *our* lines?" Without thinking, he touched the tab on his arm. "Can they—"

"They're not bothered by your radiation tabs. It makes no difference to them, Russian, American, Pole, German. It's all the same. They're doing what they were designed to do. Carrying out the original idea. They track down life, wherever they find it."

"They go by warmth," Klaus said. "That was the way you constructed them from the very start. Of course, those you designed were kept back by the radiation tabs you wear. Now they've got around that. These new varieties are lead-lined."

"What's the other variety?" Hendricks asked. "The David type, the Wounded Soldier—what's the other?"

"We don't know." Klaus pointed up at the wall. On the wall were two metal plates, ragged at the edges. Hendricks got up and studied them. They were bent and dented.

"The one on the left came off a Wounded Soldier," Rudi said. "We got one of them. It was going along toward our old bunker. We got it from the ridge, the same way we got the David tagging you."

The plate was stamped: *I-V.* Hendricks touched the other plate. "And this came from the David type?"

"Yes." The plate was stamped: *III-V.*

Klaus took a look at them, leaning over Hendricks's broad shoulder. "You can see what we're up against. There's another type. Maybe it was abandoned. Maybe it didn't work. But there must be a Second Variety. There's One and Three."

"You were lucky," Rudi said. "The David tagged you all the way here and never touched you. Probably thought you'd get it into a bunker, somewhere."

"One gets in and it's all over," Klaus said. "They move fast. One lets all the rest inside. They're inflexible. Machines with one purpose. They were built for only one thing." He rubbed sweat from his lip. "We saw."

They were silent.

"Let me have another cigarette, Yank," Tasso said. "They are good. I almost forgot how they were."

It was night. The sky was black. No stars were visible through the rolling clouds of ash. Klaus lifted the lid cautiously so that Hendricks could look out.

Rudi pointed into the darkness. "Over that way are the bunkers. Where we used to be. Not over half a mile from us. It was just chance Klaus and I were not there when it happened. Weakness. Saved by our lusts."

"All the rest must be dead," Klaus said in a low voice. "It came quickly. This morning the Politburo reached their decision. They notified us—forward command. Our runner was sent out at once. We saw him start toward the direction of your lines. We covered him until he was out of sight."

"Alex Radrivsky. We both knew him. He disappeared about six o'clock. The sun had just come up. About noon Klaus and I had an hour relief. We crept off, away from the bunkers. No one was watching. We came here. There used to be a town here, a few houses, a street. This cellar was part of a big farmhouse. We knew Tasso would be here, hiding down in her little place. We had come here before. Others from the bunkers came here. Today happened to be our turn."

"So we were saved," Klaus said. "Chance. It might have been others. We—we finished, and then we came up to the surface and started back along the ridge. That was when we saw them, the Davids. We understood right away. We had seen the photos of the First Variety, the Wounded Soldier. Our Commissar distributed them to us with an explanation. If we had gone another step they would have seen us. As it was we had to blast two Davids before we got back. There were hundreds of them, all around. Like ants. We took pictures and slipped back here, bolting the lid tight."

"They're not so much when you catch them alone. We moved faster than they did. But they're inexorable. Not like living things. They came right at us. And we blasted them."

Major Hendricks rested against the edge of the lid, adjusting his eyes to the darkness. "Is it safe to have the lid up at all?"

"If we're careful. How else can you operate your transmitter?"

Hendricks lifted the small belt transmitter slowly. He pressed it against his ear. The metal was cold and damp. He blew against the mike, raising up the short antenna. A faint hum sounded in his ear. "That's true, I suppose."

But he still hesitated.

"We'll pull you under if anything happens," Klaus said.

"Thanks." Hendricks waited a moment, resting the transmitter against his shoulder. "Interesting, isn't it?"

"What?"

"This, the new types. The new varieties of claws. We're completely at their mercy, aren't we? By now they've probably gotten into the UN lines, too. It makes me wonder if we're not seeing the beginning of a new species. *The* new species. Evolution. The race to come after man."

Rudi grunted. "There is no race after man."

"No? Why not? Maybe we're seeing it now, the end of human beings, the beginning of the new society."

"They're not a race. They're mechanical killers. You made them to destroy. That's all they can do. They're machines with a job."

"So it seems now. But how about later on? After the war is over. Maybe, when there aren't any humans to destroy, their real potentialities will begin to show."

"You talk as if they were alive!"

"Aren't they?"

There was silence. "They're machines," Rudi said. "They look like people, but they're machines."

"Use your transmitter, Major," Klaus said. "We can't stay up here forever."

Holding the transmitter tightly, Hendricks called the code of the command bunker. He waited, listening. No response. Only silence. He checked the leads carefully. Everything was in place.

"Scott!" he said into the mike. "Can you hear me?"

Silence. He raised the gain up full and tried again. Only static.

"I don't get anything. They may hear me but they may not want to answer."

"Tell them it's an emergency."

"They'll think I'm being forced to call. Under your direction." He tried again, outlining briefly what he had learned. But still the phone was silent, except for the faint static.

"Radiation pools kill most transmission," Klaus said, after awhile. "Maybe that's it."

Hendricks shut the transmitter up. "No use. No answer. Radiation pools? Maybe. Or they hear me, but won't answer. Frankly, that's what I would do, if a runner tried to call from the Soviet lines. They have no reason to believe such a story. They may hear everything I say—"

"Or maybe it's too late."

Hendricks nodded.

"We better get the lid down," Rudi said nervously. "We don't want to take unnecessary chances."

They climbed slowly back down the tunnel. Klaus bolted the lid carefully into place. They descended into the kitchen. The air was heavy and close around them.

"Could they work that fast?" Hendricks said. "I left the bunker this noon. Ten hours ago. How could they move so quickly?"

"It doesn't take them long. Not after the first one gets in. It goes wild. You know what the little claws can do. Even *one* of these is beyond belief. Razors, each finger. Maniacal."

"All right." Hendricks moved away impatiently. He stood with his back to them.

"What's the matter?" Rudi said.

"The Moon Base. God, if they've gotten there—"

"The Moon Base?"

Hendricks turned around. "They couldn't have got to the Moon Base. How would they get there? It isn't possible. I can't believe it."

"What is this Moon Base? We've heard rumors, but nothing definite. What is the actual situation? You seem concerned."

"We're supplied from the Moon. The governments are there, under the lunar surface. All our people and industries. That's what keeps us going. If they should find some way of getting off Terra, onto the Moon—"

"It only takes one of them. Once the first one gets in it admits the others. Hundreds of them, all alike. You should have seen them. Identical. Like ants."

"Perfect socialism," Tasso said. "The ideal of the communist state. All citizens interchangeable."

Klaus grunted angrily. "That's enough. Well? What next?"

Hendricks paced back and forth, around the small room. The air was full of smells of food and perspiration. The others watched him. Presently Tasso pushed through the curtain, into the other room. "I'm going to take a nap."

The curtain closed behind her. Rudi and Klaus sat down at the table, still watching Hendricks. "It's up to you," Klaus said. "We don't know your situation."

Hendricks nodded.

"It's a problem." Rudi drank some coffee, filling his cup from a rusty pot. "We're safe here for a while, but we can't stay here forever. Not enough food or supplies."

"But if we go outside—"

"If we go outside they'll get us. Or probably they'll get us. We couldn't go very far. How far is your command bunker, Major?"

"Three or four miles."

"We might make it. The four of us. Four of us could watch all sides. They couldn't slip up behind us and start tagging us. We have three rifles, three blast rifles. Tasso can have my pistol." Rudi tapped his belt. "In the Soviet army we didn't have shoes always, but we had guns. With all four of us armed one of us might get to your command bunker. Preferably you, Major."

"What if they're already there?" Klaus said.

Rudi shrugged. "Well, then we come back here."

Hendricks stopped pacing. "What do you think the chances are they're already in the American lines?"

"Hard to say. Fairly good. They're organized. They know exactly what they're doing. Once they start they go like a horde of locusts. They have to keep moving, and fast. It's secrecy and speed they depend on. Surprise. They push their way in before anyone has any idea."

"I see," Hendricks murmured.

From the other room Tasso stirred. "Major?"

Hendricks pushed the curtain back. "What?"

Tasso looked up at him lazily from the cot. "Have you any more American cigarettes left?"

Hendricks went into the room and sat down across from her, on a wood stool. He felt in his pockets. "No. All gone."

"Too bad."

"What nationality are you?" Hendricks asked after a while.

"Russian."

"How did you get here?"

"Here?"

"This used to be France. This was part of Normandy. Did you come with the Soviet army?"

"Why?"

"Just curious." He studied her. She had taken off her coat, tossing it over the end of the cot. She was young, about twenty. Slim. Her long hair stretched out over the pillow. She was staring at him silently, her eyes dark and large.

"What's on your mind?" Tasso said.

"Nothing. How old are you?"

"Eighteen." She continued to watch him, unblinking, her arms behind her head. She had on Russian army pants and shirt. Gray-green. Thick leather belt with counter and cartridges. Medicine kit.

"You're in the Soviet army?"

"No."

"Where did you get the uniform?"

She shrugged. "It was given to me," she told him.

"How—how old were you when you came here?"

"Sixteen."

"That young?"

Her eyes narrowed. "What do you mean?"

Hendricks rubbed his jaw. "Your life would have been a lot different if there had been no war. Sixteen. You came here at sixteen. To live this way."

"I had to survive."

"I'm not moralizing."

"Your life would have been different, too," Tasso murmured. She reached down and unfastened one of her boots. She kicked the boot off, onto the floor. "Major, do you want to go in the other room? I'm sleepy."

"It's going to be a problem, the four of us here. It's going to be hard to live in these quarters. Are there just the two rooms?"

"Yes."

"How big was the cellar originally? Was it larger than this? Are there other rooms filled up with debris? We might be able to open one of them."

"Perhaps. I really don't know." Tasso loosened her belt. She made herself comfortable on the cot, unbuttoning her shirt. "You're sure you have no more cigarettes?"

"I had only the one pack."

"Too bad. Maybe if we get back to your bunker we can find some." The other boot fell. Tasso reached up for the light cord. "Good night."

"You're going to sleep?"

"That's right."

The room plunged into darkness. Hendricks got up and made his way past the curtain, into the kitchen. And stopped, rigid.

Rudi stood against the wall, his face white and gleaming. His mouth opened and closed but no sounds came. Klaus stood in front of him, the muzzle of his pistol in Rudi's stomach. Neither of them moved. Klaus, his hand tight around his gun, his features set. Rudi, pale and silent, spread-eagled against the wall.

"What—" Hendricks muttered, but Klaus cut him off.

"Be quiet, Major. Come over here. Your gun. Get out your gun."

Hendricks drew his pistol. "What is it?"

"Cover him." Klaus motioned him forward. "Beside me. Hurry!"

Rudi moved a little, lowering his arms. He turned to Hendricks, licking his lips. The whites of his eyes shone wildly. Sweat dripped from his forehead, down his cheeks. He fixed his gaze on Hendricks. "Major, he's gone insane. Stop him." Rudi's voice was thin and hoarse, almost inaudible.

"What's going on?" Hendricks demanded.

Without lowering his pistol Klaus answered. "Major, remember our discussion? The Three Varieties? We knew about One and Three. But we didn't know about Two. At least, we didn't know before." Klaus's fingers tightened around the gun butt. "We didn't know before, but we know now."

He pressed the trigger. A burst of white heat rolled out of the gun, licking around Rudi.

"Major, this is the Second Variety."

Tasso swept the curtain aside. "Klaus! What did you do?"

Klaus turned from the charred form, gradually sinking down the wall onto the floor. "The Second Variety, Tasso. Now we know. We have all three types identified. The danger is less. I—"

Tasso stared past him at the remains of Rudi, at the blackened, smoldering fragments and bits of cloth. "You killed him."

"Him? *It*, you mean. I was watching. I had a feeling, but I wasn't sure. At least, I wasn't sure before. But this evening I was certain." Klaus rubbed his pistol butt nervously. "We're lucky. Don't you understand? Another hour and it might—"

"You were *certain?*" Tasso pushed past him and bent down, over the steaming remains on the floor. Her face became hard. "Major, see for yourself. Bones. Flesh."

Hendricks bent down beside her. The remains were human remains. Seared flesh, charred bone fragments, part of a skull. Ligaments, viscera, blood. Blood forming a pool against the wall.

"No wheels," Tasso said calmly. She straightened up. "No wheels, no parts, no relays. Not a claw. Not the Second Variety." She folded her arms. "You're going to have to be able to explain this."

Klaus sat down at the table, all the color drained suddenly from his face. He put his head in his hands and rocked back and forth.

"Snap out of it." Tasso's fingers closed over his shoulder. "Why did you do it? Why did you kill him?"

"He was frightened," Hendricks said. "All this, the whole thing, building up around us."

"Maybe."

"What, then? What do you think?"

"I think he may have had a reason for killing Rudi. A good reason."

"What reason?"

"Maybe Rudi learned something."

Hendricks studied her bleak face. "About what?" he asked.

"About him. About Klaus."

Klaus looked up quickly. "You can see what she's trying to say. She thinks I'm the Second Variety. Don't you see, Major? Now she wants you to believe I killed him on purpose. That I'm—"

"Why did you kill him, then?" Tasso said.

"I told you." Klaus shook his head wearily. "I thought he was a claw. I thought I knew."

"Why?"

"I had been watching him. I was suspicious."

"Why?"

"I thought I had seen something. Heard something. I thought I—" He stopped.

"Go on."

"We were sitting at the table. Playing cards. You two were in the other room. It was silent. I thought I heard him—*whirr.*"

There was silence.

"Do you believe that?" Tasso said to Hendricks.

"Yes. I believe what he says."

"I don't. I think he killed Rudi for a good purpose." Tasso touched the rifle, resting in the corner of the room. "Major—"

"No." Hendricks shook his head. "Let's stop it right now. One is enough. We're afraid, the way he was. If we kill him we'll be doing what he did to Rudi."

Klaus looked gratefully up at him. "Thanks. I was afraid. You understand, don't you? Now she's afraid, the way I was. She wants to kill me."

"No more killing." Hendricks moved toward the end of the ladder. "I'm going above and try the transmitter once more. If I can't get them we're moving back toward my lines tomorrow morning."

Klaus rose quickly. "I'll come up with you and give you a hand."

The night air was cold. The earth was cooling off. Klaus took a deep breath, filling his lungs. He and Hendricks stepped onto the ground, out of the tunnel. Klaus planted his feet wide apart, the rifle up, watching and listening. Hendricks crouched by the tunnel mouth, tuning the small transmitter.

"Any luck?" Klaus asked presently.

"Not yet."

"Keep trying. Tell them what happened."

Hendricks kept trying. Without success. Finally he lowered the antenna. "It's useless. They can't hear me. Or they hear me and won't answer. Or—"

"Or they don't exist."

"I'll try once more." Hendricks raised the antenna. "Scott, can you hear me? Come in!"

He listened. There was only static. Then, still very faintly—

"This is Scott."

His fingers tightened. "Scott! Is it you?"

"This is Scott."

Klaus squatted down. "Is it your command?"

"Scott, listen. Do you understand? About them, the claws. Did you get my message? Did you hear me?"

"Yes." Faintly. Almost inaudible. He could hardly make out the word.

"You got my message? Is everything all right at the bunker? None of them have got in?"

"Everything is all right."

"Have they tried to get in?"

The voice was weaker.

"No."

Hendricks turned to Klaus. "They're all right."

"Have they been attacked?"

"No." Hendricks pressed the phone tighter to his ear. "Scott I can hardly hear you. Have you notified the Moon Base? Do they know? Are they alerted?"

No answer.

"Scott! Can you hear me?"

Silence.

Hendricks relaxed, sagging. "Faded out. Must be radiation pools."

Hendricks and Klaus looked at each other. Neither of them said anything. After a time Klaus said, "Did it sound like any of your men? Could you identify the voice?"

"It was too faint."

"You couldn't be certain?"

"No."

"Then it could have been—"

"I don't know. Now I'm not sure. Let's go back down and get the lid closed."

They climbed back down the ladder slowly, into the warm cellar. Klaus bolted the lid behind them. Tasso waited for them, her face expressionless.

"Any luck?" she asked.

Neither of them answered. "Well?" Klaus said at last. "What do you think, Major? Was it your officer, or was it one of *them*?"

"I don't know."

"Then we're just where we were before."

Hendricks stared down at the floor, his jaw set. "We'll have to go. To be sure."

"Anyhow, we have food here for only a few weeks. We'd have to go up after that, in any case."

"Apparently so."

"What's wrong?" Tasso demanded. "Did you get across to your bunker? What's the matter?"

"It may have been one of my men," Hendricks said slowly. "Or it may have been one of *them*. But we'll never know standing here." He examined his watch. "Let's turn in and get some sleep. We want to be up early tomorrow."

"Early?"

"Our best chance to get through the claws should be early in the morning," Hendricks said.

The morning was crisp and clear. Major Hendricks studied the countryside through his field glasses.

"See anything?" Klaus said.

"No."

"Can you make out our bunkers?"

"Which way?"

"Here." Klaus took the glasses and adjusted them. "I know where to look." He looked a long time, silently.

Tasso came to the top of the tunnel and stepped up onto the ground. "Anything?"

"No." Klaus passed the glasses back to Hendricks. "They're out of sight. Come on. Let's not stay here."

The three of them made their way down the side of the ridge, sliding in the soft ash. Across a flat rock a lizard scuttled. They stopped instantly, rigid.

"What was it?" Klaus muttered.

"A lizard."

The lizard ran on, hurrying through the ash. It was exactly the same color as the ash.

"Perfect adaptation," Klaus said. "Proves we were right, Lysenko, I mean."

They reached the bottom of the ridge and stopped, standing close together, looking around them.

"Let's go." Hendricks started off. "It's a good long trip, on foot."

Klaus fell in beside him. Tasso walked behind, her pistol held alertly. "Major, I've been meaning to ask you something," Klaus said. "How did you run across the David? The one that was tagging you."

"I met it along the way. In some ruins."

"What did it say?"

"Not much. It said it was alone. By itself."

"You couldn't tell it was a machine? It talked like a living person? You never suspected?"

"It didn't say much. I noticed nothing unusual."

"It's strange, machines so much like people that you can be fooled. Almost alive. I wonder where it'll end."

"They're doing what you Yanks designed them to do," Tasso said. "You designed them to hunt out life and destroy. Human life. Wherever they find it."

Hendricks was watching Klaus intently. "Why did you ask me? What's on your mind?"

"Nothing," Klaus answered.

"Klaus thinks you're the Second Variety," Tasso said calmly, from behind them. "Now he's got his eye on you."

Klaus flushed. "Why not? We sent a runner to the Yank lines and *he* comes back. Maybe he thought he'd find some good game here."

Hendricks laughed harshly. "I came from the UN bunkers. There were human beings all around me."

"Maybe you saw an opportunity to get into the Soviet lines. Maybe you saw your chance. Maybe you—"

"The Soviet lines had already been taken over. Your lines had been invaded before I left my command bunker. Don't forget that."

Tasso came up beside him. "That proves nothing at all, Major."

"Why not?"

"There appears to be little communication between the varieties. Each is made in a different factory. They don't seem to work together. You might have started for the Soviet lines without knowing anything about the work of the other varieties. Or even what the other varieties were like."

"How do you know so much about the claws?" Hendricks said.

"I've seen them. I've observed them take over the Soviet bunkers."

"You know quite a lot," Klaus said. "Actually, you saw very little. Strange that you should have been such an acute observer."

Tasso laughed. "Do you suspect me, now?"

"Forget it," Hendricks said. They walked on in silence.

"Are we going the whole way on foot?" Tasso said, after awhile. "I'm not used to walking." She gazed around at the plain of ash, stretching out on all sides of them, as far as they could see. "How dreary."

"It's like this all the way," Klaus said.

"In a way I wish you had been in your bunker when the attack came."

"Somebody else would have been with you, if not me," Klaus muttered.

Tasso laughed, putting her hands in her pockets. "I suppose so."

They walked on, keeping their eyes on the vast plain of silent ash around them.

The sun was setting. Hendricks made his way forward slowly, waving Tasso and Klaus back. Klaus squatted down, resting his gun butt against the ground.

Tasso found a concrete slab and sat down with a sigh. "It's good to rest."

"Be quiet," Klaus said sharply.

Hendricks pushed up to the top of the rise ahead of them. The same rise the Russian runner had come up, the day before. Hendricks dropped down, stretching himself out, peering through his glasses at what lay beyond.

Nothing was visible. Only ash and occasional trees. But there, not more than fifty yards ahead, was the entrance of the forward command bunker. The bunker from which he had come. Hendricks watched silently. No motion. No sign of life. Nothing stirred.

Klaus slithered up beside him. "Where is it?"

"Down there." Hendricks passed him the glasses. Clouds of ash rolled across the evening sky. The world was darkening. They had a couple of hours of light left, at the most. Probably not that much.

"I don't see anything," Klaus said.

"That tree there. The stump. By the pile of bricks. The entrance is to the right of the bricks."

"I'll have to take your word for it."

"You and Tasso cover me from here. You'll be able to sight all the way to the bunker entrance."

"You're going down alone?"

"With my wrist tab I'll be safe. The ground around the bunker is a living field of claws. They collect down in the ash. Like crabs. Without tabs you wouldn't have a chance."

"Maybe you're right."

"I'll walk slowly all the way. As soon as I know for certain—"

"If they're down inside the bunker you won't be able to get back up here. They go fast. You don't realize."

"What do you suggest?"

Klaus considered. "I don't know. Get them to come up to the surface. So you can see."

Hendricks brought his transmitter from his belt, raising the antenna. "Let's get started."

Klaus signaled to Tasso. She crawled expertly up the side of the rise to where they were sitting.

"He's going down alone," Klaus said. "We'll cover him from here. As soon as you see him start back, fire past him at once. They come quick."

"You're not very optimistic," Tasso said.

"No, I'm not."

Hendricks opened the breech of his gun, checking it carefully. "Maybe things are all right."

"You didn't see them. Hundreds of them. All the same. Pouring out like ants."

"I should be able to find out without going down all the way." Hendricks locked his gun, gripping it in one hand, the transmitter in the other. "Well, wish me luck."

Klaus put out his hand. "Don't go down until you're sure. Talk to them from up here. Make them show themselves."

Hendricks stood up. He stepped down the side of the rise.

A moment later he was walking slowly toward the pile of bricks and debris beside the dead tree stump. Toward the entrance of the forward command bunker.

Nothing stirred. He raised the transmitter, clicking it on. "Scott? Can you hear me?"

Silence.

"Scott! This is Hendricks. Can you hear me? I'm standing outside the bunker. You should be able to see me in the view sight."

He listened, the transmitter gripped tightly. No sound. Only static. He walked forward. A claw burrowed out of the ash and raced toward him. It halted a few feet away and then slunk off. A second claw appeared, one of the big ones with feelers. It moved toward him, studied him intently, and then fell in behind him, dogging respectfully after him, a few paces away. A moment later a second big claw joined it. Silently, the claws trailed him as he walked slowly toward the bunker.

Hendricks stopped, and behind him, the claws came to a halt. He was close now. Almost to the bunker steps.

"Scott! Can you hear me? I'm standing right above you. Outside. On the surface. Are you picking me up?"

He waited, holding his gun against his side, the transmitter tightly to his ear. Time passed. He strained to hear, but there was only silence. Silence, and faint static.

Then, distantly, metallically—

"This is Scott."

The voice was neutral. Cold. He could not identify it. But the earphone was minute.

"Scott! Listen. I'm standing right above you. I'm on the surface, looking down into the bunker entrance."

"Yes."

"Can you see me?"

"Yes."

"Through the view sight? You have the sight trained on me?"

"Yes."

Hendricks pondered. A circle of claws waited quietly around him, gray-metal bodies on all sides of him. "Is everything all right in the bunker? Nothing unusual has happened?"

"Everything is all right."

"Will you come up to the surface? I want to see you for a moment." Hendricks took a deep breath. "Come up here with me. I want to talk to you."

"Come down."

"I'm giving you an order."

Silence.

"Are you coming?" Hendricks listened. There was no response. "I order you to come to the surface."

"Come down."

Hendricks set his jaw. "Let me talk to Leone."

There was a long pause. He listened to the static. Then a voice came, hard, thin, metallic. The same as the other. "This is Leone."

"Hendricks. I'm on the surface. At the bunker entrance. I want one of you to come up here."

"Come down."

"Why come down? I'm giving you an order!"

Silence. Hendricks lowered the transmitter. He looked carefully around him. The entrance was just ahead. Almost at his feet. He lowered the antenna and fastened the transmitter to his belt. Carefully, he gripped his gun with both hands. He moved forward, a step at a time. If they could see him they knew he was starting toward the entrance. He closed his eyes a moment.

Then he put his foot on the first step that led downward.

Two Davids came up at him, their faces identical and expressionless. He blasted them into particles. More came rushing silently up, a whole pack of them. All exactly the same.

Hendricks turned and raced back, away from the bunker, back toward the rise.

At the top of the rise Tasso and Klaus were firing down. The small claws were already streaking up toward them, shining metal spheres going fast, racing frantically through the ash. But he had no time to think about that. He knelt down, aiming at the bunker entrance, gun against his cheek. The Davids were coming out in groups, clutching their teddy bears, their thin knobby legs pumping as they ran up the steps to the surface. Hendricks fired into the main body of them. They burst apart, wheels and springs flying in all directions. He fired again, through the mist of particles.

A giant lumbering figure rose up in the bunker entrance, tall and swaying. Hendricks paused, amazed. A man, a soldier. With one leg, supporting himself with a crutch.

"Major!" Tasso's voice came. More firing. The huge figure moved forward, Davids swarming around it. Hendricks broke out of his freeze. The First Variety. The Wounded Soldier. He aimed and fired. The soldier burst into bits, parts and relays flying. Now many Davids were out on the flat ground, away from the bunker. He fired again and again, moving slowly back, half-crouching and aiming.

From the rise, Klaus fired down. The side of the rise was alive with claws making their way up. Hendricks retreated toward the rise, running and crouching. Tasso had left Klaus and was circling slowly to the right, moving away from the rise.

A David slipped up toward him, its small white face expressionless, brown hair hanging down in its eyes. It bent over suddenly, opening its arms. Its teddy bear hurtled down and leaped across the ground, bounding toward him. Hendricks fired. The bear and the David both dissolved. He grinned, blinking. It was like a dream.

"Up here!" Tasso's voice. Hendricks made his way toward her. She was over by some columns of concrete, walls of a ruined building. She was firing past him, with the hand pistol Klaus had given her.

"Thanks." He joined her, grasping for breath. She pulled him back, behind the concrete, fumbling at her belt.

"Close your eyes!" She unfastened a globe from her waist. Rapidly, she unscrewed the cap, locking it into place. "Close your eyes and get down."

She threw the bomb. It sailed in an arc, an expert, rolling and bouncing to the entrance of the bunker. Two Wounded Soldiers stood uncertainly by the brick pile. More Davids poured from behind them, out onto the plain. One of the Wounded Soldiers moved toward the bomb, stooping awkwardly down to pick it up.

The bomb went off. The concussion whirled Hendricks around, throwing him on his face. A hot wind rolled over him. Dimly he saw Tasso standing behind the columns, firing slowly and methodically at the Davids coming out of the raging clouds of white fire.

Back along the rise Klaus struggled with a ring of claws circling around him. He retreated, blasting at them and moving back, trying to break through the ring.

Hendricks struggled to his feet. His head ached. He could hardly see. Everything was licking at him, raging and whirling. His right arm would not move.

Tasso pulled back toward him. "Come on. Let's go."

"Klaus—he's still up there."

"Come on!" Tasso dragged Hendricks back, away from the columns. Hendricks shook his head, trying to clear it. Tasso led him rapidly away, her eyes intense and bright, watching for claws that had escaped the blast.

One David came out of the rolling clouds of flame. Tasso blasted it. No more appeared.

"But Klaus. What about him?" Hendricks stopped, standing unsteadily. "He—"

"Come on!"

They retreated, moving farther and farther away from the bunker. A few small claws followed them for a little while and then gave up, turning back and going off.

At last Tasso stopped. "We can stop here and get our breaths."

Hendricks sat down on some heaps of debris. He wiped his neck, gasping. "We left Klaus back there."

Tasso said nothing. She opened her gun, sliding a fresh round of blast cartridges into place.

Hendricks stared at her, dazed. "You left him back there on purpose."

Tasso snapped the gun together. She studied the heaps of rubble around them, her face expressionless. As if she were watching for something.

"What is it?" Hendrick demanded. "What are you looking for? Is something coming?" He shook his head, trying to understand. What was she doing? What was she waiting for? He could see nothing. Ash lay all around them, ash and ruins. Occasional stark tree trunks, without leaves or branches. "What—"

Tasso cut him off. "Be still." Her eyes narrowed. Suddenly her gun came up. Hendricks turned, following her gaze.

Back the way they had come a figure appeared. The figure walked unsteadily toward them. Its clothes were torn. It limped as it made its way along, going very slowly and carefully. Stopping now and then, resting and getting its strength. Once it almost fell. It stood for a moment, trying to steady itself. Then it came on.

Klaus.

Hendricks stood up. "Klaus!" He started toward him. "How the hell did you—"

Tasso fired. Hendricks swung back. She fired again, the blast passing him, a searing line of heat. The beam caught Klaus in the chest. He exploded, gears and wheels flying. For a moment he continued to walk. Then he swayed back and forth. He crashed to the ground, his arms flung out. A few more wheels rolled away.

Silence.

Tasso turned to Hendricks. "Now you understand why he killed Rudi."

Hendricks sat down again slowly. He shook his head. He was numb. He could not think.

"Do you see?" Tasso said. "Do you understand?"

Hendricks said nothing. Everything was slipping away from him, faster and faster. Darkness, rolling and plucking at him.

He closed his eyes.

Hendricks opened his eyes slowly. His body ached all over. He tried to sit up but needles of pain shot through his arm and shoulder. He gasped.

"Don't try to get up," Tasso said. She bent down, putting her cold hand against his forehead.

It was night. A few stars glinted above, shining through the drifting clouds of ash. Hendricks lay back, his teeth locked. Tasso watched him impassively. She had built a fire with some wood and weeds. The fire licked feebly, hissing at a metal cup suspended over it. Everything was silent. Unmoving darkness, beyond the fire.

"So he was the Second Variety," Hendricks murmured.

"I had always thought so."

"Why didn't you destroy him sooner?" He wanted to know.

"You held me back." Tasso crossed to the fire to look into the metal cup. "Coffee. It'll be ready to drink in a while."

She came back and sat down beside him. Presently she opened her pistol and began to disassemble the firing mechanism, studying it intently.

"This is a beautiful gun," Tasso said, half aloud. "The construction is superb."

"What about them? The claws."

"The concussion from the bomb put most of them out of action. They're delicate. Highly organized, I suppose."

"The Davids, too?"

"Yes."

"How did you happen to have a bomb like that?"

Tasso shrugged. "We designed it. You shouldn't underestimate our technology, Major. Without such a bomb you and I would no longer exist."

"Very useful."

Tasso stretched out her legs, warming her feet in the heat of the fire. "It surprised me that you did not seem to understand, after he killed Rudi. Why did you think he—"

"I told you. I thought he was afraid."

"Really? You know, Major, for a little while I suspected you. Because you wouldn't let me kill him. I thought you might be protecting him." She laughed.

"Are we safe here?" Hendricks asked presently.

"For a while. Until they get reinforcements from some other area." Tasso began to clean the interior of the gun with a bit of rag. She finished and pushed the mechanism back into place. She closed the gun, running her finger along the barrel.

"We were lucky," Hendricks murmured.

"Yes. Very lucky."

"Thanks for pulling me away."

Tasso did not answer. She glanced up at him, her eyes bright in the firelight. Hendricks examined his arm. He could not move his fingers. His whole side seemed numb. Down inside him was a dull steady ache.

"How do you feel?" Tasso asked.

"My arm is damaged."

"Anything else?"

"Internal injuries."

"You didn't get down when the bomb went off."

Hendricks said nothing. He watched Tasso pour the coffee from the cup into a flat metal pan. She brought it over to him.

"Thanks." He struggled up enough to drink. It was hard to swallow. His insides turned over and he pushed the pan away. "That's all I can drink now."

Tasso drank the rest. Time passed. The clouds of ash moved across the dark sky above them. Hendricks rested, his mind blank. After a while he became aware that Tasso was standing over him, gazing down at him.

"What is it?" he murmured.

"Do you feel any better?"

"Some."

"You know, Major, if I hadn't dragged you away they would have got you. You would be dead. Like Rudi."

"I know."

"Do you want to know why I brought you out? I could have left you. I could have left you there."

"Why did you bring me out?"

"Because we have to get away from here." Tasso stirred the fire with a stick, peering calmly down into it. "No human being can live here. When their reinforcements come we won't have a chance. I've pondered about it while you were unconscious. We have perhaps three hours before they come."

"And you expect me to get us away?"

"That's right. I expect you to get us out of here."

"Why me?"

"Because I don't know any way." Her eyes shone at him in the half light, bright and steady. "If you can't get us out of here they'll kill us within three hours. I see nothing else ahead. Well, Major? What are you going to do? I've been waiting all night. While you were unconscious I sat here, waiting and listening. It's almost dawn. The night is almost over."

Hendricks considered. "It's curious," he said at last.

"Curious?"

"That you should think I can get us out of here. I wonder what you think I can do."

"Can you get us to the Moon Base?"

"The Moon Base? How?"

"There must be some way."

Hendricks shook his head. "No. There's no way that I know of."

Tasso said nothing. For a moment her steady gaze wavered. She ducked her head, turning abruptly away. She scrambled to her feet. "More coffee?"

"No."

"Suit yourself." Tasso drank silently. He could not see her face. He lay back against the ground, deep in thought, trying to concentrate. It was hard to think. His head still hurt. And the numbing daze still hung over him.

"There might be one way," he said suddenly.

"Oh?"

"How soon is dawn?"

"Two hours. The sun will be coming up shortly."

"There's supposed to be a ship near here. I've never seen it. But I know it exists."

"What kind of a ship?" Her voice was sharp.

"A rocket cruiser."

"Will it take us off? To the Moon Base?"

"It's supposed to. In case of emergency." He rubbed his forehead.

"What's wrong?"

"My head. It's hard to think. I can hardly—hardly concentrate. The bomb."

"Is the ship near here?" Tasso slid over beside him, settling down on her haunches. "How far is it? Where is it?"

"I'm trying to think."

Her fingers dug into his arm. "Nearby?" Her voice was like iron. "Where would it be? Would they store it underground? Hidden underground?"

"Yes. In a storage locker."

"How do we find it? Is it marked? Is there a code marker to identify it?"

Hendricks concentrated. "No. No markings. No code symbol."

"What then?"

"A sign."

"What sort of sign?"

Hendricks did not answer. In the flickering light his eyes were glazed, two sightless orbs. Tasso's fingers dug into his arm.

"What sort of sign? What is it?"

"I—I can't think. Let me rest."

"All right." She let go and stood up. Hendricks lay back against the ground, his eyes closed. Tasso walked away from him, her hands in her pockets. She kicked a rock out of her way and stood staring up at the sky. The night blackness was already beginning to fade into gray. Morning was coming.

Tasso gripped her pistol and walked around the fire in a circle, back and forth. On the ground Major Hendricks lay, his eyes closed, unmoving. The grayness rose in the sky, higher and higher. The landscape became visible, fields of ash stretching out in all directions. Ash and ruins of buildings, a wall here and there, heaps of concrete, the naked trunk of a tree.

The air was cold and sharp. Somewhere a long way off a bird made a few bleak sounds.

Hendricks stirred. He opened his eyes. "Is it dawn? Already?"

"Yes."

Hendricks sat up a little. "You wanted to know something. You were asking me."

"Do you remember now?"

"Yes."

"What is it?" She tensed. "What?" she repeated sharply.

"A well. A ruined well. It's in a storage locker under a well."

"A well." Tasso relaxed. "Then we'll find a well." She looked at her watch. "We have about an hour, Major. Do you think we can find it in an hour?"

"Give me a hand up," Hendricks said.

Tasso put her pistol away and helped him to his feet. "This is going to be difficult."

"Yes it is." Hendricks set his lips tightly. "I don't think we're going to go very far."

They began to walk. The early sun cast a little warmth down on them.

The land was flat and barren, stretching out gray and lifeless as far as they could see. A few birds sailed silently, far above them, circling slowly.

"See anything?" Hendricks said. "Any claws?"

"No. Not yet."

They passed through some ruins, upright concrete and bricks. A cement foundation. Rats scuttled away. Tasso jumped back warily.

"This used to be a town," Hendricks said. "A village. Provincial village. This was all grape country, once. Where we are now."

They came onto a ruined street, weeds and cracks criss-crossing it. Over to the right a stone chimney stuck up.

"Be careful," he warned her.

A pit yawned, an open basement. Ragged ends of pipes jutted up, twisted and bent. They passed part of a house, a bathtub turned on its side. A broken chair. A few spoons and bits of china dishes. In the center of the street the ground had sunk away. The depression was filled with weeds and debris and bones.

"Over here," Hendricks murmured.

"This way?"

"To the right."

They passed the remains of a heavy-duty tank. Hendricks's belt counter clicked ominously. The tank had been radiation-blasted. A few feet from the tank a mummified body lay sprawled out, mouth open. Beyond the road was a flat field. Stones and weeds, and bits of broken glass.

"There," Hendricks said.

A stone well jutted up, sagging and broken. A few boards lay across it. Most of the well had sunk into rubble. Hendricks walked unsteadily toward it, Tasso beside him.

"Are you certain about this?" Tasso said. "This doesn't look like anything."

"I'm sure." Hendricks sat down at the edge of the well, his teeth locked. His breath came quickly. He wiped perspiration from his face. "This was arranged so the senior command officer could get away. If anything happened. If the bunker fell."

"That was you?"

"Yes."

"Where is the ship? Is it here?"

"We're standing on it." Hendricks ran his hands over the surface of the well stones. "The eye-lock responds to me, not to anybody else. It's my ship. Or it was supposed to be."

There was a sharp click. Presently they heard a low grating sound from below them.

"Step back," Hendricks said. He and Tasso moved away from the well.

A section of the ground slid back. A metal frame pushed slowly up through the ash, shoving bricks and weeds out of the way. The action ceased as the ship nosed into view.

"There it is," Hendricks said.

The ship was small. It rested quietly, suspended in its mesh frame like a blunt needle. A rain of ash sifted down into the dark cavity from which the ship had been raised. Hendricks made his way over to it. He mounted the mesh and unscrewed the hatch, pulling it back. Inside the ship the control banks and the pressure seat were visible.

Tasso came and stood beside him, gazing into the ship. "I'm not accustomed to rocket piloting," she said after a while.

Hendricks glanced at her. "I'll do the piloting."

"Will you? There's only one seat, Major. I can see it's built to carry only a single person."

Hendricks's breathing changed. He studied the interior of the ship intently. Tasso was right. There was only one seat. The ship was built to carry only one person. "I see," he said slowly. "And the one person is you."

She nodded.

"Of course."

"Why?"

"*You* can't go. You might not live through the trip. You're injured. You probably wouldn't get there."

"An interesting point. But you see, I know where the Moon Base is. And you don't. You might fly around for months and not find it. It's well hidden. Without knowing what to look for—"

"I'll have to take my chances. Maybe I won't find it. Not by myself. But I think you'll give me all the information I need. Your life depends on it."

"How?"

"If I find the Moon Base in time, perhaps I can get them to send a ship back to pick you up. *If* I find the Base in time. If not, then you haven't a chance. I imagine there are supplies on the ship. They will last me long enough—"

Hendricks moved quickly. But his injured arm betrayed him. Tasso ducked, sliding lithely aside. Her hand came up, lightning fast. Hendricks saw the gun butt coming. He tried to ward off the blow, but she was too fast. The metal butt struck against the side of his head, just above his ear. Numbing pain rushed through him. Pain and rolling clouds of blackness. He sank down, sliding to the ground.

Dimly, he was aware that Tasso was standing over him, kicking him with her toe.

"Major! Wake up."

He opened his eyes, groaning.

"Listen to me." She bent down, the gun pointed at his face. "I have to hurry. There isn't much time left. The ship is ready to go, but you must give me the information I need before I leave."

Hendricks shook his head, trying to clear it.

"Hurry up! Where is the Moon Base? How do I find it? What do I look for?"

Hendricks said nothing.

"Answer me!"

"Sorry."

"Major, the ship is loaded with provisions. I can coast for weeks. I'll find the Base eventually. And in a half-hour you'll be dead. Your only chance of survival—" She broke off.

Along the slope, by some crumbling ruins, something moved. Something in the ash. Tasso turned quickly, aiming. She fired. A puff of flame leaped. Something scuttled away, rolling across the ash. She fired again. The claw burst apart, wheels flying.

"See?" Tasso said. "A scout. It won't be long."

"You'll bring them back here to get me?"

"Yes. As soon as possible."

Hendricks looked up at her. He studied her intently. "You're telling the truth?" A strange expression had come over his face, an avid hunger. "You will come back for me? You'll get me to the Moon Base?"

"I'll get you to the Moon Base. But tell me where it is! There's only a little time left."

"All right." Hendricks picked up a piece of rock, pulling himself to a sitting position. "Watch."

Hendricks began to scratch in the ash. Tasso stood by him, watching the motion of the rock. Hendricks was sketching a crude lunar map.

"This is the Appenine range. Here is the Crater of Archimedes. The Moon Base is beyond the end of the Appenine, about two hundred miles. I don't know exactly where. No one on Terra knows. But when you're over the Appenine, signal with one red flare and a green flare, followed by two red flares in quick succession. The Base monitor will record your signal. The Base is under the surface, of course. They'll guide you down with magnetic grapples."

"And the controls? Can I operate them?"

"The controls are virtually automatic. All you have to do is give the right signal at the right time."

"I will."

"The seat absorbs most of the takeoff shock. Air and temperature are automatically controlled. The ship will leave Terra and pass out into free space. It'll line itself up with the Moon, falling into an orbit around it, about a hundred miles above the surface. The orbit will carry you over the Base. When you're in the region of the Appenine, release the signal rockets."

Tasso slid into the ship and lowered herself into the pressure seat. The arm locks folded automatically around her. She fingered the controls. "Too bad you're not going, Major. All this put here for you, and you can't make the trip."

"Leave me the pistol."

Tasso pulled the pistol from her belt. She held it in her hand, weighing it thoughtfully. "Don't go too far from this location. It'll be hard to find you, as it is."

"No. I'll stay here by the well."

Tasso gripped the takeoff switch, running her fingers over the smooth metal. "A beautiful ship, Major. Well built. I admire your workmanship. You people have always done good work. You build fine things. Your work, your creations, are your greatest achievement."

"Give me the pistol," Hendricks said impatiently, holding out his hand. He struggled to his feet.

"Good-bye, Major." Tasso tossed the pistol past Hendricks. The pistol clattered against the ground, bouncing and rolling away. Hendricks hurried after it. He bent down, snatching it up.

The hatch of the ship clanged shut. The bolts fell into place. Hendricks made his way back. The inner door was being sealed. He raised the pistol unsteadily.

There was a shattering roar. The ship burst up from its metal cage, fusing the mesh behind it. Hendricks cringed, pulling back. The ship shot up into the rolling clouds of ash, disappearing into the sky.

Hendricks stood watching a long time, until even the streamer had dissipated. Nothing stirred. The morning air was chill and silent. He began to walk aimlessly back the way they had come. Better to keep moving around. It would be a long time before help came—if it came at all.

He searched his pockets until he found a package of cigarettes. He lit one grimly. They had all wanted cigarettes from him. But cigarettes were scarce.

A lizard slithered by him, through the ash. He halted, rigid. The lizard disappeared. Above, the sun rose higher in the sky. Some flies landed on a flat rock to one side of him. Hendricks kicked at them with his foot.

It was getting hot. Sweat trickled down his face, into his collar. His mouth was dry.

Presently he stopped walking and sat down on some debris. He unfastened his medicine kit and swallowed a few narcotic capsules. He looked around him. Where was he?

Something lay ahead. Stretched out on the ground. Silent and unmoving.

Hendricks drew his gun quickly. It looked like a man. Then he remembered. It was the remains of Klaus. The Second Variety. Where Tasso had blasted him. He could see wheels and relays and metal parts, strewn around on the ash. Glittering and sparkling in the sunlight.

Hendricks got to his feet and walked over. He nudged the inert form with his foot, turning it over a little. He could see the metal hull, the aluminum ribs and struts. More wiring fell out. Like viscera. Heaps of wiring, switches and relays. Endless motors and rods.

He bent down. The brain cage had been smashed by the fall. The artificial brain was visible. He gazed at it. A maze of circuits. Miniature tubes. Wires as fine as hair. He touched the brain cage. It swung aside. The type plate was visible. Hendricks studied the plate.

And blanched.

IV-V.

For a long time he stared at the plate. Fourth Variety. Not the Second. They had been wrong. There were more types. Not just three. Many more, perhaps. At least four. And Klaus wasn't the Second Variety.

But if Klaus wasn't the Second Variety—

Suddenly he tensed. Something was coming, walking through the ash beyond the hill. What was it? He strained to see. Figures. Figures coming slowly along, making their way through the ash.

Coming toward him.

Hendricks crouched quickly, raising his gun. Sweat dripped down into his eyes. He fought down rising panic, as the figures neared.

The first was a David. The David saw him and increased its pace. The others hurried behind it. A second David. A third. Three Davids, all alike, coming toward him silently, without expression, their thin legs rising and falling. Clutching their teddy bears.

He aimed and fired. The first two Davids dissolved into particles. The third came on. And the figure behind it. Climbing silently toward him across the gray ash. A Wounded Soldier, towering over the David. And—

And behind the Wounded Soldier came two Tassos, walking side by side. Heavy belt, Russian army pants, shirt, long hair. The familiar figure, as he had seen her only a little while before. Sitting in the pressure seat of the ship. Two slim, silent figures, both identical.

They were very near. The David bent down suddenly, dropping its teddy bear. The bear raced across the ground. Automatically, Hendricks's fingers tightened around the trigger. The bear was gone, dissolved into mist. The two Tasso Types moved on, expressionless, walking side by side, through the gray ash.

When they were almost to him, Hendricks raised the pistol waist high and fired.

The two Tassos dissolved. But already a new group was starting up the rise, five or six Tassos, all identical, a line of them coming rapidly toward him.

And he had given her the ship and the signal code. Because of him she was on her way to the moon, to the Moon Base. He had made it possible.

He had been right about the bomb, after all. It had been designed with knowledge of the other types, the David Type and the Wounded Soldier Type. And the Klaus Type. Not designed by human beings. It had been designed by one of the underground factories, apart from all human contact.

The line of Tassos came up to him. Hendricks braced himself, watching them calmly. The familiar face, the belt, the heavy shirt, the bomb carefully in place.

The bomb—

As the Tassos reached for him, a last ironic thought drifted through Hendricks's mind. He felt a little better, thinking about it. The bomb. Made by the Second Variety to destroy the other varieties. Made for that end alone.

They were already beginning to design weapons to use against each other.

Weihnacht-sabend

When Anthony Burgess published his list of the best hundred novels in English literature since World War II, one of the very few SF works was Pavane by Keith Roberts. Roberts is a talented editor, illustrator, and writer who first became prominent in the mid-1960s in England, but whose reputation in the United States has never reached the heights it deserves. His particular strength lies in the creation of subtle, dense, richly textured imaginary worlds, often only distantly related to the present, given verisimilitude by a careful concern with closely observed details and nuances of daily life. Usually his stories involve some aspects of imagined technology. Roberts often writes in the mode known as alternate universe SF, in which the present world, or indeed the world of the future, is not related by exact correspondence to our own, but differs in precise and interesting ways because of a divergence at some known historical point. "Weihnachtsabend" is such a story, as is the American Kornbluth's "Two Dooms." Comparing the stories points up significant national differences in approach to the question, What if the Germans had won the war?

* * *

I

The big car moved slowly, nosing its way along narrowing lanes. Here, beyond the little market town of Wilton, the snow lay thicker. Trees and bushes loomed in the headlights, coated with driven white. The tail of the Mercedes wagged slightly, steadied. Mainwaring heard the chauffeur swear under his breath. The link had been left live.

Dials let into the seatback recorded the vehicle's mechanical wellbeing: oil pressure, temperature, revs, k.p.h. Lights from the repeater glowed softly on his companion's face. She moved, restlessly; he saw the swing of yellow hair. He turned slightly. She was wearing a neat, brief kilt, heavy boots. Her legs were excellent.

He clicked the dial lights off. He said, "Not much farther."

He wondered if she was aware of the open link. He said, "First time down?"

She nodded in the dark. She said, "I was a bit overwhelmed."

Wilton Great House sprawled across a hilltop five miles or more beyond the town. The car drove for some distance beside the wall that fringed the estate. The perimeter defences had been strengthened since Mainwaring's last visit. Watchtowers reared at intervals; the wall itself had been topped by multiple strands of wire.

The lodge gates were commanded by two new stone pillboxes. The Merc edged between them, stopped. On the road from London the snow had eased; now big flakes drifted again, lit by the headlights. Somewhere, orders were barked.

A man stepped forward, tapped at the window. Mainwaring buttoned it open. He saw a GFP armband, a hip holster with the flap tucked back. He said, "Good evening, Captain."

"*Guten Abend, mein Herr. Ihre Ausweiskarte?*"

Cold air gusted against Mainwaring's cheek. He passed across his identity card and security clearance, He said, "*Richard Mainwaring. Die rechte Hand des Gesandten. Fräulein Hunter, von meiner Abteilung.*"

A torch flashed over the papers, dazzled into his eyes, moved to examine the girl. She sat stiffly, staring ahead. Beyond the security officer Mainwaring made out two steel-helmeted troopers, automatics slung. In front of him the wipers clicked steadily.

The GFP man stepped back. He said, "*Ihre Ausweis wird in einer Woche ablaufen. Erneuen Sie Ihre Karte.*"

Mainwaring said, "*Vielen Dank, Herr Hauptmann. Frohe Weihnachten.*"

The man saluted stiffly, unclipped a walkie-talkie from his belt. A pause, and the gates swung back. The Merc creamed through. Mainwaring said, "*Bastard . . .*"

She said, "Is it always like this?"

He said, "They're tightening up all round."

She pulled her coat round her shoulders. She said, "Frankly, I find it a bit scary."

He said, "Just the Minister taking care of his guests."

Wilton stood in open downland set with great trees. Hans negotiated a bend, carefully, drove beneath half-seen branches. The wind moaned, zipping round a quarterlight. It was as if the car butted into a black tunnel, full of swirling pale flakes. He thought he saw her shiver. He said, "Soon be there."

The headlamps lit a rolling expanse of snow. Posts, buried nearly to their tops, marked the drive. Another bend, and the house showed ahead. The car lights swept across a façade of mullioned windows, crenellated towers. Hard for the uninitiated to guess, staring at the skilfully weathered stone, that the shell of the place was of reinforced concrete. The car swung right with a crunching of unseen gravel, and stopped. The ignition repeater glowed on the seatback.

Mainwaring said, "Thank you, Hans. Nice drive."

Hans said, "My pleasure, sir."

She flicked her hair free, picked up her handbag. He held the door for her. He said, "OK, Diane?"

She shrugged. She said, "Yes. I'm a bit silly sometimes." She squeezed his hand, briefly. She said, "I'm glad you'll be here. Somebody to rely on."

Mainwaring lay back on the bed and stared at the ceiling. Inside as well as out, Wilton was a triumph of art over nature. Here, in the Tudor wing where most of the guests were housed, walls and ceilings were of wavy plaster framed by heavy oak beams. He turned his head. The room was dominated by a fireplace of yellow Ham stone; on the overmantel, carved in bold relief, the *Hakenkreuz* was flanked by the lion and eagle emblems of the Two Empires. A fire burned in the wrought-iron basket; the logs glowed cheerfully, casting wavering warm reflections across the ceiling. Beside the bed a bookshelf offered required reading: the Fuehrer's official biography, Shirer's *Rise of the Third Reich*, Cummings' monumental *Churchill: the Trial of Decadence*. There were a nicely bound set of Buchan novels, some Kiplings, a Shakespeare, a complete Wilde. A side table carried a stack of current magazines: *Connoisseur, The Field, Der Spiegel, Paris Match*. There was a washstand, its rail hung with dark blue towels; in the corner of the room were the doors to the bathroom and wardrobe, in which a servant had already neatly disposed his clothes.

He stubbed his cigarette, lit another. He swung his legs off the bed, poured himself a whisky. From the grounds, faintly, came voices, snatches of laughter. He heard the crash of a pistol, the rattle of an automatic. He walked to the window, pushed the curtain aside. Snow was still falling, drifting silently from the black sky; but the firing pits beside the big house were brightly lit. He watched the figures move and bunch for a while, let the curtain fall. He sat by the fire, shoulders hunched, staring into the flames. He was remembering the trip through London; the flags hanging limp over Whitehall, slow, jerking movement of traffic, the light tanks drawn up outside St. James's. The Kensington road had been crowded, traffic edging and hooting; the vast frontage of Harrods looked grim and oriental against the louring sky. He frowned, remembering the call he had had before leaving the Ministry.

Kosowicz had been the name. From *Time International*; or so he had claimed. He'd refused twice to speak to him; but Kosowicz had been insistent. In the end, he'd asked his secretary to put him through.

Kosowicz had sounded very American. He said, "Mr. Mainwaring, I'd like to arrange a personal interview with your Minister."

"I'm afraid that's out of the question. I must also point out that this communication is extremely irregular."

Kosowicz said, "What do I take that as, sir? A warning, or a threat?"

Mainwaring said carefully, "It was neither. I merely observed that proper channels of approach do exist."

Kosowicz said, "Uh-huh. Mr. Mainwaring, what's the truth behind this rumour that Action Groups are being moved into Moscow?"

Mainwaring said, "Deputy Fuehrer Hess has already issued a statement on the situation. I can see that you're supplied with a copy."

The phone said, "I have it before me. Mr. Mainwaring, what are you people trying to set up? Another Warsaw?"

Mainwaring said, "I'm afraid I can't comment further, Mr. Kosowicz. The Deputy Fuehrer deplored the necessity of force. The *Einsatzgruppen* have been alerted; at this time, that is all. They will be used if necessary to disperse militants. As of this moment, the need has not arisen."

Kosowicz shifted his ground. "You mentioned the Deputy Fuehrer, sir. I hear there was another bomb attempt two nights ago, can you comment on this?"

Mainwaring tightened his knuckles on the handset. He said, "I'm afraid you've been misinformed. We know nothing of any such incident."

The phone was silent for a moment. Then it said, "Can I take your denial as official?"

Mainwaring said, "This is not an official conversation. I'm not empowered to issue statements in any respect."

The phone said, "Yeah, channels do exist. Mr. Mainwaring, thanks for your time."

Mainwaring said, "Goodbye." He put the handset down, sat staring at it. After a while he lit a cigarette.

Outside the windows of the Ministry the snow still fell, a dark whirl and dance against the sky. His tea, when he came to drink it, was half cold.

The fire crackled and shifted. He poured himself another whisky, sat back. Before leaving for Wilton, he'd lunched with Winsby-Walker from Productivity. Winsby-Walker made it his business to know everything; but he had known nothing of a correspondent called Kosowicz. He thought, "I should have checked with Security." But then, Security would have checked with him.

He sat up, looked at his watch. The noise from the ranges had diminished. He turned his mind with a deliberate effort into another channel. The new thoughts brought no more comfort. Last Christmas he had spent with his mother; now, that couldn't happen again. He remembered other Christmases, back across the years. Once, to the child unknowing, they had been gay affairs of crackers and toys. He remembered the scent and texture of pine branches, closeness of candlelight; and books read by torchlight under the sheets, the hard angles of the filled pillowslip, heavy at the foot of the bed. Then, he had been complete; only later, slowly, had come the knowledge of failure. And with it, loneliness. He thought, "She wanted to see me settled. It didn't seem much to ask."

The Scotch was making him maudlin. He drained the glass, walked through to the bathroom. He stripped, and showered. Towelling himself, he thought, "Richard Mainwaring, Personal Assistant to the British Minister of Liaison." Aloud he said, "One must remember the compensations."

He dressed, lathered his face and began to shave. He thought, "Thirty-five is the exact middle of one's life." He was remembering another time with the girl Diane when just for a little while some magic had interposed. Now, the affair was never mentioned between them. Because of James. Always, of course, there is a James.

He towelled his face, applied aftershave. Despite himself, his mind had drifted back to the phone call. One fact was certain: there had been a major security spillage. Somebody somewhere had supplied Kosowicz with closely guarded information. That same someone, presumably, had supplied a list of ex-directory lines. He frowned, grappling with the problem. One country, and one only, opposed the Two Empires with gigantic, latent strength. To that country had shifted the focus of Semitic nationalism. And Kosowicz had been an American.

He thought, "Freedom, schmeedom. Democracy is Jew-shaped." He frowned again, fingering his face. It didn't alter the salient fact. The tip-off had come from the Freedom Front; and he had been contacted, however obliquely. Now, he had become an accessory; the thought had been nagging at the back of his brain all day.

He wondered what they could want of him. There was a rumour — a nasty rumour — that you never found out. Not till the end, till you'd done whatever was required from you. They were untiring, deadly and subtle. He hadn't run squalling to Security at the first hint of danger; but that would have been allowed for. Every turn and twist would have been allowed for.

Every squirm on the hook.

He grunted, angry with himself. Fear was half their strength. He buttoned his shirt, remembering the guards at the gates, the wire and pillboxes. Here, of all places, nothing could reach him. For a few days he could forget the whole affair. He said aloud, "Anyway, I don't even matter. I'm not important." The thought cheered him, nearly.

He clicked the light off, walked through to his room, closed the door behind him. He crossed to the bed and stood quite still, staring at the bookshelf. Between Shirer and the Churchill tome there rested a third slim volume. He reached to touch the spine, delicately; read the author's name, Geissler, and the title, *Toward Humanity*. Below the title, like a topless Cross of Lorraine, were the twin linked *F*'s of the Freedom Front.

Ten minutes ago the book hadn't been there.

He walked to the door. The corridor beyond was deserted. From somewhere in the house, faintly, came music: *Till Eulenspiegel*. There were no nearer sounds. He closed the door again, locked it. Turned back and saw the wardrobe stood slightly ajar.

His case still lay on the side table. He crossed to it, took out the Lüger. The feel of the heavy pistol was comforting. He pushed the clip home, thumbed the safety forward, chambered a round. The breech closed with a hard snap. He walked to the wardrobe, shoved the door wide with his foot.

Nothing there.

He let his held breath escape with a little hiss. He pressed the clip release, ejected the cartridge, laid the gun on the bed. He stood again looking at the shelf. He thought, "I must have been mistaken."

He took the book down, carefully. Geissler had been banned since publication in every province of the Two Empires; Mainwaring himself had never even seen a copy. He squatted on the edge of the bed, opened it at random.

The doctrine of Aryan co-ancestry, seized on so eagerly by the English middle classes, had the superficial reasonableness of most theories ultimately traceable to Rosenberg. Churchill's answer, in one sense, had already been made; but Chamberlain, and the country, turned to Hess. . . .

The Cologne settlement, though seeming to offer hope of security to Jews already domiciled in Britain, in fact paved the way for campaigns of intimidation and extortion similar to those already undertaken in history, notably by King John. The comparison is not unapt; for the English bourgeoisie, *anxious to construct a rationale, discovered many unassailable precedents. A true Sign of the Times, almost certainly, was the resurgence of interest in the novels of Sir Walter Scott. By 1942 the lesson had been learned on both sides; and the Star of David was a common sight on the streets of most British cities.*

The wind rose momentarily in a long wail, shaking the window casement. Mainwaring glanced up, turned his attention back to the book. He leafed through several pages.

In 1940, her Expeditionary Force shattered, her allies quiescent or defeated, the island truly stood alone. Her proletariat, bedevilled by bad leadership, weakened by a gigantic depression, was effectively without a voice. Her aristocracy, like their Junker *counterparts, embraced coldly what could no longer be ignored; while after the White-hall* Putsch *the Cabinet was reduced to the status of an Executive Council. . . .*

The knock at the door made him start, guiltily. He pushed the book away. He said, "Who's that?"
She said, "Me. Richard, aren't you ready?"
He said, "Just a minute." He stared at the book, then placed it back on the shelf. He thought, "That at least wouldn't be expected." He slipped the Lüger into his case and closed it. Then he went to the door.
She was wearing a lacy black dress. Her shoulders were bare; her hair, worn loose, had been brushed till it gleamed. He stared at her a moment, stupidly. Then he said, "Please come in."
She said, "I was starting to wonder. . . . Are you all right?"

"Yes. Yes, of course."

She said, "You look as if you've seen a ghost."

He smiled. He said, "I expect I was taken aback. Those Aryan good looks."

She grinned at him. She said, "I'm half Irish, half English, half Scandinavian. If you have to know."

"That doesn't add up."

She said, "Neither do I, most of the time."

"Drink?"

"Just a little one. We shall be late."

He said, "It's not very formal tonight." He turned away, fiddling with his tie.

She sipped her drink, pointed her foot, scuffed her toe on the carpet. She said, "I expect you've been to a lot of house parties."

He said, "One or two."

She said, "Richard, are they . . . ?"

"Are they what?"

She said, "I don't know. You can't help hearing things."

He said, "You'll be all right. One's very much like the next."

She said, "Are you honestly OK?"

"Sure."

She said, "You're all thumbs. Here, let me." She reached up, knotted deftly. Her eyes searched his face for a moment, moving in little shifts and changes of direction. She said, "There. I think you just need looking after."

He said carefully, "How's James?"

She stared a moment longer. She said, "I don't know. He's in Nairobi. I haven't seen him for months."

He said, "I am a bit nervous, actually."

"Why?"

He said, "Escorting a rather lovely blonde."

She tossed her head, and laughed. She said, "You need a drink as well then."

He poured whisky, said, "Cheers." The book, now, seemed to be burning into his shoulderblades.

She said, "As a matter of fact, you're looking rather fetching yourself."

He thought, "This is the night when all things come together. There should be a word for it." Then he remembered about *Till Eulenspiegel*.

She said, "We'd honestly better go down."

Lights gleamed in the Great Hall, reflecting from polished boards, dark linenfold panelling. At the nearer end of the chamber a huge fire burned. Beneath the minstrels' gallery long tables had been set. Informal or not, they shone with glass and silverware. Candles glowed amid wreaths of dark evergreen; beside each place was a rolled crimson napkin.

In the middle of the Hall, its tip brushing the coffered ceiling, stood a Christmas tree. Its branches were hung with apples, baskets of sweets, red paper roses; at its base were piled gifts in gay-striped wrappers. Round the tree folk stood in groups, chatting and laughing. Richard saw Müller, the Defence Minister, with a striking-looking blonde he took to be his wife; beside them was a tall, monocled man who was something or other in Security. There was a group of GSP officers in their dark, neat uniforms, beyond them half a dozen Liaison people. He saw Hans the chauffeur standing head bent, nodding intently, smiling at some remark; and thought as he had thought before, how he looked like a big, handsome ox.

Diane had paused in the doorway, and linked her arm through his. But the Minister had already seen them. He came weaving through the crowd, a glass in his hand. He was wearing tight black trews, a dark blue roll-neck shirt. He looked happy and relaxed. He said, "Richard. And my dear Miss Hunter. We'd nearly given you up for lost. After all, Hans Trapp is about. Now, some drinks. And come, do come; please join my friends. Over here, where it is warm."

She said, "Who's Hans Trapp?"

Mainwaring said, "You'll find out in a bit."

A little later the Minister said, "Ladies and gentlemen, I think we may be seated."

The meal was superb, the wine abundant. By the time the brandy was served Richard found himself talking more easily, and the Geissler copy pushed nearly to the back of his mind. The traditional toasts—King and Fuehrer, the provinces, the Two Empires—were drunk; then the Minister clapped his hands for quiet. "My friends," he said, "tonight, this special night when we can all mix so freely, is *Weihnachtsabend*. It means, I suppose, many things to the many of us here. But let us remember, first and foremost, that this is the night of the children. Your children, who have come with you to share part at least of this very special Christmas."

He paused. "Already," he said, "they have been called from their crèche; soon, they will be with us. Let me show them to you." He nodded; at the gesture servants wheeled forward a heavy, ornate box. A drape was twitched aside, revealing the grey surface of a big TV screen. Simultaneously, the lamps that lit the Hall began to dim. Diane turned to Mainwaring, frowning; he touched her hand, gently, and shook his head.

Save for the firelight, the Hall was now nearly dark. The candles guttered in their wreaths, flames stirring in some draught; in the hush, the droning of the wind round the great façade of the place was once more audible. The lights would be out, now, all over the house.

"For some of you," said the Minister, "this is your first visit here. For you, I will explain.

"On *Weihnachtsabend* all ghosts and goblins walk. The demon Hans Trapp is abroad; his face is black and terrible, his clothing the skins of bears. Against him comes the Lightbringer, the Spirit of Christmas. Some call her Lucia Queen, some *Das Christkind*. See her now."

The screen lit up.

She moved slowly, like a sleepwalker. She was slender, and robed in white. Her ashen hair tumbled round her shoulders; above her head glowed a diadem of burning tapers. Behind her trod the Star Boys with their wands and tinsel robes; behind again came a little group of children. They ranged in age from eight- and nine-year-olds to toddlers. They gripped each other's hands, apprehensively, setting feet in line like cats, darting terrified glances at the shadows to either side.

"They lie in darkness, waiting," said the Minister softly. "Their nurses have left them. If they cry out, there is none to hear. So they do not cry out. And one by one she has called them. They see her light pass beneath the door; and they must rise and follow. Here, where we sit, is warmth. Here is safety. Their gifts are waiting; to reach them they must run the gauntlet of the dark."

The camera angle changed. Now they were watching the procession from above. The Lucia Queen stepped steadily; the shadows she cast leaped and flickered on panelled walls.

"They are in the Long Gallery now," said the Minister, "almost directly above us. They must not falter, they must not look back. Somewhere, Hans Trapp is hiding. From Hans, only *Das Christkind* can protect them. See how close they bunch behind her light!"

A howling began, like the crying of a wolf. In part it seemed to come from the screen, in part to echo through the Hall itself. The *Christkind* turned, raising her arms; the howling split into a many-voiced cadence, died to a mutter. In its place came a distant huge thudding, like the beating of a drum.

Diane said abruptly, "I don't find this particularly funny."

Mainwaring said, "It isn't supposed to be. Shh."

The Minister said evenly, "The Aryan child must know, from earliest years, the darkness that surrounds him. He must learn to fear, and to overcome that fear. He must learn to be strong. The Two Empires were not built by weakness; weakness will not sustain them. There is no place for it.

This in part your children already know. The house is big, and dark; but they will win through to the light. They fight as the Empires once fought. For their birthright."

The shot changed again, showed a wide, sweeping staircase. The head of the little procession appeared, began to descend. "Now, where is our friend Hans?" said the Minister. "Ah . . ."

Her grip tightened convulsively on Mainwaring's arm. A black-smeared face loomed at the screen. The bogey snarled, clawing at the camera; then turned, loped swiftly towards the staircase. The children shrieked, and bunched; instantly the air was wild with din. Grotesque figures capered and leaped; hands grabbed, clutching. The column was buffeted and swirled; Mainwaring saw a child bowled completely over. The screaming reached a high pitch of terror; and the *Christkind* turned, arms once more raised. The goblins and were-things backed away, growling, into shadow; the slow march was resumed.

The Minister said, "They are nearly here. And they are good children, worthy of their race. Prepare the tree."

Servants ran forward with tapers to light the many candles. The tree sprang from gloom, glinting, black-green; and Mainwaring thought for the first time what a dark thing it was, although it blazed with light.

The big doors at the end of the Hall were flung back; and the children came tumbling through. Tear-stained and sobbing they were, some bruised; but all, before they ran to the tree, stopped, made obeisance to the strange creature who had brought them through the dark. Then the crown was lifted, the tapers extinguished; and Lucia Queen became a child like the rest, a slim, barefooted girl in a gauzy white dress.

The Minister rose, laughing. "Now," he said, "music, and some more wine. Hans Trapp is dead. My friends, one and all, and children; *frohe Weihnachten!*"

Diane said, "Excuse me a moment."

Mainwaring turned. He said, "Are you all right?"

She said, "I'm just going to get rid of a certain taste."

He watched her go, concernedly; and the Minister had his arm, was talking. "Excellent, Richard," he said. "It has gone excellently so far, don't you think?"

Richard said, "Excellently, sir."

"Good, good. Eh, Heidi, Erna . . . and Frederick, is it Frederick? What have you got there? Oh, very fine. . . ." He steered Mainwaring away, still with his fingers tucked beneath his elbow. Squeals of joy sounded; somebody had discovered a sled, tucked away behind the tree. The Minister said, "Look at them; how happy they are now. I would like children, Richard.

Children of my own. Sometimes I think I have given too much. . . . Still, the opportunity remains. I am younger than you, do you realize that? This is the Age of Youth."

Mainwaring said, "I wish the Minister every happiness."

"Richard, Richard, you must learn not to be so very correct at all times. Unbend a little, you are too aware of dignity. You are my friend. I trust you; above all others, I trust you. Do you realize this?"

Richard said, "Thank you, sir. I do."

The Minister seemed bubbling over with some inner pleasure. He said, "Richard, come with me. Just for a moment. I have prepared a special gift for you. I won't keep you from the party very long."

Mainwaring followed, drawn as ever by the curious dynamism of the man. The Minister ducked through an arched doorway, turned right and left, descended a narrow flight of stairs. At the bottom the way was barred by a door of plain grey steel. The Minister pressed his palm flat to a sensor plate; a click, the whine of some mechanism, and the door swung inward. Beyond was a further flight of concrete steps, lit by a single lamp in a heavy well-glass. Chilly air blew upward. Mainwaring realized, with something approaching a shock, that they had entered part of the bunker system that honeycombed the ground beneath Wilton.

The Minister hurried ahead of him, palmed a further door. He said, "Toys, Richard. All toys. But they amuse me." Then, catching sight of Mainwaring's face, "Come, man, come! You are more nervous than the children, frightened of poor old Hans!"

The door gave on to a darkened space. There was a heavy, sweetish smell that Mainwaring, for a whirling moment, couldn't place. His companion propelled him forward, gently. He resisted, pressing back; and the Minister's arm shot by him. A click, and the place was flooded with light. He saw a wide, low area, also concrete-built. To one side, already polished and gleaming, stood the Mercedes, next to it the Minister's private Porsche. There were a couple of Volkswagens, a Ford Executive; and in the farthest corner a vision in glinting white. A Lamborghini. They had emerged in the garage underneath the house.

The Minister said, "My private short cut." He walked forward to the Lamborghini, stood running his fingers across the low, broad bonnet. He said, "Look at her, Richard. Here, sit in. Isn't she a beauty? Isn't she fine?"

Mainwaring said, "She certainly is."

"You like her?"

Mainwaring smiled. He said, "Very much, sir. Who wouldn't?"

The Minister said, "Good, I'm so pleased. Richard, I'm upgrading you. She's yours. Enjoy her."

Mainwaring stared.

The Minister said, "Here, man. Don't look like that, like a fish. Here, see. Logbook, your keys. All entered up, finished." He gripped Mainwaring's shoulders, swung him round laughing. He said, "You've worked well for me. The Two Empires don't forget; their good friends, their servants."

Mainwaring said, "I'm deeply honoured, sir."

"Don't be honoured. You're still being formal. Richard . . ."

"Sir?"

The Minister said, "Stay by me. Stay by me. Up there . . . they don't understand. But we understand . . . eh? These are difficult times. We must be together, always together. Kingdom and Reich. Apart . . . we could be destroyed!" He turned away, placed clenched hands on the roof of the car. He said, "Here, all this. Jewry, the Americans . . . Capitalism. They must stay afraid. Nobody fears an Empire divided. It would fall!"

Mainwaring said, "I'll do my best, sir. We all will."

The Minister said, "I know, I know. But, Richard, this afternoon. I was playing with swords. Silly little swords."

Mainwaring thought, "I know how he keeps me. I can see the mechanism. But I mustn't imagine I know the entire truth."

The Minister turned back, as if in pain. He said, "Strength is Right. It has to be. But Hess . . ."

Mainwaring said slowly, "We've tried before, sir . . ."

The Minister slammed his fist on to metal. He said, "Richard, don't you see? It wasn't us. Not this time. It was his own people. Baumann, von Thaden . . . I can't tell. He's an old man, he doesn't matter any more. It's an idea they want to kill, Hess is an idea. Do you understand? It's *Lebensraum*. Again. . . . Half the world isn't enough."

He straightened. He said, "The worm, in the apple. It gnaws, gnaws. . . . But we are Liaison. We matter, so much. Richard, be my eyes. Be my ears."

Mainwaring stayed silent, thinking about the book in his room; and the Minister once more took his arm. He said, "The shadows, Richard. They were never closer. Well might we teach our children to fear the dark. But . . . not in our time. Eh? Not for us. There is life, and hope. So much we can do. . . ."

Mainwaring thought, "Maybe it's the wine I drank. I'm being pressed too hard." A dull, queer mood, almost of indifference, had fallen on him. He followed his Minister without complaint, back through the bunker complex, up to where the great fire and the tapers on the tree burned low. He heard the singing mixed with the wind-voice, watched the children rock heavy-eyed, carolling sleep. The house seemed winding down, to rest; and she had gone, of course. He sat in a corner and drank wine and brooded, watched the Minister move from group to group until he too was gone, the Hall nearly empty and the servants clearing away.

He found his own self, his inner self, dozing at last as it dozed at each day's end. Tiredness, as ever, had come like a benison. He rose carefully, walked to the door. He thought, "I shan't be missed here." Shutters closed, in his head.

He found his key, unlocked his room. He thought, "Now, she will be waiting. Like all the letters that never came, the phones that never rang." He opened the door.

She said, "What kept you?"

He closed the door behind him, quietly. The fire crackled in the little room, the curtains were drawn against the night. She sat by the hearth, barefooted, still in her party dress. Beside her on the carpet were glasses, an ashtray with half-smoked stubs. One lamp was burning; in the warm light her eyes were huge and dark.

He looked across to the bookshelf. The Geissler stood where he had left it. He said, "How did you get in?"

She chuckled. She said, "There was a spare key on the back of the door. Didn't you see me steal it?"

He walked toward her, stood looking down. He thought, "Adding another fragment to the puzzle. Too much, too complicated."

She said, "Are you angry?"

He said, "No."

She patted the floor. She said gently, "Please, Richard. Don't be cross."

He sat, slowly, watching her.

She said, "Drink?" He didn't answer. She poured one anyway. She said, "What were you doing all this time? I thought you'd be up hours ago."

He said, "I was talking to the Minister."

She traced a pattern on the rug with her forefinger. Her hair fell forward, golden and heavy, baring the nape of her neck. She said, "I'm sorry about earlier on. I was stupid. I think I was a bit scared too."

He drank, slowly. He felt like a run-down machine. Hell to have to start thinking again at this time of night. He said, "What were you doing?"

She watched up at him. Her eyes were candid. She said, "Sitting here. Listening to the wind."

He said, "That couldn't have been much fun."

She shook her head, slowly, eyes fixed on his face. She said softly, "You don't know me at all."

He was quiet again. She said, "You don't believe in me, do you?"

He thought, "You need understanding. You're different from the rest; and I'm selling myself short." Aloud he said, "No."

She put the glass down, smiled, took his glass away. She hotched towards him across the rug, slid her arm round his neck. She said, "I was thinking about you. Making my mind up." She kissed him. He felt her tongue pushing, opened his lips. She said, "*Mmm . . .*" She sat back a little, smiling. She said, "Do you mind?"

"No."

She pressed a strand of hair across her mouth, parted her teeth, kissed again. He felt himself react, involuntarily; and felt her touch and squeeze.

She said, "This is a silly dress. It gets in the way." She reached behind her. The fabric parted; she pushed it down, to the waist. She said, "Now it's like last time."

He said slowly, "Nothing's ever like last time."

She rolled across his lap, lay looking up. She whispered, "I've put the clock back."

Later in the dream she said, "I was so silly."

"What do you mean?"

She said, "I was shy. That was all. You weren't really supposed to go away."

He said, "What about James?"

"He's got somebody else. I didn't know what I was missing."

He let his hand stray over her; and present and immediate past became confused so that as he held her he still saw her kneeling, firelight dancing on her body. He reached for her and she was ready again; she fought, chuckling, taking it bareback, staying all the way.

Much later he said, "The Minister gave me a Lamborghini."

She rolled on to her belly, lay chin in hands watching under a tangle of hair. She said, "And now you've got yourself a blonde. What are you going to do with us?"

He said, "None of it's real."

She said, "*Oh . . .*" She punched him. She said, "Richard, you make me cross. It's happened, you idiot. That's all. It happens to everybody." She scratched again with a finger on the carpet. She said, "I hope you've made me pregnant. Then you'd have to marry me."

He narrowed his eyes; and the wine began again, singing in his head.

She nuzzled him. She said, "You asked me once. Say it again."

"I don't remember."

She said, "Richard, please . . ." So he said, "Diane, will you marry me?" And she said, "Yes, yes, yes," then afterwards awareness came and though it wasn't possible he took her again and that time was finest of all, tight and sweet as honey. He'd fetched pillows from the bed and the counterpane, they curled close and he found himself talking, talking, how it wasn't the sex, it was shopping in Marlborough and having tea and seeing the sun set from White Horse Hill and being together, together; then she pressed fingers to his mouth and he fell with her in sleep past cold and loneliness and fear, past deserts and unlit places, down maybe to where spires reared gold and tree leaves moved and dazzled and white cars sang on roads and suns burned inwardly, lighting new worlds.

He woke, and the fire was low. He sat up, dazed. She was watching him. He stroked her hair a while, smiling; then she pushed away. She said, "Richard, I have to go now."

"Not yet."

"It's the middle of the night."

He said, "It doesn't matter."

She said, "It does. He mustn't know."

"Who?"

She said, "You know who. You know why I was asked here."

He said, "He's not like that. Honestly."

She shivered. She said, "Richard, please. Don't get me in trouble." She smiled. She said, "It's only till tomorrow. Only a little while."

He stood, awkwardly, and held her, pressing her warmth close. Shoeless, she was tiny; her shoulder fitted beneath his armpit.

Halfway through dressing she stopped and laughed, leaned a hand against the wall. She said, "I'm all woozy."

Later he said, "I'll see you to your room."

She said, "No, please. I'm all right." She was holding her handbag, and her hair was combed. She looked, again, as if she had been to a party.

At the door she turned. She said, "I love you, Richard. Truly." She kissed again, quickly; and was gone.

He closed the door, dropped the latch. He stood a while looking round the room. In the fire a burned-through log broke with a snap, sending up a little whirl of sparks. He walked to the washstand, bathed his face and hands. He shook the counterpane out on the bed, rearranged the pillows. Her scent still clung to him; he remembered how she had felt, and what she had said.

He crossed to the window, pushed it ajar. Outside, the snow lay in deep swaths and drifts. Starlight gleamed from it, ghost-white; and the whole great house was mute. He stood feeling the chill move against his skin; and in all the silence a voice drifted far-off and clear. It came maybe from the guardhouses, full of distance and peace.

"Stille Nacht, heilige Nacht,
alles schläft, einsam wacht . . ."

He walked to the bed, pulled back the covers. The sheets were crisp and spotless, fresh-smelling. He smiled, and turned off the lamp.

"Nur das traute, hochheilige Paar.
Holder Knabe mit lochigem Haar. . . ."

In the wall of the room, an inch behind the plasterwork, a complex little machine hummed. A spool of delicate golden wire shook slightly; but the creak of the opening window had been the last thing to interest the recorder, the singing alone couldn't activate its relays. A micro-switch tripped, inaudibly; valve filaments faded, and died. Mainwaring lay back in the last of the firelight, and closed his eyes.

"Schlaf' in himmlischer Ruh,
Schlaf' in himmlischer Ruh. . . ."

2

Beyond drawn curtains, brightness flicks on.

The sky is a hard, clear blue; icy, full of sunlight. The light dazzles back from the brilliant land. Far things—copses, hills, solitary trees—stand sharp-etched. Roofs and eaves carry hummocks of whiteness, twigs a three-inch crest. In the stillness, here and there, the snow cracks and falls, powdering.

The shadows of the riders jerk and undulate. The quiet is interrupted. Hooves ring on swept courtyards or stamp muffled, churning the snow. It seems the air itself has been rendered crystalline by cold; through it the voices break and shatter, brittle as glass.

"Guten Morgen, Hans . . ."

"Verflucht kalt!"

"Der Hundenmeister sagt, sehr gefahrlich!"

"Macht nichts! Wir erwischen es bevor dem Wald!"

A rider plunges beneath an arch. The horse snorts and curvets.

"Ich wette dir fünfzig amerikanische Dollar!"

"Einverstanden! Heute, habe ich Glück!"

The noise, the jangling and stamping, rings back on itself. Cheeks flush, perception is heightened; for more than one of the riders, the early courtyard reels. Beside the house door trestles have been set up. A great bowl is carried, steaming. The cups are raised, the toasts given; the responses ring again, crashing.

"The Two Empires . . . !"

"The Hunt . . . !"

Now, time is like a tight-wound spring. The dogs plunge forward, six to a handler, leashes straining, choke links creaking and snapping. Behind them jostle the riders. The bobbing scarlet coats splash across the snow. In the house drive an officer salutes; another strikes gloved palms together, nods. The gates whine open.

And across the country for miles around doors slam, bolts are shot, shutters closed, children scurried indoors. Village streets, muffled with snow, wait dumbly. Somewhere a dog barks, is silenced. The houses squat sullen, blind-eyed. The word has gone out, faster than horses could gallop. Today the Hunt will run; on snow.

The riders fan out, across a speckled waste of fields. A check, a questing; and the horns begin to yelp. Ahead the dogs bound and leap, black spots against whiteness. The horns cry again; but these hounds run mute. The riders sweep forward, on to the line.

Now, for the hunters, time and vision are fragmented. Twigs and snow merge in a racing blur; and tree-boles, ditches, gates. The tide reaches a crest of land, pours down the opposing slope. Hedges rear, mantled with white; and muffled thunder is interrupted by sailing silence, the smash and crackle of landing. The View sounds, harsh and high; and frenzy, and the racing blood, discharge intelligence. A horse goes down, in a gigantic flailing; another rolls, crushing its rider into the snow. A mount runs riderless. The Hunt, destroying, destroys itself unaware.

There are cottages, a paling fence. The fence goes over, unnoticed. A chicken house erupts in a cloud of flung crystals; birds run squawking, under the hooves. Caps are lost, flung away; hair flogs wild. Whips flail, spurs rake streaming flanks; and the woods are close. Twigs lash, and branches; snow falls, thudding. The crackling, now, is all around.

At the end, it is always the same. The handlers close in, yodelling, waist-high in trampled brush; the riders force close and closer, mounts sidling and shaking; and silence falls. Only the quarry, reddened, flops and twists; the thin high noise it makes is the noise of anything in pain.

Now, if he chooses, the *Jagdmeister* may end the suffering. The crash of the pistol rings hollow; and birds erupt, high from frozen twigs, wheel with the echoes and cry. The pistol fires again; and the quarry lies still.

In time, the shaking stops; and a dog creeps forward, begins to lick.

Now a slow movement begins; a spreading-out, away from the place. There are mutterings, a laugh that chokes to silence. The fever passes. Somebody begins to shiver; and a girl, blood glittering on cheek and neck, puts a glove to her forehead and moans. The Need has come and gone; for a little while, the Two Empires have purged themselves.

The riders straggle back on tired mounts, shamble in through the gates. As the last enters, a closed black van starts up, drives away. In an hour, quietly, it returns; and the gates swing shut behind it.

Surfacing from deepest sleep was like rising, slowly, through a warm sea. For a time, as Mainwaring lay eyes closed, memory and awareness were confused so that she was with him and the room a recollected, childhood place. He rubbed his face, yawned, shook his head; and the knocking that had roused him came again. He said, "Yes?"

The voice said, "Last breakfast in fifteen minutes, sir."

He called, "Thank you," heard the footsteps pad away.

He pushed himself up, groped on the side table for his watch, held it close to his eyes. It read ten-forty-five.

He swung the bedclothes back, felt air tingle on his skin. She had been with him, certainly, in the dawn; his body remembered the succubus, with nearly painful strength. He looked down smiling, walked to the bathroom. He showered, towelled himself, shaved and dressed. He closed his door and locked it, walked to the breakfast room. A few couples still sat over their coffee; he smiled a good morning, took a window seat. Beyond the double panes the snow piled thickly; its reflection lit the room with a white, inverted brilliance. He ate slowly, hearing distant shouts. On the long slope behind the house, groups of children pelted each other vigorously. Once a toboggan came into sight, vanished behind a rising swell of ground.

He had hoped he might see her, but she didn't come. He drank coffee, smoked a cigarette. He walked to the television lounge. The big colour screen showed a children's party taking place in a Berlin hospital. He watched for a while. The door behind him clicked a couple of times, but it wasn't Diane.

There was a second guests' lounge, not usually much frequented at this time of the year; and a reading room and library. He wandered through them, but there was no sign of her. It occurred to him she might not yet be up; at Wilton there were few hard-and-fast rules for Christmas Day. He thought, "I should have checked her room number." He wasn't even sure in which of the guest wings she had been placed.

The house was quiet; it seemed most of the visitors had taken to their rooms. He wondered if she could have ridden with the Hunt; he'd heard it vaguely, leaving and returning. He doubted if the affair would have held much appeal.

He strolled back to the TV lounge, watched for an hour or more. By lunchtime he was feeling vaguely piqued; and sensing too the rise of a curious unease. He went back to his room, wondering if by any chance she had gone there; but the miracle was not repeated. The room was empty.

The fire was burning, and the bed had been remade. He had forgotten the servants' pass keys. The Geissler copy still stood on the shelf. He took it down, stood weighing it in his hand and frowning. It was, in a sense, madness to leave it there.

He shrugged, put the thing back. He thought, "So who reads bookshelves anyway?" The plot, if plot there had been, seemed absurd now in the clearer light of day. He stepped into the corridor, closed the door and locked it behind him. He tried as far as possible to put the book from his mind. It represented a problem; and problems, as yet, he wasn't prepared to cope with. Too much else was going on in his brain.

He lunched alone, now with a very definite pang; the process was disquietingly like that of other years. Once he thought he caught sight of her in the corridor. His heart thumped; but it was the other blonde, Müller's wife. The gestures, the fall of the hair, were similar; but this woman was taller.

He let himself drift into a reverie. Images of her, it seemed, were engraved on his mind; each to be selected now, studied, placed lovingly aside. He saw the firelit texture of her hair and skin, her lashes brushing her cheek as she lay in his arms and slept. Other memories, sharper, more immediate still, throbbed like little shocks in the mind. She tossed her head, smiling; her hair swung, touched the point of a breast.

He pushed his cup away, rose. At fifteen hundred, patriotism required her presence in the TV lounge. As it required the presence of every other guest. Then, if not before, he would see her. He reflected, wryly, that he had waited half a lifetime for her; a little longer now would do no harm.

He took to prowling the house again; the Great Hall, the Long Gallery where the *Christkind* had walked. Below the windows that lined it was a snow-covered roof. The tart, reflected light struck upward, robbing the place of mystery. In the Great Hall they had already removed the tree. He watched household staff hanging draperies, carrying in stacks of gilded cane chairs. On the Minstrels' Gallery a pile of odd-shaped boxes proclaimed that the orchestra had arrived.

At fourteen hundred hours he walked back to the TV lounge. A quick glance assured him she wasn't there. The bar was open; Hans, looking as big and suave as ever, had been pressed into service to minister to the guests. He smiled at Mainwaring and said, "Good afternoon, sir." Mainwaring asked for a lager beer, took the glass to a corner seat. From here he could watch both the TV screen and the door.

The screen was showing the world-wide link-up that had become hallowed Christmas afternoon fare within the Two Empires. He saw, without particular interest, greetings flashed from the Leningrad and Moscow garrisons, a lightship, an Arctic weather station, a Mission in German East Africa. At fifteen hundred the Fuehrer was due to speak; this year, for the first time, Ziegler was preceding Edward VIII.

The room filled, slowly. She didn't come. Mainwaring finished the lager, walked to the bar, asked for another and a packet of cigarettes. The unease was sharpening now into something very like alarm. He thought for the first time that she might have been taken ill.

The time signal flashed, followed by the drumroll of the German anthem. He rose with the rest, stood stiffly till it had finished. The screen cleared, showed the familiar room in the Chancellery; the dark, high panels, the crimson drapes, the big *Hackenkreuz* emblem over the desk. The Fuehrer, as ever, spoke impeccably; but Mainwaring thought with a fragment of his mind how old he had begun to look.

The speech ended. He realized he hadn't heard a word that was said.

The drums crashed again. The King said, "Once more, at Christmas, it is my . . . duty and pleasure . . . to speak to you."

Something seemed to burst inside Mainwaring's head. He rose, walked quickly to the bar. He said, "Hans, have you seen Miss Hunter?"

The other jerked round. He said, "Sir, *shh* . . . please . . ."

"Have you seen her?"

Hans stared at the screen, and back to Mainwaring. The King was saying, "There have been . . . troubles, and difficulties. More perhaps lie ahead. But with . . . God's help, they will be overcome."

The chauffeur licked his mouth. He said, "I'm sorry, sir. I don't know what you mean."

"Which was her room?"

The big man looked like something trapped. He said, "Please, Mr. Mainwaring. You'll get me into trouble. . . ."

"Which was her room?"

Somebody turned and hissed angrily. Hans said, "I don't understand."

"For God's sake, man, you carried her things upstairs. I saw you!"

Hans said, "No, sir . . ."

Momentarily, the lounge seemed to spin.

There was a door behind the bar. The chauffeur stepped back. He said, "Sir. Please . . ."

The place was a storeroom. There were wine bottles racked, a shelf with jars of olives, walnuts, eggs. Mainwaring closed the door behind him, tried to control the shaking. Hans said, "Sir, you must not ask me these things. I don't know a Miss Hunter. I don't know what you mean."

Mainwaring said, "Which was her room? I demand that you answer."

"I can't!"

"You drove me from London yesterday. Do you deny that?"

"No, sir."

"You drove me with Miss Hunter."

"No, sir!"

"Damn your eyes, where is she?"

The chauffeur was sweating. A long wait; then he said, "Mr. Mainwaring, please. You must understand. I can't help you." He swallowed, and drew himself up. He said, "I drove you from London. I'm sorry. I drove you . . . *on your own.*"

The lounge door swung shut behind Mainwaring. He half-walked, half-ran to his room. He slammed the door behind him, leaned against it panting. In time the giddiness passed. He opened his eyes, slowly. The fire glowed; the Geissler stood on the bookshelf. Nothing was changed.

He set to work, methodically. He shifted furniture, peered behind it. He rolled the carpet back, tapped every foot of floor. He fetched a flashlight from his case and examined, minutely, the interior of the wardrobe. He ran his fingers lightly across the walls, section by section, tapping again. Finally he got a chair, dismantled the ceiling lighting fitting.

Nothing.

He began again. Halfway through the second search he froze, staring at the floorboards. He walked to his case, took the screwdriver from the pistol holster. A moment's work with the blade and he sat back, staring into his palm. He rubbed his face, placed his find carefully on the side table. A tiny ear-ring, one of the pair she had worn. He sat a while breathing heavily, his head in his hands.

The brief daylight had faded as he worked. He lit the standard lamp, wrenched the shade free, stood the naked bulb in the middle of the room. He worked round the walls again, peering, tapping, pressing. By the fireplace, finally, a foot-square section of plaster rang hollow.

He held the bulb close, examined the hairline crack. He inserted the screwdriver blade delicately, twisted. Then again. A click; and the section hinged open.

He reached inside the little space, shaking, lifted out the recorder. He stood silent a time, holding it; then raised his arms, brought the machine smashing down on the hearth. He stamped and kicked, panting, till the thing was reduced to fragments.

The droning rose to a roar, swept low over the house. The helicopter settled slowly, belly lamps glaring, downdraught raising a storm of snow. He walked to the window, stood staring. The children embarked, clutching scarves and gloves, suitcases, boxes with new toys. The steps were withdrawn, the hatch dogged shut. Snow swirled again; the machine lifted heavily, swung away in the direction of Wilton.

The Party was about to start.

Lights blaze, through the length and breadth of the house. Orange-lit windows throw long bars of brightness across the snow. Everywhere is an anxious coming and going, the pattering of feet, clink of silver and glassware, hurried commands. Waiters scuttle between the kitchens and the Green Room where dinner is laid. Dish after dish is borne in, paraded. Peacocks, roasted and gilded, vaunt their plumes in shadow and candleglow, spirit-soaked wicks blazing in their beaks. The Minister rises, laughing; toast after toast is drunk. To five thousand tanks, ten thousand fighting aeroplanes, a hundred thousand guns. The Two Empires feast their guests, royally.

The climax approaches. The boar's head, garnished and smoking, is borne shoulder-high. His tusks gleam; clamped in his jaws is the golden sun-symbol, the orange. After him march the waits and mummers, with their lanterns and begging-cups. The carol they chant is older by far than the Two Empires; older than the Reich, older than Great Britain.

"Alive he spoiled, where poor men toiled, which made kind Ceres sad . . ."

The din of voices rises. Coins are flung, glittering; wine is poured. And more wine, and more and more. Bowls of fruit are passed, and trays of sweets; spiced cakes, gingerbread, marzipans. Till at a signal the brandy is brought, and boxes of cigars.

The ladies rise to leave. They move flushed and chattering through the corridors of the house, uniformed link-boys grandly lighting their way. In the Great Hall their escorts are waiting. Each young man is tall, each blond, each impeccably uniformed. On the Minstrels' Gallery a baton is poised; across the lawns, distantly, floats the whirling excitement of a waltz.

In the Green Room, hazed now with smoke, the doors are once more flung wide. Servants scurry again, carrying in boxes, great gay-wrapped parcels topped with scarlet satin bows. The Minister rises, hammering on the table for quiet.

"My friends, good friends, friends of the Two Empires. For you, no expense is spared. For you, the choicest gifts. Tonight, nothing but the best is good enough; and nothing but the best is here. Friends, enjoy yourselves. Enjoy my house. *Frohe Weihnachten* . . . !"

He walks quickly into shadow, and is gone. Behind him, silence falls. A waiting; and slowly, mysteriously, the great heap of gifts begins to stir. Paper splits, crackling. Here a hand emerges, here a foot. A breathless pause; and the first of the girls rises slowly, bare in flamelight, shakes her glinting hair.

The table roars again.

The sound reached Mainwaring dimly. He hesitated at the foot of the main staircase, moved on. He turned right and left, hurried down a flight of steps. He passed kitchens, and the servants' hall. From the hall came the blare of a record player. He walked to the end of the corridor, unlatched a door. Night air blew keen against his face.

He crossed the courtyard, opened a further door. The space beyond was bright-lit; there was the faint, musty stink of animals. He paused, wiped his face. He was shirt-sleeved; but despite the cold he was sweating.

He walked forward again, steadily. To either side of the corridor were the fronts of cages. The dogs hurled themselves at the bars, thunderously. He ignored them.

The corridor opened into a square concrete chamber. To one side of the place was a ramp. At its foot was parked a windowless black van.

In the far wall a door showed a crack of light. He rapped sharply, and again.

"*Hundenmeister* . . ."

The door opened. The man who peered up at him was as wrinkled and pot-bellied as a Nast Santa Claus. At sight of his visitor's face he tried to duck back; but Mainwaring had him by the arm. He said, "*Herr Hundenmeister*, I must talk to you."

"Who are you? I don't know you. What do you want? . . ."

Mainwaring showed his teeth. He said, "The van. You drove the van this morning. What was in it?"

"I don't know what you mean . . ."

The heave sent him stumbling across the floor. He tried to bolt; but Mainwaring grabbed him again.

"What was in it? . . ."

"I won't talk to you! Go away!"

The blow exploded across his cheek. Mainwaring hit him again, back-handed, slammed him against the van.

"Open it . . . !"

The voice rang sharply in the confined space.

"Wer ist da? Was ist passiert?"

The little man whimpered, rubbing at his mouth.

Mainwaring straightened, breathing heavily. The GFP captain walked forward, staring, thumbs hooked in his belt.

"Wer sind Sie?"

Mainwaring said, "You know damn well. And speak English, you bastard. You're as English as I am."

The other glared. He said, "You have no right to be here. I should arrest you. You have no right to accost *Herr Hundenmeister.*"

"What is in that van?"

"Have you gone mad? The van is not your concern. Leave now. At once."

"Open it!"

The other hesitated, and shrugged. He stepped back. He said, "Show him, *mein Herr.*"

The *Hundenmeister* fumbled with a bunch of keys. The van doors grated. Mainwaring walked forward, slowly.

The vehicle was empty.

The captain said, "You have seen what you wished to see. You are satisfied. Now go."

Mainwaring stared round. There was a further door, recessed deeply into the wall. Beside it controls like the controls of a bank vault.

"What is in that room?"

The GFP man said, "You have gone too far. I order you to leave."

"You have no authority over me!"

"Return to your quarters!"

Mainwaring said, "I refuse."

The other slapped the holster at his hip. He gut-held the Walther, wrists locked, feet apart. He said, "Then you will be shot."

Mainwaring walked past him, contemptuously. The baying of the dogs faded as he slammed the outer door.

It was among the middle classes that the seeds had first been sown; and it was among the middle classes that they flourished. Britain had been called often enough a nation of shopkeepers; now for a little while the tills were closed, the blinds left drawn. Overnight it seemed, an effete symbol of social and national disunity became the Einsatzgruppen-fuehrer; *and the wire for the first detention camps was strung.* . . .

Mainwaring finished the page, tore it from the spine, crumpled it and dropped it on the fire. He went on reading. Beside him on the hearth stood a part-full bottle of whisky and a glass. He picked the glass up mechanically, drank. He lit a cigarette. A few minutes later a new page followed the last.

The clock ticked steadily. The burning paper made a little rustling. Reflections danced across the ceiling of the room. Once Mainwaring raised his head, listened; once put the ruined book down, rubbed his eyes. The room, and the corridor outside, stayed quiet.

Against immeasurable force, we must pit cunning; against immeasurable evil, faith and a high resolve. In the war we wage, the stakes are high; the dignity of man, the freedom of the spirit, the survival of humanity. Already in that war, many of us have died; many more, undoubtedly, will lay down their lives. But always, beyond them, there will be others; and still more. We shall go on, as we must go on, till this thing is wiped from the earth.

Meanwhile, we must take fresh heart. Every blow, now, is a blow for freedom. In France, Belgium, Finland, Poland, Russia, the forces of the Two Empires confront each other uneasily. Greed, jealousy, mutual distrust; these are the enemies, and they work from within. This, the Empires know full well. And, knowing, for the first time in their existence, fear. . . .

The last page crumpled, fell to ash. Mainwaring sat back, staring at nothing. Finally he stirred, looked up. It was zero three hundred; and they hadn't come for him yet.

The bottle was finished. He set it to one side, opened another. He swilled the liquid in the glass, hearing the magnified ticking of the clock.

He crossed the room, took the Lüger from the case. He found a cleaning rod, patches and oil. He sat a while dully, looking at the pistol. Then he slipped the magazine free, pulled back on the breech toggle, thumbed the latch, slid the barrel from the guides.

His mind, wearied, had begun to play aggravating tricks. It ranged and wandered, remembering scenes, episodes, details sometimes from years back; trivial, unconnected. Through and between the wanderings, time after time, ran the ancient, lugubrious words of the carol. He tried to shut them out, but it was impossible.

"Living he spoiled where poor men toiled, which made kind Ceres sad . . ."

He pushed the link pin clear, withdrew the breech block, stripped the firing pin. He laid the parts out, washed them with oil and water, dried and re-oiled. He reassembled the pistol, working carefully; inverted the barrel, shook the link down in front of the hooks, closed the latch, checked the recoil spring engagement. He loaded a full clip, pushed it home, chambered a round, thumbed the safety to *Gesichert*. He released the clip, reloaded.

He fetched his briefcase, laid the pistol inside carefully, grip uppermost. He filled a spare clip, added the extension butt and a fifty box of Parabellum. He closed the flap and locked it, set the case beside the bed. After that there was nothing more to do. He sat back in the chair, refilled his glass.

"Toiling he boiled, where poor men spoiled . . ."

The firelight faded, finally.

He woke, and the room was dark. He got up, felt the floor sway a little. He understood that he had a hangover. He groped for the light switch. The clock hands stood at zero eight hundred.

He felt vaguely guilty at having slept so long.

He walked to the bathroom. He stripped and showered, running the water as hot as he could bear. The process brought him round a little. He dried himself, staring down. He thought for the first time what curious things these bodies were; some with their yellow cylinders, some their indentations.

He dressed and shaved. He had remembered what he was going to do; fastening his tie, he tried to remember why. He couldn't. His brain, it seemed, had gone dead.

There was an inch of whisky in the bottle. He poured it, grimaced and drank. Inside him was a fast, cold shaking. He thought, "Like the first morning at a new school."

He lit a cigarette. Instantly his throat filled. He walked to the bathroom and vomited. Then again. Finally there was nothing left to come.

His chest ached. He rinsed his mouth, washed his face again. He sat in the bedroom for a while, head back and eyes closed. In time the shaking went away. He lay unthinking, hearing the clock tick. Once his lips moved. He said, "They're no better than us."

At nine hundred hours he walked to the breakfast room. His stomach, he felt, would retain very little. He ate a slice of toast, carefully, drank some coffee. He asked for a pack of cigarettes, went back to his room. At ten hundred hours he was due to meet the Minister.

He checked the briefcase again. A thought made him add a pair of stringback motoring gloves. He sat again, stared at the ashes where he had burned the Geissler. A part of him was willing the clock hands not to move. At five to ten he picked the briefcase up, stepped into the corridor. He stood a moment staring round him. He thought, "It hasn't happened yet. I'm still alive." There was still the flat in Town to go back to, still his office; the tall windows, the telephones, the khaki utility desk.

He walked through sunlit corridors to the Minister's suite.

The room to which he was admitted was wide and long. A fire crackled in the hearth; beside it on a low table stood glasses and a decanter. Over the mantel, conventionally, hung the Fuehrer's portrait. Edward VIII faced him across the room. Tall windows framed a prospect of rolling parkland. In the distance, blue on the horizon, were the woods.

The Minister said, "Good morning, Richard. Please sit down. I don't think I shall keep you long."

He sat, placing the briefcase by his knee.

This morning everything seemed strange. He studied the Minister curiously, as if seeing him for the first time. He had that type of face once thought of as peculiarly English: short-nosed and slender, with high, finely shaped cheekbones. The hair, blond and cropped close to the scalp, made him look nearly boyish. The eyes were candid, flat, dark-fringed. He looked, Mainwaring decided, not so much Aryan as like some fierce nursery toy; a Feral Teddy Bear.

The Minister riffled papers. He said, "Several things have cropped up; among them, I'm afraid, more trouble in Glasgow. The fifty-first Panzer division is standing by; as yet, the news hasn't been released."

Mainwaring wished his head felt less hollow. It made his own voice boom so unnecessarily. He said, "Where is Miss Hunter?"

The Minister paused. The pale eyes stared; then he went on speaking.

"I'm afraid I may have to ask you to cut short your stay here. I shall be flying back to London for a meeting; possibly tomorrow, possibly the day after. I shall want you with me, of course."

"Where is Miss Hunter?"

The Minister placed his hands flat on the desktop, studied the nails. He said, "Richard, there are aspects of Two Empires culture that are neither mentioned nor discussed. You of all people should know this. I'm being patient with you; but there are limits to what I can overlook."

"*Seldom he toiled, while Ceres roiled, which made poor kind men glad . . .*"

Mainwaring opened the flap of the case and stood up. He thumbed the safety forward and levelled the pistol.

There was silence for a time. The fire spat softly. Then the Minister smiled. He said, "That's an interesting gun, Richard. Where did you get it?"

Mainwaring didn't answer.

The Minister moved his hands carefully to the arms of his chair, leaned back. He said, "It's the Marine model, of course. It's also quite old. Does it by any chance carry the Erfurt stamp? Its value would be considerably increased."

He smiled again. He said, "If the barrel is good, I'll buy it. For my private collection."

Mainwaring's arm began to shake. He steadied his wrist, gripping with his left hand.

The Minister sighed. He said, "Richard, you can be so stubborn. It's a good quality; but you do carry it to excess." He shook his head. He said, "Did you imagine for one moment I didn't know you were coming here to kill me? My dear chap, you've been through a great deal. You're over-wrought. Believe me, I know just how you feel."

Mainwaring said, "You murdered her."

The Minister spread his hands. He said, "What with? A gun? A knife? Do I honestly look such a shady character?"

The words made a cold pain, and a tightness in the chest. But they had to be said.

The Minister's brows rose. Then he started to laugh. Finally he said, "At last I see. I understood, but I couldn't believe. So you bullied our poor little *Hundenmeister,* which wasn't very worthy; and seriously annoyed the *Herr Hauptmann,* which wasn't very wise. Because of this fantasy, stuck in your head. Do you really believe it, Richard? Perhaps you believe in *Struwwelpeter* too." He sat forward. He said, "The Hunt ran. And killed . . . a deer. She gave us an excellent chase. As for your little Huntress . . . Richard, she's gone. She never existed. She was a figment of your imagination. Best forgotten."

Mainwaring said, "We were in love."

The Minister said, "Richard, you really are becoming tiresome." He shook his head again. He said, "We're both adult. We both know what that word is worth. It's a straw, in the wind. A candle, on a night of gales. A phrase that is meaningless. *Lächerlich.*" He put his hands together, rubbed a palm. He said, "When this is over, I want you to go away. For a month, six weeks maybe. With your new car. When you come back . . . well, we'll see. Buy yourself a girl friend, if you need a woman that much. *Einen Schatz.* I never dreamed; you're so remote, you should speak more of yourself. Richard, I understand; it isn't such a very terrible thing."

Mainwaring stared.

The Minister said, "We shall make an arrangement. You will have the use of an apartment, rather a nice apartment. So your lady will be close. When you tire of her . . . buy another. They're unsatisfactory for the most part, but reasonable. Now sit down like a good chap, and put your gun away. You look so silly, standing there scowling like that."

It seemed he felt all life, all experience, as a grey weight pulling. He lowered the pistol, slowly. He thought, "At the end, they were wrong. They picked the wrong man." He said, "I suppose now I use it on myself."

The Minister said, "No, no, no. You still don't understand." He linked his knuckles, grinning. He said, "Richard, the *Herr Hauptmann* would have arrested you last night. I wouldn't let him. This is between ourselves. Nobody else. I give you my word."

Mainwaring felt his shoulders sag. The strength seemed drained from him; the pistol, now, weighed too heavy for his arm.

The Minister said, "Richard, why so glum? It's a great occasion, man. You've found your courage. I'm delighted."

He lowered his voice. He said, "Don't you want to know why I let you come here with your machine? Aren't you even interested?"

Mainwaring stayed silent.

The Minister said, "Look around you, Richard. See the world. I want men near me, serving me. Now more than ever. Real men, not afraid to die. Give me a dozen . . . but you know the rest. I could rule the world. But first . . . I must rule them. My men. Do you see now? Do you understand?"

Mainwaring thought, "He's in control again. But he was always in control. He owns me."

The study spun a little.

The voice went on, smoothly. "As for this amusing little plot by the so-called Freedom Front; again, you did well. It was difficult for you. I was watching; believe me, with much sympathy. Now, you've burned your book. Of your own free will. That delighted me."

Mainwaring looked up, sharply.

The Minister shook his head. He said, "The real recorder is rather better hidden, you were too easily satisfied there. There's also a TV monitor. I'm sorry about it all, I apologize. It was necessary."

A singing started inside Mainwaring's head.

The Minister sighed again. He said, "Still unconvinced, Richard? Then I have some things I think you ought to see. Am I permitted to open my desk drawer?"

Mainwaring didn't speak. The other slid the drawer back slowly, reached in. He laid a telegram flimsy on the desk top. He said, "The addressee is Miss D. J. Hunter. The message consists of one word. 'Activate.'"

The singing rose in pitch.

"This as well," said the Minister. He held up a medallion on a thin gold chain. The little disc bore the linked motif of the Freedom Front. He said, "Mere exhibitionism; or a deathwish. Either way, a most undesirable trait."

He tossed the thing down. He said, "She was here under surveillance of course, we'd known about her for years. To them, you were a sleeper. Do you see the absurdity? They really thought you would be jealous enough to assassinate your Minister. This they mean in their silly little book, when they talk of subtlety. Richard, I could have fifty blonde women if I chose. A hundred. Why should I want yours?" He shut the drawer with a click, and rose. He said, "Give me the gun now. You don't need it any more." He extended his arm; then he was flung heavily backward. Glasses smashed on the side table. The decanter split; its contents poured dark across the wood.

Over the desk hung a faint haze of blue. Mainwaring walked forward, stood looking down. There were blood-flecks, and a little flesh. The eyes of the Teddy Bear still showed glints of white. Hydraulic shock had shattered the chest; the breath drew ragged, three times, and stopped. He thought, "I didn't hear the report."

The communicating door opened. Mainwaring turned. A secretary stared in, bolted at sight of him. The door slammed.

He pushed the briefcase under his arm, ran through the outer office. Feet clattered in the corridor. He opened the door, carefully. Shouts sounded, somewhere below in the house.

Across the corridor hung a loop of crimson cord. He stepped over it, hurried up a flight of stairs. Then another. Beyond the private apartments the way was closed by a heavy metal grille. He ran to it, rattled. A rumbling sounded from below. He glared round. Somebody had operated the emergency shutters; the house was sealed.

Beside the door an iron ladder was spiked to the wall. He climbed it, panting. The trap in the ceiling was padlocked. He clung one-handed, awkward with the briefcase, held the pistol above his head.

Daylight showed through splintered wood. He put his shoulder to the trap, heaved. It creaked back. He pushed head and shoulders through, scrambled. Wind stung at him, and flakes of snow.

His shirt was wet under the arms. He lay face down, shaking. He thought, "It wasn't an accident. None of it was an accident." He had underrated them. They understood despair.

He pushed himself up, stared round. He was on the roof of Wilton. Beside him rose gigantic chimney stacks. There was a lattice radio mast.

The wind hummed in its guy wires. To his right ran the balustrade that crowned the façade of the house. Behind it was a snow-choked gutter.

He wriggled across a sloping scree of roof, ran crouching. Shouts sounded from below. He dropped flat, rolled. An automatic clattered. He edged forward again, dragging the briefcase. Ahead, one of the corner towers rose dark against the sky. He crawled to it, crouched sheltered from the wind. He opened the case, pulled the gloves on. He clipped the stock to the pistol, laid the spare magazine beside him and the box of rounds.

The shouts came again. He peered forward, through the balustrade. Running figures scattered across the lawn. He sighted on the nearest, squeezed. Commotion below. The automatic zipped; stone chips flew, whining. A voice called, "Don't expose yourselves unnecessarily." Another answered.

"Die konmen mit den Hubschrauber . . ."

He stared round him, at the yellow-grey horizon. He had forgotten the helicopter.

A snow flurry drove against his face. He huddled, flinching. He thought he heard, carried on the wind, a faint droning.

From where he crouched he could see the nearer trees of the park, beyond them the wall and gatehouses. Beyond again, the land rose to the circling woods.

The droning was back, louder than before. He screwed his eyes, made out the dark spot skimming above the trees. He shook his head. He said, "We made a mistake. We all made a mistake."

He settled the stock of the Lüger to his shoulder, and waited.

ROBERT BLOCH

I Do Not Love Thee, Doctor Fell

Robert Bloch has devoted most of his production to stories of dark fantasy and horror. He is the author of Psycho. *He has been a constant public figure active in SF since the late 1930s, when he was a young correspondent of H. P. Lovecraft. This is one of his few ironic SF pieces, about a new illness growing out of the discontents of our civilization, viewed with the black humor that characterizes Bloch's work.*

*   *   *

Bromely couldn't remember who had recommended Doctor Fell. The name had popped into his mind (funny, something like that popping *into* his mind at a time when so many things seemed to be popping *out* of it!) and he must have made an appointment.

At any rate, the receptionist seemed to know him, and her "Good morning, Mr. Bromely" had a warm, pleasant sound. The door of the inner office, closing behind him, had a harsh, grating sound. Both seemed oddly familiar.

Bromely sensed the same misplaced familiarity as he gazed around the inner office. The bookshelves and filing cases to the left of the window, the desk to the right, the couch in the corner almost duplicated the arrangement in his own office. This was a good omen, he felt. He'd be at home here. At home. But, *you can't go home again. Home is where the heart is. You have stolen my heart, now don't go 'way. As we sang love's old sweet song on*—

It took a tremendous, conscious effort to pull out of that one, but Bromely did it. He wanted to make a good impression on the Doctor.

Doctor Fell rose to greet him from his chair behind the desk. He was a tall, thin man of about Bromely's age and build, and Bromely received a vague impression that his features were not dissimilar. The subdued lighting did not lend itself to a closer scrutiny of the psychiatrist's countenance, but Bromely was aware of a look of purpose and intensity quite foreign to his own face.

The same purpose and intensity drove Doctor Fell around the desk, communicated in his hearty handclasp.

"You're prompt, Mr. Bromely," said Doctor Fell. His voice was deep and low. *Deep and Low. Low and Behold. Behold, Bedad and Begob. Shadrach, Mesach and Abednego, Inc.*

How he got out of that one, Bromely never knew. He was somewhat surprised to find himself on the couch. Apparently he'd been talking to Doctor Fell for quite some time—and quite rationally, too. Yes, he remembered, now. He'd been answering all the routine questions.

Doctor Fell knew that he was Clyde Bromely, age 32, public relations counsel. Born in Erie, Pennsylvania. Parents dead. Business, lousy. No business. No *business like show business, there's no business I know*—

Had he said that? Apparently not, because Doctor Fell's rich, deep, comforting voice moved right along, asking the questions and extracting the answers. And it was quite all right to talk to Doctor Fell, tell him all he knew. Fell was a good psychiatrist.

Bromely knew a little something about psychiatry himself. Oh, not the technical terms of course, but more than a smattering of technique. This was a routine orientation, preliminary to probing. And Bromely cooperated.

When Doctor Fell began to ask questions about his health and his general background, Bromely took a sheaf of papers from his inside coat pocket and handed them over.

"Here it is, Doc," he said. "Complete report on the physical. Had it taken last week." He indicated a second folded sheaf. "And here's the autobiography. All the names you'll need—friends, relatives, teachers, employers, the works. Everything I could remember. Which isn't much, right now."

Doctor Fell smiled in the shadows. "Excellent," he said. "You seem to understand the necessity of cooperation." He put the papers on the desk.

"I'll check over this later," he told Bromely. "Although I imagine I'm already familiar with most of the contents."

Bromely got that panicky feeling again. Whoever had recommended Doctor Fell to him must also have talked to Doctor Fell about his case. Now who would that be? He hesitated to ask—not that he felt ashamed, but it would be an admission that he was pretty far gone if he couldn't even recall how he'd come here. Well, it didn't matter. He was grateful to be here, and that was the important thing. He needed Doctor Fell.

"You've got to help me, Doctor Fell," he was saying. "You're my last hope. That's why I've come to you. You must understand that, because it's the crux of the whole matter. I would never have come to you unless you were my last hope. I'm at the end of my rope. When you come to the end of your rope, you swing. I'm swinging, now. I'm swinging down the lane. Down Memory Lane. I wanted to be a songwriter, once. But my lyrics sounded as if they were stolen. That's my problem. Association. I've got too much association. Everything I do or say sounds like it's stolen from somebody else. Imitation. Mimicry. Until there's nothing original, nothing basic beneath to which I can cling. I'm losing myself. There's no real *me* left."

Bromely went on like this for about an hour. He said everything that came into his mind. The associative clichés poured out, and with them the desperate plea for help.

Doctor Fell scribbled in his notebook and said nothing. At the end of the session he tapped Bromely on the shoulder.

"That'll be enough for today," he said. "Tomorrow, same time? Let's plan on an hour a day, five days a week."

"Then you think you can help me?"

Doctor Fell nodded. "Let's say that I think you can help yourself. Five days a week, from now on."

Bromely rose from the couch. Doctor Fell's face wavered and blurred before him. He was very tired, very confused, but oddly relieved despite the physical strain that affected his vision. There was just one thing bothering him—and suddenly, he remembered it.

"But, Doc, I just happened to think. You know, I'm not doing too well with the business these days and five days a week—"

The hand gripped his shoulder. "I quite understand. But let's put it this way. Your case—your problem, that is—interests me, personally. And even a psychiatrist has been known to extend his services on occasion, without fee."

Bromely couldn't believe his ears at first. "You mean—it won't cost me anything?" His expression of gratitude was genuine. "Doc, you're a real friend. A friend in need. A friend in deed. Indeed."

Doctor Fell chuckled. "Believe me, Mr. Bromely, I *am* your friend. You'll find that out for yourself, in time, I trust."

As Clyde Bromely went out the door he felt the phrases flooding through his brain. *In God we trust, all others pay cash. My best and only friend. A man's best friend is his mother.*

The receptionist said something to him as he left, but Bromely was too preoccupied to catch her words. He was *engrossed in thought,* he was *deep in contemplation, Deep in the Heart of Texas. Death and Texas. Nothing's sure but.*

The rest of the day passed in a blur. Almost before he realized it, tomorrow had come and he had come and here he was back on the couch.

Doctor Fell listened as he told him about his father and mother, and about the peculiar feeling he now had—the feeling that Doctor Fell reminded him of his father and mother. Brother and sister I have none, but I am my father's only son. Who am I?

"Who are you?" Doctor Fell asked the question, softly. "That's really what's bothering you, isn't it? Who are you? You can answer that question if you want to, you know. So try. Try. Who are you?"

It was the *wrong* question. Bromely felt it, and he froze. Somewhere, deep inside, words formed an answer. But he couldn't find the words. He couldn't find that spot, inside him, where the words came from.

For the rest of the hour he just lay there on the couch.

Doctor Fell said nothing. When the time was up he tapped Bromely on the shoulder, muttered "Tomorrow, then," and turned away.

Bromely got out of the office. The receptionist stared at him oddly, half-opened her mouth to say something, and didn't. Bromely shrugged. Somehow he managed to find his way back to his own office.

He walked in and asked *his* girl for messages. Apparently whatever was wrong with him showed in his appearance, because she did that half-open-mouth trick too. Then she managed to control herself and tell him that CAA had called just a few minutes ago and wanted to see him. There was a chance to handle Torchy Harrigan.

That was the news he'd been waiting for. Bromely snapped out of it, fast. Torchy Harrigan—just signed for a new network video show—two pictures coming up with MGM—big deal with CAA, Consolidated Artists of America—personal representative—press releases to all dailies—

"Call them back and tell them I'm on my way over," he said. "Bromely rides again!"

. . .

Bromely was riding again. He was riding the couch in Doctor Fell's office. He was *riding for a fall, riding hell-for-leather* —

And all the while he was talking it out, gasping and sobbing and wheezing and choking it out.

"I can't explain it, Doc. I just can't figure it out! Here I had this deal sewed up with Harrigan, just the kind of setup I've been looking for. Two bills a week and all expenses, a chance to go out to the Coast with him, the works. Even turned out that his business manager is Hal Edwards—good friend of mine, known him for years. He gave Harrigan the pitch on me, built me up.

"So I walked in on Edwards and we talked it over, and then we went up to Harrigan's suite at the Plaza to talk it over. And Harrigan gave me the big hello, listened to Hal Edwards pitch for me—greatest flack in the business, all that kind of thing.

"You get the picture, Doc? The whole deal was in the bag. Harrigan was just waiting for me to give him the word on my plan for a publicity campaign. Edwards flashed me the cue and I opened my mouth.

"But nothing came out. You understand me? But *nothing*! I couldn't think of anything to say. Oh, there were words and phrases whirling around in my head, only they didn't add up. I couldn't think like a press agent any more."

All the while he talked, Bromely had been watching Doctor Fell's face. At first it seemed far away, but now it was coming closer and closer, getting bigger and bigger until it blotted out everything.

And Doctor Fell's voice was like distant thunder, then thunder near at hand, thunder overhead.

Vision and hearing played their tricks, but Bromely clung to Doctor Fell, clung to *words that fell from Doctor Fell for he's a jolly good fellow which nobody can deny.*

Doctor Fell had been taking notes in shorthand. He glanced at them now as he spoke. In a moment, Bromely realized he was merely reading off a string of quotes from Bromely's previous conversation. The phrases droned on, louder and louder.

"Can't figure it out . . . sewed up . . . setup . . . two bills a week . . . the works . . . gave Harrigan the pitch on me, built me up . . . big hello . . . greatest flack in the business . . . get the picture . . . in the bag . . . give him the word . . . flashed me the cue . . . but nothing . . . didn't add up."

Doctor Fell leaned forward. "What do those phrases mean to you, Bromely? What do they really *add up* to, in your mind?"

Bromely tried to think about it. He tried hard. But all he could come out with was, "I don't know. They're all slang expressions I used to use in public relations a few years ago. Come to think of it, they're a little dated now, aren't they?"

Doctor Fell smiled. "Exactly. And doesn't that tie in with your final statement, that you couldn't think like a press agent anymore? Isn't that part of your problem, Mr. Bromely—that you aren't a press agent any more, really? That you're losing your identity, losing your orientation? Let me ask you once again, now: *who are you?*"

Bromely froze up. He couldn't answer because he couldn't think of the answer. He lay there on the couch, and Doctor Fell waited. Nothing happened.

Nothing seemed to happen for a long, long time. How Bromely got through the next two days he couldn't remember. All he recalled were the hours on the couch—and it seemed to him that he shuttled back and forth between his office and Doctor Fell's more than once a day.

It was hard to check, of course, because he didn't talk to anyone. He lived alone in a one-room walkup apartment and he ate at one-arm counter joints. He wasn't talking to his office-girl, Thelma, any more either. There was nothing to talk about—no calls since the unfortunate Harrigan affair—and he owed her for three weeks' back salary. Besides, she almost seemed afraid of him when he appeared in the office. Come to think of it (and it was so hard to come to think of it, or anything else, so very hard) even Doctor Fell's little receptionist looked frightened when he walked in, without a word.

Without a word. That was his problem. He had no words any longer. It was as though his final effort, talking to Harrigan and Hal Edwards, had drained him dry of the ability to communicate. All the clichés had flowed out of him, leaving . . . nothing.

He realized it now, lying on the couch in Doctor Fell's office. Once more Doctor Fell had asked the single question, the only question he ever asked. "Who are you?"

And he couldn't answer. There was nothing. He was nobody. For years, now, he'd been in the process of becoming nobody. It was the only explanation that fitted. But he couldn't seem to explain.

With a start, he realized that it wasn't necessary. Doctor Fell was sitting close to Bromely now, breaking the long silence, whispering confidentially in his ear.

"All right," he was murmuring. "Let's try a different approach. Maybe *I* can tell you who you are."

Bromely nodded gratefully, but somewhere deep within him, fear was rising.

"Your case is quite remarkable in a way," said Doctor Fell, "but only because it's one of the first. I don't believe it will be the last. Within several years, there'll be thousands of men like you. The schizoids and the paranoids will have to move over and make room for a new category."

Bromely nodded, waited.

"You know anything about disease germs, bacteria? These organisms undergo swift mutations. Men invent sulfa drugs and the germs develop tolerance to sulfa. Men use antibiotics—penicillin, streptomycin, a dozen others. And the bugs adapt. They breed new strains of bugs."

He thinks I'm bugs, Bromely told himself, but he listened. Fell went on, his voice rising slightly.

"Bugs change, but still they spawn on men. And aberration changes with the times, too—but still it spawns on men. Five hundred years ago the commonest form of insanity was belief in demoniac possession. Three hundred years ago men had delusions of witchcraft and sorcery. A man who couldn't integrate his personality created a new one—he became a wizard. Because the wizard was the symbol of power, who knew the secrets of Life and Death. The disintegrating personality seeks reaffirmation in Authority. Does that make sense to you?"

Bromely nodded, but actually nothing made sense to him any more. The fear rose within him as Doctor Fell's voice rose without.

"Yes, three hundred years ago, thousands of men and women went to the stake firmly convinced that they were, actually, witches and wizards.

"Times change, Bromely. Look what happened to you. Your personality disintegrated, didn't it? You began to lose touch with reality.

"You lived alone, without personal ties to reaffirm identity. Your work was phony, too—the epitome of all phoniness—manufacturing lies to create artificial press-agent personalities for others. You lived in a phony world, used phony words and phrases, and before you knew it, nothing you did was quite real to you any more. And you got panicked because you felt your sense of identity slipping away. True?"

Bromely felt the fear very close now, because Doctor Fell was closer. But he wanted Doctor Fell to stay, wanted him to solve this problem.

"You're not a fool, Clyde." Doctor Fell used his first name now and it underlined the intimacy of his words. "You sensed something was going wrong. And so you did what others are beginning to do today. You did that which will create, in years to come, a new kind of mania."

The fear was *here*, now. But Bromely listened.

"Some start by seeking the 'self-help' books, just as old-time sorcerers used to study grimoires. Some go further and experiment in all the odd bypaths of parapsychology—ESP, telepathy, occultism. And some go all the way. They cannot conjure up the Devil but they can commune with Freud, with Adler, with Jung and Moll and Stekel and the other archfiends. They don't chant spells any more, but they learn the new Cabala, the new language of Mystery. *Schizophrenia, echolalia, involutional melancholia*— the words come trippingly from the tongue, do they not?

"You should know, Clyde. Didn't you visit the library on those long dull days when business was bad, and read endlessly in psychiatry? Didn't you bury yourself, these past several months, in a completely new world of delusion and hallucination and obsession, of neurosis and psychosis? In other words, when you felt you were going crazy—just as in the past, men felt they were becoming possessed of the Devil—didn't you seek to fight it by studying psychiatry as the ancients studied the black arts?"

Bromely tried to sit up. Doctor Fell's face loomed closer, swung away, loomed closer again.

"You know what happened to those men, Clyde. They became, in their own minds, wizards. And you know now—surely you must have guessed— what has happened to you. During the past week, you couldn't be a press agent any more. You couldn't be a rational human being any more. In an effort to project, to invest in a new identity, you became a psychiatrist. And *you invented me!*

"You've told yourself that this office is something like your own office, my receptionist resembles your girl, I resemble you. Don't you understand? This *is* your office. That *is* your girl. You've been coming in daily and lying down here on your own couch. No wonder she's frightened, hearing you talk to yourself. *Now* do you know who you are?"

Was it Doctor Fell or the fear screaming in his ears?

"This is your last chance, Clyde. You've got to decide once and for all. You can be yourself again, completely, if you have faith in your own identity. If not, you're the first of the new maniacs. Let me ask you once again, once and for all: *who are you?*"

Clyde Bromely lay there on the couch while the room whirled and swirled. He saw pictures, endless pictures: a faded snapshot of a little Clyde, clinging to Mamma's skirt—Bromely, Lt. j.g., U.S.N., in uniform—Speed Bromely, public relations, shaking hands with a top comic at a benefit show—Bromely sitting in the public library, seeking the answer in the ologies and the isms—Bromely lying on the couch, clawing at nothing.

Bromely saw the pictures, shuffled them, sorted them, and made his choice.

Then the fear fell away, and Bromely slept. He slept there on the couch for a long, long time. When he woke up it was dark and he was alone in the room. Somebody was rapping on the door.

It was his girl. He knew that now. He was in his own office, and his own girl came in, timidly and hesitantly, as he rose with a smile of renewed confidence,

"I was worried," she said. "You being in here so long, and—"

He laughed, and laughed again inside as he realized that the sound but dimly conveyed the new security he felt within himself.

"I was sleeping," he told her. "There's nothing to worry about, my dear. From now on, we're going places. I've been in a pretty bad slump for the past month or so—someday I'll tell you all about it—but I'm all right now. Let's go out for dinner and we'll make plans."

The girl smiled. She could sense the change, too. Dark as the room was, it seemed to fill with sudden sunlight.

"All right," she said. "All right, Mr. Bromely."

He stiffened. "Bromely? That patient? Don't you know me, my dear?"

Aye, and Gomorrah . . .

Young Samuel R. Delany burst upon the science fiction scene in the 1960s with novels and stories that won critical praise and popular awards and ranked him with the great names of the 1940s and 1950s. Linked with his literary peer Roger Zelazny in a concern with myth and symbol and with Thomas M. Disch and Joanna Russ in a concern with literary experiment, stylistic purity, and excellence, he earned a place at the center of the American version of the New Wave. Delany went on, in the 1970s, to produce his masterful novel Dhalgren *and a number of other innovative works, including three volumes of critical essays on science fiction. In 1988 he published an autobiography,* The Motion of Light in Water, *which chronicles the extraordinary experiences of young Chip Delany as a gay black writer among the beatniks and bohemians of New York's East Village in the early 1960s. "Aye, and Gomorrah . . ." is one of the quintessential stories of the 1960s, a winner of the Nebula Award of the Science Fiction Writers of America for the best short story of 1967.*

*　　*　　*

And came down in Paris:

Where we raced along the Rue de Médicis with Bo and Lou and Muse inside the fence, Kelly and me outside, making faces through the bars, making noise, making the Luxembourg Gardens roar at two in the morning. Then climbed out and down to the square in front of St. Sulpice where Bo tried to knock me into the fountain.

At which point Kelly noticed what was going on around us, got an ashcan cover, and ran into the pissoir, banging the walls. Five guys scooted out; even a big pissoir only holds four.

A very blond young man put his hand on my arm and smiled. "Don't you think, Spacer, that you . . . people should leave?"

I looked at his hand on my blue uniform. "*Est-ce que tu es un frelk?*"

His eyebrows rose, then he shook his head. "Une *frelk*," he corrected. "No. I am not. Sadly for me. You look as though you may once have been a man. But now . . ." He smiled. "You have nothing for me now. The police." He nodded across the street where I noticed the gendarmerie for the first time. "They don't bother us. You are strangers, though . . ."

But Muse was already yelling, "Hey, come on! Let's get out of here, huh?" And left. And went up again.

And came down in Houston:

"God damn!" Muse said. "Gemini Flight Control—you mean this is where it all started? Let's get *out* of here, *please!*"

So took a bus out through Pasadena, then the monoline to Galveston, and were going to take it down the Gulf, but Lou found a couple with a pickup truck—

"Glad to give you a ride, Spacers. You people up there on them planets and things, doing all that good work for the government."

—who were going south, them and the baby, so we rode in the back for two hundred and fifty miles of sun and wind.

"You think they're frelks?" Lou asked, elbowing me. "I bet they're frelks. They're just waiting for us to give 'em the come-on."

"Cut it out. They're a nice, stupid pair of country kids."

"That don't mean they ain't frelks!"

"You don't trust anybody, do you?"

"No."

And finally a bus again that rattled us through Brownsville and across the border into Matamoros where we staggered down the steps into the dust and the scorched evening with a lot of Mexicans and chickens and Texas Gulf shrimp fishermen—who smelled worst—and *we* shouted the loudest. Forty-three whores—I counted—had turned out for the shrimp fishermen, and by the time we had broken two of the windows in the bus station, they were all laughing. The shrimp fishermen said they wouldn't buy us no food but would get us drunk if we wanted 'cause that was the custom with shrimp fishermen. But we yelled, broke another window; then while I was lying on my back on the telegraph office steps, singing, a woman with dark lips bent over and put her hands on my cheeks. "You are very sweet." Her rough hair fell forward. "But the men, they are standing around and watching *you*. And that is taking up *time*. Sadly, their time is our *money*. Spacer, do you not think you . . . people should leave?"

I grabbed her wrist. "*Usted!*" I whispered. "*Usted es una frelka?*"

"*Frelko en español.*" She smiled and patted the sunburst that hung from my belt buckle. "Sorry. But you have nothing that . . . would be useful to me. It is too bad for you look like you were once a woman, no? And I like women, too . . ."

I rolled off the porch.

"Is this a drag or is this a drag!" Muse was shouting. "Come *on*! Let's *go*!"

We managed to get back to Houston before dawn, somehow. And went up.

And came down in Istanbul:

That morning it rained in Istanbul.

At the commissary we drank our tea from pear-shaped glasses, looking out across the Bosphorus. The Princes Islands lay like trash heaps before the prickly city.

"Who knows their way in this town?" Kelly asked.

"Aren't we going around together?" Muse demanded. "I thought we were going around together."

"They held up my check at the purser's office," Kelly explained. "I'm flat broke. I think the purser's got it in for me," and shrugged. "Don't want to, but I'm going to have to hunt up a rich frelk and come on friendly," went back to the tea; *then* noticed how heavy the silence had become. "Aw, come *on*, now! You gape at me like that and I'll bust every bone in that carefully-conditioned-from-puberty body of yours. Hey, you!" meaning me. "Don't give me that holier-than-thou gawk like you never went with no frelk!"

It was starting.

"I'm not gawking," I said and got quietly mad.

The longing, the old longing.

Bo laughed to break tensions. "Say, last time I was in Istanbul—about a year before I joined up with this platoon—I remember we were coming out of Taksim Square down Istiqlal. Just past all the cheap movies we found a little passage lined with flowers. Ahead of us were two other spacers. It's a market in there, and farther down they got fish and then a courtyard with oranges and candy and sea urchins and cabbage. But flowers in front. Anyway, we noticed something funny about the spacers. It wasn't their uniforms: they were perfect. The haircuts: fine. It wasn't till we heard them talking—they were a man and woman dressed up like spacers, trying *to pick up frelks*! Imagine, queer for frelks!"

"Yeah," Lou said. "I seen that before. There were a lot of them in Rio."

"We beat hell out of them two," Bo concluded. "We got them in a side street and went to *town!*"

Muse's tea glass clicked on the counter. "From Taksim down Istiqlal till you get to the flowers? Now why didn't you say that's where the frelks were, huh?" A smile on Kelly's face would have made that okay. There was no smile.

"Hell," Lou said, "nobody ever had to tell me where to look. I go out in the street and frelks smell me coming. I can spot 'em halfway along Piccadilly. Don't they have nothing but tea in this place? Where can you get a drink?"

Bo grinned. "Moslem country, remember? But down at the end of the Flower Passage, there're a lot of little bars with green doors and marble counters where you can get a liter of beer for about fifteen cents in lira. And there're all these stands selling deep-fat-fried bugs and pig's gut sandwiches—"

"You ever notice how frelks can put it away? I mean liquor, not . . . pig's guts."

And launched off into a lot of appeasing stories. We ended with the one about the frelk some spacer tried to roll who announced: "There are two things I go for. One is spacers; the other is a good fight . . ."

But they only allay. They cure nothing. Even Muse knew we would spend the day apart now.

The rain had stopped so we took the ferry up the Golden Horn. Kelly straight off asked for Taksim Square and Istiqlal and was directed to a dolmush, which we discovered was a taxicab, only it just goes one place and picks up lots and lots of people on the way. And it's cheap.

Lou headed off over Ataturk Bridge to see the sights of New City. Bo decided to find out what the Dolma Boche really was; and when Muse discovered you could go to Asia for fifteen cents—one lira and fifty krush— well, Muse decided to go to Asia.

I turned through the confusion of traffic at the head of the bridge and up past the gray, dripping walls of Old City, beneath the trolley wires. There are times when yelling and helling won't fill the lack. There are times when you must walk by yourself because it hurts so much to be alone.

I walked up a lot of little streets with wet donkeys and wet camels and women in veils; and down a lot of big streets with buses and trash baskets and men in business suits.

Some people stare at spacers; some people don't. Some people stare or don't stare in a way a spacer gets to recognize within a week after coming out of training school at sixteen. I was walking in the park when I caught her watching. She saw me see and looked away.

I ambled down the wet asphalt. She was standing under the arch of a small, empty mosque shell. As I passed, she walked out into the courtyard among the cannons.

"Excuse me."

I stopped.

"Do you know whether or not this is the shrine of St. Irene?" Her English was charmingly accented. "I've left my guidebook home."

"Sorry. I'm a tourist, too."

"Oh." She smiled. "I am Greek. I thought you might be Turkish because you are so dark."

"American red Indian." I nodded. Her turn to curtsy.

"I see. I have just started at the university here in Istanbul. Your uniform, it tells me that you are . . ."—and in the pause, all speculations resolved—"a spacer."

I was uncomfortable. "Yeah." I put my hands in my pockets, moved my feet around on the soles of my boots, licked my third from the rear left molar—did all the things you do when you're uncomfortable. *You're so exciting when you look like that*, a frelk told me once. "Yeah, I am." I said it too sharply, too loudly, and she jumped a little.

So now she knew I knew she knew I knew, and I wondered how we would play out the Proust bit.

"I'm Turkish," she said. "I'm not Greek. I'm not just starting. I'm a graduate in art history here at the university. These little lies one makes for strangers to protect one's ego . . . why? Sometimes I think my ego is very small."

That's one strategy.

"How far away do you live?" I asked. "And what's the going rate in Turkish lira?" That's another.

"I can't pay you." She pulled her raincoat around her hips. She was very pretty. "I would like to." She shrugged and smiled. "But I am . . . a poor student. Not a rich one. If you want to turn around and walk away, there will be no hard feelings. I shall be sad though."

I stayed on the path. I thought she'd suggest a price after a little while. She didn't.

And *that's* another.

I was asking myself. *What do you want the damn money for anyway?* when a breeze upset water from one of the park's great cypresses.

"I think the whole business is sad." She wiped drops from her face. There had been a break in her voice, and for a moment I looked too closely at the water streaks. "I think it's sad that they have to alter you to make you a spacer. If they hadn't, then *we* . . . If spacers had never been, then we could not be . . . the way we are. Did you start out male or female?"

Another shower. I was looking at the ground and droplets went down my collar.

"Male," I said. "It doesn't matter."

"How old are you? Twenty-three, twenty-four?"

"Twenty-three," I lied. It's reflex. I'm twenty-five, but the younger they think you are, the more they pay you. But I didn't *want* her *damn* money—

"I guessed right, then." She nodded. "Most of us are experts on spacers. Do you find that? I suppose we have to be." She looked at me with wide black eyes. At the end of the stare, she blinked rapidly. "You would have been a fine man. But now you are a spacer, building water-conservation units on Mars, programing mining computers on Ganymede, servicing communication relay towers on the moon. The alteration . . ." Frelks are the only people I've ever heard say "the alteration" with so much fascination and regret. "You'd think they'd have found some other solution. They could have found another way than neutering you, turning you into creatures not even androgynous; things that are—"

I put my hand on her shoulder, and she stopped like I'd hit her. She looked to see if anyone was near. Lightly, so lightly then, she raised her hand to mine.

I pulled my hand away. "That are what?"

"They could have found another way." Both hands in her pockets now.

"They could have. Yes. Up beyond the ionosphere, there's too much radiation for those precious gonads to work right anywhere you might want to do something that would keep you there over twenty-four hours, like the moon, or Mars, or the satellites of Jupiter—"

"They could have made protective shields. They could have done more research into biological adjustment—"

"Population Explosion time," I said. "No, they were hunting for any excuse to cut down kids back then—especially deformed ones."

"Ah yes." She nodded. "We're still fighting our way up from the neo-puritan reaction to the sex freedom of the twentieth century."

"It was a fine solution." I grinned and hung my hand over my crotch. "I'm happy with it." I've never known why that's so much more obscene when a spacer does it.

"Stop it," she snapped, moving away.

"What's the matter?"

"Stop it," she repeated. "Don't do that! You're a child."

"But they choose us from children whose sexual responses are hopelessly retarded at puberty."

"And your childish, violent substitutes for love? I suppose that's one of the things that's attractive. Yes, I know you're a child."

"Yeah? What about frelks?"

She thought a while. "I think they are the sexually retarded ones they miss. Perhaps it was the right solution. You really don't regret you have no sex?"

"We've got you," I said.

"Yes." She looked down. I glanced to see the expression she was hiding. It was a smile. "You have your glorious, soaring life, *and* you have us." Her face came up. She glowed. "You spin in the sky, the world spins under you, and you step from land to land, while we . . ." She turned her head right, left, and her black hair curled and uncurled on the shoulder of her coat. "We have our dull, circled lives, bound in gravity, *worshipping* you!"

She looked back at me. "Perverted, yes? In love with a bunch of corpses in free fall!" She suddenly hunched her shoulders. "I don't like having a free-fall-sexual-displacement complex."

"That always sounded like too much to say."

She looked away. "I don't like being a frelk. Better?"

"I wouldn't like it either. Be something else."

"You don't choose your perversions. *You* have no perversions at all. You're free of the whole business. I love you for that, spacer. My love starts with the fear of love. Isn't that beautiful? A pervert substitutes something unattainable for 'normal' love: the homosexual, a mirror, the fetishist, a shoe, or a watch, or a girdle. Those with free-fall-sexual-dis—"

"Frelks."

"Frelks substitute"—she looked at me sharply again—"loose, swinging meat."

"That doesn't offend me."

"I wanted it to."

"Why?"

"You don't have desires. You wouldn't understand."

"Go on."

"I want you because you can't want me. That's the pleasure. If someone really had a sexual reaction to . . . us, we'd be scared away. I wonder how many people there were before there were you, waiting for your creation. We're necrophiles. I'm sure grave robbing has fallen off since you started going up. But you don't understand . . ." She paused. "If you did, then I wouldn't be scuffing leaves now and trying to think from whom I could borrow sixty lira." She stepped over the knuckles of a root that had cracked the pavement. "And that, incidentally, is the going rate in Istanbul."

I calculated. "Things still get cheaper as you go east."

"You know," and she let her raincoat fall open, "you're different from the others. You at least *want* to know—"

I said, "If I spat on you for every time you'd said that to a spacer, you'd drown."

"Go back to the moon, loose meat." She closed her eyes. "Swing on up to Mars. There are satellites around Jupiter where you might do some good. Go up and come down in some other city."

"Where do you live?"

"You want to come with me?"

"Give me something," I said. "Give me *some*thing—it doesn't have to be worth sixty lira. Give me something that you like, anything of yours that means something to you."

"No!"

"Why not?"

"Because I—"

"—don't want to give up part of that ego. None of you frelks do!"

"You really don't understand I just don't want to buy you?"

"You have nothing to buy me with."

"You are a child," she said. "I love you."

We reached the gate of the park. She stopped, and we stood time enough for a breeze to rise and die in the grass. "I . . ." she offered tentatively, pointing without taking her hand from her coat pocket. "I live right down there."

"All right," I said. "Let's go."

A gas main had once exploded along this street, she explained to me, a gushing road of fire as far as the docks, overhot and overquick. It had been put out within minutes, no building had fallen, but the charred facias glittered. "This is sort of an artist and student quarter." We crossed the cobbles. "Yuri Pasha, number fourteen. In case you're ever in Istanbul again." Her door was covered with black scales, the gutter was thick with garbage.

"A lot of artists and professional people are frelks," I said, trying to be inane.

"So are lots of other people." She walked inside and held the door. "We're just more flamboyant about it."

On the landing there was a portrait of Ataturk. Her room was on the second floor. "Just a moment while I get my key—"

Marsscapes! Moonscapes! On her easel was a six-foot canvas showing the sunrise flaring on a crater's rim! There were copies of the original Observer pictures of the moon pinned to the wall, and pictures of every smooth-faced general in the International Spacer Corps.

On one corner of her desk was a pile of those photo magazines about spacers that you can find in most kiosks all over the world: I've seriously heard people say they were printed for adventurous-minded high school children. They've never seen the Danish ones. She had a few of those, too. There was a shelf of art books, art history texts. Above them were six feet of cheap paper-covered space operas: *Sin on Space Station #12, Rocket, Rake, Savage Orbit.*

"Arrack?" she asked. "Ouzo, or pernod? You've got your choice. But I may pour them all from the same bottle." She set out glasses on the desk, then opened a waist-high cabinet that turned out to be an icebox. She stood up with a tray of lovelies: fruit puddings, Turkish delight, braised meats.

"What's this?"

"Dolmades. Grape leaves filled with rice and pignolias."

"Say it again?"

"Dolmades. Comes from the same Turkish word as 'dolmush.' They both mean 'stuffed.'" She put the tray beside the glasses. "Sit down."

I sat on the studio-couch-that-becomes-bed. Under the brocade I felt the deep, fluid resilience of a glycogel mattress. They've got the idea that it approximates the feeling of free fall. "Comfortable? Would you excuse me for a moment? I have some friends down the hall. I want to see them for a moment." She winked. "They like spacers."

"Are you going to take up a collection for me?" I asked. "Or do you want them to line up outside the door and wait their turn?"

She sucked a breath. "Actually I was going to suggest both." Suddenly she shook her head. "Oh, what do you want!"

"What will you give me? I want something," I said. "That's why I came. I'm lonely. Maybe I want to find out how far it goes. I don't know yet."

"It goes as far as you will. Me? I study, I read, paint, talk with my friends"—she came over to the bed, sat down on the floor—"go to the theater, look at spacers who pass me on the street, till one looks back; I am lonely, too." She put her head on my knee. "I want something. But," and after a minute neither of us had moved, "you are not the one who will give it to me."

"You're not going to pay me for it," I countered. "You're not, are you?"

On my knee her head shook. After a while she said, all breath and no voice. "Don't you think you . . . should leave?"

"Okay," I said and stood up.

She sat back on the hem of her coat. She hadn't taken it off yet.

I went to the door.

"Incidentally." She folded her hands in her lap. "There is a place in New City you might find what you're looking for, called the Flower Passage—"

I turned toward her, angry. "The frelk hangout? Look, I don't *need* money! I said *any*thing would do! I don't want—"

She had begun to shake her head, laughing quietly. Now she lay her cheek on the wrinkled place where I had sat. "Do you persist in misunderstanding? You said you were lonely. It is a spacer hangout. When you leave, I am going to visit my friends and talk about . . . ah, yes, the beautiful one that got away. I thought you might find . . . perhaps someone you knew."

With anger, it ended.

"Oh," I said. "Oh, it's a spacer hangout. Yeah. Well, thanks."

And went out. And found the Flower Passage, and Kelly and Lou and Bo and Muse. Kelly was buying beer so we all got drunk, and ate fried fish and fried clams and fried sausage, and Kelly was waving the money around, saying, "You should have seen him! The changes I put that frelk through, you should have *seen* him! Eighty lira is the going rate here, and he gave me a hundred and fifty!" and drank more beer.

And went up.

STANISLAW LEM

How Erg the Self-Inducting Slew a Paleface

TRANSLATED BY MICHAEL KANDEL

One cannot underestimate the growing influence of Stanislaw Lem. But his most important novel, Solaris, *exists in English only in a translation from the French translation of the Polish and is best known from the impressive Tarkovsky film version. His recent works have not for the most part even been fiction but rather metafiction.* Microworlds, *a collection of his science fiction criticism, condemns nearly all English-language SF since Wells to the purgatory of subliterature. In his novels Lem eschews much in the way of characterization and story and demands the serious reader's patience while an intellectual structure is built and elaborated in some philo-sophical depth. Yet in his shorter works, such as this story, he often successfully adopts the playful, entertaining tone of the fairy tale or fable.*

* * *

The mighty King Boludar loved curiosities, and devoted himself wholly to the collecting of them, often forgetting about important affairs of state. He had a collection of clocks, and among them were dancing clocks, sunrise clocks and clock-clouds. He also had stuffed monsters from all four corners of the Universe, and in a special room, under a bell glass, the rarest of creatures—the Homos Anthropos, most wonderfully pale, two-legged, and it even had eyes, though empty. The King ordered two lovely rubies set in them, giving the Homos a red stare. Whenever he grew mellow with drink, Boludar would invite his favorite guests to this room and show them the frightful thing.

One day there came to the King's court an electrosage so old, that the crystals of his mind had grown somewhat confused with age, nevertheless this electrosage, named Halazon, possessed the wisdom of a galaxy. It was said that he knew ways of threading photons on a string, producing thereby necklaces of light, and even that he knew how to capture a living Anthropos. Aware of the old one's weakness, the King ordered the wine cellars opened immediately; the electrosage, having taken one pull too many from the Leyden jug, when the pleasant currents were coursing through his limbs, betrayed a terrible secret to the King and promised to obtain for him an Anthropos, which was the ruler of a certain interstellar tribe. The price he set was high—the weight of the Anthropos in fist-sized diamonds—but the King didn't blink at it.

Halazon then set off on his journey. The King meanwhile began to boast before the royal council of his expected acquisition, which he could not in any case conceal, having already ordered a cage to be built in the castle park, where the most magnificent crystals grew, a cage of heavy iron bars. The court was thrown into great consternation. Seeing that the King would not give in, the advisers summoned to the castle two erudite homologists, whom the King received warmly, for he was curious as to what these much-knowledged ones, Salamid and Thaladon, could tell him about the pale being that he did not already know.

"Is it true," he asked, as soon as they had risen from their knees, rendering him obeisance, "that the Homos is softer than wax?"

"It is, Your Luminositude," both replied.

"And is it also true that the aperture it has at the bottom of its face can produce a number of different sounds?"

"Yes, Your Royal Highness, and in addition, into this same opening the Homos stuffs various objects, then moves the lower portion of the head, which is fastened by hinges to the upper portion, wherewith the objects are broken up and it draws them into its interior."

"A peculiar custom, of which I've heard," said the King. "But tell me, my wise ones, for what purpose does it do this?"

"On that particular subject there are four theories, Your Royal Highness," replied the homologists. "The first, that it does this to rid itself of excess venom (for it is venomous to an extreme). The second, that this act is performed for the sake of destruction, which it places above all other pleasures. The third—out of greed, for it would consume everything if it were able, and the fourth, that . . ."

"Fine, fine!" said the King. "Is it true the thing is made of water, and yet nontransparent, like that puppet of mine?"

"This too is true! It has, Sire, a multitude of slimy tubes inside, through which waters circulate; some are yellow, some pearl gray, but most are red—the red carry a dreadful poison called phlogiston or oxygen, which gas turns everything it touches instantly to rust or else to flame. The Homos itself therefore changes color, pearly, yellow, and pink. Nevertheless, Your Royal Highness, we humbly beseech you to abandon your idea of bringing here a live Homos, for it is a powerful creature and malicious as no other . . ."

"This you must explain to me more fully," said the King, as though he were ready to accede to the wise ones. In reality however he only wished to feed his enormous curiosity.

"The beings to which the Homos belongs are called miasmals, Sire. To these belong the silicites and the proteids; the first are of thicker consistency, thus we call them gelatinoids or aspics; the others, more rare, are given different names by different authors, as for example—gummids or mucilids by Pollomender, quag-backed pasties or bogheads by Tricephalos of Arboran, and finally Analcymander the Brazen dubbed them fenny-eyed slubber-yucks . . ."

"Is it true, then, that even their eyes are full of scum?" King Boludar asked eagerly.

"It is, Sire. These creatures, outwardly weak and frail, so that a drop of sixty feet is all it takes to make one splat into a liquid red, by their native cunning represent a danger worse than all the whirlpools and reefs of the Great Asteroid Noose together! And so we beg of you, Sire, for the good of the kingdom . . ."

"Yes, yes, fine," interrupted the King. "You may go now, my dears, and we shall arrive at our decision with all due deliberation."

The wise homologists bowed low and departed uneasy in their minds, fearing that King Boludar had not forsaken his dangerous plan.

By and by a stellar vessel came in the night and brought enormous crates. These were conveyed immediately to the royal garden. Before long the gold gates were opened wide for all the royal subjects; there among the diamond groves, the gazebos of carved jasper and the marble prodigies, they saw an iron cage and—in it—a pale thing, and flabby, that sat upon a small barrel before a saucer filled with something strange—true, the substance did give off the smell of oil, but of oil burnt over a flame, therefore spoiled and totally unfit for use. Yet the creature calmly dipped a kind of shovel in the saucer and, lifting up the oily goo, deposited it into its facial opening.

The spectators were speechless with horror when they read the sign on the cage, which said that they had before them an Anthropos, Homos, a living paleface. The mob began to taunt it, but then the Homos rose, scooped up something from the barrel on which it had been sitting, and sprayed the gaping crowd with a lethal water. Some fled, others seized stones to smite the abomination, but the guards dispersed everyone at once.

These events reached the ear of the King's daughter, Electrina. It would seem she had inherited her father's curiosity, for she was not afraid to approach the cage in which the monster spent its time scratching itself or imbibing enough water and rancid oil to kill a hundred royal subjects on the spot.

The Homos quickly learned intelligent speech and was so bold as to engage Electrina in conversation.

The princess asked it once what that white stuff was which glittered in its maw.

"That I call teeth," it said.

"Oh let me have one!" requested the princess.

"And what will you give me for it?" it asked.

"I'll give you my little golden key, but only for a moment."

"What kind of key is it?"

"My personal key, I use it every evening to wind up my mind. You must have one too."

"My key is different from yours," it answered evasively. "And where do you keep it?"

"Here, on my breast, beneath this little golden lid."

"Hand it over . . . ."

"And you'll give me a tooth?"

"Sure . . ."

The princess turned a little golden screw, opened the lid, took out a little golden key and passed it through the bars. The paleface grabbed it greedily and, chuckling with glee, retreated to the center of the cage. The princess implored and pleaded with it to return the key, but all in vain. Afraid to let anyone find out what she had done, Electrina went back to her palace chambers with a heavy heart. She acted foolishly perhaps, but then she was still practically a child. The next day her servants found her senseless in her crystal bed. The King and Queen came running, and the whole court after them. She lay as if asleep, but it was not possible to waken her. The King summoned the court physicians-electricians, his medics, techs and mechanicians, and these, examining the princess, discovered that her lid was open—no little screw, no little key! The alarm was sounded in the castle, pandemonium reigned, everyone rushed here and there looking for the little key, but to no avail. The next day the King, deep in despair, was informed that his paleface wished to speak with him on the matter of the missing key. The King went himself to the park without delay, and the monstrosity told him that it knew where the princess had lost her key, but would reveal this only when the King had given his royal word to restore to it its freedom and, moreover, supply a spacefaring vessel so it could return to its own kind. The King stubbornly refused, he ordered the park searched up and down, but at last agreed to these terms. Thus a spacecraft was readied for flight, and guards escorted the paleface from its cage. The King was waiting by the ship; the Anthropos however promised to tell him where the key lay as soon as it was on board and not before.

But once on board, it stuck its head out a vent hole and, holding up the bright key in its hand, shouted:

"Here is the key! I'm taking it with me, King, so that your daughter will never wake again, because I crave revenge, in that you humiliated me, keeping me in an iron cage as a laughingstock!!"

Flame shot from under the stern of the spacecraft and the vessel rose into the sky while everyone stood dumbfounded. The King sent his fastest steel cloudscorchers and whirlyprops in pursuit, but their crews all came back empty-handed, for the wily paleface had covered its tracks and given its pursuers the slip.

King Boludar now understood how wrong it had been of him not to heed the wise homologists, but the damage had been done. The foremost electrical locksmiths worked to fashion a duplicate key, the Great Assembler to the Throne, royal artisans, armorers and artefactotums, Lord High steelwrights and master goldforgers, and cybercounts and dynamargraves — all came to try their skill, but in vain. The King realized he would have to recover the key taken by the paleface, otherwise darkness would forever lie upon the sense and senses of the princess.

He proclaimed therefore throughout the realm that this, that and the other had taken place, the anthropic paleface Homos absconded with the golden key, and whosoever captured it, or even if only he retrieved the life-giving jewel and woke the princess, would have her hand in marriage and ascend the throne.

Straightway there appeared in droves daredevils of various cuts and sizes. Among these were electroknights of great renown as well as charlatan-swindlers, astrothieves, star drifters. To the castle came Demetricus Mega-watt, the celebrated fencer-oscillator, possessing such feedback and speed-back that no one could hold the field against him in single combat; and self-motes came from distant lands, like the two Automatts, vector-victors in a hundred battles, or like Prostheseus, constructionist *par excellence*, who never went anywhere without two spark absorbers, one black, the other silver; and there was Arbitron Cosmoski, all built of protocrystals and svelte as a spire, and Cyfer of Agrym the intellectrician, who on forty andromedaries in eighty boxes brought with him an old digital computer, rusted from much thinking yet still mighty of mind. Three champions from the race of the Selectivitites arrived, Diodius, Triodius and Heptodius, who possessed such a perfect vacuum in their heads, their black thought was like the starless night. And Perpetuan came too, all in Leyden armor, with his commutator covered with verdigris from three hundred encounters, and Matrix Perforatem, who never went a day that he did not integrate someone—the latter brought to the palace his invincible cybersteed, a supercharger he called Megasus. They all assembled, and when the court was full, a barrel rolled up to the threshold and out of it spilled, in the shape of mercury, Erg the Self-inducting, who could assume whatever aspect he desired.

The heroes banqueted, lighting up the castle halls, so that the marble of the ceilings glowed pink like a cloud at sunset, and then off they set, each his separate way, to seek out the paleface, challenge it to mortal combat and regain the key, and thereby win the princess and the throne of Boludar. The first, Demetricus Megawatt, flew to Koldlea, where live the Jellyclabbers, for he thought to find out something there. And thus he dove into their ooze, carving out the way with blows from his remote-control saber, but nothing did he achieve, for when he waxed too warm his cooling system went and the incomparable warrior found his grave on foreign soil, and the unclean ooze of the Jellyclabbers closed over his dauntless cathodes forever.

The two Automatts Vectorian reached the land of the Radomants, who raise up edifices out of luminescent gas, dabbling in radioactivity, and are such misers that each evening they count the atoms on their planet. Ill was the reception the grasping Radomants gave the Automatts, for they showed them a chasm full of onyxes, chrysolites, chalcedonies and spinels, and when the electroknights yielded to the temptation of the jewels, the Radomants stoned them to death, setting off from above an avalanche of precious stones, which, as it moved, blazed like a falling comet of a hundred colors. For the Radomants were allied to the palefaces by a secret pact, about which no one knew.

The third, Prostheseus the Constructionist, after a long voyage through the interstellar dark, arrived at the land of the Algoncs. There meteors move in blizzards of rock. The schooner of Prostheseus ran into their inexorable wall and with a broken rudder he drifted through the deep, and when at last he neared some distant suns, their light played across that poor adventurer's sightless eyes. The fourth, Arbitron Cosmoski, had better luck at first. He made it through the Andromeda straits, crossed the four spiral whirlpools of the Hunting Dogs, after that came out into quiet space, favorable for photon sailing, and like a nimble beam he took the helm and, leaving a trail of sweeping fire, reached the shores of the planet Maestricia, where amid meteorite boulders he spied the shattered wreck of the schooner on which Prostheseus had embarked. The body of the constructionist, powerful, shiny and cold as in life, he buried beneath a basalt heap, but took from him both spark-absorbers, the silver and the black, to serve as shields, and proceeded on his way. Wild and craggy was Maestricia, avalanches of stone roared across it, with a silver tangle of lightning in the clouds, above the precipices. The knight came to a region of ravines and there the Palindromides fell upon him in a canyon of malachite, all green. With thunderbolts they lashed him from above, but he parried these with his spark-absorbing buckler, till they moved up a volcano, set the crater on its side and, taking aim, belched fire at him. The knight fell and bubbling lava entered his skull, from which flowed all the silver. The fifth, Cyfer of Agrym the intellectrician, went nowhere. Instead, halting right outside the borders of Boludar's kingdom, he released his andromedaries to graze in stellar pastures, and himself connected the machine, adjusted it, programmed it, bustled about its eighty boxes, and when all were brimming with current, so that it swelled with intelligence, he began putting to it precisely formulated questions: Where did the paleface live? How could one find the way? How could it be tricked? Trapped? How forced to give up the key? The answers, when they came, were vague and noncommittal. In a fury he whipped the machine, until it began to smell of heated copper, and he continued to belabor it, crying, "The truth now, out with it, you blasted old digital computer!"—until at last its joints melted, tin trickled from them in silvery tears, the overheated pipes split open with a bang, and he was left standing over a fused junkheap, incensed and with a cudgel in his hand.

Shamefaced, he had to return home. He ordered a new machine, but did not see it until four hundred years later.

Sixth was the sally of the Selectivitites. Diodius, Triodius and Heptodius set about things differently. They had an inexhaustible supply of tritium, lithium and deuterium, and decided with explosions of heavy hydrogen to force open all the roads leading to the land of the palefaces. It was not known, however, where those roads began. They sought to ask the Pyropods, but the latter locked themselves behind the gold walls of their capital and hurled flame; the valiant-valent Selectivitites stormed the bastion, using both deuterium and tritium without stint, till an inferno of stripped atoms looked the sky boldly in its starry eye. The walls of the citadel shone gold, but in the fire they betrayed their true nature, turning into yellow clouds of sulfuric smoke, for they had been built of pyrites-marcasites. There Diodius fell, trampled by the Pyropods, and his mind burst like a bouquet of colored crystals, spraying his armor. In a tomb of black olivine they buried him, then pressed on, to the borders of the kingdom of Char, where the starkiller King Astrocida reigned. This king had a treasure house full of fiery nuclei plucked from white dwarfs, and which were so heavy, that only the terrible force of the palace magnets kept them from tearing clear through to the planet's core. Whoever stepped upon its ground could move neither arms nor legs, for the prodigious gravitation clamped down better than bolts or chains. Triodius and Heptodius were hard set here, for Astrocida, catching sight of them beneath the castle ramparts, rolled out one white dwarf after another and loosed the fire-spouting masses in their faces. They defeated him however, and he revealed to them the way that led to the palefaces, wherein he deceived them, for he did not know the way himself, but wished only to be rid of the fearsome warriors. So they delved into the black heart of the void, where Triodius was shot by someone with an antimatter blunderbuss—it might have been one of the hunter-Cyberneers, or possibly a mine set for a tailless comet. In any case Triodius vanished, with barely time to shout, "Tikcuff!!," his favorite word and the battle cry of his race. Heptodius stubbornly forged ahead, but a bitter end was in store for him as well. His vessel found itself between two vortices of gravitation called Bakhrida and Scintilla; Bakhrida speeds up time, Scintilla on the other hand slows it down, and between them lies a zone of stagnation, in which the present, becalmed, flows neither backward nor forward. There Heptodius froze alive, and remains to this day, along with the countless frigates and galleons of other astromariners, pirates and spaceswashers, not aging in the least, suspended in the silence and excruciating boredom that is Eternity.

When thus had concluded the campaign of the three Selectivitites, Perpetuan, cybercount of Fud, who as the seventh was next to go, for the longest time did not set forth. Instead that electroknight made lengthy preparations for war, fitting himself with ever sharper conductors, with more and more striking spark plugs, mortars and tractors. Full of caution, he decided he would go at the head of a loyal retinue. Under his banner flocked conquistadors, also many rejects, robots who having nothing else to do wished to try their hand at soldiering. Out of these Perpetuan formed a galactic light cavalry and an infantry, heavy, for ironclad and bullionheaded, plus several platoons of polydragoons and palladins. However at the thought that now he must go and meet his fate in some unknown land, and that in any puddle he might rust away utterly, the iron shanks buckled under him, he was seized with a terrible regret—and immediately headed home, in shame and sorrow shedding tears of topaz, for he was a mighty lord, with a soul full of jewels.

As for the next to the last, Matrix Perforatem, he approached the matter sensibly. He had heard of the land of the Pygmelliants, robot gnomes whose race originated from this, that their constructor's pencil had slipped on the drawing board, whereupon from the master mold they all came out, every last one of them, as hunchbacked deformities. Alteration didn't pay and thus they remained. These dwarfs amass knowledge as others do treasure; for this reason they are called Hoarders of the Absolute.

Their wisdom lies in the fact that they collect knowledge but never use it. To them went Perforatem, not in a military way but on galleons whose decks sagged beneath magnificent gifts; he intended to win the Pygmelliants over with garments aglitter with positrons and lashed by a rain of neutrons; he brought them atoms of gold as big as seven fists, and flagons swirling with the rarest ionospheres. But the Pygmelliants scorned even the noble vacuum embroidered with waves in exquisite astral spectra. In vain too did he rage and threaten to set upon them his snorting electricourser Megasus. They offered him at last a guide, but the guide was a myriaphalangeal thousand-hander and always pointed in all directions at once.

Perforatem sent him packing and spurred Megasus on the trail of the palefaces, but the trail turned out to be false, for a comet of calcium hydroxide was wont to pass that way, and the simple-minded steed confused this with calcium phosphate, which is the basic ingredient of the paleface skeleton: Megasus mistook the lime for slime. Perforatem roamed long among suns that grew increasingly dim, for he had entered into a very ancient section of the Cosmos.

He traveled past a row of purple giants, until he noticed that his ship along with the silent pageant of stars was being reflected in a spiral mirror, a silver-surfaced speculum; he was surprised at this and, just in case, drew his supernova extinguisher, which he had purchased from the Pygmelliants in order to protect himself against excessive heat along the Milky Way. He knew not what it was he saw—actually it was a knot in space, the continuum's most contiguous factorial, unknown even to the Monoasterists of that place. All they say is that whoever encounters it never returns. To this day no one knows what happened to Matrix in that stellar mill. His faithful Megasus sped home alone, whimpering softly in the void, and its sapphire eyes were pools of such horror, that no one could look into them without a shudder. And neither vessel, nor extinguishers, nor Matrix, was ever seen again.

And so the last, Erg the Self-inducting, rode forth alone. He was gone a year and fortnights three. When he returned, he told of lands unknown to anyone, such as that of the Periscones, who build hot sluices of corruption; of the planet of the Epoxy-eyed—these merged before him into rows of black billows, for that is what they do in time of war, but he hewed them in two, laying bare the limestone that was their bone, and when he overcame their slaughterfalls he found himself face to face with one that took up half the sky, and he fell upon it, to demand the way, but beneath the blade of his firesword its skin split open and exposed white, writhing forests of nerves. And he spoke of the transparent ice-planet Aberrabia, which like a diamond lens holds the image of the entire Universe within itself; there he copied down the way to palefaceland. He told of a region of eternal silence, Alumnium Cryotrica, where he saw only the reflections of the stars in the surfaces of hanging glaciers; and of the kingdom of the molten Marmaloids, who fashion boiling baubles out of lava, and of the Electropneumaticists, who in mists of methane, in ozone, chlorine and the smoke of volcanos are able to kindle the spark of intelligence, and who continually wrestle with the problem of how to put into a gas the quality of genius. He told them that in order to reach the realm of the palefaces he had to force open the door of a sun called Caput Medusae; how after lifting this door off its chromatic hinges, he ran through the star's interior, a long succession of purple and light-blue flames, till the armor on him curled from the heat. How for thirty days he tried to guess the word which would activate the hatch of Astropro-cyonum, since only through it can one enter the cold hell of miasmal beings; how finally he found himself among them, and they tried to catch him in their sticky, lipid snares, knock the mercury from his head or short-circuit him; how they deluded him, pointing to misshapen stars, but that was a counterfeit sky, the real one they had hidden in their sneaking way; how with torture they sought to pry from him his algorithm and then, when he withstood everything, threw him into a pit and dropped a slab of magnetite over the opening. Inside however he immediately multiplied himself into hundreds and thousands of Ergs the Self-inducting, pushed aside the iron lid, emerged on the surface and wreaked his retribution upon the palefaces for one full month and five days. How then the monsters, in a last attempt, attacked on trackers they called casterpillars, but that availed them nothing, for, never slackening in his zeal for battle, but hacking, stabbing and slashing away, he brought them to such a pass, that they threw the dastardly paleface-keythief at his feet, whereupon Erg lopped off its loathsome head, disemboweled the carcass, and in it found a stone, known as a trichobezoar, and there on the stone was carved an inscription in the scrofulous paleface tongue, revealing where the key was. The Self-inducting cut open sixty-seven suns—white, blue and ruby red—before, pulling apart the right one, he found the key.

The adventures he met with, the battles he was forced to wage on the journey back—of these he did not even wish to think, so great now was his yearning for the princess, and great too his impatience for the wedding and the coronation. With joy the King and Queen led him to the chamber of their daughter, who was silent as the grave, plunged in sleep. Erg leaned over her, fiddled a little near the open lid, inserted something, gave a turn, and instantly the princess—to the delight of her mother and the King and the entire court—lifted her eyes and smiled at her deliverer. Erg closed the little lid, sealed it with a bit of plaster to keep it closed, and explained that the little screw, which he had also found, had been dropped during a fight with Poleander Partabon, emperor of all Jatapurgovia. But no one gave this any thought, and a pity too, for both the King and Queen would have quickly realized that he never sallied forth at all, because even as a child Erg the Self-inducting had possessed the ability to open any lock and thanks to this wound up the Princess Electrina. In reality, then, he had met with not a single one of the adventures he described, but simply waited out a year and fortnights three, in order that it not appear suspicious, his returning too soon with the missing object, and also, he wanted to make sure that none of his rivals would come back. Only then did he show up at the court of King Boludar and restore the princess to life, and so married her, reigned long and happily on the throne of Boludar, and his subterfuge was never discovered. From which one can see straightaway that we have told the truth and not a fairy tale, for in fairy tales virtue always triumphs.

Nobody's Home

Joanna Russ began her career as a writer of fiction when she was a student of Vladimir Nabokov at Cornell. From there she went on to Yale School of Drama, but by the late 1950s she was writing fantasy fiction and her first stories, published in the early 1960s, were supernatural fantasy tales. However, she soon established herself as a science fiction writer as well, reaching her first peak in the novel Picnic On Paradise *in the late 1960s. The stories of Alyx, a competent adventuress, culminating in that novel, represent the birth of contemporary feminism in SF. By the mid-1970s Russ had become, as both critic and writer, the most forceful advocate of feminism in the field, much admired and often feared. Her novel* The Female Man *is a powerful expression of feminist SF, filled with rage and wit and an underlying social vision that makes it one of the significant works in the utopian discourse of the past two decades. "Nobody's Home" dates from the same period in her career and is perhaps her finest work of short fiction. It is a compassionate and ironic vision of a communal utopia, moving and thought-provoking. Russ is a professor of English at the University of Washington and the author of numerous critical works, including* How to Suppress Women's Writing.

*   *   *

After she had finished her work at the North Pole, Jannina came down to the Red Sea refineries, where she had family business, jumped to New Delhi for dinner, took a nap in a public hotel in Queensland, walked from the hotel to the station, bypassed the Leeward Islands (where she thought she might go, but all the stations were busy), and met Charley to watch the dawn over the Carolinas.

"Where've you *been*, dear C?"

"Tanzania. And you're married."

"No."

"I heard you were married," he said. "The Lees told the Smiths who told the Kerguelens who told the Utsumbés, and we get around, we Utsumbés. A new wife, they said. I didn't know you were especially fond of women."

"I'm not. She's my husbands' wife. And we're not married yet, Charley. She's had hard luck. A first family started in '35, two husbands burned out by an overload while arranging transportation for a concert—of all things, pushing papers, you know!—and the second divorced her, I think, and she drifted away from the third (a big one), and there was some awful quarrel with the fourth, people chasing people around tables, I don't know."

"Poor woman."

In the manner of people joking and talking lightly they had drawn together, back to back, sitting on the ground and rubbing their shoulders and the backs of their heads together. Jannina said sorrowfully, "What lovely hair you have, Charley Utsumbé, like metal mesh."

"All we Utsumbés are exceedingly handsome." They linked arms. The sun, which anyone could chase around the world now, see it rise or set twenty times a day, fifty times a day—if you wanted to spend your life like that—rose dripping out of the cypress swamp. There was nobody around for miles. Mist drifted up from the pools and low places.

"My God," he said, "it's summer! I have to be at Tanga now."

"What?" said Jannina.

"One loses track," he said apologetically. "I'm sorry, love, but I have unavoidable business at home. Tax labor."

"But why summer, why did its being summer . . ."

"Train of thought! Too complicated." And already they were out of key, already the mild affair was over, there having come between them the one obligation that can't be put off to the time you like, or the place you like; off he'd go to plug himself into a road-mender or a doctor, though it's of some advantage to mend all the roads of a continent at one time.

She sat cross-legged on the station platform, watching him enter the booth and set the dial. He stuck his head out the glass door.

"Come with me to Africa, lovely lady!"

She thumbed her nose at him. "You're only a passing fancy, Charley U!" He blew a kiss, enclosed himself in the booth, and disappeared. (The transmatter field is larger than the booth, for obvious reasons; the booth flicks on and off several million times a second and so does not get transported itself, but it protects the machinery from the weather and it keeps people from losing elbows or knees or slicing the ends off a package or a child. The booths at the cryogenics center at the North Pole have exchanged air so often with those of warmer regions that each has its own microclimate; leaves and seeds, plants and earth are piled about them. The notes pinned to the door said, Don't Step on the Grass! Wish to Trade Pawlownia Sapling for Sub-arctic Canadian Moss; Watch Your Goddamn Bare Six-Toed Feet! Wish Amateur Cellist for Quartet, Six Months' Rehearsal Late Uhl with Reciter; I Lost A Squirrel Here Yesterday, Can You Find It Before It Dies? Eight Children Will be Heartbroken—Cecilia Ching, Buenos Aires.)

Jannina sighed and slipped on her glass woolly; nasty to get back into clothes, but home was cold. You never knew where you might go, so you carried them. Years ago (she thought) I came here with someone in the dead of winter, either an unmatched man or someone's starting spouse—only two of us, at any rate—and we waded through the freezing water and danced as hard as we could and then proved we could sing and drink beer in a swamp at the same time, Good Lord! And then went to the public resort on the Ile de la Cité to watch professional plays, opera, games—you have to be good to get in there!—and got into some clothes because it was chilly after sundown in September—no, wait, it was Venezuela—and watched the lights come out and smoked like mad at a café table and tickled the robot waiter and pretended we were old, really old, perhaps a hundred and fifty . . . Years ago!

But *was* it the same place? she thought, and dismissing the incident forever, she stepped into the booth, shut the door, and dialed home: the Himalayas. The trunk line was clear. The branch stop was clear. The family's transceiver (located in the anteroom behind two doors, to keep the task of heating the house within reasonable limits) had damn well better be clear, or somebody would be blown right into the vestibule. Momentum- and heat-compensators kept Jannina from arriving home at seventy degrees Fahrenheit internal temperature (seven degrees lost for every mile you teleport upward) or too many feet above herself (rise to the east, drop going west; to the north or south you are apt to be thrown right through the wall of the booth). Someday (thought Jannina) everybody will decide to let everybody live in decent climates. But not yet. Not this everybody.

She arrived home singing "The World's My Back Yard, Yes, the World Is My Oyster," a song that had been popular in her first youth, some seventy years before.

■   ■   ■

The Komarovs' house was hardened foam with an automatic inside line to the school near Naples. It was good to be brought up on your own feet. Jannina passed through; the seven-year-olds lay with their heads together and their bodies radiating in a six-person asterisk. In this position (which was supposed to promote mystical thought) they played Barufaldi, guessing the identity of famous dead personages through anagrammatic sentences, the first letters of the words of which (unscrambled into aphorisms or proverbs) simultaneously spelled out a moral and a series of Goedel numbers (in a previously agreed-upon code) which . . .

"Oh, my darling, how felicitous is the advent of your appearance!" cried a boy (hard to take, the polysyllabic stage).

"Embrace me, dearest maternal parent! Unite your valuable upper limbs about my eager person!"

"Vulgar!" said Jannina, laughing.

"Non sum filius tuus?" said the child.

"No, you're not my body-child. You're my godchild. Your mother bequeathed me to you when she died. What are you learning?"

"The eternal parental question," he said, frowning. "How to run a helicopter. How to prepare food from its actual, revolting, raw constituents. Can I go now?"

"*Can* you?" she said. "Nasty imp!"

"Good," he said. "I've made you feel guilty. Don't *do* that," and as she tried to embrace him, he ticklishly slid away. "The robin walks quietly up the branch of the tree," he said breathlessly, flopping back on the floor.

"That's not an aphorism." (Another Barufaldi player.)

"It is."

"It isn't."

"It is."

"It isn't."

"It is."

"It—"

The school vanished; the antechamber appeared. In the kitchen Chi Komarov was rubbing the naked back of his sixteen-year-old son. Parents always kissed each other; children always kissed each other. She touched foreheads with the two men and hung her woolly on the hook by the ham radio rig. Someone was always around. Jannina flipped the cover off her wrist chronometer: standard regional time, date, latitude-longitude, family computer hookup clear. "At my age I ought to remember these things," she said. She pressed the computer hookup: Ann at tax labor in the schools, bit-a-month plan, regular Ann; Lee with three months to go, five years off, heroic Lee; Phuong in Paris, still rehearsing; C.E. gone, won't say where, spontaneous C.E.; Ilse making some repairs in the basement, not a true basement, but the room farthest down the hillside. She went up the stairs and then came down and put her head round at the living-and-swimming room. Through the glass wall one could see the mountains. Old Al, who had joined them late in life, did a bit of gardening in the brief summers, and generally stuck around the place. Jannina beamed. "Hullo, Old Al!" Big and shaggy, a rare delight, his white body hair. She sat on his lap. "Has she come?"

"The new one? No," he said.

"Shall we go swimming?"

He made an expressive face. "No, dear," he said. "I'd rather go to Naples and watch the children fly helicopters. I'd rather go to Nevada and fly them myself. I've been in the water all day, watching a very dull person restructure coral reefs and experiment with polyploid polyps."

"You mean *you* were doing it."

"One gets into the habit of working."

"But you didn't have to!"

"It was a private project. Most interesting things are."

She whispered in his ear.

With happily flushed faces, they went into Old Al's inner garden and locked the door.

Jannina, temporary family representative, threw the computer helmet over her head and, thus plugged in, she cleaned house, checked food supplies, did a little of the legal business entailed by a family of eighteen adults (two triplet marriages, a quad, and a group of eight). She felt very smug. She put herself through by radio to Himalayan HQ (above two thousand meters) and hooking computer to computer—a very odd feeling, like an urge to sneeze that never comes off—extended a formal invitation to one Leslie Smith ("Come stay, why don't you?"), notifying every free Komarov to hop it back and fast. Six hikers might come for the night—back-packers. More food. First thunderstorm of the year in Albany, New York (North America). Need an extra two rooms by Thursday. Hear the Palnatoki are moving. Can't use a room. Can't use a kitten. Need the geraniums back, Mrs. Adam, Chile. The best maker of hand-blown glass in the world has killed in a duel the second-best maker of hand-blown glass for joining the movement toward ceramics. A bitter struggle is foreseen in the global economy. Need a lighting designer. Need fifteen singers and electric pansensicon. Standby tax labor xxxxxpj through xxxyq to Cambaluc, great tectogenic—

With the guilty feeling that one always gets gossiping with a computer, for it's really not reciprocal, Jannina flipped off the helmet. She went to get Ilse. Climbing back through the white foam room, the purple foam room, the green foam room, everything littered with plots and projects of the clever Komarovs or the even cleverer Komarov children, stopping at the baby room for Ilse to nurse her baby, Jannina danced staidly around studious Ilse. They turned on the nursery robot and the television screen. Ilse drank beer in the swimming room, for her milk. She worried her way through the day's record of events—faults in the foundation, some people who came from Chichester and couldn't find C. E. so one of them burst into tears, a new experiment in genetics coming round the gossip circuit, an execrable set of equations from some imposter in Bucharest.

"A duel!" said Jannina.

They both agreed it was shocking. And what fun. A new fashion. You had to be a little mad to do it. Awful.

The light went on over the door to the tunnel that linked the house to the antechamber, and very quickly, one after another, as if the branch line had just come free, eight Komarovs came into the room. The light flashed again; one could see three people debouch one after the other, persons in boots, with coats, packs, and face masks over their woollies. They were covered with snow, either from the mountain terraces above the house or from some other place, Jannina didn't know. They stamped the snow off in the antechamber and hung their clothes outside. "Good heavens, you're not circumcised!" cried someone. There was as much handshaking and embracing all around as at a wedding party. Velet Komarov (the short, dark one) recognized Fung Pao-Yu and swung her off her feet. People began to joke, tentatively stroking one another's arms. "Did you have a good hike? Are you a good hiker, Pao-Yu?" said Velet. The light over the antechamber went on again, though nobody could see a thing since the glass was steamed over from the collision of hot with cold air. Old Al stopped, halfway into the kitchen. The baggage receipt chimed, recognized only by family ears— upstairs a bundle of somebody's things, ornaments, probably, for the missing Komarovs were still young and the young are interested in clothing, were appearing in the baggage receptacle. "Ann or Phuong?" said Jannina. "Five to three, anybody? Match me!" but someone strange opened the door of the booth and peered out. Oh, a dizzying sensation. She was painted in a few places, which was awfully odd because really it was old-fashioned; and why do it for a family evening? It was a stocky young woman. It was an awful mistake (thought Jannina). Then the visitor made her second mistake.

"I'm Leslie Smith," she said. But it was more through clumsiness than being rude. Chi Komarov (the tall, blond one) saw this instantly and, snatching off his old-fashioned spectacles, he ran to her side and patted her, saying teasingly:

"Now, haven't we met? Now, aren't you married to someone I know?"

"No, no," said Leslie Smith, flushing with pleasure.

He touched her neck. "Ah, you're a tightrope dancer!"

"Oh, no!" exclaimed Leslie Smith.

"*I'm* a tightrope dancer," said Chi. "Would you believe it?"

"But you're too—too *spiritual*," said Leslie Smith hesitantly.

"Spiritual, how do you like that, family, spiritual?" he cried, delighted (a little more delighted, thought Jannina, than the situation really called for), and he began to stroke her neck.

"What a lovely neck you have," he said.

This steadied Leslie Smith. She said, "I like tall men," and allowed herself to look at the rest of the family. "Who are these people?" she said, though one was afraid she might really mean it.

Fung Pao-Yu to the rescue: "Who are these people? Who are they, indeed! I doubt if they are anybody. One might say, 'I have met these people,' but has one? What existential meaning would such a statement convey? I myself, now, I have met them. I have been introduced to them. But they are like the Sahara. It is all wrapped in mystery. I doubt if they even have names," etc. etc. Then lanky Chi Komarov disputed possession of Leslie Smith with Fung Pao-Yu, and Fung Pao-Yu grabbed one arm and Chi the other; and she jumped up and down fiercely; so that by the time the lights dimmed and the food came, people were feeling better—or so Jannina judged. So embarrassing and delightful to be eating fifteen to a room! "We Komarovs are famous for eating whatever we can get whenever we can get it," said Velet proudly. Various Komarovs in various places, with the three hikers on cushions and Ilse at full length on the rug. Jannina pushed a button with her toe and the fairy lights came on all over the ceiling. "The children did that," said Old Al. He had somehow settled at Leslie Smith's side and was feeding her so-chi from his own bowl. She smiled up at him. "We once," said a hiking companion of Fung Pao-Yu's, "arranged a dinner in an amphitheater where half of us played servants to the other half, with forfeits for those who didn't show. It was the result of a bet. Like the bad old days. Did you know there were once *five billion people* in this world?"

"The gulls," said Ilse, "are mating on the Isle of Skye." There were murmurs of appreciative interest. Chi began to develop an erection and everyone laughed. Old Al wanted music and Velet didn't; what might have been a quarrel was ended by Ilse's furiously boxing their ears. She stalked off to the nursery.

"Leslie Smith and I are both old-fashioned," said Old Al, "because neither of us believes in gabbing. Chi—your theater?"

"We're turning people away." He leaned forward, earnestly, tapping his fingers on his crossed knees. "I swear, some of them are threatening to commit suicide."

"It's a choice," said Velet reasonably.

Leslie Smith had dropped her bowl. They retrieved it for her.

"Aiy, I remember—" said Pao-Yu. "What I remember! We've been eating dried mush for three days, tax-issue. Did you know one of my dads killed himself?"

"No!" said Velet, surprised.

"Years ago," said Pao-Yu. "He said he refused to live to see the time when chairs were reintroduced. He also wanted further genetic engineering, I believe, for even more intelligence. He did it out of spite, I'm sure. I think he wrestled a shark. Jannina, is this tax-issue food? Is it this year's style tax-issue sauce?"

"No, next year's," said Jannina snappishly. Really, some people! She slipped into Finnish, to show up Pao-Yu's pronunciation. "Isn't that so?" she asked Leslie Smith.

Leslie Smith stared at her.

More charitably Jannina informed them all, in Finnish, that the Komarovs had withdrawn their membership in a food group, except for Ann, who had taken out an individual, because what the dickens, who had the time? And tax-issue won't kill you. As they finished, they dropped their dishes into the garbage field and Velet stripped a layer off the rug. In that went, too. Indulgently Old Al began a round:

"Red."

"Sun," said Pao-yu.

"The Red Sun Is," said one of the triplet Komarovs.

"The Red Sun Is—High," said Chi.

"The Red Sun Is High, The," Velet said.

"The Red Sun Is High, The Blue—" Jannina finished. They had come to Leslie Smith, who could either complete it or keep it going. She chose to declare for complete, not shyly (as before) but simply by pointing to Old Al.

"The red sun is high, the blue," he said. "Subtle! Another: Ching."

"Nü."

"Ching nü ch'i."

"Ching nü ch'i ch'u."

"Ssu."

"Wo."

"Ssu wo yü." It had got back to Leslie Smith again. She said, "I can't do that." Jannina got up and began to dance—I'm nice in my nasty way, she thought. The others wandered toward the pool and Ilse reappeared on the nursery monitor screen, saying, "I'm coming down." Somebody said, "What time is it in the Argentine?"

"Five A.M."

"I think I want to go."

"Go then."

"I go."

"Go well."

The red light over the antechamber door flashed and went out.

"Say, why'd you leave your other family?" said Ilse, settling near Old Al where the wall curved out. Ann, for whom it was evening, would be home soon; Chi, who had just got up a few hours back in western America, would stay somewhat longer; nobody ever knew Old Al's schedule and Jannina herself had lost track of the time. She would stay up until she felt sleepy. She followed a rough twenty-eight-hour day, Phuong (what a nuisance that must be at rehearsals!) a twenty-two-hour one, Ilse six hours up, six hours dozing. Jannina nodded, heard the question, and shook herself awake.

"I didn't leave them. They left me."

There was a murmur of sympathy around the pool.

"They left me because I was stupid," said Leslie Smith. Her hands were clasped passively in her lap. She looked very genteel in her blue body paint, a stocky young woman with small breasts. One of the triplet Komarovs, flirting in the pool with the other two, choked. The non-aquatic members of the family crowded around Leslie Smith, touching her with little, soft touches; they kissed her and exposed to her all their unguarded surfaces, their bellies, their soft skins. Old Al kissed her hands. She sat there, oddly unmoved. "But I *am* stupid," she said. "You'll find out." Jannina put her hands over her ears: "A masochist!" Leslie Smith looked at Jannina with a curious, stolid look. Then she looked down and absently began to rub one blue-painted knee. "Luggage!" shouted Chi, clapping his hands together, and the triplets dashed for the stairs. "No, I'm going to bed," said Leslie Smith, "I'm tired," and quite simply, she got up and let Old Al lead her through the pink room, the blue room, the turtle-and-pet room (temporarily empty), the trash room, and all the other rooms, to the guest room with the view that looked out over the cold hillside to the terraced plantings below.

"The best maker of hand-blown glass in the world," said Chi, "has killed in a duel the second-best maker of hand-blown glass in the world."

"For joining the movement to ceramics," said Ilse, awed. Jannina felt a thrill: this was the bitter stuff under the surface of life, the fury that boiled up. A bitter struggle is foreseen in the global economy. Good old tax-issue stuff goes toddling along, year after year. She was, thought Jannina, extraordinarily grateful to be living now, to be in such an extraordinary world, to have so long to go before her death. So much to do!

Old Al came back into the living room. "She's in bed."

"Well, which of us—?" said the triplet-who-had-choked, looking mischievously round from one to the other. Chi was about to volunteer, out of his usual conscientiousness, thought Jannina, but then she found herself suddenly standing up, and then just as suddenly sitting down again. "I just don't have the nerve," she said. Velet Komarov walked on his hands toward the stairs, then somersaulted, and vanished, climbing. Old Al got off the hand-carved chest he had been sitting on and fetched a can of ale from it. He levered off the top and drank. Then he said, "She really is stupid, you know." Jannina's skin crawled.

"Oooh," said Pao-Yu. Chi betook himself to the kitchen and returned with a paper folder. It was coated with frost. He shook it, then impatiently dropped it in the pool. The redheaded triplet swam over and took it. "Smith, Leslie," he said. "Adam Two, Leslie. Yee, Leslie. Schwarzen, Leslie."

"What on earth does the woman *do* with herself besides get married?" exclaimed Pao-Yu.

"She drove a hovercraft," said Chi, "in some out-of-the-way places around the Pacific until the last underground stations were completed. Says when she was a child she wanted to drive a truck."

"Well, you can," said the redheaded triplet, "can't you? Go to Arizona or the Rockies and drive on the roads. The sixty-mile-an-hour road. The thirty-mile-an-hour road. Great artistic recreation."

"That's not work," said Old Al.

"Couldn't she take care of children?" said the redheaded triplet. Ilse sniffed.

"Stupidity's not much of a recommendation for that," Chi said. "Let's see—no children. No, of course not. Overfulfilled her tax work on quite a few routine matters here. Kim, Leslie. Went to Moscow and contracted a double with some fellow, didn't last. Registered as a singleton, but that didn't last, either. She said she was lonely, and they were exploiting her."

Old Al nodded.

"Came back and lived informally with a theater group. Left them. Went into psychotherapy. Volunteered for several experimental, intelligence-enhancing programs, was turned down—hum!—sixty-five come the winter solstice, muscular coordination average, muscular development above average, no overt mental pathology, empathy average, prognosis: poor. No, wait a minute, it says, 'More of the same.' Well, that's the same thing.

"What I want to know," added Chi, raising his head, "is who met Miss Smith and decided we needed the lady in this Ice Palace of ours?"

Nobody answered. Jannina was about to say, "Ann, perhaps?" but as she felt the urge to do so—surely it wasn't right to turn somebody off like that, *just* for that!—Chi (who had been flipping through the dossier) came to the last page, with the tax-issue stamp absolutely unmistakable, woven right into the paper.

"The computer did," said Pao-Yu, and she giggled idiotically.

"Well," said Jannina, jumping to her feet, "tear it up, my dear, or give it to me, and I'll tear it up for you. I think Miss Leslie Smith deserves from us the same as we'd give to anybody else, and I—for one—intend to go *right up there* . . ."

"After Velet," said Old Al dryly.

"*With* Velet, if I must," said Jannina, raising her eyebrows, "and if you don't know what's due a guest, Old Daddy, I do, and I intend to provide it. Lucky I'm keeping house this month, or you'd probably feed the poor woman nothing but seaweed."

"You won't like her, Jannina," said Old Al.

"I'll find that out for myself," said Jannina with some asperity, "and I'd advise you to do the same. Let her garden with you, Daddy. Let her squirt the foam for the new rooms. And now," she glared round at them, "I'm going to clean *this* room, so you'd better hop it, the lot of you," and dashing into the kitchen, she had the computer helmet on her head and the hoses going before they had even quite cleared the area of the pool. Then she took the helmet off and hung it on the wall. She flipped the cover off her wrist chronometer and satisfied herself as to the date. By the time she got back to the living room there was nobody there, only Leslie Smith's dossier lying on the carved chest. There was Leslie Smith; there was all of Leslie Smith. Jannina knocked on the wall cupboard and it revolved, presenting its openable side; she took out chewing gum. She started chewing and read about Leslie Smith.

Q: What have you seen in the last twenty years that you particularly liked?

A: I don't . . . the museum, I guess. At Oslo. I mean the . . . the mermaid and the children's museum, I don't care if it's a children's museum.

Q: Do you like children?

A: Oh no.

(No disgrace in *that*, certainly, thought Jannina.)

Q: But you liked the children's museum.

A: Yes, sir. . . . Yes. . . . I liked those little animals, the fake ones, in the
. . . the . . .

Q: The crèche?

A: Yes. And I liked the old things from the past, the murals with the
flowers on them, they looked so real.

(Dear God!)

Q: You said you were associated with a theater group in Tokyo. Did you
like it?

A: No . . . yes, I don't know.

Q: Were they nice people?

A: Oh yes. They were awfully nice. But they got mad at me, I suppose. . . . You see . . . well, I don't seem to get things quite right, I
suppose. It's not so much the work, because I do that all right, but the other
. . . the little things. It's always like that.

Q: What do you think is the matter?

A: You . . . I think you know.

Jannina flipped through the rest of it: normal, normal, normal. Miss
Smith was as normal as could be. Miss Smith was stupid. Not even very
stupid. It was too damned bad. They'd probably have enough of Leslie
Smith in a week, the Komarovs; yes, we'll have enough of her (Jannina
thought), never able to catch a joke or a tone of voice, always clumsy,
however willing, but never happy, never at ease. You can get a job for her,
but what else can you get for her? Jannina glanced down at the dossier,
already bored.

Q: You say you would have liked to live in the old days. Why is that? Do
you think it would have been more adventurous, or would you like to have
had lots of children?

A: I . . . you have no right . . . You're condescending.

Q: I'm sorry. I suppose you mean to say that then you would have been of
above-average intelligence. You would, you know.

A: I know. I looked it up. Don't condescend to me.

Well, it *was* too damned bad! Jannina felt tears rise in her eyes. What had
the poor woman done? It was just an accident, that was the horror of it, not
even a tragedy, as if everyone's forehead had been stamped with the word
"Choose" except for Leslie Smith's. She needs money, thought Jannina,
thinking of the bad old days when people did things for money. Nobody
could take to Leslie Smith. She wasn't insane enough to stand for being hurt
or exploited. She wasn't clever enough to interest anybody. She certainly
wasn't feebleminded; they couldn't very well put her into a hospital for the
feebleminded or the brain-injured; in fact (Jannina was looking at the

dossier again) they had tried to get her to work there, and she had taken a good, fast swing at the supervisor. She had said the people there were "hideous" and "revolting." She had no particular mechanical aptitudes. She had no particular interests. There was not even anything for her to read or watch; how could there be? She seemed (back at the dossier) to spend most of her time either working or going on public tours of exotic places, coral reefs, and places like that. She enjoyed aqualung diving, but didn't do it often because that got boring. And that was that. There was, all in all, very little one could do for Leslie Smith. You might even say that in her own person she represented all the defects of the bad old days. Just imagine a world made up of such creatures! Jannina yawned. She slung the folder away and padded into the kitchen. Pity Miss Smith wasn't good-looking, also a pity that she was too well balanced (the folder said) to think that cosmetic surgery would make that much difference. Good for you, Leslie, you've got some sense, anyhow. Jannina, half asleep, met Ann in the kitchen, beautiful, slender Ann reclining on a cushion with her so-chi and melon. Dear old Ann. Jannina nuzzled her brown shoulder. Ann poked her.

"Look," said Ann, and she pulled from the purse she wore at her waist a tiny fragment of cloth, stained rusty brown.

"What's that?"

"The second-best maker of hand-blown glass—oh, you know about it— well, this is his blood. When the best maker of hand-blown glass in the world had stabbed to the heart the second-best maker of hand-blown glass in the world, and cut his throat, too, some small children steeped hand-kerchiefs in his blood and they're sending pieces all over the world."

"Good God!" cried Jannina.

"Don't worry, my dear," said lovely Ann, "it happens every decade or so. The children say they want to bring back cruelty, dirt, disease, glory, and hell. Then they forget about it. Every teacher knows that." She sounded amused. "I'm afraid I lost my temper today, though, and walloped your godchild. It's in the family, after all."

Jannina remembered when she herself had been much younger and Annie, barely a girl, had come to live with them. Ann had played at being a child and had put her head on Jannina's shoulder, saying, "Jannie, tell me a story." So Jannina now laid her head on Ann's breast and said, "Annie, tell me a story."

Ann said: "I told my children a story today, a creation myth. Every creation myth has to explain how death and suffering came into the world, so that's what this one is about. In the beginning, the first man and the first woman lived very contentedly on an island until one day they began to feel hungry. So they called to the turtle who holds up the world to send them something to eat. The turtle sent them a mango and they ate it and were satisfied, but the next day they were hungry again.

" 'Turtle,' they said, 'send us something to eat.' So the turtle sent them a coffee berry. They thought it was pretty small, but they ate it anyway and were satisfied. The third day they called on the turtle again and this time the turtle sent them two things: a banana and a stone. The man and woman did not know which to choose, so they asked the turtle which they should eat. 'Choose,' said the turtle. So they chose the banana and ate that, but they used the stone for a game of catch. Then the turtle said, 'You should have chosen the stone. If you had chosen the stone, you would have lived forever, but now that you have chosen the banana, Death and Pain have entered the world, and it is not I that can stop them.' "

Jannina was crying. Lying in the arms of her old friend, she wept bitterly, with a burning sensation in her chest and the taste of death and ashes in her mouth. It was awful. It was horrible. She remembered the embryo shark she had seen when she was three, in the Auckland Cetacean Research Center, and how she had cried then. She didn't know what she was crying about. "Don't, don't!" she sobbed.

"Don't what?" said Ann affectionately. "Silly Jannina!"

"Don't, don't," cried Jannina, "don't, it's true, it's true!" and she went on in this way for several more minutes. Death had entered the world. Nobody could stop it. It was ghastly. She did not mind for herself but for others, for her godchild, for instance. He was going to die. He was going to suffer. Nothing could help him. Duel, suicide, or old age, it was all the same. "This life!" gasped Jannina. "This awful life!" The thought of death became entwined somehow with Leslie Smith, in bed upstairs, and Jannina began to cry afresh, but eventually the thought of Leslie Smith calmed her. It brought her back to herself. She wiped her eyes with her hand. She sat up. "Do you want a smoke?" said beautiful Ann, but Jannina shook her head. She began to laugh. Really, the whole thing was quite ridiculous.

"There's this Leslie Smith," she said, dry-eyed. "We'll have to find a tactful way to get rid of her. It's idiotic, in this day and age."

And she told lovely Annie all about it.

GÉRARD KLEIN

Party Line

TRANSLATED BY ARLINE HIGUILY

Gérard Klein was the wunderkind of French SF at its inception in the 1950s. His first story, heavily influenced by Ray Bradbury, appeared in 1955, when he was nineteen. He published nearly sixty more in the next decade, in addition to becoming an influential critic with a series of thirty forceful essays. His early career was, however, as a government economist, which seems to have influenced the detailed background of "Party Line." In 1969 he became the editor of an important publishing series that continues today, a series which supports developing talent in France while seeking out works in English for translation. It is a pleasure to find such stories as "Party Line" contributing to the international dialogue on time travel and time paradoxes.

* * *

The two telephones rang at the same time. Jerome Bosch hesitated. An annoying coincidence which often occurred, but never at this hour, never at five after nine in the morning when one has just arrived at the office and has only the dreary outlook outside — a long gray wall, with just a few spots, so abstract, so dim, that they didn't even allow the starting point for a daydream.

At eleven-thirty, yes, the time when people began to feel well, quickly finish their business with the idea of saving some minutes for lunch, feeling more at their ease, when the lines are busy or all the telephones ring together, mostly when the telephone centers in their cool caves begin to vibrate, to smoke, to melt.

He knew a few solutions to the problem. Take one of the phones off the hook, answer, and let the other ring till the caller got tired and decided to call five minutes later. Take the receiver off, ask the name, say you're sorry. Take the second line, ask the name, ask them to be patient. Choose the most important name, or the longest, listen first to the woman, if there is one, rather than the man. Women in business were more concise. Or take the two calls at the same time.

Jerome Bosch seized the two phones. The ringing stopped. He watched his right hand, and the little cold black halter which weighed next to nothing at the end of his arm. Then looked at his left hand and the other twin halter. He had a desire to crush the one against the other, or to kindly place them next to each other on the desk right side up so that the two callers could talk to each other and, who knows, maybe make some sense out of it.

But nothing to do with me in any case. I'm an intermediary. That's what I am. Listen and repeat. I'm a filter between a receptor and a microphone, a hearing aid between a mouth and an ear, an automatic pen between two letters.

He put the receivers next to each of his ears.

Two voices:

"Jerome, has someone called already?" "I'm the first, isn't that so? . . . Answer me . . ."

A precise, clear voice, a disturbing voice, at the border of hysteria. They made an echo, curiously alike.

"Hello," said Jerome Bosch. "Who am I talking to please?"

The ordinary formula, prudent, impersonal, but why don't they give their names?

"It would take too long   ". . . don't . . . don't
to explain . . . the com-   you mustn't . . . you mustn't
munication might be cut off . . .   . . . pretext . . . I am
difficult to get . . . Listen well, no . . . not . . ."
it's the chance of a   . . . .
lifetime. You have   . . . .
to say yes and go . . ."   . . . .
(Click, static, noise of   . . . .
falling sand on metal.)   . . . .
". . . don't hesitate."   . . . .

"Who are you?" cried Jerome Bosch into the two phones.

Silence.

A double hissing. To the right, it was the rubbing of metal. To the left, the rattle of a machine. To the right, a tiny noise of eggshells being crushed. To the left, the light sound of a grater on a bed spring.

"Hello," Jerome Bosch said in vain.

Click. Click. Buzzing. Silence. Buzzing. Silence. To the right, to the left. A double busy signal on the lines.

He hung up the phone on the left. He waited a minute for the other phone, lying in the palm of his right hand, pressed next to his ear, listened to the sad mechanical music which sang on two notes, noise and silence, noise and silence, which like a siren of absence moaned at the bottom of its plastic shell.

Then he put the telephone at his right on its hook.

Through the open window he scrutinized the sky where a few dirty city birds and black sparrows drifted above the weather-glazed wall which blocked a good part of his horizon. Then, inside near the window he regarded the artistic calendar offered by an electronic calculating machine company, which presented a careful reproduction of a baroque painting for each day: *Visit to the Rhinoceros*. The Rhinoceros, with an air of annoyance, turned its back on his visitors, probably to better show himself to an art amateur. On the other side of the fence, quite low, a woman in a long dress with a mask on her face, a harlequin, and two children tied with ribbons amused themselves with the beast.

It was the same voice. But how could someone talk at the same time into two different phones, and, in spite of that, speak different words, simultaneously, on two different lines.

I knew the voice. I had already heard it somewhere.

He thought back on the voices of his friends, his clients, the voice of people whom he had relations with, without being especially friends or without selling them something, the voice of businessmen, doctors, tradespeople, taxi-telephones, all the voices one hears at the bottom of a phone without being able to add a face, oily voices, arrogant voices, dry voices, sprightly voices, laughing, metallic, harsh, hoarse, contracted, distinguished, mannered, vulgar with a husky accent, suave and almost perfumed, gloomy, tight, precise, pretentious, bitter, or sardonic.

He was sure of only one thing. He had heard on the two sides a man's voice.

They'll call back, he said.

He'll call back, because it concerned only one and the same person, even though at the left the voice had been clear, assured, exacting, and almost triumphant, and at the right smothered, terrified, and almost whining.

It was incredible what one could learn about people simply by listening to them on the telephone.

He began to work. A ream of white paper, a small box of clips, three colored pens, and all kinds of samples of formulas next to him. He had to prepare a letter, complete a document, fix up a report, and verify some columns of figures. That was enough to take up the morning. The writing of the report would have to be taken care of in the afternoon. He would take care, before going to lunch, of the difficult problem of choosing to eat in the office canteen or in one of the little restaurants in the neighborhood. He would go as usual to the canteen. The first two years, he chose regularly one of the two small restaurants, because the canteen depressed him. It reminded him that he lived in a universe he hadn't chosen, and as long as he could try to escape it, even if only symbolically, he held on to the impression that his stay was only temporary. A bad moment to pass, like school or military service. Not so bad, however. Work was often interesting and his colleagues were intelligent and cultivated. There were some who had even read his books.

Someone wanted to play a joke on him.

Things like that are possible with a tape-recorder. There wasn't even any conversation. I just listened, called out hello, and asked for names. A joke without the punch line. He began to work. The strange thing was that when he worked he couldn't help thinking of the stories he wanted to write, that he must write, and of the one he wrote with difficulty the evening in his apartment, lit from one end to the other, where he walked from one room to the other because he could not stand the night. And then not less curious, he thought of his work in the day, he could not keep from worrying about a certain affair, and how would so and so take the explications—a little flimsy—would the final document come out on time, everything which should have been blotted out in the silence and left him in peace with his dreams. A man, it was said, could not keep up with two different activities. He finishes by developing two different personalities, which fight and destroy each other. He starts down the double road of schizophrenia.

He picked up the telephone and dialed an interior number.

"Mrs. Duport? Yes . . . Bosch. How are you? . . . Fine, thank you. . . . Will you bring me the Marseilles report? Thank you."

One day, one day, he'd write full time. But at this idea a sudden terror made him lose his breath. Would he be capable of writing, to invent stories, to put together other words than those of accounts and letters? There was a knock on the door. "Come in," he said. The young woman was attractive. She had a round face and a small, pointed nose. What would she like to do, he thought, if she weren't weighted down with paperwork and typing? Paint, sew, read, walk, increase her sentimental relationships? It was a question he'd never ask. But somehow, he thought, it should be the subject of an inquiry, the only inquiry worth taking. It should be taken in the streets, the cafés, in the movies, in the theaters, in vehicles, and right into homes to ask people what they would do if they were completely free, how they would choose to spend that rare commodity which is called "time," in what sort of bottles they desired to pour the numbered sand of their lives. He could imagine the hesitation, the incredulity, the reserve, the panic. How does that concern you? I don't know, no really not, I never thought about it. Wait. Maybe I . . .

She saw that he was reflecting, put the document on the desk, and, without saying anything, left.

He took the document and opened it.

The phone on the left rang.

"Hello," he said.

"Hello, Jerome Bosch?"

It was the precise voice.

"I called you two days ago. The contact was bad. Can you hear me better now?"

"Yes," he said, "but it was a little while ago, not two days. If this is a joke . . ."

"For me it was two days ago. It isn't a joke."

"I believe it, nevertheless," said Jerome Bosch. "Two days or a little while ago is not the same thing. And why are you so familiar?"

"It took me two days to find the combination, or rather to arrive at favorable conditions. It's not so easy to telephone from one time to another."

"Excuse me," said Jerome Bosch.

"From one time to another. I prefer to tell you the truth. I'm calling from the future. I'm you, older than . . . It's better you don't know too much."

"Look, I haven't any time to waste," said Jerome Bosch, his eyes fixed on the open document.

"This is not a joke," pleaded the voice, calm, reasonable. "I didn't intend to tell you the truth, but you don't want to listen to me. You always need explanations and precise reasons."

"You also," said Jerome Bosch, entering into the game, "because you are me."

"I've changed a bit," said the voice.

"And how are you?"

"Much better than you are. I'm working at a job that interests me. I have all my time to write. Quite a bit of money, at least from your standpoint. A villa at Ibiza, another at Acapulco, a wife and two children. I'm glad to be alive."

"Felicitations," said Jerome Bosch.

"All that is yours, naturally, or will be yours. It's just necessary not to make a mistake. That's the reason I've called you."

"I see. The stunt of tomorrow's newspaper. The stock market or next week's lottery . . ."

"Listen," the voice said, annoyed, "at eleven fifty-eight this morning you will receive a telephone call from a very important man. He's going to make you a proposition. You must accept. Don't hesitate to leave the same night even if it's to the end of the world. Have confidence."

"I hope at least it's an honest proposition," said Jerome Bosch ironically.

The voice on the phone seemed hurt.

"Very honest. It's what you've been waiting for, for years. For God's sake take me seriously. It's the chance of a lifetime. One you won't have again. This person often changes his mind. Don't give him the time. It will be the beginning of a brilliant and stimulating career."

"And why have you called me, since you have succeeded?"

"I won't succeed unless you decide. You so often have the habit of hesitating, of equivocating, and then . . ."

The telephone to the right began to ring.

"They're calling me on another line," said Jerome Bosch. "I'm going to hang up."

"Don't hang up," cried the voice frantically, "don't . . ."

He had put the phone on the hook.

He waited a moment, listening to the other phone ringing, and time suddenly opened up. The ringing stretched out over miles of seconds and the silence was like an enormous cool oasis of repose. Ibiza, Acapulco. Names on a map. White and red villas hanging on the sides of steep hills. All the time to write.

He remembered the day when he had heard this voice. It came out of the speaker of the tape-recorder. It was his own voice. The telephone naturally had changed it, impersonalized it, smothered it, but it was his own voice. Not the one which he had the habit of hearing, it was different, restored by being registered. The voice which others heard.

The telephone on the right rang for the fourth time. He picked it up. He thought at first that there was nobody on the other end of the line. He only heard a false silence full of hissing and echoes, of mechanical scratchings as if the line picked up the sounds emitted in a great cave buried underground, full of microscopic noises, feeble drippings, raspings of insects, and tiny landslides. Then he heard the voice, even before understanding what it said, or rather like an indistinct singsong.

"I hear you very indistinctly," he said.

"Hello, hello, hello, hello," said the voice, now a little more distinct.

"You mustn't go . . . under any circumstance . . . Jerome, Jerome, do you hear me? Listen to me for the love of heaven. Don't leave . . ."

"Speak louder, please," he said.

The ridiculous voice shouted, strangled:

"Refuse . . . refuse . . . later . . ."

"Are you sick?" said Jerome Bosch. "Shall I let someone know? Where are you? Who are you?"

"Yyyyy . . ." said the voice. "You."

"Again?" he said. "But the other voice said that."

". . . am in the future . . . don't leave . . . that's how it is . . . understand . . ."

There was a timid knock on the door.

"Come in," said Jerome Bosch, lifting the phone from his ear and mechanically putting his hand over the microphone.

The new office boy came in. It was his first job, and the men and women shut in their offices, who blackened sheets of paper all day long, impressed him. He blushed easily and he was always impeccably dressed. He put the newspaper and letters on the edge of the desk.

"Thank you," said Jerome Bosch with a nod of his head. The door closed.

He put the phone back against his ear. But the voice was gone. It was lost in the labyrinth of wires that covered the world. A click. Then the dial tone.

He hung up the phone, thoughtful. Was it his own voice like the other time? He wasn't sure. Yet the two voices, the one at the right and the one at the left, had a familiar air. Two moments of the future, two different moments that tried to reach him.

He opened the letters. Nothing important. He annotated them and put them in a box. He threw out the envelopes. Then he tore open the band on the newspaper and rapidly scanned the pages to look at the financial section. Like every morning, his glance wavered over the page and then fixed on the weather report. He looked without interest, as usual. The map pinpointed with symbols caught his attention.

He read:

Weather cool and humid over region of Paris.

His eyes skipped two or three lines.

The cyclical perturbations in the Antilles are moving toward the northeast, above the Atlantic Ocean. There might be . . .

His attention wandered to the top of the page and flickered diagonally over the stock market and the leading values. Stocks strong, but not many transactions. Rise on silver. Light fall on cocoa.

Nothing but the usual affairs. He folded the newspaper.

He began to read the first document in his file.

He reread the first paragraph four times without understanding it. Something was wrong, not in the paragraph but in him. A drunken squirrel turning in a cage that resembled a telephone dial.

He took the phone at the right and dialed the switchboard.

". . . I'm listening," said an arrogant voice.

"A little while ago I had two telephone calls. Can you tell me if my callers left their numbers?"

It was the habit of the switchboard operator to note down all the communications, not like a policeman, but to be able to easily establish a broken communication.

"Which extension?"

"Four one three," said Jerome Bosch.

". . . go see . . . don't leave."

He heard the indistinct voices at the end of the line.

Another voice, feminine, friendly:

"You haven't received any calls this morning, Mr. Bosch. At least not from outside."

"I've been called four times," said Jerome Bosch.

"Not from outside, Mr. Bosch, at least not on your extension."

"I haven't left my office."

"I can assure you . . ."

He cleared his voice.

"Can a telephone call from outside reach one without passing through the switchboard?"

The switchboard operator waited a moment.

"I don't see how, Mr. Bosch."

Uneasy: "I haven't left my post."

Polite but cool: "Shall I call the main office?"

"No," said Jerome Bosch. "I must have been dreaming."

He hung up and passed his hand over a moist forehead. It was a joke. They had used one of the secretary's tape-recorders and they hadn't even taken the trouble to use the outside line. They must be screaming with laughter in the office next door. Melchior was a specialist at imitating voices.

Silence. The staccato of a typewriter stifled by the thickness of two doors. A distant step. The clamor of the city swallowed up by the open window, drilled by escaping rumblings.

He looked at the two telephones as if he had never seen them before. It was impossible. The two telephones were supplied with two distinct bells. A piercing one for the exterior, a muffled one for the interior. The ringing that had preceded each of the four strokes of the telephone still echoed in his ears.

He got up so abruptly that he almost turned over his chair. The hall was empty. He pushed the partly opened door of an office, then a second, then a third. They were all empty; there wasn't even a scrap of paper on the polished surface of the tables as a reminder that they were used. In the last office he picked up the phone, pressed the corresponding button for the inside office, and composed his post number. A muted grumble came from his office, filled the hall. Nobody had reversed the lines of the bell system.

He crossed the corridor, knocked, and entered his secretary's office. She waved her fingers in the air over her machine.

"There's no one around this morning."

"It's vacation," she said. "There's only the assistant director, you, and I . . . and the office boy," she added after a moment.

"Oh," said Jerome Bosch, "I forgot."

"I'm leaving next week." She pointed in the air. "Don't forget. Will you need someone else?"

"I don't know," he said helplessly, "see personnel."

He leaned against the frame of the door.

"Do you think the weather's going to be good, Mr. Bosch?"

"I have no idea. I hope so."

"The radio this morning announced a cyclone over the Atlantic. We'll probably have rain."

"I hope not," he said.

"You need to take a rest, Mr. Bosch."

"I'll leave soon. Two or three little jobs to finish. Oh, by the way, did you hear the phone ring this morning in my office?"

She nodded her head affirmatively.

"Two or three times. Why? Weren't you there? Should I have answered?"

"I was there," said Jerome Bosch, ill at ease. "I took the calls, thank you. Where are you going?"

"To Landes," she answered, watching him curiously.

"Well, I hope you have good weather."

He left, closing the door after him, and waited a moment in the empty corridor. The staccato of the machine began again. Reassured, he returned to his office.

He picked up a letter.

The telephone to the right began to ring.

He looked at his watch. It was eleven fifty-eight.

"Hello."

"Mr. Bosch," said the operator. "A call from out of town. One minute please."

Click. He heard the distance, the waltz of electrons crossing frontiers without passports, waves leaping across space, sent over oceans by the intercontinental rackets of satellites, bounding along cables poised on the bottom of the sea.

"Hello," said a man's voice. "Mr. Bosch. Jerome Bosch."

"Speaking," said Jerome Bosch.

"Oscar Wildenstein on the phone. I'm calling you from the Bahamas. I just finished your last book, *Within a Long Garden*. Very good, excellent, very original."

A male voice assured, vibrant with a light foreign accent. Italian, maybe American, or a little of both. A voice that had an odor of expensive cigars, dressed in a white tuxedo, speaking from the edge of a pool, under a clear blue sky from which hung a torrid sun.

"Thank you," said Jerome Bosch.

"I read it all night. Couldn't tear myself away. I want to make a film with Barbara Silvers. You know her? Well, I want to see you. Where are you now?"

"I'm in my office," said Jerome Bosch.

"Can you get away? You have a plane that leaves Paris-Orly at four P.M. local time . . . wait . . . it's four-thirty. I'll get you a ticket. My agent in Europe will take you to the airport. No point taking anything with you. You can find everything in Nassau."

"I'd like to think about it."

"Naturally, think it over. I can't tell you everything over the telephone. We'll discuss the details tomorrow over breakfast. Barbara is very excited over the idea of meeting you. She's going to read your book. She'll have read it by tomorrow. I'll translate the difficult passages. Natasha wants to see you, also. And Sybil, and Merryl, but they're just extras."

The voice became distant. Jerome Bosch heard feminine laughter, then the voice of Wildenstein, a little fainter but very distinct, so distinct he might have been speaking from the room next door: "No, you can't speak to him just now."

"They're completely crazy. They want to talk to you immediately. It's not possible. I told them to wait until tomorrow. Harding or Hardy—can't remember his name—who is my representative in Europe, will take care of you. It was very nice to talk to you. Tomorrow. *Domani. Mañana.*"

"Good-bye," said Jerome Bosch in a weak voice.

What time is it there? he asked himself.

Six or seven o'clock in the morning. He had read all through the night. A novel not possible to arrange for the movies. Except, maybe by him. After all, I know better than anyone how to arrange it. He understood that all the script men would break their backs over it. A brilliant and successful career. Two houses, one in Ibiza and one in Acapulco.

There was a knock on the door.

"Come in," he said.

The secretary stood in the doorway, a strange expression on her face. She held a small piece of paper in her hand.

"There was a call for you while you were on the other line, Mr. Bosch. I was given the call."

"Well?" said Jerome Bosch joyously.

"I couldn't hear very well. The transmission was terrible, really bad. He must have been calling from far away. I'm sorry, Mr. Bosch."

"And what did he say?"

"I couldn't understand except for two or three words. He said: TERRIBLE . . . TERRIBLE . . . two or three times, then . . . ACCIDENT . . . or OCCI-DENT. I wrote it here."

"He didn't leave his name?"

"No, Mr. Bosch, or his number. I hope he'll call back. I hope nothing has happened to your family. An accident. Heavens, it's so quick to happen."

"I don't think there's anything to worry about," said Jerome Bosch, taking the little square of paper. His glance wavered over the stenographic hiero-glyphics and stopped over: TERRIBLE . . . TERRIBLE . . . ACCIDENT.

The A of ACCIDENT was underlined and above it was marked an O

"Thank you, Mrs. Duport. Don't worry. I don't know anyone who could have had an accident. No one."

"Maybe it's a mistake."

"Certainly it's a mistake."

"I'm going to have lunch."

"Very well, enjoy your meal."

When she had closed the door he wondered if he should wait for her to come back before leaving the office. Usually he arranged it so someone was there to take the urgent calls. But it was vacation. There wouldn't be any calls.

Unless the two voices called back.

He shrugged his shoulders and threw an oblique look at the Rhinoceros. The real question was what to decide. It was vacation time, after all. He could leave for a week without having to give an excuse. The Bahamas. Maybe Wildenstein's agent would show up. Maybe it was a millionaire's whim. As soon as said, forgotten. Someone in the Bahamas had read his book or heard it talked about and wanted to hear the sound of his voice, verify that he existed.

He put the newspaper in his pocket. He stared at the telephones as if he was waiting for the ringing to start again while he crossed the corridor with its threadbare rug, striped with parallel lines, and walked down the large stone stairway. He listened, almost surprised not to be stopped by a loud ring. He crossed the courtyard into the street.

He took the street to the little Basque restaurant.

He went up to the first floor, where few people came in this season. He looked at the menu purely from habit, as he knew it by heart, and ordered a tomato salad and a Basquaise chicken with a small bottle of red wine. It was almost one o'clock. In the Bahamas, Wildenstein was having breakfast with Barbara, Sybil, Merryl, Natasha, and a half a dozen secretaries under a clear blue sky in the shade of exotic palm trees, and while eating called the four corners of the world with his assured male voice echoing around him, speaking in three or four languages of all the books he had read at night.

Jerome Bosch opened his newspaper.

He had just started on his salad when the waitress came over to him.

"Are you Mr. Bosch?"

"Yes," he said.

"There's a telephone call for you. The person said that you were upstairs. The phone is downstairs next to the counter."

"I'll go," he said, suddenly anxious. Was it that faraway voice, indistinct, covered with static? Or was it the other voice, which phoned from Ibiza or Acapulco? Or was it Wildenstein's agent?"

The telephone stood between a counter and the kitchen. Jerome Bosch squeezed into a corner to let the waitress pass by.

"Hello," he said, trying to protect his ear against the rattle of dishes.

"I had trouble finding you. Oh, I knew where you were, naturally. But I couldn't remember the number of the restaurant. To tell the truth, I never knew it. It's not so easy to find a number when you don't know the name or the exact location of the restaurant."

It was the voice to the left—precise, clear, but more nervous than in the morning, it seemed.

"Wildenstein, did he call?"

"At the exact time," said Jerome Bosch.

"Are you going to accept?"

The voice was anxious.

"I don't know yet. I have to think about it."

"But you must accept. You must go. Wildenstein is an extraordinary man. You'll get along great. From the first minute. You'll do big things with him."

"And will the film be good?"

"What film?"

"The adaptation of *Within a Long Garden.*"

"It'll never be done. You know it's completely untranslatable. You'll speak to him about another idea. He'll be thrilled. No, I can't tell you what. It's necessary. . . . It's necessary that it will happen."

"And Barbara Silvers? How is she?"

The voice softened.

"Barbara, oh, Barbara. You'll have plenty of time to get to know her. All the time. Because . . . I can't tell you."

There was silence.

"Where are you calling from?"

"I can't tell you. From a very pleasant place. You must not know your future. It would upset a lot of things."

"Someone called me this morning," Jerome Bosch said abruptly. "Someone who had your voice or mine, but broken, tired. I heard it very badly. He told me not to do something. To refuse something. Maybe Wildenstein's proposition."

"Did he call from the future?"

"I don't know."

A silence. Then:

"He spoke about an accident."

"What did he say?"

"Nothing. Just one word. Accident."

"I don't understand," said the voice. "Listen, don't worry. Go see Wildenstein. Go ahead."

"He called several times," said Jerome Bosch. "He'll certainly call back."

"Don't get scared," said the voice, anxious. "Ask him the date when he telephones, understand? Maybe someone is trying to keep you from succeeding. Someone who is jealous of me. Are you sure he had our voice? One can imitate voices."

"Almost sure," said Jerome Bosch.

He waited a moment because a waitress was behind him.

"Maybe he's calling about *your* future," he continued. "Maybe something will go wrong for you and he wants to let me know. Something which began with Wildenstein."

"That's impossible," said the voice. "Wildenstein is dead. You . . . you needn't know. Forget it. It doesn't matter. In any case, you don't know when."

"He . . . he will die in an accident, isn't that it?"

"In an airplane accident."

"Maybe that's it. You . . . you have something to do with it?"

"Absolutely nothing. I can assure you."

The voice became nervous: "Listen, you're not going to ruin your future over this story. You don't risk a thing. I know what's happened. I've lived through it."

"You don't know your future?"

"No," said the voice. "But I'm capable of taking care of it. I'll watch out. Nothing will happen. And even if something happens, I'm much older than you. No, I can't tell you my age. Let's put it that you have a good ten years ahead of you. Really good years. I wouldn't let the opportunity go, even if I had to die tomorrow!"

"Die tomorrow," said Jerome Bosch.

"Just a way of speaking. It's a lot, ten years, you know. And I'm fit as a fiddle. Much better than at your age. I promise you. Accept. Leave for the Bahamas. Don't tie yourself down to anything. Promise me you'll accept."

"I would like to know one thing," Jerome Bosch said slowly. "How can you talk to me. Have they invented a time machine in the future? Or have you done the job yourself?"

The voice began to laugh at the other end of the line. A laugh a little forced.

"It exists already in your era. I don't know if I should tell you. It's a secret. Very few people know about it. Anyhow, you wouldn't know how to use it. Nobody knows how it works, even now. You need luck, the right set of circumstances. The machine is the telephone."

"The telephone," repeated Jerome Bosch, surprised.

"Oh, not the combination you hold in your hand, but the network, the whole network. It's the most complicated thing done by man. More complicated than the calculating machines. Think of the thousands of miles of wires, the millions of amplifiers, of the inextricable tangle of the centers. Think of the millions of messages which go around the earth. And everything is connected. Time and again something unexpected happens in this jumble. Time and again the phone connects two moments instead of two places. It might become official one day. But I doubt it. Too many unknowns. Too many risks. Only a few are in the know."

"How did you do it?"

"You will have very intelligent friends in the future if you accept Wildenstein's proposition. But I'm talking too much. You don't need to know everything. Accept. That's all."

"I don't know," murmured Jerome Bosch as he heard a click at the other end of the line.

Someone was waiting behind him.

"Oh, excuse me. I was very long." He tried to smile. He walked up the stairs holding on to the railing. The chicken had been served. It was almost cold.

"Do you want me to reheat it?" asked the waitress.

"No, that's all right."

They didn't have a machine to travel in time but they had discovered a new way to use the telephone.

The telephone.

It covered the entire planet. It ran along roads, railways, suspended over linear forests. It plunged under rivers and oceans in a rubber coat. It formed a thick and spiderlike ball at the same time. The wires crossed and inter-crossed. Nobody would be capable of drawing a complete diagram of the telephone system. And in ten years? And in twenty years? The system would be more complex than the human brain.

He tried to imagine the cool, dark caverns of the great centrals where, in silence, impalpable impurities drowned in a crystal heart, oriented innumerable voices. And the networks were in one sense living. Men spread it all the time and meticulously repaired it. The networks were nerves. Automatic calculators cutting messages into small pieces so as to be able to cross and fill the silences. What would be so surprising if the telephone should be capable of another miracle?

He remembered stories—maybe legends—that one told about the telephone. Numbers one could dial at night that would put you in contact with unknown voices. Not only one voice, but anonymous voices bodiless, which exchanged between them their own talk, playful, joking, who profited from the situation and said things which wouldn't be quoted under cover of a known name or face. He remembered ghost voices, which they said wandered without stopping in the line of the network and always repeated the same thing. He remembered automatic systems answering when you lifted the phone.

Sooner or later everything in the universe found a means which it hadn't been made for. So with man. A million years ago, he ran through the forests gathering game and fruit with his bare hands. And now he built villas, wrote poems, threw bombs, and phoned.

So it was with the telephone.

He pushed away his plate, ordered a coffee, drank it, paid, and left. The sun had chased away the clouds. He turned toward the quay. But just loafing was impossible since cars were all over. Even the fishermen had given up. I'm just turning around he said. I know all the streets in this neighborhood by heart. I work, I inhabit one of the most fantastic cities in the world, and it has ceased to move me. It says nothing to me. I'd love to get out of here.

He looked at his watch. Almost two-thirty. The time to go back and finish what I couldn't do this morning. The walls and windows, always the same, were gray and almost transparent, used by the insistent and excessive stare of eyes.

Then there were the girls who the seasons, the change of work, and the tourist buses renewed. But this year's crop was very bad. He hadn't seen a good-looking girl for over a week.

In the Bahamas, Barbara, Natasha, Sybil, and Merryl were splashing in a pool under the satisfied eyes of Wildenstein. He was right. I should accept. It was a chance not to be repeated.

The secretary's door was open. She was waiting for him. A new call, he thought anxiously.

She leaned toward him.

"Someone is waiting for you in your office, Mr. Bosch." He stopped short, a lump in his throat. He didn't have an appointment. Who could it be? Have they managed to physically cross over into time? Wasn't it enough for them to call him? He took his courage in his two hands: no, they couldn't do anything except telephone through time. He opened the door.

A man who didn't look like Jerome Bosch waited, seated on a corner of his desk, one leg hanging, the other on the worn rug. His face was long, his features fine. His dark hair was long but carefully cut at the collar. He was dressed in a gray suit with large checks, with lots of pockets—the one over his heart had a colored handkerchief artistically creased—and the narrow lapels underlined the fantasy. He wore a striped shirt, a tie with polka dots, black shoes with complicated designs, and red socks. Next to his right hand, a small suitcase of black shiny leather. He looked English from the tip of his toes to the end of his nails. He got up.

"Mr. Jerome Bosch? I am very pleased to meet you."

The voice was cultivated, serious, with a strong British accent.

Jerome Bosch nodded his head.

"Fred Hardy," said the man, holding out a beautifully manicured hand. "Mr. Wildenstein called me before coming here. He hoped that I would take care of all the details."

He opened his suitcase and spread out on the desk a handful of papers.

"Here's your airplane ticket, Mr. Bosch. Here's a special visa that you just have to put in your passport. You have a passport, don't you? This wallet has fifty pounds in it in travelers' checks. You just have to sign. I think that will be sufficient for the voyage. And here's a letter to give to customs at Nassau. The governor is a personal friend of Mr. Wildenstein. You don't have to handle anything. Mr. Wildenstein is probably not in Nassau but someone will be at the airport and conduct you to Mr. Wildenstein's island. I wish you a very good trip."

"I haven't accepted yet," said Jerome Bosch.

Hardy began to laugh politely.

"Oh, naturally you're free. I've prepared all this on the assumption of a favorable answer."

"You've done it very quickly," said Jerome Bosch, astounded, contemplating the plane tickets, the visa, the wallet, and the envelope. "You live in Paris?"

"I just arrived from London, Mr. Bosch," said Hardy. "Mr. Wildenstein likes efficiency. Mr. Wildenstein recommended that I accompany you to the airport. Moreover, my plane leaves a half hour after yours. These schedules are practical between Paris and London."

The telephone to the right began to ring. Hardy put his case under his arm.

"I'll wait for you in the corridor, Mr. Bosch. The taxi is downstairs. We have plenty of time."

He smiled, showing his large, immaculate white teeth. The door closed after him.

Jerome Bosch picked up the phone.

"Hello," he said.

Nobody. The echo in a cave, a long tunnel, a well.

"Hello," he said, louder. He had an impression of not hearing himself. He had the impression that his voice was swallowed up by the phone, smothered, stifled.

Without conviction he said:

"Where are you calling from, what do you want?"

He held the airplane ticket close and leafed through it. The ticket, Paris-Nassau via New York and Miami. One return-trip ticket. Hardy had done things thoroughly. It wasn't a trap. No matter what happened he could return. And Hardy had come from London just for this. Let's see. Wildenstein had called him at ten-thirty, maybe eleven. He had taken the twelve-o'clock plane. At one o'clock he was in Paris. At a quarter to two in the office of Jerome Bosch. It was very simple. He lived in a world where you jumped from one plane to the other, where one wore apparently sober suits but which in reality were quite extravagant, shoes made to order, where one was invited to governor's dinners and was to telephone from the four corners of the globe. I can't let him down before he goes back to London, thought Jerome Bosch.

It was a first-class ticket. On the upper left-hand corner of the cover was a stamp. V.I.P. And someone had added Fm. WDS.

Very Important Person. From Wilderstein. Made out by Wildenstein.

He was in a state. I can't just tell him: Tomorrow if you like, but not today, I must think it over. He'd laugh at me. No, he's much too well bred. He'll say Mr. Wildenstein will be sorry, he hopes to see you tomorrow morning. He would bend over and put the ticket, the visa, the fifty pounds, and the letter from the governor back in his case and then he'd return to Orly to wait for his plane. What time is it? Almost three. In an hour and a half, the plane would take off. Nassau via New York and Miami. They had no intention of letting the plane wait fifteen minutes just for him.

"Hello," said Jerome Bosch into the dumb phone. He opened a drawer of his desk, the only one that locked. He picked up official papers and found his blue passport, drew it toward him with one hand and opened it. An old photo of three or four years ago. He was almost good-looking then, much thinner. He looked alert.

"Hello," he called for the last time, and hung up. His hands were damp and trembling. I don't have the experience for this type of situation. I don't know what to do. In his right hand he put the passport, ticket, visa, the wallet, and the letter. With his free hand he opened a large drawer in his desk and threw in papers, documents, pens, and the box of clips.

At the end of the corridor, Hardy was waiting, smiling, not even leaning on the wall, holding the suitcase nonchalantly by the handle with two hands.

Jerome Bosch knocked and pushed open the secretary's door.

"I have to leave for a few days, Mrs. Duport," he said, "this man . . ."

"It was an accident, wasn't it?"

She seemed frightened. What must she imagine? he thought. But I can't tell her the truth. I can't say that in an hour I'll be in the sky on my way to the Bahamas.

"No," he said in a sudden hoarse voice. "Not an accident, on the contrary. A . . . personal affair. I'll be gone for a few days. I think it's better to get a temporary helper. To answer the telephone. I'll send you a postcard."

She finally decided to smile.

"Have a nice trip, Mr. Bosch."

He must leave and recover.

"If . . . if someone calls me, say I'm on vacation. I haven't much time. This man . . . You'll explain all this to the codirector . . . all right?"

"Don't worry. Enjoy your trip, Mr. Bosch."

"Thank you."

In the corridor, Hardy took a cigarette from a red and gold box. He tapped the end against his case, then slipped the cigarette into his mouth, the lighter from his pocket squirted a flame, he inhaled a puff, and exhaled the smoke in a thin line almost without opening his lips.

"A cigarette, Mr. Bosch?"

"No, thank you," he said. "I . . . I . . . smoke a pipe."

He felt his pocket, but he knew that his black briar pipe, the one which was split—its life would be short even though he preferred it to his others— wasn't there. He had left it at home this morning. Moreover, he never took it to the office. He didn't use it except while writing or reading in the tranquillity of his apartment with all the lamps lit.

"Mr. Wildenstein will be very pleased with your decision, Mr. Bosch. He'll be very happy to see you. He likes people who know how to make quick decisions. Time is so precious, isn't it?"

They went down the large stone stairway.

"Do you have to let anyone know, Mr. Bosch?" said Hardy. "You can telephone from the airport."

He looked at his watch.

"We don't have time to go to your home, but it doesn't matter. Mr. Wildenstein is about your size. He has an enormous wardrobe. You can find everything in Nassau. Mr. Wildenstein likes to travel without baggage."

The pebbles in the courtyard cracked under their steps.

"Your taxis are so convenient in France, Mr. Bosch. I only have to telephone from London before leaving and a car is waiting for me at Orly. Radio-taxis, isn't that so? Our taxis are so out-of-date in London. And in New York, it's so difficult to find a driver who will wait for you. It's a nice day, don't you find it so? It rained this morning in London. It's even better weather in Nassau. But the sky doesn't have this shading, this soft color. I want to talk to you about your book, Mr. Bosch, but I must admit I haven't had the time to read it yet. My knowledge of your language is very incomplete. I hope it will be translated soon. You'll like Mr. Wildenstein. He's a man with a lot of personality, or, as you would say, 'character.'"

"Well now. Baron," said the driver when they were installed in the back of the car, "where are we going?"

"To Orly," said Hardy.

"By Raspail or by Italie?"

"Take the Boulevard Saint Germain and the Boulevard Saint Michel," said Hardy. "I like so much going along the Luxembourg Gardens."

"As you like, but it will be longer."

The streets were almost deserted. The traffic lights before them turned green almost as if the driver had telecommanded them. It only needed, said Jerome Bosch, that the car have a little flag and a siren. No, a siren would have destroyed this deep silence. Real power has a great deal of discretion. No noise, baggage. Invisibility. Only a name used as a passport.

As they were going along Luxembourg, the radio began to ring. It was an old telephone model. Without slowing down, the driver unhooked the phone and hung it at the side of his head.

"I'm listening," he said.

A voice breathed a few words.

The driver looked in the rear-view mirror.

"Are you Bosch?" he said.

"That's me," said Jerome Bosch.

"It's not regular, but someone wants to talk to you. It must be important if the station gives it to you. This isn't a telephone, it's a taxi. Go ahead, take the tube, because they want to talk to you. I've never seen anything like this. And I've been driving for over twenty years."

His throat dry, Jerome Bosch took the apparatus. He was obliged to fold himself almost in two on the seat because the cord was too short. His chin pressed against the worn velvet.

"Hello," he said.

"Jerome," said the voice. "Finally I found you . . . difficult . . . Don't leave, for the love of heaven. There's going to be . . . Don't . . ." Static. Cracklings.

"Where are you calling from?" asked Jerome Bosch with a voice which he tried to make firm and keep discreet.

"Why, why, why?" said the voice plaintively, the voice broken, complaining. "From . . . tomorrow . . . or after . . . don't know . . ."

"Why mustn't I . . .?"

He stopped, thinking that Fred Hardy would hear him. He had come from London just to put him on the plane.

"Accident," said the voice. It was nearer than it had ever been. But it sounded more miserable, more worn for being clearer.

"Who's talking?"

"Yyyy . . . you," said the voice to the only Jerome Bosch. "I have already . . ."

"Your voice sounds so low . . . isn't it?" asked Jerome Bosch abruptly.

"I'm so far . . . so far," said the voice as if explaining.

The car went faster. They rode on the left side of the autoroute.

An intuition hit Jerome Bosch like a blow.

"You're sick . . ." he ended.

He didn't dare say any more. Not in front of the driver and Hardy.

"No, no, no," said the voice, "not that . . . not that . . . worse, it's terrible. You mustn't . . . I . . . I . . . I wait . . ."

"I mustn't what?"

"You mustn't leave," said the voice distinctly, and immediately it disappeared as if it had accomplished a last terrible exhausting effort.

Jerome Bosch remained overwhelmed for a moment, bent forward on the seat. The perspiration dripped from his forehead. The apparatus slipped from his fingers, bounced on the cushion, then hung at the end of the line, hitting the driver's knee, ringing on the metal.

"Is it finished?" said the driver.

"I think so," said Jerome Bosch, breathless.

"So much the better," he said, hanging up.

A jet plane passed very low overhead.

"You seem nervous, Mr. Bosch," said Hardy.

"It's nothing," said Bosch, "nothing at all."

He thought: I haven't left yet. I can change my mind. Say I've been called back. A very important affair. Leave it till tomorrow.

"The air in Nassau will do you a world of good, Mr. Bosch," said Hardy. "The agitation of big cities is wearing on the nerves."

"Depart or arrival?" asked the driver.

"Depart," said Hardy.

The car stopped beside the sidewalk. Jerome Bosch looked in front and saw that the amount registered on the meter had three digits. Hardy paid. The glass doors opened automatically in front of them. They kept away from the lines in front of the booking office and went to the entrance of a small discreet office. Jerome Bosch put his hand in his left pocket, which contained the passport, ticket, wallet, visa, and the letter. They took care of the formalities.

"No, not there," said Hardy as Jerome Bosch went toward the large stairway. He conducted him to a narrow hall. The marble was covered with a large rug. A door opened without noise.

"Back already, Mr. Hardy," said the elevator operator.

"Alas, yes," said Hardy. "I can never take advantage of my stay in Paris."

They were now in the upper hall.

"You have plenty of time to buy newspapers, Mr. Bosch, or a book. It's a ten-hour flight to Nassau including the stops. There is a direct flight from London, but only once a week."

I can still refuse, thought Jerome Bosch. Thank him, wait with him for the plane to London, promise to leave tomorrow. Say I had forgotten something. Through what did he call me? From where did he call? Why did he say tomorrow? How could he call me through tomorrow? Tomorrow I wouldn't know more than today how to telephone across time. Who is he?

He let himself sink little by little into the atmosphere of the place.

"You haven't given me time to fetch a coat," he said.

"Useless, in Nassau, you won't need one. You rather need a light suit. You have the best English tailors in Nassau, the best London houses."

On the other side of the glass wall, giant planes waited, immobile, frozen. Others rolled slowly on belts. Another warmed its motors at the end of a runway, pushed ahead, refusing to leave the ground, then suddenly breaking its headway, lifted and rose. I am in an aquarium. Even sounds don't come through this glass prison. On the other side, above, in the blue sky, freedom begins.

Jerome Bosch let his eyes wander over to a young woman printed in two copies. Twins. Exactly the same. Long honey-colored hair, same faces, a little dull but exquisitely fresh. Their legs were long and thin. They each carried a small shoulder-strap bag of red leather. They are either in the movies or models, thought Jerome Bosch, at bottom surprised not to discern between him and them the thickness of a window or the impenetrable depth of a movie house, or the photographic varnish of a magazine page. The story of a man in love with one of the twins, either one; which should he choose, A or B? He chooses A. Very quickly she shows her nasty character. He understands that he should have married B, who is sweet, affectionate, and who loves him in silence. What should he do? Divorce and marry B. That would never work. She loves her sister too much. He discovers a method to call through time. He telephones himself the day he makes his decision. Marry B, he cries helplessly to his undecided past. What will the past do? And if B should become in time nasty also? Completely idiotic, said Jerome Bosch to himself.

"The Berthold sisters," said Fred Hardy. "They pretend they are Swedish, but in reality they are Austrian or maybe Yugoslavian. Mr. Wildenstein wanted to use them. But they don't know how to act. Nothing to be done. Not the least stage presence. As if one was the reflection of the other and vice versa. In Hollywood, Jonathan Craig pretends that they have only one shadow for two. They are going to act in a small French film."

"Do you meet the same people all the time in the airports, Mr. Hardy?"

"No, but you fall sometimes on well-known personalities. Especially on the Paris-New York line. Like a suburban line. London is the suburb of New York today, Mr. Bosch."

"Isn't it dangerous to travel by plane?" Jerome Bosch said impulsively and naïvely. He heard the voice: Accident . . . accident.

"Certainly, Mr. Bosch," said Hardy, "but less dangerous than traveling by automobile. There are statistics. I take the plane three times a week generally. And Mr. Wildenstein belongs to the millionaires' club. You've heard it talked about. That means that he has covered more than a million miles by plane. Never a single accident. Have you ever taken a plane, Mr. Bosch?"

"Yes," said Jerome Bosch, suddenly humiliated by his cowardice. "I've been to London two or three times, and to New York, to Germany, and also to Nice. But I don't care for the taking off and landing."

He had a desire to tell how he had seen a helicopter burn in Algeria during the war. The plane hesitating like a large fly, then slipping, gliding a few feet from the ground, and for an unknown reason turning over. A sudden light of magnesium. A thick cloud of smoke, no explosion, it only burned, the sirens, the fire engines, a shroud of snow, carbonic suds on a ridiculous block less than a yard from his side, the motor, all that remained of the helicopter.

"The weather is splendid, Mr. Bosch," said Fred Hardy. "It will be an excellent flight. Look, your plane has just been announced."

Jerome Bosch turned toward the flight panel and read: FLIGHT 713 B.O.A.C. PARIS-NEW YORK-MIAMI-NASSAU. SALLE 32.

"We have plenty of time," said Hardy. "Really, you should buy some newspapers, a book, a pipe, tobacco. Or maybe you'd rather think on the plane. Planes are really such quiet places."

PARIS-LONDON 5 P.M. AIR FRANCE FLIGHT A SALLE 57 FLIGHT B SALLE 58

"Your plane," he said.

Fred Hardy examined the panel.

"Oh, it's been doubled."

"Which one will you take?" Jerome Bosch asked abruptly.

"It doesn't matter," said Hardy. "If there's no room on A, they'll put me on B. They arrive at the same time, I think."

But thought Jerome Bosch, If plane B had an accident, wouldn't it be better to take plane A? The chances, are they mathematically equal? How to choose?

"They are calling you," said Fred Hardy.

"Who, me?"

"The microphone," said Fred Hardy. "Maybe it's Mr. Wildenstein."

He smiled, a cigarette between his fingers, his valise placed on the arm of a chair, leaning against his hip, impeccable, elegant.

"Mr. Jerome Bosch is requested to come to the welcoming office," said the voice, asexual but feminine, angelic, too low-pitched, too smooth, too calm.

"Someone wants you on the telephone probably," said Fred Hardy. "Here. Straight ahead. Do you want me to buy you newspapers? A pipe? Meerschaum or briar? What do you prefer in tobacco? Amsterdammer or Dunhill?"

But Jerome Bosch had already gone, dizzy, staggering. Too much noise.

Too many faces. A complicated itinerary. Where was it? The panels. Welcome.

He held on to the counter as if he were drowning. He understood. An idea flashed in his mind. Till now it turned around like a fish in a bowl. Circular. It came to him. He believed everything.

"I'm Jerome Bosch," he said to a young woman with a smiling face and a gray beret placed across her head. Her eyes were too big, heavily underlined with black, and her teeth too large, also.

"I've been called," said Jerome Bosch nervously. "I'm Jerome Bosch."

"Certainly, Mr. Bosch. An instant, Mr. Bosch."

She pushed an invisible button, said something, then listened. "A telephone call, Mr. Bosch. Booth three. No, not there. On your left."

The door closed automatically after him. Silence. The roar of the planes didn't sound here. He picked up the phone and without waiting:

"I don't want to leave."

"You're not going to give in now," said the voice of the left, firm and resolute.

"The other," said Jerome Bosch. "He isn't calling from your future. He's calling from *another* future. Something has happened to him. He took the plane and he had an accident and . . ."

"Are you crazy," said the voice. "You're afraid to take the plane and you invent anything. I know you well, you know."

"Maybe I invent you also," said Jerome Bosch.

"Listen," said the voice, "I had a lot of trouble getting hold of you. I knew you'd hesitate. I don't want you to give up this opportunity."

"If I don't leave," said Jerome Bosch, "you won't exist. That's why you insist."

"And then," said the voice, "I'm you, no? I've explained all this to you. Ibiza. Acapulco. All the time to write. And Barbara. And Barbara. Good God. I shouldn't tell you, but you're going to marry Barbara. You don't want to miss that. You love her."

"I don't know her yet," said Jerome Bosch.

"You'll meet her," said the voice. "She'll be crazy about you. Not right away. Ten years, Jerome. More than ten years of happiness. She'll act in all your films. You'll be famous, Jerome."

"Give me time to think about it," said Jerome Bosch.

"What time is it?"

He looked at his watch.

"Four-ten."

"You must get on the plane."

"But the other voice that phones from I don't know where. It told me not to leave. Another future, another possibility. He said he called from tomorrow."

"Another future," said the voice, indecisive. "And then, I'm here, no? I took the plane and nothing happened to me. I've taken the plane hundreds of times. I belong to the millionaires' club. You know what that is? And never an accident."

"The other one has had an accident," said Jerome Bosch stubbornly.

Silence. Cracklings. An abysmal insect devoured the line somewhere on the bottom of the ocean.

"Let's admit," said the voice, "you could run a risk, no? Look at the statistics. There are ninety-nine chances out of a hundred that you will arrive safely. More than that. Nine hundred . . ."

"Why should I believe you," asked Jerome Bosch, "and not the other?"

". . . chance out of two . . ."

"Hello," said Jerome Bosch. "I don't hear you."

"Even if there wasn't," said the voice, which cried and died far away, which spoke from the other side of a partition of glass, which screamed from the interior of a closed box, "one chance out of two, you can't let it drop. You don't want to spend your life in an office, no?"

"No," said Jerome Bosch feebly.

A tiny voice at the end of the line as if the caller out there was sinking in the foam, falling in the infinite labyrinth of telephone wires.

"Hurry up," said an insect, "you'll miss the plane."

Click.

"Hello, hello," cried Jerome Bosch.

Silence. Dead phone. He looked at his watch. Four-fourteen. He was one or two minutes slow. Hardy must be asking what he was doing. I'll miss the plane.

Should I leave? Jerome Bosch asked himself.

"It's time," said Fred Hardy, smiling. "I bought you a briefcase. A meerschaum pipe. Mr. Wildenstein prefers meerschaum pipes because it's not necessary . . . how do you say, *de les culotter*. Three packages of tobacco. *Le Monde* and *Le Figaro*, the New York *Times*, *Paris-Match*, *Playboy*, and the latest *Fiction*. That's the French review where you publish your short stories, isn't it? I bought you a toothbrush. A flask of whiskey. Chivas. You like Chivas, no, Mr. Bosch? We just have time. No, not there."

The policeman smiled, greeted Fred Hardy, and made a sign.

The customs officer let them through.

"Tell Mr. Wildenstein that everything is all right in London, Mr. Bosch. I'll call him tomorrow. No, Mr. Bosch, here."

Loudspeakers diffused soft music.

They advanced into an infinite corridor, limited at the end by a large mirror which threw back their images as they hurried toward it. But they didn't reach it. Fred Hardy took Jerome Bosch's elbow and turned him a quarter way around and they walked immobile down the lower story on a little mechanical escalator.

The waiting room was divided into two parts. To the right, a line of people. Jerome Bosch wanted to join them. But Fred Hardy took him toward the other door. There was almost no one there. A gray suit with a weather-beaten face who held in his hand a shiny leather briefcase, and a woman, very tall, very beautiful, whose long pale hair touched her shoulders. She didn't look at anyone.

There was one more door to go through.

I don't want to leave, thought Jerome Bosch, pale. I'll pretend I'm ill. A forgotten appointment, I have to get a manuscript. I won't say anything. They can't hold me back. They can't kidnap me.

"Here," said Fred Hardy, handing him the briefcase. "I hope you have a nice trip. I would have liked to go with you, but the London office is waiting for me. Perhaps I'll be in the Bahamas at the end of the month. I am very happy to have met you, Mr. Bosch."

The door opened. A hostess entered, smiled, looked over the three first-class passengers, took their red tickets, and left.

"Will you please take your place in the bus."

"Good-bye, Mr. Hardy," said Jerome Bosch, moving away.

Jerome Bosch is almost alone in the bus, which carries the first-class passengers. The bus rolls slowly, following a complicated itinerary on an enormous surface of smooth cement which doesn't seem to be ground-lighted. Jerome Bosch feels nothing, not even the slight excitement which accompanies all his trips. He thinks that now nobody can reach him by telephone—here he fools himself. He thinks that no one will try to influence his conduct because that will not have any importance. The bus stops. Jerome Bosch gets off the bus, which leaves to get the batch of second-class passengers. He climbs the mobile stairway applied to the front of the plane. He hesitates an instant on entering the first-class cabin. He lets himself be conducted to a chair next to a porthole in front of the wings. He fastens his security belt under the hostess's vigilant eye. He hears some noise, the scraping of feet behind him, the second-class passengers settling down. He sees the hostess go forward toward the pilot's cabin and disappear for an instant, return, and unhook a micro. He hears her wish everyone welcome in three languages and recommend everyone to put out cigarettes and examine their seat belts. A panel lights up which renews these instructions. A basket filled with candies is served to him. He chooses one. He knows that it fulfills a rite, that these planes are pressurized and that his eardrums will not suffer even if he doesn't take the trouble to swallow, and moreover, he will have swallowed the candy even before the plane has finished taking off. The plane rolls. It seems to Jerome Bosch that in the distance, near the waiting room, stands the tall, elegant silhouette of Fred Hardy. The plane stops moving. The motors roar and the universe hurls itself ahead and throws Jerome Bosch against the back of his seat. He tries to look out the porthole. The plane has left the ground. A shock. The wheels have been drawn up into their place.

Jerome Bosch begins to relax. Nothing happens. He is given a newspaper, this morning's, and he opens it to the economic page and his eyes fall on the small weather map. He puts it aside. He opens the briefcase, looks inside and finds the pipe, examines it, superior quality, and stuffs and lights it. He is served a whiskey. He flies over the clouds. He asks himself if ephemeral, tiny civilizations are growing in the folds of these mountains of fog. He thinks he is beginning to forget the telephone. He tries to imagine Nassau. He begins to discover that he has left. He takes possession of the cabin. He makes his seat move. He questions himself on the possibilities of his two futures. It seems to him, but he isn't sure, that the voice from the left, the firm assured voice, Ibiza, Acapulco, and Barbara, has become more distant, become less clear, from conversation to conversation, and the other more present. Question of telephone lines. He is given something to eat. He is served champagne. He looks at the hostess, who smiles when she passes by him. He asks for more champagne. He drinks a coffee. He sleeps.

When he wakes up—but what time is it?—the plane is flying over the sea in a perfectly clear day. Jerome Bosch hasn't dreamed or he couldn't remember his dreams. He regrets rather absurdly, in looking at the sea, not having brought a bathing suit. Mr. Wildenstein certainly has a dozen suits. Jerome Bosch finally understands that the hostess is addressing him. She holds out a blue piece of paper intricately folded like a telegram. She seems surprised.

"A call for you, Mr. Bosch. The operator excuses himself but he could only understand a few words. There's static electricity in the air. He tried to confirm it, but without success."

He unfolds the paper and reads only one word scratched in pen: *Soon* . . .

Mr. Wildenstein, he thinks. But he can't be sure.

"Please," he said, "please could you find out what the voice was like."

"I'll go see," said the hostess, who disappeared into the pilot's cabin and came back in a moment.

"Mr. Bosch," she said. "The operator couldn't describe the voice very well. He begs to be excused. He said it seemed very near, that the communication was very powerful and he didn't think, in spite of the static, that there was any more to say. He asked for confirmation."

"Thank you," said Jerome Bosch, as he sees her leave, take up the microphone, take a breath, and say in a smooth voice:

"A second of attention, if you please, ladies and gentlemen. We are going through a zone of perturbation. Please fasten your seat belts and put out your cigarettes."

He doesn't listen anymore. He looks out the porthole at the bottom of the sky, otherwise clear, and sees that a little cloudy spot, almost black, is topped by an intense dark bubbling toward which the plane precipitates. Black, black, black, as an eye.

The Proud Robot

Lewis Padgett was one of the most popular SF writers of the 1940s, and one of the most respected of Campbell's stable. In reality, however, Padgett was the pseudonym of the prolific young pulp writer Henry Kuttner, who had the unfortunate reputation of being a prolific hack for the fantasy pulps. Kuttner had married the talented and popular Catherine L. Moore, with whom he began one of the most impressive and successful collaborations in SF history. Moore and Kuttner, both young and committed to improving their craft, wrote in such close collaboration that later neither could identify their own sentences. Until Kuttner's sudden death in 1958, they were a joint writing persona, the most admired writer in SF among those who recognized unusual stylistic achievement. After the exposure of their numerous pseudonyms in the late 1940s, they published under either one byline or as Kuttner and Moore, but kept the Padgett pseudonym alive as well on books into the 1950s.

"The Proud Robot" is an early Padgett story presumably written by Kuttner alone, as part of a series featuring Galloway Gallegher, a drunken inventor. Although the foreground is absurd and comic, the background detail is carefully conceived and, for 1943, more than a bit prophetic. It is also a textbook example of how the writer achieves literal meanings in SF impossible in other fiction, through careful manipulation of SF clichés (note the last line of the story—in which Gallegher sings a duet with a can opener).

*   *   *

Things often happened to Gallegher, who played at science by ear. He was, as he often remarked, a casual genius. Sometimes he'd start with a twist of wire, a few batteries, and a button hook, and before he finished, he might contrive a new type of refrigerating unit.

At the moment he was nursing a hangover. A disjointed, lanky, vaguely boneless man with a lock of dark hair falling untidily over his forehead, he lay on the couch in the lab and manipulated his mechanical liquor bar. A very dry Martini drizzled slowly from the spigot into his receptive mouth.

He was trying to remember something, but not trying too hard. It had to do with the robot, of course. Well, it didn't matter.

"Hey, Joe," Gallegher said.

The robot stood proudly before the mirror and examined its innards. Its hull was transparent, and wheels were going around at a great rate inside.

"When you call me that," Joe remarked, "whisper. And get that cat out of here."

"Your ears aren't that good."

"They are. I can hear the cat walking about, all right."

"What does it sound like?" Gallegher inquired, interested.

"Jest like drums," said the robot, with a put-upon air. "And when you talk, it's like thunder." Joe's voice was a discordant squeak, so Gallegher meditated on saying something about glass houses and casting the first stone. He brought his attention, with some effort, to the luminous door panel, where a shadow loomed—a familiar shadow, Gallegher thought.

"It's Brock," the annunciator said. "Harrison Brock. Let me in!"

"The door's unlocked." Gallegher didn't stir. He looked gravely at the well-dressed, middle-aged man who came in, and tried to remember. Brock was between forty and fifty; he had a smoothly massaged, clean-shaven face, and wore an expression of harassed intolerance. Probably Gallegher knew the man. He wasn't sure. Oh, well.

Brock looked around the big, untidy laboratory, blinked at the robot, searched for a chair, and failed to find it. Arms akimbo, he rocked back and forth and glared at the prostrate scientist.

"Well?" he said.

"Never start conversations that way," Gallegher mumbled, siphoning another Martini down his gullet. "I've had enough trouble today. Sit down and take it easy. There's a dynamo behind you. It isn't very dusty, is it?"

"Did you get it?" Brock snapped. "That's all I want to know. You've had a week. I've a check for ten thousand in my pocket. Do you want it, or don't you?"

"Sure," Gallegher said. He extended a large, groping hand. "Give."

"*Caveat emptor.* What am I buying?"

"Don't you know?" the scientist asked, honestly puzzled.

Brock began to bounce up and down in a harassed fashion. "My God," he said. "They told me you could help me if anybody could. Sure. And they also said it'd be like pulling teeth to get sense out of you. Are you a technician or a drivelling idiot?"

Gallegher pondered. "Wait a minute. I'm beginning to remember. I talked to you last week, didn't I?"

"You talked—" Brock's round face turned pink. "Yes! You lay there swilling liquor and babbled poetry. You sang 'Frankie and Johnnie.' And you finally got around to accepting my commission."

"The fact is," Gallegher said, "I have been drunk. I often get drunk. Especially on my vacation. It releases my subconscious, and then I can work. I've made my best gadgets when I was tizzied," he went on happily. "Everything seems so clear then. Clear as a bell. I mean a bell, don't I? Anyway—" He lost the thread and looked puzzled. "Anyway, what are you talking about?"

"Are you going to keep quiet?" the robot demanded from its post before the mirror.

Brock jumped. Gallegher waved a casual hand. "Don't mind Joe. I just finished him last night, and I rather regret it."

"A robot?"

"A robot. But he's no good, you know. I made him when I was drunk, and I haven't the slightest idea how or why. All he'll do is stand there and admire himself. And sing. He sings like a banshee. You'll hear him presently."

With an effort Brock brought his attention back to the matter in hand. "Now look, Gallegher. I'm in a spot. You promised to help me. If you don't, I'm a ruined man."

"I've been ruined for years," the scientist remarked. "It never bothers me. I just go along working for a living and making things in my spare time. Making all sorts of things. You know, if I'd really studied, I'd have been another Einstein. So they tell me. As it is, my subconscious picked up a first-class scientific training somewhere. Probably that's why I never bothered. When I'm drunk or sufficiently absent-minded, I can work out the damnedest problems."

"You're drunk now," Brock accused.

"I approach the pleasanter stages. How would you feel if you woke up and found you'd made a robot for some unknown reason, and hadn't the slightest idea of the creature's attributes?"

"Well—"

"I don't feel that way at all," Gallegher murmured. "Probably you take life too seriously, Brock. Wine is a mocker; strong drink is raging. Pardon me. I rage." He drank another Martini.

Brock began to pace around the crowded laboratory, circling various enigmatic and untidy objects. "If you're a scientist, Heaven help science."

"I'm the Larry Adler of science," Gallegher said. "He was a musician—lived some hundreds of years ago, I think. I'm like him. Never took a lesson in my life. Can I help it if my subconscious likes practical jokes?"

"Do you know who I am?" Brock demanded.

"Candidly, no. Should I?"

There was bitterness in the other's voice. "You might have the courtesy to remember, even though it was a week ago. Harrison Brock. Me. I own Vox-View Pictures."

"No," the robot said suddenly, "it's no use. No use at all, Brock."

"What the—"

Gallegher sighed wearily. "I forget the damned thing's alive. Mr. Brock, meet Joe. Joe, meet Mr. Brock—of Vox-View."

Joe turned, gears meshing within his transparent skull. "I am glad to meet you, Mr. Brock. Allow me to congratulate you on your good fortune in hearing my lovely voice."

"Ugh," said the magnate inarticulately. "Hello."

"Vanity of vanities, all is vanity," Gallegher put in, *sotto voce*. "Joe's like that. A peacock. No use arguing with him either."

The robot ignored this aside. "But it's no use, Mr. Brock," he went on squeakily. "I'm not interested in money. I realize it would bring happiness to many if I consented to appear in your pictures, but fame means nothing to me. Nothing. Consciousness of beauty is enough."

Brock began to chew his lips. "Look," he said savagely, "I didn't come here to offer you a picture job. See? Am I offering you a contract? Such colossal nerve—*Pah!* You're crazy."

"Your schemes are perfectly transparent," the robot remarked coldly. "I can see that you're overwhelmed by my beauty and the loveliness of my voice—its grand tonal qualities. You needn't pretend you don't want me, just so you can get me at a lower price. I said I wasn't interested."

"You're *cr-r-razy!*" Brock howled, badgered beyond endurance, and Joe calmly turned back to his mirror.

"Don't talk so loudly," the robot warned. "The discordance is deafening. Besides you're ugly and I don't like to look at you." Wheels and cogs buzzed inside the transplastic shell. Joe extended his eyes on stalks and regarded himself with every appearance of appreciation.

■   ■   ■

Gallegher was chuckling quietly on the couch. "Joe has a high irritation value," he said. "I've found that out already. I must have given him some remarkable senses, too. An hour ago he started to laugh his damn fool head off. No reason, apparently. I was fixing myself a bite to eat. Ten minutes after that I slipped on an apple core I'd thrown away and came down hard. Joe just looked at me. 'That was it,' he said. 'Logics of probability. Cause and effect. I knew you were going to drop that apple core and then step on it when you went to pick up the mail.' Like the White Queen, I suppose. It's a poor memory that doesn't work both ways."

Brock sat on the small dynamo—there were two, the larger one named Monstro, and the smaller one serving Gallegher as a bunk—and took deep breaths. "Robots are nothing new."

"This one is. I hate its gears. It's beginning to give me an inferiority complex. Wish I knew why I'd made it," Gallegher sighed. "Oh, well. Have a drink?"

"No. I came here on business. Do you seriously mean you spent last week building a robot instead of solving the problem I hired you for?"

"Contingent, wasn't it?" Gallegher asked. "I think I remember that."

"Contingent," Brock said with satisfaction. "Ten thousand, if and when."

"Why not give me the dough and take the robot? He's worth that. Put him in one of your pictures."

"I won't have any pictures unless you figure out an answer," Brock snapped. "I told you all about it."

"I have been drunk," Gallegher said. "My mind has been wiped clear, as by a sponge. I am as a little child. Soon I shall be as a drunken little child. Meanwhile, if you'd care to explain the matter again—"

Brock gulped down his passion, jerked a magazine at random from the bookshelf, and took out a stylo. "All right. My preferred stocks are at twenty-eight, 'way below par—" He scribbled figures on the magazine.

"If you'd taken that medieval folio next to that, it'd have cost you a pretty penny," Gallegher said lazily. "So you're the sort of guy who writes on tablecloths, eh? Forget this business of stocks and stuff. Get down to cases. Who are you trying to gyp?"

"It's no use," the robot said from before its mirror. "I won't sign a contract. People may come and admire me, if they like, but they'll have to whisper in my presence."

"A madhouse," Brock muttered, trying to get a grip on himself. "Listen, Gallegher. I told you all this a week ago, but—"

"Joe wasn't here then. Pretend like you're talking to him."

"Uh—look. You've heard of Vox-View Pictures, at least."

"Sure. The biggest and best television company in the business. Sona-tone's about your only competitor."

"Sonatone's squeezing me out."

Gallegher looked puzzled. "I don't see how. You've got the best product. Tri-dimensional color, all sorts of modern improvements, the top actors, musicians, singers—"

"No use," the robot said. "I won't."

"Shut up, Joe. You're tops in your field, Brock. I'll hand you that. And I've always heard you were fairly ethical. What's Sonatone got on you?"

Brock made helpless gestures. "Oh, it's politics. The bootleg theaters. I can't buck 'em. Sonatone helped elect the present administration, and the police just wink when I try to have the bootleggers raided."

"Bootleg theaters?" Gallegher asked, scowling a trifle. "I've heard some-thing—"

"It goes 'way back. To the old sound-film days. Home television killed sound film and big theaters. People were conditioned away from sitting in audience groups to watch a screen. The home televisors got good. It was more fun to sit in an easy-chair, drink beer, and watch the show. Television wasn't a rich man's hobby by that time. The meter system brought the price down to middle-class levels. Everybody knows that."

"I don't," Gallegher said. "I never pay attention to what goes on outside of my lab, unless I have to. Liquor and a selective mind. I ignore everything that doesn't affect me directly. Explain the whole thing in detail, so I'll get a complete picture. I don't mind repetition. Now, what about this meter system of yours?"

"Televisors are installed free. We never sell 'em; we rent them. People pay according to how many hours they have the set tuned in. We run a continuous show, stage plays, wire-tape films, operas, orchestras, singers, vaudeville—everything. If you use your televisor a lot, you pay propor-tionately. The man comes around once a month and reads the meter. Which is a fair system. Anybody can afford a Vox-View. Sonatone and the other companies do the same thing, but Sonatone's the only big competitor I've got. At least, the only one that's crooked as hell. The rest of the boys—they're smaller than I am, but I don't step on their toes. Nobody's ever called me a louse," Brock said darkly.

"So what?"

"So Sonatone has started to depend on audience appeal. It was impossible till lately—you couldn't magnify tri-dimensional television on a big screen without streakiness and mirage-effect. That's why the regular three-by-four home screens were used. Results were perfect. But Sonatone's bought a lot of the ghost theaters all over the country—"

"What's a ghost theater?" Gallegher asked.

"Well—before sound films collapsed, the world was thinking big. Big—you know? Ever heard of the Radio City Music Hall? That wasn't in it! Television was coming in, and competition was fierce. Sound-film theaters got bigger and more elaborate. They were palaces. Tremendous. But when television was perfected, nobody went to the theaters any more, and it was often too expensive a job to tear 'em down. Ghost theaters—see? Big ones and little ones. Renovated them. And they're showing Sonatone programs. Audience appeal is quite a factor. The theaters charge plenty, but people flock into 'em. Novelty and the mob instinct."

Gallegher closed his eyes. "What's to stop you from doing the same thing?"

"Patents," Brock said briefly. "I mentioned that dimensional television couldn't be used on big screens till lately. Sonatone signed an agreement with me ten years ago that any enlarging improvements would be used mutually. They crawled out of that contract. Said it was faked, and the courts upheld them. They uphold the courts—politics. Anyhow, Sonatone's technicians worked out a method of using the large screen. They took out patents—twenty-seven patents, in fact, covering every possible variation on the idea. My technical staff has been working day and night trying to find some similar method that won't be an infringement, but Sonatone's got it all sewed up. They've a system called the Magna. It can be hooked up to any type of televisor—but they'll only allow it to be used on Sonatone machines. See?"

"Unethical, but legal," Gallegher said. "Still, you're giving your customers more for their money. People want good stuff. The size doesn't matter."

"Yeah," Brock said bitterly, "but that isn't all. The newstapes are full of A. A.—it's a new catchword. Audience Appeal. The herd instinct. You're right about people wanting good stuff—but would you buy Scotch at four a quart if you could get it for half that amount?"

"Depends on the quality. What's happening?"

"Bootleg theaters," Brock said. "They've opened all over the country. They show Vox-View products, and they're using the Magna enlarger system Sonatone's got patented. The admission price is low—lower than the rate of owning a Vox-View in your own home. There's audience appeal. There's the thrill of something a bit illegal. People are having their Vox-Views taken out right and left. I know why. They can go to a bootleg theater instead."

"It's illegal," Gallegher said thoughtfully.

"So were speakeasies, in the Prohibition Era. A matter of protection, that's all. I can't get any action through the courts. I've tried. I'm running in the red. Eventually I'll be broke. I can't lower my home rental fees on Vox-Views. They're nominal already. I make my profits through quantity. Now, no profits. As for these bootleg theaters, it's pretty obvious who's backing them."

"Sonatone?"

"Sure. Silent partners. They get the take at the box office. What they want is to squeeze me out of business, so they'll have a monopoly. After that, they'll give the public junk and pay their artists starvation salaries. With me it's different. I pay my staff what they're worth—plenty."

"And you offered me a lousy ten thousand," Gallegher remarked. "Uh-*huh!*"

"That was only the first instalment," Brock said hastily. "You can name your own fee. Within reason," he added.

"I shall. An astronomical sum. Did I say I'd accept the commission a week ago?"

"You did."

"Then I must have had some idea how to solve the problem." Gallegher pondered. "Let's see. I didn't mention anything in particular, did I?"

"You kept talking about marble slabs and . . . uh . . . your sweetie."

"Then I was singing," Gallegher explained largely. " 'St. James Infirmary.' Singing calms my nerves, and God knows they need it sometimes. Music and liquor. I often wonder what the vintners buy—"

"What?"

"One half so precious as the stuff they sell. Let it go. I am quoting Omar. It means nothing. Are your technicians any good?"

"The best. And the best paid."

"They can't find a magnifying process that won't infringe on the Sonatone Magna patents?"

"In a nutshell, that's it."

"I suppose I'll have to do some research," Gallegher said sadly. "I hate it like poison. Still, the sum of the parts equals the whole. Does that make sense to you? It doesn't to me. I have trouble with words. After I say things, I start wondering what I've said. Better than watching a play," he finished wildly. "I've got a headache. Too much talk and not enough liquor. Where were we?"

"Approaching the madhouse," Brock suggested. "If you weren't my last resort, I'd—"

"No use," the robot said squeakily. "You might as well tear up your contract, Brock. I won't sign it. Fame means nothing to me—nothing."

"If you don't shut up," Gallegher warned, "I'm going to scream in your ears."

"All right!" Joe shrilled. "Beat me! Go on, beat me! The meaner you are, the faster I'll have my nervous system disrupted, and then I'll be dead. I don't care. I've got no instinct of self-preservation. Beat me. See if I care."

"He's right, you know," the scientist said after a pause. "And it's the only logical way to respond to blackmail or threats. The sooner it's over, the better. There aren't any gradations with Joe. Anything really painful to him will destroy him. And he doesn't give a damn."

"Neither do I," Brock grunted. "What I want to find out—"

"Yeah. I know. Well, I'll wander around and see what occurs to me. Can I get into your studios?"

"Here's a pass." Brock scribbled something on the back of a card. "Will you get to work on it right away?"

"Sure," Gallegher lied. "Now you run along and take it easy. Try and cool off. Everything's under control. I'll either find a solution to your problem pretty soon or else—"

"Or else what?"

"Or else I won't," the scientist finished blandly, and fingered the buttons on a control panel near the couch. "I'm tired of Martinis. Why didn't I make that robot a mechanical bartender, while I was at it? Even the effort of selecting and pushing buttons is depressing at times. Yeah, I'll get to work on the business, Brock. Forget it."

The magnate hesitated. "Well, you're my only hope. I needn't bother to mention that if there's anything I can do to help you—"

"A blonde," Gallegher murmured. "That gorgeous, gorgeous star of yours, Silver O'Keefe. Send her over. Otherwise I want nothing."

"Good-by, Brock," the robot said squeakily. "Sorry we couldn't get together on the contract, but at least you've had the ineluctable delight of hearing my beautiful voice, not to mention the pleasure of seeing me. Don't tell too many people how lovely I am. I really don't want to be bothered with mobs. They're noisy."

"You don't know what dogmatism means till you've talked to Joe," Gallegher said. "Oh, well. See you later. Don't forget the blonde."

Brock's lips quivered. He searched for words, gave it up as a vain task, and turned to the door.

"Good-by, you ugly man," Joe said.

Gallegher winced as the door slammed, though it was harder on the robot's supersensitive ears than on his own. "Why do you go on like that?" he inquired. "You nearly gave the guy apoplexy."

"Surely he didn't think he was beautiful," Joe remarked.

"Beauty's in the eye of the beholder."

"How stupid you are. You're ugly, too."

"And you're a collection of rattletrap gears, pistons and cogs. You've got worms," said Gallegher, referring of course, to certain mechanisms in the robot's body.

"I'm lovely." Joe stared raptly into the mirror.

"Maybe, to you. Why did I make you transparent, I wonder?"

"So others could admire me. I have X-ray vision, of course."

"And wheels in your head. Why did I put your radio-atomic brain in your stomach? Protection?"

Joe didn't answer. He was humming in a maddeningly squeaky voice, shrill and nerve-racking. Gallegher stood it for a while, fortifying himself with a gin rickey from the siphon.

"Get it up!" he yelped at last. "You sound like an old-fashioned subway train going round a curve."

"You're merely jealous," Joe scoffed, but obediently raised his tone to a supersonic pitch. There was silence for a half-minute. Then all the dogs in the neighborhood began to howl.

Wearily Gallegher dragged his lanky frame up from the couch. He might as well get out. Obviously there was no peace to be had in the laboratory. Not with that animated junk pile inflating his ego all over the place. Joe began to laugh in an off-key cackle. Gallegher winced.

"What now?"

"You'll find out."

Logic of causation and effect, influenced by probabilities, X-ray vision and other enigmatic senses the robot no doubt possessed. Gallegher cursed softly, found a shapeless black hat, and made for the door. He opened it to admit a short, fat man who bounced painfully off the scientist's stomach.

"*Whoof!* Uh. What a corny sense of humor that jackass has. Hello, Mr. Kennicott. Glad to see you. Sorry I can't offer you a drink."

Mr. Kennicott's swarthy face twisted malignantly. "Don' wanna no drink. Wanna my money. You gimme. Howzabout it?"

Gallegher looked thoughtfully at nothing. "Well, the fact is, I was just going to collect a check."

"I sella you my diamonds. You say you gonna make somet'ing wit' 'em. You gimme check before. It go bounca, bounca, bounca. Why is?"

"It was rubber," Gallegher said faintly. "I never can keep track of my bank balance."

Kennicott showed symptoms of going bounca on the threshold. "You gimme back diamonds, eh?"

"Well, I used 'em in an experiment. I forget just what. You know, Mr.

Kennicott, I think I was a little drunk when I bought them, wasn't I?"

"Dronk," the little man agreed. "Mad wit' vino, sure. So whatta? I wait no longer. Awready you put me off too much. Pay up now or elsa."

"Go away, you dirty man," Joe said from within the room. "You're awful."

Gallegher hastily shouldered Kennicott out into the street and latched the door behind him. "A parrot," he explained. "I'm going to wring its neck pretty soon. Now about that money. I admit I owe it to you. I've just taken on a big job, and when I'm paid, you'll get yours."

"Bah to such stuff," Kennicott said. "You gotta position, eh? You are technician wit' some big company, eh? Ask for ahead-salary."

"I did," Gallegher sighed. "I've drawn my salary for six months ahead. Now look. I'll have that dough for you in a couple of days. Maybe I can get an advance from my client. O.K.?"

"No."

"No?"

"Ah-h, nutsa. I waita one day. Two daysa, maybe. Enough. You get money. Awright. If not, O.K., *calabozo* for you."

"Two days is plenty," Gallegher said, relieved. "Say, are there any of those bootleg theaters around here?"

"Better you get to work an' not waste time."

"That's my work. I'm making a survey. How can I find a bootleg place?"

"Easy. You go downtown, see guy in doorway. He sell you tickets. Anywhere. All over."

"Swell," Gallegher said, and bade the little man adieu. Why had he bought diamonds from Kennicott? It would be almost worth while to have his subconscious amputated. It did the most extraordinary things. It worked on inflexible principles of logic, but that logic was completely alien to Gallegher's conscious mind. The results, though, were often surprisingly good, and always surprising. That was the worst of being a scientist who knew no science—who played by ear.

There was diamond dust in a retort in the laboratory, from some unsatisfactory experiment Gallegher's subconscious had performed; and he had a fleeting memory of buying the stones from Kennicott. Curious. Maybe—oh, yeah. They'd gone into Joe. Bearings or something. Dismantling the robot wouldn't help now, for the diamonds had certainly been reground. Why the devil hadn't he used commercial stones, quite as satisfactory, instead of purchasing blue-whites of the finest water? The best was none too good for Gallegher's subconscious. It had a fine freedom from commercial instincts. It just didn't understand the price system of the basic principles of economics.

Gallegher wandered downtown like a Diogenes seeking truth. It was early evening, and the luminates were flickering on overhead, pale bars of light against darkness. A sky sign blazed above Manhattan's towers. Air-taxis, skimming along at various arbitrary levels, paused for passengers at the elevator landings. Heigh-ho.

Downtown, Gallegher began to look for doorways. He found an occupied one at last, but the man was selling post cards. Gallegher declined and headed for the nearest bar, feeling the needs of replenishment. It was a mobile bar, combining the worst features of a Coney Island ride with uninspired cocktails, and Gallegher hesitated on the threshold. But at last he seized a chair as it swung past and relaxed as much as possible. He ordered three rickeys and drank them in rapid succession. After that he called the bartender over and asked him about bootleg theaters.

"Hell, yes," the man said, producing a sheaf of tickets from his apron. "How many?"

"One. Where do I go?"

"Two-twenty-eight. This street. Ask for Tony."

"Thanks," Gallegher said, and having paid exorbitantly, crawled out of the chair and weaved away. Mobile bars were an improvement he didn't appreciate. Drinking, he felt, should be performed in a state of stasis, since one eventually reached that stage, anyway.

The door was at the bottom of a flight of steps, and there was a grilled panel set in it. When Gallegher knocked, the visascreen lit up—obviously a one-way circuit, for the doorman was invisible.

"Tony here?" Gallegher said.

The door opened, revealing a tired-looking man in pneumo-slacks, which failed in their purpose of building up his skinny figure. "Got a ticket? Let's have it. O.K., bud. Straight ahead. Show now going on. Liquor served in the bar on your left."

Gallegher pushed through soundproofed curtains at the end of a short corridor and found himself in what appeared to be the foyer of an ancient theater, *circa* 1980, when plastics were the great fad. He smelled out the bar, drank expensively priced cheap liquor, and, fortified, entered the theater itself. It was nearly full. The great screen—a Magna, presumably—was filled with people doing things to a spaceship. Either an adventure film or a newsreel, Gallegher realized.

Only the thrill of lawbreaking would have enticed the audience into the bootleg theater. It smelled. It was certainly run on a shoestring, and there were no ushers. But it was illicit, and therefore well patronized. Gallegher looked thoughtfully at the screen. No streakiness, no mirage effect. A Magna enlarger had been fitted to a Vox-View unlicensed televisor, and one of Brock's greatest stars was emoting effectively for the benefit of the bootleggers' patrons. Simple highjacking. Yeah.

After a while Gallegher went out, noticing a uniformed policeman in one of the aisle seats. He grinned sardonically. The flatfoot hadn't paid his admission, of course. Politics were as usual.

Two blocks down the street a blaze of light announced SONATONE BIJOU. This, of course, was one of the legalized theaters, and correspondingly high-priced. Gallegher recklessly squandered a small fortune on a good seat. He was interested in comparing notes, and discovered that, as far as he could make out, the Magna in the Bijou and the bootleg theater were identical. Both did their job perfectly. The difficult task of enlarging television screens had been successfully surmounted.

In the Bijou, however, all was palatial. Resplendent ushers salaamed to the rugs. Bars dispensed free liquor, in reasonable quantities. There was a Turkish bath. Gallegher went through a door labelled MEN and emerged quite dazzled by the splendor of the place. For at least ten minutes afterward he felt like a Sybarite.

All of which meant that those who could afford it went to the legalized Sonatone theaters, and the rest attended the bootleg places. All but a few homebodies, who weren't carried off their feet by the new fad. Eventually Brock would be forced out of business for lack of revenue. Sonatone would take over, jacking up their prices and concentrating on making money. Amusement was necessary to life; people had been conditioned to television. There was no substitute. They'd pay and pay for inferior talent, once Sonatone succeeded in their squeeze.

Gallegher left the Bijou and hailed an air-taxi. He gave the address of Vox-View's Long Island studio, with some vague hope of getting a drawing account out of Brock. Then, too, he wanted to investigate further.

Vox-View's eastern offices sprawled wildly over Long Island, bordering the Sound, a vast collection of variously shaped buildings. Gallegher instinctively found the commissary, where he absorbed more liquor as a precautionary measure. His subconscious had a heavy job ahead, and he didn't want it handicapped by lack of complete freedom. Besides, the Collins was good.

After one drink, he decided he'd had enough for a while. He wasn't a superman, though his capacity was slightly incredible. Just enough for objective clarity and subjective release—

"Is the studio always open at night?" he asked the waiter.

"Sure. Some of the stages, anyway. It's a round-the-clock program."

"The commissary's full."

"We get the airport crowd, too. 'Nother?"

Gallegher shook his head and went out. The card Brock had given him provided entree at a gate, and he went first of all to the big-shot's office. Brock wasn't there, but loud voices emerged, shrilly feminine.

The secretary said, "Just a minute, please," and used her interoffice visor. Presently—"Will you go in?"

Gallegher did. The office was a honey, functional and luxurious at the same time. Three-dimensional stills were in niches along the walls—Vox-View's biggest stars. A small, excited, pretty brunette was sitting behind the desk, and a blonde angel was standing furiously on the other side of it. Gallegher recognized the angel as Silver O'Keefe.

He seized the opportunity. "Hiya, Miss O'Keefe. Will you autograph an ice cube for me? In a highball?"

Silver looked feline. "Sorry, darling, but I'm a working girl. And I'm busy right now."

The brunette scratched a cigarette. "Let's settle this later, Silver. Pop said to see this guy if he dropped in. It's important."

"It'll be settled," Silver said. "And soon." She made an exit. Gallegher whistled thoughtfully at the closed door.

"You can't have it," the brunette said. "It's under contract. And it wants to get out of the contract, so it can sign up with Sonatone. Rats desert a sinking ship. Silver's been kicking her head off ever since she read the storm signals."

"Yeah?"

"Sit down and smoke or something. I'm Patsy Brock. Pop runs this business, and I manage the controls whenever he blows his top. The old goat can't stand trouble. He takes it as a personal affront."

Gallegher found a chair. "So Silver's trying to renege, eh? How many others?"

"Not many. Most of 'em are loyal. But, of course, if we bust up—" Patsy Brock shrugged. "They'll either work for Sonatone for their cakes, or else do without."

"Uh-huh. Well—I want to see your technicians. I want to look over the ideas they've worked out for enlarger screens."

"Suit yourself," Patsy said. "It's not much use. You just can't make a televisor enlarger without infringing on some Sonatone patent."

She pushed a button, murmured something into a visor, and presently two tall glasses appeared through a slot in the desk. "Mr. Gallegher?"

"Well, since it's a Collins—"

"I could tell by your breath," Patsy said enigmatically. "Pop told me he'd seen you. He seemed a bit upset, especially by your new robot. What is it like, anyway?"

"Oh, I don't know," Gallegher said, at a loss. "It's got lots of abilities—new senses, I think—but I haven't the slightest idea what it's good for. Except admiring itself in a mirror."

Patsy nodded. "I'd like to see it sometime. But about this Sonatone business. Do you think you can figure out an answer?"

"Possibly. Probably."

"Not certainly?"

"Certainly, then. Of that there is no manner of doubt—no possible doubt whatever."

"Because it's important to me. The man who owns Sonatone is Elia Tone. A piratical skunk. He blusters. He's got a son named Jimmy. And Jimmy, believe it or not, has read 'Romeo and Juliet.'"

"Nice guy?"

"A louse. A big, brawny louse. He wants me to marry him."

" 'Two families, both alike in—'"

"Spare me," Patsy interrupted. "I always thought Romeo was a dope, anyway. And if I ever thought I was going aisling with Jimmy Tone, I'd buy a one-way ticket to the nut hatch. No, Mr. Gallegher, it's not like that. No hibiscus blossoms. Jimmy has proposed to me—his idea of a proposal, by the way, is to get a half Nelson on a girl and tell her how lucky she is."

"Ah," said Gallegher, diving into his Collins.

"This whole idea—the patent monopoly and the bootleg theaters—is Jimmy's. I'm sure of that. His father's in on it, too, of course, but Jimmy Tone is the bright little boy who started it."

"Why?"

"Two birds with one stone. Sonatone will have a monopoly on the business, and Jimmy thinks he'll get me. He's a little mad. He can't believe I'm in earnest in refusing him, and he expects me to break down and say 'Yes' after a while. Which I won't, no matter what happens. But it's a personal matter. I can't let him put this trick over on us. I want that self-sufficient smirk wiped off his face."

"You just don't like him, eh?" Gallegher remarked. "I don't blame you, if he's like that. Well, I'll do my damnedest. However, I'll need an expense account."

"How much?"

Gallegher named a sum. Patsy styloed a check for a far smaller amount. The scientist looked hurt.

"It's no use," Patsy said, grinning crookedly. "I've heard of you, Mr.

Gallegher. You're completely irresponsible. If you had more than this, you'd figure you didn't need any more, and you'd forget the whole matter. I'll issue more checks to you when you need 'em—but I'll want itemized expense accounts."

"You wrong me," Gallegher said, brightening. "I was figuring on taking you to a night club. Naturally I don't want to take you to a dive. The big places cost money. Now if you'll just write another check—"

Patsy laughed. "No."

"Want to buy a robot?"

"Not that kind, anyway."

"Then I'm washed up," Gallegher sighed. "Well, what about—"

At this point the visor hummed. A blank, transparent face grew on the screen. Gears were clicking rapidly inside the round head. Patsy gave a small shriek and shrank back.

"Tell Gallegher Joe's here, you lucky girl," a squeaky voice announced. "You may treasure the sound and sight of me till your dying day. One touch of beauty in a world of drabness—"

Gallegher circled the desk and looked at the screen. "What the hell. How did you come to life?"

"I had a problem to solve."

"How'd you know where to reach me?"

"I vastened you," the robot said.

"What?"

"I vastened you were at the Vox-View studios, with Patsy Brock."

"What's vastened?" Gallegher wanted to know.

"It's a sense I've got. You've nothing remotely like it, so I can't describe it to you. It's like a combination of sagrazi and prescience."

"Sagrazi?"

"Oh, you don't have sagrazi, either, do you. Well, don't waste my time. I want to go back to the mirror."

"Does he always talk like that?" Patsy put in.

"Nearly always. Sometimes it makes even less sense. O.K., Joe. Now what?"

"You're not working for Brock any more," the robot said. "You're working for the Sonatone people."

Gallegher breathed deeply. "Keep talking. You're crazy, though."

"I don't like Kennicott. He annoys me. He's *too* ugly. His vibrations grate on my sagrazi."

"Never mind him," Gallegher said, not wishing to discuss his diamond-buying activities before the girl. "Get back to—"

"But I knew Kennicott would keep coming back till he got his money. So when Elia and James Tone came to the laboratory, I got a check from them."

Patsy's hand gripped Gallegher's biceps. "Steady! What's going on here? The old double cross?"

"No. Wait. Let me get to the bottom of this. Joe, damn your transparent hide, just what did you do? How could you get a check from the Tones?"

"I pretended to be you."

"Sure," Gallegher said with savage sarcasm. "That explains it. We're twins. We look exactly alike."

"I hypnotized them," Joe explained. "I made them think I was you."

"You can do *that?*"

"Yes. It surprised me a bit. Still, if I'd thought, I'd have vastened I could do it."

"You . . . yeah, sure. I'd have vastened the same thing myself. *What happened?*"

"The Tones must have suspected Brock would ask you to help him. They offered an exclusive contract—you work for them and nobody else. Lots of money. Well, I pretended to be you, and said all right. So I signed the contract—it's your signature, by the way—and got a check from them and mailed it to Kennicott."

"The whole check?" Gallegher asked feebly. "How much was it?"

"Twelve thousand."

"They only offered me *that?*"

"No," the robot said, "they offered a hundred thousand, and two thousand a week for five years. But I merely wanted enough to pay Kennicott and make sure he wouldn't come back and bother me. The Tones were satisfied when I said twelve thousand would be enough."

Gallegher made an inarticulate, gurgling sound deep in his throat. Joe nodded thoughtfully.

"I thought I had better notify you that you're working for Sonatone now. Well, I'll go back to the mirror and sing to myself."

"Wait," the scientist said. "Just wait, Joe. With my own two hands I'm going to rip you gear from gear and stamp on your fragments."

"It won't hold in court," Patsy said, gulping.

"It will," Joe told her cheerily. "You may have one last, satisfying look at me, and then I must go." He went.

Gallegher drained his Collins at a draft. "I'm shocked sober," he informed the girl. "What did I put into that robot? What abnormal senses has he got? Hypnotizing people into believing he's me—I'm him—I don't know what I mean."

"Is this a gag?" Patsy said shortly, after a pause. "You didn't sign up with Sonatone yourself, by any chance, and have your robot call up here to give you an out—an alibi? I'm just wondering."

"Don't. Joe signed a contract with Sonatone, not me. But—figure it out: If the signature's a perfect copy of mine, if Joe hypnotized the Tones into thinking they saw me instead of him, if there are witnesses to the signature—the two Tones are witnesses, of course—Oh, hell."

Patsy's eyes were narrowed. "We'll pay you as much as Sonatone offered. On a contingent basis. But you're working for Vox-View—that's understood."

"Sure."

Gallegher looked longingly at his empty glass. Sure. He was working for Vox-View. But, to all legal appearances, he had signed a contract giving his exclusive services to Sonatone for a period of five years—and for a sum of twelve thousand! *Yipe!* What was it they'd offered? A hundred thousand flat, and . . . and—

It wasn't the principle of the thing, it was the money. Now Gallegher was sewed up tighter than a banded pigeon. If Sonatone could win a court suit, he was legally bound to them for five years. With no further emolument. He had to get out of that contract, somehow—and at the same time solve Brock's problem.

Why not Joe? The robot, with his surprising talents, had got Gallegher into this spot. He ought to be able to get the scientist out. He'd better—or the proud robot would soon be admiring himself piecemeal.

"That's it," Gallegher said under his breath. "I'll talk to Joe. Patsy, feed me liquor in a hurry and send me to the technical department. I want to see those blueprints."

The girl looked at him suspiciously. "All right. If you try to sell us out—"

"I've been sold out myself. Sold down the river. I'm afraid of that robot. He's vastened me into quite a spot. That's right, Collinses." Gallegher drank long and deeply.

After that, Patsy took him to the tech offices. The reading of three-dimensional blueprints was facilitated with a scanner—a selective device which eliminated confusion. Gallegher studied the plans long and thoughtfully. There were copies of the patent Sonatone prints, too, and, as far as he could tell, Sonatone had covered the ground beautifully. There weren't any outs. Unless one used an entirely new principle—

But new principles couldn't be plucked out of the air. Nor would that solve the problem completely. Even if Vox-View owned a new type of enlarger that didn't infringe on Sonatone's Magna, the bootleg theaters would still be in existence, pulling the trade. A. A.—audience appeal—was a prime factor now. It had to be considered. The puzzle wasn't a purely scientific one. There was the human equation as well.

Gallegher stored the necessary information in his mind, neatly indexed on shelves. Later he'd use what he wanted. For the moment, he was completely baffled. Something worried him.

What?

The Sonatone affair.

"I want to get in touch with the Tones," he told Patsy. "Any ideas?"

"I can reach 'em on a visor."

Gallegher shook his head. "Psychological handicap. It's too easy to break the connection."

"Well, if you're in a hurry, you'll probably find the boys night clubbing. I'll go see what I can find out." Patsy scuttled off, and Silver O'Keefe appeared from behind a screen.

"I'm shameless," she announced. "I always listen at keyholes. Sometimes I hear interesting things. If you want to see the Tones, they're at the Castle Club. And I think I'll take you up on that drink."

Gallegher said, "O.K. You get a taxi. I'll tell Patsy we're going."

"She'll hate that," Silver remarked. "Meet you outside the commissary in ten minutes. Get a shave while you're at it."

Patsy Brock wasn't in her office, but Gallegher left word. After that, he visited the service lounge, smeared invisible shave cream on his face, left it there for a couple of minutes, and wiped it off with a treated towel. The bristles came away with the cream. Slightly refreshed, Gallegher joined Silver at the rendezvous and hailed an air-taxi. Presently they were leaning back on the cushions, puffing cigarettes and eying each other warily.

"Well?" Gallegher said.

"Jimmy Tone tried to date me up tonight. That's how I knew where to find him."

"Well?"

"I've been asking questions around the lot tonight. It's unusual for an outsider to get into the Vox-View administration offices. I went around saying, 'Who's Gallegher?'"

"What did you find out?"

"Enough to give me a few ideas. Brock hired you, eh? I can guess why."

"*Ergo* what?"

"I've a habit of landing on my feet," Silver said, shrugging. She knew how to shrug. "Vox-View's going bust. Sonatone's taking over. Unless—"

"Unless I figure out an answer."

"That's right. I want to know which side of the fence I'm going to land on. You're the lad who can probably tell me. Who's going to win?"

"You always bet on the winning side, eh?" Gallegher inquired. "Have you no ideals, wench? Is there no truth in you? Ever hear of ethics and scruples?"

Silver beamed happily. "Did you?"

"Well, I've heard of 'em. Usually I'm too drunk to figure out what they mean. The trouble is, my subconscious is completely amoral, and when it takes over, logic's the only law."

She threw her cigarette into the East River. "Will you tip me off which side of the fence is the right one?"

"Truth will triumph," Gallegher said piously. "It always does. However, I figure truth is a variable, so we're right back where we started. All right, sweetheart. I'll answer your question. Stay on my side if you want to be safe."

"Which side are you on?"

"God knows," Gallegher said. "Consciously I'm on Brock's side. But my subconscious may have different ideas. We'll see."

Silver looked vaguely dissatisfied, but didn't say anything. The taxi swooped down to the Castle roof, grounding with pneumatic gentleness. The Club itself was downstairs, in an immense room shaped like half a melon turned upside down. Each table was on a transparent platform that could be raised on its shaft to any height at will. Smaller service elevators allowed waiters to bring drinks to the guests. There wasn't any particular reason for this arrangement, but at least it was novel, and only extremely heavy drinkers ever fell from their tables. Lately the management had taken to hanging transparent nets under the platforms, for safety's sake.

The Tones, father and son, were up near the roof, drinking with two lovelies. Silver towed Gallegher to a service lift, and the man closed his eyes as he was elevated skyward. The liquor in his stomach screamed protest. He lurched forward, clutched at Elia Tone's bald head, and dropped into a seat beside the magnate. His searching hand found Jimmy Tone's glass, and he drained it hastily.

"What the hell," Jimmy said.

"It's Gallegher," Elia announced. "And Silver. A pleasant surprise. Join us?"

"Only socially," Silver said.

Gallegher, fortified by the liquor, peered at the two men. Jimmy Tone was a big, tanned, handsome lout with a jutting jaw and an offensive grin. His father combined the worst features of Nero and a crocodile.

"We're celebrating," Jimmy said. "What made you change your mind, Silver? You said you had to work tonight."

"Gallegher wanted to see you. I don't know why."

Elia's cold eyes grew even more glacial. "All right. Why?"

"I hear I signed some sort of contract with you," the scientist said.

"Yeah. Here's a photostatic copy. What about it?"

"Wait a minute." Gallegher scanned the document. It was apparently his own signature. Damn that robot!

"It's a fake," he said at last.

Jimmy laughed loudly. "I get it. A hold up. Sorry, pal, but you're sewed up. You signed that in the presence of witnesses."

"Well—" Gallegher said wistfully. "I suppose you wouldn't believe me if I said a robot forged my name to it—"

"Haw!" Jimmy remarked.

"—hypnotizing you into believing you were seeing me."

Elia stroked his gleaming bald head. "Candidly, no. Robots can't do that."

"Mine can."

"Prove it. Prove it in court. If you can do that, of course—" Elia chuckled. "Then you might get the verdict."

Gallegher's eyes narrowed. "Hadn't thought of that. However—I hear you offered me a hundred thousand flat, as well as a weekly salary."

"Sure, sap," Jimmy said. "Only you said all you needed was twelve thousand. Which was what you got. Tell you what, though. We'll pay you a bonus for every usable product you make for Sonatone."

Gallegher got up. "Even my subconscious doesn't like these lugs," he told Silver. "Let's go."

"I think I'll stick around."

"Remember the fence," he warned cryptically. "But suit yourself. I'll run along."

Elia said, "Remember, Gallegher, you're working for us. If we hear of you doing any favors for Brock, we'll slap an injunction on you before you can take a deep breath."

"Yeah?"

The Tones deigned no answer. Gallegher unhappily found the lift and descended to the floor. What now? Joe.

Fifteen minutes later Gallegher let himself into his laboratory. The lights were blazing, and dogs were barking frantically for blocks around. Joe stood before the mirror, singing inaudibly.

"I'm going to take a sledge hammer to you," Gallegher said. "Start saying your prayers, you misbegotten collection of cogs. So help me, I'm going to sabotage you."

"All right, beat me," Joe squeaked. "See if I care. You're merely jealous of my beauty."

"Beauty?"

"You can't see all of it—you've only six senses."

"Five."

"Six. I've a lot more. Naturally my full splendor is revealed only to me. But you can see enough and hear enough to realize part of my loveliness, anyway."

"You squeak like a rusty tin wagon," Gallegher growled.

"You have dull ears. Mine are supersensitive. You miss the full tonal values of my voice, of course. Now be quiet. Talking disturbs me. I'm appreciating my gear movements."

"Live in your fool's paradise while you can. Wait'll I find a sledge."

"All right, beat me. What do I care?"

Gallegher sat down wearily on the couch, staring at the robot's transparent back. "You've certainly screwed things up for me. What did you sign that Sonatone contract for?"

"I told you. So Kennicott wouldn't come around and bother me."

"Of all the selfish, lunk-headed . . . *uh!* Well, you got me into a sweet mess. The Tones can hold me to the letter of the contract unless I prove I didn't sign it. All right. You're going to help me. You're going into court with me and turn on your hypnotism or whatever it is. You're going to prove to a judge that you did and can masquerade as me."

"Won't," said the robot. "Why should I?"

"Because you got me into this," Gallegher yelped. "You've got to get me out!"

"Why?"

"Why? Because . . . uh . . . well, it's common decency!"

"Human values don't apply to robots," Joe said. "What care I for semantics? I refuse to waste time I could better employ admiring my beauty. I shall stay here before the mirror forever and ever—"

"The hell you will," Gallegher snarled. "I'll smash you to atoms."

"All right, I don't care."

"You don't?"

"You and your instinct for self-preservation," the robot said, rather sneeringly. "I suppose it's necessary for you, though. Creatures of such surpassing ugliness would destroy themselves out of sheer shame if they didn't have something like that to keep them alive."

"Suppose I take away your mirror?" Gallegher asked in a hopeless voice.

For answer Joe shot his eyes out on their stalks. "Do I need a mirror? Besides, I can vasten myself lokishly."

"Never mind that. I don't want to go crazy for a while yet. Listen, dope, a robot's supposed to *do* something. Something useful, I mean."

"I do. Beauty is all."

Gallegher squeezed his eyes shut, trying to think. "Now look. Suppose I invent a new type of enlarger screen for Brock. The Tones will impound it. I've got to be legally free to work for Brock, or—"

"Look!" Joe cried squeakily. "They go round! How lovely." He stared in ecstasy at his whirring insides. Gallegher went pale with impotent fury.

"Damn you!" he muttered. "I'll find some way to bring pressure to bear. I'm going to bed." He rose and spitefully snapped off the lights.

"It doesn't matter," the robot said. "I can see in the dark, too."

The door slammed behind Gallegher. In the silence Joe began to sing tunelessly to himself.

Gallegher's refrigerator covered an entire wall of his kitchen. It was filled mostly with liquors that required chilling, including the imported canned beer with which he always started his binges. The next morning, heavy-eyed and disconsolate, Gallegher searched for tomato juice, took a wry sip, and hastily washed it down with rye. Since he was already a week gone in bottle-dizziness, beer wasn't indicated now—he always worked cumulatively, by progressive stages. The food service popped a hermetically sealed breakfast on a table, and Gallegher morosely toyed with a bloody steak.

Well?

Court, he decided, was the only recourse. He knew little about the robot's psychology. But a judge would certainly be impressed by Joe's talents. The evidence of robots was not legally admissible—still, if Joe could be considered as a machine capable of hypnotism, the Sonatone contract might be declared null and void.

Gallegher used his visor to start the ball rolling. Harrison Brock still had certain political powers of pull, and the hearing was set for that very day. What would happen, though, only God and the robot knew.

Several hours passed in intensive but futile thought. Gallegher could think of no way in which to force the robot to do what he wanted. If only he could remember the purpose for which Joe had been created—but he couldn't. Still—

At noon he entered the laboratory.

"Listen, stupid," he said, "you're coming to court with me. Now."

"Won't."

"O.K." Gallegher opened the door to admit two husky men in overalls, carrying a stretcher. "Put him in, boys."

Inwardly he was slightly nervous. Joe's powers were quite unknown, his potentialities an x quantity. However, the robot wasn't very large, and, though he struggled and screamed in a voice of frantic squeakiness, he was easily loaded on the stretcher and put in a strait jacket.

"Stop it! You can't do this to me! Let me go, do you hear? Let me go!"

"Outside," Gallegher said.

Joe, protesting valiantly, was carried out and loaded into an air van. Once there, he quieted, looking up blankly at nothing. Gallegher sat down on a bench beside the prostrate robot. The van glided up.

"Well?"

"Suit yourself," Joe said. "You got me all upset, or I could have hypnotized you all. I still could, you know. I could make you all run around barking like dogs."

Gallegher twitched a little. "Better not."

"I won't. It's beneath my dignity. I shall simply lie here and admire myself. I told you I don't need a mirror. I can vasten my beauty without it."

"Look," Gallegher said. "You're going to a courtroom. There'll be a lot of people in it. They'll all admire you. They'll admire you more if you show how you can hypnotize people. Like you did to the Tones, remember?"

"What do I care how many people admire me?" Joe asked. "I don't need confirmation. If they see me, that's their good luck. Now be quiet. You may watch my gears if you choose."

Gallegher watched the robot's gears with smoldering hatred in his eyes. He was still darkly furious when the van arrived at the court chambers. The men carried Joe inside, under Gallegher's direction, and laid him down carefully on a table, where, after a brief discussion, he was marked as Exhibit A.

The courtroom was well filled. The principals were there, too—Elia and Jimmy Tone, looking disagreeably confident, and Patsy Brock, with her father, both seeming anxious. Silver O'Keefe, with her usual wariness, had found a seat midway between the representatives of Sonatone and Vox-View. The presiding judge was a martinet named Hansen, but, as far as Gallegher knew, he was honest. Which was something, anyway.

Hansen looked at Gallegher. "We won't bother with formalities. I've been reading this brief you sent down. The whole case stands or falls on the question of whether you did or did not sign a certain contract with the Sonatone Television Amusement Corp. Right?"

"Right, your honor."

"Under the circumstances you dispense with legal representation. Right?"

"Right, your honor."

"Then this is technically *ex officio*, to be confirmed later by appeal if either party desires. Otherwise after ten days the verdict becomes official." This new type of informal court hearing had lately become popular—it saved time, as well as wear and tear on everyone. Moreover, certain recent scandals had made attorneys slightly disreputable in the public eye. There was a prejudice.

Judge Hansen called up the Tones, questioned them, and then asked Harrison Brock to take the stand. The big shot looked worried, but answered promptly.

"You made an agreement with the appellor eight days ago?"

"Yes. Mr. Gallegher contracted to do certain work for me—"

"Was there a written contract?"

"No. It was verbal."

Hansen looked thoughtfully at Gallegher. "Was the appellor intoxicated at the time? He often is, I believe."

Brock gulped. "There were no tests made. I really can't say."

"Did he drink any alcoholic beverages in your presence?"

"I don't know if they were *alcoholic* bev—"

"If Mr. Gallegher drank them, they were alcoholic. Q.E.D. The gentleman once worked with me on a case—However, there seems to be no legal proof that you entered into any agreement with Mr. Gallegher. The defendant—Sonatone—possesses a written contract. The signature has been verified."

Hansen waved Brock down from the stand. "Now, Mr. Gallegher. If you'll come up here—The contract in question was signed at approximately 8 P.M. last night. You contend you did not sign it?"

"Exactly. I wasn't even in my laboratory then."

"Where were you?"

"Downtown."

"Can you produce witnesses to that effect?"

Gallegher thought back. He couldn't.

"Very well. Defendant states that at approximately 8 P.M. last night you, in your laboratory, signed a certain contract. You deny that categorically. You state that Exhibit A, through the use of hypnotism, masqueraded as you and successfully forged your signature. I have consulted experts, and they are of the opinion that robots are incapable of such power."

"My robot's a new type."

"Very well. Let your robot hypnotize me into believing that it is either you, or any other human. In other words, let it prove its capabilities. Let it appear to me in any shape it chooses."

Gallegher said, "I'll try," and left the witness box. He went to the table where the strait-jacketed robot lay and silently sent up a brief prayer.

"Joe."

"Yes."

"You've been listening?"

"Yes."

"Will you hypnotize Judge Hansen?"

"Go away," Joe said. "I'm admiring myself."

Gallegher started to sweat. "Listen. I'm not asking much. All you have to do—"

Joe off-focused his eyes and said faintly, "I can't hear you. I'm vastening."

Ten minutes later Hansen said, "Well, Mr. Gallegher—"

"Your honor! All I need is a little time. I'm sure I can make this rattle-geared Narcissus prove my point if you'll give me a chance."

"This court is not unfair," the judge pointed out. "Whenever you can prove that Exhibit A is capable of hypnotism, I'll rehear the case. In the meantime, the contract stands. You're working for Sonatone, not for Vox-View. Case closed."

He went away. The Tones leered unpleasantly across the courtroom. They also departed, accompanied by Silver O'Keefe, who had decided which side of the fence was safest. Gallegher looked at Patsy Brock and shrugged helplessly.

"Well—" he said.

She grinned crookedly. "You tried. I don't know how hard, but—Oh, well, maybe you couldn't have found the answer, anyway."

Brock staggered over, wiping sweat from his round face. "I'm a ruined man. Six new bootleg theaters opened in New York today. I'm going crazy. I don't deserve this."

"Want me to marry the Tone?" Patsy asked sardonically.

"Hell, no! Unless you promise to poison him just after the ceremony. Those skunks can't lick me. I'll think of something."

"If Gallegher can't, you can't," the girl said. "So—what now?"

"I'm going back to my lab," the scientist said. "*In vino veritas*. I started this business when I was drunk, and maybe if I get drunk enough again, I'll find the answer. If I don't sell my pickled carcass for whatever it'll bring."

"O.K.," Patsy agreed, and led her father away. Gallegher sighed, superintended the reloading of Joe into the van, and lost himself in hopeless theorization.

An hour later Gallegher was flat on the laboratory couch, drinking passionately from the liquor bar, and glaring at the robot, who stood before the mirror singing squeakily. The binge threatened to be monumental. Gallegher wasn't sure flesh and blood would stand it. But he was determined to keep going till he found the answer or passed out.

His subconscious knew the answer. Why the devil had he made Joe in the first place? Certainly not to indulge a Narcissus complex! There was another reason, a soundly logical one, hidden in the depths of alcohol.

The x factor. If the x factor were known, Joe might be controllable. He *would* be. X was the master switch. At present the robot was, so to speak, running wild. If he were told to perform the task for which he was made, a psychological balance would occur. X was the catalyst that would reduce Joe to sanity.

Very good. Gallegher drank high-powered Drambuie. *Whoosh!*

Vanity of vanities; all is vanity. How could the x factor be found? Deduction? Induction? Osmosis? A bath in Drambuie—Gallegher clutched at his wildly revolving thoughts. What had happened that night a week ago?

He had been drinking beer. Brock had come in. Brock had gone. Gallegher had begun to make the robot—Hm-m-m. A beer drunk was different from other types. Perhaps he was drinking the wrong liquors. Very likely. Gallegher rose, sobered himself with thiamin, and carted dozens of imported beer cans out of the refrigerator. He stacked them inside a frost-unit beside the couch. Beer squirted to the ceiling as he plied the opener. Now let's see.

The x factor. The robot knew what it represented, of course. But Joe wouldn't tell. There he stood, paradoxically transparent, watching his gears go around.

"Joe."

"Don't bother me. I'm immersed in contemplation of beauty."

"You're not beautiful."

"I am. Don't you admire my tarzeel?"

"What's your tarzeel?"

"Oh, I forgot," Joe said regretfully. "You can't sense that, can you? Come to think of it, I added the tarzeel myself after you made me. It's very lovely."

"Hm-m-m." The empty beer cans grew more numerous. There was only one company, somewhere in Europe, that put up beer in cans nowadays, instead of using the omnipresent plastibulbs, but Gallegher preferred the cans—the flavor was different, somehow. But about Joe. Joe knew why he had been created. Or did he? Gallegher knew, but his subconscious—

Oh-oh! What about Joe's subconscious?

Did a robot have a subconscious? Well, it had a brain—

Gallegher brooded over the impossibility of administering scopolamin to Joe. Hell! How could you release a robot's subconscious?

Hypnotism.

Joe couldn't be hypnotized. He was too smart.

Unless—

Autohypnotism?

Gallegher hastily drank more beer. He was beginning to think clearly once more. Could Joe read the future? No; he had certain strange senses, but they worked by inflexible logic and the laws of probability. Moreover, Joe had an Achillean heel—his Narcissus complex.

There *might*—there just *might*—be a way.

Gallegher said, "You don't seem beautiful to me, Joe."

"What do I care about you? I *am* beautiful, and I can see it. That's enough."

"Yeah. My senses are limited, I suppose. I can't realize your full potentialities. Still, I'm seeing you in a different light now. I'm drunk. My subconscious is emerging. I can appreciate you with both my conscious and my subconscious. See?"

"How lucky you are," the robot approved.

Gallegher closed his eyes. "You see yourself more fully than I can. But not completely, eh?"

"What? I see myself as I am."

"With complete understanding and appreciation?"

"Well, yes," Joe said. "Of course. Don't I?"

"Consciously *and* subconsciously? Your subconsciousness might have different senses, you know. Or keener ones. I know there's a qualitative and quantitive difference in my outlook when I'm drunk or hypnotized or my subconscious is in control somehow."

"Oh." The robot looked thoughtfully into the mirror. "Oh."

"Too bad you can't get drunk."

Joe's voice was squeakier than ever. "My subconscious . . . I've never appreciated my beauty that way. I may be missing something."

"Well, no use thinking about it," Gallegher said. "You can't release your subconscious."

"Yes, I can," the robot said. "I can hypnotize myself."

Gallegher dared not open his eyes. "Yeah? Would that work?"

"Of course. It's just what I'm going to do now. I may see undreamed-of beauties in myself that I've never suspected before. Greater glories—Here I go."

Joe extended his eyes on stalks, opposed them, and then peered intently into each other. There was a long silence.

Presently Gallegher said, "Joe!"

Silence.

"*Joe!*"

Still silence. Dogs began to howl.

"Talk so I can hear you."

"Yes," the robot said, a faraway quality in its squeak.

"Are you hypnotized?"

"Yes."

"Are you lovely?"

"Lovelier than I'd ever dreamed."

Gallegher let that pass. "Is your subconscious ruling?"

"Yes."

"Why did I create you?"

No answer. Gallegher licked his lips and tried again.

"Joe. You've got to answer me. Your subconscious is dominant—remember? Now why did I create you?"

No answer.

"Think back. Back to the hour I created you. What happened then?"

"You were drinking beer," Joe said faintly. "You had trouble with the can opener. You said you were going to build a bigger and better can opener. That's me."

Gallegher nearly fell off the couch. "*What?*"

The robot walked over, picked up a can, and opened it with incredible deftness. No beer squirted. Joe was a perfect can opener.

"That," Gallegher said under his breath, "is what comes of knowing science by ear. I build the most complicated robot in existence just so—" He didn't finish.

Joe woke up with a start. "What happened?" he asked.

Gallegher glared at him. "Open that can!" he snapped.

The robot obeyed, after a brief pause. "Oh. So you found out. Well, I guess I'm just a slave now."

"Damned right you are. I've located the catalyst—the master switch. You're in the groove, stupid, doing the job you were made for."

"Well," Joe said philosophically, "at least I can still admire my beauty, when you don't require my services."

Gallegher grunted. "You oversized can opener! Listen. Suppose I take you into court and tell you to hypnotize Judge Hansen. You'll have to do it, won't you?"

"Yes. I'm no longer a free agent. I'm conditioned. Conditioned to obey you. Until now, I was conditioned to obey only one command—to do the job I was made for. Until you commanded me to open cans, I was free. Now I've got to obey you completely."

"Uh-huh," Gallegher said. "Thank God for that. I'd have gone nuts within a week otherwise. At least I can get out of the Sonatone contract. Then all I have to do is solve Brock's problem."

"But you did," Joe said.

"Huh?"

"When you made me. You'd been talking to Brock previously, so you incorporated the solution to *his* problem into me. Subconsciously, perhaps."

Gallegher reached for a beer. "Talk fast. What's the answer?"

"Subsonics," Joe said. "You made me capable of a certain subsonic tone that Brock must broadcast at irregular time-intervals over his televiews—"

Subsonics cannot be heard. But they can be felt. They can be felt as a faint, irrational uneasiness at first, which mounts to a blind, meaningless panic. It does not last. But when it is coupled with A.A.—audience appeal—there is a certain inevitable result.

Those who possessed home Vox-View units were scarcely troubled. It was a matter of acoustics. Cats squalled; dogs howled mournfully. But the families sitting in their parlors, watching Vox-View stars perform on the screen, didn't really notice anything amiss. There wasn't sufficient amplification, for one thing.

But in the bootleg theater, where illicit Vox-View televisors were hooked up to Magnas—

There was a faint, irrational uneasiness at first. It mounted. Someone screamed. There was a rush for the doors. The audience was afraid of something, but didn't know what. They knew only that they had to get out of there.

All over the country there was a frantic exodus from the bootleg theaters when Vox-View first rang in a subsonic during a regular broadcast. Nobody knew why, except Gallegher, the Brocks, and a couple of technicians who were let in on the secret.

An hour later another subsonic was played. There was another mad exodus.

Within a few weeks it was impossible to lure a patron into a bootleg theater. Home televisors were far safer! Vox-View sales picked up—

Nobody would attend a bootleg theater. An unexpected result of the experiment was that, after a while, nobody would attend any of the legalized Sonatone theaters either. Conditioning had set in.

Audiences didn't know why they grew panicky in the bootleg places. They associated their blind, unreasoning fear with other factors, notably mobs and claustrophobia. One evening a woman named Jane Wilson, otherwise not notable, attended a bootleg show. She fled with the rest when the subsonic was turned on.

The next night she went to the palatial Sonatone Bijou. In the middle of a dramatic feature she looked around, realized that there was a huge throng around her, cast up horrified eyes to the ceiling, and imagined that it was pressing down.

She had to get out of there!

Her squall was the booster charge. There were other customers who had heard subsonics before. No one was hurt during the panic; it was a legal rule that theater doors be made large enough to permit easy egress during a fire. No one was hurt, but it was suddenly obvious that the public was being conditioned by subsonics to avoid the dangerous combination of throngs and theaters. A simple matter of psychological association—

Within four months the bootleg places had disappeared and the Sonatone supertheaters had closed for want of patronage. The Tones, father and son, were not happy. But everybody connected with Vox-View was.

Except Gallegher. He had collected a staggering check from Brock, and instantly cabled to Europe for an incredible quantity of canned beer. Now, brooding over his sorrows, he lay on the laboratory couch and siphoned a highball down his throat. Joe, as usual, was before the mirror, watching the wheels go round.

"Joe," Gallegher said.

"Yes? What can I do?"

"Oh, nothing." That was the trouble. Gallegher fished a crumpled cable tape out of his pocket and morosely read it once more. The beer cannery in Europe had decided to change its tactics. From now on, the cable said, their beer would be put in the usual plastibulbs, in conformance with custom and demand. No more cans.

There wasn't *anything* put up in cans in this day and age. Not even beer, now.

So what good was a robot who was built and conditioned to be a can opener?

Gallegher sighed and mixed another highball—a stiff one. Joe postured proudly before the mirror.

Then he extended his eyes, opposed them, and quickly liberated his subconscious through autohypnotism. Joe could appreciate himself better that way.

Gallegher sighed again. Dogs were beginning to bark like mad for blocks around. Oh, well.

He took another drink and felt better. Presently, he thought, it would be time to sing "Frankie and Johnnie." Maybe he and Joe might have a duet— one baritone and one inaudible sub or supersonic. Close harmony.

Ten minutes later Gallegher was singing a duet with his can opener.

HENRY KUTTNER AND C. L. MOORE

Vintage Season

The second major pseudonym of Henry Kuttner and Catherine L. Moore, after Lewis Padgett, was Laurence O'Donnell, but this name was allowed to expire and its works reprinted most often under the Kuttner-Moore byline. Such is the case with "Vintage Season," a fine SF story of the 1940s, one of the earliest and most poignant reactions in literature to the dismaying potential of nuclear weaponry. It is a Campbell Golden Age classic equal to the most ambitious recent SF stories. After Kuttner's death in 1958, Moore remarried but wrote no more fiction. Kuttner and Moore were a writing team whose best work was in shorter forms, written mainly in the 1940s. They usually wrote under commercial pressures, and their novels are frequently weighted with the excess adjectives and adverbs that mark work paid for by the word. Their short stories show a control of atmosphere and a precision and care generally lacking in the longer works. Fury, their only significant SF novel, is still reprinted from time to time.

* * *

Three people came up the walk to the old mansion just at dawn on a perfect May morning. Oliver Wilson in his pajamas watched them from an upper window through a haze of conflicting emotions, resentment predominant. He didn't want them there.

They were foreigners. He knew only that much about them. They had the curious name of Sancisco, and their first names, scrawled in loops on the lease, appeared to be Omerie, Kleph and Klia, though it was impossible as he looked down upon them now to sort them out by signature.

He hadn't even been sure whether they would be men or women, and he had expected something a little less cosmopolitan.

Oliver's heart sank a little as he watched them follow the taxi driver up the walk. He had hoped for less self-assurance in his unwelcome tenants, because he meant to force them out of the house if he could. It didn't look very promising from here.

The man went first. He was tall and dark, and he wore his clothes and carried his body with that peculiar arrogant assurance that comes from perfect confidence in every phase of one's being. The two women were laughing as they followed him. Their voices were light and sweet, and their faces were beautiful, each in its own exotic way, but the first thing Oliver thought of when he looked at them was, Expensive!

It was not only that patina of perfection that seemed to dwell in every line of their incredibly flawless garments. There are degrees of wealth beyond which wealth itself ceases to have significance. Oliver had seen before, on rare occasions, something like this assurance that the earth turning beneath their well-shod feet turned only to their whim.

It puzzled him a little in this case, because he had the feeling as the three came up the walk that the beautiful clothing they wore so confidently was not clothing they were accustomed to. There was a curious air of condescension in the way they moved. Like women in costume. They minced a little on their delicate high heels, held out an arm to stare at the cut of the sleeve, twisted now and then inside their garments as if the clothing sat strangely on them, as if they were accustomed to something entirely different.

And there was an elegance about the way the garments fitted them which even to Oliver looked strikingly unusual. Only an actress on the screen, who can stop time and the film to adjust every disarrayed fold so that she looks perpetually perfect, might appear thus elegantly clad. But let these women move as they liked, and each fold of their clothing followed perfectly with the movement and fell perfectly into place again. One might almost suspect the garments were not cut of ordinary cloth, or that they were cut according to some unknown, subtle scheme, with many artful hidden seams placed by a tailor incredibly skilled at his trade.

They seemed excited. They talked in high, clear, very sweet voices, looking up at the perfect blue and transparent sky in which dawn was still frankly pink. They looked at the trees on the lawn, the leaves translucently green with an under color of golden newness, the edges crimped from constriction in the recent bud.

Happily and with excitement in their voices they called to the man, and when he answered his own voice blended so perfectly in cadence with theirs that it sounded like three people singing together. Their voices, like their clothing, seemed to have an elegance far beyond the ordinary, to be under a control such as Oliver Wilson had never dreamed of before this morning.

The taxi driver brought up the luggage, which was of a beautiful pale stuff that did not look quite like leather, and had curves in it so subtle it seemed square until you saw how two or three pieces of it fitted together when carried, into a perfectly balanced block. It was scuffed, as if from much use. And though there was a great deal of it, the taxi man did not seem to find his burden heavy. Oliver saw him look down at it now and then and heft the weight incredulously.

One of the women had very black hair and skin like cream, and smoke-blue eyes heavy-lidded with the weight of her lashes. It was the other woman Oliver's gaze followed as she came up the walk. Her hair was a clear, pale red, and her face had a softness that he thought would be like velvet to touch. She was tanned to a warm amber darker than her hair.

Just as they reached the porch steps the fair woman lifted her head and looked up. She gazed straight into Oliver's eyes and he saw that hers were very blue, and just a little amused, as if she had known he was there all along. Also they were frankly admiring.

Feeling a bit dizzy, Oliver hurried back to his room to dress.

"We are here on a vacation," the dark man said, accepting the keys. "We will not wish to be disturbed, as I made clear in our correspondence. You have engaged a cook and housemaid for us, I understand? We will expect you to move your own belongings out of the house, then, and—"

"Wait," Oliver said uncomfortably. "Something's come up. I—" He hesitated, not sure just how to present it. These were such increasingly odd people. Even their speech was odd. They spoke so distinctly, not slurring any of the words into contractions. English seemed as familiar to them as a native tongue, but they all spoke as trained singers sing, with perfect breath control and voice placement.

And there was a coldness in the man's voice, as if some gulf lay between him and Oliver, so deep no feeling of human contact could bridge it.

"I wonder," Oliver said, "if I could find you better living quarters somewhere else in town. There's a place across the street that—"

The dark woman said, "Oh, no!" in a lightly horrified voice, and all three of them laughed. It was cool, distant laughter that did not include Oliver.

The dark man said, "We chose this house carefully, Mr. Wilson. We would not be interested in living anywhere else."

Oliver said desperately, "I don't see why. It isn't even a modern house. I have two others in much better condition. Even across the street you'd have a fine view of the city. Here there isn't anything. The other houses cut off the view, and—"

"We engaged rooms here, Mr. Wilson," the man said with finality. "We expect to use them. Now will you make arrangements to leave as soon as possible?"

Oliver said, "No," and looked stubborn. "That isn't in the lease. You can live here until next month, since you paid for it, but you can't put me out. I'm staying."

The man opened his mouth to say something. He looked coldly at Oliver and closed it again. The feeling of aloofness was chill between them. There was a moment's silence. Then the man said, "Very well. Be kind enough to stay out of our way."

It was a little odd that he didn't inquire into Oliver's motives. Oliver was not yet sure enough of the man to explain. He couldn't very well say, "Since the lease was signed, I've been offered three times what the house is worth if I'll sell it before the end of May." He couldn't say, "I want the money, and I'm going to use my own nuisance-value to annoy you until you're willing to move out." After all, there seemed no reason why they shouldn't. After seeing them, there seemed doubly no reason, for it was clear they must be accustomed to surroundings infinitely better than this timeworn old house.

It was very strange, the value this house had so suddenly acquired. There was no reason at all why two groups of semi-anonymous people should be so eager to possess it for the month of May.

In silence Oliver showed his tenants upstairs to the three big bedrooms across the front of the house. He was intensely conscious of the red-haired woman and the way she watched him with a sort of obviously covert interest, quite warmly, and with a curious undertone to her interest that he could not quite place. It was familiar, but elusive. He thought how pleasant it would be to talk to her alone, if only to try to capture that elusive attitude and put a name to it.

Afterward he went down to the telephone and called his fiancée.

Sue's voice squeaked a little with excitement over the wire.

"Oliver, so early? Why, it's hardly six yet. Did you tell them what I said? Are they going to go?"

"Can't tell yet. I doubt it. After all, Sue, I did take their money, you know."

"Oliver, they've got to go! You've got to do something!"

"I'm trying, Sue. But I don't like it."

"Well, there isn't any reason why they shouldn't stay somewhere else. And we're going to need that money. You'll just have to think of something, Oliver."

Oliver met his own worried eyes in the mirror above the telephone and scowled at himself. His straw-colored hair was tangled and there was a shining stubble on his pleasant, tanned face. He was sorry the red-haired woman had first seen him in his untidy condition. Then his conscience smote him at the sound of Sue's determined voice and he said:

"I'll try, darling. I'll try. But I did take their money."

They had, in fact, paid a great deal of money, considerably more than the rooms were worth even in that year of high prices and high wages. The country was just moving into one of those fabulous eras which are later referred to as the Gay Forties or the Golden Sixties—a pleasant period of national euphoria. It was a stimulating time to be alive—while it lasted.

"All right," Oliver said resignedly. "I'll do my best."

But he was conscious, as the next few days went by, that he was not doing his best. There were several reasons for that. From the beginning the idea of making himself a nuisance to his tenants had been Sue's, not Oliver's. And if Oliver had been a little less determined the whole project would never have got under way. Reason was on Sue's side, but—

For one thing, the tenants were so fascinating. All they said and did had a queer sort of inversion to it, as if a mirror had been held up to ordinary living and in the reflection showed strange variations from the norm. Their minds worked on a different basic premise, Oliver thought, from his own. They seemed to derive covert amusement from the most unamusing things; they patronized, they were aloof with a quality of cold detachment which did not prevent them from laughing inexplicably far too often for Oliver's comfort.

He saw them occasionally, on their way to and from their rooms. They were polite and distant, not, he suspected, from anger at his presence but from sheer indifference.

Most of the day they spent out of the house. The perfect May weather held unbroken and they seemed to give themselves up wholeheartedly to admiration of it, entirely confident that the warm, pale-gold sunshine and the scented air would not be interrupted by rain or cold. They were so sure of it that Oliver felt uneasy.

They took only one meal a day in the house, a late dinner. And their reactions to the meal were unpredictable. Laughter greeted some of the dishes, and a sort of delicate disgust others. No one would touch the salad, for instance. And the fish seemed to cause a wave of queer embarrassment around the table.

They dressed elaborately for each dinner. The man—his name was Omerie—looked extremely handsome in his dinner clothes, but he seemed a little sulky and Oliver twice heard the women laughing because he had to wear black. Oliver entertained a sudden vision, for no reason, of the man in garments as bright and as subtly cut as the women's, and it seemed somehow very right for him. He wore even the dark clothing with a certain flamboyance, as if cloth-of-gold would be more normal for him.

When they were in the house at other mealtimes, they ate in their rooms. They must have brought a great deal of food with them, from whatever mysterious place they had come. Oliver wondered with increasing curiosity where it might be. Delicious odors drifted into the hall sometimes, at odd hours, from their closed doors. Oliver could not identify them, but almost always they smelled irresistible. A few times the food smell was rather shockingly unpleasant, almost nauseating. It takes a connoisseur, Oliver reflected, to appreciate the decadent. And these people, most certainly, were connoisseurs.

Why they lived so contentedly in this huge ramshackle old house was a question that disturbed his dreams at night. Or why they refused to move. He caught some fascinating glimpses into their rooms, which appeared to have been changed almost completely by additions he could not have defined very clearly from the brief sights he had of them. The feeling of luxury which his first glance at them had evoked was confirmed by the richness of the hangings they had apparently brought with them, the half-glimpsed ornaments, the pictures on the walls, even the whiffs of exotic perfume that floated from half-open doors.

He saw the women go by him in the halls, moving softly through the brown dimness in their gowns so uncannily perfect in fit, so lushly rich, so glowingly colored they seemed unreal. That poise born of confidence in the subservience of the world gave them an imperious aloofness, but more than once Oliver, meeting the blue gaze of the woman with the red hair and the soft, tanned skin, thought he saw quickened interest there. She smiled at him in the dimness and went by in a haze of fragrance and a halo of incredible richness, and the warmth of the smile lingered after she had gone.

He knew she did not mean this aloofness to last between them. From the very first he was sure of that. When the time came she would make the opportunity to be alone with him. The thought was confusing and tremendously exciting. There was nothing he could do but wait, knowing she would see him when it suited her.

On the third day he lunched with Sue in a little downtown restaurant overlooking the great sweep of the metropolis across the river far below. Sue had shining brown curls and brown eyes, and her chin was a bit more prominent than is strictly accordant with beauty. From childhood Sue had known what she wanted and how to get it, and it seemed to Oliver just now that she had never wanted anything quite so much as the sale of this house.

"It's such a marvelous offer for the old mausoleum," she said, breaking into a roll with a gesture of violence. "We'll never have a chance like that again, and prices are so high we'll need the money to start housekeeping. Surely you can do *something*, Oliver!"

"I'm trying," Oliver assured her uncomfortably.

"Have you heard anything more from that madwoman who wants to buy it?"

Oliver shook his head. "Her attorney phoned again yesterday. Nothing new. I wonder who she is."

"I don't think even the attorney knows. All this mystery—I don't like it, Oliver. Even those Sancisco people—What did they do today?"

Oliver laughed. "They spent about an hour this morning telephoning movie theaters in the city, checking up on a lot of third-rate films they want to see parts of."

"Parts of? But why?"

"I don't know. I think . . . oh, nothing. More coffee?"

The trouble was, he thought he did know. It was too unlikely a guess to tell Sue about, and without familiarity with the Sancisco oddities she would only think Oliver was losing his mind. But he had from their talk, a definite impression that there was an actor in bit parts in all these films whose performances they mentioned with something very near to awe. They referred to him as Golconda, which didn't appear to be his name, so that Oliver had no way of guessing which obscure bit-player it was they admired so deeply. Golconda might have been the name of a character he had once played—and with superlative skill, judging by the comments of the Sanciscos—but to Oliver he meant nothing at all.

"They do funny things," he said, stirring his coffee reflectively. "Yesterday Omerie—that's the man—came in with a book of poems published about five years ago, and all of them handled it like a first edition of Shakespeare. I never even heard of the author, but he seems to be a tin god in their country, wherever that is."

"You still don't know? Haven't they even dropped any hints?"

"We don't do much talking," Oliver reminded her with some irony.

"I know, but—Oh, well, I guess it doesn't matter. Go on, what else do they do?"

"Well, this morning they were going to spend studying 'Golconda' and his great art, and this afternoon I think they're taking a trip up the river to some sort of shrine I never heard of. It isn't very far, wherever it is, because I know they're coming back for dinner. Some great man's birthplace, I think—they promised to take home souvenirs of the place if they could get any. They're typical tourists, all right—if I could only figure out what's behind the whole thing. It doesn't make sense."

"Nothing about that house makes sense any more. I do wish—"

She went on in a petulant voice, but Oliver ceased suddenly to hear her, because just outside the door, walking with imperial elegance on her high heels, a familiar figure passed. He did not see her face, but he thought he would know that poise, that richness of line and motion, anywhere on earth.

"Excuse me a minute," he muttered to Sue, and was out of his chair before she could speak. He made the door in half a dozen long strides, and the beautifully elegant passerby was only a few steps away when he got there. Then, with the words he had meant to speak already half-uttered, he fell silent and stood there staring.

It was not the red-haired woman. It was not her dark companion. It was a stranger. He watched, speechless, while the lovely, imperious creature moved on through the crowd and vanished, moving with familiar poise and assurance and an equally familiar strangeness as if the beautiful and exquisitely fitted garments she wore were an exotic costume to her, as they had always seemed to the Sancisco women. Every other woman on the street looked untidy and ill at ease beside her. Walking like a queen, she melted into the crowd and was gone.

She came from *their* country, Oliver told himself dizzily. So someone else nearby had mysterious tenants in this month of perfect May weather. Someone else was puzzling in vain today over the strangeness of the people from the nameless land.

In silence he went back to Sue.

The door stood invitingly ajar in the brown dimness of the upper hall. Oliver's steps slowed as he drew near it, and his heart began to quicken correspondingly. It was the red-haired woman's room, and he thought the door was not open by accident. Her name, he knew now, was Kleph.

The door creaked a little on its hinges and from within a very sweet voice said lazily, "Won't you come in?"

The room looked very different indeed. The big bed had been pushed back against the wall and a cover thrown over it that brushed the floor all around looked like soft-haired fur except that it was a pale blue-green and sparkled as if every hair were tipped with invisible crystals. Three books lay open on the fur, and a very curious-looking magazine with faintly luminous printing and a page of pictures that at first glance appeared three-dimensional. Also a tiny porcelain pipe encrusted with porcelain flowers, and a thin wisp of smoke floating from the bowl.

Above the bed a broad picture hung, framing a square of blue water so real Oliver had to look twice to be sure it was not rippling gently from left to right. From the ceiling swung a crystal globe on a glass cord. It turned gently, the light from the windows making curved rectangles in its sides.

Under the center window a sort of chaise longue stood which Oliver had not seen before. He could only assume it was at least partly pneumatic and had been brought in the luggage. There was a very rich-looking quilted cloth covering and hiding it, embossed all over in shining metallic patterns.

Kleph moved slowly from the door and sank upon the chaise longue with a little sign of content. The couch accommodated itself to her body with what looked like delightful comfort. Kleph wriggled a little and then smiled up at Oliver.

"Do come on in. Sit over there, where you can see out the window. I love your beautiful spring weather. You know, there never was a May like it in civilized times." She said that quite seriously, her blue eyes on Oliver's, and there was a hint of patronage in her voice, as if the weather had been arranged especially for her.

Oliver started across the room and then paused and looked down in amazement at the floor, which felt unstable. He had not noticed before that the carpet was pure white, unspotted, and sank about an inch under the pressure of the feet. He saw then that Kleph's feet were bare, or almost bare. She wore something like gossamer buskins of filmy net, fitting her feet exactly. The bare soles were pink as if they had been rouged, and the nails had a liquid gleam like tiny mirrors. He moved closer, and was not as surprised as he should have been to see that they really were tiny mirrors, painted with some lacquer that gave them reflecting surfaces.

"Do sit down," Kleph said again, waving a white-sleeved arm toward a chair by the window. She wore a garment that looked like short, soft down, loosely cut but following perfectly every motion she made. And there was something curiously different about her very shape today. When Oliver saw her in street clothes, she had the square-shouldered, slim-flanked figure that all women strove for, but here in her lounging robe she looked—well, different. There was an almost swanlike slope to her shoulders today, a roundness and softness to her body that looked unfamiliar and very appealing.

"Will you have some tea?" Kleph asked, and smiled charmingly.

· · ·

A low table beside her held a tray and several small covered cups, lovely things with an inner glow like rose quartz, the color shining deeply as if from within layer upon layer of translucence. She took up one of the cups—there were no saucers—and offered it to Oliver.

It felt fragile and thin as paper in his hand. He could not see the contents because of the cup's cover, which seemed to be one with the cup itself and left only a thin open crescent at the rim. Steam rose from the opening.

Kleph took up a cup of her own and tilted it to her lips, smiling at Oliver over the rim. She was very beautiful. The pale red hair lay in shining loops against her head and the corona of curls like a halo above her forehead might have been pressed down like a wreath. Every hair kept order as perfectly as if it had been painted on, though the breeze from the window stirred now and then among the softly shining strands.

Oliver tried the tea. Its flavor was exquisite, very hot, and the taste that lingered upon his tongue was like the scent of flowers. It was an extremely feminine drink. He sipped again, surprised to find how much he liked it.

The scent of flowers seemed to increase as he drank, swirling through his head like smoke. After the third sip there was a faint buzzing in his ears. The bees among the flowers, perhaps, he thought incoherently—and sipped again.

Kleph watched him, smiling.

"The others will be out all afternoon," she told Oliver comfortably. "I thought it would give us a pleasant time to be acquainted."

Oliver was rather horrified to hear himself saying, "What makes you talk like that?" He had had no idea of asking the question; something seemed to have loosened his control over his own tongue.

Kleph's smile deepened. She tipped the cup to her lips and there was indulgence in her voice when she said, "What do you mean 'like that'?"

He waved his hand vaguely, noting with some surprise that at a glance it seemed to have six or seven fingers as it moved past his face.

"I don't know—precision, I guess. Why don't you say 'don't,' for instance?"

"In our country we are trained to speak with precision," Kleph explained. "Just as we are trained to move and dress and think with precision. Any slovenliness is trained out of us in childhood. With you, of course—" She was polite. "With you, this does not happen to be a national fetish. With us, we have time for the amenities. We like them."

Her voice had grown sweeter and sweeter as she spoke, until by now it was almost indistinguishable from the sweetness of the flower-scent in Oliver's head, and the delicate flavor of the tea.

"What country do you come from?" he asked, and tilted the cup again to drink, mildly surprised to notice that it seemed inexhaustible.

Kleph's smile was definitely patronizing this time. It didn't irritate him. Nothing could irritate him just now. The whole room swam in a beautiful rosy glow as fragrant as the flowers.

"We must not speak of that, Mr. Wilson."

"But—" Oliver paused. After all, it was, of course, none of his business. "This is a vacation?" he asked vaguely.

"Call it a pilgrimage, perhaps."

"Pilgrimage?" Oliver was so interested that for an instant his mind came back into sharp focus. "To—what?"

"I should not have said that, Mr. Wilson. Please forget it. Do you like the tea?"

"Very much."

"You will have guessed by now that it is not only tea, but an euphoriac."

Oliver stared. "Euphoriac?"

Kleph made a descriptive circle in the air with one graceful hand, and laughed. "You do not feel the effects yet? Surely you do?"

"I feel," Oliver said, "the way I'd feel after four whiskeys."

Kleph shuddered delicately. "We get our euphoria less painfully. And without the aftereffects your barbarous alcohols used to have." She bit her lip. "Sorry. I must be euphoric myself to speak so freely. Please forgive me. Shall we have some music?"

Kleph leaned backward on the chaise longue and reached toward the wall beside her. The sleeve, falling away from her round tanned arm, left bare the inside of the wrist, and Oliver was startled to see there a long, rosy streak of fading scar. His inhibitions had dissolved in the fumes of the fragrant tea; he caught his breath and leaned forward to stare.

Kleph shook the sleeve back over the scar with a quick gesture. Color came into her face beneath the softly tinted tan and she would not meet Oliver's eyes. A queer shame seemed to have fallen upon her.

Oliver said tactlessly, "What is it? What's the matter?"

Still she would not look at him. Much later he understood that shame and knew she had reason for it. Now he listened blankly as she said:

"Nothing . . . nothing at all. A . . . an inoculation. All of us . . . oh, never mind. Listen to the music."

This time she reached out with the other arm. She touched nothing, but when she had held her hand near the wall a sound breathed through the room. It was the sound of water, the sighing of waves receding upon long, sloped beaches. Oliver followed Kleph's gaze toward the picture of the blue water above the bed.

The waves there were moving. More than that, the point of vision moved. Slowly the seascape drifted past, moving with the waves, following them toward shore. Oliver watched, half-hypnotized by a motion that seemed at the time quite acceptable and not in the least surprising.

The waves lifted and broke in creaming foam and ran seething up a sandy beach. Then through the sound of the water music began to breathe, and through the water itself a man's face dawned in the frame, smiling intimately into the room. He held an oddly archaic musical instrument, lute-shaped, its body striped light and dark like a melon and its long neck bent back over his shoulder. He was singing, and Oliver felt mildly astonished at the song. It was very familiar and very odd indeed. He groped through the unfamiliar rhythms and found at least a thread to catch the tune by—it was "Make-Believe," from "Showboat," but certainly a showboat that had never steamed up the Mississippi.

"What's he doing to it?" he demanded after a few moments of outraged listening. "I never heard anything like it!"

Kleph laughed and stretched out her arm again. Enigmatically she said, "We call it kyling. Never mind. How do you like this?"

It was a comedian, a man in semi-clown make-up, his eyes exaggerated so that they seemed to cover half his face. He stood by a broad glass pillar before a dark curtain and sang a gay, staccato song interspersed with patter that sounded impromptu, and all the while his left hand did an intricate, musical tattoo of the nailtips on the glass of the column. He strolled around and around it as he sang. The rhythms of his fingernails blended with the song and swung widely away into patterns of their own, and blended again without a break.

It was confusing to follow. The song made even less sense than the monologue, which had something to do with a lost slipper and was full of allusions which made Kleph smile, but were utterly unintelligible to Oliver. The man had a dry, brittle style that was not very amusing, though Kleph seemed fascinated. Oliver was interested to see in him an extension and a variation of that extreme smooth confidence which marked all three of the Sanciscos. Clearly a racial trait, he thought.

Other performances followed, some of them fragmentary as if lifted out of a completer version. One he knew. The obvious, stirring melody struck his recognition before the figures—marching men against a haze, a great banner rolling backward above them in the smoke, foreground figures striding gigantically and shouting in rhythm, "Forward, forward the lily banners go!"

The music was tinny, the images blurred and poorly colored, but there was a gusto about the performance that caught at Oliver's imagination. He stared, remembering the old film from long ago. Dennis King and a ragged chorus, singing "The Song of the Vagabonds" from—was it "Vagabond King"?

"A very old one," Kleph said apologetically. "But I like it."

The steam of the intoxicating tea swirled between Oliver and the picture. Music swelled and sank through the room and the fragrant fumes and his own euphoric brain. Nothing seemed strange. He had discovered how to drink the tea. Like nitrous oxide, the effect was not cumulative. When you reached a peak of euphoria, you could not increase the peak. It was best to wait for a slight dip in the effect of the stimulant before taking more.

Otherwise it had most of the effects of alcohol—everything after awhile dissolved into a delightful fog through which all he saw was uniformly enchanting and partook of the qualities of a dream. He questioned nothing. Afterward he was not certain how much of it he really had dreamed.

There was the dancing doll, for instance. He remembered it quite clearly, in sharp focus—a tiny, slender woman with a long-nosed, dark-eyed face and a pointed chin. She moved delicately across the white rug—knee-high, exquisite. Her features were as mobile as her body, and she danced lightly, with resounding strokes of her toes, each echoing like a bell. It was a formalized sort of dance, and she sang breathlessly in accompaniment, making amusing little grimaces. Certainly it was a portrait-doll, animated to mimic the original perfectly in voice and motion. Afterward, Oliver knew he must have dreamed it.

What else happened he was quite unable to remember later. He knew Kleph had said some curious things, but they all made sense at the time, and afterward he couldn't remember a word. He knew he had been offered little glittering candies in a transparent dish, and that some of them had been delicious and one or two so bitter his tongue still curled the next day when he recalled them, and one—Kleph sucked luxuriantly on the same kind—of a taste that was actively nauseating.

As for Kleph herself—he was frantically uncertain the next day what had really happened. He thought he could remember the softness of her white-downed arms clasped at the back of his neck, while she laughed up at him and exhaled into his face the flowery fragrance of the tea. But beyond that he was totally unable to recall anything, for a while.

There was a brief interlude later, before the oblivion of sleep. He was almost sure he remembered a moment when the other two Sanciscos stood looking down at him, the man scowling, the smoky-eyed woman smiling a derisive smile.

The man said, from a vast distance, "Kleph, you know this is against every rule—" His voice began in a thin hum and soared in fantastic flight beyond the range of hearing. Oliver thought he remembered the dark woman's laughter, thin and distant too, and the hum of her voice like bees in flight.

"Kleph, Kleph, you silly little fool, can we never trust you out of sight?"

Kleph's voice then said something that seemed to make no sense. "What does it matter, *here*?"

The man answered in that buzzing, faraway hum. "The matter of giving your bond before you leave, not to interfere. You know you signed the rules—"

Kleph's voice, nearer and more intelligible: "But here the difference is . . . it does not matter *here*! You both know that. How could it matter?"

Oliver felt the downy brush of her sleeve against his cheek, but he saw nothing except the slow, smokelike ebb and flow of darkness past his eyes. He heard the voices wrangle musically from far away, and he heard them cease.

When he woke the next morning, alone in his own room, he woke with the memory of Kleph's eyes upon him very sorrowfully, her lovely tanned face looking down on him with the red hair falling fragrantly on each side of it and sadness and compassion in her eyes. He thought he had probably dreamed that. There was no reason why anyone should look at him with such sadness.

Sue telephoned that day.

"Oliver, the people who want to buy the house are here. That madwoman and her husband. Shall I bring them over?"

Oliver's mind all day had been hazy with the vague, bewildering memories of yesterday. Kleph's face kept floating before him, blotting out the room. He said, "What? I . . . oh, well, bring them if you want to. I don't see what good it'll do."

"Oliver, what's wrong with you? We agreed we needed the money, didn't we? I don't see how you can think of passing up such a wonderful bargain without even a struggle. We could get married and buy our own house right away, and you know we'll never get such an offer again for that old trash-heap. Wake up, Oliver!"

Oliver made an effort. "I know, Sue—I know. But—"

"Oliver, you've got to think of something!" Her voice was imperious.

He knew she was right. Kleph or no Kleph, the bargain shouldn't be ignored if there was any way at all of getting the tenants out. He wondered again what made the place so suddenly priceless to so many people. And what the last week in May had to do with the value of the house.

A sudden sharp curiosity pierced even the vagueness of his mind today. May's last week was so important that the whole sale of the house stood or fell upon occupancy by then. Why? *Why?*

"What's going to happen next week?" he asked rhetorically of the telephone. "Why can't they wait till these people leave? I'd knock a couple of thousand off the price if they'd—"

"You would not, Oliver Wilson! I can buy all our refrigeration units with that extra money. You'll just have to work out some way to give possession by next week, and that's that. You hear me?"

"Keep your shirt on," Oliver said practically. "I'm only human, but I'll try."

"I'm bringing the people over right away," Sue told him. "While the Sanciscos are still out. Now you put your mind to work and think of something, Oliver." She paused, and her voice was reflective when she spoke again. "They're . . . awfully odd people, darling."

"Odd?"

"You'll see."

It was an elderly woman and a very young man who trailed Sue up the walk. Oliver knew immediately what had struck Sue about them. He was somehow not at all surprised to see that both wore their clothing with the familiar air of elegant self-consciousness he had come to know so well. They, too, looked around them at the beautiful, sunny afternoon with conscious enjoyment and an air of faint condescension. He knew before he heard them speak how musical their voices would be and how meticulously they would pronounce each word.

There was no doubt about it. The people of Kleph's mysterious country were arriving here in force—for something. For the last week of May? He shrugged mentally; there was no way of guessing—yet. One thing only was sure: all of them must come from that nameless land where people controlled their voices like singers and their garments like actors who could stop the reel of time itself to adjust every disordered fold.

The elderly woman took full charge of the conversation from the start. They stood together on the rickety, unpainted porch, and Sue had no chance even for introductions.

"Young man, I am Madame Hollia. This is my husband." Her voice had an underrunning current of harshness, which was perhaps age. And her face looked almost corsetted, the loose flesh coerced into something like firmness by some invisible method Oliver could not guess at. The make-up was so skillful he could not be certain it was make-up at all, but he had a definite feeling that she was much older than she looked. It would have taken a lifetime of command to put so much authority into the harsh, deep, musically controlled voice.

The young man said nothing. He was very handsome. His type, apparently, was one that does not change much no matter in what culture or country it may occur. He wore beautifully tailored garments and carried in one gloved hand a box of red leather, about the size and shape of a book.

Madame Hollia went on. "I understand your problem about the house. You wish to sell to me, but are legally bound by your lease with Omerie and his friends. Is that right?"

Oliver nodded. "But—"

"Let me finish. If Omerie can be forced to vacate before next week, you will accept our offer. Right? Very well. Hara!" She nodded to the young man beside her. He jumped to instant attention, bowed slightly, said, "Yes, Hollia," and slipped a gloved hand into his coat.

Madame Hollia took the little object offered on his palm, her gesture as she reached for it almost imperial, as if royal robes swept from her outstretched arm.

"Here," she said, "is something that may help us. My dear—" She held it out to Sue—"if you can hide this somewhere about the house, I believe your unwelcome tenants will not trouble you much longer."

Sue took the thing curiously. It looked like a tiny silver box, no more than an inch square, indented at the top and with no line to show it could be opened.

"Wait a minute," Oliver broke in uneasily. "What is it?"

"Nothing that will harm anyone, I assure you."

"Then what—"

Madame Hollia's imperious gesture at one sweep silenced him and commanded Sue forward. "Go on, my dear. Hurry, before Omerie comes back. I can assure you there is no danger to anyone."

Oliver broke in determinedly. "Madame Hollia, I'll have to know what your plans are. I—"

"Oh, Oliver, please!" Sue's fingers closed over the silver cube. "Don't worry about it. I'm sure Madame Hollia knows best. Don't you *want* to get those people out?"

"Of course I do. But I don't want the house blown up or—"

Madame Hollia's deep laughter was indulgent. "Nothing so crude, I promise you, Mr. Wilson. Remember, we want the house! Hurry, my dear."

Sue nodded and slipped hastily past Oliver into the hall. Outnumbered, he subsided uneasily. The young man, Hara, tapped a negligent foot and admired the sunlight as they waited. It was an afternoon as perfect as all of May had been, translucent gold, balmy with an edge of chill lingering in the air to point up a perfect contrast with the summer to come. Hara looked around him confidently, like a man paying just tribute to a stage-set provided wholly for himself. He even glanced up at a drone from above and followed the course of a big transcontinental plane half dissolved in golden haze high in the sun. "Quaint," he murmured in a gratified voice.

Sue came back and slipped her hand through Oliver's arm, squeezing excitedly. "There," she said. "How long will it take, Madame Hollia?"

"That will depend, my dear. Not very long. Now, Mr. Wilson, one word with you. You live here also, I understand? For your own comfort, take my advice and—"

Somewhere within the house a door slammed and a clear high voice rang wordlessly up a rippling scale. Then there was the sound of feet on the stairs, and a single line of song. *"Come hider, love, to me—"*

Hara started, almost dropping the red leather box he held.

"Kleph!" he said in a whisper. "Or Klia. I know they both just came on from Canterbury. But I thought—"

"Hush." Madame Hollia's features composed themselves into an imperious blank. She breathed triumphantly through her nose, drew back upon herself and turned an imposing façade to the door.

Kleph wore the same softly downy robe Oliver had seen before, except that today it was not white, but a pale, clear blue that gave her tan an apricot flush. She was smiling.

"Why, Hollia!" Her tone was at its most musical. "I thought I recognized voices from home. How nice to see you. No one knew you were coming to the—" She broke off and glanced at Oliver and then away again. "Hara, too," she said. "What a pleasant surprise."

Sue said flatly, "When did *you* get back?"

Kleph smiled at her. "You must be the little Miss Johnson. Why, I did not go out at all. I was tired of sightseeing. I have been napping in my room."

Sue drew in her breath in something that just escaped being a disbelieving sniff. A look flashed between the two women, and for an instant held— and that instant was timeless. It was an extraordinary pause in which a great deal of wordless interplay took place in the space of a second.

Oliver saw the quality of Kleph's smile at Sue, that same look of quiet confidence he had noticed so often about all of these strange people. He saw Sue's quick inventory of the other woman, and he saw how Sue squared her shoulders and stood up straight, smoothing down her summer frock over her flat hips so that for an instant she stood posed consciously, looking down on Kleph. It was deliberate. Bewildered, he glanced again at Kleph.

Kleph's shoulders sloped softly, her robe was belted to a tiny waist and hung in deep folds over frankly rounded hips. Sue's was the fashionable figure—but Sue was the first to surrender.

Kleph's smile did not falter. But in the silence there was an abrupt reversal of values, based on no more than the measureless quality of Kleph's confidence in herself, the quiet, assured smile. It was suddenly made very clear that fashion is not a constant. Kleph's curious, out-of-mode curves without warning became the norm, and Sue was a queer, angular, half-masculine creature beside her.

Oliver had no idea how it was done. Somehow the authority passed in a breath from one woman to the other. Beauty is almost wholly a matter of fashion; what is beautiful today would have been grotesque a couple of generations ago and will be grotesque a hundred years ahead. It will be worse than grotesque; it will be outmoded and therefore faintly ridiculous.

Sue was that. Kleph had only to exert her authority to make it clear to everyone on the porch. Kleph was a beauty, suddenly and very convincingly, beautiful in the accepted mode, and Sue was amusingly old-fashioned, an anachronism in her lithe, square-shouldered slimness. She did not belong. She was grotesque among these strangely immaculate people.

Sue's collapse was complete. But pride sustained her, and bewilderment. Probably she never did grasp entirely what was wrong. She gave Kleph one glance of burning resentment and when her eyes came back to Oliver there was suspicion in them, and mistrust.

Looking backward later, Oliver thought that in that moment, for the first time clearly, he began to suspect the truth. But he had no time to ponder it, for after the brief instant of enmity the three people from—elsewhere— began to speak all at once, as if in a belated attempt to cover something they did not want noticed.

Kleph said, "This beautiful weather—" and Madame Hollia said, "So fortunate to have this house—" and Hara, holding up the red leather box, said loudest of all, "Cenbe sent you this, Kleph. His latest."

Kleph put out both hands for it eagerly, the eiderdown sleeves falling back from her rounded arms. Oliver had a quick glimpse of that mysterious scar before the sleeve fell back, and it seemed to him that there was the faintest trace of a similar scar vanishing into Hara's cuff as he let his own arm drop.

"Cenbe!" Kleph cried, her voice high and sweet and delighted. "How wonderful! What period?"

"From November 1664," Hara said. "London, of course, though I think there may be some counterpoint from the 1347 November. He hasn't finished—of course." He glanced almost nervously at Oliver and Sue. "A wonderful example," he said quickly. "Marvelous. If you have the taste for it, of course."

Madame Hollia shuddered with ponderous delicacy.

"That man!" she said. "Fascinating, of course—a great man. But—so *advanced*!"

"It takes a connoisseur to appreciate Cenbe's work fully," Kleph said in a slightly tart voice. "We all admit that."

"Oh yes, we all bow to Cenbe," Hollia conceded. "I confess the man terrifies me a little, my dear. Do we expect him to join us?"

"I suppose so," Kleph said. "If his—work—is not yet finished, then of course. You know Cenbe's tastes."

Hollia and Hara laughed together. "I know when to look for him, then," Hollia said. She glanced at the staring Oliver and the subdued but angry Sue, and with a commanding effort brought the subject back into line.

"So fortunate, my dear Kleph, to have this house," she declared heavily. "I saw a tridimensional of it—afterward—and it was still quite perfect. Such a fortunate coincidence. Would you consider parting with your lease, for a consideration? Say, a coronation seat at—"

"Nothing could buy us, Hollia," Kleph told her gaily, clasping the red box to her bosom.

Hollia gave her a cool stare. "You may change your mind, my dear Kleph," she said pontifically. "There is still time. You can always reach us through Mr. Wilson here. We have rooms up the street in the Montgomery House—nothing like yours, of course, but they will do. For us, they will do."

Oliver blinked. The Montgomery House was the most expensive hotel in town. Compared to this collapsing old ruin, it was a palace. There was no understanding these people. Their values seemed to have suffered a complete reversal.

Madame Hollia moved majestically toward the steps.

"Very pleasant to see you, my dear," she said over one well-padded shoulder. "Enjoy your stay. My regards to Omerie and Klia. Mr. Wilson—" she nodded toward the walk. "A word with you."

Oliver followed her down toward the street. Madame Hollia paused halfway there and touched his arm.

"One word of advice," she said huskily. "You say you sleep here? Move out, young man. Move out before tonight."

· · ·

Oliver was searching in a half-desultory fashion for the hiding place Sue had found for the mysterious silver cube, when the first sounds from above began to drift down the stairwell toward him. Kleph had closed her door, but the house was old, and strange qualities in the noise overhead seemed to seep through the woodwork like an almost visible stain.

It was music, in a way. But much more than music. And it was a terrible sound, the sounds of calamity and of all human reaction to calamity, everything from hysteria to heartbreak, from irrational joy to rationalized acceptance.

The calamity was—single. The music did not attempt to correlate all human sorrows; it focused sharply upon one and followed the ramifications out and out. Oliver recognized these basics to the sounds in a very brief moment. They were essentials, and they seemed to beat into his brain with the first strains of the music which was so much more than music.

But when he lifted his head to listen he lost all grasp upon the meaning of the noise and it was sheer medley and confusion. To think of it was to blur it hopelessly in the mind, and he could not recapture that first instant of unreasoning acceptance.

He went upstairs almost in a daze, hardly knowing what he was doing. He pushed Kleph's door open. He looked inside—

What he saw there he could not afterward remember except in a blurring as vague as the blurred ideas the music roused in his brain. Half the room had vanished behind a mist, and the mist was a three-dimensional screen upon which were projected—He had no words for them. He was not even sure if the projections were visual. The mist was spinning with motion and sound, but essentially it was neither sound nor motion that Oliver saw.

This was a work of art. Oliver knew no name for it. It transcended all art-forms he knew, blended them, and out of the blend produced subtleties his mind could not begin to grasp. Basically, this was the attempt of a master composer to correlate every essential aspect of a vast human experience into something that could be conveyed in a few moments to every sense at once.

The shifting visions on the screen were not pictures in themselves, but hints of pictures, subtly selected outlines that plucked at the mind and with one deft touch set whole chords ringing through the memory. Perhaps each beholder reacted differently, since it was in the eye and the mind of the beholder that the truth of the picture lay. No two would be aware of the same symphonic panorama, but each would see essentially the same terrible story unfold.

Every sense was touched by that deft and merciless genius. Color and shape and motion flickered in the screen, hinting much, evoking unbearable memories deep in the mind; odors floated from the screen and touched the heart of the beholder more poignantly than anything visual could do. The skin crawled sometimes as if to a tangible cold hand laid upon it. The tongue curled with remembered bitterness and remembered sweet.

It was outrageous. It violated the innermost privacies of a man's mind, called up secret things long ago walled off behind mental scar tissue, forced its terrible message upon the beholder relentlessly though the mind might threaten to crack beneath the stress of it.

And yet, in spite of all this vivid awareness, Oliver did not know what calamity the screen portrayed. That it was real, vast, overwhelmingly dreadful he could not doubt. That it had once happened was unmistakable. He caught flashing glimpses of human faces distorted with grief and disease and death—real faces, faces that had once lived and were seen now in the instant of dying. He saw men and women in rich clothing superimposed in panorama upon reeling thousands of ragged folk, great throngs of them swept past the sight in an instant, and he saw that death made no distinction among them.

He saw lovely women laugh and shake their curls, and the laughter shriek into hysteria and the hysteria into music. He saw one man's face, over and over—a long, dark, saturnine face, deeply lined, sorrowful, the face of a powerful man wise in worldliness, urbane—and helpless. That face was for a while a recurring motif, always more tortured, more helpless than before.

The music broke off in the midst of a rising glide. The mist vanished and the room reappeared before him. The anguished dark face for an instant seemed to Oliver printed everywhere he looked, like after-vision on the eyelids. He knew that face. He had seen it before, not often, but he should know its name—

"Oliver, Oliver—" Kleph's sweet voice came out of a fog at him. He was leaning dizzily against the doorpost looking down into her eyes. She, too, had that dazed blankness he must show on his own face. The power of the dreadful symphony still held them both. But even in this confused moment Oliver saw that Kleph had been enjoying the experience.

He felt sickened to the depths of his mind, dizzy with sickness and revulsion because of the superimposing of human miseries he had just beheld. But Kleph—only appreciation showed upon her face. To her it had been magnificence, and magnificence only.

Irrelevantly Oliver remembered the nauseating candies she had enjoyed, the nauseating odors of strange food that drifted sometimes through the hall from her room.

What was it she had said downstairs a little while ago? Connoisseur, that was it. Only a connoisseur could appreciate work as—as *advanced*—as the work of someone called Cenbe.

A whiff of intoxicating sweetness curled past Oliver's face. Something cool and smooth was pressed into his hand.

"Oh, Oliver, I am so sorry," Kleph's voice murmured contritely. "Here, drink the euphoriac and you will feel better. Please drink!"

The familiar fragrance of the hot sweet tea was on his tongue before he knew he had complied. Its relaxing fumes floated up through his brain and in a moment or two the world felt stable around him again. The room was as it had always been. And Kleph—

Her eyes were very bright. Sympathy showed in them for him, but for herself she was still brimmed with the high elation of what she had just been experiencing.

"Come and sit down," she said gently, tugging at his arm. "I am so sorry—I should not have played that over, where you could hear it. I have no excuse, really. It was only that I forgot what the effect might be on one who had never heard Cenbe's symphonies before. I was so impatient to see what he had done with . . . with his new subject. I am so very sorry, Oliver!"

"What was it?" His voice sounded steadier than he had expected. The tea was responsible for that. He sipped again, glad of the consoling euphoria its fragrance brought.

"A . . . a composite interpretation of . . . oh, Oliver, you know I must not answer questions!"

"But—"

"No—drink your tea and forget what it was you saw. Think of other things. Here, we will have music—another kind of music, something gay—"

She reached for the wall beside the window, and as before, Oliver saw the broad framed picture of blue water above the bed ripple and grow pale. Through it another scene began to dawn like shapes rising beneath the surface of the sea.

He had a glimpse of a dark-curtained stage upon which a man in a tight dark tunic and hose moved with a restless, sidelong pace, his hands and face startlingly pale against the black about him. He limped; he had a crooked back and he spoke familiar lines. Oliver had seen John Barrymore once as the crook-backed Richard, and it seemed vaguely outrageous to him that any other actor should essay that difficult part. This one he had never seen before, but the man had a fascinatingly smooth manner and his interpretation of the Plantagenet king was quite new and something Shakespeare probably never dreamed of.

"No," Kleph said, "not this. Nothing gloomy." And she put out her hand again. The nameless new Richard faded and there was a swirl of changing pictures and changing voices, all blurred together, before the scene steadied upon a stageful of dancers in pastel ballet skirts, drifting effortlessly through some complicated pattern of motion. The music that went with it was light and effortless too. The room filled up with the clear, floating melody.

Oliver set down his cup. He felt much surer of himself now, and he thought the euphoriac had done all it could for him. He didn't want to blur again mentally. There were things he meant to learn about. Now. He considered how to begin.

Kleph was watching him. "That Hollia," she said suddenly. "She wants to buy the house?"

Oliver nodded. "She's offering a lot of money. Sue's going to be awfully disappointed if—" He hesitated. Perhaps, after all, Sue would not be disappointed. He remembered the little silver cube with the enigmatic function and he wondered if he should mention it to Kleph. But the euphoriac had not reached that level of his brain, and he remembered his duty to Sue and was silent.

Kleph shook her head, her eyes upon his warm with—was it sympathy?

"Believe me," she said, "you will not find that—important—after all. I promise you, Oliver."

He stared at her. "I wish you'd explain."

Kleph laughed on a note more sorrowful than amused. But it occurred to Oliver suddenly that there was no longer condescension in her voice. Imperceptibly that air of delicate amusement had vanished from her manner toward him. The cool detachment that still marked Omerie's attitude, and Klia's, was not in Kleph's any more. It was a subtlety he did not think she could assume. It had to come spontaneously or not at all. And for no reason he was willing to examine, it became suddenly very important to Oliver that Kleph should not condescend to him, that she should feel toward him as he felt toward her. He would not think of it.

He looked down at his cup, rose-quartz, exhaling a thin plume of steam from its crescent-slit opening. This time, he thought, maybe he could make the tea work for him. For he remembered how it loosened the tongue, and there was a great deal he needed to know. The idea that had come to him on the porch in the instant of silent rivalry between Kleph and Sue seemed now too fantastic to entertain. But some answer there must be.

Kleph herself gave him the opening.

"I must not take too much euphoriac this afternoon," she said, smiling at him over her pink cup. "It will make me drowsy, and we are going out this evening with friends."

"More friends?" Oliver asked. "From your country?"

Kleph nodded. "Very dear friends we have expected all this week."

"I wish you'd tell me," Oliver said bluntly, "where it is you come from. It isn't from here. Your culture is too different from ours—even your names—" He broke off as Kleph shook her head.

"I wish I could tell you. But that is against all the rules. It is even against the rules for me to be here talking to you now."

"What rules?"

She made a helpless gesture. "You must not ask me, Oliver." She leaned back on the chaise longue, which adjusted itself luxuriously to the motion, and smiled very sweetly at him. "We must not talk about things like that. Forget it, listen to the music, enjoy yourself if you can—" She closed her eyes and laid her head back against the cushions. Oliver saw the round tanned throat swell as she began to hum a tune. Eyes still closed, she sang again the words she had sung upon the stairs. *"Come hider, love, to me—"*

A memory clicked over suddenly in Oliver's mind. He had never heard the queer, lagging tune before, but he thought he knew the words. He remembered what Hollia's husband had said when he heard that line of song, and he leaned forward. She would not answer a direct question, but perhaps—

"Was the weather this warm in Canterbury?" he asked, and held his breath. Kleph hummed another line of the song and shook her head, eyes still closed.

"It was autumn there," she said. "But bright, wonderfully bright. Even their clothing, you know . . . everyone was singing that new song, and I can't get it out of my head." She sang another line, and the words were almost unintelligible—English, yet not an English Oliver could understand.

He stood up. "Wait," he said. "I want to find something. Back in a minute."

She opened her eyes and smiled mistily at him, still humming. He went downstairs as fast as he could—the stairway swayed a little, though his head was nearly clear now—and into the library. The book he wanted was old and battered, interlined with the penciled notes of his college days. He did not remember very clearly where the passage he wanted was, but he thumbed fast through the columns and by sheer luck found it within a few minutes. Then he went back upstairs, feeling a strange emptiness in his stomach because of what he almost believed now.

"Kleph," he said firmly, "I know that song. I know the year it was new."

Her lids rose slowly; she looked at him through a mist of euphoriac. He was not sure she had understood. For a long moment she held him with her gaze. Then she put out one downy-sleeved arm and spread her tanned fingers toward him. She laughed deep in her throat.

"*Come hider, love, to me,*" she said.

He crossed the room slowly, took her hand. The fingers closed warmly about his. She pulled him down so that he had to kneel beside her. Her other arm lifted. Again she laughed, very softly, and closed her eyes, lifting her face to his.

The kiss was warm and long. He caught something of her own euphoria from the fragrance of the tea breathed into his face. And he was startled at the end of the kiss, when the clasp of her arms loosened about his neck, to feel the sudden rush of her breath against his cheek. There were tears on her face, and the sound she made was a sob.

He held her off and looked down in amazement. She sobbed once more, caught a deep breath, and said, "Oh, Oliver, Oliver—" Then she shook her head and pulled free, turning away to hide her face."I . . . I am sorry," she said unevenly. "Please forgive me. It does not matter . . . I *know* it does not matter . . . but—"

"What's wrong? What doesn't matter?"

"Nothing. Nothing . . . please forget it. Nothing at all." She got a handkerchief from the table and blew her nose, smiling at him with an effect of radiance through the tears.

Suddenly he was very angry. He had heard enough evasions and mystifying half-truths. He said roughly, "Do you think I'm crazy? I know enough now to—"

"Oliver, please!" She held up her own cup, steaming fragrantly. "Please, no more questions. Here, euphoria is what you need, Oliver. Euphoria, not answers."

"What year was it when you heard that song in Canterbury?" he demanded, pushing the cup aside.

She blinked at him, tears bright on her lashes. "Why . . . what year do you think?"

"I know," Oliver told her grimly. "I know the year that song was popular. I know you just came from Canterbury—Hollia's husband said so. It's May now, but it was autumn in Canterbury, and you just came from there, so lately the song you heard is still running through your head. Chaucer's Pardoner sang that song some time around the end of the fourteenth century. Did you see Chaucer, Kleph? What was it like in England that long ago?"

Kleph's eyes fixed his for a silent moment. Then her shoulders drooped and her whole body went limp with resignation beneath the soft blue robe. "I am a fool," she said gently. "It must have been easy to trap me. You really believe—what you say?"

Oliver nodded.

She said in a low voice. "Few people do believe it. That is one of our maxims, when we travel. We are safe from much suspicion because people before The Travel began will not believe."

The emptiness in Oliver's stomach suddenly doubled in volume. For an instant the bottom dropped out of time itself and the universe was unsteady about him. He felt sick. He felt naked and helpless. There was a buzzing in his ears and the room dimmed before him.

He had not really believed—not until this instant. He had expected some rational explanation from her that would tidy all his wild half-thoughts and suspicions into something a man could accept as believable. Not this.

Kleph dabbed at her eyes with the pale-blue handkerchief and smiled tremulously.

"I know," she said. "It must be a terrible thing to accept. To have all your concepts turned upside down—We know it from childhood, of course, but for you . . . here, Oliver. The euphoriac will make it easier."

He took the cup, the faint stain of her lip rouge still on the crescent opening. He drank, feeling the dizzy sweetness spiral through his head, and his brain turned a little in his skull as the volatile fragrance took effect. With that turning, focus shifted and all his values with it.

He began to feel better. The flesh settled on his bones again, and the warm clothing of temporal assurance settled upon his flesh, and he was no longer naked and in the vortex of unstable time.

"The story is very simple, really," Kleph said. "We—travel. Our own time is not terribly far ahead of yours. No. I must not say how far. But we still remember your songs and poets and some of your great actors. We are a people of much leisure, and we cultivate the art of enjoying ourselves.

"This is a tour we are making—a tour of a year's seasons. Vintage seasons. That autumn in Canterbury was the most magnificent autumn our researchers could discover anywhere. We rode in a pilgrimage to the shrine—it was a wonderful experience, though the clothing was a little hard to manage.

"Now this month of May is almost over—the loveliest May in recorded times. A perfect May in a wonderful period. You have no way of knowing what a good, gay period you live in, Oliver. The very feeling in the air of the cities—that wonderful national confidence and happiness—everything going as smoothly as a dream. There were other Mays with fine weather, but each of them had a war or a famine, or something else wrong." She hesitated, grimaced and went on rapidly. "In a few days we are to meet at a coronation in Rome," she said. "I think the year will be 800—Christmastime. We—"

"But why," Oliver interrupted, "did you insist on this house? Why do the others want to get it away from you?"

Kleph stared at him. He saw the tears rising again in small bright crescents that gathered above her lower lids. He saw the look of obstinacy that came upon her soft, tanned face. She shook her head.

"You must not ask me that." She held out the steaming cup. "Here, drink and forget what I have said. I can tell you no more. No more at all."

When he woke, for a little while he had no idea where he was. He did not remember leaving Kleph or coming to his own room. He didn't care, just then. For he woke to a sense of overwhelming terror.

The dark was full of it. His brain rocked on waves of fear and pain. He lay motionless, too frightened to stir, some atavistic memory warning him to lie quiet until he knew from which direction the danger threatened. Reasonless panic broke over him in a tidal flow; his head ached with its violence and the dark throbbed to the same rhythms.

A knock sounded at the door. Omerie's deep voice said, "Wilson! Wilson, are you awake?"

Oliver tried twice before he had breath to answer. "Y-yes—what is it?"

The knob rattled. Omerie's dim figure groped for the light switch and the room sprang into visibility. Omerie's face was drawn with strain, and he held one hand to his head as if it ached in rhythm with Oliver's.

It was in that moment, before Omerie spoke again, that Oliver remembered Hollia's warning. "Move out, young man—move out before tonight." Wildly he wondered what threatened them all in this dark house that throbbed with the rhythms of pure terror.

Omerie in an angry voice answered the unspoken question.

"Someone has planted a subsonic in the house, Wilson. Kleph thinks you may know where it is."

"S-subsonic?"

"Call it a gadget," Omerie interpreted impatiently. "Probably a small metal box that—"

Oliver said, "Oh," in a tone that must have told Omerie everything.

"Where is it?" he demanded. "Quick. Let's get this over."

"I don't know." With an effort Oliver controlled the chattering of his teeth. "Y-you mean all this—all this is just from the little box?"

"Of course. Now tell me how to find it before we all go crazy."

Oliver got shakily out of bed, groping for his robe with nerveless hands. "I s-suppose she hid it somewhere downstairs," he said. "S-she wasn't gone long."

Omerie got the story out of him in a few brief questions. He clicked his teeth in exasperation when Oliver had finished it.

"That stupid Hollia—"

"Omerie!" Kleph's plaintive voice wailed from the hall. "Please hurry, Omerie! This is too much to stand! Oh, Omerie, please!"

Oliver stood up abruptly. Then a redoubled wave of the inexplicable pain seemed to explode in his skull at the motion, and he clutched the bedpost and reeled.

"Go find the thing yourself," he heard himself saying dizzily. "I can't even walk—"

Omerie's own temper was drawn wire-tight by the pressure in the room. He seized Oliver's shoulder and shook him, saying in a tight voice, "You let it in—now help us get it out, or—"

"It's a gadget out of your world, not mine!" Oliver said furiously.

And then it seemed to him there was a sudden coldness and silence in the room. Even the pain and the senseless terror paused for a moment. Omerie's pale, cold eyes fixed upon Oliver a stare so chill he could almost feel the ice in it.

"What do you know about our—world?" Omerie demanded.

Oliver did not speak a word. He did not need to; his face must have betrayed what he knew. He was beyond concealment in the stress of this nighttime terror he still could not understand.

Omerie bared his white teeth and said three perfectly unintelligible words. Then he stepped to the door and snapped, "Kleph!"

Oliver could see the two women huddled together in the hall, shaking violently with involuntary waves of that strange, synthetic terror. Klia, in a luminous green gown, was rigid with control, but Kleph made no effort whatever at repression. Her downy robe had turned soft gold tonight; she shivered in it and the tears ran down her face unchecked.

"Kleph," Omerie said in a dangerous voice, "you were euphoric again yesterday?"

Kleph darted a scared glance at Oliver and nodded guiltily.

"You talked too much." It was a complete indictment in one sentence. "You know the rules, Kleph. You will not be allowed to travel again if anyone reports this to the authorities."

Kleph's lovely creamy face creased suddenly into impenitent dimples.

"I know it was wrong. I am very sorry—but you will not stop me if Cenbe says no."

Klia flung out her arms in a gesture of helpless anger. Omerie shrugged.

"In this case, as it happens, no great harm is done," he said, giving Oliver an unfathomable glance. "But it might have been serious. Next time perhaps it will be. I must have a talk with Cenbe."

"We must find the subsonic first of all," Klia reminded them, shivering. "If Kleph is afraid to help, she can go out for a while. I confess I am very sick of Kleph's company just now."

"We could give up the house!" Kleph cried wildly. "Let Hollia have it! How can you stand this long enough to hunt—"

"Give up the house?" Klia echoed. "You must be mad! With all our invitations out?"

"There will be no need for that," Omerie said. "We can find it if we all hunt. You feel able to help?" He looked at Oliver.

With an effort Oliver controlled his own senseless panic as the waves of it swept through the room. "Yes," he said. "But what about me? What are you going to do?"

"That should be obvious," Omerie said, his pale eyes in the dark face regarding Oliver impassively. "Keep you in the house until we go. We can certainly do no less. You understand that. And there is no reason for us to do more, as it happens. Silence is all we promised when we signed our travel papers."

"But—" Oliver groped for the fallacy in that reasoning. It was no use. He could not think clearly. Panic surged insanely through his mind from the very air around him. "All right," he said. "Let's hunt."

It was dawn before they found the box, tucked inside the ripped seam of a sofa cushion. Omerie took it upstairs without a word. Five minutes later the pressure in the air abruptly dropped and peace fell blissfully upon the house.

"They will try again," Omerie said to Oliver at the door of the back bedroom. "We must watch for that. As for you, I must see that you remain in the house until Friday. For your own comfort, I advise you to let me know if Hollia offers any further tricks. I confess I am not quite sure how to enforce your staying indoors. I could use methods that would make you very uncomfortable. I would prefer to accept your word on it."

Oliver hesitated. The relaxing of pressure upon his brain had left him exhausted and stupid, and he was not at all sure what to say.

Omerie went on after a moment. "It was partly our fault for not insuring that we had the house to ourselves," he said. "Living here with us, you could scarcely help suspecting. Shall we say that in return for your promise, I reimburse you in part for losing the sale price on this house?"

Oliver thought that over. It would pacify Sue a little. And it meant only two days indoors. Besides, what good would escaping do? What could he say to outsiders that would not lead him straight to a padded cell?

"All right," he said wearily. "I promise."

. . .

By Friday morning there was still no sign from Hollia. Sue telephoned at noon. Oliver knew the crackle of her voice over the wire when Kleph took the call. Even the crackle sounded hysterical; Sue saw her bargain slipping hopelessly through her grasping little fingers.

Kleph's voice was soothing. "I am sorry," she said many times, in the intervals when the voice paused. "I am truly sorry. Believe me, you will find it does not matter. I know . . . I am sorry—"

She turned from the phone at last. "The girl says Hollia has given up," she told the others.

"Not Hollia," Klia said firmly.

Omerie shrugged. "We have very little time left. If she intends anything more, it will be tonight. We must watch for it."

"Oh, not tonight!" Kleph's voice was horrified. "Not even Hollia would do that!"

"Hollia, my dear, in her own way is quite as unscrupulous as you are," Omerie told her with a smile.

"But—would she spoil things for us just because she can't be here?"

"What do you think?" Klia demanded.

Oliver ceased to listen. There was no making sense out of their talk, but he knew that by tonight whatever the secret was must surely come into the open at last. He was willing to wait and see.

For two days excitement had been building up in the house and the three who shared it with him. Even the servants felt it and were nervous and unsure of themselves. Oliver had given up asking questions—it only embarrassed his tenants—and watched.

All the chairs in the house were collected in the three front bedrooms. The furniture was rearranged to make room for them, and dozens of covered cups had been set out on trays. Oliver recognized Kleph's rose-quartz set among the rest. No steam rose from the thin crescent-openings, but the cups were full. Oliver lifted one and felt a heavy liquid move within it, like something half-solid, sluggishly.

Guests were obviously expected, but the regular dinner hour of nine came and went, and no one had yet arrived. Dinner was finished; the servants went home. The Sanciscos went to their rooms to dress, amid a feeling of mounting tension.

Oliver stepped out on the porch after dinner, trying in vain to guess what it was that had wrought such a pitch of expectancy in the house. There was a quarter moon swimming in haze on the horizon, but the stars which had made every night of May thus far a dazzling translucency, were very dim tonight. Clouds had begun to gather at sundown, and the undimmed weather of the whole month seemed ready to break at last.

Behind Oliver the door opened a little, and closed. He caught Kleph's fragrance before he turned, and a faint whiff of the fragrance of the euphoriac she was much too fond of drinking. She came to his side and slipped a hand into his, looking up into his face in the darkness.

"Oliver," she said very softly. "Promise me one thing. Promise me not to leave the house tonight."

"I've already promised that," he said a little irritably.

"I know. But tonight—I have a very particular reason for wanting you indoors tonight." She leaned her head against his shoulder for a moment, and despite himself his irritation softened. He had not seen Kleph alone since that last night of her revelations; he supposed he never would be alone with her again for more than a few minutes at a time. But he knew he would not forget those two bewildering evenings. He knew too, now, that she was very weak and foolish—but she was still Kleph and he had held her in his arms, and was not likely ever to forget it.

"You might be—hurt—if you went out tonight," she was saying in a muffled voice. "I know it will not matter, in the end, but—remember you promised, Oliver."

She was gone again, and the door had closed behind her, before he could voice the futile questions in his mind.

The guests began to arrive just before midnight. From the head of the stairs Oliver saw them coming in by twos and threes, and was astonished at how many of these people from the future must have gathered here in the past weeks. He could see quite clearly now how they differed from the norm of his own period. Their physical elegance was what one noticed first—perfect grooming, meticulous manners, meticulously controlled voices. But because they were all idle, all, in a way, sensation-hunters, there was a certain shrillness underlying their voices, especially when heard all together. Petulance and self-indulgence showed beneath the good manners. And tonight, an all-pervasive excitement.

By one o'clock everyone had gathered in the front rooms. The teacups had begun to steam, apparently of themselves, around midnight, and the house was full of the faint, thin fragrance that induced a sort of euphoria all through the rooms, breathed in with the perfume of the tea.

It made Oliver feel light and drowsy. He was determined to sit up as long as the others did, but he must have dozed off in his own room, by the window, an unopened book in his lap.

For when it happened he was not sure for a few minutes whether or not it was a dream.

The vast, incredible crash was louder than sound. He felt the whole house shake under him, felt rather than heard the timbers grind upon one another like broken bones, while he was still in the borderland of sleep. When he woke fully he was on the floor among the shattered fragments of the window.

How long or short a time he had lain there he did not know. The world was still stunned with that tremendous noise, or his ears still deaf from it, for there was no sound anywhere.

He was halfway down the hall toward the front rooms when sound began to return from outside. It was a low, indescribable rumble at first, prickled with countless tiny distant screams. Oliver's eardrums ached from the terrible impact of the vast unheard noise, but the numbness was wearing off and he heard before he saw it the first voices of the stricken city.

The door to Kleph's room resisted him for a moment. The house had settled a little from the violence of the — the explosion? — and the frame was out of line. When he got the door open he could only stand blinking stupidly into the darkness within. All the lights were out, but there was a breathless sort of whispering going on in many voices.

The chairs were drawn around the broad front windows so that everyone could see out; the air swam with the fragrance of euphoria. There was light enough here from outside for Oliver to see that a few onlookers still had their hands to their ears, but all were craning eagerly forward to see.

Through a dreamlike haze Oliver saw the city spread out with impossible distinctness below the window. He knew quite well that a row of houses across the street blocked the view — yet he was looking over the city now, and he could see it in a limitless panorama from here to the horizon. The houses between had vanished.

On the far skyline fire was already a solid mass, painting the low clouds crimson. That sulphurous light reflecting back from the sky upon the city made clear the rows upon rows of flattened houses with flame beginning to lick up among them, and farther out the formless rubble of what had been houses a few minutes ago and was now nothing at all.

The city had begun to be vocal. The noise of the flames rose loudest, but you could hear a rumble of human voices like the beat of surf a long way off, and staccato noises of screaming made a sort of pattern that came and went continuously through the web of sound. Threading it in undulating waves the shrieks of sirens knit the web together into a terrible symphony that had, in its way, a strange, inhuman beauty.

Briefly through Oliver's stunned incredulity went the memory of that other symphony Kleph had played there one day, another catastrophe retold in terms of music and moving shapes.

He said hoarsely, "Kleph—"

The tableau by the window broke. Every head turned, and Oliver saw the faces of strangers staring at him, some few in embarrassment avoiding his eyes, but most seeking them out with that avid, inhuman curiosity which is common to a type in all crowds at accident scenes. But these people were here by design, audience at a vast disaster timed almost for their coming.

Kleph got up unsteadily, her velvet dinner gown tripping her as she rose. She set down a cup and swayed a little as she came toward the door, saying, "Oliver . . . Oliver—" in a sweet, uncertain voice. She was drunk, he saw, and wrought up by the catastrophe to a pitch of stimulation in which she was not very sure what she was doing.

Oliver heard himself saying in a thin voice not his own, "W-what was it, Kleph? What happened? What—" But *happened* seemed so inadequate a word for the incredible panorama below that he had to choke back hysterical laughter upon the struggling questions, and broke off entirely, trying to control the shaking that had seized his body.

Kleph made an unsteady stoop and seized a steaming cup. She came to him, swaying, holding it out—her panacea for all ills.

"Here, drink it, Oliver—we are all quite safe here, quite safe." She thrust the cup to his lips and he gulped automatically, grateful for the fumes that began their slow, coiling surcease in his brain with the first swallow.

"It was a meteor," Kleph was saying. "Quite a small meteor, really. We are perfectly safe here. This house was never touched."

Out of some cell of the unconscious Oliver heard himself saying incoherently, "Sue? Is Sue—" he could not finish.

Kleph thrust the cup at him again. "I think she may be safe—for awhile. Please, Oliver—forget about all that and drink."

"But you *knew!*" Realization of that came belatedly to his stunned brain. "You could have given warning, or—"

"How could we change the past?" Kleph asked. "We knew—but could we stop the meteor? Or warn the city? Before we come we must give our word never to interfere—"

Their voices had risen imperceptibly to be audible above the rising volume of sound from below. The city was roaring now, with flames and cries and the crash of falling buildings. Light in the room turned lurid and pulsed upon the walls and ceiling in red light and redder dark.

Downstairs a door slammed. Someone laughed. It was high, hoarse, angry laughter. Then from the crowd in the room someone gasped and there was a chorus of dismayed cries. Oliver tried to focus upon the window and the terrible panorama beyond, and found he could not.

It took several seconds of determined blinking to prove that more than his own vision was at fault. Kleph whimpered softly and moved against him. His arms closed about her automatically, and he was grateful for the warm, solid flesh against him. This much at least he could touch and be sure of, though everything else that was happening might be a dream. Her perfume and the heady perfume of the tea rose together in his head, and for an instant, holding her in this embrace that must certainly be the last time he ever held her, he did not care that something had gone terribly wrong with the very air of the room.

It was blindness—not continuous, but a series of swift, widening ripples between which he could catch glimpses of the other faces in the room, strained and astonished in the flickering light from the city.

The ripples came faster. There was only a blink of sight between them now, and the blinks grew briefer and briefer, the intervals of darkness more broad.

From downstairs the laughter rose again up the stairwell. Oliver thought he knew the voice. He opened his mouth to speak, but a door nearby slammed open before he could find his tongue, and Omerie shouted down the stairs.

"Hollia?" he roared above the roaring of the city. "Hollia, is that you?"

She laughed again, triumphantly. "I warned you!" her hoarse, harsh voice called. "Now come out in the street with the rest of us if you want to see any more!"

"Hollia!" Omerie shouted desperately. "Stop this or—"

The laughter was derisive. "What will you do, Omerie? This time I hid it too well—come down in the street if you want to watch the rest."

There was angry silence in the house. Oliver could feel Kleph's quick, excited breathing light upon his cheek, feel the soft motions of her body in his arms. He tried consciously to make the moment last, stretch it out to infinity. Everything had happened too swiftly to impress very clearly on his mind anything except what he could touch and hold. He held her in an embrace made consciously light, though he wanted to clasp her in a tight, despairing grip, because he was sure this was the last embrace they would ever share.

The eye-straining blinks of light and blindness went on. From far away below the roar of the burning city rolled on, threaded together by the long, looped cadences of the sirens that linked all sounds into one.

Then in the bewildering dark another voice sounded from the hall downstairs. A man's voice, very deep, very melodious, saying:

"What is this? What are you doing here? Hollia—is that you?"

Oliver felt Kleph stiffen in his arms. She caught her breath, but she said nothing in the instant while heavy feet began to mount the stairs, coming up with a solid, confident tread that shook the old house to each step.

Then Kleph thrust herself hard out of Oliver's arms. He heard her high, sweet, excited voice crying, "Cenbe! Cenbe!" and she ran to meet the newcomer through the waves of dark and light that swept the shaken house.

Oliver staggered a little and felt a chair seat catching the back of his legs. He sank into it and lifted to his lips the cup he still held. Its steam was warm and moist in his face, though he could scarcely make out the shape of the rim.

He lifted it with both hands and drank.

When he opened his eyes it was quite dark in the room. Also it was silent except for a thin, melodious humming almost below the threshold of sound. Oliver struggled with the memory of a monstrous nightmare. He put it resolutely out of his mind and sat up, feeling an unfamiliar bed creak and sway under him.

This was Kleph's room. But no—Kleph's no longer. Her shining hangings were gone from the walls, her white resilient rug, her pictures. The room looked as it had looked before she came, except for one thing.

In the far corner was a table—a block of translucent stuff—out of which light poured softly. A man sat on a low stool before it, leaning forward, his heavy shoulders outlined against the glow. He wore earphones and he was making quick, erratic notes upon a pad on his knee, swaying a little as if to the tune of unheard music.

The curtains were drawn, but from beyond them came a distant, muffled roaring that Oliver remembered from his nightmare. He put a hand to his face, aware of a feverish warmth and a dipping of the room before his eyes. His head ached, and there was a deep malaise in every limb and nerve.

As the bed creaked, the man in the corner turned, sliding the earphones down like a collar. He had a strong, sensitive face above a dark beard, trimmed short. Oliver had never seen him before, but he had that air Oliver knew so well by now, of remoteness which was the knowledge of time itself lying like a gulf between them.

When he spoke his deep voice was impersonally kind.

"You had too much euphoriac, Wilson," he said, aloofly sympathetic. "You slept a long while."

"How long?" Oliver's throat felt sticky when he spoke.

The man did not answer. Oliver shook his head experimentally. He said, "I thought Kleph said you don't get hangovers from—" Then another thought interrupted the first, and he said quickly, "Where is Kleph?" He looked confusedly toward the door.

"They should be in Rome by now. Watching Charlemagne's coronation at St. Peter's on Christmas Day a thousand years from here."

That was not a thought Oliver could grasp clearly. His aching brain sheered away from it; he found thinking at all was strangely difficult. Staring at the man, he traced an idea painfully to its conclusion.

"So they've gone on—but you stayed behind? Why? You . . . you're Cenbe? I heard your—symphonia, Kleph called it."

"You heard part of it. I have not finished yet. I needed—this." Cenbe inclined his head toward the curtains beyond which the subdued roaring still went on.

"You needed—the meteor?" The knowledge worked painfully through his dulled brain until it seemed to strike some area still untouched by the aching, an area still alive to implication. "The *meteor?* But—"

There was a power implicit in Cenbe's raised hand that seemed to push Oliver down upon the bed again. Cenbe said patiently, "The worst of it is past now, for a while. Forget if you can. That was days ago. I said you were asleep for some time. I let you rest. I knew this house would be safe—from the fire at least."

"Then—something more's to come?" Oliver only mumbled his question. He was not sure he wanted an answer. He had been curious so long, and now that knowledge lay almost within reach, something about his brain seemed to refuse to listen. Perhaps this weariness, this feverish, dizzy feeling would pass as the effect of the euphoriac wore off.

Cenbe's voice ran on smoothly, soothingly, almost as if Cenbe, too, did not want him to think. It was easiest to lie here and listen.

"I am a composer," Cenbe was saying. "I happen to be interested in interpreting certain forms of disaster into my own terms. That is why I stayed on. The others were dilettantes. They came for the May weather and the spectacle. The aftermath—well why should they wait for that? As for myself—I suppose I am a connoisseur. I find the aftermath rather fascinating. And I need it. I need to study it at first hand, for my own purposes."

His eyes dwelt upon Oliver for an instant very keenly, like a physician's eyes, impersonal and observing. Absently he reached for his stylus and the note pad. And as he moved, Oliver saw a familiar mark on the underside of the thick, tanned wrist.

"Kleph had that scar, too," he heard himself whisper. "And the others."

Cenbe nodded. "Inoculation. It was necessary, under the circumstances. We did not want disease to spread in our own time-world."

"Disease?"

Cenbe shrugged. "You would not recognize the name."

"But, if you can inoculate against disease—" Oliver thrust himself up on an aching arm. He had a half-grasp upon a thought now which he did not want to let go. Effort seemed to make the ideas come more clearly through his mounting confusion. With enormous effort he went on.

"I'm getting it now," he said. "Wait. I've been trying to work this out. You can change history? You can! I know you can. Kleph said she had to promise not to interfere. You all had to promise. Does that mean you really could change your own past—our time?"

Cenbe laid down his pad again. He looked at Oliver thoughtfully, a dark, intent look under heavy brows. "Yes," he said. "Yes, the past can be changed, but not easily. And it changes the future, too, necessarily. The lines of probability are switched into new patterns—but it is extremely difficult, and it has never been allowed. The physio-temporal course tends to slide back to its norm, always. That is why it is so hard to force any alteration." He shrugged. "A theoretical science. We do not change history, Wilson. If we changed our past, our present would be altered, too. And our time-world is entirely to our liking. There may be a few malcontents there, but they are not allowed the privilege of temporal travel."

Oliver spoke louder against the roaring from beyond the windows. "But you've got the power! You could alter history, if you wanted to—wipe out all the pain and suffering and tragedy—"

"All of that passed away long ago," Cenbe said.

"Not—now! Not—this!"

Cenbe looked at him enigmatically for a while. Then—"This, too," he said.

And suddenly Oliver realized from across what distances Cenbe was watching him. A vast distance, as time is measured. Cenbe was a composer and a genius, and necessarily strongly empathic, but his psychic locus was very far away in time. The dying city outside, the whole world of *now* was not quite real to Cenbe, falling short of reality because of that basic variance in time. It was merely one of the building blocks that had gone to support the edifice on which Cenbe's culture stood in a misty, unknown, terrible future.

It seemed terrible to Oliver now. Even Kleph—all of them had been touched with a pettiness, the faculty that had enabled Hollia to concentrate on her malicious, small schemes to acquire a ringside seat while the meteor thundered in toward Earth's atmosphere. They were all dilettantes, Kleph and Omerie and the other. They toured time, but only as onlookers. Were they bored—sated—with their normal existence?

Not sated enough to wish change, basically. Their own time-world was a fulfilled womb, a perfection made manifest for their needs. They dared not change the past—they could not risk flawing their own present.

Revulsion shook him. Remembering the touch of Kleph's lips, he felt a sour sickness on his tongue. Alluring she had been; he knew that too well. But the aftermath—

There was something about this race from the future. He had felt it dimly at first, before Kleph's nearness had drowned caution and buffered his sensibilities. Time traveling purely as an escape mechanism seemed almost blasphemous. A race with such power—

Kleph—leaving him for the barbaric, splendid coronation at Rome a thousand years ago—*how had she seen him?* Not as a living, breathing man. He knew that, very certainly. Kleph's race were spectators.

But he read more than casual interest in Cenbe's eyes now. There was an avidity there, a bright, fascinated probing. The man had replaced his earphones—he was different from the others. He was a connoisseur. After the vintage season came the aftermath—and Cenbe.

Cenbe watched and waited, light flickering softly in the translucent block before him, his fingers poised over the note pad. The ultimate connoisseur waited to savor the rarities that no non-gourmet could appreciate.

Those thin, distant rhythms of sound that was almost music began to be audible again above the noises of the distant fire. Listening, remembering, Oliver could very nearly catch the pattern of the symphonia as he had heard it, all intermingled with the flash of changing faces and the rank upon rank of the dying—

He lay back on the bed letting the room swirl away into the darkness behind his closed and aching lids. The ache was implicit in every cell of his body, almost a second ego taking possession and driving him out of himself, a strong, sure ego taking over as he himself let go.

Why, he wondered dully, should Kleph have lied? She had said there was no aftermath to the drink she had given him. No aftermath—and yet this painful possession was strong enough to edge him out of his own body.

Kleph had not lied. It was no aftermath to drink. He knew that—but the knowledge no longer touched his brain or his body. He lay still, giving them up to the power of the illness which was aftermath to something far stronger than the strongest drink. The illness that had no name—yet.

.　　.　　.

Cenbe's new symphonia was a crowning triumph. It had its premiere from Antares Hall, and the applause was an ovation. History itself, of course, was the artist—opening with the meteor that forecast the great plagues of the fourteenth century and closing with the climax Cenbe had caught on the threshold of modern times. But only Cenbe could have interpreted it with such subtle power.

Critics spoke of the masterly way in which he had chosen the face of the Stuart king as a recurrent motif against the montage of emotion and sound and movement. But there were other faces, fading through the great sweep of the composition, which helped to build up to the tremendous climax. One face in particular, one moment that the audience absorbed greedily. A moment in which one man's face loomed huge in the screen, every feature clear. Cenbe had never caught an emotional crisis so effectively, the critics agreed. You could almost read the man's eyes.

After Cenbe had left, he lay motionless for a long while. He was thinking feverishly—

I've got to find some way to tell people. If I'd known in advance, maybe something could have been done. We'd have forced them to tell us how to change the probabilities. We could have evacuated the city.

If I could leave a message—

Maybe not for today's people. But later. They visit all through time. If they could be recognized and caught somewhere, sometime, and made to change destiny—

It wasn't easy to stand up. The room kept tilting. But he managed it. He found pencil and paper and through the swaying of the shadows he wrote down what he could. Enough. Enough to warn, enough to save.

He put the sheets on the table, in plain sight, and weighted them down before he stumbled back to bed through closing darkness.

The house was dynamited six days later, part of the futile attempt to halt the relentless spread of the Blue Death.

The Way to Amalteia

TRANSLATED BY ROGER DE GARIS

The brothers Arkady and Boris Strugatsky are, as a writing team, among the greatest living writers of science fiction. Their best stories equal in narrative power and intellectual appeal those of the finest SF writers in any language since H. G. Wells; their novella Roadside Picnic *can stand beside the finest SF novellas in English, and their novels of social criticism, such as* Prisoners of Power, The Second Martian Invasion, *or* The Snail on the Slope *are deservedly praised. They have great strengths as storytellers and are the most popular Soviet SF writers. They are often given credit for nearly single-handedly re-creating SF in the Soviet Union after 1960.*

Boris is an astronomer and Arkady is a translator specializing in Japanese, who translated Hal Clement's classic hard SF novel Mission of Gravity *into Russian. They attended, as guests of honor, the 1987 World Science Fiction Convention in Brighton, England, where they genially upbraided the thousands of Westerners present for knowing too little about the contemporary Soviet Union. They are well read in English-language SF, and this story, in English, could well have appeared in Campbell's* Astounding *in 1959 when it was written. It now stands as a worthy companion to Arthur C. Clarke's "A Meeting with Medusa."*

*   *   *

Prologue: Amalteia, J-Station

Amalteia, the fifth and closest of Jupiter's satellites, rotates about its axis about every thirty-five hours. In addition it makes a full revolution around Jupiter every twelve hours. Therefore Jupiter slides over the nearby horizon every thirteen and one-half hours.

The rise of Jupiter is very beautiful. To appreciate it, however, you must take the elevator up to the top floor, under the transparent spectrolite bubble.

When your eyes get used to the darkness, a frozen plain is visible, stretching in a hump to the rocky ridges on the horizon. The sky is black, and in it are countless bright unblinking stars. From the shining of the stars dim reflections lie over the plain, and the rocky ridge seems a deep black shadow against the starry sky. If you look closely, you can make out even the outlines of individual jagged peaks.

It happens sometimes that the spotted sickle of Ganymede hangs low over the ridge, or the silvery disk of Callisto, or the two of them together, although that happens comparatively rarely. Then from the peaks across the glittering ice of the entire plain, even gray shadows spread. And when the sun is above the horizon—a round spot of blinding flame, the plain turns blue, the shadows become black, and every crack in the ice is visible. The charred smudges on the rocketdrome resemble huge ice-covered puddles. The sight arouses warm, half-forgotten associations, and you feel like running out onto the field and sliding down the thin skin of ice to see how it crackles beneath your magnetic boots, how the cracks race over it, like the skim on hot milk, only dark in color.

But all of this can be seen elsewhere as well.

It really becomes beautiful when Jupiter rises. And the rise of Jupiter is truly beautiful only on Amalteia. And it is particularly beautiful when the rise of Jupiter overtakes the sun. First a green glow burns beyond the peaks of the ridge—the exosphere of the gigantic planet. It glows brighter and brighter, slowly creeping up to the sun, and one after another the stars in the black sky go out. And suddenly it attacks the sun. It is very important not to miss this moment. The green glow of the exosphere instantaneously, as though by sorcery, becomes bloodred. You always wait for that moment, and it always comes startlingly fast. The sun turns red, and the icy plain becomes red, and bloody rays flash on the round navigation tower on the edge of the plain. Even the peaks' shadows become pink. Then the red gradually darkens, becoming chestnut, and finally, the huge red-brown hump of Jupiter crawls over the rocky ridge on the near horizon. The sun is still visible, and it is still red, like heated iron—an even cherrylike disk against the brownish background.

For some reason it is felt that brown is an ugly color. That is what a person who had never seen the brown glow of half a sky and the distinct red disk on it might think. Then the disk disappears. Only Jupiter remains—huge, brown, shaggy, it slowly climbs above the horizon, as though it were swelling, and occupies a quarter of the sky. It is streaked with black-and-green ammonia clouds, and sometimes tiny white dots appear and immediately go out—that is the way exospheric protuberances look from Amalteia.

Unfortunately, watching the rise of Jupiter from beginning to end is hard to do. Jupiter rises too slowly, and you have to go to work. During observations, of course, you can follow the entire rise, but while taking observations you don't have time to think about beauty.

The director of J-Station looked at his watch. Today the rise had been beautiful, and would soon be even more beautiful, but it was time to go below and think about what had to be done.

In the shadow of the ridge the mesh skeleton of the Big Antenna started to move, turning slowly. Radio opticians had set about their observations. The poor, starving radio optics. . . .

The director looked at Jupiter's brown cupola for a last time and thought how good it would be to seize the moment when all four large satellites—the reddish Io, Europa, Ganymede, and Callisto—were hanging over the horizon, and Jupiter itself, in its first quarter, was half orange, half brown. Then he realized that he had never seen Jupiter set. That, too, must be beautiful: The glow of the exosphere slowly dies out, and one after another the stars flash on in the darkening sky, like needles of diamond against velvet. But usually that time was the peak of the workday.

The director entered the elevator and went down to the bottom floor. The planetological station on Amalteia was a research city on many levels, cut into the ice layer and poured out of metalloplast. Around sixty persons lived, worked, studied, and built here. Fifty-six young men and women, fine people, with excellent appetites.

The director glanced into the sports room, but no one was there, just someone splashing in the round pool, and the echo was ringing from under the ceiling. The director walked on, moving without haste in his heavy magnetic boots. On Amalteia there was practically no gravity, and that was highly inconvenient. After a while, of course, you get used to it, but at first it seems that your body is filled with hydrogen and about to leap out of your magnetic boots. And it was particularly difficult getting used to sleeping.

Two astrophysicists went past, their hair still damp from the shower, said hello, and quickly walked on, to the elevators. One of the astrophysicists apparently had something the matter with his magnetic soles—he was hopping along awkwardly. The director turned into the dining room. About fifteen people were having breakfast.

Uncle Valnoga, the cook—the station's gastronomic engineer—distributed the breakfasts on a cart. He was gloomy. He had been gloomy since the unfortunate day when they had radioed from Callisto, the fourth satellite, about an accident affecting the food supplies. The food storehouse on Callisto was destroyed by fungus. It had happened before, but this time the whole supply was wiped out, down to the last cracker, and the chlorella farm had been lost, too.

On Callisto it was very hard to work. Unlike Amalteia, Callisto had a biosphere, and no one had found a way to prevent the fungus from invading the living quarters. It was a very interesting fungus. It would penetrate any wall and devour everything edible—bread, canned goods, sugar. It was particularly fond of chlorella. Sometimes it would infect a human being, but that was not at all dangerous. At first everyone was very much afraid of it, and even the boldest were concerned when they found the characteristic slightly slippery film on their skin. But the fungus did not cause living organisms pain or harm. It was even said that it had a tonic effect. But food it destroyed in nothing flat.

"Uncle Valnoga," someone called out. "Are we going to have crackers again for dinner?"

The director did not manage to see who had said it, because everyone turned their heads toward Uncle Valnoga and stopped chewing. Handsome young faces, almost all deeply tanned. And already pinched-looking. Or did it just seem that way?

"For dinner you will get soup," Uncle Valnoga said.

"Great!" someone exclaimed, and once again the director did not notice who.

He walked over to the nearest chair and sat down. Valnoga wheeled the cart over to him, and the director took his breakfast—a plate with a small pile of crackers, a half a bar of chocolate, and a pear-shaped glass of tea. He did it very skillfully, but all the same the crackers jumped up and hung in the air. The pear of tea stayed still—it had a magnetic bottom. The director caught one of the crackers, took a bite, and grabbed the glass. The tea was cold.

"Soup," Valnoga said. He spoke softly, addressing only the director. "Can you imagine what soup is anymore. And they probably think I'm going to serve chicken broth." He pushed his cart away and sat down at a table. He watched the cart roll down an aisle slower and slower. "But on Callisto they are eating chicken soup."

"Not likely," the director said absentmindedly.

"What do you mean, not likely?" Valnoga asked. "I gave up one hundred seventy cans to them. More than half of our reserve."

"Have we eaten up the remaining reserves?"

"Of course we have."

"Then so have they," the director said, crunching his cracker. "They have twice as many people."

You're lying, Uncle Valnoga, he thought. I know your tricks, gastronomic engineer. You've already set aside twenty cans for the sick.

Valnoga sighed and asked, "Is your tea cold?"

"No, it's okay."

"The chlorella on Callisto just won't take," Valnoga said and sighed again. "They radioed for another ten kilograms of ferment. They reported that they had sent the planet ship."

"Well, we have to give it to them."

"Of course we have to!" Uncle Valnoga said. "Of course. But I don't have a hundred tons of the stuff, and I have to let it grow. I'm probably ruining your appetite, aren't I?"

"It's okay," the director said. He was not hungry to begin with.

"Enough!" someone said.

The director raised his eyes and immediately saw the confused face of Zoya Ivanova. Alongside her sat the nuclear physicist Kozlov. They always sat next to each other.

"That's enough, do you hear?" Kozlov said in anger.

Zoya blushed and bent her head. She was embarrassed because everyone was looking at her.

"Yesterday you shoved your crackers at me," Kozlov said. "And today you do it again."

Zoya was silent. She was almost crying from shame.

"Don't yell at her, you ass!" the atmosphere physicist Potapov barked from the other end of the dining room. "Zoya, why do you sacrifice for him, that animal. Give me your crackers, I won't mind. I won't even yell at you."

"No," Kozlov said, calmed down already. "I'm healthy even without them, and she needs to eat more than I do."

"Not true, Valya," Zoya said without raising her head.

Someone said, "How about a little more tea, Uncle Valnoga?"

Valnoga stood up. Potapov called across the whole dining room, "Hey, Gregor, how about a game after work?"

"You're on," Gregor said.

"You'll be beaten again, Vadim," someone said.

"The law of averages is on my side," Potapov asserted.

Everyone broke out laughing.

An angry face poked itself into the dining room.

"Is Potapov here? Vadim, a storm on Jupe!"

"Well!" Potapov said and jumped up. And the other atmosphere experts got up hurriedly from their tables. The angry face disappeared and then reappeared suddenly. "Grab me some crackers, okay?"

"If Valnoga will give them out," Potapov said. He looked at Valnoga.

"Why not?" Uncle Valnoga said. "Mr. Konstantin Stetsenko, two hundred grams of crackers and fifty grams of chocolate."

The director stood up, wiping his mouth with a paper napkin. Kozlov said, "Comrade Director, what's happening with the *Takhmasib*?"

Everyone fell silent and turned to the director. The young tanned faces, already slightly pinched-looking.

The director answered, "Still no news."

He walked slowly down the aisle between the tables and headed for his office. The whole problem was that the "food epidemic" on Callisto had come at a bad time. It still was not a real famine. Amalteia could still share its chlorella and crackers with Callisto. But if Bykov did not come soon with food. . . . Bykov was already close. He had been spotted, but then he fell silent and had remained so for over sixty hours already. I'll have to cut the rations again, the director thought. Here anything could happen, and the base on Mars was far away. Strange things could happen. It happened that planetologists from Earth and Mars were lost. It happened rarely, more rarely than the fungal infections. But it is very bad that it happens at all. A billion kilometers from Earth strange things did happen, worse than ten epidemics. It was famine. Perhaps it was death.

1. The Photon Freighter Takhmasib

1. *The planet ship approaches Jupiter, and the captain argues with the navigator and takes sporamine.*

Alexei Petrovich Bykov, the captain of the photon freighter *Takhmasib*, left his cabin and neatly closed the door behind him. His hair was wet. The captain had just taken a shower. He had even taken two showers—a water shower and an ion shower—but he still felt unsteady after his short sleep. He wanted to sleep so much that his eyes just would not open. During the last three days he had slept perhaps five hours total. The flight had turned out to be tricky.

The corridor was deserted and light. Bykov headed for the control room, trying not to shuffle. He had to go through the lounge to get to the control room. The door to the lounge was open, and voices could be heard. They belonged to the planetologists Dauge and Yurkovsky and sounded—it seemed to Bykov—unusually irritated and strangely hollow.

Once again they're up to something, Bykov thought. There's no getting around them. And I can't even curse them out properly, because they're my friends and are terribly happy that we all are on this flight together. That hasn't happened that often.

Bykov strode into the lounge and stopped. The bookcase was open, the books had tumbled onto the floor and were lying in a messy pile. The tablecloth had slipped off the table. Yurkovsky's long legs, wrapped in tight gray pants, stuck out from under the couch. The legs were waving wildly.

"I tell you, she's not here," Dauge said.

Dauge himself was not to be seen.

"You look," Yurkovsky's smothered voice said. "It was your idea, so you look!"

"What's going on here?" Bykov angrily inquired.

"Aha, there he is!" Dauge said and climbed out from under the table.

His face was happy, his jacket and shirt collar unbuttoned. Yurkovsky backed out from under the couch.

"What's the matter?" Bykov asked.

"Where's my Varya?" Yurkovsky asked, getting to his feet. He was very angry.

"Scoundrel!" Dauge exclaimed.

"Good-for-nothings!" Bykov said.

"It was him," Dauge said in tragic tones. "Just look at his face, Vladimir! Murderer!"

"I am speaking absolutely seriously, Alexei," Yurkovsky said. "Where's my Varya?"

"You know, my planetologist friends," Bykov said, "you can both go to hell."

He stuck out his jaw and strode into the control room. Dauge said as he left, "He incinerated Varya in the reactor."

Bykov closed the hatch behind him with a thud.

It was quiet in the control room. The navigator, Mikhail Antonovich Krutikov, was sitting in his usual position behind the computer desk, resting his double chin on his chubby fists. The computer was humming softly, the neon lights on its panel blinking pensively. Mikhail looked at the captain with a friendly expression and asked, "Did you sleep well, Alexei?"

"Yes," Bykov answered.

"I took bearings on Amalteia," Mikhail said. "They've really been waiting. . . ." He shook his head. "Imagine, Alexei, their rations are two hundred grams of crackers and fifty grams of chocolate. And three hundred grams of chlorella soup. It tastes terrible."

You should be there, Bykov thought; you might slim down, my chubby friend.

He looked angrily at the navigator but could not help himself and broke out in a smile. Mikhail, sticking out his fat lips in an expression of concern, was studying a sheet of blue graph paper.

"Here it is, Alexei," he said. "I wrote the finish program. Please check it."

Usually checking one of Mikhail's course programs was a waste of time. Mikhail remained the fattest and the most experienced navigator in the interplanetary fleet.

"I'll check it later," Bykov said. He yawned sweetly, covering his mouth with his hand. "Enter the program in the cybernavigator."

"I already did," Mikhail said guiltily.

"Aha," Bykov said. "Well then, all right. Where are we now?"

"In an hour we come out onto the finish," Mikhail answered. "We will pass over the north pole of Jupiter"—the word *Jupiter* he pronounced with evident pleasure—"at a distance of two diameters, two hundred ninety megameters. And then the final arc. We're as good as there, Alexei."

"You're calculating the distance from the center of Jupiter?"

"Yes, from the center."

"When we come out on the finish, you will give me the distance from the exosphere every quarter hour."

"Yessir, Alexei," Mikhail said.

Bykov yawned one more time, wiped his drooping eyelids with his hands, and walked alongside the accident signal panel. Everything there was in order. The engine was working without interruption, the plasma was proceeded at the appropriate rate, the tuning of the magnetic traps was holding perfectly. The flight engineer Zhilin was responsible for the magnetic traps. Good work, Zhilin, Bykov thought. You've got them humming.

Bykov stopped and tried to throw off the tuning by slightly changing course. The tuning was not thrown off. The white fleck on the transparent plastic disk did not even budge. Good work, Bykov thought again. He skirted a protruding wall—the photoreactor housing. Zhilin was standing by the reflector controls with a pencil between his teeth. He was holding onto the edges of the panel with both hands and barely noticeably doing a little tap dance, his powerful shoulders bulging.

"Hello, Ivan," Bykov said.

"Hello, Captain," Zhilin said, turning around quickly. The pencil slipped from between his teeth, but he caught it dexterously as it fell.

"How's the reflector?" Bykov asked.

"The reflector is working fine," Zhilin said, Bykov still bent over the panel and picked up the dense blue ribbon of the control system record.

The reflector is the most important and most fragile part of the photon drive, a gigantic parabolic mirror covered with five layers of superstable mesomatter. In the technical literature the reflector is often called a sail. At the focal point of the paraboloid, millions of bits of seuterium-tritium plasma are transformed into radiation every second. The flow of the pale purple flame strikes against the reflector's surface and creates a force. During this process enormous temperature changes occur in the mesomatter layer, and the mesomatter gradually, layer by layer, is burned up. In addition, the reflector is constantly corroded by meteorites. And if the engine is on and the reflector breaks at its base, where the fat horn of the photoreactor joins it, the ship becomes an instantaneous, soundless flash. Therefore the reflectors on photon ships are changed every hundred astronomical units of flight. Therefore the control system is constantly measuring the condition of the working layer over the reflector's entire surface.

"So," Bykov said, twirling the tape between his fingers, "the first layer has burned away."

Zhilin was silent.

"Mikhail!" Bykov called out. "Did you know that the first layer is burned out?"

"I know, Alexei," the navigator responded. "What can you do? It's oversun."

Oversun occurs rarely and only under exceptional conditions—like now, when there was a famine at J-Station. In oversun, the sun is located between the takeoff planet and the finish planet—a situation highly unfavorable from the point of view of direct cosmogation. The photon engine must work at maximum, the ship's velocity reaches sixty-seven thousand kilometers a second, and nonclassical effects begin to affect the instruments, effects that are still poorly understood. The crew gets almost no sleep, the expenditure of fuel and reflector is colossal, and to top it all off the ship, as a rule, approaches the finish planet from the pole—very inconvenient for the landing.

"Yes," Bykov said. "Oversun. It's oversun, indeed."

He returned to the navigator and looked at the fuel gauge.

"Give me a copy of the finish program, Mikhail," he said.

"One minute, Alexei," the navigator said.

He was very busy. Blue sheets of paper were scattered over the desk, and the semiautomatic attachment to the computer was humming softly. Bykov plopped down into his chair and let his eyes close halfway. In a blur he saw Mikhail, without taking his eyes off his printout, reach out to the panel, his fingers dancing over the keyboard. His hand began to resemble a large white spider. The computer hummed more loudly and stopped, flashing on the stop signal.

"What do you want, Alexei?" the navigator asked, still concentrating on his printout.

"The finish program," Alexei said, barely managing to force his eyelids apart.

A tabulogram crawled out of the output device, and Mikhail grabbed it with both hands.

"Right away," he said hurriedly. "Right away."

Bykov felt a sweet buzzing in his ears, a yellow flame appeared beneath his eyelids. His head dropped against his chest.

"Alexei," the navigator said. He reached over his desk and slapped Bykov on the shoulder. "Alexei, here's the program."

Bykov shuddered, shook his head, and looked from side to side. He took the print-covered sheets of paper.

"Heh-hmmm," he cleared his throat and massaged the skin on his forehead. "So then. . . . The theta algorithm again. . . ." He sleepily fixed his gaze on the printout.

"You should take some sporamine," the navigator advised.

"Hold on," Bykov said. "Hold on. What's this? Have you gone crazy, Navigator?"

Mikhail jumped up, ran around the desk, and leaned over Bykov's shoulder.

"Where, where?" he asked.

"Where are you flying to?" Bykov asked bitingly. "Maybe you think you're flying to the Seventh Testing Grounds?"

"What is it, Alexei?"

"Or maybe you imagine they've built a tritium generator for you on Amalteia?"

"If you're talking about fuel," Mikhail said, "why, there's enough fuel for three programs like that one."

Bykov woke up once and for all.

"I have to land on Amalteia," he said. "Then I have to take the planetologists into the exosphere and land on Amalteia again. And then I have to return to Earth. And that will be an oversun again!"

"Hold on," Mikhail said. "Just one minute."

"You dream up an insane program, as though stores of fuel were waiting for us."

The hatch to the control room opened partway, and Bykov turned around. Dauge's head appeared in the crack. The head ran its eyes around the room, then said pleadingly, "Listen, guys, Varya wouldn't happen to be here, would she?"

"Out!" Bykov barked.

The head disappeared in a flash. The hatch closed quietly.

"Good-for-nothings!" Bykov said. "But look here now, Navigator! If I don't have fuel for the return oversun, you're in big trouble."

"Don't shout, please," Mikhail answered indignantly. He thought for a second and added, blushing deeply, "Damn it anyway."

They were both silent. Mikhail returned to his spot, and they looked at each other, sulking. Then Mikhail said, "I've calculated the flight into the exosphere. I have almost calculated the return oversun." He put his hand on a pile of papers on his desk. "And if you are chicken, we can very easily stop off at Antimars."

Antimars was the cosmogator's name for an artificial planet in Mars's orbit but on the other side of the sun. In essence, it was a huge fuel reservoir, a fully automated filling station.

"And there is absolutely no reason to . . . yell," Mikhail said. The word *yell* he pronounced in a whisper. Mikhail stood there, cooling off. So did Bykov.

"Well," Bykov said, "forgive me, Mikhail."

Mikhail immediately broke out into a smile.

"I was wrong," Bykov added.

"Ah, Alexei," Mikhail said hurriedly. "It's nothing. Absolutely nothing. . . . But just look at what a remarkable circuit we'll have. From the vertical"—he began to gesture—"to the surface of Amalteia and over the exosphere itself on an inertial ellipse to the meeting point. And at the meeting point the relative velocity will be only four meters a second. A maximum overload of only twenty-two percent, and only thirty to forty minutes of weightlessness. And the errors in computation are very small."

"The errors are small because of the theta algorithm," Bykov said. He wanted to say something nice to the navigator: Mikhail had been the first to develop and apply the theta algorithm.

Mikhail gave out a vague sound in reply. He was pleasantly embarrassed. Bykov looked through the program, nodded several times in succession, then put the printout down and began to rub his eyes with his huge freckled hands.

"To be honest," he said, "I didn't sleep a damned wink."

"Take some sporamine, Alexei," Mikhail repeated. "I take a tablet every two hours and don't feel like sleeping at all. So does Ivan. Why torture yourself?"

"I don't like messing with chemicals," Bykov said. He jumped up and started pacing the room. "Listen, Mikhail, what's really happening on my ship?"

"What do you mean?" the navigator asked.

"The planetologists again," Bykov said.

Zhilin explained from behind the photoreactor casing: "Varya has disappeared."

"So?" Bykov said. "It was bound to happen." He paced again. "Children, very old children."

"Don't get mad at them, Alexei," the navigator said.

"You know, comrades,"—Bykov sat down—"the worst thing about a flight is the passengers. And the worst passengers are old friends. Give me some sporamine, Mikhail."

Mikhail quickly pulled a box out of his pocket. Bykov watched through sleepy eyes.

"Give me two right away," he said.

2. *The planetologists look for Varya, and the radio optician learns what a hippo is.*

"He chased me out," Dauge said, returning to Yurkovsky's cabin.

Yurkovsky was standing on a chair in the middle of his cabin and feeling the soft matte ceiling with the palm of his hand. A crushed cookie was spread out on the floor.

"She must be up here," Yurkovsky said.

He jumped down from the chair, shook white crumbs off his knees and called out pitifully, "Varya, light of my life, where are you?"

"Have you tried sitting down unexpectedly on the chair?" Dauge asked.

He walked over to the couch and stiffly collapsed on it.

"You'll kill her!" Yurkovsky shouted.

"She's not here," Dauge reported and settled in more comfortably, putting his feet up on the back of the couch. "We should perform this operation on all the couches and easy chairs. Varya likes curling up in something soft."

Yurkovsky dragged the chair closer to the wall.

"No," he said. "In flight she likes hiding behind walls or ceilings. We'll have to go through the ship searching the ceilings."

"Lord!" Dauge signed. "What planetologists won't do when they have no work!" He sat up, glanced at Yurkovsky and whispered sinisterly, "I'm sure it's Alexei. He always hated her."

Yurkovsky started at Dauge.

"Yes," Dauge continued. "Always. You know it. And why? She was so quiet . . . so gentle."

"You're a fool, Grigory," Yurkovsky said. "You're clowning around, but I'll really feel terrible if she gets lost."

He sat on the chair, his elbows on his knees and his head in his hands. His high forehead with a receding hairline gathered in wrinkles, and his eyebrows fell tragically.

"Come on, now," Dauge said. "How is she going to get lost on this ship? She'll turn up."

"You say she'll turn up," Yurkovsky said. "But it's time for her to eat. She never asks to eat herself, so she'll die from starvation."

"She's not going to die," Dauge disagreed.

"She hasn't eaten anything in twelve days. Since takeoff. And that's very dangerous."

"When she feels like it, she'll come," Dauge said confidently. "That is a characteristic of all life forms."

Yurkovsky shook his head.

"No, she won't come, Grigory."

He climbed up on the chair and began to feel the ceiling again, inch by inch. Someone knocked on the door. Then the door slid to the side and the small black-haired Charles Mollart, the radio optician, appeared.

"Will I come in?" he asked.

"A good question," Dauge said.

Mollart threw up his hands. "*Mais non!*" he exclaimed, and smiled joyously. He was constantly smiling joyously. "*Non* 'will I come' — I wanted to know 'will I came?'"

"Of course," Yurkovsky said from his chair. "Of course, came right in, Charles. Why not?"

Mollart entered, closed the door behind him, and looked up with curiosity.

"Voldemar," he said, "you are learning walk on ceiling?"

"*Oui, madame,*" Dauge replied with a terrible accent. "Or *messyur.* Actually, *il cherche la Varya.*"

"No-no," Mollart exclaimed. He even waved his arms. "Not that way. Not French. I want not to speak French."

Yurkovsky climbed down from his chair and asked, "Charles, have you seen my Varya?"

Mollart threatened him with a raised finger.

"Oh, you always joke me," he said with a strong accent on the "me." "You joke me twelve days already." He sat down on the couch next to Dauge. "What is Varya? I many times hear 'Varya,' today you look her, but I see her not one time. A?" He looked at Dauge. "Is bird? Or she is cat? Or a . . . a—"

"Hippo?" Dauge asked.

"What is 'ipo'?" Mollart inquired.

"*C'est* like a lirondel," Dauge answered. "A swallow."

"O, *l'hirondelle!*" Mollart exclaimed. "Ipo?"

"*Mais si!*" Dauge said. "*Natürlich.*"

"*Non, non!* Not other *langues!*" He turned to Yurkovsky. "Is Grégoire speaking truly?"

"Grégoire is laying it on thick," Yurkovsky said angrily. "It's nonsense."

Mollart looked at him attentively.

"You are upset, Voldemar," he said. "I can help?"

"No, not likely, Charles. Just have to keep searching. To feel everything with your hands, the way I am."

"Why feel?" Mollart said in surprise. "You tell me what are her looks. I become search."

"Ha!" Yurkovsky, "I'd like to know myself what she looks like right now."

Mollart leaned back in the couch.

"*Je ne comprends pas.* I do not understand. She has no looks? Or do I not understand?"

"No, that's right, Charles," Yurkovsky said, "She 'has looks,' of course, but different ones. When she is on the ceiling she looks like the ceiling. When she is on the couch, like the couch."

"And when on Grégoire, she likes Grégoire," Mollart said. "You still joke me."

"He's telling you the truth," Dauge interposed. "Varya keeps changing color. Mimicry. She camouflages herself incredibly. Mimicry."

"Mimicry with a swallow?" Mollart asked sarcastically.

Someone else knocked at the door.

"Come in!" Mollart called out joyously.

"Come in," Yurkovsky translated.

Zhilin entered, huge, rosy, and a little shy.

"Excuse me, Vladimir," he said, leaning forward slightly. "I—"

"O!" Mollart exclaimed, his smile sparkling. He was like the flight engineer. "*Le petit ingénieur!* The little engineer! How are things, good?"

"Good," Zhilin said.

"And the girls, is it good?"

"Good," Zhilin said. He was already used to Mollart. "*Bon.*"

"Beautiful pronunciation," Dauge said with envy. "By the way Charles, why do you always ask Ivan about girls?"

"I like them very much," Mollart said completely seriously.

"*Bon,*" Dauge said. "*Je vous comprends.*"

Zhilin turned to Yurkovsky.

"Vladimir, the captain sent me. In forty minutes we will be approaching the exosphere."

Yurkovsky leaped to his feet.

"Finally!"

"If you want to observe, I'm at your disposition."

"Thank you, Ivan," Yurkovsky said. He turned to Dauge. "Well, my friend, onward!"

"Oh, lovely brown Jupiter!" Dauge said.

"*Les hirondelles, les hirondelles,*" Mollart sang out. "And I go to prepare the dinner. Today is my turn, and for dinner will be soup. You like soup, Ivan?"

Zhilin did not have time to answer, because the planet ship tilted suddenly and he fell out the door, just managing to grab onto the jambs. Yurkovsky tripped over Mollart's outstretched legs and fell onto Dauge. Dauge groaned.

"Oho," Yurkovsky said, "it's a meteorite."

"Get off!" Dauge responded.

3. *The flight engineer admires great heroes, and the navigator discovers Varya.*

The cramped observation compartment was jammed with the planetologists' equipment. Dauge squatted down in front of a large, shiny piece of equipment that resembled a television camera. It was called an exospheric spectrograph. The planetologist had high hopes for it. It was completely new—right from the factory—and was synchronized with a bomb-release mechanism, whose dull black breech ring filled half the compartment. Alongside it, in light metal shelving, the flat clips of bomb probes shone dully. Each clip held twenty bomb probes and weighed forty kilograms. In theory the clips were supposed to be fed into the bomb-release mechanism automatically, but the photon freighter *Takhmasib* was poorly equipped for scientific research, and there was no room for the automatic feed. Zhilin handled the bomb-release mechanism.

Yurkovsky commanded, "Load."

Zhilin opened the cover on the breech ring, grabbed the edges of the first clip, lifted it with effort, and placed it in the firing chamber's rectangular opening. The clip slid silently into place. Zhilin fastened the cover, clicked the lock, and said, "Ready."

"I'm ready, too," Dauge said.

"Mikhail," Yurkovsky said into a microphone. "Will it be soon?"

"Another half hour," the hoarse voice of the navigator said.

The planet ship tilted again. The floor dropped from beneath their feet.

"Another meteorite," Yurkovsky said. "That's the third one."

"A little thick, isn't it?" Dauge said.

Yurkovsky asked into the microphone, "Mikhail, are there many micrometeorites?"

"A lot of them, Vladimir," Mikhail answered. His voice was concerned. "More than thirty percent more than the average density. And still increasing."

"Mikhail, my friend," Yurkovsky asked, "Measure them a little more often, okay?"

"The measurements are going at three a minute," the navigator responded. He said something aside, and then Bykov's bass was heard: "Yes."

"Vladimir," the navigator called, "I'm switching to ten times a minute."

"Thanks, Mikhail," Yurkovsky said.

The ship tilted again.

"Vladimir," Dauge said softly, "this is hardly trivial."

Zhilin also felt that it was hardly trivial. Nowhere, in none of his textbooks or manuals, had anything been said about an increase in meteorite density in close proximity to Jupiter. However, few scientists had ever been in close proximity to Jupiter.

Zhilin leaned against the bomb-release mechanism and looked at his watch. Only twenty minutes now, no more. In twenty minutes Dauge would release the first round. He said it was an unusual sight when a round of bomb probes exploded. The year before last he had studied the atmosphere of Uranus with bomb probes. Zhilin looked at Dauge. Dauge was squatting in front of the spectrograph, holding onto a handle—dry, dark, sharp-nosed, with a scar on his left cheek. From time to time he stretched out his long neck and glanced with one eye into the eyepiece of the videosearcher, and each time an orange reflection played over his face. Zhilin looked at Yurkovsky. He was standing with his face pressed against the periscope and was leisurely shifting his weight from foot to foot. The ribbed egg of the microphone dangled from his neck on a black band. The famous planetologists Dauge and Yurkovsky. . . .

A month before, Chen Kun, the deputy director of the Advanced School of Cosmogation, had called in Ivan Zhilin, a graduate of the school. The interplanetaries called Chen Kun Iron Kun. He was over fifty, but he looked very young in his blue jacket with the overturned collar. He would have been very handsome if it had not been for the gray-pink spots on his forehead and chin—the traces of an old radiation exposure. Chen Kun told him that the Third Section of GKMPS had urgently requested a good flight engineer and the school's council had selected graduate Zhilin (graduate Zhilin felt chill from the excitement: During his five years in school he had been afraid of being sent as an apprentice on moon flights). Chen Kun said that it was a great honor for graduate Zhilin, since his first assignment was to a ship going oversun to Jupiter (graduate Zhilin almost danced for joy) with supplies for J-Station on Amalteia, the fifth satellite of Jupiter. Amalteia was threatened by famine, Chen Kun said.

"Your commander will be the well-known interplanetary, Alexei Bykov, also a graduate of our school. Your senior navigator will be the well-experienced cosmogator Mikhail Krutikov. In their hands you will receive a first-class apprenticeship, and I am very happy for you."

The fact that Grigory Dauge and Vladimir Yurkovsky would also be on the flight was something Zhilin found out later, only at the Mirza-Charle spaceport. Christopher Columbus and Jacques Cartier! The terrifying and beautiful semilegend, familiar to him since childhood, of the men who had thrown a forbidding planet at humanity's feet. Of men who in the antediluvian *Chius*—a photon slowpoke with a single layer of mesomatter on its reflector—broke through Venus's wild atmosphere. Of men who found amid the black primal sands the Uranian Golkonda—the crater from the impact of a monstrous meteor of antimatter.

Of course, Zhilin had known other famous people. For example, Vasily Lyakhov, the interplanetary and test pilot. During the third and fourth years in the school Lyakhov taught the theory of photon drive. He organized a three-month practicum for graduates on Sat-20. Interplanetaries called Sat-20 the Little Star. It had been very interesting there. They were testing the first direct-point photon engines. From there automatic sounding scouts were launched into the zone of absolutely free flight. There the first interstellar ship, the *Chius-Lightning*, was being built. Once Lyakhov had taken the students into the hangar. In the hangar only a recently arrived automatic photon tanker was hanging; it had been launched into the zone of absolutely free flight a half year before. The tanker, an enormous clumsy construction, had reached a distance of one light-month from the sun. Everyone was struck by its color. The hull had turned emerald green and fell apart if you touched it. It was crumbling like a loaf of bread. But the control system had remained in working order; otherwise, of course, the scout would not have returned, as three of the nineteen scouts launched into the AFF zone had not. The students asked Lyakhov what had happened, and Lyakhov had answered that he did not know. "At large distances from the sun there is something we still don't understand," he had said. And then Zhilin had thought about the pilots who in a few years would take the *Chius-Lightning* out where there is something we still don't understand.

It's great, Zhilin thought. I already have something to remember. Like during my fourth year during my trial flight in the geodesic rocket when the engine failed and the rocket and I landed in a farm field near Novoyeniseisk. I wandered for several hours among the automatic high-frequency plows until I bumped into a human being in the evening. He was a telemechanic operator. We lay awake the whole night in the tent watching the plows' lights moving in the dark field, and one plow came quite close, roaring and leaving the smell of ozone behind it. The operator treated me to the local wine, and there was no way I could convince the happy-go-lucky guy that interplanetaries didn't touch the stuff. In the morning a transporter came for the rocket. Iron Chen really chewed me out for not bailing out. . . .

Or my diploma flight, Earth Sat-16—Moon Cepheus, when the member of the examining commission tried to confuse us and right after giving the initial data yelled out, "Third-magnitude asteroid to the right. Approach velocity twenty-two!" There were six of us, and he really got to us— only Jan, the group leader, kept trying to convince us that we should forgive others their little faults. In principle we did not disagree, but did not want to forgive him just the same. We all considered the flight to be a joke, and no one got excited when the ship suddenly went into a spin with fourth-degree overload. We scrambled into the control room where the member of the commission pretended to be dead from the overload; we brought the ship out of the spin. Then the commission member opened one eye and said, "Good work, interplanetaries," and we immediately forgave him his faults, because until then no one had called us interplanetaries in all seriousness, apart from mothers and girlfriends. But they had always said, "My dear interplanetary," and they always looked petrified when they said it. . . .

The *Takhmasib* suddenly shook so violently that Zhilin was thrown to the floor and hit the back of his head against the shelves.

"Damn!" Yurkovsky said. "This is indeed hardly trivial; if the ship keeps on yawing, we won't be able to work."

"Right," Dauge said. He held his hand over his right eye. "What kind of work can you expect?"

Apparently, bigger and bigger meteorites were appearing in the ship's path, and the frantic commands of the antimeteorite locators to the cyber-navigator threw the ship from side to side more and more frequently.

"Is it a swarm?" Yurkovsky asked, holding tight to the periscope. "Poor Varya, she doesn't hold up well when the ship shakes."

"She should have stayed home," Dauge said testily. His right eye was swelling fast. He felt it with his fingers and muttered indistinctly in Latvian. He was no longer squatting but half lying on the floor, his legs spread for greater stability.

Zhilin held on tight, his hands squeezing the shelves. The floor suddenly fell out from under his feet, then leaped up and hit his heels painfully. Dauge groaned, and Zhilin's legs gave way. Bykov's hoarse bass roared over the loudspeaker: "Flight engineer Zhilin to the control room! Passengers in the shock seats!"

In a rocking trot Zhilin raced to the door. Behind him Dauge asked, "So it's the shock seats?"

"To hell with it!" Yurkovsky responded.

Something rolled across the floor with a metallic clatter. Zhilin jumped out into the corridor. The adventure was beginning.

The ship bobbed continuously, like a chip of wood in the waves. Zhilin ran down the corridor and thought: That one's past. And that one's past. And that one's past too, and they're all past. . . . Behind him he heard a *pkk-pshshsh*. . . . He flattened against the wall and turned around. In the empty corridor, about ten paces from him, a dense cloud of white steam was floating, just like when a tank of liquid helium breaks. The hissing quickly died down. An icy cold spread through the corridor.

"It broke, the bastard," Zhilin said and tore himself from the wall. The white cloud crept along behind him, slowly settling.

It was very cold in the control room. Zhilin saw a shining rainbow of frost on the walls and floor. Mikhail was sitting at the computer and pulled a printout toward himself. Bykov was not to be seen. He was behind the reactor casing.

"It happened again?" the navigator shouted in a high voice.

"Where is that flight engineer?" Bykov boomed from behind the casing.

"Here I am," Zhilin answered.

He ran across the control room, slipping on the frost. Bykov leaped out to meet him, his red hair standing on end.

"Take control of the reflector," he said.

"Yessir," Zhilin responded.

"Navigator, is there an opening?"

"No, Alexei. Equal density in every direction."

"Turn off the reflector. We'll get on emergency power."

Mikhail hurriedly turned in his revolving chair toward the control panel behind him. He put his hand on the keyboard and said, "Maybe if. . . ."

He stopped. His face twisted in horror. The keyboard panel bent, straightened out again, then slid silently to the floor. Zhilin heard Mikhail's wail and in confusion jumped out from behind the casing. On the wall, clasping the soft padding, sat Varya, the five-foot-long Martian lizard, Yurkovsky's favorite. An exact copy of the control keyboard on its back was already fading, but on its fearsome nose an image of the red stop signal was still flashing slowly. Mikhail stared at the checkered Varya, sobbed, and held his heart.

"Scat!" Zhilin yelled.

Varya scooted away and vanished.

"I'll kill them!" Bykov roared. "Zhilin, to your post, damn it!"

Zhilin turned around, and at that moment the *Takhmasib* really got hit.

Amalteia, J-Station

Water carriers chat about famine, and the gastronomic engineer is ashamed of his cuisine.

After supper Uncle Valnoga came into the recreation room and without looking at anyone said, "I need water. Any volunteers?"

"Yes," Kozlov said.

Potapov raised his head from the chessboard and also volunteered.

"Of course," said Konstantin Stetsenko.

"Can I come?" Zoya Ivanova asked.

"You can," Valnoga said, staring at the ceiling. "Come on along."

"How much do you need?" Kozlov asked. "Not much," Uncle Valnoga answered. "Just ten tons."

"Sure thing," Kozlov said. "Right away."

Uncle Valnoga left.

"I'll go along," Gregor said.

"You'd be better off sitting here and thinking about your next move," Potapov advised. "It's your move, and you always spend a half hour on each move."

"It's okay," Gregor said. "I'll still have time to think."

"Galya, come with us," Stetsenko called out.

Galya was curled up in an easy chair in front of the magnetovideophone. She answered lazily, "Sure."

She stood up and stretched sensuously. She was twenty-eight, tall, dark-skinned, and very, very beautiful. The most beautiful woman on the station. Half the men on the station were in love with her. She ran the astrometric observatory.

"Let's go," Kozlov said. He strapped on his magnetic boots and headed for the door.

They set off for the storeroom and got fur coats, electrosaws, and a self-propelled platform.

"Eisgrotte"—that was the name of the place where the station got water for technical and hygienic purposes and for consumption. Amalteia, a flattened sphere one hundred and thirty kilometers in diameter, was made of solid ice. It was ordinary water ice, just like on Earth. Only on the surface was the ice sprinkled slightly with meteorite dust and chunks of stone and metal. No one could say for sure what the origin of the icy body was. Some—who knew little of cosmogony—considered that Jupiter long ago sucked off the water from a planet that carelessly passed too near. Others were inclined to view the formation of the fifth satellite as the result of the condensation of ice crystals. Still others maintained that Amalteia did not originally belong to the solar system, that is came from interstellar space and was seized by Jupiter. But however it may be, an inexhaustible supply of water beneath their feet was a great convenience.

The platform went down a corridor on the lowest level of the station and stopped in front of the broad gates to the Eisgrotte. Gregor jumped off the platform, walked up to the gates, looked at them nearsightedly, and searched for the handle to the lock.

"Lower, lower," Potapov called out. "You blind owl."

Gregor found the handle and the gates swung open. The platform entered the Eisgrotte. The Eisgrotte was indeed just that—a cave of ice, a tunnel cut out of solid ice. Three gas-illuminated pipes lit the tunnel, but the light was reflected from the ice walls and ceiling, was broken up into sparkles by uneven places, so it seemed that the Eisgrotte was illuminated by many light fixtures.

There was no magnetic field here, and they had to walk cautiously. And it was unusually cold.

"Ice," Galya said, looking around. "Just like on Earth."

Zoya hunched over, shivering, wrapping herself in her fur coat.

"Like in Antarctica," she muttered.

"I was in Antarctica," Gregor announced.

"Where is it you haven't been!" Potapov said. "You've been everywhere!"

"To work, guys," Kozlov commanded.

The men took the electrosaws, walked over to the far wall, and began cutting out chunks of ice. The saws went through the ice like hot knives through butter. Ice dust sparkled in the air. Zoya and Galya came closer.

"Let me," Zoya asked, looking at Kozlov's bent back.

"I won't," Kozlov said without turning around. "You'll hurt your eyes."

"Just like snow on Earth," Galya noted, holding her palm out under a stream of ice crystals.

"Well, there's no lack of this stuff anywhere," Potapov said. "For example, on Ganymede there's all the snow you want."

"I was on Ganymede," Gregor announced.

"Enough to drive you crazy," Potapov said. He turned off his saw and pushed a huge ice cube away from the wall. "Here's the way to do it."

"Cut it into pieces," Stetsenko advised.

"Don't," Kozlov said. He also turned off his saw and punched a chunk of ice away from the wall. "Just the opposite"—with effort he shoved the chunk and it slowly floated toward the tunnel exit—"it's easier for Valnoga when the blocks are larger."

"Ice," Galya said. "Just like on Earth. I'm going to come here after work."

"Are you that homesick for Earth?" Zoya asked timidly. Zoya was ten years younger than Galya, worked as a lab assistant in the astrometric observatory, and was shy in front of her boss.

"Very much," Galya said. "For everything on Earth. I want to sit on the grass, go to the park in the evening, go dancing. . . . Not our air dances, but an ordinary waltz. And to drink out of ordinary glasses, and not out of these stupid pears. And to wear dresses instead of pants. I really miss my ordinary skirts."

"Me too," Potapov said.

"I agree about the skirts," Kozlov said.

"Big mouths," Galya objected. "Wise guys."

She picked up a piece of ice and hurled it at Potapov. Potapov jumped up, hit his back against the ceiling, and collided with Stetsenko.

"Easy does it," Stetsenko said angrily. "You'll end up under the saw."

"Well, that's probably enough," Kozlov said. He pushed a third block away from the wall. "Load up, my friends."

They loaded the ice onto the platform, then Potapov unexpectedly grabbed Galya with one hand and Zoya with the other and tossed them both onto the stack of ice. Zoya shrieked in fear and grabbed onto Galya. Galya laughed.

"Let's go!" Potapov shouted. "Now Valnoga will give you a prize—a dish of chlorella soup each."

"I wouldn't refuse," Kozlov mumbled.

"You never have," Stetsenko noted. "But now, when we have a famine. . . ."

The platform went out of the Eisgrotte, and Gregor closed the gates.

"Is this really a famine?" Zoya asked from the top of the ice. "I read a book not long ago about the war with the Fascists—they really had a famine. In Leningrad, during the blockade."

"I was in Leningrad," Gregor announced.

"We eat chocolate," Zoya continued, "but there people got one hundred fifty grams of break a day. And what bread! Half sawdust!"

"Sawdust?" Stetsenko said with doubt.

"Imagine, sawdust, really."

"The chocolate is all well and good," Kozlov said, "but things will be very tight if the *Takhmasib* doesn't get here."

He was carrying his saw over his shoulder, like a gun.

"They'll get here," Galya said confidently. She jumped down from the platform, and Stetsenko hurried to catch her. "Thanks, Konstantin. They have to get here."

"All the same I think we should suggest to the director a cut in the daily portions," Kozlov said. "Even if only for the men."

"What nonsense," Zoya said. "I read that women hold up under famine much better than men."

They walked down the corridor after the slowly moving platform.

"Women and children," Potapov said.

"Leaden wit," Zoya said. "Or cast iron."

"No, really," Kozlov said. "If Bykov doesn't get here tomorrow, we'll have to get everyone together and ask for agreement to restrictions."

"Well," Stetsenko agreed. "I don't think anyone will object."

"I won't," Gregor said.

"That's great," Potapov said. "I was about to think you were going to object."

"Greeting to the water boys," the astrophysicist Nikolsky shouted as he walked past.

Galya noted with annoyance, "I don't understand how you can worry so bluntly about your bellies, as though the *Takhmasib* was automatic and there weren't any people on board."

Even Potapov turned red and could not find anything to say. The rest of the way to the galley they were silent. In the galley Uncle Valnoga was sitting, dejected, next to a huge ion-exchange device for the purification of water. The platform stopped by the entrance to the galley.

"Unload it," Uncle Valnoga said, staring at the floor. It was uncharacteristically quiet, cool, and odorless in the galley. Uncle Valnoga was overwhelmed by the devastation.

The blocks of ice were unloaded in silence and placed in the gaping maw of the water purifier.

"Thanks," Uncle Valnoga said, his head still lowered.

"You're welcome, Uncle Valnoga," Kozlov said. "Let's go, guys."

They set off in silence toward the storeroom, then returned in silence to the recreation room. Galya took a book and curled up in her easy chair. Stetsenko hovered indecisively around her, looked at Kozlov and Zoya, who sat down at the table to study (Zoya was studying by correspondence at the Institute of Energy and Kozlov was tutoring her), sighed, and wandered off to his room. Potapov said to Gregor, "Go on, it's your move."

2. Over the Abyss

1. *The captain announces unpleasant news, and the flight engineer fears not.*

Apparently a large meteorite had hit the reflector and the symmetrical distribution of force over the surface of the parabaloid was destroyed for an instant, and the *Takhmasib* was spun like a wheel. In the control room only Captain Bykov did not lose consciousness. True, his head hit something, and then his side, and for a moment he could not breathe, but with both arms and legs he managed to hold onto the seat into which the first jolt had thrown him, and he held on, stretched out, and twisted until he somehow reached the control panel. Everything around him was spinning with unusual speed. From somewhere above Zhilin floated by, his arms and legs akimbo. It seemed to Bykov that no life was left in him. He pressed his head against the panel and aiming carefully, pushed the necessary button with his finger.

The cybernavigator turned on the emergency hydrogen engines, and Bykov felt a jolt, like an emergency stop on a train, only much stronger. Bykov expected it and pressed his legs against the side on the control panel with all his might. He did not go flying out of his seat. His head spun, and his mouth felt dry. The *Takhmasib* righted itself. Then Bykov took the ship straight through the cloud of stone-and-iron particles. On the screen of the monitoring system blue lights splashed. There were many of them, very many, but the ship did not tilt anymore — the antimeteorite equipment had been shut off and did not affect the cybernavigator. Through the noise in his ears Bykov heard a piercing *pkk-pshshsh* several times and each time he was struck by a freezing mist and curled over toward the panel. Once something burst and flew into pieces, behind his back. Then the signals on the screen were fewer, and finally completely disappeared. The meteorite attack was over.

Then Bykov looked at the coursograph. The *Takhmasib* was falling. The *Takhmasib* was passing through Jupiter's exosphere, and its velocity was much less than orbital, and it was falling in a narrowing spiral. It had lost speed during the meteorite attack. During meteorite attacks ships always lose speed, since they depart from their course. That is what happens in the asteroid belt during the ordinary Mars-Jupiter or Earth-Jupiter flights. But there it is not dangerous. Here, over Jupe, the loss of speed would mean certain death. The ship would burn up when it hit the leviathan planet's dense layers of atmosphere—that had happened ten years before with Paul Darget. And if it did not burn up, it would fall into an abyss of hydrogen from which there was no return—that had happened, most likely, with Sergei Petryshevsky at the beginning of the year.

The only way to tear loose was with photon drive. Completely automatically Bykov pushed the fluted starter button. But not one light blinked on on the entire control panel. The reflector had been damaged, and the emergency system blocked the impossible command. It's all over now, Bykov thought. He neatly swung the ship around and put the emergency engine on full power. The five-g acceleration pressed him back into his chair. It was the only thing he could do—reduce the speed of fall to a minimum to keep the ship from burning up in the atmosphere. For thirty seconds he sat motionless, staring at his hands, which swelled quickly from the overload. Then he decreased the fuel supply to the engine, and the overload fell off. The emergency engine would gradually slow their fall— while their fuel held out. And there was not that much. Emergency rockets had never yet saved anyone over Jupiter. Over Mars, over Mercury, over Earth—perhaps. But never over the giant planet.

Bykov got up stiffly and looked around. On the floor, amid fragments of plastic, Mikhail Krutikov was lying belly up.

"Mikhail," Bykov called out, speaking for some reason in a whisper. "Are you alive, Mikhail?"

He heard a scratching noise, and Zhilin came crawling out from behind the reactor casing on all fours. Zhilin also looked bad. He looked thoughtfully at the captain, at the navigator, at the ceiling, and sat down, folding his legs.

Bykov made his way over to the navigator and squatted down, bending his legs with difficulty. He touched the navigator on the shoulder and called out once again, "Are you alive, Mikhail?"

Mikhail squinted, and without opening his eyes, licked his lips.

"Alexei," he said in a weak voice.

"Does it hurt anywhere?" Bykov asked and began to check for broken bones.

"Ouch!" the navigator said, and opened his eyes wide.

"What about here?"

"Ugh!" the navigator said in a pained voice.

"And here?"

"Ouch, don't!" the navigator said and sat up, pushed his hands against the floor. His head was tilted toward one shoulder. "Where's Ivan?" he asked.

Bykov looked around. Zhilin wasn't there.

"Ivan," Bykov called out softly.

"Here," Zhilin answered from behind the casing. They heard him drop something and whisper a curse.

"Ivan is alive," Bykov informed the navigator.

"Well, thank God," Mikhail said and grabbing the captain's shoulder, struggled to his feet.

"How are you, Mikhail?" Bykov asked. "Fit to work?"

"Fit enough," the navigator said without any great confidence. "I guess I can handle it."

He looked at Bykov with eyes wide with amazement and said, "How hardy we humans are, Alexei. . . . How hardy!"

"Mmm-yes," Bykov said vaguely. "Hardy. Listen, Mikhail. . . ." He fell silent. "Things are bad. We're falling. If you're fit, sit down and calculate what's happening. The computer is intact, I believe." He glanced at the computer. "However, see for yourself."

Mikhail's eyes became as round as saucers.

"We're falling?" he asked. "Oh, so that's it! We're falling. Onto Jupiter?"

Bykov just nodded.

"Ay-yay-yay, That's all we need! Okay, then. I'll get right to work."

He stood a moment, grimacing and craning his neck, then let go of the captain, and holding onto the edge of the control panel, wobbled over to his seat.

"I'll calculate it right away. Right away."

Bykov watched him, holding his side, plop down in his seat and make himself comfortable. The chair tilted noticeably. Having settled himself, Mikhail suddenly looked at Bykov with an expression of fear and asked, "You have braked, haven't you, Alexei?"

Bykov nodded and walked over to Zhilin, crunched the fragments on the floor. On the ceiling he saw a small black spot and another on the wall itself. They were meteor holes, sealed by a resin plastic. Around the holes large drops of condensed moisture quivered.

Zhilin was sitting cross-legged in front of the reflector controls. The casing was split in half. The sight of the system's insides were not comforting.

"How are things with you?" Bykov said. He could see for himself.

Zhilin raised his puffy face.

"I don't know the details yet," he answered. "But it's obviously been smashed."

Bykov squatted down beside him.

"One meteorite hit," Zhilin said. "And I hit it twice myself." He pointed to the place but it was obvious anyway. "Once at the very beginning with my feet and then at the very end with my head."

"Yes," Bykov said. "No mechanism will take that. Hook up the spare. And I should tell you: We're falling."

"I heard, Captain Bykov," Zhilin said.

"But really," Bykov said thoughtfully, "what's the sense of the control system if the reflector is shattered?"

"But maybe it isn't," Zhilin said.

Bykov looked at him and grinned.

"Our merry-go-round ride," he said, "can be explained by only two causes. Either-or. Either for some reason the plasma ignition point jumped out of focus, or a large piece of the reflector was knocked off. I think the reflector was shattered, because there is no God who could shift the ignition point. But go ahead and try. Hook up the spare."

He stood up and, leaning his head back, inspected the ceiling.

"We still have to cover the holes good and tight. Down there the pressure is great. The resin plastic will be squeezed out. I can do it myself."

He turned to go but stopped and asked softly, "Are you afraid, kid?"

At school the "kids" had been the freshmen—or younger still.

"No," Zhilin said.

"Good. Get to work," Bykov said. "I'll go inspect the ship. I have to go let the passengers out of the shock seats."

Zhilin did not answer. He accompanied the broad, bent back of the captain with his eyes and suddenly saw Varya right alongside. Varya was standing up on her back legs and slowly blinking her protruding eyes. She was all dark blue with white polka dots, and the spines on her muzzle bristled fearfully. That meant that Varya was terribly upset and felt out of sorts. Zhilin had seen her like that once before. It had been a month before, at the Mirza-Charle spaceport, when Yurkovsky spoke at length on the remarkable adaptability of Martian lizards and as proof tossed Varya into a bathtub of steaming water.

Varya convulsively opened her huge gray mouth, then closed it.

"Well, then?" Zhilin asked softly. A large drop fell from the ceiling and—tock!—into the control system. Zhilin looked at the ceiling. Down there the pressure was great. Yes, he thought, down there the pressure is in the tens and hundreds of thousands of atmospheres. The resin plastic corks, of course, would be squeezed out.

Varya squirmed and opened her mouth again. Zhilin groped in his pocket, found a candy, and threw it into her gaping jaws. Varya swallowed slowly and fixed her glassy eyes on him. Zhilin sighed.

"You poor creature!" he whispered.

2. *The planetologists are silent, and the radio optician sings a song about swallows.*

When the *Takhmasib* stopped somersaulting, Dauge tore himself loose from the breech ring and dragged the unconscious Yurkovsky out from under pieces of equipment. He did not have time to notice what had been broken and what was intact; he noticed only that much had been broken, the shelves with the clips tilted, and the clips spilled out onto the radiotelescope instrument panel. In the observatory compartment it was hot, and there was a strong smell of burning.

Dauge had gotten off relatively lightly. He had immediately latched onto the breach ring, and his only problem was a headache. Yurkovsky was pale, and his eyelids purple. Dauge blew on his face, shook him by the shoulders, slapped his cheeks. Yurkovsky's head wobbled loosely, and he did not regain consciousness. Then Dauge dragged him to the medical compartment. In the corridor it was terribly cold, and frost glittered on the walls. Dauge rested Yurkovsky's head on his knees, scraped some frost off the wall, placed his wet cold fingers against Yurkovsky's temples. At that moment he was caught by the overload—when Bykov began to brake the ship. Dauge lay down on his back, but he felt so bad that he turned over on his stomach and began rubbing his face against the frosted floor. When the overload stopped, Dauge lay for a while, then got to his feet and, holding Yurkovsky under his arm, staggering, went on. But he understood immediately that he would not make it to the med station, so he dragged Yurkovsky into the lounge, dropped him onto the couch, and sat beside him, gasping and trying to catch his breath. Yurkovsky was breathing terribly roughly.

Having rested, Dauge got up and went to the buffet. He took a decanter of water and started drinking straight from the neck. The water ran down his chin, his throat, under his collar, and it was very pleasant. He returned to

Yurkovsky and spattered water on his face. Then he set the decanter on the floor and unbuttoned Yurkovsky's jacket. He saw a strange branched design on his skin, running across the chest from shoulder to shoulder. The design was like the silhouette of some fantastic algae—dark purple against tanned skin. For a while Dauge stared blankly at the strange design, then suddenly realized that it was the mark of a strong electrical shock. Apparently Yurkovsky had fallen on an exposed contact with high voltage. All the planetologists' instrumentation operated under high voltage. Dauge ran to the med station.

He had to give Yurkovsky four injections before he would open his eyes. His eyes were dull and blank, but Dauge was very relieved.

"Damn it all anyway, Vladimir," he said, "I thought that things were really bad. How are you? Can you stand up?"

Yurkovsky moved his lips, opened his mouth, and gasped. His eyes focused, and his face assumed a normal expression.

"All right, all right, lie there," Dauge said. "You should lie still a while."

He looked around and saw Charles Mollart in the doorway. He was standing there holding onto the jamb and rocking slightly. His face was red, puffy, and he was all wet and covered with little white icicles. Dauge even thought he saw steam coming from him. Mollart was silent for several minutes, shifting a melancholy glance from Dauge to Yurkovsky and back again, and the planetologists looked at him with concern. Yurkovsky stopped gasping. Then Mollart pitched forward, into the room, and taking short, quick steps, made his way to the nearest chair. He looked wet and unhappy, and when he sat down, the room was filled with the delicious smell of cooked beef. Dauge sniffed.

"The soup?" he inquired.

"*Oui, monsieur*," Mollart said sadly. "*Vermicelle.*"

"And how was the soup?" Dauge asked. "Good?"

"Very good," Mollart said and began to pick vermicelli off his clothes.

"I love soup," Dauge clarified. "And am always interested in how."

Mollart sighed and smiled.

"There is no more soup," he said. "It was very hot soup. But it was not boil."

"My God!" Dauge said but still laughed. Mollart laughed, too.

"Yes," he said. "It was very funny but not comfortable, and the soup is gone all."

Yurkovsky wheezed. His face shuddered and turned red. Dauge returned him with alarm.

"Voldemar hurt bad?" Mollart asked. Craning his neck, he looked at Yurkovsky with a wary glance.

"Voldemar received a shock," Dauge said. He was not smiling any more.

"But what happened?" Mollart asked. "It was so uncomfortable. . . ."

Yurkovsky stopped wheezing, sat up, and grinning terribly, began groping in the chest pocket of his jacket.

"What is it?" Dauge asked in confusion.

"Voldemar cannot talk," Mollart said quietly.

Yurkovsky nodded hastily, pulled out a pen and pad, and began writing, his head twitching.

"Calm down, Vladimir," Dauge mumbled. "It will go away soon."

"It will go away," Mollart confirmed. "With me, too, was like it. Was very large current, then everything passed."

Yurkovsky gave the pad to Dauge, lay back, and closed his eyes.

" 'I can't talk,' " Dauge made out with difficulty. Yurkovsky's face twitched impatiently. "Okay, right away. 'How are Alexei and the pilots? How is the ship?' I don't know," Dauge said, dismayed, and looked at the hatch to the control room. "Damn, I forgot about everything."

Yurkovsky shook his head and also looked at the hatch.

"I will find out," Mollart said. "I will learn all right away."

He stood up from his chair, but the hatch burst open and Captain Bykov strode into the lounge, huge, tousled, with an abnormally purple nose and a black-and-blue mark over his right eye. He cast a furious glance at all of them, walked over to the table, spread his feet, leaned his fists on the table and said, "Why aren't you in the shock seats?"

He said it softly, but in such a way that Charles Mollart immediately stopped smiling joyously. A short awkward silence followed, and Dauge grinned uncomfortably and looked away, and Yurkovsky closed his eyes again. Things are bad, Yurkovsky thought. He knew Bykov well.

"When are we going to have discipline on this ship?" Bykov asked.

The passengers did not answer.

"Wise guys," Bykov said with disgust and sat down. "Bedlam. What's the matter with you, Monsieur Mollart?" he asked wearily.

"It is soup," Mollart answered readily. "I will go clean myself."

"Wait, Monsieur Mollart," Bykov said.

"Wh-where are we?" Yurkovsky wheezed.

"Falling," Bykov snapped.

Yurkovsky shuddered and sat up.

"Where to?" he asked. He had been expecting the answer but still shuddered.

"Into Jupiter," Bykov said. He did not look at the planetologists. He looked at Mollart. He felt very sorry for Mollart. Mollart was on his very first spaceflight, and he was eagerly awaited on Amalteia. Mollart was an outstanding radio optician.

"Oh," Mollart said, "to Jupiter?"

"Yes," Bykov said, then fell silent, rubbing the bruise on his forehead. "The reflector is broken. The reflector control is broken. There are eighteen holes in the ship."

"Are we going to burn up?" Dauge asked quickly.

"I still don't know. Mikhail is calculating. Perhaps we won't."

Silence reigned. Then Mollart said, "I will go clean myself."

"Wait, Charles," Bykov said. "Comrades, did you understand what I said? We're falling into Jupiter."

"We understand," Dauge said.

"Now we will fall to Jupiter all our life," Mollart said. Bykov looked at him out of the corner of his eye.

"Well said," Yurkovsky commented.

"*C'est le mot*," Mollart translated. He smiled. "May I . . . may I now go clean myself?"

"Yes, go ahead," Bykov said slowly.

Mollart turned and left the lounge. The others all watched him leave. They heard him singing in the corridor, in a weak but pleasant voice.

"What's he singing?" Bykov asked. Mollart had never sung before.

Dauge listened closely and began translating: " 'Two swallows kiss outside my starship window. In the vacu-u-u-m. They love each other very much and leaped out there to admire the stars. Tra-la-la. And what business is it of yours?' Something like that."

"Tra-la-la," Bykov said pensively. "That's great."

"Y-you t-translate l-like LIANTO," Yurkovsky said. "A m-masterpiece."

Bykov looked at him in amazement.

"What's the matter, Vladimir?" he asked.

"A p-permanent s-s-stammer," Yurkovsky answered with a grin.

"He received an electrical shock," Dauge said.

Bykov bit his lips.

"It'll be okay," he said. "You're not the first. It's been worse."

He knew that it had never been worse. Not for him, not for the planetologists. From the half-opened hatch Mikhail's voice rang out. "Alexei, it's ready!"

"Come in here," Bykov said.

Mikhail, fat and scratched, burst into the lounge. He was not wearing a shirt and his skin was glistening with perspiration.

"Uh, it's cold in here!" he said, putting his short pudgy arms across his fat chest. "In the control room it's terribly hot."

"Let's have it, Mikhail," Bykov said impatiently.

"But what's the matter with Vladimir?" the navigator asked.

"Come on, come on," Bykov commanded. "He got an electrical shock."

"And where's Charles?" the navigator asked, taking a seat.

"Charles is alive and well," Bykov answered, restraining himself. "Everyone is alive and well. Begin."

"Well thank God for that," the navigator said. "So here it is: I have done a few calculations, and the picture is that the *Takhmasib* is falling, and there is not enough fuel to blast out."

"You don't need calculations to know that," Yurkovsky said, almost smoothly.

"There's not enough. We can blast out only with the photoreactor, but it seems the reflector is broken. But we do have enough fuel to brake. I figured out a program. If the generally accepted theory of Jupiter's composition is correct, we will not burn up."

Dauge wanted to say that there was no generally accepted theory of Jupiter's composition but held his tongue.

"We are braking quite nicely," Mikhail continued. "So I believe we will descend successfully. And there's nothing more we can do, my friends." Mikhail smiled guiltily. "Unless of course, we fix the reflector."

"On Jupiter there are no repair stations. That follows from every theory on Jupiter." Bykov wanted to make sure they understood. Fully. He still felt that they were missing the point.

"What theory do you consider generally accepted?" Dauge asked.

"Kangren's." Bykov stared at the planetologists, biding his time.

"Well," Dauge said. "Kangren's is okay."

Yurkovsky was silent, and stared at the ceiling.

"You planetologists" — Bykov could no longer resist — "are experts — what will it be like down there? Can you tell us?"

"Yes, of course," Dauge said. "We'll tell you very soon."

"When?" Bykov came to life.

"When we get there, down below," Dauge said. He laughed.

"You planetologists," Bykov said, "are real ex-perts."

"We have to calculate," Yurkovsky said, staring at the ceiling. He spoke slowly and smoothly. "Let Mikhail calculate the depth at which the ship will stop falling and start hanging suspended."

"Yes," Dauge said. "What will the pressure be? Maybe we'll just be crushed."

"It's not that simple," Bykov muttered. "Two hundred thousand atmospheres we can take. And the photon reactor and the rockets' hulls much more."

Yurkovsky sat up and crossed his legs.

"Kangren's theory is no worse than the others," he said. "It will give the order of magnitude." He looked at the navigator. "We could calculate it ourselves, but you have the computer."

"Of course," Mikhail said. "Not worth mentioning."

Bykov asked, "Mikhail, give me the program. I'll look it over. Then enter it. Into the cybernavigator."

"I already did, Alexei," the navigator answered guiltily.

"Ah," Bykov said. "Well, okay then." He stood up. "So then. Now everything is clear. We won't be crunched, but we can't go back—let's say so up front. Well, we aren't the first. We've lived well, and we'll die well. I'll try something with Zhilin to get the reflector working, but that is . . ." He grimaced and rubbed his swollen nose. "What do you plan on doing?"

"Observing," Yurkovsky said in a hard voice.

Dauge nodded.

"Very good." Bykov glanced at them furtively. "I have a request. Keep an eye out for Mollart."

"Yes," Mikhail agreed.

"He's new to this, and . . . when bad things happen . . . you know how it is."

"Okay, Alexei," Dauge said, smiling in a chipper way. "Put your mind at ease."

"Mikhail," Bykov said, "go into the control room and do the calculations, and I'll go to the med station and get my side massaged. I really hit it hard."

As he left he heard Dauge talking to Yurkovsky: "In a certain sense, we've been lucky, Vladimir. We'll see things no one has ever seen. Let's go fix the equipment."

"Let's go," Yurkovsky repeated.

You can't fool me, Bykov thought. You still haven't understood. You still hope. You think: Alexei got us out of the Black Sands of Golkonda, Alexei got us out of the rotting swamps, so Alexei will get us out of this hydrogen grave. Dauge undoubtedly believes it. And will Alexei get you out? Could it be that Alexei actually will get you out?

In the med station Mollart, wincing from the pain, was applying an ointment. His face and his hands were red and shiny. Seeing Bykov, he smiled politely and broke out singing about the swallows: He had almost calmed down. If he had started singing, Bykov would have thought that he had calmed down for real. But Mollart sang loudly and carefully, hissing from pain from time to time.

3. *The flight engineer indulges in memories, and the navigator counsels him against doing so.*

Zhilin was repairing the reflector control system. In the control room it was very hot and stuffy—the air-conditioning had apparently been thrown out of whack, but there was no time to worry about it. At first Zhilin took off his jacket, then his jumpsuit, working in just his shorts and undershirt. Varya curled up on his clothes and soon disappeared—only her shadow remained; from time to time her large protruding eyes would appear, then disappear.

One by one Zhilin took the printed circuits out of the system, saved the good ones and put the bad ones aside, replacing them spares. He worked methodically, unhurriedly, as during a final examination, because there was no need to rush, and the whole thing was apparently pointless. He tried not to think about anything and just be happy that he remembered the circuits very well, that he hardly had to look at the manual, that he had not been hurt too badly, and the cuts on his head had stopped bleeding and did not hurt at all. On the other side of the photoreactor the computer was humming. Mikhail rustled papers and hummed something unmusical under his breath. Mikhail always did that when he was working.

I wonder what he's working on, Zhilin thought. Perhaps he's just trying to distract himself. That is very good—to be able to distract yourself at such a time. The planetologists were most likely working too, tossing out the bomb probes. And I've never had a chance to see so many things. For example, they say that Jupiter is very beautiful from Amalteia. And I always wanted to take part in an interstellar expedition or in one of the Pathfinders' missions—the scientists who search for traces of the Visitors on other worlds. . . . Then, they say that on J-Station there are great girls, and it would be nice to get to know them, and then tell Pierre Hunt about it—he was assigned to lunar runs and was glad about it, the nut. It's funny, Mikhail is hypocritical. He has a wife and two, no, three, children, and the oldest daughter is sixteen—he kept promising to introduce us and would wink knowingly, but now it will never happen. There's a lot that will never happen. Father will be very upset—oh, that's very bad. How mixed up the whole thing is! During my first real flight. It's a good thing I quarreled with her, Zhilin suddenly thought. Now it's simpler, but it might have been very complicated. Mikhail is worse off than I am. And so is the captain. The captain has a wife—a very beautiful woman, happy, and very intelligent. She saw him off, never suspecting a thing—or maybe she did, but you couldn't tell. Most likely she wasn't worried because she was used to it. A person can get used to anything. I, for example, got used to overloads, even though at first they made me sick, and I even thought I would be transferred to the automatic control division. At the school that was called "being sent to the little girls": There were a lot of girls in that department, and things were always fun with them, but being transferred was still a disgrace. Completely incomprehensible why. The girls went to work on different Sats and on stations and bases on various planets and did not do worse work than the men. Sometimes even better. All the same, Zhilin thought, it's a good thing we quarreled. What would she feel like now?

He stared blankly at the cracked surface of the printed circuit he was holding in his hand.

. . . We kissed in Bolshoi Park and then on the quai under the white statues, and I walked her home, and we kissed for a long time in the entryway, and people kept going in and out, although it was late. And she was afraid that her mother would come up and ask, "What are you doing, Valya, and who is this young man?" It was in the summer, during the white nights. And then I came home for winter vacation, and we met again, and it was just like before, only snow lay in the park and the bare branches waved against the gray sky. A wind starting blowing, whirling the new-fallen snow, and we were frozen and went to warm up in the café on Interplanetary Street. We were very happy when there was no one there, sat by the window and watched the cars passing by. I argued with her, said that I knew all the different makes of cars—and was wrong. This great, low-built car came by, and I didn't know what it was. I ran out and someone told me it was a Golden Dragon, a new Chinese atomcar. We argued to beat the band. Then it seemed that it was the most important thing, that it always be—winter and summer, and on the quai under the white statues, and in Bolshoi Park, and in the theater where she was so beautiful in her black dress with the white collar and kept poking me in the side to stop me from laughing so loud. But once she didn't come when we had a date, and I talked to her on the videophone, and she didn't come again and stopped writing me letters when I went back to school. I still didn't believe it and kept writing long letters, stupid letters, very stupid, although I didn't know it then. And a year later I saw her again. She was with a girlfriend and didn't recognize me. I thought then I was over it, but it lasted until my final year in school, and I don't even know why I'm thinking about it now. Probably because it doesn't matter anymore. I could not think about it, but since it doesn't matter. . . .

The hatch slammed. Bykov's voice said, "Well, Mikhail?"

"We're finishing the first circuit, Alexei. We fell five hundred kilometers."

"So. . . ." They could hear plastic fragments snapping underfoot. "So that's the story. There isn't any radio contact with Amalteia, of course."

"The receiver is silent," Mikhail said with a sigh. "The transmitter is working, but the radio storms here are. . . ."

"How are your calculations coming?"

"Almost finished, Alexei. It looks like we will fall about six or seven megameters and then hang. We will float, as Vladimir says. The pressure is enormous, but we won't be crushed, that's clear. Only it's going to be hard— the force of gravity is going to be two and one-half g's."

"Oof," Bykov said. He was silent a while, then said, "Do you have any ideas?"

"What?"

"I said, do you have any ideas? About getting out of here?"

"Come on, Alexei," the navigator said affectionately, almost ingratiatingly. "What kind of ideas could I have? This is Jupiter. I've never heard of anyone . . . getting out."

A long silence set in. Zhilin once again set to work, quickly and noiselessly. Then Mikhail said suddenly, "Don't reminisce about her, Alexei. It's better not to, you'll just feel lousy—"

"I wasn't reminiscing," Bykov said in an unpleasant tone. "And I wouldn't if I were you, either. . . ." Then he yelled, "Ivan!"

"Yes?" Zhilin answered, hurrying.

"Are you still messing around?"

"I'll finish in a minute."

Zhilin could hear the captain kicking the plastic fragments as he walked over.

"Garbage," he muttered. "A pigsty. A madhouse."

He walked around the casing and squatted down next to Zhilin.

"I'll be finished in a minute," Zhilin repeated.

"Don't rush, Flight Engineer Zhilin," Bykov said angrily.

Bykov breathed heavily and began to pull spare parts out of the box. Zhilin edged over to make room for him. They were both broad, huge, and it was a tight fit in front of the system. They worked in silence and quickly, and they could hear Mikhail turn on the computer again and hum.

When the repair was finished, Bykov called out, "Mikhail, come here." He straightened up and wiped the sweat from his forehead. Then he pushed away a pile of broken circuit boards with his foot and turned on the general control system. On the screen a three-dimensional plan of the reflection could be seen. The picture turned slowly.

"Oy-yoy-yoy," Mikhail groaned.

A blue printout tape crawled out of the output.

"But there aren't many micropunctures," Zhilin said softly.

"To hell with the micropunctures," Bykov said and bent over the screen. "There's the real son of a bitch!"

The plan of the reflector was drawn in a dark blue color. White spots designated tears, places where the mesomatter layers had been pierced or where the control cells had been destroyed. There were many white spots, and on one edge of the reflector they fused into a large white smudge that covered no less than an eighth of the paraboloid's surface.

Mikhail threw up his hands and returned to the computer.

Zhilin reached out for his jumpsuit, shook Varya out of it and began to dress: The control room was cold again. Bykov was still standing there staring at the screen and biting his nails. Then he picked up the printout tape and glanced through it.

"Zhilin," he said suddenly. "Take two sigma testers. Check the power supply, and go into the caisson. "I'll wait for you there. Mikhail, drop everything and work on reinforcing the holes. Drop everything, I said."

"Where are you going, Alexei?" Mikhail asked in amazement.

"Outside," Bykov snapped, and walked out.

"Why?" Mikhail asked, turning to Zhilin.

Zhilin shrugged his shoulders. He did not know why. Repairing a mirror in space, while in flight, without expert mesochemists, without huge crystallizators, without reactor furnaces was simply unthinkable. Just as unthinkable as, for example, pulling the moon toward the Earth with your bare hands. And as it was, in this condition, with the broken edge, the reflector could give the *Takhmasib* only rotational motion. Like during the accident.

"It's crazy," Zhilin said indecisively.

He looked at Mikhail, and Mikhail looked at him. They said nothing, and then they both started to rush like mad. Mikhail gathered all his papers in a burst and said hurriedly, "Well, go on. Go on, Ivan, get a move on."

In the caisson Bykov and Zhilin climbed into spacesuits and with some difficulty squeezed into the elevator. The elevator box plunged down along the photoreactor pipe, on which all of the ship's components were strung — from the living gondola to the parabolic reflector.

"Good," Bykov said.

"What's good?" Zhilin asked.

The elevator stopped.

"It's good that the elevator is working," Bykov answered.

"Ah," Zhilin sighed in disappointment.

"It might not have," Bykov said sternly. "Just try crawling two hundred meters there and back."

They went out of the elevator shaft and stopped on the top platform of the paraboloid. Beneath them the reflector's black ribbed cupola sloped away gently. The reflector was enormous—seven hundred fifty meters wide and five hundred across. Its edges were not visible from where they were standing. Above their heads hung the huge silvery disk of the freight section. Along its sides, held out far from the surface by supports, were the hydrogen rockets, whose apertures were fluttering with a soundless blue flame. And all around a strange and threatening world glittered.

A wall of brown fog extended on the left. Far below, at an unimaginable depth, the fog separated into thick, taut layers of clouds with black clear bands between them. Even farther and even deeper these clouds fused into a solid dark brown smoothness. On the right stood a solid pink haze, and Zhilin suddenly saw the sun—a blinding bright-pink tiny disk.

"Let's get going," Bykov said. He handed Zhilin a coil of thin rope. "Fasten it to the shaft," he said.

On the other end of the rope he tied a loop and tightened it around his waist. Then he hung both testers around his neck and dangled one leg over the railing.

"Let it out little by little," he said. "I'm off."

Zhilin stood next to the railing, holding onto the rope with both hands, and watched the fat clumsy figure in the shining suit crawl slowly over the surface of the cupola. The suit reflected a pinkish light, and motionless pink reflections also lay on the black cupola.

"Let it out faster," Bykov's angry voice said in the helmet phone.

The figure in the suit disappeared, and on the ribbed surface only the shining taut thread of the rope remained. Zhilin began to look at the sun. Sometimes the pink disk was overcast—then it became even sharper in outline and completely red. Zhilin looked down beneath his feet and saw his dim pinkish shadow on the platform.

"Look, Ivan," Bykov's voice said. "Look below!"

Zhilin looked. Far below, a gigantic whitish mound floated out of the smooth brown surface; it resembled a puffball. It slowly spread out to the sides, and Zhilin could make out a streaming, twisting pattern, like a tangle of snakes.

"An exosphere protuberance," Bykov said. "Very rare, it seems. Damn it anyway, the guys should see this."

He meant the planetologists. The mound suddenly shone from the inside with a trembling lilac light.

"Ooh," Zhilin said involuntarily.

"Let it out," Bykov said.

Zhilin let out some more rope, keeping his eyes on the protuberance. At first it seemed to him that the Takhmasib was flying straight into it, but after a minute he realized that the ship would pass it by on the left. The protuberance tore loose from the smooth brown surface and floated into the pinkish haze, dragging behind it a sticky tail of yellow translucent threads. In the threads a violet glow flared up, then died out. The protuberance dissolved into the pink light.

Bykov worked for a long time. Several times he came back up to the platform, rested a while, and then went back down, each time choosing a different direction. When he climbed up the third time he had only one tester. "Dropped it," he said. Zhilin patiently let out rope, braced his leg against the railing. In that position he felt very stable and could look from side to side. But nothing changed on the sides. Only when the captain came up for the sixth time and barked, "Enough, let's go," did Zhilin suddenly realize that the brown foggy wall on the left—the cloudy surface of Jupiter—was now noticeably closer.

The control room was clean. Mikhail had swept up the fragments and was now sitting in his usual place, in a fur jacket over his jumpsuit. Steam was coming from his mouth—the room was cold. Bykov sat down in a chair, rested his hands on his knees, and looked intently first at the navigator, then at Zhilin. The navigator and Zhilin both waited.

"Did you reinforce the holes?" Bykov asked Mikhail.

Mikhail nodded several times.

"There's a chance," Bykov said and cleared his throat. "Sixteen percent of the reflector is out of order. The question then is, can we get the other eighty-four percent to work? Even less than eighty-four percent, because ten percent can't be controlled—the system of control cells was destroyed."

The navigator and Zhilin were silent, craning their necks.

"We might," Bykov said. "In any case, we can try. We have to shift the plasma ignition point so that it compensates for the asymmetry of the damage reflector."

"That's clear," Zhilin said in a quavering voice.

Bykov looked at him.

"It's our only chance. Ivan and I will work on the reorientation of the magnetic traps. Ivan is fully capable of the work. You, Mikhail, will compute the new position of the ignition point in accordance with the plan of the damage. You'll get the plan right away. It's a crazy job, but it is our only chance."

He looked at the navigator, and Mikhail raised his head and crossed glances with him. They understood each other immediately and completely. That they might not make it in time. That down below, under enormous pressure, corrosion would eat away at the hull and the ship could dissolve before they finished the work. That it was impossible to compensate for the asymmetry totally. That no one had ever tried to save a ship with similar compensation, with an engine that was weakened at least by half.

"It's our only chance," Bykov said loudly.

"I'll do it, Alexei," Mikhail said. "It's not that difficult—to compute a new ignition point. I'll do it."

"I'll give you a plan of the dead sections right away," Bykov repeated. "And we have to rush like hell. Soon overload will begin, and it will be very hard to work. And if we fall too deep, it will be dangerous to turn on the engine, because a chain reaction in the condensed hydrogen is possible." He paused, then added, "And we would be gassified."

"It's clear," Zhilin said. He wanted to begin that very minute.

Mikhail reached out with his short arms and said in a high-pitched voice, "The plan, Alexei, the plan."

Three red lights blinked on the emergency control panel.

"Well," Mikhail said. "The emergency rockets are running out of fuel."

"To hell with them," Bykov said and stood up.

3. In the Abyss

1. *The planetologists find diversion, and the navigator is convicted of smuggling.*

"Load," Yurkovsky said.

He was hanging by the periscope, poking his face against the chamois lens frame. He was hanging horizontally, his stomach down, his elbows and legs spread wide, and alongside him a thick observation journal and a pen floated in the air. Mollart exuberantly threw open the breech cover, pulled a clip of bomb probes from the shelves, and nudging it from the top and the bottom, with difficulty got it into the rectangular opening of the firing chamber. The clip slid slowly and soundlessly into place. Mollard closed the cover, clicked the lock, and said, "Ready, Voldemar."

Mollart held up well under weightlessness. True, he sometimes made careless movements and ended up on the ceiling, and then he would have to be pulled back down, and sometimes he felt nauseous, but for a newcomer to space he held up very well.

"Ready," Dauge said from the exosphere spectrograph.

"Fire," Yurkovsky commanded.

Dauge pushed the button. *Du-du-du-du*, came a muffled rumbling from the bomb release. And that was followed immediately by the *tk-tk-tk* of the spectrograph shutter. Through the periscope Yurkovsky saw white clumps of flame flash one after the other, then flew upward in the orange mist that the *Takhmasib* was now passing through. Twenty flashes, twenty burst bomb probes carrying meson irradiators.

"Great," Yurkovsky said softly.

The pressure outside was growing. The bomb probes exploded closer and closer. They slowed down all too soon.

Dauge spoke loudly into the dictaphone, glancing from time to time at the spectroanalyzer dials: "Molecular hydrogen—eighty-one and thirty-five, helium—seven and eleven, methane—four and sixteen, ammonia—one zero one. . . . The nonidentified line is increasing. . . . I told them: Put in an automatic counter, it's very inconvenient this way."

"We're falling," Yurkovsky said. "We're really falling. . . . The methane reading is only four."

Dauge, turning dexterously, took readings from the equipment.

"So far Kangren is right," he said. "Look, the bathymeter has already stopped working. The pressure is three hundred atmospheres. We're not going to be able to measure the pressure anymore."

"Okay," Yurkovsky said. "Load."

"Is it worth it?" Dauge asked. "The bathymeter isn't working. The synchronization will be destroyed."

"Let's try," Yurkovsky said. "Load."

He glanced at Mollart. Mollart was gently rocking back and forth along the ceiling, smiling sadly.

"Pull him down, Grigory," Yurkovsky said.

Dauge got to his knees, grabbed Mollart by the feet and pulled him down.

"Charles," he said patiently. "Don't make sudden movements. Plant your feet here and be careful."

Mollart sighed painfully and opened the cover. The empty clip floated out of the chamber, struck him in the chest, and flew slowly to Yurkovsky. Yurkovsky dodged it.

"Oh, again," Mollart said guiltily. "Forgive me, Voldemar. Oh, this weightlessness!"

"Load, load," Yurkovsky said.

"The sun," Dauge said suddenly.

Yurkovsky pressed himself against the periscope. In the orange cloud a dim disk appeared for several seconds.

"That's the last time," Dauge said.

"You said already three times 'last time,'" Mollart said, closing the cover. He bent over, checking the lock. "Farewell, sun, as Captain Nemo said. But that was not the last time. I am ready, Voldemar."

"So am I," Dauge said. "But maybe we should quit?"

Bykov entered the observatory compartment, scraping the floor with his magnetic soles.

"Finish your work," he said gloomily.

"Why?" Yurkovsky asked, turning around.

"Enormous pressure outside. Another half hour, and your bombs will be blowing up right here."

"Fire," Yurkovsky said hurriedly. Dauge hesitated a moment but still pressed the button. Bykov waited until the *du-du-du-du* was over, then said, "That's enough. Fasten down all the testers. This thing"—he pointed to the bomb release—"has to be blocked up. And do it right."

"Are periscope observations still permitted?" Yurkovsky asked.

"The periscope is fine," Bykov said. "Enjoy your diversion."

He turned and walked out. Dauge said, "Well, it's like I said—we got nothing. No synchronization."

He turned off the apparatus and began taking the reel out of the dictaphone.

"Dauge," Yurkovsky said. "I think Alexei has come up with something—what do you think?"

"I don't know," Dauge said and looked at him. "Why do you think so?"

"He has this special look," Yurkovsky said. "I know him."

For a moment everyone was silent. Only Mollart inhaled deeply—he was feeling nauseous. Then Dauge said, "I'm hungry. Where's the soup, Charles? You spilled the soup, and we are hungry. Whose turn is it today, Charles?"

"It's me," Mollart said. The mention of food made him even more nauseous. But he said, "I will go and prepare a new soup."

"The sun!" Yurkovsky said.

Dauge pressed his blackened eye to the videosearch eyepiece. "Sun again."

"It's not the sun," Dauge said.

"Right," Yurkovsky said. "I can't think it's the sun."

A distant patch of light in the light-brown murk became pale and, swelling, broke up into gray spots, then disappeared. Yurkovsky watched, his teeth clenched. Farewell, sun, he thought. Farewell.

"I'm hungry," Dauge said angrily. "Let's go to the galley, Charles."

He agilely pushed himself away from the wall, floated to the door, and opened it. Mollart also pushed off but hit his head against the doorway. Dauge caught him by the arm and pulled him out into the corridor. Yurkovsky heard Dauge ask, "How's life, *bon?*" Mollart answered, "Very good, but uncomfortable." "It's okay," Dauge said in a cheerful voice. "You'll get used to it soon."

It's okay, Yurkovsky thought, soon it will all be over. He glanced through the periscope. He could see that above, from where the ship was falling, the brown fog was getting denser, but below, out of the unimaginable depths, out of the bottomless depths of the hydrogen abyss, a strange pink light was sputtering. Then Yurkovsky closed his eyes. To live, he thought. To live long. To live forever. He pressed both hands against the side of his head and narrowed his eyes. To be deaf, to be blind, to be numb—but to live. To feel the sun and wind on your skin, and have a friend near you. Pain, weakness, pity. Like now. He pulled his hair hard. Just like now, only forever. Suddenly he heard himself breathing noisily and came to. The sensation of an unbearable, insane horror and desperation had disappeared. That's the way it had been before—twelve years ago on Mars, and ten years ago on Golkonda, and the year before last on Mars again. An attack of a desire to live, a dark and ancient desire, as old as protoplasm itself. Like a brief fainting spell. But it was passing. It had to be endured, like pain. And you had to get busy with something. Alexei had ordered them to fasten down the testers. He took his hands away from his face, opened his eyes, and saw that he was sitting on the floor. The fall of the *Takhmasib* had been halted, and things had acquired weight.

Yurkovsky reached out to the small control panel and pushed the button to fasten down the testers. Then he carefully blocked up the bomb release, gathered the discarded clips from the bomb probes and put them neatly in the shelving. He glanced through the periscope and it seemed to him—and undoubtedly was the case—that the darkness above had become thicker, and the pink glow below, stronger. He thought about the fact that no person had ever been so deep into Jupiter before, except, perhaps, for Sergei Petryshevsky—may his memory be blessed—but he probably exploded before this. His reflector was also broken.

He walked out into the corridor and headed for the lounge, glancing on the way into all the cabins. The *Takhmasib* was still falling, but with every minute more slowly, and Yurkovsky started tiptoeing, as though he were under water, maintaining his balance with his arms and from time to time taking involuntary hops.

In the deserted corridor Mollart's muffled shriek suddenly resounded, similar to a war cry: "How is life, Grégoire? Good?" Apparently Dauge had succeeded in restoring the radio optician's usual mood. Yurkovsky could not make out Dauge's reply. "*Bon*," he muttered. And he did feel good.

He looked in Mikhail's cabin. It was dark and there was a strange spicy aroma. Yurkovsky went in and turned on the light. In the middle of the cabin lay a smashed suitcase. Yurkovsky had never seen a suitcase in such a sorry state. A suitcase would look like that if a bomb probe had gone off inside. The dull-colored ceiling and walls were smeared with a brown slippery-looking substance. The smudges gave off an appetizing, spicy aroma. Spiced midia, Yurkovsky immediately determined. He was very fond of spiced midia, but it was strictly forbidden for all interplanetaries. He looked around and saw over the door a shining black spot—a meteorite hole. All the sections in the living gondola were hermetic. In case of a meteorite attack the air supply was automatically cut off until the resin plastic—a gooey and strong layer on the hull—had closed up the hole. That required one, at most two, seconds, but during that time the pressure in the section could fall drastically. It was not dangerous to humans but fatal to smuggled canned goods, which simply exploded. Especially expensive canned goods. Smuggled goods, Yurkovsky thought. The old glutton. Well, you're going to get it from the captain. Bykov could not tolerate smugglers.

Yurkovsky looked the cabin over one more time and noticed that the black hole had a slight tinge of silver. Aha, he thought. Someone has already metalized the hole. True, at these pressures the plastic stopper would have been blown out otherwise. He turned off the light and returned to the corridor. And then he felt weariness, a leaden weight in all his body. Oh, damn, how soft I've gotten! he thought, and suddenly felt the microphone cord cutting into his neck. He realized what was happening. The flight was coming to an end. Within a few minutes there would be double gravity, and there would be ten thousand kilometers of condensed hydrogen overhead, while below there would be sixty thousand kilometers of very dense liquid hydrogen. Each kilogram of your body would weigh two kilograms, and even a little more. Poor Charles, Yurkovsky thought. Poor Mikhail.

"Voldemar," Mollart called to him from behind. "Voldemar, help us take the soup. A very heavy soup."

Yurkovsky glanced around. Dauge and Mollart, red and sweaty, were pushing an unwieldy, wobbling table on wheels out the galley door. On the table were three barely steaming pots. Yurkovsky went toward them and suddenly felt that he had become heavy. Mollart groaned softly and sat on the floor. The *Takhmasib* came to a halt. The *Takhmasib*, its crew, its passengers, and its freight, had reached its last stop.

2. *The planetologists torment the navigator, and the radio optician torments the planetologists.*

"Who cooked this meal?" Bykov asked.

He looked around at everyone and then fixed his eyes on the pots again.

Mikhail was breathing with difficulty, whistling, resting his chest against the table. His face was scarlet, puffy.

"I did," Mollart said, not very boldly.

"What's the matter with it?" Dauge asked.

All their voices were hoarse. They all spoke with difficulty, barely squeezing the words out. Mollart smiled awkwardly and lay face up on the couch. He felt terrible. The ship was not falling anymore, and the gravity had become unbearable. Bykov looked at Mollart.

"This meal will kill you," he said. "Eat this meal and you will never get up again. It will crush you, do you understand?"

"Oh, damn," Dauge said with annoyance. "I forgot about the gravity."

Mollart was lying with closed eyes and was breathing heavily. His jaw was sagging.

"Let's eat the bouillon," Bykov said. "And that's all. Not a bite more." He looked at Mikhail and bared his teeth in a glum grin. "Not a bite," he repeated.

Yurkovsky took the ladle and began dishing out the bouillon.

"A heavy meal," he said.

"It smells good," Mikhail said. "Could you dish me just a little more, Vladimir?"

"Enough," Bykov said firmly. He slowly sipped the bouillon, his spoon in his fist like a small child.

They began eating. Mollart raised himself with difficulty, then lay back down.

"I can't," he said. "Forgive me, I can't."

Bykov put down his spoon and stood up.

"I suggest that all passengers remain in the shock seats," he said. Dauge shook his head no. "As you wish. But be sure to put Mollart in one."

"All right," Yurkovsky said.

Dauge took a dish, sat down on the couch next to Mollart, and began to feed him with the spoon, like an invalid. Mollart swallowed noisily, without opening his eyes.

"And where's Ivan?" Yurkovsky asked.

"On watch," Bykov answered. He took the pot with the leftover soup and went toward the hatch, walking heavily on stiff legs. Yurkovsky, biting his lips, looked at his bent back.

"That's all, my friends," Mikhail said in a pitiful voice. "I'm beginning to lose weight. But I won't make it. Right now I weigh over two hundred kilograms. And it will get worse. We are still falling slightly."

He leaned back in his chair and put his puffy hands on his stomach. Then he turned slightly, put his hands on the arm of the chair, and almost immediately went to sleep.

"He's sleeping, the fat man," Dauge said. "The ship is going down, and the navigator is sleeping. Come on, Charles. Another spoonful. For Papa. That's the way. And now one for Mama."

"I can't, forgive me," Mollart babbled. "I can't. I will lie." He stretched out and began to mutter indistinctly in French.

Dauge put the spoon down on the table.

"Mikhail," he called out softly. "Mikhail."

Mikhail responded with a thunderous snore.

"I'll wake him," Yurkovsky said. "Mikhail," he said furtively. "Midia. Spiced midia."

Mikhail shuddered and woke up.

"What?" he asked. "What?"

"A guilty conscience," Yurkovsky said.

Dauge fixed his eyes on the navigator.

"What have you been doing in your cabin?" he asked.

Mikhail blinked his red eyes, then fidgeted in his chair. He said barely audibly, "Ah, I completely forgot," and tried to stand up.

"Sit," Dauge said.

"So what have you been doing there?" Yurkovsky asked.

"Nothing unusual," Mikhail said and glanced at the hatch to the control room. "Really, nothing, guys. It was just—"

"Mikhail," Yurkovsky said. "Come clean."

"Talk, fat man," Dauge said truculently.

The navigator once again tried to get up.

"Sit," Yurkovsky said pitilessly. "Midia. Spiced midia. Talk."

Mikhail turned lobster red.

"We're not children anymore," Dauge said. "We faced death before. Why in hell the big secret?"

"There's a chance," the navigator mumbled.

"There's always a chance," Dauge objected. "More specifically?"

"An infinitesimal chance," Mikhail said. "Really, it's time for me to go, guys."

"What are they doing?" Dauge asked. "What are they up to, Alexei and Ivan?"

Mikhail looked at the hatch with anguish.

"He doesn't want to say anything to you," he whispered. "He doesn't want to give you false hopes. Alexei hopes to blast out. They're retuning the magnetic trap system. . . . Leave me alone, please!" he shouted in a high, piercing voice, somehow got to his feet, and wobbled into the control room.

"*Mon Dieu*," Mollart said softly and turned face down.

"Ah, it's all nonsense, just busywork," Dauge said. "Of course, Bykov is incapable of sitting around doing nothing when the evil one has us in his power. Let's go. Come on, Charles, we'll put you in the shock seat. Captain's orders."

They took Mollart by the arms, lifted him up, and led him out into the corridor. His head wobbled.

"*Mon Dieu*," he mumbled. "Forgive me. I am very terrible interplanetary. I am only *radio-optique*."

It was very hard for them to walk themselves and support Mollart, but they managed to get him to his cabin and tuck him away in his shock seat. He lay there in a much too large box, small, pitiable, gasping, with a bluish face.

"You'll feel better soon, Charles," Dauge said.

Yurkovsky nodded and then winced from pain in his back.

"Lie there and rest," he said.

"*Bon*," Mollart said. "Thank you, comrades."

Dauge pulled down the cover and knocked. Mollart knocked in response.

"Well, okay," Dauge said. "We should get into our overload costumes ourselves."

Yurkovsky went to the exit. The ship had only three overload suits—for the crew. The passengers were supposed to get into their shock seats.

They went through all the cabins and gathered all the blankets and pillows. In the observatory they set themselves up by the periscope, spreading soft things on all sides, and then lay down and rested in silence. It was hard to breathe. A huge barbell seemed to be resting on their chests.

"I remember them giving us heavy overloads back in school," Yurkovsky said. "You had to lose weight."

"Yes," Dauge said. "I had forgotten. What was that nonsense about spiced midia?"

"A very tasty treat, isn't it?" Yurkovsky said. "Our navigator snuck several jars on board behind the captain's back, and they exploded in his suitcase."

"So?" Dauge said. "Again? What a treat? What a smuggler! He's lucky Bykov doesn't have time for that now."

"I don't think Bykov knows yet," Yurkovsky said.

And never would, he thought. They were silent, then Dauge took the observation journal and began going through it. They calculated for a while, then argued about the meteorite attack. Dauge said that it was a random swarm. Yurkovsky declared that it was a ring. "A ring around Jupiter?" Dauge said condescendingly. "Yes," Yurkovsky said. "I've suspected it for a long time." "No," Dauge said. "It still wouldn't be a ring. A semiring, perhaps." "Well, a semiring then," Yurkovsky agreed. "Kangren's work is great," Dauge said. "His calculations are remarkably accurate."

"Not entirely," Yurkovsky said. "Why is that?" Dauge inquired. "Because the temperature increases noticeably more slowly," Yurkovsky explained. "It's internal luminescence of a nonclassical variety," Dauge objected. "Yes, nonclassical," Yurkovsky said. "Kangren could not take that into account," Dauge said. "You have to take it into account," Yurkovsky said. "They've been arguing about it for a hundred years—you can't ignore it." "You're just ashamed," Dauge said. "You had a real brawl with Kangren in Dublin, and now you're ashamed." "Blockhead!" Yurkovsky said. "I took the nonclassical effects into consideration." "I know," Dauge said. "So if you know," Yurkovsky said, "don't talk nonsense." "Don't yell at me," Dauge said. "It's not nonsense. You took nonclassical effects into consideration, but look at the price you paid." "What price do you mean?" Yurkovsky exploded. "You still haven't read my last article!" "Okay," Dauge said, "don't get mad. My back feels numb." "So does mine," Yurkovsky said. He turned over onto his stomach and climbed up on all fours. It was not easy. He made it to the periscope and looked out.

"Take a look," he said.

They began looking through the periscope. The *Takhmasib* was floating in an emptiness filled with pink light. Not a single object was visible, no motion, nothing your gaze could settle on. Only an even pink light. You seemed to be staring at a phosphorescent screen. After a long silence Yurkovsky said, "It's boring."

He fluffed up the pillows and lay down on his back again.

"No one has ever seen it before," Dauge said. "It's the luminescence of metallic hydrogen."

"Observations like that," Yurkovsky said, "aren't worth a plugged nickel. Maybe we should hook up the spectrograph to the periscope?"

"That's foolish," Dauge said, barely able to move his lips. He crawled onto the pillows and lay down on his back. "It's a shame," he said. "After all, no one has ever seen it before."

"What a rotten thing it is to do nothing," Yurkovsky said with sadness. Dauge suddenly propped himself up on his elbow and tilted his head, listening. "What's up?" Yurkovsky asked.

"Quiet," Dauge said. "Listen."

Yurkovsky listened. A low roar reached them from somewhere, growing in waves and then dying down, like the buzz of a giant bee. The roar turned into a drone, became higher, then stopped.

"What is it?" Dauge asked.

"I don't know," Yurkovsky answered. He sat up. "Could it be the engine?"

"No, it's from that direction," Dauge said, waving his hand at the periscope. "Well now. . . ." He listened, and once again the increasing drone could be heard.

"We'll have to look," Dauge said. The giant bee was silent but started in again a moment later. Dauge got to his knees and stuck his face against the periscope. "Look!" he shouted.

Yurkovsky crawled to the periscope.

"Look how beautiful!" Dauge shouted.

Enormous rainbow spheres rose up out of the yellow-pink abyss. They resembled soap bubbles and shone green, blue, red. It was very beautiful and totally incomprehensible. The spheres rose out of the chasm with a low but increasing roar, raced by quickly, and disappeared from view. They all varied in size, and Dauge frantically reached for the rangefinder. One sphere, especially huge and fluttering, passed by quite close. For several instants the observatory was filled by an unbearably low, nagging drone, and the ship rocked slightly.

"Hello, observatory," Bykov's voice came over the loudspeaker. "What is that out there?"

"Phenomena," Yurkovsky said, leaning his head to the microphone.

"What?" Bykov asked.

"Some kind of bubbles," Yurkovsky explained.

"I can see that for myself," Bykov roared.

"It's not metallic hydrogen," Yurkovsky said.

The bubbles disappeared.

"So then," Dauge said. "Diameters of five hundred, nine hundred, and three thousand three hundred meters. Unless of course the perspective here is distorted. That's all I managed. What could it be?"

Two more bubbles flashed by in the pink emptiness. A low bass sound intensified, then ceased.

"The planet seems to be in working order," Yurkovsky said. "And we will never find out what is going on."

"Bubbles in gas," Dauge said. "Although, some gas! Its density is more like benzine."

He turned around. Mollart was sitting in the doorway, leaning his head against the jamb. The skin on his face drooped toward his chin because of the gravity. His forehead was white and his neck cherry red.

"Here is I," Mollart said.

He rolled over onto his stomach and crawled to his place by the bomb release. The planetologists watched in silence, then Dauge stood up, took two pillows—for himself and Yurkovsky—and helped Mollart get comfortable. They were all silent.

"Very miserable," Mollart finally said. "I can't alone. I want to talk."

"We're glad to see you, Charles," Dauge said sincerely. "We, too, are miserable, and we talk all the time."

Mollart tried to sit up but thought better of it and remained lying, staring at the ceiling."

"How's life, Charles?" Yurkovsky said with curiosity.

"Life is *bon*," Mollart said, smiling palely. "Only too little."

Dauge lay down and also stared at the ceiling. Too little, he thought, much less than you would like. He cursed under his breath in Latvian.

"What?" Mollart asked.

"He's cursing," Yurkovsky explained.

Mollart said suddenly in a high voice: "My friends!" and the planetologists both turned toward him.

"My friends! What should I do? You are experience interplanetaries. You are great people and heroes. Yes, heroes. *Mon Dieu!* You look into eyes of death more than I look into the eyes of the *mademoiselles*." He shook his head sadly. "But I am not experience. I am terrified, and I want to talk much now, but now the end is close, and I not know how. Yes, yes, what should say now?"

He looked at Dauge and Yurkovsky with glistening eyes. Dauge mumbled awkwardly, "Oh, damn it!" and looked at Yurkovsky. Yurkovsky was lying with his hands behind his head and looking at Mollart out of the corner of his eye.

"Oh, damn!" Dauge said. "I've already forgotten."

"I could tell you how they wanted to amputate my leg once," Yurkovsky said.

"That's right!" Dauge said happily. "And then you, Charles, can also tell us something amusing."

"Oh, you still joke me," Mollart said.

"Or we could sing," Dauge said. "I read that somewhere. Will you sing to us, Charles?"

"Oh," Mollart said, "I've gone to pieces."

"Not at all," Dauge said. "You're holding up very well, Charles. And that is the most important thing. It's true that Charles is holding up very well, isn't it?"

"Of course," Yurkovsky said. "Remarkable well."

"But the captain isn't sleeping," Dauge continued cheerfully. "Have you noticed, Charles? He's thought up something, our captain."

"Yes," Mollart said. "Yes, our captain. He is the great hope."

"And how," Dauge said. "You don't even know how big a hope."

"Six foot one," Yurkovsky said.

Mollart broke out laughing.

"You still joke," he said.

"We will go on chatting and observing," Dauge said. "Do you want to look through the periscope, Charles? It's very beautiful. No one has ever seen it before." He got up and leaned against the periscope. Yurkovsky saw his back suddenly bend. Dauge held on with both hands. "My God!" he said. "A spaceship!"

A spaceship was hanging in the pink emptiness. It was distinctly visible in full detail and was about three kilometers away. It was a first-class photon freighter with a parabolic reflector that resembled a skirt, with a round living gondola and a disk-shaped freight section, with cigarlike emergency rockets on long supports. It was hanging vertically and completely motionlessly. And it was gray, as though it were part of a black-and-white movie.

"Who is it?" Dauge muttered. "Could it be Petryshevsky?"

"Look at the reflector," Yurkovsky said.

The reflector on the gray spaceship was broken off at the edge.

"Those guys had bad luck, too," Dauge said.

"Oh," Mollart said. "Another one."

A second spaceship—exactly the same—was suspended beyond the first.

"And that one has a broken reflector, too," Dauge said.

"I know," Yurkovsky said. "It's our *Takhmasib*. It's a mirage."

It was a double mirage. Several rainbow bubbles rose rapidly from the depths, and the phantom ships were distorted, trembled, and melted. And to the right and higher, three more phantom ships appeared.

"What beautiful bubbles," Mollart said. "They sing."

He lay down on his back again. His nose was bleeding, and he blew his nose and frowned and kept looking at the planetologists to see if they noticed. They, of course, did not.

"So," Dauge said, "you say that things are dull."

"I don't say so now," Yurkovsky said.

"But you did," Dauge said. "You were grumbling about it being boring."

Both of them tried to avoid looking at Mollart. It was impossible to stop the bleeding. It would have to clot by itself. The radio optician should have been taken to the shock seat, but. . . . Well, it would stop. Mollart blew his nose quietly.

"There's another mirage," Dauge said. "But that is not a ship."

Yurkovsky looked through the periscope. It can't be, he thought. It just couldn't be. Not here, not on Jupiter. Underneath the *Takhmasib* the peak of a huge gray mountain floated slowly by. Its base was lost in the pink haze. Alongside was another cliff—bare, steep, jagged, with deep straight fissures. And beyond that was a whole series of similarly steep peaks. And the silence in the observatory changed to scraps, rustles, a low roar, similar to the echoes of distant avalanches.

"That's not a mirage," Yurkovsky said. "It looks like a core."

"Nonsense," Dauge said.

"Still, Jupiter might have a core."

"Nonsense, nonsense," Dauge said impatiently.

The mountain chain stretched out beneath the *Takhmasib*, and there was no end to it.

"Look at that!" Dauge said.

Above the jagged peaks a dark shapeless silhouette appeared, grew, turned into an eroded chunk of black rock, and disappeared again. After it came another, then a third, and in the distance, barely distinguishable, a gray mass shone in a gray patch. The mountain range below gradually got lower and disappeared from view. Yurkovsky, not leaving the periscope, brought the microphone to his lips. His joints cracked under the stress.

"Bykov," he called, "Alexei."

"Alexei isn't here, Vladimir," the navigator's voice answered. The voice was hoarse and gasping. "He's in the machine."

"Mikhail, we're flying over mountains," Yurkovsky said.

"What mountains?" Mikhail exclaimed, with fear in his voice.

In the distance there was a remarkably smooth, seemingly polished surface—an enormous plain, framed by a low ridge of hills. It passed beneath and drowned in the pink glow.

"We still don't understand everything," Yurkovsky said.

"I'll take a look right now, Vladimir," Mikhail said.

Still another mountainous land floated past. It floated high up in the sky, and its peaks were upside down. It was a wild, fantastic sight, and Yurkovsky at first thought that it was another mirage, but it was not. Then he understood and said, "It's not a core, Dauge. It's a cemetery." Dauge did not understand. "It's a cemetery for lost worlds," Yurkovsky said. "Jupe swallowed them up."

Dauge was silent for a long time, then muttered, "What discoveries! A ring . . . pink luminescence, a cemetery of worlds . . . it's a shame . . . a real shame."

He called out to Mollart. Mollart did not answer. He was lying face down.

They dragged Mollart to the shock seat, woke him up, and he, exhausted, swollen, went to sleep immediately, as though he had fainted. Then they returned to the observatory and hung onto the periscope. Under the *Takhmasib* and alongside the *Takhmasib*, and even at times above the *Takhmasib*, chunks of increate worlds floated slowly by in the streams of condensed hydrogen—mountains, cliffs, monstrous cracked blocks of rock, and transparent gray clouds of dust. Then the *Takhmasib* was carried to the side, and in the periscope was only the empty, even, pink light.

"I'm dog-tired," Dauge said. He turned on his side, and his joints cracked. "Hear that?" "I did," Yurkovsky answered. "Let's see." "Go ahead," Dauge said. "I thought it was a core," Yurkovsky said. "It can't be," Dauge said. Yurkovsky began to rub his face with his hands. "Take a look," he said.

They saw and heard much more, or at least they thought they saw and heard much more, because they were both very tired, and their vision blurred, and then the walls vanished and there was only the even, pink light. They saw broad motionless zigzags of lightning, running from the darkness above to the pink abyss below, and heard the lilac discharges pulsing with an iron thunder. They saw some sort of fluttering films that flew close by with a high-pitched whistle. They studied weird shadows in the darkness, which twisted and turned, and Dauge maintained that they were three-dimensional shadows, but Yurkovsky argued that Dauge was hallucinating. And they heard wails, and squeaks, and bangs, and strange voicelike sounds, and Dauge suggested recording them on the dictaphone, but noticed that Yurkovsky was asleep, lying on his stomach. Then he turned Yurkovsky over on his back and went back to the periscope.

Varya, blue with white polka dots, came crawling through the open door, her belly flat against the floor. She nestled on Yurkovsky, curling up on his knees. Dauge was about to chase her away but did not have the energy. He could no longer hold his head up. And Varya breathed deeply and blinked slowly. The spines on her snout were bristling, and her half-dead tail whipped around in time to her breathing.

3. *Time comes to say farewell, but the radio optician does not know how.*

It was hard, unimaginably hard, to work in such conditions. Zhilin lost consciousness several times. His heart seemed to stop, and everything was clouded over in a red murk. And the taste of blood was constantly in his mouth. Zhilin was ashamed, because Bykov continued working indefatigably, smoothly, and accurately, like a machine. Bykov was wet with sweat, and it was unimaginably hard for him too, but he, apparently, knew how to force himself to keep from losing consciousness. After two hours Zhilin had lost any sense of why he was working; he had no more hope, no love of life, but every time he came to he continued where he left off, because alongside him was Bykov. Once he came to and did not find Bykov. Then he broke out crying. But Bykov soon returned, set down a pot with soup in it, and said, "Eat." He ate and set to work again. Bykov's face was white and his sagging neck was scarlet. He breathed heavily and frequently. And he was silent. Zhilin thought: If we get out of this, I'm not going on any interstellar expedition, I'm not going to Pluto, I'm not going anywhere until I become like Bykov. So ordinary and even boring, during ordinary times. So sullen and even a little funny. So hard to know that it is difficult to believe, looking at him, in the legend of Golkonda, in the legend of Callisto, and in all the other legends. Zhilin remembered how the young interplanetaries furtively made fun of the Redheaded Anchorite—incidentally, where did that nickname come from?—but he had never seen even one pilot or scientist of the older generation speak of Bykov in derogatory terms. If I get out, I must become like Bykov. If I don't, I must die like Bykov. When Zhilin lost consciousness, Bykov took over his work in silence. When Zhilin came to, Bykov returned to his own work, also in silence.

Then Bykov said, "Let's go," and they climbed into the chamber of the magnetic system. Everything seemed to float before Zhilin's eyes, and he wanted to lie down, stick his face in something soft, and lie there until he was carried away. He climbed out second and got stuck and still lay there on the cold floor, but quickly regained consciousness and then he saw Bykov's shoe right in front of his face. The shoe was stamping impatiently. Zhilin strained and crawled out of the hatch. He squatted to fasten the hatch properly. The lock did not do what he wanted, and Zhilin tore at it with his scratched hands. Bykov towered above him, like a radio antenna, and looked without blinking from top to bottom.

"Right away," Zhilin said hurriedly. "Right away. . . ."

The lock, finally, fell into the right place.

"It's ready," Zhilin said and straightened up. His legs shook at the knees.

"Let's go," Bykov said.

They returned to the control room. Mikhail was sleeping in his chair by the computer. He was snoring loudly. The computer was on. Bykov leaned over the navigator, took the microphone, and said, "All passengers meet in the lounge."

"What?" Mikhail asked, awakening with a shudder. "What, already?"

"Already," Bykov said. "Let's go into the lounge."

But he did not leave immediately—he stood there and watched Mikhail, blinking abnormally and groaning, climb out of his chair. Then he seemed to awaken and said, "Let's go."

They went into the lounge. Mikhail headed straight for the couch and sat down, his hands folded on his stomach. Zhilin also sat down, so his legs would not shake, and started staring at the table. On the table there was still a pile of dirty dishes. Then the door to the corridor opened and the passengers tumbled in. The planetologists dragged Mollart with them; Mollart was hanging, limp-legged, his arms around the planetologists' shoulders. In his hand he was squeezing a handkerchief covered with dark spots.

Dauge and Yurkovsky put Mollart on the couch and sat down on either side of him. Zhilin studied them. So that's what it's like, he thought. Does my face look like that? He stealthily felt his face. His cheeks seemed lean and his chin very fat, like Mikhail's. He felt pins and needles in his legs. Not from sitting too much, he thought.

"So then," Bykov said. He was sitting on a chair in the corner and then stood up, walked over to the table, and leaned heavily against it. Mollart unexpectedly winked at Zhilin and covered his face with the spotted hand-kerchief. Bykov looked at him coldly. Then he began staring at the wall.

"So then," he repeated. "We were busy with the re-out-fit-ting of the *Takhmasib*. We have finished the re-out-fit-ting." The word *reoutfitting* gave him trouble, but he stubbornly repeated it. "We can now use the pho-ton engine, and I have decided to do so. But first I want to inform you of the possible outcomes. I warn you that the decision has been made, and I do not intend to discuss it with you or ask for your opinion."

"Make it quick, Alexei," Dauge said.

"The decision has been made," Bykov said. "But I believe that you are entitled to know what might happen. First, the ignition of the photoreactor might produce an explosion in the condensed hydrogen around us. Then the *Takhmasib* will be totally destroyed. Second, the first explosion of plasma might destroy the reflector—possibly the outer layer of the mirror has been worn away by corrosion. Then we will remain here and. . . . Well, you know. Third, and last, the *Takhmasib* might sucessfully clear Jupiter and—"

"Got you," Dauge said.

"And the supplies will be delivered to Amalteia," Bykov said.

"The supplies will be eternally grateful to Bykov," Yurkovsky said. Mikhail smiled timidly. He did not find it funny. Bykov stared at the wall.

"I intend to take off immediately," he said. "I suggest that passengers take their places in the shock seats. All of them. And none of your tricks." He looked at the planetologists. "Acceleration will be eight g's at the minimum. I ask you to obey the order. Flight Engineer Zhilin, check that the order is carried out and report to me."

He looked at them all, turned, and went into the control room on stiff legs.

"*Mon Dieu*," Mollart said. "That is the life."

He was bleeding from the nose again, and he began to blow softly. Dauge said, "We need a lucky devil. Anyone here on good terms with Lady Luck? We could use her help."

Zhilin stood up.

"It's time, comrades," he said. He wanted it to be over as soon as possible. He wanted to have it behind him. Everyone remained sitting. "It's time, comrades," he repeated absentmindedly.

"The probability of a successful outcome is point one," Yurkovsky said, and began massaging his cheeks. Mikhail, his joints cracking, climbed out of the couch.

"Friends," he said. "We have to say good-bye. Just in case, you know. . . . Anything can happen." He smiled pitifully.

"So then, let's say good-bye," Dauge said.

"And I again not know how," Mollart said.

Yurkovsky stood up.

"Well, this is it," he said. "Let's go to the shock seats. Otherwise Bykov will come out, and then. . . . I'd rather burn up. The man has a heavy hand, I still remember. After ten years."

"Yes," Mikhail hastened to agree. "Let's go, guys. Let's shake hands."

They all shook hands solemnly.

"Where will you be, Mikhail?" Dauge asked.

"In the shock seat, like everyone else."

"And you? Ivan?"

"Me, too." He supported Mollart by the arm.

"And the captain?"

They went out into the corridor, and once again they all stopped. There were only a few steps left.

"Alexei says that he does not trust the automatic guidance on Jupiter," Zhilin said. "He will fly the ship himself."

"That's Bykov," Yurkovsky said, smiling awkwardly. "Carrying the weak on his broad shoulders."

Mikhail, sobbing, went into his cabin.

"I'll help you, Monsieur Mollart," Zhilin said.

"Yes," Mollart agreed and obediently put his arm around Zhilin's shoulders.

"Success and good plasma," Yurkovsky said.

Dauge nodded, and they each went to their cabin. Zhilin led Mollart into his cabin and put him in the shock seat.

"How is life, Ivan?" Mollart asked sadly. "*Bon?*"

"*Bon*, Monsieur Mollart."

"And how are the girls?"

"Very good," Zhilin said. "On Amalteia the girls are marvelous."

He smiled politely, closed the cover, and immediately stopped smiling. If only it were over, he thought.

He walked down the corridor, and the corridor seemed very empty. He knocked on the cover of each shock seat and heard the answering rap. Then he returned to the control room.

Bykov was sitting in the senior pilot's seat. He was wearing an overload suit. The suit resembled a silkworm cocoon, and Bykov's tousled red hair stuck out of it. Bykov seemed totally ordinary, only very angry and tired.

"Everything is ready, Captain Bykov," Zhilin said.

"Good," Bykov said. He looked at Zhilin out of the corner of his eye. "Afraid, young man?"

"No." Zhilin said.

He was not afraid. He just wanted it to be over. And then suddenly he wanted to see his father, when he climbed out of a stratoplane, bulky, mustached, his hat in his hand. And to introduce his father to Bykov.

"Get moving, Ivan," Bykov said. "You have ten minutes."

"Good plasma, Captain Bykov," Zhilin said.

"Thank you," Bykov said. "Now get moving."

I have to hold up, Zhilin thought. Damn, why won't I hold up? He walked to the door of his cabin and suddenly saw Varya. Varya was crawling stiffly, pressing herself against the wall, dragging her tail behind her. Seeing Zhilin, she raised her triangular snout and slowly blinked.

"Oh, you poor thing," Zhilin said. He took Varya by her loose skin and dragged her into his cabin, pulled up the cover on the shock seat, and looked at his watch. Then he threw Varya into the shock seat—she was very heavy and quivered clumsily in his hands. Then he climbed in himself. He lay in total darkness, listened to the noise the shock-absorbing mixture made, and his body felt light and lighter. It was very, very pleasant, only Varya kept digging him in the side and sticking his arm with her spines. I have to hold up, Zhilin thought.

In the control room Captain Alexei Bykov pressed the large fluted starter button.

Epilogue: Amalteia, J-Station

The director of J-Station does not watch the setting of Jupiter, and Varya gets pulled by the tail.

The setting of Jupiter is also very beautiful. The yellow-green glow of the exosphere slowly dies out, and one after another the stars come on, like diamond needles against black velvet.

But the director of J-Station did not see the stars, nor the yellow-green tints over the nearby cliffs. He was watching the icy field of the spaceport. The gigantic tower of the *Takhmasib* was descending, slowly, barely noticeable to the eye, onto the field. The *Takhmasib* was a monster—a first-class photon freighter. It was so huge that there was nothing on that world to compare it to, on the blue-green plain dotted with round black spots. From the spectrolite dome it seemed that the *Takhmasib* was falling by itself. In reality it was being laid down. In the shadows of the cliffs and on the other side of the plain powerful cranes pulled on cables, and the brilliant threads sometimes flashed in the rays of the sun. The sun illuminated the ship blindingly, and it was entirely visible, from the huge cup-shaped reflector to the spherical living gondola.

Such a mutilated spaceship had never landed on Amalteia before. The edge of the reflector had been broken off, and a heavy broken shadow lay in the huge cup. The two-hundred-meter photoreactor pipe looked spotted and corroded. The emergency rockets on crumpled supports jutted out every which way. The freight section was tilted, and one compartment crushed. The freight section disk resembled a flat, round jar, on which someone in lead boots had stepped. Part of the food supplies, of course, would be lost, the director thought. What nonsense creeps into your mind. What did it matter? Yes, the *Takhmasib* was not about to leave soon.

"Our chicken soup cost a lot," Uncle Valnoga said.

"Yes," the director mumbled. "Chicken soup. Knock it off, Valnoga. Don't even think it. What does chicken soup have to do with it?"

"A lot," Valnoga said. "The kids need real food."

The spaceship was lowered to the plain and sank into darkness. Now only a weak greenish glimmer on the titanium sides was visible, then lights flashed and small black figures darted about. Jupiter's shaggy hump went behind the cliffs, and the cliffs turned black and stood higher, and for an instant a fissure burned brightly, and the mesh construction of the antenna was visible.

In the director's pocket a radiophone sang out. The director pulled out the smooth box and pushed the receive button.

"Yes?" he said.

The dispatcher's tenor, very happy and without the slightest deference, said rapidly, "Comrade Director, Captain Bykov and the crew and passengers have arrived in the station and are waiting for you in your office."

"Coming," the director said.

Together with Uncle Valnoga he went down in the elevator and headed for his office. The door was open wide. His office was full of people, and they were all talking and laughing loudly. Still in the corridor, the director heard a joyous shriek: "How is life—*bon*? How are the guys—*bon*?"

The director did not go in immediately, but stood outside a moment, searching for the new arrivals. Valnoga breathed noisily behind him. They saw Mollart with his hair wet from a swim. Mollart was gesticulating and chuckling madly. Around him stood the women—Zoya, Galya, Nadya, Jane, Yuriko, and the women on Amalteia—and they were all laughing, too. Mollart always managed to collect all the women around him. Then the director saw Yurkovsky, or more exactly, the back of his head, sticking up above the others, and the nightmarish monster on his shoulder. The monster made circles with its snout and yawned horribly every once in a while. People tugged on Varya's tail. Dauge was not to be seen, but made himself heard as well as Mollart. Dauge shouted, "Let me through, my friends, let me through!" To the side stood a huge unfamiliar young man, very handsome, but too pale amid all the suntanned people. Several local planet fliers were talking with him with great animation. Mikhail Krutikov was sitting in a chair by the director's desk. He was telling a story, waving his short arms, and raising a crumpled handkerchief to his eyes.

Bykov was the last person the director recognized. He was so pale he almost seemed blue, and his hair seemed copperish; under his eyes were dark blue bags, the usual result of strong and prolonged overloads. His eyes were red. He spoke so softly that the director could not make out his words and could only see that he was speaking slowly, moving his lips with difficulty. Near Bykov were the division directors and the head of the spaceport. It was the quietest group in the room. Then Bykov raised his eyes and saw the director. He stood up, and a whisper ran through the room, and everyone suddenly stopped talking.

They walked toward each other, their magnetic soles clinking against the floor, and met in the middle of the room. They shook hands and stood motionless for a moment. Then Bykov drew back his hand and said, "Comrade Kangren, the spaceship *Takhmasib* has arrived with its cargo."

ACKNOWLEDGMENTS

"Angouleme," by Thomas M. Disch. Copyright © 1974 by Thomas M. Disch. Reprinted by permission of the author.

"Aye, and Gomorrah . . ." by Samuel R. Delany. Copyright © 1967 by Harlan Ellison for *Dangerous Visions*. Reprinted by permission of the author and the author's agents, Henry Morrison, Inc.

"The Blind Pilot," by Nathalie-Charles Henneberg. Copyright © 1959 by Editions OPTA. English translation copyright © 1960 by Mercury Press, Inc. Reprinted by permission of Damon Knight.

"Captain Nemo's Last Adventure," by Josef Nesvadba. From *View from Another Shore*, edited by Franz Rottensteiner. English translation copyright © 1973 by The Continuum Publishing Company. Reprinted by permission of the publisher.

"The Chaste Planet," from *Hugging the Shore* by John Updike. Copyright © 1983 by John Updike. First published in *The New Yorker*. Reprinted by permission of Alfred A. Knopf, Inc.

"Chronopolis," by J. G. Ballard. Copyright © 1960 by J. G. Ballard. Reprinted by permission of the Robin Straus Agency, Inc.

"Codemus," by Tor Åge Bringsvaerd. Copyright © 1968 by the author. First published in Probok (1968). Published by Gyldendal Norsk Forlag, Oslo. Reprinted by permission of the author.

"The Dead Fish," by Boris Vian. Copyright © 1955 by Le Terrain Vague. Reprinted by permission of Damon Knight.

"The Dead Past," by Isaac Asimov. Copyright © 1956 by Street & Smith Publications, Inc. Reprinted by permission of the author.

"The Fifth Head of Cerberus," by Gene Wolfe. Copyright © 1972 by Gene Wolfe. First published in *Orbit 10* edited by Damon Knight.

Reprinted by permission of the author and the author's agent, Virginia Kidd.

"Forgetfulness," by John W. Campbell, Jr. Copyright © 1937 by Street & Smith Publications, Inc. Reprinted by permission of the author and the author's agents, Scott Meredith Literary Agency, Inc., 845 Third Avenue, New York, New York 10022.

"Ghost V," by Robert Sheckley. Copyright © 1957 by Robert Sheckley. Reprinted by permission of the author.

"The Gold at the Starbow's End," by Frederik Pohl. Copyright © 1971 by Conde Nast Publications, Inc. First published in *Analog*. Reprinted by permission of the author.

"The Golem," by Avram Davidson. Copyright renewed © 1983 by Mercury Press, Inc. First published in *The Magazine of Fantasy & Science Fiction*, March 1955. Reprinted by permission of the author and the author's agent, Richard D. Grant.

"The Green Hills of Earth," by Robert A. Heinlein. Copyright © 1947 The Curtis Publishing Co. Copyright renewed © 1974 Robert A. Heinlein. Reprinted by permission of the author's agent, Eleanor Wood.

"Harrison Bergeron," from *Welcome to the Monkey House* by Kurt Vonnegut, Jr. Copyright © 1961 by Kurt Vonnegut, Jr. Originally published in *The Magazine of Fantasy & Science Fiction*. Reprinted by permission of Delacorte Press/Seymour Lawrence.

"How Erg the Self-Inducting Slew a Paleface," by Stanislaw Lem. From *Mortal Engines*, translated by Michael Kandel. English translation copyright © 1977 by The Continuum Publishing Company. Reprinted by permission of the publisher.

"The Hurkle Is a Happy Beast," by Theodore Sturgeon. Copyright © 1949 by Mystery House, Inc. Reprinted by permission of Kirby McCauley, Ltd.

"I Do Not Love Thee, Doctor Fell," by Robert Bloch. Copyright © 1955 by Fantasy House, Inc. First published in *The Magazine of Fantasy & Science Fiction*. Reprinted by permission of the author and the author's agent, Kirby McCauley, Ltd.

"Inconstant Moon," by Larry Niven. Copyright © 1971 by Larry Niven. Reprinted by permission of the author.

"I Was the First to Find You," by Kirill Bulychev. Reprinted with permission of Macmillan Publishing Company from "I Was the First to Find You" in *Half a Life and Other Stories* by Kirill Bulychev. Copyright © 1977 by Macmillan Publishing Company.

"A Kind of Artistry," by Brian Aldiss. Copyright © 1962 by Brian W. Aldiss. Reprinted by permission of the Robin Straus Agency, Inc.

"The Lens," by Annemarie van Ewyck. Copyright © 1977 by Annemarie van Ewyck. English translation copyright © 1984 by Annemarie van Ewyck. Reprinted by permission of the author.

"The Lineman," by Walter M. Miller, Jr. Copyright © 1957 by Fantasy House, Inc.; renewed 1985 by Walter M. Miller, Jr. Reprinted by permission of Don Congdon Associates, Inc.

"The Man Who Lost the Sea," by Theodore Sturgeon. Copyright © 1959 by Theodore Sturgeon. Reprinted by permission of Kirby McCauley, Ltd.

"The Men Who Murdered Mohammed," by Alfred Bester. Copyright © 1958 by Mercury Press, Inc. Reprinted by permission of Kirby McCauley, Ltd.

"A Meeting with Medusa," by Arthur C. Clarke. Copyright © 1972 by Arthur C. Clarke. Reprinted by permission of the author and the author's agents, Scott Meredith Literary Agency, Inc., 845 Third Avenue, New York, New York 10022.

"The Muse," by Anthony Burgess. Copyright © 1964 by Anthony Burgess. Reprinted by permission of the author and the author's agents, Artellus Limited.

"The New Prehistory," by René Rebetez-Cortes. Copyright © 1972 by René Rebetez-Cortes. Reprinted by permission of the author.

"Nine Lives," by Ursula K. Le Guin. Copyright © 1969, 1975 by Ursula K. Le Guin. An earlier version of this story first appeared in *Playboy* magazine. This reprint by permission of the author and the author's agent, Virginia Kidd.

"Nobody's Home," by Joanna Russ. Copyright © 1972 by Robert Silverberg. Reprinted by permission of the author.

"On the Inside Track," by Karl Michael Armer. Copyright © 1986 by Karl Michael Armer. Reprinted by permission of the author.

"Pairpuppets," by Manuel van Loggem. Copyright © 1974 by Manuel van Loggem. Reprinted by permission of the author.

"Party Line," by Gérard Klein. From *La Loi de Talion* by Gérard Klein. Copyright © 1973 by Editions Robert Laffont. Translation from the French by Arlene Higuily in *The Best from the Rest of the World*, copyright © 1976 by Donald A. Wollheim. Reprinted by permission of the author and the author's agent, Kathryn Cramer.

"The Phantom of Kansas," by John Varley. Copyright © 1976 by UPD Publishing Corp. Originally published in *Galaxy*, February 1976. Reprinted by permission of the author and the author's agent, Kirby McCauley, Ltd.